As a general rule, except when weather threatened the harvest, Pierre-Edouard did not work on Sundays. Instead he made use of this day to survey his property quietly, noting the fine growth of the crops, the vigour of the trees and vines. He loved these walks, and took great pleasure in them.

Sometimes Mathilde and the children accompanied him. Then, whilst the children galloped ahead, they remembered the paths walked and the years gone by since that morning in September 1917 when they had met, up there among the broom and juniper bushes of the White Peak. Pierre-Edouard had never for a moment regretted that day, the sudden urge which had thrown them together and united them for all time with an oft-renewed fervour. Their love grew stronger and deeper, quickened afresh by the daily round of work on the land they loved, enlivened by the births of their children and the happiness and vitality they brought with them . . .

Claude Michelet was born in Brive in Limousin in 1938. He still lives on his land at Marcillac, close to Brive, where one of his six children now farms with him. In addition to this trilogy, he is the author of many other works, including a biography of his father, Edmond Michelet, who was a minister in General de Gaulle's government.

# Firelight and Woodsmoke
## Applewood
## Scent of Herbs

• • • • • • • • • • • • • • • • • • • • • • • • • • • • • • • •

OMNIBUS EDITION

# CLAUDE MICHELET

Translated by Sheila Dickie

ORION

An Orion paperback
First published in Great Britain in this omnibus edition
in 1995 by Orion
an imprint of Orion Books Ltd
Orion House, 5 Upper St Martin's Lane, London WC2H 9EA

Published by Orion in separate volumes as:
*Firelight and Woodsmoke* Copyright © 1979 Editions Robert Laffont, S.A., Paris
*Applewood* Copyright © 1980 Editions Robert Laffont, S.A., Paris
*Scent of Herbs* Copyright © 1990 Editions Robert Laffont, S.A., Paris
Translation copyright © 1993, 1994 by Sheila Dickie

A CIP catalogue record for this book is available
from the British Library

ISBN: 1 85797 668 1

Typeset by Deltatype Ltd, Ellesmere Port
Printed in Great Britain by Clays Ltd, St Ives plc

# THE DUPEUCH FAMILY

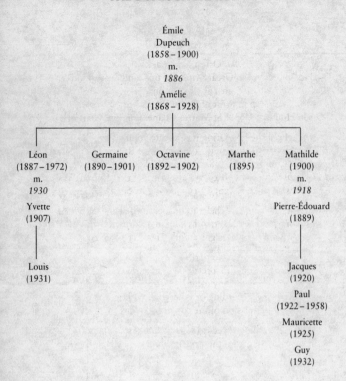

Émile
Dupeuch
(1858–1900)
m.
*1886*
Amélie
(1868–1928)

| Léon | Germaine | Octavine | Marthe | Mathilde |
|---|---|---|---|---|
| (1887–1972) | (1890–1901) | (1892–1902) | (1895) | (1900) |
| m. | | | | m. |
| *1930* | | | | *1918* |
| Yvette | | | | Pierre-Édouard |
| (1907) | | | | (1889) |
| | | | | |
| Louis | | | | Jacques |
| (1931) | | | | (1920) |
| | | | | Paul |
| | | | | (1922–1958) |
| | | | | Mauricette |
| | | | | (1925) |
| | | | | Guy |
| | | | | (1932) |

# THE VIALHE FAMILY

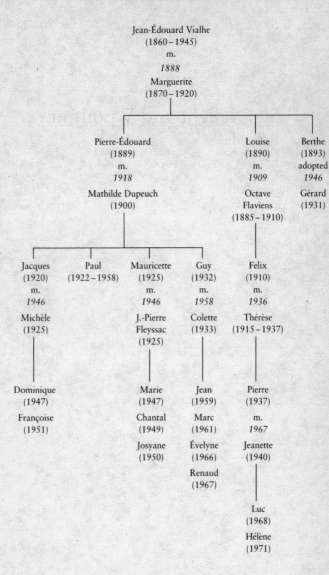

Jean-Édouard Vialhe
(1860–1945)
m.
*1888*
Marguerite
(1870–1920)

Pierre-Édouard
(1889)
m.
*1918*

Mathilde Dupeuch
(1900)

Louise
(1890)
m.
*1909*

Octave
Flaviens
(1885–1910)

Berthe
(1893)
adopted
*1946*

Gérard
(1931)

Jacques
(1920)
m.
*1946*

Michèle
(1925)

Paul
(1922–1958)

Mauricette
(1925)
m.
*1946*

J.-Pierre
Fleyssac
(1925)

Guy
(1932)
m.
*1958*

Colette
(1933)

Felix
(1910)
m.
*1936*

Thérèse
(1915–1937)

Dominique
(1947)

Françoise
(1951)

Marie
(1947)

Chantal
(1949)

Josyane
(1950)

Jean
(1959)

Marc
(1961)

Évelyne
(1966)

Renaud
(1967)

Pierre
(1937)
m.
*1967*

Jeanette
(1940)

Luc
(1968)

Hélène
(1971)

# Firelight and Woodsmoke

*To Bernadette*

The People of Saint-Libéral

*Il y a deux choses auxquelles il faut se faire, sous peine de trouver la vie insupportable: ce sont les injures du temps et les injustices des hommes.*

Sébastien Chamfort

*There are two things to which we must adapt, lest we find life unendurable: they are the injuries of time and the injustices of man.*

# PART ONE

## *The House of Vialhe*

# 1

THEY abandoned the sunken path and the shelter of the thick brambles. The east wind burst in their faces, seared their cheeks and lashed their bare legs; cold prickly tears appeared like pearls between their clenched eyelids.

The three children crossed towards the far edge of the plateau and slipped between the juniper bushes. The snow squeaked beneath their steps, stuck to the nails of their clogs and gave them huge, heavy white soles; they stopped frequently, knocked their feet together to shake off the frozen blocks, then trotted on.

The eldest led the way; he walked without hesitation and as fast as the undergrowth, snowdrifts and rocks would allow. Behind him came a young lad, his hand outstretched behind him, holding a little girl firmly by the hand. Her face was reddened with cold, she was sniffing noisily and almost running to keep up.

'There it is,' pointed out the eldest. They were approaching a juniper bush.

The thrush was stiff, frozen, hard as stone. The wind gave it the appearance of life, making it revolve on a necklace of horsehair hanging from a low branch. The snare must have trapped it early in the morning, at the hour when the pale sun broke between two clouds of snow. Attracted by the black laurel berries neatly arranged in a little trench of pressed snow, it had pecked up to the fatal fruit, in front of which Léon Dupeuch had placed the noose. At twelve years old, Léon was already a creditable trapper. His snares deceived even the wiliest hare.

'It's a lovely little songster,' he said, unhooking the bird. 'With the others that makes seven, and they're worth at least fifteen sous each. That makes . . .'

He hesitated, his brows furrowed, then, discouraged, he turned to his companion.

'Five francs twenty-five,' said Pierre-Edouard Vialhe, puffing himself out a little.

Pierre-Edouard Viahle was considered one of the best pupils in the village, and the schoolmaster was sure he would get his school certificate one day. He was only ten and a half, still plenty of time before he would have to face that exam, but he was preparing for it already.

'Blimey! How do you do it?' groaned Léon jealously. 'I don't understand all those numbers!'

Pierre-Edouard shrugged his shoulders. 'Hurry up, it's late; we must get back,' he said, examining the sky.

'We're going to get into trouble,' whimpered his sister, and suddenly, without a sound, began to cry. She regretted having insisted on following them.

'You're just a little girl, Louise!' Léon had teased her. 'What use would you be to us up there!'

'I'm nine and I am *not* a little girl. I want to go!'

'All right, come,' her brother had said. He was kind, was Pierre-Edouard; he almost always did everything she wanted. But this time it would have been better if he had not given in to her demands.

She was frightened and cold. What was she going to tell her mother as an excuse for this escapade? First of all their parents did not like them to leave the village; secondly they wouldn't like to know that Louise and Pierre-Edouard were with Léon Dupeuch. Although Léon was good fun, they said he was not well-bred; that he would rather be out in the wilds than in school; that everything he found – even a stray hen – became his property; that his poaching would lead him to prison one day – and above all, that his parents were worthless.

No one really knew where they'd come from, they weren't from this region. They had been seen arriving eight years ago, from the area of Brive, more than thirty kilometres away. Strangers ... Tenant farmers on one of the solicitor's farms, they cultivated three hectares after a fashion: two cows, six sheep, a pig and some poultry. They lived poorly, spoke little, and did not join in the community life of Saint-Libéral-sur-Diamond. Therefore, no one trusted them.

'We must go,' insisted Pierre-Edouard.

'Hang on! Let me get my trap ready for tomorrow. In weather like this, other birds are bound to come down from the north; my father says the cold spell will last as long as this moon.'

'I know, Grandfather told me that, too. Come on, let's go – it'll be dark, they're bound to punish us!'

Without hurrying, Léon delicately attached a new circlet to the middle of the juniper branch, which he curved down to the ground and held there with a big lump of frozen snow. The ring of horsehair was at just the right height. If a bird put its head through,

4

it was done for. The slightest shake would free the branch and the victim would be suspended, without even having swallowed the bait.

Léon got up at last, and blew on his numbed hands. 'I hope the wind won't get up again and bring more snow, that will spring the whole thing. You crying again?'

Louise sniffed fiercely, pulled her cloak tight around her and took her brother's hand. 'Hurry up,' she urged. 'They're bound to have called us in by now.'

Pierre-Edouard agreed, and began to step out. They were not far from the village; they could make out the columns of smoke, down there on the side of the hill. At any other time they would have reached it in less than a quarter of an hour; they only had to zigzag down between the trees to rejoin the path and the first houses. But the snow made rapid progress impossible. In places the wind had driven it up to fifty centimetres deep; elsewhere the frost had solidified the long streams of water which poured in torrents from the moorland. There were many tricky spots which they had to negotiate with care, making progress difficult and slow.

It had been bitterly cold for a fortnight. It had come all of a sudden, without warning.

'You see, mon petit, it's to finish the century,' Pierre-Edouard had been told by his paternal grandfather. 'It hasn't been a very good one. It's dying as it lived, meanly . . .'

It had all begun on 10 December, a Sunday. The wind, which until then had kept the humidity of the west, had veered round to the north. It didn't stay there long, just long enough to change the colour of the clouds, which threatened snow now, instead of rain. And then, as suddenly as it had quit the west, the wind shifted to a full easterly, and settled there. The thermometer at the Mairie had registered minus 10° that Sunday, then minus 12° the next day, and eventually, on Tuesday, minus 16°. That was when the snow arrived; not a single flake melted on the frozen land. Since then it had held, frozen to the heart, during several awful nights. 'There'll be more!' declared Grandfather.

Pierre-Edouard stumbled, almost went sprawling, and let go of his sister's hand.

'We'll be told off,' she repeated between two hiccups. She was still crying silently, and two long candle-drips of mucus flowed down to her chapped lips.

'Blow your nose!' ordered her brother. 'No, perhaps they won't have noticed today . . .'

He had taken a risk, agreeing to this escapade with Léon.

5

Normally he would never have dared to vanish for so long, and go so far; he had too much respect for his father's belt, that terrifying thong of leather which whistled as it swept down on his bare legs and thighs.

But today was different. First of all it was Sunday, and then it was Christmas Eve; the adults were preparing for the celebration supper after Midnight Mass and the next day's holiday. With a bit of luck, no one would have noticed their disappearance.

They had left at about two thirty, and had immediately climbed towards the vast plateau which dominated the village. Passing close to the source of the Diamond – the stream which ran down to Saint-Libéral, springing from a cave on the side of the hill – they could not resist the temptation to break the huge ice stalactites which hung from its vault. Then they set off again, each sucking a delicious candle of ice, so cold that it stopped your breath and burned your tongue.

The climb through the wood had warmed them up and their cloaks seemed too hot, almost unnecessary. Already Léon had pushed back his hood and undone his muffler. But an icy blast greeted them on the plateau. Up here there was nothing to stop the wind; only the path bordered by hedges and some clumps of bushes gave intermittent shelter.

Pierre-Edouard loved this great stretch of land; he felt at home here, in his fields. He knew them by name, at least those which belonged to the Vialhes. Here the piece called Longue, with its old nut trees; over there, next to Caput Hill, the Peuch field; further on the Malides – a crop of wheat; further still the Perrier patch, and finally, right at the end, hidden by the White Peak, the Big Field, sown with rye.

The boy also knew to whom the other fields belonged, the position of each boundary; he knew everyone who worked there, landowners and tenants, and whether they paid in money or kind. Almost all lived in Saint-Libéral, and almost all had other strips of land spread across the hillside to which the village clung. Down there the Vialhes owned more meadows and woods, and also a nascent vineyard and a big plot for vegetables, set on the open escarpment, exposed to the rising sun and well protected from late frosts. The slope was so steep that everything had to be done by hand, but the yield justified the labour. With fifteen hectares, eight cows, a dozen ewes, two goats and three sows, the Vialhes were among the more substantial landowners in the commune. Only the solicitor and the château had more land, and perhaps some of the leased farms belonging to people from Terrasson, Objat or Ayen.

'We'll get told off,' said Louise once more.

'Your sister's just like my jackdaw!' joked Léon. 'She always says the same thing.'

Pierre-Edouard did not rise to the bait – not because of the comparison, which he did not mind, but because he did not want that ugly bird introduced into the conversation. Everyone knew that the only sentence the Dupeuchs' jackdaw could repeat (ad nauseam) was 'Pig of a priest! Pig of a priest!'

'A disgrace!' said Grandmother Vialhe. 'That's why you shouldn't associate with the Dupeuch boy, my dears.'

Pierre-Edouard knew perfectly well that it was not Léon but his father who had taught the bird this vulgarity, but it was still an irritating subject. Pierre-Edouard went to catechism classes, and Mass, and would soon make his First Communion. Léon didn't do any of that and prided himself on it, an attitude which upset Pierre-Edouard; embarrassed him, too, for it gave his parents good reason to forbid him to see his friend.

'We won't be there before dark!' admitted Pierre-Edouard.

The shadow was advancing quickly, densely. It was climbing up the valley, already drowning the village. Up there on the plateau it was still almost daylight, but the wood into which the children had plunged was growing darker minute by minute.

'Stop crying, you! We'll get there,' he said, shaking his sister.

'It'll take ten minutes,' declared Léon, 'if that.'

They were right in the centre of the wood when the howling transfixed them. It seemed to come from the plateau – more exactly, from the spot where Léon had stretched his last snare, close by the White Peak. The cry, long and wavering, echoed again.

'A wolf,' breathed Léon. 'My God, a wolf!'

'Quick, quick!' whispered Pierre-Edouard. 'We must run. You be quiet!' he ordered his sister.

She was not saying anything; besides, she was paralysed with fear.

'No,' said Léon. 'Just the opposite, we must make a noise. My father told me that. Make lots of noise. It'll be frightened of us!'

His voice was barely audible.

'Run,' insisted Pierre-Edouard. And he leapt down to the left through the snow.

Another howl reached them and this one did not come from the plateau; it rose up from the valley, flowing out of the darkness and echoing on the sides of the hill, an interminably long cry, which froze their blood.

'Quick, quick!' stammered Léon. 'Let's run *and* make a noise.

They're there, they're after us! They've smelt us! Make some noise, Pierre, make a noise, for God's sake.'

'What with?'

'Talk, talk loudly,' begged Léon in a whisper.

'I don't know what to say,' murmured Pierre-Edouard. However, he raised his voice and stammered out his last geography lesson.

'La Corrèze; administrative centre Tulle, other towns Brive and Ussel . . . La Corrèze is a region which . . . which is part of Limousin. It is irrigated by three rivers, the Dordogne, the Vézère and Corrèze. It, it . . . I don't know any more!'

'Go on, go on,' begged Léon. 'They're coming!'

They reached the path as a fresh howl rose from the plateau and impelled them on their way.

'Say something! We're not near the houses yet, they can still eat us!' gasped Léon.

'Throw away the thrushes! That's what they can smell,' ordered Pierre-Edouard.

'You must be mad. I've got more than five francs' worth!'

'Throw them away, I'm telling you,' insisted Pierre-Edouard, shaking him, 'otherwise they'll get us!'

'All right,' groaned Léon. He opened his rucksack without slowing down, drew out fists full of birds, and threw them over his shoulder.

'Talk, Pierre-Edouard, talk!'

'Hail Mary, full of grace, the . . . Oh, I can't any more, it stops me running,' sobbed the boy.

'The Lord is with thee,' piped up Louise. She sniffed and, still crying, continued in a high-pitched tone: 'Blessed are those . . .'

At last they arrived at the first house in the village, but they went on running, right to the church square.

'Bye!' shouted Léon, crossing to the alley which led to his place.

Pierre-Edouard and Louise slowed down, drew breath, and walked to their home at the end of the main street, on the way out of the village. After blowing their noses, they slid quietly into the comforting warmth of the cowshed.

The milking had already been done and the animals were ruminating. They could make out their father, tying up a calf in the darkest corner of the barn, where the feeble glow of the paraffin lamp hardly penetrated.

'Where have you been?' asked Jean-Edouard.

'Over there . . .' said Pierre-Edouard, attempting a vague gesture. He took a fork and rearranged the straw.

'Go in,' he whispered, to his sister. 'Say that you were here with

8

me. And I'll come in soon, with Father; Mother will think we've never left him.'

'And before that, where were we?'

'Playing in the square, sliding on the overflow from the wash-house . . .'

Louise pushed open the double door and slipped between its two wings into the main room. The dog, flopped down as close to the hearth as possible, his nose in the dying embers, turned his head towards her. His eyes shone golden, reflecting the flames, and he gently wagged his tail. Seated on the wooden settle, grandfather was delicately peeling chestnuts.

'There you are, poppet. Come and give me a kiss.'

She went up to him, placed her chapped lips on his rough, prickly cheek and settled beside him; she was still shivering.

'You're cold?'

'A bit. Where's Mother?'

'She's seeing to the pigs.'

'And Grandma?'

'Gone to the grocer's. She wanted to take you, but you weren't there.'

'And Berthe?'

'With Grandma.'

Berthe was only seven; she was much too little to follow the big boys. Good thing she wasn't with us, contemplated Louise; we wouldn't have been able to run, and the wolves would have caught us. She shuddered at the thought.

'Have you caught a cold? Where have you been?'

'I was with Pierre-Edouard . . . Hey, will you roast me some chestnuts?'

'Here,' said the old man. He bent down towards the hearth, moved aside the warm cinders with his fingertips, and revealed some fifteen chestnuts roasted in their skins. 'I knew you'd want some.'

He took several steaming nuts, rubbed them between his clasped hands so that the charred, cracked skin fell off, and stretched them out on his palm to the little girl. The wall-clock struck six as Jean-Edouard came in, his son behind him.

'Have you heard the news?' called out Jean-Edouard, approaching the fire. 'The wolves have come!'

'He's made Pierre talk!' thought Louise, and her throat felt dry. Punishment was imminent.

'Who said so?' asked the older man.

'Go out into the yard, you can hear them!' Jean-Edouard took down the paraffin lamp and lit it. A harsh, white light replaced the gentle warm glow of the fire. 'Delmont came to find me in the byre,' he explained. 'He's just met the doctor, who saw one on the way back from Ayen; it crossed the road right in front of him. Then we heard them.'

'How many?'

'At least three. Two on the plateau, towards the peaks, and another sounding off towards Yssandon. I bet they're coming from the north. With this cold it's not surprising.'

'Three, that's nothing,' said the old man. 'Remember '78, in February, there were at least fifteen prancing around us every night, even after gobbling up Marjerie's dog at Perpezac!'

'I know, I know, but I thought things had calmed down since the big round-up two years ago – no, three; it was '96. We're going to have to do something about them, I don't like those animals.'

Steps sounded outside and then the tap of clogs against the steps. Grandmother entered, pressing her granddaughter close to her.

'You know?'

'We know,' said Grandfather. 'You're not going to tell me that three wolves curdle your blood. You didn't hear any more?'

'No,' she agreed, taking off her woollen cloak, 'but the little one was frightened. Go and warm yourself, darling, there's no danger now. Go on.'

Louise glanced at her sister. Berthe was sucking a stick of liquorice given her by their grandmother. She breathed in long, wet slurps.

'I heard the wolves!' she crowed. 'I heard the wolves and you didn't, so there!'

Louise shrugged her shoulders and munched a chestnut. One day, one day, she'd tell that little brat that she had not only heard them, but had almost been devoured, and Pierre-Edouard and Léon too! For after all, their adventure on the plateau and White Peak was a much bigger thing than going to the grocer's and back! She stuck out her tongue at her sister and popped in another chestnut.

Pierre-Edouard was struggling painfully against sleep. Already the myriad tapers which surrounded the crib seemed like a gigantic single sun, an enormous warm sphere. Beside him, among the thirty catechism-class children, a few were already asleep, supported against each other on their benches. They wavered, leaned forward, sat up suddenly and then resumed their slumber.

Pierre-Edouard rubbed his eyelids and envied his sisters, who had stayed at home in their grandfather's care. They must be asleep; he pictured them in bed, and dozed off for a few seconds. The scraping of chairs being pushed back awoke him; everyone else was standing up for the Preface. He rose with a jump, and calculated in his head that he would have to endure at least another half hour of the service – ten minutes to get to the end of this second Mass, and, if everything went well, about twenty minutes for the third and last Mass of Christmas Night.

Three Masses was really too many; especially as the first one had been sung, and the sermon had lasted an eternity! The priest always took advantage of the big feast days, when parishioners filled the church, to give his flock a good telling off, for, according to him, they did not visit the House of the Lord often enough. He addressed himself mainly to the men, who preferred to spend their Sundays at the bar, or hunting, or – mortal sin – at work, rather than in the glorification of God.

Pierre-Edouard did not like this sort of scolding; he felt himself on the side of the men. Admittedly, his father did not go to Mass every Sunday, far from it, and nor did his grandfather, but at least they kept Easter. They were not like some others who never practised their faith, never even entered the church for funerals.

He turned round, looking for his father in the congregation. Of course he was there, in the third row, with his mother and grandmother. In front, in the pew reserved for them, stood the squire, his wife, two daughters and their governess. He saw, too, the doctor's wife, the solicitor and his family, the baker's wife and children; all the familiar faces of the community.

He was suddenly aware that his father was frowning in his direction, and hurriedly looked to the front. This was no time to step out of line.

He hardly dared believe in the fabulous luck which had enabled them to return from their expedition without damaging consequences. However, the slightest mistake might reveal that he did not have an easy conscience. He loved his father, but he feared him. He was intimidated by his great bulk, his burliness, his enormous hands and stern face intersected by a thick black moustache. And then, he seemed so old – not as old as Grandfather, but almost. He didn't know his parents' exact age, and did not remember ever having had the courage to ask them.

He realised with pleasure that the second Mass was drawing to a close, and Father Feix was already restarting the prayers at the foot of the altar.

*

'The little fellow's asleep,' said Marguerite as she collected up the plates. They had all just celebrated the Eve of Christmas with a hearty meal, except of course the two girls, whom nothing and no-one could wake. Head on the table, Pierre-Edouard was sleeping beside his plate on which a small piece of white sausage lay congealed.

The men rose, went over to the hearthside carrying the tobacco-pot of red stoneware; they rolled their cigarettes which they lit with tapers.

'Did you talk to the others?' asked Grandfather.

At sixty-nine, despite a lifetime of work on the land, seven years of military service and a year at war, despite the rheumatism which bowed him to the earth, Edouard Vialhe controlled the fate of his farm and his family with a heavy hand. Nothing escaped him; although he found it more and more difficult to do his share of the work, he kept an eye on every detail.

Only son of Mathieu-Edouard and Noémie Vialhe, he had inherited from them the basis of the existing property: eight hectares, gathered together patiently by a whole line of Vialhes who, from generation to generation, had handed on the land, the knowledge, and the Christian name Edouard as their heritage. To his eight hectares he had been able to add one more on his return from military service, and his wife Léonie had brought two good hectares of grazing as part of her wedding settlement in 1859. Born the following year, their only son, Jean-Edouard, had been a great help with the farm work, and above all had made a good deal in marrying Marguerite when he was twenty-eight. Ten years his junior, pretty as a jenny wren, her dowry had included four hectares of excellent land.

The only complaint one could make was that their daughter-in-law had three children; to think, that fat-head Jean-Edouard did not know how to cast his seed more wisely! One day those three kids might quarrel and divide the land. God forbid that an old man should live to see such a destruction of their assets!

'Well, did you talk to them?'

'Yes, we're going to hunt them down.'

'When?'

'Tomorrow.'

'Tomorrow's Christmas,' protested his mother. 'Couldn't you make it a day of rest?'

'Listen,' argued Jean-Edouard, 'we're not going to let the wolves settle in this country again! I have children and I have animals.

Everyone in the village is agreed on tomorrow, they'd even prefer to go right away. Anyway, the mayor has decided.'

'That rascal!' grumbled Grandmother. She did not really mind that the leading citizen of the community was totally indifferent to religion; it did not matter to her that the mayor would eventually burn in hell. But he had dragged her son on to the local council – that she could not forgive!

Secretly she was very proud of his role, but she refused to admit that a free-thinker like the mayor could also be open-minded enough to invite Jean-Edouard, a man who went to Mass at least three times a year, to sit with him in council. She always feared he was up to no good; that the mayor and those other republican atheists might lead her son into a trap. She was not aware that the mayor had chosen Jean-Edouard as his deputy firstly because he knew how to read and write, and secondly because he was an excellent farmer, who would co-operate in getting a buying syndicate off the ground, one of his long-term ambitions.

'He may be a rascal, but he's a good mayor,' cut in the old man. 'Come on, let's get to bed.'

Everyone rose and Marguerite, helped by her husband, undressed Pierre-Edouard in front of the fire. He did not wake, even when she slipped on his nightshirt which had been warming by the flames, nor when she laid him in the big bed where his two sisters were already asleep.

# 2

JEAN-EDOUARD swallowed the last mouthful of bread and home-made pâté of his morning snack and emptied his glass of wine. Then he carefully wiped his knife on his thick black corduroy trousers, closed it and slipped it into his pocket.

'The wind's still in the east,' warned his father from his seat opposite on the other side of the fireplace. 'You'll have to approach them through the château pinewood, otherwise they'll outwit you.'

'I know. Anyway, there's nothing to say that they're still up there. They travel, those animals . . .'

He left the hearth and plunged into the darkness of the room, not considering it necessary to light the lamp. He opened the drawer of the dresser, fumbled in it, found the box he was looking for and took from it a fistful of cartridges, then returned to sit by the fire.

'What are you waiting for?'

'Jeantout and Gaston. They're supposed to pick me up.'

The daylight was slowly sharpening; the clouds, thick and low, lingered on the edge of the plateau, hiding the peaks. The door banged, and Marguerite entered.

'You're still here?'

She had come from attending to the cows, and the smell of the byre floated into the room with her. She put down the milkpail on the table.

'Help me put the pig bucket on the fire.'

He rose, grasped the enormous pot full of kitchen waste mixed with turnips, bran mash and water, and hung it on the chimney hook.

'I thought you were going on this hunt,' she repeated.

'I am going. Look, there they are,' he said, catching sight of his neighbours through the window. He slipped on his heavy hunting jacket and took down his gun.

'Try to be back by midday, won't you? It *is* Christmas,' she reminded him. 'And . . . take care.'

About fifteen men were grouped in front of the mairie, stamping about in an attempt to warm their feet. Jean-Edouard and his companions joined them, shaking hands.

The village was waking up and from all the cowsheds, those opening on to the main street and its seven side alleys, came familiar sounds: the low mooing of cows calling their calves, the hiss of milk on buckets, the raking of forks on flagstones, cries of famished pigs, clucking of poultry already scratching about on the dung heaps, gentle plaints from ewes and goats.

Houses were opening up with a great banging of shutters and heavy whorls of smoke rose from the chimneys; the air smelled of fires re-lit, of cut wood and dried broom. The bedroom lights in the inn came on one by one, and in the big saloon downstairs some customers were already seated at tables: three pedlars trapped by the snow, a wood-merchant and a mattress-maker. Only a few still slept: those in professions needing no animals, and shopkeepers, who would not be opening up on Christmas day.

The church clock was showing two minutes to eight when the squire appeared at the end of the main street. Muffled up to his ears, his gun on his shoulder, he was stepping with care on the frozen snow. Behind him, holding back four good-sized dogs with great difficulty, came Célestin, the man-of-all-work at the château. The squire mingled with the group, shook hands and joked.

'Time, it's time!' he trumpeted. 'His worship the mayor is late, he's been overdoing the celebrations.'

Jean Duroux was a good-looking forty-year-old, with a cheerful disposition and easy manner, who revelled in his role as Lord of the Manor. He had been born here, and was on friendly terms with all the men of his age.

Son and grandson of ships' chandlers, the death of his father had left him heir to the château, with ninety hectares of good land and forests surrounding it, and to property in Brest, Rouen and Paris. Not lacking for money, he considered it an unnecessary bore to try to make any more. His days slipped by pleasantly, surrounded by his wife, his two daughters, the governess, Célestin and several servants. Twice a year he assembled his household, loaded them all on to the train at Brive or Terrasson, and left for two months in Paris or Biarritz.

There was only one shadow on his happiness: his name lacked any trace of nobility. He cleverly repaired this deficiency by introducing himself as Jean Duroux de Saint-Libéral; great was his joy when, on arriving in Paris or Biarritz, he heard them announcing Monsieur de Saint-Libéral!

Who was ever going to check up that Saint-Libéral-sur-Diamond was a country town in the lower Corrèze, and that he, Jean Duroux, was only one among the 1092 citizens of the commune who could claim that title? He would have been shocked to find that at the markets of Tulle, Seilhac, Brive, or Turenne, all the men used the same strategem, not out of boastfulness or vanity, but simply to give an address and show their origin.

The people of Saint-Libéral ignored his little deceit; if he was The Squire to them, someone from another world, they all agreed that he was not stuck-up.

'You've got a new rifle,' remarked Jeantout, who had been eyeing the weapon since the squire had arrived.

'Oh yes,' admitted the owner, drawing the double-barrelled gun from his shoulder. He held it out, turned it over, then broke the barrels. 'Nice piece, isn't it? It's the best there is at the moment; I bought it in London. Look, hammerless, Anson and Deeley system, twelve-bore, central percussion of course. Three breech bolts, chokebore on the left barrel, English shoulder-piece. It's a little heavy, perhaps, but nevertheless a wonderful thing! Best of all I can use cartridges with B powder – no more smoke, and unrivalled power. As to the coupling . . .'

They drank in his words, and if the technical terms went over their heads, it only served to demonstrate just how old-fashioned their own rifles were. The most modern were only some Lefaucheux with exposed hammers and pin-fire cartridges. A few still sported muzzle-loading flintlocks, and they all used black powder, of which the most minor inconvenience was that it gave off a thick cloud of smoke on ignition.

'It must have cost something,' murmured one of the admirers.

'A bit . . . Fifty louis.'

The amount left them speechless. A thousand francs for a rifle! The price of three good cows! Crazy!

'That's impossible,' blurted out Jean-Edouard incredulously. He could not begin to understand how someone could lay out a sum like that for a rifle, however beautiful it was.

'Well, I wouldn't like it,' joked Jeantout. 'I wouldn't be able to take aim. With the big hammers at least you can frame the target,' he said, bringing his old gun to his shoulder and tracking an imaginary partridge across the sky.

But no one was listening to him; they were deflated by the enormity of the price. When the mayor arrived he found them reverently passing from hand to hand the weapon which Jean Duroux had kindly lent them.

'Beautiful gun!' It was his turn to admire. He felt its weight, put it

16

to his shoulder, then handed it back to the owner, whistling quietly when he was told its price.

Antoine Gigoux had been elected mayor at the age of forty-two, and had fulfilled his mandate for more than twenty years. He managed the community with the same care he devoted to his farm. Affable to all, he exercised, when necessary, the good-natured but firm authority of a paterfamilias. He climbed the steps of the Mairie and raised his arm to call for silence.

'Before leaving, I would remind you that hunting is forbidden when snow is on the ground. So, no games. I don't want to hear gunshots after hares mistaken for wolves . . . Only aiming at a wolf is allowed, or possibly a fox. And also, to do it properly, I should have permission from the préfecture, but I'll take that responsibility. Tulle's a long way off, the prefect won't hear us! Right, we'll get into groups, how many are we?'

He counted quickly and then pointed to the village policeman: 'Octave, you take five volunteers, good shots, and go to the sunken roadways. Put three on the cutting and three on the Coombe. Get a move on, you're not tired out already! The rest of us will beat across the peaks and the plateau with the dogs. If all goes well and if they're still up there, we should get a fair shot by about eleven o'clock. Let's go, and don't fire at each other!'

'And don't shoot at my dogs, either!' advised Jean Duroux, stroking his animals.

'Your dogs have never seen wolves, have they?' asked the mayor as they started off.

Jean Duroux could not protest at the familiar 'tu' the mayor used in addressing him; they would make fun of him if he did. But he could not adopt the same familiarity, because he was so much younger than the mayor; so he attempted to maintain his superior position by an exaggeratedly affected way of speaking. The forced informality of his manner did not deceive anyone, least of all Antoine Gigoux.

'Not seen wolves, my dogs? See here, my friend, you remember our hunt three years ago? I already had Trompette and Tambour then, and there was no holding them! The two others are younger, but they are very keen after foxes.'

'And what are they called, Bugle and Fifi?' quipped the mayor.

'Of course not! Their year letter was A, so that one is Ardent and . . .'

'And the other is Angry,' suggested a joker behind his back.

'And that one is Aramis,' continued Jean Duroux, ignoring the laughter.

He adored guns, hounds and hunting and could talk forever once he started on one of these topics. They listened willingly enough, for no one could deny that he was one of the best hunters in the area, perhaps even in the whole region, a dog-handler without equal and a crack shot.

'Yes,' he continued, 'this cross of fox-hound and Poitou dog is really a success. Just look at that neck, those solid hindquarters, the stance! And wait till you see them point or spring . . .'

All the hunters were grouped around him, and measured their pace to fit his.

'You haven't got that other one any more?' asked one of them. 'The big fellow with mournful eyes, like a beaten wife, who almost tripped over his own ears?'

'I expect you're talking about Faraud, my deerhound? Yes, I've still got him, but he's almost blind – fifteen's a lot for a dog. I miss him, there was none better after hares.'

They left the village and plunged into the pinewoods, up the steep pathway beside the château, which they could see perched higher up the slope. It overlooked the town and the whole valley from its sheltered position on the south-facing cliff. From up there you could see almost ten kilometres on a clear day; you could make out the Monédières, the foothills of Cantal, and the greater part of the Vézère valley in the foreground.

The castle had been built at the beginning of the century by a distant cousin of Marshall Marbot, on the remains of a medieval stronghold. Not very imposing, more like a large family house than a château, it owed its title to its position and the size of the estate, rather than to its architecture. Solidly fashioned from blocks of light sandstone, its side wing looked like a keep from the distance; capped with a solid roof of slate and enhanced by a series of terraced gardens, it was very attractive.

Grandfather Duroux had bought it for a song in about 1825. The proprietors, who had been forced to retreat to Paris at the time of the White Terror of 1815 and 1816 –particularly threatening in this area – had never dared to return to face a population whom they considered implacably hostile. They did not realise that no one wished them the slightest harm. The blaze of anger shown by the villagers was nothing but a flash in the pan, as ephemeral as the fistful of agitators who came from Périgord to unleash reprisals, which had been truly bloody. Once those wanting revenge had left in search of other victims, the village had returned to its habitual calm, and no one even thought of going to break the casements or empty the cellar of the uninhabited house for ten years.

Grandfather Duroux had not mentioned this to the vendors, and had paid a derisory sum for the entire estate. This masterly stroke, known to all, assured him of unquestioned esteem in this rural environment, where money was scarce. Those who knew how to buy or sell at maximum profit were always respected.

The prestige of the new proprietor had flowed down to his descendants, and guaranteed Jean Duroux the respect due to the richest man in the commune. Only a few older people, like the mayor, the priest, the doctor or even old man Vialhe, treated him a little lightly, but all the others deferred to him.

Jean-Edouard shivered; the cold was winning. He was startled to find himself dreaming of a blazing fire and a good bowl of hot wine.

He had arrived at one of the posts designated by the mayor a quarter of an hour ago, and had placed himself beside a huge chestnut tree, leaning up against the enormous trunk. He could make out the immobile silhouette of Jeantout thirty paces away, and further off that of Gaston. Ears pricked, he waited for the howling of the dogs which would herald the start of the drive.

The wolves must still be up on the plateau, for he had seen no sign of them in the snow during his long trek from the town. Besides, wolves had well-marked paths for climbing to the plateau or coming down from it, possibly as many as five or six, which they alternated according to the wind. What always amazed Jean-Edouard was that the hares, foxes and even wild boar followed almost the same tracks. An undeniable imperative seemed to draw them back, generation after generation.

'Good God,' he thought, 'what are they doing? They must have had time to get up there by now!'

He pictured the hunters emerging at the other end of the plateau and fanning out in extended order after releasing the hounds. The right-hand group would comb over the White Peak, the fields and chestnut groves that surrounded it; those on the left would be beating over the Caput Hill and the whole stretch of plateau where the Vialhe fields lay, in all three good kilometres' walk to reach the cutting which he was guarding.

This cutting, the remnant of old iron workings, bit into the plateau as if hewn by a giant axe-blow, thirty metres long and forty wide. Not a single tree remained undamaged in that hollow. Every one without exception had been struck by lightning, some several times over. Fireballs flashed into the cutting at each storm, attracted by the red iron-ore in the soil.

Jean-Edouard still recalled the terror which had nearly driven him mad when he was still just a boy, minding the flocks with Jeantout and Gaston. One stormy day they had rushed to shelter in an old half-collapsed mine tunnel, where they endured, dumb with terror, for half an hour whilst the lightning crashed incessantly around them. He still remembered the monstrous thunderbolts which ricocheted from rock to rock before exploding in huge showers of dazzling sparks. Cowering in their hole, the three boys had thought that the priest's frequent threats might have come true: they really were in the depths of Hell.

'What the devil's keeping them?' he grumbled. Now he was not only freezing but longing for a smoke, and there was no question of that. You might as well fire a shot to warn the wolves they were expected!

The little troop of beaters topped the crest of the White Peak, then descended towards the chestnut grove which began at the foot of the steep escarpment.

The White Peak and its twin, Caput Hill, still bore the traces of the espaliered vines which had covered them to their summits twenty years earlier. The thick bed of snow could not blot out the undulations in the earth formed by the thousands of ridges where vines had once grown.

Their raised profile was silent witness to the dirty white earth, full of flints, heavy with impenetrable chalk, a geological curiosity isolated in this plateau of good red soil; the peaks had rejected any other crop but vines. Ever since the phylloxera infection had ravaged and destroyed the French vines, it had lain fallow, supporting nothing but juniper, box and Spanish broom.

Before the attack of the American disease, the vines on the peaks had guaranteed a considerable income to the majority of farmers in the village. Every time they returned to these places, long since uncultivated, each felt a weight of sadness, arising from the many failures which had rewarded their attempts to replant with American vines.

The soil rejected them. It alone was to blame. This vine was impervious to the parasite, and developed properly when planted in other fields of the commune. Its wine was found to be drinkable. Of course, it was not as good as the old one, far from it: it lacked strength, bouquet, dignity; it was neuter. But it was a good cropper and the young vines grew well.

Here, the plantations of Riperia or Rupestris wilted mysteriously during their first year; they vegetated, produced puny shoots and sickly leaves, then died. No one had succeeded in keeping one of these vine stocks alive for more than three years. Tired of slaving away in vain, the men had gradually abandoned cultivation on the slopes. The walls of the hundreds of terraces, no longer maintained, soon succumbed to the pressure of the earth; rainstorms scoured out gullies and frost insidiously undermined them. Split open and collapsed, the terraces failed to retain the soil; up till then it had been preserved by the painstaking work of men, who carried back up baskets full of the earth which trickled down each winter.

Since then the peaks had been barren, and the children of the village could not understand why those places had such unlikely names as High Vineyard, Beautiful Vines, the Trellises, or Low Vines . . . For nearly twenty years these designations had been meaningless, and already new names were developing: Quarry Meadow, Stonefield, Turnstones, the Junipers . . .

Just as the beaters reached the chestnut groves, one of them called out to Jean Duroux. Célestin still followed him, holding back the dogs with more and more difficulty.

'Here!' cried the man, and was immediately surrounded by the rest of the band.

There was a trail. It led from the steep escarpment which plunged from the very edge of the plateau to the valley across woods and rocky scree.

'A young one,' commented Jean Duroux, 'not more than two years old. By the way, I'd like to know whose children have been playing around here. Have you seen? Three kids, and not very old by the size of their clogs.'

'I noticed the footprints,' said the mayor. 'I expect it was Séraphine's kids who came through here; they're into everything.'

Séraphine lived two kilometres away, in a tumbledown cottage at the place called Calvary. The widow of a farm labourer who had died four years ago, she had somehow survived since then, thanks to the warm welcome most of the local farmers gave her. To save her the shame of begging, she was given work according to the season: some fleeces to wash in the Diamond, hemp to be dressed, linen to rinse in the stream. Wielding her sickle, she joined in the harvest; the farmers turned a blind eye to the stalks she sometimes forgot – there had to be some ears of corn for her kids to find when they went gleaning . . . Lively as squirrels, they were out of doors in all weathers, picking up a forgotten turnip here, a few chestnuts there.

'They're brave, those kids,' commented the squire. 'Good, this animal is heading right into the chestnut trees. I'll let the hounds go, but first I'd like to know where the other two are.'

'Here!' called one of the hunters, who had followed the trail up to the wood.

They joined him.

'That one's a big old wolf,' explained Jean Duroux. 'Not young, that animal, look at his pads! He's coming from the same direction and heading the same way. Look, the young one has caught up with the older one's trail, and he doesn't like it! See how he's peed on it to try to mask the smell! You know what I think? We'll find the she-wolf's tracks a bit further on. It's time for her to come on heat, I bet that animal has lost her mate and she's calling the male.'

They entered the dark chestnut grove. The hounds wailed mournfully at the end of their chains.

'Peace, my beauties, peace! Be patient.'

At last they found the third trail.

'And here's our little hussy,' announced Jean Duroux. He stroked his dogs and then released them. They sprang away, mad with excitement.

'Perhaps we should get into line?' suggested the mayor.

'If you think so,' conceded the squire. 'Listen, I don't want to disappoint you, but the hunt's over.'

They looked at him, waiting for an explanation. No one doubted he was right; they simply wanted to understand.

'That female is out searching, she may be fifty kilometres from here by now,' explained Jean Duroux. 'Look, see her tracks, she's running hard. No wavering, straight ahead, and I'll bet she crossed the wood at the same pace. She's heading for the Forest of Cublac and she must have left the plateau by way of my acacia copse.'

'And why didn't she wait for the others? She was calling them, right enough!'

'Yes, but this isn't her patch, she's only here by chance. I tell you, she's recently lost her mate – no territory and doesn't know where to settle down. Well, she won't get a chance here! Now, if we were dealing with a pair and their cubs, with a bit of luck we'd have been able to find them here; the wood's quiet, full of game, they could stay here several days. But with a baggage who's asking for it . . . Let's go on anyway. We'd better tell the others, they must be freezing down there on guard!'

Jeantout and Gaston, blue with cold, had joined up with Jean-Edouard. Cross at having waited around for nothing, they were smoking furiously as they hopped from foot to foot to warm themselves a little.

'I'd like to know what they're playing at, up top! They should have been here by now!' fumed Gaston. 'The wolves certainly aren't there, so what are we waiting for!'

'They'll come soon,' said Jean-Edouard, clapping his arms energetically round his body. The yapping of the hounds suddenly reached them.

'Damn! To your positions!' shouted Jeantout, tossing away his cigarette.

He dashed off, followed by an even more furious Gaston.

'Never seen the like! What kind of work is this! They've had a little chat with them, those wolves, before chasing them?'

He stumbled on a root and measured his length.

'Damn and blast!' he muttered as he got up. 'Oh hell,' he said, looking at his snow-covered clothes and rifle.

Chilled and disheartened, he shrugged his shoulders towards his two companions, who tried to stifle their wild laughter. At that moment the animal emerged ten paces from him.

They mayor and the squire were advancing side by side when the hounds belled.

'So, you and your explanations!' threw out the mayor.

'My dear fellow, you don't know my dogs,' said Jean Duroux with irritating calm. 'Listen to Trompette, can you hear him?'

'Yes, and with our walking pace and guns over our shoulders, we've let the beast go. Bravo! I'll remember your lectures on wolves!'

'I hope so! See here, my friend, what you lack is a good knowledge of the canine race. I would remind you that wolves and foxes are part of that noble family, and dogs too, of course, not forgetting jackals and coyotes, but that's beside the point . . .'

'And so what?' groaned the furious Antoine Gigoux.

'Well, good old Trompette isn't going for a wolf, but a fox. Difference in size, isn't there?'

'It's a fox he's put up?'

'Of course, what do you think it is! With the noise we've been making since we found the tracks, no wolf would have stayed around. This fox is from round here; he'll just go to ground in some bushes, hoping that we'll pass by without getting wind of him, but with Trompette he doesn't stand a chance. I hope the marksmen on guard don't miss him.'

'Unless they've gone home,' muttered the mayor. 'We've certainly taken long enough to make ourselves heard!'

'Yours! Yours!' yelled Gaston. 'Shoot, dammit! There! There!'

Jean-Edouard raised his gun, but he could see nothing.

Then suddenly he spied the fox, which made a half-turn at full speed and climbed back up the side of the cutting. He fired, and the cloud of smoke hid his target.

'Again! Again!' urged Gaston.

But the animal was long gone; they caught a glimpse as it reached the crest, ran along it for a second and then disappeared into the coppice.

'And you, why didn't you fire?' shouted Jean-Edouard.

'I don't intend to blow my head off. Look at this. It made you laugh when I fell, but look at my gun barrels. Stuffed with snow, they are! That happened to my father once; he took a shot and almost blew his brains out with it!'

'Did you hit it?' asked Jeantout.

'What do you think? It was too far! And him telling me "Yours, yours!" and not telling me where, the silly ass!'

'Oh, well, the others will laugh. Look, there are the dogs. By God, how they point! They can't track in this snow, they're scenting on the wind.'

'I should have had Duroux's rifle,' mutterd Jean-Edouard. 'It's no good with my old pop-gun . . .' He was annoyed, and looking for excuses. 'It's true,' he insisted, 'he was more than forty metres away. And you, you had to go and try to break your neck!'

'Sorry; I did it on purpose, of course! And you, if you can't see properly, you should get some spectacles!'

'Come on, you two, leave it be!' said Jeantout. He winked in the direction of Jean-Edouard, clumsily mimed the incident of the fall, and let out a shout of laughter under the wrathful eye of Gaston.

# 3

LÉON got up as gently as possible, taking great care not to rustle the hay. He slid out of the warm hole where three little shapes slept huddled together, muffled under an old coverlet.

He knew very well what was going on in the house; he was the oldest, after all, and he had understood immediately when he saw the doctor arrive at about nine o'clock in the evening: this New Year's Eve would see one new member to increase the Depeuch family. But for that, the only bedroom in the house had had to be cleared.

Their closest neighbour, called on by the doctor to help out, had suggested to Léon that they should settle down by the hearth in her house, but the boy hated that woman; he found her more disagreeable and ill-tempered than an ailing sow. Rather than accept her offer, he preferred to take his three little sisters to the stable. There he took care of them. He hollowed out a nest in the big stack of hay which had been put ready for tomorrow's feeding time, in the area which separated the two cows from the ewes. The little ones had immediately fallen asleep, reassured by the animals' quiet breathing.

Léon half opened the barn door and listened. He remembered the last birth, two years earlier, and knew that the baby would be there when his mother's groans died away. But it was impossible to catch the slightest sound above the howls of the tempestuous wind and rain.

It had been bucketing down since the day before yesterday; the rain was unusually warm for the time of year, and had drowned all traces of the snow. The town was now saturated with water, and the Diamond rose hour by hour, swelled by streams from the plateau and slopes. They said the miller had been forced to take hasty refuge in his own loft; but then he did live at the bottom of the valley.

Léon closed the door and the barn returned to complete darkness. He felt his way towards the pile of hay and settled down in the warmth; he had made up his mind to wait for the birth, to stay alert for as long as was necessary. Five minutes later he was asleep.

'Here's another one who won't end up in the priesthood!' cried the doctor, dangling the tiny child at arm's length. He held the chubby, shining body by the feet and smiled as he observed the furious grimaces of the baby, who was yelling at the top of its voice.

'Wash her,' he ordered, passing the child to the neighbour. 'And you, get rid of that for me,' he said, pushing an armful of bloodstained linen towards the father.

Then he bent towards the mother, who was still spreadeagled across the bed. With a long caressing stroke he soothed her; her belly was still contracted and tense, yet it relaxed beneath his massage.

'If all women gave birth as easily as you . . .' he murmured, pressing gently on the abdomen. 'Wait, I'll deliver the afterbirth and then it will be over.'

At sixty-five, despite thirty-eight years in practice, Doctor Fraysse still felt a great joy – and even a sense of wonder – at each birth. God knows he had seen enough of them, and all sorts!

Since he was an excellent physician, the mothers gladly forgave him his familiarity – he addressed them with the intimate 'tu' from beginning to end of the birth. And if some husbands were occasionally shocked, the squire for instance, he explained with a smile. 'It is possible, dear friend, that you got her in that condition by saying "vous" to her; everyone to his own taste and methods. For my part, I need intimacy to finish your work; believe me, this is not the most attractive stage, I need tenderness and trust. I need to speak gently to your wife, or to bawl her out if necessary. And that's not possible with: "Madame would it please you to, if I might ask . . ." But if it really worries you, I can do without you. And now my friend, let's go, just us two, and see how this little fellow is getting on. And don't worry, all will be well, you listen to me.'

He had adopted this custom of using 'tu' in the field hospital to which he had been posted during the war.* There, in the tents, when they bought him cartloads full of wounded, he searched and probed, wielded scalpel and saw on the crushed bodies, and he noted how pain and labour were alike in many ways – the same anxiety, the same rattle in the throat, the same convulsions, panting breath and sweating, the same waiting for relief. And in both cases, the same comfort brought by a friendly calm voice, a fatherly gesture, a caress.

'It's over,' he said, placing the placenta in a basin. 'There you are, my dear, everything's all right. You've been very brave; I'm going to bind up your stomach with these two towels and then you can rest. Not sleep, you understand. You remember, don't go to sleep straight away; you must watch in case there's any serious bleeding. But don't

---

* The Franco-Prussian War, 1870–71

worry, I'll stay a while; I'll have to do the dressing for your daughter. By the way, what is she to be called?'

'Mathilde,' murmured the mother.

'Lovely name. Here, Emile, hold your wife up while I fix these towels for her. And I must say, you know, between us, five is quite a lot, isn't it? I would very much like not to have to come back next year . . . But that's your business.'

'I would have liked another boy,' said Emile, as he replaced the pillows.

'Bah, you'll get sons-in-law!'

'Well, yes . . . Say, would you like a glass of punch? It's all I can offer you.'

'Fetch something to eat as well,' suggested his wife in a weak voice. 'You forget that it's time to celebrate the New Year!'

'My God, that's right! A new century, too!' exclaimed Emile.

'Yes, by heavens!' cried Doctor Fraysse, feeling in his waistcoat pocket. He took out his watch. 'Half past midnight! There's my first customer this century! Well, that must be celebrated! And I shall provide the toast! Emile, you slip over to my place, they'll be bringing in the New Year. 1900 – that's quite something! Tell my wife to give you a well-filled basket and a bottle of champagne. Ask for a bottle of Bordeaux for your wife too, that will revive her. And don't forget to tell them to wait for me, I'll be there within the hour. What's the matter?' he demanded, when he saw the father's look of dismay.

'I can't,' said Emile, 'I'd never dare go and ask for all that. We've already kept you from the celebration . . . No, no, I can't!'

'No, we can't accept that,' his wife reiterated, 'we'd be too ashamed. We're not well off, we could never repay you, so . . .'

'Oh in God's name, you two make me tired! Madame Lacoste, have you finished with that little girl?'

'I'll bring her to you,' called out the neighbour, who was finishing bathing the baby in the next room.

'Did you hear what I asked Emile to do?'

'Doctor, I'd rather you and Madame left now . . .'

'Give me that child, I'll deal with her. Slip over to my place, since this big ninny is making a fuss. Go on – and get the basket well filled, I'm so hungry I could swallow a whole bullock raw!'

'Don't go, Germaine!' begged the mother. 'You know we can't repay him.'

'That's enough from you, you should rest. Go on, Madame Lacoste, you must always do what the doctor says! Hurry up. And remember to tell them to wait for me!'

The dog barked as it heard the neighbour returning, then recognised her and calmed down. Léon woke with a start and listened. It was still raining. He nearly fell asleep again, then suddenly noticed he was not in his own bed. He gently pushed aside one of his sisters who was snuggled up against him, got up, and felt about to retrieve his clogs.

The damp cold gripped him as soon as he reached the yard. He ran to the house and flattened his ear against the door. Nothing, no more groans; the baby had been born. He pressed the latch, pushed first on the top half of the stable-door, and hesitated a minute.

'Come in!' said his father.

The light surprised and dazzled him. For a brief moment he did not recognise the room; the doctor's big hurricane lantern spread an unaccustomed brightness, illuminating all the dark recesses never revealed by the family's oil-lamp with its thin wick.

He saw then the food and bottles on the table, and wondered where the devil his father could have got them from – surely not from the chest or cupboard? He knew their contents too well.

Eventually he noticed his mother through the open door. He went towards her hesitantly; he hardly recognised her either. He was accustomed to her looking fat and weighed down; now she seemed quite slight and thin.

'At least look at your little sister,' said his mother.

He glanced in disappointment towards the cot; he would have preferred a brother. Three sisters were too many already.

'Here, come and eat with us!' cried the doctor.

Léon treasured the astonishing memory of that first night of the century all his life; the first thing he described to Pierre-Edouard when he met him next day was this remarkable New Year Party.

'And I even drank champagne, I did!'

He had to explain to his friend what the champagne was like – its taste, colour, the strangely-shaped bottle and the curious cork which could not be put back once it had been pulled out.

'The doctor told me that it was done specially so you can't re-cork the bottle, so you have to drink it all up! That's what I did with the doctor and Ma Lacoste. My father didn't want to drink any.'

'Why not?'

'He was too ashamed.'

'And was it good?'

'It's prickly and full of bubbles which make you burp . . . And of course it's expensive. My father told me it might be worth more than ten francs a bottle! It made him ill! And on top of that, you know, the doctor didn't want to be paid for his work.'

'Who was sick?'

'No one, he just came to get my sister born. He said it was free because it was his first customer of the century. That's something, that is!'

The birth of Mathilde Dupeuch filled all the conversations in the village during the following weeks. Since Madame Lacoste had been a privileged participant in this famous party, she recounted all the events of New Year's Eve.

She did not like the Dupeuch family, so she transformed their poverty into misery and the doctor's gesture into the munificence of a lord. She managed it so well that many finished by believing that Dupeuch had begged the doctor to take pity on them. They had not thought much of him beforehand; now they despised him.

Despised, but envied too, for the town council had decided to honour the first-born child of the century by opening a savings account for her, with a deposit of fifteen francs. Many were convinced that Emile would drink it away before she was three months old; that was pure slander, as everyone knew he was an abstemious man.

On top of that, the solicitor's wife proposed herself as godmother, since Emile was one of her tenants; she also added ten francs to the account and had a whole heap of clothes, which had once belonged to her daughters, carried over to the Depeuchs'.

Then a letter from the préfecture announced that, as Mathilde was the first-born of the century in the whole département, the general council had voted unanimously to deposit fifty francs in the newly-opened account.

Emile, pale with shame at being the focus of the whole community and the subject of whispering which weighed heavily on his conscience, became convinced that all this generosity was simply aimed at showing up his poverty.

Poverty alone he could bear. What else could he do, since he was responsible for others? He worked, he didn't drink, he had owed no one anything before that cursed night. True, he earned little, very little; but the few sous which enabled him to support his family were the result of his own work, and they weren't dying of hunger. None of them had ever gone begging.

But his pride prevented him from accepting all these gifts passively; to preserve his honour he should have offered the donors something in return; perhaps not the equal amount, but at least the best part of the value received. It was impossible. He realised that for the rest of his life, whatever he did, the community would remember him as the man who had been fed by his kids, the one who had accepted everything and given nothing in return . . .

Léon bumped into his father's dangling legs when he entered the barn on the evening of 16 January. Emile had been dead for two hours.

By his side lay the savings book, torn to pieces, the pile of clothes given by the godmother, and an unopened bottle of Bordeaux.


'And what's to become of the five little ones?' asked Marguerite, putting down the soup tureen in the middle of the table.

Jean-Edouard made a dismissive gesture; they had discussed it at the town council, and no one had found a solution.

'She'll just have to go back home!' pronounced old Léonie. For her the matter was plain; she had always said that Dupeuch was good for nothing. He had simply confirmed that by destroying himself, like a heathen.

'The solicitor is letting her keep the farm,' announced Edouard. 'He told me this evening. With Léon, she can manage: they only have two cows to look after!'

'You should have told me,' remarked his son. 'At the council meeting we did want to make a collection . . .'

'That's the limit!' cried his mother indignantly. 'With all the money the little one got, just for being born! And the solicitor's wife is her godmother!'

'And also,' continued Edouard, with an irritated look in his wife's direction, 'the doctor is going to take on Léon to work in his garden, which will give him a few sous.'

The old man began to eat his soup, noisily sucking in the thin slices of soaked bread, then wiping his moustache on his lapel. 'He is strange, the doctor. He's saying everywhere that it's his fault . . .'

'What's his fault?' asked Jean-Edouard.

'The business with Emile.'

'And how could it be his fault?'

'We'll find out sooner or later.'

'Perhaps the little one looks too much like him,' commented the old woman ironically, without raising her head from her plate.

She was bringing up an old piece of gossip from twenty years ago. At that time the doctor was still unmarried, and some rumours had been attached to him. It was said that he had shown marked attention to certain female patients, and two or three had even boasted of having received – and refused, of course – unmistakable advances.

Finally the doctor heard the story and laughed about it, as if it were a good joke. He considered the matter so banal – and silly – that he had never felt the need to silence this slander, which was repeated from time to time. 'Especially in the spring!' the doctor was convinced. 'I have a few patients who need a good dose of extract of water-lily root, it's excellent for soothing the over-heated . . .'

'You be quiet!' ordered Edouard. 'The children are listening! What tales you're telling again! With a wife like his, do you think he needs Amélie Dupeuch! That little scrap, thin as a rake and smelling of the cowshed! Just be quiet!'

'Well, why did he say that it was his fault?' insisted Jean-Edouard. The old man shrugged.

'Well, I know,' said his daughter-in-law. 'Yes, it was Germaine Lacoste who told me . . .' She fell silent, hesitating because of the children. Then she thought it would be good to keep them in the picture; forewarned, they might later avoid repeating the same mistake (even the sin) of the Dupeuch family.

'Yes,' she recommended. 'Germaine had a good look, she was at the birth – the child was marked by bad luck, just under the left breast, a patch like a crescent moon . . . And besides, she'll be blind; she opened her eyes straight away!'

'And so what?' remarked Jean-Edouard mockingly.

'Well, she *has* brought bad luck with her. Already her father . . . But it is to be expected that it would happen like that, you remember the Chasse Volante . . .'

'Oh yes,' murmured her mother-in-law, 'that one in March, about the 25th, that would be just the right time . . .'

They all remembered, even Pierre-Edouard. That evening, the sound of the flight had woken him; a terrible sound, full of cries and howls which fell from the sky. It had passed over the village, and the wails had echoed so close that he had rushed to his parents' bed. Then his mother had explained that he was hearing the cries of all the condemned souls of the village; they returned to circle above the cemetery, cursing those who did not pray for their sins to be forgiven, and she had recited her rosary immediately.

'That's all nonsense!' protested Jean-Edouard violently.

'Don't say that,' commanded the old woman, 'your wife is right! That evening, if the Dupeuchs had been praying instead of . . . they

31

wouldn't have had this punishment nine months later! And the mark on the little girl is the result – it's the sign of mortal sin, and a bad omen!'

'Nonsense!' insisted Jean-Edouard. 'And besides, why should that be the doctor's fault, eh?'

'You know he doesn't like salt to be put in the water for the first bath, nor a piece of blessed boxwood. He says it's dirty! Well it may be, but it's the only way to guard against bad luck. That's why it's his fault!'

Jean-Edouard served himself a generous helping of cauliflower with bacon and looked at his father, but the old man would not take sides.

'Rubbish,' repeated Jean-Edouard. 'The next flight of game-birds I hear, I'll go out and bring one down for you with a shot from my gun!'

'You wouldn't do that!' begged his wife.

'I will if you go on reciting all that nonsense in front of the children. It's only good to frighten them, they're old wives' tales!'

'That's what the teacher told us,' said Pierre-Edouard in a small voice. Caught in the crossfire, between two beliefs, he did not know where to position himself; he was hesitating before publicly choosing which camp to join.

'And what did he tell you, that teacher?' interrogated his grandmother.

'Well . . . It was just after the last . . . Chasse Volante, that time in the autumn . . . He said we . . . shouldn't believe that they were the souls of the damned . . .'

'There you have it!' cried the old lady in triumph. 'He doesn't believe in God or the Devil!'

'Let him speak,' murmured Grandfather. 'Tell us, mon petit, what the teacher said?'

Pierre-Edouard looked anxiously at his mother, then at his grandmother, and held himself ready to dodge the blow he felt was imminent.

'He said they were birds flying by, wild geese and – something else, I don't remember any more what, he talked about a route.'

'The heathen!' muttered Grandmother. 'Birds! Honest birds can't see at night! It's only birds of ill-omen, like tawny owls and barn owls, which fly and call at night! Anyway, even if they were birds, they'd still bring bad luck. But they're not birds!'

'Yes, they are,' cut in Jean-Edouard. 'I've been told they're birds too, and I believe it.'

'Who told you?' questioned his wife.

'The squire. He knows about these things, he does!'

The two women were silenced: one could not accuse the squire of being a heretic. He accompanied his wife to Mass every Sunday, except when he went hunting or fishing; he kept Easter, and he invited the priest to dine at the château twice a year, on Corpus Christi and on 15 August, the feast of the Assumption.

'Well, he's wrong!' insisted the older woman. 'You mark my words, you'll see other misfortunes happening because of that baby.'

Father Feix had been priest in St Libéral for thirty-five years. He understood perfectly the mentality of his parishioners, their vices, faults, and good qualities, for he was the son of peasants who kept a smallholding in a neighbouring village. He was strict with himself, and did not compromise when he felt the authority of the church he represented was in danger. His moral code was inflexible and he guided his flock with a firm hand; when he passed judgement, which he did only after long reflection and prayer, none dared to contradict him openly.

So he had forbidden his congregation to patronise the grocer's shop belonging to Jean Latreille. Since losing his wife, Jean had been living openly with a little servant girl; he was old enough to be her father! Ma Eugenie's bar was off limits as well, for her bed was open to all; forbidden, too, were the Saturday night dances the Chanlat couple organised at the inn. The sort of dances they did there could only corrupt the young, by exciting lust and impurity.

Despite this narrowness of outlook, Father Feix knew he was supported and loved by all his faithful flock. Certainly an anticlerical tendency, originating in the towns, had been developing in the village for some time. But it had not come to open warfare, and the few atheists in the community were neither insolent nor malicious; moreover, all paid him the respect his position merited. Only those whose dissolute life he had openly condemned turned aside as he passed and kept their hats on their heads. But the others – the mayor, for example, the doctor and the two teachers, man and wife – never refused to speak to him when the occasion arose.

Emile Dupeuch's suicide deeply saddened him and, but for his cassock and responsibilities, he would have been among the first to offer his support to the family of the deceased. But the sinful manner of the death called for perpetual condemnation; he therefore allowed two weeks to pass before visiting Amélie Dupeuch.

Despite the bitter cold of this month of February, he found her in the little garden behind the house. She was planting onions with the help of Léon. He knew that Amélie was a good Christian. During her husband's lifetime she had attended Mass as often as possible, made sincere confessions, and had had the two children born in the village baptised, even though her husband had been indifferent in religious matters. She had apologised for the jackdaw and its insulting call; she had also apologised for Léon, who modelled his attitude on that of his father, and cultivated a condescending contempt for all that holy stuff. Thank heavens that Emile had been tolerant; it hadn't mattered to him if his wife practised her religion, as long as it did not interfere in any way with the daily work.

The priest advanced down the line of digging, stopped and smiled sadly.

'Well, my poor Amélie, what a misfortune, what a misfortune! I would have liked to come earlier, but you know how it is . . .'

She knew. She understood the penalty for suicide. Emile had been buried like a dog, and besides refusing a religious ceremony, the priest had publicly expressed his total disapproval and indignation. If he had come earlier someone might have thought that he was absolving the sin. At the same time, to avoid exacerbating the situation, Amélie had refrained from visiting the church.

'After all,' he continued, 'time heals all . . . With regard to that, I hope to see you at Mass again soon. Another thing, I spoke to that good lady Madame Lardy; she's still prepared to be godmother to your little girl. Of course we shall have to do that as quietly as possible, you do understand, don't you?'

She understood. During Emile's life their situation had forced her to be modest and discreet. By destroying himself her husband had prevented her from ever escaping this position; she would always be the widow of the man who had committed suicide, and her children the orphans of the one who hanged himself.

'And then,' continued Father Feix, 'you'll have to send me this boy now, to learn his catechism. You don't want him to stay a heathen. You'll come, Léon, won't you?'

'No, I won't come! Never!' growled the child.

'Don't speak to the priest like that,' said his mother sharply. 'You'll go to catechism classes as of Sunday!'

But she knew very well that he would do no such thing, and no one could force him to give way. Since he had become head of the family, Léon took his role seriously and kept his own counsel. She needed him too much to run the risk of striking him. He was only twelve years old, but when he knocked against his father's legs that evening he became as hard and cold as a man toughened by a half-century of ordeal and affliction.

'You will do what your mother asks, won't you?' repeated the priest.

'I'll do what I have to do,' said the lad, without lowering his eyes. He spat between clenched teeth, turned round and continued his work.

# 4

PIERRE-EDOUARD Viahle sat the examination for his school certificate on 11 July 1902. He needed all his strength to face this test, for he was paralysed by fright and discomfited by his Sunday suit.

Of the five candidates defending the honour of the community of Saint-Libéral-sur-Diamond that day, he was the one who was expected to do well. And knowing that so many hopes rested on him did not help to calm him. He was scarcely able to enjoy all the marvellous treats which accompanied this expedition: first of all a journey in old Lamothe's horse-trap, then lunch in a restaurant.

The five candidates climbed into the conveyance, accompanied by their master Monsieur Lanzac, who was taking the place of parents busy with their work, and settled down for the journey to the county town. Pierre-Edouard and his friends were familiar with this stretch of fifteen kilometres; they had all walked to market in company with their fathers. But only Jacques Bessat and Edmond Vergne could boast – and they made the most of it – of having ridden in the old rattletrap before.

Jacques was an old hand; his grandparents lived in Ayen, and he went to see them several times a year. As for Edmond Vergne, not only was he familiar with the great trek, he could also outline the programme for the entire day, including the menu awaiting them at the restaurant: noodle soup, sausage and pickled pork with lentils.

It was no credit to him that he could play the fortune-teller, for this was the second time he had sat for the certificate. His father worked in the post office at Saint-Libéral and was determined that his son should win this diploma, which would open the door to an administrative post.

Pierre-Edouard was greatly impressed by old Lamothe's dexterity as he guided the horses, two magnificent beasts with huge hind-quarters, shoulders heavy with muscles and hooves larger than soup plates, topped by shining well-brushed hair on their pasterns. But he could not really enjoy the journey; he could not manage to forget that every turn of the wheels brought him closer to the formidable test.

With an anguished expression, he surveyed the countryside. All around was the same destruction as at Saint-Libéral, everywhere the same carnage – rows of peas fallen and plastered in mud; cereal and fodder beaten flat to the ground, as if crushed by giant feet; fruit trees torn down with leaves already wilted, their fruit still green but dull and withered.

All around men, women and children were busy; here raking yellow, dusty hay, which still smelled of water and the beginnings of mould; there harvesting with difficulty the mangled ears and crushed straw of cereal crops; in other places, trying to gather up a few remnants of peas and some plums spared by the hail.

It had been a year of storms. The first had come at the end of April, proving Grandfather Vialhe once more correct, for he had predicted it from the month of March onwards: 'Look at the birds, they're building low: that's a sign of storms.' And truly the magpies were not constructing their nests in the tops of the poplars or the oaks, but rather halfway up, and sometimes even in the big blackthorn bushes, two metres from the ground.

After some warning rumbles at the end of April, the heat built up throughout May; a damp, suffocating mugginess. Every evening the thunderstorms grumbled in the distance, turned, rolled away and broke over the mountains of Auvergne or Cantal; the nights were full of flashes. In the morning the sun emerged, looking washed out, from a dirty haze in which threatening blanched clouds of cumulo-nimbus were already discernible.

Once June arrived they should have attacked the hay and scythed it, despite the constant menace which hung over them from midday onwards. On the morning of the 12th it rained, the warm drops of the tail-end of a storm, which made the earth steam and filled the atmosphere with a thick and unhealthy humidity.

Everyone felt the threat growing; animals and humans alike were irritated by the stings of horse-flies and, despite the heat of the long days, the hay was not drying well.

On Midsummer's Eve a dark cloak of cloud unfurled over the whole valley of the Vézère, pushed along at a great pace by a boiling, turbulent wind. The village was spared this assault, but they could see the columns of rain hanging like long, black twisted ropes from the clouds.

However, this deluge was not enough to change the weather, and the next day they were all aware that the storm was still imminent. They sensed it, they felt it lying in wait, just beyond the horizon. It gathered its forces for almost a week; it broke each evening, distant but oppressive.

In the fields and meadows they struggled against the weather: exhausting days without rest. The men rose two hours before dawn to mow and harvest; the women, the old men and children busied themselves turning the hay and binding the sheaves.

During the hottest hours, when the draught cattle could no longer bear the pace of work or the temperature, they gathered the burning sheaves and packed them into stacks, and collected the hay into pot-bellied heaps which were later loaded onto the carts; in the evening, when the animals had been rested, they could drag the towering heaps to the haylofts, which were as hot as ovens.

On Monday the 30th, the sun rose with a copper glow. Already in the west the storm clouds were swelling with iridescent outcrops, burnished by a warm, constantly shifting wind. There were no preliminary rumbles, nothing; a dense silence in which the slightest everyday sound, the swish of the scythes or the creak of the carts, sounded menacingly loud. Towards midday the crickets fell silent, the hens took refuge in the barns, and the myriad swallows suddenly left the sky empty.

At St Libéral, they waited. A presentiment, a fear, kept the men at home. Standing at their thresholds, they surveyed the gigantic cap of bronze clouds with darkened edges which topped the peaks. They were ready for the worst, but the magnitude and suddenness of the attack took their breath away.

A thunderclap of incredible violence exploded above the village. At the same time a shower of sparks set the plateau aglow in the area of the cutting, where the ore-bearing ground always attracted thunderbolts. Almost at the same moment, as if released by the ribbon of lightning, the clouds of hail vomited their load. Real pebbles of ice, as big as a fist, fell with a roar like a stream in spate, and the noise was such that it overwhelmed the sound of the bell which the perspiring sacristan was swinging with whirling arms to frighten away the storm.

In a few seconds everything was white. A cat, mad with fright, fled from some cellar and sped along the main street in search of shelter; half-pound hailstones knocked it to the ground, battered it, buried it.

The hail pelted down for three long minutes. It broke everything, flayed the trees down to the sapwood, reduced the vines to skeletons, overturned and hammered all the crops. In the village only the thatched roofs withstood this unprecedented assault, which cracked the more substantial coverings of slate; at the Vialhes' they later counted a hundred and eighty Travassac slates which had been broken like glass in the mutilated roof, despite being nearly as thick as a man's finger.

The cumulus clouds moved away eventually, but were immediately replaced by an opaque stormcloud, heavy with rain and iridescent with electrical charges. Darkness enveloped St Libéral, and in every house people grouped themselves around the holy candles they had lit at the first clap of thunder.

After the hail came flood and fire. A dazzling flash of light dodged among the spouts of water, caught the edge of the Peyrou barn with one of its claws, and set it alight in a few seconds. The building, laden with hay still warm from the fields, blazed like a bundle of dry broom, spouting thirty-metre flames towards the sky. Peyrou himself had to be held down by his son-in-law to prevent him throwing himself into the furnace. The old man wanted to untie his beasts; they were found later, four cows and six ewes, burnt to death.

The pandemonium lasted for an hour, and then the devils of the air moved on. At last the silence returned, and the alarm bell echoed, dismally throbbing through the coolness.

Peyrou's barn was nothing but a heap of smoking embers, and it would have been useless to waste time trying to salvage any debris. In contrast, all around were flooded cellars, roofs torn off by the wind or split open by the fall of trees or the weight of hailstones. The drumbeat of the village constable, calling them to arms, mingled with the alarm bell.

One by one, silent and haggard, all the able-bodied men gathered in the square. Even the priest and the squire offered their labour to clear the rubble, empty the basements, work and go on working until night fell, so as not to remain inactive in the face of such a catastrophe.

It was not until the next day that the men dared to go out to the fields, and the destruction was such that more than one cried silently, alone, in the middle of his plot of devastated maize or tobacco. For some it spelled ruin; complete, with no hope of recovery, the end of a life dedicated to the land. In one single hour this thunderstorm was going to push them out of the village, forever. They would have to escape, disperse, some towards Terrasson, some to Brive or Tulle, but all of them towards a town which would perhaps offer them a chance to survive.

The Vialhes' property was severely affected, but by luck some of their lands were untouched, for the hail had fallen in a narrow corridor; certainly everything had suffered from the water-spouts and the wind, but the losses were more easily recovered than elsewhere.

To provide for the most needy, the mayor requisitioned all the craftsmen – the masons, carpenters, thatchers and slaters – and directed them to the most urgent repairs. He was a peasant himself, so he knew that the farmers would have to save what they could of the crops still standing; and they had to work fast, for mildew threatened. Furthermore, there could be other storms.

The horse-trap quickly climbed the last long slope before the descent into Ayen. Pierre-Edouard sat with glazed eyes and felt the panic seize him – he was no longer able to recite the seven-times table. He saw he was lost, almost ready to give in to despair.

'We'll soon be there,' warned the teacher. 'Remember my advice, now!'

Pierre-Edouard had not forgotten it. Firstly, well presented work with perfect handwriting; no spots or rubbings-out, careful punctuation and, when necessary, well formed, graceful capital letters. Then, modest behaviour, decorum: no hands in pockets or fingers in noses, stand up straight to answer questions, clasp the hands behind the back to relax the voice and not constrict the breathing; always think before answering and beware of this sort of trap: 'So, you are certain that the revocation of the Edict of Nantes took place on 18 October 1685. You're sure?' Or again, 'You have just told me that six times seven are forty-four?' After having reflected with mature consideration: 'Yes' or 'No, sir'.

Finally, and this was one of the secret weapons revealed by their teacher, never hesitate to make some mention of Alsace and Lorraine, whenever the opportunity arose. It was quite easy, especially in history or geography. There was nothing to prevent them, for instance, speaking of the real – or provisional – frontiers of France, and of her natural and historic frontiers. Nor was it forbidden to recall that Alsace had been linked to France by the Treaty of Munster in 1681, and that Lorraine had been French territory since 1766.

Pierre-Edouard remembered all that, but he was still searching for the seven-times table when they arrived at the district capital.

First they had to solve a problem of area, a silly rigmarole about one hectare and twenty ares of land to be divided among three heirs: two-fifths to the eldest, one-and-a-half fifths to each of the other two. Pierre-Edouard managed it very well, and nothing showed in the copy he handed in of the unorthodox way he achieved it.

In fact, at home he was used to calculating area in strips of ten square metres, not in hectares or ares, so he naturally converted; one hectare equals 10 strips, twenty ares are worth 2 strips: 12 strips altogether. The rest was obvious.

In history and geography there was no question about Alsace and Lorraine, but about the reign of Henry IV and the Aquitaine Basin, and it would hardly have been sensible to make any allusion to Strasbourg or the course of the Rhine.

Then, by a stroke of luck – or their master's perfect knowledge of the programme – the dictation offered was one of those they had studied three weeks earlier. Pierre-Edouard immediately recognised the text by Victor Hugo, remembered the pitfalls, and only made one-and-a-half mistakes.

Later, when it was all over and they were seated on the terrace of the restaurant waiting for the results, he showed the rough copies he had carefully kept to the teacher, and anxiously awaited the verdict.

'Well, my boy, if you didn't make any mistakes in copying out, you will have your certificate. Very good; very, very good.'

An hour and a half later the results were published, and Pierre-Edouard approached the notice-board with trembling steps and dry throat. But he did not know where to look for his name, and it was the teacher who announced to him that he was first among the candidates from St Libéral, and third in the district. It was more than a success, it was a triumph!

Edmond Vergne had also passed, but only just. As for the others, it was a débâcle . . .

When they returned to the village, the teacher insisted on accompanying his pupil right to his home, and seeing them pass you could not tell who was prouder and happier, the teacher or the pupil!

Grandfather Edouard was alone, seated in front of the house; since the thunderstorm, he had been tortured by rheumatism. All the rest of the family was harvesting the wheat in the Malides field, up on the plateau.

'Well, there it is!' said Monsieur Lanzac. 'Pierre-Edouard passed, and passed well. I'm very proud of him!'

The old man looked at them and then made a movement which amazed his grandson, who knew how painful it was for his grandfather to hold himself upright: he got up. His wrinkles deepened in a smile, and Pierre-Edouard could hardly believe his eyes when he noticed that the old man's eyelids were edged with tears. And his astonishment grew when he spoke, not in patois, which had always been his customary language, but in French, the French which he only employed in exceptional circumstances.

'No, no,' he assured them, 'I'm not going senile, it's nothing . . .' He swallowed his saliva and gave a faint smile: 'You know, you are the first of all the Vialhes, the first ever, to get a diploma . . . Me, I don't know how to write, and can hardly read. And you, you have a diploma, a real state diploma! Wait a minute . . .'

He went limping into the house and they could hear him rummaging in his bedroom. He returned carrying three glasses on the tips of his fingers and a bottle of ratafia under his arm. He put them all down on the bench, sat down, plunged his hand into his waistcoat pocket and took out a napoléon worth twenty francs. When he held out the coin, his grandson shook his head. He could not accept such a large gift.

'Yes, yes, take it, it would give me so much pleasure. It's for you, you deserve it. Go on, take it.'

Pierre-Edouard stretched out his hand towards the shining napoléon which lay on the calloused palm among the dark wrinkles. When he touched the skin, dry and hard as old leather, Edouard Vialhe closed his fist and shook his grandson's hand slowly.

'The first of all the Vialhes . . . You're a man now. We shall drink your health and your teacher's, and he shall dine with us tonight. We have had enough misery these past few days; we must make ourselves a bit of happiness.'

Pierre-Edouard took off his Sunday clothes, slipped into his everyday wear, and climbed up towards the plateau singing to himself.

He announced his news from as far away as possible, and his cry of joy was echoed by his mother, grandmother, and sisters. As for Jean-Edouard, he leant on his scythe, regarded his son and whistled his satisfaction. He too was flushed with pride.

But there was work to be done, and it was a long time till nightfall. When Marguerite heard that the teacher would be there for dinner she held out her bundle of withies to her son: 'You take over for me here, we must receive him properly!'

Pierre-Edouard worked until dusk. He followed his father, step for step, and tied up the sheaves with practised movements. First of all he gathered the swathes cut by the scythe in to his chest and made a round-bellied heavy sheaf, which he bound with a fistful of damp rye straw. Then, turning the sheaf onto the ground, he pressed his knee onto its creaking stomach and with both hands twisted the withy, making sure that it held by slipping the ends under the belt of straw.

His sheaves were as fine, heavy and thick as those made by a full-grown man.

His sisters gleaned behind him. Finally, at the end of the procession came his grandmother. She gathered the sheaves into stooks of thirteen, arranging them head to head in a cross with four arms; each arm of three sheaves overlapped and the last sheaf capped them to protect the whole. And everywhere on the plateau, there was the same patient persevering labour.

Jean-Edouard often stopped to draw the grindstone from the box lined with damp grass which hung at his belt and re-sharpen his scythe. The steel sang under his strokes.

When at last they stopped, darkness already covered the whole valley. The teacher was waiting for them, sitting in front of the house with the old man. The table was laid, the air was fragrant with chicken broth and goose preserved with mushrooms.

'No, it's impossible,' said Jean-Edouard. 'Besides I already said no to Monsieur Lanzac, and that was only yesterday evening!'

'I know, I heard that he was dining with you,' affirmed Father Feix, 'and I suspected he would suggest some sort of plan of his own . . .'

Jean-Edouard passed his finger along the edge of the blade. He had just been sharpening his scythe and preparing to set off for the plateau when the priest arrived.

'You must understand,' insisted Father Feix, 'your lad is a brilliant fellow, a good, well-behaved boy, you have no right to squander his talents. Remember the parable of the talents? God will ask you one day what you made of your son.'

'I need my son. He works like a man, and if you think we can do without workers, after this last disaster!'

'I know, but it wouldn't cost you anything! I guarantee you that I'll come to some arrangement with the bishop, so that you don't have a penny to pay.'

'Oh, yes, and that teacher, he wants to make arrangements with some school inspector or other! I'm going to tell you straight, no disrespect intended, you seem to me just like recruiting sergeants! It's no! The boy is not going to a seminary, nor to any kind of school in Tulle. He'll be staying here; that point is settled! Look here, just ask my wife what she thinks about it!'

'Well, you too, Marguerite; you're of the same opinion?' asked the priest.

The young woman had just come from seeing to the pigs. She dried her hands on her apron and came nearer.

'Yes, Father,' she said, blushing just as she used to do when she stumbled over her catechism in class, 'I agree with Jean-Edouard. We don't want all these arrangements, we need the boy too much.'

'But you're only thinking of yourselves, aren't you? And him, his future, what about that?'

'He doesn't want it either,' said Jean-Edouard. 'He has no desire to be a teacher, nor a priest!'

'But it's not a question of making a preacher out of him! I am simply saying that concentrated study at the seminary would do him a great deal of good. And if, later on, he wanted to turn to the priesthood . . .'

'Monsieur Lanzac said exactly the same thing, only it wasn't a question of ending up as a priest, but as a teacher!'

'You're not going to compare the institution which I'm suggesting to you with some lay school, where all Christian ideas are forbidden!'

'The result's the same,' interrupted Grandfather, who had just dragged himself to the doorstep. 'You want to take our boy away from us. That's not good what you're doing there, not good at all!'

'Well, what use is his school certificate to him?' shouted Father Feix angrily. 'It's pointless to push him this far if you're then going to stop him!'

'He can use it to say: "I have my diploma",' retorted the old man. 'The point is that he can read, write, count, walk with his head high! And you think that's not enough? Why do you want to add other diplomas, which will turn his head and make him forget his father and mother? And his land! No, no, I don't want this boy taken away from me and spoiled in your towns. He too is a Vialhe, an Edouard, an eldest son, and you want to deprive him of his land? And the farm, what would become of it without him? Give it to the girls? Never! The land has belonged to the Vialhes for more than a century, and it's going to stay like that!'

'Well!' sighed the priest, 'you are all consummate egoists. I am disappointed in you, Marguerite; yes, most of all in you . . . And Grandmother, what has she to say about it?'

'The same as me,' cut in the old man. 'And I'd like to see her say anything different!'

'Well, I can see that you're all in it together; I won't go on. But you'll regret it one day. You'll say: "Ah, if only we had listened to the priest!" But it will be too late! Well, too bad; *I* shall have a clear conscience!'

Father Feix mopped his streaming brow and departed with a flourish of his cassock.

44

Pierre-Edouard now emerged from the house. He had heard everything and feared at one point that his parents would give in. He had no desire to leave the house and village to go to these distant schools they were proposing to him. School was finished. He was thirteen years old and had his certificate; he felt a man now.

Father Feix nodded to several old ladies who were gossiping under the lime trees in the square, and went into the presbytery. The heavy door banged shut behind him.

He was in a very bad mood, and angry with himself for falling into the temptation of wrath once more, coming within a fraction of succumbing to it. Of course he had managed to control himself in front of the Vialhes, but it would have taken very little to make him explode, and offer some thoughts which had little to do with Christian charity.

He poured himself a large glass of his own infusion and forced himself – as a mortification and despite being very thirsty – to drink slowly. He lived modestly and soberly, and kept the wine from his small trellis for Sundays and Holy Days. In the high season he prepared a refreshing and invigorating drink based on the leaves of the ash tree; in autumn he made a light wine from apple juice, and in winter he drank water.

He mopped his brow and neck, which were dripping with sweat, unbuttoned the neck of his cassock, turned back his sleeves and went out in the little garden. Here the heat was unbearable. The plot was encircled by walls which stored and reflected the sun's warmth; it only cooled down late in the evening, and the rows of vegetables needed watering every day.

He quickly returned to the presbytery, appreciating its coolness, and settled himself in a rattan chair to continue reading his breviary. But he had to make a great effort to banish all traces of anger from his mind; this anger had laid siege to his thoughts for months, and the slightest irritation brought it to the attack.

But how could he remain passive in the face of the madness and scandal shaking the whole country, threatening the Church and the Faith? Thanks to the generosity of the squire he had a subscription to the newspaper *The Cross*, and read it from the first to the last line. He also kept himself informed on events in the region by reading *The Cross of Corrèze*, which the solicitor's wife gave him. So he was well-informed, and from the first he had followed the rise of atheism and freemasonry with disquietude. Neither his congregation, nor the village in general, had really been affected by this disease, but he had nevertheless felt a certain change of attitude amongst some parishioners.

The mayor, for example, was more proud and self-confident than ever before, and pinned back the ears of his electors by recounting, for the thousandth time, the story of his interview with the President of the Republic! If you believed him, Eric Loubet and he had become inseparable friends! The mayors' banquet must have taken place almost two years ago, but Antoine Gigoux never ceased to tell of its splendour. And as time passed he skated over the fact that he had been only one of more than 20,000 mayors privileged to be received by the President . . . The priest forecast that in a few more years he would be saying that he had lunched with him tête à tête!

Father Feix was not jealous of the aura now surrounding the first citizen of the community, but he deplored the infatuation, not to say devotion, centred on Antoine Gigoux. He was indisputably popular, so it was easy for him to direct the municipal administration in a modern and dynamic way. With the help and wisdom of Jean-Edouard, he had started a buying syndicate, where most of the farmers came for their supplies.

Already there was a rumour that the council were going to organise a market, to take place twice a month in the church square. Father Feix had been told that the soundings of cattle dealers, street-traders and pedlars had been favourable, and only the cost of installing a weighing machine for the animals was holding up the start.

The priest was wary of this innovation. Certainly it would bring some money into St Libéral and everyone would feel the benefit of that, but there was a risk that it would radically change the way of thinking in the community. Moreover, and worst of all in his view, all this was being done for the glory of the Republic – that Republic which was revealing its true nature as the months passed. It was the face of the Antichrist.

He had been indignant first about the law concerning congregations, then scandalised by the unjust case brought against the Assumptionists in the previous year. Since then he had boiled with anger. And how could he calm down! The last elections, on 6 and 20 May, had fostered the atheistic aims of the government, rather than putting the brakes on them. Now they had the power to continue their campaign against the Faith until the end of their term of office. Since the Republican faction held 367 out of 587 seats they could do anything, and they were making the most of it!

Not content with defeating men like Barrès, the Socialists had just chosen a leader worthy of themselves, the renegade Emile Combes; further encroachments on the power of the Church were to be expected, for he had a malicious hatred of it. It all stank of decay and decomposition; like the treason and immorality spread by that horrible Jew Dreyfus and all who supported him!

Father Feix often reproached himself for falling into pessimism and despair; so, as soon as he felt the flame of the second virtue dying, he hurried to revive it – with prayer, of course, but also, he had to admit, with a burst of anger which propelled him, still raging, out of the presbytery. Then he went on his rounds among the faithful and exhorted them to resist and fight on.

But there too, what disappointments, what disillusion! To his way of thinking his parishioners lacked fire, passion and spirit. He found them too passive, too soft. Only a few women supported him, but the others, all the others, continued their humdrum lives without taking sides; not against him, but not with him, indifferent. So the mayor could influence them as he pleased, helped by the teacher, who passed *La Petite Republique*, that dreadful rag full of lies and slanders, all around the village.

Even the squire was spineless; he did not want to quarrel with anyone, took care not to reveal his opinions openly, and kept friends on both sides. He wanted to stand for election to the *Conseil Général*, so he reconciled chalk and cheese to arrive at this goal. As for the solicitor – careful not to annoy any of his clients, he smoothly played down his political position; even if he secretly shared the priest's concern, in public he played the role of Pontius Pilate.

Doctor Fraysse was a free-thinker who spoke frankly, and the priest almost preferred his mocking attitude to that of his lukewarm, faint-hearted supporters. The doctor did not conceal his opinions, and seemed to be highly delighted by the turn of events. He counted the blows of the combatants and amused himself freely by reading out articles from the *Petit Journal*, but he was never malicious. The priest even forgave his recent greeting: 'Ah, tell me, what are they doing to you? If I were in your place I wouldn't put up with it!' Basically the doctor was not a threat; he was not an ally, but not an enemy either, rather an honest irrelevance. He jokingly gave his judgement on a dispute which did not affect him. Besides, since Father Feix had never expected his support, he was not disappointed in him.

He did not feel the same about the Vialhes. That family was slipping away from him, he could feel it. Jean-Edouard was getting out of hand, taking over authority, restrained only by old Edouard's grasp. But the latter was in his decline, his physical pain, his age, relegating him to a secondary role. Of course he still directed the farm and the family with his voice, but the real owner, the master, was now Jean-Edouard. His capabilities won him the respect of all: it was he who used the first fertiliser, he who boldly established a plantation of a hectare of walnut trees on the plateau, he who, it was said, was soon to own a mechanical reaper; he, finally, who managed the buying syndicate.

Jean-Edouard was not really in opposition to the priest, not yet . . . He respected religion, went to church at Easter, but more and more he kept his distance. The proof was in the way he had been received an hour ago! Jean-Edouard had dared to compare the Church's behaviour with that of the teacher, what a sorry state of affairs!

And after all, wasn't that the best solution: to send little Pierre-Edouard, who was so talented, to study seriously at a seminary? Wasn't that the only way to foster his intellectual and moral development? And most of all, wasn't this the opportunity to score a point against the anti-clerical movement, and reassert his shaky authority in the village?

But the Vialhes had refused his offer; even Marguerite had rejected it. Luckily, they had also refused the teacher's tempting but underhand proposition. Perhaps all was not lost . . .

He closed his breviary and immediately reproached himself for allowing his thoughts to stray in this way, so far from spiritual meditation. But wasn't the aim of his work to strive to protect his flock? To guard them against the attacks which he knew assailed them from so many directions?

# 5

Jean-Edouard finally decided to buy a mowing machine in April 1905, having thought about it for a long time. He had planned the purchase years ago, but had to postpone it as a result of several bad harvests.

After the catastrophic storm of June 1902, he was unable to recoup the losses caused by the hail; the accounts showed a deficit in the years which followed as well. A late frost in the spring of 1903, and again in 1905, destroyed practically all the vegetables and fruit, which provided a substantial part of the farmer's income in a normal year. They had coped, but there was no question of making new investments.

In the community, the shortage of money was reflected in the buying syndicate, and it had taken all Jean-Edouard's persistence to prevent its closure. But the number of subscribers continued to diminish. In three years twelve farmers had left the village, compelled by force of circumstance to seek work in the town. Luckily the fortnightly market had developed rapidly, and the country folk came from far and wide to buy and sell in the market-place of St Libéral. It was a great comfort to Jean-Edouard and the rest of the town council, and it also brought prosperity to the tradesmen.

For the Vialhes, Grandfather's increasing demands added to the difficulties caused by the capricious weather. The old man could no longer move without terrible pain and effort; his attacks of rheumatism were so severe that they often had to call out Doctor Fraysse, or his colleague, the young Doctor Delpy, who was to take over the surgery and clientele before the end of the year. At two francs fifty a time, with potions and other medicines on top, it came to ten francs nearly every visit.

Jean-Edouard never begrudged his father the cost of the care he needed. His father had worked his time; from now on he had a right to rest, and nothing would be spared to see that he enjoyed it as much as possible. He kept himself informed about the work on the farm, made them take him to the looseboxes from time to time to see the calves or the sheep; he worried about the condition of the soil and the growth of the fruit trees.

On the day of the first market he had wanted to get to the square at all costs. There, gripping his walking stick in one hand, the other on his grandson's shoulder, he had slowly made the round of the rails where the cows and calves were tethered. He was very proud that his son was one of the architects of this creation; very proud, too, to tell several old acquaintances from nearby villages that his son had the best yields in the community, thanks to his knowledge and use of fertilisers.

But Jean-Edouard knew his father was rapidly weakening. It now took both his wife and Marguerite to get him up in the morning, and it was seldom that a week passed without a visit from the doctor. Because of all this he had been forced to delay buying a reaper. Yet it had become essential; his father could not work any more, his mother and Marguerite were kept busy looking after him and the animals. Jean-Edouard had only himself and his son to count on.

At sixteen, Pierre-Edouard was a fine young man. Tall and well-formed, he could work almost as well as an adult, but he still did not have quite the staying power or work output. The periods of heavy work were becoming harder. At forty-five Jean-Edouard was still at the height of his strength, but he could see ahead, and knew that his power and endurance would fade and decrease. Occasionally, after a day of reaping or harvesting, he would feel a stabbing pain shooting through his kidneys, an indication that his body was rebelling against such arduous work.

He endeavoured to take on a farm labourer, a sturdy, honest man, but it was no use. Those who were looking for a job preferred to work in the town, and the others plied for hire in the farms on the plain near Brive, Larche or Terrasson, where the work was less strenuous than on the slopes of St Libéral. Only a few day-labourers stayed in the village, and he didn't want them at any price. He could not do with them pottering about, demanding their pay each evening; they got drunk straight away and took two days to sleep off their wine. Besides, he did not want men like that sitting at his table, looking at his wife, and at Louise too.

Louise was turning into a really beautiful girl. She would soon be fifteen, and already had the manners and affectations of a young lady, which worried her father a little. She was lively and coquettish and just as proud of her little breasts – hardly bigger than nuts! – as Pierre-Edouard was of his shadow of a moustache!

Brother and sister had a close relationship which allowed them to understand each other's feelings without speaking. They never quarrelled but always supported each other, uniting in adversity.

They excluded their little sister completely from their secret conversations —after all, she was only twelve, cried for no good reason, and was completely spoiled by her grandmother. Besides, Berthe often told on her older brother and sister, happily reporting their actions and movements, and more than once had got them into real trouble with their parents by doing so.

Jean-Edouard's anger was uncontrollable the moment he thought that someone was contesting his authority. He had submitted to his father until he was forty, and he intended to impose *his* will for as long as he could. He was head of the family, master of the land, the leader, who thought and acted for the Vialhe household, and no one ever questioned his decisions. So no one reacted when he announced, during supper on the evening of 23 April, the plan for the following day.

'I'm going to Brive tomorrow, it's market day.'

Louise glanced at her brother, requesting his help. She was dying to go to Brive with her father. She still did not know the town which her brother had talked about so often. He had all the luck!

Pierre-Edouard had already been to Brive twice with his father — once in 1904, for the onion market which took place in August, and another time for the 'King's Market', the most important one in the area, which took place each year in the week of Epiphany. And he had talked to his sister about all the splendours of the great city, and the marvels of the journey by train.

Best of all, he had had the luck to see petrol-driven cars motoring along during the journey; he jauntily assured her that he was not afraid of them! But she thought he was showing off a bit, because their father had also spoken of these encounters, with quite terrifying descriptions! He was sure that these machines would never come into the country, for the noise and the flames surrounding them would make the cows go dry, madden the sheep, and drive the pigs wild. Despite this, Louise was prepared to suffer these distressing experiences for the sake of finally getting to the great town.

'Please, father, may I go with you?' she ventured to ask.

'You stay here to help your mother and look after the livestock. Pierre-Edouard will accompany me!'

It was still pitch dark when they set out, and St Libéral lay silent and asleep. They had a good two hours' walk to the station at La Rivière-de-Mansac; the train passed there at 6.10, coming from Terrasson. It would get them to Brive three-quarters of an hour later, after connecting with the villages of Larche and St Pantaléon.

They were just reaching the last houses when a silhouette started out of an alleyway.

'Is that you, Léon?'

'Good morning, Monsieur Vialhe. Hi, Pierre!'

'You're going to the market at Brive?'

'That's right.'

'Well, we'll go along together.'

In contrast to Pierre-Edouard, who was still coasting through adolescence, Léon Dupeuch was a man, and few people realised that he was only eighteen. He was stocky and rugged, with a deep voice and a thick black moustache which accentuated his stern features. Through his confrontation with death at too young an age, he had acquired a cold look and the maturity and cynicism of an old man, mixed with harshness, icy humour and a curt manner.

After his father's death he had buried two of his sisters, one after the other. Tuberculosis, said the doctor; a curse, whispered the women, who remembered the mark Mathilde bore. This last child was not blind at all, contrary to all predictions; she was now a little scrap of a girl, five years old; the only person, they said, who knew how to make Léon laugh. He never forgot to bring her back some treat from each of his journeys.

Two years ago he had been taken on as a scout by a cattle-dealer from the village of Malemort, a place on the other side of Brive on the road to Tulle, as well as still keeping busy with the meagre smallholding belonging to the solicitor. His judgement was infallible. At a glance he could estimate to the pound the weight of a calf or cow on the hoof; although he had earlier been confused by calculations, he now knew what should be offered for an animal, almost to the centime.

His work consisted of hurrying among the lines of animals as soon as the bell announced that the market was open, to spot the beasts he wanted and to enquire the price. He immediately offered a much lower amount – or, worse still, shrugged his shoulders, disclaimed any interest in buying, and hurried towards other clients. In this way he gauged the mood of the market and the tenacity of the stockmen, and he had a marvellous knack of casting doubt into the minds of sellers.

Once he had finished his tour of the market he began the circuit again, still just as blasé, just as haughty, and on his heels came the buyer, more agreeable, more flexible and a tiny bit less mean. He was a faithful pilot fish for a shark in a blue overall, indicating by a secret look which prey seemed easy to take . . .

But he could also be a formidable seller when he offered a lot of heifers bought by his employer in Seilhac or Treignac, or bullocks acquired in Turenne. He haggled over every sou of the price, fought over each centime, and often displayed such strength of character that even his own employer admired him – and *he* was a real skinflint!

Léon was paid by the head – bought or sold – and made a good living, but he knew that the majority of the inhabitants of St Libéral saw him as a complete scoundrel. The farmers instinctively distrusted cattle-dealers, and that was what he was in the process of becoming. There was really absolutely no doubt that, the way he was going, he would be his own master within five years, for he had shown proof of his skills.

On top of that, many could not forgive him for still being an incorrigible poacher, just as he had been in his youth. Everyone knew that he was laying snares, but no one had ever been able to surprise him doing it. It was understood that he hunted without a licence, but to catch him red-handed . . . The village policeman and even the gendarmes from the Ayen force had all tried and failed!

Finally, everybody disapproved of his power over women – and in this particular matter his fame spread beyond the village. You could imagine that he fascinated them with his cold-blooded stare, like a viper. Certainly he was far from having as many conquests to his name as he was credited with, but there too he had a certain savoir-faire.

Strangely enough he had remained friends with Pierre-Edouard, though they seldom met; sometimes their paths crossed by chance, or, like this morning, they met on the same road. Then a sort of brotherly understanding revived between them, with a hint of mutual admiration – the younger admired his elder's experience, and the latter valued the cheerfulness and erudition of his friend. But both knew that the Vialhe parents would not have liked these chance conversations, however rare they might be.

They kept going at a good pace for an hour, and none of them considered it necessary to talk during that time. Jean-Edouard had nothing to say to this fellow Léon, whom he distrusted; Pierre-Edouard did not dare say the first word. As for Léon, he kept quiet, as was his custom. Nevertheless it was he who broke the silence.

'Tell me, Monsieur Vialhe, is it true, this story about the railway?'

'They're talking about it . . .'

For those whose business it was to talk about it *were* talking! Jean

53

Duroux took his role seriously, since he had been elected general councillor. It was thought that he was going to stand as candidate for the legislature. He let the rumour spread without confirming or denying it.

On the other hand he had got it into his head that the railway should pass through St Libéral, and he was doing everything possible to achieve this aim. He wanted the line leaving La-Rivière-de-Mansac to climb up to Brignac; from there it should ascend to Perpezac-le-Blanc, then reach St Libéral before turning away towards Ayen and Juillac. The villages it would pass were far from agreeing to this ambitious project; even before the route of the line had been settled, they were talking about woodlands cut in half, farms broken up and fields and pastures destroyed.

Cliques had formed, and even within the inner circle of the town council of St Libéral you could reckon with two factions. Antoine Gigoux himself hesitated over which party to join. He had recently been re-elected, and it was known that this would be his last term of office, but he wanted to finish in a dignified way so as not to damage his son's chances – it was no secret that he hoped for the succession.

As for Jean-Edouard, he was one of the warmest proponents of the project. If one day the railway came to the village, he would be able to consign to it all the fresh vegetables and fruit which he now had to deliver to the wholesale market at Objat. Moreover, he would be able to get to Brive or Tulle in a reasonable time. But he did not have very high hopes; politics was behind all that, everything depended on politics. Jean Duroux tried his best to keep in with the deputy, and even with the prefect, but no decision would be taken before the next electoral campaign, and it promised to be hotly contested!

Jean-Edouard often wondered when this stupid quarrel between Church and State would at last stop. He was fed up with being the target of both sides. The fact that he went to Mass three or four times a year earned him sarcastic comments from some of the anti-Church faction in the village – there were not many of them, but they grew increasingly vociferous – and his membership of the town council, which had a left-wing mayor, attracted public censure from Father Feix. He would not quickly forget the dreadful scene the priest had made when he had first been re-elected as vice-chairman.

'You're an ally of those barbarians and Freemasons! You approve of the dissolution of parishes! You're hounding poor monks who have been chased out of their monasteries! You are lining up with those who demand accounts from us, it's despicable! Your duty as a Christian is to resign!'

What the priest could not begin to understand was that Jean-Edouard, like the majority of men in the community, had very little interest in a quarrel which he didn't really understand. He did not feel concerned about the ins and outs of these laws, these decrees, these expulsions. From his point of view, none of it was worth fighting over. Besides, in the village there were only a few hardliners who tried, in vain, to whip up opinion against Father Feix. Apart from this handful of trouble-makers, no one wished the priest any harm at all. They knew he did his work well, that he was poor – he gave away all he received – and they respected him.

But he was asking for more, the poor man! He was calling the faithful to arms; he clamoured for their support, practically demanded that they loudly condemn the attitude of those up there in Paris who had the responsibility for governing the country.

It was really senseless; people had quite different things to worry about, and more serious ones too! They were not going to get mixed up in a dispute which hardly affected them, certainly not just to please him!

Of course, by means of sermons, visits and discussions, the priest had succeeded in convincing many women. And that, quite frankly, was displeasing! Jean-Edouard had been forced to speak severely to his own mother and even Marguerite, to stop them filling his ears with this rubbish. To make matters worse, he had recently had to put some idiot in his place, a silly ass who felt secure, surrounded by fellow drinkers on the terrace of Ma Eugenie's bistro, who thought it was clever to stand in his way and bray. He didn't play the donkey for long! Jean-Edouard had shot him into the middle of the road with a boot to his backside and once there, stretched him out for the count with a single backhander. All the same, he didn't want to have to lay hands on his wife to get some peace and quiet.

'Well, do you think it'll come, this railway?'

'You bet!'

'So then you'll pass your time scouring all the market places!'

'You have to look for the money where you can find it . . .'

'Maybe, but you're not going to get hold of mine!'

'Well, I'm showing a lot of beautiful heifers at the market. They're five months in calf, and I'm sure you'll find the one you're looking for among them,' countered Léon, solely for the purpose of discovering the reason for his neighbour's journey to Brive.

Jean-Edouard gave a quick laugh; what an obvious trap!

'You're still a bit young to catch me out! Keep your old goats, and spare your tongue too! Come on, walk faster, or we'll miss the train.'

The market was not yet open when they sat down at a table outside Gaillard's bistro, but Guierle Square was humming with a thousand sounds: the lowing of worried cows, the cries of calves separated from their mothers, the squeals of pigs, the shouts and oaths of men.

The bistro was directly opposite the market-place, and Jean-Edouard and his son noticed Léon, twenty paces away in the bay reserved for cattle merchants. He was busy with his animals, combing them, brushing their hair first one way and then the other, preparing them.

Jean-Edouard noted that they actually were very fine heifers. They were classic examples of the Limousin breed, well-covered, with plump hindquarters, and their light red coats shone from the damp brush Léon was wielding with energetic strokes.

These animals would be resold for at least 325 or 330 francs each, which really put them out of his reach. Besides, it was obvious that the beasts had been specially brought on – they hadn't put on all that meat by eating hay, more likely artichokes and barley-meal! They were in too fine fettle to be put out for the winter, as whoever bought them would soon find out . . . Put to grass, those heifers would lose twenty kilos in a month!

And finally, maybe they were in calf, but could you prove that it was five months? With those traders you could expect anything; they were ready to sell their mothers and fathers so long as they made a profit!

But if Jean-Edouard distrusted the cattle-dealers, he was even more suspicious of the salesmen for agricultural machinery. Confronted with the dealers he felt an equal, and was quite capable of detecting the faults and good points of a beast; the animals presented no difficulties for him, and he conducted negotiations without ever losing his grip on the situation. But the machinery salesmen had him at their mercy.

They were not offering a familiar commodity, but instruments with mysterious workings. Lacking technical knowledge, he had to accept as Gospel whatever they confidently asserted, for they were initiated into these mysteries.

Jean-Edouard knew nothing about these machines. If, for example, he did understand how the horse-driven threshing machine worked, the one the contractor brought to St Libéral each year in the high season, he was still incapable of starting it himself; even less of repairing it, should it break down. The same went for the mowing-machine he wanted to buy.

His choice had been made since the last King's Market. That day he had compared the models and prices at great length, but he knew his judgement was based on a few superficial details – colour, or the shape of the seats! – rather than on mechanical criteria. He was confused by the complexity of the machines; he felt vulnerable, and wary of the traps the salesmen might lure him in to.

Nevertheless, he forced himself to hide his worry and to stroll about. Followed by Pierre-Edouard, he sauntered through the machinery park, stopping in front of a vine-grower's cart, looking at a drill, fingering a harrow, to return eventually to the mowing-machine. He slowly walked all round it, pretending to be passionately interested in the crank-head, the pinions of the big gear wheel, or the blades of the cutting-bar.

'So, have you made up your mind this time?' asked the salesman, coming up to him. He recognised the customer who had questioned him for more than an hour at the last King's Market.

'Possibly . . .' admitted Jean-Edouard. 'But I would like to be sure that it cuts well, and won't break down . . .'

And what he had dreaded actually happened: the salesman immediately launched into a long and detailed explanation, loaded with technical terms and barbarous names.

'And look, with this gearing, the wheels drive the transmission shaft, on top of which is a disc-crank which, in turn, by the motion of the driving-rod, gives an alternating movement to the blade which slides along the cutting bar . . .'

Jean-Edouard nodded in agreement, and turned to his son.

'Do you understand?'

'Yes, it's not complicated,' declared Pierre-Edouard. He hesitated, a little frightened by his audacity, and asked: 'If you want to regulate the cutting height, how do you do that?'

'Quite simple,' the salesman was delighted to reply. 'You just have to operate the trimmer, here. Look, here, you have a screw which slides in this groove; with that you can raise or lower the blade.'

'And to take out the blade, you use that too?'

'That's right. I see you're mechanically minded.'

Pierre-Edouard blushed with pride. It was true that this machine fascinated him, and no less true that he understood perfectly how it functioned.

'And you say you could fit a board to it for the sheaves?' murmured Jean-Edouard, who felt excluded from the conversation.

'Yes,' explained the salesman, still addressing himself to Pierre-Edouard. 'Look, you fix the board here and hold it in the high position by means of this pedal; the stalks fall there. When you think the bundle is thick enough, you release the pedal, the board drops, the sheaf slips off and all the followers have to do is pick it up. But if you prefer, we have real reaping and binding machines,' he finished, turning to Jean-Edouard.

'No, no, that would definitely be too expensive for us. Even your mowing machine . . . How much does it come to now?'

'The same price as last time, three hundred and sixty-five francs.'

'It's much too expensive!' declared Jean-Edouard.

'Not at all; it's *not* expensive! You have here one of the best machines currently available! We pride ourselves on several decades of experience, and have won the premier prizes in all the exhibitions of Europe and America! Just ask around, everyone will tell you that the McCormick reapers are the champions.'

'Sure! You sell them, you're not going to tell me anything different! Come on, give me fifteen francs off and we can go on talking, okay?'

'Impossible, I'd lose by it!'

'Go on,' persisted Jean-Edouard. 'Fifteen francs, what's that to you!'

He felt at home again. Now that it was a question of price rather than mechanics he could fight on equal terms, and he made the most of it. He knew that the dealer would not lower his price, but he was sure he could get some other concessions.

The discussions became long and bitter, and threatened to break down. Jean-Edouard was encouraged by a group which had formed around him, and felt honour-bound to beat the salesman down. But the latter knew that his reputation was at stake. At last the moment arrived when Jean-Edouard sensed that his opponent would not give ground in front of witnesses.

'Good, let's go and settle it over a glass,' he said wearily. 'And you, you wait there for me,' he threw at his son.

He returned a quarter of an hour later, and Pierre-Edouard knew straight away that he had won.

'Well there it is,' said his father, in high spirits. 'She's costing me dear, but I got him to give me a spare blade. Also, he's going to deliver it to the house, and then he'll show me how to start it. And to top off the bargain, he's giving me two litres of oil for the gears! You see, you must always bargain. Now, this machine, is it true that you understand how it works?'

'Yes. You know, it's not at all complicated.'

'Obviously!' replied Jean-Edouard. He was firmly convinced it was very complicated, but there was no need for his son to know that.

There was a crowd to watch the machine working, one month later. Almost all the men of the village, and some of the women too, were squeezed together along the edge of one of the Vialhes' meadows, not wanting to miss a single moment of the show.

Once more, the salesman turned to Pierre-Edouard with the necessary explanations. The young man listened to chapter and verse, made him repeat several details, mentioned some of the problems which could arise – like meeting a mole-hill or scraping the blade badly – and hoisted himself into the seat. He was confident, but still felt very excited. He looked at his father, whose job it was to lead the animals.

Jean-Edouard stood firm between the two cows, the goad under his arm; he gave an appearance of calm which he was far from feeling. He was worried that some incident might make him appear ridiculous in everyone's eyes. He knew that his purchase had inspired jealousy. Some of the men, especially the older ones, were convinced that this engine could never produce such good work as a scythe in expert hands; others insinuated that the grass would not regrow so well after a machine had been over it.

It was all nonsense; they had said virtually the same things when he had spread the first phosphate fertiliser – some of them had even predicted that he would scorch all his land with it. He knew that the reaper did good work; he had seen two of them in operation on the plain at Larche, and had been able to judge the quality of the cut. But it remained to be proved to the sceptics that he, Jean-Edouard Vialhe, could do just as well as the big landowners on the plain. He looked questioningly at his son, and saw that he was ready. Taking a step forward he called to the animals.

The experiment would have been a disaster if it had not been for his great experience with cattle. The team panicked at the un-accustomed noise clacking away at their backs, and almost bolted; it was only by pressing against the cows' horns and calming them with his voice that he succeeded in controlling them.

As for Pierre-Edouard, he did not turn a hair, but simply knocked the big tufts of grass out of the way with his whip; if they were cut too fast, the blade was in danger of getting jammed.

Gradually, the animals slowed down as they got used to the noise; at last they found the right pace. Behind the reaper appeared a long ribbon of cut grass jumping with grasshoppers.

Jean-Edouard went up to the end of the meadow and stopped the animals. Already the curious neighbours were swarming along the break opened by the cutter, and all they could do was nod in admiration and exclaim in astonishment. Followed by his son, he walked along it in his turn to inspect the work.

What a marvel! A regular cut, flush with the ground, one metre-twenty wide; a long swathe cut in a few moments which a good scytheman could not have lined up in less than twenty minutes!

He looked at his neighbours, and knew that his demonstration had succeeded. Even his fiercest critics, those who had been poking fun and nudging each other three minutes earlier, were won over, convinced; they all knew, consciously or otherwise, that they had been present at a great event. From now on, thanks to machines of this sort, the work on the land would never be the same.

'Well,' asked the salesman, advancing towards Jean-Edouard, 'are you satisfied? Is that all right?'

'Yes indeed! You'd have to be hard to please not to like it!'

'Say,' added the dealer, lowering his voice, 'if by any chance you have the slightest problem, let me know straight away. Yes,' he insisted, as he saw Jean-Edouard's look of astonishment, 'two or three of your neighbours are interested in this reaper, and I think . . . Well, your machine should be a credit to the brand name, okay?'

'You don't waste much time, do you?'

'Say what you like, agricultural equipment's the future. The time will come when you won't be able to do a thing without it.'

'That would surprise me, the price you're selling it at!'

'You'll see, you'll see . . . Good – anyway, when you next come to Brive, drop in and see me. I'll give you a few blade sections, and a set of cogs to replace any that might get broken on the stones.'

'You'll *give* them to me?'

'But of course! I tell you, I want this reaper to go like clockwork. You're the first buyer in this area, I owe you that.'

Jean-Edouard nodded his head. Yes, once more he was the first in the area. By using fertiliser he had already amazed everyone. Today he had raised himself to the ranks of the leaders in farming, thanks to this machine, and he would have to do everything to keep that position.

'Okay,' he said. 'I'll keep an eye on it.'

'And above all, listen to what your son says. He has a feel for machinery, that lad.'

'I know,' cut in Jean-Edouard, somewhat drily. 'But as you say, he's only a lad.'

# 6

PIERRE-EDOUARD set the plough down sideways on the headland, the strip left at the end for turning; stopped the animals with a word, and looked back. He could be proud of his work. He had begun ploughing the morning before and the field of nut trees looked good. The furrows were perfectly straight and of even depth, worthy of a master ploughman, and Pierre-Edouard knew his father would be satisfied, even if he wouldn't say anything.

The field was really superb and rich with promise: the rows of young trees were encircled by a shining brown wave of ploughed soil. One day, in twenty years' time, it would be a fertile plantation where you could pick walnuts by the cartload.

'Are you dreaming?' called out Louise, who was spreading manure thirty paces from him.

He shrugged, and moved towards her.

'If you won't let me take a breather, at least let the beasts have a rest!'

'I'd like to get back down before nightfall, that's all.'

'Oh yes, and I know why,' he said teasingly. 'But if father found out about it . . .'

'So what, I'm not doing anything wrong!'

He shook his head with a knowing look and returned to his team. At his command the animals turned on the headland, lined themselves up on the unploughed land, and resumed their slow march. They knew Pierre-Edouard well: for several months it had been he who had commanded them.

His father's time was more and more taken up by municipal responsibilities; since a good number of the local inhabitants seemed to have gone mad, someone had to try to make them see reason. And this had been going on for more than a year, since September 1906 to be exact.

From the beginning of the electoral campaign, the deputy standing for re-election had taken over the planning of the railway track as if it were his idea, cutting the ground from beneath Jean Duroux's feet. The squire, a good sport, had supported him, weighing in with all his influence as a general councillor to bring the plan to fruition, but it was whispered that he had retired from the electoral contest on the promise of a seat on the senate . . .

Once re-elected, the deputy had to put his promises into action, show that he was a man of his word, and since then, the village had been in a fever of excitement. The critical mission of talking round the opponents of the scheme had fallen to Jean-Edouard, who also had to control the absurd demands of the landowners affected by the route of the railway, and keep them within reasonable limits. This thankless task made him more enemies than friends.

Already the 'anti-train' lobby had completely broken off negotiations; they maintained that the railway, and especially the navvies and the railway yard which would come with it, would corrupt the whole community. Several older people were of this opinion, including a handful of women cunningly indoctrinated by the priest – who was to be pitied, for it was obvious that he was campaigning for a lost cause.

A final quarrel had taken place between Father Feix and Jean-Edouard in December 1905, when the priest, devastated at the separation of Church and State, had rushed to Jean-Edouard to demand his resignation. He was beside himself with rage, and had gone so far as to say that all those who supported this government, whatever their status, were liable to be excommunicated. Jean-Edouard had shown him the door. Since then neither he nor his son had set foot in the village church, and to make their point they had since celebrated Easter at Yssandon or Perpezac. But the priest and his little band of allies hardly bothered Jean-Edouard. They did not own any land affected by the line, and so offered only verbal opposition.

In contrast, almost all the landowners affected by the route were fighting a fierce campaign to secure the maximum compensation. Moreover, they had succeeded in getting the whole area on their side by appearing to show that they were fighting for the good of everyone, and that if they gave in, nobody would have any protection from the designs of private companies.

During the preceding spring the company had sent one of the engineers to obtain their permission. The poor fellow had not managed to get a single signature! It might have been possible to initiate procedures for compulsory purchase, but the outcome was uncertain; moreover, this could take years, constantly delayed by litigants who would enjoy running from one law court to another.

To crown it all, the general mood of the country was frankly hostile at the beginning of the year, which led the authorities to proceed with extreme caution. The whole wine-growing area of the Midi was in turmoil, and nothing should be done to inflame tempers and to incite the people of Corrèze to imitate the Midi. Certainly the farmers of Perpezac, St Libéral or Ayen had no real reason for espousing the wine-growers' cause. The battle being fought further south was not theirs, and they had very little in common with the wine-growers, but you had to reckon with a tendency to revolt which lay dormant in every countryman. It was therefore important to proceed with caution.

To avoid all risk of discontent, the company changed its tactics and brought its alternative plan into effect. The original route had the merit of being the shortest and most logical, but the inconvenience of running slap into this block of landowners; so they threw that in the bin and decided, with the agreement of the Ministry of Bridges and Roads, simply to follow the lane which already curved between all the towns and villages the railway wished to reach. It was much further in kilometres and involved some ridiculous bends, but when the sums were done, it worked out less expensive than the inflated compensation which the rebellious landowners demanded.

There remained one difficulty; the road was not wide enough. They would have to increase its breadth by several metres, and to do that they would once more have to win over the wayside landowners. These proprietors were not in such a strong position, and could not count on popular support. They could not decently invoke the sacred rights of ownership, nor complain of their fields being divided; the road had passed that way for centuries, and no one had ever complained of any inconvenience from it. Nevertheless, someone had to persuade them to give up the few square metres needed to put down the rails.

The company, on its guard after the first setback, asked each commune concerned to appoint a mediator to be responsible for collecting signatures. So it was that Jean-Edouard, accompanied by an engineer and a surveyor, launched into the campaign for authorisation.

Here there was opposition from a quarrelsome fellow who refused to let them cut down a couple of stunted oaks or three crooked chestnut trees, there an indignant farmer deprived of a metre and a half of grazing; elsewhere the protests of workers who stood to lose the tip of a vegetable plot, or half a row of vines.

Jean-Edouard had to reassure each one that compensation would be paid, and that it would not be trifling. Often the engineer and surveyor had to take measurements and put in poles to show exactly where the route would pass, to demonstrate it more clearly than on the paper plan; so once again it was a long, troublesome business.

In more than six months, not a week had passed without the engineer arriving to fetch Jean-Edouard so that he could smooth out some disputed point. However, these trials were coming to an end; almost all the landowners had now signed, and the two or three stubborn ones who needed a lot of coaxing would eventually give in too.

Already, teams of specialists were marking out the ground plan. If all went well, the building-yard would open before the end of the year.

Pierre-Edouard stuck his whip in the ground, slipped between the cows, which were damp with sweat, and unhitched his plough. Night was coming on, and it was high time to go down and take care of the animals. Today his father had again gone off, grumbling, to try to overcome old Treilhard's resistance; he was refusing to let the track cross his land on the pretext that it would cut him off from a spring, which was pure invention. Pierre-Edouard knew full well that if his father had the misfortune to suffer another setback, the slightest delay or smallest mistake would cloud his temper. Even at eighteen, he still dreaded a parental scene. The era of slaps or the belt had passed, but the bitter comments which had taken their place were not to the young man's taste.

For the moment he accepted the criticisms without comment, even if they were unjust, but he had a feeling that the day would come when he would stand up to his father. Already he was as tall as his father and almost as strong, but he still confined himself to passive defence; the more Jean-Edouard raised his voice, the more he kept quiet.

Louise did not hesitate to answer back, but all she usually gained from it was a couple of smacks. As for Berthe, she was still a sly one, with a marvellous knack of diverting her father's or mother's admonishments towards her older brother and sister.

He moved to the animals' heads and set off down the path to the village. Despite his good advice, Louise had already left half an hour ago. He was worried about her. He loved her dearly, and for several months had been seriously troubled on her account; but she did what she wanted!

Louise pushed the rebellious lock of brown hair back under her scarf; it was always escaping and falling in her eyes. She patted her dress to brush off a few stalks of hay, confirmed that her clogs were clean, grasped the can of milk and went out.

She climbed back up the main street and crossed the square. Already her heart was pounding and her mouth was dry. She pushed open the door of the inn and went in. He was there, as he had been every evening for the last six months.

'Well, little Louise, always on time!' teased the innkeeper's wife. She agreed with a smile.

Every evening held the same fascination. She would go in, hold out the milk, and she had less than two minutes to look at him. She watched him in the big mirror which decorated the corner of the room behind the bar. She could see him between a bottle of gentian bitters and a flagon of plum brandy.

He was always there, moving slowly around the billiard table; calculating his shots, thinking, hesitating, and then playing. She guessed whether he had won the point or not from the sound of the balls.

Tall, slim and well-dressed, he smoked small cigars, which he raised to his lips with a charming air of refinement, allowing her to admire his hand, a delicate white hand with long supple fingers and immaculate nails. Sometimes he gently stroked his small black moustache with his forefinger, especially when he was considering which combination to play. His face was then tense with concentration and his dark stare became more definite, more penetrating beneath his folded lids.

One evening his eyes were attracted to the mirror and met hers; the memory of this meeting still made her blush every time she thought of it.

She knew everything about him. She had gleaned her information here and there, with the patience and care of a spider, and she guarded it like a treasure. He was an assistant surveyor and had been lodging at the inn for six months. It was he who often came with the engineer to fetch her father to win over an opponent. It was he who was now busy marking out the line.

From her father she had learned his name, Octave Flaviens, and his age, twenty-five. From the innkeeper's wife she knew where he came from: a town in the north, Orléans. From one of the servants she discovered all his favourite dishes; he didn't like leeks but adored creamed carrots! Thanks to the second servant, who looked after the bedrooms, she knew that he read *Le Petit Parisien*, and big books as well; that he received very little post and, unlike many others, had never tried to kiss her. If he had, Louise would have forgiven him and slapped the little slut!

Yes, she knew all about him. She lived with him, breathed in time with him, walked in his footsteps, slept with him. But she had never spoken a word to him, and was nowhere near doing even that!

It was enough to come each evening to deliver the milk, to open the door and see him.

Jean-Edouard dipped the ladle into the soup tureen and made a sign that they should pass their plates up. He filled them and then looked at his mother.

'And father?'

'That's all right, he's already eaten.'

Old Edouard was steadily losing strength and rarely left his bed now. But occasionally he had a fancy to sit by the fireside or, if it was fine, in the sun outside the door. Then he was supported as far as the settle or the bench where he remained, murmuring and sighing, feebly moving his huge hands which were now useless, quite deformed and stiffened by arthritis. He did not complain; he was waiting.

'Did old Treilhard sign?' asked Marguerite.

'Yes, but what a cunning old fox he is! He wanted to make me believe he was being cut off from his spring!! What a joke, the spring's on the other side! All the same, if I hadn't been there he would have fooled the engineer and his spear-carrier!'

Louise trembled; she hated her father speaking of Octave like that. Octave was *not* a spear-carrier; he was an assistant surveyor, a professional! But her father always appeared to be making fun of him. He probably found him too distinguished, too handsome.

'If he's conceded, is it finished, can the line go through?'

'Yes; the Deschamps and the Moulys have signed as well, they were the last.'

'So you don't need to get involved in it any more?'

'No.'

'All the same, the mayor can't hold a candle to you! Basically, you've done his work!'

'Better that job than the one that's coming. From now on, I just wish them luck . . .'

'And who'll deal with it?'

He made a dismissive gesture and did not reply. He had completed his task, and was satisfied that he had managed it well, but he knew that many held a grudge against him. He was accused of betraying the country folk by siding with the company. Some people would never believe that he had not been paid an inflated price for the few square metres which he, too, had been forced to give up. Of course it was not true; he had received no more than his due. But that did not prevent malicious tongues from insinuating that he had banked a small fortune!

He knew all the lies that were being told behind his back. From now on he would have to take a back seat for the sake of some peace, let his part be forgotten, and let the other members of the town council worry about the problems. And there would be plenty of them!

Now that the work could begin, the urgent business was to lodge and feed the dozens of workers who would occupy the town – it was said there would be more than a hundred! Dormitories, canteens and bars would have to be provided. All that would bring a lot of money into the community, but also a lot of trouble for those in charge of organising it.

Already, before anything had been decided, Jean-Edouard knew that the mayor was being accused of favouritism. One of the carpenters in St Libéral was his brother-in-law, and it was whispered that he had exclusive rights to the work. Other rumours insisted that if the station was sited next to the bar and grocery store belonging to the Delmonds, that was because their cousin Gaston was a member of the town council . . .

All this was idle gossip, but Jean-Edouard knew that some people were taking advantage of the situation, and that this malicious nonsense would leave its scars. If he wanted to follow Antoine Gigoux as Mayor one day – as time passed, he became more and more convinced that Gigoux's son, who also wanted the office, was a total pudding-brain – he would have to drop into the background for a while; devote his time to his farm and the syndicate and nothing else. The day would come when everyone would feel the benefit of the train and he would be thanked for playing the role of mediator who had made the route possible. On the other hand, they would find it more difficult to forgive allegedly corrupt officials, and even the most scrupulous administrators would have great difficulty in ridding themselves of that defamatory label.

He cut himself a thick slice from the ham, then pushed it back into the middle of the table.

'You say you'll be finished by tomorrow night?' he asked his son.

'Definitely.'

'Good, then while you're finishing the ploughing, I'll do the sowing. Is the drill up there?'

'Yes.'

'You, you'll come with me,' he decided, looking at Louise. 'We'll take Grey and Saddleback, it will do them good.'

Besides the two old working cows, Red and Ribbon, they had trained a pair of young animals. They were strong and very hardy but still a bit lively, too nervous and fearful to plough comfortably. Grey especially was wayward, like a goat; she sometimes tried to go off on her own, forgetting the yoke – as strong as an ox, she would side-step a metre or two, pulling her companion with her. She was not yet ready for the plough, which demanded a perfectly regular and straight walk. On the other hand, a day pulling the drill would calm her, accustom her to his voice and signals.

'Saddleback is missing a shoe,' warned Pierre-Edouard.

'My God, couldn't you have told me earlier?'

'I told you when she lost it, last week.'

'You told me! You told me!' shouted Jean-Edouard . . . Yes, now he remembered, and was furious at having forgotten. 'And now what? Why didn't you take her to be re-shod? I have to tell you everything! Huh, if I'd worked like that for my father!'

Pierre-Edouard held his peace. He was not in the wrong, and knew it; it was not his job to decide when to take the animal to the smithy. He had done his duty by warning his father; the rest was not his business.

'All right,' conceded Jean-Edouard, 'we'll go and get her shod at daybreak. Bloody hell! It's a bit rough when I have to think of everything round here!'

Jean-Edouard snuffed out the candle and slipped between the sheets, which were already stiff with cold; the temperature was already so low, for mid-November, that a severe winter was expected. He crept towards his wife, appreciating her warmth. Marguerite murmured a little as she felt her husband's icy feet against her calves, and really shivered when he hugged her.

'Are you asleep?'

'No.'

They were obliged to whisper in each other's ears to prevent the two girls hearing their conversation. The house only had two bedrooms, a communal living room, and a loft. When Pierre-Edouard was fourteen they had to give him a corner of his own; it was not proper to let him continue to sleep in the same room as his sisters and parents. So he had his bed in the living room; the grandparents had the first bedroom, Jean-Edouard, Marguerite and the two girls the second. A screen separated the beds, but it was not enough to stop sounds travelling.

Jean-Edouard continued to feel cold, however much he pressed against his wife, who was snuggled up in a ball.

'You know,' he said, 'I'm glad to have finished with all that business of the signatures. Are you listening to me?'

'Yes, yes.'

'Now all we have to do is wait and prepare ourselves . . .'

'Yes . . . Tell me, do you really think there will be so many people?'

'Perhaps even more! Believe me, it will bring fantastic opportunities, and it will last! Just consider – we're in a position halfway between La Rivière and Ayen; all the workmen on the track will gather here, and for a long time!'

'How long?'

'The engineer told me we could count on two years. According to him, the line should be open at the end of 1909. Trust me, it'll bring prosperity to everyone with a bit of go. If we get busy, we can make any amount of money – and honestly. Money no one can begrudge us. We'll give Louise a proper dowry and find her a good match. I'd be pleased with a fellow like Léonard Bouyssoux.'

'The Bouyssoux from the Heath?'

'Yes.'

'He's old . . .'

'No he isn't! He's not even thirty. Best of all, he's an only son, and Heath Farm is magnificent . . . Well, we'll talk about it later.'

'I'd have thought he was older than that.'

'And so what! I was a good twenty-eight and you hardly eighteen when we got married, and it's good, isn't it?'

'With us, it wasn't the same. And you say we should sow at least twenty strips of potatoes?'

'Yes, and haricot beans, broad beans and cabbage, and you must raise as many chickens and hens as you can, and then I'll buy two extra sows . . .'

'And are you sure you can sell all that to the men on the line?'

'Yes.'

'You're really sure?' she persisted.

It was his secret; he had not talked to anyone about it and still did not want to reveal it, even to his wife. One day, when accompanying the engineer to La-Rivière-de-Mansac, he had made the acquaintance of the steward who worked for the company, a man burdened with the taxing job of feeding an army of famished labourers every day.

He had quickly seen how he could turn this meeting to his own advantage. A man who had so many stomachs to satisfy must always be on the look-out for assorted supplies. Jean-Edouard tested the water.

'And where do you buy your produce – let's say vegetables, for instance?'

'Where I can find them, mon ami! And it's not always easy, believe me, I have to chase around! A ton of tatties here, five hundredweight of beans there – if you knew the time it takes me! Look, when I began to work for the railway building-yards, in the '90s, I started on the section of the main line between Uzerche and Brive. Well, believe it or not, I had to get potatoes sent from the Seine area! Yes, no means of making my living from thereabouts, unless I spent all my days traipsing round the farms!'

Jean-Edouard listened, fascinated.

'If you like, I'll provide them for you, the tatties . . .'

'And why not!'

'You'd take several tons?'

'Of course!'

'And beans?'

'Everything that's edible and not too expensive.'

'So cabbage, too?'

'Naturally.'

'And meat?'

'Yes, pigs or barren cows.'

He could hardly believe his ears. It was providence that had set this man in his path!

'Do you really mean it?' he persisted.

'It's as real as the train that's coming through your way.'

'Let's shake on it. I'll grow it and you buy it.'

'Mind you, I buy at wholesale prices.'

'Understood.'

'Well, let's shake on it, then.'

Their hands had touched; that was worth the same as a signature.

Since then he had been designing his plan of cultivation. The fellow wanted provisions? He should have them!

'Answer me,' repeated Marguerite, turning to him. 'You're sure we're not going to grow all that for nothing?'

'I know what I'm doing!'

He placed his broad hand on his wife's hip and pulled her towards him.

'We could never manage to hoe and weed all that,' she insisted, 'and to lift all the potatoes, think about that too?'

'Don't worry,' he said, tightening his embrace.

# PART TWO

*The House Divided*

# 7

THE opening of the railway construction yard turned life in the village upside down, to the jubilation of its opponents. But revenge had a bitter taste for Father Feix and his few sympathisers; what use was it to have predicted all the disasters which were now unleashed on St Libéral? What good to say 'I told you so!', for the enemy was within!

It had come in the form of more than a hundred workers, whom the community were responsible for housing. And as soon as dormitories and canteens had been built on the edge of the village, they were literally swamped every evening by a motley crowd of bellowing and bellicose men divided by region or race: Italian navvies, men from Brittany and the Auvergne to place the sleepers and carry the rails, team leaders from Paris or Lyons. Added to these main groups were a certain number of men taken on locally; also two Poles accompanied by a woman – they lodged, all three together, in a sort of shepherd's caravan – and finally a huge Senegalese, who terrified the children.

As soon as they finished work, this whole mass took over the two bistros in St Libéral, invaded the bar at the inn, laid siege to the shops, fought, got drunk, whistled and called after the women and girls, and created a shocking din until the early hours.

Saturday nights were the worst; the village belonged to the newcomers, and the young people from round about were virtually barred from the dances at the inn.

The Chanlat couple, hustled and barracked, overcome by the activities and the arrogance of the strangers, resigned themselves to seeing their establishment turned into a dance-hall. Some of the Parisians made fun of the hurdy-gurdy and barrel-organ, and told them bluntly that these were as dated as ox-drawn carts; they should keep up with the times. The old folk-dances gave way to the fashionable *java*.

But although a whole host of men wanted to dance, there were not enough partners for them. There was no question of the local girls sullying themselves with the strangers; only a few not very respectable women of doubtful reputation were content to be passed from arm to arm – like Ma Eugenie, whose bed never had time to cool down! Added to these four or five hussies were the two inn servants and the Polish woman who, they quickly discovered, was the sister of the two jabberers, and the consoler of all the unmarried men. That was definitely too few women for the hundred lively fellows quartered at St Libéral, and even if a certain number of them sometimes went down to Brive or Terrasson on a spree, there were still too many left without dancing partners. It was unusual for the dances to end without fisticuffs.

The village policeman was completely powerless – and also extremely angry, since four laughing Italians had dispatched him, little drum and all, into the middle of the village wash tank. He warned the mayor that henceforth he would not set foot outside his house after six o'clock in the evening. The village therefore became accustomed to regular visits from two policeman from the Ayen force. They arrived at a trot, let themselves be seen, paraded about the square, let their mounts have a breather, inquired of Antoine Gigoux how things were going, and then went home again. But they were never there on Saturday evenings, about ten o'clock, when the first blows were struck in the big hall of the inn or outside in the square.

To this constant din, the brawling and shouting that disturbed the life of St Libéral, was added another no less serious scourge. The workmen had hardly been there a week when not a single hen was safe outside a firmly shut henhouse guarded by dogs! Usually all the hens were left free to peck around outside the buildings, and so the farmers' wives blamed foxes for the first disappearances, but they quickly realised that these thieves had broad shoulders – unless Reynard had lost two paws and learnt Italian . . .

Their raids made huge gaps in the winged tribes of the region; even geese and turkeys disappeared without trace. The band of Italians –with a good percentage of French mixed in – were very well organised, and did not stop until they had cleaned up everything. These vultures even managed to wipe out all the guinea-fowl, a very shy bird, by trapping them like partridges, either by laying snares or with vicious hooks concealed in a piece of cooked potato!

The people of the community, disheartened by such an accumulation of irritations, at first avoided all contact with the invaders; many regretted having opted for the railway-line. But very soon many also realised the benefits they could derive from this mass of consumers. Of course, the workers had their canteens, but they

76

were not above supplementing their normal fare; their fowling raids were proof of that.

By tacit but unanimous agreement, there was a sudden rise in prices. A dozen eggs jumped to one franc forty, a litre of wine to seventy centimes, and a bottle of plum-brandy was worth up to four francs. To make up for their losses from pilfering, the farmers' wives offered a pair of young chickens at six francs, and demanded the same price for a couple of ducks. Thus, as Jean-Edouard had thought, everyone profited from the railway-yard; but for a long time he remained the only one to have planned ahead on a grand enough scale to transform a small business into a great enterprise.

Since the village had been taken over every evening by workers in festive spirits, there was no question of Louise going to deliver the milk to the inn. For now the inn overflowed with drinkers; their salacious comments, not to mention evil propositions, prevented any nice girl from going near the place. Certainly she was prepared to brazen it out and shut her ears for the sole joy of looking at the handsome Octave Flaviens for a brief moment, but she had to accept her mother's decision and allow Pierre-Edouard to replace her.

She did not even attempt to plead her cause, certain that to persist would arouse suspicion. It was, of course, impossible to breathe a word to her parents of the emotions which this young man had awakened. She had therefore to show extreme prudence, without which, she knew, the drama could become a tragedy. The Vialhe household were not about to allow a chit of seventeen to fall head over heels in love with a stranger, an outsider!

Naturally, Pierre-Edouard had known for a long time what was going on, but he had never spoken to her openly about it; he simply let her know by a few remarks that he was not deceived. But he would keep quiet; and she was not worried about him. On the other hand she distrusted Berthe; the little one had a sharp eye and a mind quick enough to interpret the slightest sigh.

Curiously, although Louise had remained an adolescent for a long time, as though her body were tentatively searching out the most beautiful shapes, Berthe became a woman in a few months, and only her childish behaviour betrayed her fifteen years. She had already been whistled at by several of the louts who hung about the main street even in broad daylight.

Louise merited such demonstrations of admiration too but, unlike Berthe, she took no pride in being noticed. Her beauty, style and daintiness were not for street fowl: they could peck around beneath her feet, they did not exist. Only Octave counted.

She continued to love him with a silent and patient love. A love which grew stronger and more idealised day by day, until she convinced herself that it was too great, too beautiful, too pure not to be returned! She could not imagine that the young man could be indifferent to her attention; no, he remained silent and reserved out of discretion.

She was convinced that he was suffering as much as she was from their separation, and she was deeply affected when it became impossible to see him every day. She lived through a dreadful week while she pondered the best means of re-establishing their meetings. At the same time she undertook a novena to seek aid from Saint Eutrope, the patron saint of the parish.

The saint heard her — at least Louise believed so — for the innkeeper's wife let it be known that she would prefer to receive her milk in the morning than the evening. Louise saw in this a sign from heaven, a sort of miracle; God was blessing her love! In fact, Madame Chanlat was monopolised every evening by the swarms of drinkers, and had no time to deal with the milk. Swept along by a whirlwind of glasses to rinse, beermugs to fill, measures of rum to pour, she forgot to boil the milk two evenings in a row; it curdled and had to be given to the dogs. So she wanted to have it in the morning. At dawn the inn was peaceful; only the customers who slept at the establishment breakfasted quietly in the corner.

Louise cleverly questioned the servant, found out what time Octave ate, and suggested to her mother, quite innocently, that she should save Pierre-Edouard the trouble of delivering. Marguerite saw no objection to letting her take over the job again at that time of day.

With her heart thumping, quite pink and glowing with happiness, Louise pushed open the door of the inn, went in, and almost let go of the milk-can. He was there! He was no longer far away at the other end of the room, in the corner by the billiard table, but there, standing at the bar. Alone, completely alone in the huge saloon, he was breakfasting off a bowl of coffee into which he dipped a slice of buttered bread as big as a hand.

They looked at each other intensely for several seconds and she knew, quite definitely, that he was pleased to see her again. She searched for something to say, found nothing, and simply nodded to him.

Then he spoke. He did it with such ease, so naturally, that she felt all her shyness evaporate. They spoke to each other from the first as if they had always known each other, as if they were continuing a conversation which had started months ago.

'Well, Mademoiselle Louise, so you've come back to see us at last? Do you know that I missed your evening visits very much?'

'I did too, but . . .'

'Yes, I know; from six o'clock on, this inn turns into a real slum; you're right to avoid it. Your father is well, then?'

'Very well, thank you.'

He nodded, drank a mouthful of coffee, and glanced in the direction of the kitchen to make sure they were still alone.

'Tell me,' he continued, lowering his voice, 'don't you think this is a funny way to do things? It's good to see each other for two minutes a day, but wouldn't you like to meet somewhere quieter? I'm sure we've got lots to say to each other . . .'

'Of course . . .' she murmured, suddenly frightened by the speed with which this first real meeting had developed. Accustomed to being quiet, to waiting, she felt herself at a loss, out of her depth. Even in her wildest dreams she had never dared to imagine she would one day experience such an adventure.

'What are you afraid of?' he persisted, 'your parents? They wouldn't stop you from talking, surely?'

'That depends who to . . . And they would never want me to meet you, I know that.'

'Well, they won't find out about it, so there!'

'Listen,' she suddenly decided, 'every afternoon, I look after the animals on Combes-Nègres, there . . .'

He considered this, then smiled. Since he had been doing the surveys for the line he knew the village inside out.

'Yes, I know, that's the meadow on the slope just beyond the path down to the mill; the stream flows through it.'

'That's it,' she whispered. 'Look out, here's Madame . . .'

'Oh, Louise! Have you been here long?' asked Madame Chanlat as she came into the saloon.

'No, no, just arrived this minute,' Louise assured her without turning a hair.

She forced herself not to look at Octave, to feign complete indifference. She somehow knew that from now on she would have to hide this intrigue, to lie, to deceive, to pretend, all day long.

Pierre-Edouard straightened up, leant on his hoe and breathed out. He was aching all over. Despite that, he was still a good fifteen metres ahead of his father. He turned his tool upside down, stuck the handle in the earth, rested his behind on the flat steel and rolled a cigarette.

He and his father had begun hoeing the potatoes three days ago, and already the first rows looked different; the tops of the plants were magnificent, rich, a deep green. You felt they were full of life, but two hectares, that was really an awful lot of hoeing! And as if that were the only task to be completed! No – besides this huge area laid down to potatoes, his father had also planted out innumerable leeks, cabbages, lettuces and onions, sown interminable lines of carrots, broad beans and haricot beans, four strips of lentils and the same of turnips!

Almost all the land on the plateau was planted with crops like these, as well as their field called The Gardens, on the slope by the village. Only the Long Piece and the Big Field were given over to cereals. At least those did not require any work, for the moment . . . But the rest! He would not forget this spring in a hurry.

The outstanding event, the one he would always remember, was that Saturday in May when he came of age. From now on he was eligible for military service, and he was proud of it.

This promotion helped to dim the haunting memory of the ridiculous exhibition he had been forced to make of himself. He saw himself once again in the great hall of the Mairie in Ayen, just as naive and awkward as Jacques Bessat, Edmond Vergne and his other friends from the village. They were all even more frightened than they had been on the day they had sat their examination together.

'Right,' Jacques Bessat had cried, unbuttoning his shirt. 'After all, they can't cut them off.'

But his heart was not in it, and his remark only raised a few thin giggles among the dozens of young men crowded in there.

'Get on with it! Are you scared of catching cold?' bellowed the fat, apoplectic warrant-officer.

'Have you seen his ugly mug, looks just like my backside!' came an anonymous whisper. 'If he keeps still, we won't be able to find him among all our bums!'

This joke corresponded exactly to their image of military life and galvanised them: they larked around and teased each other as they undressed. But once they were naked they all looked at each other with a false air of confidence; none of them dared to check openly, by comparing, whether or not their organs seemed a normal size and shape. And they did not know what to do with their hands.

They were weighed, measured, examined, questioned. Pierre-Edouard had filed in front of the authorities, shown his feet (not at all flat) and his teeth (in good condition). He had also stated, and proved, that he knew how to read, write and count, and that he had his school certificate. He noticed that the mention of this diploma resulted in a satisfied nod from the non-commissioned officer who was making notes.

He heard himself declared fit for service, dressed again in a hurry and at last found himself outside, where he was set upon by the pedlars of cockades and ribbons, of fanciful military-style caps and paper flags. Already Jacques Bessat and Edmond Vergne were decked in various bits and pieces, and shouting some ribald song to which they only knew half the words. No matter, their hearts were in it!

Then they joined a group of happy conscripts, squeezed into an enormous cart hired for the occasion, and rattled off in the direction of Tulle; a bottle mysteriously appeared from nowhere and circulated from mouth to mouth.

They disembarked outside the préfecture during the course of the afternoon and, still bawling, began a tour of the bars. Later, after quite a few glasses, they arrived at the door of a brothel and entered it as an occupying force; to see what they could see! But only three of the dozen dared to follow the women, the others assuring each other in loud voices that, no, really the ladies were too ugly. As for Pierre-Edouard, he was obliged to make a hasty exit in search of air; the last four brandies had been too much for him . . .

Much later, towards midnight, they met up again in the cathedral square, where they 'sang' a hymn before setting off in procession for the Corrèze. They had thrown plenty of stones into the river, tried unsuccessfully to push a huge charabanc into it too; then the group had separated, scattered, and disappeared into the night.

So the St Libéral conscripts began their journey home. They had a thirty-five-kilometre walk ahead of them before reaching their beds; Pierre-Edouard arrived home just as his father was coming out to see to the animals.

'I'm okay!' he called. Then he staggered as far as the barn, where he curled up in the straw and slept until evening.

'The chores won't get done by themselves!' yelled Jean-Edouard. 'You won't get to the end by standing there with your nose in the air.'

'I'm doing my bit, it seems to me!' retorted Pierre-Edouard.

He slowly lit his cigarette so as not to give the impression of knuckling under too quickly, then took out his knife and carefully scraped the blade of his hoe, on which the red sticky earth had built up.

'Not finished messing about yet!' railed his father, within an inch of exploding.

Since the beginning of the year Jean-Edouard had been in a sombre mood. First of all he took it badly when many blamed him for what had happened since the yard had opened, even though he had expected it. To listen to all those loud-mouths in the village, you would think he was responsible for the behaviour of the workmen. And then there was a great deal of jealousy; he was reproached for not having shared his idea of large-scale planting to provision the canteens of the company.

It was true that he had kept his secret well, even going so far as to buy a large quantity of his seed from a merchant in Objat, and not from the syndicate in St Libéral, despite being its chief founder. So he avoided alerting the others; they did not see him acquire such a weight of seed.

Then he had sown and planted everything as discreetly as possible and avoided talking about his work with his neighbours. Of course they had understood in the end, when the plants came up, that Vialhe was on to a big thing. By then everyone had seen what a huge opportunity the yard offered; but they were too late, at least for this year, to compete significantly with his production. He expected to be copied the following year, but for that he already had a plan, and just thinking about it made him laugh to himself.

But these small sources of satisfaction were not enough to cheer him up. What had put him in such a bad mood was the amount of work he had undertaken: he was worried that he would not be able to carry it through successfully. He and his son were far from finishing the hoeing of the two hectares of potatoes, and already all the other plantings needed the same attention. If they didn't get it, the results would be of poor quality, not to say rotten, and the loss would be obvious. And that was what they were smirking about in the village.

He tried to set the whole family to the hoeing, but Marguerite was tied to the house by the care his father needed, and could only leave it in short bursts. That left the two girls; they came sullenly, preferring to spend their time looking after the animals. Anyway they didn't get much done and complained all the time, especially Berthe, who often contrived to stay at home, saying it was to keep her grandmother company – and it was true that Léonie was growing weaker . . .

\*

Since he had given up his practice, Doctor Fraysse could at last devote himself to those hobbies which forty-five years of professional life had prevented him pursuing. On market days, when the patients flocked in, he still sometimes helped his young colleague. Occasionally he was called to a difficult labour, or to treat a few obstinate old men who refused the attentions of the new practitioner and threatened to waste away if they were not cured by the 'real doctor'. But apart from these few cases, which allowed him to do some of the work he still loved, his time was his own and he made good use of it.

Late in life he had discovered a real vocation as a gardener, and out of the neglected patch in front of his house he had created a garden worthy of admiration. He was not content to grow vegetables in profusion, but joined beauty and utility by interplanting flowers between the rows of carrots, cabbages or leeks. His gladioli, zinnias, lupins and blue hydrangeas were the most beautiful in the village. As for his roses, they had furnished the ground for a cautious reconciliation, even a sort of friendship, with Father Feix. It was the old priest who had taught him the art of pruning and grafting the buds.

He could indulge in fishing too, his great passion. From now on he was free to spend a whole day, his fly-rod in his hand, wading up the Diamond, aiming his fly expertly at the foot of the big alder trees, where the trout hid among the roots. He was a fine fisherman, and amazingly knowledgeable about the habits of the salmon family; he would never have let anyone else concoct all the different sorts of artificial flies which he used according to the weather, the temperature and the season. It was a great joy to him to prepare a collection of flies – wet or dry.

He was an enthusiastic botanist, and his retirement allowed him to undertake the construction of a herb garden, something he had dreamed of since his youth. He collected the multitude of species which abounded in the region and classified them with great care, and added to them a collection of medicinal plants, a professional idiosyncrasy which greatly amused his young successor. These herbs, weighed and measured to the exact gramme, gave great pleasure to several old patients who preferred an infusion of poppies, juniper or yarrow to the medicine prescribed by Doctor Delpy.

He relished every second of all these pastimes, as well as the game of billiards he played against Antoine Gigoux every night at the inn. He was not one to be scared away by the invasion of the establishment by the railway men. He even took a certain amount of pleasure, tinged with nostalgia, in plunging into this rowdy atmosphere of Gauloises and coarse laughter, which reminded him of certain memorable evenings in his student life.

Besides, this daily visit enabled him to keep himself up to date with everything that happened in the community; the progress of the work, the health of several old acquaintances, the marriages and births.

Often, between sips of gentian bitters, he and the mayor would recall past times, vanished friends, those who had left. The teacher frequently came up in their conversation. He had retired about a year earlier and returned to his native Ussel; his departure was mourned by everyone, and deprived the two players of an agreeable partner.

A young couple fresh from college now occupied the school, and they were applying modern educational methods which lacked the paternal friendliness of the well-loved former teachers. Previously, when Monsieur Lanzac or his wife heard the children speaking dialect to each other, they merely interrupted them and suggested they use French. And when a pupil, at a loss for words, spoke of the 'burn', the 'cloggie' or the 'shippon' they would gently reprove him; 'Say the stream, the cobbler, the cowshed; that way everyone will understand you, even northerners!'

Now there was no question of the children getting away with such linguistic aberrations; the new teachers pretended not to understand the dialect, and fought against its use at every turn.

The mayor was delighted with their zeal, and equally appreciative of their political militancy. The doctor was less enthusiastic.

'They're too fanatical for me. Especially him; his political opinions are too blatant!'

'They're not fanatical, they're socialists!'

'And so what? So am I!'

'Oh! You . . .'

'Exactly! But I never mixed up my profession with my politics! I looked after everyone; Royalists, followers of General Boulanger, anarchists – even the good nuns! And I never tried to make them change their opinions. Whereas your two young ones, they manage to get politics into arithmetic!'

'Who told you that?'

'Come on, it's an open secret, everyone's talking about it! No, believe me, if you let them go on like that, they'll be more tyrannical than the priests, and that's saying something! You know me, I approved when we broke the power of the clergy; I hope I don't have to fight any secular despots in the future . . . Go on, it's your turn to play, and if you win this point, I pay for the game. But I think I'm safe . . .'

That afternoon in May the air was sweet, just right for a stroll. Doctor Fraysse set off down the path to the mill, walking slowly, on the look-out for a rare plant.

It was quite by chance, because his eye was drawn to a magnificent growth of stinking hellebore in the shade of the hedge, that he noticed Louise and Octave about thirty paces away.

They were seated on the other side of the meadow at the foot of a chestnut tree, ignoring the animals which grazed not far from them. The young people must have been speaking in low voices, for the doctor could hear nothing. He noted merely that they were sweetly holding hands, so he smiled and went his way without a sound.

It was only later, when he thought over the encounter, that his conscience troubled him. He knew Jean-Edouard well and regarded him highly, but he also knew what his reaction would be if he learned that Louise was letting the young assistant surveyor flirt with her.

As a good paterfamilias, Jean-Edouard kept his girls on a short rein and saw that no young fellows came hanging about around his house. Besides, everyone knew that neither Louise nor Berthe would be married to the first comer, such was the reputation and standing accorded by his land and livestock. They would make good marriages, and it was almost certain that, at least for the elder one, her father already had a plan in mind. There was no doubt that Octave Flaviens did not feature on the list of possible future sons-in-law! His situation was respectable but no more; worst of all he was a stranger to the area – and a townee to boot! – so the doors of the Vialhe house were definitely closed to him.

The doctor knew all this; he was fond of Louise, whom he had delivered, and the young Flaviens was likeable. He often played billiards with him, and although he found him rather lightweight, a little colourless, he judged him to be honest, hard-working and well-bred. So he worried about the future of these two young people.

His anxiety grew as the days passed, for several times, and without setting out to look for them, he saw the two lovers sitting in the same place, each time just as quiet and reserved. And it was this modest behaviour which made him realise that Louise's and Octave's feelings went far beyond a simple flirtation. Truly, if Octave were a commonplace seducer, he would have already arrived at his goal and achieved the conquest, or else Louise would have sent him packing long ago.

The doctor considered the matter, hesitated, weighed the pros and cons, then came to a decision and positioned himself one day on the path which Louise took to guide her animals to the grazing. As he had expected, the girl soon arrived behind her flock, chivying cows and ewes when they browsed too long on the edges of the path.

'Good day, Doctor!' she cried as soon as she saw him.

'Good day, Louise. Well, you're growing more and more beautiful. Almost a woman, aren't you?'

She blushed, smiled, and made to continue on her way.

'Wait,' he urged, 'leave the animals, they won't do any damage. You see, this is embarrassing for me, but I must speak to you, and please don't take it amiss. What I want to say is – Listen, Octave is a good boy and you're a good girl; I think it's charming that you meet each other. Don't deny it, I've seen you together . . .'

'We're not doing anything wrong!' she defended herself vehemently.

'I know. Anyway, that's not the problem. What you have to understand is that I have seen you. Of course, I haven't told anyone. But suppose someone else discovers you and tells your father all about it? He'll see red, you'll lose your good reputation and your Octave will have to leave at the double and think himself lucky if your father doesn't thrash him! Have you thought of all that?'

'We're not doing anything wrong,' she repeated, 'and it's not nice of you to spy on us!'

'Good God, you idiot girl, I don't give a damn what you do! What are you thinking of, you silly goose! I'm talking to you to save you trouble. Consider the gossip there'll be in the village if others get to hear of it!'

'We want to get married!' she raged back.

'You've spoken to your father about it?'

'No.'

'Why not?'

'He doesn't like Octave, and then . . . Well, he's got other plans for me,' she admitted, her eyes full of tears.

'Has he told you about them?'

'Not him; my mother has.'

'Who is it?'

'Léonard Bouyssoux.'

'Oh yes, him from Heath Farm . . .'

He knew the young man in question, and prevented himself from adding that he considered Léonard an absolute fool. Whatever Louise's plans were, Léonard Bouyssoux had the best chance of getting her to bed. Next to him, Octave did not count, at least in Jean-Edouard's eyes. She would doubtless be Bouyssoux's wife within two years, so it was pointless to tell her what he thought of her future husband . . .

'And you, of course, don't want that?'

'I'm going to marry Octave, and no one else!'

'Well, that's not my business. All I want you to understand is that you must take more care. Don't spoil everything by letting some gossip surprise you with jealous scandal-mongering. That's all I wanted to tell you, the rest is none of my business.'

He moved away and cut across the meadow to return to the village. It was then that he noticed Octave, concealing himself clumsily behind a clump of bushes. He ought to have gone to talk to him, but he shrugged his shoulders and continued on his way.

# 8

Léonie Malcroix, young Doctor Delpy's housekeeper, could not resist the pleasure of relaying the news. The story had been doing the rounds for some time, but no one had been able to guarantee its authenticity until that day. Léonie was very proud to capture the attention of all fifteen women who were working around the wash-house when she came to dip her linen in the fresh water of the big stone basin.

'This time, it's really happening!' she announced, as she untied the sheet which she had stuffed with her employer's hankies, shirts and underpants. 'Yes,' she continued, girding herself in an oil-cloth apron, 'he's gone to fetch it from Brive, he'll come back tonight with . . .'

'Pity us,' commented her neighbour, 'that's all we need!'

'Doctor Fraysse would never have entertained such an idea!' added another gossip. And all the housewives agreed.

No one disputed the young doctor's professional ability, nor his kindness, but many distrusted the new-fangled ideas which he expressed, and practised on the sick.

One of his latest fancies was to send some of them to a colleague in Brive who owned a mysterious and worrying machine. It seemed the patient was made to enter a sort of box – part metal, part glazed – which filled almost the whole of a small, dark room; the machine lit up suddenly with a glare which hurt the eyes, but it was said that it allowed you to see what illness the patient was suffering from. One of the fascinations of this mechanism was that it was absolutely painless. As for its usefulness, Doctor Delpy said it was marvellous. He maintained that it had already enabled him to save several people, and to reduce some complex fractures. All the same, old Doctor Fraysse had never felt the need for this cupboard-thing to treat people, and he had done it more cheaply!

Another of Doctor Delpy's ideas was that children should not spend too long in the cowsheds; that they should not rake out the dung, nor play with the animals, nor drink unboiled milk. To listen to him you would think they caught chills from goats, chest infections from cows and worms from dogs!

All that was easy for him to say, but who was going to look after the flocks if you started listening to rubbish like that? The children's work was to take the animals to the grazing, to watch them, to clean out the litter – exactly as their parents had done before them, and they weren't dead yet!

Doctor Delpy had other fads of that kind; he maintained that the brandy given to children when they had an attack of worms could poison them, even kill them! As if half a glass of liquor mixed with a good spoonful of fresh soot could harm anyone, if it was taken on the first day of the new moon! A good plum brandy was certainly less dangerous than the doctor's latest eccentricity – the acquisition of an automobile, which, according to Léonie Malcroix, would make its debut in St Libéral that very evening.

A motor vehicle had already passed through the village. Its arrival had created panic at first, to the great satisfaction of the madman driving it, one of the company engineers. The monstrous machine, in which four people were imprisoned, had climbed the main street, and none of the bystanders would be quick to forget the infernal noise, the clouds of dust it raised, the confusion and fear aroused as it passed, among humans as well as animals.

Luckily, the monster had simply dashed through. It had been seen taking the road to Ayen at mind-boggling speed, vanishing as quickly as it had appeared. It had not been seen again, and no sensible person wished for its return.

Only a few thoughtless young people were happy about the doctor's purchase, looking forward to, if not sitting in the vehicle, at least the opportunity to touch it, to look at it, to admire it. Pierre-Edouard was one of these scatterbrains who approved, and professed themselves proud to belong to a village which was going to have a car.

Nevertheless, almost all the villagers, whether for or against, happened to find themselves in small groups in the main square that evening when an urchin, sent out as a scout, arrived at the gallop and warned them that he had heard the machine breasting the last rise. Instinctively all the gawpers moved away from the road, left the verges empty, ranged themselves against the houses or around the trees; some cautious ones even climbed onto the steps of the Mairie, while others sheltered under the church porch.

And suddenly, the noise was there. Every eye was on the turning from which the engine would emerge. First of all came a dog; maddened and trembling, it shot into the square in a crazy zigzag race, stopped for an instant and then, with rounded back and tail between its legs, plunged into an alley. Then the automobile appeared.

Magnificent! Red coachwork with silver edges, long copper bonnet, enormous lamps and gold velvet upholstery, it throbbed with a final deep-throated roar which seemed to propel it into the centre of the square, where it stopped, surrounded by fumes and smoke, but silent at last.

Doctor Delpy took off his goggles, pushed back his helmet with ear-flaps, so that it hung around his neck, unbuttoned his heavy coat and jumped down to the ground. They were astonished to see him so dashing, so alert, not at all disturbed by his experience. He took out his pocket-watch, did a quick calculation, and smiled.

'Fifty-two minutes from Brive, you can't do better than that! And of course I lost a lot of time because of the construction work!' he threw out as an aside.

He added more, but the words were lost in the general hubbub. Already he was surrounded by enthusiasts, who questioned him excitedly, silencing the grumblers and old fogeys who beat a retreat, still moaning and prophesying dire calamities.

The triumphant doctor replied graciously to the multitude of questions, gave all the technical details, and expounded on the exceptional performance of his Renault. He even invited the mayor and Doctor Fraysse to take a seat, and gave them a lap of honour. The manoeuverability of the machine, its responsiveness, the security provided by its brakes – it was all delightful.

As the inquisitive villagers slipped away one by one to their various tasks, they were succeeded later in the evening by the railway company workers. They glanced at the vehicle without interest. For them an automobile was not a rare beast; they had seen others, and better ones too! One of them was so disrespectful as to press the fat bulb of the horn, which emitted a piteous cry.

'It's time to put it away; these fellows are so cheeky, they're capable of starting it!' remarked Doctor Delpy, emptying his aperitif glass.

He bade goodbye to the major and Doctor Fraysse, who were sitting with him on the terrace of the inn, turned the motor with a firm hand and set off.

'Well, it really is fantastic, progress,' commented Antoine Gigoux. 'Just think, St Libéral with a car! Who would have believed that ten years ago!'

'You'll have to get used to it; there'll soon be another one,' predicted Doctor Fraysse.

'Are you going to buy one?'

'You must be joking! At my age! Besides, what use would it be to me? No, but I bet you an aperitif that our squire will want to keep up with the times. Just wait till he comes back from holiday and you'll see . . .'

And sure enough, one evening six weeks later Jean Duroux entered the village at the wheel of a Panhard and Levassor sparkling with chrome. But only a few boys rushed to admire it. The adults did not react; they were accustomed to cars.

All summer the Vialhes worked non-stop to keep up their productivity, and it was a good growing season. The first sales of vegetables were already beginning to repay them for their perseverance.

Jean-Edouard and his son maintained an inhuman work-rate for several months. Caught between haymaking, reaping, picking the plums and delivering them to Objat, hoeing and collecting the various crops, the two men lived only to work. They rarely slept more than a few hours at night, only occasionally allowed themselves a quarter of an hour siesta, and they even broke the Sabbath – greatly scandalising Father Feix – unable to rest until they had done their all to make each square metre produce its maximum.

Exhausted and dazed, they often went whole days without speaking to each other; the only words they addressed to the women, when they came to help, were to demand food or drink, or to indicate the pressing tasks to be accomplished.

At last September came, and with it harvest time. They could slacken their pace then, and take a breather. Of course the potato-digging would take many more days, but they were encouraged by the certainty that their crops were no longer in danger; that the money was there under the faded potato-haulms, in the dry bean-pods, in the abundant rows of vegetables.

Until that moment they had feared the worst, worried about everything – drought and hail, floods, disease, parasites, all the natural disasters they could do nothing to prevent. Now, since the heavens had spared them, since they had only to bend down to collect the reward of their sweated labour, they could at last allow themselves a few moments respite, a more human life style, and a more balanced rhythm of work. They could also resume contact with the life of the village, and pause to chat with neighbours once more.

Jean-Edouard's ideas had excited great jealousy, but now admiration and esteem grew, as many saw the considerable amount of work accomplished by the Vialhes. A few neighbours even came to help them occasionally during the course of the summer; just like that, spontaneously, for an hour or two, to show that they were happy and proud to be on good terms with the most courageous and astute farmer in the commune, with the one who had first understood that the railway could bring prosperity.

Some even took the opportunity to try to get Jean-Edouard to disclose his plans; that was a waste of time! He certainly had an idea, but he would not reveal it. However, it was obvious that as soon as the next growing season began many farmers would launch into the cultivation of vegetables and attempt to dispose of their produce at the company canteens. But they all knew that if there were too many practising this system there would be a slump. Well, how could they prevent over-production?

'Miladiou, you can tell *me*, can't you?' said Jeantout, when he came one evening to hoe with Jean-Edouard.

'If I tell you, it'll be all over the place!'

'But I won't say a word! Besides, it's not me that's going to compete with you; I haven't got enough land, as well you know!'

'I'm not stopping anyone having ideas, doing the same as me . . .'

'You want to make me think you're going to plant the same crops? Do you take me for a fool? Next year Pierre-Edouard will be in the army; you couldn't grow that much all by yourself!'

'We'll see . . .'

'That's right, and when we see, it'll be too late to copy you and queer your pitch!'

'Possibly . . .'

'You're a bloody swine!' commented Jeantout. But his tone was so admiring that this could not be taken as an insult.


Eventually Jean-Edouard overheard two or three comments at the inn and learned that his daughter was spending time with Octave Flaviens; he was so tired by the last months of work, so drained, that even he was surprised at his own reaction.

Most of the village already knew. The two young people had been seen making eyes at each other in all the corners best-known for their supposed seclusion. Their latest nest was one of the caves which opened on to the old mine cutting, probably where he had once sheltered from the storm with Gaston and Jeanout, that half-collapsed tunnel where lovers took refuge, all naively believing the sanctuary was known only to them. 'But,' as Gaston said, 'if I could find as many gold napoléons as virgins had been deflowered in that hole, I'd be as rich as Rockefeller!'

Contrary to the general expectation, Jean-Edouard did not explode into one of his customary rages, but his suppressed anger was no less terrible. He returned home, went about his business without a word, and waited for dinner-time.

When the whole family was seated at the table, he served the soup as usual and began to eat. It was only after he had mixed some wine with his bouillon, drunk it to the last drop and wiped his moustache on the back of his arm, that his enormous hand came down on Louise's shoulder and transfixed her, whilst the other hand, the open palm shining and lined with callouses, smashed against her cheek.

'That'll teach you to run around! And that,' he added, striking once more, 'is to remind you that we don't like sluts! And now, get your things together. Tomorrow I'm taking you to Tulle, to your cousins. They'll make you work, that will keep you busy! You can come back when I've sent that little upstart of a spear-carrier packing, and believe me, that won't take long . . .'

Louise rushed from the table and took refuge in the bedroom. The door slammed behind her, and they heard the sound of the key hastily turned.

'What's going on?' stammered Marguerite, surprised by the speed of events and disturbed by her husband's icy calm.

'What's going on is that you don't look after your daughter properly – she's been running after that miserable little surveyor for months!'

'And you think that . . .' murmured Marguerite, completely devastated.

'I don't know anything at the moment, but I'll find out tonight.'

'And if by any chance she were . . .'

'We'll deal with that.'

'No,' Marguerite tried to reassure herself, 'I don't believe there's any harm done . . . I would have noticed, I know about these things . . .'

'What's she done?' asked old Léonie. She had become completely deaf, and did not understand what the scene was about.

Jean-Edouard did not bother to reply, but looked at his second daughter.

'What are you laughing at?'

'I knew about it, I did!' crowed Berthe.

She did not have time to dodge the awful blow which threw her against her brother.

'That's to teach you to connive with her,' growled her father. 'And so you know what to expect as well, in case you were by any chance

93

thinking of copying your sister some day. And you, did you know too?' he shouted at his son.

'If you think I've had time to bother about that . . .' replied Pierre-Edouard, without lowering his eyes.

'I asked whether you knew!'

'Yes, and so what?' For the first time in his life, Pierre-Edouard openly defied his father. For a moment Jean-Edouard was powerless, then he recovered and clenched his fists fiercely.

'My God! So you don't care if she disgraces herself with that squirt? You don't care if everyone laughs at us? Well, answer me, in God's name!'

'No one laughs in front of me,' stated Pierre-Edouard quietly, 'and I don't see what disgrace there would be if Louise married Octave . . .'

Jean-Edouard was nonplussed, stunned by the calm way his son had just expressed such a stupid, incredible hypothesis that it left him speechless.

'But . . . but you're raving!' he mumbled at last. 'There's no question of that happening; have you gone mad or something?'

He poured himself a glass of wine, which he emptied in one go, then pushed back his plate and got up.

'Good God! Just wait while I have a word with that little beast,' he snarled as he marched towards the door. 'Marry her! I swear you *must* have gone mad!'

He went out into the night.


Jean-Edouard threaded his way between the drinkers, managed to make a space for himself at the bar, and ordered a plum brandy. The inn was packed, full of shouting workers and merry-makers pressed around the tables where players were laying down their cards.

At the billiard table Octave Flaviens and Doctor Fraysse were quietly playing a game, oblivious to the uproar around them.

Jean-Edouard leant towards the barmaid. 'Go and tell the doctor I would like to see him, and I'm waiting for him outside.' He paid for his drink, emptied his glass in one gulp and went out.

All that crowd confused him, and made the scheme he had in mind useless. In his plan, he entered an almost deserted inn, caught the fellow by the ear, sent him out with a kick up his backside and gave him ten minutes to pack his bag; all this punctuated by a few slaps around the face, not to mention a cuff or two round the head, and the matter was sorted out!

But the thirty or so drinkers gathered in the saloon put that out of the question. He was not going to make a spectacle of himself, become a laughing stock in front of strangers! Besides, a good number of them were capable of taking the lad's side, just for a laugh.

'What's the matter?' asked the doctor as he joined him.

'I'd like you to tell that little brat with you to come and see me.'

The doctor took a long puff on his cigar, and its glowing end lit up his worried face. 'People have been telling you things . . .'

'You're damn right they have!'

'You're not going to make a fool of yourself?'

'I'll do what I have to do! Would you please tell that fellow to come here, I have a few words to say to him . . .'

'Okay, but I'm coming out with him. I don't trust you and your words . . .'

He went back into the inn, leaving Jean-Edouard even more furious at the certain knowledge that everyone knew about his daughter's misconduct. The proof was that the doctor had immediately understood.

'You want to see me?'

The young man's confident voice surprised him; it was not that of a guilty man caught in the act.

'Yes, and I've a good mind to smash your face to teach you to respect my daughter!' he shouted, advancing on Octave.

'Let him speak!' ordered the doctor, stepping between them.

'First of all,' retorted Octave, 'I would ask you not use "tu" to me, we are not related in any way. Secondly, if you touch me, I shall be forced to lay a charge, and I have a witness. Finally, I would like to take advantage of this opportunity to assure you that I have never shown any disrespect towards your daughter.'

'Good God, don't take that tone with me! You've been seen together, and I know where too!'

'And so what? Talking isn't forbidden, nor dishonourable!'

'That's what you say, and I know how it ends up! Well listen carefully – either you get out of here, and right now, or I'll lay charges myself! My daughter's a minor, I have the law on my side. You'll see how we get rid of hangers-on!'

'You're being absolutely stupid,' the doctor intervened. 'Anyone would think you wanted to make yourself a laughing stock!'

'You go back to your flowers and leave me in peace; I know what I'm doing!'

'No, you don't know anything! There's no law preventing two

young people from talking to each other, and you have no rights over Monsieur Flaviens!'

'Except the right to thrash him if I see him around Louise, is that clear?'

'Listen,' said Octave, 'I don't know what I've done to you, and it doesn't matter now. But I would like to give you a warning too: I'll wait as long as I have to, until she comes of age if necessary, but I shall marry Louise.'

'Well, you could wait for ever for that, you little squirt!' yelled Jean-Edouard. He was about to rush at the younger man, then he controlled himself and strode away.

Marguerite was waiting for him, sitting by the fireside. He noticed her eyes reddened with tears and the damp handkerchief held tightly in her hands.

'Well?' she asked feebly.

'Oh, the filthy beast!' he growled. 'Where are the children?'

'Pierre's gone off to sleep in the barn. He left his bed for Berthe – she couldn't get into the bedroom, Louise had locked the door. She's only just opened it.'

He approached the corner of the room where the bed was tucked away, and bent over Berthe. 'Are you asleep?'

'Leave her,' interrupted his wife.

'Yes, it doesn't matter if she does hear; she'll learn from it,' he said, coming back to the settle.

'Well?' asked Marguerite again.

'How should I know!' he growled, angrily poking the smouldering logs.

'You want to take her to Tulle?'

'Yes, at least there she won't see him any more.'

'Our cousins will have a good laugh . . .'

'We don't have to tell them the whole story. I'll say that she asked to go away somewhere . . .'

'And why should she do that?'

'Because she can't step into the street any more without being whistled at by all the ruffians from the railway company! Because every evening they come around the house making a racket, that's why!'

Marguerite, unconvinced, shook her head and began to cry silently. She was sure that their relatives would not be deceived; that they would laugh at her expense, only too happy at this turn of events.

These cousins were fruit and vegetable merchants, grander and richer than the Vialhes; they behaved in a crushingly superior manner whenever they met, which was only once or twice a year. They kept on good terms despite that, but Marguerite was convinced that her cousin had no love for her; that she was jealous that Marguerite had three fine children while she herself was childless.

'Stop blubbering!' he ordered. 'It's decided.'

'And what about him, what did he say?'

'Don't talk to me about that worm – I think I'd have knocked him out cold if the doctor hadn't been there!'

'He knows? Him as well?' she moaned.

'You bet! Him and everyone else! That little slut has dragged us into an ugly situation. Oh, the little baggage! If ever old man Bouyssoux hears about it! And he certainly will . . . But I'll go and see him, as soon as possible. The best thing would be to bring the wedding forward a bit. But not too much, we don't want people to start talking. I think Easter would be a good time, what do you think?'

'Yes, that would be fine. I haven't finished the trousseau, but after all . . .'

'What a good thing we found out before that little turd touched her! Think back, could she be . . .'

'Don't say that! No, no, she can't have . . . It's not possible, she wouldn't have done that to us, in any case!'

'Then she really would have been in trouble! Good,' he said, getting up. 'Tulle tomorrow, old Bouyssoux the day after, and the wedding in six months. And while we're waiting, let's go to bed.'

'Don't hit her again,' begged Marguerite, 'your cousins will see the marks . . .'

He shrugged, and went into the bedroom. He marched towards his daughter's bed, carrying the oil-lamp at arm's length, and noticed with satisfaction that she had obeyed him: her bundle was ready.

'I know you're not asleep. Well listen. All this, I'm doing it for your own good, in six months you'll thank me for it. And now go to sleep, we'll have to take the six o'clock train to La Rivière. I'll explain to you tomorrow what we're going to tell our relatives.'

Pierre-Edouard watched the moving rays of the oil-lamp until they showed that his parents were in their bedroom, then he slipped out of the stable and set off down the main street.

Despite the late hour there were still many drinkers in the bar of the inn, but none paid any attention to his arrival. A glance around showed him that Octave Flaviens was not there; without hesitating he climbed the stairway which led to the bedrooms, walked to the door of number seven and knocked.

'What is it?' grunted Octave.

'I've come on behalf of Louise,' whispered Pierre-Edouard.

He heard bare feet slapping on the tiles, then the lock grated and a hand half opened the door.

'Oh, it's you!' murmured Octave, raising his lamp to face-level. 'Come in. You must excuse me, I was already in bed.'

He was rigged out in a shirt which stopped at mid-thigh and revealed lank, hairy legs; he looked a bit ridiculous, and Pierre-Edouard wondered how his sister could be in love with a man like that. Without his well-cut clothes, which set him off to advantage, he looked weak and puny, almost pitiful. 'He's as thin as a green woodpecker,' thought Pierre-Edouard. 'One blow from Father would smash off his head.'

'Well?' asked Octave, sitting down on the edge of the unmade bed. He felt around on the bedside table, picked up his box of cigars and held it out. 'Do you smoke?'

Pierre-Edouard helped himself, and contemplated the man for whom his sister had risked so much; he felt a surge of pity at his weakness and dishevelment. He felt so strong in contrast to Octave, so powerful that he almost felt the need to protect him, to comfort and help him as he would a younger brother.

'Well?' asked Octave again.

'My father is taking her to Tulle tomorrow morning, to our cousins. They live in Rue de la Barrière, you can't miss it. They're fruit-merchants, it's written on the house.'

'What went on at your place?'

'It wasn't too bad.'

'Did he hit her?'

'Not much, just a cuff or two. Nothing really . . .'

'You think that's nothing?' broke in Octave. 'Two blows! And . . . after that, she didn't run away!'

'Run away? And where would you want her to go? Besides, if she'd done that I wouldn't give much for her chances when father found her!'

'Don't say that! And what else did she say to you then?'

'Well, not much; she spoke to me out of the window, and it was difficult, because our mother might have heard. Just . . . she'll expect to see you in Tulle, that's all . . .'

'Of course,' murmured Octave, rolling his cigar between his

fingers. 'Tell me, do you really think your father would be opposed to our marriage?'

'I rather think so, yes.'

'But why?'

'He has other plans, I believe . . .' Pierre-Edouard evaded. 'But then, perhaps you'd better know,' he expanded suddenly. 'He wants her to get married at Easter, I heard just now; I was listening at the door.'

'Get married? But this is barbarous! We're not in the Middle Ages! She has a right to some say in the matter, after all!'

'Huh! It's the custom,' explained Pierre-Edouard, shrugging his shoulders. 'Right, now it's time I went back.'

'She didn't say anything else?'

'Yes, she sends you a kiss . . .' admitted Pierre-Edouard, very embarrassed to relay such a message.

'Will you see her again before she leaves?'

'Yes, but she'll be with Father, so . . .'

'Too bad. Thank you for coming,' said Octave, holding out his hand. 'I'd like to say that I think we'll get on very well, when we're brothers-in-law.'

Pierre-Edouard shook the hand that was offered but kept quiet. Brothers-in-law? That certainly wasn't the road he saw them going!

# 9

DESPITE Marguerite's fears, the relatives in Tulle did not seem to suspect the real reasons which forced Jean-Edouard to entrust his daughter to them. In fact, they were overwhelmed with work, hardly had time to ask questions, and were also undoubtedly delighted to take on an extra employee at little cost to themselves.

And Louise played the part to perfection, according to her father's instructions. She was lively and smiling and deceived everyone with amazing ease; she declared she was delighted to get away from the unpleasant atmosphere in St Libéral for a while, and glad to work with her cousins.

Jean-Edouard was not entirely taken in, but he was somewhat reassured. He convinced himself that his daughter would eventually be beaten at her own game: her false cheerfulness would soon be followed by the eclipse of this silly love-affair. As night fell he reached St Libéral in high good humour, happy to have resolved so satisfactorily – and with all necessary speed – the problem which he had only taken in hand twenty-four hours earlier.

To close the matter finally, he went into the inn even before going home; he ordered an absinthe and asked to see the young assistant surveyor. It was very satisfying to hear from the landlady that Octave had left that same morning: from now on he would be staying at the hotel in La-Rivière-de-Mansac.

'He was a proper gentleman,' sighed the landlady, 'I'm sorry he's gone. Aren't you?' she asked, with an ironic smile which annoyed him.

'He'll be closer to his work,' he retorted. 'That'll be better for him. And for everyone . . .'

Old Bouyssoux made him wait on the doorstep before inviting him in. Standing at the foot of the steps, they first discussed the weather, the crops, the flocks, the year in general, the condition of the vines, and the start of the hunting season.

Bouyssoux complained of his aches and pains, and envied the youth and health of his visitor; twelve years older, he abused the privilege of age quite shamelessly. What's more, he knew all about the reasons behind this approach, and took great pleasure in testing Jean-Edouard's patience.

'Now, come on in,' he said at last. 'You're in luck, I'm all alone; we won't be interrupted. My wife and son are picking potatoes. I can't bend any more, my back . . .'

They sat down at the table and the old man filled their glasses.

'It's like this,' said Jean-Edouard. 'I've come back to see what you think of the idea I mentioned to you last spring . . .'

The old man slowly rolled a cigarette and stuck it under his grey moustache.

'Well,' he said, 'it's okay with me, but it's my son . . .'

'How do you mean, your son?'

'Well . . . there's been talk in the village; living out here, we don't know exactly what's going on.'

'I've sorted that matter out.'

'That's what I heard,' agreed the old man, happy to demonstrate that news reached him very quickly in spite of the three kilometres which separated him from the village. 'Yes, that's what I heard . . . But you have to understand my Léonard. He's a serious fellow, and very proper. He wouldn't like to take on a brat that didn't belong to him . . .'

'My God!' Jean-Edouard pounded his fist on the table in fury. 'That's not how the Vialhes behave! And you know it!'

'Well I know that your daughter hasn't been very wise . . . You got her out of that, it's true, and that's good. The other little suitor has gone off to rub up against someone else, that's good too . . . But how are you going to prove to me that a third thief hasn't already taken his place, eh?'

'I forbid you to talk like that!' shouted Jean-Edouard, leaping up. 'If you're going to take it like that, you can tell your son to find another girl! I'll keep my daughter, she won't be losing much!'

'Don't sound off like that! What I've been saying, it's just to make sure . . . And when were you thinking of for this marriage?'

Jean-Edouard pretended to reflect on it; he emptied his glass, it was his turn to roll a cigarette. Bouyssoux waited. He passed the time by calculating how many months ahead Vialhe would risk setting it; he had come to an understanding with his son on a date beyond which, if there were a birth, it would be impossible to withdraw without dishonour.

'I talked to my wife,' he said at last. 'We thought it would be fine if we had it – well, let's say at Easter. Is that all right with you?'

'In God's name, why couldn't you have said that earlier! If it's at

Easter, you must be sure of your daughter! Well, why did you let me go on talking, eh?'

'Just to see what sort of stories are being spread about us, and to prove to you that the Vialhes have always been respectable.'

'Okay,' grumbled the old one, cross at being lectured. 'And as a dowry?'

Once more, Jean-Edouard pretended to reflect.

'As dowry, first of all she has a full trousseau,' he said as he lit his cigarette with exasperating slowness. 'And then I'll give her . . . Now, let's say . . . eight thousand francs.'

'Phew!' exclaimed the old man, surprised at the size of the sum. 'So it's true you're making all that money with the railway company!' He nodded, but continued very quickly: 'Eight thousand francs, that's good, but for land?'

'No land.'

'How's that, no land? We'll see about that!'

'Nothing, not a single square metre. The land – that's not to be divided, that's to be kept; you won't see any of the Vialhes' plots given to anyone outside the family in a hurry! The trousseau, eight thousand francs, the girl; nothing more. And, for your part, how do you propose to set up the young people?'

'Well, I . . . The boy will get everything, one day, he's an only child . . .'

'One day, yes, but what about now?'

'Bah, we'll manage something . . .'

'No, no,' insisted Jean-Edouard, now that he was confident of success. 'It must be arranged beforehand, and in front of a solicitor. I'd like my son-in-law to have land in his own name, and animals of his own and some implements too!'

'Oh, oh! How you do go on! I'm not going to move out into the barn! *You* give them some land!'

'Never. It's staying in the Vialhe name. Come on, let's see what you're going to put in the basket for them . . .'

They argued for another two hours and finally agreed. Everything was arranged down to the smallest detail, and it was even accepted that Louise would spend two months in Tulle; time for her to forget, and to prove to everyone that there was no reason for hurrying.

When she returned, Léonard could come and court her. He would call on his intended for almost three months, which was perfectly proper and would silence all the malicious tongues. Then would come the wedding, and Jean-Edouard would do everything to make it one of the finest in the area.

*

Jean-Edouard took the situation in hand with such speed and energy that the laughter changed to respect; those who, three days earlier, had been telling jokes behind his back were the first to admit that he managed his family with as much intelligence and astuteness as he cared for his farm.

The admiration reached its peak in the weeks that followed, as he was seen each day coming down from the plateau with carts full of superb potatoes. Incredible rumours circulated about the weight of the crop sold to the railway company, and the amount of money this represented.

He let them talk, convinced that it was better to be envied than pitied. But, contrary to what his neighbours thought, he did not dispose of all his potatoes to the steward. He sorted them and kept several tons of the poorer ones; this reserve stock was part of his plan of action for the year to come.

At the end of October, with all the crops in, he ploughed his fields and sowed them with cereals. People were slightly amazed, but pleased to see him give up his vegetable production, and grateful to him for giving his fellow farmers the chance to try their luck in his place.

'And after all,' said a few jealous souls, 'he's made enough this year! Besides, when his son goes, he's going to be virtually on his own, what else could he do?'

But those who knew him well recognised that he was planning a new project. It was quickly executed, and once more took everyone by surprise. Of course everyone had been asking questions since the beginning of November; that was when Jean-Edouard, his son, the carpenter and two labourers began erecting a huge lean-to shed against the barn wall. At first the neighbours thought that Vialhe was putting up a tobacco drying-shed, but his fields, covered in oats, wheat and barley, destroyed this hypothesis. It was Jeantout who was the first to understand.

'You old devil, I see what you're up to,' he said, after examining the building. 'How many are you going to put in it? Go on, you can say it, nobody can compete with you!'

'You guessed it then, this time?'

'By Our Lady . . . oh, I should have thought of it earlier, I knew you wouldn't rest on your laurels. It doesn't matter, the idea is fantastic. But with that amount of space you're going to keep a bloody horde of them!'

'Forty here, thirty there,' explained Jean-Edouard, indicating with his head. 'And over there I'll have room for six sows and the boar.'

'Got to think it out and be brave enough to do it,' commented Jeantout.

'Well, yes! This year vegetables, next year pigs.'

'And the company will buy them from you?'

'You bet! You don't think I'm going into this blind, do you?'

No, Jeantout did not think that. He was sure his neighbour had worked it all out in advance.

'And when are you going to begin?'

'Now. For a start I'm going to buy forty young porkers at the next fair in Brive, plus six breeding sows and a male, and after that I'll rotate my stock.'

'But that's going to take a lot of feeding!'

'That's been thought of,' said Jean-Edouard, walking to a shed. 'See here,' he said as he opened the door.

Jeantout looked at the huge pile of turnips and beets, and whistled in admiration.

'Yes, with all that, you've got something to start with. But after that, what will they eat, in the summer?'

'What rubbish you talk; my cereal crops, of course! And then – listen, and I'll tell you what's going to happen. You're all going to grow spuds next year and a whole heap of vegetables. The railway company won't be able to take it all, there'll be too much of everything . . .'

'And then what?' asked a worried Jeantout.

'Then you'll be quite happy to sell me your surplus for the same price the catering manager would give you. Believe me, my pigs aren't going to die of hunger. The steward has promised me all the left-overs from his kitchens, as well.'

'You're a cheeky devil,' muttered Jeantout enviously. 'My God, you'll earn hundreds and thousands again, and we get damn all . . .'

'I'm not stealing from anyone,' said Jean-Edouard drily.

'Well no, but . . .'

'But what?'

'Nothing . . . So you think it's not worth planting spuds? There'll be too many?'

'Listen,' Jean-Edouard lowered his voice, 'you do what you want, but if I were you, I'd lay off the potatoes and the rest. There's only one thing I'd grow . . .'

'What? Well, tell me, dammit!'

'Yes, and then you'll talk about it, and everyone will copy you, and then you'll come whining to me again!'

'Are you mad? Go on, say it, what is it?'

'Salad stuff.'

'Salad? You're making fun of me!' cried Jeantout, who was quite plainly disappointed in his friend.

'All right, do what you like, but don't come and complain afterwards! This year, I could have sold twenty times more than I'd grown. You have no idea how much salad they eat in the summer, no idea. I couldn't supply enough, not by a long way, even though I had a bloody great square of it planted!'

'Basically, it's not so stupid, but I'd have to be sure I could get rid of it . . .'

'If that's the only problem, I'll speak to the catering manager.'

'You'd do that?'

'Why not?'

'Oh well, then . . .' muttered Jeantout in an embarrassed way. 'Listen,' he said suddenly, 'I have to tell you, there are plenty of us who've had it up to our eyes with the mayor and his son. He's too old and his lad is too bloody stupid. So, next time, it's you we're counting on, you know that?'

Jean-Edouard hid his satisfaction with a shrug.

'We'll see . . . What's definite is that with the railway we'll need a mayor who stirs himself to bring a bit of life into this community . . . I've got some ideas about that too, believe me . . . We'll talk about it another time. But for the moment, you mustn't say anything, it's too early, the elections are too far away. But don't worry, I'll do the right thing when the time comes . . . As I'm sure I can trust you to do,' said Jeantout, contemplating the new pig-unit.

For the first three days Louise thought she would go mad, and she had to call on her reserves of energy and willpower so as not to break down. To avoid thinking too much, she threw herself completely into the work, and astonished her relatives with her strength, courage and ability.

The apple and walnut season was at its height. She very quickly learned to sort the apples according to size and quality and to line them up in their boxes; as soon as they were closed and labelled they were sent off to Paris, Lyons and even London. She did not balk at bleaching the nuts, and burnt her hands mixing the fruit in baths of chlorinated water to remove marks of dirt or mildew.

In the beginning the dozen employees who worked for the wholesaler regarded the new arrival with a jaundiced eye; her relationship with the bosses made her suspect, and conversations stopped when she approached. In less than two days, Louise had won over all her working companions. Without quite understanding why she was there, without recognising her as one of them, the workers still appreciated her company, approved of her good manners, and laughed at her jokes. None of them guessed that she was always on the point of bursting into tears and that her shouts of laughter masked sobs.

Her cousins were kind to her and, having no reason to distrust her, left her completely free to wander the town as she pleased during the infrequent breaks from work. Of course it went without saying that she was not allowed out after nightfall; this was an unnecessary instruction, as she had no desire to go out then.

At last the long-awaited Sunday arrived. Even though she had not been able to arrange anything, nor to speak to Octave, she felt certain that this day would not pass without him appearing. She did not know where or how he would give a sign of life, but she was sure he would succeed in getting news to her.

During busy periods her cousins worked on Sunday mornings. Nevertheless, because they knew the Vialhes' religious convictions, they promised her that she could take her day of rest; besides, her aunt would also take an hour off to go and hear Mass, and it would be a pleasure to accompany her to the Cathedral.

She got up early, mad with impatience, dressed and did her hair with great care. She had not brought many things in the bundle she had put together in such haste on the night of the row, but she did possess a black skirt finely edged with lace, new stockings and an attractive pale blue blouse; she cleaned her sabots and polished their pale leather straps.

When she was ready she mooched about the house, aimlessly waiting for the time of the church service. She didn't dare go into the depot, where her cousins were working with four or five women who had volunteered in order to earn a few extra sous; so she pushed open the door and went out into the street.

It looked such a beautiful day, a wave of bitterness rose in her heart. In weather like this it would be a joy to go and mind the animals in the warm hours of the afternoon, to sit down at the foot of a chestnut tree and, in feverish anticipation, to watch the path by which Octave would arrive. Why hadn't they listened to the doctor and been more circumspect! She almost began to cry, and realised that only the presence of witnesses would strengthen her self-control. She went into the depot, kissed her cousins, greeted the workers, made a joke and even began sorting apples.

'Leave that,' said her aunt, 'you'll get yourself all dirty. We're about to go now anyway.'

'All right, I'll wait for you outside.'

She was proud of having overcome that crisis of despair, and went out singing.

*

Louise was greatly impressed by the ceremony of the High Mass. Used to the little church of Saint-Libéral, she was amazed by the immense nave, the iridescent cloth of the celebrant's chasuble; by the red-and-white surplices of the six choirboys, the richness of the chandeliers and the candlesticks resplendent with enormous candles. She started at the first thunderous chord of the great organ, and her bewilderment made her aunt smile beside her.

It was as she turned round furtively to see whence this flood of music gushed that she saw him. He was there, just behind her. She mastered the impulse to hold out her hand, controlled herself in time, but felt herself turn pale and forced herself to stare at the back of the priest bending over the altar.

She was deliriously happy to know that he was there, but, wondering how she could meet and talk to him, she did not really follow the remainder of the service; if she complied with the movements, the genuflexions, the signs of the cross and responses, it was purely out of habit.

So, for her sake, he had come to take part in the Mass. She felt overwhelmed with gratitude, for on this point they were completely divided. She had been terribly upset when Octave had declared that he did not believe in God or the Devil; she could not understand how he, who was so intelligent, so good, could call himself an atheist.

'Take note, Louise, that I am not forcing anyone to agree with my point of view. I am in favour of liberty. You're free to believe whatever you like, so don't bother about my ideas.'

This tolerance had lessened her sorrow, but she secretly promised herself that she would reform his opinions. In any case he had assured her that, to please her, he would in principle accept a religious marriage, and he had no objection to the baptism of their children.

'I was baptised and it didn't kill me, so do what seems best to you for our little ones. But, as for me, I don't see what I'd do at a Mass!'

And yet he was there. She sensed him behind her back and noted from the sound of his chair that he was rising and kneeling at the correct moments.

'Are you coming?' asked her aunt, touching her arm. She jumped, realised that Mass was over, and panicked at the idea of having to leave again without having spoken to him.

'If you would permit it,' she whispered, 'I'd like to look around the cathedral . . .'

'Of course; you'll get back alone all right. See you soon.'

She was amazed to have found an alibi so easily, and remained seated in her chair for a few moments without daring to move. At last she turned round. Octave was still there, standing, impeccably dressed, apparently deeply immersed in an act of prayer. He lowered his head imperceptibly to greet her, then whispered: 'You go out first, I'll join you . . .'

She obeyed like a sleep-walker; emerged on to the courtyard and made an effort to admire the stained glass window at the entrance.

'Come,' he said, as he rejoined her, 'let's walk on the embankment.'

'And what if we're seen together?'

'We're not in Saint-Libéral. Here two people in love are not forbidden to be together. Come on, let's walk, you're not in any danger.'

She smiled at him and held out her hand.


Father Feix knocked his clogs against the steps to remove the sticky earth, and pushed the door of the presbytery open. Despite the damp cold of this late November morning, he had just spent two hours digging a large bed in his garden, and he was aching all over.

He went up to the fire, which was almost out, and stretched out his swollen fingers in their worn mittens to the embers. He moved the logs closer, worked the bellows, made the flames spring up and lifted his cassock to try to warm his legs. But he knew really that nothing would rid his body of these recurring attacks of pins and needles which ceaselessly and coldly reminded him that he was old, worn out, miserable.

Of course Doctor Fraysse gave him some pills from time to time, recommended infusions or herbal teas, but neither of them was convinced that these treatments had any effect.

Father Feix felt that his time was up and that his years – perhaps even months – were numbered. He did not rebel against it, did not complain, continued his ministry as best he could; but sometimes, when weariness overcame him, he began to wish secretly that death would release him. What good did it do to try and manage a church in the heart of a community which no longer recognised it!

Everything was changing too fast, evolving in a direction which he felt was wrong. The village had become a sink of debauchery where the railway-workers crowded in and got drunk. There was dancing on Saturday nights until three o'clock in the morning, the licensees were making fortunes, and, although the village had at first cold-shouldered the strangers, more than half the inhabitants were now doing business with them. Already the young people were daring to patronise the inn and they danced too, girls and boys, until all hours . . .

And what could one do about that, since everyone seemed to enjoy this immorality? What good did it do to dwell on what he felt in his heart, to repeat it to the few old ladies who still came to Mass? It was not these poor simple souls who needed to be convinced, but the others, those who no longer came to the services.

He left the fire's gentle warmth and went to the entrance to pick up the paper the postman had just slipped under his door. The sight of an envelope on top of *The Cross of Corrèze* intrigued and even worried him. It was years since he had received a letter.

He picked it up, examined it, went to sit down by the fire, ripped it open nervously and read it. He was vexed with himself for the rest of his life for his first, fleeting reaction, and he never forgave himself for having, for at least ten seconds, greatly failed in Christian charity. But the fact is that a wave of self-satisfaction surged over him when he realised how events had proved him right. He recovered himself quickly, begged God's forgiveness for the base thoughts which had just been guiding his spirit, and re-read the letter. The page trembled at his finger-ends.

He slipped the paper into his pocket and rose, went out and walked over to the church. There, kneeling at the foot of Saint Sacrement, he prayed for a whole hour, despite the intense cold which took hold of him as the minutes passed.

One o'clock was chiming as he rose again. He had eaten nothing for lunch, but did not even consider that as he headed bravely towards the house of Doctor Fraysse.

# 10

DOCTOR Fraysse and his wife were drinking their coffee when their maidservant showed Father Feix in. The doctor, astonished at this visit, almost upset his cup, and remained dumbfounded for several seconds.

'What's happened?' he asked, getting up. 'This is the first time you've ever come to my house. Something must have . . .'

'That's right,' admitted the priest. 'Excuse me for disturbing you, but I must speak to you. And it's not about pruning roses,' he added with a sad smile.

'Well, let's go into my study.'

'No, no,' said his wife. 'You stay here by the fire, you'll be more comfortable.' She went out and shut the door.

'This is what brought me,' said the priest, holding out the letter.

'Please sit down,' invited the doctor, as he put on his pince-nez. He read, sighed and then made a face.

'Ah, that unpleasant episode,' he murmured. 'The little fools, I warned them . . .'

'Yes; it's because Louise told me you knew that I've come to see you. I don't know what to do, and yet they're counting on me,' he said sadly.

'Don't get in a state, let's just think about it. Young Louise and her Octave have been seeing each other every Sunday for almost two months. Between ourselves, that big ninny Jean-Edouard should have known that the matter wouldn't be so easily dealt with. Well. . . !

'To summarise, next Monday Louise is supposed to return to her family, and everyone knows that poor simpleton Léonard Bouyssoux is going to be there the same evening to begin courting her. Today is Saturday, and Louise tells us that this evening she will leave her relatives' home to join her lover, God knows where! And all in order to get married without delay. Between you and me, she's not telling us why they're in such a hurry . . .'

'You think that . . .'

Doctor Fraysse paused, and smiled.

'*Caro autem infirma*, as your Gospels say, I believe . . . Yes, the flesh is weak. But in their case, and from what I've seen of them, I hesitate to give an opinion. Anyway, that's not the question.'

'Perhaps there's time to send a telegram to warn the relatives,' suggested Father Feix timidly.

'Oh, no!' interrupted the doctor. 'The young people have confided in you, you wouldn't betray them?'

'And if it's for Louise's good?'

'Don't make me laugh! You know Léonard. Can you see that imbecile with Louise?'

'After all, it is her parent's choice, and . . .'

'And nothing!' the doctor cut him off. 'Look here, I promised not to get mixed up in this affair, but I see that you may force me to!'

'Well, I don't know what to do.'

'Jean-Edouard must be told everything, and made to understand that basically young Flaviens is a good match. It's true, after all; he may become an engineer in the end! Or almost . . .'

'Jean-Edouard is capable of doing something stupid! You must remember that the wedding is planned for Low Sunday. Also, the girl's a minor, she can do nothing without his consent . . .'

'I know. She can do nothing, except . . . There it is, we have only to tell him that she's pregnant . . .'

'Oh, no!' protested the priest. 'That's impossible, I refuse to tell a lie!'

'Bloody hell!' raged the doctor. 'Who's talking about lying? She's spelt it out – "For we are going to get married as soon as possible." '

' "We are going to", and not "We have to". It's a nice point!'

'Bravo! I didn't know you were such a Jesuit! In fact you're quite ready to punish her for *not* having sinned, as you call it! Here is a girl who, as far as we know, is a virgin, an unwritten page, and who, because of that, risks finding herself in the arms of an idiot she doesn't want! And your blessing is enough to make his taking her legal, and blessed by God. Dammit!'

'I beg you, don't swear; you know perfectly well that I don't know what to do.'

'Excuse me,' said the doctor, getting up. He walked to the side table, uncorked a bottle of plum brandy and filled two glasses: 'Here, this might give us inspiration.'

'No, no, thank you, not just now . . . I haven't had time to eat, and I fear that alcohol on an empty stomach . . .'

'You should have told me!' cried the doctor. He strode to the door, opened it and called to the maid: 'Adèle! A plate of something for the Father's lunch, and at the double!'

It was after Father Feix's lunch, after coffee and brandy, that they decided to go together to tell Jean-Edouard. It was understood that the doctor would assume responsibility for any lies which might be necessary in the course of what would be a very difficult interview.

They found Jean-Edouard in the new piggery; if he was intrigued by their visit, he gave no indication of it.

He had bought about forty weaners at the last market, and was lavishing great care on them. He leant his fork against the wall and advanced towards his visitors.

'Well, Father, you've come to bless my new pigsty? What an excellent idea. I expect it was Marguerite who asked for this . . .'

Every year, Father Feix went round the barns to bless the flocks. It was an old custom which his parishioners considered very important, almost as important as Rogation Day, the ceremony in which he blessed the fields, begged mercy from the Lord, and asked for fair weather and good crops as a reward for man's work.

'Listen, Jean-Edouard, if you wish, I'll come back another day for the blessing, but I'm pleased that you asked me,' said the priest in confusion.

'Well, so what brings you both here?' asked Jean-Edouard with a frown.

The priest felt wretched at having to announce the news, and he turned to the doctor to beg for help.

'Good God,' grumbled the doctor, 'it's not a tragedy, after all, it's not the end of the world! All right,' he gulped, and decided to take it on himself. 'Louise has written to me; she's left her cousins' house, she's going to marry Octave Flaviens, and you will no doubt be a grandfather within a short time. That's what we've come to tell you. Okay, it's not very amusing, but it isn't a catastrophe! At the end of the day what matters is that your daughter should be happy!'

Both he and the priest were astonished at Jean-Edouard's reaction. They had expected shouts, threats, even a brandished shotgun; they saw only pallor and silence. Such a heavy silence, so oppressive, that the priest felt he ought to break it.

'I understand how you feel, you know. You see, I could exult and say: "I told you the railway would bring misfortune!" But no, believe me, I'm as hurt as you. Louise is my daughter too; I baptised her, I taught her the catechism, and I was looking forward to marrying her. But there it is, it's the will of God which has thwarted your plans; it must be accepted whatever it brings. . .'

Jean-Edouard looked at them, but did not seem to see them. He took up his fork, arranged the pig's bedding-straw, then put down the fork again and patted his pockets in search of his tobacco; his fingers were trembling so much as he shaped the cigarette that the paper split. He added another paper and rolled it.

'Well, so that's it,' he said at last. 'Okay, fine . . .' He lit his cigarette and breathed in a lungful. 'Okay,' he repeated. 'She marries her spear-carrier. But since it is you she's written to' – he looked at the doctor – 'tell her that the Vialhe family no longer recognises her as one of them. She's chosen, and that's that.'

'Don't be a fool!' cried the doctor. 'I understand that you're disappointed, but that's not a good enough reason for disowning your daughter! Good God, do I have repeat it? It's not a tragedy! Well, don't overdramatise it, don't insult the future!'

'I said it was over, and I'm not going back on it.'

'Listen,' it was the priest's turn to try, 'no one is asking you to give her a party right now. But she is your daughter, and her children will be your grandchildren! You have no right to . . .'

'I said that's that; don't offend my ears with your rights! The kids she has will be. . . what was it, just now? Oh yes, Flaviens. They will never be Vialhes, I don't want to know them. Let that be fully understood; that she should never venture to set foot in the house. The door will be closed, you tell her that.'

He took up his fork again and foraged in the litter.

'Oh, yes!' he continued, stopping his work, 'she'll need authorisation. I'll get it to you – you, the go-between!' he shouted in the direction of the doctor. 'You're surprised I thought of it? Well, let me tell you, one disgrace is enough. I don't want anyone to be able to say that there are bastards from a Vialhe girl, here or anywhere else. There never have been, and that little slut is not going to start!'

'I'm sure your feelings will change later on,' ventured Father Feix, 'but still, I'd like you to reassure me that you won't go for your son-in . . . well, the husband of your daughter. You're bound to see him again, his work here isn't finished.'

'No, I shan't see him. And even if he were standing between you two, I still wouldn't see him! He can come in peace, the village doesn't belong to me. But if by any mischance either he or she set foot on my property, my house or my land . . .'

'Good, all right,' interrupted the doctor. 'Well, I think time will heal all. Now we'll leave you, but believe me, it gave us no pleasure to come . . .'

Jean-Edouard watched them disappear, crushed the cigarette between his fingers, and cried.

*

He had dry eyes when he went into the house half an hour later, but Marguerite immediately knew from his expression that something had happened.

'Where are the children?' he asked.

'Berthe is bringing in the sheep, Pierre-Edouard's bedding down the cows.'

'Call them immediately. Now, by God!' he shouted, as she hesitated.

As soon as they arrived, he announced the news to them, and they knew that it was pointless to say anything whatsoever.

'And you,' he said, looking at Berthe, 'get it into your head that I'll have my eye on you. You're not going the same way as her. If I see you so much as look at a man, I'll split your skull! Now get back to work, I've still got things to do . . .'

By nightfall he had sorted everything out. His first visit was to old Bouyssoux. With him two or three sentences were sufficient to bury all their plans. Plus one last sentence, a warning: 'And if you want to laugh, wait until I've left, and gone some distance too. I'll smash the face of anyone who laughs, even old men . . .'

He strode away and returned to the village. Once there he went into the mairie. Ten minutes later he had resigned from the council and as president of the syndicate.

As he passed by the doctor's house he delivered the paper which permitted his daughter to be legally married as a minor; everything was within the law, including the mayor's stamp as witness to his signature.

It was dark when he returned to the house. His mother, wife and two children were waiting to dine with him. He took his place and served the soup.

'The day after tomorrow is the market at Objat,' he said, stirring his bouillon. 'We'll buy those six young sows and the male we need. Since I have no need to go to Tulle,' he said, looking at Marguerite, 'we might as well make the most of it.'

There was a lot of talk throughout the village, and even beyond, but no one dared to reveal to any member of the Vialhe family that they were aware of the misfortunes which had befallen them. Of course some people were vastly amused and considered that this event was exactly what was needed to take Jean-Edouard down a peg or two; and if by any chance he were in the mood to climb on his high horse again, they would always be able to ask casually after his daughter and the baby!

But those who laughed and rejoiced did so discreetly. They knew that Jean-Edouard would be merciless.

Besides there were many who, even if they envied and didn't much like him, admired his attitude, not only towards his daughter (that was his personal problem), but also in resigning and withdrawing from all public life; that proved he was aware of the dishonour, and had chosen the right solution. Others in his situation might have tried to cling to power, but who could respect the opinion of a town councillor (canvassing to be mayor, too) and a president of the syndicate who was not even capable of looking after his own daughter?

The conduct of his wife was also beyond reproach. In one instant Marguerite had aged ten years, and it was no secret that this affair tormented her day and night. It was enough to see her pass down the main street, upright and dignified, with no attempt to conceal her tear-filled eyes. None of the gossips dared let slip the slightest allusion to it in front of her either.

As for old Léonie, she was so deaf that one could not be sure that she knew what was going on; in her conversations there was no sign of awareness. That left Grandfather, but he had not left his bed for months now and had become incoherent; he did not need to be worried by what had happened to his granddaughter.

Only Pierre-Edouard and Berthe showed chinks in the armour of their perfectly correct behaviour. The young man was pitied most of all, for everyone knew that he adored his sister and suffered from her absence and her banishment; it was felt he was within an ace of defying his father and openly taking Louise's side. Some hoped secretly that he would do that, just so that they could enjoy the confrontation. They felt sorry for Berthe too, for it was obvious that her father forbade her any excursions. For the whole month of December the behaviour of the Vialhes was secretly observed, then the gossips grew weary of it and busied themselves with the end-of-year celebrations.

Pierre-Edouard lived sadly during his last days of liberty. He had received his call-up papers, and knew that he must join his regiment on 7 January.

It was not leaving for the army which embittered him, but going away without seeing Louise again, and without the smallest sign of life from her. Even Octave Flaviens stayed out of sight; you would think he had left the railway and the area.

And now he was being sent into exile, to the back of beyond, without even knowing whether his sister was married or not. His posting had arrived the week before Christmas, and he had been quite happy to get it. It unlocked the doors of his house, allowed him to escape the oppressive and unhealthy atmosphere where every word might be misinterpreted by his father, or the slightest gesture taken as a sign of rebellion.

Nevertheless, despite being glad to sally forth, he had been vexed by his assignment. He had naively believed that, like most of the young men in the area, he would be sent to Tulle, to Limoges, to Périgueux, possibly to Bordeaux – and why not even to Brive! – in some infantry regiment or other. He was way off the mark, and had looked at the piece of paper uncomprehendingly for several seconds, the time it took him to search his memory for the location of Besançon – where the devil was it?

'Where are they sending you?' his father asked.

'Fifth artillery regiment in Besançon . . .'

'And where's that?'

'In Doubs, a long way off. Up there, dammit!'

'Oh well! We won't be seeing much of you . . .'

His father had said nothing more, but Pierre-Edouard knew that he was angry. He had hoped that his son would be in a garrison close by, and would return frequently to give him a hand.

Since then Pierre-Edouard had made the best of a bad job; he was going to see something of the country, and then, the artillery was an important branch of the service. So he would have set off with a light heart, if it had not been for Louise . . .

Her absence was deeply felt on Christmas Day, a dreadful day, sad enough to bring tears; neither he nor Berthe knew what to do, what to say. Finally he took his gun and climbed to the peaks, but those places reminded him too much of his sister – their adventure in the snow, Léon's thrushes, the wolves . . .

And now, this afternoon of New Year's Eve, he was killing time as best he could by splitting wood with huge blows of the axe. He brought down the heavy chopper on a billet of chestnut wood which exploded, then prepared another log.

'Keeping warm?'

He lifted his head and saw Léon, who had just spoken to him from the roadway.

'Yeah . . .'

He had not seen Léon for several weeks, and felt embarrassed to have to start a conversation, which he had no doubt would inevitably touch on Louise.

'Got time to come out?' asked Léon, having made sure that there was no one else about.

'Well, look here. . . .' muttered Pierre-Edouard, pointing to the pile of wood.

'Don't muck about. Put that down and come on. I've got news of your sister.'

Pierre-Edouard stuck his axe in the chopping-block and slipped on his jacket. 'Wait for me; I'll fetch my gun, we'll make the rounds.'

He bounded towards the house, returned with his 12-bore (with central percussion, a present from his grandfather on his sixteenth birthday) and caught up with his friend, who was already climbing up through the wood towards the plateau.

'Have you seen her? How is she?'

'At first sight, like someone in love . . .'

'Don't play the fool or I'll tan your hide!'

'Keep your hair on! Dammit, it's very good to be in love! Yes, I met her, and him too. They came to see me this week at Tulle market.'

'My God! The market was on Tuesday, now it's Thursday – you could have told me earlier!'

'Hey, I've got work to do too! If you want to know, I was in Limoges yesterday.'

For the last two years Léon had been his own master, and was doing very well in his particular line of business. He was exempt from military service as the family bread-winner, and despite his youth had plunged into cattle-dealing. He still rented his farm, but the solicitor had entrusted him with several hectares of excellent pasture land as well, and he made the maximum profit from this.

'Well, what did she say to you?'

'They're getting married on the second of January, at Aubazine. The day after tomorrow, that is. And they'd really like you to be there.'

Pierre-Edouard felt a sudden wave of joy. His sister was getting married, she wanted him there too; it was reasonable, normal, that was how one should live, not under a burden of sorrow and bitterness.

'I'll be there,' he said. 'You bet I'll be there! How is she?'

'I told you, like someone in love.'

'And . . . Does it show much?'

'That she's in love? Yes, of course! If she weren't your sister . . .'

'Stop fooling! Does it show much that . . . well, that she's expecting a baby?'

'Are you joking or what?' Léon guffawed. 'Your sister, a baby?

And where would she put it? Flat as my palm she is, a fine girl and as pretty as a picture! Ha! She tricked you all!'

'Don't say that!' cried Pierre-Edouard, catching his arm. 'I tell you, Father said so. I don't know where he got it from, but it was he who told me. Besides, why do you think he let her get married, eh?'

'Listen,' said Léon, smiling, 'as far as I know, you and girls, you haven't got very far, you need a bit of help to learn a thing or two . . . But I know what I'm talking about when it comes to these things, if you don't mind me saying so. Your sister wanted Octave, so she went off with him, that's all. But that doesn't mean to say that it's gone any further. Besides, I've listened to them, they're still saying "vous" to each other, can you imagine it? Hardly credible, is it? And, believe me, she's looking after her reputation; in that way, she's a Vialhe! . . . He's rented a room for her with an old lady who's half blind, so she didn't check your sister's age, and he lodges in the Station Hotel when he goes to Tulle! Yes sir! At the Hôtel de la Gare! She told me so and I believe her, because I've got an eye for it, and I can tell the difference between an innocent girl and a woman . . .'

'Well!' Pierre-Edouard was flabbergasted. 'That's how it is . . . And, I thought . . .'

He was suddenly very proud of his sister; very proud that she knew how to control her life, without mistakes, sticking to her idea of marriage, to her idea of honour. She was going to be able to get married in white, and no one could deny her that right.

'What time is the wedding?' he asked.

'Eleven o'clock.'

'Thank you for everything. Now I must go back.'

'Look,' Léon stopped him, 'she's invited me, but it's really not my business; I don't want to go.'

'That was good of her, too,' murmured Pierre-Edouard. 'Yes, you must accept, you must come. Then there'll be at least one inhabitant of Saint-Libéral who can one day tell them how it all really happened. No one will ever believe me.'

'If you imagine that people would rather believe a cattle-dealer. . . ! Well, all right, I'll come. That'll double the crowd, eh? And we can make the journey together.'

# 11

'TOMORROW we'll go back for some more wood – we'd better make the most of you while we've got you. When I'm alone . . .' Jean-Edouard announced on the evening of 1 January.

The day had been just as bleak and gloomy as Christmas Day; to keep busy, Jean-Edouard and his son had spent most of the afternoon cutting firewood.

'No,' said Pierre-Edouard, 'I shan't be here tomorrow.'

'What?' growled his father.

'I'm going to Brive,' said Pierre-Edouard. 'I have something to do.'

He had not breathed a word to anyone about what Léon had told him; not even to Berthe, who would not have known how to hold her tongue.

'Miladiou! I don't like your manners,' grumbled Jean-Edouard. 'No, you're in the wrong place! You're not a soldier yet! Tomorrow we're going to get wood, whether you like it or not!'

'Then you'll have to go on your own.'

'And what are you up to in Brive?' questioned his father, forcing himself to control his temper.

'We're having a dinner, all the fellows in my class,' said Pierre-Edouard, without batting an eyelid. He knew that his father would soon find out that he was lying, but he didn't care; he'd be a long way off when the deception was revealed.

'A dinner! A dinner!' muttered Jean-Edouard. 'And that's going to take all day? Hah, you lead a fine life, you young ones! All right then, you'll come with me,' he said, looking at Berthe. 'You haven't got a dinner, have you?'

The girl shook her head, lowered her eyes and kept quiet; she knew that her only defence was to remain mute.

It was still dark when Pierre-Edouard climbed into Léon's dog-cart. Léon touched the horse, and it started off at a gentle trot. They took the road which descended towards Perpezac and Brignac and soon arrived at the railway workings.

'They're getting on fast now,' Pierre-Edouard remarked.

'Yes, another three kilometres and they'll have reached us. But it seems it wasn't all easy going among the rocks over Ferrière way; that's what held them up. But that's all right for your father – the longer it takes the more profit he makes!'

'They say you're not losing by it either,' said Pierre-Edouard drily.

'Huh! I sell them a few surplus cows from time to time, some sausages perhaps, but I'm not making a lot of money out of that, believe me.'

'Your horse goes well,' observed Pierre-Edouard, after several minutes' silence.

'Yes, we'll soon be in Brive. I won't be long there, I must just pop in to the abattoir to check on two carcasses. Don't worry, we won't miss the train . . .' He fell silent, spat out his cigarette, then continued. 'You know, it gives me a funny feeling to be going to your sister's wedding.'

'Me too; I can hardly believe it. Time passes quickly, doesn't it? You remember the wolves?'

'You're asking me do I remember? You made me throw away my thrushes; I lost more than five francs!'

They got off the train at Aubazine station at 9.20. There Léon, who really seemed to know everyone, borrowed a horse-cab. The cab had no hood and they had to muffle up, for it was bitterly cold.

'Go on!' cried Léon, shaking the reins, 'be brave, old girl! Talk about an old nag!' he observed, as the animal slowed down for a breather on the long hill which led to the village. 'We'd be quicker on foot! It's going to take us almost an hour to cover these four kilometres. Still, we are sitting down!'

'Yes, but we're freezing. Push the old crock on so that we get there!'

'Don't be funny; if I push her, she'll kick the bucket! I know her well, I sold her to him . . .'

'You managed to sell an old hack like that!'

'Easy,' claimed Léon. 'Give her to me for an hour and I'll make her ten years younger.'

'Oh yes?'

'Of course! Two litres of oats in four litres of dry white wine, a good grooming with sugar to make her coat shiny, a dab of polish on her hooves, two drops of vinegar under her eyelids to make her eyes sparkle, a good layer of lime on her teeth, and to finish off, a quarter of a peeled onion stuck up her backside – that way a horse'll prance around like a three-year-old stallion!'

'You're a dreadful scoundrel!' exclaimed Pierre-Edouard. 'But next day, don't you ever have any trouble?'

'Well, no. For proof, you saw how the buyer greeted me. Besides, he can't complain, the beast isn't dead yet! And then, to tell the truth, the day after the sale I'm not there . . .'

Freezing rain mixed with snow was falling when they finally arrived in Aubazine. A heavy pall of fog sprawled down from the Pauliac mountain and darkened the whole village.

Léon went straight to the inn, gave the horse and cart over to the stable boy, and rushed into the dining-room, where a huge fire was crackling.

'Two mulled wines, and in big bowls!' he ordered, sitting down by the fireside.

Their drinks were just being served when Louise and Octave came into the room. Pierre-Edouard stood a few seconds without moving, then he went to his sister and hugged her.

'You know,' he said, 'you showed us a thing or two, and it's not over yet. Oh, I can tell you, you really did it!'

'Don't say it, I know . . .'

'Who told you?'

'Doctor Fraysse. He wrote to Octave,' she explained, controlling her tears, 'and if he talks to you about it, you can tell Father that I shan't be coming back. Never.'

'Come, come,' interrupted Octave, 'we'll see about that later on. Today is a special day! Here,' he said, turning to a tall fellow who had just come in, 'I'd like to introduce my witness. And you, Louise, have you asked Monsieur Dupeuch if he agrees?'

'Me?' said Léon with feeling. 'Witness? But why not Pierre-Edouard instead?'

'He's still under twenty-one,' explained Octave.

'So you'll accept, Léon,' insisted Louise. 'It would please me, and it will always remind me of our adventures in Saint-Libéral, you remember?'

'Yes,' muttered Léon, his throat tightening. It was the first time anyone had ever spoken to him with such spontaneous kindness.

'Fine,' he said at last. 'If you want me to, but . . . Thank you for thinking of me.'

The formalities at the Mairie were extremely brief, and they realised that the mayor had been forewarned by his colleague in St Libéral; he was carrying out his duties because he could not really do otherwise, but his attitude showed just how much he too disapproved of this marriage.

The church was hardly more welcoming, and the young vicar responsible for the ceremony sped through the blessing in a trice. Then he reminded them in a few words of the mutual duties of husband and wife, and could not prevent himself from glancing slyly and inquisitively at Louise's extraordinarily flat stomach when he talked about the Christian education of children. At the end he offered a short prayer at the altar of the Blessed Virgin, had the registers signed, and disappeared into the darkness of the nave.

At the meal the atmosphere was no more cheerful. It was obvious that Louise, despite the happiness which shone from her eyes, could not forget all she had endured and sacrificed to achieve this pitiful, almost clandestine, ceremony on a dark and freezing day.

As for Octave, he was attentive to his wife's every movement, but he too was deeply hurt at not being able to offer his young wife a big, jolly family festival, a feast spiced with song, laughter and discussion, a dance enlivened by some cheerful lasses and fellows – all the things that go to make a happy wedding.

During the meal, Louise informed her brother that they had found lodgings in Terrasson, and were going to live over there for as long as Octave was needed on the railway. Afterwards they would leave for Orléans, her husband's home town.

'And I'm going to work too,' she said. 'Octave didn't want me to, but I really don't see why I should stay idle, just waiting for him to come home. Later, when a baby is expected, we'll see.'

'She had to say it,' thought Pierre-Edouard. 'She doesn't want any suspicion that the child came before the husband!' He glanced at Léon, and smiled at his dumb-show which neatly declared: 'You see, I told you so!'

'But what will you do?' he asked.

'Some sewing for one of Doctor Fraysse's colleagues. It was he who recommended me.'

'He's a good man,' agreed Pierre-Edouard. Then he announced his imminent departure on army service, and the conversation dragged a little; Octave and his friend talked of their own service, evoking memories of interest only to themselves.

With the dessert Léon insisted on treating them to champagne. Everyone scolded him for such extravagance, but he persisted, opened the bottle and filled the glasses himself. With a mock clumsy gesture – which fooled no one – he managed to break Louise's glass, so that the sparkling wine spilt on to her white bodice.

'There,' he said, 'that brings good luck. Here's to the young couple!'

A little later, when it was already beginning to get dark, it was he who gave the signal to leave.

'Yes, you'll have to excuse us! We mustn't miss the train, and with that old nag to get us there . . .'

Louise and Octave accompanied them to the stable.

'So that's it,' said Pierre-Edouard, after kissing his sister. 'Good luck, and . . .'

He shook his brother-in-law's hand, and climbed into the cart.

'See you soon!' called Louise.

He nodded yes, and forced his mouth into the ghost of a smile. He was convinced that months, probably even years, would pass before that wish came true.

During his last two days at home Pierre-Edouard barely opened his mouth, but no one paid any attention to that: less and less was said in the Vialhe house. He could not forget that spoiled wedding, where everything rang false, when everyone was forced to appear pleased; he could not forgive his father for being the indirect author of that travesty of a ceremony which reeked of sadness.

Then it was the day of his departure.

'Come back as soon as you can,' his father advised. 'You know that there's no lack of work here!'

'And be careful,' added his mother.

He went to kiss his grandfather, but could not be certain that the old man recognised him; then he brushed his lips on the faded cheek of his grandmother, who innocently asked him where he was going. Finally he kissed his parents and his sister, picked up his modest suitcase of pressed cardboard, and opened the door.

'I wanted to tell you,' he called before leaving, 'on Saturday I was at Louise and Octave's wedding. They are very happy and they're not expecting a baby yet! Léon can tell you all about it, he was a witness. . .'

He slammed the door violently behind him, and strode away.

For several years Father Feix had hardly managed to sleep more than four hours a night. So, instead of lying awake and chilled, tossing in his bed, he preferred to delay his time of going to bed as long as possible. He sat down by the fireside, where he could at least gather a little warmth for his legs and hands, which were always frozen.

Once installed on the settle, he first took up his breviary. Then he embarked on *The Cross of Corrèze*, which he read and re-read from first to last line. Towards one o'clock he recited his rosary five times, to which he added the litany of the Most Blessed Name of Jesus and of the Virgin Mary. Then, since sleep still evaded him, he meditated while drinking a large bowl of lime-blossom tea.

All this brought him to two o'clock when, sleepy or no, he went to lie down; he never failed to thank the Lord on waking if he had managed to doze until six.

So he was quickly at the door when there was a knock towards eleven o'clock, that night of 18 January. He opened it, and recognised Jean-Edouard.

'It's my father, he's just going . . .'

'Wait for me so that you can light my way; I'll be right with you.'

He threw his heavy cloak around his shoulders, fetched his holy oils and joined his visitor. They were soon at the Vialhes'.

Unconscious, emaciated, hardly recognisable, old Edouard was in agony, his nostrils already pinched; only a tenuous breath, barely perceptible, showed that he was still alive. Nevertheless, Father Feix estimated that he had time to administer Extreme Unction in full, and while reciting the prayers he anointed the gaunt body six times, touching the eyes, ears, nostrils, mouth, hands and feet of the dying man. Around the bed, Jean-Edouard, Marguerite and Berthe murmured the responses. As for old Léonie, crouched by the fire in the living-room, she was crying silently, staring at the flames which danced at her feet without seeing them.

When he had finished the last orison, the priest moved away from the bed.

'Listen, my child,' he said to Berthe, 'you go and look after your grandmother; he doesn't need you any more. Go on, I'm going to stay here.' He knelt at the foot of the bed and began his vigil.

The old man passed away at three o'clock – without a sound, without a gasp, in a silence hardly disturbed by the sputtering of the two candles placed on the bedside table. The priest gave the final blessing, and then made way for Marguerite and her daughter as soon as they came in to lay out the corpse.

'Do you want me to walk back with you?' suggested Jean-Edouard, who had followed him into the living-room.

'No, stay here,' advised the priest.

He approached old Léonie, shook both her hands, then walked towards the door.

'You would be doing a good deed if you informed Louise. Do you want me to do it?' he asked.

'Don't bother with that,' cut in Jean-Edouard, 'I know what I have to do.'

The priest went out, and already behind him he heard the plaintive wailing of the three women; it was only a discreet quavering at the moment, on the surface of their lips. But soon, when the village awoke, when day dawned, they would howl like animals, wail with open mouths, as if to empty out their pain, their sorrow, and so that everyone in St Libéral would know that death had struck at the Vialhes'.

The burial attracted a huge crowd. Since the morning of the death Jeantout, delegated by Jean-Edouard, had toured the countryside to announce the news at every farm; even the most remote received a visit.

And the people came, for the Vialhes were known by everyone, and because the deceased had always been a good man, esteemed and respected. Relatives who had not been seen for years wanted to be part of the obsequies; even the ones from Tulle came, and God knows, Jean-Edouard had good reason to refuse to receive *them*! Nevertheless he welcomed them, greeting them as if nothing had happened, as if it were not from their house that his daughter had run away.

Naturally, when the whole family came out of the house to walk behind the hearse, everyone noticed Louise's absence. Pierre-Edouard was not there either, but that was different.

And yet, when they found themselves in the cemetery after the Mass, by the open grave where four men were slowly lowering the coffin, everyone saw the modest wreath placed among the rest. It was the smallest, no doubt the cheapest; a few artificial flowers interwoven with a purple ribbon, and on it, for what it was worth, the letters in silver:

> *To our late lamented Grandfather.*
> *Octave and Louise, his grandchildren.*

The death of his grandfather made Pierre-Edouard very sad. He had always had a great affection for him, and often remembered the old man's joy on the day he got his certificate. He did not remember the same emotion being shown when Louise and Berthe achieved the diploma in their turn, nor that they received a napoléon of twenty francs, as he had. He had never wanted to spend that napoléon; he kept it carefully like a good luck charm.

He learned of the demise of his grandfather by telegram, brought to him by the post orderly during a drill session.

'What is it?' demanded the sergeant, having ordered 'at ease'.

'Nothing, Sergeant,' he stammered, embarrassed to have to announce news which concerned only himself in front of all his comrades.

'As you like! But if it's your girlfriend making a date, make her wait — you're nowhere near in the mood to give her a smacker!'

The quip roused several perfunctory laughs, and he forced himself to smile as well.

He did not ask permission to go to the funeral; he had been enrolled for too short a time to hope that they would grant him leave. All his class were confined to quarters for months to come, and would not even have the right to go into town until after their basic training and vaccinations. And finally, he had no desire to return to St Libéral in such circumstances, no desire to immerse himself in civilian life again for forty-eight hours. He had struggled enough getting used to his new state, and knew that any absence, however brief, would only make things more difficult.

Taken in hand on arrival by an old NCO with enormous moustaches and legs like barrel-hoops, Pierre-Edouard and his friends had been forced to submit to all his bullying without saying a word.

'From now on,' the artillery sergeant had bellowed, having lined them up as best he could on the parade-ground, 'From now on, you're no longer "Gentlemen", but lowly gunners, crewmen, riflemen! You've been chosen to serve in the best division in the world, and it's a great honour for a load of no-hopers like you. But to be an artilleryman's an achievement, and I'll make you achieve it; *I* shall, you swine. And if anyone's not happy, he can always ask to be transferred to the foot-sloggers, those despicable infantrymen, only good for cannon-fodder! Now, everyone to the stables! For now you're going to collect horse-dung for me. You're going to learn that before touching a gun you have to know how to look after the ones that pull them, look after the horses and ride them! And when your backsides are as leathery as old drumskins, then perhaps we'll let you have a look at a seventy-five!'

Since then there had been nothing but fatigue duties in barracks, room and equipment inspections, parade sessions and musket-drill, on top of cleaning the stables, grooming the horses and polishing the harness.

Pierre-Edouard, accustomed to work in the fields, was not overburdened by the work rate required here; it was far less than he had to bear when hoeing on the plateau! On the other hand, he had difficulty in getting used to military discipline, which allowed the stupidest idiot, just because he was a brigadier, to use any means to break the spirit of the strong-willed.

So he adopted the habit of silence, sank into the mass of recruits, and did nothing – either good or bad – which might draw attention to himself.

When Father Feix's old housekeeper came, as she did every morning, into the main room of the presbytery, and saw the old priest on the settle in front of the cold hearth, she thought he had fallen asleep there on returning from Mass. In fact, as Doctor Delpy confirmed shortly afterwards, he had been dead for more than five hours. Dead, alone by the fireside, where he sat each evening.

His passing shook the parish; the parish he had served for almost half a century, in which he was the most respected figure, even by those who disliked him, criticised or complained about him, for everyone in the community was obliged to him in some way. He had baptised and taught the catechism to all those under forty, married half of the couples; with very few exceptions, every household had received him at least once to administer the last rites to someone who lay dying, or to conduct a burial.

Thus his death saddened the whole community – and worried them, for they wondered who would replace him as head of the parish. In any case, whoever the new priest was, it would take him years to get to know his parishioners; their old secrets, their quarrels and ancestral feuds, the subjects never to be mentioned to someone or other – in short, everything which had made Father Feix part of every family, who had the right to give his opinion even if his advice was not followed. They even went so far as to forget his outbursts against the Republic, and his grim opposition to the railway line.

So, despite the spring workload in this month of April, there was a crowd on the day of the burial. Few of the men actually went into church, and if no one was surprised at the attendance of the squire, the solicitor and Jean-Edouard, there was a lot of talk amongst those waiting in the square, at the inn or in the bistros, when the mayor and Doctor Fraysse entered.

As luck would have it, a dozen navvies from the railway were already installed at the bar of the inn when the wheelwright, Fernand Fronty, walked in, followed by several friends, to empty a jar while awaiting for the coffin to emerge. 'My God!' shouted one of the drinkers brazenly, 'you're making a great fuss over a priest. It's only one old crow less!'

'Take that back!' ordered the wheelwright, marching right up to him.

Fernand Fronty had never set foot in the church since his first and probably last communion twenty-five years earlier, and everyone knew of his profound indifference to all things religious; he had barely greeted Father Feix when he passed him in the street. Yet his reaction surprised no one. The priest was what he was, but he was theirs, and those lousy foreigners had no right to say anything about him. When they insulted him, they insulted the whole community.

'Take it back!' repeated Fronty, grabbing the drinker by the shirt.

Sober, the man would certainly have complied after one glance at the wheelwright's breadth of shoulder. But he did not notice the huge arms, shaped by twenty years of daily exercise with the plane, axe and sledge-hammer, nor the fist, as big as a ham, which held him by the collar.

'Damn the crows!' he yelled. 'They're all . . .'

No one ever found out what they were, for the wheelwright's backhander propelled him unconscious into the middle of the room. His companions hesitated for a second, and then very wisely put their noses into their glasses; it was really too early in the day to organise a good fight. Besides, they were still clear-headed enough to make an accurate assessment of Fernand's strength.

'Miladiou!' he commented, taking his place at the bar, 'I'm not going to let that worm insult our priest! All right?' he asked pointedly, smiling threateningly at the other workers.

They nodded hastily in agreement, and cleared off as soon as their companion was fit to walk.

Jean-Edouard retreated into isolation, but that did not mean that he neglected his farm; quite the opposite. His daughter had brought him dishonour and forced him to abandon his political ambitions, therefore he had nothing to lose and no one to plan for.

So, to demonstrate that he was still a force to be reckoned with, he anticipated Jeantout in salad cultivation. God knows why, as he had no need to do it to earn money. His pig-rearing was going well. He supplied the railway company and also sold his surplus at the main markets of the area, in groups of ten or fifteen bacon pigs, fattened on the scraps from the canteen.

He planted out half a hectare of lettuce simply for the pleasure of it; he gave over the field called The Gardens to this, for it had the best aspect and gave the earliest crops. A further advantage was that he gave responsibility for the crop to Berthe. While she was busy with that, she would not think of acting like her sister!

Jeantout was angry at this spiteful act, but he said nothing. He knew only too well that his neighbour was just looking for an excuse to explode in fury.

Jean-Edouard was not content with earning a lot; he wanted his money to bear fruit as well. To achieve this he didn't mind falling out with the mayor and the squire when he did them out of two hectares of good land on the plateau. It had been put up for sale by the solicitor, who now also wanted to buy a car. These fields bordered on the property of Antoine Gigoux and Jean Duroux, and it suited the two men very well to come to a secret understanding, hold down the price, and divide the land.

Jean-Edouard got wind of the affair, went to Monsieur Lardy and put a bag of napoléons on the table; twenty minutes later he was the owner of the two hectares. In the same way he snapped up a hectare of meadowland set in the valley, not far from the mill, under the very nose of Léon Dupeuch. He heard mention of it one morning at St Libéral market; the business had almost been done, and because he had already signed the private contract Léon had committed the error of talking far too much.

Jean-Edouard immediately went to Perpezac and found the seller – an old spinster who drove a hard bargain, but was so grasping that she was very happy to renege on her signature and follow this generous new buyer all the way to the lawyer's office. Jean-Edouard placed his pieces of gold on the table without a qualm, pocketed the deeds to the property, and returned to tell Léon.

'God damn it!' growled Léon, 'that's not the way an honest man behaves! I could take you to court!'

'You won't do that, you'd lose money by it. And as for honesty, that's not something a cattle-dealer can talk about!'

'Okay,' said Léon, 'you've conned me, but don't worry; I'll short-change you, one day . . . And I'll find other pastureland easily, whereas you'll have to look a lot further before you find Louise again . . .'

Ten years earlier Jean-Edouard would have knocked him cold. But he was suddenly aware of his age, and realised that Léon was perfectly capable of beating *him* up.

'You'll be sorry you said that!'

'Oh yes,' jeered Léon, 'I'll be sorry, like Louise is sorry about

Léonard, that old decaying bit of rubbish you found! You know what they say? Since then he's made do with his goats! Oh, he was lovely, the future Vialhe son-in-law!'

And he burst into insolent laughter.

When he announced his latest purchase to Marguerite, Jean-Edouard said nothing of his visit to Léon. Neither of them had talked about Louise since she left, and that worm Léon was not going to break their silence on the subject with his spiteful words.

He had expected that Marguerite would try to make him relent, but to his great astonishment she had never said anything which could be interpreted as a plea for mercy. He knew that she adored Louise, but she had been so delighted with the planned marriage, so proud of the advantageous match awaiting her daughter, that she could not forgive her the destruction of the project, nor the shame she herself had since suffered.

She was not about to forget that her daughter had deceived her in four ways. First she had compromised herself with a stranger; secondly, she had pretended to accept her parents' decision; then she had led them to believe that she had got herself into trouble; and lastly she had used that miserable lie to marry a good-for-nothing, a poor man without land. No, she would not plead for her daughter, never. To allow her to return one day would be to accept that she was right to behave like a tramp; well, Louise had done wrong, and if God was good, the future would give proof of it!

'That makes ours one of the finest farms,' she murmured, musing on the new purchase, 'but it will give us more work, and already . . .'

He shrugged his shoulders — work didn't frighten him, and in eighteen months Pierre-Edouard would be back; what luck that the 1905 law had reduced army service to two years! It wasn't like in his time; he'd had to do five years, enough to drive you mad!

# PART THREE

*The Confrontation*

# 12

THE inauguration of the line took place on Saturday 31 July 1909; from now on it would join Saint-Libéral-sur-Diamond to La-Rivière-de-Mansac.

Once more the work had been delayed, halted less than a kilometre from the village as the result of a substantial landslide caused by the very wet spring. On a stormy night in May the rush of water had carried away twenty metres of the line, both rails and sleepers, and gouged a huge gully in the road. It had to be filled in and the repair strengthened and reinforced with stonework. Eventually the building work could be restarted, and the line linked up to the brand-new station at St Libéral.

The arrival of the first train was the excuse for celebrations to which the whole community was invited, and everyone agreed that the town council had arranged matters well.

With the help of the squire, who was still a general councillor, Antoine Gigoux had managed to get the district prefect and their Parliamentary deputy to attend; the latter had the honour of cutting the tricoloured ribbon which barred the track. The united brass bands of Brignac, Perpezac and St Libéral played the Marseillaise, and the train arrived just as the final chords rang out.

The convoy entered, beribboned, whistling, at full steam, covered in flowers and flags and crammed with workers and urchins; puffing into St Libéral, it halted at the little station amidst cheers, applause and cries of joy.

After the photos, in which everyone wanted to be included, there were kisses, congratulations and slaps on the back; then many settled into the carriages for a short but exciting journey in reverse, and a triumphant return.

A gigantic banquet had been planned, at which the workers and the villagers were to sit side by side, fraternise, and reconcile their differences. In the evening they all danced in the square; a great deal of drinking went on too . . .

At midnight a superb firework display came shooting from the engine, thanks to the generosity of the squire. The sparks rose high in the sky and announced the news: St Libéral was connected to the rest of the world!

No member of the Vialhe family joined in the festivities. Nobody cared whether they did or not. Who still remembered that it was partly Jean-Edouard's perseverence and his mediation which had brought the train this far?

Pierre-Edouard distinguished himself in the tests which marked the end of the corporals' training course – his captain, on the strength of his school certificate and his general air of intelligence, had officially entered him in the list of candidates for his first stripes.

Pierre-Edouard obeyed orders and acquitted himself well. The 75 gun, 1897 model, soon had no secrets from him, and on the day of the test he managed to fire at a fine rate of fifteen shots a minute – and better still, to place all the shells within the prescribed circle. (Admittedly, he had promised his gun-crew of six the greatest binge of their lives if they helped, proving their goodwill by their speed.) When he was questioned on the theoretical working of the Schneider 75, he was able to explain the functioning of the hydraulic brakes and the melignite shells, both time- and percussion-fused.

That evening he joined a happy band of successful examination candidates who strolled through Besançon bawling out 'The Artillery-man of Metz' and various coarse jokes. They visited several bars then, still singing and reeling more and more dangerously, they set off for Ma Fifine's brothel, determined to finish the evening by proving to the women that artillerymen were the best and fastest shots! Unluckily they came across a police patrol in the town; the officer in charge was a surly fellow, narrow-minded and possibly envious of them, who dispatched them summarily to sleep it off at the police station.

During his first six months serving the flag, Pierre-Edouard had heard very little news of St Libéral. It was true that he himself did not know what to write in the few letters he occasionally sent to his family. What could he say that would interest his parents? That he had some very good friends, among them a workman from Paris, a farrier from Orléans, a farmer from Brie and another from the Chartres area? That would not matter to them, he thought. Or should he write to them about the only man from the Corrèze apart from himself in the regiment? This was a Sergeant-Major, the worst sort of non-commissioned career officer, an evil drunkard, like an old diseased boar, who delivered his orders and insults in patois after a drink or two! A disgrace to the whole of the Corrèze! No, that really was not something to describe to his parents!

As for asking for news of the village and the farm, he knew the main facts; the death of Father Feix, the arrival of the train, the flourishing market for pig-rearing and the purchase of more land.

This acquisition really cheered him up; he remembered the location of the plots perfectly. But he thought with longing of all the days that separated him from the moment when he could at last harness his plough there, goad the animals, and mark his first furrow in this new Vialhe land.

What he would really have liked to ask for in his letters was news of Louise, but it was unthinkable to risk it. He was sure that his father had not forgiven him for attending his sister's wedding. To beg for news of the outlaw would be considered a grave insult.

He had indeed tried to write to her directly by addressing his letter to Octave Flaviens, care of the railway company. But he had received no reply, and he presumed that the message had got lost. Or possibly (but he refused to believe it) that his sister had decided to sever all ties . . .

Almost a year had passed before he could at last return to the village to spend his regulation leave. He arrived on Christmas Eve by the evening train, very conscious of the impression he made on his fellow-travellers, with his beautiful artillery uniform enhanced by the two broad red stripes of a corporal.

'You must be the Vialhe boy?' asked an old peasant who climbed on at Perpezac station.

'Certainly am, Monsieur Mathou,' he agreed, without taking his eyes off the passing countryside. His heart was full as he followed in the train the route which he had taken so often on foot and knew in every detail.

'Well, so you're a soldier! I was just saying to myself that it's been some time since we saw you!'

'Yes, indeed!' he said. 'It's been a while.'

'Bah! It goes quickly nowadays, not like in my time! Well, there you are, on leave I suppose? You'll find some changes in the village. And your father, how's he?'

'Fine, I think,' he said in astonishment.

'We hardly see him. It's true he's had some problems . . .'

'What problems?' he asked anxiously. The last letter, dated a month ago, had given no cause for concern.

'Oh, didn't you know? Ah, the poor chap! He lost forty pigs in a week, and I've heard say they were damned fine animals, worth more than two hundred livres each! A touch of swine-fever and it was all over. It seems he only managed to save a dozen, and they don't look too bright!'

'Well,' thought Pierre-Edouard, 'he must be in a fine old mood . . .' But still he was relieved; for a moment he had feared that one of the family was ill.

It was almost dark when the train stopped at St Libéral station. Pierre-Edouard jumped down to the ground, gazing around, trying to make out what had changed in his world.

Apart from the station, which was completely new and had been only foundations when he left, he noticed the additions made at the inn; a big extension – bedrooms probably – had been attached to the main building. The bakery had been enlarged as well. The grocery had been repainted. The butcher's shop, previously quite small, now opened onto the main street, with a large window in which hung strings of sausages and enormous hams. He walked down the street and noticed an unfamiliar motorcar in front of the solicitor's house. So he had bought one, too!

He met several people who hesitated for a moment before returning his greeting. And suddenly, there, at the end of the street, already engulfed in darkness but still discernible, he saw his home. He hastened his step.


'But you should have let us know!' repeated his mother for the twentieth time.

He had told her repeatedly that leave was always in danger of being revoked, but she stuck to her point and rather held it against him for arriving unexpectedly like this.

'You see, we hadn't got anything planned for Christmas Eve, but with you here it'll be different!'

'I hope so,' he agreed as he bent to the hearth to rearrange the logs. 'Father's not here?'

'He had to go to Objat to fetch some medicine for the pigs. I'd better tell you that . . .'

'I know,' he interrupted, 'Old Mathou talked to me about it. And Grandma, where's she?'

'Oh, poor thing, leave her. She's already in bed.'

'And Berthe?'

'In the cowshed.'

'I'll go there.'

He went out, the dog frisking with delight around his legs. He

136

pushed the door to the cowshed with his foot, entered and savoured the rich smell of the animals. Berthe was milking the old cow, Grey. She jumped, then put down her bucket and rushed to hug him.

'There, there!' he said, as he stroked her hair. Then he held her away from him and looked at her.

'You're not very plump,' he ascertained, 'but you've grown very pretty all the same. Well, anything new here?'

'Nothing,' she said, shrugging.

'And Louise,' he murmured, 'have you any news of her?'

'The last I heard she was in Terrasson, but I don't know any more. You know, I can't go out . . .'

'So they're still the same, the parents?'

'What do you think? Look out, here's Father.'

He heard a horse's hooves and was amazed. 'He's bought a horse and cart?'

'Yes, last summer.'

'And he didn't even write to tell me that,' he muttered, a little annoyed.

He went out and walked towards his father, who was just getting down from the trap. Jean-Edouard turned round and examined the silhouette marching towards him; it was now completely dark.

'Oh, it's you!' he said at last. 'You should have let us know! But you've arrived just in time; you can help me inject the pigs.'

By Boxing Day, Pierre-Edouard knew that he could no longer get along with his father. He was saddened by this, for he had really hoped to establish a good relationship with him, one man to another. But it was impossible. And yet he was not questioning his father's authority as head of the family and master of the land in any way – if only his father would not take advantage of him, but accept that he was now more than twelve years old!

Indirectly, it was Louise who was again responsible for the row. On the morning of the 26th, Pierre-Edouard went to visit old Doctor Fraysse, and found out the address of the doctor at whose house she was working. He was so pleased with this information that he decided to go to Terrasson straight away; he returned home and changed.

'Where are you going like that?' called out his father.

'To town.'

'That's it – to town? Let me tell you you're not in the barracks here! There's plenty of work to be done. And if you want to spend your days in town you'd better put up in a hotel!'

'Listen, I've a right to enjoy my leave!'

'That's right, and I only have the right to work while I wait for you! You haven't even been to see the land!'

'I will, there's plenty of time. But now I'm going into town!'

'Which one?' questioned Jean-Edouard, who felt vaguely that his son's activities must have something to do with Louise. And he suddenly remembered that, a year earlier, Pierre-Edouard had told him he was going to Brive for a dinner with his school class. A dinner? Oh yes! Except it was a wedding!

'Which town?' he asked again.

'That's none of your business,' said Pierre-Edouard, marching towards the door.

'Miladiou!' grumbled his father, 'go on talking to me like that and you won't need to set foot here again!'

'Ah, well!' called back Pierre-Edouard, shrugging, 'then all you'll have to do is chuck Berthe out, and you'll be happy at last!'

Jean-Edouard sprang at him, grasped him by the arm and almost hit him.

'All right,' he said as he released him, 'go where you like. After all, I've been working alone for twelve months, and I've not been doing too badly!'

He passed in front of his son and set off towards the piggery.

Pierre-Edouard took three and a half hours to reach Terrasson. Twenty kilometres on foot held no fears for him, and at least these were accomplished without a full pack on his back, without a gun, without cartridge pouches, and with shoes which were not killing him. After having a snack at the first bistro he came to, he found the doctor's house with no difficulty and rang the bell.

He shuffled from one foot to the other, hardly knowing what to say to the old lady who, in three words, had just destroyed his happiness. Louise had been gone for a month. The railway construction yard was being closed, and Octave had returned to Orléans.

'But she is all right, as far as you know?' he asked at last.

'Yes, but . . . Are you a relative?'

'Her brother.'

'I should have guessed,' exclaimed the old lady, 'she looks like you. Yes, she's very well, and has no problems at all with her pregnancy.'

'Ah! she's expecting . . .'

'Yes, in January.'

He calculated immediately that the baby would arrive a full year after the wedding. Who would dare to gossip now!

'And you haven't got her address?'

'Yes, of course I have!'

This news lifted his spirits again; he had not come in vain.

He looked forward to the end of his leave with relief – not that he felt the slightest enthusiasm for the idea of returning to life in the barracks, but the atmosphere in his family was growing daily more oppressive.

And this despite having devoted all his time to the work on the farm, apart from his escapade to Terrasson. He found that he enjoyed returning to this work, but his father was so despotic that Pierre-Edouard could not accept all his strictures with good grace.

His father ruled and supervised everything, ordered the family by voice and gesture, as if he feared for his position as patriarch – which he now was in fact, since the death of the old man – and the slightest complaint unleashed a thunderbolt of recrimination. Pierre-Edouard noticed in amazement that his mother supported her husband totally, rather than trying to moderate his severity.

It was true that his parents needed to present an impenetrable defence to the attacks from without. Pierre-Edouard soon became aware of village opinion; as far as his parents were concerned they were consumed by envy, by jealousy, sometimes even by hate. Previously Jean-Edouard had been admired; now he was criticised remorselessly. He was not forgiven for his success, his money, his purchase of land, his ruthlessness in trampling on anyone who got in his way.

Added to this, many were angered at having to admit that, once he had left the buying syndicate, it had survived only six months before sinking without trace. Last but not least amongst their complaints, since his resignation the town council had staggered from one crisis to the next; no one could ignore the accumulation of mistakes, the energy wasted in disagreements, which increased the electors' dissatisfaction. Some even predicted that Antoine Gigoux, ageing fast, would not stay until the end of his term of office; that he was preparing to resign in favour of his son. Now, many of the electors did not want to hear any mention of that candidate. They knew he was supported and encouraged behind the scenes by the young teacher, who was the new secretary at the Mairie, and they foresaw that they would be landed with a town council which many considered too left-wing. The opposition had rested their hopes on Jean-Edouard and he had betrayed them, as if he wanted the whole world to be punished because his daughter had run away.

Certainly no one could overlook the offence; what she had done was unforgiveable. But all in all, was that any good reason to make everyone suffer for it? Many who had admired him a year earlier for his noble attitude as an honest man ill-used by circumstance, now felt that he had made too much of what was essentially a private matter.

A few days in St Libéral were enough for Pierre-Edouard to gauge the resentment many neighbours felt towards his father, and, by association, all the members of the family. Even Léon reproached him curtly with his father's dishonesty, and he had a lot of difficulty in convincing Léon that he didn't know anything about the meadow business.

The discovery of all the bitterness surrounding the name of Viahle, added to the heavy, tense atmosphere of mourning which he found at home, spoiled his leave. He was almost happy to climb into the train one morning to return to Besançon. Only the knowledge that Berthe was utterly miserable prevented him from humming to himself as the train moved off.

He had not heard her speak more than three or four times during the whole of his visit. Mute and obstinate, the young girl submitted to all the work and trials imposed by her parents. She did not complain but retreated into complete silence. She seemed to be awaiting some miracle which would at last allow her to live.

The railway workers finally left the village at the beginning of February 1910. Their departure created a void in the life of St Libéral. They had been there for two and a half years; everyone had grown accustomed to their presence and, above all, to the trade they brought. Not everyone had known how to squeeze the maximum from this mass of consumers, as Jean-Edouard had done, but everyone had profited in one way or another from this lucky windfall. Its disappearance affected the economy of the community, and very soon they came to speak nostalgically of the good times when the railway yard had been open. This feeling, tinged with regret, was not solely due to the loss of substantial profits.

In two and a half years a tide of fellow-feeling had flowed between the strangers and the indigenous population; many were saddened to know that those long winter evenings of story-telling in the inn were gone forever. They used to gather in groups in the bar and listen open-mouthed to the fabulous tales recounted by some of the old navvies, who had toured the whole of France and North Africa. One of them, an old foreman in his sixties, had even been gangmaster on the cutting of the Panama Canal in 1886; thanks to him, life in the Americas was depicted in snippets during the course of the evenings. Since then a few privileged listeners had continued to narrate to others the old man's marvellous adventures. True or false, they also formed part of the good times when the railway yard was open.

With the departure of the workers, the peace and silence which had been forgotten for more than two years returned. St Libéral rediscovered its life, its customs, its humdrum daily round, hardly disturbed by the train passing through twice a day. And it was during this re-adjustment to the intimacy of village life that the new priest arrived.

Since the death of Father Feix the community had lacked a priest; Masses and various ceremonies had been provided by a curate from Objat. He was a likeable man, he could not be faulted, except that he was a stranger. He was accepted as such and tolerated simply because the Bishop had assured the parish that they would shortly have their own priest.

Months passed without an appointment being announced, despite the respectful enquiries from some of the faithful. It was necessary for the squire and the solicitor to take the matter in hand, and visit the bishop's palace to plead the community's cause.

Father Paul Verlhac arrived a month later, by the evening train. He was young and full of energy and had fought his first campaign as a soldier of Christ as curate at Tulle and then at Uzerche. His nomination to St Libéral raised him to the rank of priest, and he was very proud of this title. But he foresaw that he would need a lot of tact, patience and humility to become the really good shepherd he wished to be. So he began his ministry with great discretion.

They were grateful to him for his circumspection. A few spiteful tongues maintained that he was hiding his cards, some even whispered that he had a troubled past – that his departure from Uzerche was the result of some unpleasantness (there was talk of women, and also of notorious drunkenness) – but the majority of parishioners accepted the young priest, who bravely undertook the responsibilities of his new role and began to get to know the flock slowly and cautiously, like a farmer cultivating a new plot.

Pierre-Edouard agreed to join the training detachment for non-commissioned officers mainly to fill his increasingly boring days. A military career held no attraction for him, but the theoretical and practical courses required for the training were less dull than the everyday drudgery imposed on the troopers. In the end he was quite pleased to be forced into intellectual tasks.

He quickly absorbed the basics of trigonometry and geography necessary to a good artilleryman, and turned with pleasure to the field exercises and various manoeuvres. These excursions allowed him to escape from the barracks for a while, and to explore a landscape and agricultural system which had nothing in common with the Corrèze.

Having no news of his parents, he conducted a correspondence with Louise instead, and was deeply moved to learn that she had chosen him as godfather to her son. Little Félix was now four months old, and would be baptised as soon as Pierre-Edouard was allowed leave to visit Orléans.

Louise recovered slowly from a difficult confinement; she had undergone a caesarian section which almost cost her her life. She seemed to be very happy and very much in love, but he wondered whether it was not rather forced, for she never mentioned her parents, Berthe or their neighbours. To read her letters you would think that nothing had happened before she ran away; that she had absolutely no interest in any part of what had been her life for eighteen years; that the only things that mattered from now on were her husband and her son.

He was a little saddened by this rejection. How could she pretend to have forgotten her childhood, her farm, everything? He remained bound to his land, body and soul; he missed it, as he missed the work, the animals, the plough, the long days of toil.

However, he knew that he had to reckon with his father's character; as the date of his discharge approached, he worried more and more about his future, and dreaded the resumption of their stormy relationship.

# 13

THE electors of St Libéral did not pay much attention to the voting for the Legislative Assembly in May 1910; they were absorbed in the spring farmwork, and a little sleepy and indifferent in their newfound peace and old re-adopted customs. Perhaps they would have reacted differently if Jean Duroux had stood as a candidate, but he was busy with the preparations for his elder daughter's wedding and had other things to worry about: he let it be known that his mandate as general councillor was sufficient; he had abandoned any other political ambitions.

So the men voted without great feeling or conviction; they knew that electoral gifts would not reach the area for a long time. They were all benefitting from the railway line, and expected nothing more.

But if the elections were quiet and quickly forgotten, another important event enlivened the summer. It brought further disruption to the lives of all the farmers, and there were many who considered it more significant than the opening of the railway.

The news emerged one morning at St Libéral market and had spread around the whole region before sunset: Teyssandier of Brignac had just bought a steam-driven threshing machine and was going into big business!

Everyone knew Teyssandier; he already visited all the most important farms of the canton each summer, set up his thresher and team, and dealt with the sheaves to the slow rhythm of two pairs of oxen who walked tirelessly around the mill. But his machinery was so archaic (he had inherited it from his father, who had acquired it in the '70s), so cobbled together, so temperamental in its functioning, he only agreed to get it going beside the big cornstacks, where size justified moving the engine into place and laboriously starting it up.

Many of the small farmers could not make use of that machine, and had to thresh their whole harvest with a flail. Those were exhausting days which left them all, women as well, with sore shoulders and arms, burning hands, and ears filled with the penetrating drumming of the ash staves hitting the straw-covered floor. So they were glad to learn that henceforth, thanks to this modern machine with its greatly improved output, Teyssandier would call at most of their smallholdings. And if they were really too small to justify the journey, there was nothing to stop the farmers from bringing their wheat sheaves to the machines.

So it was with impatience to see this marvel at work that they completed the harvest. Only a few moaners and a few old women maintained that all these machines would be the death of good workmanship, the ruin of the labourer, and would one day put the small farmer out of business. Moreover these old-timers stated quite positively, and quite mistakenly, that a threshing machine, however modern, could never produce such fine grain as that threshed by hand and cleaned on the wind, any more than a mowing-machine was capable of reaping a meadow as clean as a well-sharpened scythe wielded by a good workman!

No one listened to those old crabs; it was they who had put up the fiercest opposition to the train, who swore at the cars and insulted the passengers, who held that fertiliser was a concoction of the devil. And it was they who cried it was a lie, or a demonic invention, when they were assured that normal men, neither the excommunicated nor the damned, could climb into an aeroplane and rise into the air like crows. However, although not a single person in the village had been involved in such a miracle, many believed in it. The newspapers had talked about it for a long time, and besides, the squire had seen one of these flying engines during a journey to Paris, and he was no liar.

So the whiners and the grumblers were left to their old-fashioned ideas, and the threshing-machine was welcomed.

Teyssandier's acquisition forced Jean-Edouard out of his isolation, and the haughty silence he had affected towards his neighbours. But it was with anger in his heart that he undertook the necessary steps which allowed him to re-establish good relations with those he needed as friends.

He should have been the first to rejoice about the new machine; his harvest was one of the largest in the community, only exceeded by that of the squire. A thresher worthy of the name therefore had a job to do at his place, and he undertook to feed it as it deserved. But if he was secretly delighted at this purchase by the contractor, his happiness was spoiled by one problem which he could not solve alone; the manpower necessary for the efficient working of the machine . . .

He had to find at least a dozen strong men at whatever cost, who would be ready to help at the right moment. And those to whom he should have turned were the neighbours he no longer spoke to, and who might perhaps turn him down with a shrug of the shoulders. But he needed twelve men.

God knows he had counted and re-counted the jobs! The result was always twelve approaches, twelve visits during which he would be asking for favours. He needed one man to throw the sheaves from the rick to the thresher. Two other hands there, one to untie them, the other to feed the machine, then a fourth to watch over the sacks as they filled and tie them up when full. After that; three fellows to lift the hundred-kilo sacks up into the loft. Finally a minimum of three men to hump the threshed straw to the barn, where the two last ones would stack it. He himself would spell each of them in turn.

There was no way out of it; he had to call for help, say to Jeantout, for example: 'I need you, I'll come and give you a hand in return. . .' He had to invite all those people to come and work for him, to drink his wine, to eat at his table; he was obliged to open his house to them.

He imagined for a short while that he could do without their services, prove to everyone once again that he was clever and strong enough to succeed alone, without anyone's help. But he realised what a ridiculous spectacle he would make of himself, trying to thresh his whole harvest with a flail; it really was impossible. Perhaps he might have risked it if he had been twenty years younger and had Pierre-Edouard to help. . . But now; no, it was unthinkable.

He was so afraid of being refused that he could not get over the welcome he received. Even Jeantout, who had good reason to bear a grudge against him, did not refuse to come and help. But if no one made any reference to his past attitude and behaviour, he was sensitive enough to divine that no one had forgotten it. He had expected they would try to teach him a lesson by rejecting his request, but quickly understood that he had under-estimated his neighbours. No one prevaricated, everyone agreed directly, without any discussion, without even doing him the honour of making him beg, without giving him the opportunity to justify all the improprieties in his behaviour, which had mounted one upon another since Louise's flight.

It was not by refusing to come to his aid that his colleagues made their point; it was by agreeing. From now on he would stand indebted to them, would owe them a favour and feel himself at a disadvantage with them, until he had discharged the debt of work. And his worst fears would be realised if no one ever did ask for his help. Then, in everyone's eyes he would be shown up as a person to be ignored, a person so untrustworthy that he could not even be taken on to work . . .

On the surface he showed no visible sign of this humiliation; only Marguerite and Berthe felt how deeply he was distressed. It was Berthe above all who felt the repercussions of her father's mortification. She seemed to have resigned herself to the persecution which was her daily lot. She knew that whatever she did, her father would always find some reason to vent his anger on her. Nor was her mother any gentler with her and, although she did not add to her husband's constant bad temper, she at least made it clearly understood that she agreed with him on every point. The girl's only defence was to enclose herself in total silence, to suppress any sign of rebellion or tiredness, to dull the mind slowly into a state close to autism.

Even the arrival of the threshing-machine left her indifferent. It was nevertheless an exceptional event.

They learned that Teyssandier – who really knew the country well – was to begin his campaign of threshing in the hamlets scattered in the hills; in Fage, Peuch and Abeille Peak. He knew that up there the sun beat down fiercely, and the harvest was ripe well before that in the plain. Then he would turn to the Heath and the farm of old Bouyssoux, and finally he would reach St Libéral. Fate decreed that the first farm he came to on this route would be the Vialhes'.

Jean-Edouard was not the only one to have to call on his neighbours for help; Marguerite also had to appeal to several acquaintances to prepare the meals for the hard day's work. Teyssandier, his helper and a young labourer were added to the twelve men recruited by her husband, and it would not do to be stingy with the food for these fifteen fellows – sixteen, counting Jean-Edouard!

So, helped by Berthe and three neighbours, Marguerite installed herself in the kitchen twenty-four hours before the day of the threshing. She knew that the whole family, and she especially, would be judged by the manner in which they fed their guests. If one single person considered that she had stinted the quantity or the quality, everyone would say that the Vialhes had lost their sense of hospitality and their good manners, as well as their daughter. It would be whispered that they had grown mean, more disposed to get work on account than to feed those who, out of the goodness of their hearts, had come to their aid.

So, even if it meant they all died of indigestion, she would prove to them that the Viahle household was just as prosperous and well-run as ever, despite the unhappiness it had suffered. In short, she was upholding her rank.

She therefore sacrificed numerous chickens, prepared an enormous pot-au-feu, a brawn and some calves' feet. To these first provisions she would add, in due course, clear soup with noodles, two sorts of pâté, ham, pickled pork, tomato salad, cucumbers and lettuce, kidney beans, salsify in a glaze, cheeses; then would come a variety of fruit and jam tarts, and finally *merveilles*, those lightly fried cakes which she cooked to perfection.

Would any worker dare to say that he was still hungry? Anyway, she would be watching closely to make sure no one toyed with their food, refused a dish, turned their nose up at a chicken leg or a slice of cherry tart, and if they all fell under the table exhausted, so much the better!

Apart from the cooking she dressed the dishes, polished the plates and cutlery, laid the table; even her mother-in-law had to bestir herself and join in the work.

Old Léonie was now isolated by total deafness and did not understand the reasons for this great to-do, and so she murmured vague queries as she began to shell an enormous heap of kidney beans. Completely cut off from the world, several times during the day she ventured a question, but in vain – no one took the trouble to answer her any longer, except with a shrug. What good was it trying to communicate with the poor woman, when even a gun-shot would not make her blink? It was equally useless to put the answer down on paper; she could neither read nor write.

Despite this she persisted in talking, ceaselessly asking questions on a subject which tormented her like a thorn beneath a nail. She had seen Pierre-Edouard in uniform during his leave, and had deduced that he was completing his military service. But where was Louise? Why had she been away for so long?

Old Léonie tipped a handful of beans into the stew-pan and looked at her daughter-in-law. An idea came to her.

'All this, would it by any chance be for Louise's wedding?'

For the first time, and because it all seemed quite reasonable, she openly expressed the fruit of her silent thoughts. She had been there at that meal during which Jean-Edouard had slapped the girl. She had not seen her since then, and had patiently formulated an explanation for that scene. Her granddaughter had certainly been at fault and had been sent away; that was quite proper. She had to get married quietly, probably at Rocamadour, that was where all the girls in a hurry went. But now, after such a long time, she could return and no one would take exception to it. So it would be for her, her husband and child that they were preparing the feast . . .

Nevertheless, in her role as grandmother she would have to appear shocked, to tell Louise that it was wrong to have eaten her Easter eggs during Lent. That was not how it was done in respectable families, she would tell her, and then it would not be mentioned again.

'Well, that's good, isn't it? She's coming back?' she repeated.

Marguerite blushed and glanced at her daughter, and at the three neighbours who were silently plucking the chickens.

'Isn't that so? Answer me!'

Marguerite shook her head violently, but her furious look did not stop her mother-in-law, who suddenly saw the light:

'Well then, if it isn't that . . . What is it? Where can she be, Louise, eh? I'd have known if she were dead, wouldn't I? Poor little thing!'

Her daughter-in-law hesitated, certain that her neighbours were eagerly watching her reaction – then she confirmed it. And her nod of agreement was a challenge to the whole community, to all the gossip, all the speculation. Who would now dare to speak of Louise again? It was high time that this whole affair was finally forgotten; high time for an end to the questions about whether she and Jean-Edouard would one day forgive Louise. Now the matter was closed. The neighbours would pass on the news, and everyone would know that the Vialhes had cut themselves off from their daughter.

She ignored her mother-in-law, who now began to cry silently, without stopping her work of shelling the beans. Marguerite grasped a chicken and pushed it towards Berthe.

'Go on, stop dreaming! Hurry up, time's getting on!'

Instinctively the neighbours quickened the pace of their work as well, as if humbled by such resolve, such hardness of heart.

Marguerite reported the scene to Jean-Edouard; on reflection she was not sure whether she had acted wisely, but he agreed with her completely.

Curiously enough he felt comforted, relieved of a burden he had been carrying for a long time. From now on, as Marguerite had said, there would be no further misunderstandings; everyone would know once and for all where they stood. He felt stronger, more secure, certain that the weaklings would no longer pity him, the cowards no longer make excuses for him and commiserate with him, the jokers no longer smile at his expense.

Once again he would show them, all of them, what it was to be a Vialhe! He discovered that he no longer felt worried at the idea of collecting the thresher and the steam-engine from the Heath.

Teyssandier had decided that each hirer should go and fetch the equipment from its last work-place. So Jean-Edouard would go to old Bouyssoux; when the work was finished, someone else would come and take delivery of the engine from him.

That evening, when there were still two good hours of daylight left, he connected up his two pairs of cows, called to them and made his way to Jeantout's place. He had asked him, and Gaston as well, to accompany him with their own cows; four pairs of animals would not be too many to pull that heavy equipment. It seemed that the steam-engine was a formidable weight, and six cows had sometimes been needed to get it up the steeper slopes.

Dinner was in full swing when he arrived at the Bouyssoux farm; the atmosphere was jolly, laughter rang out and pitchers of wine were doing the rounds, as the men called for them and held out their glasses.

Jean-Edouard had not spoken a word to Bouyssoux since he had broken off the marriage. Each man sedulously avoided the other, and even took care that they did not have to greet each other at the market in St Libéral. Today, however, they would have to speak . . .

'Good evening, everyone!' called out Jean-Edouard, as he approached the table under the shade of a large umbrella pine.

All the men fell silent, and even the tipsy heads cleared in a flash as they understood that the slightest remark could precipitate a scene. Everyone knew that old Bouyssoux considered Jean-Edouard, and all the Vialhes, his enemies; his slanders were circulating round the whole region. One of his least malicious lies was that Jean-Edouard and his whore of a daughter were responsible for his son not getting married. (His Léonard had not, in fact, been able to find a good match anywhere.)

'Well, did it do a good job?' asked Jean-Edouard. Sober, Bouyssoux would not have fallen for this trick, but his mind was dulled by fatigue, noise and dust, and he was drunk on the strong wine which he had been taking since daybreak. He jumped feet first into the trap.

'Did a good job?' he exclaimed. 'And how! I told them, everyone,' he shouted, with a sweep of the arm towards the workers, ' "Yes Sir," I told them: "Have a good look, you won't see another harvest like this one at the Heath in a hurry!" We were threshing all day! And that machine, it can deal with any amount!'

Jean-Edouard nodded, and turned towards Teyssandier.

'Good, we can take it? I wouldn't like to be too late getting back; we need to be able to set it up this evening and start as early as possible tomorrow morning. Because at my place,' he said, addressing Bouyssoux, 'it will be working for two full days! Well, yes!' he added, as if apologising. 'I sowed more than thirty plots of oats, so it will take more than one little day to swallow all that, even if it's a very greedy machine . . . Let's go. Jeantout and Gaston are going to manage the thresher; I'll take charge of the steam-engine . . .'

Already he was backing his animals up in order to harness them to the steam-engine.

'My God!' cried the old man with a false laugh, 'you don't think you're going to pull that boiler with your two pairs of animals! I bet it won't move a single metre!'

Jean-Edouard smiled.

'You'll lose again, Bouyssoux. Everybody knows that your draught animals are hardly as strong as the sick goats which give your son so much pleasure . . . And everybody knows that mine are as strong as oxen! But then of course, our place isn't like yours, we don't ration their food . . .'

He called the four animals by name, gently touched their horns with his goad, and set off without even turning round. The animals braced themselves, joined forces and dragged the heavy machine after them.

A murmur of admiration ran through the crowd of helpers. Say what you like, Jean-Edouard, he was really something!

From five o'clock in the morning Teyssandier and his two aides were busy about the steam-engine; they filled it with water, stoked and lit the boiler, greased the belt-pulleys and stretched the drive belts.

The neighbours arrived in small groups and wandered around it at a distance, frightened of the machine, nodding their heads as its mysteries were revealed.

The thresher impressed them more than the steam-engine, which after all was rather like the locomotive that passed through the village twice a day. The thresher, on the other hand, was nothing like the antique model which Teyssandier had brought out for so many years.

It was enormous, magnificent, with orange paintwork and the name of the genius who manufactured it spread out in huge letters: MERLIN-VIERSON. It was worrying, too: full of pulleys, gears, belts which crossed over, valves and grids, slide-valves and trapdoors.

It was said to be capable of threshing ten quintals in an hour; but if they were not mistaken, that meant this new-fangled quintal of a hundred kilos, not the measure used in the country, which reckoned a quintal as the sum of five times ten kilos. This colloquial unit of measurement created a lot of trouble between the generations. The young people, instructed by the teacher, said that a quintal weighed a hundred kilos, and that its name did not come from the old French word 'quinte', as the ignoramuses thought, but from Arabic 'quintar'. What a fuss and complication! For their elders, a quintal would always be fifty kilos. So, whatever some people said, it was actually *twenty* 'quintals' that the thresher dealt with in an hour, and that really was a lot!

At about a quarter past six Marguerite called everyone and offered the first refreshment of the day. The men were a little intimidated, for it was a long time since any of them had entered the Vialhes' house; nevertheless they did justice to the soup, to the pâté, the ham and the soft cheese; but they talked little, not daring to restart a dialogue which had been broken off so long ago by the master of the house. A feeling of unease hung over them, and it was with relief that they left the table to gather around the threshing machine.

The engine had got up steam and was humming like a bread oven; its tall chimney spat out thick black wreaths of smoke, and terrifying jets of steam forced open the valves.

Teyssandier explained the work to each man, and advised them to beware of the belts and pulleys, which he warned were capable of slicing off a head or an arm.

Everyone took his place, a little tense, alarmed at the thought of serving such a monstrous machine, and full of admiration for its owner who dared to go right up to it. The piercing whistle, so unbearably shrill, surprised them all. They recoiled.

Teyssandier manipulated the valve, and the engine emitted a great cry from the boiler, which was ready for work. And this wave of sound broke over the village, echoed on the surrounding hills, announced as far as Yssandon and Perpezac, and even further, that a day's work was beginning at the Vialhes'. With a slight movement he released the great lever which freed the gigantic driving-wheel.

At first there was nothing but a low murmur followed by a long hissing of the belts as they stretched, and a clicking of the cogs as they engaged. Then he increased the pressure.

Suddenly the noise enveloped them, its intensity throwing them into a panic. They recoiled a step or two further. The speed and uproar grew, the machine changed its rhythm and began to whirr regularly, and already all the dust and chaff which had collected in its innermost workings shot out in all directions, stinging their eyes and throats.

'Right!' shouted Teyssandier as he climbed on to the machine. 'It wants some wheat!'

Jean-Edouard was the first to get a grip on himself; he nimbly scaled the rick, grasped a sheaf and threw it on to the deck of the thresher. It was immediately untied by the labourer and the wheat stalks spread out in front of Teyssandier, who pushed them slowly but deftly towards the metal beater drums, which were vibrating like humming tops. They swallowed them with a greedy crunching, and all the men listened to the progress of the corn and the straw as it passed through the entrails of the thresher.

And everyone wanted to admire the first blond grains, taking them in their cupped hands as soon as they dropped, shining and clean, out of the drum. Jeantout drew out a big fistful, examined it and passed it to Jean-Edouard, who leaned down from the top of the mill, wanting to see it too. He admired the grain, smiled, then spat on his hands and signalled for another sheaf.

Then all the men took up their positions, for they were all in a hurry now to be part of this revolution of steam-threshing.

They worked until midday, and the heap of grain in the Vialhe granary grew higher. Marguerite came round many times to pour the men frequent large glasses of chilled wine, which they all swallowed eagerly, for the heat was intense and the dust awful.

They had gradually grown accustomed to the noise, and when Teyssandier stopped the engine's transmission the silence could almost be felt. The thresher ran on, still whirring round for a short while, then its note changed, grew softer, murmured and finally stopped.

Now they looked at each other, grey with dirt and streaming with sweat; they were astonished, and laughed, at being able to speak without having to yell. Reeling with exhaustion, they all went to the well and doused themselves with big buckets of fresh water. So there was already good-natured banter as they sat down around the table.

Immediately – even though they had been dreading this reunion, and each had solemnly vowed to remain silent to avoid the dangers of hazardous conversation, even though Jean-Edouard himself had been prepared for silence – they all began to talk.

There was so much to say about the machine! And so much to laugh about, when comparing its results with threshing by flail! Such shouts of laughter at the way Jean-Edouard had snubbed old Bouyssoux the previous evening! However, that was a thorny subject which threatened to get out of hand. . . But everyone agreed with

Jean-Edouard; he had done a bloody good job, putting that old sod in his place, that's how you should speak to that savage at the Heath!

As the dishes and glasses flowed by, they renewed the bonds of friendship and esteem. Jean-Edouard did not forget for one second that he was under an obligation to his neighbours from now on, that he owed them, all of them, the good turn they had done him; but he did not feel inferior to them any more. Quite the opposite, in fact.

He realised that all these men were at heart very proud to have been chosen as workmates. He was honest enough to admit that he too had always felt flattered when someone came to beg a favour. Was that not proof that you could rely on him, that his level-headedness, his strength and knowledge were recognised? He looked at his companions, understood that he had chosen them for their good qualities; by his approach he had paid tribute to them, and they were grateful to him for it.

He had been mistaken in believing he could detect a malicious plan when they had accepted so promptly. Jeantout, Gaston and the others were not there to teach him a lesson, at least not in the way he had expected. They were there because they were happy to meet again, as before, in his home. Happy to prove that mutual help and good neighbourliness were the right thing at all times. Yes, that was the real lesson, and it was no shame to learn it.

# 14

A heavy, cold and clammy drizzle soaked the town and transformed the rays of the gas lamps into the dim glow of candle-ends.

Pierre-Edouard had lost his way in an area far from the one he was looking for. Angry with himself, and angry with this unknown and unprepossessing town, he decided to ask the way yet again.

An old strawberry seller, who was sorting his unsold wares before covering his cart, assured him that he was on the right road; another two hundred paces and he would see the Cloister of St Aignan on his right. The alley which he had been trying to locate for more than two hours lay just behind it; he could not mistake it or overshoot, it ended in the River Loire.

He slowed down and searched through the mist for signs of a bar. He had need of a glass of something to give him courage, so as not to turn right round and set off at a run for the station.

He had looked forward to his reunion with Louise all summer, but now it was turning into a nightmare. God knows how he had counted the days that remained until little Félix's christening! Instead of that celebration, planned for the last Sunday in October, a telegram had arrived the previous day; it was now fingered into fragments at the bottom of his pocket. Four words had made his heart pound and now caught at his throat, slowed his steps, killed all his courage; 'Octave dead, come . . . Louise.'

He pushed open the door of an estaminet, ordered a Calvados, and emptied it in one gulp.

'Hi there, soldier,' chaffed a drinker, 'I heard you like that better than facing the guns!'

He did not reply, but his expression was enough to stifle any further remarks. He held out his glass to be refilled, swallowed it down with one flick of his wrist, paid and went out.

The bedroom smelt of gas lamps, unchanged baby, medicine, death. At first he did not recognise Louise. He had left a girl, fresh, plump and pretty, and now a tired woman, aged and thin, was clasped in his arms.

What to do, what to say? Nothing except to stammer: 'Come, come,' as he stroked the head resting on his shoulder.

He gently pushed his sister away and greeted the old lady seated beside the bed. Obviously Octave's mother. Then he looked at the dead man.

A shock, and then suddenly a glimpse into the past. Octave in his bedroom in the inn, back there in St Libéral . . . He relived the scene and remembered the slight young man, so slim, frail and defenceless, with his nightshirt flapping at his thighs, revealing his skinny legs; the hands too delicate, too white, which fingered the little cigar.

In death Octave looked more emaciated, pale and pitiful, but he was recognisable, and the fingers entwined with a rosary were indeed those which had offered him the box of cigars. Yes, truly Octave had changed less than Louise . . .

He made the sign of the cross, collected his thoughts for a few moments, and then returned to his sister.

'How did it happen?'

She shrugged her shoulders and wiped her eyes. 'Galloping consumption . . .'

'And why didn't you tell me anything about it?'

'What good would it have done . . . Besides we didn't know, we thought it was asthma . . . And when the doctor told us, two months ago, it was already too late. There it is . . .'

He should have raged at her, told her that she had really been blind and stupid not to suspect it earlier! That the emaciation and pallor of her husband were obvious signs; that he himself had been filled with compassion at the sight of Octave, quite pitiful in his nightshirt two years ago. But he remained silent.

'You have at least told our parents?'

'No.'

'You must,' he insisted. 'I'll do it, if you like.'

She shrugged her shoulders.

'And Félix?'

'He's sleeping, over there.'

'I'd like to see him.'

He had been prepared for the sight of a sickly baby, rather puny, like his father; he was surprised at the strength and size of the child – an enormous infant with plump cheeks and chubby hands all dotted with dimples.

'My goodness!' he gasped. 'Don't get angry with me if I tell you that's a real Vialhe you've got there!'

'I know. And at his birth he was just as difficult and uncooperative as a Vialhe . . . That's not meant for you!' she apologised hastily.

He pretended not to have heard.

'Our parents are going to be proud of him, you'll see. They'll be mad about him!'

'Certainly not!'

'Why's that? You don't think they'll leave the door closed to you now? We'll see about that!'

'Open or closed, it makes no difference. I won't be returning.'

'But you're mad! So what *do* you propose to do?'

'I'll manage . . .'

'But him!' he pointed with his forefinger towards the baby. 'You've got to bring him up, feed him, look after him!'

'Exactly! He's mine, all that's left to me, and I'm keeping him,' she said forcefully.

And suddenly he recognised her again; stubborn, sure of herself, strong and resolute. Once again, she intended to lead her life as she thought fit.

'You must understand,' she explained in a firm voice, 'if I come back to the village, everyone will insinuate – even tell me outright – that Octave's death was a punishment from Heaven. And besides, our parents would want to take charge of the little one, and I won't have that!'

'But,' he repeated, 'what are you going to live on?'

'I told you, I'll manage,' she replied sharply.

'My God,' he grumbled, 'you're worse than a mule! Well, I'll tell the parents, we'll see . . .'

'Tell them if you like, I don't think it's worth discussing any further. By the way, the baby has been christened . . .'

'But I thought that . . .' he said in disappointment.

'Yes, I know, don't worry. In the register, you are the godfather. It was Octave who wanted the ceremony brought forward . . .' He looked at her and saw her eyes fill with tears. 'Yes,' she continued, 'he knew it would make me happy to know he was baptised before . . . before he went away, you know . . . And yet he didn't really believe in it . . . It was just to make me happy. So he was baptised a month ago. He's called Félix Octave Pierre . . .'

'You were right,' he murmured, 'it was best to do it.' He cleared his throat, and continued with a sigh: 'Your husband – I have to say it, your husband was a gentleman.'

Pierre-Edouard wrote to his parents as soon as he returned to Besançon. His sister had made him promise that he would reveal neither her address nor her plans; he kept his word and limited himself to reporting the tragedy in a few short words. Then he mentioned his nephew and, as he wanted them to know whose side he was on, he did not hesitate to tell them that he was very proud to be little Félix's godfather, and very proud to have known Octave Flaviens as well.

He waited almost a month for the reply, and understood when he read it just how right Louise had been. Of course his parents regretted Octave's death, but should it not be seen as a sign from Heaven, a cruel but just punishment for Louise's improper behaviour? Naturally, if she asked, she and her son could return to the farm; there was plenty of room and work for them. They would not turn her away, and no one would mention the past, for everyone in the family and the village would realise that she had paid the price for her transgression.

But if she wished to return to the fold, it would have to be done discreetly, modestly, in all humility. As for the child, they would look after it, of course ... Finally, Pierre-Edouard himself should understand, once and for all, that he was free to feel as he liked about his sister – on condition that he kept his feelings to himself and never tried to preach to his parents again.

Having said that, they were looking forward to showing the community what two strong, industrious men could make of land which only needed to be broken in.

He crumpled the letter and threw it away in fury; it did not even merit a reply. Besides, what would he say? Every line, every word, clearly showed that his father – supported by his mother – remained obdurate as head of the family, and intended to continue as such.

But Pierre-Edouard's doubts grew stronger; would it be possible for him to bear his father's tyranny without reacting? It was only two and a half months until his release. Since he had become a non-commissioned officer, he knew how intoxicating power and command could be, although he had never abused his modest authority; he knew it would be almost impossible to return to the humiliation of passive obedience.

Once more Marguerite acted adroitly; so cleverly that Jean-Edouard had to congratulate her. Thanks to her the Vialhe family rapidly regained the prestige they had lost when Louise ran away.

Since the threshing, proper relations had been re-established with all their neighbours. Gradually all Jean-Edouard's meanness and spite were forgotten, but their memory was not swept away completely, and everyone knew that the slightest thing could break the bridges of friendship once more. The proof of this lay in Jean-

Edouard's continued refusal to take charge of the buying syndicate, and insistence that he would not take on the role of mayor; many had hoped he would stand at the next elections.

One single step taken by Marguerite was sufficient to rekindle the esteem and sympathy of the majority of the community. Two years earlier they had been objects of pity, because of their unhappiness. Then, as the months passed, this had turned to dislike when they seemed to want to make the whole village feel the burden of their misery. But now the neighbours were sorry for them with good reason; pitying and forgiving, for this time it was a serious matter . . .

Despite being new to the parish, Father Verlhac had begun to discover the character of his flock; he also knew many secrets and gradually, with tact and patience, learned the family histories.

As far as the Vialhes were concerned, public rumour had alerted him to their unhappiness from the moment he had arrived in the village. He knew of Louise's love affair and of her parents' attitude to it; although he personally disapproved of their harshness, he had not yet found the right opportunity or excuse to broach the subject with Marguerite or Jean-Edouard. So he thought that Heaven had come to his aid when he saw Marguerite waiting for him as the church emptied after Angelus; she asked to speak to him.

'Is it urgent?' he asked, for he had decided that he wanted plenty of time for an interview in which he hoped to persuade the Vialhes to forgive their daughter.

Marguerite nodded, and he noticed her downcast expression, her sombre appearance.

'It's about saying Masses for someone who has died . . .'

He thought a moment, and remembered that Grandfather Vialhe had been dead less than two years. 'For your late lamented father-in-law, no doubt? I didn't know him, but I've heard well of him. It's good of you to be concerned about his salvation.'

'No, Father, it's not for my father-in-law, it's for our poor son-in-law . . .' murmured Marguerite. For the first time in her life she used the word 'son-in-law' to describe Octave.

Father Verlhac was out of his depth; he had not yet sufficient understanding of human cunning to comprehend all the clever, calculating hypocrisy in Marguerite's request. Old Father Feix would never have swallowed a bait like that; he knew his faithful flock too well, and would have immediately seen through this stratagem. Besides, Marguerite would never have tried that game with him.

But Father Verlhac was young, more inclined to see good than bad. He never entertained the slightest suspicion, so it was in good faith that he became the tool of his parishioner in her carefully prepared plan.

'Your son-in-law has died?' he exclaimed. And he was really very sad.

Marguerite assented with a sorrowful sniff, gave a few details, recalled with great discretion and humility the reasons for their silly quarrel, which had taken place so long ago, lamented the sad fate of her daughter and little Félix, then offered the young priest the fee for twenty-four masses, one a month for two years.

'It's simply that we've suffered so much unhappiness already, Father, that – well, we don't want to talk about it, you know what people are like . . . I know some will say that we're pleased about this tragedy . . . So if you just announce on Sunday that you're saying Masses for our poor son-in-law, that will be enough. The neighbours will know that we don't want to be visited, we don't want to talk about all our misfortunes, and that'll be that.'

'Of course,' agreed the priest, 'I understand. Take heart, my dear woman; I shall pray for you, and for him . . .'

Thus the whole community learned of the loss the Vialhes had suffered. Everyone was genuinely sorry for them. How could you hold a grudge against people like that, who were victims of one tragedy after another! Besides, everyone greatly appreciated their discretion and their gesture. With these twenty-four Masses they showed Christian forgiveness towards the young assistant surveyor, including him in the parish and the family at the same time; for each month during those two years Father Verlhac would announce, as was the custom: 'Mass for the soul of Octave Flaviens, son-in-law to the Vialhes.' In addition, each Sunday for a year he included the deceased in all the Masses, when he remembered the dead of the parish.

Thanks to this posthumous reconciliation one could at last talk about Louise quite safely. She was no longer a fallen woman, a runaway, but a poor and pitiable widow. Her loss ennobled her, and surrounded her parents with an aura of respectability.

The wedding of Jean Duroux's elder daughter was an unforgettable event. It was remembered for years and impressed everyone just as much as the festivity and rejoicing organised when the railway line was opened.

It was gorgeous. Even the weather co-operated for one day, although it had been frightful since the beginning of the month;

the squire led his daughter to the Mairie beneath a pale October sun.

Only the chief attendants – twelve bridesmaids and their escorts – and the closest relatives could fit into the little hall, where Antoine Gigoux welcomed the husband and wife-to-be, and fought to control a paralysing bout of stage-fright.

The remaining friends – at least twenty more ladies and gentlemen, so well dressed it was difficult to tell who was the richest – gathered on the steps of the Mairie and clapped each time the fiancés said 'I do'.

The inhabitants of St Libéral, intimidated by such splendour, squeezed into the main square and held their breath. They were overwhelmed. Jean Duroux had hired the whole of the inn for the chauffeurs and valets, and they had revealed (in confidence, of course) the lofty station of the guests. There were more than a dozen counts present, three dukes, several lords – among them a Scotsman in his ceremonial kilt, who so transfixed the spectators that they did not dare to laugh – not forgetting two former government ministers, three deputies and two prefects. And to watch over the security of these important persons, all the gendarmes of the Ayen force were on parade, in their best uniforms.

The wedding party crossed the square and proceeded towards the church. They were received by Father Verlhac, also very intimidated by the archbishop who was present, a cousin of the young groom. He was to undertake the blessing of the rings, receive their vows and deliver the address.

For more than three weeks Father Verlhac had not known which way to turn. First of all he had to clean the church from top to bottom, take out and beat the old carpets, scour the chandeliers, the censor, the little handbell; wax the pews and chairs, dust down the statues, scrape off the rivulets of wax which surrounded the Virgin's feet, hunt the spiders' webs hiding in the copper lights.

He also had to repair the best altar cloths and ornaments, wash, iron and starch the eight red chasubles for the choirboys, and their surplices, heavy with lace.

Finally, to avoid any mistakes, he had rehearsed the high nuptial Mass with the choir, a complex ceremonial to be performed before a congregation more used to cathedrals than to the simplicity and poverty of his church.

The crowd entered and Father Verlhac immediately noticed a ripple pass through the congregation, a sort of embarrassment, a hesitation in taking their seats. He panicked and turned to the archbishop, silently begging for help. The prelate reassured him with a smile, and leaned towards him.

'It's nothing, my son. They are accustomed to an usher showing them to their seats, according to their rank and relationship to the couple. Here there is no one to guide them and they don't know where to sit! It's much better this way; it's very good for them to be reminded from time to time that they are all equal before God. Let them be, they'll get settled eventually!'

Father Verlhac forced a timid smile, and turned to examine the altar for the last time. He heard the scraping of chairs and a gentle hubbub, then all fell silent. The congregation was finally seated.

'You see,' whispered the prelate, 'God takes care of these matters so well! The old man, there, on the right, in the morning coat, he's a former government minister, a Freemason of course, who voted with both hands for those villainous anti-clerical laws. You know who is beside him? One of my cousins, a knight of Saint Sepulchre, who was received and blessed by our Holy Father the Pope less than a month ago! Amusing, isn't it?'

The ceremony was perfect, and if Father Verlhac was distracted for a moment no one noticed it; he promised himself a severe penance when he caught himself, his heart full of joy and amazement, estimating the value of the collection. Truly, the baskets of coins and notes were a disturbing sight for such a poor priest as he! Never had he imagined such alms; enough to help him forget all his money worries for a long time – and God knew how serious those worries were.

A peal of bells sounded as the newly-married couple stepped out of the church; the square was dark with people and all the village boys were there. Generously the young groom threw them a handful of sweets, among which twinkled the occasional ten-franc coin. A few punches were exchanged as these heavenly gifts were collected up, but that did not disturb the general good humour.

Perspiring with happiness, Jean Duroux was savouring his triumph. Helped by his daughter he had at last made his dreams come true. His son-in-law, a well-bred fellow of thirty-five, was from the true nobility – from the Napoleonic Empire admittedly, but with a real coat-of-arms, won with great honour by his ancestors, who had made history for France by distinguishing themselves at the battles of Marengo, Jena or Austerlitz! His son-in-law even boasted of his great-grand-uncle the cardinal, who, he maintained, had been advisor and friend to his Holiness Pope Pius IX!

Despite that, he was a straightforward person, and not proud, as the villagers quickly concluded. He willingly shook them by the hand and inquired about the progress of the farmwork, the health of their animals and relatives, without any haughtiness. He loved hunting too, and he won the respect of all the men when they learned from Célestin that he was in the habit of letting off both barrels at partridges, and that his gun was even more beautiful and more expensive than the squire's.

Added to all these qualities, he had a solid fortune judiciously invested in the Land Banks of France (in bonds of 500 francs which earned 3% per annum), in the Orléans Railway Company (also at 3%), in sugar refineries in Egypt (at 4%) without forgetting the Consolidated Russian Loan (of 1901, at 4%) and his stocks in the Electricity Company of Moscow (at 5%); so Jean Duroux's great happiness was easily understood. One could also very well understand why he had not hesitated to augment his daughter's 300,000-franc dowry with one of his properties in Brest and two of the tenant farms belonging to the château estate.

The whole wedding party lined up in front of the church, set their smiles and posed patiently for the photographers. That done, the guests climbed into the gleaming automobiles which would take them to the château, but Jean Duroux, with his daughter and son-in-law, joined a group of men in their Sunday best who were waiting in front of the inn.

They were almost all there; Gaston, Jeantout, Léon and a great many other farmers, besides the smith, the butcher, the baker, the miller, the postman, the village policeman and the station-master, the carpenters and the masons and, strutting amongst them, the gendarmes from Ayen, their shiny uniforms bursting with pride.

The only ones missing were the solicitor, the two doctors, the mayor and the priest, but everyone knew that they were invited to the wedding breakfast, and were probably already in the château, mixing with high society. All the men gathered in the square were very proud to know that the others were up there, as representatives of the community.

Jean-Edouard was not there. He had excused himself, and everyone agreed that his recent sad loss was good reason for his absence.

Jean Duroux invited them to go in. He had very honourably and thoughtfully decided to offer a drink to all those who wished to share his joy; so, while the bells pealed, they all joked and squeezed into the saloon of the inn. There the squire treated them to champagne, to everyone's amazement, for there were many who admitted that they had never drunk it before.

As for Léon, the sparkling wine transported him back ten years; to that first night of the century, when his sister had been born. What a lot had happened since then! And how he had come up in the world!

He was in a fair way to becoming one of the more important stock-dealers in the area. He did not have what you would call really close friends, and some people did not trust him completely, but at least he was respected: for his money, to be sure, but also for his acknowledged skills and his perfect eye for judging an animal.

Everyone clinked glasses, wished the couple every joy, congratulated the happy father of the bride, and in a welter of compliments and good wishes, accompanied their hosts to the huge red Renault, which set off to the cheers of the crowd.

At the château the celebrations went on for three days, and in the evenings everyone in the village could hear the strains of the orchestra the squire had hired. And everyone approved of the marvellous fireworks which were the crowning glory of the wedding night – that sumptuous wedding which figured long and large in the history of St Libéral.

# 15

1911 began with rain. One would have thought all the water in the sky had been chucked down during the previous year, and that after the floods – even Paris had been up to its belly in water – the sun would appear. But the rain was still there, persistent, penetrating and glacial.

However, Pierre-Edouard and his friends faced it cheerfully. What did spouts of water matter now? They were free at last, released from military service, to return to the civilian life which had been interrupted two years ago.

The exhilaration of freedom, girls, good wine – what joy! And the Devil take the barracks, the uniform and the fatigue details; damn all those cowardly NCOs and officers who had wasted twenty-four months of their youth; they wished they might never see them again, with their stripes, their hellish rules and their bloody guns!

Pierre-Edouard and his companions dispersed throughout Besançon, still quite amazed that they could lark about without the risk of being apprehended by a patrol of the Military Police. They were still careful, however, for they were under military jurisdiction until their demobilisation papers had been stamped by the police in the capitals of their respective cantons. They plunged into the nearest bar to change into their old civilian clothes – they would put their uniforms on again for the train journey.

Pierre-Edouard realised that he had grown appreciably. His jacket was tight across his shoulders, but he was delighted to put it on. Thanks to it he could push behind him First-Sergeant Vialhe of the 2nd Battery, 3rd Unit, 5th Artillery Regiment of Besançon, and at last became Pierre-Edouard Vialhe again, of Saint-Libéral-sur-Diamond! That was worth a round of drinks, or even several! As the highest in rank, he ordered the first . . .

Night was coming on as the band of happy revellers – some of them staggering dangerously – made their way tunefully towards the station. There, after weighty slaps on the back, a last exchange of addresses and promises to meet up again one day, the little group separated, dispersing on to the various platforms to wait for trains to Paris, Strasbourg or Nancy.

As for Pierre-Edouard, he had to cut short the protestations of friendship and jump nimbly into the Lyon train as it ground out of the station.

The day after his return, Pierre-Edouard set about rediscovering his world, and it was with delight that he strode across the fields, the meadows and the woods of the farm. Everything was in good order, well-kept, and the thirty-one walnut trees on the big field had grown luxuriantly, a perfect line of white trunks.

As for the animals, they were superb, shining with health – only the horse was not up to standard; he found its coat dull and eyes sad, and made a note to speak to his father about it. But in his happiness he quickly forgot the animal and gaily set about renewing old friendships with people in the village, the neighbours, Léon, anyone who called out to him and offered a drink to celebrate his return.

He immediately noticed that their attitude to his parents had changed. The village no longer criticised them, but sympathised with them, and the feeling was genuine. He guessed that this was connected with Octave's death and was astounded, but he said nothing, although he was determined to get to the truth of the matter.

He could not believe the extent to which his parents had managed to draw a veil over Louise's flight, nor that Octave's death had led them to absolve the fault. For, if that were the case, what was the meaning of that letter which had made him so furious?

When he returned home he observed more clearly what was going on. Back in the family he was aware of a strange feeling; a sort of false bonhomie that was overdone and did not ring true. At first sight the atmosphere did indeed seem to be less tense; his father appeared less imperious and his mother less worried. But that only highlighted Berthe's downtrodden expression, and his grandmother's total bewilderment; everyone was ill-at-ease.

He guessed that the whole business of Louise was poisoning their relationships, and was inwardly revolted by the idea of spending his whole life on guard, of biting his tongue so as not to show his parents the grief that would no doubt afford them a certain mean satisfaction.

He decided to lance the abcess immediately. He was of an age to feel he should not have to pretend and deceive if he wanted to write to his sister, send a postal-order to his godson, or pin his photo above his bed. False alibis, secret meetings, news via intermediaries and accomplices – that was schoolboy stuff; he was a man, and intended to make that fact known. He started to open the wound during the evening meal.

'Have you any news of Louise?'

His father started, surprised by the attack, then he reddened and his breathing quickened.

'Miladiou!' he scolded after a pause. 'What gives you the right to ask questions like that? Louise does as she pleases, it's not our business! Anyway we don't know anything, and we don't need to know!'

His voice rose; he got up.

'After all, she didn't even tell us . . . well, about the death of that man, did she? Nothing! It was you who told us! So why are you starting to interfere now, you fool! Do you think we give a damn! She doesn't want to come back and live as an honest woman? All right! Let her manage as best she can! She doesn't even want to write? All the better, we don't have to answer! And I warn you, I don't want to hear any more talk about this! Do you understand?'

Pierre-Edouard rummaged in his pocket, took out his wallet, pulled a photo from it and threw it on the table.

'I shall talk about it if I wish to,' he maintained calmly. 'Louise is my sister and' – he pointed to the snapshot – 'he is my godson. And one day he'll come back here, with Louise, whether you like it or not!'

'But, but . . .' stammered his mother, peering at the photo, 'we wrote to you to tell her that she could come back whenever she wanted! Just think, we are having twenty-four Masses said for . . . well, for him, you know.'

'Oh, so that's it!' Pierre-Edouard suddenly understood why the neighbours had changed their opinions. 'That's it . . . So you're making good use of him? Outside you pretend and here . . . Here, no one is allowed to talk about it! Bloody hell!'

'What do you mean, make use of him!' shouted his father. 'We're to blame for having Masses said?'

'No, I don't give a damn about the Masses.'

'Well, what *are* you complaining about?'

'Me? I'm not complaining. I merely think that Louise was absolutely right about what she could expect if she came back.'

'And now she has the right to judge us!' exclaimed Jean-Edouard, banging on the table. 'No, you tell me, who made off with the first fellow who came along? The good-for-nothing. Who was it who disgraced us for two years? Just so, two years for the whole community to laugh at us, eh?'

'And now, is there no disgrace any more?' Pierre-Edouard asked quietly. 'Now she's a widow, is there no more shame? Is that it? Octave had to die so that it could be forgotten, so that people would respect you and pity you? Hah! Would you like me to go to the neighbours and tell them what the Vialhes' daughter is doing, would you like me to go and explain to them, just to amuse them a little? You'll see if they don't laugh to your face, you and your Masses!'

'What is she doing?' Jean-Edouard was suddenly very worried. He expected the worst.

'Charring, in God's name! The Vialhes' eldest daughter is a charlady! Their land is the best in the whole commune, and she's a charlady! She washes floors to earn a pittance! But she still prefers that, she knows only too well what to expect if she comes back. She doesn't want any of your "I told you so! If you'd listened! It served you right, what happened! It's God's punishment . . ." Damn it, she was right to stay where she is!'

'Where is she?' demanded Jean-Edouard.

'I'm not going to tell you. Don't worry, it's a long way away, no one here will find out!'

'Tell me where she is!' commanded his father, marching towards him.

Pierre-Edouard rose, and suddenly noticed that he was taller, sturdier, stronger than his father. He shook his head.

'I'm not going to tell you; not you, nor anyone else. And if you want to hit me, do it, but remember that I'll go out that door and I won't come back for a long time . . .'

They stood looking at each other, sizing each other up.

'Very well, keep it to yourself.' Jean-Edouard finally turned away. 'But listen here, I won't say it again; don't ever dare to lecture me again. Never, do you understand? I wrote as much to you before! Tonight you didn't take any notice of that, but I think you've drunk too much to celebrate your return, so we'll overlook it for once. But that's the last time. Next time you'll feel the back of my hand . . .'

Pierre-Edouard shook his head, doubting whether such a threat would be carried out. He had just discovered that his father was no longer invulnerable; that he could be resisted, that he was almost an old man and whatever he did, he would soon have to let go the reins which had grown too heavy for him. The reins which he, Pierre-Edouard, would take up.

Jean-Edouard was not about to give up his place, and it took his son only two days to understand that.

First of all, although Jean-Edouard was still wary of taking part in community affairs, everything demonstrated that he had regained his status; he alone was spoken of as the next mayor. Then Pierre-Edouard had to admit in all honesty that he managed his farm and livestock with skill, knowledge and great experience. Finally, despite appearing to give way during their stormy discussion, absolutely nothing had changed in his attitude or conduct.

It was obvious that he lost his temper less readily and less violently than before, but his looks and silences were enough to maintain his authority; it was enough to see Berthe walking with her head down and back bowed to understand that he set great store by obedience; that an order was not to be repeated twice, and that the only way to live in peace while he held sway was to fit in with his wishes.

Pierre-Edouard could no longer do that. Everything urged him to react, to give his opinion, even to criticise, and each time there was a confrontation.

The first serious quarrel came when Pierre-Edouard, ferreting about in the barn, noticed the reaper, and saw immediately that it had been misused and poorly maintained. Several points on the bar were broken, the pinions were dry and unevenly worn down; finally, to compound this negligence, his father had not folded back the blade after the last cut of the season, and there it was, jammed in a mass of rust. There were even two sections missing, broken off by some stone.

'Bloody hell!' exclaimed Pierre-Edouard, as he entered the stable where his father was feeding the cows. 'Have you seen the state of the reaper?'

'What about the reaper? It's January, and it's a long time till we'll need it!'

'And a good thing too! It's little better than a wreck! It was practically new when I left, and now it's just a heap of iron.'

'Come right out with it, then – I don't know how to look after it!'

'Too right! It wouldn't have cost you much to stick some oil in the gears! And to change the broken points and to bloody well take off the blade! Now it's rusted away and it's your fault!'

'You're beginning to annoy me,' observed his father drily. 'So you're not happy? Well, go and clean the machine and leave me in peace! Go and scrape it off, that way you'll be earning your supper at least! You've done damn-all for two years, it's high time you put something into the business!'

Pierre-Edouard controlled himself, shrugged his shoulders, and went back to the reaper. He spent the whole day on it, got it moving with plenty of oil, changed the parts, tightened the nuts, greased the gear-wheels. But it did not calm his temper in the slightest.

He was still in a black mood next morning, when he came out into the yard and saw his father harnessing the horse to the cart; he remembered the poor impression the beast had made on him.

'Are you going far with him?'

Jean-Edouard felt like telling him to mind his own business, but he deigned to reply.

'To the miller; he still owes me three sacks from the last grinding.'

'To the mill! With that horse! Have you had a good look at him?'

Jean-Edouard sensed a dispute in the offing. He had indeed noticed that the horse was limping, but he was sure it was no more than a shoe loosely nailed, nothing to prevent his journey.

'I know,' he said, 'he's limping a bit, it's nothing.'

'But – bloody hell! You can see he's suffering damnably!' Pierre-Edouard burst out. 'I swear he is! How long has he been lame, to have got such a dull coat and sad eye? And you want him to do ten kilometres, in this rain and on the stony roads!'

'Exactly, and he won't die of it!' maintained his father, tightening the girth.

He was slightly embarrassed. He specialised in cows, ewes and pigs; he did not know much about horses, found them difficult to understand, with their delicate temperaments and digestion. But it was not for his son to teach him about an animal which he'd already kept for two years! So he interrupted when Pierre-Edouard tried to examine the sore limb.

'Let go that paw and shut up!' he rasped.

'It's not a paw,' said Pierre-Edouard automatically. Horses held no mysteries for him. Each battery of 75s used a minimum of sixty horses; sixty beasts to be cared for constantly, groomed, watched for the slightest sign of a wound, infection or weakness.

'What you're holding on to isn't a paw? Well what is it then?'

'A hoof,' replied Pierre-Edouard distractedly, busy feeling the sole.

He took out his knife, scraped away the mud and earth and touched the heel. The animal started and tried to break free.

'Stop mucking about and let me get going,' said his father, shaking him.

'Dammit, shut up!' shouted Pierre-Edouard, completely forgetting who he was talking to.

'Are you speaking to me?' growled his father, and dispatched a violent blow to his ribs.

'Yes, you! Your horse has a sore – probably infected, because it's oozing magnificently. A fine cock-up, and he's been lame for a good long time. And you couldn't be bothered to pay attention to it! Look at his action, your mount! He's been suffering for weeks, it hits you in the eye, doesn't it? But if it amuses you to kill him, go on then, take him on a tour of the countryside, gallop him to the mill so that everyone will see that you don't know a thing about horses!'

'And you, you worm, you think you know about them?'

'More than you, but that's not difficult! You can hardly tell a horse from a donkey . . .'

'Good God! I don't expect to meet asses like you! And now get out of the way so that I can get going, clear the decks! By Heaven, will you leave that animal alone!' he yelled as he lunged towards his son, who was already unharnessing the horse.

'Listen,' said Pierre-Edouard, as he unbuckled the straps, 'I'll take care of him for you, it's not difficult. I'll use copper sulphate, the same as for foot rot with the ewes.'

He took another blow to the stomach, shook himself but continued to unharness the mount. It was then that he felt a cuff to the ear, not a heavy blow, one which he would have ignored a few years earlier. But this was one too many; it came too late.

He turned briskly, placed his hand on his father's shoulder and held him at arm's length.

'I warned you the other night. One thump and I'm out the door. Is that what you want? Well, we're in agreement.'

He slapped the horse's rump and it set off limping towards the stable.

'You can see that he is lame in the right hind leg,' he said, sticking his hands in his pockets. He gazed at his father for a long time, then turned and marched towards the house.

An hour later he was on the road to Brive. He was lucky to be overtaken by Maître Lardy's car, just before Perpezac; the solicitor recognised him, stopped, and drove him into the town. On the way Pierre-Edouard had no inhibitions about explaining that he had quarrelled with his father and left home.

That evening the solicitor related the story to his wife; the dining-room door was open, and the maid heard it all. The next day, before the midday bell had sounded, the whole village knew that Pierre-Edouard, the Vialhes' eldest son, had got into a fight with his father, packed up and taken to the roads.

Some of them were convinced that the quarrel had erupted over a natural son he had fathered on a barmaid in Besançon. Others were sure that he had left for North Africa. Actually, nobody knew where he was going, not even Pierre-Edouard himself.

Strangely enough he left, if not happy, at least content. Content and liberated. He had long foreseen that his relationship with his father would be problematical. He had prepared himself to accept what came, but he was unaware that even he had limits of endurance . . .

Two days had been sufficient to demonstrate the gulf which separated him from his father. So, what was the good of perservering? He had no more illusions; he would never be able to submit to his father's fist. Their complete disagreement on the subject of Louise was only one among many; even without her the rift would have opened up.

Although he was relieved to escape the foul atmosphere in the house, at the same time his heart was heavy at leaving his land, his farm, St Libéral – everything which had been his life, the things he had dreamed of during those two years in the barracks.

Of course he knew that one day he would return as master; that the farm, the fields, and the animals would be his. But he had naively believed that the time was approaching, almost upon him, when his father would stand down; that had suddenly faded into the distant future. He would have to wait patiently for several years before being able to stamp his ways without hindrance on the Vialhe lands, which were his of right.

That did not mean that he had the slightest wish for his father to die; that thought did not even occur to him. He had simply become a man, with the intentions and impulses of a man. Emerging from boyhood, he rose against an old man of fifty-one who did not understand that he was fairly of an age to accept a share in the decisions and the activities. Jean-Edouard could not yet prepare himself for his role as grandfather, and begin to fade discreetly out of the picture.

Indeed, everything showed that his father continued to insist on being recognised as the sole decision-maker. Well, what good would it do to stay? It would be better to leave, try his luck elsewhere, discover new horizons and wait . . .

Meanwhile, he had to live. He had about a hundred francs in savings, plus the napoléon from his grandfather, which he hoped he would not have to use. One hundred francs was not a fortune, but at least he was assured of several months of peace. That was if he kept himself to one meal a day – and there were plenty of cheap cafés which offered one for twelve sous – if he was content with a hunk of bread and a glass of water in the evenings, and spent the night in the stable, and most of all, if he economised on tobacco – at eight sous a packet, you could earn a living by re-using cigarette butts!

Anyway, he had hopes that he would not have to wait long before finding work. Naturally there was no question of him staying in the area; he did not want to run the slightest risk of accidentally coming nose to nose with his father at some market or round a corner in Brive or Tulle. Besides, he foresaw that his first jobs would not perhaps be exalted, and he declined to sully the family reputation. No one had any need to know that the Vialhes' eldest son was reduced to working for others, when his father owned one of the finest farms in the community. It would become known if he stayed in the region. Sooner or later some pedlar would recognise him and prattle about it.

On the other hand, if no one knew where he was, he had a good chance that they would make up some mysterious but honourable situation for him. Hadn't he heard in the village that Louise had inherited a pension of 1,000 francs from her husband; that her parents-in-law were in no want, which explained why she preferred to bring up her son close to them?

He had not denied it. Why tell all those gossips that Octave's illness had eaten up all the household money; that instead of well-to-do parents-in-law, Louise had a mother-in-law who only survived thanks to her modest work as a seamstress? What good would it do to tell them that Louise had left Orléans and was now working in a château, a huge edifice, isolated in a fishing and shooting region somewhere on the other side of Chateauroux, in a country of mist and rain, a sad corner in the depths of a huge dark forest.

Of course she was not a charlady, as he had told his parents in that burst of anger; she did not scrub the floor nor empty the night-soil buckets. Better than that! She was the sewing-maid, and had no complaints about her work, nor her employers, and she was lucky to be able to keep her son with her. But she was a long way from a pension of 1,000 francs and rich parents-in-law!

As for him, if he were clever enough to get himself forgotten, they would doubtless soon be saying that he had found a good position. Perhaps they'd even be a little jealous of him.

He did not hesitate for long. Perhaps he subconsciously knew where he would go when he decided to leave the house. The idea must have been already there, as a possible escape route if agreement with his father could not be effected. Now he had to act on it.

He bought ten-sous' worth of bread and some sausage, and took the road for Paris. If it did not rain too much, if it didn't snow, he could reach his goal within about twelve days. It would have taken him two fewer in summer, but the January nights were too long and came on too early to allow him a daily walk of twelve hours. Not that he was scared of the dark, but he did not want to run the risk of finding himself on a strange path, without a farm in sight to shelter him, at eight o'clock in the evening. It really was too cold to sleep out under the stars.

Just as Louise's story had enlivened the village, so did Pierre-Edouard's, but it too faded quickly and was forgotten; it was discussed for several days and then dismissed from conversation and memory.

Few sought to analyse the compulsion which had propelled Pierre-Edouard so quickly into the outside world. He was not the first to want to fly the nest for a while; that type of quarrel between father and son was relatively common, and of no consequence.

It was after all quite normal for a young man to let off steam, make the most of his newly-attained adulthood and try to stand on equal terms with his elders. It was also quite normal for the latter not to let their toes be trodden on, to give reminders that they were still the boss.

In standing up to his father Pierre-Edouard had been surveying the terrain, to see whether his young strength was sufficient to supplant that of the head of the family; it was proof that he had character and was a son worthy of his father. He would return in a while, only too happy to find his home again – including the paternal scolding – his work, his place at table and somewhere to rest. They would pretend to believe it if he said he had discovered America. They would even accept his explanation for returning to the cradle without smiling – the father's health just before the harvest always gave cause for worry, and excuses for the young prodigals – and no one would speak about the little adventure again.

So nobody criticised Jean-Edouard's attitude; on the contrary. Besides, he exhibited absolutely no sign of being discouraged or resentful. He even assured Gaston that he had got quite used to his son's absence during the last two years, and was perfectly capable of doing without him.

'Well,' said Gaston, 'you'll see him back in a little while! These young people, they're all the same, they lose their tempers at the slightest thing. We'll see him again within six months, I'll be bound.'

'No doubt,' agreed Jean-Edouard, but he didn't believe a word of it. He knew that his son had not left on impulse; his decision had been a considered one. The break was definite; he would not return until he was sure of having control of everything.

Although he hid it carefully, that made him furious. Had not he himself been forced to wait more than forty years to be the boss? Had not he too suffered the questions, the advice, sometimes even the orders, of his own father, right to the end? So what right had that boy to call him to account, try to teach him his job?

Truly the cuff he'd received had been well earned! And if by any chance he was of a mind to return shortly, tail down and pockets empty, he would not enter the house until he had apologised. Just as Louise would have to apologise if she one day reappeared.

But this comforting scene was only a dream. Neither of them would ever give him the satisfaction of humbly begging his forgiveness. They were too stubborn for that, too proud. Too Vialhe, perhaps . . .

His bad mood was exacerbated by Marguerite's attitude. She had supported him in the conflict with Louise, and on that matter she always saw things from his point of view. Now she did not conceal that she was not entirely on his side in the latest battle. Of course, she said, Pierre-Edouard had behaved badly and spoken rudely; but hadn't he himself shown a lack of patience and understanding as well? And what was to become of them now, without the strong arms of their son?

Yes, indeed, that was a big worry. Until now he had waited patiently for that good pair of hands, waited and worked as best he could, without accomplishing all that was necessary to get the maximum yield. He could no longer farm alone. It was too hard, and he was no longer twenty years old . . .

Only a fellow like Pierre-Edouard could have helped him to manage all the work of the farm for optimum output. And because he was counting on his return, he had sown a hectare more of seed than the previous year, set aside and prepared a fine area for cultivating tobacco, maize, peas; even spread phosphates on the meadows to increase their yield, as a result of which he had acquired three extra cows.

And now he found himself alone again, defenceless, with all that work waiting for him, which he could never satisfactorily complete.

He gave himself until April to come to a decision. By that time, if Pierre-Edouard had not returned, he resolved to take on a labourer.

It was the only solution. He discussed it with Marguerite, who agreed enthusiastically.

'We'll put him up in the corner of the stable. With lodging and food, what will that cost, a farmhand?'

'Not too much,' he was sure. 'We'll see. It'll depend on his work ... But with two packets of tobacco a week, some old clothes occasionally, we might get away with four francs a week. And that's paying too much, definitely. Just think, a few years ago, any workman would be happy to get supper, a pile of straw and a few sous a month!'

Pierre-Edouard reached Meaux eleven days after leaving Brive. He had been lucky on the way, and taken advantage first of a weaver's cart, then a wine-merchant's dray. These conveyances were slow, especially the one loaded with barrels, but they still allowed him to gain a day.

Passing Chateauroux he should have made a detour to go and see Louise, but the journey of almost fifty kilometres deterred him. Besides he would have had to leave the main road, plunge into the forest of Niherne, cross part of the Lancosme woods, then venture into the Brenne, that region of lakes and marshes, where he feared he might get lost, or at the very least find himself alone and without shelter at nightfall. He decided it was more sensible to forgo this excursion and continue on the main road.

He arrived at Meaux during the course of the afternoon, reckoned that he could reach his destination before evening, and quickened his pace. Once he had reached Villeroy he had no doubt that he would easily find Moureau Farm – a farm of 180 hectares belonging to the parents of his regimental friend, Jules Ponthier, about which he had heard stories for the last two years. A farm so beautiful and so large that it made his fifteen hectares of land seem quite pathetic!

Happy to be so close to his destination, he stepped out, covering the last fifteen kilometres in less than three hours. Night was falling as he passed through Villeroy and was shown the right direction; he set off down the track which led to Moureau Farm. From the distance he admired the huge buildings surrounded by ploughed fields which stretched to the horizon. There had to be work here.

As soon as he crossed the threshold of the huge covered gateway which opened on to the farm yard, he was frozen to a statue by three enormous long-haired dogs who launched themselves at him with menacing expressions and impressive howls. He had not reckoned with this and waited patiently, certain that someone would be disturbed by the chorus of barking.

'What is it?' shouted a woman, coming out of the cowshed at last. She approached, and quietened the dogs.

'I'd like to see Jules Ponthier.'

'Which one, the father or the son?'

'The son.'

'Don't move, I'll call him.'

Jules emerged and walked to meet him.

'Well, brigadier, you've got bloody good guards!' shouted Pierre-Edouard.

'It's you! What a surprise! What are you doing here? Now, if you'd told me!'

They clapped each other on the shoulder and greeted each other.

'But what are you doing here?' asked Jules again. 'I thought you'd gone home!'

'Oh . . . No, you see . . . I went home and I left again. But it would take too long to explain it to you. Now, I'm looking for work. There you have it. I hope you have something I can do,' said Pierre-Edouard, sitting down on one of the big stones which marked the entrance way.

'Bloody hell,' muttered Jules, 'there's a turn-up! I'm not boss yet, you know . . . And at this time of year . . . To tell the truth we've got enough gangers . . . You have to understand the ploughing is over. And we have plenty of carters as well . . .'

'Are you mucking me about? You're not going to tell me that you can't find me a job?'

'Well, I'd like to take you on, but . . . Hell, you must see, I'm not the boss yet,' repeated Jules.

'So there's nothing for me to do but set off again? That's it, is it? I've covered more than five hundred kilometres for nothing? With friends like you . . .'

'All right,' sighed Jules, 'come on, I'll try anyway. But don't blame me if it doesn't work out, okay?'

They stepped into the hall, where Pierre-Edouard was aware of a long table, piled with about thirty plates and as many glasses at one end. Then he recognised the woman who had received him at the gate, stirring up the fire beneath a kitchen range; she must be Jules' mother. Finally he saw his comrade's father, seated in the inglenook; a man of about sixty, tall, with a harsh face, grey moustache and tufted eyebrows.

'Who is it?' grumbled the old man.

'Pierre-Edouard Vialhe; you remember, I talked about him, a friend from the regiment.'

'Oh, yes. So what does he want?'

'Well . . . He's looking for work, and he thought that –'

'Work? At this time of year? Where's this friend of yours from? Paris? Doesn't he know that no workers are taken on in the country in the winter?'

'Yes, I do know,' said Pierre-Edouard, 'but I thought . . . I can do whatever you like, hard work has never frightened me.'

'Dammit, I tell you there's nothing! There's no shortage of fellows looking for supper and a roof over their head at the moment! But in this house we don't feed people for nothing!'

'Listen,' pleaded Jules, 'we could put him with the team digging the drainage ditches. One man more wouldn't be in the way, and you know that swine of a Polack is drunk after lunch, and all the fellows take advantage of that.'

'I know, but even if it's only for the morning, the Polack works like two men, and when it comes to the hoeing, there's no better team-leader.'

'But I'm sure Pierre-Edouard would be very useful here,' insisted Jules. 'You know, he's capital with horses. When it comes to ploughing, he'll hold the plough better than most, I'm sure of it.'

'You know how to plough?' asked the old man.

'Of course,' interrupted Jules. 'He's got land too.'

'So why did you leave it?'

'Our holding is too small,' lied Pierre-Edouard, who was certain that if he gave the real reason for leaving, this man would turn against him – he was too like his own father! 'There wasn't enough for us all. But I know how to plough, to sow, to milk, everything . . .'

'All right, we can only try him,' decided the mother, coming over. She gave him a long look, sizing him up. 'You'd better not turn your nose up at the supper, you . . . Fine, we'll take you, but only because Jules keeps on about it! We'll take you on to clear out the ditches. In the spring, if you're still here, we'll see what you can do . . .'

Pierre-Edouard glanced towards the old man. He had dissociated himself from the conversation. Obviously what happened next did not concern him.

'Well, that's settled,' continued the woman. 'You begin tomorrow. We'll put you up, we'll feed you and you will have – well, let's say twenty sous a day! And that, I must say, is good pay, considering that we don't need you! After all, we're not going to throw out a friend of Jules, are we?'

Pierre-Edouard agreed in silence, still in a state of shock at his reception, and most of all at the derisory sum which would reward his daily labour of ten or twelve hours. Twenty sous a day, thirty francs a month – and that only if they paid on Sundays, when no work was done, so that was extremely unlikely – twenty sous a day was the price of half-a-dozen eggs!

# PART FOUR

*Exile*

# 16

THE municipal election campaign split the community into wildly opposing factions. It re-awakened old disputes, grudges and jealousies. It was grim, sometimes even violent, and left many with lasting scars of bitterness, defeat and frustration.

As soon as it was established that Antoine Gigoux was withdrawing from the contest and promoting his son in his place, a delegation rushed to Jean-Edouard, to beg him to throw himself into the fray. He prevaricated, referred to his personal difficulties, his busy work programme – of course he was now employing a labourer, but if he wasn't watching him all the time . . . He made them go on asking for a long time before he eventually agreed to enter the lists and lead the team who could and should soon settle into the Mairie, if all went well. Certainly they had to bear in mind that the electors had the right to split their votes, were free to cross out such and such a person and replace him with a candidate of their choice, but despite that Jean-Edouard had high hopes of retaining a comfortable majority of supporters on his ticket.

But he knew it would be hard work to oust the opposing party. The Gigoux lad might be worse than useless; he still had the advantage of his father's solid reputation, and was supported by the schoolmaster's enthusiasm, eloquence, electoral and political skills. And he had several loudmouths, like the wheelwright, on his side, and allies among the shopkeepers – including the Chanlat couple, who did not stint the free drinks in their pub for anyone who was lukewarm or undecided.

'No matter, we should be able to make them squirm!' maintained Jean-Edouard. 'I'm going to re-open some old files . . . First of all, the dormitories and canteens for the railway navvies. We know very well who built them all; it was Gigoux's brother-in-law . . . Then there's the organisation of the market. Before I resigned, I asked for an extra train to run on market days to carry the animals. Nobody listened to me, no wonder the market is going downhill. And then the syndicate, have you seen what's become of it? It just happens that since it closed the miller has started to sell seed, soon he'll start on fertilisers . . . Well, after all, everyone knows he's Madame Gigoux's cousin! As for the local taxes, there again it's high time to stick our noses in, and it'll smell, all right . . . I tell you we must take matters in hand before it's too late! By the way, I hope the priest will support us?'

'Well, by God!' asserted the baker, 'you don't think he could be for Gigoux? Then we'd have to inform the bishop that his priest is red!'

No one took this up, not grasping the implications. Besides, they all knew that the Gigoux lad and his friends were far from being red, hardly even pink, just faintly socialist . . .

'Yes,' concluded Jean-Edouard, 'the priest will be for us, definitely. We must win.'

But two days after this call to arms, the news broke. A real bombshell! Jean Duroux was standing as candidate and throwing all his weight into the contest — as an honest, popular man, the squire, and a general councillor.

This blow beneath the belt disconcerted the fighters already in the ring; it demoralised young Gigoux's friends as much as it did Jean-Edouard's. They very nearly threw in the towel when they discovered that Doctor Fraysse was supporting the squire and almost all the names on his list; it was a good list on the whole, including some decent people, shopkeepers and farmers who were irreproachable.

However, one particular name made Jean-Edouard start and fly into a rage; he calmed down very quickly. Now he knew where to direct his attack, and it would be vicious. Jean Duroux had made a big mistake when he accepted Léon Dupeuch in his team, an error which could cost him the mayoralty. St Libéral was not about to elect a cattle-dealer like Léon; that good-for-nothing, that swindler, that scum of the markets, that ill-bred son of a suicide!

It was Léon they should attack, and without mercy; destroy him in such a way that the mud flying from that fight would stick to all those who had welcomed him into their group as well, starting with the squire . . .

It was not out of political ambition that Léon had decided to throw himself into the race for the town council. Politics did not interest him, and he rarely even followed the contests at second-hand when he happened on a newspaper from time to time. As for the administration of the town, he took it as it came, and was quite prepared to see young Gigoux — fool though he was — succeed his father.

But Jean-Edouard's candidature had touched him like a whiplash, reawakened all the anger he had suppressed when he had been so dishonestly cheated out of the meadow by the mill. Since then he had hated Jean-Edouard, considering him a lucky devil, a tyrant, a brute and false to the core, all at the same time. Much as he liked Pierre-Edouard, the mere sight of his father turned his stomach.

After all, he knew every detail of the real reasons which had impelled Pierre-Edouard to leave. Not only was he aware of all the background to the story but, to make matters worse, he knew where and how his friend was living since his exile.

He had been very surprised, but also deeply touched by this proof of trust, when he had received a long letter from Pierre-Edouard two months earlier. This letter was not a long list of complaints – though it said plenty about his father's attitude – but was written solely to ask for news, and not just any news; only about the land, the buildings, the animals . . . Pierre-Edouard wanted to watch over his estate from afar through a third party; he was relying on Léon . . .

The latter was in a quandary as to how to reply, since he hardly knew how to write his name; but, very conscious of the honour his friend had done him, he had dictated a long letter to his young sister, little Mathilde. At eleven, she was writing so well that she could perhaps become a school-teacher one day, said the good nuns at Allassac, to whom he had entrusted her education.

Pierre-Edouard had not shown any further sign of life, but Léon knew that other letters would arrive during the following months; for instance, there was no doubt that Pierre-Edouard would be worrying about the haymaking and the harvest at the moment.

So he was inspired by two grudges – one over the meadow, the other in support of his friend – when he decided to make old Vialhe bite the dust. He immediately saw that young Gigoux would not be up to Jean-Edouard's weight; the latter had regained all his prestige and pride. He was a good speaker, a good administrator, an excellent farmer. Only someone like Jean Duroux could beat him. So he would have to convince the squire . . .

That was much easier than Léon had anticipated. Deep down Jean Duroux was only waiting for one thing; to be asked, to be assured that the community needed him. Léon pleaded on behalf of his fellow citizens, and was just as convincing as he could be in the marketplace.

He deliberately skated over young Gigoux's candidature, and got busy illustrating all the dangers which lay behind the election of Jean-Edouard: an honest man, he had no doubt, despite his trade in provisions with the steward of the railway company . . . And then wasn't it a bit worrying that this mayor-to-be, called on to represent and serve all the citizens of the community, was opinionated and stubborn, narrow-minded even, to the point where he had maliciously ejected not only his unhappy daughter, but also his son and heir? If he were to act with such obstinacy once he was elected, some fine injustices would result . . .

'Yes,' agreed Jean Duroux, 'and I haven't forgotten the rude way he stole that land on the plateau right under my nose. Do you remember? The piece belonging to the solicitor; I was to have shared it with Gigoux. He behaved quite improperly that time!'

'Who do you think you're telling! He did exactly the same to me over the meadow by the mill. Oh, I don't bear any grudges, but it just shows you!'

'That's right, it all comes back to me now. Yes, definitely, I believe I shall have to stand as a candidate. But who will support me?'

'Everyone in the village, for certain! But I thought that these people would suit your views,' said Léon, taking a list from his pocket.

Jean Duroux studied it and nodded his head. 'Yes, very good. But you're not on it. Why not?'

'No wish to, really. Besides, I don't know about that sort of thing.'

'Now don't make a fuss; I'll put you in for a position, see, in third place. With you in charge, I'm sure the market in St Libéral will quickly become the biggest in the whole area!'

With every passing day the electoral campaign intensified; public meetings, combative debates, home visits followed one another at a frantic pace.

Direct attacks and poster campaigns were countered with false innuendoes, dark predictions and lies. All the dirty linen was brought out; the outgoing party was openly blamed for the poor management of town business and alleged bribes they had taken. But there was also talk about those who had grown so rich so quickly as a result of the railway line . . . In the end they even attacked the sumptuous wedding the squire had provided for his daughter; a scandalous waste of money at a time when the working classes and peasants had such difficulty in making a living! More than three hundred thousand francs for that chit of a girl, whilst a worker hardly earned eight francs a day! And the wedding itself had cost hundreds and thousands!

Sometimes, usually at the end of an evening, after the generous rounds paid for by the candidates, threats were uttered, fists were clenched, blows were even struck . . .

Two days from the ballot none could say for certain who would win. Then Léon revealed his trump card.

Until then he had wisely restricted himself to quiet but effective persuasion; and he was allowed to talk because he spoke gently, without malice or insults. He politely demolished his enemies' arguments without ever getting worked up; softly, just as he would demonstrate to a farmer that his cow was too thin or too worn out. Better still, he knew that all discussions needed to be punctuated from time to time with a good joke, which lightened the mood and encouraged agreement and sympathy to his view. So people were glad to listen to him, and even his fiercest critics were disconcerted by his calm, his self control, his good humour.

So everyone took him seriously when he made an announcement during a small informal meeting: he had it on very good authority that his colleagues, the stock-dealers, would no longer set foot in the village unless they had the promise of an extra train on market days.

'But,' called out one of his audience, 'that's exactly what old Vialhe wants! Good God, he's been saying it often and long enough!'

'Yes,' conceded Léon, 'but Duroux says the same . . .' He stopped, smiled, and looked around at the small group in a friendly way.

'Between ourselves, lads, do you know what it takes to get an extra train twice a month? Eh? You have to make representations to the Railway Company . . . And who will the company listen to? Gigoux? He's much too timid; I don't see him arguing with those gentlemen . . . Vialhe? You know him, he'll play the bully-boy and get thrown out! Then there's our squire. He's a general councillor and he knows everyone, did you see the guests at the wedding? He knows how to talk to people like that, he's accustomed to it . . . Believe me, there's no one but him will be able to get that train for the animals. That's what all my colleagues said to me, just the day before yesterday at Tulle market. They're counting on the squire becoming mayor, because if he doesn't they won't get their train, and you – well, you can say goodbye to the market at St Libéral . . .'

Léon paid for the drinks and left the bar, certain that he had sown the seeds of doubt and fear. Shortly afterwards he entered the inn, espied a group of drinkers, and repeated his confidential news to them.

Father Verlhac was well aware that a false step could reduce his status to nothing, so he confined himself to prudent neutrality. He let it be known that electoral prejudice was not part of his pastoral role; he was vicar to all of them and intended to remain so. It was therefore no use relying on his endorsement.

Despite this, he was secretly hoping for the defeat of Gigoux's son.

Not that he was a bad fellow, far from it; but he was poorly advised by the secretary at the Mairie – who happened to be the teacher, a blatant sectarian and anticlerical, with whom the priest could never agree.

The teacher behaved absolutely correctly as regards the children, and (as far as the priest knew) never tried to turn them against the catechism. Despite this praiseworthy impartiality, his secular and materialistic teaching was so divorced from Christian and Roman faith that the two men could never have anything in common. They were not enemies; they avoided each other.

When he thought of Jean-Edouard the priest experienced a sort of vague embarrassment; he could not make out his true character, and wavered between classifying him amongst his good, reliable parishioners, or in the opportunist category.

To this was added the indefinable impression that he had been used by the Vialhes. There was something suspicious going on in that family, and the more he thought of the Masses paid for by Marguerite the more his unease grew. What sort of people were they, who had services read for their late son-in-law – and attended them without fail – whilst their door remained firmly closed to their own daughter? And they had turned their eldest son out so quickly that he, the parish priest, had not even had time to meet him! Really there were too many mysteries or sordid tales for one to have complete confidence in Jean-Edouard Vialhe . . .

That left the squire, and the priest admitted to himself that this was his preferred candidate. Jean Duroux fulfilled all the necessary conditions for a good mayor. He was honest, stable yet liberal, and enjoyed an excellent reputation throughout the country. He was even counted among the men admired by the bishop; one would wish to support him – though very discreetly, of course.

The priest asked no more than to help him a little, and not only through prayer, but his position forbade him from proclaiming aloud where votes should be cast. It was useless even to make delicate allusions, to try to influence his female parishioners. The ballot did not concern them, and they had only one desire: for it all to be over and peace to return finally!

Despite all this, and because he could not bear to be inactive, he decided to lend a hand – and he knew how to do it without getting his fingers dirty.

Father Verlhac waited until the day before the ballot. Then, at about half past eleven, he watched out for the squire to arrive, sure that the latter would not fail to appear in the village at the aperitif time.

As soon as he caught sight of the squire, shaking hands, greeting each elector, raising his hat even to the women working in the communal wash-house, he strode out of the presbytery towards him. He knew that he was immediately the focus of attention for everyone in the square and main street.

'Sir,' he cried as he approached, 'I apologise for disturbing you in the midst of your work, but never fear, it's not the candidate I wish to see, everyone knows that I don't concern myself with politics. My request is purely personal . . .'

Jean Duroux, only too happy to be seen in conversation with the priest, hurried to fall into step, and they entered the presbytery together. The door closed behind them.

'Well, it's this,' began the priest, after inviting his visitor to be seated. 'You will be aware that the bishop is to honour us with his presence in three months' time. He is coming to confirm fourteen of our children.'

'I know,' said Jean Duroux, who did not see where this was leading at all.

'Sir, I have a very serious problem to put to you. You know custom has it that when His Lordship comes into the area, he should be received with all due respect?'

'I know, I know,' interrupted Jean Duroux, looking at the pendulum clock.

'For several years my brothers in neighbouring parishes had an understanding, they undertook this heavy burden. Knowing the age, poor health, and indeed poverty, of my late-lamented predecessor, they invited His Lordship to them for the midday meal. But this year, the awe-inspiring privilege falls to me again . . .'

'And what's the problem?'

'The problem?' repeated the priest, indicating the room with a wave of his arm. 'Do you believe that I can receive him here with dignity? I have nothing, sir; just two bench seats, three plates, four glasses, two of them chipped, a cracked dish, two miserable pots, a few twisted knives and forks . . . Oh! I'm not complaining, it's quite enough for me. But for His Lordship the Bishop . . .'

'But what the devil are you getting at?' asked Jean Duroux. 'Do you want me to send you over some china and a few good bottles? Listen, you can count on me,' he said, getting up to leave.

'No, no, sir, it's simpler than that. You know everyone understands your feelings for us – I mean for the Church – and that's why I have turned to you. I know that you are personally acquainted with the bishop. I know that he respects you a great deal, he told me so when he appointed me here . . . So I thought, excuse my boldness, I wondered, whether it would be at all possible for you to invite His Lordship to dine with you on that day . . . He would surely understand the situation, and would be delighted.'

'Good Heavens!' cried Jean Duroux, as he too understood, 'that's a brilliant idea! But of course he must be my guest! I'll write to him this very afternoon! He can't refuse, can he?'

'I believe not,' said the priest, fetching out a bottle of pale yellow wine. He filled two glasses, one of which really was chipped; he held out the other to the squire.

'I don't think he will refuse,' he continued, 'and I believe, in the utmost confidence of course, that he would hope to be received by the mayor of St Libéral . . .'

'I'm counting on it,' confirmed Jean Duroux. He emptied his glass and turned towards the door.

'I'm sure,' he paused a moment, 'you would have no objections if I were to announce this good news to a few friends?'

'One hides nothing from true friends . . .'

'Between ourselves,' murmured the squire, returning a few paces, 'you have no fear that His Lordship would disapprove of this . . . this scheme?'

'Personally, I see no scheme! Only the jealous may perceive it as a political move, but everyone knows that I don't go in for politics . . .'

'You're a stout fellow, Father. I know several bishops who lag far behind you in diplomacy!'

'I have no ambitions in those circles, and believe me, if I could have received the bishop here . . . But it really is impossible, isn't it? Everyone will understand that, even the agnostics!'

It was very soon understood that Father Verlhac had been in some embarrassment (and all the witnesses were in agreement on this point), and had passed on a message from the bishop; it was a favourable response to an invitation from the château which had been expressed some two months earlier . . .

All this was seen for what it was, but nevertheless it proved that Jean Duroux really was somebody. The reds might well shout that the squirearchy were past it, that true republicans did not like the nobility, let alone bishops and priests and their silly flocks; it was no use, many of the undecided opted for Jean Duroux. He had once again proved that his arm was strong and influential. After all, who else in the village could boast of having a bishop to dine?

The day of the election was quiet. Passions had calmed. Already many considered that the die was cast. Here and there, in the bars or the inn, they were taking bets on how many votes this man or that would get.

The hours dragged on towards the counting of the votes. That took a long time, for almost all the papers contained crossings-out, split votes or names which appeared on no list at all. There were also several spoiled papers. One raised a few worried laughs through clenched teeth: 'I vote for my donkey, he's cleverer than the lot of you!'

At about nine o'clock the results were at last announced. More than two-thirds of the candidates on the squire's ticket were elected in the first round; Jean Duroux collected almost eighty per cent of the votes. Léon, too, had a very good score.

The applause rang out, the men congratulated each other, the losers were silent and the remainder of the results were declared. They applauded heartily when they learned that Jean-Edouard, Jeantout and Gaston had also gained an absolute majority. As for the others, including Gigoux, there was nothing to stop them continuing as candidates; there remained two seats to be decided.

The inn was invaded to toast the outcome at the expense of the newly-elected councillors. Jean Duroux perched himself on a table and improvised his first speech as mayor. It was impeccable, moderate, assured them that he was delighted to welcome into his team men of the calibre of Jean-Edouard, Gaston and Jeantout; thanks to them it would be possible to get down to work immediately, for they already had a good knowledge of council administration.

Jean-Edouard, squeezed in at the back of the saloon, was boiling with rage. He had lost thirty-four votes compared to the previous elections; his total did not allow him to hope for the position of deputy mayor. And what really made him raging mad was to see, over there, in the front row, that swine Léon, who had been given twenty-nine votes more than him by this electoral dunghill!

There was one consolation in the midst of this débâcle: that imbecile young Gigoux had suffered a real rebuff, and if by any chance he was elected at the second ballot it would still not be on his vote!

Despite his defeat and his urge to tell all those idiots around him what he thought of them, he clinked glasses, feigned happiness and good humour, even accepted congratulations from old friends. He too paid for a round of drinks, and was among the last to leave the saloon.

Once alone, he was at last free to express his torment. 'So,' he reflected, 'you can put it all down to the family; one reckless daughter and one disrespectful son . . .'

Marguerite was waiting for him by the fireside; she rose as he entered, saw his face, and thought he had been defeated.

'Well?' she asked timidly.

'It's Duroux and his nest of fleas!'

'And you?'

He shrugged his shoulders. 'Elected, but with thirty-four votes fewer than last time! Just think, that muck-heap Léon got more than me!'

'You're elected? Well don't complain! You know, you've come from so far behind that I was afraid they'd beat you. They're so jealous of us, they bear such a grudge against us!'

He looked at her, nodded, and finally smiled.

'You're right, perhaps they do bear a grudge; perhaps they're jealous of us. Well, they haven't seen the last of it! I'll show them, I'm not finished yet! I promise you, they're not about to see a Vialhe give in!'


Pierre-Edouard leant on his hoe, turned and smiled. Once more the Polack was beaten; the quickest worker with the hoe had met his match. He was still more than twelve paces behind in thinning the beets.

The young man rolled himself a cigarette and surveyed the vast field where eighteen men were working, bent towards the ground. Some of them were more than thirty metres behind him.

They were walking along bent double, aching all over; some of them were even working on their knees to be closer to the ground, to assuage the pain which ravaged their backs and stabbed at their kidneys. They had bound up their knees with rags and plaited straw, and resembled grotesque misshapen dwarves. They hobbled between the rows, their tools in front of them, hopping on their straw-covered stumps to which the heavy clay clung in damp clods.

And all of them repeated the same movements a thousand times, combining thorough weeding with an effective thinning of the young beet-plants, which were growing so densely that their roots could not develop properly.

This operation, rendered necessary by direct sowing, had been a great surprise to Pierre-Edouard when the master had sent them into this vast field a fortnight ago. He was sorry to have to chop into the young plants; in his heart it seemed such a waste to cut away so many like weeds, leaving only one plant every twenty-five to thirty centimetres.

Down in St Libéral they did things differently. First of all a single row was sown, taking great care not to squander the precious seeds, those tiny grains from which four or five red and green shoots would soon sprout. When the plants reached fifteen centimetres in height, and their roots were already swelling, they were delicately and lovingly drawn out and replanted behind the blade of the plough, in that strip of fresh soil which opened up behind the slow steps of the cows.

But down there at home, on the plateau, you considered yourself fortunate if you had planted out three hundred square metres of beet, three plots . . .

Here, of course, in this country, where everything was of monstrous proportions, it was impossible to farm like that. The field in which the men had been breaking their backs for two weeks was forty-eight hectares, four hundred and eighty plots. It was crazy!

There was no way out; he had to get used to the sight of these immeasurable sweeps of land, to this plain, to ploughing furrows that sometimes stretched for half a kilometre. At first Pierre-Edouard had felt he could never grow accustomed to such excess. Everything was too big, too vast; even the farm buildings overwhelmed him with their bulk.

From the first evening there had been one amazement after another: first of all that gigantic table, around which the twenty-two farm workers gathered at a quarter to seven. They waited standing up until the master and mistress had taken their places, one at each end of the table; only then did they sit down.

Jules signalled to him with a wave of the hand to find a space between a stripling who stank of horse manure and an old man of at least fifty-five, whose dry and wizened hand trembled as he retrieved the foul quid of tobacco from his cheek, where it had deformed his face like an abcess.

At the end of the table, the master cut thick slices of bread from a grey loaf and passed them around. Then a serving-maid appeared, a dim-looking girl with sunken breasts and bony hips, who placed a cauldron of broth in front of the lady of the house. Just as the master had distributed the bread, so the mistress shared out the soup, a mixture of bacon fat, cabbage, potatoes and bread.

Pierre-Edouard observed that no one touched his plate; he took care not to plunge his spoon into his own. He was mesmerised by the ceremony, as well as by the silence, and waited in absolute stillness until all had received their rations.

The master was served last, and he then tapped on his plate with the blade of his knife; that was the signal, the men could eat at last. There was little conversation during this astonishing meal; just a few murmurs here and there, a few grunts, a few belches and the slurping of soup as it was swallowed with famished greed. 'Hey you, Polack!' shouted the proprietor suddenly. 'Tomorrow you'll have this young fellow to dig the ditches with your team. It seems he knows how to work . . . He far did you get today?'

'Seventy-two paces,' announced the man, in a strong accent.

'My God! You've done nothing! That's twelve fewer than yesterday. Do you think the soup's for free here?'

'It's all full of stones there . . .'

'Tell me, are you trying to teach me about my own land? Go on like that and you can do without your booze in the morning!'

Pierre-Edouard learned later that the Pole was paid only ten sous a day in money: to make it up, he had the right to a litre bottle of brandy every morning and two litres on Sundays. The master profited by it, and would have gladly paid all his workers in this sort of money. The alcohol cost him nothing. It was an appalling vitriol, 72% proof, which only the Pole had the power to swallow without flinching.

'No more booze, no more work; I'll be off!' grumbled the foreman.

His boss shrugged, and turned towards the head carter.

'And that manure, how many cartsful?'

'Nineteen.'

'Couldn't you manage twenty, eh? Well, it'll do . . .'

He wiped his plate with a crust of bread, gulped down the morsel, wiped his moustaches and snapped shut his clasp-knife. The blade clicked, the meal was over.

Since then Pierre-Edouard had grown accustomed to this ritual. Nobody ate before the master, and nobody ate after him either. But that evening he was still astonished at such strictness as he followed the men to the dormitory.

He entered a building attached to the stables: a single room, dark, with a low ceiling and walls black with grime. Here and there, in an unbelievable muddle, the men had established their corners, their lairs. It was an incredible accumulation of old packing-cases, upturned to serve as tables, cobbled together as cupboards, set up around mean wooden bedsteads with shapeless torn mattresses.

Pierre-Edouard was about to cut and run, to return to the open road and march south until he reached exhaustion point. However, he controlled himself; he was dead beat. He decided to spend the night under shelter and make off at daylight.

'Hey, mate! There's an empty corner over there by the partition,' one of the men showed him. 'Don't worry if you hear a ringing in your ears in the night; the stallion's just the other side, and he likes to lash out at the planks! Where are you from?'

'From the Corrèze. Limousin, you know?'

'No work down there?'

'Not much,' he explained, holding out his tobacco pouch.

The man seemed astonished at such generosity; he hesitated, and then rolled himself a cigarette.

'What's your name? Me, I'm Moïse Coutôt. I'm from near Lagery, in Champagne, not very far away.'

'I'm Pierre-Edouard Vialhe.'

'Do you know about farming?'

'Yes.'

'You'll see, the Pole's a real pig. Towards midday he gets in a foul mood with the drink. He sobers up just in time for supper.'

'And the owners?'

'Oh, them! Huh – like all masters, want work, always work, but to get any money out of them . . . Well, they're masters, that's all. They treat you like dirt, but there are worse. You'll see, it's not bad here.'

'Good . . . And Jules?'

'Do you know him already?'

'You bet, I did two years' army service with him! And he told me that things were good here.'

'Oh, I see! Jules, he's one of us – works just the same, has to do his share like everyone else. You know, with this mistress it's no good thinking you'll get any supper if you haven't earned it. You have to admit she's quite something, that woman!'

'But she doesn't give the orders, does she?'

'God dammit, no! But she has the money, and the land belongs to her too; make no mistake, the master only came here as a son-in-law, a while back. Well, that's what I've been told.'

Pierre-Edouard shrugged; he couldn't care less about all these trivialities. At dawn, he'd be on his way.

He had stayed. In the morning, when he was already making up his bundle, Moïse came towards him.

'Come on, hurry up and get your breakfast, the others are already there.'

How could he explain that he was going to leave, hit the road again? The other man would immediately understand that he was giving in, like a baby; perhaps he would even think that he was frightened of work, that really he was only one of those fireside boasters who drifted around looking for bread, but not for work.

And Jules would think the same; Jules, who had done everything to get him taken on. Besides if he fled, left, where would he go? To Saint-Libéral? His pride would not let him.

No, it was impossible to leave immediately. At the end of the month, that would do all right, but not this morning. Anyway, he owed them for supper and the night's shelter, and never let it be said that a Vialhe stole his bed and board! He threw down his bundle and followed his companion.

And then, gradually, he had grown accustomed to the life, accustomed to seeing nothing unusual in the twenty-seven enormous Percheron horses, the fifty-two dairy cows, hundred sows and twenty-eight ewes the farm accommodated.

They had cleaned out the ditches until winter's end, and he had shown them straight away that he knew how to handle the tools. Then, one morning in spring, he found himself with the handles of a plough in his palms once more.

He had never ploughed with horses, and the Dombalse plough which he had to guide was much wider and heavier than the little plough of his youth, the one he'd used to turn over the Vialhe earth so long ago.

'You're sure you know how to plough?' asked the master ploughman when he arrived at the gate of the field.

'Yes,' Pierre-Edouard assured him.

He knew he was being watched, weighed up by the men around him – eleven ploughmen all in a line, each behind his implement, whip furled under the arm, waiting for the master ploughman, Octave, to start. It was for him to open carefully the first furrow, a perfectly straight furrow of the correct depth which would serve as a guide to the rest.

Octave spat out a long jet of tarry saliva, stained black from the quid of tobacco which he chewed all day, and turned to look back towards the farm which lowered in the distance through the morning mist. He surveyed the track which led to it, making sure that the farmer was not coming towards them with long silent steps.

'Well, if that's the case, since you know how to plough, you begin!'

It was a trick he played on the young ones. Their confusion, even panic, and the mess they made of the few metres he let them cover, gave him a good laugh, to start with; and then he could sound off and bawl out the novice; that gave him a chance to reinforce his authority, and make them understand that nobody could take his place as master ploughman.

Pierre-Edouard spotted the catch at once, saw the sly looks of his work-mates and their stifled laughter. One glance at his plough made him shake his head. 'You must take me for an idiot!'

Behind his back, one of his neighbours had surreptitiously loosened the anchor screw. The way it was set, the plough would only have scratched the surface and zigzagged all over the place.

He adjusted the machinery and checked that no other joker had tampered with the harness or the horses. Only then did he grasp the handles, raise the rear wheel of the Dombasle, urge on the horses, and guide them, lining up the ploughshare.

'Go on,' he cried. 'On, my beauties!'

He braced himself against the plough and began his first furrow. He knew immediately that he could steer it right to the end of the field, as straight as a ruler and perfectly regular.

It was a pleasure to work land like this. The soil was fine, aerated, just damp enough; it sang as it slipped past the mould-board. He had fought his first battles with the soil of the plateau – good earth, but heavy, compacted, difficult to separate from the sub-soil; sometimes it stuck to the metal blade, often fell unevenly, exhausting man and beast.

But here, what a delight, what joy! Even the stones were no trouble; they grated briefly on the metal and then disappeared.

'Stop!' he heard from behind.

'Go and get stuffed!' he shouted over his shoulder.

'In God's name, stop, I tell you! The master's coming, I'll get into trouble!'

And now Octave was running beside him. 'Give me the handles and go to the end of the line, he can't see us yet! You must know,' Octave squirmed, 'this is my place; if he finds you here, he'll think we spend all our time fooling around!'

Pierre-Edouard looked round and saw that the men, one by one, were setting their ploughs to the field. He ran to the driverless team and pushed it into plough-land.

Everything was as it should be when the master arrived. From that day forward Pierre-Edouard was respected: not only could he plough like the boss, he was a good fellow too. It was better not to think what might have happened if the farmer had caught him opening the first furrow! Octave could have lost his job; he was paid a considerable salary, a hundred sous a day, and not for playing the fool or wasting time. That's why he made the others work strongly and steadily for ten hours a day.

Pierre-Edouard threw away his cigarette and smiled at the Pole, who had at last caught up with him.

'Little squirt! Think it's funny to get ahead of me?' shouted the man, as he wiped the sweat streaming from his face. 'I've a good mind to smash your face. What's the master going to say when he finds out I'm not the ace any more, eh?'

'He won't see anything, and the work's done anyway!'

'Yes, but what about me, what does that make me to all those lazy sods?' asked the Pole, gesturing in the direction of the men toiling away behind him.

'It makes you a good Pole! Besides, they don't care, they don't even understand what you say to them! So, keep talking!'

For the last two weeks the farmer had been taking on day-labourers for the thinning. They had arrived in little groups, jabbering away in some lingo or other. Only Pierre-Edouard managed to understand their speech. That was no sign of great talent: the Limousin dialect had common roots with Catalan, Piedmontese, Italian and Spanish; those languages from the lands full of sunshine, but full of misery too, whence the poor fellows set out, travelling from farm to farm, according to the season and work available, hiring out their strength for a bowl of soup and a few pence. They were only happy when they heard the chink of coins. As for their supper, it was served in the barn; there was no question of opening the house to those foreigners!

'You, tell them to work faster,' ordered the Pole.

He took a flat bottle from his back pocket, reviewed the level of the liquid remaining in it, then plunged the neck into his toothless mouth. 'Tell them, go on, damn you!' he repeated, after having his drink. 'Do you want a sip?' He offered the bottle.

'You're mad! Keep your poison.'

'Well tell them, go on!'

'No, I don't care if they do nothing! I'm not paid to make them work, and you're not either. Does that bother you?'

'The master will bawl us out tonight, and how!'

'Then let him bawl! Anyway, he always bawls at us, that ass, it's his little weakness! You know something, I don't understand that fellow. He's richer than anyone should ever be allowed to be, he has land as far as the eye can see, he has cows, ewes, everything, and he spends his time bawling at everyone! To listen to him, you'd think nothing was ever right and he's surrounded by a team of shirkers. Even poor Jules gets told off! What an idiot that Jules is! If I were him . . . And Madame, she's just the same. When she serves the soup, you always have the impression that she's disembowelling some poor animal with each ladleful! My God, they're real beasts, those people! And to cap it all they make out they're "gentry" – huh, never pleasant, never a smile, nothing. Beasts, I tell you! You know, Polack, down our way, we're not rich like here, although we work just as hard. We're not rich, no, but we still know how to laugh! Listen, for instance, once in the village . . .'

'There's the master!' whispered the Pole.

'So what? We can still talk, can't we?' grumbled Pierre-Edouard. But he held his tongue and went back to his work in silence.

# 17

THE new town council kept its promises. It took Jean Duroux less than a month to arrange for the railway company to lay on an extra train, just as the stock-dealers demanded.

At a stroke, the market took on an unprecedented importance, and the financial rewards were enjoyed by all the electors. This success was partly due to the judicious manipulation of the railway system, but it was equally Léon's creation, for he had taken great trouble to attract as many of his colleagues as possible to the village.

He also lured in several wholesalers from Brive, Objat and Tulle who specialised in veal, for he guaranteed that the farmers of St Libéral produced the best white veal in all Corrèze. At the same time he spread the message to the breeders, as he toured the regional markets, that they would benefit by coming to sell at St Libéral, where, according to him, good beasts fetched the highest prices in the département.

Soon everyone for forty kilometres around knew that St Libéral market was by far the best! Twice a month hundreds of calves were lined up in the market-place. These Limousin calves were lovingly reared in the darkest corner of the stable, fed exclusively on milk, to which the best breeders secretly added raw eggs. They were groomed and coaxed and fussed over to extremes, to produce the fine red-blond coat called 'leveret's fur' which was the guarantee of tender, melting flesh of palest pink, almost white.

St Libéral market had established a solid reputation within less than two years: it reached its peak when machinery as well as animals began to be displayed. There were also three special fairs each year, one of them with prizes, where not only cash but rosettes were also awarded; magnificent blue, red or green badges that were the pride and joy of the winners, and brought great honour to the stables where they were displayed.

The prize-fair was established on the feast of Saint Eutrope, the patron of the parish, and the council decided to supplement it with an agricultural show, which would attract a considerable crowd of exhibitors, stall-holders and the curious. Even the gypsies, the basket-makers, the tumblers, the showmen with bears and monkeys, set up their caravans close to the village. They would probably have camped there all winter if the village policeman had not forced them to take to the road again once the fête was over, for there was a local bye-law expressly forbidding this.

The Deputy himself deigned to appear during the course of the day. It was eight months until the elections for the legislative assembly, scheduled for late April 1914, and it seemed sensible to him to support and praise such a dynamic council, such a united team, a living example of democracy and fraternal republican unity.

All these achievements intensified Jean-Edouard's hatred for Léon – that good-for-nothing, the illiterate whom Jean Duroux had dared to choose as his deputy! Léon had succeeded in no time at all in executing all Jean-Edouard's plans for the town; if only the electors had placed him at least second, or failing that third! – first was asking too much, in competition with the squire. Then it would have been he, Jean-Edouard, who received the credit for all this.

Instead it was Léon who, having pillaged his ideas and projects, reaped the benefits. Léon who, confident of his popularity, was now directing the syndicate which Jean-Edouard had revived and which, thanks to him and him alone, improved its business turnover each year.

Nobody could dispute that. This success was his, and, if it didn't outdo the squire's achievements at least it equalled them, proved that its architect was not the stubborn narrow-minded diehard some jealous people liked to call him.

Besides these humiliations, Jean-Edouard had family problems. First of all there was his mother's health. The poor woman was going on seventy-nine, and had become worse than a child. She never stopped talking, quite incoherently, all day long; she soiled her bed and could not feed herself any more; for long periods she became obsessed by an idée fixe which she repeated obstinately until the family was exhausted. She wanted to see Louise, and would go on about it for days and nights. She would call for her at the top of her voice, sometimes at two o'clock in the morning, and attack Berthe when she tried to calm her down. It was impossible ever to leave her alone in the house; the poor woman was capable of setting fire to it.

So she took up all Berthe's time every day. Luckily the girl cared for her without a murmur – indeed, without a word; you could easily have believed that Berthe had lost her power of speech.

Another worry for Jean-Edouard was Marguerite, who was in

the middle of the change of life; her character was affected by it, and her moods changed like April winds. Sometimes she was happy and full of go, then she fell quickly into the darkest despair and reproached him for driving Louise away, accusing him of being wicked and cruel to prevent her knowing her grandson.

From here she would go on to defend Pierre-Edouard, to justify his actions, to approve of his departure; it was sickening. Sickening and tiring. And he had to bear all this under the bovine gaze of Abel, the labourer he had employed for the last two years.

Not a bad old man, Abel; he was nearly sixty, and a relatively good worker when watched, but he had no ideas or initiative; he was stupid to the point of waiting an hour by a broken plough-stilt without knowing whether he should change it or not. Abel was such an idiot that he talked to all and sundry about Grandmother's madness, Marguerite's scenes, and the master's bursts of anger . . .

And how could he remain calm when everything conspired to infuriate him? Especially the postcards, always addressed to Berthe, which that worm Pierre-Edouard sent twice a year, one for New Year and the other for her Saint's day.

Jean-Edouard regarded these messages as deliberate provocation. The words were nearly always the same. 'I hope you are well; Louise and Félix are well, I am very well.' They sounded like a challenge to him, an insult which he had to suffer passively, for the writer never put his address. The cards were posted at Meaux – what was he doing at Meaux, the fool, when there was so much work at the farm! – and even the pictures and captions seemed deliberately chosen to defy him.

Jean-Edouard saw red when he deciphered the golden, flowing letters on shiny paper to read 'I'm far away but I am thinking of you . . .' Set in the centre of a heart or a bunch of flowers, they must have leapt to the eye of the postmaster and the postman, those two gossips.

'The little toad!' he muttered. 'The day he comes back I'll show him I'm thinking of him too! He'll get such a thrashing!'

But he was all the more furious, for he knew in his heart of hearts that his son would never take that from him again. And then, would he ever come back?

He doubted it sometimes, and felt a dark mood of discouragement. He saw old age approaching, and the terrible tiredness which accompanied it; fatigue often undermined his strength and effectiveness already. And that fool Abel would not be able to manage the farm if he were unlucky enough to fall ill . . .

Now that he was considered worthy to be called a ploughman, Pierre-Edouard did not regret having stayed on Moureau Farm. He had eventually got used to his employers' taciturn natures, to their severity, their miserliness and their total lack of humour. He had even managed a good laugh when he thought of the sleep they must have lost when they were forced to raise all their workers' salaries.

They hadn't had any choice in the matter: in June 1912, just after the haymaking and a week before the corn harvest, more than two-thirds of the men, including himself, had packed their bags and threatened to leave the Ponthiers to manage their eighty hectares alone.

By this time day-labourers were no longer touring the farms; either they had been taken on for the season, or they had followed the example of others and fled to the towns, for work which they heard could pay eight or ten francs a day.

The farmers were trapped; with what they held most dear under attack – their harvest, and with it their money – they gave in, and old Ma Ponthier, whey-faced with anger and humiliation, opened her purse and laid out the coins. Since then, as a ploughman Pierre-Edouard had earned two francs seventy a day in summer and two-twenty in winter. That was very different from the twenty sous he had received in the beginning!

Naturally the mistress had immediately tried to cut down on their food; the gruel grew thinner, the slices of bread less heavy. But, she was warned, probably by the farmgirl, that eighteen men were about to leave – this time without notice – and she felt obliged to thicken her stew, to make it more substantial, so that the food was at least nourishing, if nothing special.

Pierre-Edouard always wondered whether the slut had spoken out because she enjoyed telling tales, or for fear of seeing her customers depart. She would climb into the hayloft for fifteen sous, and enjoyed the attentions of three-quarters of the workmen; she easily earned twenty-five francs a month, a nice little nest-egg.

Pierre-Edouard had always refused to touch that sack of bones. There were plenty of pretty girls elsewhere, and for free! All one had to do was go and seek them out . . .

With the help of Moïse, who had worked in the area for more than ten years, Pierre-Edouard explored the country for thirty kilometres around; he spent his Saturday evenings and Sundays at the little dances at Yverny, at Puisieux, Nantouillet and Villeroy. Once he and Moïse even dared to go as far as Sevran. But there were too many townies over that way, too many factory-workers, too many smoothies – the dancers would not deign to look at two miserable peasants like them.

Another time they pushed on as far as Coulommiers, where the young bucks of the area very quickly objected to their success with the girls, to their way of doing the polka or schottische, and most of all to Moïse's remarks. He inexplicably but implacably hated the people of the Brie region, quite unreasonably holding them responsible for all the miseries of the dog's life he led; Pierre-Edouard had even heard him insult a Percheron mare with the words 'Bloody bitch of a bastard from Brie!'

'All cunning devils,' he announced, 'not one better than the other, and proud as priests with it! By God, they're not like the fellows round our way! Anyway we've got wine, whereas they can only make cheese!'

Pierre-Eduard took care not to ask Moïse from Champagne why he had left his own area to live in enemy territory. But that evening, when attacked by a dozen men from Coulommiers, he had been forced to take sides – and to hit out hard to get away.

'I told you they were all hooligans and sons of pigs! You saw the dirty fellows! Twenty to one! Hooligans, cheats! And their girls, no better than rotten beets, at least that's what they smell like!' bellowed Moïse, as soon as they had shaken off their pursuers.

He had a nose like a tomato and was snorting like a worm-ridden horse. Pierre-Edouard agreed with his companion for once; any inclination to impartiality was overridden by a rapidly swelling left eye. They climbed on their bicycle and set off for the farm. For Moïse actually owned an old bike, a strong machine on to which he had fixed a luggage-carrier, where Pierre-Edouard perched when they set off on their adventures. On the return journeys, Pierre always steered, because Moïse could not hold his wine, still less spirits, but always mixed them anyway. So he would climb on the back with great difficulty, his clogs trailing on the ground, and grasp instinctively for the driver's belt. Despite this grip he often fell off heavily, and each time he simply curled up and continued his sleep on the ground. Pierre-Edouard had to kick him in the ribs and help him up, otherwise he would certainly have ended these nights in a ditch.

During his first year at the farm, Pierre-Edouard went out with Jules as well. But since Jules had started hanging around a girl from Yverny – a big lusty wench, plump as a brood-mare, whose father farmed a hundred and fifty-eight hectares – he couldn't be relied on any more.

Besides, Pierre-Edouard had never really rediscovered the friend he had known in Besançon; one of the boys, always among the first to have a laugh, pay for a round, or pass under Fifine's red light, always yelling the same overworked joke which he considered witty: 'We gunners have had enough of breach-loaders; we want to unload our breeches!'

Yes, that Jules had been left behind in some bar in Besançon; he had nothing in common with the Ponthiers' son. He worked like the other labourers, and never carried tales to his father about the two or three shirkers among them, but now that he was back under the thumb of his parents the spark had simply gone out of him.

Besides that, he had never understood why Pierre-Edouard had come to work on the farm, accepting such killing work for such a miserable wage.

'But, for God's sake, why do you stay here?' he often exclaimed. 'If it were me, with a school certificate; well. . . !'

'Well, what?'

'I would be . . . in Paris, you'd see! You could get a job in government! Or I'd have re-enlisted; you could have been a company sergeant, or even a warrant officer!'

'Are you sick or something? And what would I do in the government or the army?'

'Well, nothing, that's the point! And at least you'd be earning a penny or two, and doing damn all for it!'

'Money, money, you make me tired with your money! What I want is my land.'

'Your land? Perhaps it's all disappeared since you left, perhaps your father's sold up . . .'

'Don't worry, that won't happen. I'm keeping an eye on it . . .'

Thanks to Léon, he had three long letters a year packed with information, stories and every particular about the life of St Libéral, the farm, the state of the land, the crops and the yield. Léon even gave him news of the livestock: 'Your father has sold the bay mare, she was old, at least eighteen; I believe he got 215 francs for her, that's good, I wouldn't have taken her at that price, it was Fleyssac of Objat who bought her.' Or again: 'The plums are fine, your father must have picked at least two tons from what I can see from the roadway . . .' Then: 'Berthe is all right, but she's not happy, she needs to go out and enjoy herself a bit, but . . .'

Pierre-Edouard had been pleasantly surprised when he read the first letter. After he had sent his, he began to have doubts, and reproached himself at the thought of Léon struggling to read it and suffering torments to write a reply, if he even attempted it. But in place of the laborious essay he had expected, he received a polished epistle, without spelling mistakes, in good French; the handwriting was a little childish, to be sure, but well joined-up, perfectly readable, with capital letters and punctuation where required. He supposed that Léon had set himself to writing late in life, just as he had learned his arithmetic, for the sake of his profession.

As a result of this he felt close to St Libéral, to his land and his animals, despite the distance which separated him from the village. If necessary he could leave at a moment's notice, return home and set to work immediately. He knew exactly which crops had been sown on which fields, the precise number of cows, ewes and pigs. But he was waiting, in the certain knowledge that it was still too early to return and live on equal terms with his father.

Pierre-Edouard accepted his lot patiently, thanks to this correspondence. Besides, he recognised that he was experiencing and learning about a completely different form of agriculture from that of his youth, however awful the work, the weariness and discouragement.

The Ponthiers were hard, grasping people, but the farmer knew how to cultivate the land, how to care for and enrich it. He rotated the crops wisely and manured the land generously; as for spreading fertiliser, it had nothing in common with the methods which had brought Jean-Edouard Vialhe such renown. At St Libéral his father had used phosphates almost exclusively, and in very small quantities, since they were expensive. Sometimes he added guano from Peru, but very sparingly and carefully.

Here, old Ponthier spread not only phosphates, but also potash and sulphate of ammonia in ample measures. In addition he used selected wheat seed each year, usually 'Good Farmer' or 'Reliable Early', which he had sent direct from Vilmorin (in St Libéral everyone sowed seed taken from the previous year's crop); so his seedlings were beautifully uniform, rarely affected by diseases such as rust or blight, and delivered the finest, highest yields Pierre-Edouard had ever seen. He, who had been so proud when his father had harvested a dozen bushels from a hectare – an enormous quantity for the Corrèze – was speechless when he realised that his master was harvesting twenty-three! Enough to make the farmers of St Libéral cry with shame!

As for the buxom cows of Normandy, they were much fatter and better built than the few milkers of St Libéral, and easily produced eight to ten litres more milk each day. They did have mangers full of beets, clover, barley and molasses, however.

Even the pigs raised by his father did not compare favourably with the ones here. The black-spotted Limousin breed demanded little special feeding; they happily accepted potatoes, cooked beets, mouldy corn, chestnuts and even acorns, and produced finer meat than this Craon race, fattened on full-cream milk and barley flour by the mistress. But what a difference in shape, in growth and in weight! Here the porkers bordered on 200 kilos at barely fifteen months, whereas at St Libéral they hadn't reached 150 kilos at that age. And what did the butchers demand? Animals with some weight on them, of course! Pierre-Edouard was dreaming of a Craon-Limousin crossbreed with the flavour of the one and the yield of the other, hoping that he would be able to realise this idea some day.

Then there were the three huge reversible ploughs, called Double Brabants, which the farmer purchased for the 1912 ploughing season; they were mechanical marvels, so easy to manipulate that a sturdy lad of twelve could drive them. Pierre-Edouard had not yet had the honour; only Octave and the two oldest ploughmen were privileged to use them. The other ploughmen had to be content with the old Dombasle and to hold on tight to the handles, whilst that lucky devil Octave and his two colleagues walked along, practically with their hands in their pockets, beside their new machines.

And those were not the only implements which fascinated him. Besides the mechanical reaper, which he already knew about, he discovered the huge rake which turned the swathes of hay in no time, spread it out carefully to dry in the sun, and did the work of ten men. As for the reaping and binding machine, he had seen one at work on a neighbouring farm, and his employer intended to purchase one for the 1914 harvest. He had boasted of it – even telling them the price, 885 francs – and announced that, thanks to this machine, they would never be able to blackmail him again on the eve of the harvest!

'On that day, you wretches, I won't need to stop you going through the door – I'll even help you on your way! Because from then on, you can wait for a pay rise forever!'

This malicious comment did not stop Pierre-Edouard from dreaming of the day when he, too, would reap the corn with a fine machine like that, but on his own land.

While he was waiting he did not waste a crumb of all he observed. He developed his knowledge, he stored it away, he refined it. One day he would make use of it.

Léonie Vialhe passed away peacefully, at the age of seventy-nine, on Tuesday 28 April 1914. Her death was welcomed as a release by Marguerite and Berthe, for she had required constant care and had sunk to a near-vegetable state in recent years. Although Jean-Edouard was also deeply relieved, he was nevertheless affected by losing the last tie with his youth. From now on he was the oldest in the family, whether he would or no; he had become the patriarch, who would, quite logically, be the next to go . . .

While still alive his mother had provided a measure of security, a constant which, quite illogically, had given him confidence, a defence against his own old age. His fifty-four years seemed nothing compared to the seventy-nine of his mother; once she had gone, he found that they suddenly weighed more heavily. And the fact that twenty-five years separated him from his mother was no comfort. It passed so quickly, a quarter of a century, and was so quickly filled! Twenty-five years ago, that's when he had married Marguerite, as if it were yesterday . . . And since the past years had flown by so fast, should he not expect to see the years to come gather pace?

It took him more than two weeks to overcome this lowness of spirit. He reasoned with himself. Of course he was no longer young, but he was still strong, despite the pains which ravaged his kidneys and back during the heavy work, despite the constant tiredness, despite his whitening hair and moustache.

Spring burst forth all around him, and swept away the dark thoughts.

Winter was really over, you could see the grass growing. Jean-Edouard decided to put his cows out to pasture. They had been confined to the cowshed since November and, although they had been fed as much as they could eat, they needed sunshine and fresh grass now. They had already been mooing for several days, stretching their muzzles towards the door and refusing their hay. It needed all his attention, and Marguerite and Abel to help him, when he untied them each morning and evening to let them drink, lest they slip away and make for the fields.

So on the 16 May he decided to let them loose in the least exposed meadow, the one with the earliest growth, Combes-Nègres. He untied the ten animals, drove them into the courtyard and opened the gate.

What a rush, what speed! The cows charged forward frantically, lowing with pleasure, running happily between jumps, spinning round and kicking out their legs. They left the village and at last stopped to sniff each other slowly and carefully to get to know each other again, to test their strength by clashing horns briefly, until the dog snapped at their heels and put a stop to that.

But when they reached Combes-Nègres there was a serious settling of accounts, for Jolie, a fat, ten-year-old Limousin, was challenged by an impetuous heifer – a fine beast, heavy and well-built, who had claimed the bull's attentions a month earlier.

Jean-Edouard saw the battle commence; sent off the dog, and ran to separate the combatants himself as well. Nothing worked; neither old Miro's fangs, nor his volleys of blows and shouts. The two adversaries were firmly entangled, head to head and bellowing; they arched their backs and put all their energy into the struggle, pushing each other to and fro to regain lost ground.

Suddenly the heifer lost her footing, for she was less experienced in fighting; she turned her side towards her rivals' horns as she slipped round. Jolie butted her violently under the belly and propelled her to the edge of the ravine. Her hooves gave way beneath her weight and she fell down about three metres. From above Jean-Edouard clearly heard the crack as she fractured her right tibia.

He tumbled down the scree towards the beast, and swore as he saw the huge swelling stretching the skin on her thigh. He climbed back on to the path, drove the other cows into the meadow, and left for the village at a run.

'And you say he won't be back until this evening?' Jean-Edouard fumed.

'Well, yes, Monsieur Vialhe. But if you like I can help you!'

'Little squirt,' he grumbled to the butcher's young assistant, 'I could cut you in two with a blunt knife, and you want to slaughter an animal! So where is he, your master?'

'At Brive. He's at a wedding today, and I'm keeping the shop.'

'Huh, it's well-equipped with you there!' shouted Jean-Edouard as he left.

He would have to go as far as the post office to contact the butcher in Ayen. Thanks to the telephone (a recent installation and Jean Duroux's great pride) he could call the post office in Ayen and request the operator to alert the butcher. But would he feel like coming, and if so, when?

The injured beast needed to be slaughtered immediately. Each passing minute reduced his chances of getting any money for her; if the pain and shock were to make her feverish, only the knacker would be happy. She needed to be slaughtered now.

Jean-Edouard had killed a great number of pigs in his life; he didn't like it, but he did it expertly. Executing a cow was a different matter: you couldn't play around, you needed to know the right technique. Was there anyone in the village capable of undertaking such an operation, apart from that idiot of a butcher who wasn't there? Who could stun it, bleed it, skin it and divide the carcass, and all at the bottom of a ravine? Nobody, except Léon. That was almost a part of his job, and since he dealt with cattle there was a fair chance he had already had to do it. But to be forced to call on him for help!

Jean-Edouard's soul revolted as he set out at a run and slipped down the alley which led to Léon's place. He reached the house, knocked and examined the building. It was quite new, large and well built. There was no sign of the hovel in which the cattle-dealer had spent his youth. That fellow had certainly made his fortune quickly! 'And with our money . . .' he thought, as he banged on the solid oak door.

'Don't exhaust yourself, I'm here,' announced Léon, coming out of the stable. 'What brings you here?'

'An accident. I have a heifer who's just broken her thigh-bone.'

'So what? I only buy them in good condition.'

'I know that, dammit! But she needs to be slaughtered, and the butcher's gone off for the day!'

'That's a nuisance, but I don't see what I can do about it.'

'Oh, for goodness sake, don't play the fool! You must help me. You know how to slaughter. Come on, get your gear and come quickly. We can't let the animal suffer! I told Abel to get the neighbours; there'll be several of us, we'll help you.'

'It's not my job, and I don't see why I should do anything for you, except perhaps thank you for taking the meadow by the mill.'

'Good God! You don't want to bring up that old business again, do you?'

'Why not?'

Jean-Edouard was beside himself with fury, but realised just in time that one word out of place would lead to the total loss of his heifer.

'Well, all right, I went a bit too far there, I admit. Let's forget it.'

'Damn it all! You're quick to forgive yourself!' Léon mocked him, slowly rolling a cigarette. 'Hey,' he shouted towards the stable, where one of his workmen was grooming a horse, 'a rope, the big pulley and the set of knives too, ask my mother for them. He'll follow us,' he explained. 'Well, where is this animal?'

She had not moved. Around her stood Abel, Jeantout, and Gaston; Marguerite was there too, sitting by her head, soothing her with words and caresses and crying silently.

'Well, what do we do?' asked Jean-Edouard.

'Not so fast, not so fast,' recommended Léon, feeling the animal with expert hands. 'Not good, that leg, she'll lose several kilos. And she isn't plump. Not thin, but lacking a bit ... You can see for yourself, you won't get much for her ... And then some of the tenderloin will be missing. What do you want for her?'

'Heavens, how do I know! I thought that ...'

'Yes, yes,' interrupted Léon. 'That I was going to slaughter her and you'd toss me a coin and perhaps a bit of sirloin, and sell the rest to the butcher! That won't work. Here's what we'll do: I'll buy her, I'll slaughter her and sort it out from there. Any other ideas and it's good evening to you! Well, what's your price?'

'That's not how it's usually done!' countered Jean-Edouard, and felt encouraged by murmurs of agreement from his neighbours.

'I don't care what's usual! It's not my usual job to slaughter animals, and if you don't like it, Monsieur Vialhe, I'm off!' Léon assured him with a smile. He had him hooked and wasn't about to let him off the line. He had waited for a chance like this for a long time.

'All right,' sighed Jean-Edouard at last, 'Four hundred and fifty francs, that's what I want.'

'Oh, fine, you should have said straight away you were dragging me up here for a good laugh!' exclaimed Léon, as he scrambled back up the slope. 'Take good care of yourselves, all of you!'

'Name your price!' yelled Jean-Edouard.

Léon stopped halfway up, shrugged his shoulders and assumed a disgusted expression.

'What do you want me to say. . . ? You can see she's not fat, and I shouldn't be surprised if she weren't feverish already.' He went back to the animal and lifted one eyelid.

'Hullo! Look at that eye, it looks feverish, I'm telling you! But the longer we leave it . . . So, just to help you out, I'll give you . . . Let's see, what does she weigh, not heavy, is she? Let's say eighteen pistoles!' He instinctively employed an old form of coinage peculiar to cattle-dealers. 'Sixty crowns, if you prefer . . .'

'Good God!' Jean-Edouard was choking and his hands began to tremble. 'A hundred and eighty francs, for that animal! Do you want me to knock your block off! Swindler! It wasn't enough to run against me in the elections! You have to steal from me as well!'

'Come, come, Monsieur Vialhe, at your age, it doesn't do you any good to get in a temper! I told you I wouldn't forget the meadow by the mill . . . You see, today, the tables are turned. It's my decision. Come on, shake on a hundred and eighty francs! I've got other things to do. It's agreed, eighteen pistoles?'

'Dammit, she's worth four hundred and fifty!' insisted Jean-Edouard.

'Perhaps she was a short while ago, before she fell, but now . . . I'm beginning to wonder whether even eighteen pistoles . . . I'm giving it away . . . I'm sure if we wait a bit she'll go down to fifteen, or twelve . . .'

Jean-Edouard looked at his neighbours, who had moved away in embarrassment. They didn't want to take sides. Of course Léon was openly taking advantage of the situation, but they all remembered the meadow by the mill . . . That time it was Jean-Edouard who had behaved badly. So . . .

'Give me the money,' he said at last.

He counted the francs and put them in his pocket.

'Leave that,' he ordered Marguerite, and drew her away, helping her to climb the embankment. Before they reached the path they were startled by the dull thud of the poleaxe splitting the skull.

# 18

PIERRE-EDOUARD tore open the little blue envelope with trembling hands. The postman had walked out to meet him as he was coming back from the wheat field; he had been using a scythe to cut a pathway for old Ponthier's new binder.

'Here,' he said giving him a coin, 'I can't offer you a drink, my flagon's empty.'

'Don't apologise, lad.' The postman wiped his forehead. 'I know how it is. It's not good, is it?'

'What?'

'The telegram.'

'No.'

'It's very rarely good news . . .'

Pierre said goodbye and hurried across the fields towards the farm. Just before reaching it he read the message again: '*Félix very ill, come. Louise.*'

He looked at the date, 15 July. The plea had been sent that very morning, and perhaps since then . . . He went straight to the dormitory, stuffed his few belongings into an old bag, and strode towards the owner's house.

'What do you want? And where are you going with your bag?' called his boss from the barn where he was working.

'I'm leaving,' he announced as he approached.

'What do you mean, leaving? In the middle of the harvest! I believe you haven't sobered up yet from yesterday! Or are you trying to repeat the trick you played two years ago? If that's the case, you can go!'

Pierre-Edouard shrugged. 'I have to go, my sister has sent for me . . .'

'Oh yes? Just like that, she clicks her fingers and you go? And the harvest, have you thought of that?'

'Shut your mouth,' growled Pierre-Edouard, advancing a step towards him, 'you can stuff your harvest! I'm off, and you owe me a fortnight's pay!'

'Listen, you little bastard, if that's how you want it – we'll pay you, oh yes, but I advise you not to come back. Never! If you try, I swear I'll set the dogs on you!'

'Don't worry, there's no danger of that! I've had enough of working for you and killing myself in your bloody fields! You won't see me back here in a hurry! Come on, give me my money and I'm off.'

'Go and see the mistress, and go to the devil!'

'Comes to the same thing!' shouted Pierre-Edouard as he walked away.

The farmer's wife counted out his money exactly and pushed the coins towards him. 'When I think we took you on to please Jules!' Her voice grated between clenched teeth. 'And you leave right in the middle of harvesting; that's not the way decent people behave!'

'Don't talk to me about decent behaviour; seek the beam in your own eye!' He put his money in his wallet and left. Coming out of the yard he spotted his workmates in the distance, building up a huge stack of barley; he waved to them and took to the road.

'If you want work, it's no use going to the château; you need the farm, son, over there, behind the trees,' the gardener warned him, looking him up and down.

'No, it's not that, I've come to see my sister. Louise, Louise Flaviens; she works here, at the castle,' explained Pierre-Edouard.

He had been travelling all night, changed trains three times, and to complete the journey he had hired the services of a good man who owned a tilbury.

'Oh well, yes, I wondered . . . You do look like her, that's true. I expect you know that your nephew's almost done for?'

'Do you know anything about it? That's why I've come,' asked Pierre-Edouard.

'The doctor came by this morning – he comes every day, but he don't tell me nothing.'

'But you would know if, well, if . . .'

'If the little fellow had gone? Of course, my wife would have told me!'

Pierre breathed easier. 'Where's my sister's room?'

'Up there, in the attics.' The man waved his arm towards the roof. 'You go through the servants' entrance, turn right as soon as you get into the courtyard, the door at the bottom of the first tower. Climb up there and you'll find the servants' quarters.'

Pierre-Edouard thanked him and strode towards the Château de la Cannepetière; doves fluttered around one side of the enormous building, whilst more of them were resting in the centre of a formal garden, with beautiful banks of rose bushes and avenues of chestnut trees where peacocks called.

He heard the cough long before reaching the top storey: a harsh and terrible cough, which seemed to use up all the breath and rose to wheezy rasp, as painful as the death-rattle of a cock strangled at the highest pitch of its final cry. He ran up the last few steps, and darted towards the room where he could now hear a panting gasp between hollow gurgles. He entered without knocking.

'Yes, yes, honestly, he's getting better,' Louise explained a little while later, 'but yesterday morning I thought that . . . So I sent for you. It's silly, I'm ashamed of myself.'

'You did the right thing,' he said as he stroked the child's damp forehead.

He smiled at him, spoke to him softly, awkwardly; he was moved to discover in Félix, not the baby he had known, but a little man with a turned-up nose, bright eyes and curly blond hair. And he talked, wanted to know everything, his eyes following Pierre-Edouard everywhere, so happy to meet him at last.

'But what is the matter with him? Tell me, what have you got?' he asked the child.

'Whooping-cough,' the little invalid spoke feebly. 'It's there, it's burning,' he explained, touching his chest and throat.

'Yes, but it's getting better, the doctor just said so. You'll soon be well,' Louise comforted him, 'and now you've seen your godfather.'

The child smiled, but was immediately overwhelmed by a long fit of coughing; it was exhausting and terrifying, and left him panting and out of breath.

'Good God, what a dreadful infection!' said Pierre-Edouard. 'What are you giving him for it?'

'The doctor left some medicine, some syrup; and I make him an infusion – do you remember the one Granny gave us to get rid of colds, with mallow, poppies, hollyhocks and honey?'

He went one better: 'And she used to make mustard plasters!'

'I've made them for him.'

'And they sting,' murmured the child.

'Yes, but it helps you get better too,' Pierre-Edouard assured him. 'The more it stings, the more it cures! And how are you?' he asked his sister.

She had changed during the intervening three years; she had put on weight and looked happy again. She did seem tired, worn out by the disturbed nights and the bedside vigil; despite that, she appeared in better form than at their last meeting.

They talked for a long time. He passed on to her all the details of home life faithfully transmitted to him by Léon; named the neighbours and relatives who had come to Grandmother's funeral – he spoke of it all so minutely that you would have thought he had arrived straight from St Libéral. Finally, he told her about his departure from Moureau Farm.

'It's my fault,' she reproached herself. 'I made you lose your job.'

'It's no great loss! Now I've left, I'm wondering how I could have stayed there so long. Three and a half years, just think!'

'Why don't you go back home now? Perhaps father . . .'

'No, he hasn't changed; Léon told me. And for that matter, why don't you go back yourself?'

'Oh, me . . . that's different. You know, I don't miss it any more. I'm settled here – my employers are kind, and I have good accommodation, good food, good wages. Just think, I get thirty francs a month now; that's good, you know! The best part is that I can keep the little one with me. And then . . .' She faltered and blushed as her brother gazed at her questioningly. 'Yes, I was going to write to you about it, and then Félix fell ill. I'm going to get married again.'

'Well, what a surprise!' he whistled.

He had never imagined that his sister would have been able to cut herself off from the memory of Octave, that she would want to start her life anew. A wave of anger flooded through him. My God! She had created the whole mess, upset the entire family, quarrelled with her parents, only to jump into the arms of another man four years after the first one had disappeared! Perhaps his father was right when he maintained that she was too quick and easy!

'Do you mind very much?' she asked sadly.

He pulled himself together, reproaching himself for his first reaction. Basically his burst of anger was just as stupid and unjust as his parents' reaction had been so long ago. Just as she had done five years earlier, Louise was doing the opposite of what others wanted and expected, without asking his opinion, without realising that she was free to make different plans. For he had firmly placed her among the widows who wore mourning and sadness all their lives, who accepted their fate passively and discreetly. He had never imagined that she could one day fall in love with someone other than Octave, and be happy with his usurper.

'Yes, I can see you hold it against me,' she continued. 'Oh, I know, you helped me so much with Octave.'

'No, I don't mind, but you gave me a shock. I would never have thought . . .' He fell silent. What had he thought? That his sister was the sort who would submit to her fate? That was poor judgement of her character!

'You know,' she reminded him, 'I'm only twenty-three. Do you think it's fun to be alone all the time? Of course, I have Félix. But after all, is it wrong to want to live with a man? Is it wrong to want to keep house for him, to cook his meals, to wait for him, to love him, to sleep at his side, to grow old with him? Do you think it's wrong?'

'No, no!' he assured her quite sincerely, 'there's nothing wrong in that! You're quite right. I simply wasn't expecting it, that's all. Anyway, it's none of my business. You know, what matters is that you should be happy. And him too,' he said, pointing to the child.

She smiled. 'He will be, don't worry. Jean liked him straight away. And then, you know, life is strange – Jean lost his wife three years ago, she died in childbirth and their little girl didn't survive either. So, when we met . . . You see, we can share our sorrow, that's what it is. I know that for him it won't be the same as with his first wife, and for me it's like that too; it will never be the same as it was with Octave. But we can't change what's happened, life's like that . . .'

'I understand. What does he do?'

'He's a forester. He earns a good living. And the baron is going to let us have a cottage, in the middle of the forest. It'll be good there, it even has a garden.'

'And is he young?'

'Thirty-two, that's not so old. You know, I've talked to him a lot about you. I'm sure you'll get on very well.'

'Why not . . . And when are you getting married?'

'We had chosen the 25th, before the boy was ill. Well, since he's getting better we won't postpone it.'

'The 25th of which month?'

'Of this one.'

'Good heavens, so soon!'

'Why wait longer? We've known each other for two years.'

'And you never told me . . .'

'It's not easy in letters. I was going to write, I swear it, just before the boy's illness. You believe me, don't you? I wouldn't have got married again without telling you beforehand!'

'I believe you. But you know, on the way here, I didn't think you'd be announcing your wedding for next week.'

'Yes. This way, if things turn out badly, at least we'll be married.'

'What could turn out badly?'

'The situation. Jean says we might be going to have a war. Well, you'd know more about that, eh?'

'Huh! I don't think it'll come to that, it's just a political matter, that's all.'

'Jean thinks it'll happen; he reads the paper every day. It seems that it's been very bad since the assassination of that poor prince, or king, I don't remember which . . .'

'Go on! I read the paper too, sometimes. Well, all right, there's been this assassination, down there, devil knows where; so what does it matter to us? Besides, in the train I read in someone else's paper that the President has just set out for Russia. Do you think he would go trundling off so far away if it was as serious as Jean says? Go on, I know why he told you that; because he's in a hurry to get you to the registry office!'

Despite his great age, Doctor Fraysse had not changed his habits at all. He pushed open the door of the inn, as he did every evening, to compete with Antoine Gigoux at billiards. They chose and prepared their cues, began to play, and took up the conversation where they'd left off the night before.

'So you're still ready to take on the Prussians?' joked the former mayor.

'My dear Gigoux, I'll tell you once more, it's not for old men like me to decide; I can't attack anything much these days, sad to say. But your mockery and scepticism won't stop the war. I'll take a bet with you on that!'

'But of course it'll be stopped! Jaurès is right, we must create a great international peace movement. That's what all sensible people are hoping for!'

'I'll tell you something; your Jaurès is a fine one. I won't go so far as those who think that he's sold out to the Germans, but I do say he's a lying swine!'

'You have no right to say that! Nobody has ever done as much as he has in the cause of peace.'

'Eternal peace, yes; the peace of the graveyard! When I think he was against the three-year military service, and for disarmament! In the name of God, Gigoux, open your eyes a little! You don't see that the Austrians and the Germans are just dying to start a war! Go and talk about peace to Franz-Josef or the Kaiser! Really, you are stupid; it would be laughable if it weren't so sad!'

'You're nothing but a warmonger! It's a good thing everyone's not like you!'

'Warmonger, me? I would remind you that I've spent my whole

life looking after people. Are you telling me I've been trying to finish them off for the fun of it!'

'Well no, I didn't mean to say that!' Antoine Gigoux apologised.

'I know. But your blindness worries me.'

'My what?'

'You see nothing, my poor Gigoux. You and a few others, including our dear teacher, dream of world peace. I do, too. But I know that some dreams never come true. We're going to have war, I can feel it; there's no other way out. And believe me, it doesn't make me happy. I know what it's like, you see; I was there in '70. It's abominable, war . . . And that's what I tell all the young people in the village, the ones who really want to fight. The poor things, if they only knew what it was like!'

'So you see why we must campaign for peace!'

'Of course, of course,' sighed the doctor, 'but go and explain that to the mad dogs who are growling at your heels! They won't even give you time to speak, and once you've been bitten you'll have rabies too, and goodbye to your lovely dreams of universal peace! Look, there's our squire and his town council come to drink to some new decision they've made. Don't make that face, my old friend; after all, your son was only beaten by twelve votes. Anyway, that's all in the past.'

'Have you heard the news?' asked Jean Duroux coming up to them. 'Austria has just mobilised eight divisions. This time I fear the worst . . .'

'And why is it the worst?' called out Léon. 'We're going to smash their faces, for sure. We've been talking about it long enough!'

'Especially you,' spat Jean-Edouard. 'It's all very well for you to talk; everyone knows you're excused military service!'

'Come, come, my friends,' Jean Duroux intervened. 'We haven't come to that yet! I have complete confidence in our government; I'm sure that every effort will be made to avoid conflict.'

'May God hear you,' murmured the old doctor, and his serious tone made an impression on everyone.

Pierre-Edouard grasped the fat bundle of rye, swiftly bound it up, placed the sheaf behind him and gathered a fresh armful. Beside him eleven other men were busy with the binding; they were walking at the heels of a dozen men with scythes who swung their long blades in almost perfect harmony to lay low the tall stalks.

Pierre-Edouard could not get over his good fortune. First of all he had had no trouble in finding a job at the farm belonging to the château, thanks to Louise of course, and at an incredible salary – two francs ninety a day, twenty centimes more than at the Ponthiers' for the same work. Secondly, little Félix was much better; he was cheerful again, and the colour had come back into his cheeks. Lastly, he had been able to witness his sister's marriage the previous day.

The quiet ceremony was celebrated first at the town hall and then in the church at Mézières-en-Brenne twelve kilometres away. Today Louise, Jean and Félix had moved into their little forest cottage, a real love nest, perched in the middle of the woods more than six kilometres from the château.

He had not been able to help them settle in; the weather augured ill, the air felt stormy, the harvest must be got in. It was a Sunday, but this was a serious matter. The farm manager had offered a bonus of a franc to those who would work, and they had all come.

In the three and a half years on Moureau Farm, Pierre-Edouard had got used to vast spaces, to great plains interspersed occasionally by a few pretty woods. So he was like a fish out of water, astonished by this new landscape which had been his home for the last ten days.

Here were no huge stretches of good rich soil; there were fields, big ones, but poor and sandy, full of puddles, divided by a maze of deep ditches and surrounded by woods or by moors of heather and bracken. A poor region, where even the rye seemed to have difficulty in growing – he had noticed that as he grasped it. Watery land, too; he could not get over the number of pools and marshes.

And amidst it all a profusion of game, which had to be respected despite its depradations; these losses did not seem to bother the farm manager. For instance in this field of rye, which was not all that marvellous anyway, Pierre-Edouard reckoned that the toll taken by fallow and roe-deer or wild boar was more than forty sheaves; they had wallowed in it like pigs, which made the reapers' work all the more difficult.

'But the baron has twelve hundred hectares, a thousand of them forested; he values them more than the soil,' explained his new brother-in-law. 'And then he doesn't need it to live off. Besides, hunting is his great love. I'll show you his pack of hounds, it's really something . . .'

And Pierre-Edouard was speechless when he saw the seventy-five English crossbred hounds sheltering in the kennels. Then he began to laugh quietly, at the thought of the three or four dogs which were Jean Duroux's pride and joy back home in the village.

He had to force himself not to give Jean a chilly reception when

Louise introduced them. He could not stop thinking of Octave, his quiet air, his gentle voice. But he was quickly convinced his sister had not been mistaken in her choice.

'Well, so you're Pierre-Edouard! Christ Almighty! Louise talks of nothing but you. Thanks to her I've known you for two years; I'm glad to shake you by the hand. It seems you muddled through together, down there in the Corrèze!'

Yes, he had been won over by this tall, well-built fellow, a handsome man who watched and waited on Louise and was full of affection for Félix. Jean maintained that sooner or later he would come with his wife to the Corrèze, to explore the area she had talked about so much. And Louise approved of this plan. He joked readily, too:

'You haven't got any trees down there in the Corrèze, have you? It's too poor.'

'No trees! We have the most beautiful chestnut trees in the world!' protested Pierre-Edouard and his sister.

'Go on! A few twisted saplings, some miserable aspens, a few broom brushes. No, I couldn't earn a living down there. I need trees; you've seen the oak plantations we have here?'

These really were beautiful and well maintained; it was Jean who looked after them, and he was more than a little proud of them.

'Of course, compared to the forest at Tronçais, it's pathetic,' he added, suddenly becoming serious. 'But if I'd stayed there, where I worked for five years, I'd never have got to know your sister, that's my consolation.'

He had found consolation, for that and his other losses, and so had Louise: what more could one ask?

Pierre-Edouard dexterously bound another sheaf and looked up at the sky; the storm was receding. He felt completely happy, content to be there doing work he enjoyed, amongst companions who seemed to have accepted him, despite the fact that he didn't understand half of what they were saying – they had such dreadful accents! Happy to be able to say: 'I'm all right here. There's Louise, Félix and Jean; the pay is good and I like the country, and if I want to, I can stay, and that's what I'm going to do! Tomorrow I'll write to Léon.'

He gathered another sheaf and began to whistle. Life was beautiful.

# PART FIVE

*The Red Furrows*

# 19

JEAN-EDOUARD was struck by the silence when he stepped out into the main street; such a heavy silence, so deep, that he was quite frightened by it. It made him want to talk, to say something, anything, just to reassure himself that it was possible to disturb the abnormal peace, the unbearable, unnatural calm which oppressed the whole region. Even the animals seemed beaten into a sort of stupor; nothing moved, all animation suspended.

'It's not possible, God help us!' he murmured. 'It's as if the whole village has died since they left . . .'

They had left in a state of happy madness, a sort of collective hysteria, after several days of sheer lunacy!

First of all there was a dramatic scene on 1 August, with the teacher as principal actor, standing out in the centre of the square: the teacher waving his newspaper, running from side to side towards onlookers attracted by his cries. The teacher, a man normally so calm, was crying, really crying, huge tears which shone on his cheeks. The poor man held out the paper and stammered between hiccups and pathetic sobs:

'They've killed him, like an animal! They've murdered the only man who could have saved us, all is lost! They've killed Jaurès!'

And then the same day, towards five-thirty in the afternoon, when everyone was still in a state of shock from the morning's news, the postmaster rushed out of his office waving a telegram and shouting:

'Mobilisation order! Extremely urgent! First mobilisation day, Sunday August the second.'

So there was a state of alarm, a frenzy. The men ran to and fro, as if there were a fire, finding out the news. The cries, of joy, of hate! And all those words!

'We must leave immediately!'

'And the harvest, you idiots, what's to become of it?'

'Shut up!'

'Call the train, quick, quick. They're expecting us!'

And by evening the first departure, the first farewells. Then on Sunday all the young people streamed away, the lifeblood of the village. On the next and following days the older men left; obedient to the instructions on the coloured pages of their military handbooks, they went to present themselves to their units on the second, third or seventh mobilisation days.

Then there was silence in the village; emptiness, paralysis. And still there were others who had not yet joined up; there were still several fathers of families, and the older men, between forty and fifty-one, who would be called up in the following days. But they were not making any noise, they were making ready.

Jean-Edouard walked up the main street towards the Mairie.

'I was expecting you,' said Jean Duroux, shaking his hand. 'Well, how many of us are left at the final count?'

'From the council? Four – no, five with Dupeuch; you, Gaston, Jeantout, myself and then Léon. We can't count André and Jacques, they're leaving the day after tomorrow.'

'We shall have to get ourselves organised. Just think! No postman, no policeman, no butcher nor baker, no one left. Even Doctor Delpy, our priest and the teacher have gone . . .'

'Yes, and almost all the farmers in the community. What are we going to do? We're already behind with the harvest, with this weather. Have you seen how much there is still to bring in and thresh?'

'I've seen . . . but, you know, everyone agrees that it won't be for very long, a month or two perhaps. No more.'

'And everyone is wrong!' maintained Doctor Fraysse, coming into the room. 'Believe me, I see it as a long drawn out affair, this war. A year, maybe more. No, I'm not a defeatist!' he insisted, catching Jean Duroux's disapproving look. 'I'm simply telling you that it will be terrible and long. I know them, the Prussos! I saw them in '70. They only attack when they're sure of themselves. Oh, they won't win this time! President Poincaré is no Napoleon, luckily! But they won't be on their knees in two months, as you're saying. And that's what brings me here. You can inform everyone who's still here that I'm starting work again.'

'But you can't . . .' The squire was worried. 'Well, I don't have to tell you that it's hard work.'

'I know, I'm seventy-nine, and so what? You'll just have to find me a horse and cart. But I think Léon could provide that.'

'You can take my team, for free,' interrupted Jean-Edouard. 'It's just as good as anything that old swindler might sell you. Strutting about pretending to be a gentleman, when everyone else of his age is serving the flag!'

'He has a family to support,' argued Jean Duroux, 'and we should be glad that a few men like him are staying here. We're going to need them.'

'And the old folk,' the doctor agreed. 'You're going to have to work with all the former members of the council, like Antoine Gigoux. And with the women too.'

'Yes, we're going to organise all that. But I'm still convinced that it will all be over soon.'

Saint-Libéral came to life again, soberly, at a gentler pace. There really were too many hands missing for the bubbling activity of pre-war years to revive; the incessant toing and froing as from a hive in the honey-making season, the powerful rhythm of men at work.

Jean-Edouard demonstrated his remarkable flair for organisation, and it was partly thanks to him that the community emerged from its paralysis. He very quickly established teams of all the able-bodied men, women and children, who went out into the fields to finish the harvest, to bring in the sheaves and store the produce under cover.

It was amazing to see the stiff old men, sometimes leaning on young boys, but remembering and repeating the swing of the scythe by instinct. The women doing men's work; harnessing the animals, leading the teams, handling scythe and sickle, grinding the flour, cutting the meat, lighting the fire at the forge; they took over as heads of families with a hitherto unsuspected authority and power!

Jean-Edouard worked without respite; he was everywhere at once, and many were grateful to him for the loan of his mechanical reaper to cut the last patches of corn. He went round the farms where he knew there were no menfolk, always followed by Abel, whose grin grew more and more vacuous, and by Berthe – who, everyone agreed, had grown into a beautiful girl. He did not pause until the last sheaf was safely in, and proved once more that however dreadful the tragedies which beset him, he was not defeated by them, but rather made stronger and more determined. It was as if he had been waiting for just such a test to show his true mettle.

Inspired and intoxicated with fanatical energy, he was avenging all the wrongs he had suffered for the last five years; the slights, the family set-backs, the mayor's chain which had been denied him. They had thought him weakened and discouraged, but he came to the top stronger than ever; became again the man who had fought like a lion for the railway, the syndicate, the market, for all that was dear to his heart and that he believed he should do.

Jean-Edouard fulfilled his role wonderfully, admittedly helped by Jeantout and Gaston, and the squire also rose to the occasion. He gave his time unstintingly, and drew up a list of the worst affected families, where there were no men, the father long dead and the son away, where only women and children remained. He made sure that help went to them first, and sometimes even gave money from his own pocket to the most needy.

And then to him, as the elected mayor of the community, fell the most terrible task of all, the one which left him a changed man. What a shock when he opened the telegram announcing the first death from among the villagers, the first martyr, whose death was to drive all the mothers and wives mad with fear, though they crossed themselves every day! This death was going to destroy the unity of a family which he, Jean Duroux, had to visit without delay; it was he who must plunge them into black despair!

For a fleeting moment he was tempted to delegate the burden to a third party, to one of his assistants, or to the old doctor. But he pulled himself together immediately, wished that Father Verlhac could have accompanied him, and went out.

With hesitant step and hunched shoulders he made his way towards the inn. The first death was that of André Chanlat, the son of Jacques and Léonie, the innkeepers. He fell on the twenty-fourth day of the war. He was thirty-one and had two children.

Berthe stuffed her things into the big sack of coarse blue cloth she normally used to carry the dirty linen to the wash-house, and set it down against the door. Then she put on her Sunday clogs and smoothed her dress, all the while keeping an eye on the town square which was black with people.

Almost all the villagers were there for the funeral service, conducted by the old priest from Yssandon, in memory of André Chanlat. His death had caused general confusion and consternation. Despite the absence of body or coffin, which made the ceremony seem vaguely unreal, the mayor and town council had decided to honour the sacrifice made by this young father.

Berthe looked at the clock and then half opened the door. Presently she heard the whistle of the train; it always whistled as it started round the last bend just before the village, then it slowed down and came up beside the main street at walking pace.

She grasped her bundle, went out without a backward glance, ran towards the track and hid in the ditch. The funeral procession filed slowly past. She stood up suddenly, jumped into a compartment and threw herself down in it.

She had calculated that few people would be curious enough to turn round to watch the train pass. If she had judged it right, they should all be giving their attention to Jean Duroux and the funeral oration which he was delivering at that very moment — a very beautiful speech, no doubt, very sad. As for other travellers, it was highly unlikely that anyone would get on at St Libéral station. Who could possibly need to go to La Rivière or Brive, since the war had started? And if anyone did get into her compartment, what could they say? She had a right to take the train, hadn't she?

The carriages crossed the square, slid into the station and stopped with a metallic squeak. She held her breath and forced herself to count to three hundred. If she did not hurry, the train would leave again when she reached that number; it never stopped more than five minutes.

It set off sooner than she expected, almost without a sound, without a cheery whistle, as if the driver were in a hurry to get away from a place marked by death, as he could tell from the black flag hanging above the door to the inn.

Berthe breathed more easily. She had succeeded. She had overcome all the difficulties and completed the first stage — by far the hardest part — of a plan she had been hatching for years, an idea which had sustained her, allowed her to survive without going mad when she had to submit to her father's inflexible will, her mother's sternness, her grandmother's senility.

At last she could begin to live, to laugh, without fearing her father's anger or her mother's scoldings. God knows Louise and Pierre-Edouard had had good reason to leave! And how she had counted the days which separated her from freedom!

It would have been a terrible mistake to have fled earlier, an irretrievable error which would have condemned her to continue that joyless, aimless, and loveless existence. She knew her father too well; she dared not leave him whilst he had any hold over her. That identity card, which he had used and abused, had been in his hand only the day before yesterday; she had been about to escape from him and he hadn't even realised it! For yesterday, 25 August 1914, Berthe had attained her majority.

She was twenty-one, yes, but cautious as a wild-cat, with a strong intelligence refined by years of observation, of silence, of rebellion hidden under a false passivity.

She knew that her father would not hesitate to use any means to force her to return home, if she gave him half a chance; to send a couple of policemen to the station at Brive, for instance, to welcome her as she alighted from the train. Not to stop her — he no longer had the right to do that – but to keep her there for an hour or two, to give him time to get there himself. Convinced of his rights, his duty even, he would place a hand on her shoulder and take her back to the house, whether she would or no . . .

But she was cleverer than him, more cunning; she had been contemplating her departure for such a long time that she had studied every detail, each minute possibility that, if neglected, might bring her plans to naught.

The note she had slipped under her parents' bedcovers would not be found for hours. For the moment, everything depended on her parents not noticing her absence for a while. And even if they returned early to the house, there was no immediate evidence that she had fled. They would probably think she was in the cowshed, or the vegetable plot.

Later, of course, at suppertime . . . But by then it would be much too late; nothing could be done to try to catch her. Yes, every passing minute told her that she had won.

When the train arrived at La Rivière-de-Mansac, she jumped down onto the platform, barely pausing, for she saw the other line of carriages, the ones which would take her away forever. She knew that she had five minutes to spare to buy a ticket. It was relatively easy to travel without paying between St Libéral and La Rivière, but that was not advisable on the main line. Confident, with the easy tread of a seasoned traveller who knows exactly where she's going and is surprised at nothing, she moved towards the ticket-office.

If her father set out to look for her, it would be at Brive. But he, who believed he saw and knew it all, hadn't thought of everything. He had not taken account of the women who gossiped around the village wash-house, where Mother Bouchard, the cobbler's wife, explained that her husband always had to leave the day before for Thenon market, where he had a thriving clientele, because there was no proper connection in the morning. He always caught the 18.16 for Périgueux . . .

Jean-Edouard and Marguerite noticed Berthe's absence far sooner than she had expected, and she would doubtless have swiftly devised an alternative plan if she had realised that her departure would be discovered even before the train set her down at La Rivière-de-Mansac.

It was Marguerite who had the first suspicions. She too had put on her Sunday clogs, to go to the funeral. She took them off as soon as she got home and slid them into their usual place under the stairs, then frowned when she noticed that her daughter's good clogs had disappeared.

'Well she must be mad, poor Berthe!' she cried to Jean-Edouard, who was changing into his work-clothes in their bedroom. 'Call her! What's got into her, putting on her best shoes to clean out the cowshed! I'll teach her how much they cost, I will!'

Five minutes later they were forced to face the facts: Berthe was not in the cowshed, nor in the garden; nor was she minding the animals, for Abel had led them up on to the stubble fields on the plateau.

A strange presentiment led Marguerite to open the wardrobe, and she stood dumbstruck for a moment; most of Berthe's things had gone. All that was left were a few old rags, some skirts and aprons worn threadbare.

'Jean!' she cried feebly. 'Look, she's taken everything, all her things; she's done it to us, her as well . . .'

'Bloody hell!' he swore. Then he controlled himself: 'What in God's name are you trying to say? Who could she have gone with? There are only old men left around here! Well, she won't have left alone, she's not capable of it. Besides, where's she supposed to have gone to, eh?'

'I don't know, do something, we have to find her . . .'

'My God, yes, I'm going to find her! What's that girl thinking of? That she decides what happens here, like the others did! Just you wait, she'll get a good hiding . . . Come on, come with me, we must ask everyone. Somebody must have seen her . . .'

'But then everyone will know! What will they think of us?' protested Marguerite.

'I don't care! We need all the neighbours to help us. Come on, hurry up, we'll question them.'

It was Jeantout's mother who very soon told them. She had been unable to walk for years, and her only pleasure was to watch the main street; she had seen the girl climb into the moving train.

Jean-Edouard ran to the post-office to telephone the police station at Ayen, and explained the situation in a few words.

'And it's most important that you tell your colleagues at Brive to keep her there until I arrive!' he said to the sergeant at the other end, whom he had known for years. 'What's that? What's it got to do with her age, anyway? She's my daughter, isn't she? She's . . .'

Suddenly he realised, and his voice fell; his energetic shout dwindled to a barely audible whisper. 'She was twenty-one the day before yesterday,' he finally admitted. 'Oh, I see . . . Right.'

Some of the villagers who saw him returning from the post-office thought that he had just learned of the death of his son.


Berthe arrived in Paris the following morning. She was deafened and exhausted by a night on the train, and came staggering out of the Gare d'Austerlitz almost on the point of giving up. Despite her strength of character, her desire to change her life – to *live* – she was ready to climb back onto the train and return to St Libéral's peace and quiet.

She knew no large towns except Brive, so she was frightened, almost petrified, by the noise, the crowds, the crush of cabs and taxis, the terrifying roar of the overhead railway which passed just above her, the continuous rumbling of military convoys. Through her confusion she suddenly became aware of the incredible madness which had impelled her to flee, which was now forcing her to act independently. She remained paralysed by fear for a long time, frozen to the spot in the middle of the pavement.

Then she gradually came to her senses, collected her thoughts, and began to resolve the problems she was faced with one by one.

First of all, she was glad that she had not left without some money. The 832 francs which she had hidden under her skirts really belonged to her. It was made up of small coins her grandparents had given her long ago, which she had carefully kept for years, and the savings which old Léonie had patiently accumulated, stored in her chest between two piles of linen.

'These savings,' her mother had told her as they returned from the burial service, 'will be yours, for your dowry. For the time being I'll look after them, you don't need them just now. But never fear, they'll come to you on your wedding day.'

She had taken the hoard from her parents' wardrobe just before leaving. The nest-egg was somewhat diminished by the cost of the journey – 25 francs 75 – but it was still significant, and made the future less bleak. This money would guarantee her bed and board for several months.

She urgently needed to find work, however. Convinced that a town as huge as Paris would provide opportunities for every sort of job, she tossed her bag over her shoulder and set off down the Boulevard de l'Hôpital.


At St Libéral there was little talk about her flight, and few sympathised with her parents. What was the departure of one girl, compared to the slaughter which stained the countryside red and laid the young men to rest in the stubble!

Already the village was coming to terms with another death – a lad of twenty-three, killed three days after the Chanlats' son – and six wounded, two of them in a serious condition. So what did it matter that little Berthe had run away to live her own life? It was simply proof that her father was as hard as ever, just as strict, and that he had not learned his lesson from what had happened with Louise and Pierre-Edouard!

And if she had left to join up with a boyfriend (some of the women were convinced of this), one could only hope that the lass would make the most of it and enjoy her man! Make the most of it while he was alive and strong, fit to make her happy night and day, to show her how beautiful life had been before . . . Before men had gone mad and begun to massacre each other indiscriminately, killing kids of twenty as well as fathers of families.

The Vialhes' closest neighbours, friends such as Jeantout, Gaston, the mayor and the old doctor, even took the trouble to show Jean-Edouard that Berthe's departure was of no consequence and held no dishonour. They all reminded him that she was an adult and free to lead her life as she wished, even if it was a trial to her parents to accept this at first.

'Of course it's all right,' said Jean-Edouard ironically, one evening when the squire was trying to reason with him. 'I've lost my third and last child, and I'm supposed to be singing!'

'I didn't say that! You haven't lost anything at all. Your children are still alive! Talking of which, have you had any news of Pierre-Edouard?'

'Yes, at least he's written to us. He's at the front, I don't know where. You know how it is, they're not even allowed to say where they are. And you, your son-in-law?'

'He's okay; he can't say where he is either, somewhere up there, like all the rest . . . So you mustn't torment yourself about Berthe. She's in no danger, her . . . By the way, did you know that Léon had signed up?'

'I don't believe it, that little twerp? For what? The supply corps, I bet! I thought he was exempt from service?'

'Only as head of a family. He's realised that his sisters can manage on their own now. One has got a job in Brive, and Mathilde is nearly fifteen. No, he's not in the supply corps, he's in the infantry. He left yesterday to join the 126th at Brive . . .'

Jean-Edouard nodded, but with an unhappy expression; it did not please him to have to admit that Léon had done the right thing.

'But then, if he's gone as well,' he said suddenly, 'there are no young men left at all in the community! Only the old ones like us!'

'Well yes, nothing but old men . . .'

'What will become of us? Just think of the grape-picking, the ploughing, the sowing, everything! How are we going to get all that work done?'

'With the women, my friend, with the women. You'll have to get used to the idea: if this war continues, and I'm afraid that it will, it's the women who are going to take the place of the men. Everywhere. In the fields and on all the farms . . .'

'That's never been done before!' protested Jean-Edouard. 'My God, there have been other wars and that's not been done! Can you see women doing the ploughing? Perhaps the harvest and the easy jobs, but not the ploughing! Go on! This war won't last because the other side needs the men, just as we do, to work the land, to produce food. When there's no corn, then they'll have to stop their bloody war, or they'll die of starvation! That's what'll happen, and your idea of women doing the ploughing, that's not going to happen tomorrow, that's never been done!'

Jean Duroux shrugged his shoulders. 'And a girl who jumps into a train the day after she's twenty-one, have you seen that before, in the past? Don't get in a state, I'm not saying that to annoy you, you know me. But believe me, our world, the real world we lived in until last month, doesn't exist any more. I'm afraid it's dead and gone forever.'

Berthe wandered about for five days, feeding on crusts and sleeping each night in a different room. Each evening found her with less energy and less courage than the previous day.

The capital was in a frenzy, preparing for a siege or even for street-fighting, and she wandered the streets without knowing where she was going, along the most miserable thoroughfares of the poor areas and the prosperous avenues of the 7th district. She even had to reject amorous admirers, attracted by the fresh complexion and graceful, slender figure of the little girl from the country. But no one offered her any honest work.

Paris was at fever-pitch and in a torment. Day after day the front gave way, collapsing on all sides. Already hundreds of thousands of Parisians were fleeing to the provinces in the south and west, leaving others to worry about stopping the barbarian hordes who, they were convinced, burned everything in their path, cut off children's hands, massacred old men and violated women and girls.

232

The most fantastic rumours spread like flies from a decaying carcass: it was said that the governor of Paris had just been assassinated by a spy, that Joffre had committed suicide, that the government was about to flee to Bordeaux, that von Kluck was at Montdidier and making straight for Compiègne, Senlis and Paris, that more than five hundred thousand Parisians had already left town . . .

Truth and falsehood were closely interwoven in stories which played on the popular imagination, creating an overcharged atmosphere, close to delirium. They changed hourly, and exacerbated the cowardice and defeatism of some and the anger, energy and patriotism of others.

How could she find work in the midst of such madness! Berthe was discouraged and worn down by the lonely days of walking, but on the sixth morning she set out again on her search. In vain she offered her services at several laundries, grocery stores, butchers' and even bars. In vain she asked the caretakers of fine-looking flats if any of the tenants were in need of a maid, a cleaner, a cook?

By chance she started down the rue Saint-Jacques; a crowd blocked her way in front of the Val-de-Grâce church. A long convoy of lorries was just arriving – on some of them you could still see the names of the grand stores underneath the red crosses, for they had been delivery vans only a month earlier – and the wounded were being carried out of them by the dozen: pale bodies, drained of blood, which groaned, dressed in red trousers on which the blood had made dark patches, their blue-grey greatcoats smeared with mud and torn by purple holes made by shrapnel or a bullet, their heads sticky with sweat, grime and powder, their limbs dislocated, smashed, sometimes missing.

Berthe was seized by an impulse; it inspired her, propelled her forwards. Here there was work for her, work which she did not find repugnant, which she knew how to do. Had she not cared for her grandmother all those years?

'Let me through,' she commanded as she cleared herself a way through a crowd of onlookers.

She reached the front and strode towards the ambulances. An old policeman wanted to push her back. She drew herself up and eyed him scornfully: 'I work here, can't you see I'm a nurse!'

The man muttered a vague apology, and watched her move towards the stretchers.

# 20

PIERRE-EDOUARD groaned, kicked out fiercely at a great gangling fellow who had just stepped on his stomach, and tried to get back to sleep. The straw in the wagon stank of sweat and horse manure and urine.

He turned over and stuck his elbow in the chest of his neighbour, who protested softly. The train had been on the move for hours, jolting and grinding along. Added to this were the snorts and whinnies of the horses on the other side of the wagon, who sometimes delivered great kicks to the boarding separating them, just to stretch their legs.

Pierre-Edouard, unable to sleep again, got up and walked to the wide-open doorway. Here sweet fresh air came into the wagon and made the atmosphere almost fit to breathe. Dead tired, he leaned out, his face to the wind, examining the night. It was inky black and revealed nothing about which direction the convoy was heading. Anyway, what did it matter . . .

He wanted to smoke, and started to take out his pipe and tobacco pouch, then remembered the ban. Of course, with all that straw . . . He made do with sucking the stem of the short pipe between his teeth. He had changed over to a pipe since the beginning of the war; it was the only way to smoke without the worry that he would reveal his position to the enemy lines. And even when extinguished it gave some relief from the desire to smoke, and to a certain extent it helped with the awful pain in his head and ears caused by the hellish noise of a battery of 75mm guns in full action.

He went back to his sleeping place on tiptoe, but stepped on a body.

'For God's sake! Try to be more careful!'

'Don't swear at me, Jules,' he retorted peaceably, as he snuggled down in the straw.

Jules! What a face he had made, poor Jules, on meeting him back in the barracks! Yet it was logical that it should happen like that. Weren't they both from the same regiment, the same squad, the same battery? One little point made Pierre-Edouard happy: he had worked for almost four years under the authority of Jules' father –

and what authority! – only to find Jules, no longer son of the boss but a simple bombardier, under *his* orders. The orders of a farm worker on twenty sous a day!

Pierre-Edouard nursed no grievance against his colleague; he knew he wasn't responsible for his brute of a father nor his bitch of a mother. And anyway, it was all so far away, so childish even, that the memory of life before the war was softened, like those of childhood! He had not believed the war would really happen, had thought it impossible, yet all of a sudden he had been tossed into the middle of a battle, into the slaughter, down there in Alsace. Now the train which had left Alsace the previous evening was taking them to an unknown destination.

Alsace! How happy they were to tread the soil, what ecstasy to be among the first liberators of the area! They were greeted with kisses, hugs and tears of joy; all the people vowed they owed them an eternal debt of gratitude! That had not lasted long.

The 5th Artillery Regiment, under Colonel Nivelle, had been incorporated into the 7th Army Corps of General Dubail's 1st Army, then assigned to the Army of Alsace under General Pau. On the extreme right wing, they had pushed towards Thann from the morning of 7 August. It was a baptism of fire for Pierre-Edouard and all the others, an unforgettable initiation into a murderous folly which spurred them on to kill, to go on killing, faster and faster, speeding up the firing rate, pushing it to the furthest limits of endurance for both guns and men. It transformed them from peaceable chaps, hardly capable of killing a hen, into a species of happy barbarians who shouted for joy when their shrapnel burst among the cavalry or infantry or, best of all, in the middle of the enemy gun-emplacement. That 77 Battery loomed over them, surrounded them with its missiles, launched its red and black scrolls into the sky; as the ammunition spun away and exploded, it tossed pieces of shredded corpse all around.

Then there was the constant and exhausting repositioning, the parts to be put on to the guns, the line of fire to be adjusted, the horses to be brought back under control when they took fright and kicked, the guns and ammunition wagons to be hitched on in haste as they bent low under enemy fire: advance, retreat, turnabout. Mulhouse was liberated, then re-taken, bombarded, destroyed. Then the advance towards those places with difficult names – Buetwiller, Guewenheim, Burbach, Munster.

Finally, on the evening of 22 August, when they had reoccupied

Mulhouse, came the incredible news – denied by the officers but discussed and spread about by the soldiers and warrant-officers – that the British Army was in retreat, forcing the French to give way in turn, to withdraw, to let the enemy retake the land so dearly bought . . .

'We don't even know where we're going!' thought Pierre-Edouard in a sort of stupor. He searched for somewhere to lay his head, felt around for his kitbag but did not find it, and so rested against Jules' back and fell asleep.

The 5th Artillery Regiment disembarked next day in Amiens. On 25 August, Colonel Nivelle informed his men that the 7th Army Corps was now under the command of General Maunoury of the 6th Army, and they would be in charge of the northern defence of Paris . . .

Pierre-Edouard had to make an effort not to fall asleep; despite the jolting gait of his mount and the clanking of the whole artillery convoy, it was difficult to stay upright in the saddle which had been torturing his buttocks for the last four hours.

On the previous evening, 3 September, the 7th Army Corps had begun its march to the south east; they left the defensive positions they had occupied between Mesnil and Dammartin just as the northern horizon pulsated with the ominous red light of Senlis and Creil in flames.

The long artillery convoy entered a sleeping village – or was it deserted? Pierre-Edouard looked without interest at the tumble-down cottages, then suddenly woke up.

'Well, well, well!' he murmured, gazing into the shadows. 'There's no mistake, we're in Nantouillet!'

He urged on his horse and caught up with Jules, who was with the ammunition chest thirty metres ahead.

'Hey, Jules, have you seen where we are?'

'Yes, at Nantouillet. We're just passing old Lachaud's café . . .'

'Bloody hell, if I'd known . . .' whispered Pierre-Edouard. 'Just think, we're heading straight for Monthyon!'

'Yes, and the farm's over there, just to the right,' said Jules, indicating the plain with outstretched arm. 'My God, I wonder whether . . .'

'No, no,' Pierre-Edouard reassured him, 'they haven't got this far yet. You can see, everything is peaceful here.'

'Maybe, but they're banging away hard enough over by Meaux . . . Hey, why are we stopping? They're not going to make us camp here in the open!'

'Dismount, dismount,' was whispered along the line.

'I think we're going to finish the night here,' said Pierre-Edouard. 'Really, we could have pushed on as far as your place; it would have done me good to see your father's face, after he ordered me never to set foot in his house again! All right, I'm only joking. Basically he's a good fellow, your father, I've nothing against him.'

The morning of the 4th was heavy and oppressive. The 6th Army took up its position, reinforced its defences, closed off the routes which led straight to the capital. On the left wing they linked up with the English army of Marshal French, which was hidden between Lagny and Signy to block the Marne valley.

There were agonising hours of waiting before the great push which was to overrun and decimate von Kluck's 1st Army, which had been threatening Paris on the east side. They knew from continuous aerial observation that his 2nd, 3rd and 4th Corps were boldly deployed between Betz and Meaux.

Two groups from the 5th Artillery Regiment set out at about four in the afternoon and advanced to Plessis. Pierre-Edouard and Jules saw Moureau Farm on their right, less than two kilometres away: the fields, the massive buildings, the huge corn stacks which they themselves had constructed, only six weeks earlier.

'It's too bloody, too bloody . . .' said Jules, examining each plot of his own ground on the horizon.

'Don't worry, we'll be back,' Pierre-Edouard comforted him, for he too was affected by the sight of familiar ground.

All the villages and hamlets he could make out over there in the distance, Neufmontier, Peuchard, Saint-Souplets . . . All those places he had visited with Jules, or with Moïse, his bicycle and his famous binges; where he had danced, flirted with the girls, lived – without appreciating just how lucky he was to live, to dance, drink, have fun, work; a gift from heaven, a present fit for a king.

In the evening they camped at Cuizy, which was swamped by a flood of light infantry, Algerians, cavalry; a solid mass of armed men.

The order to attack reached them on the night of 5 September, at 2.55 a.m., accompanied by an unequivocal message:

'No more looking to the rear! A troop which can no longer advance should hold its ground, at whatever cost, and die in position rather than retreat. No weakness will be tolerated.'
JOFFRE

Since the death of the Chanlat boy, Jean Duroux and his friends in the council no longer dared to finish their discussion at the inn. The establishment had a gloomy atmosphere and a large photo – draped with black crêpe – of the deceased in his hussar uniform, hung in the middle of the main wall; it interrupted the drinkers accusingly, cut short any desire to tarry there, to imbibe and debate as if nothing had happened.

Besides, how could they let the Chanlat couple and their children overhear the normal run of their conversations: the war, the news of a son, a nephew, a brother . . . Gaston alone, who only had two unmarried daughters, was not affected by it. But the others – Duroux, Jeantout, Jean-Edouard, even Antoine Gigoux – just lived for the next letter, the one that told them all was well. And they comforted each other, passed on vague snippets of information which a soldier occasionally managed to slip into his missive. The censor was thorough.

As for the papers, full of news which they endlessly dissected – they began to realise that these were controlled, muzzled and one-sided; the articles, so idiotically soothing, even euphoric, were nothing but a collection of lies and rubbish. Who could still believe what some of the scribes triumphantly maintained – that German weapons were no good, that their shells did not explode, that the Boche (the name was just emerging) did not know how to fight, that they were as timid as rabbits, that they were so hungry there were thousands of them queuing up for a mess-tin of soup! That good soup which the fine Frenchmen offered them without bitterness . . .

'Yes, but who to believe, what to believe?' asked Jean Duroux that evening, as he emerged from the Mairie with his councillors. Old habits die hard, and all four turned instinctively towards the inn; then suddenly stopped, embarrassed, as if caught in the wrong, as if people would think they had forgotten.

'Go on, don't be as stupid as the Boche!' called out Doctor Fraysse from his garden. He was delicately pruning the withered blooms from a huge climbing rose; he slipped the secateurs into the front pocket of his gardening apron and came towards them. 'I've been watching you for more than two weeks, you are silly! Do you want the Chanlats to close the inn? Don't you think the village is sad enough without that?'

'Not at all!' retorted the mayor. 'But if you think it's jolly . . .'

'Who's talking about jollity! For the time being all we can do is try to make a living, to keep going. The Chanlats need you, need all of us, to be there, to talk and play billiards. And I made Gigoux promise that he would come and play billiards with me, starting this evening. Come on, the Chanlats have enough troubles as it is, without you treating them as if they had an infectious disease as well!'

'It's not like that!' protested Jean Duroux. 'It's out of respect for them, they're in mourning.'

'I know what I'm talking about!' The old doctor was carried away. 'I understand human beings better than you! I tell you they need us. *Need*, have you got it? To live! To live, by God! So as not to die of sorrow! And if they're left all alone, that's what will happen! Come on, we'll all go together, like in the good old days. While we're on that subject, Duroux, is there any news?'

Jean Duroux regularly telephoned his daughter in Paris, where she had bravely remained. Her information was therefore more recent, but no more trustworthy, than that which arrived in letters to the village.

'Not much,' replied the mayor. 'Here's what the headlines of the Paris papers said this morning: "Seventh September. Yesterday a counter-attack started along the whole front, a brilliant success for our troops." You have to admit that it's pretty vague – and besides, we don't even know where the front is exactly!'

Pierre-Edouard spurred on his mount, jumped the swollen corpse of a horse which had opened like a rotting fruit, and made sure that the gun and ammunition chest were following. He shouted encouragement but could not hear his own voice, such was the pandemonium.

All around them shells were falling like a shower of hail, across devastated fields and charred haystacks. Their fiery explosions mixed with the smoking trails of the cannon-balls, and throbbed like clouds of wasps whose nest is disturbed by a ploughshare.

And everywhere bodies, countless bodies; poor disfigured corpses biting the earth with bared teeth, their arms stretched wide, or gently laid out, backs on the golden stubble, as if to follow the sweet passage of the clouds with fly-filled eyes – pitiful remains which the wheels of the gun-carriages mutilated a second time as they charged over them at full gallop.

Five batteries of guns, among them Pierre-Edouard's, were forcing their way towards Puisieux, which lay under a dark cloud of enemy dust, where they were killing each other in a pitiless hand-to-hand battle. Huge waves of spiked helmets were hurling themselves constantly at this objective, in vast grey squadrons. Puisieux could only be saved by fire from the twenty 75mm guns charging to its relief.

Twenty cannon and their ammunition chests, almost three hundred horses driven at full speed in a mad charge, rushing into the heat of the battle, to a cauldron of molten metal, a dead heap of ruins which had to be defended.

The convoy plunges into the conflict, into the thick reeking fog of burnt powder, stones, earth and shattered bodies. Orders stream out, precise, according to the regulations; instructions seem superfluous, ridiculous, for already the men are busy, unhitching the horses, unloading the ammunition, preparing the weapons. But the orders serve their purpose; they reassure, they prove to everyone that the battery team is complete, that every man is at his post, aware of his role, ready to fulfil it to the best of his ability, just as they did during exercises, a long time ago, on the firing range.

Fast, faster, for every second counts, for it depends on you to get the barrel ready for firing, ready to belch out, to stem the flood which rises, advances, swells, which is going to annihilate you; for those men who are running towards you, yelling, are going to overwhelm you, massacre you. They are so close that all the scientific theory – the positioning, the drift, the correction of the trajectory – is reduced to nothing. There is only one order which flies along the line of barrels:

'Set to zero! To zero, for God's sake, light the fuses and fire at will! Watch the recoil!'

And suddenly the salvo, resounding, rolling out, swelling, speeding away.

'Watch out, it's slipping!' shouted Pierre-Edouard. 'Christ, hold on to that cannon, it's running back!' The spade was thrust into the ground, a hole was dug and the gun carriage steadied.

Firing began again, methodically.

Pierre-Edouard whirled round and looked at the bugler who was shaking him. The man had his mouth open, he must be bellowing an order.

'What?' he yelled.

'Stop firing!'

Finally he understood the order from afar, a faint murmur smothered by the surrounding noise. Then with a tired wave he signalled to his men to hold their fire; turned towards them, reeling with fatigue, and leant against the left wheel of the red-hot cannon. Like many of his comrades his nose was bleeding, and a thousand bells were ringing in his skull.

In front of him, across the ravaged fields and shattered

undergrowth, stretched the bodies of men, as far as the eye could see; cut off in mid-charge, at point-black range, little patches of grey, crouching low, insignificant. Above them, an occasional tracer rocket left a trail of fire.

'What we've done to them! Just look what they've taken, the buggers!' exclaimed the second loader, leaning against the other wheel.

Pierre-Edouard smiled faintly and kicked at some clods of earth; then he wiped his nose and blew into his empty pipe. In front of him the loader was lighting a cigarette.

'Lend me a fill of tobacco.'

The man stretched his arm across the gun. A dry crack halted his movement. His cap flew up like a butterfly taking wing. Numbly Pierre-Edouard watched his companion slide gently across the wheel. The bullet had punched a hole in the top of his skull. The smoke from the cigarette he had just lit drifted gently from his half-open lips.

'My God, now I've seen it all!' he cried, as he knelt beside his colleague.

He thought he really had seen all there was to see since the previous day; every impossibility, every monstrosity. Seen everything, even taxis crammed full of armed men making their way towards Nanteuil: a fleet of taxis, hundreds of vehicles going up to the forward line, a staggering spectacle, crazy, which made him and his friends shout for joy.

Joy, yes. They had needed that so badly after the carnage, the bombardment, the corpses; after the explosion of one of the guns, struck by an 150mm shell, a monster fired by a cannon so far away that they could do nothing about it, it was out of range, far beyond the five kilometres reached by the 75mms.

Seen everything, even farms burned down, like that of Jules' future father-in-law, close to Yverny. Its blackened walls were still smoking and between them, amongst the rubble and hay cinders, they could make out the charred skeletons of the tethered cows. Even huge stacks of corn which crackled into flame like torches dipped in resin; even whole waves of men laid low with one blow, wiped out by grapeshot and shells.

Days as long as centuries, with the capture of Neufmontier, Monthyon, Saint-Souplets and Villeroy as well, so close to Moureau Farm. It had been bombarded too, the roofs damaged, but it was still standing, at least it had been three hours earlier . . . How could you know what might happen in three hours, when a man could die in less time than it took to exhale the smoke of his last cigarette . . .

He felt someone shaking him; he closed the dead man's eyes and straightened up.

'Got to go,' said a bombardier.

'Where to?'

'I don't know.'

'You never know anything!' he shouted intemperately, and then immediately regretted giving way to anger.

How could he have known six months earlier, when he was dancing with the girls in the inn, that he would be back in Puisieux on 7 September, twenty feet from the ruins of the inn, not to laugh and drink and tease the girls, but to kill men at point blank range? Men of his own age, who surely must have wanted to drink and laugh and make love, as he had done?

Ever since that impulse had driven Berthe towards the ambulances, she had lived surrounded by the smell of death, of infected wounds and blood. But nothing repelled or disgusted her. Not that she was insensitive to the suffering of others, far from it; it was just because, for the first time in her life, she felt she was something more than the obedient daughter who had docilely submitted to paternal authority and had been obliged to supress her own wishes and ideas. At last she had a feeling of being alive, even if it was amongst cries and pus and gangrene. She had the confidence that she was doing a job no one had forced on her, which she had chosen to do – and scores of women and girls from every background and area had chosen, like her, of their own accord, to wash, dress, bandage and feed these men.

For the first fortnight she did not dare go out of the Val-de-Grâce Church. She was so afraid that she would not have the strength to go back in again that she preferred to live there, in that world of suffering, nibbling a sandwich at intervals, sleeping a few hours in the dormitory, but always available, ready at any time of day or night to run to the side of a wounded or dying man.

Years of looking after the old woman had accustomed her to the most disagreeable tasks. Nothing offended her, and she quickly got to know her companions. The volunteer nurses were always full of good will, although the sights and smells and the atrocious wounds sometimes made them feel sick or faint. They appreciated her strength of character, her calmness, her kindness and spontaneity.

Then she made friends with a young hat-designer who came there each evening after work, and who suggested to her quite straight-forwardly that Berthe should share her room, in rue Servandoni. She accepted, but could not rest until she too had started making hats for ladies to pay her rent. It took her more than a year to perfect her skills, and then she put them to use with great taste and foresight; she kept one step ahead of the fashions, and presented the elegant ladies with exactly what they wanted when they wanted it.

She rapidly became more Parisienne than a native of Saint-Germain, and was soon recognised as an exceptional stylist. None of this prevented her from continuing her work as a nurse every morning. It never occurred to her to give that up; she had chosen it, and nobody was going to stop her seeing it through.

Despite Jean-Edouard's predictions, the women did begin ploughing. They had to, for everything indicated that the war would be long; the men would not be back for the sowing. So if they were to find anything to harvest, the ground would have to be cultivated . . .

Everyone set to, children and old folk – even the squire's wife was to be seen behind the harrow, guiding it and shaking it out in the freshly sown fields, although she had never touched a farm implement in her life before.

When the time came for school to start again in the autumn, a new problem arose. The teacher's wife alone could not provide education for eighty-seven children. The solicitor's wife volunteered her services, as if nothing had happened; as if the fiancés of her two daughters had not been killed one after the other, one boy from Saint-Robert lost on the Marne, the other, from Allassac, fallen in Lorraine.

Thanks to her, the school was well organised, and in October the playground rang with the laughter and shouts of children. They no longer played longtag, prisoner's base or hopscotch; it was the capture of Château-Thierry or the taxis at the Marne. Since three further deaths had plunged the village into mourning, eight of the schoolchildren were now fatherless.

The squire's son-in-law, a lieutenant in the 5th Dragoons, was seriously wounded on 25 October. They learned later that he had taken part in the battle of Yser and had fallen at Dixmude, hit in the stomach by an exploding 105.

As soon as he heard the news, Jean Duroux rushed to see Jean-Edouard. He found him picking nuts, saw him suddenly go pale, and remembered that five times already he had been the unhappiest of messengers, the one each family feared to see coming.

'No, no,' he stammered, 'it's not for you, it's not Pierre-Edouard . . .'

243

'Who is it, then?' asked Jean-Edouard in an expressionless voice.

'My son-in-law. Wounded. My daughter's just telephoned; I'm leaving for Paris straight away, for a long time possibly. So you'll have to take my place at the Mairie, there's only you . . .'

'And Jeantout, and Gaston? Or why not old Gigoux, he's used to it all . . .'

'Don't argue, I don't have the time. You'll have to take my place. I'm going to tell the others, I know they'll agree with me. Now go and put your wife's mind at rest, she's crying up there at the window. She must be thinking that I've come – the same as you did.'

'Yes,' murmured Jean-Edouard, 'and from now on I'll have to make these visits . . . By God, it will be heavy, your sash of office!'

Jean-Edouard devoted all his energy to this new task. He attempted to pull the village out of the economic quagmire into which it had sunk since the departure of the men. The markets had lapsed since the beginning of the war and he tried to get them going again, but it was no use. Too many of the stock-dealers were at the front, and those left behind (the old men and the cowards) soon learned that their best interests lay in quietly touring the farms and picking off their prey one by one. The women were easier to dupe if you could discuss it with them alone, inside the barn. Gathered together in the market place they would surely have been as cunning as the men, but isolated, often ignorant of dealing, confused by and unprepared for the high inflation and worried by rumours of requisitioning, they were easy prey.

In order to limit the exploitation of innocent people, Jean-Edouard decided to fix a list to the door of the Mairie each week, giving the current price for each commodity. Besides that he organised, together with Jeantout and Gaston, deliveries of beasts to the markets at Brive or Objat, which were still continuing. They gathered together the stock to be sold and haggled over the price, hoof by hoof, as keenly as if they were their own property.

He tried to keep the syndicate going too, but in vain, for the deliveries of fertilisers grew gradually worse. Besides, who could afford fertiliser? Its price had doubled since the beginning of the war.

Then it came – what he had most feared, and it made him ill for days – a brief telegram announcing the death of Edouard Duffraisse, one of the carpenter's sons. Within a fortnight he had to make three further visits, and each time he left a home full of tears.

The village counted nine dead by the end of the year.

# 21

Spurting out of the thick pall of smoke that lay over the ground, two green rockets streaked across the sky.

'Lengthen the range!' ordered Pierre-Edouard, eyes glued to his binoculars. 'Faster, for God's sake!' he commanded, as he ran to one of the guns of his battery, where shrapnel was just being cleared out of the mouth of the loading-chamber. He adjusted the barrel and the level and corrected the angle of fire.

'Prepare for ranging fire!' he shouted, as he examined again the battle lines on hill 196 between Beauséjour and Mesnil. The 122nd and 142nd Infantry had been trying to capture it since morning, at the cost of terrible slaughter.

He located the explosion of the first shells, too short . . . 'Lengthen it, in the name of God! We're still hitting our own men!'

Further away, he hoped beyond the French lines, the fat red blossoms of shells glowed.

'Good, keep that trajectory, but watch the air-hole! In twelves! Faster!'

He did not even hear the 210mm shell, was hardly aware of the fantastic sound of the explosion. He felt himself thrown into the air, saw a huge expanse of sky, and then was buried under a big red wave.

For the third time since the beginning of the month, Jean-Edouard inscribed a birth in a fine round hand, a new citizen of the commune of St Libéral.

'Jean Marie Léon Mouly, born 14 March 1915 at 12.40pm – better put one o'clock' suggested Doctor Fraysse, bending over his shoulder to read. 'A fine boy,' he commented, 'another one. It's crazy the number of births I'm expecting this month. And that's nothing compared to next month; that will beat all the records! Really, I'd never have thought that the announcement of a war would act as such an effective aphrodisiac,' he said, smiling: Jean-Edouard looked at him questioningly. 'Yes, I didn't think it would turn all the poor fellows on like that, and their wives too.'

'Well, they made the most of it before leaving, and that's understandable, because since then . . .'

'Anyway,' said the doctor, more seriously, 'however many births we have, they'll never fill the gaps left during the last eight months . . . You know, I'm almost sorry not to have died earlier, then I would have avoided seeing this catastrophe.'

'Come, come, don't say that. Besides, we need you.'

'Not much. Since the war started, no one's ill any more! It doesn't occur to people to think about their little aches and pains. Even the old folks are hanging on, they want to see victory! By the way, you know the village is going to have to help Marty's widow; she still hasn't received her pension.'

'I know, I've been dealing with it, I wrote to the préfecture, but everything's in such a muddle! If the squire were here, he'd have got them moving, but me . . .'

'Poor Duroux, I don't think we'll see him for a while.'

The squire had returned once to the village, a lightning visit to sort out some business, but had left for Paris again immediately; his son-in-law was still in a critical condition.

Jean-Edouard closed the Register of Births, then sorted through his desk and held out a pamphlet to the doctor:

'Look, instead of paying out war widows' pensions, this is what they dream up, the fools! All this writing just to remind me about daylight saving and to put the clocks forward an hour! What use is that rubbish!'

'It's a good idea in the towns,' the doctor admitted. 'It reduces electricity consumption. But here, you're right, it's ridiculous. They should know that we don't have electricity!'

'It's like their posters for war loans; I don't know where to put them all! Here, look at this: "For France, invest your gold! Gold fights for Victory!" They're not satisfied with just taking all our young men; they want to beggar us as well! I tell you, it'll all end badly . . .'

'But you've contributed, like everyone else!'

'Of course, but against my better judgement . . . Do you know what a seventy-five millimetre shell costs? Go on, have a guess! . . . Fifty-two francs!'

'Where did you get that from?'

'I went to see André Lachaud in the hospital. He was next to a boy who'd been working in munitions.'

André Lachaud was the first man from the village to be seriously wounded – he had fallen on 18 August, and would soon be returning home. For him the war was over, but so was fishing: he had lost both arms.

'Yes,' repeated Jean-Edouard, 'fifty-two francs for a shell! I don't earn that much every day, that's for sure. That's the price of a young calf! And it seems they fire off thousands of these a day! They ought to come and calve the cows, they wouldn't be able to do it!'

'It would be good to speak to these people face to face . . . By the way, have you any news of Pierre-Edouard?

'Yes, yes, he's okay. He writes from time to time, just a few lines to reassure his mother. Nothing, really . . . She writes the replies; I've nothing to say to him.'

'You're not going to tell me that you still bear a grudge against him?'

'I told you, I've nothing to say to him. If you must know, he never asks about the farm, or the animals and the crops. He doesn't care! So we're not about to come to any understanding. And then, I don't know whether he'll ever want to come back here . . . He must have found a good job up there near Paris. It doesn't surprise me, he's got his school certificate, so . . . The farm's not good enough for him now.'

'And Louise? And Berthe?' insisted the old doctor, who was the only person who dared ask these questions.

'Nothing,' admitted Jean-Edouard with a shrug. 'Come on, don't let's talk about that any more. That's all in the past now.'

Pierre-Edouard tried to struggle, but his arms were too heavy, too weighed down to make the slightest movement. He attempted to speak, but felt as if he were blowing into a huge bowl of milk; very creamy, thick, sweet, warm milk. So he gave up and waited. But his brain was working.

His first thought was that one of the guns in the battery had exploded; that had become quite a common occurrence. The staff at headquarters had done their best to hush up the business, but all the artillerymen knew that almost two hundred 75mm cannon had blown up since the end of December . . . more than sixty a month, along the whole front. And it wasn't the sort of accident you could conceal for long, because at least six men were blown to pieces with each explosion. Naturally there was talk of sabotage, in order to keep up morale; but it wasn't that, it was just poor workmanship and the terrific firing rate demanded of the guns. They heated up, and then shattered suddenly like the glass shade of a paraffin lamp. That's what must have happened.

Pierre-Edouard felt someone moving him, pawing at him, whispering very far above him.

'It's the adjutant, get his dressing pack . . .'

Adjutant? Well that wasn't him. He was battery sergeant-major. At least . . . No, he *was* adjutant, had been for a week, to replace the last one who had been cut in two by a fragment of a 150mm shell as big as a fist and sharp as a razor (after the adjutant, it had gone through one horse and stuck in the neck of the next!).

He felt someone cleaning his face, then his eyes, and a finger was inserted into his mouth to clear that big lump of milky curds which was bothering him. He struggled and retched.

'Don't choke me, dammit!' he spat out. He opened his eyes, and saw his comrades through a vague pink blur. Even Jules was there.

'You great oaf, Jules! What are you up to here?' he stammered out.

'Blimey, you had a close shave,' explained Jules, crouching down besides him. A 210. Seven dead, and we thought you were done for too . . .'

'What have I bought?'

'At least a month behind the lines!' joked the orderly, sponging away the blood still trickling down.

'Don't muck me about! What happened to me?'

'A fine hole in your head, you can see the bone; another on your forehead, a third on the cheek. It's still pouring blood, but it shouldn't be too serious.'

'And why am I seeing red everywhere?' he asked anxiously.

'It's nothing, blood and mud. We'll clean that up.'

'Hey, if my gob's blown to pieces, I'll frighten off the girls.'

'Don't you believe it! They love that, the girls do. The more bashed up you are, the keener they are. It excites them . . .'

He tried to raise himself, managed to kneel, then darkness swallowed him.

He spent a month in a hospital behind the lines. As soon as he was able, he wrote a long letter to Léon, reproaching him for sending no news since the beginning of the war. Then he wrote a note to his mother, brief as usual; he did not feel there was any point in mentioning his wounds to her.

Having done that he filled his free time with interminable games of cards and tried, like all his companions, to seduce some of the young nurses. But they were much less sociable than front-line gossip maintained, and only one or two allowed liberties without alerting the whole building: out of charity, almost, they allowed a touch on the bodice or a pat on the behind. He was not upset. He tried his luck, not really to gain anything, rather in line with the tradition that all wounded men (as far as they were able) were representatives of the men on the front when it came to girls.

The doctors' fears of a skull fracture proved unfounded. His wounds healed quickly; even the gash across his cheek didn't leave too bad a scar; just a furrow, a ridge, a souvenir.

He went back to the front and found his regiment; the battery was pouring a constant bombardment on the localities of Gussainville, Maizeroy and Les Eparges, twenty kilometres south-east of Verdun.

Three days later, Jules had to be evacuated; he had a fragment of shrapnel in the stomach and another in the chest. If all went well, if no infection set in, he would be back on his feet in a couple of months . . .

Pierre-Edouard accompanied him to the ambulance. 'Jammy devil,' he said, forcing a smile, 'you'll be home for the harvest, what a stroke of luck! Give my regards to your old folks, and the Polack. And tell him to drink a few to our health. We'll be needing it.'

After this war, which was supposed to last a month, had lasted a year, headquarters at last decided to allow home leave. Pierre-Edouard received his in September 1915. Six days, what could you do in six days? He could not decide, and very nearly set out for St Libéral. He'd had no reply from Léon, and was worried about the farm and the livestock. Of course his mother sent him some news, but it was brief, incomplete and vague. The poor woman filled her letters with exhaustive suggestions, advice, and tirades against Berthe and Louise, those runaways; complaints about how busy his father was, getting behind with the work; how expensive everything was; about the cursed war which would not finish.

Afraid to go back to the same sad atmosphere as before – it would probably be worse, since Berthe's departure – he decided to spend his leave in Paris. Then the return would be less painful than if he had to wrench himself away from the land he missed more and more – the Corrèze, the only land which mattered to him.

He arrived in Paris on 3 September, found a room in a hotel close to the Gare de l'Est, immediately ran a bath and washed himself. He scrubbed his skin almost raw, as if to erase the memory of the rats and lice, all the vermin crawling about at the front. When at last he was clean, he lay down and slept for fifteen straight hours.

The next day, rested but confused by the bustle, even gaiety, which animated the capital, he strolled along the boulevards, from café to café, with a dreadful feeling of being out of place in this crowd of thoughtless, happy people, the women sporting blue, white and red ribbons or dressed up as nurses, the plump and shiny young men. You could see straight away that the war, the killing war, did not concern them; they were profiting from the other war, the one that brought in good returns, and they were proud of it.

His amazement, and his bitterness, reached its climax when his gaze fell on the window of a chocolate shop in the Boulevard de la Madeleine, called the 'Marquise de Sévigné'. He thought he was dreaming. There before him, for the delectation of the customers, lay a 75mm shell. In the name of God, a shell, in aluminium foil banded with copper, painted in the colours of France, filled with decorative chocolates. Price: 15 francs for the small one, 20 francs for the large one! And there was more; a little ammunition box made of cardboard, with a gun in relief on it, filled with twenty-four tiny chocolate shells. Price: 8 francs 50 . . .

'Well, that's the limit!' he murmured. He could not come to terms with such insensitivity. Shells stuffed with chocolates! And why not a bottle of perfume in the shape of a grenade or a gas mask?

'Bloody civilians, eh?' spoke out a staff-sergeant from beside him; he too had been drawn by the window display.

'You can say that again! The bastards, they deserve a faceful of real shells!' he exclaimed, in relief at sharing his indignation. 'You're from the 120th line regiment?' he asked, after examining his neighbour's badges.

'Well, yes.'

'Were you at Mesnils, at the beginning of March?'

'Rather!'

'We were too.'

'Oh, you artillerymen,' said the other, 'you're set up behind the lines! Just right for shooting at our backs. Can't even be bothered to adjust your guns, idle sods, just like at headquarters . . . All right, I was only joking,' he apologised as he saw Pierre-Edouard stroking the scar on his cheek. 'All the same, it's true, you know; sometimes, you shoot like shit. You could be more careful, eh?'

'We do our best, but . . . Come on, let's go and drink to the health of the united gunners and infantry!'

'And after that we'll go and look for some women. It would give me very great pleasure to have a go at one of these bloody civilian women!'

They set off for Montmartre chatting like two old friends.

As he walked away from the hospital where he had just closed his son-in-law's eyes after eleven months of suffering, Jean Duroux was struck down by a heart attack.

He fell in rue de Bellechasse, a few metres from his apartment. He was fifty-five. They buried him in the family mausoleum in the cemetery of Montparnasse.

The news of his death reached St Libéral two days later. The whole community was affected by this latest bereavement, which was announced in the village square by the policeman's wife. Jean-Edouard, who was mayor from now on, consulted Doctor Fraysse, his friends and some of the old men before deciding not to organise a funeral service.

The custom had been abandoned since the beginning of the year, and only the first three deaths in the war had earned this honour. How could they continue the tradition, when it had to be repeated every month? It was impossible; it was digging a knife into the wound and accentuating the atmosphere of sadness and suffering which prevailed in the village. In thirteen months of war the community had lost eleven men, killed randomly at the front.

Thus no ceremony marked the death of Jean Duroux; his was just one death among many. Besides, the old curate from Yssandon did not want to be bothered by that sort of service; he was in charge of several parishes and really did not have the time to run from one village to the next every time a man fell at the front. The squire's departure grieved everyone, but there was already so much distress, so many tears, that little was said about it. Each person was enclosed in his private sorrow, his personal worry.

When the first soldiers came home on leave and the wounded were invalided out of the army, the people of Saint-Libéral found out about the real war, the one which the newspapers had been carefully hiding. Though the men from the front talked little; they seemed like strangers to everyone, not quite right in the head, as if drunk. Nevertheless, they said enough to increase the general malaise.

Everything got worse. Prices went mad, and whatever one did money was slow to come in. Everyone did their best, but for lack of manpower some plots had to be left fallow; all those, for example, which had been cultivated without machinery before the war, and there were many of them. They were the fields on steep slopes where the plough could not be used, but which had yielded the best and earliest crops before 1914, the spring vegetables which had brought renown and wealth to the region. And these plots were not the only ones which had to be abandoned; others, although suitable for ploughing, were also covered with weeds. There had been no time to turn the soil just when it needed doing.

Of course the men on leave lent a hand, but what could they do in a few days, poor fellows? And besides, they were already so tired, so worn out, they needed their rest!

Léon came back on 10 September, but was hardly seen by anyone. He slept like a log at first, like the others, and then strode alone across all his land, trailed around the markets at Brive and Tulle, and left again without bothering to set foot in the Mairie. Jean-Edouard did not forgive this slight.

A week after returning from his leave Pierre-Edouard received a long letter from Léon, several pages of neat writing. Thanks to this he got to know the farm again; but he was upset to learn that his father had left the Malides field fallow, and all the market-garden plots, due to lack of manpower and time.

Having said that, the animals were all right, they were in fine form. According to Léon they were fetching incredible prices; he had seen two-year-old heifers, just in calf, sold for 625 francs each at Brive market! A year earlier they had been worth 200 francs less. As for calves, he had seen them starting at 150 francs, even not particularly good ones! That was crazy, but hadn't everything gone crazy since the war started?

In the postscript he learned that his friend had been at the front for more than a year, and could therefore send no further news. If it was important for Pierre-Edouard, he could always write to Léon's sister Mathilde, who would inform him just as well. Perhaps he should know that it was she who had been writing the letters from the very beginning . . .

'What a cheat!' thought Pierre-Edouard, laughing to himself. 'And I'm an ass, thinking that he had learned to write! I was amazed at the beautiful letters, as if written by a professional. What a damned swindler that Léon is!' But he did not hold it against him, and resolved from then on to correspond with little Mathilde, the kid Léon had seen born.

Two days later a brief note from Louise left him speechless, on the verge of tears. Jean, the quiet forester who so loved his trees, was dead, somewhere in a corner of Champagne.

Across the whole front the second winter began, and there was no guarantee that it would be the last.

1916, 1917; terrifying years, months of ceaselessly repeated night-mares, days and nights of horror. Ghastly slaughter from the mustard gas which seeped into their cold guts and froze them rigid in an endless winter, sinister waves of gas sinking down into the stinking, muddy trenches, heralding a spring without hope . Like false storm clouds, it spread a greenish layer over the heavy dusting of flies on the battlefield as it sweltered in a heatwave which ripened no harvest; a stealthy mist which merged almost invisibly with the drizzle of autumn and the fog of November. Vile gas, corroding everything, spreading its deadly putrefaction everywhere.

Pierre-Edouard suffered it all; knew despair, exhaustion and that overwhelming depression which paralyses the spirit, binding him in a strait-jacket of numbed fatalism, leaving only the most basic urges alive: to eat, sleep, survive; forget the past and obliterate the idea of any future, existing only in the present.

He even forsook the memories and ideas which he had once liked to evoke: his fields, his land, Saint-Libéral. All that was too far away, too emotional, untouchable; in another world, an inaccessible universe. If he continued to send news occasionally to his mother, he never wrote to Léon's sister, for the idea of worrying about his land, his animals or his crops seemed ridiculous, childish. Such things had no significance in the face of death; death which had made Louise a widow for the second time and continued, all around him, to cut down his comrades.

The months rolled by, punctuated by the lunatic battles. Eix and Douaumont in February; the forest of Caillette and Thiaumond in April. Then the Somme, in June, with engagements at Monacu farm and at Cléry; finally, at the end of the month the biggest, the longest, artillery bombardment ever undertaken by the French, lasting six days without a break. There was shelling on an unprecedented scale to prepare for a formidable charge on 1 July. At 7.30 a.m. assault troops were thrown forward on a forty-five kilometre front towards Bapaume and Péronne.

And then nothing; they were bogged down in another winter, long months when the unusually cold weather froze the two armies into the hardened mud of their trenches. In February 1917 the temperature fell to minus 20°, paralysing the men, the horses, the whole war.

It was a short respite, broken by the squalid butchery of the Chemin des Dames and on the Craonne plateau. After that, neither Pierre-Edouard nor his colleagues were proud to have had a colonel called Nivelle at the beginning of the war.

In October, while the rumours of mutinies and executions drifted to and fro, Pierre-Edouard was granted leave again. He was so in need of rest, of silence, of peace, that he set off for Saint-Libéral without a second thought.

# 22

FEW people recognised him. There was no trace left of the young man who had taken to the road one morning in January 1911. Then they had thought that he would soon return, quiet and repentant. He had not reappeared until today, almost seven years later, formed, sculpted and hardened; a mature man with none of the youthful traits they remembered.

He arrived on the morning train and was immediately struck by the silence in the village; by the emptiness of the main square, the lack of movement, the absence of men. He passed several women, some in mourning, who returned his greeting shyly, self-consciously, as you respond to a stranger who is friendly for some unknown reason.

Coming to his own home, he was surprised by the state of the yard; its untidiness, the dirt in little piles everywhere, the tools left scattered about. Before, everything had always been put away, the yard clean, swept by his grandfather and grandmother, who made a point of showing passers-by and neighbours a well-kept farm. Now it was obvious that nobody had time to rake up the cow-pats, to lift the dung-pile onto a cart, to put each implement in its place.

The house was empty. There nothing had changed; he put down his bag and went back out, to the stables, where he found a wizened old man, with the thick lips of a simpleton, who would not look him in the eye. He recognised the labourer Léon had mentioned.

'Are you Abel?'

The man stepped back, sheltering behind his pitchfork, and only just managed to swallow his saliva.

'Answer me, then! I'm not going to hit you, you're too thin. Well, where are my parents?'

'You're not the Vialhes' boy, from back then?' stammered the old man.

'Of course. Where are my parents?'

'You're older than I'd have expected. Hey, if you come back, I'm going to lose my job, aren't I?'

'You're even stupider than I was told! Where are my parents?'

'On the plateau, the Peuch field; they're ploughing. Say, is

254

it true you were at the war? Is it finished then, since you've come back?'

Pierre-Edouard muttered something rude and went out. Soon afterwards he strode up the track which climbed to the high fields, and felt himself reborn.

A curious relationship was established between himself and his father. It wasn't good, it wasn't bad – it was neutral.

Jean-Edouard still considered his son a rebel and had not forgiven him for leaving, but he could not keep his vow to take him in hand again; too many years had passed, too many things had happened. But since he was also secretly delighted that Pierre had returned safe and sound – and, though he'd never admit it, very proud of the warrant officer's stripes, the chevrons for war service, the Croix de Guerre with two stars shining on it – he considered it prudent to confine himself to gruff enquiries, to avoid any outburst, of either bitterness or pleasure.

In fact, although he did not want to accept it, his son disconcerted him, even amazed him, as a man can astonish and surprise you, when you think you know him well and he suddenly reveals a totally unknown side to his character and takes your breath away.

For his part Pierre-Edouard was far too weary, too tired to want to start any discussion at all, let alone the slightest argument. It seemed childish to cross swords with his father. So he too adopted a manner bordering on indifference.

Although he was prepared for it, the death of several of his friends in the village affected him deeply. Jacques Bessat and Edmond Vergne, dead; dead also André Duplat, the Delpy brothers, Edouard and Jacques, Serge Traversat, François Laval, and many more; it was enough to make you cry.

He was not feeling affectionate towards his mother, either. He found her just as whining and tearful as in her letters, complaining all the time that Berthe had gone and she had no news of her, that Louise never wrote; moaning about the mountains of work, the rise in the cost of living and all those lovely gold coins which his father had been forced to exchange for paper money.

'What are you moaning about?' he cried on the first evening, during supper. 'Berthe's not at the front, so she's not in any danger, is she? You've lost your gold? That's just too bad – better than losing your arms, or your legs, or anything else! As for Louise, let's talk about that! There you are crying into your soup about silly things, and what about her! She's been widowed for the second time! Yes, she remarried, she was perfectly entitled to. Her husband died two years ago in Champagne. And now she's alone! And there you are, happy as a draft-dodger, and *you're* complaining? My God!'

Jean-Edouard was present at this little scene, but he did not open his mouth to silence his son; instead his anger was turned viciously on Abel, that malign idiot, who had the cheek to snigger and dribble into the soup he was slurping at the end of the table.

Pierre-Edouard carefully avoided showing himself around the village. There were too many women in mourning whom he might offend, too many worried wives and mothers who would want reassurance and information; he did not have the courage to talk to them.

So he turned his steps towards the woods, the peaks and the plateau. There, in the silence and sweetness of autumn, he forgot the hails of bullets; he regained his strength, recovered his soul, learned to enjoy days without alarms, gun barrages and disembowelled comrades.

On the third day of his leave, his wanderings took him as far as the White Peak, where Léon had dragged him with Louise seventeen years earlier, to check the snares for thrushes – the thrushes which they'd had to throw to the wolves! He smiled and gazed down on the plateau where, far away, his father and mother were ploughing the Peuch field. Neither of them had wanted to accept his offer of help.

'We'll manage by ourselves, we're used to it. Have a rest, go on,' his father had said.

He hadn't pressed it. Besides he did not feel that basic urge to work, that keenness which had propelled him to labour happily behind the plough before the war . . .

Fifty metres below him, at the base of the peak, he noticed seven or eight cows clambering among the remains of broken-down blackberry bushes, amid the scrub and broom where the blackbirds were singing. They were beautiful Limousins, whose rounded shapes owed nothing to the poor pasture over which they ranged so erratically. A dog jumped around, brought them together, tried to herd them towards a meadow still covered in clover. But the cows were skittish, and galloped into the bushes, where they delighted in scratching themselves to get rid of the flies.

'That piece of clover used to belong to the squire,' thought Pierre-Edouard. Then he was entertained by the appearance of a small figure, which ran through the broom bushes hurling insults at the cows. He got up, tumbled down the slope, cut off the animals and turned them towards the meadow.

'Thank you, Pierre!'

The voice was breathless but light; he turned. For a moment he stood stock still, astonished, in front of the girl who was smiling at him. From up there, he had taken her for a boy.

She looked good enough to eat; a brunette, rather small but well formed, with bright deep brown eyes, a little nose, slightly tilted, cheeks rosy from the fresh air and a very sweet smile framed by vivid red lips. He noticed her breasts, modest, but filling her bodice nicely, admired the slim waist, liked the soft curve of her hips beneath the heavy skirt and blue apron.

'You know me?' he asked eventually.

'Oh, yes!'

'Well, I don't know you. Are you from the village?'

'Of course.'

'That's it,' he said, after staring hard at her, 'I know! You're Gaston's youngest daughter, little Françoise.'

She gave a clear little laugh which made her eyes sparkle with a mischievous gleam. 'Françoise is twenty-five! Do you think I'm that old?'

'So whose daughter are you?' he asked, using the formal 'vous' as she had done, without realising that he was now addressing her as an adult.

'I am Léon's sister.'

'My goodness! Is it really you, Mathilde?'

He looked her over anew and nodded his head. Mathilde! He had not seen her since he had left to do his army service, and remembered her as a chubby-faced urchin, almost a baby.

'You really didn't recognise me?' she wanted to know.

'Good heavens, no! How could I? So it was you who wrote the letters! But where were you seven years ago, when I came back from conscription?'

'With the nuns, at Allassac. Léon wanted me to be educated,' she said with a smile.

'And with good reason! Tell me, you used to say "tu" to me, have you forgotten?' He used 'tu' again himself.

She blushed a little. 'No, I haven't forgotten, but then I didn't know . . .'

He drew nearer and put his hand on her shoulder. 'So it's you, Mathilde,' he repeated. 'So . . . You know, you're really very pretty now,' he added earnestly, 'yes, very pretty. And I'm very glad to get to know the person who has been writing me such beautiful letters at last. Talking of which, where's Léon? How is he?'

'Fine. He was home on leave in August. He's a corporal,' she added proudly, 'and he's got a medal, too!'

'That doesn't surprise me. And where is he?'

'When he was here he told me that he was close to Rheims. It's very dangerous up there, isn't it?' she asked with sudden anguish.

He recalled that Léon had been like a father to her; the head of the family, a sort of god who had brought her up, returned from each market with a trinket for her, who adored her. He pulled her gently towards him and stroked her hair.

'Dangerous, up there? Don't you believe it! It's one of the least exposed sectors, almost the quietest on the front.' Neither voice nor eyes betrayed his lie. 'Up there, they have champagne instead of plonk! You don't realise how lucky Léon is!'

'But the newspapers say . . .'

'The papers say all sorts of things, as usual. Go on, don't you worry about him. He's got his wits about him, he'll have found a good corner!'

'He's not a shirker!' she protested, with an offended look.

'Not at all! The proof is, he's got a medal.'

'That's true.' She was suddenly calmer, and examined his face intently. 'And you, where you are, is it very dangerous?' she asked, placing her hands on his shoulders.

'No, it's quiet there too . . .' he murmured, moved by her closeness.

His eyes darted towards her bodice and he became obsessed with a thought which seared through him, quickening his breath and heartbeat. He tried to chase away the seventeen-year-old memory, of that evening when his mother and grandmother had talked of Mathilde and of the birthmark she bore on her breast – but which one? the left of the right? – a mark like a little crescent moon. He forced himself to blot out the disturbing picture.

As a child he had imagined that sign, a little brown sickle on the smooth body of a baby, but today . . . Today it was right before his eyes, there, a few centimetres away, the sweet furrow which separated the tiny round breasts, one of which – but *which* one, for God's sake! – was decorated with a beauty spot . . .

She increased his agitation without even realising it.

'All the same' – she gently stroked her finger across his cheek – 'you've been wounded. Forgive me, you didn't have that mark before. You can tell it's recent.'

He turned his head a little and grazed the back of her hand with his lips. Her skin was sweet, fresh as spring water. He pulled himself together and moved away a little.

'You know, you're more dangerous than a battery of four-twenties!' he joked, in a tone which he hoped sounded relaxed. 'It's lucky that you're Léon's sister! Hey, look at your cows, they've run away!'

'Huh, they won't go far. Besides, they never leave our land.'

'How do you mean, your land? These fields belong to the château!'

She shook her head. 'No, since she was widowed the squire's daughter has let them to us.'

'Well, I *am* surprised. But now I think about it, where's the rest of Léon's herd? He's got more than seven cows, hasn't he?'

'Yes, and he's got two farmhands, old fellows, and then there's my mother and me; we manage. Tell me, you're not going back straight away?'

'You mean this morning? Oh, I can help you look after the animals if you like,' he assured her with a smile, 'but what will people say if they see us together?'

'There's nobody about, and besides, everyone knows I'm sensible!'

'Sensible?' he asked, with mock solemnity. 'Well what are you doing here then, right next to me?'

'I'm not in any danger with you. I know you, you see . . . I wrote the letters, but I read yours as well. Because Léon doesn't read very well, either . . .'

'Oh, I understand! Just wait till I see him again, your lout of a brother, I'll give him what for!' he grumbled in embarrassment, remembering that he had shared news of some of his conquests with her brother. He was sure he had even named names, and described some of their attributes.

She saw that he was upset, and guessed why intuitively. 'Oh, I bet you're thinking of all those girls!' she cried gaily, 'but that's all old stuff. And at that time I was so young! Besides, you know, that doesn't worry me, I still trust you. I'm not a silly little girl, so there's no danger!'

He felt a fool, awkward and clumsy. He was much more upset than he liked to admit, disturbed by this little slip of a woman with dark eyes who in a few minutes, with a few words, had aroused feelings he'd never experienced before, of unexpected sweetness. It bore no relationship to what had pushed him into the arms of Justine, the petite Parisienne he had bedded during his last leave, or that hot little number, Françoise.

'That's right,' he murmured at last, as he stroked her eyelids gently with the tip of his finger, 'you're right, there's no danger.'

Then he kissed her lightly on the cheek, and took her hand. 'Come on, let's go and look after your cows, that'll do me good.'

Going back was terrible, worse than anything he had feared. He knew full well that each end of leave was torture to the spirit, a terrible tearing apart which some did not survive. Those were the unhappy ones who sprang forward like madmen at the height of a bombardment, to meet the burning blow which would release them from this uncontrollable nightmare, this cancer which undermined them from within.

The train was barely a hundred metres out of St Libéral before Pierre-Edouard succumbed to the deepest despair. The evening before, when he had realised that Mathilde was even more upset than he was at saying goodbye, only her vulnerability had strengthened him, forced him to pretend to be unconcerned and cheerful although he was a million miles from such feelings.

He had almost succeeded in making a joke, had been rolling his eyes at her, when she had lain down, warm and tender, under the trees on the White Peak and pulled him to her, against her, on to her, in an embrace full of ardour, a total surrender. At that moment he could have done anything, got everything – and spoiled everything, easily, which would have made his self-reproach even more violent.

For although Mathilde was still the virginal girl whom he had loved at first sight a few days earlier, yet he knew that now, for her as well as for him, the waiting would be longer and more terrible. Wasn't life hard enough without adding the pangs of separation, just for the fun of it?

At the front, he had noticed how vulnerable those married and engaged comrades were to the absence of the wife, the fiancée, the children, the girl-friend, to that emptiness. It was they who frantically awaited the arrival of the post orderly, who read and re-read the letters from which flower-petals, curls of hair, ribbons or photos sometimes slipped; they who were gnawed by anxiety and pain when deprived of news, sometimes to the point of despair.

Until today he had not known this form of torment, and neither had Mathilde – for although she worried about her brother, she did not await Léon's return in the same way as she awaited his own.

And it was for that he blamed himself; for dragging her into this madness. With her he had forgotten about the war, had pretended to believe that the future belonged to them. Instead, he should have done his best to prevent the kindling of that flame in her, the passion which from the first moment had impelled them irresistibly towards each other.

But it was too late to step back, to erase from his mind the memories which revolved round her, the centre of his universe. He did not even want to; all his being strove wildly to remember. And already, there floated before his eyes the slight silhouette of a girl, her face, her hands. And her laugh rang out.

When the school-leavers of 1918 were called up it was a fresh blow to Saint Libéral, and the crop planting was further restricted.

Gradually the fields which had been abandoned for several years returned to the wild; grew shrubs, ash, oak and hornbeam. Elsewhere bracken, broom and ferns took over the places once cleared by men, encroached on the fallow plots, and invaded the meadows no longer trimmed by scythes.

Production fell appreciably in the community, as it did in the country as a whole. Paradoxically, money flowed as never before, because of galloping inflation fuelled by shortages. The beginning of the war had harmed the economy, but its continuation inspired a new dynamism. Everything was saleable, because everything was in short supply.

From 1916 onwards, this situation had encouraged Jean-Edouard to sow wheat on every available field – at least, on those he had time to cultivate. Like everything else, the price of wheat had reached giddy heights, despite being taxed (in theory anyway) at 33 francs on every 100 kilos. From 25 francs for 100 kilos in 1914, it climbed to the fabulous sum of 50 francs after the 1917 harvest, and they said it would reach 75 francs before the end of 1918.

For men of Jean-Edouard's generation, accustomed to counting in sous and centimes rather than in millions of francs, this flood of money felt like a crisis. Besides, however large the sums written on them, these new banknotes were not, in their eyes, worth anything like the gold coins of which successive subscriptions to the war effort had relieved them.

Of course Jean-Edouard had not donated all his gold; he had preserved a precious store of twenty-franc gold napoléons. Nevertheless, his conviction that paper money was worthless inspired him to search for more land. But who would sell land in the middle of a war! He alerted the solicitor as to his needs, and waited.

He had to be patient until May 1918. About the 15th of the month, the elder daughter of the late lamented Jean Duroux informed Monsieur Lardy that she wished to sell the two small-holdings which formed her dowry, as quickly as possible; there were fourteen hectares, of which four and a half were good land situated on the plateau. Many years later, they learned that the unhappy widow had sold all her assets before marrying an American officer and following him to his country.

As soon as he received the letter, Monsieur Lardy went to tell Jean-Edouard.

'You say she's selling her two smallholdings?' asked Jean-Edouard, as he distractedly rearranged the papers and circulars piled on his desk.

'Both of them, yes. So, as you told me you were looking for land . . .'

'Yes, but not fourteen hectares! What would I do with it? I haven't time to plant the land I've got already!'

'Pierre-Edouard will come back soon. This war can't last much longer.'

'Oh, Pierre-Edouard, if I have to depend on him! And anyway, I haven't enough cash to buy fourteen hectares.'

'Well, it's a bargain. I don't understand why she's selling. It's really bad timing, if she'd come to me I would have told her so. But she wants it done quickly, so . . .'

'How much?'

'Roughly 1,900 francs a hectare. A gift, isn't it?'

Jean-Edouard fiddled with his pen-holder and made a face. 'It's enough, I tell you. When I think I paid 1,250 francs for the lot you sold me before the war!'

'No jokes, please; you know very well that everything has doubled or tripled in price since then, except land. That's how it is: who wants to buy in times like these!'

Jean made a quick decision. 'Fine, I'll take the fields on the plateau. You say there are forty-five chains? That'll do. But I can't manage the rest.'

'You're making a mistake. It's a bargain, I assure you.'

'Maybe, but I haven't enough money.'

'Go on . . . I understand that you don't want to break into your reserves, but in that case, why not borrow? You couldn't make a better investment.'

'No,' Jean-Edouard interrupted him drily, 'the Vialhes don't eat borrowed bread. When we buy, it's with our own money. I'm not about to get involved in borrowing, that's the way to ruin a family. I prefer to have less, but use my own money. I don't want to owe anything to anyone.'

'Pity, I think it's silly not to take it. Well, that's your business. Good, I'll make note of your offer and see who might be interested in the remainder. In any case, I have to warn you in all honesty that the land you're interested in will go to the highest bidder.'

'Of course,' agreed Jean-Edouard with a smile. 'If you can find anyone else who wants it.'


The 150mm shell fell less than fifty metres from the battery; a second missile came within twenty metres. 'They've picked us out, the next ones will be for us and we'll get it in the neck . . .' mused Pierre-Edouard as he crouched behind a rough shelter.

It was always the same: all went reasonably well whilst they could fire from concealed positions, but if by any chance an aeroplane or observer on the ground picked out the source of the shots from the smoke, then all hell was let loose. Then the enemy held the trumps. In the push towards Compiègne they had infiltrated the Matz valley and were now encamped on the Lataule plateau. From up there, they could see everything . . .

'Now they've had time to adjust their range,' thought Pierre-Edouard, 'it won't be long before it's raining down thick and fast.'

He touched the little photo Mathilde had sent him, which lay in the pocket next to his heart. That was his last movement, his last thought, before an enormous sun exploded in front of him. It was 2.30 p.m.


That same day, 9 June, and at the same hour, Monsieur Lardy arrived at the Mairie to inform Jean-Edouard of the results of his negotiations. Since his first visit three weeks earlier everything had changed, and in a way that he could not have foreseen; the situation had taken an incredible turn. In thirty-five years at his job the solicitor had never experienced such a change of direction. Nor had he ever discussed matters with such a young negotiator. He was still amazed – and admiring – at the way little Mathilde had managed the business! He reflected yet again how much the war had changed things by giving women the opportunity to take responsibilities.

'Well?' asked Jean-Edouard.

'She's not giving in, and as far as I can tell she's prepared to raise her bid as well . . .'

'Hell and damnation, the little worm! That little slut! She's worse than her brother! You told her that I would go to 2,150 francs a hectare?'

'Naturally, but she immediately announced that she would offer 2,200.'

'But she's mad! And where's she getting her money from, for goodness sake?'

'It's not hers, you know that, it's her brother's. And he's got plenty; the war hasn't stopped his herds from growing . . .'

'What a swine! My God, that thief!'

Jean-Edouard had been in a temper for a whole week. At first, when the solicitor told him that Mathilde had announced her intention to buy, he had thought it was a hoax.

'You're joking? Anyway, she can't do anything, she's under twenty-one.'

'Indeed, but she's become emancipated since Léon left.'

'So what?'

'So she has a perfect right to act in her brother's name, and that's what she's doing.'

He was struck dumb, amazed that a girl no taller than three goats' tails had the audacity to carry through such an operation, alone.

'Bloody hell!' he argued obstinately, 'I don't know much about the law, but surely she can't sign anything! It would have to be Léon who did that! Since he isn't here, and the sale is urgent, well . . . Look, if you want, I'll sign right away, and pay!'

'It's not as simple as that. Besides, the signature is not a problem. When he left, Léon gave power of attorney to his mother . . .'

'Dammit! He thought of everything, that dungheap!' And that made him furious as well. Léon really had planned everything. And now the solicitor was proving just how he had underestimated his adversary, and just how formidable this little scrap of a woman Mathilde was – perhaps even more dangerous than her brother, because she was better educated.

'You see,' explained the lawyer, 'Mathilde explained it all to me. When he left, Léon gave her the task of surveying everything being sold in the neighbourhood and buying the best. So, you can imagine that she's keen to do business, and she's persistent.'

'A girl doing a man's business! It's scandalous,' grumbled Jean-Edouard. 'All right,' he made a sudden decision, 'go and tell that little worm that I'll go to 2,250. I don't want to go and see her myself or argue with her; I'd box her ears, just to teach her about life! Who does the little pisser think she is? A man? Tell her 2,250, we'll see who wins in the end! I'll see them back in the hovel they should never have left!'

'Listen, I'll give you some advice; let her have the land. Don't get worked up, let me speak. I'm telling you how it is, I've just come from her place. Believe me, that little Mathilde will go to 2,500 if need be, further even, but she'll get the land.'

'Then I'll go higher!'

'She'll match it at the last moment, and that poor Duroux woman will choose her rather than you.'

'What do you know about it? My money is as good as hers, isn't it?'

'Yes, only I have to admit to you . . . Mathilde has written to her, to the widow; she told me so. And she told me that the Duroux girl would prefer to sell to her, she has a right to choose . . .'

'She dared do that! She dared to write! Oh my God!' Jean-Edouard exploded; he was beside himself.

'Yes, she did. My poor fellow, these women are astonishing, and when it comes to agreeing things behind our backs . . . Well, there it is. You're free to continue, but you won't win. Oh, but she agrees to let you have the three acres which lie between your fields.'

'Oh, good!' said Jean-Edouard sarcastically, 'now she's dividing it up! In God's name, what does she take me for? Just a minute, I'm beginning to think that you're advising her!' he shouted suddenly. 'That's it! Did you think we had forgotten your wife is her godmother? It's true, isn't it? She *is* the godmother of that suicide's daughter?'

'My dear friend, you're talking absolute rubbish,' the solicitor interrupted him drily. 'So, will you buy that field?'

'No; I don't want any favours from that slut!'

'You're wrong, it's not a favour. You see, she knows how to read a land register, that little one does. That land is enclosed by yours, so it's of little interest to her, as she'd have to cross yours to get to it . . . But it's up to you if you want to let Léon settle down in the middle of your property!'

'All right, all right.' Jean-Edouard was beaten, and white with anger. 'I'll buy that patch, since they're so keen to let me have it. But I'm buying it right away. And you can tell that little bitch and her dungheap of a brother that I won't forget them. One day I'll make them regret all their double-dealing . . .'

The deeds were signed next day. Mathilde immediately wrote to Pierre-Edouard to announce that Léon had just bought three hectares of land for her dowry, those fine fields on the plateau, stretching up to White Peak, where they had met during his leave, their own land . . . Then she wrote to her brother to inform him, and to thank him for his generosity.

Neither of them received this news. On 11 June 1918, Léon was mown down by a volley from a Maxim gun, during the battle for Piave on the Italian front. The first shot broke his right fibula, the second his left tibia, just below the knee, and the third tore off his left hand.

# 23

MATHILDE was terribly shocked when she learned that her brother had fallen on the Italian front. However, the fact that she knew he was alive was a comfort to her, however badly he might be injured. Yes, he was wounded, but from now on he would be protected; the war could no longer kill him.

The next day she received another dreadful blow, delivered by the postman in conversation with her mother:

'What a massacre!' he said as he put down the newspaper. 'Yesterday your poor Léon, today the Vialhes' boy . . .'

'What about him?' asked her mother.

'I'm not sure; you know old Vialhe, he's not very forthcoming. It was poor Marguerite who told me, seems he's almost done for. At least according to what she was saying . . .'

Mathilde almost ran to the Vialhes' house to find out, to relieve the weight of anxiety which was crushing her. But she was sure that they would throw her out; they would be rude to her and would not tell her anything.

So her long wait began, every minute a torture, made more painful by her mother's remarks. The poor woman had known right from the beginning that her daughter was seeing Pierre-Edouard. When the letters appeared, sometimes as many as four a week, she understood that this was a serious, lasting attachment and she was worried, nervous at the thought of how his parents would react.

'I told you that he wasn't for you,' she bleated as soon as the postman had gone. 'People like the Vialhes don't marry the daughters of smallholders! You see, even God doesn't wish it . . . If you knew how we lived before . . . before Léon started earning some money! And to them, we'll always be poor. You'll see, they'll start talking about your poor father . . .'

'I don't care! Pierre-Edouard doesn't need them!'

'That's what he says . . . Suppose his father were to disinherit him! Look what he did to his daughters!'

'Too bad! Léon will help us, I know he will. But as long as . . . How do we know . . .'

She had to be patient for five more days and nights of fear and despair. She watched for the postman every morning, ran to him as he took out the letters, and then returned like a sleepwalker to endure the endless wait while in her mind she became convinced that her fiancé had died. But, she told herself, she would have heard that. The Vialhes would talk about it! Unless they were so madly proud that they kept their grief to themselves . . .

At last, on the sixth morning, the letter arrived. A few words, practically nothing, just what had to be said.

She ran to the church and lit ten fat candles in front of the statue of the Virgin Mary, ten in front of Joseph, and ten more for Saint Eutrope. And there, seated amidst all those flames, she let herself go and cried for the first time in six days, half crazy with happiness in the warm flickering light of the candles.

Pierre-Edouard had only vague memories of his first days in hospital; he remembered distant conversations without knowing who was speaking, nor where they were. Who was the seriously injured person they were discussing at his bedside? Only later did he realise that the first conversation had taken place on the day he arrived. A strange argument . . .

'I tell you we must amputate . . . look at this mess.'

'Cut, cut, that's all you know about! There's no question of amputating!'

'But look, my dear fellow . . .'

'Fellow? You must be joking! I'm not your fellow-butcher!'

'I order it! I shall refer the matter to the authorities!'

'Get out, or I'll write to Clemenceau!'

'Do you know him?'

'Of course! He was talking to me only this morning, he said: "Fernand, I am relying on you not to turn all our wounded men into legless, armless cripples! Don't listen to the army doctors, they round up their pay with commissions from all the artificial limb makers in France . . ." '

'You and your stupid jokes! Do you think this is the time for a laugh? This lad will get gangrene; we must amputate, and quickly . . .'

'Out of the question. I'll take full responsibility.'

'Sister, you are witness to this. And you too, my dear?'

'But of course they're witnesses, and if you want a signed bit of paper, tell them I'll put it into verse for them. Go on, sister, prepare this chap for theatre; I'm in charge here.'

'Fine, I wash my hands of it.'

'What an excellent decision, I've been waiting two months for this hygienic result! . . . Now, just between us two, my boy . . .'

And later a strange awakening, a sort of rebirth, to the sound of a warm voice.

'Right, to sum up. We'll say: simple fracture of the right tibia, no problem. Simple double fracture of the left femur with tearing of the right anterior quadriceps and the vastus externus, and perforation of the vastus internus. Small tear in the large sartorial muscle. That's all. You know, my boy, you've been very lucky! Just a fraction higher and you'd be a capon singing soprano!'

Pierre-Edouard opened his eyes and looked at the man seated beside him, gently stroking his forehead. He was immediately reassured by the grey-blue eyes smiling at him through pince-nez, by the curved mouth beneath the little moustache, and by the sound of the voice continuing its monologue.

'Just imagine, they wanted to cut off your leg! Can you credit it! What idiocy, a lovely leg like that, with such strong bones! No, no, don't worry, it's still there, really well mended, a miracle! And in a few months you'll be able to gallop about – and without limping, I've laid a bet on it with my eminent colleague, the local butcher . . . So tell me, is the Diamond still full of crayfish and trout?'

'At home? You know it?' gasped Pierre-Edouard in one breath.

'Of course I know it. And good Doctor Fraysse too. It was he who showed me the Diamond, what a fine stream! And I know his colleague very well too, my friend Doctor Delpy. He used to send me patients a long time ago, to be x-rayed. No, don't talk. Later on you must tell me where you lost your l. No, not your elbow.' Pierre-Edouard was looking anxiously at his arms, so the doctor repeated it: 'The l in your name. You see, I'm called Vialle as well, but with two 'ls; Fernand Vialle, of Brive, currently on holiday in the Amiens area on account of a war . . .'

A wave of warmth and happiness flooded through Pierre-Edouard and overwhelmed him, his eyes filled with tears of gratitude. He knew, for certain, that the doctor was not making it up; one day soon he would be running up the mountains, just as the man had said.

Who in Limousin hadn't heard of Doctor Vialle! A man not yet fifty whose reputation had spread throughout the département; a man who put his inspired talents as a bone-setter at the service of medicine, for whom no fracture held any mysteries or was too complicated to deal with!

'Now don't get excited, I'll come and see you tomorrow. And then we'll talk patois, I'd like that. *Ora, chaut durmir.*'

Pierre-Edouard nodded agreement, smiled and shut his eyes. Twenty-five years earlier, his mother had told him nearly every night: '*Ora, chaut durmir.*'

St Libéral, bled white by four years of massacre, was subjected from July onwards to a vicious attack of the illness which had already hit the whole of Europe. Old Antoine Gigoux was the first victim. He was carried off within three days; he was just beginning his eighty-first year.

His death was swift, but it did not alarm Doctor Fraysse; he was very upset to lose his old friend, but consoled by the thought that now Antoine Gigoux could at last rejoin his son. The doctor had witnessed just how much the loss had affected the old mayor, when his only son had been killed on the Eastern Front in 1917. He was consumed by a grief which no one and nothing could relieve, and as the months passed he had slipped deeper into lassitude and depression. So the doctor did not pay too much heed to the cause of death.

But the death of the miller did alarm him; made it clear to him that this was a real epidemic. This man was sixty-three years old, still in his prime, healthy and strong as an ox, yet he was laid out in less than a week by this illness they called the Spanish 'flu, but which was really a sort of plague.

'That's all we needed!' exclaimed Jean-Edouard when the doctor informed him. 'What should we do?'

'Who knows? Plague, you see . . .' muttered the doctor, shaking his head. He was tired and discouraged, as he felt each time after closing the eyes of one of his patients. Besides, although he was in excellent health the years weighed heavily now; he was already eighty-three.

'What do you want me to tell you?' he murmured at last. 'Epidemics, believe me, I've seen some! But to know how to stop them . . .'

'Well, we can't leave it like that! We must warn people, there must be precautions that can be taken!'

'You're a real fighter, aren't you?' said the doctor with genuine admiration, 'and you're right. And how's Pierre-Edouard?'

'All right, coming on better than we could have hoped.'

'What good luck that he landed with my friend Doctor Vialle, eh?'

'Yes, indeed. But what do we do about this plague, then?'

'All right,' the doctor decided, 'you must publish a warning. Everyone must read or hear it. Go on, get writing . . . Start how you like, but don't put them in a panic. I'll give you the treatment, if you can call it that . . . Avoid getting chilled or overheated, especially after heavy work. Drink only water which contains a weak solution of permanganate to disinfect it, or brandy – that's right, use what you've got! Every morning on waking, after each meal, and at night on going to bed, rinse the mouth with half a glass of lukewarm water containing five or six drops of Thymol, I'll send for several bottles of it. In the morning on rising, put a little dab of Goménol vaseline in each nostril, I'll get some of that too. Finally take a gentle purgative every two weeks. That's it. Strictly between you and me, I don't really believe in it, but as you say, we have to do something . . .'

By evening the proclamation was made public, and many women came to the Mairie to read the order, then went to the doctor to obtain the drugs prescribed. But in the following months the Spanish 'flu claimed four new victims, among them a child of six.

Caught between the plague and the never-ending war, the community of St Libéral slipped into apathy and despair. The weeds and bushes gained ground on all sides.

Just as the end of peace had seen a mass departure of all the young people of the village, the end of the war was greeted by the return of the wounded to the fold – at least, of those who were in a condition to come home.

From mid-October onwards they began to reappear one by one from the various hospitals; those whom death had disdained to take and the army no longer wanted either, now they were so badly injured, crushed, gassed, useless . . .

Léon arrived at St Libéral station one evening at the end of October. He had not informed anyone of his return and, limping a little, turned to walk home alone. He stopped several times on the way to catch his breath and to relieve his right arm of the weight of his suitcase. He could not change hands; he had only one.

Peace had finally arrived, but it had been so long in coming, and had cost so dear, that it did not inspire the excitement in the village that it did in the towns. In St Libéral, a community where everyone knew everyone else, where everyone was a neighbour, there were too many missing, too many losses, too many families in mourning – those who had been spared could not decently express their pleasure.

Of course there was happiness; some songs, some hugs and kisses, and the wine flowed freely; but joy, pure joy with warmth and peals of laughter, no. That was masked by the shadow of the forty-three men the war had cut down, stifled by the black skirts and shawls of the twenty-seven widows, proscribed by the grave faces of the forty-nine orphans.

Pierre-Edouard had to wait until 22 November 1918 before he was finally discharged. He had been convalescing for two months at a hospital in Treignac, slowly learning to walk again. But if he still had a slight limp, he knew that although the broad, deep scars on his legs would not disappear, this uneven gait would; Dr Vialle had assured him of it, and he believed him.

At Treignac he had received a visit from his parents. It was a strange interlude: a father who did not know what to say and a mother full of lamentations. His father had hardly dared to speak of the future except in vague conditionals: 'If you come home, there's plenty of work . . . If you were there, we could clear the land; it's dreadful how the brambles have taken over . . .'

As for his mother, she spent her time listing all the dead in the village, telling him about the widows and orphans, the sadness of the times.

He had said nothing. What was the use . . . He had not spoken of any of his plans, nor had he tried to get them to understand that if he returned to the farm it would be organised according to his ideas; everything led him to believe that this would lead to immediate and serious conflict with his father.

Neither had he spoken of Mathilde; she was his secret. Besides, he could guess what his parents' reaction would be, how they would oppose the addition to the Vialhe family of the daughter of a good-for-nothing, the sister of a lout. He had no desire to start an argument which he knew he could not win. He had a plan with regard to Mathilde, and he would keep to it.

His parents only came to see him that once, and he had to admit that it was better so; they had become strangers to him.

He got out at Brive station towards three o'clock in the afternoon; as he was still in uniform, with all his fine medals, the other passengers kindly helped him down from the compartment. He thanked them, and limped towards the connecting train for St Libéral.

Then, suddenly, he saw her – Mathilde. She was there, ten paces away, so small, so beautiful, a miracle. Mathilde, running towards him and throwing herself into his arms. And he, overcome by happiness, stupidly repeating: 'You came, you came . . .'

And her replies merged, got muddled up and overtaken by the questions, for there was so much to say, to explain, to listen to!

'You came . . .'

'I wanted to be the first to welcome you.'

'But how did you get here, there's no train at this time!'

'By cart, Léon let me . . .'

At last they came out of the station and climbed into the trap, all the while talking, touching, holding on to each other.

'Give me the reins.'

She smiled, snuggled up against him and let herself be driven.

It was dark by the time they at last reached St Libéral.

'If your parents are expecting you on the train they'll be worried; it came in an hour ago!' said Mathilde.

'It doesn't matter, I didn't tell them I'd be back today.'

'But you told me.'

'Of course. If you hadn't come to Brive, I wanted to visit you first. That's why I didn't say anything to my parents.' He directed the cart down the main street and set the horse into a trot.

'Where are you going?' she asked, suddenly anxious.

'To my house.'

'But . . . what about me?'

'You're coming with me.'

'But your parents, they'll . . .'

'No, they won't,' he reassured her. 'I'll bring home whoever I like.'

He guided the horse right up to the front steps and got down, pulling a face at the stabbing pain from his scars.

'Give me your hand,' he said.

He felt her trembling, so he put his arm around her shoulders, pushed open the door and went in. As he had expected, his mother and father were seated at the table.

'Here I am again,' he said. 'There's no need for me to introduce Mathilde to you, you know her, but I brought her this evening to tell you that we'll be getting married before Christmas.'

Nothing which followed surprised him – he had foreseen it all. His parents' cold welcome, their silence whilst Mathilde was there. And his father waiting for him by the fire when he came back alone at midnight, after taking her home and enjoying a drink with Léon.

'You can't have believed that we'd agree?' cried Jean-Edouard as soon as he stepped in.

Pierre-Edouard carefully filled his pipe and lit it with a spill. 'No,' he said at last. 'I knew all along you'd be against Mathilde. But I don't give a damn.'

'You don't give a damn? Really? The war and your wounds don't give you all the rights, you know!'

'The right to tell you to stuff it? Yes they do!' he said calmly, sitting on the settle.

'Bloody hell! You're making a mistake, if you think in this family – '

'No; you're making the mistake about your son, and about your daughters too! Talking of them, Louise wrote to me; she's well, and so is Félix.'

'Damnit, don't try to get at me with that old story! We're not talking about that, but about this girl you want to bring into my house, this daughter of – '

'Take note of what I am going to say,' interrupted Pierre-Edouard gravely. 'One single insult, just one, and this time it'll be me that lashes out . . . And you can tell mother that, too . . .'

'You wouldn't dare!' Jean-Edouard taunted him, rising.

Pierre-Edouard sighed, and pushed a few twigs into the fire. 'Yes I would,' he said quietly. 'What do you think? Do you think I've come back from my first communion? Of course I'll slap the face of the first person who shows any disrespect to my wife!'

'Your wife? Already? Well, you bastard, you haven't wasted any time!'

'Think what you like, I don't give a damn about that either. Not a damn.'

'All right,' cut in Jean-Edouard, 'you don't give a damn about anything! Well marry the kid, I wish you joy! Marry her, but don't count on my roof for shelter. There's no question of that. I'll never let her live in my home! Never, do you understand? And if I'm not mistaken your mother will agree with me! What did you think, that we would let a Dupeuch lay down the law here, in our house?'

'Don't worry, I never believed that. I know you too well.'

'So then, it's settled; you can marry her tomorrow if you like, but you'll never bring her over the threshold. I'll fling her out if you do!'

'Fine,' said Pierre-Edouard, getting up, 'I wanted to hear you say it. That way we know where we stand . . . Goodnight.'

He picked up his case, limped towards the door and went out into the darkness.

Léon was still sitting beside the fire, waiting for him.

'Right, it's all sorted out, don't let's talk about it any more,' Pierre-Edouard announced. 'Tell me, what did that?' he said, stretching a finger towards the stump under his friend's left sleeve.

'That? A bloody Maxim gun. And you, what was it?'

'One of those stupid one-fifty-millimetre jobs!'

They were still talking at dawn, when Léon's mother got up as usual to light the fire.

The return of the survivors brought an increase in activity and work, which the whole village was in sore need of. First of all the men who had left school between 1892 and 1897 returned at the year's end, then in the following months came the younger ones.

Life began again; St Libéral finally emerged from its dangerous sloth. Everything seemed to return to normal, everyone tried hard to resume the old pre-war habits, but no one was fooled. They all knew that the customs, the mentality, the general climate had changed to such an extent that it was practically impossible to take up the old life they had left behind on 1 August 1914.

It was not only 1,300,000 men who had died in the war; it was a whole epoch, a century. It became obvious through thousands of little instances, and every day brought proof that they were entering a new era.

The young soldiers returned in a very different frame of mind from that which had previously been the great strength of rural society; this civilisation had been based on, even constrained by, a patriarchal system, whose legitimacy very few had ever questioned. Now disputes broke out on all sides, for the old guard felt they held authority almost as a divine right, while the young men not only questioned their autocracy, but ridiculed it unmercifully, made a joke of it and, since they lacked the power to change it, fled it.

This war had been their first opportunity to leave their little world, and they had learned more than just how to kill; they had also discovered that beyond their village or canton there was the world, with other ways of working and living. So there were many who repacked their bags and left, refusing to bow to the dictatorship of the head of the family. The company and the friendship of a whole variety of townspeople had taught them that there were other ways of earning your bread than by ploughing; they had exchanged ideas as well as wine and tobacco, compared their work and their wages.

As for the older combatants, those who had already been their own masters before the war, they also found it hard to adapt to new ways, to accept the idea that women could fill their places and manage the farms as well as they had. A new way of thinking had emerged there too, a different mentality, and if many wives stepped back and resumed the position they had occupied four years earlier, it did not fool anyone. No one could forget that they were capable of filling the men's jobs if necessary. And the band of widows was there too, to remind the men that they were not indispensable.

The years of shared misery created a close bond amongst all the former soldiers in the village. Everyone was amazed to see how warmly those who had been at the front now greeted Father Verlhac. Even the schoolteacher was not pretending when he expressed admiration, respect and friendship for him. They all knew that the priest had been a stretcher-bearer for four years, but only those who had seen combat could appreciate the importance, the self-sacrifice and the courage of the stretcher-bearers.

Jean-Edouard felt pushed aside, isolated amongst these men who had faced the guns together, but he continued his work as mayor with undiminished vigour. No one challenged him for the sash of office bequeathed by Jean Duroux; they knew that he had made good use of the power it gave him.

Nor did anyone criticise his attitude towards his son. That quarrel was of no further interest; it was no longer a boy set against his father, but simply two men who chose to differ. And such a disagreement concerned nobody but the parties involved, like an everyday dispute between two neighbours; it was wiser not to take sides.

The young woman leaned against her companion's shoulder and shivered. She raised the fur collar of her coat against the keen wind which whipped across the gangway of the big white steamship; there were few passengers prepared to brave the cold of this arctic region.

Only the announcement that an iceberg was drifting by not far from the ship brought a few of the curious out of the well-heated saloons; they rushed to the rails, admired the sparkling mountain of ice and then returned, numb with cold, to their bridge or whist tables, their conversations, their cups of tea and glasses of champagne.

The young woman and her companion reached the poop-deck and gazed in silence at the ribbon of silver created by the wake, stretching to the horizon. The man stroked her face, pushing aside the wild curls which the wind drove across her eyes.

'Then you're sure, you don't want to marry me?'

'No, I don't.'

'But why not?'

'I've told you a thousand times.'

'I'll end up believing that you hate men!'

'Idiot!' she murmured. 'You didn't always speak like that, but I'll make you suffer for having said it. No, I don't hate men, but what they can become. Husbands, for instance . . .'

'And what if I make you a nice little baby, handsome and charming like me?'

'All the more reason not to marry! First the husband, then the father! No, thank you very much! Let's go in now, I'm cold.'

That was just an excuse. She wasn't going to tell him everything, explain the whole tale to this kind Canadian doctor whom she had known for six months.

Besides, would he believe it? Probably not. Who could imagine that the young milliner who kept a shop in the rue du Bac, who employed eight workers, designed hats for all Paris and was now going to present her models in America, was young Berthe Vialhe? What was left of the peasant from the Corrèze who had spent her childhood and adolescence minding the flocks, cleaning the stables, doing the washing, working like a slave?

There was nothing left. Berthe Vialhe no longer existed, swallowed up by the famous label sewn in her hats. It was a madly chic signature, with a good ring to it, like a tinkling mountain stream: Claire Diamond.

Louise gently tucked in the child who had just fallen asleep, kissed him and left the bedroom.

Quietly she slipped down the corridors which wound between the attic rooms of the castle, and went down the servants' staircase to the first floor. Here she took the grand staircase to the first floor, and entered a long corridor of shining parquet which smelled deliciously of wax. On either side the heavy panelling was decorated with trophies of death, with stags and roe deer, boars' heads, wolves and foxes.

The surroundings no longer impressed her; she had grown accustomed to them, accustomed to the splendour of the private town house in the rue du Passy, the palatial hotels in Biarritz and Deauville and Nice. It was three years since she had become the companion to the old baroness, and luxury no longer astonished her.

She had Jean to thank for this position – or rather, his disappearance. At his death, mad with grief, she had wanted to leave the castle, to draw a veil over the past for a second time. But then the young baroness took an interest in her future. Perhaps she was troubled by this first death amongst her employees; perhaps it was to relieve her conscience, to redeem herself in the eyes of her servants – her husband had been declared unfit for military service and had not changed his way of life one iota, everything continuing as it had before the war; she needed to prove that he really was concerned about the fate of his people . . .

So it was that the young baroness suggested she become lady companion to her mother-in-law. Not a very demanding old lady; she did not ask much, just to be able to talk to someone, to have her cups of verbena or lime tea served at set times, to have a few pages read to her each evening from *The Imitation of Christ*.

Louise had accepted. Since then her life had flowed by smoothly and silently, without great joy but without great pain. She expected nothing from life, but accepted it without bitterness, because of Félix.

Félix didn't pay any attention to his mother's mourning attire, and wasn't surprised by the first white hairs, not knowing that she was only twenty-seven. Only Félix still knew how to make her laugh.

# PART SIX

*Coste-Roche*

# 24

It was snowing thick and fast when they eventually reached the dilapidated building on the night of Saturday 21 December. It was a two-roomed thatched cottage about three kilometres from the village, just past the cutting leading to the old mine-workings, on the edge of the parish, on the south slope of the plateau, at the place called Coste-Roche.

It was part of the tiny farm Pierre-Edouard had rented from the solicitor for a token sum – fifty francs a year. Five years ago fifty francs would have been the price of three sheep, but since the war you could get that much for four hens! However Pierre-Edouard had insisted that Monsieur Lardy accept the money; the solicitor was only too glad that someone was prepared to take on the cottage and the two hectares surrounding it, and was prepared to let it for nothing, as a wedding present to his wife's god-daughter.

He was a little embarrassed, really, for the house had been empty since 1914 and was in a very poor state; apart from the half-hectare field which lay close to the building and could be ploughed, the rest of the land was covered in weeds, scrub and wood.

Pierre-Edouard fixed up the house within three weeks, helped by Léon and his two labourers. Once it no longer rained through the rye-straw of the roof, the doors and shutters closed firmly, and the two rooms were scoured with lots of water and lime-washed, so that they were clean and neat, it was just right for a young couple.

Pierre-Edouard thanked Léon, who was already turning his cart, pushed open the door and went in. The huge oak-stump he had put on the hearth at the beginning of the afternoon was only half burned. The fire ate slowly into it, with tiny flames, opening out wide holes in the heart of the wood where scarlet embers threw out a lasting warmth.

He hung up the oil-lamp and turned down the flame, for the light of the fire reflected by the whitened walls was almost enough in itself. He looked at Mathilde, who was taking off her heavy black cloak, on which the snowflakes were already melting.

The snow had begun to fall just as they were going into the Mairie. Gaston, the deputy mayor, was waiting for them, confused and ashamed at having to stand in for Jean-Edouard, who had not been seen since the previous evening. Gaston was torn between his friendship with his neighbour and sympathy for Pierre-Edouard and Mathilde, but he managed it all very well, despite his embarrassment. He didn't make any mistakes; he kissed the bride and reassured Pierre-Edouard that it would all come right in the end.

In the church the ceremony was quiet but full of happiness, conducted by Father Verlhac, who obviously approved of the young couple's behaviour and rejoiced to see them happy. He even accepted their invitation to the inn, to drink the health of the newly-weds, and once more wish them much joy and happiness.

Pierre-Edouard and Léon had invited several friends to dine with them at the inn afterwards. The meal was simple, light-hearted without being boisterous; there were none of the rude jokes and coarse laughter which often punctuated wedding banquets. There were too many absentees that evening, and André Chanlat looked down on them from his frame of black crêpe.

'You're not cold, are you?' worried Pierre-Edouard.

'No, not at all, it's very cosy,' she said, holding out her hands to the fire.

He moved nearer to her; put his hands on her hips and kissed her on the neck, just below the ear. 'Are you happy?'

Yes, she was happy, but she asked: 'Will you sit with me for a moment on the settle?'

'Of course.' He took the ledge opposite her in the deep inglenook.

'Well, here we are . . .' she said, pushing the log which threw off sparks.

He saw that she was tense, a little sad and worried. 'Are you frightened of me?' he asked jokingly.

She shook her head in dissent, and blushed a little.

'No, it's not that; I don't know how to say it. It's a strange feeling, knowing we're married at last. And then . . . I want you to know that . . . if . . . Well, if you had wanted to, that's to say . . . Well, you could have, before this evening, you know . . . I wouldn't have minded, I would have understood . . .'

'I know.'

'Well, why didn't you want to? I'd have done whatever you wanted . . .'

'I know that.'

'So it's right what I thought, it was my fault if . . . well, if I deprived you, because I didn't have the courage to ask. And now you resent me for having made you wait . . . And I . . . I don't know what to do, anyway . . . so.'

She was frustrated and tense, close to tears.

'You know, you are a funny little girl! But you've got it wrong. Of course we could have, ever since I came back, and it's been hard watching you and waiting, believe me . . . But one day on the White Peak you said to me: "I'm not a little girl, I trust you". You were right to say that.'

He poked the log, pushed several bits of bark back into the embers. 'So,' he continued, 'that was it. I'm like that. If – well, if we'd taken in the harvest too early, I'd have enjoyed it, of course, just at that moment, but I would have been sorry later. And you too; you'd have been disappointed that I couldn't wait a month. And today, you and I would both have known that your white dress wasn't quite white . . . Whereas now it's different; we're married, we're not putting the cart before the oxen, it's all proper, just as it should be. Do you understand? Now we'll always remember that there was a before and after this evening.'

She gazed at him intently and smiled, her eyes dancing with happiness.

'I knew you'd say that. At least, I was hoping, and I'm so pleased you did. And that we waited till this evening. Everything's perfect.'

She got up, hesitated a moment and then continued. 'I have something else to tell you. I've got a birthmark, not a bad one, but a mark, on . . . well, on my chest. You see, it's not very nice, and I wanted to tell you, so that you wouldn't be surprised . . . . . . It's not funny! It's true! It's not something to laugh about, you idiot!' she insisted, seeing that he was shaking with uncontrollable laughter.

'Oh, you, you really are something!' The words tumbled out as he wiped the tears of laughter from his eyes. 'I know you've got a mark! I've known since you were born! What's more, everyone in the village knows too. A mark like a crescent moon. But I have to admit that I don't remember which side it's on!'

She stood for a moment in amazement, a little annoyed; then she smiled and crinkled her eyes mischievously at him.

'Oh, so it's like that! Everyone knows! Well in that case, it's time you saw it, and found out which side it's on . . .'

The snow fell all night. In the morning Pierre-Edouard pushed the door half open and saw that the drifts were up to fifteen centimetres. He closed the flap silently and made up the fire by throwing a big bundle of broom onto the still smouldering embers; they ignited instantly, blazing like a torch. Then he filled the fireplace with several hefty logs and turned back towards the bed.

Mathilde was still sleeping. He tenderly watched her gentle breathing, admired her delicate face, still so young, so fresh – the delicious curve of her half-open mouth, the mischievous snub nose, the fine tracery of long eyelashes against her cheeks. Then he thought of the little shape like a crescent moon which lay there beneath her left breast, two fingers from the nipple.

So, because it was Sunday, because it was such bad weather you wouldn't put a dog out in it, because he was happy as never before, and life was beautiful, he slipped gently back into the warm bed.

Mathilde did not wake, but instinctively stretched her arm towards him, as if already used to him being there; she touched his chest and her body came to rest confidingly against his.

The snow lasted for two weeks, making any outdoor work impossible, keeping people by their firesides. Pierre-Edouard and Mathilde, completely cut off in their cottage, experienced the happiest time of their lives.

Despite the cold they climbed several times to the plateau, for the pleasure of looking down on that fine expanse below, of surveying their fields, the ones Mathilde had stolen from under Jean-Edouard's nose and which Léon had given them, the deeds signed by the solicitor, on the day of their marriage. The three hectares had lain fallow for years, but only needed hard work and proper treatment to turn into good rich plough-land again.

'And down there,' Pierre-Edouard pointed, 'those are our fields. Well, my father's . . .'

'The Long Field, with its twenty-eight walnut trees . . .'

'No, thirty-one! I should know, I planted them with my father in 1901!'

'Twenty-eight,' she repeated. 'Three died in February 1917. The frost . . . And,' she continued, outlining the other fields from above, 'then there's the Peuch, the Malides, the Perrier, the Great Field! I know each one! Léon set me to watch them when you wrote for news . . .'

'So, he didn't bother at all, that peasant! When I thought all the information came from him!'

'What an idea!' she laughed. 'He didn't have time for that. But I know your father's fields. And I can even tell you which ones he's growing grain on for three years out of four.'

'Yes, I'm aware of that,' Pierre-Edouard frowned. 'It's so stupid, it exhausts the soil. Well, that's his business . . . Tell me if I remember it right; these plots here are called Monteboeuf, la Combille and au Bourdelet?'

'Yes, that's what it says in the land register.'

'Well, we'll give them new names, to remind us. That one we'll call "Léon's Letters", this one "Mathilde's" and over there, below the White Peak, "The Meeting Field". Would you like that?'

'Of course,' she replied, laughing, 'and one day our grandchildren will say we were crazy to give the fields names which are quite meaningless. How funny!'

He smiled, kissed her on the nose, and pulled her down onto the vast white sheet of the plateau.


He took long paces but strode slowly and smoothly in a perfectly straight line, governed by the straw markers which divided the ploughed field.

He was sowing, with broad regular sweeps which produced a fine golden lace springing from his wide palms as they opened; the waves of grain twisted and rustled as they settled on the ground, then seemed to take flight again with the next full swing of his arm, shooting out against the blue sky.

March had come in warm and damp; conditions were right earlier than usual for the spring sowing. Pierre-Edouard had lost no time since borrowing Léon's plough and oxen ten days ago. Already The Meeting Field was a beautiful sight, a fold of brown furrows where it now rained barley seeds.

What a joy to rediscover the technique of ploughing again, the movements and habits coming back to him instantly, without hesitation. What a pleasure to hear the coarse, gritty song of the earth again as it cracked, opened and curled over, hissing behind the mould-board. With complete happiness he contemplated the stretch of shining furrows he had created, one moulded to the next; neat, straight, perfectly cut.

Of course it had taken time to get his eye in again, adjust his stride to the size of the fields and the pace of the oxen, so much slower than the horses on Moureau Farm. The earth was harder, tougher, less giving and less uniform than the rich provident earth of old Ponthier. But he had known that for a long time. And here it was all better, because he was at home, on his land, in his realm, and the barley he was to harvest would be his own.

And in the evening, instead of the table of twenty-five men, waiting in silent attention, watching the movements of their employer, ready to rise at the click of a clasp knife being snapped shut; instead of the fatty, burnt soup of Ma Ponthier, the old warhorse; instead of the huge shed and revolting nests from which rose, from time to time, one of the scullery-maid's clientele, already undressed – instead of all that, he would be with Mathilde again.

He would have soup lovingly prepared by her, the intimacy of a meal alone together, and then, when the door and shutters were closed, the fire stoked up for the night, he would have her, fresh and soft as a spray of lily of the valley, impassioned and twining like a tendril of honeysuckle; the spontaneous welcome of her warm body, so well known already, yet rediscovered each time.

They needed all that – the complete understanding, harmony of purpose, and a taste for hard work – to overcome together the daily trials. There were plenty of them!

Gradually the little nest-egg saved from four years' wages melted away, but it allowed them to equip their household and live for three months.

The money vanished in the purchase of fifteen hens: 150 francs. A two-month-old piglet to fatten: 135 francs. The bran and grain needed for these animals: 100 francs; the barley and potatoes for sowing: 250 francs. In everything – in the sacks of fertiliser which he needed this year for lack of manure, in the modest outlay for food, the bread at two francs twenty a kilo, the milk at eighty sous a litre, the vegetables and occasionally meat.

These days, 1000 francs was no longer an enormous sum. Fifteen to twenty years earlier it would have bought him three fine cows: now, for the same amount, all he could buy were three eight-month-old piglets! What madness!

Sometimes, when Mathilde saw him looking worried, she reminded him of her savings book. 'You know, I was given seventy-five francs when I was born!'

'I remember, everyone talked about it at the time. It was a good sum then, but . . .'

'Wait! There's interest added in the book, and then Léon kept it up for me, before the war. By now I must have 345 francs. With that we could buy two six-week-old calves, keep them for eighteen months and sell them ready to breed, and . . .'

'I can tell you're related to a cattle dealer! No, keep your savings, you never know . . .'

'Well then,' she continued, 'I'm sure Léon would give us a loan. Would you like me to ask him?'

'No, he's already done enough for us. Think of the land he gave as your dowry! I don't want to borrow any money from him, nor anyone else. It's me who's got to feed you, not your brother.'

The worry about money made him touchy, but the land too was a constant source of concern. There, only an arm's length away, stretched the Vialhe holdings, his land: all those beautiful fields which his father could no longer maintain as they deserved, which he was depleting with his inefficient system of crop rotation. But the Vialhe land was forbidden to him. The best he could hope for was that one day, in ten or fifteen years perhaps . . . Just so long as his father had not sold it all by then.

Although normal life had resumed in St Libéral, there was a feeling of stagnation and depression. As mayor, Jean-Edouard was made aware of this almost every day.

His son had not been the only one to leave, slamming the door behind him. Plenty of other young people had copied Pierre-Edouard, but instead of staying in the parish they had moved to the towns, and for good; there was no doubt of that.

This exodus had diminished the ageing, dispirited population. In 1900 there had been 1,092 inhabitants; in 1914 there were 979 and now, 701 . . .

Already one of the two grocers' had closed down. Before the war there had been four carpenters; now there were only two, and they had just as much difficulty making a living as the three remaining stonemasons and the last slater. No one had come to replace the old miller, and they knew that the solicitor would be closing his office at the end of the year. The tenants of smallholdings were disappearing everywhere, no longer able to survive on a farm of three or four hectares. Weeds and bushes took over where they left.

The buying syndicate was moribund. As for the fortnightly markets, Léon had fought to get them going again, but they did not attract half the numbers who had flooded into St Libéral before the war. He had to do away with the special markets, and it looked as if they might soon be down to one market a month . . .

Nothing was going well anywhere else, either! The newspapers spoke of nothing but strikes, demonstrations, those Bolsheviks who were upsetting everyone. And to make matters worse, someone had tried to assassinate Clemenceau! What a disgrace, what depravity!

For Jean-Edouard life grew more difficult. He was assailed by lassitude, not so much physical as spiritual fatigue. Marguerite's grumpiness and bad temper increased daily; she was growing old ungracefully, and hated her isolation and solitude. Since she could not vent her anger on her own daughters, who now seemed to have disappeared completely, she turned all her bitterness on her daughter-in-law. That little serpent, with her air of innocence, she must have displayed all her charms to turn Pierre-Edouard's head – the fool, preferring to live up there in the wilds at Coste-Roche, instead of down here, working the farm. Huh, they would come to no good, those two . . . !

Jean-Edouard was basically in agreement with his wife, but the daily repetition of these complaints exasperated him. Of course Mathilde was worthless, it ran in the family, didn't it? Of course she'd gone the whole way to get that idiot Pierre-Edouard to marry her; she had her eye on his land, that was obvious, clear as the Diamond!

He knew all that, he was convinced of it, but, unlike Marguerite, he did not chew it over constantly. What good did that do? The damage was done, they had made the break; why harp on it, why stir up anger and bitterness? He didn't need that; it came back to him anyway, every time he saw his son or daughter-in-law – that kid! A week earlier, she had called out to him like a challenge, in front of everyone, a ringing: 'Good morning, Mayor!' and it had echoed defiantly along the main street. Then she had walked away, perfectly well aware of the impression she had created, confident of her youth, her cheeky little face, her hip-swinging walk. He would have liked to hit her!

He preferred his son's attitude to her defiance. At least he didn't speak. He said nothing, except when he had the gall to come and get supplies from the syndicate, and even there he found an opportunity to teach his own father a lesson: he criticised the seed varieties on offer, made a face over the heaps of phosphates, demanded some unknown fertiliser, talked of products with unpronounceable names – in short, behaved as if he alone knew more than all the farmers in the community; more than his own father, what's more! It was disgusting! After that, Jean-Edouard let one of the employees serve him and answer his questions!

But it was all so tiring and depressing; and the farm work was getting more difficult and demanding. He did it without wanting to, it gave him no pleasure. He was in his sixtieth year and felt his strength and drive fading; even that urge and need for a fight, which had supported him for so long, was going. His sash of office as mayor weighed heavy, too; he was tempted to lay it aside for good at the next elections, which were due to take place at the end of the year.

*

288

Pierre-Edouard was absorbed in his work, earthing up the potatoes he had planted six weeks earlier in the field next to the little cottage, and he did not notice Mathilde at first.

She was just tackling the final bend which led steeply up to Coste-Roche, and would be home in five minutes. He was suddenly aware that she was loaded up like a pack-mule; besides two big rounds of bread and the week's groceries, she was carrying the twenty-five kilos of buckwheat seed he had ordered. He thrust his hoe into the ground and ran down to meet her.

She saw him leaping and zigzagging through the broom bushes; relieved to put down the load which she had carried for almost three kilometres, she sat down to wait for him. She was worn out and perspiring, for the June sun was beating down.

'Bloody hell!' he shouted as he reached her. 'I didn't tell you to *bring* the buckwheat, I told you to order it. I would have fetched it! That was a bit silly of you, in this heat!'

'So, now you don't have to go to the village! And anyway, I've carried loads like that before!'

'Just content yourself with carrying that,' he said, gently placing a hand on her stomach.

Pierre-Edouard had been very attentive for the last fortnight, since Doctor Delpy had confirmed that the child would be born in January; he made sure she didn't do the heavy jobs – and that wasn't easy, because there were plenty of them.

'Anything new down there?' he asked, sitting down beside her.

'I saw your father.'

'And of course, as usual, you said "Good day, Mayor!" to him.'

'Naturally,' she giggled, 'except I nearly said "Good day, Grand-father!" After all, he is going to be a grandfather, isn't he? Perhaps that will make him happy.'

He filled his pipe and lit it. 'I doubt it. Don't forget he's been one for a long time, and it doesn't seem to have changed anything!'

'I saw Léon too, guess what he told me . . .'

He pulled on his pipe and shrugged his shoulders.

'Do you remember the Treilhes? The ones at Ayen?' she asked.

'Yes, the carriers.'

'They're selling their farm. Since she's been widowed, poor Marie can't find a tenant for the land. Just think, twelve hectares . . . You know what we must do, don't you?' she asked, and carried right on. 'We must buy the two hectares on the plateau, close to our land.'

'Have you gone mad? You know we haven't a penny!'

289

'We'll have to find it,' she insisted, 'and we must buy. That way we'll have five hectares, a nice little farm!'

'No,' he said drily. 'Don't talk to me about a nice farm! No house, no cowshed, no livestock, not even tools to work with! That's all we need to be ruined. You'd better forget that idea.'

He was aware that he was dashing her hopes, and was sorry for it, but the facts were plain to see: they had no money left. Apart from the 345 francs in Mathilde's savings book, and his grandfather's napoléon, the tiny sum still available would just tide them over until they got some small returns from the sale of the barley, maize and vegetables they were growing. There were also the hens and rabbits Mathilde was rearing and the small pension awarded for his war wounds, but even all added together it didn't come to much.

'All the same,' she replied stubbornly, 'we have to buy. Léon told me so.'

'What business is it of his! No, listen, instead of dreaming, why not agree to what he suggested to me?'

'You're going to borrow from him?'

'Not at all! But two months ago he suggested I go and help him on market days. Well, I'll go and do that. That way I'll earn a bit, we'll save, and one day we'll be able to buy land.'

'And the fields on the plateau will have been sold long since,' she replied bitterly. 'Well, you never told me that Léon suggested you work for him! Why didn't you say anything?'

'Because it depressed me,' he said. 'Really, I can't bear the thought of it. I'm not a cattle dealer, I don't enjoy swindling people! But I've got to put my mind to it. Soon there'll be three of us, have you thought of that? And even if I work myself to a standstill we can't survive on our thirty miserable strips of land. When I think that just next door my father is leaving half his land fallow, dammit all!'

She saw that he was downcast and demoralised, and snuggled up to him. 'Well, there you have it, that's why we must buy! I don't want you to go running round the markets four or five times a week! I don't want that, do you hear? We have to buy those two hectares, and we're going to!'

'And how much do they want for the land?'

'They're rather expensive,' she spoke softly. 'Prices are rising fast . . .'

'How much?'

'Three and a half thousand a hectare, but perhaps if you haggled a bit . . .'

'Okay, don't let's talk about it any more. Come on; it's past midday and I'm hungry.'

Mathilde had been in bed for more than an hour when he finally returned to the house. He had been taking advantage of the long June evening to work in the vegetable plot. It was late, and already the setting sun was giving way to stars, which outshone the last rays on the horizon and accentuated the dark of the night sky.

Before going into the house he drew up a full bucket of water, undressed and washed himself. The water ran down his body, fresh and delicious, after that stifling day. He filled another bucket and tipped it over his head, shaking himself. Then, having washed off the accumulated dust and sweat of twelve hours' labour, he went in and shut the door.

It was dark, but he did not light the lamp; he moved noiselessly towards the bedroom and slipped into bed. Mathilde had thrown off all the covers because of the heat, and only the coarse linen sheet lay partly over her. He felt her bare back and shoulders, worried that she would catch cold, for the night would be cool if it stayed clear. Gently, he pulled up the sheet.

'Leave it, it's too hot!'

'You're not asleep! I was being so careful not to wake you . . .'

'That was kind of you. I'm thirsty . . .'

'Now you tell me!'

He sighed, but got up and walked to the sink. She heard him feeling around for a glass.

'You could have lit the lamp . . .'

'So that we can feed the mosquitoes? Anyway, I've found it,' he said, coming back. He stumbled into a stool, and swore like a muleteer.

'Have you hurt yourself?' she asked, though a chuckle escaped.

'What do you think? I like stubbing my toes, you know that! Here, have a drink. All right, can I get into bed now? Anything else you need? Sure you wouldn't like a few cherries? I could go and fetch some for you from the plateau, it's only a couple of kilometres . . .'

'Don't be silly! Come to bed.'

He kissed her and stretched out beside her. Outside, the barn owl which nested in the loft above the stable gave a long screech.

'Why does it do that?' asked Mathilde.

'That must be the male,' he explained seriously. 'I think the female has sent him for a glass of water, and he's knocked into something on his way back.'

She pinched him unexpectedly on the behind, then sat up.

'Where are you going?'

'Nowhere,' she said, drawing up her legs and winding her arms round her knees. 'You know, I've been thinking about what Léon told me, this morning . . .'

'Oh no! Not at this hour of the night! I'm fond of your brother, but I don't want him in my bed!'

'Listen to me,' she insisted, 'and consider the way he's done things.'

'What now? He's sold a milch-cow without an udder by swearing that she gives twelve litres a day?'

'No,' she continued, 'I'm serious. Listen; before the war, when he bought all the grazing land he could and had the house built, you know what he did? He borrowed. He told me this morning . . .'

'Your brother took a loan? Well, well! and I thought he earned enough to pay for it himself. The devil, pretending to be rich on other people's money!'

'Don't be stupid! You're talking like an old man, you sound like your father! It's not a sin to borrow, is it? And anyway, he's paid it back!'

'All the better! Since the money isn't worth anything now, he hasn't been wasting his time, the crook!'

'That's true,' she admitted frankly, 'but he told me it's going to go on like that . . .'

'What is?'

'Money will lose value each year . . . You don't see gold coins any more now, he told me that was a bad sign. Well, according to him, this is a good time to borrow, and if you want to he'll stand guarantee for you at the Crédit Agricole. He knows the people in Tulle . . .'

'My God! You plotted all this with him this morning, didn't you?' he groaned, wanting to sound angry, but a note of admiration crept in.

'And why not? He's my brother, isn't he? He's got a right to talk to me!'

'Bloody hell, you make a fine pair! My word, if I hadn't got you out of there you'd have ended up worse than him!'

'No, I wouldn't. Anyway, you can't be cross with me for worrying about how we're going to manage, someone has to . . .'

'Oh no, tell me right out then, I'm a spendthrift!'

'It's not that, but Léon says that you're not interested in money . . .'

'Your brother is beginning to annoy me! Anyway, what does he know about it? Has he been to look in my wallet?'

'No, but he told me that you once made him throw away more than five francs' worth of birds for no good reason! And he hasn't forgotten. To him, that's proof enough!'

He burst into laughter, sat up and hugged her to him.

'Five francs!' he repeated with a hiccup, 'Five francs! And for no good reason, he tells you, the idiot! Well, if I remember rightly, we had the wolves on our tail. If you'd seen him run! He'd have been glad to pay a couple of guineas to get away!'

'Don't laugh!' she struggled in his embrace and beat him with her fists. 'It's serious, what I'm talking about. Light the lamp!'

'Look, it's late; I want to sleep, I've been on my feet since four!'

'You can sleep afterwards; light the lamp!'

He sighed, fumbled for the matches and struck one. Very soon the flame of the oil lamp flickered across the room. Mathilde got up and grasped the lamp; its slender shadow danced on the white walls.

'Shut the window to stop the mosquitoes!' he suggested.

He smiled as he watched her trot across the room, admiring her body, which was improved by the rounding of early pregnancy. Later it would look ungainly, out of proportion, but at the moment her shape was changing day by day; the slim, graceful girl was growing confidently into a complete woman, in harmony with herself. It showed in the slight swelling of her breasts, the enveloping, protective curve of her hips, in certain gestures even: the instinct which led her to place her hand on her stomach as a protective wall – although it was still quite flat, a smooth soft stomach like a pigeon's breast – where their son, or their daughter, was growing, the baby who was going to be born for its mother's twentieth birthday.

She went to the sideboard, opened it, took out a sheet of paper and a pencil, and sat down at the table.

'I want to go to sleep!'

'Wait, it will only take a minute,' she replied, starting to write.

She came back to the bed. 'There,' she explained. 'That's what we need to borrow, and that's what it will cost us in repayments each year . . .'

He took the piece of paper, read it, and choked.

'Eleven thousand francs! Are you out of your mind? And why eleven thousand francs? You told me that they were selling at three and a half a hectare; there are two hectares, that makes seven thousand! What's the extra for?'

'Simple; it's to buy two sows and eight ewes, and for tools; Léon will still let us borrow his oxen.'

'But look what we'd have to repay each year!'

'Well we'll have twenty years to do it!' she said, and twined her arms around his neck. 'And after all, the repayments are only four good piglets each year! And if we have two sows, we'll have at least a dozen piglets to sell!'

'Stop it, sweetheart!' he said seriously, 'we're not there yet. Let me look at your sums . . .'

He picked up the paper again and studied it. She saw he was hesitating, that he was not yet convinced, so she tried tenderness, taking his hand and placing it on her stomach.

'Look, think of this too.'

'I am! I don't want him to have a father who's imprisoned for debt!'

'There's no danger of that. If necessary, I'd sell my land! So, you've decided? You agree? We can't let this one get away! So it's yes?' she whispered, leaning closer to him.

He gazed at her for a long time and considered the two hectares which he could perhaps own, thanks to her. Those two hectares were their chance, a lifebelt thrown to the drowning; they needed them. She had done it all, she had taken the lead with firmness and energy, as in everything she undertook. So he didn't feel outwitted and beaten by her charm and her deliciously persuasive weaponry; he knew that it was thanks to her, to all the things he loved in her, that he would achieve his goals and fulfil his potential.

'I'm very proud of you,' he said at last.

'It's yes?' she asked, kissing him.

'I'd like to meet the person who could say no to you at this moment. I couldn't . . .'

# 25

THE sale and division of the Treilhes' farm aroused little interest. The business dragged on, for the heavy burden of summer work interfered with the discussions and calculations which are a vital precursor to every transaction. Then came the preparations for the elections to the town council and to the chamber of deputies in the autumn; this distracted everyone, so that the various purchasers managed to buy all the fields close to the village without actually tearing each other apart.

Thus Jeantout's son, Maurice, got his hands on several plots which lay within the family land – he was one of the few young men who had not fallen out with his father. Léon bought meadows for grazing; other farmers divided the remainder between them.

No one coveted the two hectares Pierre-Edouard and Mathilde wanted; the land was a long way from the village, had lain fallow for years, and lay directly between the property of old Vialhe and his daughter-in-law – in other words, right in the middle of a family quarrel. No one wanted to be involved in that!

Everyone knew that Jean-Edouard had easily enough money to push up the price by bidding for it; but no one had forgotten, either, how Mathilde had won the first round with her masterly purchase eighteen months earlier. So they were anticipating a really good feud.

Marguerite rinsed the potato with a twist of her hand, dispatched it brusquely into the bowl of water, seized a fresh tuber and peeled it nervously. Jean-Edouard noticed how tense and edgy she was, and anticipated a fresh attack.

But the more agitated his wife became, the calmer he appeared. He carefully divided the thick slice of bread into tiny strips and let them fall into his bowl, then poured in the chicory coffee and a little milk and stirred it.

'So you're going to let them do it to you!' griped Marguerite.

He tipped a spoonful of sugar into the bowl and stirred again. 'Let them do it? No one's bothering me!' he said, without raising his voice.

'Oh, so you think that, do you? You're going to let them set up right in the middle of your property! So that every time they go to work on their land, that little slut can make fun of us and show off. You've got to buy that land, do you hear me!'

'No,' he said, and sucked in a noisy spoonful of coffee and soggy bread.

'And why not?'

'Because I can't even cultivate all the ground I've got now. I'm ashamed enough of that, without adding to it!'

'You only have to find a worker, or even two, if that's what it needs!'

'No I don't; it's nice and quiet since old Abel left to hang about somewhere else!'

'Well I'm telling you that it has to be bought, whatever you say!' she shouted suddenly, banging the table with the handle of her knife.

'You still haven't got enough land? Tell me, don't you think there'll be enough space to bury us in? My God! What do you want with another two hectares! I'd be better off selling than buying!'

'You must take them, do you hear,' she repeated. This had been her obsession for several years now – to acquire. It didn't matter what – land, money – just to hoard it, for the satisfaction of being able to say that they were rich; richer than their neighbours, and therefore more respectable.

He had shared this passion in his time, but at least when he bought land it was to increase the Vialhe holdings; for the honour of the Vialhes, to leave a substantial property for his descendants, larger than the one he had inherited from his father. But Louise had left, Pierre-Edouard had left, Berthe had left; so what was the good of buying land of which they now had no need? So that his son would get it back when he died? No, thank you, that was too easy, it went against the grain. If Pierre-Edouard wanted the two hectares, let him take them, but at least he'd have to pay for them out of his own pocket.

'If you don't buy them everyone will say that the little slut has made a fool of you again, and no one will believe that you never intended to acquire them. Or they'll say that Pierre-Edouard has got you on a tight rein!'

'Well, let them talk! I don't give a damn!' he swore, swallowing another lump of bread.

And it was true, he didn't care. He didn't care because in his view none of that mattered any more; because manners, ideas, principles even, all the ways of doing things since the war, had nothing in common with what he had known and revered for more than sixty years. In this new world children had no respect for tradition, or authority, or filial duty; in this world money, good money in fine gold coins, had been replaced by worthless paper. This mad world threatened by social revolutions and political struggles, this world turned upside down, no longer interested him. He felt like a stranger who had lost his way.

And Marguerite could go on wailing and moaning and raging as much as she liked, he would not listen to her. Just as he did not listen to those (and there were many of them) who clamoured for him to seek a further term of office as mayor.

The general election in November 1919 and the municipal elections which followed it did not unleash any strong feelings in St Libéral. It was a far cry from the fights, manipulations and struggles of former times.

There again the climate had changed. Even Father Verlhac did not hide his preference, although he did not go so far as to suggest voting for anyone in particular; he was even seen discussing politics with the teacher, and without them coming to blows! Nobody took offence. Why should the priest have to keep quiet? After all, they'd allowed women to speak, very nearly given them the right to vote!

This idea had been rejected by the Senate, who had no doubt that the Church would take advantage of the opportunity to influence its female devotees, but the women did not hesitate to express their opinions and defend their candidate just the same. And it was they who placed Jean-Edouard Vialhe first on the list of candidates at St Libéral. They had seen him at work during the war, knew how he had devoted himself to his mayoral duties, and vigorously encouraged the men to vote for him.

Two old hands were re-elected with Jean-Edouard, Léon and Jeantout, but the majority were young ex-soldiers, like Jeantout's lad, Maurice, and Jacques, the grocer's son; even Dr Delpy was elected. Everyone knew he was not convinced that he wanted to be a councillor, but they knew that he had done his duty and more during the war.

As for Jean-Edouard, he was surprised to find himself elected with such a majority; surprised and deeply moved. Although he believed and felt he had been overtaken and tossed aside by a new era in which he had no role, they had nevertheless chosen him; they wanted him to lead the community. Him, the old man, the patriarch.

He saw the electors' decision as an affirmation of his whole life and all his decisions; he was astounded, but elated too, and felt his strength return in a way he would never have believed possible. He was re-invigorated to fight on and to prove to everyone that they had been right to choose him.

He had only one regret, which no one would have guessed but which Marguerite never failed to remind him of. He regretted having once dropped his guard, not having taken up the challenge and affirmed his power as head of the family, when he had allowed his son to buy those two hectares, which he had undervalued through weariness and weakness.

But it was too late to go back, to undo what he now saw as a humiliation. Pierre-Edouard and Mathilde were already the owners. They had signed the deeds of purchase more than a month earlier, in one of the last transactions undertaken by Monsieur Lardy. Since then his office had been closed, and Saint-Libéral had no solicitor.

Once more the wave of pain lanced her lower body, spreading out like a tongue of flame to the base of her stomach; seared her kidneys and left her short of breath, waiting for the next agonising current to flow through her.

Despite this, Mathilde did not wake Pierre-Edouard. He was sleeping the deep sleep of a man broken by the effort of a whole day spent clearing the land, their new land up on the plateau. The night before, a violent pulling in her loins had driven her to shake her husband awake; but that had been a false alarm, just a warning, and she had been cross with herself for disturbing his rest. But tonight . . .

Then she considered how she had taxed her own strength during the previous day. She had been seized by a frenzy of activity, heightened by annoyance that she had mistaken the signs of labour, and thrown herself into cleaning their little house; attacking their few pieces of furniture until they were gleaming; scrubbing out the crib which had lain ready for two weeks; sweeping the floor of beaten earth with a fierce care; hunting down the spiders in their webs who played hide and seek with her between the thick beams blackened by centuries of smoke. Yes, perhaps she had done too much.

She calculated furthermore that, since it was the night of 6 January, the baby wasn't due yet, although it would be coming soon. Tomorrow, perhaps . . .

She placed her hands on her stomach and noticed immediately that a change had taken place. The warm ball of life which distended her skin and an hour earlier had pushed against her breasts, had sunk down. It was no longer perfectly oval in shape, soft and relaxed; it was humped in the middle, like a huge misshapen fist, hard and knobbly.

A new pain shot through her like electricity, from her feet to the nape of her neck; so she gently shook Pierre-Edouard. He woke up straight away, instantly alert.

'It's the real thing this time?' he asked, as he lit the oil lamp.

'I think so, yes. I'd like you to go and fetch Doctor Delpy.' She raised herself painfully on to her elbows and sat up, her back against the wooden headboard. They distinctly heard a rustling like torn tissue paper, followed by the sound of an egg being cracked on the corner of a table and dripping onto the floor.

'That's it; the waters are about to break, I can feel it. Hurry, go and get the doctor.'

'Good God,' he said, hurriedly dressing, 'you should have woken me earlier!' He did not panic, but an insidious fear gripped him and tightened his chest.

'But I'll have to leave you here all alone, with no one for three kilometres in any direction. Are you sure you wouldn't rather I stayed?'

He was aware that he was asking a stupid question. They had discussed this birth for long enough, and he had been the first to admit that he did not feel equal to the task alone. This time it was not a cow or a ewe to be helped through labour. It was Mathilde, his love; her softness already changing and opening for the delivery. And in that, he really did not know how to help her.

He dressed carefully, for the frost was biting outside. 'Lie down,' he suggested as he tried to cover her.

'Leave me alone, I'm all right as I am; go quickly!'

'I don't like to leave you alone . . .'

'Hurry up, it'll be okay.'

He stoked the fire with four enormous blocks of oak, then lit the big hurricane lantern and rushed out.


The burning sensation was overwhelming her stomach, cutting off her breath; her face and breast ran with sweat. It went away; it returned, all-powerful, all-consuming.

Instinctively Mathilde regulated her breathing, perhaps because she had seen so many ewes in labour: she deliberately changed to short rapid breaths which increased in tempo, until the pain blurred and settled down in the centre of her being, like an animal pretending that it was tamed, but ready to spring out again. She watched the clock anxiously, the big copper pendulum scything away each second with a broad stroke.

Pierre-Edouard had left twenty minutes ago; he would have run all the way along the track, he must be knocking on the doctor's door by now. Perhaps he was already on the way back with him, and soon she would hear the sound of the motor. Miraculous car, which could drive right up to the house bearing someone who would take away this fearful burning which was tearing her apart, destroying her!

A fresh flame of pain lit up in the small of her back. She bit her thumb in order not to cry out and she didn't cry, but she tasted her own blood through her teeth.

And the pain returned, settled in and did not leave her. Then she cried out for Pierre-Edouard, all the time, in the plaintive tones of a lost child calling for help, stubbornly repeating the name, trying to banish her fear with the sound of her own voice; talking, talking, as if to keep away the beast of death she sensed lurking nearby.

Pierre-Edouard ran like a madman; at least, he tried to run. Less than two hundred metres from the house an evil patch of ice had sent him rolling head over heels into a ditch full of brambles. He wasn't much hurt, but the glass of the lantern had exploded like a miniature grenade, leaving him in complete darkness.

There was no moon, no stars, nothing to help his dash down to the village. He ran on nevertheless, now mad with worry and overwhelmed by the certain knowledge that Mathilde needed help; up there she was alone, quite lost, and needed him more than ever before.

He tripped on a bump, fell full-length again, and slid three metres. He was up in a bound, without heeding the dull pain from his scarred legs. He set off again, ice and stones from the path embedded in his palms; he wiped them on his jacket as he ran.

At last he reached the first houses of the village. Everyone was asleep, but suddenly the dogs gave voice, alerted by the sound of his steps echoing in the alleyways. In the main square he quickened his pace and threw himself on the doctor's door, pounding it with his fist until a light appeared.

'Who is it?' demanded the old maidservant through the closed door.

'Open up, in God's name! It's me, Vialhe, my wife is having a baby! We need the doctor, quick!'

'Oh, you poor man, you'll have to wait. He left less than an hour ago to deliver Madame Bonny's baby up in the hills, not far from Perpezac . . .'

'But, good God! What shall I do?' he cried.

And suddenly he saw himself as a widower, saw himself returning to the cottage to find lifeless she for whom he would have given his life . . . But four years of war had made him into a fighter, and a decisive man. He clenched his teeth and ran towards Doctor Fraysse's house.

The door was opened almost immediately.

'What's the matter with you?' asked the old doctor, as he wrapped himself in his dressing-gown. 'Was that you yelling just now?'

'Yes, Delpy's not at home and Mathilde is in labour up there, all alone!'

'All right,' commented the old man. 'Well, go and fetch Madame Traversat, she's a good midwife.'

'No, I don't want her! She's the one who pulled Gaston's little girl about, she even dislocated the baby's shoulder, I don't want that butcher! *You* must come. You can't refuse!'

The doctor sighed, and objected mildly: 'Look, I'm eighty-five, it's not right at my age to be running about at two o'clock in the morning, especially when it's as cold as this!'

'You must come! You wouldn't leave her like that!'

'Of course I wouldn't. Well, it'll make me feel younger to help a woman I delivered twenty years ago. Besides,' the old man murmured, as if to himself, 'I owe it to her. No, you wouldn't understand, that's an old story, from your father's time. Go on, find a cart for us while I get dressed. And don't worry; a first birth always takes a long time.'

Pierre-Edouard rushed off into the darkness, ran to his brother-in-law's house, and hammered on the door fit to wake the dead.

'Who's the idiot who wants a blast from my shotgun?' shouted Léon suddenly from behind the shutters.

'Shut up! It's me, Pierre, I need your horse. Hurry up, it's for Mathilde!' he yelled, as he ran towards the stable.

Despite the darkness he found the horse and brought it out. He was already putting on the horse-collar when Léon arrived with a lamp.

'What's going on?'

'It's a mess! Mathilde is giving birth and Delpy's devil knows where! He promised he'd be there, the old cheat! So I woke up Doctor Fraysse. Lift the shafts! And you, back, back!' he directed the horse. 'Go on, back!'

'Do you want me to follow you? Do you want me to tell my mother to come?'

'No, no! What use would that be? Your mother's ill, what could she do! Bye!' He jumped into the cart, and whipped the nag into a gallop towards Doctor Frayssse's house.

The doctor was waiting for him, bundled up to the ears. He held his little black bag tightly, as if it were an object of great value, and the sight of it comforted Pierre-Edouard a little. The old doctor heaved himself painfully into the trap and tucked the cover over his knees.

'Off you go, young man. I'm ready, I'll hold tight.'

Pierre-Edouard lashed the horse's flanks and urged it on; the noise of the iron wheels grinding on the cobblestones echoed through the village. But he was forced to slow down a little when they reached the rough track which climbed up to Coste-Roche.

'Don't tip us out!' cried the old man. 'That wouldn't help. And calm down a bit!'

'Me, calm down? My God! It's almost two hours since I left! Tell me, what do you think . . . Is she in danger?'

'No, no, your little Mathilde is well made, just the right size; the child will come easily, I'm sure of that. But tell me, why didn't you ask her mother to come and stay with you? That's the usual thing.'

'I know! But my mother-in-law had some trouble with her heart a week ago, she's in bed!'

'Oh, I didn't know that. Slow down, I tell you, we've got time.'

'No we haven't! Mathilde is alone up there! All alone, remember that!'

'Of course. But you know, at moments like that you're always alone, even when the room is full of people . . . Well, that's what I feel, anyway. Take care, this curve is deceptive . . . So which would you prefer, a boy or a girl?'

'Oh, I don't care about that! All I want is to help Mathilde! Good God, if you knew . . . Oh, you wouldn't understand!'

'Yes, I know what she is to you, and you to her. You don't need to say it. You only need to look at you two to know that you're like the fingers of a hand; better still, like the eyes in a face; one never moves without the other. Don't go so fast, we'll tip over.'

'I'm frightened,' Pierre-Edouard admitted, without reining in the horse, 'frightened we'll arrive too late. Like I was afraid in the war; I'm scared to death like when they were firing on us, and I'm not ashamed to admit it.'

'I'm glad to hear it; only fools have no fear. But it's no good getting in a panic.'

'I'm not in a panic, that's not my way! But to think of her alone up there . . . Tell me, do you think she'll be in a lot of pain?'

'Maybe, but she's brave, your Mathilde.'

'I know, but that doesn't make it all right. Oh Lord, let us get there in time!'

'We will. And you'll see, she may keep us waiting all night!'

Mathilde called once more for Pierre-Edouard, overwhelmed by pain and tormented by the living thing which she sensed was there, by the lump which was tearing her apart, which she could not expel. But he had been gone an hour already, and anxiety gnawed at her: something must have happened. Perhaps he had tumbled into the ravine, perhaps he had broken his leg again . . .

So she was going to be alone there all night. Nobody would come to help her, no one would rescue her from this tearing pain which seemed to be splitting her in two; she felt herself opening like an over-ripe melon which bursts in the sun.

She repeated her cries, gasping, perspiring, exhausted; but they were growing weaker.

Pierre-Edouard encouraged the horse, urged it up the last slope.

'We're coming, we're coming, we're there,' he spoke gently, as if to his wife.

'Did you think to heat any water?' asked the doctor. 'No, of course not! Well you must do that as soon as we arrive. Damn it, what an idea to live so far away from everyone else! When I think . . .'

'I know, I should be in the village, with my father! Well, we're not, that's all there is to it!'

'I'm not blaming you, it's none of my business. Ah, we've got here anyway!' The old man could just make out the low outline of the cottage.

Pierre-Edouard jumped to the ground, grasped the rug which had protected them and threw it over the horse's back; the poor animal was sweating. He should take it out of the harness and rub it down, but there was no time; he hoped the rug would prevent it from catching a fatal chill, and rushed towards the farmhouse, dragging the doctor with him.

They went in. The house was warm and quiet, an uncanny silence hardly disturbed by the tick of the pendulum and the crackle of the fire. At the back, in the bedroom, by the flickering light of the lamp, they saw the little figure lying still in the middle of the bed, curled up beneath the covers.

Pierre-Edouard ran to her and stopped, petrified by the sight of her wan face, her closed eyes shadowed with fatigue, her pinched nose and pale lips. He did not dare stretch out his hand to touch her forehead, where her hair lay in damp wisps, stuck down by sweat.

'Push,' commanded the doctor. He brushed Mathilde's cheek with his finger, then pulled back the covers.

'Oh my God!' he exclaimed in a low voice.

The baby was there, all plump and shiny with dampness, stretched out calmly on its stomach on top of its mother. Its sticky head nestled almost between her breasts, and in that narrow cleft a little turned-up nose snuffled happily. But the reddish cord still twined beneath the baby's legs and joined it to its mother.

The doctor grasped the child by its feet, and saw the torn hanky which the young woman had managed to tie to the cord low down on her belly. Then he laid the little creature down between Mathilde's legs, and began to attend to her.

'Is she. . . ?' asked Pierre-Edouard weakly. He looked just as pale as she did, and was quite unable to move.

'No, of course not! What do you think! She's sleeping. Well, almost. But I shall have to get her working again,' the doctor explained as he prepared his syringe. 'Go on, go and heat some water, find some clean sheets, make some coffee. Get a move on!'

'Are you sure. . . ?'

'Don't worry, just do what I tell you. And get the cot ready for your son.'

'Oh, it's a boy,' he murmured, as he gradually became aware of his surroundings again. Transfixed by the pallor and stillness of his wife, he hadn't even thought to look at the child when the doctor picked it up.

'Get going, everything's all right. Look, she's already stirring.'

The burden which had weighed him down, almost crushed him, during the preceding two hours now disappeared. He crouched at the head of the bed and whispered into his wife's ear, his face close to hers, speaking a thousand sweet nothings which only she could hear. And his hand stroked her forehead and warmed her icy cheeks.

Mathilde tossed restlessly; her hands reached to her stomach and felt around there, searching; she panicked when she found nothing, and awoke with a start.

'Where is he?' she cried, lifting her head a little.

She saw the two men smiling at her, felt Pierre-Edouard's caresses. Then she sank back onto the pillow, exhausted.

'He's handsome, isn't he?' she sighed.

'Beautiful!'

'I want to see him.'

'See, here he is,' said the doctor, resting the child on her breast. He had finally divided the child from his mother, and a crêpe bandage was tied around its belly. The baby was upset and howled in rage, its tiny fists clenched and beating clumsily on his mother's breasts.

'He cried a little while ago,' she explained in a weak voice. 'I called for you, and he answered. That gave me courage. He was born at a quarter past two. You're not cross that I didn't wait for you?'

'Are you mad? It's my fault,' he apologised.

'I couldn't keep him in, he wanted to come, he pushed. I felt his head with my hands, I wanted to help him. He came, and yelled angrily straight away. I remembered that you're supposed to tie the cord, so I used what I could find and then I laid him on my body and he calmed down. After that I can't remember any more.'

'You worked like a heroine,' the old doctor reassured her. 'I congratulate you. Pierre-Edouard should be proud of you.'

'But I was a bit frightened,' she admitted, 'I thought you'd had an accident. Then I thought I'd be all alone . . . But next time you must be there, all right? Promise?'

'I promise, I'll be there. I was really frightened too.'

Pierre-Edouard marched down towards the village whistling in time with his steps like an artilleryman, despite the frosty night and the aches in his legs.

He was madly happy, ready to stop the first person he saw to relate what had happened that night; to tell of his wife's courage, to describe his fine son, a strong fellow of three kilos! To measure his weight Doctor Fraysse had wrapped him in a napkin and hung him from the hook of the spring balance Mathilde which used to weigh the rabbits and chickens.

Yes, he was ready to hug the whole world! But what a nightmare, what a fright! Now all that was over, finished, there was nothing but joy.

Towards seven o'clock Doctor Delpy had arrived, apologising to his colleague and to Pierre-Edouard, who could no longer feel cross that he hadn't been there during the night. All that was forgotten, banished by the little cries which emanated from the crib, and by Mathilde's smile. After accepting a cup of coffee, Doctor Delpy had taken Doctor Fraysse back down in his car. Pierre-Edouard did not know how to thank him enough, and the old doctor kissed Mathilde as if he were her grandfather, congratulating her.

'It's I who must thank you, my children. This is definitely my last delivery, and what's more I've done nothing! But I am glad that I came to welcome this baby. You've given me the nicest of presents. I'm very, very pleased.'

Shortly after they had left Léon arrived, all worried, not knowing what he was going to find. He knocked discreetly on the half-door with the metal claw which had replaced his left hand six months since.

What a pleasure to open the door to him, to drag him into the bedroom, to invite him to admire the mother and baby! He was going to be the godfather of this child; just as Louise had earlier chosen Pierre-Edouard in place of Félix's grandfather, Pierre-Edouard and Mathilde had asked Léon and his mother to be godparents to their son. Jean-Edouard would doubtless have refused anyway.

Then Léon had gone back down with his horse; once Pierre-Edouard had emerged from his trance he had taken it out of its harness, led it into the stable, and rubbed it down vigorously to warm its blood and dry the lather of sweat which had frozen in a hard layer on its coat.

Pierre-Edouard reached the village at about eleven o'clock, and realised straight away that Léon had announced the good news. He thanked all the people who congratulated him, bought a round of drinks for three or four friends, then marched toward the Mairie.

# 26

PIERRE-EDOUARD had not spoken to his father for several months. This was not out of rancour or bitterness; he simply had nothing to say to him. But the breach did not worry him, and he was ready to forget all about it on condition that his father recognised once and for all that he was no longer a little boy . . .

Anyway, as time passed he felt more inclined to smile at his father's attitude, the image he had of his role as head of the family. All that was so outdated, and so confounded by the paths chosen by his own children, that it was almost laughable.

Just one thing prevented Pierre-Edouard from contacting his parents again: their hostility to Mathilde. He would not accept that, he would not forgive that, and nothing could be done so long as his father and mother refused to recognise her as a full member of the Vialhe family.

But these thoughts did not oppress him, that morning of 6 January, and he was still whistling as he walked into the Mairie. 'Wow, you're here already?' he said, a little surprised to see his father.

He had thought he would find the secretary, then remembered that it was Tuesday, and the teacher would be busy with the children.

'Does that surprise you? I am the mayor, aren't I?'

'I know. Well, here I am, I expect you've heard the news. You know why I'm here?'

'I've been told. Anyway, it seems you made so much noise last night that the whole village heard the news . . . The whole village apart from us.'

'It's not my fault you live a long way from the main square.'

'All the same, you could have come and fetched your mother . . .'

'I didn't think of that,' he admitted.

And it was true, the idea had never even occurred to him. He took out his pipe and filled it, hoping that his father would not make a scene about a little thing like that. Besides, what would he have gained by bringing his mother to Mathilde's bedside? Nothing, except possibly a long list of complaints and bitter comments.

'Well, one could say that you were at fault . . .'

'Okay, if that makes you happy,' he said between puffs.

His father shrugged his shoulders, looked down at the register, grasped his pen and dipped it carefully into the ink.

'Let's get on; notify me about this child,' he said, starting to write: 'Today, 6 January 1920 at . . . at what time?'

'Quarter past two,' said Pierre-Edouard, and continued: 'Jacques Pierre Léon Vialhe was born.'

'Bloody hell!' said his father. He laid down the pen and briskly pushed the register away. 'Hell and damnation! You're renouncing your ancestors now, eh?'

'Which ancestors?'

'Dammit! Your great-great-grandfather was called Edouard Benjamin, your great-grandfather was Mathieu Edouard, your grandfather was Edouard, your father Jean-Edouard, and you're Pierre-Edouard, and you want to baptise him Jacques Pierre Léon! Are you ashamed of the Edouards? Huh, I've seen it all, now! And calling him Léon, like a Dupeuch!'

'So what? You don't want me to call him Mathilde, do you? He's as much Dupeuch as he is Vialhe! And it's just too bad if you don't like it!'

'No, I don't like it! A Vialhe son should be called Edouard!'

'You're beginning to annoy me with your Edouards. He'll be called Jacques Pierre Léon, and that's that, dammit, that's it! And if you don't want to write it, I'll wait till the secretary is here!'

He found the whole scene grotesque, all the more so because none of it was intentional. It had not occurred to him to christen his son Edouard, simply because his second name was rarely used now: Mathilde simply called him Pierre. And perhaps it was a subconscious decision too, because Edouard signified first and foremost his father, with his impossible character, his moods and his stubbornness.

'Well, it wouldn't cost you much to add Edouard!' Jean-Edouard persisted.

'And why should I do that? For what reason? The Edouards, all the Edouards, were born down there, at your place, in the house where I was born! They were born at home, under their own roof, on their own property! But this one, my son, was born all alone on the edge of the parish, because of your damned stupidity – yes, your stupidity! And if his mother had died, it would have been because of you! So don't give me your Edouard Vialhes; all they're good for is throwing children out of the house, and what's more they don't even bother to look after their land properly! The Edouards are finished! So you write: Jacques Pierre Léon!'

'You little bastard,' his father swore, 'you're getting rid of Edouard and putting Pierre instead of it, eh? That's it, isn't it?'

'Exactly!' Pierre-Edouard agreed, without thinking what he was saying, 'you've got it right! I'm doing that so that all my descendants will remember it, so that they'll know that you have to wait for a Pierre to come along before anything changes in this damned family!'

'Very well,' Jean-Edouard spoke quietly, and picked up the pen again: 'you can go on behaving like an idiot, but you'll do it alone. I've heard enough.'

Pierre-Edouard looked at him and noticed how he had aged. He seemed to have shrunk, and his hand trembled as he formed the letters.

'Oh, what the hell!' he recovered his previous euphoria suddenly, and began to laugh. 'Add Edouard, if it makes you happy. It's all nonsense anyway! Wait! After Léon, first add Libéral, then Edouard last of all. Perhaps the one will calm the other down. There: Jacques Pierre Léon Libéral Edouard Vialhe – and if the Edouards raise their ugly heads after all that lot, I'll be very surprised!'

'Don't be so full of yourself,' said his father, as he carefully applied the blotting-paper to the page in the register. 'Don't think you're so wonderful, or so clever. We'll see what you manage to do, you and your kids . . . We'll talk about it again some time . . . If they're as bloody-minded as you and your sisters, they'll lead you a merry dance. And when that happens I shall have a good laugh, believe you me!'

Pierre-Edouard skilfully manipulated his hoe to raise a little mound of earth around the young green shoot; then he looked behind him and thought once again that he had set himself an impossible task, far too great. He had overestimated his strength, and that of Mathilde.

However willing and strong, she could not work at his pace. But she was determined, got down to work and always appeared slightly apologetic that she could not keep up with him. And he, anxious and distressed to see her straining and exhausting herself, tried to relieve her by moving even faster; by earthing up the greatest number of tobacco plants as quickly as possible, doing the work of two men all by himself.

Despite that, the ridging of this field seemed to last an eternity; it ate up all their time and forced them to work fifteen hours a day. For tobacco was not the only crop which needed attention; there was maize too, potatoes, beets and all the other vegetables.

Added to that there were the animals to care for; feeding the two sows, the hens, ducks and rabbits, watching the eight ewes and their lambs; and for Mathilde there were the demands made by the baby, nursing it, washing its nappies, mending and preparing the meals. Pierre-Edouard was now regretting starting to grow tobacco.

As a former soldier with a war wound, he had obtained permission to plant 3,800 seedlings; he had thought he could manage that many. That way they would improve their finances and relieve the worry caused by lack of money and rising prices. Tobacco growing brought a good return, but what a drudgery it was!

First of all he had prepared a bed of good fertile earth beside the barn, where the spring sunshine warmed it; he had to sieve it and lightly enrich it with horse manure. Then he had sown the minute seeds — he had been told that a gramme weight held 12,000 of them — which he had to mix with ash to spread them at the correct density.

Then came the supervision of the seed bed; watering it, protecting it from night frosts, the first thinning of the seedlings. Later he had meticulously divided the field into strips with string and had transplanted 3,800 plants: no more, no less, for the inspector of the tobacco department was not joking when he said he inspected the plantations rigorously. The official measure was 38,000 plants to the hectare; he was cultivating a thousand square metres, so he must have 3,800 plants.

Now that the stems had reached fifteen centimetres he had to earth them up, to make them stronger and promote the development of ancillary roots.

What was worrying Pierre-Edouard was all the other work this crop would require. It was high time he started on the first thinning, cutting back the small, worthless leaves which would weaken the plant. After this first tidying-up came the pruning, during which he had to choose the seven best leaves and cut off all the rest. Then followed the pollarding, which severed the main stalk, the one carrying the flower; finally, when the leaves measured twenty centimetres, it was necessary to disbud the whole plant once more. And each of these painstaking processes had to be repeated for 3,800 plants . . .

Later, during the winter, when the tobacco was quite dry, there were other tasks which were physically less demanding because they could be carried out indoors, but still it was slow, laborious work. He had to grade the leaves by size, colour and quality, tie them into bundles of twenty-five leaves each, and finally into bales of a hundred bundles. Then, and only then, would he and Mathilde get any reward for their trouble, would at last be paid for their broken backs, aching kidneys, their hands stained yellow and stinking from handling 26,600 leaves.

He turned once more to look at Mathilde. She was far behind him but kept on doggedly, bent over the soil, bowed down with weariness and the heat. So he called to her: 'Hey, time's up!' although the sun gave the lie to this.

She straightened up, and it was pitiful to see her face so red, running with perspiration. Like him, she looked up at the sun and shook her head.

'No,' she said, wiping her forehead, 'I've still got some time to go. Anyway, he's not crying.'

'Time's up,' he insisted, walking towards her. 'Go on, go and sit over there, go and feed him. Go and rest.'

'But there's no need!'

'Don't argue,' he replied, taking her hoe. 'You're working too hard, you'll lose your milk.'

'I'm no weakling! I've got milk and your greedy son knows it! How do you think he puts on so much weight, by feeding on air? Everyone takes him for ten months old, and he's only six months!'

He took her arm and drew her to the edge of the field, towards the huge chestnut tree which sheltered the baby. His basket hung from the low branches of the tree and there he lay, gazing at the shimmering leaves, entranced to see them move in the wind, lulled by his own movements as they swayed the light crib.

'You see how good he is!' she said, bending over him. The baby, happy to see his mother again, wriggled; he trembled with happiness and blew several large bubbles.

'Now that you're here, stay here,' he said. 'You should rest, you're doing too much; let the tobacco go to the devil!'

'You won't say that when it affects our income!'

'Oh, money! No, I've taken on too much for us two. Years ago my father grew tobacco, but there were at least five or six of us to take care of it! Everyone joined in, and the work got done! Whereas here . . .'

'And that's why you've made me sit down!'

He looked at her, delighted to see her still so petite, so young. She had not lost her figure through the pregnancy; she was good enough to eat, like a bunch of cherries.

'Don't argue,' he said, pointing to the baby. 'He needs you and your milk, and he comes before the tobacco, and before any other work too!'

'I'm not made of glass! Years ago my mother had to do a man's work and . . .'

'Yes, I know; mine too, years ago. But that was a long time ago and now it's different. I don't want you to look like your mother – nor like mine, for that matter. Go on, rest a bit, and if I see you out in the field before half an hour is up there'll be trouble.'

'You'll beat me up, eh?' she teased.

'Of course,' he assured her as he walked back to his work. 'That's the only tradition which should be preserved.'


Pierre-Edouard re-counted the 725 francs which he had just received from the sale of six lambs. The animals were really not bad looking, and he had managed to dispose of his lot quite well. He would certainly have gained more by keeping them three or four weeks longer, but it was September and the acorns were dropping: he had no way of controlling the ewes and lambs. As soon as the barn door was opened the animals tried to escape into the woods to stuff themselves with acorns; they devised a multitude of tricks to escape Mathilde's watchful eye, to dash over to the oak-wood and indulge themselves. A small quantity of acorns did them no harm, but too large a dose could poison them as surely as a handful of arsenic. That was why he had just sold six of the ten lambs his ewes had produced; the other four were ewe-lambs, which he wanted to keep to increase his flock.

He came out of the bar where the buyer had been dealing with his customers, and looked around for Mathilde. She should be at the other end of the square, with the women who were selling their chickens and vegetables. Mathilde had nothing to sell this morning, but he would bet she was over there anyway, showing off her son to a bevy of soft-hearted housewives.

He walked up between the lines where the calves were lowing, and noticed how few there were. Really, the market was nothing like it had been in days gone by! On the other side, the cows were just as scarce. Only Léon and one of his colleagues had brought in some heifers, but buyers were few and far between.

Pierre-Edouard greeted and talked to the men he knew as he made his way to the lot of animals offered for sale by his brother-in-law.

'Well, you old devil, still looking for a sucker?'

'I don't want to talk about that,' retorted Léon, giving him a friendly cuff. 'It's a real misery, nobody's buying!'

'Are you surprised? With the prices you're asking?'

'It's not that, it's like this everywhere. You'd think the whole world was as mad as that poor fellow, who is president, Deschanel.'

'Is it true he's resigned?' Pierre-Edouard enquired. He didn't come down to the village very often, and didn't take a newspaper.

'You're a bit behind the times! That was a week ago! Wait, it was market day at Seilhac, the twenty-first, that was it. Huh, that'll show the cowards, they should have elected Clemenceau! My God, when I think that they preferred that simpleton to him! It was incredible! Can you wonder that things aren't going well?'

Pierre-Edouard agreed. He didn't take much interest in politics, but he shared his brother-in-law's sense of outrage. Clemenceau, Foch, Joffre, Pétain, those were real men. But the others, all the others – what a pack of good-for-nothing opportunists!

'Have you seen your godson?' he asked, as he offered his tobacco-pouch.

'Yes,' smiled Léon. 'Beautiful, isn't he? A sturdy boy! You know, my colleague here told me he looks like me!' he added, pink with pride.

'Now that has upset me!' exclaimed Pierre-Edouard with a laugh. 'That's all we need! One of you is quite enough in this area!'

Still laughing, he turned suddenly, for someone had just tugged his sleeve.

'Well, well, Jeantout, what brings you here?'

'Your father wants to see you.'

'My father?' he mumbled. 'What does my father want me for? . . . Answer me, what for!' he insisted, noticing now the old man's haggard expression. 'What's happened?'

'It's your mother . . .'

'What about my mother?'

'Go home, go!'

'No, you explain,' ordered Pierre-Edouard, suddenly anxious, 'I wasn't expecting – What's the matter with my mother?'

'She's dead.'

'Oh my God!' he cried out, quite stunned by the news. 'But how can that be? Mathilde saw her only this week!'

'They had to take her down to Brive last night, she had perimonitis . . .'

'Peritonitis. And?'

'Well, it was too late . . . She died in the night. They've just brought her back to your place.'

He nodded to show that he understood. He felt infinitely sad, sad enough to cry. But the tears had been left behind, somewhere at the front; the well had run dry after the death of too many comrades.

In a flash he saw his mother again. Not the old embittered woman of the final years, but as she was earlier, in the good times, when the whole family sat around the dining table every evening, with Louise teasing and joking, Berthe telling tales and himself laughing in his corner. He saw her young again, gentle and attentive, and was sorry that it was too late to tell her that he loved her very much, despite everything; that Louise and Berthe loved her dearly as well, that it wasn't her fault that they had all three left home. It wasn't anything to do with her, she wasn't responsible for the Vialhe character, she was only the intermediary; they had inherited it from their father.

'I'll go there. But I must tell Mathilde.'

He moved through the crowd, which parted for him in silence, for the news had flown from mouth to mouth. Already everyone knew that Jean-Edouard Vialhe was now a widower, and alone . . .

They handed over little Jacques to his godfather and climbed the main street, walking towards the house which they were going to enter for the first time since their marriage. But without happiness or rejoicing, only in sadness and affliction.


'There she is,' said Jean-Edouard, opening the door to the bedroom. He was crying, silently, discreetly, almost as if he were ashamed of it.

Marguerite looked younger; her severely lined face was smoother, only the finer wrinkles etched by her smile remained. She was wearing an old nightdress, dragged on hastily by some nurse. She looked pitiful lying there, all dishevelled, her arms spread out, her feet bare.

'Leave us, Father,' said Mathilde, as soon as she could gather her thoughts. 'Leave us, we'll take care of her. I'll take care of her,' she repeated. 'It's my job.'

And she steered him towards the door, gently, leading him to the settle where she made him sit down.

'You're not cold, are you? Shall I warm you up a bit of coffee?'

He shook his head and fixed his gaze on the dead fire. He did not move when she furtively took out her hanky to wipe the tears that formed droplets at the end of his white moustache. Then, softly and silently, she returned to the bedroom.

'Pierre, go and fetch Jeantout's wife, she'll help me. Then after that you can be with your father.'

'No, there's no need for Jeantout's wife. I've seen more of death than you'll ever see. Come on, you help me; we'll dress her in her

314

Sunday best. The clothes used to be in here,' he said, as he opened the big wardrobe.

They were still there.

For four days Pierre-Edouard and Mathilde took over the management of the house and the stock, received the neighbours and distant cousins, and organised the nightly vigil.

On the first morning, as soon as they had dressed the corpse, prepared the bedchamber, covered the mirrors and tidied the house, Pierre-Edouard ran to the post office and sent a telegram to Louise. He could not tell Berthe, for he had no address.

Louise arrived by train the following morning. She was so deep in the grip of sorrow that she could scarcely draw breath, yet as she walked across the village her heart softened, for at each step she rediscovered the world of her youth; the church square which had changed so little, the inn where once Octave . . . the main street where the hens pecked about as always, and the ducks still dabbled in the pools of liquid which flowed out of the dung heaps.

She saw several women she knew by name, but she did not stop. Who would recognise her? She had left twelve years ago! And yet, as soon as she passed, the whispers and stifled exclamations burst forth:

'Louise is back! Yes, yes, we recognised her easily! She's a lady now. She's well-dressed and all that, but you can tell, it's still Louise Vialhe! You see, she's not a bad girl after all . . .'

'You should have brought Félix.' Pierre-Edouard was rather reproachful.

'No, he's had enough of death for his age. And after all, he didn't know her,' whispered Louise.

They were both at their mother's bedside, but they still kept on talking in low voices. They had so much to say to each other!

'And how is my Félix?'

'Very well. And your son?'

'Oh, him; nothing worries him! You'll see, he's a true Vialhe. He's with my mother-in-law; I'll take you there.'

'And your wife?'

'She's resting at her mother's home too, she wanted to take the whole of the night vigil.'

'When I think that it's little Mathilde! She was just a kid when I left.'

'Well, yes . . .'

'So, did you manage to come to some arrangement with Father?'

'No, you know what he's like. He didn't want to see Mathilde, so that was it!'

'Poor old man, he's completely lost. I don't even know if he recognised me when I kissed him just now.'

'Of course he did, don't let it worry you. I'm sure he's very pleased that you've come back. But he won't say so . . . and I'm sure he would have loved to see Berthe again too, but I couldn't tell her; I don't know where she is, the tearaway! I would have loved her to have been here, for all three of us to be together . . .'

'I told her.'

'You know where she's staying? How the devil – ?'

'We write from time to time. She began it, during the war.'

'Oh yes,' he remembered, 'I gave her your address when I left here. Do you think she'll come?'

'I don't know, but at least she's been told. She knows that mother has gone.'


That same evening, soon after the train had passed, the door of the Vialhes' house was pushed open, but no one recognised Berthe.

Even Pierre-Edouard wondered for a minute who the beautiful young lady could be, dressed in the latest city fashions, with an elegant feathered hat perched on her short blonde hair, her face delicately made up and her hands fine. She walked without hesitation towards the bent old man by the fireside, and leant over him.

Jean-Edouard recoiled instinctively, then hesitated and examined her face steadily, narrowing his reddened eyes.

'Well, well,' he said, 'if your mother could see you!'

But he allowed her to kiss him, and they all saw him grasp his daughter's shoulders in return.


'There,' said Pierre-Edouard, the day after the funeral, 'everything's sorted out, it's all tidy. I've asked Ma Coste, and if you like she'll come in each day to make your supper and do the housework.'

He held Mathilde close to him, and little Jacques stretched out from her arms and babbled, waving his tiny fists at the fire.

'So you're leaving again, you too, like your sisters . . .' murmured Jean-Edouard.

He said it without bitterness; his tone of voice was not reproachful. He was stating a fact. As he had been forced to state that Louise

316

and Berthe were free to act as they saw fit, live as they pleased, with whomsoever they wished.

'Times have changed,' he said, following this train of thought. 'So you're going back up there, to Coste-Roche? All right . . .'

He hesitated and cleared his throat. 'I just want to say, your wife, now I know her – she's a good daughter . . .'

He could not bring himself to speak to Mathilde, his voice failed him. He had reiterated for far too long that his daughter-in-law was worthless to be able to change from one day to the next, and speak to her without constraint. Even now he could not express, even to his son, all that he wished to say. He tried to start a conversation, but half-heartedly, knowing that he was avoiding an argument.

'If you wanted,' he tried again, 'if you wanted . . . Now, you could stay here, in this house, on our land . . .'

'I know, but we won't be doing that.'

'Well, I'm sure . . .'

'Don't think that we hold it against you, that's not it at all. Let bygones be bygones – that's how I see it, anyway, and Mathilde too.'

'But you're leaving all the same?'

'Yes, we're leaving.'

Pierre-Edouard sensed that his father was within a hair's breadth of giving in, that he was weakening, almost broken; it would take very little to defeat him, to extract all the concessions he could demand and to push him into the abyss of despair. But that would be to humiliate him, to trample on his pride. That pride which still held him back, prevented him from saying: 'I would like you to stay; I ask it of you. I need you, your wife, your child too; please stay. From now on you are head of the family.' It would have been easy at that moment to crush the old man with the tear-filled eyes forever . . .

Pierre-Edouard looked at his father, saw that he was beaten and miserable, took pity on him and tried to explain.

'You must understand – I know we could move in here now, right away. But if we did that, sooner or later you would think that we'd taken advantage of you, when . . . Well, of mother's death, of the whole situation, you see. That we imposed the decision on you and made use of your . . . of your pain . . .'

Jean-Edouard nodded his head slowly and spat into the fire. 'Yes, you know me well now,' he admitted at last. 'Perhaps better than I thought . . . You're right to want to go. But if one day – well, we'll see, all right?'

'That's right,' murmured Pierre-Edouard, as he gently pulled Mathilde to him. 'One day perhaps, later . . . We'll have to leave it a bit, let time decide, as always . . .'

Jean-Edouard did not move as the door closed behind them.

# Applewood

A Mes Enfants

La plénitude des arbres séculaires émanait de leur masse, mais l'effort par quoi sortaient de leurs énormes troncs les branches tordues, l'épanouissement en feuilles sombres de ce bois, si vieux et si lourd qu'il semblait s'enfoncer dans la terre et non s'en arracher, imposaient à la fois l'idée d'une volonté et d'une métamorphose sans fin.

André Malraux
*Les Noyers de l'Altenburg*

The richness of the century-old trees emanated from their size, but the energy of the twisted branches springing from the enormous trunks, the dark leaves spreading from the wood, so old and so heavy that it seemed to be burrowing into the ground rather than rising from it, imposed at the same time the idea of ceaseless strength and growth.

André Malraux
*The Walnut Trees of Altenburg*

# PART ONE

*Saint-Libéral-sur-Diamond*

# 1

THEY ran quickly and silently, darting like the agile lizard which passes in a grey blur across a sunny old wall. The grass rustled against their bare legs, and their tousled hair captured occasional petals from the drift falling from the plum and cherry trees across the whole countryside. Warblers, stonechats and dunnocks were chirruping from each tiny bush, announcing the spring on every side; they sang on the peaks and hillsides and in the woods which surrounded the village of Saint-Libéral. The oft-repeated call of the cuckoo echoed the monotonous chant of the hoopoe. As far as the eye could see the fruit trees shook their haloes, like angels preparing for a wedding. The air smelled of pollen, honey and fertile, fresh earth.

The two children jumped nimbly over the Diamond. The white pebbles on the bed of the stream had been washed and rewashed by the winter floods and were now revealed beneath the spring cascades of water so pure, so limpid, that it seemed almost invisible.

They cut across a damp pasture, already bright with buttercups reflecting the sun, with the purple tears of wild orchids and the white tracery of Queen Anne's Lace. An angry blackbird shot out of the dark bushes as they slipped through a hedge and crept along the edge of a meadow. They lay on their stomachs among the vetch and then rose slowly to their elbows and watched, their hearts thumping.

The men were working about three hundred metres away; a large group of them were busy around a tall metal derrick.

'You'll see, they're going to lift it,' whispered the older boy.

'I know,' cut in his brother.

And down below, suspended from a rope hauled by the workers, rose a tall column of white concrete, straight and slender as a Lombardy poplar – magnificent! It joined the others which were already fixed in concrete and rose in a perfectly straight line, scaling the heights and plunging into the ravines, disappearing out of sight. These were the advance guard of the approaching electricity line which would soon throw light into the houses of Saint-Libéral.

The work had started in October 1929, but the site had been deserted all winter. First of all the holes meant for the pylons had filled with water as fast as they were dug out, and then a period of bitter frost prevented any concreting, for each pole had to be solidly embedded and immovable.

'Did you see, they've put on the saucers,' remarked the younger boy.

The two lads had watched over the work impatiently as it slowly advanced. They made sure they came twice a week, on Sunday afternoons and on Thursdays; it was now Thursday 24 April 1930.

'They're beautiful,' agreed the older one, gazing at the four glass insulators which decorated the top of a pylon nearby. It had been put up a week ago, there in the middle of the meadow, only fifteen paces from them.

'Bet you I can knock one off,' whispered the little one.

Jacques Vialhe turned quickly and gave his brother a cuff.

'You're mad, don't do it!'

'Bet you!'

'No, come away! Anyway, we must go and look after the animals.'

They had left them up on Combes-Nègres, four hundred metres away. In theory the cows would not leave the pasture, too happy enjoying the freshly growing grass, but you never knew with them! If old Pig left to go exploring, for example, it would be enough to set the whole herd off after her. Jacques felt worried; he imagined the Limousin cows spreading out into the fields, vineyards and orchards which adjoined Combes-Nègres, and the inevitable punishment which would result from this lack of care. He was ten years old and would be held responsible. But just at the moment, the cows' behaviour worried him less than his brother's.

Paul was two years younger than him, but almost as tall and strong. He was driven primarily by a spirit of audacity, of sheer nerve which bordered on madness. For him life had no real meaning, was not worth living, unless he could enliven it by doing everything which the grown-ups tried to proscribe. Such as, among other things, going secretly one night to the public wash-house and diving in to pull out the plug, just to enjoy the cries of the housewives, faced with a huge empty basin and piles of dirty linen next morning. Or again – this impious deed had taken place two weeks ago – taking advantage of his role as altarboy to climb into the bell tower on Maundy Thursday and wrap rags and old sacks round the clapper of the big bell; he experienced several minutes of intense pleasure as he watched the consternation of the faithful worshippers on Easter morning, when, instead of the cheerful call of the great bell in the Gloria, they heard only the muffled rumbling of bronze in bandages!

Of course these little jokes attracted paternal retribution, that was only fair. But it was less fair that the blows fell indiscriminately; Paul had all the outrageous ideas and carried them out, but Jacques always shared the beating which followed.

To be quite frank he readily admitted that, although Paul was the inventor and instigator of the pranks, he himself was the craftsman; without the string which he had given Paul, the rags and sack would never have stayed around the clapper of the big bell . . .

Though an accomplice, Jacques, unlike his brother, was always aware of the enormity of the crimes committed, and above all of the inevitable consequences. So he did his utmost to dissuade Paul. It was a waste of time! His brother, crouching in the vetch, was already stretching out his catapult in the direction of the four insulators which challenged them.

'Don't be a fool!' begged Jacques, without also, as he should have done, grabbing Paul's arm. The pebble hummed away, just missed the insulator, bounced off the concrete and shot into the sky.

'Amateur!' cried Jacques.

This was not true, for no one could teach Paul anything about catapults.

'Amateur yourself! The pebble was no good,' explained the marksman. He searched his pockets and smiled as his fingers met a fine round stone, the size of a pigeon's egg.

'I could blow it up with the first shot!' said Jacques, fingering the handle of his weapon, which hung around his neck.

Once more, Paul envied his brother's magnificent catapult. It was a superb tool: the boxwood fork had a perfect angle of curvature – not any old V-shaped fork, but two slender branches moulded into a perfect half oval. The bands fixed to them were of white rubber, easy to pull but with incredible strength and power. It was Uncle Léon, Jacques' godfather, who had given him this little marvel, with strict instructions not to use it for any mischief . . .

Jacques now felt in his own pockets, and suddenly in his palm he held a shiny steel marble.

'Oooh,' breathed Paul, 'where's that from?'

'My godfather. He gave me a dozen of them, they're ball bearings.'

'Give me one, just one!'

'Uh, uh,' replied Jacques, as he slid the projectile into the leather pouch of his catapult. He crouched, tensed his arm, and closed his left eye. The dry crack of the elastic was almost overtaken by the shattering noise as the insulator exploded under the impact; lumps of glass scattered over several metres. It was a fine shot!

'Did you see that?' said Jacques, beginning to smile. But he was already gripped with panic. What stupidity, he thought. 'Come on, we'd better get going,' he said briskly.

'Let me shoot!' protested Paul. 'Look, I'm aiming for the third one.' And that insulator vanished into thin air just like the other. 'And I haven't even got ball bearings! Never mind, I can still bust a few things . . . '

'Let's go!' insisted Jacques. 'The cows will have gone off somewhere!'

Paul gazed covetously at the untouched insulators. They were so tempting!

'Okay,' he sighed, 'but we'll come back, eh?'

'You must be mad! When our parents find out . . . '

'And how will they know, we're not the only ones who can shoot!'

Jacques shrugged his shoulders; that was his brother's reasoning! Of course other kids in the village had catapults, and used them in the same way – and at the same targets, if they got the chance – but those lucky devils had parents who were blind, easy to deceive, who believed the most shameless lies. That was by no means the case for them, the sons of Pierre-Edouard and Mathilde Vialhe. Their parents knew everything, and straight away. They were not fooled by any lies or subterfuges. They were in charge.

Jean-Edouard Vialhe sat in the sun in front of the house, and smiled as he watched the little girl holding out her plump hands towards him. Mad with impatience, she moved from one side to the other, clinging to his trousers, clambering on his clogs, and trying desperately to get hold of the object he was making for her; her big eyes shone with desire and wonder.

'Give it to me, Pépé, give it to me!' the little one repeated.

She came up to his knee, was covered in delightful dimples, and was amazingly precocious. Mauricette was five years old and understood perfectly how to control the whole household. Obstinate and fiery as a true Vialhe, but quiet and coaxing like her mother, she got what she wanted from her elder brothers, Jacques and Paul, who were always kind to her and indulged her every whim.

'God knows how those rascals got the devilment in them,' thought Jean-Edouard, 'especially the second one! It's incredible what they dream up, those kids! And it's not that they haven't been properly brought up!'

He smiled as he thought how that did not prevent the two young imps from adding to their escapades and adventures; the deeds were reprehensible, of course, but they had the gift of making you laugh until you cried.

He had decided right from the start never to intervene in the organisation of the farm or the conduct of the family. He had not taken this decision easily or happily, but he had kept to it for eight years. Nor did he regret it: it was better so, more sensible and peaceful. He was respected as the older man and he had never, in all the eight years, experienced the least lack of due deference. As for everything else – his authority, the management of the farm and the family – he had willingly given that up once and for all in favour of his son, for he understood that this was the only way to remain on good terms with him.

This abdication had been painful, and during the years following the death of his wife he had struggled to delay the inevitable decision. For two years, alone on the farm, he had tried to get to grips with things, to accustom himself to the miserable loneliness, to his own unhappiness, his weakness even. For he could see how everything was going downhill; first of all the animals, but above all the land, which he became less and less able to tend alone. And when his neighbours, like Jeantout and Gaston, had kindly come to help him, he had felt mortified each time, for everyone knew that his own son Pierre-Edouard was up there on his miserable steading at Coste-Roche, just waiting for the word to return and take his place as head of the family.

Yes, Pierre-Edouard was just waiting for one word: 'Come.' But it still remained to be spoken, and for that Jean-Edouard had to climb up to the cottage and say: 'I will step down. From now on, you are the boss.'

How simple that seemed in hindsight, now that everything had returned to normal, eight years later! But at the time it was an admission that he was stepping aside to let his son take over, that he accepted almost all Pierre's past opinions; that he would forget all their years of quarrelling, his son's snide comments, the fact that he took his sisters' side, and finally his marriage. He had condemned this union from the start, when Pierre-Edouard returned from that terrible war at the end of 1918, and presented them with a *fait accompli* by introducing Mathilde.

It had not been easy to forget all that, or to admit to himself that not all the faults had been on Pierre-Edouard's side: that he himself and his obstinacy had contributed to the sad situation; he, one of the most able farmers in the village, had neglected his land and let his farm go to ruin, simply because he had quarrelled with his eldest son.

Just as he had fallen out with his two daughters! They, unlike Pierre-Edouard, had left the Corrèze and never returned.

All this had held him back, for two years, from going to see his son. At first he had hoped that Pierre-Edouard would return of his own accord, and that he would gradually let him take the reins, discreetly, as the years passed. But that did not allow for the Vialhe character. Pierre-Edouard was too proud, and too wise, to ask anything of his father. So, after two years of waiting and reflecting in solitude, it was he who had to take the first step.

The announcement of the expected birth of a second child, Paul, had made up his mind; even stimulated him. He had harnessed the horse and driven it up to Coste-Roche, on the slope leading to the plateau, on the edge of the parish. Then, once he had taken that first step, it all seemed plain and simple, and they talked without embarrassment or constraint.

'I know you're expecting another child; that's good, it's very good. But this one should be born at home, under our roof – well, your roof, if you prefer . . . '

Jacques, the eldest of the Vialhe grandchildren, had seen the light of day here, in this pitiful hovel where the young family were living.

'You want it to be born at our place, is that what you're saying?' Pierre-Edouard needed to get it clear.

'Yes, you come back. You can see very well that I'm just struggling along since your dear mother died. You've seen the fields . . . '

'Yes, I have, they're dreadful, they need a bit of effort put into them . . . '

A few years earlier a comment like that would have made his blood boil, but now he just shrugged his shoulders.

'No, there's no lack of effort, but at sixty-two, however hard I work it's not worth a quarter of what you could do. You're young, and so's your wife; that's what it needs. I can't cope with it any more. So there it is; come back, set up home there. And don't worry, I know what you're like, I won't give you any excuse to grumble about me. When you're living there you can do as you think fit with the land and the animals, just whenever and however you think best. It won't be my business any more . . . '

He had kept his word. It had not been easy, and he had often felt the urge to interfere with his son's ideas and ways of doing things. But he had always managed to remain silent, to keep the ironic and bitter comments to himself although they were on the tip of his tongue. It was much better like that. Besides, he had been forced to recognise that Pierre-Edouard was an excellent farmer and a good son, Mathilde the best of daughters-in-law, and the three grand-children adorable rascals.

However, even with them he had to adjust to a new sort of relationship. In his time, children would never have dared to be so familiar with their parents, and certainly not with their grand-parents, as to address them as 'tu'. But nowadays the young ones did not say 'father', they said 'papa'. The word grandfather meant nothing to them, replaced by the strange-sounding Pépé! As for the formal 'vous', that was reserved for strangers, outside the family.

'Now, Pépé, give it to me, yes!' insisted the little girl, pulling at his waistcoat.

'I'll give it to you in exchange for a smacker,' he said, turning his cheek towards her.

She placed a wet kiss on his rough cheek, and wrinkled her nose. 'You prickle, you should shave off those scratches,' she said, rubbing her tiny forefinger over her little pink chin with its smiling dimple. 'Go on, give it to me, you promised!'

He held out the willow basket which he had just woven, and was touched to see her so happy with such a simple gift. She slipped her arm jauntily through the handle of bent chestnut twigs and trotted happily into the house.

Pierre-Edouard glanced in the direction of Paul, who was greedily eating his soup. Then he looked at Mathilde, sitting opposite him, and smiled at her discreetly; she responded by winking in agreement.

'Why have you been playing about with the reaper?' he asked his sons.

They lowered their noses to their plates and contemplated the globules of fat on the clear soup with great interest. They were amazed that their father was so quickly aware of their activities. It was Paul, yet again, who had had the absurd idea to check whether the reaper was equipped with any bearings which could be extracted to provide some fine missiles for their catapults. Their efforts had been in vain: the ball bearings were completely inaccessible. But who the devil could have seen them when, having returned from their expedition to the building site and brought the cows back home, the two of them had slipped into the barn? Their parents? Surely not; at the time when Paul was attacking the impenetrable gearing with a hammer, they were planting potatoes on the Meeting Field, up on the plateau, more than a kilometre away! Who could it be then? Pépé? No, he was busy with the animals and certainly would not have heard anything; he had grown a little deaf in his old age. Mauricette?

She had not left her grandfather's side, she was so delighted to help him bed down the animals by proudly carrying a handful of straw in her brand-new basket.

'Well?' Pierre-Edouard asked again, and wrinkled his brow quizzically. 'What did you want with the reaper, eh?'

'Oh, nothing!' Jacques assured him.

'No, nothing!' his brother confirmed.

'Well, why were you messing about with it then – just for fun? Don't you know that's dangerous? If the cutter falls on your head it'll crush you! I've already told you that.'

'And how do you know that we touched it?' Paul ventured to ask; his father's gift for being everywhere simultaneously filled him with admiration.

'I know, that's enough, and Maman knows too.'

'Did you see us?' Jacques had a turn at trying to find out.

'Just as if we were there!' his mother assured him, ruffling his hair. 'Go on with you,' she responded to his air of amazement, 'it's not so difficult. Look at your nails, you mucky pups, they're black with oil!'

'Damn!' groaned Paul, sorry now that he had put so much effort into washing his hands. Really, if that was the outcome it was enough to put you off soap and water for life! He looked at his fingers; of course, they should have cleaned their nails as well! Annoyed, he made a note to watch out for tell-tale signs like that the next time he went in search of ball bearings.

'Guess what,' Jacques told them, 'Godfather came by just now, he said he wanted to see you both at his place this evening.'

'Great!' cried Paul, 'we're going to Uncle Léon's.'

'Oh no you're not,' interrupted his mother, 'you're going to bed. Anyway, he said he wanted to see us two; that's the two of us, Papa and me.'

'And why doesn't Uncle Léon ever come to our house?' asked Paul.

'Don't you bother about that, just eat up.' Pierre-Edouard changed the subject.

The matter of Léon was the only sticking point on which Jean-Edouard had consistently refused to make the slightest concession. Too much bitterness, hatred even, had built up between himself and his daughter-in-law's brother. The two men had avoided each other and not spoken for years. If Léon paid one of his rare, fleeting visits to the house, Jean-Edouard would pointedly leave the room to go and shut himself in his bedroom. This behaviour, embarrassing for everyone, quickly made Léon understand that he was not welcome; that the old man could never forgive his actions and his attitude in times past.

Furthermore, Jean-Edouard could not forgive Léon for succeeding to the mayoralty at the elections in May 1925. At the time Jean-Edouard had let it be known that he was retiring from the contest, that he was not even interested in the humbler position of councillor. But there was no doubt that his political strategy would have been different if he had suspected that Léon Depeuch would succeed him. And masterfully, since, no sooner elected, he had moved heaven and earth to get water laid on, just as the electors had demanded. However, blinded by his resentment towards Léon, he refused to accept that his enemy was the best choice for Mayor of Saint-Libéral. He was as obstinate as he was prejudiced, and finally convinced himself that the electors would reject Léon – that lout, that crook, that faithless and lawless stock-dealer who had amassed a veritable fortune by plundering the market places all around! When it came to these elections he had really hoped that his son would throw himself into the fray. Unfortunately Pierre-Edouard did not feel attracted by the sash of office; he was not interested in the job, and had only reluctantly accepted the position of deputy which the new mayor had offered him.

These reasons were quite sufficient to justify Jean-Edouard's lasting animosity, but his anger was also fuelled by the solid friendship which allied his son to that toad Léon. An old friendship, forged in their youth, and now reinforced by family ties since Pierre-Edouard's marriage to Mathilde. An unshakeable friendship, which was a constant source of irritation to him.

Léon was aware of all this; he felt no need to turn the knife in the wound, poison the abscess of hatred, and so he restricted his visits to the Vialhes as much as possible. But that did not prevent him from maintaining a very good relationship with his sister, brother-in-law, nephews and niece; his house was always open to them.

# 2

LÉON poured coffee into the wide earthenware bowls, and replaced the coffee-pot on the wood-burning stove. Since his mother had died fifteen months earlier – Mathilde was still wearing her mourning black – he had lived entirely in one room of the vast mansion which he had had built just before the war. Unmarried and engrossed in his work, he lived away from home more often than under his own roof. He took all his meals at the inn, often slept in Brive or Tulle, even in Limoges or Paris, and never bothered with housekeeping as such. So the single room which he used had become a real slum; but it was a slum without any dust, for Mathilde cleaned it every week, upset to see it turned into a pigsty.

The room was therefore clean but cluttered, invaded – drowned, almost – by an accumulation of strange objects; of washing, paperwork, dishes. Even the grand fireplace, where he never lit the fire, was full of calving-ropes, harness and wooden yokes.

'Well, what's new?' asked Pierre-Edouard, as he searched the sideboard to try to unearth the sugar tin. At last he found and opened it: it was full of nails. 'So that's your sugar?' he teased.

'Ask your wife! It's she who tidies it away, it seems that sugar should be in a sugar bowl! Look, it's over there, on the chair, in the pot marked Heather Honey.'

'You wanted to see us?' Pierre-Edouard continued as he returned with the container.

'Yes, sit down. Here,' said Léon, pushing a bottle of plum brandy towards him, 'help yourself, take a good drop, you're going to need it . . . ' He sat down as well, looked at them both, and smiled at his sister. 'It's amazing, you never look any older! Of course you're still young, only thirty! Ah, if only I were still thirty!'

He deftly unstrapped the prosthesis on the end of his left arm – a souvenir of the battles on the Piava river – laid the metal claw on the table, and rubbed the swollen, purplish stump which had replaced his fist.

'*Miladiou*, it doesn't half itch in the evenings!' he grumbled as he scratched himself.

'Come on, stop mucking about,' demanded Pierre-Edouard,

'you didn't ask us here to talk about your fleas!'

He knew his brother-in-law well, and guessed he was feeling embarrassed and inhibited.

'Have you done something stupid?' Mathilde was worried. She had a secret horror, a fear, of seeing her brother entangled in some unsavoury dealings over animals, for he was not overburdened with scruples. He had an enormous turnover of stock, a lot of money passed through his hands, and he probably amassed a tidy sum from one year to the next. He was certainly as cunning as a fox, but you could never be sure: he swam with sharks, and perhaps one day he would meet one more ruthless than himself.

'Hey, what do you take me for! Stupid? Would I do something I shouldn't? No, that's not my style. Now, as it happens,' he turned to his brother-in-law, 'I've rented six more hectares on the plain at Varetz, not far from Castel Novel; good pasture land, you must come and have a look at it.'

'Okay,' Pierre-Edouard agreed, and stirred his coffee. Now he was sure it must be something serious, important, and Léon was trying to delay his confession with red herrings.

'So,' he tried again, 'you're not going to have us stay the night, are you? What's up?'

Léon shrugged, and poured himself a generous slug of brandy.

'I'm going to get married,' he said with a smile.

'Oh, so that's it . . .' Pierre-Edouard gasped. He was as surprised as he had been twenty years earlier, when his newly-widowed sister Louise had announced her intention to remarry just as abruptly.

'Now,' he hesitated, 'you're not teasing?'

'Tell us, Léon, is it a joke?' Mathilde was not sure either, just as flabbergasted as her husband.

'My God! Anyone would think you were upset about it! I'm not that old!'

'We're not at all upset!' protested Pierre-Edouard. 'Quite the opposite! But you always told us that you didn't want a wife.'

'Well, yes, I know, I always preferred other people's . . . but a fellow can change his mind, can't he? I'm fed up with running after the girls! Oh, don't look at me like that, little sister. Just because your husband keeps you happy, it doesn't mean it's like that for all wives! Basically I was doing the poor lasses a favour; thanks to me they've known a little affection . . .'

'So that was it,' she interrupted, 'you did it all out of kindness! That's very fine, you should try explaining it to the priest like that, it'd make him very happy . . .'

Mathilde was a good Christian. She never missed Mass on Sundays, and made sure that her boys attended catechism classes regularly. She felt a little sad that Pierre-Edouard so rarely accompanied her to the service, but she knew that in his own way he too had respect for religion. He took Communion at Easter, and got on well with Father Verlhac, who did them the honour of coming to share the family dinner three or four times a year.

But as far as her brother was concerned, she had good reason to be worried about his religious practices. Not that he was violently anti-clerical – he was on the best of terms with the priest – but that was no proof of Faith; all the former soldiers in the parish got on well with the cleric because he too was a war veteran. Apart from this relationship, Léon was totally indifferent to Church matters; he did not deride religion or argue about it but he declared 'I don't give a damn about all that!'

'Go on, no more kidding, is it a joke?' Pierre-Edouard insisted.

'Not at all! For God's sake, what's so extraordinary about it? Dammit, I'm not so old! Do you feel old yourself?' he asked his brother-in-law. 'No? Well then! Okay, I'm two years older than you, but it's no big deal to be forty-three! Think of that moron Léonard Bouyssoux at the Heath; he was over forty before he got married! And Gaston's second son-in-law, how old was he, eh? And Doctor Delpy, he was over fifty! So what?'

'That's not the problem,' his sister interrupted, 'it's just that we hadn't pictured you with a wife, that's all. Besides, who is she? Is she from round here?'

'No; well, yes . . . ' he explained, fiddling with the prongs of his false hand. 'Bloody hell,' he burst out suddenly, 'you don't seem to like it very much! No, but it's true, you've given me the hump!'

'You've got it wrong,' Pierre-Edouard reassured him earnestly. 'We're surprised, that's all; put yourself in our shoes, we didn't expect to have a sister-in-law.'

'Who is she?' asked Mathilde again.

'You don't know her; she's from Brive, Chantalat's daughter . . .'

'Chantalat! The biggest wholesale butcher in the Corrèze! Well, my friend,' exclaimed Pierre-Edouard, 'you *are* aiming high!'

'What do you know about it! It's not like that . . . '

'I hope not!' Mathilde interrupted. 'How old is she?'

'Well . . .' he muttered in embarrassment. 'All right, she's twenty-three. Oh, I know what you're going to say! She's too young. She'll like going to dances. She'll need lots of dresses, and then I'm old enough to be her father, and so on and so on! Well, maybe I am, but

336

so what? I don't care! You can say what you like, I shall marry her anyway!'

'Don't get upset,' said Pierre-Edouard, putting a hand on his arm, 'we won't say anything.'

'Maybe you won't, but they'll be gossiping in the village!'

'It'll soon pass,' Pierre-Edouard tried to comfort him. 'And after all, as you say, you're not the first person to marry someone younger than yourself!'

'Yes, I know,' said Léon gloomily. 'And I know better than you what young people need . . . so there! All I ask of her is that she gives me a child, a child like yours.' He was embarrassed to show a new side to his character. 'I'd like to have a son – yes, a son! And if he'd like to study, I'll pay for it. If he wants to be a doctor or even a government minister, then he'll be one! I've had enough of being alone with my pile of money! I don't know what to do with it all! The more I pay out, the more I get back, and it's no real use to me! Look, here, I've leased all the land and grazing belonging to the château and to the solicitor, that's sixty-two hectares, plus forty on the Rivière plain, another twenty-two at Larche, eight at Daudevie and six more at Varetz! I employ ten workers and I pay them well! I have a turnover of hundreds of calves, cows, bullocks and horses every year! And what's it all for? To live in this dump!' He waved his arm at the room. 'To end up all alone like a bad-tempered old boar! No, it can't go on like this. So, I'm going to get married, we'll have a child, and then it'll be worth earning some money.'

'You're right,' said Mathilde, 'and what's her name?'

'Yvette. She's not very pretty – no, she wouldn't hold a candle to you. She's not a beauty, but she is kind and gentle, and she has lovely eyes. And then, she's not marrying me for my money, she's got more than me! Just think, Chantalat's only child! So it's all settled, we're getting married in Brive on the twelfth of July, it's a Saturday. You will come, won't you? And the children too?'

'Of course,' said Mathilde.

'Good, so Pierre-Edouard will be my witness. I was really worried that you'd be cross with me, especially you,' he said, looking at his sister, 'you've always watched me like a cat watches her kittens! Well, I was worried that you wouldn't want to have anything to do with a sister-in-law. So, if you think it's a good idea, will you help me?'

'What with?'

'To sort things out here, get the house ready, all that. You see, I don't know much about women – well, what I mean is, what I know isn't any good for . . .'

'I understand,' Mathilde interrupted. 'Don't worry, we'll prepare a fine home for her. And you'll see, everyone in the village will be pleased to know that their mayor is settling down at last.'

Jacques turned over again in bed and envied his brother, who was deep in untroubled sleep, curled up at his side. He pushed him away roughly, and heard the familiar and irritating sound of greedy sucking. Not only did Paul fall asleep as soon as he got into bed, he also still sucked his thumb, despite being eight years old.

Jacques concluded that this babyish habit, and the fact that he could fall into sweet dreams in a few moments, proved that his brother lacked a conscience. Father Verlhac maintained that the guilty were tortured and often lay awake half the night. Not so! The priest was wrong, and that devil Paul was proof of it! It wasn't he who was gnawed by remorse, or the sneaking anxiety it engendered; *his* sleep was as calm and peaceful as a new-born babe's!

Yet, there were plenty of things to worry about and to dread in the next few days. For Jacques had no doubt that the damage they had caused would be discovered tomorrow, perhaps had been already. The workers putting up the line could not fail to notice how the insulators had been broken. They would naturally report this crime to the Mayor, and then it would not be Godfather or Uncle Léon, but a very strict grown-up who would instruct Alfred, the town sergeant, to investigate the matter immediately. 'Alfred wouldn't set the world on fire,' thought Jacques, remembering an expression his father had used, 'it's true that he's a fool, and he can't run because of losing a foot in the war, but still, he knows that we mind the cattle on Combes-Nègres and it's not far from the building site . . . No, it was a stupid idea to take my shooter!' He cursed himself again.

Then he thought that Paul would have broken the insulators anyway, and he would have been accused of aiding and abetting him. So, if you weighed it all up, at least he would deserve whatever he got . . .

He heard his grandfather going to bed on the other side of the partition. The springs creaked a little and then silence fell in the bedroom again, the only sounds the gentle breathing of little Mauricette, who lay beside her parents' bed, and the vulgar snuffling of that lucky devil Paul.

Jacques wondered what time his parents would return. They often went to see Léon after dinner; normally he was not aware of their return, for the noise they made going to bed and the light of their paraffin lamp did not wake him. But would it be the same, soon, when they turned on the electricity?

Everything was ready for it. Already a porcelain shade hung from the ceiling of the bedroom, and when the moment came his father would connect one of the bulbs which now stood in the top of the wardrobe. There were six of them, and according to his father each would be as bright as twenty-five candles! What a marvel that such a little sphere of glass could emit such a light! Six bulbs, one for each of the two bedrooms of the house, another for the main room, one to light the yard in winter and the last two for the barn and piggery.

A lot of the villagers considered this a waste of money – one had to have plenty to spare to install electricity for the animals! But Pierre-Edouard replied that, since the electricians were coming to do work at his place, he might as well make the most of the opportunity.

True, the installation must have been expensive. Jacques did not know exactly what the final cost was, but the few conversations which he had happened to interrupt or overhear made him think his father must have paid out at least 1,500 francs. That was considerable, the price of a young heifer. Jacques was proud of this extravagance, and regarded his friends at school with a certain air of condescension, for their parents were content with the minimum provision necessary and, for the sake of economy, would continue to milk by the light of an oil-lamp, or even with a candle, as they had done in the past! He even knew some, real barbarians these, who had refused to allow the electricity into their homes; they proclaimed that it would attract lightning towards the houses of those who had clamoured for this foolish innovation!

This was stupid, and the schoolmaster had told them so; he had even explained how electricity worked! Naturally you should not touch the wires, or put fingers or nails into the sockets; that was obvious, anyone could understand it! Of course – this thought depressed him – you should not break the insulators with catapult shots either . . .

He heard the front door creak, and the footsteps of his parents. He turned towards the wall, covered his nose with the sheet, and pretended to be asleep.

Just as Jacques had anticipated, the foreman of the work-team from the Gas Fusion company, which held the contract to install the line, stormed over to the mairie early next morning, described the damage, and demanded immediate action.

'You must understand,' he explained to Léon, 'if we do nothing there won't be a single insulator left when we come to attach the wire! It's bound to be some local kids up to mischief!'

'From this community? You have no proof,' Léon retorted, for he felt allegiance to his villagers and their offspring. 'But never fear, I'll look into it.'

But he had plenty of other things to do, and forgot the incident. Towards the end of the morning he noticed the children coming out of school, and this jogged his memory. He smiled when he saw his godson, Jacques, followed by his brother, who was kicking along an old tin with great thuds of his clogs. Then he rememberd the foreman's complaint, and called to his nephews.

There was no cause to suspect them in particular among the forty or so children dispersing across the square – except that Paul had a certain reputation. When he saw their faces he knew that he was on the right track. He forced himself to adopt a formidable expression, although he really had no wish to treat them harshly. He loved the two boys, knew that their parents kept them on a short rein, and did not want to be responsible for the punishment awaiting them, if they actually were guilty. And he had his own memories too. What had he *not* done, at that age! And Pierre-Edouard as well, always with his sister Louise in tow, had never been slow to join in Léon's outrageous escapades then.

'Well, young fellows,' he called to them, 'how's it going at school? Yes, I'm sure it's fine, you both work well . . . And my catapult, is that working well?'

It was Paul who saved the situation. Jacques had made Paul swear he would not whisper a word to anyone of the conversation overheard the previous evening, at a time when he was supposed to be asleep; now he was annoyed that he had confided in Paul, and blushed from head to toe.

'Hey, uncle, is it true that you're going to get married?' asked Paul with an innocent expression.

'Who told you that?' Léon was startled. He had asked his sister and brother-in-law to be discreet; he intended to announce the news himself during the next meeting of the town council. 'Well, who told you?'

'It was Jacques,' blurted out the boy as he cleared out his nose with an experienced forefinger. He scrutinised the digit and then licked it clean. 'It's great you're getting married, we'll go to the wedding!'

'Bloody hell, where did you get that from, eh?' asked Léon, examining his godson.

'It was yesterday evening, I wasn't asleep when my parents came back from your place,' Jacques admitted, and hung his head. 'But we haven't told anyone,' he reassured his uncle.

'Honest,' added Paul, 'we haven't said anything yet . . . '

'Oh no? You're two rascals who'd be quite capable of breaking some insulators on the electricity line, wouldn't you? You haven't heard anything said about that by any chance, have you?'

'Well . . . ' Paul took evasive action. 'Tell us, is it true that you're going to buy yourself a car?'

'My God!' exclaimed Léon with a great guffaw, 'you'll get by okay, you've got the gift of the gab all right! Fine,' he said and suddenly became serious, 'I don't want to know which little scamps broke the insulators – it couldn't have been you, could it, eh? The Mayor's nephews couldn't do that! What would people think of me then, eh? And your parents! If they found out they'd tan your backsides pretty quickly . . . Go on, get out of here, and make sure you're not caught hanging about near the electricity pylons, or someone might get suspicious . . . Understand?'

'Yes, yes,' they chorused back.

'But you won't say anything to Papa, will you?' begged Jacques.

'No, I won't,' his godfather reassured him. 'This time, and this time only, I think it was those ragamuffins from Perpezac or Yssandon who came and did it, so that won't concern your father . . . '

Pierre-Edouard shrugged his shoulders, folded his newspaper and got up.

'I must go,' he said, glancing at the big pendulum clock.

It was his duty to attend the meeting of the town council, and he was sorry to give up this peaceful April evening for it. The children had been in bed for the last half-hour and were already quiet. His father had also gone to his bedroom, and only the hissing of the fire and the clicking of Mathilde's knitting-needles disturbed the peace and quiet of the room.

'I'll wait up for you,' said his wife from the settle.

'That's nice of you. Do you want the newspaper?'

'Oh no, I make do with watching your face as you read it!' she joked.

'You may be better off with that! I wonder what will come of it all!'

He slipped on his jacket, bent over Mathilde to kiss her, and went out.

It was fresh, almost cold, and the sky was quite clear, punctuated by a reddish arc, the first quarter of the new moon.

'If it doesn't cloud over, that russet moon will cause some losses,' he thought as he started down the main street.

There was no need for natural forces to add to their troubles and make things even more difficult. The country was in crisis; if Pierre-Edouard shrugged his shoulders as he read the paper, it was because there was nothing else he could do. All those idiotic politicans quarrelling over their share of the cake were not worth anything more. Because anyone with any sense was fed up with ministers who came and went; since the sad departure of Poincaré they had been led by a series of puppets – Briand, Tardieu, Chautemps. All those time-servers had achieved was a fall in the price of corn; six months ago it had dropped from 161.50 francs a quintal to 139.50. They really had something to be proud of! Proud of the slump in the price of meat too, and the growing difficulties which beset the farmers on all sides!

Despite this, Pierre-Edouard would not be drawn into militant political action, although he was never slow to give his opinion. He mistrusted those who made a living out of politics – and a good living – too much to want to imitate them and support one party or another.

He reserved the right to praise or criticise whoever he saw fit, whatever their political colour, and he exercised this right freely. Up till now he had managed to remain on good terms with all his friends, whether they were liberal and apolitical, like Dr Delpy; on the right, like his next-door neighbour Maurice, Edouard Lapeyre or even Pierre Delpeyroux; moderate like his brother-in-law Léon; or frankly leftist like Martin Tavet, Jean Bernical or Louis Brousse. All these men were members of the town council and did their best to promote the well-being of the community of Saint-Libéral-sur-Diamond.

Exclamations and laughter exploded from the mairie and echoed along the main street: Pierre-Edouard realised that his brother-in-law had just announced his impending marriage, and quickened his pace. Now he was in a hurry to see the expression of the prospective bridegroom of forty-three, and in a hurry to join in the jokes which would probably take up a good part of the meeting. He pushed open the door of the mairie and was himself greeted with shouts.

'You knew about this, did you?' cried Maurice.

'Only since the day before yesterday, no longer,' he confessed.

'Are we all here?' bawled Léon. 'Perhaps we ought to get down to a bit of work!'

'The doctor can't come,' Pierre Delpeyroux informed them, 'he's gone to the Mazière farm, it looks as if the father won't last the night . . .'

The mood darkened immediately, and the men nodded their heads. Old Firmin Mazière was eighty-seven, the patriarch of the village and well liked by everyone. He had never harmed anyone, was a good neighbour and an honest man. He was one of the last who could still recall the old way of life and evoke memories of an age when there were almost 1,300 people living in the parish of Saint-Libéral; when every patch of land was lovingly tended, when the village could feed everyone who wanted to take the trouble to work, and young people had no need to leave for the towns.

Alas, a bygone era! Today there were only 594 inhabitants, and the land left fallow extended further each year, just as the exodus of the young also gathered strength. Nothing could halt this flight, for nothing could relieve the poverty which forced them from their homes.

'Say what you like, old Mazière was a fine man,' Léon continued. And everyone agreed.

After the meeting they all repaired to the inn, for Léon's engagement had to be suitably celebrated, and there they learned of Mazière's death. He had passed away an hour earlier. The landlady had the news from the doctor, whom she saw returning from the house of the deceased.

'He died just as we were talking of him,' remarked Martin Tavet.

'Bah,' their hostess interrupted, 'he was old enough, wasn't he? What can I get you?'

No one said a word, but gave their orders without commenting on Suzanne's thoughtlessness and lack of respect; such a remark would never have been tolerated when the Chanlats were running the place. The Chanlat couple were local; they knew everyone, and they respected the dead. But with Suzanne, they would have to overlook it . . .

After all, she was an outsider, born in Tulle, and then, everyone agreed that she was slightly crazy. You would have to be, to buy an inn which was on its last legs – the bedrooms had remained desperately empty during the three years of her ownership. But she hadn't balked at the amount, had paid the asking price, cash on the nail. Since then business had been neither good nor bad, but Suzanne did not complain. As a war widow, she had a good pension anyway.

Her first husband had been killed on the Marne in September 1914 when she was only eighteen; his faded portrait adorned the wall on the left side of the mirror behind the bar. However, they were all of the opinion that this unfortunate private was not the one who had made her fortune. On the contrary, she was beholden to her second husband, a sergeant-major; he had just found time to give her a daughter before stupidly stepping on a mine in August 1918. Since then she banked a regular income to live on and raise her daughter, thanks to the good man whose photo and medals hung on the right of the mirror; the modest takings from the inn were almost superfluous.

But the two bereavements she had suffered before she was twenty-three had left another legacy, besides the pension. She was seized by terrible bouts of melancholia, when she dissolved into tears, and all the unmarried men in the area were seized by an insatiable urge to console her. These crises of despair were invariably followed by a period of euphoria during which she sang like a blackbird, willingly served anyone, and even gave credit to all those who wanted to share in her happiness.

In fact it was an open secret that she changed her partner every four or five months; she drowned her sorrows in curaçao for a week or so, and revived again as soon as she could lay her hands on a sympathetic man who had his health and strength. Yes, she was a foolish woman and her remarks were often indiscreet, but all her customers were fond of her. As for the women of the village, they considered her a dangerous and depraved female.

'Come on, give us another of those,' demanded Léon, holding out his empty glass.

'Well now, it's my turn, in honour of your marriage,' announced Suzanne, with a touch of bitterness in her voice. She cherished unmistakable but unreciprocated feeling for Léon, who had always rebuffed her advances. He was very circumspect in the matter of his conquests; although a terrible skirt-chaser, he had the prudence of a fox and, like them, did not hunt on his home patch.

'I bet you haven't heard the latest news, have you?' added Suzanne. She paused to increase the suspense, and was satisfied when she noticed that everyone was listening; she drew herself up –you were forced to admire her bust, everyone said as much.

'Yes,' she continued, 'I had it from Maître Chardoux, from his own lips, he stopped by this evening on his way back from the château . . . '

'And so what?' asked Léon.

Everyone knew that Maître Chardoux took care of her ladyship's affairs. Since she had been widowed during the war, the old lady had not returned to the village. She was living in Paris with her second daughter, and left to her solicitor the business of renting the land and maintaining the château, which had been empty for nearly fifteen years. The arrival of the solicitor in Saint-Libéral was therefore nothing unusual.

'And so what?' mimicked Suzanne. 'Well, her ladyship is going to come back to live here soon, and her daughter too . . .'

'Incredible!' cried the men.

They were pleased at this decision, for everyone was sad to see the great building deteriorate from year to year, when it had once been so full of life. Nothing was more forlorn than the closed shutters overgrown with ivy and wild vines, the steps overrun by briars and nettles, the terraced gardens invaded by scrub, the old trees in the orchard smothered in old man's beard and honey-suckle.

If the squire's wife returned, all that would be brought back to life, renovated, and the village would be enhanced in the process. Furthermore, the restoration would give the craftsmen some work – the tiler, the joiner, the stonemason; there was so much to do to repair the neglect of years! Then the lady would certainly need a housekeeper, a gardener, and perhaps even a steward, as before. Her return really was good news.

# 3

As a general rule, except when weather threatened the harvest, Pierre-Edouard did not work on Sundays. Instead he made use of this day to survey his property quietly, noting the fine growth of the crops, the vigour of the trees and vines. He loved these walks, and took great pleasure in them.

Sometimes Mathilde and the children accompanied him. Then, whilst the children galloped ahead, they remembered the paths walked and the years gone by since that morning in September 1917 when they had met, up there among the broom and juniper bushes of the White Peak. Pierre-Edouard had never for a moment regretted that day, the sudden urge which had thrown them together and united them for all time with an oft-renewed fervour. Their love grew stronger and deeper, quickened afresh by the daily round of work on the land they loved, enlivened by the births of their children and the happiness and vitality they brought with them.

There had been difficulties enough, and worries still beset them, but these did not daunt them or weaken their resolve; instead each problem drew them together, strengthened their unity, as comrades in adversity support, encourage and complement one another.

Pierre-Edouard entered the field called the Meeting. He was alone on his walk on this the first Sunday in June, for Mathilde had preferred to remain at home to look after Mauricette, who was feeling low after a persistent cold. As for Jacques and Paul, as soon as High Mass was over, they had joined their Sunday School friends in a game of rugby, with Father Verlhac as referee, and would return elated but covered in bruises.

He stopped in front of the field of potatoes, took out his pipe and filled it while contemplating the vast expanse of the plateau and the pattern of fields. Here, at least, the land was clean and in good heart. The slopes where the gradient demanded hand digging and manual cultivation were quite a different matter.

Abandoned since the war for lack of manpower, most were now covered with brushwood and undergrowth. It was a pity to think that beneath the saplings a fine rich loam lay hidden, just right for spring vegetables and fruit trees; but what was to be done about it?

No one had the time or opportunity to work as in the past. Just a few plots, the more accessible ones between the briars and gorse, displayed a variety of vegetables in rows: peas, onions and salad greens. But this area dwindled from year to year; it was enough for a grandfather or grandmother to die for the tiny oasis which they tended with such care to perish with them.

Fortunately, it was a different matter on the plateau. The fields were level, easy to plough, and the soil was productive when well cared for. Many of the farmers of Saint-Libéral owned plots up here. But the best pieces, the largest, were undoubtedly those of the Vialhe family.

Over there the Big Field, covered in wheat; then the Malides, where winter barley was growing; further on the Perrier field, with its lines of young but vigorous plum trees, and to the right the Long Piece with its twenty-eight walnut trees; these were nearly thirty years old, and had grown into magnificent specimens. Nearer to him lay the land called the Letters, which had belonged to Léon and then Mathilde, and in front of him the patch called the Meeting.

Eight years ago all this land had been neglected, the soil exhausted by his father's poor system of crop rotation. Pierre-Edouard had taken it in hand and restored it. Rough work, to which he and Mathilde had devoted time and effort unstintingly – and now their labours were bearing fruit.

From his time on a farm near Paris, Pierre-Edouard had brought back modern ideas and techniques. Some had made his neighbours laugh, but eventually they were forced to admit that he knew what he was doing. They had been compelled to acknowledge that the seeds and fertilisers he used gave excellent results, and that his methods of work were an improvement on theirs.

Now no one disputed his position as the best farmer in the community, just as his father had been before him. Year in, year out, he managed a return of seventeen quintals – an old measure, approximately equal to a hundredweight – of corn from each hectare; that was about eight more than the average yield in the area. As for his pure-bred Limousin cows, they compared well with the championship animals which Léon exhibited at the agricultural shows all around. He also raised pigs, a dozen sows and a boar which everyone admired. The breeding stock had been ordered from the farm where he had spent four years before the war, following the quarrel with his father. These Yorkshire piglets were fatter, longer and faster growing than the black and white local breed common to the area.

All this justified the decision, taken by the majority of the farmers, to entrust him with the office of president of the farmers co-operative society, the buying syndicate. He had therefore replaced his father at the head of this organisation and everyone benefited from his professional skill and judicious advice.

However, there was a cloud on the horizon, a threat to the future. Although Pierre-Edouard had earnestly requested it, his father had never set his affairs in order. Most of the land – seventeen hectares of it – the farm and the outbuildings, were still in Jean-Edouard's name, and while he was alive they would remain so. Of course Pierre-Edouard was in charge; it was he and he alone who managed the farm and ran it in his own way, just as he managed the five hectares which were his and Mathilde's own property.

There was nothing to prevent his sisters from one day reclaiming their share of this inheritance. He would have preferred it to happen during his father's lifetime, if only to know where he stood, resolve the uncertainty of his situation.*

But Jean-Edouard would never give in. He had probably forgiven his daughters their past behaviour, but not so fully that he would allow them to benefit from his prosperity while he was still there!

Pierre-Edouard was therefore making economies, to prepare for the day when his father died and his sisters would exercise their rights to the property. He did not mind paying them compensation, that was a legitimate principle, but his fear was that Louise or Berthe would refuse the money, would choose the land. They might force him to divide up the Vialhe estate, which for almost two centuries had increased in size and beauty. It was his pride, and he intended to pass it on to one of his sons, whichever he judged best able to succeed him. But for the time being, the farm was not even in his own name!

He reassured himself: his sisters would not want land, what could they do with it? Especially Berthe! You could say she had been successful, but what a life she led! You might get the flavour of it by looking at some of the postcards she sent each year: London, New York, Rio, Berlin, Rome. She had widened her field of operations and, without abandoning her first great success – her remarkable talent as a milliner – had expanded into haute couture, and now toured the world to present her collections or to open new showrooms.

Pierre-Edouard was full of admiration for her, but he also had his reservations. He admired her because he knew what she had suffered

*In France all children inherit equally if the father dies intestate.

on the farm until that day in August 1914 when she had at last attained her majority and taken to the road. What a change since then! What boldness and business sense, to know how to set up an enterprise like that! But he could not accept the way of life she had chosen; it embarrassed him. A life of luxury, of a liberated woman, who preferred to remain unmarried and seek *affaires*, rather than the calm and ordered role which befitted a worthy daughter of the house of Vialhe. Berthe really threw him off-balance.

It was not the same with Louise. Despite the distance which separated them and the fact that they had not seen each other for ten years, he still felt the same bond with her that had linked them all their youth.

She also wrote regularly, as did her son Félix, who was Pierre-Edouard's godson. Louise continued as governess in the château in Brenne, where she looked after her employer's three children, and never complained. As for Félix, he was completing his military service; he was in Morocco and enjoying it. After his discharge he would become a forest warden, like the stepfather whom he had hardly known but greatly admired, to the point of sharing the same love of trees and the forest.

Louise, Berthe and himself: what paths they had travelled in the last twenty years!

Pierre-Edouard lit his pipe, tamped the tobacco with his thumb, and walked on into the potato field. They were fine strong plants; he had earthed them up during the week and they were in good order.

He bent down and fingered the leaves. He was pleased with his choice of seed potatoes; for the first time he had chosen 'Early Round', a variety similar to 'Orléans Yellow', which was supposed to do well in this area and produce fifteen to twenty tons a hectare. He straightened a slightly withered shoot, stared at the plant and suddenly swore: 'My God, they've arrived . . . '

He took a few steps and immediately saw them: dozens of yellow and red beetles with ten black stripes running down the body. He could not be mistaken – the colony which was currently devouring his potatoes was that dreaded parasite, the Colorado beetle!

It was not really a surprise. For years all the farmers had been expecting just such an attack; for years they had discussed the inexorable approach of these destructive insects. The beetles had made their first appearance in 1920 in the Bordeaux area, and caused such losses that the whole farming community of France had been worried. But that had not prevented the pests from spreading further each year, from reaching Charentes, the Dordogne, Vienne and Haute Vienne and then, two years ago, part of the Corrèze. Up till now nobody in the village had been affected by this curse, this catastrophe. Now it was fact; the Colorado beetles were there.

Pierre-Edouard bent down again, turned over several leaves and pulled a face as he saw dozens of minute yellow eggs stuck to the underside of the foliage. On some of the plants the sticky, obese larvae were already crawling about, orangey-red caterpillars with black patches.

'Now we're for it!'

The most fantastic stories were told about Colorado beetles. Some people were certain that they came from America, secretly despatched by the government over there in order to ruin French farmers, so that the Americans could export their surplus potatoes. Other rumours swore that the blow had been struck by the Germans as revenge for their defeat. The latest gossip pointed to the pesticide salesmen, who were supposed to have come by night and shaken out sacks of insects from aeroplanes over the areas which were not yet infested.

This rubbish was not worth listening to; Pierre-Edouard knew, from reading about it in one of the farming reviews, that it was much simpler than any of that. It was true that the infestation had begun in 1920 in the Gironde area, true that it had originated in America, but it was accidental, not deliberate; the pests had been imported in a cargo of potatoes. All the rest was lies, and those who accused the Germans were ignorant, because it was well known that the beetle – discovered in 1824 in Colorado – had first appeared in Germany in 1876! However, it *was* true to say that they were very poorly equipped to defend themselves against this invader.

Pierre-Edouard strode swiftly through the field. He then cut across the plateau and hurried towards the village.

Just as he had expected and hoped, plenty of men were taking a drink at Suzanne's. He went in and leaned towards Maurice.

'Go and tell the men who are at Lamothe's to come here. Yes, yes, it's important, they must come!'

The Lamothe daughter kept the other bistro in the village. She had followed in the footsteps of her mother, Ma Eugènie, whose reputation had been more than questionable in the early 1900s. It was enough to make you believe that vice was hereditary, for Noémie Lamothe was even more slatternly than her mother, according to the old men, and that was saying something...

Thirty-five years old, with a bold eye, not ugly, but careless of her appearance, she survived thanks to a small but loyal clientele of old bachelors who did not mind the tittle-tattle and preferred to visit her rather than a brothel. It was closer to home, friendlier and cheaper; the only inconvenience was that you could not be in a hurry – the wench was hard to satisfy and took her time. Compared to that slut, the beautiful Suzanne almost passed for a saint. Two or three episodes a year practically raised her to the rank of a decent woman.

Pierre-Edouard elbowed his way to the bar and ordered a Pernod. He was just finishing his glass when the half-dozen customers from Noémie's rounded up by Maurice entered the auberge.

'Good God! What's up with you?' complained Mathieu Fayette. He was furious because Maurice had fetched him back from halfway up the staircase which led to Noémie's bedroom. 'Well, what do you want?' he repeated. 'I've got other things to do besides coming to your meetings!'

This comment was greeted with coarse laughter and plenty of improper suggestions, but Pierre-Edouard did not feel like laughing.

'I don't want to call a meeting! I've just come down from the plateau and look, lads, up there it's covered in Colorado beetles . . .'

'God damn it!' cried the men.

'I told you,' shouted one of the drinkers, 'it's you who brought them here, with your blasted special seeds! They're not on *our* plants, those pests won't touch *us*!'

'Don't talk rubbish,' interrupted Pierre-Edouard. 'On my way back I crossed your potato field; it's worse affected than mine! And covered in blight as well! I told you to spray with copper sulphate, but as usual you don't listen to anything!'

'The beetles are on my land?' the heckler was reduced to murmuring.

'Yes, on your land! On Maurice's too, on Bernical's, my brother-in-law's and yours, Edmond; I didn't see any on yours, Pierre, that was the only one.'

They were all struck dumb by the news. Eventually, Louis Brousse spoke out: 'But we must do something!'

'Well, yes,' replied Pierre-Edouard quietly, 'but what? I know we need lead arsenate, but I haven't any in the store – the pest control officer gave me some, but I passed it on to Léon.'

'Why didn't you keep it! It's your business to have some in the co-op!' cried one of the group.

'Go and get lost!' Pierre-Edouard shouted at him. 'If you want my job, you can have it. You don't think I was going to keep that poison in stock? It's full of arsenic, that stuff!'

'So we must contact Léon,' suggested Maurice.

'It's Sunday, who knows where he'll be!'

'He'll have gone off to look under the leaves with his lady-friend,' cried a joker.

But there was little laughter in response to this comment, for they were all thinking about the beetles eating their crops.

Father Verlhac was the first to launch an attack on the pests. As soon as he heard the news, that is to say just after lunch, he went to Pierre-Edouard and explained his idea. He was not the first to think of it; he admitted that it came from reading an article in the *Pélerin*. In the badly affected areas, the schoolchildren had collected up the insects and leaves bearing eggs, and this had slowed down the infestation.

'But they'll trample on all the plants!' exclaimed Jean-Edouard. 'Your cure will be worse than the illness!'

He had been considering the best way to stop the invasion ever since his son had told him what he had seen. He had never been the sort to give up, and he intended to fight this battle too. He had experienced so many of these struggles between man and nature in his lifetime! The Colorado beetles were a new plague; they had to survive it and beat it if possible.

'Yes,' he repeated, 'your kids will crush everything.'

'I'm not so sure,' said Pierre-Edouard, 'if we explain it carefully, it might work. If we put one or two of them in each row, with a box to throw the pests into, that's not so complicated!'

'No,' said Paul, 'but what if they pinch our fingers?'

'Stupid! They don't sting!' his brother snapped at him. 'That's right, isn't it, Papa, they can't hurt us?'

'No, only the potatoes.'

'So, what's the decision?' asked Father Verlhac.

'We'll do as you suggest, but we'll have to contact the teacher first so that he can get all the kids together; it's a matter of explaining carefully how to do it.'

'All right, I'll go and see him.'

The relationship between the priest and Charles Deplat, the primary school teacher, was most peculiar. The two men were almost the same age, getting on for fifty, and had arrived in the village in the years just before the war. There followed a long period of stealthy observation and of extreme circumspection; each did his best not to provide any ammunition for the other to attack him.

The four years of war had changed all that, and when they met again it was not as enemies but as brothers-in-arms. Brothers sometimes have little family quarrels, of course; ideological differences, nothing of consequence, they were settled in battles of words. One would wave the latest article by Herriot or Briand, the other defended his position every inch of the way by quoting long tirades from the latest Papal Encyclical, *Divini illius Magistri* – concerning Christian education – or, if it was a really serious matter, denounce him in the words of Léon Daudet!

When, at the end of arguments, they resorted to calling each other Bolshevik, Communist lackey, Fascist or Royalist, reconciliation was in sight. This was usually sealed with a glass of aperitif, in which each combatant toasted the health of his own party.

'To the socialists of the world and long live the class struggle!' the teacher would gravely announce.

'To the Christians martyred by you Reds, and long live God!' responded the priest.

The whole village understood this mild guerilla warfare and found it amusing, except the hardline militants who made themselves ridiculous by fiercely advocating either Marx or Christ! The former accused the schoolmaster of complacency in confronting the enemy, the latter – a few men and a horde of bigoted women – scolded their pastor, for he not only consorted with a disciple of the Devil, he also encouraged vice and debauchery by drinking at Suzanne's, the fallen woman. They had even written to the bishop deploring the laxity of their priest.

Father Verlhac knew their opinion of him, but he did not worry about it any more than he did about his best cassock. All that concerned him was that through the rugby team, which he organised with the help of the teacher, the boys continued to come and see him, even after their First Communion.

It had the desired effect, and that was only a start! He was still laughing at the underhand blow he had just dealt the anti-church faction; he had secretly purchased a magnificent miniature film projector, bleeding himself white to pay for it. Thanks to this machine and some good films, he was confident, as soon as electricity was connected in the village, of increasing the number of children within his realm of influence. His acquisition had enraged the teacher, furious that he had not been the first with such a brilliant idea! The two men had called each other names, and then drank together to seal a truce.

The priest found the teacher in his garden. He was weeding a long row of carrots, with the help of his wife; the clergyman was sorely tempted to criticise them for working on a Sunday. He swallowed his words, remembering that he had come with the aim of setting the children to work; this idea, worthy of an arch-pagan, was all his own.

An hour later, all the children were on the plateau. There were also many men and women curious to see what the beetles looked like and what damage they caused. After they had expressed their horror and outrage, they augmented the teams spread out in the various plots and joined the hunt.

They worked until evening, filling their buckets or tins and then going to empty them into a basin half-full of paraffin. When it began to get dark and they were about to go back down to the village, Pierre-Edouard had an argument with several of the women who wanted to keep what they had collected – to feed their hens, they explained.

'No, no! In the first place I don't know whether chickens eat these creatures, and secondly they can fly, so if you take them to the village, some are bound to escape and you'll have spread the plague a bit further, is that what you want to do?'

'Pierre-Edouard is right,' agreed the teacher as he wiped his fingers, sticky and yellow from crushing many insects, on the grass. 'We must not spread these evil creations of our good Lord!' he called out in the direction of the priest.

'Of the Devil, my friend, of the Devil,' the priest firmly stated. 'You're in a good position to know that Satan is the ruler in this world . . . '

'Yes, yes,' interrupted Pierre-Edouard, not in the mood to referee the slanging match he felt was imminent. He was tired but more, very worried, for after a few steps through the rows of potatoes, he could already see that many of the beetles had escaped being collected.

'Yes,' he repeated, 'we don't give a damn whether they come from God or the Devil! All I know is,' he took out his lighter, 'I'm going to set fire to the horrible mess. Mind out!' he shouted, as he lit a handful of dry grass.

The bowl instantly blazed up with a clear, high flame, the wing cases and bodies sparkling and sputtering as they burned.

'There's a good job done,' he announced, 'but we must spray the plants, starting tomorrow. My God, we didn't need this! Come on, I must get back.'

They fell into step with him and strode down towards the village, which was already bathed in darkness.

A council meeting took place as early as possible the following morning, to implement a proper plan of action.

'Do you know where you can get this preparation?' asked Léon, turning to his brother-in-law, 'because the amount you gave me won't be enough.'

'In Objat.'

'And do you know what we need?'

'Yes, lead arsenate and lime.'

'Well, go and get some straight away. Since we've decided to treat the fields, there's no point in waiting till the evening train for delivery. Take your cart and get going. My God, how long have I been saying that I should buy a car! To think I missed that old one belonging to Monsieur Lardy!'

The former solicitor, who had retired ten years ago, had sold his Renault six months earlier, but Léon had carelessly missed the chance to buy it. Now only the doctor owned a motor-car, and he certainly would not have time to run over to Objat on a Monday morning!

'I'll take your tilbury instead,' Pierre-Edouard informed him. 'My mare won't get there and back without losing at least one of her shoes, they're so worn down at the moment. And now I think of it, we must count how many sprayers we've got, we'll need to use them all.' Not all the farmers had spraying-machines. Only those with good-sized vineyards had bought one of these devices for spreading the copper sulphate, and there was no guarantee that they were in working order.

'Yes, I'll get Alfred to see to that, starting this morning. Come on, get going, you should have left already! And don't forget,' he called out, 'I bought my horse from the army, he's just as idle as an adjutant!'

Everyone laughed, for they all knew that Pierre-Edouard had ended the war with that rank.

Pierre-Edouard returned during the afternoon; no horse could dawdle along with him, who had broken in plenty of them. As soon as he emerged into the main square he noticed a row of at least twenty spraying-machines in front of the fountain, and carts lined up with barrels of water and tubs on them, to prepare the mixture. The men were waiting, sitting under the lime trees or on the terrace of Suzanne's bar.

'You didn't hang around,' Léon said admiringly, patting the sweat-soaked flanks of his horse.

'He's a fine beast, I suspect you don't now how to talk to him,' replied Pierre-Edouard as he jumped down.

'He's a good-for-nothing, I told you,' maintained Léon stubbornly as he began to unload the boxes, 'but if you like I'll let you have him at cost price!'

'Keep talking!' cried Pierre-Edouard as he set off home, 'I'm going to get a bite to eat, I didn't have time earlier. I'll join you up there. Oh, and if it's any comfort to you, we're not alone; it seems there are beetles right across the plain. They multiplied in that humidity, that's why there are so many all at once.'

They worked until darkness fell, taking turns to carry the heavy, metal machines; the straps cut into their shoulders, and their right arms, which had to pump continuously, swelled up, and the weight rested agonisingly on the small of the back.

Towards eight o'clock, while it was still light, the women came up with food. The men ate hungrily but with wrinkled noses, for their hands and clothes were impregnated with the chemicals, and a revolting smell hung over the plateau. Then they resumed their dogged march to and fro, walking with the slow step of exhausted foot soldiers.

When they finally stopped, all the potatoes on the plateau had received their dose of poison. They returned to the village believing that they had won the battle.

But a week later, the beetles appeared in the fields on the edge of the village. In a fortnight they reappeared on the high ground. The men repeated the treatment. They knew that from now on they would have to reckon with this pest. It seemed ineradicable, like midges, lice or mosquitoes. So they might as well get used to it; it was just another enemy to fight.

# 4

SINCE the new moon in mid-June the weather had been superb, warm, just right for the haymaking. The whole village set to work in haste, to try to make up for the days lost at the beginning of the month, when it had been too stormy. They rose at dawn to the whetting of the scythe and the scratching of the reaper blades on the sandstone grinder, and they fell asleep late at night while the chains rattled on the well-coping and the water gushed from the last buckets the workers poured over themselves. The air grew balmy, and as the last swathes were cut their slightly bitter, coarse smell mingled with the heavy perfume of drying hay which transpired in the relative cool of the barns.

Pierre-Edouard was washing his face one last time in front of the well, his chest bare and trousers rolled up to the knee; he dried himself roughly with his sweat-soaked shirt, and smiled as he watched his sons. For once they were not being stingy with the water; they usually ran away from the tap over the sink, but now they seemed to be enjoying washing themselves. They really had sweated themselves out, helping him to load the last cartful of hay.

'Come on,' he called to them, 'you've watered yourselves enough now. Maman and Pépé will have finished seeing to the animals, you'd better get dressed, it's supper-time.' He walked into the main room and his bare feet slapped on the tiles. 'Good God, it's as dark as an oven in here!' He felt along the plaster moulding above the fireplace in search of matches.

He pulled down the paraffin lamp hanging above the table, lit it and was pleased to see that everything was ready for the meal; the table laid, the lettuce ready to be tossed, the jugs filled. As for the soup, it was simmering gently on the dying embers of the fire. He poured himself half a glass of wine, topped it up with water and swallowed it in one, then he slipped on his clogs and went out again to join Mathilde in the stable. Beside the well, the children were still splashing about in fits of giggles.

'You got everything under cover?' asked Jean-Edouard, as he poured a measure of wine into the bottom of his soup bowl.

'Yes, and I had help!' said Pierre-Edouard, lifting his chin towards Jacques and Paul.

'You do as you think best,' continued his father, 'but if I were you I wouldn't mow tomorrow, the sun set in a watery haze . . . '

'I saw it. But don't worry, I don't need that to tell me that a storm's coming . . . '

'Your leg?' asked Mathilde.

She was resting on the settle and gently stroking Mauricette's head; the child had fallen asleep on her lap.

'Yes,' he replied, 'since midday.'

He had been seriously wounded during the final months of the war, and bore a long deep scar on his left thigh which reacted to the slightest change in the weather with a nagging pain. It did not hurt enough to incapacitate him, just enough to warn him.

'Well, we'll see what tomorrow brings; anyway we've done most of it,' he said, sliding a portion of omelette on to his plate. He served his sons, and then suddenly pointed his fork towards the paraffin lamp. 'Speaking of tomorrow, do you remember?'

The children nodded. Of course they remembered! The electricity was going to be connected, they had been looking forward to the day for ages!

'It's an important date,' continued Pierre-Edouard. 'Have a good look at this paraffin lamp; we won't be needing it after tomorrow.'

'So we could smash it!' cried Paul, full of excitement at the thought of such a fine target.

'And what for?' growled his father. 'All you ever think of is destroying things! No, we won't smash it up, we don't need that!'

'Well, if it isn't any use any more . . . ' Paul tried again.

'Be quiet! Then eat up and get to bed, there's school tomorrow!'

'Yes, and we won't be able to see the electricity when it comes on,' Jacques complained.

'Yes, you will,' Mathilde reassured him, 'I'm sure the teacher will test it in school. What time are they connecting us?' she asked her husband.

'At eleven o'clock. And afterwards there's a reception at the mairie and everyone is invited – especially former town councillors,' he added casually.

He knew his father would not deign to appear, particularly if it involved congratulating Léon! But at least he could not say that he had not been informed about it!

'Right, I'm going to bed,' observed Jean-Edouard drily.

He leaned towards his grandsons, offered his grey stubbly cheek to be kissed, and then went into his room. The door slammed behind him.

Mathilde looked at Pierre and shrugged her shoulders almost imperceptibly; the gulf between her brother and her father-in-law could not be bridged, and even the inauguration of the electricity supply would not change that.

Everyone in the village was happy to have electricity at last, so they came in great numbers to celebrate its arrival. A few pessimists gravely foretold that this step forward would cost them their eyesight, but the majority of the inhabitants were proud of the brand-new posts beside the main road, and the transformer on the edge of the village, just beyond the railway station.

But the heavens were not propitious. The clouds were already dense and low as dawn broke, and all those who had hay on the ground were in a bad mood as they rushed to the meadows to try to gather the drying fodder into tall heaps. It was no use: the first shower came pattering down at about nine o'clock, short but violent, and drenched all the crops. It also soaked all the workers, who came back angrily cursing the clouds. Towards ten o'clock the thunder rolled over Terrasson.

'Bah, the morning storm doesn't deter the traveller,' cried Léon to the men who had already arrived at the town hall.

'No,' replied Louis Brousse seriously, 'but it rots the hay . . . '

He was reproaching himself bitterly for having cut a large part of his meadow the previous evening, and he almost regretted paying 1,850 francs for his reaper. For he too, like many others, had finally given in to the temptation to mechanise. What alternative was there? Seasonal workers were few and far between now, and the occasional young man who offered his services hardly knew how to use a scythe, let alone sharpen it without ruining the blade! It was really sad. A far cry from the teams of mowers of twenty years ago who cut the majority of the hay-meadows in the village. Nowadays only the steeply sloping fields echoed to the swish of the scythe; the rest was ruled by machinery.

He had nothing against the machines. They were efficient – too efficient perhaps, for they made it all too easy and encouraged you to work on, each swathe calling to its brother as it fell! That was what made Louis Brousse so cross with himself: he had not known when to stop. Now, because of that wretched machine which mowed so quickly, half his meadow was soaking up the water! He would not have suffered such damage if he had stuck to his good old scythe. The effort required for the work meant that a man was never tempted to mow more than he could bring in. He cut a section, turned it, gathered it up and stored it under shelter. Then he took up his blade again and set quietly to mowing a fresh portion of grass. Pacing oneself like that, the amount of hay spoiled never caused any loss of sleep, even if a storm came. Whereas now more than half a hectare had been exposed to the downpour . . .

'Have you got hay on the ground?' Léon asked him.

'You could say so! All the top part of my holding!'

'Everyone has got some on the ground,' said Bernical, 'that's the way it is with the mechanical reapers, nothing comes in half measures!'

'That's just what I said,' grumbled Louis Brousse, 'we're fools to let ourselves be controlled by machines!'

He shrugged his shoulders and moved to the window, pensively watching the rain pour down.

The storm broke at ten to eleven. It was not one of those huge terrifying onslaughts which leave you breathless and counting anxiously as you await the next peal of thunder. It was quiet, frightened no one, and moved away after five or six warning flashes.

Unfortunately one of these broke the circuit in the transformer, which made Léon look ridiculous. As eleven o'clock struck, having said a few well-chosen words on the benefits of scientific progress, he intended to illuminate the hall of the mairie. He lowered the switch and the assembly looked up towards the porcelain lamp-shade.

'Bloody hell, what's up! It's not working!' murmured Léon, flicking the little copper switch up and down to no avail. 'Well now,' he called to the chief engineer, 'so that's your electrical magic? It doesn't seem much of a miracle!'

'The storm must have blown a fuse in the transformer,' explained the engineer. 'It will be quickly repaired.'

He sent off one of his men immediately to have a look at the transformer. The expert returned very soon and confirmed the diagnosis.

'So, this time is it going to work?' asked Léon. 'Yes? Good, let's go.'

He moved the switch and swore when he observed that nothing had happened; a murmur of discontent rumbled around the hall.

'*Miladiou*! Are you trying to make a fool of me, or what?' groaned Léon.

'The problem must lie here,' declared the engineer crossly. 'Are you sure your meter is switched on?'

'What an idea! I'm not stupid!'

'Let's make sure, all the same,' suggested the engineer, and strode to the little cupboard which concealed the black box. But he had to believe the evidence of his eyes. The meter was working.

'Very well, very well,' he said, forcing a smile. He ran his hand through his hair and scratched his head. 'The whole sector must be out,' he pronounced authoritatively, 'because of the storm. It happens sometimes . . . '

'That's not much use,' cried one of the men. 'If the light goes out every time a cloud farts sideways, it wasn't worth all that expense!'

'That's right,' added his neighbour, 'say what you like, that doesn't happen with a candle.'

'Just the opposite,' joked Maurice. 'At my house my wife lights the Candlemas candle as soon as she hears a peal of thunder!'

'So, what shall we do?' asked Léon. 'Will it take a long time?'

'No, no,' the engineer reassured him, 'my colleagues must be mending it already, believe me.'

'We-e-ell, all right.' Léon was somewhat sceptical. 'Fine, we'll drink to it anyway,' he decided, and turned to the table laden with bottles and glasses. 'Come along, help yourselves,' he invited.

But however much they clinked their glasses and told jokes, their hearts were not in it. They felt frustrated and soon began to slip away.

'Ah, now it's working!' Léon noticed after everyone had left.

'Simply an accident,' the engineer tried to reassure him.

'Yes, yes,' added Pierre-Edouard, 'and it'll be more use this evening, your electricity. You'll see then, it'll be fine.'

The current was actually switched on at about half-past twelve, although it had been expected at eleven, and most people were not even aware of it, for they had very wisely switched off at the meter because of the thunderstorms rumbling around the hills. So it was not until night-time that everyone could at last appreciate the advantages of electric lighting. Alas, the electricity was cut off again less than an hour and a half later; it was greeted with cries of protest from every household.

Days later they learned that the tiny storm at Saint-Libéral had erupted violently elsewhere; branches had fallen on the wires and caused short-circuits. Very disappointed, the villagers retired to bed grumbling.

But they were so little used to the whole business of switches that many left theirs on. When the supply was finally reconnected at about midnight, a large part of the village suddenly lit up. The customers cursed progress as they were woken from their sleep to get up and switch off those blasted bulbs: stupid things which did not work when you needed them and lit up without a by-your-leave! That never happened with a paraffin lamp.

The return of the squire's wife did not pass unnoticed. A rich elderly lady was expected, the embodiment of luxury and comfort, but it was an old woman of very modest appearance who got down from the evening train in Saint-Libéral on Wednesday 25 June.

Helped by her daughter, she climbed carefully down from the carriage and waited patiently while the porter unloaded her luggage and piled it on the dusty platform.

Apart from their trunks and cases – of beautifully polished leather, with a few old labels from grand hotels to recall past splendours – nothing else gave the impression that the two passengers had once known the leisured and gilded existence of those who could live on their unearned income. Even the station manager, who remembered full well the lady of pre-war years, hesitated before approaching this elderly woman; he hardly recognised her as the widow of the late lamented Jean Duroux. And then he was amazed to see her climbing into Julien's charabanc a little later; she settled down amongst the luggage and endured, without batting an eyelid, the jolts and creaks of the dilapidated cart which was commonly used to transport calves and pigs.

Hardly had this outfit set off up the road to the château than the station-master, still in a state of shock, ran to Suzanne's, where he was sure the regulars would be fascinated by the incredible news: the lady of the manor had returned, but instead of arriving in a beautiful motor-car as everyone expected, she had just disembarked from the railcar, like an ordinary village wife coming back from market at Objat!

'Well, that's hard to believe,' murmured one of the drinkers. 'And you say they climbed into Julien's cart?'

'I swear they did!'

'Well, well,' sighed the man, 'then we really will have to accept that she has no money left! But look here, you knew that, didn't you?' he asked, turning to the back of the room, where the former solicitor was playing billiards all alone.

Maître Lardy shrugged, struck another ball, then replaced the cue and came to the bar.

'Yes, I knew that,' he admitted. 'Oh, I can tell you, I'm not bound by professional confidentiality any longer, anyway it's not a secret. You'll soon see, the lady doesn't own much any more . . . '

'But how the devil's that!' asked the man.

They could not begin to understand how the Duroux family's solid fortune could have disappeared without trace.

'Ah, my dear fellows,' the solicitor exhaled slowly, 'the really hard task these last ten years hasn't been earning money, but keeping it!'

'But good God!' his neighbour persisted, 'the squire in his time owned property and, and . . . what do you call them, those bits of paper?'

'Stocks and shares,' the old notary laughed sarcastically. 'Of course he did. And his widow is proof positive that no one can be protected from injudicious investments . . . His property? Sold at the end of the war! As for his shares, they lost four-fifths of their value in ten years! And then there were the Russian loans . . . No, believe me, the fine times at the château are over, well and truly finished. All that Madame Duroux has left are the farm rents paid by Léon and, I think, the income from a small flat in Paris. She can still live off that, but she'll have to be careful . . . '

'My God! You could have told us earlier! She owes me money!' cried Edouard Feix. He was a slater, and had just spent a fortnight renovating the roof of the château; now he feared that he would not be paid.

'Complain to my colleague in Terrasson, he's looking after the last remains of Madame Duroux's estate,' Maître Lardy reminded him.

'I know,' grumbled the other, now annoyed that he had undertaken more than 500 francs'-worth of repairs. 'Tell me, do you think she'll still be able to pay me?'

'Of course. Don't make it worse than it is, she's not a beggar yet!'

'Maybe not yet,' agreed one of the customers, 'but all the same, if you'd told me that one day she would travel up to the château in Julien's cart! Well!'

The return of the squire's wife and her daughter enlivened the village gossip for several days. A few evil tongues made the most of the station-master's and Julien's reports, assuring everyone that the old lady was not only completely ruined but also burdened with debt, and the shopkeepers should beware of demands for credit which would not be long in coming.

But that malicious tittle-tattle did not circulate for long after it was discovered that Edouard Feix had his bill for 518 francs settled without any difficulty. Roger Traversat, the carpenter, who had repaired a few shutters and several square metres of parquet flooring lifted by the damp, promptly climbed up to the château, politely presented his invoice, and pocketed the 1,027 francs he was owed. Then everyone had to admit that even if the lady no longer enjoyed her former riches, she still had enough to live on, provided she confined herself to a modest way of life.

So they became accustomed to seeing her walking into the village to make her necessary purchases of groceries. Always accompanied by her daughter, she never failed to greet all the elderly people whom she had known in former times. Often she stopped for a little chat, asked for news of such and such a one, or enquired after the health of those whom she remembered. But many of these were missing, carried off by the war, old age or illness. Then she would shake her head and murmur: 'How time passes . . . ' and continue her walk.

A devout Christian, she attended Mass every morning, naturally resuming her place in the old pew reserved for the lords of the manor; it still stood between the fourth and fifth rows of chairs, to the left of the altar. No one had dared to sit in that stall since the departure of the Duroux family fifteen years earlier.


'Are you ready? asked Pierre-Edouard, pushing open the door of the bedroom. He went in, smiled, then strode over to Mathilde, picked her up in his arms and twirled her round.

'You're crazy! We're not the ones getting married!' she protested with a laugh, 'you'll spoil my things!'

He kissed her on the neck, enraptured. She looked ravishing in a beautifully cut, diaphanous blue dress which suited her perfectly.

She had made the outfit herself, following an example shown in *Petit Echo de la Mode*; not content to copy it exactly, she had improved it by using some remnants of tulle to add delicate touches to the cuffs, collar and bodice. For the first time since her mother's death she had left off her mourning dress, in honour of her brother, and felt quite young again.

'You'll look much more beautiful than the bride,' he assured her as he turned her round at arm's length. 'Right, this is too important to be late, are the children ready?'

'Of course, but they're hanging about outside and . . . I hope they haven't got dirty!'

'Yes, it's time to go, come on, into the gig,' he said, holding out his hand to her.

The cart was waiting by the door, and Mathilde noticed that

Pierre-Edouard had polished the harness; the horse-collar shone like the sun, the copper rivets glowed, and even the bit had been rubbed with fine sand and sparkled in the horse's mouth.

'Wait for us! Wait for us!' shouted the children, running out of the barn.

'What have you been up to in there?' Pierre-Edouard frowned at them, but then smiled at their sheepish expressions, and with one arm lifted up little Mauricette – pink from head to foot in her pink dress – and placed her on the seat of the cart.

'Climb in, I'll be back in a minute,' he said and moved towards the stable. 'We're going now,' he called to his father.

Jean-Edouard loaded a forkful of dung onto the wheel-barrow and nodded. 'All right.'

'I expect we'll be back very late.'

'Yes, of course. Go on, don't worry, the house won't be empty, the animals will be seen to, I'm here . . . '

'Good. Right then, we're going,' repeated Pierre-Edouard, and went out.

Once again he was a little embarrassed not to be able to share this happiness, just because Léon was involved. If only his father could forget his old grudges, and stop adopting a frosty expression whenever there was any mention of Léon! It was getting boring, and annoying, because Mathilde could not even invite her brother in. And the children were not stupid, they asked more and more often why their uncle never came to spend an evening at their house.

'We'll have to find a way,' he thought, 'especially now that he'll have a wife! Bloody hell, she'll be our sister-in-law!'

But it was a difficult problem to resolve, for no one could force his father to open his home to someone he disliked. The house belonged to him; he had the right to let Léon know that his presence was not welcome.

The big Mathis automobile slid along the kerbstone and stopped in front of the entrance to the mairie. Behind it a sparkling eight-cylinder Amilcar drew in to park, then a Morris-Léon-Bollée, and finally two Renault Vivasix.

The curious positioned on every street corner, and the customers who paraded the length of the market stalls in Place St Martin, all nodded their heads like experts. Marriages took place frequently at Brive, especially on Saturday afternoons, but a wedding with so many guests and such luxurious vehicles was a rare sight.

All the bystanders joined in a good-natured conspiracy which inspired each to chatter spontaneously to his closest neighbour; soon they were all informed as to the identity of the husband and wife to be. A lively commentary ensued on the age of the bride, the price of her dress, the size of her dowry and her father's estate. The naïve might exclaim at the great difference in age between the bride and the groom, and the cynics ramble on as Léon took his young fiancée's arm in his and entered the mairie, but the majority of onlookers declared unanimously that successful, lasting marriages were based on similarities of position in life, on alliances of wealth and eventually, as a result of these, on mutual esteem. For love and fresh water is fine for giddy girls or the thoughtless, but not for serious people who know how hard life can be, what things cost and what dangers lie in wait for marriages based solely on blind passion.

'The mayor must be blind!' cried one joker. 'Or otherwise he'll have to put a paper bag over his head tonight. Blimey, that's no Mistinguett he's marrying! What a beanpole!'

This observation was cruel and unjust. Certainly Yvette Chantalat was no Venus, but she was really not ugly, as the connoisseur of female beauty had just implied. Not ugly, but dull and faded, too thin and puny; despite her magnificent dress, which had been designed to show off her best points, everyone suspected it concealed a fleshless backside and a charmless façade.

In spite of all this, she radiated a sort of goodness and kindness which was attractive. It derived from her gaze, so sweet, so serene, and also from her infectious smile – delicate, sometimes tinged with an air of sadness – which seemed to be apologising to the world. A little as if the young girl knew well enough that she was not beautiful, but she could not remedy that and would have to be accepted as she was.

Léon had the honesty to declare quite openly to her that he was not looking for a beauty or a fortune, but simply a good honest wife, and for that reason she had accepted his offer of marriage. She was grateful for his candour, and had chosen him because he was the only man who had not lied to her. There were other suitors circling around, hypocrites who declared they were madly in love with her, with her charm, with her elegance – some even dared to vow her beauty!

How could those idiots think that she would be taken in by their monkey-tricks? All those dowry-hunters in love with her? Get away! Self-interested or morally corrupt, yes! The youngest of them was two years older than Léon, and she knew via her father that he was a spendthrift and gambler, to such an extent that he had run through a fine fortune within a few years of inheriting it from his parents! As for the others who had been trying their luck since her eighteenth birthday, they were no better!

But Léon was different. Her father and he had known each other for many years; they often worked together, and respected each other. And then Léon had behaved very delicately, almost prudishly, had hardly allowed himself more than an occasional kiss; but he had been very attentive, and had promised to do everything to make her happy. What more could she hope for, when no boy her own age looked at her without sneering?

# 5

PIERRE-EDOUARD looked at Mathilde, caught her eye and smiled at her. But he was feeling for her, because he guessed that she was ill at ease. The banquet was in full swing and, judging by the menu, it would not be possible to leave the table for at least three or four hours.

After High Mass at St Martin's and the photo session on the church steps, the whole wedding party was taken to the Truffe Noire hotel, where Chantalat senior provided drinks for his numerous friends and relations before they repaired to the dining room.

Pierre-Edouard and Mathilde soon realised that they did not belong to the same class as the other guests; that they were nothing but peasants who had strayed into a world which rather despised them. This world was one of meat trading, money, big business. Lots of wholesale butchers, transport agents and stock dealers were there, and to Pierre-Edouard they were the enemy who all, or almost all, owed their plump bellies, florid countenances, flamboyant dress and flashy, painted wives to the dirty tricks which they had played on him and all the other farmers. What's more he was not rich, not to them, and that was a definite fault.

Even Léon and Mathilde's own sister was judging them with a critical eye. She had married, eleven years earlier, an employee from the préfecture, the local seat of government. He was an elegant man, no doubt a good husband and father, but he was haughty and bumptious, proud of being an official, and he enjoyed reminding everyone that his frequent professional promotions were due entirely to his own abilities and achievements.

Pierre-Edouard had no liking for this bureaucrat, whom he regarded as an idler paid to do nothing. He loathed his pedantic style and his way of wrinkling his nostrils and feigning disgust on the rare occasions he condescended to visit Saint-Libéral, and there encountered muddy gutters, cow-pats and dung-heaps; anyway, he had not set foot in the village since the death of his mother-in-law two years earlier.

Mathilde and her sister were completely alienated from each other because of him. Now, since the announcement of his marriage, this sister had grown closer to Léon; she felt that her brother was making a good move, an alliance that raised him to the ranks of suitable people, with whom the wife of an official might possibly associate without demeaning herself.

Even their only son, a lad the same age as Jacques, had adopted the same habits, and behaved like the worthy heir of his pretentious father. Pierre-Edouard, watching the child, suddenly felt anxious for him.

He was sitting right at the end of the table, between Jacques and Paul, who had immediately realised that their cousin was an arsehole, but that they were not going to give him the chance to fart over them. From there it was a small step to dreaming up a few innocent little tricks to enliven the day . . . Pierre-Edouard knew his sons well, and feared they might be planning to settle some accounts.

He looked back towards Mathilde and pitied her, suffering the imbecilities of a fat, red-faced man who was already well away and trying to whisper down her neck. The wedding party had been at table for two hours, and the men were already taking off their jackets and loosening their ties.

Jacques and Paul were busily stuffing their faces, drinking hard and beginning to feel their ears turning pink. They were enjoying to the full the freedom allowed them there, right at the end of the table, where they ate what they wanted, when they felt like it, and as much of it as they desired. They frequently poured themselves half glasses of Sauterne, but with natural caution diluted it with fresh water.

The foie gras garnished with truffles had been served with a Château-Yquem as sugary as a fruit cordial, and almost as heavy; the children loved it so much that Paul cleverly spirited away three half-bottles while the courses were changed.

Jacques and Paul were good trenchermen, but quite frankly their cousin's observations were beginning to exasperate them. This fellow from Tulle was upsetting their digestive systems, if not exactly their appetites, his remarks irritating them like horseflies in August. What did it matter to them that he had a bicycle, a wrist-watch and a fountain pen? And what was this sixth form and this Lycée which he was to attend in October? It was the beginning of the holidays, and the idiot was talking about going back to school! A real imbecile!

'I'm going for a pee,' said Paul, getting up.

He winked to his brother, who instantly announced that he too was dying to go.

'He's a bloody fool, that one!' declared Paul, after they had admired the cleanliness and sophistication of the toilets. 'And he doesn't even know how to fire a catapult!' he added, as he admired the bubbles he was making in the lavatory bowl.

'And I have a red bicycle with a headlamp and a wrist-watch too!' Jacques imitated him in a sing-song voice. 'I bet he can't tell a magpie from a crow!'

'We'll have to get him drunk,' decided Paul.

'Don't be a dummy!' his brother warned him. 'They'll tan our backsides!'

'Oh, no, they won't.' Paul was sure of himself. 'We'll have a competition to see who can drink the most.'

'You must be mad! We'll get tiddly too!'

'Oh no! Listen, you talk to him, and meanwhile I'll fill my glass three-quarters full of water with a drop of wine to colour it, and then I'll fill his glass. While we're drinking, you do the same – lots of water and hardly any wine – and then we'll begin again. He won't be so full of himself after a few of those . . . '

'But what if the grown-ups see us at it?'

'Huh, they're too busy drinking themselves! Come on, we'll miss the guinea-fowl. So we'll do that, okay?'

'We'll get another hiding,' Jacques forecast fatalistically.

Their cousin's pride was a great help to them. He quickly saw through their game but believed that he was stronger than them; he resolved to show these country bumpkins how they drank in the towns.

'Hey, look at that! You're swallowing that like milk!' exclaimed Paul in false admiration, when the second glass had been emptied in one go.

'You'd better stop now, or you'll be ill,' Jacques sweetly advised, attacking a wing of guinea-fowl.

'Ill, me? Let me tell you, my father gives me wine with the dessert every Sunday, and livelier than that one!' their cousin assured them, as he filled his glass.

He drank, but his sudden pallor allerted the brothers, who decided to provide themselves with a convincing alibi; they rose and sauntered out into the courtyard of the hotel.

A few stifled cries, then some laughter – the scene they had prepared had been enacted. They returned with innocent expressions, their spirits revived by the fresh air, to find that the boy had disappeared; his place setting had been removed and a waiter was wiping up under the table.

'I hope you're not going to do the same?' demanded a fat lady.

'What happened?' asked Jacques.

'What happens to children who are too fond of wine!'

'Oh, I'm not surprised!' exclaimed Paul, 'he did nothing but drink from the moment he sat down. We told him he'd be ill, eh Jacques, didn't we tell him?'

His brother firmly agreed. But one look from his father assured him that their game had not escaped him; he was amazed when Pierre-Edouard winked at him and smiled conspiratorially.

It was a beautiful evening, warm and echoing to the chirp of the crickets, and in a sky sparkling with stars shone the pale arc of a quarter moon.

Leaning against Pierre-Edouard, gently rocked by the swaying cart, Mathilde dozed a little. Behind her, stretched out on a rug, the three children were sleeping soundly. Overcome by fatigue and their overloaded digestive systems, they had drifted off even before the carriage left the suburbs of Brive.

Now the horse was trotting smoothly across the Larche Plain; it knew the way and was making good progress without too much effort. Lulled by the regular rhythm of movement and the beat of the hooves on the ground, Pierre-Edouard felt his own eyelids grow heavy, and would gladly have copied the children, whose deep breathing he could hear behind him. But he reckoned that they would be on the road for at least an hour before reaching Saint-Libéral, so he filled and lit his pipe. The high flame from his fat copper lighter disturbed Mathilde's doze; she sat up and examined the shadows.

'Where are we?' she asked, staring wide-eyed about her.

'Just coming to Daudevie. Were you asleep?'

'Nearly. What a day!'

They had not been able to speak privately since the morning, and now had a lot to say to each other.

'It was a really fine wedding, after all,' she admitted with a yawn.

'Yes, and what a meal!'

'Oh, that . . . Old man Chantalat was certainly generous!'

'But it must have cost him a fortune . . . Tell me, weren't you bored between those two fat pig-dealers?'

'No, and how did you get on?'

'I was all right. You have to experience all sides of life,' he said with a shrug.

'We were a bit out of place, weren't we? I hope you weren't ashamed of me?'

'Don't be silly. You were the most beautiful woman there, by a long chalk!'

'Well, I'm sure I was the only one who had made her own dress. It wasn't too obvious?'

'Don't be daft,' he said, pulling her close to him, 'anyone would think you hadn't seen the old goat and the fat sausage on either side of me! They may have had beautiful outfits and all that jewellery, but I swear they were jealous of you!'

'Do you think so? Well, Léon's married at last . . . Tell me, do you think he'll turn out like them?'

'How do you mean?'

'I was thinking of those people there . . . Well, you can see perfectly well that they don't live like us, so I was wondering whether Léon . . . '

'No, no,' he reassured her, 'anyway, he won't be leaving Saint-Libéral.'

'That's true. And what did you think of Yvette?'

'I think she's very nice,' he said with sincerity.

But he did not tell her what else he was thinking. He was having difficulty in accepting the idea that his brother-in-law could find contentment with such a thin and unattractive wife, especially after tumbling so many pretty girls in the straw. And yet he seemed to be, not exactly in love, but very tenderly disposed towards her, and very considerate. Hadn't he thought to install a real bathroom in his house in Saint-Libéral, like they had in the towns, with an indoor toilet! Apart from the doctor, he was the only person in the village to enjoy such a luxury. Despite having water piped in, the other houses only had one little tap above the sink.

The other point which proved how far he was prepared to go to please his wife was this honeymoon trip – to Paris, of all places! That set him apart from the rest. Only the idle rich – a type unheard of in Saint-Libéral – could afford such an expensive adventure. Léon had justified it to Pierre-Edouard –who had not requested any explanation – by demonstrating that he could make use of his time in the capital to contact some of the wholesale horse-dealers in La Villette.

On the other hand it was probable, and in line with his character, that all this generosity was a demonstration; a bid to prove to the world that he had no need of his wife's dowry, but owed his prosperity to his own ability and hard work. Yes, perhaps it was his pride which forced him to compete with a show of wealth.

But if that was the case he had a lot to do, for that little Chantalat was really rich! Everything proclaimed it, starting with the car given to her by her father on her twenty-first birthday, which she drove with amazing competence. Pierre-Edouard only knew two women drivers, his new sister-in-law and Dr Vialle's second daughter. The man who had saved his leg in 1918 still lived in Brive, and Pierre-Edouard visited him every Christmas without fail, taking four pairs of chickens, or a leveret, or six woodcock; it was during one of these calls that he saw the girl driving a motor car. And to think that his sister-in-law had the same prowess! That had spurred on Léon. How else to explain his sudden haste to pass his driving test? He had talked about buying a car for a long time, but had never seriously addressed the problem of getting a licence until a few months ago. It was enough to see his fiancée at the steering wheel; he immediately decided to take the test.

There again he had reacted typically. Pierre-Edouard knew him well; that would not be the last proof of his pride. The Dupeuchs attached importance to the ideal of honour; such an inflexible ideal that Léon and Mathilde's father had died of it, thirty years earlier . . .

They had just passed through Brignac when a pair of headlights lit up the cart from behind. Pierre-Edouard turned round, screwed up his eyes at the approaching car, and directed his horse on to the verge. The B2 overtook them and continued in the direction of Perpezac-le-Blanc.

'I would say that's the doctor's car,' remarked Mathilde.

'Yes, it's his,' agreed Pierre-Edouard, who had recognised the number plate.

'I didn't know he had patients so far away.'

'Perhaps he's just spent the evening with friends, in Brive or in Larche.' Pierre-Edouard skated round the subject.

Mathilde had great faith in the doctor, and he did not want her to know what Léon had confided to him six months earlier, first extracting a promise that he would not repeat it to anyone. It was a sad story, which would spoil the doctor's reputation if it became known, make him a laughing stock and probably force him to move. A doctor could not treat people who made fun of him behind his back, or even despised him.

Pierre-Edouard really liked Dr Delpy. Of course he did not have the style and renown of his predecessor, Dr Fraysse, who had died eight years earlier and was still mourned by the village; nevertheless, nobody questioned his professional competence, his dedication or his honesty. He was one of the village personalities, who gave very good advice on town business and even on family matters. It was

373

therefore important not to say anything which might lower his public standing. Otherwise spiteful gossip would take over and make his life hell.

Two years earlier he had married a beautiful, distinguished young woman, the widow of one of his colleagues in the Saint-Yrieix area. Unfortunately he was seventeen years older than her. In addition, although she had done all she could to persuade him, he refused to abandon his patients in Saint-Libéral and open, as she had begged him to, a practice in Tulle; he was a country doctor and intended to remain one. 'Besides, as I told her, at my age you don't change your way of life!'

A wise principle, which he should have considered before he sacrificed his comfortable bachelor life at the age of fifty-two! His loyalty to the people of Saint-Libéral deserved their respect, and called for discretion concerning his misfortunes. If Léon had talked of what he knew to his brother-in-law it was only so that he could help, whenever necessary, to scotch the unpleasant rumours which had been circulating the countryside for the last year.

Already several vicious gossips – the sort who raise frigidity to a virtue and want to make it universal and compulsory – those nasty pieces of work were suggesting that the doctor's wife was possibly not looking after her sick mother when she was away two weeks in every month . . . Other equally evil and no less sterile minds whispered that the young woman was getting on very well with a young lawyer in Tulle, said to be her cousin . . . The sad part of the story was that the lying devils were not far from the truth.

It was Léon who, one day, had discovered and understood everything when his business had led him as far as Limoges. For it was not in Tulle but in Limoges that this warm and dimpled blonde spent a fortnight each month. Léon had seen her in the rue du Clocher, looking in the window of Demerliac, the jeweller's; a very handsome man had his arm round her waist. Léon did not know whether he was a lawyer, but he was certainly not her cousin. No family ties, however close, could give a couple such an air of perfect harmony, nor drive two people to hold each other so close, exchange such burning gazes full of understanding and promise; still less to talk so intimately.

The young woman was so completely preoccupied by her companion that she did not see Léon, who was blushing two metres away and already looking for an excuse, as though he were the guilty party! He had made off as fast as he could and, when he got back, warned Pierre-Edouard that the matter was serious. He had decided straight away to do all he could to keep it a secret, and always changed the subject when some mean spirit happened to make a ribald comment about the number of trips undertaken by the doctor's wife.

Since then, still without seeking to know, Léon had also learned – from one of his business contacts – that the poor doctor went to Brive to console himself in the arms of a sympathetic mistress, whom he had visited for a long time before his marriage and who held no grudge against him for his short-lived defection. So the doctor had probably not been visiting the sick, but his lady-friend.

'Tell me,' asked Mathilde suddenly, 'do you believe that, that he . . . well, goes to Brive to see women?'

Pierre-Edouard had never lied to his wife and hoped he would never have to. So before replying he tried to find out what prompted her to ask such a question.

'Who told you that rubbish?'

'Oh, it was at the wash-house, you know how it is, people talk . . . But it was Germaine who was saying it most. And she's positive that his wife is deceiving him, too. It's not true, is it?'

Mathilde had lofty ideals when it came to conjugal fidelity; Pierre-Edouard shared her ideals, but knew that some of his friends did not attach quite the same importance to them; he did not stick his nose into their business, that was their problem, not his. But he knew that his wife was too frank, too honest, too innocent perhaps, to be able to conceal her feelings if he revealed the whole story to her. Of course she would not pass judgement, as many did. Despite her disappointment she would say nothing, but he knew that she would be quite unable to speak frankly and naturally to the doctor, let alone his wife, as if nothing had happened. Her attitude to them would change because her good opinion of them had been destroyed, and she would be unhappy.

'And did you believe her, silly old Germaine?' he asked, as he filled his pipe.

'No.'

'Well, go on that way, then. You know gossip is like a blow-fly, it comes from carrion and loves to foul up everything. I suppose that's what it's meant to do.'

Twelve years earlier Pierre-Edouard had entrusted Mathilde with the management of their finances, and it was a point of honour with her to acquit herself well as guardian of the purse. She kept careful accounts and knew to within about twenty sous the exact total of their available funds. Economical without being mean or grasping, she saw to it that the volume of their investments grew as much as possible, in anticipation of the day when Pierre-Edouard would have to compensate his sisters.

Over the course of the years she had calculated what they had lost through the weakness of the currency, so that she had no confidence in bank notes. As soon as she could, she entrusted her small savings to Léon, who transformed them, by means of various discreet transactions, into honest-to-goodness gold coins. Pierre-Edouard made fun of her little precautions, like the provident ant in the fable stocking up for winter, but at heart he was very happy to have a wife with such foresight, and very relieved that thanks to her he was rid of the burden of doing the accounts.

One morning at the end of October, the day of the monthly market in Saint-Libéral, Mathilde drew several notes from the box which she kept at the back of her wardrobe, took her shopping bag, called Mauricette who was playing in the yard, and set out towards the main square.

She was pleased to see that there was a good turn-out of animals and numerous buyers and sellers, altogether a fine crowd. That would gladden the hearts of all those in the village who had been worrying for years about declining markets. Some had been so sparsely attended that the town council had considered abolishing them, although in former days the markets had stimulated the finances of the whole town. They were convenient too, not only for the farmers, who were saved the difficulties of taking their produce to Objat, Brive, Tulle or Terrasson, but also for the housewives, who found what they needed to buy, thanks to the stall-holders.

Mathilde pushed her way towards a group of horse-dealers in black overalls who were haggling in front of the inn, reached her brother and pulled his sleeve.

'Oh, it's you,' he said, turning round. He kissed her and Mauricette, and then guided her towards a quieter corner. 'I've some news,' he blurted out. 'It's not a cold that's making Yvette feel tired!'

She smiled, and marvelled that a man of his age could be so naïve as to confuse a touch of 'flu with the obvious signs of early pregnancy. She had seen her sister-in-law the previous evening and known then that the young woman was expecting; the symptoms were unmistakable to a mother. But she did not want to tell her brother that she had guessed, and allowed him the pleasure of announcing the great news.

'This time it's definite!' he said triumphantly. 'Yvette is expecting a baby! Just imagine, it will be born in May!'

He beamed proudly at her.

'Are you sure?' she teased him. 'I haven't noticed anything, and I see Yvette every day.'

'Yes, of course. The doctor said so,' he insisted. Then he saw that she was joking and began to laugh. 'Huh, so you're making fun of me, are you? Well, never mind, I'm really happy!'

'And so are we!'

'Look, you'll keep an eye on her, won't you? Make sure she doesn't do anything silly, eh? And at the birth, you'll come and help her?'

'But of course. And don't worry, it's not an illness!'

'Yes, yes, I'm really happy,' he repeated. 'Just imagine, I'm going to have a baby!'

'I expect Yvette's happy too?'

'Oh yes, and how! Really I could never have hoped . . . You know,' he admitted, 'she's a truly wonderful wife. Yes, she is. At the beginning I was a bit worried, you knew that, she doesn't come from here, and her family, well . . . So I said to myself she'll have difficulty in getting used to it, and everything. Well, it's not like that at all. She, she – I don't know how to put it, but I think she likes it here.'

'And I'm sure of it; she told me so.'

'Really?'

'Truly,' she assured him.

'Well, I owe that to you; you welcomed her as a sister, and your kids are always popping into our place! It seems they were needing an aunt!'

'They did. Yvette spoils them with sweets and cakes!'

'That's because she loves them. Well, I'd better be getting back to work. Is Pierre-Edouard around?'

'Yes, he should be at the syndicate.'

'Now, will you come to our house tonight to celebrate?'

'With pleasure. You know, I'd like to be able to invite you to my home too, but . . . '

'Don't worry about it, it's not worth quarrelling with your father-in-law over a little thing like that, it isn't important.'

'That's not how Pierre-Edouard feels, nor me,' she admitted a little sadly. Then she shrugged and moved on.

'How much are these?' asked Mathilde, brandishing a pair of woollen stockings.

'Nine francs fifty,' replied the trader.

'Oh well, I like knitting, and it's obviously worth doing,' she remarked, and put them down again. 'And the men's shirts?'

'The pure wool American ones are eighteen francs fifty, the wool-mixture is thirteen francs, or linen at twelve francs fifty.'

'But,' she protested, 'the last ones I bought from you cost two or three francs less! And that was only two years ago!'

'You're talking ancient history, dear! Haven't your chickens gone up in the last two years? The last one I bought cost me six francs a pound!'

'Not that much!' she protested. 'But if you want to talk about chickens I'll talk about our wheat; that's lost more than twenty francs a quintal in two years! And this, how much is it?' she asked, pointing to a pair of children's shorts with the Petit Bateau trade mark.

'Eight francs fifty.'

'And you think that's worth more than two pounds of chicken! Anyone can tell you don't breed them,' she cried, as she continued to rummage on the stall.

She chose what she needed with great care and held out her purchases to the trader, but alerted him with one of those special smiles she had.

'I'm a good customer of yours, you should give me a discount. Look how much I'm buying.'

The man shook his head, and began to add it up in a low voice: 'Two shirts at twelve-fifty, three Petit Bateau at eight-fifty, two boys' shirts at eleven . . .'

'What! Eleven francs for those shirts?' she interrupted. 'But they're not worth it, the children will have them in shreds within two months!'

The man shrugged and continued his counting. 'One hundred and thirty francs twenty-five,' he announced, 'let's say one-thirty because you're sweet.'

'Oh no, no,' she said, pretending to leave, 'unless perhaps you add this,' she decided, picking up a zip fastener twenty centimetres long. She was in the process of making a sweater for Pierre-Edouard, and realised that a zip would finish it off nicely.

'You must be joking! That cost me almost seven francs! It's the very best!'

'Well, that's all I can afford!' she said quite insincerely, a lie worthy of her cattle-dealer brother.

'No, no! Okay, the zip, I'll let you have it for five francs, but I'm losing by it. All right, a hundred and thirty-five francs for the lot. And look, I'll throw in these sweets for your little girl, and for you, this nice pair of suspenders. They're pretty, aren't they? They cost me more than a franc, your husband will like them! The lucky devil, what a fine time he'll have taking them off . . . '

'I don't need *them* to give him a fine time! Oh, all right, a hundred and thirty francs and we're quits,' she said, briskly seizing the pink suspenders, which went to join the zip fastener at the bottom of her bag.

'Now come on! You're taking all my profits!' protested the salesman.

'Far from it,' smiled Mathilde, offering her money. 'So, it's agreed? Because I can always buy from the fellow next door if you prefer . . . '

'Fine,' the tradesman capitulated, and took what he was owed. 'But if all my customers were like you . . . '

'Well, then life would be less expensive,' she assured him as she moved away, 'and then everyone would get on better.'

# PART TWO

*The Ungrateful Land*

# 6

THE harvest was at its height when Mathilde realised that her fourth pregnancy had just started. She had suspected as much for a week, and the wave of giddiness which swept over her, as she was tying sheaves in the Peuch field, confirmed it.

She was forced to lean against a plum-tree and wait for the galaxy of stars twirling in her brain to disperse. Her dizziness disappeared quite quickly, but was replaced by nausea which gave her the feeling of having her stomach between her teeth, whilst an icy wave washed across her back.

She breathed slowly, calmly, made herself take a few steps and felt better. Then, so that no one should become aware of her condition, she took up the sheaf she had dropped and bound it with a flick of the wrist. She saw that, luckily, nobody had noticed her moment of weakness.

Twenty paces ahead worked her father-in-law and Paul, with little Mauricette chirruping along beside them, whilst right at the end of the field Pierre-Edouard and Jacques were guiding the reaping-machine. As for Léon's farm-hand, whom Pierre-Edouard hired for the heavy work, he was even further away, busy opening a corridor for the machine with the scythe.

The wheat crop was not bad, and anyone but Pierre-Edouard would have been quite satisfied, but not he. He found it a poor return. 'When you think what I put down, it's hardly worthwhile! No, what we should do is plough deeper, like they do up in the north, but that's impossible with our cows. Like it or not, I should buy a pair of oxen; with those and my new Brabant swivel, I could plough it beautifully!'

This statement had almost caused an outbreak of hostilities between himself and his father. Old Jean-Edouard, with the confidence of seventy-one years' experience, had questioned the efficacy of deep ploughing.

'Ten, twelve centimetres, that's quite enough. After that you bring up cold earth that's never seen the sun and is no use for anything! Believe me, I know this soil. And then, oxen – they eat enough for four cows and don't give any milk or calves. Really, anyone would think you had money to burn!'

'In any case, it's *my* money,' grumbled Pierre-Edouard, 'and as for knowing the soil . . .'

The dispute had been cut short, for Mathilde calmed her husband with a smile. He had stated his case and she accepted that he planned to buy oxen; she knew him well enough to realise that he would carry out his project. Besides, he was sure to be right. She picked up a new sheaf, and then suddenly thought how the arrival of a baby would upset their lives for the next year.

Firstly, despite her determination and strength, her ability to work would gradually lessen during the final three months, and Pierre-Edouard needed her help to get through all his work. Then, and this was the most worrying thing, there were the problems of accommodation. There were already five of them sleeping in the same room, and it would be difficult to fit in another child, especially a baby whose crying would be sure to wake the other children during the night.

She recalled the pathetic squalling of a new-born baby, and smiled to herself over the fond memories.

'We'll put the boys in the main room,' she planned, 'after all, that's where Pierre slept when he was their age. Anyway, if there's another baby it's his fault, and if he's forgotten when he made it, I'll remind him! But I'm sure he won't have forgotten,' she decided, laughing silently to herself.

It was impossible that he could have forgotten. There are moments in a couple's life which are engraved for ever on their minds. They shape the memories which lend such secret and confiding tenderness to the looks exchanged by very old couples much later in life, at least by those who are still united in love.

The day of Louis' birth was one of those events which mark the calendar, such is the happiness and celebration surrounding them. Léon's son was born a week after Paul Doumer was elected as the new President of the Republic. Léon and Yvette's joy, as they leant over the cradle, was so great that Pierre-Edouard and Mathilde had shared it, adopted it and made it their own. When night came, the happiness was still with them. It was so beautiful on that May evening, so good to walk beneath the stars, to embrace and whisper to each other like two lovers who happen to find a soft nest of moss by a path and lie down to enjoy an hour of perfect love . . .

Pierre-Edouard could not have forgotten that evening; it was impossible. No more than he could forget all those evenings up there at Coste-Roche, in their little cottage, where they could live and love without thinking about the children who now slept or didn't sleep within two metres of them in the same room; without worrying about that moonbeam which cast an indiscreet ray of light through the heart-shaped hole in the shutter, so that the little ones would observe you with an astonished and curious eye if they awoke; not to mention the squeaking springs whose rattling might amuse or wake her father-in-law, whose expression in the morning would seem weighted with meaning.

But *that* night! Ah! that night, even the moon was welcome, when it later softly illuminated the peaceful, relaxed face of Pierre-Edouard, asleep under the Milky Way.

'Are you certain?' asked Pierre-Edouard, watching her closely.

Mathilde had waited till night fell, until children and grandfather were in bed and the workman had disappeared down the path which led to the village. Then she had told him, in two words. She looked at him and thought she discerned a shadow of annoyance in his expression, but it was only the effect of tiredness after a full day of harvesting.

'I hope you're not cross with me?' she questioned, nonetheless.

'Oh no,' he said, smiling. 'We'll have to tighten our belts a bit more, that's all.' He looked her up and down and drew her to him. 'And I bet you're going to tell me that it was all because of that evening in May, when the moon was so beautiful?' he murmured.

'Well, yes. I was sure you'd remember it.'

'Are you sorry?'

'No, not at all, quite the opposite. And you?'

'No, I'm not sorry either. We're not so old, we're still of an age to make tomorrow's children. Just imagine, this baby will only be sixty-eight in the year 2000; that's fantastic when you think about it!'

'So it's all right,' she repeated. 'You're not cross with me?'

He shook his head, then stroked her cheek with the back of his hand.

'No, I'm actually very happy. You see, this little one will force us to fight on. We felt younger when we made it. I reckon the good Lord must have seen us. With that moon he would have had to be blind not to! Yes, he must have seen us, all young and in love, so he sent us this child to keep us young and in love. And I'm also happy because it will just show your brother!' he joked. 'Since he's had a son, he thinks he's the only one who knows how to make them!'

Pierre-Edouard did not turn to his brother-in-law when he decided to buy a pair of oxen, for fear of spoiling their friendship; they both knew that you should never mix business and pleasure. Léon owned several pairs, beautiful beasts grazing his pasture, probably good workers too.

'But,' as he said to Pierre-Edouard, 'you're right, I'd prefer to sell them to someone else. One never knows, eh; suppose they went lame or something? That'd make trouble between us, and I don't want that.'

'Me neither, but what you can do is take me to the market at Turenne and help me choose. Two pairs of eyes are always better than one.'

On the appointed day, one fine morning in September, the two men climbed into Léon's Renault – a beautiful piece of engineering which he drove with ease and confidence, despite his false arm. It was a second-hand model in excellent condition which had cost him nearly 4,000 francs, but he did not regret the purchase. Thanks to this comfortable fast car, he no longer had to catch the train at impossible times in order to reach the markets when they opened. An end to the white nights at station buffets, waiting for connections to Treignac, Meymac, Bugeat or Saint-Privat! From then on he got behind the wheel and proceeded to the other side of the département with no trouble at all. Now he was often managing to research the markets of Lot or Creuse or Haut-Vienne.

They reached Turenne three-quarters of an hour before the market opened, which allowed them time to take a cup of coffee and then saunter around the market-place and have a look at the animals.

'It's a small market,' observed Léon. 'If you'd seen the last one with fat stock, the one on the Thursday after Passion Sunday, there must have been more than a thousand animals, and good ones at that!'

'Yes but I'm not looking for fat stock. Look over there; those two aren't bad.'

'Keep moving,' ordered Léon, pulling him away. 'I know that salesman, he's a colleague – a wide boy, and I know what I'm talking about! Cast an eye over those over there. Tough-looking, eh?'

They circled the animals, two superb Limousins with short heads, wide foreheads crowned by pale broad horns, thick necks, strong shoulders, solid well-muscled limbs, with wide hocks and short cannon-bones.

'A bit heavy, really,' Pierre-Edouard criticised them, 'and still quite young; seven or eight, do you think?'

'Have to look at their teeth, but I think you're right. We'll come back and look at them, all the same. I may well buy them myself.'

They strolled about for another ten minutes, looking at the other yokes of oxen, and Pierre-Edouard identified a pair of young ones among them which seemed to him outstanding. So, as soon as the drumbeat announced the beginning of the market, Léon and he sauntered carelessly around these animals. Prudently, the seller left them to it. He was a little old man with thin lips and a crafty expression. He knew what his animals were worth, but did not intend to sing their praises just at the moment.

'Well,' said Pierre-Edouard, after observing them for several minutes, 'they're a bit thin, aren't they? Especially this one,' he said, feeling the animal's rump.

Léon joined in the game. 'That one! Oh dear, oh dear, it's been suffering! That one hasn't always had enough to eat, it'll never reach eight quintals. And then, you see, there's a risk of a lop-sided team, because his partner will push harder . . . '

'That may be so, but he's eighteen months older!'

'Quite possibly . . . How old?' Léon asked the seller.

'You only have to look, my friend!' said the little old man, calmly rolling a cigarette.

Léon grasped the beast's muzzle, separated the lips and shook his head. Then he studied the second animal's teeth.

'That one is getting on for five,' he said, pointing to the first one, 'and he's only just three and a half . . . '

'That's not true!' cried the owner, forced to break his silence by such an outrageous statement.

'How's that, not true?' repeated Pierre-Edouard. 'That one has the corner teeth developing, and this one is just getting his second intermediates! So?'

'It's not true!' repeated the old man, who now took his turn at opening the animal's mouth. He pushed his nicotine-stained index finger in towards the row of teeth. 'Where are these corner teeth you can see? Are those them, there? No! It's just the second intermediates coming through! My oxen are forty months old, both of them!'

'I'm not so sure, I'm not so sure,' insisted Léon, who knew very well that the good man was telling the truth, to within two or three months.

'All the same,' slipped in Pierre-Edouard, 'they're not very heavy for their age.'

'Not heavy? Just you see here!' protested the seller. 'Those oxen, they'll reach thirteen quintals.'

'Oh, oh, my friend!' cried Léon with a laugh, 'now you're joking!'

He stepped back and measured them with narrowed eyes.

'Look, I bet if you took them to the weighing-machine, they wouldn't make eleven quintals. But I put them at . . . one thousand and sixty-five, no more!'

'How did that go again?' the old man asked sarcastically, shrugging his shoulders. But he was furious; he had weighed his animals two hours earlier and knew that Léon had a formidable eye for a beast. He had guessed right, to within two kilos!

'I hope they're docile?' asked Pierre-Edouard.

'Of course, isn't it obvious that they're trained?'

'Get them to walk a bit.'

The man obediently called the animals, who followed him quietly.

'What do you think of them?' Pierre-Edouard whispered in Léon's ear.

'They're good, very good. Look, they move forward together, and in a straight line, and believe me at ten years old, if they're well treated, they'll be on the verge of eighteen quintals.'

'That's what I thought. Well, how much do you want for them?' he asked, as soon as the owner had brought back the team.

The old man pretended to consider it; pushed his beret on to the back of his head, scratched his bald patch, spat and then sighed.

'5,250 francs – including the yoke of course . . . '

'Hah!' Léon exploded with a great laugh. 'Look, we'll take them without the yoke! A good ash yoke, with attachments and everything, is worth eighty francs, and you're asking us a thousand for it! You're not going to tell us that those little oxen are worth what you're asking!'

'Yes, I am, they're worth it, absolutely! 5,250 francs, no less!'

'Well then, no sale,' warned Pierre-Edouard.

'So, you're not the only ones at the market, are you?' was the seller's riposte.

'That's right,' Léon admitted gently, 'but shall I tell you something? Your bullocks there, at a thousand and sixty kilos, what would they give in meat, eh? They're thin, you know, you wouldn't get fifty-five per cent of the live weight in meat, let's say at a pinch fifty-three per cent, that would give you . . . call it five hundred kilos. And do you know what meat is worth, at La Villette? Eight francs fifty . . . So you see what that makes them? 4,250 francs, not a sou more, and that would be a good price! Believe me, I'd be amazed if you got more, but you can always try. Have a good day!'

'I'll shepherd him, the fool!' he continued, when they were thirty paces from the man.

Turning a seller into a shepherd was one of his specialities. All he had to do was draw two of his colleagues into the game and ask them, in return for doing the same for them some time, to go and negotiate with the chosen victim, and come to an understanding with him – or almost. In this case, since the old man was asking for 5,250 francs, that meant he would be ready to accept 4,900. So someone had to feed him the bait with an offer of 4,800 and then disappear for ever. Then the second accomplice would come along and offer 4,100 francs. The seller would laugh in his face, certain that he could do much better, but would be a little worried not to see that pleasant, honest buyer returning, and sorry, now, that he had let him go. For already, in his mind, 4,800 was a very good price that he ought to guard, as a shepherd watches over his ewes . . .

There would follow two hours of torture during which the trickster would periodically badger him, hovering around like a marauding wolf, but always making the same ridiculously low offer, sapping his resolve to hold out.

Towards midday, as activity in the market slackened and the seller found himself alone, cursing himself for having missed a good deal, it would be easy to strike a bargain. Remembering too late that a bird in the hand is worth two in the bush, the man would welcome any customer whose offer was nearer to the price suggested by the first 'wolf'; the original price was long forgotten.

'Yes,' continued Léon. 'I noticed Chassaing and Delmond – I'll prime them, and we'll shepherd him, the ass! How much do you want to part with?'

'4,300,' said Pierre-Edouard, 'but I don't like your system very much. Don't you think we should simply bargain with him?'

'No, you don't know a thing about it! These old guys, you've got to squeeze them! 4,300, you say? They're worth it; you could even go to 4,400, but more than that would be too much. Good, wait there; I'll prime my colleagues and come back to you.'

Pierre-Edouard watched him walk away and shook his head as he filled his pipe. Léon was a bloody good dealer!

Once the trap had been set, Pierre-Edouard and Léon strolled about the market, pretending complete lack of interest in the coveted animals.

Léon put in a bid for the first pair which they had seen before the fair opened, just for the fun of it and to have something to do, but the seller was greedy. Besides, Léon discovered a weakness in the rear hoof of one of the beasts. The heel had split, and though the scar was hardly visible and looked well on the way to complete recovery, there was no guarantee that it would not open up on the first stone it struck.

'Keep your oxen,' said Léon as he left, 'their feet are too fragile for my liking.'

Dealing tailed off earlier than expected, so it was towards half-past eleven when Pierre-Edouard and Léon returned to circle around their quarry. The old man, now realising that he was out-manoeuvered, glared at them vengefully. He feared the worst.

'So you're still here?' commented Léon genially.

'Seriously, now, do you want to sell, or have you just come out to give your animals some fresh air? asked Pierre-Edouard, offering his tobacco pouch and cigarette papers.

The old man rolled himself a cigarette, lit it and shrugged.

'If I don't sell today, I'll be here at the next market.'

'That's easy to say, but very rarely worth the trouble,' Léon intervened. 'So, how much?'

'4,800, that's the lowest I'll go!'

'No, no,' said Pierre-Edouard, 'we have to talk seriously, the market's nearly over and I have to get home. So let's shake on 4,250, and I'll pay for lunch.'

'You're mad! Animals like that!'

'*Miladiou*, we're not going to argue about it; you must know the price is too high, since they're still here! All right, I'll add five pistoles and it's done!' proposed Pierre-Edouard, holding out his hand.

'The devil take me if I'll let them go at that price!' protested the seller, turning away.

'Come on, you'll have to come to an agreement,' said Léon. 'How about we split the difference? All right, let's say he adds eight pistoles. Come on, shake on it.'

'No, twelve!' insisted the man. 'Not one less!'

'I'll go for twelve,' Pierre-Edouard conceded. 'That brings them to 4,370 – a high price for those little oxen!'

But he was delighted with his purchase.

Most of the inhabitants of St Libéral shared the feeling of unease which affected the country during the autumn, but few of them realised the seriousness of the crisis. Probably only the old solicitor and the doctor understood the significance of, for example, the complete financial collapse in Germany, the crash of the Viennese bank Kreditanstalt, and the forty per cent devaluation of the English pound following the abandonment of the gold standard in Britain.

For in St Libéral they were only vaguely aware of the existence of the Bourse, so when they learned that the market was falling it did not appear to be a catastrophe. In the eyes of most people, there did not seem to be any connection between strangely named shares and the price of a quintal of wheat.

Nevertheless, there was a sense of foreboding, without any perception of what the danger was, and the atmosphere in the village grew sombre. Since Léon had a sixth sense about this sort of thing, and perhaps also because he remembered the Wall Street crash – without really knowing what had happened, except for the waves of bankruptcies and suicides, which in themselves told him enough – he toured all the markets in the region and filled his pastures and sheds with heifers, young bullocks and other animals which could be fattened up. That stock, he was hoping, would not lose its value. Then he suggested that Pierre-Edouard do the same. But his brother-in-law was not worried about his savings; they were meagre, and therefore less vulnerable.

However, Pierre-Edouard also smelt danger, and made a substantial investment in supplies of seed and various fertilisers; he decided to plant as much land as he could, and set to ploughing. This season he could at last plough to a proper depth, as he had long wanted to do.

His oxen, Red and Fawn, were perfectly trained, despite being so young, and their strength was promising. They pulled the Brabant plough without apparent difficulty, and if Pierre-Edouard did not set it quite as deep as he would have liked – he did not want to exhaust his team – he improved on his previous ploughing by at least four good centimetres. Though they seemed to move so slowly, he succeeded in turning over a third of a hectare of land in a single day, thanks to these oxen – one whole plot more than with his cows.

Even Jean-Edouard had to admit that the exposed soil was of a fine consistency, with a promising, fresh appearance and a respectable colour. He gladly helped his son to sow the seed, then to harrow all the plateau fields, which were planted, according to their aspect and yield, with wheat, winter barley and rye on the poorest plots.

When all the crops were sown, Pierre-Edouard, following an old custom, fixed a small cross, shaped roughly out of straw, in the middle of each field. Mathilde attached importance to this practice. She saw it firstly as a sort of tribute to the land and to the work, and also as a discreet appeal to Heaven, a little wink at the Lord, as if to say to him: 'Look, we've done all we should do, as well as we could; now it's up to You to do the rest.'

*

Guy Vialhe, a strong baby of over seven pounds, saw the light of day on Wedneday, 24 February 1932. He had not caused his mother any problems for nine months, and now he was born just as easily. He announced his arrival quietly, towards eight o'clock in the morning, as his elder brothers were having breakfast before going to school, and he welcomed them back with his squalling when they returned at midday.

The boys might have believed in a miracle considering the speed of the birth, but they were accustomed to seeing animals coupling and to long hours watching calves and lambs being born. You go off in the morning, leaving your mother by the fireside, and you come back to find her in bed with a totally red baby beside her; it howls worse than a stuck pig, and your father is leaning over it with a soppy expression.

'Well, that was quick!' murmured Jacques.

'Hm, yes, it was!' echoed Paul, trying to sound as though everything was normal.

He was very shy, not sure whether it was quite proper to see his mother in bed. Especially as Mauricette, jealous as a broody hen, clung to her mother's nightdress and had pulled it half-open to reveal two breasts heavy with milk.

'Come and give me a kiss,' Mathilde told them. She hugged them and ruffled their hair.

'He's sweet, your little brother, isn't he?' asked Pierre-Edouard.

'Yes, yes,' they lied in chorus, for they really could not say what they were thinking. Just imagine, their brother was as ugly as a freshly skinned leveret!

And yet even their grandfather, who was talking to the doctor at the back of the room, seemed to think he was superb. As for their Aunt Yvette, busy changing the marvel, it was quite obvious she had gone completely mad, with her 'gouzi-gouzi' and ridiculous fussing. Her behaviour was so bizarre that the two boys did not even realise it was the first time she had entered their house.


The non-Communist Socialists campaigned fiercely during the first round of elections to the legislative assembly, and were well received by the electors in Saint-Libéral. Many had appreciated the moderate speeches made by Léon Blum. At least he did not have his eye on people's private property; he had given a guarantee to all the farmers that his party would help them to keep their land.

That was certainly more reassuring than the proletarian revolution proposed by others. Even when the Reds in St Libéral proclaimed that they too would respect the property of small farmers, many people mistrusted their word. St Libéral might be a long way from the centre of the world, but they still read the newspapers and what they knew of the Soviet experience was food for disturbing thoughts.

It was towards five o'clock in the afternoon, two days before the second round of the elections should have taken place as normal, that the dreadful news broke. Yvette Dupeuch was the first to know. Six months earlier Léon had given her a big wireless, on which she picked up the programmes from Radio Limoges *and* those from Paris. Her receiver, the only one like it in the village, was the envy of all – the doctor owned one, but it was a crystal set with comparatively poor reception. The next-door neighbours were happy when Yvette opened her window; then they all enjoyed the tunes, concerts and songs broadcast by the beautiful machine – for free.

Léon was in the stable when his wife came to inform him of the crisis. He put down his brush and currycomb, and leaned on the horse he had been grooming.

'My God, it reminds me of poor old Jaurès . . . '

Then he went out to tell his brother-in-law. As he entered the courtyard he bumped into Jean-Edouard, who gave him a baleful look and turned his back.

'Is Pierre there?' asked Léon.

'What's that to you?' muttered Jean-Edouard, moving away.

*He's a bloody fool, that old man*, groaned Léon inwardly. He hesitated, nearly decided to leave, and then suddenly called out: 'This is a fine time to have the sulks! They've just murdered the President of the Republic!'

'What's that you said?' whispered Jean-Edouard, turning back.

'A Russian shot him, not two hours ago, in Paris. He's not dead, but it's just like when . . . '

'Ah, well, yes . . . like Sadi Carnot . . . A Russian, you said? That doesn't surprise me, those Bolshevik pigs!' The old man was carried away; for him, all Russians were Reds, after 1917.

His feelings towards those whom he accused of making a pact with the Germans in the middle of the war were such that no one could get him to see that Gorguloff, despite being Russian, was a White, an anarchist and, to cap it all, mentally deranged.

'That's what I'm saying!' he insisted, 'a real Bolshevik! And clear out of my way, you and your newspapers!' He pushed away the ones his son shoved under his nose the following morning.

And that evening he cursed all the Marxists in creation as he turned on his heel, walked into the house and slammed the door.

'He'll never accept me, the queer old fish!' grumbled Léon, left standing in the middle of the farmyard.

So it was not until it grew dark, when Pierre-Edouard came down from the plateau where he had been planting maize, that he learned the news. It saddened him. He respected the President of the Republic for, as he explained to his sons during dinner:

'A man who has lost four sons out of five in the war can't be a bad man. He must be an honest man, because he could have protected them from having to enlist if he'd wanted to. Yes, four sons out of five. And now it's him they're firing at . . . Well, perhaps he'll survive it . . . '

In the early morning, the village discovered that Paul Doumer had rendered up his soul at sunrise, at exactly 4.37 a.m.

The financial crisis, which everyone had been expecting for several months, spared no one in Saint-Libéral, not even Léon. During the summer of 1932 the price of wheat fell sharply from the level it had been at for the last two years, about 140 francs to 117 a quintal – and those who could get rid of it at that price were well content, for it fell again in the months that followed. As for meat, the rate fell by twenty per cent.

For many small farmers, who were already finding it difficult to make a living and could not economise further, it was truly terrible. They sank into miserable poverty, and did not even have the solution of seeking a living in the towns, for unemployment was already rife there.

The whole commercial life of the village was affected, and Saint-Libéral fell into a torpor; soon there was very little cash in any household. As a logical reaction, the only thing that might save them, the farms tried to turn in on themselves, become self-sufficient, undertaking nothing which required the slightest capital outlay. For the few sous which did come in were essential to settle the vital bills – the local taxes, the fire insurance, the electricity, the medical expenses in families where someone was sick. And then, for many farmers, there were also the annual interest payments on loans.

All the shopkeepers and craftsmen in the village suffered from the scarcity of money; a few could save their businesses, come what may – some charitable ones even gave credit – but others could not keep afloat for long, and they disappeared.

So it was that Jean Breuil, one of the two carpenters, went away, and also Edouard Feix, the last slater. And then one evening, having carefully swept up the golden shavings which drifted across the floor of his workshop, put away all his tools, placed his last pair of sabots on the shelf, the old clog-maker climbed stiffly up to his attic, where the walnut logs were stored. He rolled one of them into the middle of the room, sat down on it, placed his chin over the mouth of his old Flobert – a 12-bore with pin-fire cartridges and black powder – and blew out his brains.

His death distressed the whole community, for the old man, who was going on for eighty, had been part of the life of the village. As he had been a widower for ten years and had no children, the town council arranged a civil funeral, attended by a thoughtful crowd. Everyone approved of the presence of Father Verlhac, who, disregarding the precepts, came to pray by the open grave; then, turning to the congregation, explained to them that this old man had the right to prayers, despite his suicide, for despair, loneliness and poverty had prompted him to an irrational act which should be forgiven.

No one ever knew that this charitable impulse, denounced to the bishop by several devotees, earned him a scolding the following week from an elder of the Church who would not compromise over the regulations.

On top of these deaths and failures, the schoolteacher retired, and he and his wife left the village. He had held his post in Saint-Libéral since 1906; they had integrated into the community, and if some felt they were politically biased to the left, all were unanimous in recognising their professional competence as above criticism. Thanks to them, and the twenty-six years they had devoted to teaching, numerous inhabitants now possessed a School Certificate. Added to that were the many services rendered, the good advice and even the helping hand which they had never hesitated to offer.

Everyone was sorry to see them go. Few men therefore missed the leaving party organised by the council, and all were moved to hear the warmth and emotion in the teacher's voice when he thanked them.

'As for you, Father,' he concluded, 'you know that we don't work in the same way, neither with the same weapons nor the same aims. Nevertheless, I must say that I've always found you an honest and outspoken opponent, and I can admit – for everyone is aware of it – that you were my enemy when we first knew each other, but have become my friend, as has everyone else here. To conclude, I hope that my young successor, who has won his teaching spurs in Objat, will find as much happiness here as I have done, and that everyone will give him the welcome he deserves.'

The new teachers, Jacques and Germaine Sourzac, arrived at the beginning of September. It was soon obvious that he too was a radical Socialist, more politically committed than his predecessor and more extreme in his views. But the situation was so bad, the mood so bitter, that his acid comments and opinions passed unnoticed. No one needed him to tell them that things were not going well!

During the course of his life, Pierre-Edouard had often been forced to struggle against discouragement, tiredness and pessimism, but he had never doubted his vocation until this slump came. Following a poor harvest, a storm or a severe frost, he had experienced the dragging depression which haunts the lives of all those who wrestle with nature, but he had reacted by telling himself that next year would perhaps be better.

Even at the beginning of their marriage, when he and Mathilde had fought to survive on their tiny farm, they had continued the battle by telling themselves that the future would smile on them. The poverty they suffered was the natural reward of those who lacked land and so could not produce more, but it would be over as soon as they could increase their output.

But those times, when all you had to do was work your fingers to the bone to develop and increase the crops, were long gone. Since the market had fallen there was no point in killing yourself to get the harvest in; you still had to sell, and count yourself lucky when the prices covered the expense of production.

This situation worried Pierre-Edouard; its illogicality made him doubt his vocation. For the first time, he began to question what use and value there was in his profession.

For several months he drifted in a haze of discouragement, scepticism and bitterness. Finally he reacted, with all the strength and aggression of a Vialhe, but he never forgot the lesson of those chaotic years, when he fought against real poverty, despite full storage lofts and generous harvests.

The threat hanging over the whole farming world forced him to open his eyes to the future facing his own children. Up till then – faithful to long family tradition – he had nurtured the hope that the most capable of his sons would succeed him. The crisis threw everything into disarray, showing him that this sequence was not as reliable as he had thought. The one who inherited the farm would not necessarily be the lucky one; it might be a millstone.

This realisation shook him. However, because he had never given up, he refused to despair, and did not abandon the idea of one day leaving in the hands of Jacques, Paul or Guy that land which had fed the Vialhes for almost two centuries.

But he was prudent. He surmised that owning land was no longer a sufficient advantage, and he decided, in agreement with Mathilde, to do his best to equip his sons for the battle of life: this crrisis might be only the forerunner of worse to come.

All these worries, all these doubts, forced Pierre-Edouard and Mathilde to throw themselves into the struggle. For a while they drifted in despair, sleepwalking through the minimum work necessary, but their awakening was sudden and violent.

The spirit which had helped them surmount the first trials, fourteen years earlier, took hold of them again. They joined forces and plunged into the thick of battle.

Mathilde was the first to react. One evening at the end of that sad year, 1932, when the children were asleep, Grandfather was ensconced on the settle reading *La Montagne* – they had subscribed to it for the past two years – and Pierre-Edouard was flicking through a back number of *Chasseur Français*, Mathilde pushed a school exercise book covered in figures towards him.

'Do you want to discourage me completely?' he reproached her, glancing at the rows of figures.

'Of course not. Look, here . . . '

He did as she asked, remembering fondly that evening more than twelve years ago when, as now, she had shown him the results of her calculations and suggested what he should do to extricate them from their difficulties.

'Fine,' he said, having surveyed her accounts, 'and so what?'

'So what? Come on, look here, don't you see?' she replied, pointing to one column with her forefinger. 'Don't you see that the only product to hold its price is tobacco?'

'I've known that for a long time; there's no need to tell me!'

'Yes, you know, but you don't draw the right conclusions!'

On the settle, Jean-Edouard nervously turned the pages of his newspaper. He admired his daughter-in-law, respected her, but he could not accept her meddling in a subject which, in his opinion, was no business of hers. Pierre-Edouard was the head of the farm, and his wife, however charming, should not stick her nose in. But as he had sworn never to get mixed up in this sort of discussion, he resumed his reading; he was startled to hear his son's reply.

'All right, dear,' joked Pierre-Edouard, 'you should know by now that you married an idiot! So what should we do? Your ideas are bound to be better than mine!'

'We must plant three or four times as much tobacco!'

'Oh, that's all? We put in ten thousand this year, and you'd like to do forty thousand? A hectare, eh? Nothing puts you off, does it?'

'That's the only thing which gives any results,' she repeated. 'First you'll have to get permission to increase your production, but that's no problem, Léon will get it for you – he's already done battle with the new director of the Tobacco Board. Then we'll have to get down to it, starting this year!'

'*Mais miladiou*!' he grumbled, 'anyone would think you didn't know the work involved! That's what's preventing me doing it! If it were up to me I'd have planted another 25,000 at least two years ago! Bloody hell, there are only three of us here! And that's only because Father is willing to help us! Tell me, don't you think we work long enough hours as it is?'

'We'll *have* to manage it!' she insisted. 'We can't go on like this. All you have to do is take on some day labourers – Léon would like nothing better than to loan you two or three of his workers.'

'Sure! At ten or twelve francs a day, plus food! And where am I going to find money like that? By selling our wheat, perhaps? Nobody wants it!'

'We must grow more tobacco,' she repeated. 'It's the only way out, think about it.'

He thought about it. But it was a whole month later before he took the step; he was almost pushed into it by other events.

First of all, in January, there was a gloomy meeting of the town council during which Léon announced the closing down of the shuttle connection which had replaced the main-line trains since 1924. This decision, supposedly taken following a very serious accident – there had in fact been deaths – was actually for economic reasons.

The railway line, which had opened Saint-Libéral to the world at the beginning of the century, made possible the markets, the shows, and trade with other areas, was running at a loss. Without it, Saint-Libéral would sink back into loneliness and isolation. A bus was promised to replace the train, but that was no use to transport the tons of plums, cherries, peas and beans produced in the commune to Brive and Objat. They would have to load up their carts as in the old days, and set off in the middle of the night so as not to miss the opening of the wholesale markets. Or buy a van, but nobody could afford one of those.

All the villagers took the closure of the line as a personal insult. They also saw it as proof that those up there in Limoges or Paris who had taken this decision could not care less about the consequences, were completely indifferent to the future of the village; it could die, for all they would worry about it.

What was Saint-Libéral to the smart men in suits? Nothing. It was only a hamlet in a remote corner of the Corrèze. Whether it lived or died did not concern them; did they even know of its existence?

The second event which shook Pierre-Edouard was the deterioration of the political situation, and the certain knowledge that this had caused the terrible impasse in which he was stuck, like millions of his colleagues, unable to find a way out.

After Herriot was overthrown on 14 December 1932, Paul-Boncour was the next to fall, only six weeks later. It was Léon who announced this news to him when they met out hunting on Sunday, 29 January. But it was nothing unusual: it was only the fifth government to flounder in eighteen months.

'My God!' swore Pierre-Edouard. 'When are they going to stop fooling about! It's incredible, we'll never get out of this!'

Léon shrugged, and looked down at his dog, who was wagging his tail and stretching his nose towards an oak spinney.

'Look out,' he alerted Pierre. 'He might flush out a woodcock.'

But it was only a blackbird, which shot out at knee height, piping its alarm call.

'Yes,' Léon replied eventually, 'they're in a complete muddle up there, it'll all end in disaster . . . '

'But what's to become of us? Bloody hell, we've got to live! I've got four kids, after all!'

'All you have to do is plant more tobacco!' joked Léon.

'Oh, so Mathilde's been talking to you about her plans! She's a fine one, your sister . . . '

'Yes, when she wants something, it's quite something . . . but her idea holds up.'

'Maybe . . . Maybe, and tobacco's the only way to get anything out of the State!'

When he returned home at midday, he had taken the decision.

'All right,' he said, 'we can't go on like this. If we get permission, we'll sow 40,000 tobacco plants this year.'

'I knew you'd come round to it,' said Mathilde, putting the soup tureen on the table. 'You'll see, we'll get out of this.'

And her smile warmed his heart.

The following evening, Saint-Libéral learned that Germany had chosen a new Chancellor, one Adolf Hitler. But nobody took any interest in the news.

'Besides,' as one of Suzanne's customers put it, 'what's all the fuss about that pig of an Austrian; *he* won't give us back our trains or improve the price of wheat!'

When spring came the whole village saw that Pierre-Edouard had decided to launch an offensive; instead of submitting passively to the effects of the crisis (and there was no end in sight) he was preparing to tempt fate.

The old men smiled, and reminded the younger ones that Pierre-Edouard had something to live up to; at the beginning of the century his father had also amazed everyone with his determination to work hard and take risks. He had realised what profit could be made from the building of the railway line, and had put the work in hand to benefit from it. And the greybeards, who still remembered and admired the enterprise which had made him rich, had no doubt that his son knew what he was doing, that his plan was considered, matured, with every detail thought out.

Despite that, they were absolutely astonished. They knew the Viahles, they were ready for anything. But even Jean-Edouard could not believe his ears when his son announced that he would not be growing a single grain of wheat while the prices remained so low.

'No more wheat? You can't be serious! The wheat, that's the . . . that's the pride of the farm!'

'Huh, pride! I don't give a damn about that; it's costing me too dear, your pride!'

'My God! Think of the neighbours! What will they say?'

'I don't give a damn about the neighbours either.'

'And your bread? Eh? What about your bread?'

'What about my bread? I'll buy it, that's all!'

'But, good God, it won't be your own!'

'Oh, so you think that the baker keeps our flour separate from his? Oh well! I suppose he puts more chalk in it!'

Up till then the Vialhes, and all the farmers in the village, had got their bread by bartering their flour for it. Since the death of the miller the water-mill at St Libéral lay silent, so they took their grain down to the factory-mill at Brignac, collected their flour and their bran and returned, happy in the knowledge that they would not lack bread in the year to come. By deciding not to grow wheat any more, Pierre-

Edouard was flouting an ancient tradition; to his father it was worse than insulting, it was criminal.

'*Per moun arme!*' Jean-Edouard swore an old oath. 'On my word, while I live, this farm will provide a portion of wheat! I'm seventy-three years old, but in the name of God, I am still capable of holding the plough and sowing my wheat!'

It was the first time that he had protested since he had handed over the farm to his son. He had closed his eyes to many things, but this was going too far. It was Mathilde who saved the situation.

'Now, now, Father, don't worry. Remember, the wheat has been sown for this year, you've seen it; the "Dattel" crop is doing well and so is the "Good Farmer", and there's almost four hectares of it! What Pierre means is that he won't drill in the autumn, unless the market improves. If it climbs back up, he'll sow, that's a promise – just enough for us, but he'll sow it. If the price stays down he'll keep back double the amount of corn for our flour, that's all. And perhaps things will be looking better the year after.'

'But why don't you want to sow any more wheat?' grumbled Jean-Edouard, a little reassured but not convinced.

'Because I'm losing money on it!'

'And what are you going to put in its place?'

'It doesn't matter what – maize, tatties, tobacco, barley, that's what's selling least badly.'

'Never mind that.' His father was stubborn. 'No wheat on the farm, it's hardly a proper farm!'

'We'll talk about it again when it's time to sow,' said Pierre-Edouard, shrugging his shoulders, 'but I'm telling you, if wheat doesn't recover its price, I won't sow a single handful!'

'Yes, Father, we'll talk about it another time,' Mathilde interrupted, placing her hand on her husband's arm. 'Just now Pierre wants to plant our land with potatoes, maize and tobacco, not forgetting vegetables. It'll be a lot of work for us.'

When Mathilde spoke of 'our' land, she meant the fields which belonged specifically to them, to Pierre-Edouard and herself – the Meeting Field, Léon's Letters, Mathilde's, the Peaks. The Vialhe fields she only ever referred to as '*the*' land, and everyone understood.

'So besides 40,000 tobacco plants, you want a hectare of potatoes and the same of maize, and vegetables as well! You must be mad, you'll never manage it!' predicted Jean-Edouard, who knew full well just how much work such areas required.

'Yes, we will,' Pierre-Edouard assured him. 'We'll manage it because we have no choice.'

There were many in the village who shared Jean-Edouard's scepticism. Some felt that Pierre-Edouard was aiming too high, embarking on work of such a scale that he would never accomplish the hoeing of such areas with only his wife and father to help him. The old man might be strong, but you could see his age. As for Mathilde, she was a plucky one, but she had plenty to keep her busy; her little one was now thirteen months old and took a lot of looking after – the other children too, not to mention the cows, ewes, pigs and the fowl in the yard.

'Well then,' Maurice interrupted one evening at Suzanne's when the conversation turned to Pierre-Edouard's plans, 'he'll take on Léon's workers, that's how he'll do it! I'm not worried about him!'

'Maybe, but labourers are only good at eating up the profits.' Bernical was sure of it. 'No, he'll break his back, that's for sure!'

'And that would please you, eh?' joked Louis Brousse.

They all knew that, while Bernical was not a bad man, he was envious and resentful by nature; he saw every neighbour's success as a personal affront, so he had plenty to vent his spleen on when it came to the Vialhes.

'Me?' he replied. 'I don't give a damn! He can do what he likes, it's his farm!'

'All the same,' continued Maurice, 'I know him well, I'm sure he'll come out of it all right. And his idea of not wanting to plant any more wheat, it's not so stupid as all that. Believe me, he's right about that too.'

'So why don't you do the same?' asked his neighbour.

They all knew the answer. Although he was getting on for forty-two and remained on good terms with his father, Maurice was not the owner. At the farm it was his father, old Jeantout of seventy-two, who took all the decisions, and it would be like that until he died. Maurice was not going to copy Pierre-Edouard; even if the price of wheat fell further, it would never be said that Jeantout's land grew no wheat. He too felt that a farm was judged by its wheat-store.

Nicolas arrived in Saint-Libéral one evening in May 1933. He walked in long strides, with the supple, rhythmic gait of one accustomed to the high road; he marched like a man who was not afraid of 50 kilometres at a go, or a journey of 500 leagues. And at his back, swinging from a stout elm cudgel across his shoulder hung the bundle which is common to all those who can tie up their fortune and all their belongings in a simple linen cloth.

He stopped in the middle of the square and looked slowly around him. The few old women chatting under the lime trees noticed that he looked like a hawk, one of those spirited birds of prey whose gaze mesmerises.

Tall and well built, he had a haughty air and a severe expression accentuated by a generous shock of white hair; an angular, scraggy face with sparkling pale blue, almost grey, eyes. Dressed in black corduroys, worn but very clean, and a blue shirt open to reveal a powerful tanned chest, he was impressive, with his noble bearing, his stature and his haughty manner of narrowing his eyelids and throwing back his white mane as he looked about him. After he had examined each house and glanced coldly in the direction of the gossips, he turned on his heel and marched towards the mairie.

Alfred, the town sergeant, who was sipping an absinthe at Suzanne's, had noticed the stranger's arrival and did not know quite how to classify him. The bundle denoted a tramp, but the figure demanded respect. These two totally contradictory facts provoked an uncontrollable outbreak of sweat on his balding forehead. He pushed his kepi on to the back of his neck, mopped his brow, then, to restore his confidence, fingered the shining copper badge proudly pinned over his heart. He stepped out into the square and called to the newcomer.

The man turned round and, from the steps of the mairie, looked down at the representative of law and order hobbling towards him.

Alfred, whom the fortunes of war had assigned to St Nazaire in 1917, had lost a foot while helping to unload an American cargo ship. But he was very proud of his pegleg, exhibited it with great complacency and used it to convince the younger generation that he had received this wound during the terrible battles of Mort-Homme. The old men sniggered at this blatant lie and assured everyone gravely that Alfred was the one who had received the most 'sardines' during the war, those coveted chevrons which were the pride of all the veterans. The wicked men knew that foolish Alfred had received a crate on his foot, accidentally released from a crane; the crate contained a ton of sardines in oil.

'There's no one at the mairie at the moment!' he advised, as he struggled up the four steps.

He fiddled with his badge again, and stared hard at the stranger to try to discover what his business was. For Alfred, the human race was divided into two groups, the good and the bad. The former were clean, hard-working, honest and had the right to be addressed respectfully; they did not wander the byways or frequent places of ill-repute, and could produce their papers in good order at a moment's notice. The latter were quite the opposite.

His examination of the tall fellow who stood before him plunged him into agonising confusion. This person was definitely a tramp, for he carried the bundle of a poor man and had arrived on foot. But he had the bearing of a colonel in a cavalry regiment, and his gaze penetrated your brain, which absolutely contradicted the first impression; a traveller would never give him the feeling that he should stand up straight and prepare to salute. Racked by doubts, Alfred opted for the cautious approach.

'Are you by any chance looking for someone?'

'Mayor!' said the other, after a moment's hesitation.

'The mayor? He's not there yet.'

'Where I find mayor?' insisted the man, in a strong accent which sounded picturesque to Alfred's ear.

*He's a dago!* he thought, and this discovery put him at his ease. Everything fell into place; the suspect, despite his grand manner, was indeed a poor beggar, and it would give him real pleasure to accompany this interloper to the parish boundary and use his boot too, if necessary! He drew himself up and frowned, which accentuated the sluggishness of his bovine expression.

'What do you want with the mayor then, eh?'

'Where he, mayor?' repeated the other.

*He doesn't understand a thing, the mug!* Alfred was in control: 'Come on, show me your papers,' he ordered abruptly. And to intimidate his victim he took a step forward, hoping that this would provoke action. 'Move a muscle and I'll clap you inside for assaulting a police officer. Articles 228 and 230 of the penal code!' he recited in delighted anticipation. 'Right, these papers, where in hell are they!'

'Oh, papers!' said the man, fumbling in his jacket. He took out a well-used wallet, but its fine leather and gold initials caught the sergeant's eye.

*I bet he stole that*, he rejoiced inwardly, and pictured himself arresting the fellow.

'Give me those,' he ordered, eagerly seizing the identity cards which the stranger held out to him.

He glanced over the writing, furrowed his brow, then laboriously spelt out in a low voice: 'Nicolas Kra-jha-lo-vic, born 30 June 1893 at . . . at Kra-gu-je-vac, Serbia. Dammit, a Russian! Well, what's he up to here, this Cossack! Eh? What are you wandering around here for? What a turn up!' he said, scratching his head. He turned round towards the square to enlist the women as witnesses, for they had strolled nearer.

Heaven granted that Father Verlhac emerged at that moment from the presbytery, to go to recite the Angelus. He saw the gathering and came over.

'What's going on?' he asked the sergeant.

'There's this Russian, looks a bit fishy to me, wants to see Léon.'

'A Russian?'

'Well, yes, see here,' said Alfred, holding out the papers to him.

The priest studied them, and smiled. 'He's no more Russian than you! He's a Serbian – or to be more precise, a Yugoslavian for the last two years.'

'Oh well, it's all the same, isn't it?' protested Alfred, in annoyance.

The priest shrugged his shoulders and turned to the man.

'Do you speak French?' The stranger looked confused. He continued: 'German? Italian?'

Then, suddenly, the man launched into a long speech, a mixture of Italian, German and French. The priest listened, asked a few questions, and turned to Alfred.

'He wants to see Léon because he's looking for work. He's come from Marseilles, on foot. He left his country in 1930 and he's spent two years in Italy; his papers and his residence permit are all in order.'

'Oh, all right,' said Alfred, quite cast down. 'Well, he'll just have to wait for the mayor, it's not my business then.' And he went off grumbling to himself.

Léon arrived half an hour later. He had chanced upon Father Verlhac and been alerted to the situation, so he called upon the few scraps of Italian he had learned during the war and tried to find out what this strange creature wanted. But the man, before replying to the question, pointed his finger at Léon's metal hook.

'War?'

'Yes,' said Léon. 'Why?'

'Me too, war,' said the man, opening his shirt.

'My God! They really made a mess of you!' gasped Léon as he viewed a deeply scarred hole the size of a man's fist carved in the man's stomach.

'Demis-Kapou,' explained the stranger, buttoning up his shirt. Then he clicked his heels and cried out: 'Long live Franchet d'Esperey, Marshal of France!'

'Well, you're a card!' murmured Léon, quite won over. 'So you're looking for work? Any sort of work? Yes? Well, old chap, I can't give you any, I've got all the workers I need! But come on, I know who might be able to find you something.'

# 7

PIERRE-EDOUARD untied the young calf, who bounded immediately to his mother and butted her stomach, furiously and clumsily, with his head. Pierre-Edouard guided him to the udder swollen with milk and pushed his muzzle towards a teat; the calf snatched at it greedily and sucked long and appreciatively. His tail quivered almost in time with the rhythm of his swallows and a thick foam bubbled out at the corners of his lips.

'You're a fine one, you are,' Pierre-Edouard said again, leaning against the cow, 'I do need a worker, but not just anyone! I don't know this fellow! It may be that he's never touched a tool in his life!'

'Don't be stupid,' said Léon, 'did you see his hands? You can't believe that they got calloused like that by resting his backside on a chair as a clerk?'

'Mmmm.' Pierre-Edouard gave him that. 'Perhaps he does know how to grip a handle.'

He sucked on his unlit pipe and sighed. He was exhausted and not in the mood for taking decisions. He had spent the day hoeing in the company of Mathilde, his father and two of Léon's hands, and now he could feel the drag of tired muscles in his back and sides.

'What do you think?' he asked Mathilde.

The young woman shrugged her shoulders evasively, and continued her work. She was milking briskly, and the powerful jets of milk hissed into the bucket which she gripped between her knees.

'He seems to be honest, and one more man wouldn't come amiss,' she said at last.

'Well, you could always give him a try,' insisted Léon, 'you'll soon see whether he's up to it!'

Pierre-Edouard sized the man up and reckoned that his height, his bearing and, most of all, his serious manner, spoke in his favour. His quietness too: since he had entered the cowshed, the stranger had not said a word. He had simply greeted them by bowing his white head in their direction, then he had stood still and straight, with an almost haughty expression, as if what Léon was saying to explain his presence did not really concern him. But his intense blue eyes contradicted his distant attitude; it was evident that despite his apparent passivity, he was trying to understand what they were saying.

'Are you sure that he's only forty?' asked Pierre-Edouard.

'Yes, according to his papers. Of course, with his white hair . . . I think he must have had some dreadful . . . '

'Yes, but he can't speak French, it's not very practical! And then you know, I haven't even space to house him!'

'Bah, you've got a loft, haven't you, and straw and hay? Eh, would that do for you?' asked Léon, turning to the man: 'To sleep!' he indicated the loft with a wave of his arm.

'You really wish to work?' asked Pierre-Edouard more formally. Unlike his brother-in-law he found it difficult to adopt a familiar tone, address a stranger as 'tu'. 'All right, twelve francs a day, plus food, of course; will that do?'

'No,' said the man, at last breaking his silence.

'Oh-ho!' cried Léon, 'you're not going to turn up your nose at that! Twelve francs is excellent pay!'

'No, not twelve francs,' repeated the stranger. 'Eight francs and four of those,' he explained, pointing to the bucket of milk.

And as neither Pierre-Edouard nor Léon understood, he moved to a corner of the shed and signalled to them to follow. Intrigued, they moved closer. The man made sure that Mathilde could not see, and then unbuttoned his shirt.

'For this, four!' he said, pointing to the terrible scar gouged in his stomach. He smiled, and lifted the neck of an imaginary bottle to his mouth. 'Drink only milk, four!' he repeated, buttoning up his shirt.

'*And* he's a cripple,' said Pierre-Edouard, 'he won't make much of a worker!' But he was impressed by the stranger's sense of decency: the man had not wanted to expose himself in front of a woman, that was in his favour. 'You want four litres of milk and eight francs a day?' he asked, after some thought.

'Yes, yes! Four and eight francs!'

'Well, you won't be the loser,' slipped in Léon to his brother-in-law, 'at sixty centimes a litre!'

'All right, agreed,' Pierre-Edouard confirmed it, 'and you sleep in the loft, but no smoking there! Understood? No smoking, forbidden!'

The man smiled and shook his head.

'Never smoking.' He felt around in his pocket, brought out a little black horn with a silver cap at one end, and shook it.

'He takes snuff,' explained Léon, 'he won't set you on fire. Good, I'll leave you. You know, if I'd had work for him, I'd have kept this fellow. I'm sure you'll be pleased with him.'

'Maybe,' conceded Pierre-Edouard. 'We'll have to see how it goes. And what's his name?'

'Me, Nicolas,' said the man, 'You, boss, she, madame,' he said, pointing to Mathilde. Then he looked at Léon and added: 'And he, Mayor.'

'Good for you, Nicolas,' said Pierre-Edouard, and held out his hand to seal their agreement.

As soon as he heard from Jacques, who had listened to this conversation, that his son had taken on a guy with white hair, and a foreigner to boot, Jean-Edouard could not contain his disapproval. It was bad enough to have to seat Léon's workhands at the table – they had to be fed, after all – but to break bread with someone who did not even speak French, whom you knew absolutely nothing about; what if he were a good-for-nothing? So he gave Pierre-Edouard a frosty welcome when he came in, and pretended not to see Nicolas at all as he followed him into the room.

'I told you that you were aiming too high!' was his immediate reproach, 'and now you see, you have to take on foreigners to finish the hoeing!'

'Well, what does it matter, if he works! Anyway, it's me who's paying him, isn't it?' retorted Pierre-Edouard, who was too tired to be diplomatic.

'Suit yourself! But don't come complaining afterwards! Those sort of people, they're all thieves, drunkards and idlers! That's why they're on the road, you'll see.'

'And so what? I had to take to the road too!' remarked Pierre-Edouard drily.

This barb found its mark. His father hated to be reminded of certain events which he would have preferred forgotten.

'Fine, if you're going to take it like that!' he said, getting up. And to underline his anger, he ostentatiously left the room and shut himself in his bedroom.

'Old gentleman not happy . . . ' commented Nicolas apologetically.

'It'll pass!' muttered Pierre-Edouard. *Unless you give him cause to complain*, he added to himself.

Nicolas won over the whole Vialhe family in less than a week; even Jean-Edouard was converted. He would not acknowledge it straight away, for he hated to admit his mistakes, but everyone knew that he accepted, even appreciated, the newcomer when, one evening after supper, he took a packet of snuff out of his pocket and pushed it towards Nicolas.

'He doesn't smoke . . . ' he explained.

Pierre-Edouard nodded; he understood. Unable to share his tobacco pouch as a mark of esteem and friendship, his father had found this device. Modest though it was, his gift was generous in spirit. It announced loud and clear that he recognised the white-haired foreigner as a real man of the soil – dependable, conscientious, and whose strength commanded admiration.

That was the opinion of everyone who had watched him at work. To see him handling a hoe, you could believe that he had done nothing else all his life. Yet other signs – his impeccable table manners for example, or his even more refined behaviour towards Mathilde – proved that he had not always earned his living in the fields.

It was only as the months passed, gradually, as a result of his efforts to learn French, that Nicolas revealed a minute section of his history. A few facts, a few remnants of an existence which remained shrouded in mystery and secrecy, were all that he deigned to reveal.

Thus one day he admitted to Pierre-Edouard that back there, in his country, he had been for more than ten years steward of a beautiful estate, so vast that it took two whole days in the saddle to ride around it all!

'So why d'you leave, then?' asked Pierre-Edouard, who had finally adopted the familiar form of address for convenience.

'Politics, bad thing, very bad thing . . . ' explained Nicolas, before enclosing himself in an impenetrable silence.

Several weeks passed before he revealed a few more snippets of information. Yes, he had been steward; a fine, enjoyable position which he had inherited from his father. And no one had ever questioned his ability, for the lands which he managed gave their maximum yield and all the peasants under his orders loved and respected him. He was happy and his young wife, fifteen years his junior, could live like a princess.

Politics had spoiled everything, destroyed everything. Nicolas had never accepted the rule imposed by Alexander I. Immediately in conflict with the government of Pasic, he had even gone so far as to join the resistance, the Croatian Nationalists – although they were sworn enemies of the Serbs – had plotted with them, done all he could to overthrow a regime he detested.

What followed was unfortunately nothing unusual: his house surrounded in the middle of the night, gunfire suddenly ringing out, his wife shot in the neck as they fled and he, heartbroken and inconsolable at her death, forcing his mount on, setting course southwards, leaving behind his whole life and all he owned. Exile, in Albania at first. Then Italy, and there again a prudent flight, away from a police state which showed no sympathy towards penniless foreigners. Finally France, and now Saint-Libéral – but for how long?

'As long as you like!' Pierre-Edouard reassured him.

The story he had just heard made a deep impression on him. All the more so because Nicolas had, as he confided in him, never lost his slightly detached, rather ironic smile, as if the meagre memories he was quietly relating were not really his own but those of another man, whose pitiful life had undergone such dramatic changes that you had to be amused by it, or weep at it. But he was not a man to cry over spilt milk. The talented steward, the determined conspirator, even the refugee, were long dead. Now he was nothing but an emigrant, a man for ever cut off from his roots, a simple farm labourer. Only his hawk-like gaze, amazing white hair and wallet with gold initials testified to another and very different past.

Adopted by the Vialhes, he was also accepted by the people of Saint-Libéral. It quickly became known that he was sober, quiet, pleasant and did not run after women. And on the day old Jean-Edouard admitted that, without him, Pierre-Edouard and Mathilde would never have been able to pursue their intensive crop cultivation, he became a full member of the community.

Nicolas was the one who made it possible to plant, among other things, a hectare of tobacco; the revenue from this helped them to confront the crisis, and implement the other project which they had planned for many months – ever since Pierre-Edouard had realised that the land would no longer provide an unassailable haven for his sons.

Jacques accepted his parents' decision without saying a word, but Paul, as was his wont, protested enough for two and fought like ten men. They had been warned at the beginning of the year that, barring accidents, they would start the next school year as boarders in Brive, so the two boys had had plenty of time to get used to the idea. This had not prevented them from praying for frost, hail and storms to destroy the 40,000 tobacco plants on which their fate depended.

Unfortunately for them, the weather was exceptionally mild, good for growing things. The plum trees were weighed down with fruit, and even the twenty-eight walnut trees on the Long Field played their part in helping Pierre-Edouard and Mathilde to pay for their sons' boarding school.

It was enough to make you lose faith in the Lord! Paul was on bad terms with Him anyway, since overhearing a conversation between his father and Abbé Verlhac. For it was he who had encouraged their parents, he who had pointed out the new school due to open in October. Paul considered this such a terrible betrayal that he no longer felt at all guilty when he swigged the communion wine and munched the unconsecrated wafers after Mass; these reprisals were mere trifles compared to the perfidy of Father Verlhac.

Furthermore, he was furious with himself. Why had he not realised earlier that his zeal and competence at school just strengthened his parents' determination to see him continue his studies! He had landed himself with all those good marks and was beginning to regret it; the only result – a fine reward in his opinion – was to speed his entry into the sixth form at Bossuet School in Brive. As for Jacques, he had just been awarded his School Certificate with excellent marks, and would join the fourth form at the same establishment.

Jacques was just as upset as his brother at the idea of having to leave his parents, the farm and the village, everything which shaped his world. But in contrast to his younger brother, he accepted it in principle; fate had decreed the catastrophe and there was no use fighting it. Sometimes his brother irritated and worried him with his obsessive search for a means of escape from the boarding-school which was to be their prison.

'Well, what if we were to be ill?' Paul suggested to him on one of those September afternoons when the skies are such clear blue and the air so mild, that it seems nothing in the world can be better than to lie on your back on the warm moss, gazing up at the heavens while the cows you are minding graze around you.

'It wouldn't make any difference,' Jacques shrugged. 'Anyway, they'd soon see that it wasn't true.'

'Then we'll have to leave here before term starts!'

'Are you mad? Where would you go?'

'Papa left, that time!'

'Yes, but he was old, he was at least twenty-one!'

'It's a real pity that Pépé isn't in charge. If it were up to him, we'd stay here!'

The announcement that his grandsons were going to boarding-school had put Jean-Edouard in a rage; he could not help showing his feelings, and thumped the table like in the old days. It was to no avail; Pierre-Edouard would not give in.

'If they study, they'll be no use on the land!' cried the old man. 'The priest and the teacher wanted you to study, a long time ago, and we refused! And if your grandfather and I had listened to them, those smooth talkers, you wouldn't be here today!'

'Yes I would, and I'd be managing just as well, probably better. There are a lot of things that pass me by, which I might understand if I'd studied a bit longer!'

'It's a waste of time when you're working on the land. And then, they'll get ideas in their heads in the town. You'll see, they'll never want to come back to the farm!'

'They'll come back here if they want to. I say we must give them something else besides the land. Don't you see that it's betraying us! It can't feed its own people any longer! It's staring you in the face! You've seen the price of wheat? So? Is that what you want for them, poverty?'

'*Lo diable m'estel*! It's better to live poor at home than rich amongst strangers! What have your children done to you that you want to get rid of them? And you,' he cried to Mathilde, 'don't you care about your children being abandoned in the town?'

'Yes, of course I do. But they won't be unhappy. You must understand, Father, they have to study. One day you'll be proud to have a grandson who's an agricultural engineer, or even a teacher!'

'Huh, I don't give a damn for that! They'll be so posh they won't want to know me. Or you either. That's what'll happen, I can see it: children who despise you, and your land lying fallow!'

'We haven't come to that yet,' Pierre-Edouard had interrupted him. 'Anyway, if neither Jacques nor Paul want the farm, Guy will take it over.'

'Bloody hell! He's not even two yet, your heir! A lot of things can happen between now and him learning how to plough! You're still young, but that doesn't mean you can't fall ill! Who'd do the work then, eh? Jacques at least could be a help to you already, he's strong, he has a taste for the work and he's the oldest . . . He should follow you. When I was his age I was doing a man's work, almost, and so were you, not learning all that nonsense in schools, in the town!'

'Times have changed. Our children are clever enough to study and they're going to do it, and that's that!'

'It'll bring you nothing but misery, making your sons forget where they come from. You'll see, nothing but misery, I tell you, you're asking for bad luck!'

'Good God! Do I have to listen to this? Tell me, do you know what year it is? It's 1933! It's time you realised that! How do you think we

413

got electricity, cars, aeroplanes, radios, all that! You think they appear all by themselves? People who studied invented all those things!'

'Huh, for all the good they do us!'

'You didn't always say that! In your day, you had the finest, most up-to-date farm in the area, and that's still the case, because I've continued it, to the best of my ability. And whoever comes after me will do the same, and the farm will be more efficient and modern, just so long as he's capable of working it.'

'No need to go to school to do that!'

'Yes there is. Anyway, I don't know why I'm bothering to argue. Say what you like, it won't change a thing!'

So the argument ended there, but Paul, who had overheard the whole conversation from his bedroom, had felt a surge of affection for his grandfather. He had the right arguments! Unfortunately, it was not him making the decisions!

# 8

MATHILDE had to call on all her reserves of strength not to weaken or show her distress when she accompanied her sons to the school. The journey from Saint-Libéral to Brive was sad, for it was obvious that Pierre-Edouard's heart was heavy, too. He pretended to be light-hearted and flippant, tried to joke with Jacques and Paul, made believe that he was jealous of their fine uniforms, but nobody was fooled; it was a mournful occasion. Even the gentle trot of the mare sounded funereal as each click of the hooves, each tinkle of the bells attached to the collar, each creak of the cart-axles marked the passage of time, the progress towards the town, to school and the approaching separation which, in less than two hours' time, would divide the family unit; until that day they had never been apart.

Pierre-Edouard and Mathilde felt it deeply; a page was about to be turned. From now on, life in the house would never be quite the same again. Two voices would be missing, and in the evening, at supper-time, the two empty places would leave a gap at the table which would affect them all. Not forgetting Mauricette's plaintive questions about her brothers, and grandfather's disapproving silence.

Despite this, Pierre-Edouard and Mathilde did not regret their decision, or the various sacrifices which it had forced on them. If all went well, the time would come when the children would thank them. At the moment they were bravely controlling their tears, and probably did not understand why they had to be sent away to the town. But one day they would appreciate all the advantages acquired during their years of study. Then, strengthened by a good education, they would be free to choose whatever job they wanted – perhaps even farming . . .

Night was coming on as the cart left the rue de Bossuet and set off towards Estavel. Mathilde turned round and strained to hear the racket made by the pupils in the playground, where they were supposed to be getting into line. A bell rang, and the murmuring of children's voices petered out into silence.

'That's it . . . ' sighed the young woman.

Pierre-Edouard looked at her, and despite the shadows he could see her lips trembling, and the tears shining in her eyes. He pulled her to him and hugged her.

'Come on, come on, they'll be fine there, it's not a barracks! And,' he continued, 'we'll be coming to see them all the time. Léon and Yvette will visit too.'

'I'll miss them, I miss them already . . .'

'Me too, but we can't always follow our feelings.'

'I know,' she said, wiping her cheeks briskly with the back of her hand. 'You know,' she continued, 'I'm afraid your father won't get over this . . .'

'Go on, don't be silly!'

'No, it's true, I know him well. To him, this separation is dreadful, he loves them so much, our children!'

'He'll do the same as us, he'll get used to it.'

'No, because he's convinced that there's no point in sending them to this school. He's sure that neither of them will want to take over the farm in the future. So, you know what we should do to comfort him a bit? We should sow a square of wheat, just to please him.'

'Bloody hell! Have you seen the market price? 117 francs last year, 85 francs this year! I'm not going to sow even a handful!'

'Yes you are; you're going to plant it, to please me.'

'But you agreed! It's you who keeps the accounts, you know very well that it's a waste of time and money!'

'That doesn't matter; we must sow a bit, just to comfort your father. Because if you take away our children *and* his plot of wheat, I'm convinced it will kill him. You know very well that for him, only wheat counts. Promise me you'll sow the Léon's Letters field. After all, that's my land,' she said with a smile, 'I have the right to do what I want with it!'

'The whole field?' he protested.

'No, half of it, just the five strips where we had potatoes. We carried lots of manure on to it, it won't take much effort to get a beautiful crop.'

'You've been working it all out, as usual. Oh, you, honestly!'

'So, you promise? Then we could tell your father straight away, it would cheer him up.'

'All right,' he said with a laugh, 'anyway, I'm getting used to it, it's always you who wins! I'll send Nicolas to plough it, starting tomorrow.'

She kissed him on the cheek and hugged him to her.

'Tell me, about Nicolas, do you reckon on keeping him on long-term?'

'Oh, don't try to tell me that he costs us too much! I'm keeping Nicolas, and I won't change my mind about that!'

'You are stupid, you know,' she joked. 'I'm not suggesting you get rid of him! I know we'd never find anyone better. Everyone envies us, even Léon's sorry to have let him come to us!'

'Well then, why are you talking about him?'

'Winter's coming . . . '

'Yes, so what?'

'Well, you can't leave him to sleep in the hay! The poor man will freeze out there. And I feel ashamed; someone may say that we don't know how to look after our workers. So you're going to build a room in the shed, beside the calf boxes. It won't take many planks for him to have a home and be in the warm. We'll bring down the old bed from the attic, and that way Nicolas will be comfortable.'

He nodded and smiled.

'You really are something; you think of everything. Me, I'd never even have thought that our trusty Nicolas would be frozen, and I hadn't seen that my father needs to be consoled by sowing a square of wheat for him. You understood straight away what had to be done, and you're right. I'm just an old fool, I do believe.'

Jacques threw himself into his studies to escape the terrible depression which threatened to engulf him, but Paul reacted in quite a different way. He changed from one day to the next; whereas at school in Saint-Libéral he had always been noted for his lively spirit, now he retreated into a deep silence from which nobody could draw him out. With stubborn bad temper, he methodically undermined any hope that he might be considered an outstanding pupil.

Cunning and guileful, he nevertheless took care not to attract the masters' attention by sinking into idleness; his marks were never bad, not even poor, just absolutely average.

As he was bored to tears, and working way below his capabilities, he expended his excess energy at games, and by causing trouble and picking fights. He hit out hard and fast, and never hesitated to take on the big boys who were more than a head taller than him; he collected plenty of knocks, but built himself a fine reputation as a fighter.

Ignoring his brother's warnings, he became the instigator of, and chief actor in, all the escapades which could be devised by a child who refuses to fit in, a lad much too proud to cry in public, but who, every evening, wept out his soul into his pillow, clenching his fists and teeth so that his neighbours guessed none of it.

417

It was he who slipped into the refectory one evening towards midnight, silently collected up all the bowls set out for breakfast, and stuffed them all into the lavatory pans. He who slashed the teachers' bicycle tyres one night a week later. In memory of his adventures in Saint-Libéral, he also succeeded in climbing up to the bell on a subsequent evening; he unhooked the rope which he then tied across the stairway leading to the masters' rooms, at ankle height.

Vigorous enquiries were made by the disciplinary prefect, but they led nowhere. No one suspected him except Jacques, who immediately detected a familiar little spark of revenge in his brother's eye. Paul did not deny it.

'But you're crazy!' protested Jacques. 'If they catch you, they'll expel you, and then Papa will . . . '

'That's all the same to me, at least I'll be at home! Anyway they won't catch me, they're all a load of sissies!'

And then one evening, about a week before Christmas, he could take it no longer. As soon as he was sure that the dormitory monitor was sleeping, he got up, dressed and left. Holding his shoes in one hand, he bounded along the corridors, hurtled down the stairs, and jumped down into the courtyard from one of the classroom windows.

Once outside, he put on his shoes and ran silently to the street wall, which he nimbly climbed. The soil of the kitchen garden which lay behind the school softened his fall. He was free.

Free but terrified, worried sick and deathly cold. It was freezing hard, and the ridged earth cracked beneath his feet like glass. Here and there, the raucous barking of dogs greeted him from sleeping farms as he passed. He had been running for more than fifteen minutes, and could already make out the dark shape of the railway embankment ahead of him. He turned towards the Estavel bridge and at last reached the road.

The darkness frightened him, as did the distance to Saint-Libéral, more than thirty kilometres. But he swallowed his tears, tried not to think that he would have to run all night to see home again, and set off along the macadam.

In the hour that followed, he had to stop running three times to crouch in the ditch as cars passed. He was on the slope down to Saint-Pantaléon, and about to cross the bridge which spanned the bend in the road, when another car appeared behind him. He attempted to hide on the verge, but the beam of the headlights suddenly engulfed him, blinding him.

Petrified, cowering against a blackberry bush, he ducked his head between his shoulders and tried, in a last desperate reflex, to hide his face in his hands. The headlights passed over him, swept across the archway of the bridge and stopped there, a huge yellow stain curdled by a few wisps of mist. A door clicked and the beam of a torch investigated the corner where the boy was sobbing convulsively, paralysed with fear.

'You, upon my word! What are you up to here? Well, if anyone had told me . . . '

Paul felt a hand placed on his shoulder, and blinked towards the lights which were dazzling him.

'God in heaven, you're freezing, poor child! Come on with me! Do you recognise me, at least?'

Paul nodded, sprang towards his rescuer, and clung to his chest.

'Come, come.' Dr Delpy calmed him by gently stroking his hair. 'Come on, let's go and warm you up in the car. I'll give you a sugar cube with a few drops of mint spirit on it, that'll buck you up. And after that you can tell me, if you like, what you're doing on this road at one o'clock in the morning. Okay?'

'Oh, yes!' said Paul.

He was ready to confess everything, to explain everything, just so long as the doctor did not leave him there, alone on the road which seemed it would never reach Saint-Libéral.

'I understand,' the doctor comforted him, after Paul had finished his story.

He gave the boy's knee a friendly pat, and nodded. Say what you like, this boy snuggled up beside him had brains.

The car purred along gently and a pleasant warmth suffused Paul's legs, all wrapped in a rug. The car was approaching the hill up to Perpezac-le-Blanc.

'And what will your father say?' asked the doctor, after a little while.

'Oh well, he's bound to beat me,' forecast Paul. But his tone of voice showed quite clearly that this very logical result was nothing compared to the three months of hell he had just endured, or the two traumatic hours of flight.

'Yes, he's bound to beat you, as you say; what's more, you deserve it, don't you? No, what's worrying me is waking up your parents at this time of night, because of your grandfather, you understand? At his age this sort of excitement is not recommended, and as he's just had a bad attack of bronchitis . . . '

'I could go to Uncle Léon's,' suggested the boy.

'If you think he'd be happy to be got out of bed in the middle of the night!'

'Well then, I'll go to the cowshed, I'll sleep with Nicolas. Mama told me that he's built himself a room next to the calf-boxes.'

'That's not a bad idea, that's what we'll do. You see, I'd take you to my place, but you know my old Marthe, she's not happy just to keep house for me! She tells everyone everything she sees, so if she finds you with me tomorrow, the whole village will know about it. You don't want it all to come out, do you? Think how ashamed your parents would be!'

'That's true, people would be only too pleased . . . It's better if I go and sleep with Nicolas.'

Despite the knowledge that punishment would follow, Paul trotted along the main street of Saint-Libéral with a joyful heart. The dogs barked as he passed, but he knew them all and quietened them with a word. The squat shape of his house came into view at the end of the street; he smiled and hurried on.

He was pushing open the door of the cowshed without a sound when suddenly a beam of light transfixed him, and a fist grasped him firmly. He jumped with fright.

'Well, well!' said Nicolas with a smile, putting down the heavy stave he was brandishing. 'It you, my little fellow! And what you do here? I thinking to catch a thief!'

'I'll explain it to you,' whispered Paul, moving into the barn. He took several steps, and then could not resist the temptation to stroke old Moutonne. The cow, resting on a bed of dried chestnut leaves, stretched out her damp nose towards the hand which was patting her.

'She's had her calf?' asked Paul.

'There,' Nicolas pointed.

'Oh, he's super!' cried the child admiringly, hugging the little animal's curly head.

'What you do here?' asked Nicolas once more. 'You left town, eh? Not good, that! Boss will use his belt!'

'Well yes, but I must explain it to you. Say, it's quite good, this room of yours!' commented Paul as he reached the sanctuary. He tested the springs, sitting on the still-warm bed. 'You're nicely set up here!' He suddenly noticed a photograph pinned to one of the boards of the partition, and nodded to it: 'What a beautiful lady, and dressed so finely . . . '

'Yes' murmured Nicolas.

'That's a beautiful house behind her too, is that where she lives?'

Nicolas nodded in confirmation but his eyes grew steely.

'Tell why left!' he commanded.

'Well, you see . . . ' began Paul.

He reached the point where the doctor had made him take some sugar with mint when he suddenly collapsed into sleep. So the tall man with white hair bent over him, slid him between the sheets, straightened the blankets and the plump eiderdown, and furtively, with the back of his hand, stroked the downy cheek of the sleeping child. Then he seated himself on a stool, took out his snuff-horn and settled down for a sleepless night.


'But, good God, man, I don't understand a thing you're telling me!' moaned Léon, passing his hand through the opening of his nightshirt.

He scratched energetically, yawned and stretched. He had just got up when Nicolas irrupted into his kitchen.

'Me knowing you always first up in village,' Nicolas had apologised, then embarked on an improbable tale which totally baffled Léon, in his sleepy state.

Léon went to the stove, poked it, pushed three logs into the grate and put a pan of coffee on the top plate.

'Go on, tell me while the coffee's warming,' he urged as he took out two bowls.

'Little fellow here, leaving the town, boss not happy for sure!'

'Bloody hell, if I didn't know that you only drank milk I'd think . . . Which little fellow?'

'Paul!'

'My God!' Léon started. 'You mean to say my nephew has run away from school?'

'That's right!'

'Well, what a turn up! And where is the hooligan?'

'With me.'

'Dammit, there'll be trouble!' murmured Léon, nervously rubbing his stump. He grabbed his false arm and tied it on quickly, lacing the straps and pulling them tight with his teeth and good hand. 'Dear, oh dear,' he worried on, 'what's to be done? If it were only my sister it'd be all right, but Pierre-Edouard! He'll tan his backside with his belt! Okay,' he suddenly made a decision, 'it's not five o'clock yet, I've got plenty of time to take him back to Brive. Over there I'll sort things out with the priests, and when I come back I'll explain what happened to my brother-in-law, no one'll be any the wiser, and the kid will be out of his way! Go on, fetch that wretched Vialhe boy, hurry up, he must be here before his father gets out of bed.'

'Right!' said Nicolas as he went out.

He returned soon afterwards carrying the child, still asleep, in his arms.

'Devil of a boy, all the same!' whispered Léon. 'Since you've got him, follow me, we'll put him in the car.'

They laid him on the back seat and covered him up again with a rug. The child curled up, pursed his lips like a baby searching for its thumb, but remained asleep.

He woke as the car reached the suburbs of Brive, and sat up with a start.

'Hallo, young fellow me lad!' cried Léon.

'Oh, it's you, Uncle,' murmured Paul, without quite understanding the situation. Then he began to remember, and recalled all the adventures of the night. 'Where are we going?' he said at last.

'Where you should never have left, of course!'

'And Papa?'

'He's still asleep, I expect.'

'And he didn't say anything?'

'What should he have said? He didn't see you. Come on, don't worry, I'll explain it all to him gently.'

'You're taking me back to school . . . ' Paul realised. He had always known that it would end like this, that his father would not give in to blackmail. Thanks to his uncle – and he didn't quite understand how he had miraculously intervened – he was avoiding the worst thrashing in his life, for the time being.

'What time do you get up at this school of yours?'

'Seven o'clock.'

'Well, we're in time . . . ' murmured Léon, 'it's just six.'

Now that he was almost there, he was not sure how to extricate himself from this bizarre situation. Basically, the principal of the school could misinterpret his intervention. Paul was only his nephew, not his son; it was not for him to bring him back, to explain, to plead his case.

He didn't even know this priest anyway! And apart from Father Verlhac he was not really very fond of priests; they were not straightforward people, they did not speak frankly to your face, but always used speeches or sermons or roundabout ways of saying things! So what was he going to say to them?

'So you really hate it in this school, eh?' he asked as he slowed down.

'Oh, yes!' sighed Paul. 'If you only knew, Uncle!'

'Come on, don't cry. Look, if you promise me that you won't leave again, I'll try to get your father to understand that you really are very unhappy, perhaps that'll make him reconsider the matter. You promise, no more running away, eh?'

'Promise,' stammered Paul, swallowing his tears, 'and you give me your word that you will explain to Papa? Oh, if you only knew, those walls are horrible, I . . . sometimes I wish I was dead.'

'Don't talk stupid,' interrupted Léon quickly. 'Come on, shake on it,' he said, holding out his hand. 'Word of a Dupeuch, if you're a good boy, I'll speak up for you, okay?'

'Shake, word of a Vialhe,' said the child, touching his uncle's huge palm with his little hand. And his gesture made it a binding pledge.

'By the way, how did you get out?' asked Léon casually.

'Over the back wall, it's easy.'

'If I could be certain . . . You say they wake you at seven o'clock?'

'Yes.'

'We've still got three-quarters of an hour . . . Really, if you manage to get back in without being seen, no one would be any the wiser, eh? You go back the way you came and there'll be no trouble . . . '

'Well, yes, but . . . but from this side I can't climb the wall, it's too high . . . '

'Huh, if that's all! And which way is it to the back of this blasted school?'

'Turn down there, into the lane, then we'll have to go on foot at the end and cross the gardens.'

'That'll be easy as pie . . . Come on, that's decided, we'll go that way. And make sure you don't get caught, otherwise I'll look a fool, won't I?'

Paul slipped into his bed at twenty to seven, his return accomplished as easily as his leaving. He could hardly believe his luck, and felt overwhelmed with gratitude towards the doctor, Nicolas, and most of all his uncle, who had saved him by giving him a leg up to climb back over the wall.

Pierre-Edouard was deeply disturbed by what Léon told him when he returned. He didn't lose his temper – what good would that do, anyway! But his disappointment, his sorrow even, was such that Léon was disarmed, at a loss. He had been prepared to argue fiercely against the cold anger which he thought would overwhelm his brother-in-law when he knew the whole story. Instead, he saw a worried man before him; Pierre-Edouard looked almost demoralised.

'What shall we do with that kid?' he muttered, nervously fiddling with his pipe. 'When I think that we're bleeding ourselves white to pay for his schooling, and he thanks us by jumping the wall! But why did he do it?'

'He hates it so.'

'Oh, I know that! And his mother, don't you think she hates it too! But we're doing it for him!'

'Well, yes . . . But it seems he's not the sort to study.'

'That's rich, coming from you! You who want your son to be a gentleman! He'll have to go away to school too, will your son! So what'll you do if you see *him* running off in the middle of the night?'

'I don't really know,' admitted Léon.

'Whatever happens, his mother mustn't find out about this, you hear, not a word! She couldn't live with it, she'd make me take him away.'

'So you're going to leave him there in spite of this?'

'At least for this year, yes; after that I'll see. But for the time being, he has to make the best of it at boarding-school; it will teach him that a Vialhe doesn't give up.'

'And if he bunks off again? The doctor won't always be around to pick him up, or Nicolas to tell me, and me to take him back! Have you thought of that?'

'He won't leave again. He gave you his word, he'll keep it; or else he's not a Vialhe.'

'Yes, but it's me who's not keeping mine; I promised him I'd speak for him.'

'I'll talk to him. I've got the whole Christmas holidays to do it, he'll understand.'

'You must try to understand, as well. I think he's very unhappy, you know, it wasn't just an impulse.'

'That's why he must at least finish the year. If we give in to him, he'll be ruined; he'll think that running away is a good solution for the rest of his life.'

'You may be right, but it makes me very sorry for him.'

'Me too . . . Well, thank you for doing what you did last night, it was for the best.'

'I thought you'd fly off the handle and do something you'd regret.'

'Fly off the handle? Yes, probably, but you're wrong even so.

Because, you know, after I'd calmed down, I don't know whether I'd have had the guts to take him back to Brive.'

# 9

FACED with a constantly deteriorating economic and political situation, it was in a mood of despair close to fatalism that the inhabitants of Saint-Libéral began 1934.

Most of them had given up trying to understand the way the government people, up there in Paris, were managing affairs of State. Only the schoolmaster, encouraged by a few party faithful, tried to shake them out of their apathy and overall discouragement. Almost every evening he held forth in the main bar of the auberge, but his tirades fell flat; the drinkers shrugged their shoulders, preferring to pay court to Suzanne, who was still beautiful and kind.

They were fed up with all this politics, whether right or left; fed up with all the various movements, with the leagues which were supposed to be attacking each other in the towns. It would all come to no good; it smelt of corruption and scandal. And the price of wheat continued to fall.

Even Father Verlhac no longer took the trouble to challenge the vengeful suggestions made by the young teacher, content to shrug his shoulders when echoes of his new adversary's oratorical salvos reached his ears. Disheartened by the extremism that, whichever way he turned, was the norm amongst those purporting to be the saviours of the country; exasperated by the appeasement of some and the fanaticism of others, the priest wished to stand aside from the fray in the future. And, since the adults seemed to be quite beyond saving, he turned all his efforts towards the young people; at least they were not yet corrupted by politics.

Thanks to his Pathé-Baby film projector, he was in contact with most of the children in the village. Already he was in the process of forming a small group of adolescents inspired by the aims and ideals of the Young Christian Farmers movement. The results were concrete, obvious and refreshing. So the teacher could go on haranguing the bar customers, even try to discredit the Church by associating it with such contradictory movements as the royalist Camelots du Roi, the nationalist Croix de Feu, the new isolationism of Marcel Bucard – the priest did not care.

One evening at the beginning of January, when Dr Delpy had

invited him to take an aperitif at Suzanne's, he contented himself with putting his lay rival in his place in public, by reminding him about the Stavisky swindle.

'Stavisky was closer to the ministers, government bigwigs and other politicians of the radical left than to any poor country priest.

'Besides,' he continued wickedly, '*we* don't encourage our friends to commit suicide . . . '

Luckily, Dr Delpy defused the situation and prevented imminent warfare. He grasped the two men and steered them towards the billiard table, placed a cue in one hand, a glass in the other, and rolled the balls into the middle of the table.

'Come on, settle the matter graciously on the green baize. Politics isn't worth fighting about, you don't see me getting mixed up in it! No indeed! So!'

It was a pleasure to see how happy he was. His wife had been away from Saint-Libéral since August, but had returned on Christmas Eve. She was in mourning for her mother, who had died on 20 December; had stayed at home since her return, and was quietly reintegrating into the community. She helped her husband, visited a few chronic invalids or new mothers. Via Marthe, the doctor's maid, everyone knew that the joy of their reunion was not feigned. And since nobody, apart from Léon and Pierre-Edouard, really knew what her movements had been during their long separation, they finally accepted that, when all was said and done, perhaps she really had been visiting her mother for years. The tittle-tattle, rumours and other whispering by the gossips did not completely stop straight away, but at least they became more sporadic and discreet; they cooled down for lack of fuel to fan the flames.

Only Léon knew the details of the story. He heard, from a horse-butcher in Limoges – who had it from a charcutier who was a neighbour of the admirer – that the gallant gentleman had simply abandoned the doctor's wife for a much younger mistress.

'What luck that her mother died just at the right time, how convenient for everyone!' Léon had whispered in his brother-in-law's ear.

'Yes, but the doctor can't be fooled by it!'

'Of course not, he's not crazy! Never mind, he doesn't go to Brive any more: I know that for a fact, too . . . '

'Of course!' continued Pierre-Edouard ironically. 'You and your sister are conspiring to keep people talking!'

'Did Mathilde know about the doctor?'

'No, I don't think so, it wasn't that I was thinking of . . . '

'What then?'

'Paul's running away – she found out about it almost at the same time as I did.'

'How the devil could she?'

'He dropped his hanky in the cowshed. You know all their clothes are marked, so when she found that hanky on her way to do the milking, she started to ask herself a few questions, then she asked Nicolas some more . . . He ended up spilling the beans. Anyway, I think he was relieved to tell her about it.'

'Poor Nicolas, you should have seen him, he was just as unhappy as your kid! And what are you doing about Paul?'

'What I told you. He understands that he has to finish this year and take his School Certificate. After that we'll see.'

It was still completely dark when Pierre-Edouard disappeared into the cowshed and carefully closed the door behind him. He shivered; this February morning was cold and sharp as a knife. A mean east wind brought flurries of snow and howled over the village; it rattled the shutters, lifted the slates and seared the faces of all who left the warmth of their beds to care for their animals.

'Good morning, Nicolas!' called Pierre-Edouard.

'Good morning, boss!' said Nicolas, coming out of his recess. He held a bowl of milk which he raised to his face as if to drink a toast.

'Your good health!' cried Pierre-Edouard, filling his first pipe of the day.

This way of starting the day had become a ritual for them. Nicolas got up at least an hour before his boss. He lifted the manure and renewed the cows' litter, then he drew a litre of milk for his breakfast, which he enjoyed while washing and dressing. Pierre-Edouard would arrive and set the calves to sucking, then feed the cows which Mathilde would later milk.

'Terribly cold this morning,' commented Pierre-Edouard lighting his pipe.

'Yes, outside dungheap quite hard.'

'We'll have fun trying to break the ice on the pond so that the stock can drink. Did you see how thick it was yesterday? I'm sure it'll be worse today!'

'Winter . . . ' observed Nicolas.

'That's right, I expect you've seen some! And so have I. Here, give me the halters for the calves.'

The door suddenly banged behind him, and he turned in surprise. Mathilde was usually quieter than that.

'Oh, it's you!' he said, seeing his brother-in-law. 'What brings you here?'

'My God! Do you know what I've just heard on the wireless?' shouted Léon. 'They're fighting like madmen up there, in Paris!'

'What's that you're saying?'

'I'm telling you! Seems there are twenty dead and more than six hundred injured! And you know what? Those bloody gendarmes fired on the ex-servicemen! Just imagine, they dared do that to us! And when I think that only yesterday I sent Auguste over to La Villette! He's such a fool, he may well have been dragged into all this.'

'Tell me what's happening, I don't understand!'

And Léon related what he had heard on the news. The demonstrations in Paris the day before, the crowds threatening the Chamber of Deputies, demanding the resignation of everyone they accused of being involved in the Stavisky affair and other scandals.

'They lost their nerve and fired into the crowd. The bastards!' he finished in an angry shout.

'*Crédiou*, they should all be hanged,' growled Pierre-Edouard. 'I've been saying that for a long time! It wasn't worth fighting a war for four years if this is what happens! But what's Auguste got to do with it?'

Auguste was one of Léon's workers, the most capable and sensible of them.

'I had twelve steers to deliver, but I didn't want to leave because the child's got chickenpox; all right, it's getting better now, but you never know. So I sent Auguste with the animals. I bet he'll have stuck his nose into it up there, just for fun . . . '

'Come on, you know Paris; La Villette isn't the Place de la Concorde!'

'Okay, but I know my fellow Auguste, he's as curious as a magpie!'

'His sort don't put themselves in the front line,' Pierre-Edouard reassured him. He grasped the pitchfork and sighed: 'And you say there are twenty dead?'

'Yes, and six hundred injured.'

'It'll get worse before it gets better, that's for sure; something will have to give one way or the other. What a day, and there'll be worse to come.'

Auguste came back that same evening. The village was still in a state of shock and the men, especially the ex-servicemen, were growling and snarling. He was bombarded with questions and an audience surrounded him as he took his place at the bar of the inn.

But he had seen absolutely nothing, heard nothing, suspected nothing, for at the time of the fighting, he was happily sipping brandy in a bordello on the rue Blondel. He smilingly accepted the insults which this admission provoked.

'Old reprobate!' cried Léon. 'I don't send you to Paris to go to a brothel. You won't get back there for a long time!'

Auguste let them have their say, then held up one hand. True, he hadn't seen anything of the demonstrations: 'But I can do better than that!' he assured them, puffing out his chest. He had travelled all the way back with one of the demonstrators, a fellow from Toulouse.

'And do you know what really happened?' he began.

From him, the men of Saint-Libéral learned all about it. Their hearts pounded with the crowd which massed in the Place de la Concorde at six o'clock; they shook with rage when charged by the horses of the mounted police; their knuckles whitened when the first shots rang out. But they laughed when they learned that Edouard Herriot had only just escaped being thrown into the Seine!

They turned pale when Auguste described how the dignified column of veterans of the National Union of Ex-Servicemen, walking peacefully down the Champs-Elysées, their chests weighed down with medals and the 'Marseillaise' on their lips, were attacked by the forces of law and order.

'Then,' explained Auguste, 'came the great battle, that's when the blood really flowed. And it seems that's just the start of things.'

The men shook their heads, emptied their glasses and left the inn; they were angry and worried.


The death of the former solicitor, Maître Lardy, surprised no one. He was known to have been ill for a long time, a broken man since the death of his wife five years earlier. He had also been afflicted by the constant presence of his two daughters. They had both lost their fiancés, one after the other, during the war, and had never recovered from this ordeal, since when they had aged badly. They were so clouded by sorrow, so embittered by sadness, that life with them was a perpetual torture, a calvary.

Maître Lardy died on the morning of 30 April. Pierre-Edouard and Mathilde were the first to visit his bedside. For them it was more than a duty, it was a mark of recognition and respectful affection. All those who saw them go by, and push open the gateway to the garden of the former office, approved their action.

No one in the village had forgotten that the notary's wife had been Mathilde's godmother, or that Maître Lardy had been the one who, sixteen years earlier, had let the cottage at Coste-Roche to Pierre-Edouard for a peppercorn rent.

It was two days after the funeral, which was attended by a considerable crowd, that Maître Chardoux, the solicitor from Terrasson, summoned Pierre-Edouard and Mathilde. As executor of his dead colleague's will, he advised them that the latter had left his wife's god-daughter the tiny smallholding of Coste-Roche, its cottage and the two hectares of wasteland surrounding it.

'But you aren't obliged to accept it!' he added in honeyed tones.

Pierre-Edouard frowned. He did not like this solicitor, his cunning flattery and his shifty looks. 'And why should we not accept it?' he asked sharply.

'Oh well, according to what I hear the house and land are in such a state, they won't even be worth the expense involved in the inheritance! If you accept them, that is!'

'Of course we accept!' interrupted Pierre-Edouard. 'And I suggest you get in touch with my solicitor, Maître Lachaume of Ayen, to settle things properly and as quickly as possible.'

'I must remind you that this concerns Madame; it is her agreement I require,' insisted Monsieur Chardoux, as he pulled each finger in turn to make the joints crack.

'We both feel the same way,' replied Mathilde, 'so do as he says.'

'Very well, I will undertake what is necessary,' said the notary, getting up. 'I understand that you accept this . . . legacy, and the expenses it will bring! I admit that I find your attitude strange, but after all, that's your problem, isn't it?'

'Exactly,' said Pierre-Edouard before they left, 'but it isn't a problem at all, it's a gift – a very fine gift.'

'The notary couldn't understand, could he?' commented Mathilde with a smile.

Pierre-Edouard and she had just covered the three kilometres which separated Coste-Roche from Saint-Libéral. Now they were there, side by side, in front of the house, their house. It was almost a ruin, surrounded by brambles, nettles and bushes; even the little field which Pierre had cleared long ago was a pitiful sight. It was in the process of becoming a tangled thicket, an anarchic profusion of young ashes, elders, hornbeam and gorse; already honeysuckle and old man's beard had taken over, throwing their invasive tentacles in all directions.

'Well, well,' commented Pierre-Edouard, 'it is in a terrible state, but I'm still pleased to be here!'

'Me too,' murmured Mathilde, gripping his hand tightly.

This house, with its thatch slipping off on all sides, was theirs: the place which had welcomed them on their wedding night, that snowy evening in December 1918; which had seen the birth of Jacques and had sheltered them, happy and in love, for four years. Four often difficult years, when they were close to poverty; hard, tiring, testing times – but now, with hindsight, they seemed the richest, finest, happiest years of their life.

Pierre-Edouard slashed a path through the nettles and fool's parsley which blocked the entrance. He pushed open the door. The room smelled musty, damp and dusty. Mathilde hurried in, opening the window and the shutters.

'Look,' said Pierre-Edouard, pointing to the fireplace, 'our chimney hook is still there. It was a good thing we left it, it's been waiting for us.'

'You know you should never take down a pot-hanger, that brings bad luck,' said his wife, as she pushed open the door to the bedroom.

'Our room . . . ' she murmured, 'do you remember?'

'Of course.'

'It's a pity we can't live here. Here we'd have our own home, whereas in the village . . . '

'I know, I know,' he said, and put his arms around her shoulders, 'but you know we can't move house just because my father won't put the farm in our name!'

'Of course not. But promise me that we'll do this house up whatever happens. Then if one of the children wants it one day at least *he* will have some walls to call his own.'

'Agreed, we'll do that. But you know, the notary in Terrasson may be proved right. What with the fees on the inheritance, the roof to be repaired and all the rest, it'll cost us a lot, this present!'

'That doesn't matter,' she said. 'It's our house, we'll sort it out. That way we can come here for lunch, or even a siesta in the summer, when we're working on the plateau; it won't be so far as going right back down to the village.'

'The siesta's a good idea,' he joked, and kissed her on the neck. 'All the siestas you like, so long as we take them together, as we used to, eh!'

While replacing a joist in the loft of the small cowshed, Nicolas made a discovery which delighted him. For the past two months, Pierre-Edouard and he had got in the habit of going up to Coste-Roche every Sunday to effect whatever repairs they felt qualified to complete themselves.

The price demanded by the roofer to replace the thatch with a strong layer of slate had sent Pierre-Edouard reeling. The Ayen tiler asked for 3,840 francs, the price of a good pair of cows. It was much more than Pierre-Edouard could pay. So they had postponed this work until they had enough money, and made do with repairing what they could themselves.

Helped by Nicolas, who turned out to be an excellent craftsman, he had first patched up the thatch by blocking the holes with sheets of corrugated iron. It was not beautiful but it worked; it no longer rained into the house.

Now they were on to the roof of the barn. Pierre-Edouard was down in the yard, trimming a rafter with his axe, when he heard Nicolas's laugh, followed by a monologue in Serbian.

*Fine*, he thought, *now he's talking to himself!*

Then he noticed his companion leaning out of one of the holes in the roof and waving to him to come up and join him.

'What do you want?'

'Come, come! Good thing!' called Nicolas with a beaming smile.

Pierre-Edouard stuck his axe in the log and went over to the barn, pulled himself up into the loft, and almost poked his head into an enormous swarm of bees which, between midday and two o'clock had chosen to make their home in the old barn.

'*Miladiou*,' he gasped as he hurriedly dropped back down. 'Are you quite mad?' he called out, after retiring about ten metres. 'Does that amuse you? Wait while I fetch some sulphur matches, you'll see how I take care of those devils!'

'Not devils!' Nicolas corrected him. 'Nice creatures!'

'Come down!' Pierre-Edouard ordered. 'If they go for you, you won't even have time to run to the doctor's!'

'Not wicked! Me know!'

'Know or not, I'm telling you to come down!' he insisted. 'We can't go on with the work while they are there!'

He was frightened of bees, which he considered just as nasty and dangerous as wasps or hornets. He was going to smoke the swarm to sleep with sulphur, destroy it and make sure that none of the horrid beasts escaped punishment; they had given him such a fright.

'Well, are you coming?' he called out again.

'Yes.' Nicolas gave in, and his white head disappeared under the rotting straw of the roof.

Pierre-Edouard heard him humming gently; the man was definitely mad!

'Good thing,' said Nicolas, when he reappeared a few moments

433

later. 'Me put them in . . . ' he searched for the word 'in box,' he explained with a smile, 'and after we have good honey, great!'

'You want to put them in a hive?'

'That's right, in a box.'

'And you know how to do it?' asked Pierre-Edouard with great scepticism.

'Of course! Me, over there,' explained Nicolas, with a jab of his thumb to the east, 'lots, lots of bees on the estate, all full of little boxes. So take that one and do same, easy!'

'Well, you'll have to do it without me, mate! I'm not setting foot in the barn while they're there! But how will you do it?'

'Easy! No one keep bees in village?'

'Oh, no! At one time, yes, the last teacher had a dozen hives, but since he left . . . We don't trust those beasts, you know, they're treacherous.'

'So no one? Damn nuisance, but I fix it all alone!' confirmed Nicolas, whose progress in the French language was picturesque. 'Madame will lend veil perhaps, like women at burials? And puffer too?' asked the tall fellow; his vocabulary was also enriched by dialect words.

'You mean a mourning veil and the bellows? Yes, we'll find those for you; is that all you need?'

Nicolas nodded, and consulted the big watch which filled his waistcoat pocket.

'Too late this evening, me come tomorrow, all right?'

'Well, yes. We would have wasted the morning anyway trying to kill them, horrid things! But you manage it yourself, and too bad if they sting you; you can't count on me to help you.'

Despite this resolve, Pierre-Edouard did accompany Nicolas back to Coste-Roche. He was curious to see how Nicolas set about it, and at the same time he did not want to be considered cowardly in the eyes of this man whose confidence disconcerted him.

He had watched with interest on the previous evening as Nicolas prepared his equipment and hive. Now they were climbing up to Coste-Roche. On his shoulder Nicolas carried a large hollow log of chestnut wood. He had closed off the two ends of it with boards, leaving only a narrow opening at what was to be the bottom of the hive for the insects to pass through. Inside the trunk he had carefully arranged and firmly fixed slender rods of hazel wood on which the bees would build their combs, so he assured Pierre-Edouard.

Nicolas had improvised a smoke pump by adding an old tin can to the end of the bellows, and Pierre-Edouard was carrying this. They entered the little courtyard at Coste-Roche.

'Sh,' said Nicolas, after putting down the log. He listened, smiled, and pointed to one of the holes in the roof. 'Still there,' he said, 'already working!'

From where they were, they really could hear the buzzing of the thousands of insects busy up there. They went closer.

'Bloody hell!' muttered Pierre-Edouard, looking up at the bees who were pouring out of the opening. 'We'll be eaten alive!'

'No,' Nicolas reassured him, picking up the bellows.

He filled the smoke chamber with a mixture of nutshells, chestnut peelings and a few old scraps of jute sacking, and set the kindling alight with a spark from his tinder box. When the fire was crackling, he smothered it with a lid and activated the bellows. Thick white smoke poured from the hole he had punched in the tin.

'Good smoke,' he said, sending a plume of it on to his hand, 'not hot, just good, as it should be.'

'Yes,' replied a worried Pierre-Edouard.

'Put muslin,' said Nicolas. He took the mourning veil given to him by Mathilde, covered his hat with it, and tied it round his neck.

'Oh, you look magnificent with that on!' Pierre-Edouard teased him.

'You too put veil, boss.'

'You're joking, aren't you? Me, I'm staying here, or better still going a bit further away!'

'Me need you,' insisted Nicolas, 'to hold box . . . '

'No, no, you can go to damnation alone!' protested Pierre-Edouard. But he could see even through the black veil that Nicolas' eyes were mocking him; he angrily took out the second veil which he had stuffed in his pocket, and covered his head with it.

'You, my fine fellow, if I get a single sting, you'll hear from me!' he grumbled as he rigged himself out. He rolled down his shirt sleeves and did up the buttons. 'My God, if I'd known, I would at least have brought a coat! And you're going in with bare arms, are you?'

'That's right,' Nicolas smiled, 'and if the bees come and land there,' he said pointing to his hands, 'not be afraid, not touch, not squeeze, do nothing, they go away. Now we work?' he said, grasping the hive.

'Yes, but you go first . . . My word, you won't catch me doing this again! If anything goes wrong, I'm telling you, I'm off!'

Nicolas climbed the old ladder, hauled himself into the loft and began to laugh.

'And it makes you laugh!' groaned Pierre-Edouard, as he gingerly poked his head through the trap door.

A humming greeted him; he looked up fearfully at the swarm hanging behind a rafter.

'Well, you don't say! That's what you want to put in the box? I wish you luck!'

'Come here,' said Nicolas, paying no attention to the hundreds of insects which were already hovering around him.

*My God*, thought Pierre-Edouard, *I can't let it be said that this fellow saw me lose my nerve.* And he pulled himself into the loft.

Nicolas lifted the flap which covered the trunk, and held out the open hive.

'Hold just underneath,' he explained, 'me take down.'

Pierre-Edouard controlled himself, forced himself to keep calm, not to look at the myriad bees surrounding him, circling him in a maddening dance. Nicolas smoked the swarm, and the buzzing tone changed to a deep humming, whilst the thousands of insects collected around the queen suddenly began to quiver. Then he gently slid a lath the width of his hand along the underside of the rafter and pushed at the tip of the swarm, which broke off with a dry crack. The brown ball and the framework of combs which had been constructed since the previous day fell into the tree-trunk. *At least four kilos*, thought Pierre-Edouard.

'Hell and damnation!' he yelled suddenly, 'my hands are covered in them!' He tensed, expecting to be stung.

'Don't move,' said Nicolas, and directed a thick cloud of smoke towards him, 'they will go away, the queen calls,' he explained with a smile.

'You won't catch me doing this again,' cried Pierre-Edouard, anxiously watching the bees running over his fingers.

They left one by one, and made for the little slit in the hive. All the insects which had escaped when they dislodged the swarm were disappearing through it in a constant stream.

'That's it,' said Nicolas, 'wait a little for them all to come, and then we go away.'

'It's finished?' asked Pierre-Edouard, withdrawing towards the trapdoor.

'Yes, finished. Easy, eh?' called Nicolas with a smile.

'The bees weren't the only ones to be trapped,' grumbled Pierre-Edouard as he quickly climbed down.

He sighed with relief when he reached the courtyard and lifted his veil. At that moment, a bee caught in the material stung him on the ear. He howled like a muleteer, span round in a circle, jumped up and down and cursed Nicolas whose white head appeared through a hole in the roof laughing like a madman.

'Never again, do you hear! Go away, you idiot! You and your tricks, you won't catch me doing this again!'

But it was he who discovered a new swarm as he walked down from the peaks three days later, hanging from the branch of a flowering acacia.

'Hey,' he called to Nicolas as soon as he got back to the farm, 'I've found a new swarm by the path to the peaks, shall we go and get it? It would be a pity to let it go off again, wouldn't it? Come on, hurry, you told me they make off when the sun passes its highest point.'

'Good thing!' rejoiced Nicolas. 'Boss like bees too!'

'Like them? That's going a bit too far! But they are beginning to interest me all the same, those beasts of yours.'

In that season Nicolas and he gathered nine more swarms, and from then on Pierre-Edouard spoke of his hives with pride.

# PART THREE

*The Wind from the South*

# 10

PAUL groaned, turned over under the blankets, and tried to escape the hand which was energetically shaking him.

'Come on, get up! It's four o'clock!' whispered Jean-Edouard.

Paul opened one eye and regarded his grandfather grudgingly. He did not deserve any credit for getting up at such an unearthly hour! Wasn't he always telling the family that he was bored lying in bed after four o'clock! How could you be bored in a nice warm bed in the middle of the night!

'Come on!' insisted Jean-Edouard, 'you must get up, otherwise he'll have to come here to fetch you, and I don't want that to happen!'

The young boy sighed, sat up and rubbed his eyes. He was in a very bad mood and, as every time he was torn from his dreams at such an hour – that is, three or four times a week – he almost regretted that he had succeeded in convincing his parents that he was not the studious type. His obstinacy had displeased his father. However, he had given in. The teachers at Bossuet had testified that his son, like a caged lion at the beginning of the year, had become over the months as miserable and pitiful as a young badger on a chain.

'All right,' his father had decided, 'you have your School Certificate; I didn't go any further, so I won't make you. Besides, nobody can force a donkey to drink when he's not thirsty! But believe me, from the point of view of work you won't gain anything by changing! I'm going to put you through the mill, I am! You'll see what it's like, working on the land!'

'That's not what I want to do . . . '

'What? It seems to me that you don't have any choice! It's the farm or school, you decide!'

'I want to be like Uncle Léon . . . '

'Oh my God! That's all I need! Don't you think one stock-dealer in the family is enough? Tell me, don't you know that people like that live off our backs?'

'Not Uncle Léon!'

'He does, just like the others!'

'But he's your friend!'

'Well yes, but he was that before he became a shark.'

'You still care for him, even so. I want to be like him.'

'Well, well, that's all we needed,' his father had sighed, 'and that makes you laugh, of course!' he added as he looked at Mathilde.

'Why not? That for once the Dupeuch blood should prevail over the Vialhe . . . '

'Huh, that's really funny, what you're saying. So you don't mind if your son becomes one of those louts who earn their living off our backs!'

'Don't exaggerate. Anyway, we need them, stock-dealers.'

'Yes, more's the pity! All right, okay, I'll go and talk to Léon, and if he wants to accept you as his assistant, you won't find a better master than him. But believe me, with him you won't be laughing every day.'

Six months on, Paul had had plenty of time to realise how right his father was. With his uncle there was no question of idling around market stalls, or of balking at cleaning out the stable or grooming the animals. Added to that were three or four markets each week, when he had to leave his bed at impossible times.

On those mornings he envied his brother Jacques. At least he could sleep to his heart's content and, whatever he said, his studies were less tiring than this apprenticeship with Uncle Léon.

'Here,' said his grandfather, setting a bowl of milk on the table, 'have a quick breakfast, it'll be a long day. Where's that one going today?'

Jean-Edouard made it a point of honour never to say 'Léon' or even 'your uncle'. To him he would always be 'Dupeuch' or 'that one'.

'We're going to Dorat.'

'Dammit! You'll never get there! In my time, we would have set off the day before. Still, that one has his car! And what's he trading in, so far away?'

'Buying horses.'

Jean-Edouard shrugged. He had always rather despised those animals; he thought them too delicate, too sensitive and, whatever certain people might say, in his opinion not as good as a fine pair of oxen, or even a couple of working cows.

'Horses,' he grumbled, 'what an idea! Well, just listen to me, young fellow. Remember, those animals are vicious, mind you don't get kicked! Come on, eat your breakfast and get on, that one will be fed up waiting for you.'

Father Verlhac had known the news for a month, but he waited until

Sunday, 10 January 1935, before communicating it to his parishioners.

What he announced threw them into consternation. It was during Mass, at the end of his sermon, that he revealed what he could no longer conceal. He ended his homily and made the sign of the Cross, but instead of climbing down from the pulpit, he grasped the rim and leaned towards his flock.

'Brethren, what I am about to tell you seems to me like one of those April showers which we shall soon see. They make you sad because they still smell of winter, of frost and cold; they cheer you up because with them spring is reborn. Today my heart is heavy, but my soul is joyful. It is joyful, for the Lord has judged me worthy to serve him further. But my heart is heavy, for the Lord's decision forces me to leave you . . .

'Do not complain, one does not grumble in the house of the Lord! Yes, brethren, I am going to have to leave you after twenty-five years of life together. One evening in April when I was thirty-one, I discovered my new parish, and this church dedicated to Saint Eutrope. Today, at the age of fifty-six, I must start a new life, launch out on a new mission. Monseigneur the Bishop has honoured me with the onerous task of serving at his side, as diocesan chaplain for Action Catholique. It is a weighty but uplifting responsibility.

'However, as I told you, if my soul is joyful, my heart is heavy. After twenty-five years you have all become my friends. Thanks to you, I have been a part of this extended family which is our parish, and I have felt at home here. You have all invited me into your homes. I have baptised your children, blessed your flocks and your fields, shared your joys and sorrows. You have given me a great deal.

'Now I must leave, but I did not want to part without receiving an assurance that my place would not remain empty. Next Sunday you will be introduced to your new priest, Father Delclos; I know that you will make him welcome, he deserves it. As for me, I must take up my new post on February the first. So you see, this still leaves me with almost a month in which to bid you farewell. And now, let us celebrate together the Holy Sacrament. I will pray for you; do you pray for me, I am in need of it.'

The news took off as soon as Mass ended. It spread rapidly through the whole parish, reaching the farthest farms and upsetting everyone, even the anti-clerical types, even the Reds, like Bernical, Tavet and Brousse.

Some of the women had eyes reddened by tears as they told their menfolk. In the bar at Suzanne's or Noémie Lamothe's the men were silent at first, dumbfounded over their aperitifs. Then came anger. This priest was theirs, even if he was pigheaded, made biting comments and gave sarcastic replies, even if he made a great fuss, with his *dominus vobiscum* and his *pater nosters* which some of them did not believe in, he was still a good priest, an honest and trustworthy man. 'They' had no right to take him away!

'Oh my God!' moaned one drinker. 'They've done away with the train and the shuttle, and now they're taking away our priest! Bloody hell, what'll be left here for us!'

'Better tell Léon, and fast! Better put a stop to it!' bellowed another customer.

'Okay, let's all go!'

They went to him, and found Léon just as distressed and at a loss as to what to do as they were. His wife attended church, and she had told him as soon as Mass ended.

Pierre-Edouard was informed by Mathilde, and he too felt the blow. He was not in the habit of attending church frequently, but he did go four or five times a year. Besides, Father Verlhac was a friend, a support, an occasional confidant: that was what saddened him. It was he who had married them, who had baptised all their children, and who several times a year accepted a seat at their table as one of the family.

'Come on,' he said to Mathilde, as he pulled her to him to comfort her, 'life goes on. You know, I think he was too good for us, that's why they're taking him away from us. If he'd been like some people, whose names I won't mention, they would have left him here! Now don't make a face like that, think of the children – all the children in the village, they'll be the greatest losers. We'll lose by it too, but we've known other priests. But still, they could have left him with us, a priest like that, they won't give us another like him in a hurry, you can be sure of that! And you say his replacement has already been named?'

'Yes, he'll be here next Sunday.'

'Well, well, he'll need to tread very carefully; it won't be easy to take over, and with the council elections in four months' time, he'll be walking on eggs . . . '

All the children and young people in the parish were heart-broken by the announcement of Father Verlhac's imminent departure. All those who could – that is to say those who were not at work with their parents – gathered in the presbytery, in its youth club room, that

444

Sunday afternoon, but they were dispirited and almost embarrassed.

Already they felt less at home; the priest forced himself to make a few jokes, promised he would not forget them, he would even come back occasionally, but it did not do any good. They remained withdrawn, hardly touched the ball and gave affected laughs almost out of politeness, when the priest projected several spools on his Pathé projector. Neither *Félix the Cat* nor *Jack and the Beanstalk*, nor even a documentary about aviation really cheered them up; they felt betrayed.

Even Paul was quite distraught. For several months he had shown a certain reserve towards Father Verlhac and had pointedly kept his distance from religion; now he almost repented having avoided the presbytery and the club. He had missed the opportunity of a warm friendship freely offered, and now the offer was being withdrawn. So to mask his sadness, he tried to show off.

'Well then, when you're gone,' he carelessly commented, 'we'll be able to go dancing without any worries!'

'I never prevented you from going,' the priest reminded him with a smile. 'If my information is correct, it was your father who forbade it! I don't think he'll change his mind just because I'm leaving, quite the opposite, I expect! You know, Paul, at your age you're still a bit young to go round the dances, to pretend to be a man! What you should do is take over these meetings. I'm sure you and your friends could liven them up. Would you like me to talk to my replacement?'

'Certainly not! It's all just kid's stuff to me . . . '

'So why did you come today?'

'Well . . . ' Paul was embarrassed, 'to be with my friends, to see, you know! Yes,' he repeated it with a show of confidence, 'to come one last time. Say what you like, the new priest, he'll never be able to get us all together!'

'And why not?'

'Because he's not from here! He's a stranger to the village, we don't know him! And I, I' – he controlled the trembling in his voice with difficulty – 'I don't want to get to know him at all! So you see, it'll never be the same again!'

Father Verlhac smiled but said nothing. Paul, taking such pains to hide his sorrow, Paul was right. A page was about to be turned. It was turning for him, a simple country priest who suddenly had to confront a new world; it was turning for all his parishioners, for the whole village. Paul saw it clearly; it would never be the same, for anyone.

*

445

The arrival of Father Delclos amazed everyone. One Saturday 16 January, towards midday, he appeared in Saint-Libéral at the wheel of a B2, which made a great impression on all the watchers even though it was wheezing and dilapidated. In the village no one was accustomed to seeing a priest who owned a motor-car; this ancient Citroën, despite its well-worn state, was an unmistakable sign: it represented wealth.

In Saint-Libéral, no one knew of a country priest rich enough to buy himself a motor-car.

The priest jumped down with a thump – he was stocky, almost squat, and extremely corpulent – opened the rear door, and helped an old lady to climb out.

'Bloody hell! A married priest!' whispered one joker, who was drinking his gentian-bitters at the inn. 'Yes, yes really, lads, come and see!' he said. 'Hey, look, look!' he insisted, as he pushed aside the red-and-white checked curtain which covered the glass in the door.

'Idiot! If that were his wife he'd certainly have chosen someone younger and plumper!' joked one of his friends. 'And look how he's helping her – it's his mother, I bet!'

Without letting go of the old lady's arm the priest climbed the few steps up to the presbytery; he was about to push open the door when the heavy portal swung open to reveal Father Verlhac.

From the inn the men took in every detail of the scene. So it was learned that the new incumbent had just arrived, with his car, his mother and a considerable load of suitcases. It was decided that he must be extremely rich for, early in the afternoon, a removal van stopped in front of the presbytery and unloaded a great deal of furniture: armchairs, beds, and even two woodburning stoves which were much admired by all the onlookers.

'That's not a priest, that's a bishop!' commented Martin Tavet sarcastically, as he helped the blacksmith to shoe two of his cows at the other end of the square.

'You'll always find a stone in the hoof,' replied the smith, placing the iron on the anvil. He formed it, put down his hammer and spat onto the hearth of the forge. 'Dammit, it'll be a change from Verlhac; he wasn't our sort, but at least he wasn't proud! Did you see him, when he looked at us just now? My God! A bishop, did you say? He thinks he's the Pope, he does!'

Father Verlhac took the offensive two days before he was due to leave. The day was drawing to an end when he knocked on the Vialhes' door and entered.

'So, it's your last visit?' Pierre-Edouard asked him. 'May I offer you a glass of white wine?'

'If you like.'

'Will you stay for supper?' suggested Mathilde. 'Look, we're just about to sit down, so if you'd like to . . . '

'Bless me, I suppose I should eat, and it would give me great pleasure to do it with you – though it may be a long evening,' added the priest in an enigmatic tone.

Pierre-Edouard frowned, but kept his counsel and filled the glasses. It seemed that Father Verlhac had something important to tell him. Since he had come before the meal, he obviously wanted to be sure he would find them still up. He was long familiar with the customs of the village, and knew that the Vialhes went to bed early in the winter – as did everyone, unless they were going to spend the evening with neighbours, to help them make up bales of tobacco or play a game of cards.

'To your good health, all of you,' said the priest, raising his glass. 'I must talk to you after the meal,' he warned Pierre-Edouard. 'Is that possible?'

'Of course, start right now if you like.'

'No, it would take too long.'

It was a peculiar dinner; the atmosphere was strained and conversations stopped short. It was only at the end of the meal that old Jean-Edouard went onto the offensive, ignoring any pretence at diplomacy.

'Tell us, Father, who is this bird who's taking your place, eh? Where's he from, the old crow? You know what he said to me the other day in the square? – "At your age, Monsieur Vialhe, you should be in church every day, you have nothing else to do, think on it, you must prepare yourself, nobody lives for ever!" – And his turkey of a mother nodding her head in approval! We don't say things like that around here. He'll have to change his tune. Dammit, he won't be seeing me in his church! I'll go and take communion in Perpezac or Yssandon at Easter, in Ayen even, if need be, but certainly not here!'

'Come, come, Monsieur Vialhe, he said that as a joke! He's not a bad man! It's just that he's not accustomed to country people, you know, he's always been a town vicar, you must understand that.'

'Well, I shall be going to Perpezac as well,' said Mathilde suddenly, 'and that will be every Sunday too!'

'Now, now! You as well?' sighed the priest. 'And what has he done to you?'

447

'That's my business!' she said, collecting up the plates. 'But believe you me, he won't be seeing me again in a hurry!'

The priest looked at Pierre-Edouard, but he only made a face indicating ignorance, and shrugged his shoulders. Mathilde had told him a week ago that Father Delclos was an old cabbage-face, but she had not said any more.

She had not spoken to anyone and was not about to do so, she was so ashamed at what the priest had suggested. He had the audacity to say that he hoped a good Christian woman like her, still young too, would not be content to bring only four children into the world. Especially as her last little one, if his information was correct, was already three years old!

'Three years, my child! He is weaned now! So I hope that you will soon be welcoming another little angel, for I have no doubt that you love your husband and he loves you!'

Mathilde had gasped in surprise and turned her back on the priest, swearing to avoid him like the plague from that moment.

'And what about you, Nicolas,' joked Father Verlhac, 'has he said anything to you?'

'No, no,' Nicolas smiled as he rose, 'people don't speak to me unless I want, and that fat pope, I don't want he speak to me.'

'Well, *we* must have got on with each other,' said the priest, 'because we often talked to each other.'

'For you, it's not the same,' said Nicolas, making for the door. He bade them all goodnight with a nod of his head, and went out.

'All right,' said Jean-Edouard, 'I'm going to bed as well.' He held out his hand to the priest. 'We shall miss you, you must come back to see us.'

'Of course, Monsieur Vialhe, and above all, keep your faith!'

'Come on, children, time for bed!' called Pierre-Edouard. 'Paul, you'd better go and sleep in our room with the little ones. You see,' he explained to the priest, pointing to the bed at the end of the room, 'he usually sleeps there, but as you wish to speak to me and it seems to be a serious matter . . . '

'I'll leave you to it,' announced Mathilde in her turn.

'Oh no,' said Father Verlhac, 'I need you, and your brother too. He'll be coming at nine o'clock, I've arranged it with him.'

'He's coming here? What if my father-in-law hears him?'

'And what if he does? I'm here to keep the peace, aren't I?'

Nine o'clock was striking on the long-case clock as Léon pushed open the door.

'Have you explained to them?' he asked the priest.

'No, I was waiting for you.'

'What is going on, you conspirators! This is beginning to irritate me!' said Pierre-Edouard, bringing out the bottle of plum brandy. 'Now are we allowed to know what it's all about?'

'Yes,' said the priest. 'In three months' time there will be council elections. Martin Tavet will offer a list of Red candidates and it will be accepted!'

'Bloody hell!' exclaimed Pierre-Edouard with a laugh. 'And that's why you're making all this fuss? Really, it's not worth it. Besides, Tavet won't be elected, he's too stupid.'

'He will be elected! The teacher is behind them and believe me, he's a worker, that one! He's already begun to canvass door to door . . . '

'Well, I thought he was a radical!' Pierre-Edouard was astonished.

'You're behind the times, my friend,' said the priest, 'he took his party card after last year's disturbances.'

'All right, so what?'

'So if we let them agitate, Léon will be beaten, and you too, and all the others like you who wait around without doing anything!'

'Don't exaggerate,' interrupted Léon, 'our council *does* work!'

'Yes, but Tavet has got the credit for what you have achieved so far, because he's a council member at the moment. He's already telling everyone that the water and electricity are thanks to him, and they have you to blame for the loss of the trains!'

'People aren't that stupid!' said Pierre-Edouard. He was not worried, but he was annoyed. If, as the priest assured him, the Reds took control in the town hall, life would not be much fun in St Libéral; as for the farmers' co-operative, he would have to hand over the presidency to one of those second-rate admirers of Stalin.

'The reverend is right,' said Mathilde, 'something must be done, and I'm sure that he has an idea.'

'Yes,' said the priest. He rolled himself a cigarette, dipping into Pierre-Edouard's tobacco pouch. 'Our young people have no meeting-place, they don't know where to go any more; my colleague has installed his mother in the room which I had given them. So there it is, you have three months in which to build a village hall. It will be their club room, their library too, they could meet together there. I shall leave behind my projector and screen, my books and everything I can think of. That's what needs doing, and quickly, and all the while you'll be telling everyone that it's your idea, it's thanks to you moderates and those who'd like to vote for a sensible list of councillors.'

'Three months, that's not long,' said Léon. 'And then we need money, land, to vote for it in council, all that!'

'Right now, you're in the majority on the council; make the most of it. As for money and land, get a move on!'

'It would be in our interests to get a move on, it really would,' commented Pierre-Edouard. 'But tell me, Father, why are you bothering about all this when you'll be gone the day after tomorrow?'

'It's given me a new lease of life. You see, you weren't here when I arrived, you didn't follow the elections in 1911. I can tell you now that those elections were partly engineered by me, with Léon, and in opposition to your father. We got the squire elected and he was a very fine mayor; and so was your father, later on. Now that I'm going away, I want to leave everything in good order. I want the people of Saint-Libéral to continue to live in some sort of peace. Most of all, I don't want the young people to be let down. You must be elected; that will be my leaving present.'

Father Verlhac had got it right. Two days were enough to convince Pierre-Edouard that the opposition were losing no time. Almost every evening Jacques Sourzac, the teacher, with Tavet, Brousse and friends alongside, held the stage at the auberge; and his remarks carried weight, made an impression, sowed doubts. He spoke of the flight from the land, caused by poverty, and his statistics, which were undeniable, impressed everybody.

'Don't forget, my friends, and consider this well. Less than a century ago the rural population, the wealth of the nation, represented seventy-five per cent of the total population of France. In 1926 it was no more than fifty per cent; this year, it won't reach forty-eight per cent! More than thirty-five thousand workers have left their land every year since 1931! And, look at this, in a region neighbouring ours, in the Creuse, there are eleven thousand two hundred and sixty-six miserable souls who have had to seek refuge elsewhere between 1921 and 1931!

'It is essential that we act. This government has been corrupted by the Jews, and it's vital that we convince them that the people of France no longer recognise their own kind among the elected, up their in Paris and in our town halls, stuffing themselves and growing fat on the sweat of the proletariat. From now on we must act to take over the positions which have been held for too long by unworthy men − by stock-dealers! Then next year, we shall win the general election!'

All these arguments and figures, which he declaimed clearly and passionately, produced a substantial effect on people who were inclined to admire and follow a man who could speak so definitively.

It was therefore essential to counter-attack as soon as possible; to destroy by one means or another this fascination, almost infatuation, felt by the electors when they listened to the teacher's commanding discourses. In order to triumph they had to gain the upper hand.

There was no time to lose. It was not for nothing that Léon was a stock-dealer, Pierre-Edouard a worthy representative of the Vialhes and Dr Delpy a liar, as was fitting.

The first problem to be resolved was of the administrative kind. It was essential that the vote for the construction of the youth club should be carried only by those associated with Léon. Better still would be if their adversaries pronounced themselves totally opposed to the project. There was no doubt that they would vote against it, unless . . . unless they felt they were in the minority. In that case they would join the bandwagon and later on take all the credit.

The framework of the conspiracy was to make them believe that the majority would not agree to the project, then there would be a vote. At the very next council meeting Pierre-Edouard launched the attack.

'You know, I've been thinking . . . Our young people have no room for their youth club now. Here, in the mairie it's much too small, we should build them a shelter . . . '

'Have you gone mad?' said Léon, shrugging his shoulders.

'What do you mean?' insisted Pierre-Edouard. 'It's no big deal: four walls, a roof and they'll be happy!'

'They don't need that to keep entertained, there's plenty of space out in the country!'

'Besides,' slipped in the doctor, 'those film shows the priest organised weren't very healthy – I mean for their eyes, of course. The faculty of medicine is unanimous in the opinion that the light from cinema projectors strains the retina, over-stimulates the crystalline lens and contracts the pupil. Furthermore . . . '

'Yes,' interrupted Léon, who was afraid that the doctor was overdoing it, 'anyway if they want something to do, they can always work! Isn't that so?' he said, addressing Tavet.

'The idea of a non-religious youth club for the children is quite a good one, but we should see about that later,' proposed Tavet, who had already decided to revive the idea on his own account as soon as he was elected.

'That's it, we'll see later,' agreed Léon.

'And besides, we have no money,' the doctor reminded them.

With a glance, Pierre-Edouard reassured himself that his friends Maurice, Edouard, Jacques and Pierre Delpeyroux were playing their parts; they seemed as undecided as a cow who has found some chervil in a clump of clover.

'We only need to vote for or against the project,' he remarked. 'That's the best way. I'd like to know who agrees with me . . .'

'You've certainly got plenty of time to waste!' protested Léon.

'Considering that it's growing late already,' put in the doctor, consulting his pocket-watch.

'No, but seriously! I have the right to demand a vote on it!' interposed Pierre-Edouard.

'Yes, yes,' Léon soothed him, in a humouring tone. 'Come on then, we'll take a vote to please you, then we'll go home to bed.'

Even the teacher, who was present at the meeting, fell into the trap. He was convinced that neither Léon, nor the doctor, nor Maurice or Edouard would come down in favour of the project, so he acquiesced when Tavet quietly signalled 'no' to him with a flick of his finger.

'Results,' said Léon shortly afterwards: 'For the immediate construction of a youth club, eight votes.'

'Swine!' yelled Tavet, standing up with a great crash of his chair. 'Dungheap! You were against it, and so was the doctor!'

'Against the project,' announced Léon imperturbably, 'five votes. Project adopted.'

'It's a fiddle!' bellowed the teacher.

'Young man,' the doctor looked him up and down with a scornful eye, 'as for fiddling elections, go and ask your comrade Stalin how he feels about that, and you'll learn something!'

'You were against it,' grumbled Bernical. 'It was dishonest of you!'

'Me? Did I say I was against it? Did you hear me say that? I said that excessive film-watching was harmful to the eyes!'

'Yes, and it sounded as if you were against it!' Brousse reproached him. 'And Léon did the same!'

'I never said that I would vote against it!' protested Léon, in the offended tone of an honest man whose word has been questioned.

'All right,' groaned Tavet, 'you made fools of us. Build your club-thing, it won't stop us from beating you hollow at the next elections!'

'We'll talk about that later, my little fellow,' said Pierre-Edouard placing a hand on his shoulder, 'we'll talk about that later . . .'

Léon and his friends lost no time. A plot of land was found the very next day: it was common ground presently occupied by an old bakery which had been abandoned thirty years ago. Situated on the edge of the village, it was ideal for a youth club.

The excavations began three days later, and everything went very fast after that, for Léon let it be known that he would make a gift to the community of a barn which was threatening to collapse; the metal-work and a fair number of the slates were still usable. The people of St Libéral suddenly developed a great enthusiasm for this building which would be the pride of the village, for besides the youth club, it would serve as a village hall, and dances could be held there in the evenings after weddings.

Many electors who had been tempted by the teacher's fine words suddenly changed their minds about him. Of course he spoke well, was learned, had an answer for everything; but that was just it, he was a talker, and words are like the wind.

Léon and his friends were working on something tangible, concrete. A building, it was constructed, it was finished off, it was not described in fine sentences, nor in statistics, it was there for all to see! And in *what* there was to see, they were not disappointed.

They saw Léon, Pierre-Edouard and Nicolas, Maurice and the others, often many young people too, lending a hand with the work, mixing the cement, chiselling the stones into shape, fixing the laths, nailing on the slates. It was hard work, more honest and healthy than fine speeches, politics and all that rubbish! That really was proof that Léon was a good mayor, and that he and his friends were worthy to be chosen by the majority of the electors in the community.

The youth club was inaugurated with due solemnity two days before the first round of the elections, and Father Verlhac made a brief appearance in the village for the occasion. He made good use of his time by visiting several families, and even agreed to bless the smart little hall – only because he was pushed into it, and his colleague was taking an afternoon rest. 'Youth Club of Saint-Libéral-sur-Diamond, 1935' was inscribed in letters of gold on the front of the building for all to read.

Two days later, Léon and seven of his party were re-elected with a commanding lead. At the second round Martin Tavet and his comrades resumed their seats as well, mainly because nobody was particularly interested in the election any more. 'But,' as Léon commented when he offered a round of drinks to everyone at Suzanne's, 'with five against eight, my dear old Martin, you haven't got enough weight. Come on, your good health anyway, and no hard feelings.'

# 11

'It's incredible, the number of doves flying over!' cried Pierre-Edouard in delight, as he gazed after a huge flock of wood-pigeons which were skimming over the White Peak.

'I told you to bring your gun!' said Mathilde.

'Yes, but you know how it is; if I had carried it, I'd never have come away from up there,' he said, pointing to the peak rising 200 metres from the Peuch field where he and Mathilde were pulling beets, with the help of Nicolas. The crop was magnificent, and Pierre-Edouard was justifiably proud of it. This year he had given up growing the fodder variety 'Eckendorf' with its swollen, fat, round roots, more full of water than nourishment, and had planted only the 'Pink-collared White' sugar-beets, which were much richer and better for the animals.

Once again Jean-Edouard had raised his eyebrows when faced with this innovation; but Pierre-Edouard had not even attempted to explain his new choice – what good would it do! The old man would not have been convinced. Pierre-Edouard was constantly surprised by his father's reactions. Thirty years earlier he had been a pioneer, but as he grew older he had become just as conservative and stubborn as his friend Jeantout, which was saying something!

Pierre-Edouard did not understand this reactionary attitude – or maybe his father really believed that he held the key to the secrets of modern agriculture, and was content as things were. That was more worrying, for his agricultural methods had aged too. Pierre-Edouard was constantly aware of this; he only needed to read the professional journals which arrived at the farmers' co-operative. Everything was always changing, and at great speed. From one year to the next new products appeared – fertilisers, pesticides, graded seeds, tools, growing methods – and he was convinced that it was essential to move with the times, to innovate. He was a thoughtful man, and sometimes wondered whether he too would be capable of adapting to the new techniques applied by his successor, if one of his sons did take his place one day; he hoped he could.

'Hey, look!' he called out once more. 'What a flock coming over! Hundreds of them, and all within range!'

Mathilde lifted her head and admired the huge billowing blue cloud which beat by against the south-east wind. The wind had risen from the south on the morning of St Luke and had been blowing for four days; everyone knew that the autumn rains would start before it died away. This rainfall would be mild at first, almost summery, would green the pastures and bring out the mushrooms, if the moon were favourable; at first it was welcome, but it would soon turn cold, even freezing. Then one night, after a blast of wind from the north, the first frosts would attack and the fog would arrive. It was therefore important to get the crops in while there was no rain in the sky.

Mathilde looked at her husband and shrugged her shoulders with a smile. He was sorry to be in the fields, annoyed that he was not crouched behind a juniper bush up there on the White Peak, waiting with bated breath for the approaching flocks and aiming for them swiftly as they came within range.

The doves had been coming over since the beginning of the month. At first there were only a few isolated, scattered flocks which flew high because of the fine weather, putting them out of danger from bullets. But in the last four days there had been a real surge. The flocks followed one another with the regular rhythm of a pendulum, and it was torture for a huntsman without a gun, for they were flying low; the wind kept them close to the ground.

'Dammit, I'm going up for some pigeons tomorrow morning, beets or no beets!' Pierre-Edouard warned her as he tossed two roots into the cart.

'Do you want me to go and fetch the gun?' suggested Nicolas. His hands were covered in red earth, and he wiped them on his trousers.

'Oh, no, it's not worth it,' said Pierre-Edouard, taking out his pipe and tobacco.

For his part, Nicolas took out his snuff-horn and poured a portion on to the hollow which he formed on the back of his hand by lifting his forefinger and stretching out his thumb; he filled his nostrils.

'But just look! Look at that!' repeated Pierre-Edouard in great excitement, 'and they pass over there every year, on the dot, in the same place, in spite of the gunfire. And it may be thousands of years that they've been flying over that peak! I'd love to know why! It's probably a landmark for them, a signpost to the south . . . Where you come from, are there wood-pigeons flying over there too?'

Nicolas nodded his white head and sneezed.

'Yes, lots. And then there are geese, ducks and . . . '

He spread his arms to show the wingspan and indicated a

lengthened nose, then he squealed comically. Although he had made enormous progress, his French still lacked certain words.

'Oh, I see,' said Pierre-Edouard, 'cranes! Do you hear that?' he asked, turning to Mathilde. 'They have flocks flying over there too!'

'Stupid!' she said with a laugh.

He had long ago related to her the anecdote which had made such an impression on him as a child: his grandmother and mother discussing the bad luck which Mathilde had brought with her when she was a baby, for she had been conceived one night when a flight was passing over. But at that time neither his mother or grandmother had wanted to accept the explanation of what it really was. It was the Wild Hunt, the souls of the damned crying out, not birds! They believed this quite sincerely! What was even more astonishing – it was, after all, 1936 – Pierre knew a certain number of old people – and young ones too – who still crossed themselves when a flock of birds flew over.

'Well, I'm very fond of flocks of birds,' continued Pierre-Edouard in a serious tone which was meant to fool Nicolas, 'they leave beautiful traces behind them . . . '

'Have you quite finished?' cried Mathilde, turning red, but her eyes sparkled with amusement and understanding.

This story of her birthmark, supposedly due to the Wild Hunt and therefore a sign of misfortune, was the subject of jokes each time Pierre-Edouard rediscovered his youth in the arms of his wife; she carried a tiny blemish in the shape of a crescent moon on her left breast, and he delighted in it. 'I could easily put up with it,' he would assure her as he kissed her, 'if bad luck only left this sort of reminder!'

'Come on,' Mathilde urged him, grasping the neck of an enormous beet, 'if you want to go after pigeons tomorrow, we'll have to finish pulling all these today!'

'Yes,' he agreed, getting down to work again. 'All the same, that Nicolas has been giving me ideas . . . '

'What ideas?' asked Mathilde, fooled by his serious and measured tone.

'Well,' he said, telling the most incredible lie, 'it was he who started talking about the Wild Hunt, wasn't it?'

They worked all morning and afternoon. In the evening, when the mist was settling in the hollows and the beet field was nothing but bare earth, Mathilde suddenly noticed little Mauricette at the edge of the plateau, calling as she ran towards them.

'What's happened?' she wondered anxiously. She lifted her skirts and ran towards her daughter.

'What's the matter?' murmured Pierre-Edouard, frowning. Mauricette had no business to be up on the plateau at that time! Something really unusual must have happened for her grandfather to have sent her like that, with night about to fall. He watched his daughter with concern as she met Mathilde, and tried to hear what they were saying; he felt reassured as they hurried back towards him.

'Well, what's the matter?' he called out.

'Tell him,' said Mathilde, stroking her daughter's cheek.

'Pépé told me to come,' explained Mauricette. 'There's a tall gentleman and a beautiful lady who arrived on the evening bus. They're at our house, waiting in the yard. Pépé didn't want to let them in without you there.'

'What's all this about? And you don't know who this gentleman is?'

'No.'

'And Pépé doesn't either?'

'I don't know.'

'And it's me he wants to see?'

'Yes, he said: "I want to see Monsieur Pierre-Edouard Vialhe." He has one of those accents! I'm not sure, I could hardly understand him.'

'All right, we must go down. Hey, Nicolas, we're going on ahead! You finish picking up the odds and ends and bring the cart down.'

'Understand boss. Nothing serious, then?'

'No, probably not. Come on,' Pierre-Edouard took his daughter's hand, 'take me to see this gentleman.'

It was incredible! Pierre-Edouard understood immediately why his father had called for help, and above all why he had not wanted to open his door to the visitor. Apart from his size and build, the man watching them smilingly was the image of Octave. Octave, whom old Jean-Edouard had never forgiven for marrying his daughter Louise in the teeth of his expressed opposition. Octave had died two years after their marriage, leaving a son, Félix, and Pierre-Edouard was his godfather.

'Good God, it's you, Félix?' murmured Pierre-Edouard, spreading his arms to embrace him.

'That's me,' said the man, as they greeted each other.

'Well, well! It must be . . . wait a minute, it was in 1914, that's twenty-two years! Yes, I haven't seen you for twenty-two years, but

457

I'd have picked you out in a crowd! It's amazing, the likeness! Such a surprise, enough to give me a heart attack!'

They laughed, and then introduced their wives.

'This is Mathilde, your mother must have mentioned her!'

'This is Thérèse, we were married four days ago.'

'You should have told us beforehand, you young devil, and your mother too!'

'We wanted to surprise you . . . '

'If that was the idea, you certainly succeeded! Come on, let's go in.'

'Well . . . ' said Félix, 'I don't know whether . . . Grandfather will agree to that. I think he recognised me too, and . . . '

'I'll say he recognised you! Everyone who knew your father and saw you walking by would think they'd seen a ghost! Come on, don't worry about your grandfather, he puts on a fierce act, but it's not serious.'

They were climbing the steps to the front door when it suddenly opened to reveal Jean-Edouard ensconced on the threshold. He stood in silence, hands in pockets, legs firmly planted, and regarded them, his gaze resting longest on Félix. Then he nodded his head.

'Good,' he said at last. 'I see that I wasn't dreaming, you really are Louise's son? It's Félix, isn't it? I didn't want to let you in before because I thought my head was playing tricks with me. I'm seventy-six now, you know, so . . . Now that I'm sure I wasn't dreaming, you may come in.' His voice broke a little, and trembled. He cleared his throat and stood aside to let them pass.

'Come in,' he repeated, 'after all, you belong here. Even though,' he whispered as he turned away, 'I swore that you would never come in here, but we're not savages! And then, it's all so old now, so long ago . . . ' He paused a moment and considered. 'Twenty-seven years! It would be inhuman to harbour a grudge over such a timespan, especially for no more than childish mischief . . . '

'I believed in this Popular Front too,' agreed Pierre-Edouard, 'as did almost everyone else around here as well. Only Léon predicted disasters ahead, and he wasn't entirely wrong, because since then . . . '

They had been seated by the fire since finishing their meal. Paul and Mauricette, exhausted, had very soon followed their little brother, who had been asleep for a long time; Pierre-Edouard, Mathilde, Félix and his wife were chatting like old friends.

First they had talked of Louise, who was still governess at the château in Indre where Félix was now a forester. Then Pierre-

Edouard had spoken of Berthe, and brought out her latest postcard, from London this time – and this was in front of his father, who had always condemned the life she had chosen.

The old man had spoken very little. It made him happy just to watch this grandson whom he had previously rejected; he was delighted to discover the build of the Vialhes in this man, the character, too, and the vitality. And Pierre-Edouard watched his father surreptitiously and realised how moved he was, how affected by this unexpected reunion.

Jean-Edouard had said nothing since his first words of welcome, but to anyone who knew him those were astonishing, revolutionary even. For despite their simplicity, not to say roughness, they marked the end of a long period of disagreement and half-hearted forgiveness. Now, after twenty-seven years, came reconciliation. Then Jean-Edouard rose:

'I must go to bed. Tell me, will you be staying a few days?' he asked Félix and his wife.

'Yes, until Sunday, if you don't mind,' explained Félix, rising as well.

'Don't get up. In that case, you should know that my other grandchildren, who are only kids compared to you, well, they say "tu" to me. You must do the same – and you too, *petite*,' he added, looking at Thérèse. 'Right then, until tomorrow.'

He went into his room but came out again shortly afterwards, carrying a bottle which he placed in the middle of the table. 'It's plum brandy from 1910, the year of your birth. It should be good!'

'There's no doubt about it,' Pierre-Edouard commented a little later, 'Father is just like this brandy, he's mellowed with age . . . '

'Yes, when I tell my mother about it she won't believe me, after all the stories she's told me,' murmured Félix, as he savoured the smell of the brandy.

'That's understandable. It wasn't always much fun for her, you know!'

'I know . . . '

Then the conversation moved on, and now they were discussing politics, the war in Ethiopia and the more worrying one which had rocked Spain for the last two months, followed by the May elections and the success of the Popular Front.

'For us there's at least one good thing: the Wheat Office,' said Pierre-Edouard, filling his pipe. 'With that we're protected from those grasping grain merchants. Those scoundrels have almost ruined us, it's time it was stopped! But apart from that I think

Léon was right; I don't believe this Popular Front will work miracles.'

'The situation was so complicated,' Félix attempted to explain. 'Blum did what he could.'

'I know, but that was no excuse for devaluing our money! What are we left with now? And then all these strikes, all the unemployed! What are they thinking of? A forty-hour week, paid holidays! My God, let them come and do a turn here, they'll soon see whether we only work forty hours. Me, I do their forty hours in three days, and your aunt does too! And we're not asking for holidays on top of it! Oh, don't think I begrudge them their holidays. That's not it, but what I don't understand is that they're all demanding more money for less work. If I want to earn more it's always the other way round; I have to work longer hours to earn more. And that's not likely to change!'

'It's not so simple,' repeated Félix. 'You see . . . Thérèse will explain it to you better than I can,' he said, turning to his young wife.

She blushed and agreed. Everything in this house was very alarming, except Mathilde, who seemed to be so gentle. But the men! She could not say which of the two was the more intimidating!

'Until we were married, Thérèse worked in a shirt factory at Châteauroux – that was no joke, you know,' explained Félix, placing his hand over his wife's.

'I'd agree with that,' said Pierre-Edouard. 'It's never a joke to have to work for someone else, I know a thing or two about that too. I've taken it easy, too, occasionally. And with my workmates, we even had a sort of strike – oh, yes we did! But when we'd got what we wanted, we didn't go on asking for the moon! Whereas nowadays the more that's given, the more some people want! It's no wonder that prices go shooting up as a result. In the end it'll all finish with a crash, I've been saying that for five years and more!'

'Paying the workers better won't cause a crash!' insisted Félix.

'No doubt. Besides, it doesn't worry me if they *are* paid more, all the better for them. Mark you, we can discuss these things, but it's all political manœvering and that kind of stuff! All through history, we peasants and workers have never been anything but the losers, it's always the same everywhere! Here, have another drop of brandy and tell me a bit more about what you do up there in your forest; that's more interesting than talking about all this rubbish!'

Félix and his wife stayed two days in Saint-Libéral. They slept at the inn, and on the first evening Pierre-Edouard accompanied them there feeling quite nostalgic.

'Did you know that your father had lodgings here?' he asked, as they entered the saloon bar of the auberge.

'Yes, it seems that he and my mother met each other here.'

'Here and elsewhere, yes . . . Good evening, Suzanne, I'm sure you've been waiting for these young people? Here they are, now you can shut up shop.'

'May I get you something? It's on the house,' she suggested, as her eyes slid fondly towards Félix.

Pierre-Edouard smiled: really, good old Suzanne never gave up. Despite her forty-one years, she was still just as greedy for men!

'No, not for me. We've seen the bottom of enough glasses this evening,' Pierre-Edouard thanked her. 'So which room are you giving them?'

'As many as they like, if it makes them happy! No one comes here any more, you know. I often wonder why I stay on, I'd do better to close down!'

'Come, come, don't complain; I'm bringing you some customers, you look after them well. All right,' he said, turning towards Félix, 'you can have all the rooms you want, but if I were you I'd take number seven.'

'Why number seven?' asked Félix, although he was sure he knew the answer.

'That was your father's room. Come on, I'll take you up, I haven't been up there for almost thirty years!'

When he came down again a few moments later, he found a melancholy Suzanne sipping at a huge glass of curaçao.

'Youth is beautiful,' she commented, with a nod in the direction of the stairs. 'They're both good-looking, especially him, and so young . . . '

'All right,' Pierre-Edouard cut in, 'you look after them; they'll be here until Sunday. When they leave, don't give them the bill, eh? Even if they insist on it, I'll come by on Monday and settle with you, okay?'

'I understand, but . . . Who are they really?'

'Oh, that's right, you weren't here then. He's my nephew – and from tomorrow on, I bet you'll hear talk of his father and my sister too! I'd be very surprised if the over-forties had forgotten them!'

For two days Pierre-Edouard and Félix strode over the Vialhe lands. Félix wanted to see everything.

'And the Caput, which hill is that? And the mine-cutting, how do we get there? And the source of the Diamond, where is it? Oh, I'd like

461

to go to Combes-Nègres, too. You see, my mother talked to me so often of these places, I feel I know them by heart. That's why I want to see them all. When I was a kid, I hoped for a long time that we'd come back and live here one day! So now I'm catching up with my dreams.'

'Your mother came back once, you know, at the beginning of this month sixteen years ago.'

'Yes, for Grandmother's burial. But she didn't want me to come with her.'

'And why hasn't she been back since then? No one was stopping her!'

'I think she was afraid – of people, the neighbours, Grandfather too, of course. And then she had no work here, because you know her pension as a war widow . . . '

'Never mind that, she could come and spend a few days!'

'Yes, but she was afraid of doing that as well. Afraid that she might not have the courage to leave again. If you knew how she loves this land! I think she must have talked to me about it every day. So I've learned to love it too, almost as much as her. And when I was coming here, I was worried that I'd be disappointed. You know very well how rarely the reality is as beautiful as what you imagined. Now I'll be able to tell her that her country is even more beautiful than she told me. Christ! Up here on this peak, it's as if we're right up in the sky. You don't need to raise your eyes to look at the clouds, you don't feel them hanging over you like you do at home. Here, you are their master. You're master of everything, up here! That's what's made you so strong. You Vialhes have grown used to seeing everything from above, even the sky, right from when you were little.'

'You are a funny fellow,' murmured Pierre-Edouard. 'Listening to you, I understand why my sister fell in love with your father – he must have talked the way you do, she couldn't have resisted that. Come on, we should go down, Léon's expecting us for lunch; you'll see, he's an original too! Your mother must have spoken of him, I'm sure!'

When the time came for Félix and his wife to leave, Jean-Edouard planted himself on the threshold as he had done when they arrived, and looked at his grandson.

'You should come back,' he said to him, 'now you know the way. I ought to tell you something else. When you were born I didn't want to recognise you as a Vialhe grandson; now that I've seen you, and I've heard you, I know I was wrong. You have the Vialhe blood. There, that's all. Oh, and if, when you see your mother . . .

462

tomorrow, you say? Right, well tomorrow then, you simply say this to her: "Your father would like to remind you that he is now seventy-six." She'll understand . . . And then you tell her as well: "The stones in the Diamond are just the same as when you were here, but the water and the sand have worn them down a bit, they're less cutting than they were, so since time has succeeded in smoothing down the stones . . . " All right, off you go now, both of you, and when you have a son bring him here as soon as possible. But remember, I'm seventy-six . . . '

# 12

It had become a habit. For four years, Jacques Vialhe's class-mates had resigned themselves to watching him run off with almost all the top prizes. So, at the end of 1936, the day before the Christmas holidays began, when the headmaster strode into the class to announce the results of the end-of-term exams, all eyes turned to Jacques. Some were admiring, some disheartened, others jealous.

There were actually, among the other serious contenders, the sons of a lawyer and of a surgeon from Brive, two youths who literally worked themselves up into a rage at having to cede first place to that bloody country bumpkin, that strapping lout, who not only beat them in physics, chemistry, French and maths, but also overwhelmed them with his size, his strength and his self-confidence. It was abnormal, unnatural almost, that it should be this peasant and not one of them taking the lion's share.

They were from well-established families, with a good education and breeding. They already had their positions in the little clique of Brive society. He was nothing but a yokel, with mud on his boots; logically he should never have left the plough or the cow's backside! Instead of which, he always passed them at the post and, despite his background, would almost certainly earn a distinction when he sat for the baccalauréat exams in six months' time.

The headmaster cleared his throat and began to read out the prize-winners. And the marks rang out: French 16 out of 20, first Jacques Vialhe, English 17 out of 20, first Jacques Vialhe . . .

Jacques was standing to hear the results, and his face shone with pleasure and pride. His parents would be happy again, very happy. And even his grandfather would celebrate! The old man had eventually accepted his choice of studying in preference to farming. Besides, the path chosen by Paul was a great comfort to him; at least he was staying close to the land. Thanks to him there would be no break; some day or other, when he grew tired of running around the market-places, he would return to take up the position which was his. Reassured about the future of the farm, Jean-Edouard no longer had any reason to criticise the path chosen by his grandson Jacques. On the contrary, for there was another Vialhe coming to the forefront in a completely different manner, in a new sphere!

'Total average: sixteen out of twenty, first Jacques Vialhe,' the headmaster finally announced. 'We can wish you at least a good holiday; you've earned it. Which isn't the case for everyone in this class . . . '

Jacques sat down and his thoughts flew towards Saint-Libéral where he would return that same evening. His holidays – he knew already how he would spend them. First of all he would work with his father and Nicolas – and he was not put off at this thought, quite the opposite. He used up his energy by chopping wood; it was a healthy job which gave him an appetite, developed his muscles, allowed him to use all his strength, testing it to the limit when he used the sledge hammer to split the thick logs of oak or the knotted trunks of chestnut trees.

Then he would go hunting as well; it was a matter of proving to his godfather that the gun he had given him on his sixteenth birthday – a twelve-calibre Darne – was in good hands. Finally, in the evening, he would meet his little group of friends in the youth club.

Gathered there, happily reunited, they would discuss things, sort out the world, build the fairer, finer and more honest future they all wanted. They would comment on the articles in *La Jeunesse Agricole*. Best of all, Jacques would find Marie-Louise there, the daughter of Pierre Labrousse. Like him, she would soon be seventeen and was a boarder in Brive, at the Notre Dame school. Like him, she was taking her baccalauréat at the end of the year. She too was a farmer's daughter and not ashamed of it; everything fitted.

They had gone to school together in Saint-Libéral, sat and passed their school certificates on the same day. Then they had lost sight of each other, for Jacques had remained a child, small in stature and young-looking in comparison to others, whereas in a few months Marie-Louise grew attractive and graceful, with the mind of a young lady. Jacques had been rather annoyed. He was acutely aware of the difference in height which separated them and made him look ridiculous; he did not want to be taken for Marie-Louise's little brother! So he restrained himself from meeting her for two years.

Everything had changed in the last year. Now it was his turn to grow taller and stronger, and Jacques had become, not quite a man, but still a fine-looking youth. He was already a head taller than the girl; he now found her charmingly fragile, and felt ready to protect her.

They were glad to meet again, to exchange opinions on Shakespeare, Barrès, Victor Hugo. They amused themselves by conspiring together in a display of erudition, to enjoy the admiration of their friends in St Libéral who had only achieved School Certificate.

At this stage, neither she nor Jacques had yet confessed that they nurtured plans for a common future. But both felt that the time was fast approaching when their mutual feelings would force them to exchange the serious promises that knot the first ties of love.

Although Jacques felt big and strong, sure of himself, he was aware that his age was against him, even if he thought it quite respectable. Furthermore in Saint-Libéral, and in his family too, although it was quite acceptable for a man of twenty-five to go out with a girl of seventeen with marriage in prospect, nobody seriously considered that a boy of his age could suffer more than mild, passing fancies. Whereas he *was* serious, in everything. So, to avoid his attraction to Marie-Louise becoming the subject of teasing, he preferred to remain silent and wait. This did not prevent him from dreaming about the girl every day, and gazing with feeling at the tiny passport photo which she had given him six months earlier.

'And this one, what do you think of him?' Léon asked his nephew. 'First of all, how old is he?'

Paul walked around the horse, examined it, opened its mouth. 'He doesn't look bad,' he said at last, 'and he's getting on for eight years old, roughly . . . '

'You don't know a thing,' sighed Léon. 'It's a sorry nag, with every vice, and your eight years are more like twelve! Didn't you see that all his teeth were worn down! Good God! When I think that your father could still teach me a thing or two about horses! He knows about them, does your father! But you – away from cows, you're lost in a fog!'

Paul accepted the rebuke in silence, but shrugged his shoulders. He had no affection for horses; they were not to be trusted, too quick to respond with a kick or even a bite. And according to his uncle, they were more often than not riddled with hidden faults, which were to be avoided like the plague!

'Let's go and see him in the ring,' suggested Léon.

Paul stuffed his hands in his pockets and followed. It was cold enough for wolves on that Tuesday, 5 January 1937, and on the market field at Dorat a freezing wind blew straight from the Auvergne, burning your ears and making it hard to breathe.

Paul would have gladly avoided this chore of going to buy horses for his uncle to sell again two days later at the Kings' Market in Brive.

With all these markets sending him to the far corners of the region, he had not been able to enjoy the time his brother was spending at home as he would have liked. That lucky devil Jacques was on holiday, and he was probably stalking woodcock in the acacia thickets by the château at this very moment.

For the last two weeks the woods of St Libéral had been swarming with woodcock. Paul was not yet old enough for a firearms licence, but he liked to accompany his father or brother when they went to scour the woods. Sadly he only had the pleasure of taking the role of beater when Léon gave him some free time, which was to say, not very often. He did not resent his uncle's strictness at work; he would just have liked to stay with his brother, especially during the Christmas holidays.

The two boys still got on very well together, although their relationship had changed. Jacques now took the role of elder brother; it was he who decided how they spent their time. There was no longer any question of dragging him into escapades, or rowdiness at the inn. He said no and it meant no. And Paul obeyed him, not ashamed to admit that his brother impressed him, intimidated him almost. He would be taking the baccalauréat; knew English and maths, talked about everything with ease and confidence, had his own opinions about politics, the war in Spain, Italian Fascism, the phenomenal resurgence of Germany. And to cap it all, Jacques would discuss all this with his father, seriously, with the newspaper on hand to analyse some situation or other.

Paul had his own opinions too, but they were still vague, blurred and difficult to express. The respect he felt for Jacques was increased when his brother confided in him that he wanted to continue his studies and become a veterinary surgeon, eventually setting up a practice in Saint-Libéral. Veterinarian – that was the height of ambition, and Paul never for a moment considered that his brother might fail. He would succeed, just as he had succeeded in conquering his depression earlier at Bossuet, as he succeeded in always being at the top of the class!

Naturally, in comparison to him, Paul felt a little over-shadowed, rather mediocre. Jacques did not do anything to draw attention to himself; he did not show off. It was just that, at the moment, he was preparing to obtain outstanding marks in his exams.

Meanwhile Paul was nothing but an apprentice stock-dealer. Even if he earned a good wage – for Léon was generous – he felt the gap widening between himself and Jacques. He now knew that he would not be a stock-dealer all his life, but he kept this to himself. One day he would have to escape; to find an exciting, stimulating job. And it would not be on the farm, as his grandfather believed, nor with his Uncle Léon. Both occupations lacked appeal, romance. One day, when he was stronger and more secure, he would go out into the world. For the time being he remained silent and waited, and gave his parents and uncle every satisfaction – apart from the matter of his relationship with horses.

'Well, are you coming!' Léon called to him from the edge of the ring where the sellers were trotting their horses at the request of prospective buyers. 'Look,' his uncle explained to him, 'I asked the fellow holding the bay to show me his paces; we'll be able to judge him.'

The dealer handed the animal to a groom, who moved up towards them from the end of the ring; he held the animal by the halter and trotted beside it.

'Stop!' Léon called to him when he had covered fifteen metres. 'I don't want your old nanny-goat! She's limping on her left fore! Did you see his technique?' he asked his nephew. 'No? . . . Oh,' he called to the groom, 'go on, perhaps I made a mistake. Look, watch the devil,' he whispered to Paul, 'just look at it, my God! Can't you see how the groom is limping too, and with the same timing! That way, it gives the impression that the man and the animal are both normal. We call that the limping-horse trot. Hah, the fool, to try that on me! Good God, there's no one alive who can teach me how to doctor a nag, I know all their tricks! That'll do,' he said to the groom who had just stopped opposite him, 'you can go on with the circus, but you'll have to find a different stool-pigeon! Come on, let's go,' he said to Paul, 'we'll go and look at that lot of cart-horses; from a distance they look good, but we'll have to check them out from close to. Remember, you can never check anything too much. Come on, tell me what you think of this one, for instance. If you give me a good answer I'll let you lead the bidding and you can have that one. Come on, kid, talk like a man.'

The inhabitants of Saint-Libéral would probably not have reacted at all to the fall of the Blum government if it had not been for the opinions expressed by Father Delclos.

Everybody in the village had better things to do than bother about politics on 22 June 1937; many of the men were disappointed to see the fine dreams inspired by the Popular Front end so sadly, but the seasonal work left them no time to hold a post mortem on what was, after all, an everyday occurrence. They had become accustomed to seeing governments succeed one another for some time. It was not worth losing precious moments discussing Blum when the hay-making demanded fifteen hours work a day. The weather was fine, warm, just right for cutting hay; they had to make the most of it. Hard work made the week fly by.

The bomb exploded on Sunday, 27 June. The sky had been dangerously overcast as the last quarter of the moon approached. The wind had veered, and the swallows swept up the main street in a constant stream, skimming the ground with their russet throats. Faced with these portents, it was not wise to do any mowing, so a number of men were taking advantage of the respite from work to take a little rest and enjoy an aperitif at Suzanne's.

Even Pierre-Edouard and Léon were sitting on the terrace of the inn, in the sweet-smelling, cool shade of the old lime trees. Pierre-Edouard was the first to realise that something unusual was happening in the church.

High Mass had begun almost half an hour before the heavy clang of the church door echoed all around the square, swinging shut behind the doctor and his wife.

Since her return to the fold, the doctor's wife had attended services punctiliously, behaviour that contributed greatly to her rehabilitation in the eyes of the village women. Sometimes she was even accompanied by her husband, an indisputable sign of perfect conjugal harmony.

The couple had not yet reached the bottom of the steps before the door banged once more and Pierre-Edouard was amazed to see Mathilde also emerge. She had in fact continued to visit the church in Saint-Libéral, despite what she thought of the priest; it was after all much more practical than going to Perpezac-le-Blanc every Sunday. She only went over there for confession, a move which was extremely vexing to Father Delclos, but which she had no intention of changing for any reason.

'Now what?' said Pierre-Edouard, putting down his glass and getting up. 'What's going on over there? Hey! Mathilde, I'm here! Has Mass finished already?'

The doctor suggested that his wife and Mathilde go home, and marched towards the inn. He was red with anger, but smiling all the same.

'What's going on?' asked Pierre-Edouard again.

'Oh, my dear fellow, I've never heard such rubbish, it was more than I could bear! Nor could your wife. Really, I think that poor priest has gone mad, or he's an idiot from birth – both, probably! Suzanne, a cherry brandy!'

'He wanted you to serve Mass, perhaps?' suggested Léon ironically.

'If that were all! Listen to this! I don't expect you know that we're celebrating the sixth Sunday after Pentecost; I didn't until twenty minutes ago. I have nothing against the day's reading from the Gospel, I quite like it actually. Well, you and the Gospel ... But Pierre-Edouard will remember it, I'm sure; it's the loaves and the fishes. You see what I'm saying? Five thousand hungry people, five loaves and two fish for everyone, and despite that the whole crowd eat their fill and there are even left-overs! Well, you could argue about that, make allowances for poetic licence, but that's not the problem. Just imagine, this miserable priest thought it good to draw a parallel between this parable and the fall of Blum, I ask you! Yes, he did! Basically, he explained to us that God had no need for social reform, for forty-hour weeks or paid holidays to feed his people! That the previous government's materialism was an insult to the faith; in short, we should thank the Lord for having relieved us of it and pray that he install a regime devoted to order and morality! It was laughable, sad but laughable!'

'That's why you walked out, and Mathilde too?' questioned Pierre-Edouard.

'Oh, no, that was simply stupid. It was after that he went beyond the limit, when he announced quite boldly that all those who voted for the Popular Front last year were virtually public sinners! Well, that was too much. I made off, and he won't see me again in a long time!'

'So that's how it is!' grumbled Louis Brousse unexpectedly; he and other customers had drawn nearer while the doctor was holding forth. 'He's all right, the bastard! He's so fat himself, he doesn't give a damn if the people die of hunger!'

And suddenly, shouts rang out. At a stroke all these men felt the shame of their defeat. They had previously accepted the failure of policies they believed in, but if the priest was rejoicing, that was proof that the reactionaries were gaining ground.

In no time at all the group found their numbers swelled by new arrivals, and the shouts redoubled. In the heart of the crowd factions were attacking each other, opinions and insults exploded.

'Don't do anything stupid!' called Léon suddenly. 'You're not going to fight about rubbish like that!'

'If you're on the priest's side, you'd better say so straight away!' Martin Tavet shouted at him, his face blue with rage. 'That wouldn't surprise me anyway, you've always chosen the strongest side, where the money is! Perhaps you're one of the top two hundred families?'

'If you go on like that you'll get my hook in your face!' threatened Léon, brandishing his false hand.

'Stop it,' said the doctor. 'Let them bellyache, it'll blow over – and they're half right anyway! Look, there's our teacher, that's all we need.'

Jacques Sourzac quickly found out what was going on, and was happy to joke about it at first. Then he exploited the occasion by giving the radicals and other socialists – never mind the reactionaries – a piece of his mind; they were all responsible for the failure of the Popular Front, being too lukewarm and flabby to surmount a crisis.

'But history will judge their mistakes and their weaknesses! Today the important thing is to respond to the attacks of the bourgeois clergy. Let us defend ourselves! Mass is being sung, it seems; well, let *us* sing, we, the proletariat!' he cried, climbing up the steps of the church. And he intoned the 'Internationale'.

'The priest isn't the only one who's mad!' said Pierre-Edouard, shrugging his shoulders. 'I suppose it's because there's a storm brewing, it taxes the brain! Leave them, Léon, let them bawl, the lot of them; they'll calm down soon enough! I'm going to see my little Mathilde, I must congratulate her. She knows how I voted, that's why she walked out.'

As Pierre-Edouard predicted, the demonstration did not last long, mainly because very few men knew the words to the 'Internationale', and many people did not want to get mixed up with the band of hot-heads led by the teacher. That did not prevent the priest from being shouted down when he felt obliged to come out and curse the blasphemers who were disturbing the sacred Mass. Then everything returned to a peaceful torpor in the expectation of the warm showers all the signs indicated.

Curiously enough, Father Delclos emerged from this incident with enhanced stature, at least in the eyes of those who shared his ideas on the subject of moral codes – and there were more of them than the anti-clericals thought. The priest was reinforced in his position, sure of his adherents, and he made the most of it by asserting his authority and leading his flock along the path to salvation.

As, once, had done his predecessor Father Feix – but he had been a saintly man, all those who had known him agreed, for he at least lived frugally – Father Delclos marked out and condemned every-thing which could weaken Christian moral values: dancing, of course, but also the cinema, the wireless and the reading of novels, which, he said, excited the imagination of young people and might lead them into depraved acts. Uncompromising with regard to the respect which he felt was his due, he never forgave the doctor, nor his wife, and still less Mathilde, for the insult they had inflicted on him. As a result he never spoke to them again.

In July, Jacques passed his baccalauréat with very good marks. The whole Vialhe family took great pride in his success, and even old Jean-Edouard did not deny himself the pleasure of remarking that only his grandson had managed to survive the test – without in any way gloating over the failure of the other candidate from the village. No one dared to remind him that a short while ago he had fiercely opposed Jacques continuing with his studies. He himself seemed to have forgotten completely his previous position on the subject.

What was remarkable was his action the day after the results appeared, after he had read and re-read twenty times the name of Jacques Vialhe inscribed near the top of the list printed in the newspaper. All alone, despite his seventy-seven years, he took the bus which stopped every day except Sundays in the main square, and went all the way to Brive.

There he strolled slowly, stick in hand, black felt hat jammed tightly on his skull, along the streets Puy-Blanc, Toulzac, Carnot and Hôtel-de-Ville. Indecisively he retraced his route, sauntered around St Martin's Square, and stopped once more in front of a shopkeeper's display window.

In order to consider his problem carefully, he went as far as Chez Pierre and ordered a dozen snails and a half-bottle of white wine. When he had wiped his plate clean, emptied his glass and rolled a cigarette, he finally made a decision, and shortly afterwards he pushed open the door of Maigne the jeweller.

He had hesitated for a long time, not over the present he wished to give, just its shape. He preferred big watches, round, solid and long-lasting, those plump fob watches which slip into your waistcoat pocket when you are twenty and your grandchildren are pleased to inherit sixty years later. But Jacques was young, progressive, he had his baccalauréat; so a wrist-watch was what he needed.

The business was quickly concluded, since Jean-Edouard did not quibble over the price. He pushed away the little things made of steel which the jeweller first offered, even refused a silver-plated watch with a shrug of the shoulders.

'It's that one I want!' he said, pointing his calloused forefinger towards a Zenith. He examined it, turned it between his fingers, held it up to his ear. 'It's not working!' he protested.

'Of course not, it needs to be wound up.'

'Well, yes . . . Fine, I'd like it gift-wrapped. It's for my grandson, he's just passed his baccalauréat with very good marks. And it's even printed in the newspaper!' he explained, as he took out his wallet and counted the 1,750 francs which the Zenith cost. It was a superb piece of engineering, in a rectangular gold case; a watch which could even be read at night, with a tiny hand to count the seconds and a crocodile-leather strap which made it look very superior.

'There you are,' he said that evening, holding out the box to Jacques, 'it's for you. Now that you're a scholar and have your name in the newspaper, that will remind you of your grandfather. Come on, give me a kiss, or even two. You know, my boy, on days like this, I wish your grandmother were still here, she'd be so happy. Well, I'm happy for both of us . . . '

'Bloody hell!' exclaimed Pierre-Edouard when he saw the gift. 'Your grandfather is really doing you proud! That's worth thousands, a jewel like that!'

'Yes, indeed, Father,' said Mathilde, 'you shouldn't have, it's too fine, it's embarrassing.'

'Get away with you, both of you, it's not your money I've spent, it's mine! Come on, my boy, put it on quickly, I want to see it on your wrist. Yes,' he gave his opinion when Jacques had complied, 'there's no doubt about it, that's the latest thing, it's fine. But you know, to me, a contraption like that around my arm would get in the way of work.'

Léon learned of his godson's success when he returned from Lyons, where he had been negotiating over a large number of army reject horses. He too was as proud of Jacques' success as if he had been his own son. Furthermore, as soon as he was informed of the magnificent present given by Jean-Edouard, he determined to go one better: a matter of marking the occasion and of annoying that old relative who stubbornly refused to address one word to him and kept his door closed to him.

First of all he bought a beautiful wallet in fine leather with the initials of his godson on it. Having done that, and enhanced it with the neat sum of a thousand francs, he slipped a note into it – which he got his wife to write, conscious that his own writing was too basic and rough to satisfy a baccalauréat.

Towards evening, when he was sure that all the Vialhes would have returned to the farm – the harvest of winter barley was at its peak and required all hands – he went up to the Vialhes' and found the whole family in the process of unloading a cart full of sheaves.

Even old Jean-Edouard was there, sitting in front of the house and regarding the grain-laden sheaves with evident satisfaction. He gave Léon a dirty look but remained silent; the yard was not the house, it was almost neutral territory.

'Hey!' called Léon to his godson. 'Put down your fork and come over here a minute! Here,' he said, when Jacques had greeted him, 'this is for you. Go on, open it quickly,' he suggested, lowering his voice and smiling. 'A wallet is like a woman, not to be judged just by the outside! In my time I always used to check by feeling . . . '

'What are you telling him?' asked Mathilde, coming closer. She knew her brother well, and suspected that his whispering would be to conceal something risqué. 'Oh my! You must be mad to give presents like that!' she said when she saw the wad of notes. 'What's he supposed to think now, that money like that grows on trees!'

'Well, so what,' said Léon, 'he earned it with his work! Anyway, it's not very much for that. I can prove that, because even if I put in a thousand times as much, they wouldn't give the baccalauréat to *me* in exchange for it, so there!'

'And this, what's this? asked Jacques, taking out the sheet of paper.

'Read it, read it out, nice and loud, so that everyone can hear!' suggested Léon, glancing mischievously towards Jean-Edouard.

'Voucher for a trip to Paris,' Jacques announced clearly, and as soon as he had read the note he flung his arms around his godfather's neck. 'Oh my, is it really true? To Paris? And I could see the International Exhibition? And everything?'

'You bet! Why do you think I'm sending you up there? To run after the girls? You'd better not, your mother would have a fit!'

'It's too much,' said Pierre-Edouard, leaning on the handle of his fork. 'You and Father, my word, you've really gone too far. Really, you're treating him like a prince!'

'Showing us up, us and our present!' said Mathilde, putting her arms around her son's shoulders.

But she was smiling, and everyone knew that she was only joking; that she was happy and proud to see him so well rewarded.

'You,' said Léon, 'you've paid for his studies, that's worth more than any present! Isn't that enough for them, have they given you something else as well?' he asked Jacques.

'Yes, a bicycle, a Saint-Etienne, with pneumatic tyres, a lamp and three gears!'

'I knew it,' said Léon, giving him a friendly cuff.

'But we haven't even had time to go and fetch it,' bemoaned

Pierre-Edouard, 'what with the haymaking and the harvest, and everything, you know! Well, as soon as we can, we'll go and buy that bicycle! Well, well, you'll be going to Paris!' he said to his son, 'you'll see, it's beautiful. One day I must take your mother there. But even so, will you wait until we have finished harvest before you go?'

'Of course,' promised Jacques, 'but ... Look,' he continued, turning to his uncle and shaking the wad of notes, 'with this I could pay for Paul's ticket, if you'd give him a few days off. I'd like him to come with me, because all alone, it wouldn't be so good as if I had his company. You'll give him some leave, won't you?'

'Of course I will,' said Léon, moved. 'You really are a fine lad, and your brother too. And he deserves this trip as well, because you know he works, and hard! Oh, I know he's not like you, but believe me, it's still work and it's not much fun some days.'

For the whole month of July Jacques remained at his post, helping with the harvest. He was strong and capable now, and had the stamina to make his help valuable in getting it all in.

The yield was beautiful, even abundant, and for the first time in years Pierre-Edouard was not in agony waiting to know what income he would derive from his grain, since the Wheat Office had come into operation.

He had been cautious, and only sown one hectare of 'Dattel' wheat, preferring to plant the other fields with barley, oats, rye and maize, for although those cereals sold less well than wheat, they could always serve as fodder for the animals. If wheat stayed at a good price – as the new Chautemps government assured him it would – then he resolved to sow at least three hectares the following autumn. This news cheered old Jean-Edouard, bucked him up no end; three hectares of wheat, that was proof that the farm was still hale and hearty.

So Jacques worked through all the harvest, and gladly. He was happy to have his bac, happy to have his presents. He rode up to the plateau on his bicycle, and was madly excited at the prospect of exploring Paris with Paul.

Only one shadow clouded his horizon and almost gave him a guilty conscience about feeling so cheerful: Marie-Louise Labrousse had failed. He felt really sorry for her. However, she had the right to retake in September, and so he used every opportunity to go to her house to help her revise the syllabus.

The two young people worked diligently under the eye of an ancient grandmother, who could neither read nor write and who gloried in their knowledge, emitting little cries of delight when they juggled with logarithms. Already there was talk in the village that the Vialhes' son and the Labrousse girl were really made for each other.

# 13

JACQUES and Paul were driven to the station at Brive by their uncle, accompanied by Pierre-Edouard and Mathilde; weighed down with advice, food and luggage, they climbed into the third-class carriage which would take them to the capital in less then eight hours.

'I hope you haven't forgotten anything,' repeated Mathilde, worried to see them launched into the unknown in this way. 'And if your aunt isn't at the station, get someone to show you the way properly so that you can walk to her house!'

'Of course, of course,' Jacques reassured her, 'she lives in the Faubourg Saint-Honoré, it's not complicated!'

'And tell her the eggs are fresh, she can eat them soft-boiled!' insisted Mathilde; besides two chickens trussed ready to roast, four jars of duck confit, three pots of goose liver and two kilos of honey, she had added three dozen eggs at the last moment. In her eyes this was the least she could do to thank her sister-in-law Berthe, who had said she would be delighted to welcome her unknown nephews when they had written asking.

'And tell your aunt that we'd like to see her,' suggested Pierre-Edouard. 'It's true,' he said, turning to Léon. 'She's always got one foot on the aeroplane, ready to go to America, and it's nearly twenty years since she's been back to see us!'

'And above all,' said Léon, winking at his nephews, 'don't run after those little Parisienne girls; they're dreadful, and your mother will blame me afterwards!'

'I'd like to see them chasing girls!' protested Mathilde. 'Especially Paul, at his age!'

'Well, at his age, I, I tell you . . .'

'We know,' interrupted Pierre-Edouard with a laugh. 'Go on then, children, we'll leave you now, the train's about to leave.'

'I've put some napkins in for your midday snack,' Mathilde told them as she kissed them, 'put them on your laps so that you don't make a mess. And in the bottle it's a mixture, the wine's already diluted, don't add any water when you don't know where it's come from! And most important of all, don't lose your aunt's address, and be very polite to her,' she repeated, before jumping on to the platform.

'Tell me,' slipped in Pierre-Edouard as he put his arm around her, 'Jacques is going on eighteen and Paul sixteen; don't you think they're big enough to look after themselves?'

'Yes, of course, but . . . Well, just so long as everything is all right. It's so far away, Paris!'

Jacques and Paul regarded their Aunt Berthe, whom they knew to be forty-three years old, as almost an old lady. So when they arrived at the Gare d'Austerlitz they scanned the crowd to try to find an elderly lady who resembled their father. In her letter Berthe had written: 'I will wait for them at the barrier, and I will recognise them.' The two boys remembered this sentence well, but it did not prevent a little worry creeping in. There were so many women with greying hair!

'Anyway, if we don't find her, we'll go to her place,' decided Jacques, grasping his case and marching towards the ticket-collector.

They handed in their tickets and plunged into the crowd at the exit.

'Well, I suppose so,' said Paul. 'It's all very well Aunty saying it, but she hasn't recognised us, or else she hasn't come! What shall we do?'

'We can always look at the map of Paris, there's one over there. I'd be surprised if we couldn't find our own way!' said Jacques making for the display board. They were absorbed in careful study of the map when a voice, clear but with a sardonic lilt, made them jump.

'*Disia mé, dronles, ont'vol anar? Chas mé béleu? Ané, vene mé far lou poutou!*'

They turned round quickly and tried to see who had just addressed them in pure Saint-Libéral dialect. Two metres away an elegant lady was smiling at them; she was blonde and shapely, so refined and well dressed that Paul could hardly believe that such a vision could speak patois. So he instinctively asked in return: '*Que setz-vos? Tanta Berthe?*' without daring to look at the smiling lady.

'Well of course!' she exclaimed, holding out her arms, 'who else would speak Corrèze dialect here! You must be Jacques, the oldest,' she said as she kissed him, 'and you are Paul. Well, well, you really do look like Pierre-Edouard, don't you?'

She smelled deliciously fragrant, and her cheeks were as soft as a peach fresh off the tree.

'Is that why you were sure that you'd recognise us?' asked Jacques nervously.

'Yes,' she said with a smile, 'but by this too,' she added, tugging at her nephew's jacket. 'Oh, don't worry, you're both very, very well

dressed, and I'm sure you are the most elegant young men in Saint-
Libéral, but for here . . . Come on, let's go, we'll remedy that straight
away. You shall see, my dears; I am going to show you Paris, and
soon you'll wish you could stay for ever.'

Jacques and Paul experienced a week of perpetual amazement. At
first they felt very intimidated, both by Berthe and by the luxury of
her flat in the Faubourg Saint-Honoré – it lay above her couture
house – but they very quickly fell in step with her and adopted this
life, a bit crazy in their eyes, of seductive comfort.

For her everything seemed simple, easy, natural; so the boys were
delighted to be carried along by the events which she organised,
apparently with immense pleasure. She had been very touched by the
provisions Jacques presented to her from his mother.

'That's truly kind,' she murmured, gently fingering the eggs and
chickens. 'They're beautiful, they smell of the farm . . . Oh, confit de
canard! The real thing, from home! You tell your mother that she is
very, very kind. Yes, yes, you wouldn't understand . . . now, you talk
to me for a change; tell me everything, what's happening in Saint-
Libéral?'

They had talked until midnight, for she wanted to know everything, to hear about everything, as if, beneath her effervescent gaiety,
she was concealing deep down a few nostalgic tears.

The whirl of activity began the very next morning. Berthe first
conducted her nephews to the Boulevard des Capucines and pushed
them into the shop at number twelve, called 'Old England'. There,
despite their feeble protests, she kitted them out from head to foot,
and went into raptures when the two brothers emerged from the
fitting rooms, dressed in comfortable golfing clothes and blushing
with embarrassment.

'That's exactly what you need! Before, you looked like little boys
dressed as grandfathers; now you're young men. You look magnificent!' she exclaimed, walking around them. 'Ah, a little alteration
needed here!' she said, taking a tuck in Paul's jacket. 'It can be done
right away. Here, pass me the pins.'

'Certainly, Madame Diamond,' said the salesman dancing
attendance. He waited for her to mark the place, helped Paul take off
the jacket, and went off to the workroom.

'What did he call you?' whispered Paul. 'The Diamond, that's our
stream, at home!'

'Well, yes,' she explained, as she tried to tie on him, 'didn't you
know that it's the name of my couture house?'

479

'Oh no, we didn't know,' chorused the boys.

To tell the truth, they knew next to nothing about her. They strongly suspected that she led a life which their parents would regard as less than exemplary, as the few allusions which their father occasionally made to her eccentric life-style were unmistakable in tone. Nobody in the family had ever mentioned that her unmarried life might nevertheless be filled with masculine company. At the Vialhes' it was not the sort of subject you touched on, especially in front of the children. Although Jacques and Paul were young, they were sufficiently aware to understand, for instance, that the elegant gentleman who had driven them from the station to the Faubourg Saint-Honoré in his II CV Citroën the evening before, was more than a friend to their aunt.

'Or if he is her friend,' Paul murmured in his brother's ear just before falling asleep, 'he's a close friend . . .'

'Yes, that's obvious. Anyway his photo is all over the place here – but, after all, we don't care, do we? I think it would be better not to tell our parents about him though, okay?'

'Of course not! They wouldn't understand!'

Apart from this discovery, their aunt's life remained a closed book to them.

'There, I think that will be better,' said the salesman, returning with Paul's jacket, 'if the gentleman would like to try it.'

'Perfect,' said Berthe, taking out her chequebook. 'Good, I'll take these four shirts and these ties as well, and don't forget the caps! Your berets don't go with these clothes at all,' she explained with a smile.

She made out a cheque, and Jacques happened to see the amount; it seemed to him so exorbitant that he protested.

'Really, Aunt' he tried, genuinely embarrassed, 'it's . . . it's much too much, you shouldn't! Maman won't be at all happy, you know, and Papa even less so!'

'Now you be quiet,' she said, taking his arm, 'I have every right to give myself a treat, haven't I? Anyway, it's not as expensive as you think! And now, let's go and conquer Paris!'

In one week of Parisian life, Berthe dragged them along at such a pace that they lost all sense of time. They saw everything, or almost everything, and they were so full of enthusiasm that it was a joy for Berthe to help them discover new marvels.

For the first three days they made their way around the International Exhibition. Everything delighted them; they wanted to see it all, to visit every pavilion which stood on the banks of the Seine from Les Invalides to L'Île de Cygnes.

The foreign pavilions were grouped around the Chaillot Palace and at the foot of the Eiffel Tower, which stretched towards the sky like a sparkling arrow in a blaze of floodlights every night. Like everyone else, they were very impressed by the imposing construction crowned with a black eagle which was the German pavilion. But to their great astonishment, this was the only place where their aunt tried to hurry them through their visit.

'Don't let's linger there,' she said, 'it doesn't smell good. Believe me, my dears, I know that country well. I used to go there often at one time, and I did very good business there. But that's all over. Come on, let's go on to the island to see the Colonial Centre, it's much jollier!'

'You don't like the Germans, either! You're like Papa, then?' teased Paul.

She smiled and shook her head.

'The Germans? Yes I do, but not all of them.' She ruffled his hair. 'Come on now, and if you like, before we do to the colonies we'll take in Great Britain; it's over there, on the other side of the bridge.'

Three days at the Exhibition then, during which they also visited the Palace of Discovery, the planetarium and the upper platforms of the Eiffel Tower as well as the foreign and French creations, including all the regional exhibits. For Jacques' sake they sauntered through the Museum of Modern Art on the quai de New York. Finally, as a relaxation, they strolled slowly in the amusement park set up on the esplanade in front of Les Invalides. And every evening, although they were very tired, their aunt dragged them to the cinema. So they saw Pagnol's trilogy and also *Lost Horizon* and *The Story of a Cardsharp*.

When they had had their fill of the Exhibition, Berthe next led them round Paris. They saw everything, or at least believed they did: the Louvre, Saint-Chapelle, Notre-Dame and the Arc de Triomphe; also the Jardin des Plantes and les Halles, which made a great impression on them.

On Sunday morning Berthe did not have the heart to shock them by missing church, so she took them to eleven o'clock Mass at the Madeleine, where they were amazed by the pomp and ceremony of the High Mass.

Then came the eve of their departure. Jacques and his brother had grown so fond of their aunt that they wanted to show their appreciation in some concrete way; they clubbed together to give her a present. But what should they choose? Her flat was already full of pictures, vases and knick-knacks.

'Must be something to keep,' said Paul.

'Yes, but what?'

'Uncle Léon says that all women love jewellery.'

'Huh! Do you see yourself going and buying something like that? All alone? You'd look a right fool!'

Their aunt had accompanied them to help them chose the other presents for the family; she was so self-assured! So they had acquired a tobacco pouch decorated with views of Paris for their grandfather, a liqueur flask in the shape of the Arc de Triomphe for their parents, and also a fine scarf for their mother. There was a penholder with pictures on it for Mauricette, a big pencil box showing the Eiffel Tower for Guy, the Sacré-Coeur Church in a globe for Uncle Léon and his wife. Not forgetting Nicolas, they found a frame for the photo which was turning yellow on the wall of his room. But in this last case, they would have to manage without their aunt if the gift were to be appreciated. Where would be the surprise and delight if she helped them to choose and knew the price!

'Can you see yourself going into a jewellery shop?' repeated Jacques.

'Bah, the people in there can't by any worse than the butchers I meet with Uncle! Whatever we do we mustn't try around here; you heard what Aunt Berthe said: this is the most expensive area. You'll come with me, won't you?'

Eventually they set off on foot together for a jeweller's in a street in the St Martin district, and bought a small brooch in Limoges enamel. It was a modest gift, but they realised that their aunt's pleasure when they gave it to her was in no way feigned.

'But why? Why? You shouldn't have!' she said, pinning the brooch to her bodice. 'Oh, you remind me of your father, he always had a way of making thoughtful gestures. You have made me very happy. Now you are going to promise me that you'll come back, won't you?'

'Well, we'd love to,' said Paul, 'but what about you, why don't you ever come to see us?'

'Oh,' she replied, 'it's not so simple as all that, but I'll get organised one day, that's a promise, I . . . Listen, tell your father that I may be getting married soon . . . to a colleague. Or better still, don't say anything to him, I'll write to him.'

'Is it by any chance the gentleman who drove us in his car?' asked Jacques.

'That's right.'

'He seemed very nice, I'm sure Papa would like him.'

'I'd be very surprised if he did! But that isn't the problem,' she added quietly.

Jacques and Paul could not stop singing Berthe's praises and talking of the wonderful holiday they had spent with her, right up to the start of the school year which was to see the departure of Mauricette, whose turn it was to be sent to board in Brive. Furthermore they talked of her in such affectionate terms that even their grandfather, who was inclined to judge her severely, finished by simply shrugging his shoulders whenever the conversation returned to his daughter. He made do with mumbling the same response each time: 'Really! I never knew that plonk could turn into fine wine as it aged, unless it were a special plonk in a magic barrel!'

However, everyone knew that his surly comments masked the pride he felt in knowing that his daughter had succeeded so brilliantly; she was, after all, a Vialhe. She was now a true Parisienne, rich and famous – even the shopkeepers addressed her by name, that proved it! So Pierre-Edouard and Mathilde only smiled when the old man himself brought the conversation round to his daughter again, all the while looking as if butter would not melt in his mouth.

'And you say she calls herself Diamond? What an idea! Why not Vialhe!'

Pierre-Edouard had to bite his tongue in the effort not to remind him that twenty-three years earlier, if he could have, Jean-Edouard would have erased his daughter's name from the civil register without blinking an eyelid!

Nobody in the Vialhe family ever forgot that Monday, 25 October 1937; and for many years afterwards Pierre-Edouard recalled all the details of the events each time he strode over the Coste-Roche field which he had been sowing that day.

With the help of Nicolas, he had succeeded in clearing the plots surrounding the tumbledown cottage of Coste-Roche for the second time – that land which he and Mathilde had cultivated sixteen years earlier and which had been turned to scrub by fifteen years of neglect. He had energetically rooted out this invasion, and was planting oats on the reclaimed ground when Mathilde's call halted his work. Instead of flying out in a fine spray, the fistful of grain he was holding fell onto the ploughed earth in an awkward heap.

'What's happened?' He put down the seed sack which hung round his waist. Then he caught sight of Mathilde running up the rough track which climbed to Coste-Roche, despite the steep gradient and the stones.

'Bloody hell!' He rushed towards her. 'It has to be a catastrophe! What is it?' he called from a distance as soon as he thought she would hear him. 'Father? The children? Léon? What?'

'No,' Mathilde stopped, and used her apron to wipe the beads of sweat from her forehead.

'Well what then?' he demanded as he reached her.

'Louise telephoned . . .'

'Yes?'

'Oh, it's not fair! It's not fair!' she blurted out, suddenly throwing herself against him and beginning to cry. 'It's not fair,' she repeated.

'Tell me!' he ordered, shaking her.

'Thérèse, Félix's little Thérèse, she had her baby in the night . . .'

'Oh,' he murmured, 'and it didn't live?'

'It's not that, it's she who died, it's her, you see . . .'

'God be damned! What harm have they ever done, in heaven's name? It always strikes them! Always! But why?' he cried suddenly. 'First Octave! Then Jean! And now this young girl! Bloody hell, why?'

'Calm down,' she wiped her tears, 'it does no good to curse heaven about it.'

'Who did she call to tell us?'

'The Post Office.'

'What else did she say?'

'Don't you think that's enough? She said the mother died of a haemorrhage, the baby is beautiful, but Félix is beside himself. That's all she said.'

'All right,' he decided immediately, 'I'm going there. I should be up there – Félix will need me, and Louise too, I'm sure. I'll leave right away.'

'But . . . how?'

'Is your brother at home today?'

'Yes, I saw him an hour ago.'

'Well, he'll take me. I know him, he won't refuse. I'll manage on my own for getting back, and Nicolas will deal with things here. Come on, don't let's waste any time!'

Léon did not hesitate for a second.

'Of course I'll drive you there,' he said, as soon as he was put in the picture. 'We mustn't leave Félix all alone, nor your sister, if it turns out they don't have any close friends up there. Pack your case, I'll come for you in ten minutes.'

484

'Have you told Father?' Pierre-Edouard asked Mathilde before they went into the house.

'No, I didn't have time.'

'But you think we should . . .'

'How can we avoid it?

'You're right.' He pushed open the door.

His father was on the settle, fashioning a basket from willow wands; he looked up at his son.

'What are you doing here at this time of day? Have you finished sowing up there already?'

'No. Listen, Father, we've just heard a, a . . .'

'Who's died?' Jean-Edouard demanded fiercely. 'Come on, tell me, tell me right out!'

'Félix's wife. She had her baby and she's dead. So I'm going there right away.'

'Poor kid,' murmured the old man, twisting a willow shoot in his hands without noticing it, 'and I told them to bring the baby as soon as they could . . . You're right to go. Go and take care of them, go on! Your wife and I will look after the farm, with Nicolas.'

A quarter of an hour later, Pierre-Edouard and Léon were on the road to Limoges. At first they travelled without saying anything; then, gradually, since they could not spend the whole journey brooding over their sorrow, a dialogue was established.

'We should be there in three and a half hours, but of course it'll be dark by then,' said Léon, glancing at the clock on the dashboard.

'Yes, I hope I remember the way! Well, we can always ask. She goes well, your car.'

'She should do! But she's still running in.'

'What is it, what make?' asked Pierre-Edouard, who was quite ignorant when it came to cars.

'I told you when I bought it,' Léon reproached him cheerfully. 'I've had it less than a month and you've already forgotten. It's a Renault, six cylinders, six-seater, a hundred and thirty-five kilometres an hour! Okay, it cost me 46,000 francs and it swallows fifteen litres every hundred kilometres, but at least we're sitting in comfort!'

'That's true . . . But still 46,000 francs! I'd prefer to put the money into something else!'

'Bah! Money is for using! Not for when you're dead. Oh, sorry . . .'

'Well, no, you're right.' Pierre-Edouard lit his pipe. 'I don't really know what I'm going to say to poor Félix, nor to Louise either . . .'

485

'Nothing. You must just be with them, that's all. Words have never comforted anyone, but being there does.'

Pierre-Edouard had left the Château of Cannepetière on 2 August 1914, the day of the general call-up; he had never returned since then. In broad daylight he would have found the way, but night fell even before they arrived in Châteauroux. They were therefore forced to stop several times to ask directions.

It was nine o'clock before they finally reached the château. The caretaker explained to them that Félix did not live there, but in his forester's cottage, more than six kilometres away.

'Oh, yes, that's right,' Pierre-Edouard remembered, 'Louise and Jean moved there when they got married. We have to take the lane just past the outbuilding and turn left down the forest track, is that the one?'

'Well yes, that's just about right,' said the man, surprised at his accuracy.

'Let's go,' said Pierre-Edouard, 'and don't worry about your car; if it hasn't rained too much, we'll make it.'

It took them almost twenty minutes to reach the keeper's cottage, because the road was pitted with deep ruts and Léon was obliged to drive at walking pace.

'As you said, it's a good thing it hasn't been raining; if it had, we'd be in a mess!' he grumbled. 'My God, what an idea to live this far off the beaten track!'

They eventually perceived a faint light, which twinkled from a hollow in the forest.

'It's over there,' said Pierre-Edouard.

The nearer they drew, the more depressed he felt at the idea of seeing his sister again under such circumstances. Once before in their lives their reunion had taken place beside a death-bed, in a pitiful attic, in Orléans. And that time too, there had been a baby sleeping on one side of the room; Félix had been that baby. As Mathilde had said, it was not fair.

Léon stopped in front of the house and turned off the engine; a dog yapped faintly.

'Right, I must go in . . .' murmured Pierre-Edouard.

'I'll come with you, unless you prefer to go alone.'

'No, come on.'

He knocked on the door and, when nobody responded, pushed it open and went in.

What shocked him immediately was the sight of an old woman

asleep, sitting huddled in a corner by the kitchen range. An old woman with white hair whose eyes were closed, the rims reddened with tears, the lids a network of fine blue veins; her hands were clasped instinctively on her stomach, gripping a useless rosary. As he drew near he recognised her.

'It can't be Louise?' whispered Léon behind him.

'Yes it is!'

Then he noticed the cradle, in a corner of the room dimly lit by a little paraffin lamp. He leaned over the baby, quite pink but still wrinkled; sleeping with its mouth half open.

'And Félix? He should be here!' Pierre-Edouard said in surprise.

'With, well, with his wife, next door perhaps?' suggested Léon.

Pierre-Edouard picked up a candle, lit it, and pushed open the door. Thérèse was there, alone. On the bedside table, next to a saucer of holy water with a sliver of box-wood soaking in it, a small candle-end was alight; a tiny flame, but still enough to show the pretty, child-like features of the young woman, only her dreadful pallor betraying her true state.

'He's not there,' said Pierre-Edouard, turning back towards Louise.

He gently placed his hand on her shoulder, and his fingers felt the bones through lean flesh. She lifted her head.

'Oh, it's you . . .' she said. 'I was sure you would come.' Then she noticed Léon. 'You came too; thank you.'

'Where is Felix?' asked Pierre-Edouard.

'Félix? Oh, poor boy, he went out into the forest a little while ago.'

'But good heavens! This isn't the time to be going out into the forest!' protested Pierre-Edouard, 'especially with . . . Well it's not, anyway!'

'You don't understand,' she said. 'The little one, we were up with her for two whole nights, but she was alive then. Two nights of labour, it was long, too long, especially when you're all alone. So she finally fell asleep, that's all. She couldn't go on, you see? And nor could we. That's why you found me asleep and Félix out in the forest, to revive ourselves a bit, and because to be there with her, when she looks as if she's just fallen asleep, it's . . . it's enough to drive you mad.'

'Which way did he go?'

She shrugged her shoulders.

'Into the forest, it's big . . . Or maybe he's by the pool.'

'But my God! He shouldn't be left alone! He could . . . Well! In the name of God, Louise, stir yourself! First things first, where's this pool?'

'That way, about five hundred metres, at the end of the path which goes to the right at the bottom of the garden.'

'Stay here,' said Pierre-Edouard to León. 'I'm going to see if I can find him.'

As ill luck would have it, the moon was in its last quarter and gave only a feeble light. However, Pierre-Edouard gradually became accustomed to the darkness. He knew before he reached it that he was close to the pool; he could smell the mud and hear the rustling of the cat's-tails and reeds in the breeze.

He drew nearer, climbed the embankment, and jumped when a pair of teal flew off with a great clatter of wings and water. It took him another five minutes of searching to find Félix. He was there, leaning back against the pillar of an old shooting butt; he hardly turned his head as his uncle approached him.

Pierre-Edouard waited without moving. He did not know what to do or to say, convinced that he would blurt out something stupid if he spoke, or make an awkward gesture if he moved. So he waited patiently. Since his back was aching from the strain of the journey, he sat down beside his nephew, filled his pipe and lit it.

By the flickering light of the flame he saw that Félix was crying. Like a man, without a sound, without a sob, just an abundance of tears which had been held back for too long and now flowed over, rolled down and disappeared into the stubble of a two-day-old beard.

Ten minutes passed, and soon the grebes and coots reappeared from the shelter of the irises and rushes where they had hidden in fear at the sound of footsteps.

'You've got a fag?' Félix asked at last.

Pierre-Edouard held out his pouch and his papers, and clicked his lighter when his nephew stuck a cigarette between his lips.

'Why?' asked Félix, after the first few puffs. 'Why her? We loved each other so much! You know, she was . . . Oh, how can I say it? . . . She was me. You can't understand, you can't know. We two were, were like a tree and its bark! You know very well that a tree can't live without the bark! And that the oak dies if the lightning burns its skin! You know that! So! And now there's nothing for me but to die! Answer me that!'

'Well, I've seen a young walnut tree,' said Pierre-Edouard after a pause, 'which should have died when the goats ate its bark. But it's still standing. Oh, it suffered, and more than that; yes, it suffered, but it began to grow again despite that. Of course I helped as best I could.

I made a plaster of clay and dung and tied it all on with an old sack. It didn't prevent the tree from weeping, but at least it stopped the sun from burning it and killing it. That walnut tree still bears the scars. In May, when the sap rises, it still weeps a bit, but it doesn't want to die and every year it gives its portion of nuts.'

'But I couldn't do that. Without her, it can't be done. You understand, to go back into the house and not see her ever again, not hear her, nothing, emptiness, it can't be done!'

'You know,' Pierre-Edouard spoke after a very long silence, 'I knew a young woman, still a child, and one day the house was empty for her too. She wanted someone again and once more the day came when she found the house empty . . .'

'Yes,' murmured Félix, 'yes, but it's not the same!'

'It's always the same. If you really love someone it's always the same, for everyone, in every case! But you think you're the only one because it's so overwhelming, so unbearable, that you think another case like yours can't possibly exist. You see, one night, I too felt the anguish of losing Mathilde. I was with an old doctor who said to me, speaking of us, believe me I remember it well, "You two are like the eyes in a face, one doesn't turn without the other." He was right. But since then I've also learned that a face can still live even if it has lost an eye. And believe me, a child doesn't give a damn if his father or mother is blind in one eye, especially if that's all he's ever known. That's not to say that the kid isn't missing anything, but it's just that to him, the most beautiful face is the one that bends over him and smiles at him, even if it only has one eye. You know that better than I do, after all you didn't know your father.

Félix remained silent, then he rolled himself another cigarette.

'You've seen it, the baby?' he asked eventually.

'Yes, is it a boy?'

'Of course; she always said to me it would be a boy.'

'And what are you going to call him?'

'Pierre.'

'That's good,' said Pierre-Edouard, getting up. 'Now I'd like to go in, because I'm cold. Are you staying here?'

Félix drew on his cigarette and got up too. 'Perhaps I'd have stayed if you hadn't come, but now . . .'

'Come on then; you'll see Léon, he's there as well.'

'I didn't think you'd come so quickly,' Félix admitted as he gazed at the pool. 'If I'd known, I would have waited for you at the house. No, I would never have thought . . .'

'Well, that's because you don't know me very well. Your mother was certain that I would come.'

'Why?'

'Because she learned earlier than any of us that a burden is borne more easily when there are plenty to carry it. And because she knows that with us, the Vialhes, the living always gather around the dead. To make a united front, you understand. When there are several of you, you can keep each other company. Even if it doesn't ease the pain, at least it gives you the feeling that you're doing something.'

That night Pierre-Edouard and Léon kept the vigil over the dead body; that allowed Louise and Félix to sleep for several hours. In the small hours Léon had to leave for Saint-Libéral; Pierre-Edouard went out to the car with him.

'I'll come back the day after tomorrow,' promised Léon, 'and if Mathilde would like it, I'll bring her for the funeral, and I think Yvette will come too. That way they'll be a bit less lonely.' He nodded towards the house.

'Safe journey, and thank you.' Pierre-Edouard stifled a yawn. 'Oh, now I think of it, tell Nicolas to begin ploughing the Malides field, then we can plant it when I get back. And tell Mathilde that the baby is a big boy and he's called Pierre. Off you go, cheers!'

Louise had risen and was making coffee when he returned to the house. It seemed to him that his sister looked less old and worn now that she had rested. Even so, with her white hair and lined face she looked almost sixty. *And yet she's only forty-seven*, he calculated, *it's not such a great age, after all!*

'Léon has gone back?' she asked.

'Yes, he's got some work to do, but he'll be back the day after tomorrow.'

'I was sure you would come,' she said, as she slowly poured the boiling water into the earthenware filter. She lowered her voice. 'What do you think about Félix?'

He made an evasive gesture.

'I can't say really. Last night he was too tired for me to tell; we'll see soon enough, when he wakes. And you, how are you? I'm not talking about what's just happened, but in general?'

'Oh, me . . .' She made a dismissive movement of her shoulders. He saw that she was crying, without a sound, without even changing her expression; only a slight trembling of her lips, and the blinking of her eyelids as the tears escaped, betrayed her vast sorrow.

490

He moved towards her, pulled her to him and held her against his shoulder.

'Go on,' he said, as he gently stroked her hair, 'cry as much as you like, there's no shame in that. Cry as much as you can, but afterwards – afterwards you'll go and tidy yourself up, comb your hair properly and dress in your Sunday best. That's what you have to do, for Félix, and for the baby too, and for your own sake even.'

'First I must go and milk the goat for the baby; a good thing she's there, that nanny-goat!'

'I'll take care of her; you drink your coffee and after that, go and make yourself beautiful. You're good at that, I know; you just have to have the will.'

For two days, Pierre-Edouard watched over his sister and his nephew. When Félix saw his mother rejuvenated by a change of clothing and a little make-up, he became aware of his own miserable appearance – his cheeks blue with stubble, his clothes crumpled, he looked like a tramp going downhill. He felt obliged to react.

Once he was clean and changed, it was towards the forest that he turned his steps, and his uncle was at his side. Pierre-Edouard listened for hours, hardly saying anything himself, to all the confidences which were retold loudly and disjointedly. The confidences, secrets even, all centred on the dead young woman. In this way Félix gradually poured out his sorrow. Instead of burying it within himself like a cancer, he scratched the wound until it bled and squeezed out his misery, drop by drop. His distress was very little diminished, but discouragement and depression gave way initially to resignation, and then later to stoicism.

Two days later, Félix and his mother were surrounded by the Vialhe and Dupeuch families as they accompanied the coffin to the little cemetery of Mézières-en-Brenne. Even Jacques and the Paul were there, on either side of Mathilde. Only Berthe was missing – she was out of the country, and so Pierre-Edouard had not been able to tell her – and old Jean-Edouard, who was too old to make the journey.

He was at least represented by an enormous wreath which trembled on the side of the hearse and on which could be read:

To the granddaughter whom I would have liked to have got to know better.

Everyone appreciated this nice touch, but only Louise knew its real worth. This wreath was a discreet thank-you from her father to her after twenty-eight years; one day in January 1909 she had been newly married, banished from her family, and had not been able to attend her grandmother's funeral, so she had expressed her feelings via her modest offering of flowers. Today, Jean-Edouard remembered.

# 14

PIERRE-EDOUARD made use of a fine crop of walnuts, which realised a decent price, to execute a plan which he had cherished for several years. When winter came he undertook the modernisation of all the farm buildings with the help of Nicolas; they were sorely in need of it.

First of all he attacked the cowshed. It was old, dark and impractical, with wooden stalls and uneven flagstones which made cleaning difficult. He wanted it functional, airy, modern.

He enlarged the access, removed the wooden mangers and replaced them with low cement feeding troughs. He concreted the floor and rendered the walls. He even installed a tap, and was sorry he could not afford to buy those automatic drinking troughs he had seen in advertisements sent to the syndicate.

Despite this drawback and his father's criticisms – that the new building was too light, the cement too cold and the animals too cramped – he could now line up eight cows on each side; his shed was the finest and most modern in the village. Over the years other farmers frequently came to him to use his as a model when they were trying to renovate their cowsheds.

After that he went on to the sheepfold, which he refitted likewise from top to bottom. Then he passed on to the pigsties, which his father had built to undertake pig breeding when the railway line was being constructed. Here again, he demolished the ancient wooden boxes which had been chewed by the sows and rotted by dung, and were only held together by extensive and frequent reinforcement with chestnut planks. He built concrete sties fitted with troughs which were easy to fill, and provided ventilation by replacing the tiny skylights with wide frame windows which could be opened.

'Well, well,' remarked Mathilde when everything was finished, 'the animals and Nicolas are better accommodated than we are . . . Nicolas's room may still be in the cowshed, but it's almost nicer than ours!'

Pierre-Edouard noticed her rather injured air, and sighed.

'I know, even the pigs are more comfortable than we are, but how do you think I can undertake alterations in a house which doesn't belong to me? It would be stupid. Besides, if I know him, my father would never let anyone touch his walls.'

'You're right,' she said, 'but you know there are days when I'd almost like to go up to Coste-Roche and set up house there again, be at home, in our own place. But I know that's impossible. Never mind; when you've got a bit of money, promise me you'll get the roof fixed up there. We must think of our own children – one day they'll get married, and we wouldn't want them to have to live with us, that's not good for anyone.'

'Have you had words with Father?'

'Oh, no, not at all. But you know how it is; he has his little fads, his own set ways and times of doing things and his ideas too, and he still doesn't want to accept Léon, which is pure spite when all's said and done.'

Pierre-Edouard regarded the annexation of Austria with a very jaundiced eye. He kept himself sufficiently well informed about current affairs to realise that a crisis was looming, quite apart from the deplorable vacillations of the French politicians. Already the franc was worth almost nothing and prices rose unremittingly; but it had been the same old story for several years now.

What worried him, and Léon too, was the power and consequence being assumed by a nation which had been beaten and vanquished twenty years ago. Pierre-Edouard did not like the shows of force in Germany, nor the Italian's bravado and least of all that Franco fellow's fascism, for there was no longer any doubt that he was gong to win the war. There was no need to be a first-class politician to predict that. Léon was already employing two Republican Spaniards who had fled from reprisals and had recently arrived in Saint-Libéral. According to them, terrible atrocities and frightful massacres were taking place in their home country, and that was thanks to help from those Germans who were as proud as ganders, and those Italians who were as arrogant as peacocks.

'Mark you,' Léon said to him one night in April, when they were taking an aperitif at Suzanne's, 'for the time being they're leaving us in peace: after all, Ethiopia, Spain, Austria and Czechoslovakia, it's none of our business. All right, it has a nasty smell about it, but it's a long way off!'

'You're damn right it's a long way off!' said Delpeyroux, joining in the conversation. 'To me their Cze-losco-vakia, I don't even know where it is! I'm not in a hurry to fight for people when I don't even know where they live!'

494

'Yes,' said Pierre-Edouard, 'it's a long way off, but Hitler and Mussolini are our neighbours, both of them. I don't trust neighbours who move the boundary markers to gain a few furrows.'

'Neither do I,' said Léon, 'but just so long as it's not round here.'

'That's right, it never does any good to mind other people's business; all the same, those neighbours, I don't trust them.'

'Neither do I if it comes to that,' agreed Léon. 'Shall I tell you something? Well, in 1918, with the Huns, we stopped too soon; we should have given them a real hammering! It's true that I couldn't have gone on and neither could you, but . . .' He finished by banging his metal hook on the zinc of the bar.

Thinking that he was calling for another round of drinks, Suzanne filled their glasses and then smiled at Léon.

'You're into politics again, are you? I've heard that's all you're interested in nowadays; that's not much fun for us women!'

'Mm, yes.' Pierre-Edouard ignored the interruption. 'We weren't exactly fit in 1918, but I'm not so sure that we are today either!'

'I wouldn't go so far as to say that,' protested Delpeyroux. 'We've got the Maginot line, and that's the real thing! It's unbreachable – that's what my wife's cousin told me, and he spent four months of his service on it. Unbreachable! And then we've got aeroplanes too!'

'Yes,' added Léon, 'it's true what he says, we're prepared.'

'Listen, you two,' said Pierre-Edouard in a grave tone: 'in 1914 I found myself on the front without knowing a thing; I didn't even believe there would *be* a war on the thirty-first of July, the day before German mobilisation! So you can imagine what a fool I felt on the first of August! But this time I want to be able to see it coming, if the balloon goes up. It won't stop it happening, but at least I won't look so stupid.'

That year, the 'Ice Saints Days' lived up to their name and their cruel reputation. On 11 May Saint Mammert arrived with a white frost; on the twelfth Saint Pancras did the same, and on the thirteenth, a Friday to boot, Saint Servais succeeded in destroying the few flowers which had escaped his colleagues' attentions.

In Saint-Libéral it was a bitter blow for those who made a profit from plums, cherries and spring vegetables. A year without fruit would mean less money, and nothing could replace that loss.

It was hard for the Vialhes. Pierre-Edouard had drawn heavily on his savings to modernise the farm buildings, and he had hoped that five or six tons of plums would replenish his nest-egg. But what could you do against Heaven's will? So he shrugged his shoulders over the blackened petals and twisted pistils and even tried to comfort Nicolas, who was concerned for the bees which were hampered by the cold.

'Well, old fellow, that's the way it is. You should know that, considering how long you've been here. One year it's all right, the next it isn't. If the nuts yield well, the plums freeze, and if the tobacco is good, it's the wheat that's poor! Come on, let's go, we mustn't let it stop us from going to spray the potatoes; they're just pushing through and the Colorado beetles are gobbling them up already. The frost doesn't kill those filthy pests, that would be too easy!'

The weather remained dreadful until the middle of June, as if it had been set off course by the late frosts. Torrential showers, which washed everything away and drowned the crops, were followed by low temperatures which stopped the grass from growing and delayed the development of the cereals and vegetables.

Towards 15 June warmer weather arrived, and Pierre-Edouard began haymaking, relying on the fact that there were still two weeks left until the change of moon. It was a good thing that he seized the opportunity, for those who delayed setting to work then had to wait until the end of July to bring home any dry hay.

In the midst of all these anxieties, only Jacques' success in his second baccalauréat exams brought a ray of happiness into the Vialhe household; and it brought pride too, for as soon as he had the results Jacques announced to his parents that he intended to sit the entrance exams for the Veterinary College, either at Maisons-Alfort or at Toulouse – always providing that they could pay for his studies.

'Blimey,' muttered Pierre-Edouard, happy with his choice but worried about the cost of it all, 'you're aiming high. Well, I hope we'll be able to pay for it.'

'We will!' decided Mathilde.

'We will! We will! We'll have to see! It certainly won't be with what we've made out of plums this year!'

'Oh, I know,' she said, 'but I also know what I myself have managed to put aside over the years. What did you expect?' she asked her husband with a smile. '*I* was never in the habit of throwing thrushes to the wolves!'

'That's enough,' he interrupted. 'You're not going to bring out your brother's hoary old tale, are you?'

That was exactly what she did every time she wanted to tease him, and both of them really enjoyed the banter; it brought back their youth.

'Joking apart,' she said, 'you must find out, dear, exactly what it will cost us. We'll do all we can, but it shouldn't be to the detriment of your brothers and sisters, you understand?'

'Absolutely.'

'And how many years will it go on?' asked Pierre-Edouard.

'Four.'

'Really! Your mother was very well advised when she saved them, her . . . her thrushes! Four years of study, that'll cost a pretty penny! Especially if every year is ruined like this one!'

'We'll manage!' cut in Mathilde.

'All right, all right, we'll manage . . . in the meanwhile, you must understand that this year we can't give you a big present for your bac like we did last year. Before we had that frost I was thinking of buying you a wireless set. Oh, not a big one, but still a set that we could all have enjoyed. Well, we'll see later on, maybe.'

'Don't worry about that! Uncle Léon is going to get me one next time he goes to Brive . . .'

'There you are!' cried Pierre-Edouard triumphantly, laughing, 'and afterwards your mother will say that I'm the one who throws money out of the window! Well, I see that you've started smoking a pipe, so you can have this.' He took a box from his pocket. 'I brought you this, it's a strong one, a real briar. By the way, did the Labrousse girl get her bac too?'

'Yes, and with a good grade.'

'That's great. Well, you must ask her to come to our house one day. I think she's rather sweet, don't you?'

After his sixteenth birthday, Paul felt that he was a man at last. He had put on weight and grown taller in the last few months, was strong and well proportioned; he had to shave at least twice a week, and was very proud of the fact. He was also very proud of the lingering looks he attracted from the village girls.

Where they were concerned he assumed an air of self-confidence which he by no means felt; he pretended to be blasé, almost cynical, all the better to conceal a sort of instinctive reserve which held him back and prevented him from going the whole way. They saw in him the reliability, high standards and honesty of the Vialhes together with his uncle's imagination, and the dissolute, disreputable, unscrupulous streak which Léon used to his own advantage – although he had settled down since his marriage.

Some evenings Paul was burning to respond without further ado to the advances he provoked from, among others, the tantalizing Suzanne, but he banished the wicked idea by reminding himself that

497

the landlady of the inn was old enough to be his mother. Besides, he was secretly dreaming of a *grande amour*, and he didn't want to do anything which might spoil the way he pictured it would happen. He was torn by these conflicting emotions, but it was a point of honour to him that he should never let his state of mind show.

Only Jacques guessed the extent of his inner torment, but he knew that his brother's pride and sense of propriety prevented any exchange of confidences. The only secret Paul was willing to discuss was the plan which he had nurtured since their wonderful trip to Paris.

'You know,' Paul had confessed to him six months earlier, 'I don't want to be a stock-dealer all my life.'

'That's what Papa's counting on; he's hoping you'll come back to farming. That would be better really.'

'Well, he's wrong there, I don't want anything to do with the farm!'

'But why not?' Jacques had protested. 'Someone's got to take it on!'

'It's up to you then! But you want to be a vet instead!'

'Yes, but I can make that choice!'

'All right, we all know you're very clever! But if you think I've got to stay here because I haven't passed exams, that's where you're wrong!'

'But you don't have any choice!'

'We'll see, but let me tell you, I shall be off to Paris just as soon as I can. Up there, that's really living! Look at Tante Berthe, do you think she passed any exams?'

'Maybe not,' grumbled Jacques. 'One piece of advice though; don't tell Papa any of this rubbish, or he'll soon make you think otherwise!'

'I know, but that won't stop it happening. I'll wait, and one day I'll do it, you'll see. We'll talk about it another time . . .'

And he really did talk about it; he built his castles in Spain, cherished his project, nurtured it. Jacques listened patiently, but he felt so much more mature than his brother that he had to control himself so as not to demonstrate to Paul that his idea was just childish nonsense, a dream. For him, a brilliant scholar, life did not depend on daydreams; it had firm foundations and was to be lived in reality. Already he was methodically organising his life, with persistence and effort; he loved Paul's imagination and spirit, but he did not consider it a sensible line to conduct.

Old memories were awakened amongst the veterans and those who remembered 1914 when the call-up came for the reservists and soldiers on leave to join the Maginot Line. The news came on Sunday 4 September and led to a lot of talk, but taken altogether things were quite reassuring – it was a far cry from total mobilisation – and as nobody in the village was directly affected by it, the conversations turned on ways of preserving the peace rather than making war.

Nobody felt particularly belligerent, especially not those who had left twenty-five years earlier, shouting like men possessed, that they would not stop until they reached Berlin. They knew what war was really like and, although they enjoyed the chance to talk about their four years in the trenches yet again, what they said about it did not encourage anyone to plunge into such a hell on earth.

Thus everyone tried to reassure themselves, and the many men who got out their guns were only doing so in preparation for the opening of the hunting season. Despite that the worry ate at them, because the news was so alarming, especially to those who were the right age to bear arms.

On Friday, 23 September came the announcement of partial mobilisation; it affected about a million men and this time several reservists in the village had to leave. All those with a number 2 or 3 on their military records had to report to their barracks.

Nevertheless, many people in Saint-Libéral continued to believe that a war was impossible, as if it were enough to deny the evidence to render it null and void. Besides, the veterans of 1914 confirmed that real conflict did not begin like this. This mobilisation was more like a grand army exercise; simply a warning, a deployment of forces intended to impress any possible adversary, to prove that they were ready to defend themselves, but equally ready to discuss the matter and do everything to avoid a fight which nobody wanted.

Despite this rather forced optimism, there was a crowd that night in the church in response to Father Delclos' exhortations; during the afternoon he had called on all his parishioners to come and pray for peace, and it was best to have all the winning cards in your hand at times like these. Everyone believed that peace had been preserved when they learned, a week later, that Chamberlain, Daladier and Hitler had met in Munich and arrived at a lasting and fair agreement.

Although they were reassured about the future, Pierre-Edouard and Mathilde were not happy to see Jacques leave for the Veterinary College at Maisons-Alfort. After his departure, which came immediately after Mauricette had returned to her boarding-school in Brive, the house seemed even emptier and the table looked bigger, for Paul was also often away. The first days were the worst and Guy, feeling lost between his parents, grandfather and Nicolas, never stopped demanding that his brother come back, and also the sister whom he adored.

'They'll come back in the holidays,' Mathilde reassured him during supper.

'It's a long time until the holidays.'

'Don't complain! You're not unhappy at school, and you only have to walk down the main street to get there!'

'Well yes, but I liked it better when Mauricette was here to go with me. When I'm big, do I have to go away too?'

'You're eight years old; you've still got time to think about it, haven't you? Finish your dinner and get to bed quickly.'

'But you'll leave the door open so that I can listen to the wireless?'

'All right.'

That had become the custom at the Vialhes'. Ever since Léon had given Jacques a radio, the whole family gathered around the receiver every evening. Old Jean-Edouard was absolutely captivated by it. To him this musical box was a constant source of wonderment, and the fact that his old enemy Léon was indirectly the architect of this miracle did not diminish his admiration of it one jot. He who had previously gone to bed as soon as he had swallowed his soup now settled down comfortably by the fireside, placed his packet of coarse tobacco and his old pipe on the little hollow in the andirons, and blissfully appreciated the programmes from Radio-Paris and Poste-Parisien. Often Pierre-Edouard and Mathilde retired to bed before him, exhausted by their day's work.

'You won't forget to turn off, eh?' Pierre-Edouard advised him each time.

The reminder was unnecessary. The old man never forgot to pull out the plug before going to bed; he considered that much less complicated than turning all those knobs.

'A good thing Jacques didn't take away his wireless, with that here at least we're not bored,' declared Guy as he got up from the table.

He kissed his parents, grandfather and Nicolas, and retired to bed.

'You see, that's how you know you're getting old,' whispered Pierre-Edouard in Mathilde's ear a little later, 'when the children go away and the last one is bored with you! It's a good thing we've got the wireless, as he said!'

They had just gone to bed in their turn, and were curled up together waiting for sleep to come.

'Do you feel old, then?' teased Mathilde, stroking his chest.

'That depends on the night . . . All the same, I do miss the kids. I hope it was right for Jacques to enter that college, and I hope most of all that we can pay for his four years of study.'

'But of course we'll be able to. Oh, I know it bothers you, it does me too, but you'll see, we'll get there. That's not what's worrying me.'

'What's wrong?'

'Paul.'

'What about Paul?'

'Léon tells me that he's changed, he's less cheerful. He works hard, but according to Léon not really interested in what he's doing.'

'That's all we need!' groaned Pierre-Edouard. 'Bloody hell, he was the one who chose the job!'

'Perhaps he's realised that he's made a mistake,' she defended him.

'It's a fine time to think of it! Well, if he wants to come back to the farm he could be useful. Deep down, I always thought it would end up like that.'

'You'll have to talk to him,' she insisted. 'I've noticed myself that he's changed recently.'

'It's his age, it'll pass. Or he's got a crush on some girl . . .'

'Don't talk about things like that, he's still too young! Anyway, he's sensible, I know he is!'

'Do you think he'd come and tell you!' he teased, and wound his arms around her.

'You will speak to him, promise?'

'All right, and if he wants to work with me, there's no shame in that, quite the opposite. Now come on, we must go to sleep.'

He kissed her and turned over.

'Basically that was true, what you said just now,' she sighed after a moment's silence.

'What did I say?'

'That you were getting old! Well, as the child said, it's a good thing we have a wireless,' she said with a laugh.

'That's enough of that!' He embraced her fiercely. 'And I'll prove to you that you get the best shafts from old ash trees!'

From a distance Pierre-Edouard indicated to Paul to move forward a few steps then, with a wave of the arm, showed the direction in which he thought the bird would move. He waited for his son to take up his position in the right-place, and then advanced into the huge bushes of box and broom which clung to the slopes of the Caput Peak.

On this chilly Sunday morning in November, he and Paul had been tracking the same woodcock for almost two hours. They had flushed it at the other end of the plateau, in the acacia wood by the château. They greeted it with two useless volleys and it zigzagged between the trunks before heading towards the chestnut grove, to go to ground in the heart of a huge sloe bush, just before reaching the chestnuts.

When they put it up again it had surprised the hunters by flitting like a butterfly – never leaving the shelter of the brushwood – as far as the Vialhes' chestnut copse. From there it took flight again, this time as straight as a die, and flew swiftly towards the Caput, where Pierre-Edouard believed it was hiding in the thickest broom bushes.

Methodically Pierre-Edouard began to beat the undergrowth, always ready to raise his gun. He was forced to hunt without a dog, for the one he owned, a fine mongrel with a trace of griffon in him, was excellent when hunting mammals but a disaster area when it came to birds. He tracked partridge, quail, rail and woodcock as if they were hares or rabbits, with much bounding and barking; the lovable idiot simply tried to cath the birds by the tail as soon as he spied them! He was such a loudmouth that it was no use hoping to shoot a woodcock; he flushed them all before they were within range of the guns.

Pierre-Edouard slipped behind a clump of broom and then a gentle whirr of wings alerted him to the escaping woodcock, invisible behind a curtain of branches but heading straight for Paul. He did not even have time to warn his son before he heard the dry crack of a 16-bore gun.

'Did you get it?'

'Yes!' cried Paul triumphantly. 'Direct hit! It dropped like a stone. I nearly missed seeing it; good thing I heard it getting up!'

'Bravo!' Pierre-Edouard joined him. 'It's a fine one!' he cried appreciatively, as Paul waved the golden bird at arm's length.

He took the woodcock, weighed it in his hands and ruffled its warm feathers. A drop of cherry-red blood hung like a pearl from the end of its long beak, and splashed on to the white pebbles which were scattered on the ground.

'Poor beast,' he murmured. 'You see, now we've had the hunt and got it, we should be able to bring it back to life, don't you think?'

'Well . . . yes,' Paul hesitated, 'but they're delicious to eat as well. So . . .'

'That's true,' Pierre-Edouard admitted. 'They are very good and your mother cooks them marvellously; all the same, that's what cost him his life, nothing is perfect. Come on, it's time we were getting back.'

A little later, as they were walking down to the village, he asked: 'By the way, it seems your work with Léon isn't really to your liking, is that right?'

'Did Jacques tell you that?' demanded Paul with a scowl.

'Jacques? Oh no, it was your mother.'

'So Uncle Léon has been complaining about me?'

'Not that either – just the opposite, he's very pleased with you. But he thinks you seem to be bored, is that right?'

Paul shrugged his shoulders but remained silent.

'All right,' continued Pierre-Edouard, 'we'll assume you mean yes. So, listen to what I suggest, then at least you'll be able to choose. Here it is: if you like you can come back to the farm. We'll work together and we won't talk about running around the markets any more, okay?'

Paul stopped, stared at the ground and kicked a stone.

'It's not that,' he said seriously. 'The markets – it's true, I am fed up with them, but . . . Oh, bloody hell, it's not easy to say! . . . I don't want the farm either, you've got to understand that as well.'

Pierre-Edouard gazed at him and shook his head. He was terribly disappointed. He had thought Paul would accept his offer with pleasure; was looking forward to initiating him in his profession, to teaching him all the secrets, to sharing the happiness it brought.

'*Miladiou*,' he murmured at last, 'I didn't expect that, and neither did your mother.' He took out his tobacco pouch and nervously filled his pipe. 'But good God, what do you want to do then? Eh? It's not as if you've got any diplomas! Well, answer me then, have you any idea?'

'Not yet,' confessed Paul.

And it wasn't really a lie; although he knew very well that he wanted to go to Paris, he still did not know what he would be doing there. He was annoyed with his father, for catching him unawares, for forcing him to reveal part of his plan, for it was still vague and incomplete. He sensed that he was still too young to embark on his own venture, yet he was not so naïve as to believe that it would be easy to make it happen.

'So, if I understand you correctly,' said Pierre-Edouard bitterly, 'you know what you *don't* want, but you don't know what you *do* want?'

Paul shrugged his shoulders once more and lowered his head. Despite his disappointment, turning gradually into anger, Pierre-Edouard restrained himself: he pictured himself at the same age, or almost, and remembered how brutally his father had kept control of

503

the family at that time. Above all he remembered the results of this, and he softened his approach.

'All right,' he sighed, 'we won't beat you for that. I won't hide the fact that I was counting on you to help me with the farm and to take it over later; your mother was hoping you would too, and your grandfather as well. You tell me you don't want to, and I can't force you. Anyway, it wouldn't do any good; to work on the land, you have to love it, because if you love it, you forgive it all the tricks it plays on you. So if it doesn't appeal to you, leave well alone. Besides, you're still young, you may change your mind; so, before you embark on anything else, think about it a bit, wait a bit. And above all don't be in a hurry to destroy things; you'll find out that it's easy to break something and afterwards it takes a long time to mend it. Believe me, I know that.'

'I'd like to go and work in Paris,' said Paul suddenly.

'In Paris? And what would you do there? Don't you think there are enough unemployed up there? And why Paris! Your stay with Berthe must have turned your head!'

'It's not the town which attracts me,' protested Paul, 'but Paris itself. You know, it's big, it's all happening, it's exciting. It's full of new ideas, you can do anything there!'

'Huh, any sort of mischief!' Pierre-Edouard was disconcerted by his line of argument. 'Anyway,' he cried angrily, 'you didn't think your mother and I would let you leave, did you?'

'Well, no,' admitted Paul. He continued to scratch the ground with the toe of his boot, then he lifted his head and took a chance: 'And when I'm eighteen, may I leave then?'

The question stung Pierre-Edouard.

'Leave! Leave! Are you unhappy here? Don't you like your family? Are you bored? Come on, tell me, now we've got this far!'

'It's not that.' Paul felt his courage evaporating. 'It's not that at all!' he repeated furiously. 'But here! Here it's always the same, always the same work, the seasons and the days go by and nothing changes! Here there's no . . . no life! That's how it is! I want to live where there's something happening!'

'Well,' sighed Pierre-Edouard, 'after all, each to his own. You asked me if you could leave when you are eighteen, and I'll tell you – yes. But I'll make one condition: that you at least know what you are going to do in your bloody Paris!'

'I'll find something, I'll manage!' Paul suddenly felt cheerful again.

'You'd better!' grumbled his father. 'But while you're waiting, in the next two years, will you stay with Léon or come to us?'

'I think I'll stay with Uncle Léon. You know with him I can save a bit of money that'll be useful to me in two years' time.'

'Seen like that, of course, I can't give you what he gives you, what with the cost of your brother and sister . . .'

'If you like, I could help you out.'

'No, no, we're not that badly off.' Pierre-Edouard put a hand on his shoulder, and gazed at him at length. 'You really are a strange one. You see, I thought I knew you, but I was wrong. When you know someone, you understand, and I don't understand you. But it doesn't matter, it isn't important. So we'll do it like that, all right?'

'All right.'

'But don't talk about any of this to your grandfather. I can take it on board, it's fine by me, but it might kill him. He was counting on you for the land . . . And don't say anything to your mother either; I'll tell her. And now let's go home; she'll be getting worried about us by now.'

# PART FOUR

*The Hour of Decision*

# 15

THE thermometer fell to minus ten after several sharp frosts at the beginning of December, and then winter arrived with snow. Unfortunately it did not lie long, so that there was nothing to protect the cereal crops, already weakened by those early frosts, from the terrible cold of January 1939.

On the plateau which overlooked Saint-Libéral, huge stretches of wheat froze, only the strips protected by curtains of trees or hedges managing to survive. On the Vialhes' land seventy per cent of the wheat and oats perished, and four walnut trees on the Long Field cracked open one terrible night, split to the heart-wood by the biting cold. Four superb trees, luxuriant, gloriously strong and healthy – they were still young, only thirty-eight years old; they should have lasted two hundred years. One night was enough to kill them.

'Done for,' murmured Pierre-Edouard a month later, as he stroked the rough bark of one of them. 'Poor old thing, just like the wheat! We're in trouble!'

He had just surveyed the extent of the losses on the cereal fields, and he knew already that he would have to sow spring wheat and oats in March. To set his mind at rest he had gone to check the walnut trees – a sad surprise.

'Well?' asked Mathilde when he returned to the house.

He moved to the fire and held his hands out to the flames.

'We'll be resowing, that's all – oats, wheat, maize, doesn't matter what it is, we'll be sowing it again! But that's not the worst.'

'Oh?' she breathed a sigh.

'Four walnut trees, the ones at the bottom of the field, split like old turnips.'

'Like in 1917. The frost killed three of them in the same place . . .'

'I know,' he said, 'that sort of hollow is as cold as death. So that's it, four nut trees less. We planted thirty-one, we've got twenty-four still. At this rate our grandchildren won't need to quarrel over how to divide them up, there won't be any left . . . But by God, I'll plant more, as often as it takes!'

He felt weary and discouraged. It was easy to proclaim that he would resow, but he remembered all the work, all the effort expended the previous autumn, and to no avail.

'Well, we can't do anything about it, that's life,' he said, slipping down onto the settle. He looked at Nicolas, who was opposite him. 'And the bees? I bet they're all dead too?'

'No, no,' said Nicolas with a smile, 'they're humming, all humming!'

'Are you sure?'

'Sure! I put my ear to the hives and I tap with my finger, they are purring away!' Nicolas assured him very proudly.

He had a right to be proud, for it was he who had covered the twenty-five hives with a huge straw hood long before the first cold spell; thanks to his precautions the swarms had triumphed over the frost.

'Well, that's one good thing; the state we're in. I thought they'd all have died. Where's Father?' he asked Mathilde.

'He's resting.'

'Oh, again . . .'

For several months now, old Jean-Edouard had taken to lying down for a rest at ten o'clock in the morning, and this habit worried Pierre-Edouard and Dr Delpy as well. Both of them were relying on the spring to help the old man give up this dangerous practice. As the doctor had said: 'At that age, when you take to your bed you're finished. Young people who stay awake and old ones who sleep already have one foot in the grave . . .'

Jean-Edouard was not ill, but from month to month he was shrinking, growing weaker and more bent. And, much more alarming, he grew a little confused; he rambled, was not always sure whether it was 1939 or 1919, and called for his wife. Luckily these episodes did not last long, but they were distressing for everyone.

'It's not worth telling him about the wheat and the walnut trees,' said Pierre-Edouard. 'He won't go up to the plateau to check anyway.'

'He knows about the wheat already,' announced Mathilde. 'Pierre Delpeyroux came by just now to borrow your wedges for splitting wood, he doesn't know where he's put his. Your father was there and Pierre explained to him that the whole plateau was frosted.'

'What did Father say?'

'The same as you: we'll resow.'

During the month of February, the bell never seemed to cease tolling in Saint-Libéral. It rang first to announce to everyone that Pope Pius XI had begun his eternal life. Father Delclos organised a service attended by the usual female parishioners and a few kids from the confirmation class. Nobody noticed that he prayed very little for the deceased and a great deal for his successor, whom the Conclave was soon to elect. He implored the Holy Ghost that the next inheritor of Saint Peter's key should not attack the wrong enemy, and above all, would recognise the true perils which menaced the Church.

Nobody in Saint-Libéral knew that Father Delclos, an active supporter of the nationalist *Action Française*, had been heartbroken when it was condemned; he hoped that this change of Pope would restore the disciplines of Maurras to their rightful position – he considered them the true defenders of the Faith and of France.

After Pius XI, four old people succumbed in less than ten days; although they had succeeded in surviving the rigours of winter, they had no defence against the damp, penetrating cold which permeated everything. So they faded away: old Germaine Meyjonade from the hamlet Fonts-Perdus, then Célestin Pouch from the locality of Ligneyroux, and then Jeantout, whose death affected the whole Vialhe family, for he had always been their friend and was their nearest neighbour.

Finally, on Saturday, the squire's wife died. Everyone in the village was sad, for she represented a wealth of memories and with her death a whole era disappeared; the great and good era of the château, of wealth and display, and the pride which everyone felt in it. For the château was the jewel of the village, even if its inhabitants did not belong to the same world as everyone else in Saint-Libéral; the association honoured and benefited them all.

So they all thronged to the funeral of Madame Duroux, firstly out of politeness, then for friendship's sake, and finally out of respect. It was no secret that she and her daughter had lived in straitened circumstances, close to poverty, for several years. But they did not attempt to hide their indigence and nobody considered them to have fallen in rank; even when ruined, the lady of the manor inspired respect to her dying day.

'And what will her daughter do?' asked Mathilde, on the way home from the funeral.

'What do you expect her to do,' said Pierre-Edouard. 'She'll stay there, probably.'

'The American could at least have helped them!' said Mathilde, referring to the second daughter who had emigrated to the USA in 1918.

'It's a long way off, America,' he explained, pushing open the door. 'Look, the postman's been.' He noticed a letter which had been pushed under the door.

'Is it from Jacques?'

'No,' he said, turning over the envelope, 'it's from Berthe, and not a postcard, a letter! What a surprise, that must have taken some effort.'


'She's mad, I tell you!' groaned Pierre-Edouard, shaking the sheet of blue paper which he had just read, 'raving mad! No, but I ask you, at her age, it's almost embarrassing!'

'That remains to be seen,' said Mathilde, joining him on the settle. 'For twenty years I've listened to you saying she runs around too much, she needs a good hiding; today she announces that she's getting married and you make a fuss about that?'

'But bloody hell! You don't get married at forty-five! And especially not to a German!'

That was what was really making him angry. It was bad enough to have a sister whom you were not always proud to know, but a German brother-in-law! That was the limit, the end of the world!

'Anyway, I don't want to see them, either of them! She hasn't been here for over twenty years, she might as well keep up the record,' he decided. He read the letter again and shrugged his shoulders. 'And she wants Jacques and Paul to attend the wedding! No, I swear, she's cracked. Why are you laughing?'

'Well, you don't want me to cry, do you?' She pushed a few twigs into the fire. 'You sound so like your father when you talk like that, that I wonder whether it wouldn't be better to cry!'

'Don't exaggerate,' he grumbled. 'All I am saying is . . . Anyway, she doesn't need my permission, does she?'

'Fat chance she'd have! You'd refuse it!'

He filled his pipe, sat down again, and read the letter once more.

'Come on, admit it, she must be a bit crazy!' he repeated in a quieter tone. 'And then, this marrying business, why doesn't she do it straight away? You'll tell me there can't be any hurry, considering how old she is, but why wait till October, what's that all about?'

'She explains it all there; she has her winter collection to show in America. And then you can see, from what she says, that he has business to settle beforehand as well.'

'Well, why does she tell us so soon? Just to annoy us?'

'Listen,' she smiled at him, 'don't try to look more stupid than you really are, and stop questioning everything she does. You know perfectly well why she's written to you.'

'Well, I suppose so. Okay, she'd like to come and show us her chap, but I'd like to know why? Twenty years without showing her nose around here and all of a sudden, hey presto here I am, and with a Boche into the bargain! Can you fathom it?'

'Yes; she's happy and she wants everyone to share it.'

'Oh?'

'That must be the reason.'

'But what are we going to tell Father?' he asked, with a nod towards the bedroom.

'The truth, that's all.'

'And the children?'

'The same. After all, there's nothing to be ashamed of in getting married.

'That depends on how old you are and who you marry . . .' he muttered again.

'Come on.' She got up and stroked her fingers through his hair. 'Don't play at being Grandpa Vialhe; I can cope with one, but two is beyond a joke. You'll write to your sister and tell her that we're all very happy to hear her news.'

'Happy! Happy! We'll see about that!'

'Yes we are. And then if they come, you'll be very nice to them, especially him.'

'It's easy to talk,' he said with a smile. 'What if he's one I missed in 1914! Mind you, he may have missed me too, so I suppose we're quits!'

'That's right,' she approved. 'Look, here's the paper. Come on, write to your sister, I know you're dying to really.'

As soon as it was possible to get back on to the land – that is to say, as soon as the March wind and sun had dried the soil – Pierre-Edouard attached his Canadian cultivator, urged on his oxen, and began to remedy the damage done by the winter.

He had bought this lightweight plough three years earlier, and did not regret having paid 435 francs for it. Thanks to this, with the nine triangular tines which smoothed over the furrow ridges, it was possible to resow without a complete reploughing. Nevertheless this extra working of the soil, plus the sowing, the harrowing, and of course all the other normal seasonal work, filled his days and those of all his farming neighbours. None of them paid much attention to the election of the new Pope. So it was Pius XII; good for Pius XII! As for the re-election of President Lebrun, it was scarcely mentioned in Saint-Libéral.

From March to July, Pierre-Edouard worked without a break to try to recoup the losses caused by the frost. As he could no longer count on any help from his father, nor afford to engage any seasonal workers, he threw himself into the fray with only Nicolas to support him. Whenever she could, Mathilde came to his aid. She was there to plant the potatoes and the beets, to thin out the tobacco seedlings, sow the maize and to hoe. But her own burden of work was so onerous that she could not help him as often as she would have wished.

She had been very disappointed to learn that Paul would not be returning to work on the farm, but she felt, like Pierre-Edouard, that it would be pointless to force him. Besides, he was doing everything he could to make up for his rejection of the land. He was a good son, he gave his father practical help whenever he had the time. He was kind, respectful and hardworking, but he had no enthusiasm for the work of caring for the land.

Pierre-Edouard and Mathilde had no more illusions. The day would come, and soon, when Paul would politely apologise, perhaps even with some embarrassment at having to break the bonds which held him despite himself, and would ask: 'And now, may I go?' And since there was nothing they could do to persuade him to stay, they would watch him on his way and wish him good luck.

'But you'll see,' Pierre-Edouard had said to comfort Mathilde. 'I don't know what he'll do, but he'll make a success of it. And as for the farm, it'll be Guy who takes it on, that's how it'll be. We'll wait patiently until then, all right?'

'And what if he doesn't want it either?'

'Well, if he doesn't, that will be the end of the Vialhes,' he murmured, shocked at this unexpected realisation. 'Yes, the end of the Vialhes.'

Berthe had twice fixed a date to visit Saint-Libéral since she had informed them of her engagement, and twice cancelled it on the eve of her arrival. She pleaded pressure of work, business affairs in need of delicate negotiations, and other problems which her fiancé Helmut was having great difficulty in resolving. So Pierre-Edouard shrugged his shoulders when a card posted in New York arrived at the end of August and informed him that his sister would be passing through Saint-Libéral in the first week of October. Just before her wedding, which was to be on the tenth.

'You'll see, something else will get in the way,' he predicted, holding out the card to Mathilde.

'Jacques will have gone back by then,' she said. 'He'll be sorry, he was so looking forward to seeing her again.'

Pierre-Edouard and she had been amazed when they saw how happy Jacques and Paul were to hear that their aunt was engaged.

'And you'll see,' cried Paul, 'her fiancé is a great chap! Now we can tell you, she warned us about this two years ago!'

'It gets better and better!' grumbled Pierre-Edouard. 'So you both knew about it and I, her brother, don't have any right to hear first.

'Well . . . She told us that you might not agree with what she's doing.'

'And she was right! Well, don't let's talk about that any more. But if she comes, and him too, it won't stop me asking this German what he thinks of the German-Soviet Pact. It's not a girl from the Corrèze he should be marrying, he needs a Cossack!'

'Come, come,' Mathilde soothed him, laughing, 'it's nothing to do with him!'

'Of course it is! Everybody is concerned in this treachery! That's what Tavet and his gang were trying to tell me the other night at Suzanne's! That little teacher doesn't look too happy at the moment; I can tell you, your brother gave him a piece of his mind, they almost came to blows!'

'I know, but I don't think it helps anyone to quarrel about that sort of thing!'

'Yes it does! They got us all in a stew about the Nazi peril, and now they're buddy-buddy with Hitler! Well, right now, the Russians and the Germans and all that lot, I've had them up to here! And I'm not changing my opinions just because my sister has gone and got herself one of them! Just the opposite! All this will leave to no good, you'll see, as I shall enjoy telling my sister's Boche to his face!'

The inhabitants of Saint-Libéral fell asleep one evening, deafened and dead tired amidst the dust raised by the mechanical thresher, which had been working its way around the farms of the village for a fortnight, and awoke to find themselves in the middle of a war.

On the morning of 1 September, they were catapulted from their beds by the announcement that German troops had entered Poland. Then, at 10.30 a.m., whilst many were still trying to play it down and reassure themselves, the second piece of news reached them. It was a direct hit and shocked everyone: general mobilisation.

'This time,' said Pierre-Edouard, 'this time I knew it would come, it couldn't end any other way, but what a mess! Right, we've got to beat them back again!'

'But this call-up doesn't affect you? You're not going to leave, are you?' Mathilde was suddenly worried.

'Me? No, I'm too old. Besides, with four kids and my wound . . .'

'And Jacques? He's not twenty yet!'

'Oh, him . . .' Pierre-Edouard turned to his son. They looked at each other, then exchanged a conspiratorial smile.

'I'm going to enlist,' said Jacques. 'It's the only thing I can do.'

'I absolutely agree,' said Pierre-Edouard.

'But . . . What about the college?' Mathilde protested feebly.

But she knew already that his decision was not rash, nor a thoughtless impulse following the recent events; it was considered and irreversible.

'College can wait. Anyway, the exemptions from call-up are bound to be cancelled, so sooner or later . . .'

'Of course,' she said, and turned away.

Two days later, when the village was empty of men and the threshing machine lay abandoned in Delpeyroux's yard, silent for lack of hands to get it working, came the dreaded news of the declaration of war.

Bewildered, overwhelmed, taken unawares, the villagers drifted in a haze of silence for several days. There were now so few men left that it seemed impossible to start anything without them; their support, their strength, their knowledge. But the work was there to be done, decisions had to be made.

They came from Léon, who as mayor was forced to act. He had experienced the call-up in 1914 and had admired – without ever admitting it – the role played by Jean-Edouard Vialhe at that time; so he, Pierre-Edouard and a few of the widows from the Great War were the first to shake themselves and banish the dangerous stupor which was paralysing the village and would have gradually stifled it. Without considering what old Jean-Edouard might say, Léon flung open the Vialhes' door on the evening of 6 September, at supper-time. Finding the whole family seated at the table, he ignored the old man's mumbling and came straight to the point.

'We can't go on like this!'

'I was counting on you,' said Pierre-Edouard. 'Have you eaten?'

'No, no time.'

'Well, come on, sit down,' said Pierre-Edouard, pushing a plate to the end of the table. 'I thought you might come,' he repeated, when Léon was seated, 'so, what shall we do?'

'I've already counted all the farms without men; there are too bloody many!'

'I thought as much.'

'Now, you weren't here in August 1914, but your father's probably told you that he organised support teams, and that worked well; we'll have to do the same again. Just think, we haven't even finished threshing and at the end of the month we should start ploughing, not to mention the grapes! In my opinion the old men like us should get together and go from farm to farm to get through the heaviest work, and I'm damned if we won't manage to clear a bit of ground with the help of the women!'

'You can count on all of us,' said Pierre-Edouard. 'Jacques as well, he's here for some days yet. They're in such a muddle at Brive that they told him to go away and wait! With Nicolas and me that makes a few hands already; we'll get the urgent tasks done, starting with the threshing.'

'Excellent, and I'll tell Paul to join your team, because the markets, at the moment . . . So I can count on four men from here.'

'Not four, five!' cried old Jean-Edouard, 'I can work too!'

'Listen, Father . . .' began Pierre-Edouard.

'Shut up, I told you I could work and I will work. What do you think, I'm not an invalid!'

'All right, you come with us, but I thought you'd be useful here to help Mathilde . . .'

'Mauricette will take my place,' the old man interrupted him. 'Where's the threshing machine at the moment?'

'Still at Delpeyroux's,' said Léon.

'Have you warned them that we'll be threshing there?' the old man interrogated him.

'No, not yet, we needed to get organised first,' explained Léon.

'Well, what are you playing at, eating our soup instead of going to see them? Good God, in 1914 I was often up for two whole days, that's how we made a success of it!'

Léon, annoyed, pushed away his plate and got up.

'I know,' he said, 'you, you always did better than everyone else, but I just do what I can! I know you gave up your time in 1914. I only gave up a hand!' he rapped out, banging his hook on the table.

'Sit down and eat,' Pierre-Edouard cut in, 'it's not 1914 now. Today you're the mayor, and it's up to you to decide how we do things, not to worry about what others may say. And we Vialhes are going to help you. Besides, you've already heard it,' he continued in an amused tone, 'even my father has said he'll lend a hand! Come on, finish your dinner and afterwards we'll go together and tell the rest that we'll have to join forces.'

One cool morning at the end of November, Mathilde was alone in the house when the postman called. Besides the newspaper he delivered two letters. The first was from Berthe, but it was addressed to Pierre-Edouard so she didn't open it. Happy to know that she would shortly have some explanation for her sister-in-law's silence – they had heard nothing from her since the beginning of August – she put the letter on the sideboard, and hurried to open the second envelope, which came from Jacques.

Overjoyed to have some news of her son, who had been in the army for more than a month, she rested on the settle and began to read it with a smile. And her contentment increased as she took in the words. Jacques was getting on well, was in rude health, not eating too badly and had made some good friends. She felt reassured and placed the letter beside Berthe's before continuing her work with a song; the war was a long way off and seemed to have gone off the boil. It hit her in the face, however, when Pierre-Edouard came in at midday, and turned pale as he held out Berthe's missive to her.

'Read it,' he said.

'No, tell me,' she gasped, disturbed by his sudden pallor.

'Her fiancé, her German, they've arrested him.'

'What? Who has?'

'Them – the Germans, those bloody Nazis!'

'But I thought he was a German too!'

'Yes, but apparently he didn't like the government. According to Berthe he hasn't lived in Germany for the last four years; he went back in August to settle some business, and they arrested him.'

'And what about Berthe?'

'She's in Switzerland, trying to find out where he is.'

'So they haven't managed to get married,' she murmured, 'poor Berthe. What can we do?'

'Nothing, nothing,' he raged. 'We were thinking it wasn't a real war, and now you can see we're right in the middle of it!'

Up till then, Pierre-Edouard and Mathilde had been little affected by the conflict. Jacques had gone, some horses had been requisitioned, and there were a few difficulties with supplies, but otherwise it was developing in a strange way, just festering quietly. Pierre-Edouard himself admitted that he didn't understand a situation which was nothing like what he'd known in 1914. Surely the war wasn't going to peter out for lack of fighting?

What was more, several soldiers had already returned to the village on leave, which really surprised the veterans. They were brief visits, naturally, perhaps without permission, but still they had the time to give their point of view, in particular to explain that they weren't fighting, had never seen the enemy, and were bored.

Then, reinforcing the idea that the conflict was not serious, it was rumoured everywhere that lots of the soldiers who had been called up were returning to their homes and taking up their old jobs, designated as being on 'special assignment'; it seemed that the arms factory in Tulle was welcoming back workers every day. Really, the general state of mind was not geared towards war.

Pierre-Edouard folded his sister's letter and contemplated the fire.

'She finishes by saying that as you believe in God, you should say your prayers; she knows the Germans, and this war will be dreadful.' He pushed a corner of a log towards the flames. 'Dreadful,' he repeated forcefully. 'I'd like someone to explain to me why we're still not bloody doing anything! It's three months since this damned war started!'

# 16

PAUL had so often imagined exactly what he would do on the day of his eighteenth birthday that he was quite disconcerted when the date finally came round in April. All his plans and ideas, his enthusiasm, had been reduced to nothing by the war. He had pictured himself taking the train to Paris and embarking on new ventures; for the time being that was impossible. Paris at war held no attractions.

So instead of being able to realise his dream, he was forced to wait patiently. He was amazed to discover that this decision was no burden; it was almost a relief. One year earlier he could have left with few regrets, but today the situation had changed; there was such a need for men in the village, even though a few had been able to return briefly on farming leave, and Paul was aware that he had become a valued companion to his father and a comfort to his mother.

With Jacques gone he had naturally taken his place as the eldest, and nobody begrudged him it, especially not his brother, who had encouraged him in his letters not to leave the farm and above all not to anticipate his call-up, when Paul had enquired about this.

'I thought I would be of some use,' he had written. 'I wanted to fight, and the only battles I'm engaged in are gin rummy contests! Don't do what I did, one idiot in the family is enough.'

Jacques' bitterness and disappointment made a strong impression on him, so he abandoned the idea of going to enlist on his eighteenth birthday. Even without the disillusioned advice from his brother, he had understood from some of the soldiers on leave that this phoney war was not worth supporting, even with the modest gesture and voluntary enlistment as a private.

Everybody seemed to be indifferent, disheartened, even his father and Léon. They who had been so full of energy now drifted slowly into despondency; each day saw them more taciturn and bitter. Pierre-Edouard had already stopped listening to the wireless so as not to be disheartened by the communiqués and the pitiful babbling of the politicians. Only old Jean-Edouard was still an enthusiast, and persisted in searching the air-waves in the evenings. And Paul, in his bed in the corner of the room, fell asleep every evening to the sound of music.

The people of Saint-Libéral completed the spring work without any enthusiasm, locked in a disillusioned apathy; their hearts were not in it, nor their strength, too many men were away. So a great many plots of land, even whole fields, received none of that attention which transforms sad fallow lands into ploughed acres full of promise. Dock, henbane, blue thistle and other weeds multiplied in the abandoned patches, preparing the way for the bracken and broom which were always ready to spring up on bare ground. And all this land forgotten by many gradually returned to nature, to scrub, and added to the areas which had ben inexorably engulfing Saint-Libéral since the last war – the Great War – choking it with a tight collar of brushwood.

Only the Vialhe property remained as it should be; Pierre-Edouard made sure that nothing affected the beauty and wealth of his farm, despite his disillusionment. With the help of Nicolas and Paul he plunged into the work to deaden his senses; it became his sole aim and occupation. Thanks to it he was dead tired each evening and fell asleep in a trice, as if felled by a knock-out blow, without having to struggle against the sombre thoughts which lurked in his sub-conscious and would have kept him awake half the night.

However, his refusal to reflect on the events which were shaking the whole country did not prevent the war from developing. In the space of a fortnight, when he thought he had already plumbed the depths of discouragement, the news from the front undermined his morale and brought him to his knees.

First of all there was the invasion of Belgium, Holland and Luxembourg and the pathetic convulsions of those unhappy countries, already beaten and in the throes of death. Then, on 18 May, Léon returned from Brive and informed them that the town had already suffered two air raid warnings and was collapsing beneath a ceaselessly growing flood of refugees from the east and north: children, women, old people, who could no longer find house-room anywhere and hunkered down in cinemas, even the theatre and the station.

And with the passing days came the certain knowledge that everything was collapsing, cracking up, crumbling beneath the formidable thrust of an enemy who seemed invincible, and so swift! There was worry too, for no letter had arrived from Jacques to reassure his family since the beginning of the month, and finally anger, at the impotence of governments and the vacillations of the military command. The only hope amidst this anguish came with the announcement that Marshal Pétain had accepted the Vice-Presidency of the Council of Ministers.

'At last!' sighed Pierre-Edouard when he learned this news. 'With him there things are bound to change; he'll be able to turn the tables on them, like he did in 1917. But why did they wait so long to call on him!'

'You know, he's not so young any more,' suggested Léon. 'Perhaps he would have preferred not to be bothered!'

'Probably. Never mind, he's there and that's good news. He's a soldier, not a politician!

'If that's all that's needed, he's sure to get these spongers moving, but let's hope he hurries up! Oh, I think they've wasted too much time, messed around too long.'

'We can still halt them, it only takes the will. We did it before, didn't we? So what's to stop us doing it again?'

For seven months, Jacques had passively let himself be carried along by events. One week in the army was enough to teach him that there was no point in trying to understand any of the orders, counter-orders or wild decisions which governed his life as a soldier.

He had been dumbfounded right at the start by his posting, which bore no relation to his request. With his baccalauréat, he had opted for the Officers College of the Army Reserves and he had found himself a private in the 15th Regiment of Algerian Infantry in Périgueux. There he voiced his astonishment and made mild protests, and heard the reply of an old captain who was completely dessicated by the sun of the Atlas Mountains and also, probably mainly, by anisette:

'Certificates, we wipe our bums with those, they've never made good soldiers! And the *petits-bourgeois* who have them – here's where we lick them into shape!'

He remained silent, disconcerted by such a wealth of stupidity, all his illusions destroyed. Because he wanted to fight – and the rank hardly mattered to him – he completed the classes and stages to become corporal and sergeant without saying anything. He champed at the bit and got bored all winter whilst regretting that Périgueux was so far from the front; however lifeless that was, in his eyes it was the only place worthy of interest.

He was therefore happy to learn, at the beginning of April, that he was to be posted to the 22nd Border Regiment of Foreign Volunteers stationed in Dannemarie. He arrived in Alsace on 11th April and realised bitterly that, as at Périgueux, the only enemy to be killed was time. One month later torpor gave way to feverish activity, when the German breakthrough tore Jacques and his comrades from their siestas and gin rummy and hurled them into battle.

The 22nd Border Regiment returned to France in great haste, and disembarked in the middle of the night at Isle-Adam on the River Oise; they then squeezed into Paris buses which attempted, despite the incredible congestion on roads flooded with refugees, to clear a route in the direction of the Somme and the Weygand Line. Obstructed by the confusion and the accumulation of incongruous vehicles which jammed every tiny path, the convoy was forced to stop shortly after Pont-Sainte-Maxence.

So it was on foot and proceeding along the ditches – the roadway was too cluttered by the fleeing crowds – that Jacques and his comrades covered the seventy kilometres which separated them from the front.

Two days later, when he was in position in the woods close to Fonches, Jacques found the war. Suddenly. It bore no resemblance to what he thought he knew from his father's accounts. God knows, he had heard talk of the hideous rain of shells and the terror they inspired! But Jacques as a child had never imagined that fear could reach such a level; that it could be so paralysing, hellish, unbearable. And like his father before him under shelling, he wanted to be swallowed up by the earth, for it to open up and shelter him; but also like his father, he knew how to leap to it when the orders rang out, pushing the men forward, throwing them into attacks, withdrawals, counter-attacks and advances over a period of days as they moved towards the villages of Marchélepot, Saint-Christ and its bridge over the Somme, Villers-Carbonne, Briost.

They were equipped with single-loading guns, the old Hotchkiss rifle, and 25 mm cannons, never enough of them – and they were instructed to be sparing with the shells – and before them appeared the huge rumbling armoured cars of von Kleist's 4th Panzer Division, the 15-ton KW3s with their 37 mm cannon and the MG34 with 7.92 mm guns. The light infantryman following them, as jackals follow the lions, were lively and flexible: formidable enemies, for they were not encumbered with rucksacks, backpacks or other gear; they did not catch their feet in their puttees or the hem of their greatcoats; when faced with the strong but slow MAS36 handgun, they deployed the terrifyingly rapid fire of the automatic pistol, the MP40 . . .

Entrenched in the village and château of Misery on 1 June, surrounded on all sides, cut off from the world, out of breath, out of reinforcements, out of ammunition, the 22nd Border Regiment surrendered to the enemy after destroying their weapons, as recommended in the regulations.

Paul never forgot the pain and ensuing anger he felt when he saw how his father was consumed with shame and sorrow. To him, Pierre-Edouard had always represented strength, trust and honour. He was a model of energy and honesty, he was invulnerable; so Paul was wounded to the heart when he perceived that his father, once so admired for his reassuring aura of power, was sliding day by day into a lethargic and agonising melancholia.

Every bulletin, every communiqué, tortured him anew and left him pale, with clenched teeth and fists, deep in the depression which seemingly nothing could relieve. He no longer talked any more, but enclosed himself in a distant silence, only interrupted when it was time for the news by: 'The swine! The swine, they're selling us down the river!' And he no longer smiled, even when Mathilde placed her hand on his arm to calm him, with that familiar gesture which showed that she understood and sympathised.

Amidst this gloomy atmosphere old Jean-Edouard seemed quite serene, as if he had no worries for the future; he even went so far as to stay that all this was not a bad lesson for those who had, for a quarter of a century, constantly demeaned themselves and defied morals and traditions. Pierre-Edouard looked at him so fiercely that he was quickly constrained into silence. His glare was so hard and ferocious that Paul felt encouraged and comforted when he noticed it; in these fleeting moments, he recognised the father he loved.

The rest of the time he hated the whole world, for its spinelessness had succeeded in transforming Pierre-Edouard into an old man full of shame and grief. For a long time this memory of his father's humiliation burned in him; the eyes, empty of hope, reflecting such a heart-breaking mental anguish.

It was two o'clock in the morning, on the night of 15 June, when the sound of an engine followed by the barking of the dogs dragged Pierre-Edouard from his slumber. The evening before, he had gone to bed, still devastated and demoralised by the announcement that the Germans had entered Paris. Now there was nothing that could be done, nothing further to hope for.

'There's someone coming, put on the light,' whispered Mathilde, who was now also awake.

'No, let's have a look first,' he said as he got up. He slipped on his trousers and shirt, slid over to the window and looked through one of the vents in the shutter. The moon was almost full, and lit up the courtyard.

'What's that thing?' he murmured as he made out a dark humped shape in front of the gateway; several people were grouped around it.

'Who is it?' asked Mathilde.

'I've no idea; refugees probably, their car's loaded up like a carrier's cart.'

'We'll have to go out.'

'Of course,' he said, but without leaving his look-out post. He frowned as he watched a woman enter the yard. 'My God!' he cried. 'It's Louise, put on the light!'

He pushed open the shutters and called to his sister. It was not until after he had opened the door to her that he saw she was carrying little Pierre asleep in her arms.

'Tell me what's happened!' he demanded a few moments later.

'What do you want me to tell you!' Her voice was exhausted. 'We left yesterday morning with them,' she explained pointing to the four adults and three children whom Mathilde was hurrying to comfort. 'Everyone is leaving, you see, everyone! Oh, if you could only see the roads! It's crazy, crazy!' she repeated with a sigh. 'It's dreadful too, it took us a whole day to reach Limoges! It was a good thing I made them take to the lanes after that. But if you could see the main roads! And all the children crying . . .'

'I know, Léon was in Brive yesterday, it seems it's far worse than anything we've ever imagined. Just think, there are almost seventy thousand refugees in the town! And even here the inn is full! But these people,' he lowered his voice to ask her, 'who are they?'

'The steward of the château with his wife and children, and the cook and her husband. The steward was kind enough to bring us – he wants to go on to Spain and the cook wants to go to Toulouse, so as Saint-Libéral was on the way . . .'

'Yes. So everyone is running away, from what I can see! That lot will be able to move in, there'll be plenty of room for them!' he said bitterly. 'Aren't you hungry?' he asked after a moment's silence.

'Yes, but first I must put the child to bed,' she said, pointing to the baby whom she had lain on Paul's bed.

'Put him in there, Paul can spend the rest of the night in the hay. By the way, do you have any news of Félix?'

'No. And you, what about Jacques?'

'Nothing either . . .'

'And Berthe?'

'Not a word. You knew about her . . . her fiancé?'

'Yes, it's terrible.'

'Are you going to stay here?' asked old Jean-Edouard, coming nearer.

'Of course,' Pierre-Edouard cut in before she could reply, 'where else would she go?'

'Oh! I just wanted to know,' said the old man, 'because you could put the child in my room,' he pointed to Pierre. 'There's space and it's quiet . . .'

'We'll sort it out tomorrow,' decided Pierre-Edouard. 'For tonight he'll stay in Paul's bed, Louise will sleep in ours, and her friends can use the barn. I'll tell Nicolas to spread some straw.'

'I've done that,' said the old man. 'I sent him to see to it as soon as they arrived; we weren't going to leave them outside!'

Despite the hunger and thirst torturing him, and the overwhelming fatigue which made him want to stay lying in that meadow where they had been dumped like animals, Jacques got up once more and observed the little wood which lay about two hundred feet away, just beyond the field of wheat where the sentries paced.

For the two days that he had been marching – one wretched figure drowning in the sea of tramps – Jacques had been looking for a chance to escape, to flee from this apathetic flock of beaten men who were being pushed towards the north-east by a handful of guards.

Once already, on the previous day, as the column passed through the village of Nurlu a little after Péronne, he had dashed into a gutted house. He was spotted immediately, recaptured and beaten up; he had fallen into line again without for one second abandoning his plan to escape.

He took several steps and bent over a corporal who was stretched out on the clover.

'Got any tobacco left?' he asked, taking out his pipe.

'No, none at all,' replied the other, chewing a grass-haulm.

The young corporal observed him, and a ghost of a tired smile appeared. 'You,' he said, 'as far as I can see you're still trying to get out of this!'

'Dead right.'

'It's stupid, they'll catch you! Besides, I bet they won't keep us, they're too any of us!'

'Maybe, but I'm going to slip away anyway. Look, there's nothing to stop us, just a few sentries . . . Let's go together!'

'Nothing doing! I'd rather stay alive!'

Jacques shrugged and moved away to lie down and await nightfall.

He contained himself until eleven in the evening, and then crawled on his belly into the wheatfield. A quarter of an hour later he was in the wood. He took his direction from the stars, and marched due south.

It was as he tried to skirt round the little village of Avesnes-le-Sec that he ran into a German camp. A great burst of gunfire stopped him in his tracks, and was still ringing in his ears when a blow from a rifle butt knocked him out.

Under heavy guard, he rejoined his comrades in the early hours of the morning, and endured another beating before the convoy moved off in the direction of Valenciennes.

Conquering his despair he scribbled a brief note to his parents, and as they passed through Douchy-les-Mines, he took the opportunity to throw it towards an old woman sitting in front of her ruined house.

Louise's friends camped at the Vialhes' for two days; the driver's experience on their first journey made him fear the moment when he would again have to join the flood of vehicles fleeing southwards.

Huge groups of refugees now poured along the road through Saint-Libéral itself; they came from Limoges, from Châteauroux, from everywhere. They all had the wild eyes of hunted animals, and rushed to the wash-house fountain as soon as they saw it. Many also crowded into the mairie to beg for the shelter of a roof, be it only for one night. Léon, inundated with work, called for help from all the members of the town council.

To Pierre-Edouard and Maurice fell the job of feeding those who were hungry, and they were all hungry. So Pierre-Edouard found himself obliged to combat his depression, to fulfil his allotted task. That saved him. He got back on his feet, found new reserves of energy, and although the news – ever more disastrous – continued to torture him, at least he no longer greeted it with despondency and submission, but with anger and violence.

However, he succumbed to despair again when, on 17 June at 12.30 p.m., whilst the whole Vialhe family were sitting down for lunch, the trembling voice of the Marshal was heard on the wireless. Pierre-Edouard listened attentively and nodded vigorously at the end of the first sentence of the announcement, even murmured: 'Bravo, it's high time he took the reins!' Then gradually his expression changed, and suddenly his face crumpled.

Until that moment he had placed his trust, all his trust, in the old soldier, and if the Marshal had asked him to take up arms he would have resumed his place at the head of a battery of 75 mm guns without hesitation. All the hope and faith which he had entrusted to this man as guardian and saviour collapsed in a few seconds.

Paul saw him turn pale, then his face tensed. He noticed the quickened breathing and trembling lips and was appalled to think he might see him cry. He did control himself eventually and his eyes stayed dry but, when he put down the spoon he had been gripping, Paul noticed that it was twisted like a single strand of wire. Then he rose, briskly turned the knob of the radio, and sat down again.

'Why did you turn it off?' asked old Jean-Edouard. 'We would have had the other news!'

'Not interesting!' he cut him short.

'I think,' his father continued, 'I think the Marshal couldn't have done anything else. Now the war will stop, and that's better for everyone.'

'Listen,' said Pierre-Edouard sharply, 'you're free to think and say what you like, but don't do it in front of me!' he shouted, banging his fist on the table.

'Well, but what's with you?' protested the old man. 'I thought you were all for Marshal Pétain, like me!'

'Not so that he could surrender, the lump of shit!' He was yelling again. 'He's just sold us out, the old swine! And he dares talk of honour? My God! Even if he put a pistol to his head at the end of it, that speech wouldn't be honourable, the bastard!'

'Calm down,' begged Mathilde. 'As your father says, he probably couldn't do anything else. I believe we should put our trust in him.'

'It was obvious,' interrupted Louise, 'if you'd seen the refugees, like I saw them . . . It had to stop! Besides, we couldn't hold out!'

'You shut up!' shouted Pierre-Edouard, getting up. 'If you'd seen war as I saw it, you wouldn't talk of defeat! War is for fighting, not for turning tail! And we've just turned tail!' he sneered, as he opened the door.

He slammed it brusquely behind him and set off towards the peaks.

He walked for two hours, and ranged over all his land but did not really see it, such was the anger burning in his heart.

Then he climbed the White Peak and sat down at the foot of a juniper bush, took out his pipe and lit it. Gradually he calmed down, even reasoned with himself, compelled himself to find some hope, recalled Pétain's speech and tried to detect a sentence, a word, from which he might draw fresh courage. It was no use.

It was with a heavy heart that he later knocked out his pipe on the heel of his clog and walked back down to the village. There he immediately noticed that others had reacted in the same way as him, were now just as despairing, miserable and distraught; faced with a fait accompli and forced to accept it.

'Now what?' asked Léon as soon as he saw him.

'Now nothing.'

'Are you thinking what I'm thinking?'

'What are you thinking?'

'That we've been betrayed.'

'Yes.'

'But I don't know,' murmured Léon, 'whether the old fellow could have done any different. Of course I feel sick at heart, but there it is, the Boche are in Paris, so . . .'

'We should have fought! *We* fought them, and you know a thing or two about it!'

'Yes, well, maybe it's only a trick. The old man's cunning, perhaps he has a plan . . .'

'Perhaps,' admitted Pierre-Edouard, 'but he's hiding it well. At the moment all I can see is that he's telling people to lay down their arms!'

'We'll have to wait,' said Léon, 'wait and see.'

'I think we've waited too long and now we *are* seeing, and it's not a pretty sight.'

'You should be home. Mathilde came by just now to see if you were here; seems you were bleating like a calf and bawled them all out! Oh, there's nothing wrong with that; I haven't anyone to bawl out, so I broke the radio with this,' he said, waving his hook. 'All of a sudden I felt so depressed listening to it, that I wanted it to stop, I turned the knob a bit too hard . . . And now, after thinking it over, I tell myself that maybe we don't understand it all; they can't tell us everything, can they?'

'It's possible,' Pierre-Edouard admitted, 'perhaps we don't understand it all. That's what we have to hang on to, it's the only thing that gives a bit of hope.'

During an exhausting journey which took him from Valenciennes to the southern part of East Prussia, Jacques never found another chance to give his guards the slip.

After twelve days of travelling across the whole breadth of

Germany, he and his companions were unloaded in a terrible state at the station of the little village of Hohenstein, then herded under close escort towards Stalag 1B where thousands of prisoners were already milling about, where every evening they were supposed to fit five hundred men into huts designed for two hundred.

For a week Jacques endured the camp régime. Like everyone else – lest he die of hunger – he had to rise at four in the morning and queue, sometimes until two in the afternoon, to get that vital mess-tin full of soup.

Weakened, undernourished, sometimes beaten, he gradually lost all hope of escaping. Besides, where would he go? And how would he cover the two thousand kilometres which separated him from Saint-Libéral?

On the night of 29 June, Jacques and about a hundred of his colleagues were wakened by the shouts and blows of the guards and escorted to the station.

'Perhaps they're going to set us free?' suggested an optimist as the train set off.

'Don't count on it, we've got our backs towards France,' grumbled Jacques, after he had peered through the tiny slit in their cattle truck.

'And how do you know?'

'Blockhead! Look at the sun, we're heading straight for it. Have you ever seen it rising in the west?'

They arrived at Lützen during the morning and it was in lorries that they eventually reached the hamlet of Riechensee, where they were lined up in the main square.

'Labourers and peasants over here, students and office-workers over there!' bellowed the interpreter who was with several officers and NCOs.

Jacques did not hesitate for a second. He took the arm of his friend André, whom he had lost sight of at the time of the battles on the Somme and found again during their journey, and marched towards the group of manual workers.

'You're mad!' protested André. 'I'm a chartered accountant, I'll have you know!'

'Shut your face!' whispered Jacques, who guessed instinctively that the peasants' camp would be the lesser evil, perhaps influenced by the memory of the captain in Périgueux and his contempt for intellectuals.

Soon afterwards they were examined, and he felt the weight of suspicious looks directed at him by the soldiers and civilians who were there to choose the best recruits.

'You, not from land! Not earthy!' yelled the interpreter suddenly. 'Hands too white, not earthy! Nor him, him and him! Fat French toads!'

'That's a joke for a start,' said Jacques, 'it's ten months we've been hanging around doing nothing!'

'Not from land!' insisted the other man.

'Yes I am,' said Jacques. He suddenly spied an old peasant with his scythe on his shoulder, passively watching the scene as he walked towards them. 'Me, farmer,' Jacques addressed the interpreter again, 'look, watch this – bear's bum,' he added in a murmur as he held out his hand for the scythe.

The other man hesitated, then handed over his implement. Jacques passed his forefinger along the blade, made a face, drew the whetstone from the sheath hanging from the mower's belt and briskly sharpened the scythe. And his technique demonstrated such long practice that it was enough to convince the old peasant.

'*Schön, schön!*' he told the interpreter, 'good, good!'

'See, it wasn't a joke!' Jacques was triumphant.

'Well, he not from land!' decided the German, pointing to André.

'Yes he is!' protested Jacques. 'Look, he's going to mow that bed,' he suggested, pointing to a superb display of tulips.

The man looked at him in alarm, then shrugged and muttered, '*Ja*, you two from land!' and took no further interest in their fate. That same evening Jacques and André discovered the village of Kleinkrösten, situated on the other side of Lake Jagodner, where they joined old Karl's farm as agricultural labourers.

Despite his discouragement, and the additional work created by the presence of the refugees whom they had to take in, lodge and occasionally watch – some of them had an annoying tendency to pilfer the farmyard fowl, fruit and vegetables – Pierre-Edouard decided to begin cutting his hay. He was already more than a fortnight behind and now felt cross with himself: nervous exhaustion had paralysed him until then, reinforcing his deplorable inertia. He was ashamed of this weakness, and did not try to excuse it by saying that everybody in Saint-Libéral had sunk into the same depression; you could count on the fingers of one hand the men who had the courage, or the insensitivity, to throw themselves into the haymaking as if nothing had happened.

So on the morning of 20 June, helped by Paul, Nicolas, Mathilde and Louise – who assured him that it would rejuvenate her – he began to mow. It was high time: the grass was over-ripe and had a tendency of flatten, and in places the white clover was already growing mouldy.

In two weeks of unremitting work he made up the lost time and, helped by weariness, forgot a little of the shame and anger of 17 June. Nobody had talked about it again at home anyway, and the only conversations arising from the situation were concerned exclusively with the fate of the prisoners, and above all the date of their liberation. Although everyone was optimistic about this – it seemed unlikely that the Germans would want to be encumbered with two million captives – Mathilde and Louise were in a state of pitiful anxiety. Without news of either Jacques or Félix, they watched feverishly for the postman, then, when he sadly shook his head, they turned to each other for mutual support, trying to find a glimmer of hope in each other's arguments.

Once the haymaking was completed, Pierre-Edouard immediately began to harvest the grain. Then the news broke about the bombardment of Mers el-Kébir by the English fleet and the massacre, by these supposed allies, of 1,300 French sailors.

Pierre-Edouard, already completely disorientated by the political strategy being pursued since the defeat, now lost his balance; did not know where or to whom to turn, and ended up thinking that all things being equal, Marshal Pétain was the lesser of two evils; but he still did not forgive him. To him, Pétain would always be the architect of the surrender.

The note scribbled by Jacques took more than a month to arrive in Saint-Libéral. It was short and out of date, but still brought a little joy to the Vialhe household.

Comforted, but aware that her happiness was distressing to her sister-in-law, Mathilde hastened to reassure Louise that the message she awaited was probably already on its way, that patience was all that was needed. And the letter did arrive, on 27 July. It had been posted in Marseilles.

At first Louise could not understand at all and, convinced that her son was a prisoner too, wondered what right the English had to keep him there. For Félix was writing from London. It was only gradually that she came to understand. Trapped in Dunkirk, he had been lucky enough to get aboard a ship for England. 'And now,' he explained, 'I have the pleasure of being able to continue to fight, under the orders of General de Gaulle . . .'

'But what's all this about?' wailed Louise. 'And who is this general? And why the postmark from Marseilles?'

On reading the postscript, she understood: Félix had entrusted his message to a friend who was returning to France. Not knowing whether to laugh or cry, she hesitantly proffered the letter to Pierre-Edouard.

'Here, see if you understand it!'

He read it in his turn, and first frowned, then smiled.

'So this Legaule really exists! No, de Gaulle,' he corrected himself after checking what Félix had written. 'Damn Léon, he's always so well informed! Yes,' he explained, 'he mentioned something about this a week ago, but I didn't pay much attention to it because it seemed impossible. It seemed de Gaulle said in an English broadcast that he wants to go on fighting.'

'But the war's over!' protested Louise.

'Obviously he doesn't think so! Really,' he added, feeling suddenly quite happy, 'I'm very glad that there's at least one general who's ready to stuff the Boche! That at least is good news!'

'But what's to become of Félix?' insisted Louise.

'How should I know! Anyway, he's not a prisoner, not him, that's one good thing. Come on, no need to worry any more; now you know where he is, that's the main thing, isn't it?'

'Well, of course,' she agreed, 'but in the end I'd still have preferred him to come back. We could have gone back home, instead of me getting in your way here and taking your bedroom!'

'But this is your home!' he protested.

'Maybe, but I'm a nuisance.'

'Not at all,' Mathilde intervened. 'In the first place you're helping us, and little Pierre is as good as gold! And what's more, Father is crazy about him!'

'That's right,' added Pierre-Edouard, 'don't worry, you can stay here just as long as you need to. After all, we can squash up a bit, can't we? There's a war on. That's what Félix seems to think anyway.'

Absorbed in his work, Pierre-Edouard had turned his back on the current events which so disheartened him, but Paul had heard talk of the appeal from London on 25 June. One of his friends in Perpezac had been lucky enough to receive the signal, and had explained to him what this mysterious general had said.

Paul had been immediately captivated by this opportunity for adventure. To leave, to reach London, and there to fight, fight like a dog to wash away the shame which had almost made his father cry, and to forget the humiliation he had felt when he realised that he too was among the vanquished.

For a month, because he still doubted whether it was possible to continue the struggle, he kept himself informed and discreetly questioned those whom he thought might know of this momentous event. One evening he even managed to listen to the BBC, when his grandfather, feeling tired, had gone to his room much earlier than usual. He was overwhelmed. So it really was true! There were still Frenchmen who said that the war was not over; that it had only just begun, and must be continued by all those who refused to submit to the German jackboot.

He almost ran to tell his father, to get him out of bed and announce the good news to him, that very evening. But he thought better of it. His father was so bitter, so sad, that he was capable, quite unintentionally, of destroying all his arguments one by one, of banishing all his hopes and dampening his spirits. So, because he needed to pour out his feelings, to declare his enthusiasm, to hear himself say that he was right to want to go, he went to see Nicolas.

'And why are you telling me this?' asked Nicolas a little later. 'Me, I'm not French, not Italian, not German; my country is not at war. So . . .'

'But you fought for it, in your time, Papa told me that. And that's why you're here, after all!'

'That's true,' admitted Nicolas, 'I fought and I lost.' He took out his snuff-horn, poured himself a pinch, and ingested it in two sniffs. 'I lost,' he repeated, 'but I was still right to fight. One should always fight for one's country.'

'Ah, you see!' Paul exulted. 'So I have to go, don't I?'

'That's not for me to say.'

'And do you think Papa will understand if I go away?'

Nicolas shrugged.

'He's unhappy, very unhappy, he didn't even come to visit the hives with me, so . . .'

'Do you think I should tell him beforehand?'

'You're not going to make off like a thief in the night, are you? And your mother, what would she think?'

'That's true,' murmured Paul, suddenly aware of the seriousness of the decision he was about to take. 'All right, I'll tell them.'

The letter from Félix arrived the next day, and Paul saw it as a sign from heaven. That same evening, when the three beautiful stars, Vega, Altaïr and Deneb, already glowed in a triangle in the summer sky, Paul was just finishing the harvest in the Perrier field with his father; he placed the thirteenth sheaf, the one that protects the stook, then turned to his father.

'I'm going to leave,' he announced.

'Ah, *bon*,' said Pierre-Edouard, who immediately thought he understood. He pulled a stalk of wheat from a sheaf, rubbed the husks off the ear in his hand, and quietly munched the grains one by one. 'It's true,' he continued, 'you've been eighteen for quite a time now, but I had thought with all these things happening . . . And what are you going to get up to in Paris now? It's quite likely that the Boche won't even let you go there!'

'I don't want to go to Paris, I want to go to London, with de Gaulle, like Félix!'

'Oh well, that's different,' murmured Pierre-Edouard, 'that's quite different.'

And despite the darkness, Paul saw that he was smiling.

'Well, can I go?' he persisted.

'I told you I wouldn't stop you,' his father reminded him. 'But how will you get there, it's a long way to England!'

'I don't know; I'll manage.'

'That's right, you must manage it, at all costs. You must succeed! Listen, I wouldn't ever say this to your mother, because she, she's sort of happy that your brother is a prisoner. To her he's safe now, do you see? She's content, that's natural. Mothers like all their young to be in safe places. But it makes me ashamed to think of him in their clutches – yes, I'm ashamed! A prisoner, a prisoner should escape, or at least try to. I'm afraid your brother doesn't know how to get himself out of it. So *you* must succeed, for the honour of the Vialhes! Then no one will be able to say that my sons were just pushed around, like so many silly sheep. Remember, we Vialhes have always been shepherds, for centuries, never sheep. With this war lost and your brother a prisoner, I was afraid I'd find myself in with the flock; now I feel better. Well, in some ways, because . . . You know, I'm still frightened about you going . . . Look, if you like, rather than plunging into the unknown, let's try to get some leads for you. You must win, Paul my boy, you must . . .'

# 17

PIERRE-EDOUARD tentatively stretched out his hand and felt for Mathilde; his calloused fingers touched her shoulder as she lay close to him and then wandered up to her face and stroked her damp cheek.

He had been right: she was crying – silently, perhaps because of Louise tossing in her bed not two metres from them, or not to arouse the curiosity of Mauricette and Guy, who were probably not asleep either. It was seldom that Mathilde succumbed to her misery, but when it did happen it was always with great self-control, with a pathetic discretion which disarmed and demoralised him. And tonight she was crying, and he could neither do nor say anything to comfort her.

He had expected the announcement that Paul was leaving would upset her, that she would protest and try to prevent it; he guessed right as to her first reaction, but what came next surprised him. Mathilde simply said: 'That's right, that's what he should do,' but he knew she had done such violence to her feelings in uttering this short sentence, had so suppressed her true wishes, that he suffered for her. She, who already endured in silence and without complaint Jacques' absence, would now carry a double burden of uncertainty, anguish, and at times despair.

He slid towards her, pulled her to him, cuddled her on his shoulder and with his roughened hands stroked away the tears which rolled down for a long, long time.

'Your father's right,' said Léon, 'if you leave just like that, without doing your homework, you won't get very far!'

They were all three of them in the Dupeuch kitchen, and Pierre-Edouard was glad that his sister-in-law had disappeared when Léon simply said: 'It's something we have to sort out quietly . . .'

Now they had studied the map thoroughly, and always came back to the same point. Getting to the Spanish border was no problem, but crossing it illegally was another matter, and it would take a miracle to spirit him right across Spain to Portugal without getting caught, especially as the country had barely recovered from civil war.

'I've got an idea,' said Léon, 'but I can't tell you this evening whether it'll work. The best way is for me to go and see for myself, that's more reliable. At the moment I don't trust letters, let alone the telephone!'

'What's this idea of yours?' asked Pierre-Edouard.

'Quite simple,' said Léon, filling the glasses, 'I have a colleague who covers all the markets in the south-west. He sells Spanish horses as far north as Toulouse. He's a rogue – he has a whole team of pals on the other side of the border, and these blokes smuggle the horses across in great droves, at the gallop, miles from anywhere; so for the customs officers it's catch me if you can!' he said with a laugh. 'And he brings over some fine horses; I know, I've bought some from him . . . It's more than ten years since he started doing it. The war in Spain restricted him a bit, but now I've heard he's got his little business going again, which shows he knows the area and the Spaniards!'

'Well then,' Pierre-Edouard said with a smile, 'it's a comfort to me to know that you're not the only incorrigible swindler! And where does this smuggler of yours live?'

'Near Saint-Girons, but if I want to see him, I only have to go down to Auch. He usually works around that way, and I'm sure to find him there on a market day.'

'And you think he'll get Paul across?'

'Him, no; he's not crazy, it's not his way to cross the border on the quiet. But his Spanish friends will, certainly. Dammit, they've got to go back home when they've delivered a drove . . . So if you give them a little something, I'm sure they'll look after this young colt. How do you feel about that?' he asked Paul.

'Oh, that's great, but I'd rather not hang about too long; I'd really like to be off now!'

'But you could wait a couple of weeks, eh?' said Léon, toying with his empty glass.

'Yes of course,' said Pierre-Edouard, 'but how does he get to Portugal?'

'As for that, old chap, I've no idea,' Léon apologised. 'Mind you, once he's on the other side, if he get on with the fellows who got him across, perhaps they'll help him. Because they go a long way into Spain to look for those horses, so if he sticks with them . . . But listen, my boy, if this is to work, tell them you're in the business too, and prove it to them. You'll see, they'll help you. People always moan about us dealers, but so long as it doesn't hurt us in any way – that's to say, so long as we don't lose money by it – we know how to help our own.'

Paul arrived in London four months later, in the middle of the Blitz, on 12 December 1940. When he left Saint-Libéral one morning in September, he had naïvely imagined that his journey to England would be over within a month, even by the longest estimate.

He had been quickly disillusioned by Léon's colleague, one Antoine Puylebec, who laughed to see him so disconcerted when he explained that his Spanish friends never organised their expeditions in the summer; the nights were too short and too light.

'But they don't go over in winter either, there's too much snow. So I expect you'll see them towards the middle of October, or a bit earlier if it begins to turn cold.'

Paul had to grin and bear it. He had worked with Puylebec, running round the farms and markets as he had done previously with his uncle. And it was on one of these tours, during an evening stop over at a little auberge in Payssous, that he chanced to catch the eye of a young woman from whom Puylebec had just bought thirty lambs; if he wanted it, a bed was waiting for him to two kilometres away.

The first night of manhood, in the arms of a woman of whom he knew nothing but her first name: Marguerite. A long-awaited, long-imagined discovery: joy. And then disappointment and even remorse in the morning, when she told him with a laugh, as he pulled him to her again, that it was the first time she had deceived her husband, who had been a prisoner since June, and she was not disappointed. Paul had cherished different ideas about marital fidelity.

Then, on 20 October, when it had been raining for two days and low cloud capped the Pyrenees, Puylebec announced that they would be leaving together that every evening. They drove part of the night and arrived at the foot of the mountain in the early hours, at the head of a bare valley which already had a wintry look about it. The horses were there; Paul counted about forty of them.

They were medium-sized animals, soundly built, with strong well-muscled backs and loins and prominent withers; their muddy grey coats merged cleverly into the rocks.

'I'd say Barbary horses crossed with a bit of Arab,' said Paul.

'You've a good eye, boy, that's right,' agreed Puylebec.

Léon had always taught his nephew that it's better not to ask too many questions about the provenance of an animal, but he risked it.

'Tell me, I thought people were dying of starvation in Spain. So why don't they keep their horses?'

'They've got no money left, they can't pay a decent price for them;

that's why these fellows take the risk of crossing the border. Here we pay well, especially since the war,' explained Puylebec cynically, as he walked to meet the group of men who had just emerged from a mountain shelter.

'Right,' he said to Paul shortly afterwards, 'it's agreed; you'll go over with them tonight. They don't even want any money, I told them you're a colleague; you only have to help them carry their stuff.'

'Ah, *bon*? We're taking things back over?'

'You might as well . . .'

'But not horses, then?'

'Are you mad? With stockings, silk stockings and panties too, a whole heap of women's knick-knacks. Are you surprised? It's true they're dying of starvation over there and they've no money, but not all of them, my boy, not all! When nearly everyone is poor, there'll always be a few people making money out of it . . . So if the rich want their tarts to ponce around in silk with their boobs covered in lace, we'll have to give them what they want! The trouble is, with this war on we can't find enough fancy goods any more!'

'Of course,' said Paul, rather disgusted. 'Where are we now?'

'On my land, in a corner of the Neste d'Aure. Right, I'm off now. Good luck, lad, I'll tell your uncle that you're a good fellow, you've got a good eye and know how to buy. He taught you your trade well, he'll be glad to know that.'

'Sure,' murmured Paul nervously, for with Puylebec's departure, his last link with France was severed.

They crossed the frontier the following night, not far from Pic Lia, by an incredible pass where only a goat could have followed them. In the morning, after an exhausting forced march, they reached the Cinca river, crossed it, and plunged into the forest, heading for Parzân.

In a month Paul traversed the six hundred-odd kilometres which separated him from Portugal, thanks to the help of three horse-rustlers who had to return to the Salamanca area. He very quickly realised that his guides were also terrified of falling into the hands of the civil guards. So they avoided the large towns, and never entered any unfamiliar villages.

They therefore passed around Taffala, Logroño and Lerma. They avoided Palencia and Zamora too, and pointed Paul in the direction of the River Douro, advising him to follow its course downstream but at a distance, then they slipped away to the south.

A week later Paul arrived at Mata de Lobos. From there he reached

Porto, where he waited over a month before getting passage on a cargo boat flying the Turkish flag which was heading for Newport. Four times he had refused to take up a place on one of the ships returning to North Africa. Neither Tangier, Oran nor Algiers held any attractions. To him these towns were no more than dots on a map, and the Frenchmen who broadcast each evening to France were not calling from there. So why go and waste time in North Africa when it was all happening in England?

He learned – from a major, no less – when he disembarked in Newport that his persistence had probably saved him several months in some French colonial jail.

'And now, my boy,' smiled the Englishman, placing a hand on his shoulder, '*I'm* arresting you, instead. Come on, little Frenchie, follow me. Your story's . . . very beautiful, but who's to say it's true? Britain's swarming with spies at the moment?'

It took the English police a full week to find a certain Félix Flaviens – apparently with de Gaulle – to whom Paul vigorously referred them. It was Félix himself who came to identify him, and finally got him out of his cell.

Since 24 October 1940 and Marshal Pétain's meeting with Hitler at Montoire, the population of Saint-Libéral had divided into several factions.

First of all there were those who idolised the Marshal. To them the old man was the reassuring incarnation of a long-awaited leader, the saviour who exalted work, honoured the family and defended the nation. And his every move – even his shaking hands with the Nazi Chancellor – his every word, was welcomed with a fervour bordering in fanaticism. Father Delclos had immediately taken the lead amongst these new found zealots and he made sure that they were led to the worship of God via their faith in the Marshal. His pious activism, far from dividing him from his flock, actually swelled their numbers; they were mainly women and old men to start with, but also former soldiers such as Delpeyroux or Duverger.

Confronting them were a minority, the little group of floating undecideds, the wait-and-sees, the almost convinced – after all, the Marshal had some good ideas – and the sceptics too. Delpy lined up with the latter, and sneered as he shrugged his shoulders.

'The priest would have us believe we're being led by a second Saint Philippe. He'll soon be telling us he's a virgin! Bloody hell, as far as I can see he's more like a damn good prostitute, that old man!'

Finally there were the Communists, like Brousse, Bouyssoux and

Tavet, who were fierce opponents once they knew that the Vichy government was attacking them. As for Pierre-Edouard, Léon, Maurice and a few others, they remained silent. To them the Marshal was an enigma: good because he promised to work to free the prisoners-of-war, because he got rid of the dreadful Laval and preached the virtues of labouring on the land, but patently bad when he signed the armistice, shook Hitler's hand, and recommended collaborating with the enemy.

All these twists and turns, these contradictions, inclined Pierre-Edouard and Léon to think that he was playing a cunning double game, and this idea pleased them. All they knew was that the only true enemies were the Germans.


Without really believing in it, Pierre-Edouard listened to the English broadcasts every evening after Paul left. Paul had asked him to, assuring him that once in England he would get a message to him.

'All right,' Pierre-Edouard had said after a moment's thought. 'You mustn't on any account say our name, so all you have to say is: "My name is Paul from the Corrèze in Limousin; I'm well and I send my love to you all." We'll understand.'

Then Paul left, and the months passed. Mathilde, in agony following his departure, never stopped worrying for a single day; but there again she controlled herself, and succeeded in presenting a smiling face to little Guy, and to Mauricette whenever she came home from boarding-school. As for Pierre-Edouard, he was also gripped with anxiety, and each passing week reinforced his conviction that Paul had failed. He had learned from Léon how long he had had to wait before crossing into Spain, but now Christmas was approaching, and Paul had given no sign of life.

Everything else was going badly at the Vialhes'. First there was Father, who was losing all notion of time and place for longer periods, and more frequently too. He emerged from these attacks quite dazed, as if embarrassed, and resumed a state of complete lucidity for a while.

Pierre-Edouard had never understood how he knew that his grandson had left for London, but he did know, and was very proud of it – all the while criticising an action that ran contrary to what the Marshal said.

To add to Father and his wanderings, Berthe gave the Vialhes cause for worry. She had not written for more than a year, and Pierre-Edouard was beginning to believe that, like Paul, she had disappeared. To cap it all, neither Jacques nor Félix had made any further contact.

On 24 December 1940, Léon, Yvette and their son came to pass the evening at the Vialhes', as they had done almost daily for several months. It was a long time now since Jean-Edouard had last muttered when he saw Léon; he had reconciled himself to seeing his old enemy seated at the table. Besides, for the sake of listening to the wireless he could put up with anything!

'It's time,' said Léon, looking at the big clock.

'Don't worry, I haven't forgotten,' Pierre-Edouard reassured him, turning on the set.

Silence fell, reverently: they leaned towards the receiver the better to hear the messages which filtered through dreadful interference. The messages were not yet incomprehensible, as the would later become, and at the moment they simply spoke of Jean, André or Edmond who sent his love to Thérèse, Raymonde or Charlotte.

'It's funny,' whispered Léon, 'you get better reception, you must be in a better position than us; I'll have to extend my aerial.'

'Sh!' old Jean-Edouard frowned.

' "This is Pierre, from Saint-Ouen. My love to Jeanine and my parents. *Vive la France!*" '

'They say the same as the Marshal, don't they?' suggested Guy.

'Shh . . .' said his father.

' "My name is Paul, from the Corrèze in Limousin. I am well and so is my cousin Félix; we send our love." '

They remained frozen, not daring to believe what they had just heard.

' "I repeat," ' grated the voice: ' "My name is Paul, from the Corrèze in Limousin. I am well and so is my cousin Félix; we send our love." '

'That's it!' cried Pierre-Edouard, hugging Mathilde. 'That's it, dammit! He's done it, and he's even found Félix! Oh, the devil!'

They all hugged and kissed each other, and the men clapped each other on the back with shouts of laughter while the women wept for joy.

'Did you hear, Father?' called Pierre-Edouard. 'Paul's in London with Félix! Well, you've got some damn fine grandsons after all, that's the Vialhes for you!'

The old man nodded, and they all saw that he too was weeping with happiness.

'Bloody hell, we must drink to it!' ordered Léon. 'It's Christmas Eve anyway, the champagne's on me!'

'Yes,' said Mathilde, raising her voice to make herself heard, 'but we'll have a drink in a little while. First of all we're going to Midnight Mass, here, in the parish church.'

'Here?' Pierre-Edouard could not believe his ears. 'But we'd decided to go to Perpezac! You know very well that we've all fallen out with this priest!'

'Here,' she repeated, 'even if the priest is a . . .' She swallowed the word for the sake of the children, and continued: 'Even though the priest is not of the same opinion as us, even if it's donkey's years since he's seen us. For me it's the church where I was christened, where I took my first Communion, where we were married; *that*'s where I want to thank the Good Lord, and not anywhere else. Even if it costs me something – especially if it cost me something we owe it to Him.'

'I agree, you're right,' said Pierre-Edouard. 'We'll all come with you. Well, those who want to, of course . . .'

'I'll come,' said Léon, who had not set foot in a church since his wedding. 'I'll come, to let everyone in the village know that we're happy tonight!'

'I'll come too,' said Nicolas, 'if you like.'

'You mustn't feel obliged to!' said Mathilde in embarrassment. He shook his white head and smiled.

'I don't mind, I was christened too and . . . and all that. And sometimes, madame . . .' He hesitated as his accent hindered him. 'Yes, madame is right, sometimes we should think to say thank you to Him!' he finished, pointing a finger skywards.

Shortly after midnight, they pushed their way through a crowded church to the chairs in the front row which were reserved for the Vialhe family at all times. They were empty, for the old chair-woman watched carefully to make sure that all the parishioners found their own places for the services, even if they only came once a year. It gave her added satisfaction to see that the truly faithful could work out who was missing at a glance, their empty chairs betraying them . . .

When he saw the Vialhes Father Delclos could hardly believe his eyes, and was overjoyed to think that this family had finally seen the light. He secretly vowed to go and visit them as soon as he could, and made the mistake of keeping this promise. Two days later, after ten short minutes of political and theological discussion with old Jean-Edouard and Mathilde, he was firmly shown the door by the lady of the house.

'Really,' she reproached him, 'you're always interfering in things which don't concern you! But try to remember, here we don't ask Him to meddle in our private lives, nor do we mix God with politics!'

Paul swallowed his saliva with difficulty, contemplated the little hollow filled with sand which awaited him thirty metres below at the foot of the tower, and jumped. All very well for the instructor to explain that the FAM system was absolutely foolproof and that the big spring – to which his harness was attached by a cable – would break his fall; the ground was still a long way off . . .

He landed heavily, but still managed a very good roll, and got up feeling like cock of the walk.

'Good,' commented the instructor, 'but keep your legs together next time! My God! Think of a virgin and act like one!'

Paul nodded, unbuckled his harness and rejoined his comrades. He was happy, full of spirit and enthusiasm, despite the rigours of training; each day spent in the Ringway camp brought him fresh proof that he was made for this job.

Already he was experienced in hand-to-hand fighting, with guns, with explosives; he knew how to use a 303 Bren gun as well as a Thompson 45 or a Lewis machine-gun. Soon he would be making his first real jumps. First he would throw himself from a barrage balloon, which was fixed in the sky. Those who had experienced it assured him that this was more frightening and dizzying than jumping from aeroplanes; firstly because of the slow ascent in the balloon, and then because you had to launch yourself through a narrow hatch which opened in the middle of the gondola; there was the added danger of slicing off half your face if you were not careful.

Then, one day soon, he would finally clamber into the old Wittley, hook his static-line to the attachment bar and then watch the hangars and the landing-strip grow smaller below him. Once they were high in the sky, at the cry of 'Go!' from the dispatcher, he would plunge towards the ground. After six jumps during the daytime and one at night he would have his certificate in his pocket, and could go proudly on to test the value of his red beret amongst the little English girls of Manchester.

After he had finished getting in a supply of wood for the following winter, there were still two good months until the spring hoeing should begin, so Pierre-Edouard decided to give Mathilde a treat. She really needed it, for after the happiness of Christmas Eve had come the sadness of days, then weeks and months, with no letter from Paul.

Only Jacques had finally managed to send news, short but good. He was working on a farm, seemed to like it, and was eating well.

Despite that, since she had his address, his mother made up a huge parcel of food and sent it to him every month. Pierre-Edouard was almost certain that none of these arrived at their destination but let her do it; it gave Mathilde such pleasure, and he guessed that she was pining for her sons.

So, because he had promised her several years earlier, and since he had put by a good supply of poplar laths and some solid chestnut rafters, seasoned for five years, and could buy slates at an unbeatable price – he went to find and select them himself in the quarries at Allassac – he undertook to redo the whole roof of the house at Coste-Roche.

The biggest problem was to find the nails for the slates, because in this time of shortages copper nails were almost unobtainable. It was Léon who tracked down several kilos of them at an old ironmonger's in Terrasson, who demanded an exorbitant price and in addition four hens, six dozen eggs and a bottle of brandy. Pierre-Edouard gave him what he wanted and set to on the rotten roof.

He had to take the whole thing down and renew the rafters. But thanks to Nicolas, who was really capable of doing anything, and seemed to know the tricks of every trade, it was almost child's play. When the roof timbers were raised, the tie-beams, braces, struts and ridge-pole firmly jointed, they tacked on the lathes and, row by row, nailed on the slates in perfect alignment.

'There it is,' he said, when all was complete and Mathilde came to admire his work towards the middle of April. 'That was worth waiting for, wasn't it?'

'It's magnificent!' enthused the delighted Mathilde. 'When I think that you wanted to employ a roofer! You've done it just as well and more cheaply! Our house is beautiful!'

'Very beautiful, and even if it's no use to anyone at least it isn't being rained into.'

'It will be used,' she assured him. 'It will be used, one day, by . . . by one of the children, or perhaps by us, who knows?'

A week later, during the midday meal, a car stopped outside the Vialhes'. Immediately, even before Pierre-Edouard had time to look out of the window, someone pushed open the door and a woman came in. She held the hand of a boy of about ten, who smiled as the dog came to sniff at his legs.

For a few seconds Pierre-Edouard remained silent, examining the new arrival; noting her refinement, her make-up, her light-blonde hair, but also and above all, her family resemblance, which he still recognised after twenty years.

'It's you, Berthe,' he said at last, and it was not a question.

Louise also rose, ran to her sister and embraced her.

'You're here at last!' murmured old Jean-Edouard after staring at her for a few seconds, but he did not leave his chair and waited for his daughter to approach him. 'Is this your son?' he asked, pointing to the child.

'No; I'll explain,' she said, leaning over him.

He hugged her.

'You took your time,' he reproached her. 'Oh, I was always expecting you to come, but I didn't bank on it . . .'

'I would have liked to,' she said, 'and Pierre-Edouard knows that, but . . .' Her voice broke. Then she straightened up and cleared her throat: 'But I couldn't that's all there is to it!' she said briskly.

'Maybe you're hungry? And the boy too,' asked Mathilde. 'What's your name?' she bent to ask the child.

'He doesn't speak French, not yet,' said Berthe, stroking his cheek. 'Well, you see,' she explained with an apologetic smile, 'he's a German . . .'

Mathilde started slightly, looked at Pierre-Edouard, and smiled back.

'Well, first and foremost,' she said, 'he's a little boy, and if he's hungry he must eat.'

That evening, when the children and Jean-Edouard had gone to bed and Nicolas returned to the barn, Berthe talked, explained, told them everything. And often she stopped, as if to gather her strength, to control her suffering and to preserve at all costs her neutral tone; she sounded almost detached, as if what she was saying did not concern her. It was, however, horrifying.

First there was Helmut, the man she was supposed to marry, the German who, after his divorce in 1933, had fled a regime which he knew to be appalling. But he had not fled far enough, nor cut the ties to his country sufficiently, for he had kept two couture houses, although only by appointing managers.

'And that's how we got to know each other,' explained Berthe, 'that was in '34. And during the summer of '39, when the bad smell over there had begun to grow stronger, he wanted to go back to see to the sale of his businesses. That's when they arrested him . . . He wanted us to go and set up in America after we were married. Yes, he knew this war was going to be terrible . . .'

She fell silent and took out her cigarette-case.

'And now what?' asked Pierre-Edouard.

'He's dead, I heard two weeks ago ...' she said, lighting a cigarette.

And her brother was filled with compassion for he saw that her hands were shaking.

'Are you sure?' he persisted.

'Yes; I found out from her sister, who still lives over there. I was writing to him every week. They put him in a camp, I don't know where, but not far from Munich it seems, and he's dead. His sister even received his ashes in a little wooden box, an old cigar box.'

'I see ...' murmured Pierre-Edouard, 'but why were you in Switzerland?'

'Because of the boy, Gérard; he was at a boarding-school in Zurich since his father's divorce. Helmut asked me to look after him if anything happened to him, he had custody of him. So, now I know there's nothing else I can do, rather than leave the kid all alone over there, I thought he'd be better off here, in a family.'

'You're right,' he said. 'It was the right thing to do, and we'll manage, but . . .' He hesitated.

'Yes?' continued Berthe.

'We'd better not say he's a German; the people in the village wouldn't understand, and we don't need to explain the whole thing to them, do we? It's none of their business. We'll say he's a little orphan from Alsace whom you picked up during the evacuation. That way no one will bother us with stupid questions. And then he'll have to learn French, that's the most important thing. That way it'll be easier for everyone.'

'There's another thing,' said Berthe. 'As soon as he's settled in, I'll have to leave you, because I can't spend my life here, I've got things to do in Paris.'

'You want to go back up there?' protested Pierre-Edouard.

'Yes; even during the war women like to dress up – well, some of them do. I know, my assistant has written to me that the business is running along very nicely, but I must still go back. Of course if the boy is an embarrassment to you, I'll take him with me.'

'No, we'll look after him,' said Mathilde.

'If you like,' intervened Louise, who had remained silent until then, 'I'll take care of him. I thought I could move into Coste-Roche with little Pierre, we'd be nice and quiet up there. I'd love to have Gérard, he'd be company for me. And then it would give you a bit more room.'

'I've already told you that you're not in the way!' protested her brother.

'I know,' she said, 'but all the same, with Berthe and the child,

547

we'll be eight of us for two bedrooms, and nine when Mauricette comes back in the holidays!'

'Fine,' continued Pierre-Edouard after a moment's reflection. 'I hadn't thought of that, but it's a good idea; we'll do that. And we'll get the kitchen garden sorted out at Coste-Roche straight away, then you'll have some vegetables handy. But there's still a problem! There's not a stick of furniture up there!'

'If that's all it is, I'll take care of that,' said Berthe, 'I'll buy everything that's needed.'

A week later Louise, her grandson, Berthe and Gérard were able to move into Coste-Roche, where they lacked for nothing, except electricity.

Berthe allowed herself three weeks' rest, then she returned to Paris by train. She knew that petrol was almost impossible to find in the occupied zone, and anyway her car would probably be requisitioned if she made the mistake of attracting attention to it. She therefore stored her little white Peugeot at the back of the barn, where Pierre-Edouard and Nicolas placed it on blocks, spread a tarpaulin over it and covered that with straw.

'I'll come back as soon as I can,' said Berthe to her brother, before boarding the bus which would take her to the station at la Rivière de Mansac.

'Whenever you like, you know the way.'

'I entrust the boy to you.'

'Don't worry about him. You've seen how it is already, he and Guy make a fine pair!'

'Well, see you soon.' She kissed him, and then hesitated a moment. 'By the way,' she said, lowering her voice, 'I've been here a month and I've seen that you don't really know which way to go. On the one hand you listen to the English radio and you encouraged Paul to leave for London, and yet you think that the Marshal will manage to get us out of this, is that right?'

'And so what?' he asked, rather aggressively, for he felt he didn't need any advice.

'Well, the two don't go together. You'll have to take sides one day; I'm sure you'll choose the right one!'

'That may not be the one you're thinking of!' he said drily, irritated to hear her raising a subject which he thought was of no concern to women.

'Don't get annoyed,' she said, smiling. She climbed into the bus which had just arrived, then turned round: 'Forget what I just said; now I know that you've already chosen!'

# PART FIVE

*The Silence of Screams*

# 18

MAURICETTE was just as brilliant a pupil as her elder brother had been, and easily passed her baccalauréat in June 1942. Her success was the only event which gave the Vialhes a little happiness.

For more than a year, depression and sadness had prevailed in their household as everywhere else. Pierre-Edouard and Mathilde had tried in vain to encourage each other, for the absence of any news from Paul was torturing them, as Louise was tortured by Félix's silence. And the letters which Jacques sent, although they gave a little comfort, also proved to them that their son was not about to return, despite the promises of the Vichy government.

Added to these trials was the now certain knowledge that this war would be long and pitiless. It was now world-wide, and if it was slightly reassuring to know from the English radio that the Germans were running out of steam in Russia, it was not encouraging to learn from Radio-Paris that the Americans were making pathetically little progress in the Pacific.

But all this news, which was more or less partisan and biased according to which camp you listened to, affected Pierre-Edouard and Mathilde less than what Berthe told them on each of her visits.

She came roughly quarterly, spending a week or ten days in Saint-Libéral and then disappearing for three months. And what she related of life in the occupied zone did not restore their confidence. She spoke of the hunger and poverty raging in the capital, and of the occupying forces becoming daily more oppressive and demanding.

'Here, it's paradise! You eat your fill, the rationing doesn't affect you, but in Paris . . .'

It was true, Pierre-Edouard freely admitted it. They did not know what hunger was. They had bread, chickens, eggs and when they needed it – while they were waiting for the piglets to fatten, for example – Pierre-Edouard would sacrifice a lamb or two. Besides, when it came to meat, Léon had connections, and he made sure that his brother-in-law benefited from them. In return Pierre-Edouard supplied him with excellent honey – which conveniently replaced the rationed sugar – and with tobacco, which had also become scarce. In 1941 Pierre-Edouard had begun to cultivate tobacco for himself. It was against the law, but he didn't care. Anyway, who would know that the little field of maize behind Coste-Roche concealed, in its centre, some luxuriant tobacco plants; they weren't visible until you were right on top of them, and nobody except the Vialhes ever went up there!

'And you're making money as never before as well!' continued Berthe.

That was true too, and Pierre-Edouard was not ashamed of it. It was not his fault if everything was selling, and selling well! Some people in the village had an annoying tendency to take advantage of the situation, and demand exorbitant prices for produce which would have been used to feed pigs before the war. Pierre-Edouard was not among them. It was one thing to cultivate illicit tobacco, to slaughter stock illegally, or even to poach shamelessly on the plateau and the hills in collusion with Léon, who loved that sort of outing – since hunting had been forbidden, game was abundant – but to exploit the hunger of townspeople by raising prices, that was a step he would never take; he had always been honest and intended to remain so.

The surprising fact was that Léon also disdainfully refused to do business in this way, and Pierre-Edouard resolved to ask him one day if he did so on moral grounds or quite simply because it was much too easy to cheat like that. Almost too crude, and certainly not exciting enough, for a man who had spent forty years in his profession earning a reputation as the most formidable stock-dealer ever, to lower himself to the sort of sharp practice which any idiot could commit by coining it in with a little bunch of carrots!

'No,' insisted Berthe, 'you eat well, you're making money, you've no right to complain!'

'We're not complaining about all that, but about the boys who've gone away and show no sign of coming back!' retorted Pierre-Edouard. 'And anyway, you look as if you're getting enough grub!'

'That's true. What can I do, the Germans like their women to wear beautiful dresses, so . . .'

'And so you sell them to those bastards!'

'Wouldn't you sell them your calves if they wanted to buy them?'

'First of all I'd have to have some available when they came, and I don't think that's likely to happen . . . All right, let's talk about something else.'

All these conversations ended with him in a fury. He had difficulty in understanding how his sister could reconcile her business sense with her hatred of the enemy. Because she did hate them; it was obvious. She also made use of them, for it was through them that she so easily obtained her permits to enter the free zone, whence she set off on each journey back loaded like a mule with all provisions given to her by Mathilde.

'Basically, she's conning them all the same,' Mathilde told him in an attempt to pacify him, for she knew that he considered her attitude dubious.

'Maybe, but I wouldn't like to do that and I don't like her doing it!'

'I don't expect she's got any choice.'

'I hope not! That's all it needs, if she's doing it without being forced to! Because that's what you call collaboration, and it's not a word I like to hear around here! Yes, you're right, all things considered; every time she leaves again with her kilos of meat and butter, her dozens of eggs and her honey, when it's forbidden, then she's making fools of them!'

The visit of the Head of State to the Corrèze presented Léon with a very delicate problem. The orders from the préfecture were definite; the mayors of all the communities had a duty to recruit the largest possible number of supporters and conduct them to Brive – they would be collected by buses supplied for the occasion – to cheer the august personage.

It was energetically recommended that veterans should display all their medals and bring out their flags, that women and children should equip themselves with flowers and baskets full of rose-petals, which should be scattered over the official procession at the appropriate moment.

Everyone should be in position on the afternoon of 8 July to welcome the Marshal as he deserved. Coming from Tulle, he would arrive at Brive station by the 18.07 train, and the entire population of the cité Galliarde and its hinterland should prove to him that it deserved its name of Happy Gateway to the Midi!

Fifteen months earlier, Léon would doubtless have complied with the directives from the préfecture and, whilst considering this sort of demonstration rather childish, taken his place at the head of his people and led them to Brive. But too many things had happened since June 1940.

Now Léon no longer believed that Pétain would be their deliverer, for every concession he made to the Nazis just proved that he was incapable of resisting them. His behaviour was not a façade for a game of clever double-dealing, but the pitiful, grotesque indolence of an old man whom fate had passed by and who was, above all, extremely badly advised by his entourage.

Léon had therefore no wish to go and cheer for a man in whom he no longer had faith. He still respected him, because of Verdun, but not to the point of running to applaud him. What annoyed him was not so much the Marshal, as all the hangers-on who crowded around him. Those were the ones who were really responsible for the situation, and it was obviously in their interests that the head of state should be hailed as the Messiah; the enthusiasm he aroused gave them a free hand to act in his name.

As he knew that Pierre-Edouard shared his feelings, he sought advice from him. It was obviously impossible to hide the Marshal's impending visit from the villagers. Everyone had been forewarned; the newspaper talked of it ad nauseam. Already Father Delclos was making the children in his catechism class practise a song he had composed, with five rhymed couplets to the tune of 'Chez nous soyez Reine':

> 'Le Maréchal sauve la France
> Il fut vainqueur à Verdun
> Il guérira nos souffrances
> Nous sommes en de bonnes mains . . .'

'And you'll see,' prophesied Pierre-Edouard, 'there'll be plenty of people there, Mathilde even wants to take the children. Mind you, that's to be expected; it isn't every day they'll see a Marshal!'

'Yvette wants to go too, with the boy; she's right. But I don't want to set foot anywhere near it, because it's all just a load of rubbish!'

'You only have to be ill that day,' suggested Pierre-Edouard.

'I've never been ill in my life!'

'Then now's exactly the time!'

'That's right,' smiled Léon, 'and I'll arrange for my place to be taken by the first deputy, that's you . . .'

'There's no chance of that; I can't possibly leave the house, on account of my father. He's been completely off his trolley for the last two weeks.'

Old Jean-Edouard's mind really was wandering, recalling snippets of memories from here and there and trotting them out repetitively.

'That's true,' admitted Léon, 'it's a good excuse. All right, so it's Maurice who'll replace me.'

'Don't count on it, he's at a wedding that day, at la Bachellerie.'

'You're all leaving me in the lurch, eh!'

'No, no, Delpeyroux will be delighted to take your place, he's already polishing his medals! So if you make him your representative, as well, he'll probably burst with pride!'

'He's just the man!' Léon gloated. 'I'll get everything ready, and then at the last minute I'll cry off.'

That was what he did and nobody, not even the priest, suspected him for a moment of antipétainism. When 8 July came, he waited for the special bus to arrive and then called Delpeyroux.

'Right, you'll have to take my place.'

'Aren't you coming?'

'Uh, no . . .'

'But why not?'

'I'm ill,' said Léon, sliding his right hand into his waistcoat pocket. 'A twinge there, near the heart.'

'Oh, all right,' said Delpeyroux, perplexed but delighted. 'Okay, I'll be in charge.'

'That's right,' said Léon, lighting a cigarette, 'you take charge; with you there our people will be well represented!'

He watched the gas-powered bus depart, returned home, called his two workers and set off to the fields to reap.

Pierre-Edouard and he learned from their wives that it had been an imposing spectacle: Brive was beautiful with be-ribboned triumphal arches and had given the Marshal a magnificent welcome. They even recounted how one woman, one of those who had been able to get a place in the station, had thrown herself in a craze of rejoicing on to the track at platform number three, to kiss the rails over which the train carrying the Marshal had just passed.

The circular from the préfecture, announcing an agricultural survey which would require personal declarations, arrived on 29 September 1942 at the mairie in Saint-Libéral and aroused a general outcry amongst the farmers; even the most fervent supporters of the Marshal grumbled. Father Delclos tried to convince them that civic duty demanded they comply with the Marshal's orders – which were after all always for the common good – to no avail.

This survey was a bitter blow; it was an intolerable intrusion into people's private lives, an attack on their freedom and rights of ownership. Furthermore, it stank of an inquisition and boded ill.

Nobody was fooled. If every farmer had to declare, almost to the square metre, the size of his farm and the use he made of his land, to declare also the exact number of all his animals, including hens, ducks and rabbits, it was either to increase the taxes or to prepare for

555

requisitioning; the rise in one did not in any way prevent the implementation of the other!

'I'm not going to declare anything!' cried Martin Tavet that same evening during the council meeting.

'Just as you please,' said Léon, holding out the circular to him, 'but it's compulsory, according to the law of 20 February 1942. If you refuse they'll stick you with a fine of 800 to 10,000 francs, it's written here . . .'

'All right, then mine will be false!' warned Tavet.

'Idiot,' Pierre-Edouard whispered to him so as not to be heard by Delpeyroux, 'there's no need to say it out loud, when everyone's going to be doing it quietly.'

'Oh, I see,' said Tavet. 'So it's like that; okay.'

'Yes, but watch out,' warned Léon after the meeting, when Delpeyroux had left, 'we'll have to play it very carefully. Those fellows in the préfecture may come and check up, so I want declarations that look truer than the truth! And keep a good note of the numbers you put down, because next year it'll all start up again, I bet. No fooling around, eh? If you write down two hectares of fallow or scrubland out of ten, then make sure beforehand that you've got at least one hectare classed as grade five land on the register! Those bastards from the préfecture aren't idiots, after all; they'll compare the two, they've got nothing else to do! And the same with the stock; if you have four hectares of pasture, don't say that you've only got one cow and two goats, they won't believe you. I'm telling you, they'll be watching!'

The announcement of the American landings in Algeria made some people smile whilst others were deeply shocked; immediately afterwards came the cruel news of the invasion of the southern zone. It was a hard blow for all those who, since June 1940, had grown accustomed to living on the good side of a divided France; who had known of the war only by its shortages and by the prisoners taken. Now they would be under the same flag as those who had been subject to the occupying forces since the armistice.

'And those bastards did it today!' said Léon bitterly, on the evening of 11 November 1942.

'Of course,' murmured Pierre-Edouard, 'it's to try to live down the hammering they got in '18!'

'Well, I'm the mayor – am I going to be under their orders? Bloody hell, I resign!'

'No, no,' Pierre-Edouard calmed him, 'we've already been under their orders for two years, only we pretended not to see it. And if you resign, they'll do the same as they did in 1940 in the villages with over 2000 inhabitants; the prefect will appoint a mayor, and you can be sure he'll foist that ass Delpeyroux on us! By the way, is it true that the imbecile has signed up in the Vichy militia?'

'Yes, just this week,' replied Léon. 'It seems he's the area commander.'

'Better be even more careful what we say, now, because he'll have his eye on us.'

'It's not him who worries me,' said Léon with a shrug, 'he's not a bad fellow – but the Boche, that's a different matter! Do you think they're going to come this far?'

'Why not, it's all their country, now.'

Vigorously encouraged by his father the Delpeyroux boy was the first to leave for the Compulsory Work Service. The unanimous opinion was that the father was a good deal more enthusiastic than the son when he accompanied him to Brive in December 1942.

Two other young people from the village copied young Delpeyroux, but there were many more who, from the spring of 1943, began to disappear and lose themselves in the countryside. A rumour ran around Saint-Libéral that they had sought refuge in the woods near Cublac or even further away, fifty kilometres from there, towards Noailhac, Meyssac or Lagleygeole; in short, they had gone underground.

Father Delclos did not hestiate to label them deserters, and recommended that parents of boys who were of an age to go and work in Germany do everything to ensure that their offspring remained deaf to the call of the forest. He was wasting his time. In the course of a few months the community lost all its young people and the village, which had already been weakened since the men were in prison camps, fell into lethargy.

That year the thickets and scrubwood strengthened their encirclement, overwhelmed all the isolated plots which were difficult to reach or maintain, and clung to the previously well-kept slopes in green patches of cancerous growth.

Pierre-Edouard and Nicolas tried to struggle against nature, but from the beginning of the year they also had to battle against requisition orders.

In 1943 Pierre-Edouard was ordered to provide one cow, minimum live weight 440 kilos, five calves of at least 85 kilos, six lambs at 18 kilos, 275 kilos of potatoes, 125 kilos of wheat, 165 kilos of buckwheat, 120 kilos of rye and 23 kilos of dried beans, not forgetting 325 kilos of hay, 8 cubic metres of firewood and 224 eggs.

Of course they were offered compensation for these deliveries, but it was ridiculous, very much lower than the prices in the discreetly operated unofficial market everyone used. So for example, in April 1943 Mathilde was selling her eggs, without cheating anyone, at 33 francs a dozen. They were traded at 70 francs or more on the black market and, Berthe assured them in one of her letters, were worth 110 francs in Paris! But the Board of Supply set them at 21 francs for sixty, next to nothing. And all the official tariffs were in keeping with this, for they were based on 1939 prices!

So Pierre-Edouard did all he could to reduce these ruinous compulsory levies, arguing now that a calf and three lambs had died of diarrhoea, then that frost or drought had spoilt the crops, or again that his war-wound prevented him from cutting firewood.

In spite of this he did have to concede a few bits and pieces, if only to avoid the fines which threatened those who resisted, and which could reach twenty times the value of the undelivered goods – the price of a fine cow, for instance, if 224 eggs were not supplied! But it was with a heart full of rage that he did it. Luckily, thanks to Léon's co-operation, he did not have to draw on his cattle herd, and his Limousin cows escaped the massacre.

'It's easy,' Léon told him when the first requisition appeared, 'they're demanding a cow from you? Fine, I'll let you have one, at cost price, you pass it on to them, and I bet you'll profit by it!'

'But you won't get me to believe you paid the official price for that animal!' Pierre-Edouard was worried. 'So you'll be wasting money! They'll pay me less than you bought it for!'

'Don't talk stupid; the day's yet to come when I lose money on a cow,' Léon reassured him with a smile. 'You don't understand the system?'

'No.'

'You wouldn't have made your fortune in this job! It's quite simple. I buy the animals at the official price, if you really want to know, but only from idiots like Delpeyroux and Duverger, and I know a few others like them! You don't imagine I'm bothered about them? Anyway, if I paid the current price they're quite capable of denouncing me for economic sabotage! So I don't mess about with them, believe you me!'

'Oh, I see,' said Pierre-Edouard, laughing.

'But that's not all,' continued Léon. 'Look here, these mugs in the préfecture,' he said, pushing the official notice over to his brother-in-law, 'they really don't know a thing. They specify animals which provide at least 45 per cent meat to live weight – that's nothing, 45 per cent! But now that's the measure I use to buy from all the fools like Delpeyroux in the area! They're quite content to believe me, because it's written there!' he said with a sneer. 'Since I've been walking around with this paper in my pocket, none of the cows I've bought from them has been over 47 per cent,' he exulted. 'In fact they're all at least 52 per cent! Do you see, I'm making five per cent every time, that's how you'll make a profit!'

Actually, the cow Léon obtained, which he had bought for 6,230 francs from a notorious collaborator, netted 6,541.50 francs for Pierre-Edouard, who once again marvelled at his brother-in-law's infallible eye; the 311.50 francs difference represented exactly five per cent.

But he did not wish to keep this money, and hurried to return it to Léon.

'I don't want it,' replied the latter, 'it's your profit. You don't want it either? Fine, well, put it in poor old Jacques' savings account, that'll be fair, won't it? For once, a collaborator is giving him something!'

# 19

WHEN Pierre-Edouard came to renovate his haymaking equipment, during the month of May 1943, he was dismayed to realise that his old reaper was absolutely unusable. He had known for years that it would not last for ever and the day would come when he would have to change it; it had been working since 1905, rattling on all sides and making a horrible grinding noise. But up until then it had always done its job properly.

In order to oil the gears more easily, tighten the block on the cutting-bar and check the teeth, he brought it out into the middle of the yard, where it collapsed all of a sudden, with an ominous squeal of the drive-wheel as the axle snapped right through; the cogs, thus released, rolled to the ground.

'Bloody hell!' groaned Pierre-Edouard, seeing that the damage was irreparable.

'Busted,' commented Nicolas, passing his fingers over the worn metal.

'Yes, and it has been for a long time, that crack didn't appear today. All right, well, we didn't reckon on it, but we'll be making hay with a new reaper. It'll cost me an arm and a leg, but it's just too bad, we can't do it all with a scythe!'

Two days later, accompanied by a delighted Guy, Pierre-Edouard caught the train at la Rivière de Mansac and went as far as Brive. He made a face as soon as he emerged into the station yard.

'Look at those bastards!' he muttered, glancing towards the balconies of the Terminus Hotel, where German officers with naked torsos sprawled on chaises-longues in the sun. This sight put him in a bad mood, and the price demanded by the agricultural machinery dealer a little later did not improve matters.

'What?' he protested, '5,500 francs for a reaper? Are you ill or what?'

'Look,' the salesman defended himself, 'you are selecting our premier model, the number fifteen, you must realise. This Dollé brand is really something, with a covered gear-casing and integral sump! But if you want the old-fashioned type with the gears exposed . . .'

'When I think that the other one cost us 365 francs,' murmured Pierre-Edouard, 'and it was expensive!'

'Pardon?' said the man, thinking he had misheard.

'Yes, 365 francs!'

The dealer thought it was a joke, and laughed.

'For that price, I'll throw in two good blades, genuine prewar Swedish steel, plus two shafts and I'll add rakes, how's that for you?'

Pierre-Edouard shrugged and walked around the machine.

'I hope that at that price you'll deliver it, with the harvester?'

'Yes.'

'It's beautiful, isn't it?' Guy was in raptures as he climbed into the seat.

Pierre-Edouard watched him, smiled, and felt thirty-eight years younger. Then it was he who had accompanied his father to buy the reaper; his father who had struggled grimly to obtain a few concessions, and who had finally succeeded. He should do the same. He took out his pipe and filled it slowly.

'Fine,' he decided, as he used his fat copper lighter, '5,500 is a deal of money, so you'll need to knock a bit off . . .'

'No, no!' The saleman stood firm.

'Oh yes! You're not going to tell me you get customers like me every day . . . Look, I can still go to one of your colleagues. You say it's a Dollé? It's not a big name, that!'

'Yes it is, monsieur!' protested the sales rep, 'Dollé of Vesoul, everyone knows them!'

'I don't,' Pierre-Edouard assured him. 'Now if it was a MacCormick . . .'

'How are you going to find one of those with a war on!' sneered the other man.

'Or even a Puzenat, or an Amouroux,' he continued smoothly, 'but a Dollé . . .'

'It has gears with helicoid teeth of sharpened steel, fixed in an enclosed chamber and then tempered,' the salesman tried.

'And so what? So do the others!' said Pierre-Edouard, who had studied the brochures he sometimes received at the syndicate before coming. 'All right, you take off 350 francs and you deliver it to me, agreed?'

'Certainly not!'

'Well, too bad then,' he said, moving towards the door. 'Look,' he said, turning round, 'you could take away the old one, let's say for 300 francs, couldn't you?'

'Listen,' the salesman kept him there, 'I'll take the old one for, let's say . . . 250, okay?'

'That's not a lot per kilo for scrap iron, when you think metal's in great demand at the moment . . .' Pierre-Edouard stepped back towards him and picked up a big tin of grease. 'All right then,' he decided, 'and you add this in for me.'

'Oh! Hey! That tin costs 45 francs!'

'Come on,' Pierre-Edouard persisted. 'Tell me, is it you who'll be delivering? Good,' he continued, lowering his voice, 'well, I'll put a chicken, a few eggs and some butter on one side, just this once, okay?'

On 8 July 1943, in the evening, shortly before eleven o'clock – but because of keeping German time it was still almost light – the whole Vialhe family was seated at the table when the dog barked in the yard. Pierre-Edouard immediately switched off the radio and went to look out of the door at what had caused the animal to sound the alarm.

'Oh it's you, Doctor,' he said, recognising the visitor. 'What brings you here at this time of night?'

'Is your father all right at the moment?' enquired Dr Delpy.

'Fine, he's in good form.'

'Yes,' murmured the doctor, 'he has an iron constitution, pity about his brain, from time to time, well . . . Tell me, can I speak to you quietly somewhere?'

'Of course, but won't you come in? We're having dinner.'

'I'd prefer to stay outside, but I'd like your wife to be with us too . . .'

'I'll call her. But what's happened, is it something serious?'

'No – well, not yet, but . . . Come on, better go behind the barn,' suggested the doctor, when a worried but intrigued Mathilde had joined them. 'It's this,' he explained, 'I don't know how to say it . . . Well, anyway, I know you tend to my way of thinking.'

'Which way?' asked Pierre-Edouard prudently.

'Still not the way of the Boche, if I'm not mistaken?'

'Maybe not . . . Go on.'

'I have a problem, I'll give it to you straight. I have some friends who are looking after two kids, that lot mustn't find them, do you understand?'

'No,' said Pierre-Edouard.

'What? Yes, you do. These kids are Jews, and you know very well that the Germans are searching for them!'

'Of course,' Pierre-Edouard remembered. 'I've heard talk of it, like everyone else. But I didn't know they were looking for kids too, what do they want with them?'

'But dammit all, Pierre-Edouard, we're at war! They're arresting all of them! Bloody hell, Berthe must have talked to you about it!'

'Yes, but she never told me they were arresting children. Anyway, my sister, we haven't seen her since the Boche have been in the southern zone! That's almost nine months, and she doesn't send cards any more!'

'And these children, where are they?' asked Mathilde.

'On a farm, not very far from Varetz, but the people looking after them are afraid they may have been denounced, so the children need to disappear as quickly as possible!'

'So they're even arresting kids,' murmured Pierre-Edouard, who could not come to terms with such infamy.

Until that day, he had never concerned himself with the Jewish problem. First of all he didn't know any, had nothing against them and didn't understand why some people swore such hatred for them, and he believed, in all good faith, that the hunt for Jews was aimed solely at expelling them from France. And he was not the only one to think like that in Saint-Libéral!

'Are you in the Resistance?' he asked abruptly.

'No, not exactly. Well yes, like you, like lots of people,' explained the doctor. 'From time to time it happens that I help those who are really fighting, but no more than that; you'd do the same.'

'Yes, perhaps. Well, let's get it straight – these kids, you want us to hide them, is that it? What do you think?' he asked, looking at Mathilde.

'The same as you.'

'Well, bring them over,' said Pierre-Edouard, 'we'll trust Louise to take care of them. Up there, at Coste-Roche, they'll be safe.'

'It's because of that isolated house that I thought of you. And also because I knew you wouldn't refuse.'

'When will you bring them? We'll need to know that at least.'

'Tomorrow, probably, and quietly. On that subject, I suggest you take every possible precaution. Sheltering Jews could mean a very stiff penalty, so complete silence, all right?'

'As to that,' said Pierre-Edouard with a smile, 'I hope it won't upset them to be with a Kraut?'

'What?'

'Oh yes, the kid Berthe brought to us, little Gérard . . .'

563

'I thought he was from Alsace!' The doctor gave a muffled exclamation.

'Well, you go on thinking it, but now you know that the Vialhes know how to keep quiet.'

The two children arrived the next day; two brothers of eight and six. It was the doctor who went to fetch them, with the horse and cart which he had taken to again since petrol had become so scarce. To avoid any inquisitive eyes, he did not drive into the village, but turned off immediately up one of the tracks which climbed to the plateau.

Pierre-Edouard, Mathilde and Nicolas were waiting for him while loading a cart with wheat. As for Mauricette and Guy, they were already at Coste-Roche with their aunt Louise.

'So that's what they're arresting!' said Pierre-Edouard with a nod. 'My God, we need to shoot people who attack kids!'

'Come here,' said Mathilde, holding out her hand to them. 'What's your name?' she asked the older one.

'Louis Duval,' recited the boy without lowering his eyes, 'and my brother's called Jean, we're refugees from Lorraine and . . .'

'And you lost your parents during the exodus?' sighed Pierre-Edouard. 'Is that it?'

'Yes, sir.'

'I'm called Pierre-Edouard,' he said, squatting down to be at their height, 'and she's Mathilde, my wife. She's very kind and she's going to take you up to the house. You'll be fine up there. Come on, give me a kiss.'

'They've learnt it well,' said the doctor shortly afterwards, as he watched them walk away. 'In fact they're called David and Benjamin Salomon.'

'What does that matter to me! They're kids, that's enough,' said Pierre-Edouard forcibly, for he needed to mask the sorrow which had overwhelmed him at the sight of the two children. 'Excuse me.' He recovered himself and picked up the pitchfork to go back to Nicolas and the team.

'No offence taken, old fellow, I understand,' the doctor assured him as he climbed into his cart. 'By the way, have you heard talk of the maquis who've formed a group near Terrasson?'

'Vaguely,' said Pierre-Edouard evasively, 'but I don't think much of these young tearaways playing at war, you know, it's not serious.'

'That depends,' asserted the doctor, 'if they're well trained . . .'

'That's exactly what I'm saying! Listen, Doctor, I did four years in the war, like you; I saw what an army is, a real one. I finished up as warrant officer – believe me, it's something to command fifty twenty-year-old kids! So when I'm told they've just got hunting rifles and no real leader . . . ! If it wasn't such a serious matter, it'd make me laugh!'

'I share your point of view, but it seems that in some areas they're getting organised like a proper army.'

'Well, if it's an army, a real one, that's different.'

'And there are some Communist maquis too, I've been told.'

'I'm not getting myself worked up about them, they know what they're doing! But the others, they won't work any miracles. No, I'm telling you, I don't have much faith in them.'

'Between ourselves,' asked the doctor with a smile, 'Paul isn't in Paris, is he? He's with the maquis somewhere and that's why you're so critical of them, because he went off with them; is that it?'

'That's it exactly,' said Pierre-Edouard sarcastically, 'Paul went off with the maquis, just like the boy brought by Berthe is from the Alsace!'

'How wrong can you be . . .' murmured the doctor. 'From what I know of him, I could have sworn he'd have been one of the first to leave!'

'That's about right . . .'

'Uh-huh,' said the doctor, observing him, 'you won't be saying any more about it, eh? You're right; the way things are going now, you can't be too careful.'

'Don't take it amiss. Anyway now, with these kids you've brought, we're all for the gallows together. Paul left for London, three years ago last September,' admitted Pierre-Edouard, not without pride.

'The devil!' said the doctor, jumping to the ground and clasping his hand. 'The devil! And you haven't said a thing to anyone since then? Well I never! So there's a boy from Saint-Libéral with de Gaulle! Look here, this is fantastic news! Now I know why you didn't want to talk about Paul – oh, the lucky blighter!'

'Oh yes,' said Pierre-Edouard as he filled his pipe, 'we're like that, we Vialhes. We know it's a waste of energy to talk while you're working, so when we're working we keep quiet.'

After three years of captivity, Jacques had abandoned any idea of escape across a countryside surrounded by vast lakes and treacherous peat bogs; how could he find his way through all those thick forests? Convinced that attempts to flee were destined to fail, Jacques finally resigned himself to captivity.

It made him angry to admit it, but he sometimes felt a sort of satisfaction, not in being a prisoner, but in the work he was doing. A work which pleased him, for old Karl's farm was beautiful: rich, with twenty-four hectares of good land for potatoes and rye, with forty-five milch cows, with its big half-diesel Lanz tractor which he had very quickly learned to drive. Just as he had learned to milk the cows with the milking machines in the spacious modern cowshed.

And on this magnificent farm, he was at least the foreman, if not the boss, for since the last of the four sons of the family had returned to the front – where one of his brothers had already died – old Karl depended on him. He had complete confidence in Jacques, for he had seen immediately that he was of his own tribe: a farmer, who considered the land, wherever it lay, worthy of the best possible care.

And Jacques, working each day with André – who ended up knowing how to hold a scythe – and working well, did not have any sense of betrayal, or of labouring indirectly for the Third Reich. It was not to feed the German troops that he hoed and earthed up the long rows of potatoes, watched the rations for each cow; it was out of honesty, towards Karl, and above all towards the land.

At the beginning he had thrown himself into the work to stifle his mourning for his lost freedom, his abandoned studies, for his parents, for Marie-Louise. And the remedy did him good, for even if he was still quite often besieged by black thoughts, at least he had the daily satisfaction of completing a task which he enjoyed.

However, in the past three months he had increasing difficulty in controlling the anxiety aroused by his fiancée's last two letters. They were unclear, full of ambiguities and innuendos, almost empty of love. Enough to make you think that there in Saint-Libéral, young Marie-Louise was no longer missing him.

It was not without some difficulty that Mauricette gained entry to the teachers' training college established at Brive, since the one at Tulle had been closed by order of the Vichy government. To achieve her aim she needed to exercise all the strength and will of the Vialhes, and the obstinacy and persuasiveness inherited from her mother.

Like Pierre-Edouard she went straight to the point, but like Mathilde, she used her charm and her smile to defeat the final obstacles. A little taller than her mother, she was, at eighteen, just as sweet and graceful as Mathilde had been at the same age and, like her, she knew how to persuade those whom she wished to win over.

Nevertheless, she had to do battle with Pierre-Edouard to extract his authorisation to attend the training college. He instinctively mistrusted this sort of establishment and feared that his daughter would become just as sectarian, secular, not to say self-opinionated as, for instance, was the teacher's wife, who had taken full charge of the school since her husband had been captured.

In addition, he still had bad memories of the quarrels which had set the Church against the State at the beginning of the century, and feared that the atmosphere in the training college would be just as stupidly anti-religious as it had been then. Without being a pillar of the Church – to Father Delclos he was actually a complete infidel – he thought it had a role and a place in society, and he did not love those who wished to destroy it.

Despite all this he gave his daughter the authorisation she required, for he understood that her vocation as a teacher was sound, considered and final. He realised very soon that his worries on the subject of partisan attitudes fostered by some were not unjustified; that ostracism was still practised in the teaching profession, and that the doors were difficult to open for those who, like Mauricette, had done all their studying at independent Catholic schools; that was considered a defect.

This discovery made him furious, but far from depressing him, it spurred him on; stimulated his natural pugnacity and pushed him into action.

'So they want to play stupid games? Fine, if it comes to that, I know a few tricks,' he said when Mauricette, in tears, had recounted the scornful rebuffs she had suffered when she had presented her request to register, and above all for a grant. 'I'm going to see Léon,' he said as he went out.

He found him at the mairie, and explained the matter to him.

'With people like that, you need to go at it sideways,' decided Léon, as soon as he was informed.

'That's what I thought.'

'But I don't know anyone there.'

'Well!' Pierre-Edouard reproached him. 'You're forgetting our mutual brother-in-law, that idiot who's so proud to have become one of the pillars of the préfecture and an officer of the Vichy Militia in the Corrèze. But he hasn't forgotten us, not him, the bastard!'

Indeed, as if by chance, since the beginning of rationing, Léon's sister had remembered that her brother lived in Saint-Libéral and was a stock-dealer; that her sister Mathilde existed, and that Pierre-Edouard owned a fine farm . . .

With initial discretion, she and her husband had renewed contact; then, spurred on by hunger, they had established a firm if not sincere relationship. From then on, they came every fortnight. When they arrived on Saturday the trailer attached to their tandem jumped about behind the machine, because it was empty. But when they set off again on Sunday afternoon, the cart was weighed down with varied provisions and had a decided tendency to collapse.

Neither Léon nor Pierre-Edouard liked these two parasites, and if it were not for Yvette and Mathilde, who made it a point of honour to feed them, would happily have left them with their tongues hanging out; for they were not satisfied with being given free two-thirds of the provisions they came to fetch; they even paid for the other third at the official rate! Léon shrugged, Pierre-Edouard grumbled, but both of them let it pass.

There was only one point on which Pierre-Edouard had not given in: supplying his brother-in-law with tobacco. He knew he was a heavy smoker, and took a malicious pleasure in filling his pipe in front of him, after placing his pouch on the table, overflowing with the coarse, pungent, black tobacco which he prepared himself.

The skinflint from the préfecture drooled over it and his nostrils twitched as he saw Pierre-Edouard pulling on his pipe.

'Ah,' Pierre-Edouard would say at this point, 'I always forget that you smoke too; here, roll one,' he offered, pushing the pouch towards his brother-in-law.

The latter would roll himself an enormous cigarette, and his hand trembled as he lit it. He coughed for five minutes afterwards, for the mixture was rougher than iron filings, and as corrosive and suffocating as a sulphur match for fumigating casks!

'Aah!' he finally exhaled, his eyes full of tears. 'Your tobacco is marvellous! Could you get me a little bit?'

'No way,' Pierre-Edouard then said, as he put the pouch in his pocket, 'you can see that I've hardly enough for myself!'

'I'm prepared to pay a good price for it!' begged the addict.

'Impossible, my supplier won't do it. You understand, he grows it himself, and I don't have to tell you that that's forbidden, like the black market as well . . . So you can imagine how he's on his guard!'

They would need to play on this weakness. Léon considered for a moment, scratched his head.

'Yes,' he agreed at last, 'perhaps he could intervene, but we'll have to induce him to do it. And then, does he have enough pull?'

'Don't forget that he succeeded in getting his son repatriated. And as for inducement – if he refused, I'll kick him out, he can go and get his supplies somewhere else!'

'That wouldn't be a bad thing.' Léon was amused. 'I'm beginning to get really fed up with him, and especially as you have to be careful what you say in front of him!'

'We'll have a go at him on Saturday?' suggested Pierre-Edouard.

'Saturday, all right. But come to my house; I'll send Yvette and my sister to keep Mathilde company, that way we can discuss it man to man.'

Jacques twisted round on his seat and checked that the self-binding reaper he was towing behind the Lanz was functioning properly. The fine line of fat bales reassured him that he had everything correctly adjusted. At the beginning of the work he had experienced some difficulties with the knotting mechanism; it had really been devised to work with string made from vegetable fibre, not with this sort of paper thread which old Karl had brought back from Reichensee.

'How are you doing?' he asked André, as he passed close to him.

His friend, who was stacking the sheaves, shrugged his shoulders. He did not complain about his work – infinitely preferable to employment in a factory or at peat cutting – but he, unlike Jacques, found nothing exciting in it; he endured it while awaiting better days.

Jacques reached the end of the field, turned, and saw the owner's wife coming towards him. Every day at ten o'clock she brought them a snack, and it was not a meagre one. Since the death two weeks earlier of another of her sons, killed on the Russian Front, the little old woman was a pitiful sight, quite shrivelled up with sorrow, and silent. She gazed at things and people without seeing them and her stare, now dry from having cried to much, touched the hearts of all those who met it.

Jacques put the Lanz into neutral, jumped to the ground and thanked the old lady who held out the basket to him. Marie-Louise's letter had been slipped in between the cob loaf – made of rye and potatoes – and the cheese. He opened it, deciphered the few lines, and turned pale.

'Are you fagged out?' joked André as he came up. Then he saw the letter gripped in his friend's fingers. 'Oh,' he murmured, 'I understand . . .'

In three years of living with Jacques he had learned everything about him, and Jacques had done likewise. For several months he had suspected that all was not well with Marie-Louise.

'Right,' he tried to help, 'you'll have to fight on, my old mate.'

'She's getting engaged . . .'

'Well, you don't say . . .' whistled André.

'Big trouble?' the old woman asked quietly.

Jacques stared at her, understood that his pallor had not escaped her notice, and was moved by her solicitude.

'Mother? Father? Dead?' she continued.

He guessed she was quite prepared to comfort him, as his grandmother would have done.

'No, nobody's dead, thank you,' he said, summoning a semblance of a smile. Then he turned and strode to the tractor. 'It's only my dreams that are dead,' he hurled out as he crumpled the letter.

He climbed on to the Lanz and drove it into the rye.

As soon as he was aware of the plot, their brother-in-law protested, assuring them that he, an ordinary official, had no power to act in a realm so impenetrable as that of education.

'Don't spin me that yarn,' Pierre-Edouard interrupted. 'Official you may be, but this as well . . .' he said, placing his finger on the badge of the militia which his brother-in-law sported in his buttonhole.

'You wouldn't want me to take advantage of this . . . this responsibility, to get preferential treatment! The Marshal's Militia consists of honest people and . . .'

'Oh yes, we know that,' cut in Léon, 'but I like to come straight to the point in my business dealings, so I suggest a deal: either you get the girl into training college and get a grant for her, or tighten your belt!'

'What do you mean, my belt?'

'No more tatties, no more butter, no more chickens, nothing. You could come without your trailer, then, if you still want to come . . .'

'Well, you lousy rotten swine! That's blackmail!'

'No, no,' Pierre-Edouard calmed him down, 'we're just talking, that's all. Come on, if you look after Mauricette, on my word, I'll give you a ham.'

'You're asking too much, you two,' their brother-in-law protested feebly.

'And look here, on the day college opens, that is, if she's one of the students I'll put aside a packet of tobacco for you . . .'

'A big one?' asked the official, licking his lips.

'Er . . . Two kilos, will that do you?' asked Pierre-Edouard carelessly. 'No? All right, I'll go to four; after all, if we can't help each other within the family . . . So, a ham, four kilos of tobacco and your other provisions, as usual; is it on?'

'It's on. But tell me, if I get a favourable response early on, will you give me a bit of tobacco in advance?'

'Naturally,' said Pierre-Edouard magnanimously. He took out his pouch and drew from it enough to roll three or four small cigarettes. 'Here,' he said, 'that will help you to consider the best way to get Mauricette registered and to get her a grant.'

The young lady began her first year at teacher training college in September 1943.

The Germans entered Saint-Libéral for the first time on the morning of 14 November. Until that day the village had never entertained any occupying forces, and there were even some old people – amongst those who had not left their house or garden for years – who had never in their lives seen a single German, except in a photograph after the Great War, and who demanded to be accompanied to the Church Square to appreciate that they were really there.

One of the first to be aware of their arrival that Sunday morning was Pierre-Edouard, who was taking the opportunity while Guy was out – he was at Mass with his mother – to check that his guns were still in good condition. He was worried about the damp in the stable where he had been hiding them since the beginning of the war, and he examined them periodically to see that no spots of rust were attacking the barrels or locks.

When the order to deposit all hunting rifles at the mairie had arrived, he had not for an instant considered obeying this command. He had meticulously greased his Hamerless, like-wise Jacques' Darne and Paul's Robust, wrapped the guns in oily rags and had slid them on top of a wide beam in the cowshed.

Then, without batting an eyelid, he had carried his father's old Lefaucheux to the mairie; it was an unusable gun, eaten up with rust, and its exposed hammers had rattled about ever since their mainspring had broken, some fifteen years earlier.

'Are you sure you can manage without it?' Léon had asked, straight-faced.

'Hey, what can one do; I obey orders, I do!'

But since that time he liked to get out the guns three or four times a year; to polish them, to feel their weight, even bring them to the shoulder, for the pleasure of it.

He was about to take aim at an imaginary hare which had just bolted between the cows' hooves, right beside Nicolas' room, when he heard the deep rumble of the armoured car which preceded four lorries loaded with men.

'They're all we need!' he murmured, realising immediately what it was.

He hurried to slip the guns into their hiding place, went out into the yard, and anxiously awaited the arrival of the Germans.

The five vehicles filed past the house shortly afterwards, went up the main street and stopped in the square; the men jumped out of the lorries.

Better go and fetch Mathilde, he thought; she'll have a heart attack if she bumps into them coming out of Mass. He endeavoured to remain calm, trying to banish the memories which besieged him; to chase from his mind the crazy vision, which projected a picture of a battery of 75s, there, in the courtyard, nicely lined up between the sheepfold and the house, and himself, as in days gone by, giving the order to fire!

'From here, set to zero, with shrapnel shells, I won't let one of them get away, not one!' he thought, as he marched towards the church.

When he reached the square he saw Léon parleying with an officer. He approached them, his hands in his pockets, and waited for the Obersturmführer to move away.

'What do they want, those horrors? he asked.

'Nothing, they're passing through, that's all. I think they have a rendezvous with another convoy . . .'

'Are you sure that's all?' insisted Pierre-Edouard, noticing his brother-in-law's worried expression.

'No,' admitted Léon. 'They've been told there were some maquis around here, so it's my guess they're swaggering about a bit, a matter of letting themselves be seen. But the other young fool over there,' he added with a nod, 'also warned me that they were shooting people who were helping the terrorists. My God, I hope they go quickly: we'd have a job explaining if the kids who came through the other day appeared just now!'

A week earlier, in fact, a dozen young people had come to the village. They just paraded about a bit, kicking up a rumpus at Suzanne's, proving that they weren't frightened of anything or anybody. They had no weapons but nobody was deceived; they were certainly the maquis. Besides, they had left an hour later bellowing the 'Marseillaise'.

'I know they're a bit excitable,' Pierre-Edouard reassured him, 'but if they are around here, they must have seen them arrive, those vermin!'

'Let's hope so . . .'

'And now look, see those fine warriors, there they all are at Suzanne's!'

'You're right, but really I can't wait for them to get out of here.'

They did not leave until late afternoon, about four o'clock. After having settled in at the inn to consume their tins of rations, they then spent the afternoon nosing around the village; but without any real determination, without even going into the houses, except at Deplat's and Froidefond's, where they bought some eggs, chickens and real farmhouse bread.

Then, on the orders of the young Obersturmführer and to the shouts of the junior officers, they climbed back into the lorries and left the village.

# 20

BERTHE Vialhe was arrested on Thursday, 2 March 1944 at seven o'clock in the morning, at her home in the Faubourg Saint-Honoré.

Before taking her away, but after having put handcuffs on her, the men from the Gestapo ransacked her apartment, emptying the drawers, overturning the writing desk and cupboards, searching in vain for papers which would permit them to start hauling in other people, or compromising documents which would confirm their prisoner's guilt.

They had no need of proof to condemn her – the charges laid against her were quite weighty enough – but they liked the work well done and the dossiers watertight.

After dealing with the apartment they went down to the shop, where again, with methodical fury but great cunning – fruit of long experience – they combed through everything which might possibly hide a piece of evidence.

Leaning against the wall, her eyes closed, Berthe was at last at rest. Now she had finally reached the end of that exhausting, secret journey which had begun in September 1940 and was drawing to a close on this spring morning. Almost four years of double-dealing and contacts, of alternating between clandestine meetings and fashionable soirées, between wanted men and the lords who ruled France.

A demanding, exhausting life, full of hopes and discouragement, of occasional joy and constant fear. The life of a hunted creature which doubles back, bolts along the edge of a field, crouches, sets off again, runs out of breath, stumbles and falls.

She opens her eyes and smiled quietly to see the worried expressions of the henchmen who were in the process of leafing through her files. Files which featured the names of generals, colonels, lofty German dignitaries, not to mention the insigificant ones like commandants!

She had always known that her only defence would be there, in those notebooks, those orders, those bills, and that if she were capable of denying the charges, the others would never provide the slightest proof against her. Suspicions, yes, as many as they wanted, but certainties, no. She noted with satisfaction that the men from the Gestapo piled all the papers into a case, and hoped that they would hurry up and examine them to find there, on every page, the great names of her Nazi patrons; patrons whom she was going to exploit further.

Two men hastily grasped her, pushed her outside, and propelled her into a black II CV Citroën, which moved off down the deserted street.

Two hours later, the concierge of the block of flats opposite the shop with the sign Claire Diamond, left with her shopping bag under her arm, in the direction of the Rue de Monceau, where a shopkeeper had promised the previous day that he might perhaps be able to supply her with half a pound of turnips – not swedes, real turnips.

It was on the way back, after an hour of queuing, that she dropped in on one of her colleagues in the Rue de la Boétie. She announced to her that there were no more turnips, but that she had nevertheless found several very fine artichokes, and slipped her, as she left, a letter entrusted to her by Berthe eighteen months earlier, which she had undertaken to carry to the Rue de la Boétie should anything happen.

After many a detour, pause and change of bearer, the letter arrived in Saint-Libéral two weeks later. It had been posted two days earlier in Saint-Yrieix.

Pierre-Edouard, helped by Nicolas, was in the process of shearing his ewes when Mathilde called him.

'Yes!' he said, without stopping his manipulation of the shears. 'I'm here, you know where, don't you?'

He was annoyed because the implement was cutting badly, pulling the wool and carving steps in the fleece, a rotten piece of work.

'Come here!' repeated Mathilde from the house.

'Dammit!' he grumbled, tossing the shears to Nicolas. 'You finish it if you can!'

He wiped his sticky hands on an old sack to get rid of the woolgrease, and set off for the house, convinced that yet again his father must be calling for him at the top of his voice; then he would forbid him, as he had done long ago, to speak to that little arsehole of a surveyor who was sniffing around Louise! It was distressing, upsetting, especially when Louise was present; her little surveyor and first husband had been dead for thirty-five years! But there was nothing to be done about it, except wait patiently until the crises passed.

'Well, has he started up again?' he asked, as soon as he saw Mathilde on the steps of the house.

She shook her head and held out the letter to him; she had opened it because it was addressed to Monsieur and Madame P.-E. Vialhe.

'What's happened?' he murmured.

'Read.'

'I haven't got my glasses.'

'Here,' she said, holding them out to him.

'Oh, it's Berthe!' he said straight away. He read, and turned pale.

Dear Brother, dear Mathilde,

If one day you receive this message, it will be because I have been arrested by the Germans. I do not know why, but I have the impression that they have been watching me for some time, though as you know, I have never concerned myself with anything but fashion. Despite that, since I returned to Paris it seems that they mistrust me. It is true that I was obliged to buy material on the black market, perhaps that's the reason. Anyway, don't worry, they'll release me quickly I think. They know very well that, like you, my dear brother, I chose which side, once and for all.

Most important of all, look after the children. Guy must be a big boy now; as for Gérard, he must be able to take care of his little brother Pierre. See you soon. Kiss Louise, Father, Léon, Yvette and Louis, not forgetting Mauricette. Greetings to Nicolas and the neighbours as well. Love to you both.

Berthe.

'What's that supposed to mean?' stammered Pierre-Edouard in dismay. 'And then, when was this letter written?'

'It's not dated . . .'

'So, they've arrested her,' he said, fumbling around to find his pipe. 'Poor little thing, and she was worried whether I'd chosen the right side.'

'She was in the Resistance, wasn't she?' asked Mathilde, who needed to have confirmation of her guesswork.

'By God yes, and she'd thought of everything, even that this letter might fall into the hands of some other bastards! My, she's strong, Berthe, she's really something!'

He was so sad he could have cried, but he was proud of his sister. Proud that she had known how to do battle according to her ideals and in her own way, and above all in silence, not letting a word of these activities escape to anyone; even breaking off with her family, to prevent that lot following the trail to Saint-Libéral.

'Do you think they'll release her?' questioned Mathilde.

'No; they've got her, they'll keep her, that's the rule.'

'And what can we do?' begged Mathilde. Since the beginning of the war she had complained of not being able to *do* anything. Nothing for Jacques, or very little, and nothing for Paul either, who had been silent since Christmas 1940.

'Nothing,' he said, 'except watch over her lad, and the two others as well. That must have been written somewhere, that our job would be to look after other people's kids.'

'But what about her, can't we try anything? Through the préfecture, maybe.'

'You must be joking! Your brother-in-law, we don't see him any more, he's much too scared of being picked up by the maquis if he comes here! Believe me, in view of what's happening, he must be thinking of how to keep his backside covered, and he's not the only one!'

He pulled her to him and stroked her hair.

'Come on, it'll soon be over. They'll come back, all of them, Jacques, Paul, Berthe, Félix; the war won't last. Or else it'll kill us all.'

Scream yes, talk no. Scream like a madwoman, without restraint, because that gave some relief and most of all because you couldn't do anything else.

Because the foul water in the bathtub stifles you, drowns you until thousands of stars explode in your skull, searing your brain, and the water full of vomit and blood seeps into your lungs, corroding and crushing them.

Scream then, scream all of the time, but not talk, never, say nothing. Turn each minute gained into a century of victory, each second of biting your lips into a battle won.

Say nothing, except: I am Claire Diamond, the fashion designer; you know that, your leaders know me! And repeat that ad infinitum, until the soothing mists envelop you and you float in them, to draw strength and gain fresh energy to scream anew.

But be silent, be absolutely silent, all the time, to the end, to the finish. And so prove to yourself and prove to them, that you are the braver, the stronger, the better. And that they will never succeed in breaking down that wall, that dumb citadel where screams are only silence.

Despite the shock they felt at Berthe's arrest, Pierre-Edouard and

Mathilde overcame this new ordeal by reacting with that surge of energy and courage which spurred them on and inspired them to defend themselves each time misfortune struck.

They rejected the morbid temptation to passivity and despair and faced up to it, not only by throwing themselves into their work, but also by not attempting to conceal this fateful blow which had once again struck the Vialhe family. Instead of suppressing the news Pierre-Edouard broadcast it, not out of misplaced defiance or boastfulness, but because he reckoned that with one son a prisoner, another God knows where, a sister in the hands of the Gestapo and a nephew who had disappeared, it was his duty to show everyone that he supported these four members of his family.

A year earlier, some people in the village would have sneered when they learned that Berthe was behind bars, because prison was shameful, even when the deed was Resistance. But everything had changed in a few months. There was more and more talk of the imminent landings and the few, select resistance workers of the early days were augmented by a constantly growing wave of patriots, the more boastful and noisy for being new converts.

Already the Marshal's most fervent supporters were becoming discreet, humble, careful. For them an ill wind was blowing, and they dreaded the storm which they heard rumbling all around. Even Father Delclos was tacking between two currents. He spoke no more of politics, nor did he rant against the maquis, who now often came down to fetch provisions in the village.

They also requisitioned shamelessly. In Saint-Libéral, those who came were content to make a few restitute their ill-gotten gains: they targeted the specialists in the black market and the collaborators – Delpeyroux and his friends were their favourite suppliers, and that was only fair – but rumours abounded of real sharks who were plundering the countryside. Taking advantage of the protection afforded by their supposed membership of the French Interior Forces, they held to ransom, even tortured, and mercilessly pillaged the unfortunates who were suspected of owning anything of the slightest value.

Luckily, these predators had not yet swept down on the village. Certainly it was cowardice rather than caution, for Léon, as soon as he got wind of their extortion, had no worries about announcing good and loud at Suzanne's one evening, that anyone who didn't know the difference between the Resistance and robbery would get the worst of a hunting rifle. As for Pierre-Edouard, he had recalled that his guns were in excellent condition; that he, and Nicolas too, knew how to use them, and that even Mathilde and Guy, if need be, would know how to slide a pair of triple-o cartridges into a 12-bore.

But all these stories, all these rumours, and also the difficulty of distinguishing at first glance between the real fighters and the scum, created a climate full of suspicion and uncertainty.

This changed to terror when the news surfaced, on 31 March, that sections of Vlassov's army – a formidable horde of Germans and Georgians who had just plundered the Dordogne – were now moving towards the lower Corrèze. They arrived in a terrifying flood.

Pillaging, raping, killing, laying waste to everything, the vast cohort first shed blood in villages quite close to Saint-Libéral – Villac, Ayen, Juillac – then went on to carry death, fire and horror to Brive, Noailles, Vigeois, Tulle.

Still in despair at all these atrocities, the inhabitants of Saint-Libéral received another terrible shock when they learned, on 7 April, that Father Verlhac, who had been in the Resistance from the first moment, had been shot two days earlier, in a ditch not far from Uzerche.

On the morning of 6 June, during the maths lesson, Mauricette made sure that the lecturer wasn't watching her and quietly opened the history book balanced on her knees to re-read for the tenth time the letter she had received an hour earlier. A long and beautiful love letter, which had filled her with joy and tenderness.

Jean-Pierre was well, he loved her more and more, and when this foul war was over – partly thanks to him, of course – nothing would be able to prevent their marrying.

It was during a meeting of the Young Christian Students that Mauricette and he had bumped into each other at the beginning of the school year. The two young people, though meeting for the very first time, immediately identified with each other and very quickly loved each other. Everything drew them together and bound them closer: the same ideas about life, family and ideals in general, and the teaching vocation which they both shared.

At the end of the first term the two young people already considered themselves engaged, and both of them had told their parents, without immediately revealing quite the extent of their feelings for each other and the promises they had made.

Pierre-Edouard had frowned at first. He had only one daughter, and had no intention of letting her leave on the arm of the first young whippersnapper to turn up. Then he had tried to find out more; he was not fooled and neither was Mathilde, for the way in which Mauricette talked to them about this boy proved that she did not think of him as an ordinary friend by any means.

'And where's he from, this remarkable fellow?' he had asked with quiet amusement.

'From Uzerche, his parents keep a small shop. You'll see, he's very nice . . .'

'Oh, I see, so he's going to come here?'

'Well, I thought that perhaps during the Carnival holiday, at Shrovetide . . . he could come, well, if it's all right by you . . .'

'Of course,' Mathilde had said, 'he must come and see us. I only hope that we won't feel ashamed of our house, because, you know, town people are used to fine accommodation!'

But he had never come. Between Christmas and Carnival the rumour had spread that nineteen-year-old students, too, would have to leave for the Compulsory Work Service. Perhaps it was only a schoolboy joke, a nasty hoax, but it had hit home. Three days later Jean-Pierre joined the maquis, and disappeared into the woods near Argentat.

For Mauricette the ordeal had been cruel, and the days were sadly depressing until at last the first letter arrived. So on 6 June and for the tenth time she re-read the fourteenth letter which Jean-Pierre had sent to her since his departure.

The joy which surged through Saint-Libéral at the announcement of the landings was short-lived. It lasted four days, then was shattered when the terrible news broke on the morning of the tenth.

It was the driver of a gas-powered bus who revealed the tragedy that had taken place in Tulle the day before. He did not know many details, but maintained that the Germans of the Third Reich Division had hanged one hundred and twenty hostages, and imprisoned more than three hundred. It was not until after the Liberation that the exact number of victims in Tulle became known: ninety-nine.

Pierre-Edouard was helping the wheelwright to shoe his oxen when he learned of the tragedy. Devastated, he abandoned his team, ran home and found Mathilde hanging out the washing.

'Tell me,' he called to her, 'Mauricette's young boy-friend, which maquis did he join?'

'Somewhere near Argentat.'

'Are you sure?'

'Yes, that's what she told me, but why?' She was worried to see his defeated expression.

'Towards Argentat, that's the secret army, I think, so he couldn't have been at Tulle. Well, I hope . . .'

'What's happened?' she asked again.

'An atrocity,' he whispered, 'a real atrocity. You know, I always said those young fools would cause disaster; they think they're strong because they've got sub-machine guns and now look what happens. No,' he said, shaking his head, 'that's not the way to make war!'

'But what's going on? Tell me!'

'They wanted to liberate Tulle, all alone like big boys; it failed, of course, and the Germans came. With their tanks against those kids, it was screwed up before it started! So that lot, the Nazis, in revenge for having lost a few men and especially for having got a fright, they hanged a hundred and twenty hostages from the balconies and the lamp-posts . . .'

He saw Mathilde devastated, shook his head in despair, then clenched his fists and went off to fetch his oxen.

By the evening, they knew that the Third Reich Division was leaving a trail of fire and blood behind it along the whole length of the main roads: arson and death on the Routes Nationales 20 and 89.

But that was not all, and the inhabitants of Saint-Libéral, who thought that the peak of horror had been reached, did not believe their ears when they heard of the martyrdom of Oradour-sur-Glane. That same night, at 2 a.m., a grenade exploded in the garden of the presbytery, a blast from a Sten gun peppered the front of Delpeyroux's house, and two shots from a hunting rifle were aimed at his brother-in-law's farm. No one was injured, and nobody ever knew who was the instigator of these reprisals. But because of them, fear gripped Saint-Libéral for several months.

Berthe would not talk, ever. They could return to fetch her from her cell, take her to 84 Avenue Foch, restart the interrogation, beat her, torture her again; she would not talk. They believed she was physically broken and morally annihilated, but they were deluded. Her body was shattered but her will remained intact. That will of iron; she drew immense power and strength from it. She had patiently forged and tempered it long ago, during her youth in Saint-Libéral, when she was forced to submit meekly to her father's relentless authority. So they could give her another beating, but they would not get anything out of her.

Besides, whatever they might do, even if they were to shoot her, they were beaten. The Allies had been there, in France, for nearly three weeks now, and nobody was going to throw them back into the water. And nobody would force her to say what she wanted to conceal, either.

She turned over on her pallet and could not suppress her moans, her body was so sore; it was one mass of cuts, contusions and bruises. With the end of her fingers she gently felt the deep gashes opened by the jaws of the handcuffs; between two interrogations the wounds had no time to close, and the pain sawed at her wrists.

But because she knew that lack of action is often quickly followed by an inability to act, she forced herself to move her hands, to shift her arms and legs, to react against the suffering which tempted her into soothing but dangerous inertia, a numb lethargy. She got up, as every morning since her incarceration, then washed herself carefully. Next she began to quarter her cell, counting the paces as she went.

She took 1,850 to cover a kilometre; then would come the time for a drink of coffee. Later, if she were allowed the time – that's to say, if there were no interrogation to disturb her day – she would resume her march. In the evening she would add up 9,250 paces, then would strive to reach a total of 10,000 before finally lying down, proud to have covered at least 5 kilometres, to have conquered her weaknesses and the terrible stabbing pains which every moment provoked.

The lock clicked and the door opened, well before the usual time. Berthe thought that she would have difficulty in completing her daily five kilometres, and allowed herself to be dragged off on a long, very long, journey: Compiègne, Strasbourg, Magdebourg, Ravensbrück.

After the delight inspired by the landings, then the brutal shock of the enemy's response in the Corrèze and elsewhere, Saint-Libéral relapsed into worry, depression and pain as they waited. It was more and more difficult to know whether the war was really coming to an end, as maintained by the growing numbers of maquis in the vicinity of the village, or whether it was going to continue for a long time yet, as the occupiers were trying to prove.

The atmosphere was murky and unwholesome, like a pond in August; exhausting too, a strain on the nerves, the result of constant, depressing instability, a disagreeable mixture of hot and cold, of optimism and despair.

It was now impossible to get to Terrasson, Objat or Brive, to sell produce there, without coming upon road-blocks, one after another. At the first, manned by the maquis, you had to prove your patriotism and sometimes, depending on the men questioning you, to give up, whether you would or no, a crate of plums, a couple of chickens or a basket of peas.

At the other road-blocks, those held by the Germans on the outskirts of the towns, you needed to prove that you had no ties with the terrorists who held sway in the countryside; that was not always easy, for the Germans mistrusted anyone who looked like a farmer. They were reputed to be assassins to a man.

To avoid these constant interrogations, which infuriated him, Pierre-Edouard no longer left the parish. Despite that, simply by climbing onto the plateau to go and work there, he had been stopped several times by these armed lads. Some were polite, friendly, and some even helped him bring in the lucerne from Léon's Letters field. But others had the suspicious air and untrustworthy look of those inclined to robbery and rape.

It was their presence which made him take the decisions to bring Louise and the children back down to the village. Coste-Roche was really too isolated. It was easy prey for the bandits, and what could Louise do against them? Neither Gérard, who was now going on fourteen, nor the other children, who were younger still, could prevent the house being raided.

Louise protested. At Coste-Roche she was fine; it was quiet, and the four children she cared for loved her as a mother.

'Yes,' she confessed to her brother, 'you know, I'm happy here, and if I weren't so worried about Félix . . . And then, you, Nicolas or Mathilde, you come nearly every day, so it's all right!'

'The evil doesn't strike during the day, it comes at night!'

'But I barricade myself in at night!'

'And so what? You're three kilometres from the village, they'd have the whole night to break down your door.'

'You're exaggerating,' she said with a shrug.

'Oh, you think so? Well, those bastards have made themselves felt recently, over by Perpezac and elsewhere too. Come on, don't argue; put your things in the cart and get going!'

'And the children? What about them?' she said, nodding towards the two brothers whom the doctor had entrusted to her.

'Bah – now, you know, I don't think anyone in Saint-Libéral will be informing.'

He saw that she was not convinced, and he placed his hand on her shoulder.

'Believe me,' he said, 'you can't stay here, it's too dangerous.'

'It's a pity,' she murmured. 'Here, with the four children around me, I nearly manage to forget that we're at war. And then,' she said suddenly, 'if I come back down, how will you fit us in?'

'Don't worry about that, we've worked it out. We'll put the four kids in the main room, Mauricette with Father, and you in our bedroom. Yes, it'll be a bit of a squash, but we began the war like that, we're not going to die of it now! And then, it won't be for as long as it was before!'

July passed, and with it the harvests. In the village the dark and depressing atmosphere still prevailed, that mixture of hope and joy stifled at birth by the fear of what the morrow might bring.

Already everyone was aware that certain people – whose political orientation was well known – were using their role in the Resistance as justification, and making preprations to sweep out all those who had opposed them in the past on the town councils; it was plain and unmistakable. Moreover, Tavet, Brousse and Bernical boldly asserted that Léon, and reactionaries like him, had had their day and would soon have to go, whether they would nor no.

At first Léon let them talk; as the sneers and even threats continued to grow, he went into action on the evening of 13 August. Surrounded by Pierre-Edouard, Maurice, Edouard Lapeyre and also Delpy, he walked into Suzanne's, where he knew that Tavet and his supporters, plus several armed maquis, were holding a meeting.

'Right,' said Léon, after ordering a bottle of wine, 'so it seems someone wants to settle some old scores?' He filled his friends' glasses, turned round and gazed deliberately at the dozen or so youths who were joking and fingering their machine-guns and their grenades.

'Tell me, Tavet,' he asked quietly and with a smile, 'I didn't know that you had friends amongst the collaborators!'

'What?' growled Tavet, getting up.

'Hey!' said Léon, shrugging. 'Him, there, the little red-head, isn't he Feix's son from Meyssac? And the other one, over there, with his beret over his eyes, that must be Jeannot, Louisette's brother from La Roche-Canillac? Yes? Oh, I knew that by touring all the markets I'd end up knowing a bit about the world around me . . .'

'And so what?' cried Louis Brousse.

'Oh, nothing,' Léon reassured him. He drank a mouthful and put down his glass. 'Nothing, except that the little redhead's father has been trading with the Jerries right through the war, didn't you know that? Ask him then, the boy, why he only joined the maquis three months ago and more than fifty kilometres away from his home . . . Because from what I'm told, there are plenty of real maquis around Meyssac and Chauffour! And you, Jeannot! Don't hang your head like that! Have you told these fine pillars of the law that your sister is a whore in Brive, sometimes with the Boche, sometimes with the militia – it's so convenient, one night in the Terminus Hotel, the next at the Hotel du Parc, she only has to cross the Avenue de la Gare . . .'

'My God!' yelled Jeannot, getting up, 'I'll kill you for that!'

'Oh yes,' said Léon without moving, 'but you'd better shoot me in the back, because if I see you I won't miss.'

'In any case, they're not responsible for what their families do!' protested Martin Tavet.

'That's true,' admitted Léon, 'but it could cause a lot of gossip eh?'

'And what about you, what did you do during the war?' called out Louis Brousse.

'The same as you, old fellow, nothing, so we're quits!' He turned his back, filled his glass once more, then quickly faced them again. 'Right,' he cried, 'now we've got to know each other, the joke's over. You choose your friends where you like, that's your business. But don't muck around with us, because we could turn nasty too. You can't teach us any lessons; if anything it'd be the other way round!'

'Calm down, Léon,' the doctor intervened with a smile, 'you're not going to teach these gentlemen what all the honest people in the village already know! You're not going to tell them, for example, that your nephew Paul was one of the first to reach London, nor that Félix, Pierre-Edouard's godson, did the same thing, and least of all that Berthe is in the hands of the Gestapo . . .'

'That's true,' confirmed Pierre-Edouard, joining in the game, 'you're not going to tell them that the doctor spends more time treating the maquis than his own patients; you can be sure that Tavet knows all that!'

'Dammit,' agreed Léon, 'he also knows very well that Maurice's son has been in the maquis for a year over Terrasson way; isn't it true you know that?'

'And so what?' called a youth, brandishing his gun. 'What's that to us?'

'Nothing,' conceded the doctor, 'but you're young; if we say all this, it's so that you know that others besides your friends have fought and are still fighting!'

'And so that you know as well, and your mates too, that in Saint-Libéral we're not used to being pushed around by just anyone, even if he's wearing a fine armband, even if he has a machine-gun! Here we choose the ones we want to elect, understand, Tavet?' added Léon drily.

'We'll talk about this some other time,' promised Tavet.

'But of course,' agreed the doctor. 'As soon as the war is over we'll need to vote again, so we'll see. But meanwhile, the urgent matter is to kick out the Boche, isn't it? While we're on that subject, my children,' he said turning to the young people, 'I wonder what you're doing still here. As far as I know, all your comrades in this sector are busy encircling Brive; perhaps there's some useful work to be done over there, eh?'

'We haven't received any orders,' cried one of the youths, 'and it's not for you to give us any!'

'But I'm not giving you any, don't worry. It's just that if I were you, I'd be a bit embarrassed to be drinking shots here when my mates were exchanging shots with the enemy thirty kilometres away . . .'

'Those poor young things,' sighed Suzanne suddenly, 'they're so sweet!'

Without realising it, she broke the dangerous tension which was building up in the bar, for all the men, whatever their opinions, burst into laughter.

'Bless you, Suzanne!' spluttered the doctor. 'You're a real mother to them, a real mother hen!'

And the laughter intensified, for they all knew that Suzanne, despite her forty-eight years, had been indulging her fancies – beyond her wildest hopes – ever since the maquis had been roving the area.

'So what?' she said blushing. 'It's better than making war or politics!'

'Yes, yes,' shouted the youths.

'Vote for Suzanne!' yelled one of them.

'In the nude!' suggested another.

The doctor leaned towards Léon and Pierre-Edouard.

'That's better,' he whispered. 'Just now I was afraid that one of these crazy young men would shoot us point-blank!'

'No, no,' Léon reassured him while continuing to laugh, 'there was no danger, we were just in front of Suzanne, they were much too afraid of hitting her! You don't imagine that it's Tavet's beautiful eyes that keeps them here till this hour!'

One morning three days later, the village learned to its joy that Brive had been liberated. But the bells did not ring in Saint-Libéral, for when Léon and the members of the council went to the presbytery determined to demand – firmly if necessary – that the priest pull on his bells to announce the event properly, they found only a poor red-eyed man with a terrified expression, who announced to them between sobs that his old mother had given up her soul on the previous evening, on the Feast of the Assumption.

And the poor man was so pitiful, so helpless, that no one had the courage to celebrate in front of him for he was the very image of defeat.

# 21

AFTER Brive, the first town in France to liberate itself independently, Tulle and Ussel were next to rid themselves of their occupiers. Now at last the Corrèze was free, and neither the bombardment of Brive nor the few sporadic attempts by the enemy to recapture the place succeeded in marring the happiness of the Corrèziens.

This joy increased, the following week, with the announcement of the liberation of Paris; many then thought that the war was over. At the Vialhes', as everywhere, the events were properly celebrated. However, neither Pierre-Edouard, nor Mathilde, nor Louise were fooled by the rather forced enthusiasm which they tried to show; during these days of jubilation the absence of Berthe, Félix, Jacques and Paul weighed heavily.

And suddenly on 30 August, during the siesta, when Mathilde, Louise and Mauricette were doing the washing-up, when Pierre-Edouard and his father were sleeping and the children had gone off to hunt for crayfish in the Diamond, Léon's shout echoed round the yard. A cry of delight, followed by the sound of running and the crash of a door being flung open.

'The boy's in Paris! He's in Paris!'

'Paul? Félix?' said Mathilde and Louise simultaneously.

'Paul!' cried Léon, hugging his sister. 'He's just telephoned me! The boy's in Paris!' he repeated to Pierre-Edouard, who had just come out of the bedroom.

'I heard,' murmured Pierre-Edouard, stuffing his shirt tails into his trousers. 'Explain,' he said.

He was so agitated that he stuck his pipe between his teeth and tried to light it, although he had omitted to fill it. He became aware of his absent-mindedness and smiled apologetically.

'Explain,' he said again.

'He's been in Paris since yesterday. He telephoned as soon as he could, it hasn't been easy. But he'll call our house again this evening, at seven o'clock so you can be there, and then we were cut off . . .'

'And . . . And is he all right?' asked Mathilde.

'Of course! Just imagine,' Léon shouted to his brother-in-law, 'he's a second-lieutenant!'

587

'Damnation!' swore Pierre-Edouard. 'He's been made an officer, the devil!'

To him, who had ended the 1914 war with the rank of sergeant-major, his son's stripes had a symbolic significance. Paul had outstripped him, had done better than him; it was fantastic. He felt himself brimming with pride, pulled Mathilde to him and kissed her.

'Did you hear that,' he said to her, 'your son's an officer!'

'And that's not all,' continued Léon. 'Do you know which branch he's in? In the parachute corps!'

'My God,' said Mathilde, 'he must be mad!'

She was suddenly paralysed with fear and trembled in retrospect, to imagine that he had thrown himself from an aeroplane, and that he was perhaps going to do it again.

'He must be mad!' she repeated weakly.

'No, no!' Pierre-Edouard reassured her, as he grew prouder every moment. Then he looked at Louise, who was standing a little to one side and listening without saying anything. He saw that she was sad and smiled at her: 'We'll hear from Félix soon too, you'll see. I'm sure of it, we're on to a run of luck!'

She nodded, but turned away so that neither her brother nor Mathilde or Léon should have their pleasure spoiled by seeing her so downcast, still in such anguish. She was happy that Paul was safe, naturally, but Paul was her nephew, not her son.

In the evening, she nevertheless went to Léon's house with the others to await the promised telephone call. But they all waited in vain; the phone remained dumb.

'Well, that's it,' said Pierre-Edouard towards eleven o'clock, 'he hasn't been able to ring . . .'

He was disappointed and sorry for Mathilde; she had been so happy to think she would be able to hear her son's voice after four years of silence.

'You know,' explained Léon, 'the telephone, at the moment, works when it feels like it. Perhaps he'll call tomorrow, and then I'll come and fetch you.'

Paul did not call again, but wrote a long letter which arrived two days later. A letter which Pierre-Edouard first read out loud so that the whole family could appreciate it, and which Mathilde read and re-read alone to herself. She was now overflowing with happiness and, if it had not been for the postscript, she too was ready to believe that the war really had ended and that her sons would soon be returning; but Paul's last lines were unambiguous:

'We're setting off again this very evening, I don't know where to, but it's certainly not for a rest . . .'

Félix did not write, did not telephone; he came. He arrived by the morning bus. Dead tired, for he had journeyed through the night, he was a little disappointed to find no one at the farm but two unknown children and his grandfather, who obviously did not recognise him. The old man was sitting in front of the house and mumbling endlessly as he played with an old stick, which he turned to and fro between his hands.

'Who are you?' Félix asked the older of the two boys.

'Me, I'm called David, and he's my brother Benjamin,' explained the child, making no attempt to hide how much he admired the visitor's uniform. 'Say, you're not Paul, are you?' he asked suddenly.

'Oh no, I'm Félix.'

'Hey, it's Uncle Félix!' exclaimed the younger boy.

'But . . . I don't know you!' said Félix with furrowed brow.

'Granny Louise told us about you!' explained the little lad ecstatically.

Félix, completely at sea, decided to leave any requests for explanation until later.

'Where's all the family?'

'On the plateau,' pointed David, 'they're harvesting the buck-wheat. We're staying here to keep Grandpa Jean-Edouard company – and to look after him, too,' he added with a serious air.

'As if that explains everything,' murmured Félix. 'And are they well, at least?'

'Yes, yes!'

'All of them?' he insisted.

'Oh yes!'

'I'm going up there.'

It was just before he reached the plateau, while he was still under the chestnut trees which lined the track, that he noticed the child twenty paces from him, stalking blue tits in the bushes, his catapult in his hand.

The boy, knee-high to a grass-hopper and bronzed like a sun-ripened apricot, watched him warily as he approached. A thick fringe of chestnut hair fell over his eyes; he tossed it back with a quick flick and observed the stranger coming towards him.

Félix stopped, gazed at him, and then crouched down to be at his height. He caught his breath and bit his lips, almost surprised that the lad did not hear the wild beating of his heart, the heavy thumps booming out his happiness.

'Is it you, Pierre?' he whispered at last. 'Yes, it's you, you look so much like your mother!'

The lad frowned, and cautiously withdrew a step. Félix smiled at him and held out his hand.

'Don't be scared, please don't be scared. Nobody should be scared of their papa.'

'Papa?' the little fellow asked faintly. He hesitated again; seemed to make a huge effort, perhaps to try to remember the large silhouette which had loomed over him one morning in February 1940. Then he pronounced it again: papa, as if to get used to the word, to make it his own. And suddenly, he jumped. Félix almost fell over backwards when his son threw his arms round his neck.

Félix had to leave again the next day; but his visit, despite being so short, brought a huge measure of happiness to the Vialhe house, restoring courage and optimism in everyone. As for Louise, she looked ten years younger.

They all gathered in the evening to listen to Félix's extraordinary epic journey. He had left Dunkirk as a staff sergeant and returned a lieutenant, after having reconquered parts of Africa, Italy and Corsica.

'And now what?' asked Louise.

'Towards Germany, of course.'

'And make sure you don't do it like in 1918,' suggested Léon. 'This time, give them a good thrashing, once and for all. That way, we might avoid seeing them here again in twenty years' time!'

'We'll make sure of it.'

Three days after his departure Mauricette returned from Tulle, in tears. She had set off for the préfecture, ostensibly to attend to her registration at the training college for the following year, but in reality to meet Jean-Pierre there.

A sad meeting, for her fiancé, without trying to soften an announcement which he knew was painful, and even before reassuring her that she was and would remain his only love, had revealed to her his enlistment in the regular army, for the duration of the war. He was proud of it; she was too, of course, but so sad as well, so torn. For her, the agony was beginning.

'I've been through it, too,' Mathilde told her. 'I know that's no comfort to you, but if you want the time to pass more quickly, be brave and strong. Cry if you need to, but don't get in the habit of it, or you won't be able to do anything else and the days will seem twice as long.'

'And you know,' Pierre-Edouard tried to help, 'at least it proves he's a man, a real man, who does what has to be done, even if it costs him something; that's good. I'm glad he's not a weakling or a shirker. I'm sure he'll make a fine son-in-law.'

'But you don't even know him!' sobbed the girl.

'Yes I do,' said Pierre-Edouard, 'you've been talking to us about him for months! Oh, that's not the same, I know, and it's true we've never seen him. But if I say he'll make a good son-in-law, it's because a man who can leave a beautiful girl like you and take up his gun, now, when he doesn't have to, must be made of the right stuff. That's why I've no worries.'

The gradual liberation of France did not bring the great economic changes which everyone was hoping for. There were shortages of everything everywhere, ration coupons were necessary for the slightest requirement, inflation was spiralling upwards.

Everything was scarce, if not unobtainable, and Pierre-Edouard, who still ran the farmers' buying syndicate, could envisage a time when business would have to stop altogether.

One September morning in 1944, he was re-reading, and grumbling over, the reply from Supply Services to his request for 2 tons of chalk nitrate – he had been allocated 220 kilos, which would allow him to give about 14 kilos each to the customers who had ordered some – when his nephew Louis, Léon's son, interrupted his work.

'Hey, Uncle!' called the boy, 'Papa needs you right away, he's at Delpeyroux's.'

'At Delpeyroux's? What's he up to at that idiot's place?'

But the boy had already turned on his heel. Pierre-Edouard hurried towards the alleyway where his neighbour's farm lay and frowned on seeing the gathering in the yard and hearing Léon's remonstrations. A black Citroën was parked in front of the house.

'What's going on?' he asked.

'These fellows want to arrest him,' Léon explained to him, pointing at three young men already surrounding Delpeyroux, who was white with fear.

'Arrest him? What the devil for?'

'Well, this is nice!' sneered one of the youths. 'Another one who wants to protect a collaborator! My word, it's the whole village that needs banging in the nick, we were well informed!'

'D'you want a thump?' Pierre-Edouard hurled at him, warning him off with a wave of his fist and sliding in beside Léon.

'These are the boy's from the Liberation Committee in this département,' his brother-in-law explained, 'they've shown me their cards.'

'And that gives them the right to arrest people?'

'Well yes, so it seems. I telephoned the gendarmerie at Ayen, they told me it's legal.'

'Well now,' commented Pierre-Edouard, 'If you have to arrest all the suckers who bawled "Long live the Marshal", there won't be many people left in France!'

The young man shrugged, and pushed Delpeyroux into the car.

'We're going to have a word with your priest too,' he warned as he got in behind the steering wheel. 'He's been identified as a collaborator as well. Luckily there are some true patriots in this dump.'

Léon was shaking with anger. God knows that he held Delpeyroux in very low esteem and considered Father Delclos an old mule, but to know that one or more of his electors had been informing made him furious; he was ashamed of them. He went briskly up to the driver and grasped him by the collar with the fearsome hook of his artificial hand.

'Listen carefully, little bastard,' he cried, 'I am the mayor, and those are the town councillors, and the others there, all the ones around the car, these are the people of Saint-Libéral. We don't like informers, and we've always settled things between ourselves. All right, you've got Delpeyroux on board, okay. He's a right bastard, but we'll still come and speak for him because he's one of our own. But if by any chance you go to the presbytery, you'll see – there are about twenty of us here; well, in five minutes you'll get twenty shots in your mug. We'll keep our priest and nobody in the Corrèze needs to know that he's been behaving like a fool; we know it, and that's enough.'

'Leave me alone! Or you'll be sorry for it!' protested the man.

'One more word,' growled Léon, without letting go. 'You can see, I've only got one hand left, but watch out, my lad; my other arm is bloody long, and his too!' he said, pointing to Pierre-Edouard. 'Remember, in the village we keep things in the family. Now get out, and I advise you not to stop at the presbytery, and not to set foot here again either!'

He finally released the man, who saw his chance and drove off like a maniac. The car took the road to Brive and disappeared.

Delpeyroux spent several months in prison, then was released. As he had promised, Léon went to testify; Pierre-Edouard, Maurice and Edouard Lapeyre accompanied him. And even Tavet and Bernical went along as well, to explain that their neighbour had at least never denounced anyone nor done any great harm, although they all condemned his political decisions.

Tavet and Bernical's testimony, inspired by sixty years of neighbourliness and friendship with the accused, got them into trouble with their party officials; besides this partiality for a man who, in the eyes of the revolutionaries, deserved a dozen bullets under his skin, they were blamed for not being able to oust Léon and his friends from the mairie.

Their expulsion from the party grieved the two men deeply, but did not stop them getting themselves re-elected on the socialist ticket when the municipal elections came round a few months later. These elections gave Léon and Pierre-Edouard an equal number of votes. Léon played fair and offered the mayor's sash to his brother-in-law, who declined it. The older he grew, the less he felt attracted to politics. And the struggles which were already dividing France again, strengthened his scepticism and his condemnation of all those who, on the pretext of serving the public good, defended their own interests before all else.

A week after the arrest of Delpeyroux, a grey Peugeot stopped outside the Vialhe house, and Pierre-Edouard immediately thought that the youths of the Liberation Committee had not disbanded. He prepared to receive them coolly, but it was a woman who got out of the vehicle.

'I'm looking for Monsieur Vialhe,' she said, seeing him on the doorstep. 'Monsieur Pierre-Edouard Vialhe.'

'That's me,' he said.

'Oh, good,' she said, as she came nearer. She fumbled in her briefcase, consulted a list: 'Ah, here it is . . . Is it you who's looking after the children David and Benjamin Salomon? Is that you?'

'Maybe,' he admitted.

'Well, I've got good news; we're going to take them off your hands.'

'Who told you they were in our way?' he growled. 'And before you go any further, who are you?'

She held out a card embossed with the Red Cross.

'The two children have cousins living in Morocco, who asked us to make enquiries. It took a long time! They're ready to take in the boys. Where are they, the kids?'

'I don't know about all that,' he said brusquely. 'I only know one thing; someone entrusted the children to us, and I won't let them leave until that person has confirmed your story!'

'But, sir! I'm from the Red Cross!'

'What's that to me! I've been protecting these children for fourteen months, you don't think I'm going to let them leave with any old person!'

He was furious with this woman, who had dared to say she was going to take the children off his hands, just as coldly as a butcher coming to take delivery of a consignment of lambs! Mathilde and he had become attached to these children; they were well behaved, didn't make a fuss, and got on well with Gérard and Pierre; they were part of the family. Of course they couldn't stay in Saint-Libéral for ever, but there was a difference between that and loading them up like livestock!

'Where are they?' insisted the woman. 'I have the right to see them at least!'

'No, until I've checked up on your story, you've no rights.'

'Oh, I see,' she said, 'you probably want to be repaid the cost of their board. I should have expected it, with peasants . . .'

'Get out!' he shouted, advancing a step. 'I've never hit a woman, but it won't be long before I do!'

She took fright and ran to her car. He watched her go and shrugged. Then he smiled and thanked heaven that Mathilde had not been present at the interview. She was picking nuts with Mauricette, Louise and the children.

'She would have scratched out her eyes!' he murmured with a laugh. 'Yes, my girl, you were lucky that she wasn't here, my little Mathilde! She'd certainly have made you pay for their board, with a slap round the face probably!'

But he was worried, and set off immediately to tell Dr Delpy what had happened.

It was not until three months later, shortly before Christmas, that David and Benjamin left the Vialhe family. Beforehand, to make sure that the children would be happy in their new family, Pierre-Edouard and Mathilde had insisted that Deply get in touch with these cousins; they themselves had then written to finalise the details of the journey. The two boys were to take the train to Marseilles, where the organisation would receive them and accompany them as far as Rabat, where their cousins lived.

'So that's that,' said Pierre-Edouard when he discussed it all with the doctor. 'I'll be going with them as far as Marseilles, we're leaving the day after tomorrow.'

'You know,' commented the doctor, 'I think that you and Mathilde have done everything you could possibly have done. It's a long way, Marseilles, that's true, but I think the kids are old enough to take the train alone.'

'Possibly, but if they were my children, I'd really like someone to be there to hold their hands until they get on the boat.'

Three days later, it was with a heavy heart that he left the children in the middle of a bunch of kids who were also joining some distant cousin, ancient aunt or uncle, across the sea.

'It wasn't very nice,' he confessed to Mathilde on his return. 'They were like a litter of puppies abandoned beside a pond. Well, at least over there they'll be in their own family, that's one consolation.'

'Tell me, Uncle,' asked little Pierre during the evening meal, 'are you going to take Gérard to the boat as well?'

'And why should I take him?'

The boy shrugged.

'That's what he told me,' he explained.

Pierre-Edouard looked at the older boy, who was hiding his face and blushing.

'Gérard was just having a joke with you,' he reassured him.

'Well, why was he crying, then, when he said it?' insisted the child.

'Huh, you're imagining it! Anyway, Gérard's fourteen now, who cries at that age?'

'Well, nobody.' Pierre accepted this. But he was confused, looking first at his grandmother, then his uncle and his aunt, then at Guy, and finally at Gérard, who had now stopped eating.

'Don't worry,' Mathilde reassured him, 'Gérard will stay here until Aunt Berthe comes back, soon I'm sure. He'll be staying because he's one of the family, like a cousin, you know!'

'Ah, you see!' crowed the boy looking at Gérard. 'I knew we were cousins really!'

'But of course!' interrupted Louise. 'Now eat up if you want to grow as big as Gérard – as your cousin,' she added with a smile.

Jacques and André ran away on 20 January 1945. They had learned, the previous day, that the evacuation of Stalag 1B, to which they were still administratively attached, had begun, and that the prisoners were leaving on foot for an unknown destination.

So, instead of waiting passively for someone to come and collect them from the farm, they gathered up their modest belongings, dressed themselves as warmly as possible, and in the night left the tiny bedroom adjoining the cowshed where they had slept for almost five years.

They walked through the long byre, where they knew each cow, and emerged into the darkness. Jacques nevertheless felt some remorse as he broke open the lock to the cellar where old Karl matured his cheeses; Karl and his wife had always been good to them. What was more, with all four of their sons now killed on the Russian front, they too had suffered terribly in this ghastly war. But that was just what war was like. So Jacques and André filled their haversacks with cheeses, grabbed several kilos of onions and two bottles of schnapps, wedged the door shut again behind him, and left.

They marched in the direction of the muffled sound of cannon fire, which for weeks had indicated the position and progress of the Russian front. It was minus 30° and the snow came up to their knees; so the farm dog, who had watched their thieving with wagging tail, gave up following them as soon as they entered the forest.

Three days later, when they were at the end of their strength, dying of cold, hidden in the corner of a shed ripped open by a shell, the first Russian tank suddenly appeared. Five minutes later, hardly daring to believe that they were free at last, they fell into the arms of some huge fellows in fur hats, who not only thumped them heartily on the back but also kissed them on the lips.

The scarcity of foodstuffs still prevailing in France encouraged Pierre-Edouard to increase all his vegetable crops. He directed his efforts towards the production of quick-growing varieties, and in spring 1945 laid down big beds of potatoes, cabbages, turnips, carrots and haricot beans. At the same time he took particular care of his cattle stock, for meat was also fetching astronomical prices.

All the market rates had gone mad anyway, and Pierre-Edouard had difficulty in remembering the time, not so long ago, when he had taken on Nicolas for the sum of 8 francs a day, or 240 a month; now he paid him 1,100 francs and was not complaining.

Confronted with spiralling prices which showed no signs of abating, he was sometimes seized with panic when he considered the family settlement which he saw growing daily more imminent.

He had to be realistic. His father, although still strong, was declining fast now, and the moments were few and far between when he seemed to recapture a flash of comprehension. He was a heavy burden for Mathilde and Louise, who cared for him like a child; got him up, fed him, washed him. They looked after him without complaint, and Mathilde had even cut Delpy short when he had suggested finding the old man a room in a hospital in Brive. Pierre-Edouard had been proud of his wife's reply; it was exactly what he himself would have said.

'No, Doctor, here we don't turn old people out of their homes; we never have, and while I'm alive we never will. If he were a baby we'd gladly look after him, wouldn't we? Well then! Father's just the same. He has the right to remain under his own roof and the younger ones must look after him; that's how it is and there's no other way!'

Despite that, and in spite of all the care which his daughter-in-law and daughter lavished on him, Jean-Edouard was sinking fast. In addition to the sadness caused by his father's condition, Pierre-Edouard felt deeply worried at the thought of all the problems which would arise when he disappeared.

But there were much worse things than material worries. April arrived, and there had been no news of Jacques since December. As for Berthe, the lack of communication was agonising.

Berthe rose before her companions, as she had done every morning since arriving in the camp, slipped on her clogs and glided between the rows of three-tiered bunks on which hundreds of bodies were crammed. And, as every morning, it was with dread that she gently touched the shoulder of the one she came to waken; a shoulder as dry and thin as a juniper twig which she always feared would feel cold and stiff. She put out her hand, and sighed as she noted the warmth of the body.

'It's time,' she whispered.

So in the darkness the skeleton arose: a thin silhouette, puny and frail, of a girl of eighteen whom Berthe had been tirelessly willing to live, every day, every hour, for seven months. A life which wanted to flee, to escape, finally to leave the thirty-two miserable kilos of bones, and grant little Marie the rest she was seeking.

Berthe and she had travelled in the same convoy, suffering the same blows, and, in their accursed railway wagon, the same torture by thirst. Then they had experienced identical horror on discovering the world of the Ravensbrück camp: eleven huge blocks and sixteen small ones, populated by twenty thousand ghosts of women who were constantly urged to work twelve hours a day by other women – other plump women.

Very quickly, Berthe had sensed that Marie wanted to die; that she was letting herself slip away and that, if not supported, she would drift away before long, like the fine ash in the stinking, black smoke streaming out of the crematoria.

So, because she was inspired by a fierce will to live and to win, a will so strong that she had to share it, she had immediately taken Marie under her wing. She never left the young girl, constantly encouraged her, sometimes treating her harshly to force her to live and, against all logic, to make her believe that one day soon the nightmare would end.

And until now, Marie had survived. In some crazy way, incredibly, beginning with this duty imposed by Berthe of getting up each day before their companions, to enable them to wash in peace, before the mass of detainees surged around the tiny water taps, jostled and knocked about by the Kapos, those other women whose rags were adorned with a green triangle.

'Here,' Berthe had told her, 'everything is compulsory, we're ordered and dictated to on every side, so we must invent our own duties. They are what will save us, because we fulfil them of our own volition and when it pleases us!'

To wash at the time decided by Berthe was one of these deliberately chosen duties, and to do it despite exhaustion, cold or mortal danger. There were other principles like these: not to throw yourself like an animal at your mess-tin, for example, but to force yourself to eat slowly, despite the terrible hunger which knotted your stomach and confused your mind. Finally, the craziest perhaps, but the most subtle too, was to recite to each other long accounts of their past lives. Not tender memories – that encouraged nostalgia – but more demanding recollections, more factual.

'I will give you,' Berthe had said, 'the names of all my suppliers and their addresses, also of my clients. I will talk to you about the price of material, choosing it, the quality, the cut and how it's made up. I'll quote you all the measurements of my regular customers and explain to you how a model gown is created. You'll see, I have an excellent memory. And you, since you should have taken your bac last year, will recite to me all your lessons – all of them, you hear, I'm sure you remember them!'

And young Marie, a child lost in this hell, had acquiesced. Thus she survived, led by Berthe Vialhe's steadfast character; she rose each day a quarter of an hour before the others to wash herself, compelled herself to eat and not to guzzle, and recited her lessons in physics, maths, chemistry, Latin and Greek – Berthe understood none of it, but that was not the point.

'Come on,' whispered Berthe, holding out her hand and guiding her, 'we're going to win another day and they're going to lose it. They won't turn us into animals today either. Come on, dear Marie, you'll see, soon it'll be spring.'

Although the bells of Saint-Libéral had remained silent following the liberation of Brive, they pealed at full force on 8 May 1945. This time it really was Victory, the moment which history and mankind would remember as marking the downfall of a detestable regime and a Reich which was supposed to last a thousand years.

They danced that night in Saint-Libéral, at Suzanne's and on the main square; the prisoners were going to come back, and with their imminent return, life would begin again. Even Louise waltzed with Léon who, hugging her waist with one arm, waved a bottle of champagne in the other by jamming it in his hook – the froth spurted out in a serpentine stream.

Pierre-Edouard and Mathilde danced too. Now, they were sure, Jacques and Paul were going to come back, and even Berthe; she would return, it was not conceivable that she should not return.

*Yes, she'll come back*, thought Pierre-Edouard, smiling at Mathilde, *she'll come back, like Jacques.*

Sometimes Jacques wondered whether he had been right to escape. Since he and his companion had been found by the Russians and taken to a camp where other prisoners were kicking their heels, they were certainly not getting any nearer to France; they were actually moving further away!

Besides, the Soviet soldiers surrounding them, and the three daily roll-calls they were compelled to endure, had the familiar appearance of something extremely unpleasant. They were not prisoners, of course – not quite.

After a long detour across Prussia, interrupted by stops at Osterode and the camp at Zoldau, they had finally returned to Poland and the village of Hurle, not far from Warsaw. Then they waited. They celebrated the Victory fittingly, noticed bitterly on the following day that there was no question of repatriation, and resumed their wait.

Marie could barely walk. However, she managed to get out of the hut, leant her back against the planks and stretched out her emaciated hands towards the sun.

Free, she was free and alive. But she could not believe it yet; her mind was a turmoil of dreadful memories, horrifying sights.

Whatever she did, and despite the French and allied flags waving above the camp, the nightmare persisted; it was engrained, it sapped her strength. She closed her eyes, thought of what Berthe had said.

'Now we must be reborn. You, dear Marie, will be reborn when you can at last cry again; then I'll be sure you'll live!'

But she could not yet cry, and in the sunken hollows no tears formed; she felt herself as dry and stiff as a corpse.

A figure sat down beside her, and Berthe's hand gripped hers.

'Good news, Marie dear; we're leaving the day after tomorrow. We'll see France again at last; you're pleased, I hope?'

The girl nodded, but no smile enlivened her expressionless face. Then, because she knew that Marie could still fade away, like a flame at the lightest breath of air, Berthe continued her tireless struggle. Although she, too, was exhausted, almost finished.

'Come on,' she said, 'we'll have to resume our old habits again, we were wrong to give them up when the camp was liberated. Recite that poem for me, the one I love so much. Thanks to you I know it by heart but I like to hear it. Come on Marie dear! Come on! All right, you want me to begin?' In a voice broken with weariness she murmured:

> 'Ma petite espérance est celle
> qui s'endort tous les soirs
> dans son lit d'enfant . . .'[1]

She fell silent and clasped the girl's hand.

'Go on, I've forgotten what comes next,' she lied.

Then, at first with short gasps, slowly, gradually growing stronger and finally in a clear voice, young Marie continued:

> 'après avoir bien fair sa prière
> et qui tous les matins se réveille et se lève
> et fait sa prière avec un regard nouveau.'[2]

She stopped, moved her translucent fingers to her cheeks, and was astonished to feel tears rolling down. Then, with a rediscovered smile, she threw herself on Berthe's neck and sobbed with happiness.

---

[1] My little hope
sleeps each night in its
childish bed . . .

[2] having said its prayers
each morning it
wakes and rises
and says its prayers with
eager eyes

# PART SIX

*The Late Spring*

# 22

GUY and Gérard shot out of the mairie like two missiles and dashed towards home calling out the news Léon had just received on the telephone.

'Aunt Berthe's coming! Aunt Berthe's coming!'

The shout rolled down the main street and penetrated the seven alleyways of the village, announcing to everyone that Berthe Vialhe was at last returning.

For three weeks they had all known that she was alive, but from the newspapers they also knew what she had suffered in that camp. So, without anyone saying a word, but maybe because of Léon, who was seen to set off in the direction of the Vialhes', everyone in the village in the late afternoon of 25 May gathered together and, without even discussing it, they too marched towards the Vialhes'.

They all came; even Father Delclos – such a quiet, pathetic figure since the death of his mother – and old Léonie Lacroix, one of the doyennes of the community. Gathered in front of the doorstep, they offered Pierre-Edouard, Mathilde and Louise the gift of their presence. At first no one spoke, for there was nothing to say, but the happiness shone in their eyes.

'Thank you,' said Pierre-Edouard after a while, 'thank you for coming.' Then he turned to his brother-in-law: 'When exactly is she arriving?'

'Tomorrow in Brive, by the two o'clock train.'

'Thank you,' repeated Pierre-Edouard.

'We'll all go to meet her,' decided Léon suddenly. 'Well, if you'd like us to come with you.'

'Of course!'

'And we'll organise a reception at the mairie. The whole village must remember this homecoming!'

'Yes, you're right,' said Pierre-Edouard, 'and also . . .' He hesitated, placed one hand on Gérard's shoulder: 'And also,' he continued with emotion, 'believe me, Berthe is worthy of a fine welcome . . . Berthe, you know, is a great lady.'

The people of Saint-Libéral had all heard talk of the concentration camps, and everyone had been horrified by the photos shown in the papers, but no one had envisaged the sight which Berthe presented as she stepped down from the train.

The hurrahs and bravos, which they had all intended to shout when she appeared, died on their lips, as a tiny emaciated old lady, resembling Jean-Edouard, climbed laboriously out of the carriage. Thirty-four kilos of bones, rattling in a too-large dress, were topped by a gaunt little face with a halo of white hair, so short that you could see her scalp.

She gazed at them and shrugged slightly as if to say: 'Yes, that's how it is!' Then she finally spoke.

'What a lot of people!' she said in a clear voice.

And the sound of her voice, which they recognised, comforted them. Then, as Pierre-Edouard ran towards her, the clapping started. And it was in triumph, on the shoulders of her brothers and Léon, that Berthe was carried out of Brive station.

Much later, when darkness fell over the village, when Berthe was being talked of in every house, and at the Vialhes' the broken ties of kinship were being reforged, then, with a slight note of reproach in his voice, Pierre-Edouard said to his sister:

'You could have told us right from the beginning, you knew very well we were on your side!'

'Yes,' she smiled, 'I knew that, but I didn't want you to get too involved, because of your children – and him too,' she said, placing a hand a Gérard's shoulder. 'And if you were hiding Jews as well! I know you, you'd have approached the Resistance like your work, to be done thoroughly, without concealment. They would have caught you straight away. Look, they got me, and I was careful! So don't worry about it; we did what we had to do, each in our own way, and I think we did it well. And that's all that matters.'


After an incredible journey which took him, via Bialystock, Brest-Litovsk, Kovel, Rovno, as far as Berdichev in the Ukraine, where he had spent over a month in a camp packed with 50,000 refugees, Jacques arrived in Paris on 1 August 1945. His return journey had lasted three weeks, a long peregrination across a Poland bled white and a ravaged Germany. And then, finally, France.

After almost six years away, he was dreading the reunion with his family, for he knew that his father and mother would not be able to recognise the youth of other days in the hardened, bitter man he had become. But he was going to have to resume a normal life, although he felt morally broken; without enthusiasm, will or hope. The war and his captivity had destroyed everything which had given his life meaning before the hostilities: his studies, his vocation, Marie-Louise.

He arrived in Saint-Libéral the following evening, and was surprised to notice immediately the dilapidation of the village buildings, their obvious lack of comfort, the untidiness in all the yards, the messy dung-heaps with pools of stinking brown manure flowing out, swarming with flies.

He realised then that the five years spent on old Karl's farm had changed him. There everything was clean, orderly and convenient. He walked slowly towards the Vialhe house, and guessed from people's looks that nobody recognised him. With his old torn uniform, his bag slung across his shoulder, his hollow cheeks and wild eyes, he looked like a tramp.

Jean-Edouard Vialhe died on 10 December 1945, aged eighty-five. Existing in a cloudy world of his own for years, he had not been aware of the end of the war, nor of Berthe's or Jacques' return. He had not even recognised Paul when he visited on leave, and did not realise that Louise and little Pierre had rejoined Félix, now finally discharged, to live with him again in his forester's cottage by the Château of Cannepetière. He did not know, either, that his granddaughter's marriage was planned for Saturday, 13 July 1946.

The day before his death, Berthe helped Mathilde as usual to straighten out her father's immobile body in the bed which he now never left. The two women arranged the covers, smoothed the sheets, beat the pillow and plumped up the eiderdown, then they kissed the old man's warm forehead, wished him good night and left the room.

According to Dr Delpy, Jean-Edouard succumbed without pain, without suffering or sound, towards two o'clock in the morning. It was Berthe, sleeping in the same room as him, who realised at first light that he was no longer alive.

During the two days before the funeral, almost all the villagers made their way to the Vialhes' to pay a last visit to someone who had done so much for the community in the past. And cousins many times removed, who had not been in contact with the family for years, also came, for Jean-Edouard Vialhe was known and respected for thirty kilometres around.

Then, uniquely, all his descendants were gathered around him simultaneously: Pierre-Edouard and Mathilde, Jacques, Paul, Mauricette and her fiancé, and Guy. Also Louise, Félix and Pierre, and lastly Berthe, who at the church and in the cortège which followed the hearse to the cemetery, placed Gérard at her side and took his arm.

As for Nicolas, it was Pierre-Edouard who invited him to walk just behind them – in front of Léon, his wife and son, in front of the distant relations, in front of the neighbours. And nobody took offence at this. Furthermore, when they met again in the evening at Suzanne's to share the customary meal together, everyone considered it quite natural for Nicolas to join in.

He had the right, like the close neighbours and friends – those who had carried the pall, the coffin and the cross – like all those who during the dinner were to reminisce, sadly at first, about the old man, then to cheer up and search their memories for a reassuring anecdote, perhaps an amusing one, of which Jean-Edouard would be the focus. And none was shocked if smiles resulted. Thanks to this meal, and for its duration, Jean-Edouard lived again, and only his virtues were mentioned.


'Now, we must come to some arrangement,' said Pierre-Edouard to his sisters the following evening. He looked at Louise and Berthe, then noticed that Jacques was moving towards the door. 'Stay here!' he said to him, 'a settlement isn't a secret. Sit down – and believe me, I would have said the same to Paul and Félix, if they'd had the time to stay, and to Mauricette and Guy if they hadn't had to go back to school. The Vialhe land concerns all the Vialhes.'

Jacques took his place on the settle, where he was soon joined by his mother and Gérard. Whatever Pierre-Edouard had said, only the direct beneficiaries were left sitting at the table.

'Don't you think we should have waited a bit?' said Louise.

'No, things need to be tidied up and no one should feel disadvantaged,' Pierre-Edouard assured her.

'Bah,' said Berthe, 'all that really doesn't matter. It's you who's working it; the farm comes to you. That's quite normal.'

'Yes,' he acknowledged, 'but there has to be compensation; that's quite normal too.'

'Compensation – you gave me that in looking after Gérard and letting me stay since my return, we're quits. Besides, you know, my business is still going well, I had good managers, so your money . . .'

'No,' he interrupted, 'If I listened to you I would feel that it wasn't my property!'

'That's stupid,' stated Berthe, lighting a cigarette. 'And you, what do you say?' she asked her sister.

Louise hesitated, looked at Pierre-Edouard.

'Listen,' she said in a rush, 'I know that it will be difficult for you, but if you like, you could keep all your cash and I'll take the Combes-Nègres meadow. That's all I ask. It represents about what you'd have given me in money, doesn't it?'

He almost protested; explained that this field of more than two hectares was as necessary to him as the others, that the land should never be divided, and this pasture was excellent for stock. What was more, it contained several superb chestnut trees, and also some magnificent oaks along the edge.

Then he suddenly realised why Louise wanted this field. It was down there, right at the foot of those chestnut trees, that she and Octave had built their plans for the future forty years earlier; a pathetic future!

'Don't worry,' continued Louise, 'you could still pasture your cows there – after all, what does it matter to the animals whether the grass is yours or mine? You see, Combes-Nègres, that's . . .'

'Yes,' he broke in, 'I understand.' He looked over to Mathilde, seeking her help, but she was absorbed in contemplation of the fire and did not lift her head. 'Right,' he agreed at last, 'you shall have Combes-Nègres.'

'Thank you,' she said, placing her hand on his. 'I know that costs you more than giving money.'

He shrugged and looked at Berthe.

'All right, that leaves you. Do you want land too?' he flung out, with a degree of aggression which he immediately regretted.

'What do you want to do with Combes-Nègres?' Berthe asked Louise.

'Well, I thought one day perhaps, when I'm retired, I'd like to have a little house built there, if I can, that's all.'

'That's not so stupid,' agreed Berthe. She reflected and searched her memory: 'Tell me,' she questioned her brother, 'is the Teissonières paddock still in the same state?'

'Yes,' he admitted.

That was the only plot, of over half a hectare, which several generations of Vialhes had never been able to cultivate. It lay next to the track which climbed up to the peaks and was therefore easy to reach, but the incline and the rocks clinging to its slope made it impossible to work, even by hand. The only consolation was that the land was worth nothing: it was chalky and heavy, rejecting tools and plants. Besides, as its name indicated, it was riddled with tunnels used by badgers.

'Well, give me the Teissonières and we'll be quits,' suggested Berthe.

'The Teissonnières? But that's worth nothing! You'll never build a house on that slope!'

'Come on now,' she said with a shrug, 'I've seen much worse in America, a house can be built wherever! So is that agreed?'

'You don't mean it,' he decided. 'Louise's bit, that's worth it, but the Teissonières! If the solicitor knows where it is he'll think we're making fun of him, or that I'm swindling you!'

'Don't get involved with a solicitor,' she interrupted. 'Or at least, if you let me draft the plan, you'll see, he'll have nothing to do but copy it out and everything will be in order. Good, that's settled,' she confirmed. 'You keep the farm, Louise takes Combes-Nègres and I have the Teissonières. There, the arrangement's been made, let's not talk about it any more!'

'But . . .' he attempted again, embarrassed at the imbalance in the division.

'Let's not talk about it,' she repeated. 'Louise is happy, you are too, and so am I.' She fell silent and thought for a moment: 'And you know what,' she continued, 'we have to face up to it; if Father had made the settlement while he was alive, Louise and I would have received nothing, not even a pocket handkerchief of land! You have to admit that!'

'Yes,' he concurred, 'but if he'd suspected that I would let you have land, he would definitely have made his own arrangements before going!'

But he was laughing quietly as he spoke, and they all understood that the succession was settled.

Despite the satisfaction which it gave him to know that he was at last sole owner of the land, Pierre-Edouard was not completely happy. Firstly, despite all the conflicts and quarrels which he had previously faced with his father, his death affected him. It marked the end of a long era, and reminded him that he too was moving towards old age, weariness and loss of energy. He would soon be fifty-seven, and should be thinking of giving way to someone younger.

There was the stumbling-block. Unlike his father, who had clung fiercely to his privileges as head of the family, Pierre-Edouard was ready to share his position and responsibilities. He understood that the impetus to improve the whole farm could no longer come from him; he did not lack for ideas about future progress, only for enthusiasm, spirit and courage. Already he felt too tired to throw himself into the struggle, as he had done thirty years earlier. But he was now forced to recognise that none of his sons was going to fulfil his expectations.

Paul was much too happy in the army to consider for a moment leaving it; it was his true vocation, his reason for living. He was ready to take on the whole world, and hoped that he would be given the chance to do so.

As for Guy, he loved his studies and shone at them as his eldest brother had. He was a boarder at the lycée in Brive and, although Mathilde had been a bit shocked at Pierre-Edouard's choice of the secular system, she had quickly admitted that her husband's opinion had a solid basis.

'The Catholic school? No thank you,' he had said. 'Remember the difficulties Mauricette experienced after leaving there!'

But Mathilde knew very well that this was not the only reason; the other one was more serious and fundamental. It hinged on the attitude of Father Delclos during the war. From that time Pierre-Edouard mistrusted the clergy, was suspicious of them and not at all sure that one could have complete confidence in them.

'But think of poor Father Verlhac,' Mathilde had argued, 'he fought, and that's why . . .'

'Exactly, I'm afraid that all the good priests may have been shot! Now if there are only the ones like Delclos left, I'm not handing my son over to them!'

So Guy was at the lycée with his cousin Louis, Léon's son, and both were doing well.

That left Jacques, and with him everything was difficult. Pierre-Edouard and Mathilde had immediately seen just how the war, captivity and the break with Marie-Louise had crushed him, but they had hoped that in time things would settle down; in vain. His bitterness was so painfully obvious that nobody dared question him about his plans for the future. Did he have any at all?

During the six months and more since his return, the only comments he occasionally let fall were marked by an aggressive pessimism which pained them. When Mathilde had asked him if he was considering continuing his studies, he had laughed in her face.

'After a six-year break, at my age and after what I've experienced! Can you see me getting down to learning how to treat verminous bronchitis or foot-and-mouth disease, amongst all those kids?'

When his Aunt Berthe retorted that age was of no importance; that she herself, at fifty-one and after what she had suffered, was preparing to start work again, he had drily revealed the heart of the matter.

'Yes, indeed! You can do whatever you want, you were in the Resistance. You have some fine medals now, and all doors are open to you, as they are to everyone who chose that route! Look at the way that it's enough for any young idiot to stick on a tricolour armband for all the girls to lie down on their backs! But we fools who enlisted in 1940, where's the glory in five years of captivity? We've done nothing, right? And everyone makes sure we know it!'

'Don't talk stupid,' Pierre-Edouard had interrupted, 'nobody's blaming you for anything!'

'Perhaps it would be better if they did, at least I'd be able to defend myself.' And he had terminated the conversation by leaving the room.

Since then he had lived at the farm and worked hard, but rather like someone uninterested in the results of his efforts, almost like a wage-earner who is content to fulfil the task without being concerned about the running of the business.

Nevertheless, Pierre-Edouard had soon become aware of his skill and knowledge, but the only time he had alluded to the future of the farm, Jacques had shrugged.

'The farm?' he had said. 'You think it's beautiful, don't you? It's miserable! You're working here like at the turn of the century. All of it needs to be changed, all of it!'

'Well then, do it, for God's sake! Let's see what you can do!' Pierre-Edouard had shouted at him, annoyed at the unfairness of such a judgement.

But Jacques had turned his back, muttering to himself. Since then neither Pierre-Edouard nor Mathilde knew how to take him, but to see him so deeply embittered clouded the atmosphere for everyone.

It was Mathilde who found the original impetus to help the family out of the rut and escape the drowsiness which was engulfing the village. For despite the end of the war and the return of the prisoners, life was not going well in Saint-Libéral.

Jacques was not the only one for whom readaptation was painful; the other young people, whether they had suffered five years of captivity, two years of Compulsory Work Service, or had known the excitement of life with the maquis and the wild enthusiasm of the Liberation, could no longer accept life as it had been before the war. The routine had been interrupted, and for many the land no longer held any attraction; the work seemed so laborious to them, terribly monotnous and dull, and above all badly paid. So they succumbed to the lure of the towns.

There everything had to be rebuilt: there was no shortage of work, and even if the salaries were not as fantastic as some people said, they were secure, and so were the holidays. The young people therefore left, and the village suffered by this exodus.

It was obvious to everyone that the markets, for example, which had made the name of Saint-Libéral, were going to disappear, despite Léon's determination. Already they only attracted a few dozen sellers, and the stall-holders kept away. Like the Vialhe family, the community was not adapting well to the new-found peace.

Mathilde felt it was vital to act, and disclosed her plan. She had been nurturing it for more than twenty years, but before launching it she did the calculations, got the information, built up some practical evidence. Then, when she was confident of success, she enthusiastically revealed her project.

'Now,' she said one evening in February, having placed the soup tureen on the table, 'there's no need for us to live like animals any longer!'

'What are you talking about?' said Pierre-Edouard, surprised by her tone of voice.

'I'm saying that the settlement you made with your sisters spared you having to lay out any money. That money, if we save it, will lose value year by year, I'm sure of that.'

She poured herself two ladles of soup, waiting for her words to take effect.

'And so?' asked Pierre-Edouard.

'So we're going to make this house comfortable, we're going to extend it. I've had enough of living in a hovel where we're all on top of one another when the children are at home, where I'm ashamed to receive your sisters, and even my brother!'

Pierre-Edouard observed her, touched to see her so resolute and determined. She was always like that when it came to making an important decision, and he honestly admitted that he had never regretted having listened to her and followed the paths she had chosen. But here was a grand design; a bit too grand.

'Mustn't overdo it,' he said after a while. 'All right, we can do a bit of work, but we're a long way from building a château!'

'There's no question of that,' she interrupted. 'I don't want a château, I want to live in a proper house at last, and for that we need to extend. We've got all the space we need on the garden side.'

'Maman's right,' declared Jacques suddenly.

His father had grown so accustomed to his silence that he was astonished; as for Mathilde, she saw that she was on the right track and pushed home her advantage.

'We must add at least three bedrooms and a dining-room.'

'Not forgetting a bathroom,' added Jacques.

'Are you two in league or what?' demanded Pierre-Edouard. 'I'm not a millionaire, you know!'

'Maman's right,' repeated Jacques, looking at his father. 'You know,' he said suddenly, 'on the farm up there in Prussia, the farmer's house was as comfortable as a house in town. Yes, they even had a bathroom with a shower! And the whole farm was just as modern, so when I compare it with here . . .'

Pierre-Edouard very nearly forgot himself and shouted: 'You should have stayed there if it was better than here,' but he controlled himself, recalling the occasional comments Jacques had made about the general condition of the farm. He remembered, too, that he himself had quarrelled with his father thirty-five years earlier, because the old man would not admit that someone could do better than him in a sphere where he considered himself an innovator.

'All right,' he said at last, 'it seems German farms are more modern than ours; I've been told that already, and not just by you. But what about the money?' He sighed as he rubbed forefinger and thumb together.

'No problem,' Mathilde assured him. 'We'll put in what you'd saved for your sisters and borrow the rest; that way we could still keep a little bit in reserve.'

'You've just been telling me that money's going to lose value!'

'If it's left idle, yes, but we won't leave ours . . .'

'Oh, I see! More investment schemes with your brother!'

'And why not?'

'Right, we'll consider the matter, but why think so big?'

'Because I hope that one day,' said Mathilde, without looking at Jacques, 'I hope that you'll need it to accommodate your grand-children, and if you don't want to quarrel with your daughter-in-law, believe me, you'd better make some room!'

The work began in the spring of 1946, and proceeded at a good pace, for whenever possible Pierre-Edouard, Jacques and Nicolas helped the workmen.

Soon the new wing rose up, attached to the main body of the house; a solid construction of fine cut stone with a slate roof, a unit accessible from the old house by just one door. Mathilde had insisted on this, and opposed the demolition of the partition wall which would have enlarged the dining-room and made the new accommo-dation irrevocably part of the old.

'A door,' she had said, 'you can close it and be in your own place. Thanks to that you'll have two separate houses, if you need them; that's the best way.'

For a while, the extension of the Vialhe house provided the villagers with an interesting topic of conversation. Some found such an outlay completely senseless, others – the jealous ones – discreetly hinted that the Vialhes were investing the fruits of four years on the black market in their stonework. But no one believed those malicious tongues.

As for Pierre-Edouard, he let them talk, for he had no reply to the other argument, the only valid one, that reinforced all the criticisms: What was the use of all this outlay when Jacques remained as taciturn as ever and seemed to be retreating further into unsociable bachelordom? Neither would Paul, now in Indo-China, make use of it, nor Mauricette, who, after her marriage, would return with her husband to their small country school near Egletons. What about Guy? Nothing could be less likely: the land held little appeal for him and he did not hide the fact. So what was the good of this vast mansion? When he thought about it, Pierre-Edouard began to wonder whether, for the first time since they were married, Mathilde had been wrong.

As planned, and despite the recent bereavement which had touched the Vialhe family, Mauricette and Pierre-Edouard Fleyssac were married on 13 July 1946. The celebration was joyful but quiet, for it would have been unacceptable if Pierre-Edouard and Mathilde had provided too ostentatious a wedding only eight months after Jean-Edouard's death. All the same, because the young people thought that you should do away with all the troublesome bits of tradition and only keep the pleasing customs – even Mathilde had taken the lead by wearing mourning for only three months – they cheered the newly-weds and danced late into the night in the square.

However, those over forty, out of decency and respect for their forebear, refrained from waltzing. So Pierre-Edouard and Mathilde, seated with friends and the parents-in-law in the main room of the inn, did not see that Jacques too made the most of the celebration.

His whole evening was spent at the side of a ravishing little brunette, a friend of his sister's from Perpezac-le-Blanc. Michèle was twenty-one, as fresh and pleasing as a wild rose, and she burst into peals of laughter at the jokes he whispered in her ear.

Towards eleven o'clock when the two accordion players took a break one of the guests who had brought his gramophone and some modern records made the square of Saint-Libéral ring with unaccustomed music. All the young people shouted their delight and Michèle, who danced brilliantly, wanted at all costs to teach Jacques and frenetic steps to these newly arrived American dances which were all the rage in Paris.

Amused, he listened with good grace to his pretty partner's explanations, watched how the others were moving, and launched himself into a boisterous jive; for the first time in years, he was happy.

'You see, it's not difficult!' cried the girl triumphantly, when the record stopped with a nasty squeak of the needle.

'No, but it's tiring and loud. Look, wouldn't you like to take a walk somewhere quiet?' he asked, lighting a cigarette.

'Wait a bit, I know this record, the other side is a "slow", you'll see, it's easy. Slow, that's English for a quiet number,' she felt the need to explain.

'I know,' he said a little drily.

'Sorry,' she murmured with a blush, 'I forgot you had to give up your studies because of the war.'

The gramophone, duly wound-up by hand again, drawled out a slow rhythmic tune, a soothing melody, rather nostalgic.

'Come and dance,' invited Michèle. 'You'll see, it's quite simple.'

He embraced her, let himself be carried away by the music; felt the sweet pressure of the girl's breasts against his chest and the gentle touch of her fingers on his neck.

'You wanted to be a vet, didn't you?'

'That's right.'

She understood that he did not want to talk about it, and tried very clumsily to change the subject.

'I'd have liked to be a teacher,' she declared, 'but it was too difficult, I stopped in the third year. Still, it's better than nothing, isn't it?'

'Of course.'

'At that level, perhaps I could find a job in the town; I must find something to do, now I'm free. Yes,' she explained, 'my mother has been ill for two years, so I do her work at home. But now my father doesn't need me any more; my youngest brother is going to take up an apprenticeship in Brive.'

'The record's finished,' remarked Jacques, without for a moment letting go of the girl, 'shall we take a walk? All this noise make me feel dizzy.'

Nobody noticed that they had disappeared. Jacques led her towards the track which climbed towards the peaks. At first he was silent, then, encouraged by the darkness and the girl holding his hand, he began to talk, rather as if he were alone; to express the burden weighing on his heart, which had grown heavier since the war had destroyed his dreams. He recounted all his heartbreak, disappointment and despair; talked of the emptiness which he saw before him and which he did not know how to fill.

'I thought you were supposed to take on the farm,' she said when he fell silent. 'Well, that's what everyone around here thinks.'

'The farm?' he said bitterly. 'I'd as soon be a bishop!'

'Don't you like it?'

'No, it's not that, but you know, working with my father . . . Oh, not that he's unpleasant, poor old thing! But it's just that he's old; he has his ideas and I have mine. On the farm, you'd need to be able to start it all again from scratch, which I'd certainly like to do, but with my father that's impossible.'

'So what are you going to do?'

He stopped walking, sighed, then turned towards her and smiled at the face shining with moonlight turned up to him.

'What am I going to do?' he said at last. 'I have no idea. Perhaps leave for the town, like the others. Unless . . .'

He put out his hand and stroked the dark fringe from the girl's forehead. 'It's amazing,' he continued, 'until this evening I thought that my father being there was stopping me from taking on the farm, but I was wrong. It wasn't his presence that put me moff, but an *absence*. The most important thing was missing, do you understand?'

'Maybe.'

'Well, if you do, we'll see each other again?'

'Perpezac's not far, especially if you go over the top way . . .'

'That's right, I'll go the top way. Tomorrow then? It's Sunday. Tomorrow at two o'clock I'll be at the foot of the White Peak. Will you be there? Promise?'

She nodded and held out her hand to him.

'So you still don't want a Boche or two?' asked Léon when he arrived at the Vialhes' one evening.

'I've already told you what I think of that; me, I've seen enough of those grey-green uniforms!' said Pierre-Edouard, inspecting the cleanliness of his gun barrels.

It was the eve of the hunting season, and on the table lay his Hamerless and Jacques' Darne, in pieces.

'It's no joke,' Léon assured him. 'Following our request, I've received the reply of the departmental Office of Works and Manpower; the commune will receive seven extra prisoners of war, so if you want one . . .'

'No,' insisted Pierre-Edouard, vigorously deploying the swab, 'prisoners, I don't want any of them. I'm no warder!'

'Well, since Mouly and the others have been using them they're unhappy about it! And then, it's a good deal; bed and board doesn't even come to ten francs a day!' persisted Léon, who had enjoyed teasing his brother-in-law about this ever since the first prisoners of war arrived in the village six months earlier.

'*Miladiou*, I know!' grumbled Pierre-Edouard. 'Less than ten francs a day, okay, but what about the one who escaped from Maurice's and cost him a fine of fifteen hundred francs – not counting the pair of trousers, two shirts and the jacket he pinched when he left! Anyway, why don't you take some, eh?'

'Come on, I'm only joking,' said Léon, 'you know very well I feel the same ask you. Prisoners, I'd rather tell them how and which way to get going! All the same, do you know who's asked me for one?'

Pierre-Edouard shrugged and began to reassemble his gun.

'That rascal Delpeyroux! exclaimed Léon, laughing. 'Talk of a nerve! Well, I hope he gets a rogue who buggers off in a hurry! I'd really like it if Delpeyroux had to pay fifteen hundred francs for poor supervision! But that's not what brings me here,' he said, suddenly serious. 'Is Jacques around?'

'No, and I don't know where he is. For the last two months, as soon as work is finished, he's off!'

'I have my own ideas about that,' remarked Léon, lighting a cigarette.

'Me too, and Mathilde as well . . .'

'A girl, eh?'

'Of course, and I even know who!'

'Is she from the village?'

'No, it's the little Mas girl from Perpezac.'

'Mas?' Léon frowned. 'Oh yes, I know, it's little Michèle! The devil, he's got a good eye!'

'Yes, that's her. It was Ma Pouch, from Temple, who told Mathilde; she saw them together, over by the White Peak.'

'It doesn't sound as if you're very pleased, but she's pretty enough, that girl. He's got taste, has Jacques!'

'It's not that.' Pierre-Edouard was annoyed. 'The idiot never says anything, not a word! It's been a year since he came back, and I still have the feeling that he's just passing through!'

'That's why I'd have liked him to be here; what I've just learned might interest him. But it's you it really concerns. The squire's daughter is selling everything, even the château . . .'

'Everything?' murmured Pierre-Edouard, thinking immediately of the land on the plateau, not far from his own.

'All of it,' repeated Léon. 'She came to see me this afternoon. Yes, almost seventy hectares, thirty of them woodland – well, you know what there is!'

'Yes, yes. How much?'

'Expensive. She wants three million for the lot.'

'Bloody hell!'

'Well, yes,' said Léon, 'but I thought the land on the plateau would be just right for you. There are ten hectares up there; with those you'd have a nice little outfit.'

'Those . . .' admitted Pierre-Edouard. He thought for a moment, and continued? 'But what about you, what are you interested in? You're not going to tell me that you want to buy the château?'

'Well,' Léon looked a little embarrassed, 'I did think I might . . .'

'My God!' exclaimed Pierre-Edouard, 'but you're crazy! What do you want with that barracks?'

He was flabbergasted. All well and good that his brother-in-law should take the meadows and the woods, he could make use of them, but the château! Or perhaps it was simply to wipe out the memory of a poverty-stricken childhood: of his father hanging from the ridge beam of the barn – Léon had knocked against his legs one day in January 1900; of that sordid hovel where he'd lived, and all the humiliations he had been forced to endure, before becoming the rich and respected man he was today?'

*Yes*, he thought, *that must be it. He spent his whole life proving that he's stronger than all of us; the châeau is his revenge, his triumph! Damn it, if his father had seen this it would have driven him mad! It's incredible – Léon, the son of the poorest smallholder in the commune, Léon's going to buy the château!*

'It's incredible,' he repeated in hushed tones.

'Does it surprise you so much?'

'All things considered, no. But still, it's a bloody great sum, three million!'

'Oh, that . . .' said Léon with a shrug.

'That's right,' admitted Pierre-Edouard, remembering that Yvette's father had died fifteen months earlier, leaving them a considerable fortune.

'You understand,' explained Léon, as if he needed to justify himself, 'if we buy it, it's only for the boy. You've seen what a good student he is; maybe, he'll be a doctor or a solicitor, even a member of parliament. The château will be just the thing for him, more dignified than a plain house.

'All the same, if someone had told me you'd be sleeping in the squire's bed one day . . . !'

'The wheel turns . . . Right, these fields on the plateau; I've calculated roughly, that makes them thirty thousand a hectare. Will you take them?'

'You're crazy!' protested Pierre-Edouard, 'at that price! And look here,' he added with a touch of bitterness, 'we took out our savings to extend the house, so . . .'

Léon shrugged.

'Is Mathilde around?'

'Yes, she's doing some mending in the bedroom.'

'Tell her to come. Where money's involved, I've more faith in her than you!'

Pierre-Edouard nodded his head and called his wife.

'If only we hadn't done all this work!' sighed Mathilde, as soon as she heard the news. 'If I'd known . . .' She observed to Pierre-Edouard with an unhappy look.

'What's done is done,' he said.

'Don't make me laugh,' Léon commented sarcastically. 'You won't get me to believe that you spent everything on the extension!'

'Of course not,' admitted Mathilde.

'That would have surprised me, because you've been getting me to buy napoléons for quite a time. You must have a bloody cauldron full by now!'

'No we haven't!' she protested, 'and well you know it! We do still have a few. But I don't want to touch them, that's our savings in case we fall ill.'

'Rubbish,' said Léon. 'Believe me, the best investment is land. Thirty thousand a hectare today, and maybe three hundred thousand in ten years' time! Yes, I tell you!' he repeated at his sister's sceptical look. 'Look, remember what I paid for land on the plateau in 1918.'

'Two thousand two hundred francs,' she admitted.

'And one year later, the lot we bought together was already three thousand five hundred,' recalled Pierre-Edouard.

'All the same,' she persisted, 'thirty thousand francs, it's impossible. With the overheads, ten hectares would cost us at least three hundred and twenty thousand francs, and that's too much . . .'

'Borrow,' suggested Léon. 'It's a good time for it.'

'We already have a loan for the house,' Pierre-Edouard reminded him.

'Sort something out,' urged Léon, 'you can't let a deal like this go. I asked for two weeks to consider it. At the moment we're the only ones in on this, but in two weeks the squire's daughter will put it on the open market . . .'

'If only we knew what Jacques wants to do,' said Pierre-Edouard. 'If we were certain he'd stay, we could buy half of it on his account; that would be a good start for him.

'My God! Talk to him!' cried Léon. 'You're not going to tell me that you're frightened of him, that kid!'

'Well, no,' complained Pierre-Edouard, 'it's not that! But have you ever tried to talk about cattle-rearing with a mechanic! He doesn't care, it doesn't mean anything to him! It's like that with Jacques. He's not at home here, you see. Well, that's certainly what he feels, and I'm beginning to believe he may be right! Now, this land; we'll think about it.'

'Don't leave it too late,' advised Léon, as he headed for the door. 'And look, try and see what's up with Jacques. Really, he's beginning to get annoying, that boy!'

That evening, Pierre-Edouard waited until Nicolas had returned to his room, which was still fitted up in the stable, before rising from the table himself. He then went to turn down the radio and sat down on the settle.

Surprised at this manoeuvre, Jacques lifted his nose out of the newspaper and looked at his father. It had become almost a ritual: normally he remained seated at the table, reading and re-reading copies of *Chasseur Français* or *Rustica* while smoking a pipe or two, then went to bed.

'I must have a talk with you,' Pierre-Edouard said to him.

'Yes,' Mathilde backed him, as she plunged the plates into the washing-up bowl.

'That's convenient, because I need to talk to you, too.'

'Oh, good,' Pierre-Edouard said, somewhat astonished. 'Well, you begin.'

Jacques slowly folded the newspaper, lit a cigarette.

'I'm going to get married,' he announced.

'We knew that,' said Mathilde, smiling. 'Well, we thought so. It's little Michèle Mas from Perpezac, isn't it?' she continued, beginning to wipe a plate.

'That's right,' he agreed. He looked at his parents and his heart tightened to see them so happy, enlivened by his news. 'Yes,' he repeated, 'we're getting married next month.'

'What? Why so quickly?' demanded Pierre-Edouard, suddenly worried.

'Because time is short,' admitted Jacques, and jumped as the plate his mother was wiping shattered on the tiles.

'*Nom de Dieu!*' shouted Pierre-Edouard angrily, 'so you couldn't be bothered to wait a bit!'

He was disappointed, hurt; furious too, for what his son had just announced was a betrayal. The Vialhes of Saint-Libéral had never needed to blush for their behaviour in that respect. Even when Louise had run away to marry Octave, she had been able to marry in white, proudly, without pretence. As for Berthe, her past conduct had not been within the framework of village life.

'Look, you little sod,' he went on, 'look what your mother thinks of a marriage where time is short!'

Mathilde was crying, silently, as always. But she seemed so devastated by the revelation that Jacques felt embarrassed.

'Listen,' he urged, 'it's not a tragedy, after all! Oh, I know, it used to be something to be ashamed of, but look, it's not like that now, it's 1946, not 1920! Try to understand!'

'Be quiet,' said his mother, wiping her eyes on her apron. 'We don't need any lessons from you in understanding! Because it's you who hasn't understood how things are now!'

'All right, okay, we were too quick. But look, we're not the only ones! And now, that's how it is and it can't be changed! Anyway, we're both adults, and we'll be getting married on the twenty-sixth of October; it's a Saturday.'

Pierre-Edouard sighed, knocked his unlit pipe against the hollow of the andiron.

'Fine,' he said, 'do as you like. You said you were adults! Right, so you'll go all alone to the Mas family to explain to them that you've made a mess of things, that's all in order, is it?'

'That's what I was meaning to do,' said Jacques drily. 'I'm not in the habit of running away.'

He had never considered sending his father as a mediator, for, as soon as Michèle had told him that she was pregnant by more than a month, he had allayed her fears by assuring her that he would take total responsibility and act accordingly.

'We meant to get married on Midsummer's Day,' he'd said to her, 'but it'll be the christening then instead!'

But she had understood that he was showing off a bit, and that at heart he was contrite and upset.

'We've been stupid, haven't we?' she had continued.

'I'm the only one who's been stupid. You – you're just beautiful, that was all it took, it was bound to happen!'

'Our parents will take it badly . . .'

'Naturally, but that doesn't matter; it's our business, not theirs. And then, how do you expect them to understand!'

'Yes,' she had said, kissing him, 'I'm sure when they were young they didn't love each other as we do!'

'When is it to be, your . . . mistake?' asked Pierre-Edouard.

'End of May.'

'Right,' said Mathilde, beginning to pick up the pieces of plate, 'and apart from making babies and marrying, what else are you capable of doing? Any fool can do that, after all.'

Jacques was surprised at the coldness of her tone. He had certainly thought that she would take it badly, but that she would limit herself to simply rebuking him – it was not her way to nag.

'Yes, apart from making love, what were you thinking of doing?' Pierre-Edouard joined in bluntly. 'You're surprised to hear me talking like that? What do you think, little fool, that you were found in a cabbage patch? Good God, if your mother and I had followed our inclinations, you wouldn't have been born in 1920 but in June 1918, nine months after my leave! Only in our time, if we were thinking of the wrong side of the sheets, we considered the consequences! So, you dummy, what are you going to do, now you've made the wine before picking the grapes?'

Jacques was disconcerted. He would soon be twenty-seven and had never heard his father talk like that, nor his mother for that matter. He saw them as a couple united by great affection and long understanding, but he had always refused to imagine them as really in love, madly in love, like Michèle and himself for instance.

'Well,' he said at last, 'unless you don't want anything to do with us, we thought we could live on the farm, but . . .'

'Yes?' Pierre-Edouard pressed.

'That is . . . To prevent any difficulties, perhaps it would be better if we were independent.'

'That's exactly our feeling,' said Pierre-Edouard, and again his reply amazed his son. 'You want to take over the farm? All right, but I'm not old enough or rich enough to sit around doing nothing, so what do you suggest?'

Jacques had been turning over this problem in his mind. He had even considered going to work in the town. With his two baccalauréats, one year in veterinary college and five in captivity, he was confident of finding a job, as a civil servant for instance, in some administrative capacity.

But the idea of having to spend eight hours a day in an office, to carry out some boring task under the thumb of a departmental supervisor, had repelled him. He was not one to take orders, nor to fit in to fixed working hours, still less to wait placidly for his paid holidays and retirement.

Once he had wanted to be a veterinarian, because he liked the profession but also because he thought he could be his own master. Since this avenue was now irrevocably closed to him, it would be better to find one where he could at least keep his freedom, use his initiative, take responsibility and not be accountable to anyone but himself. The land gave him that, provided that his father understood his conditions.

'You let me work half the land as I think fit, we help each other with work, but each does as he wishes on his own ground, how's that?' he asked.

Pierre-Edouard deigned to smile.

'You're greedy, you devil! Half of it? If I'd said that to my father he'd have boxed my ears!'

'Tell him Léon's news,' interposed Mathilde.

Pierre-Edouard hesitated, wondering whether Jacques was motivated by love for the land or the need to find a job; he rejected the niggling doubts, and looked to the future.

'If you like, you could have ten hectares on the plateau, the château's fields; they're for sale. But if you want that land, you'll have to manage to buy half of it in your own name. Not got enough money? We had less than you when we got married; your mother made me take out a loan, and she was right. As for the rest of the land, we'll take care of it and make it over to you.'

'Really?' Jacques was ecstatic. 'You're not joking?'

'Really. We can't let you have the whole farm yet, because we've got to live, but you can definitely have those ten hectares belonging to the château.'

'Bloody hell, that's good news!'

'Yes,' said Mathilde, '*that* is . . .'

'Oh, and the rest too!' cried Jacques. 'You'll see, Michèle is perfect, you'll get on ever so well with her. And you can't be cross with us for ever about a little mistake like that?'

'I've already forgotten about your little mistake,' she said with a shrug, 'well, almost. And I'll forget how the people are going to laugh at us too – because, believe me, they'll enjoy that, for once the Vialhes have given them an excuse! Yes, I'll forget, but I'd be very surprised if you ever forget it! Well,' she murmured rather sadly, 'we each make our own beds to lie on, but it's no use being surprised or complaining if you feel the lumps later on.'

Léon burst into laughter when he was informed next day.

'I was afraid it would amuse you,' admitted Pierre-Edouard.

'Oh, the little beggar,' said Léon, 'who'd have thought it of him, eh? All the same, he's my nephew; I'll bawl him out a little, on principle, you know!'

'He doesn't care,' said Pierre-Edouard.

'But you and Mathilde do, I bet.'

'She's taken it badly – and then, it's so irresponsible, Dammit, everyone knows that Perpezac girls are as hot as bakers' ovens, but if you'd told me my son would go and burn himself before the loaves were ready!'

'Never mind burning himself,' joked Léon, 'he left a bun in there! I expect Mathilde's in a state!'

'Yes, and she's afraid that people will laugh at us.'

'If that's all you're worried about! You know, with the young people, things like that often happen, and just about everywhere. People soon get tired of laughing about it – and anyway, they don't dare, because they only need to have one boy or one girl to think to themselves: it could happen to us as well!'

'Maybe,' admitted Pierre-Edouard. 'Anyway, it's irresponsible,' he reiterated. 'Right, about this land; we agree, we'll buy it. Jacques has decided to stay on the farm.'

'There, you see!' Léon was jubilant. 'Everything's falling into place, now your worries are over. And I'm truly happy for all of you! So you'll take the ten hectares on the plateau?'

'Yes, we'll get the money somehow. But you're going to buy the rest, are you? Oh, I'm only saying that because I know that Maurice, Edmond too and even Edouard, would have brought a bit of it, so if we do it behind their backs, without saying anything, they'll hold it against us and for some time to come!'

'I know,' said Léon, 'I've thought about that. But if they find out about it before the sale has gone through other people will find out too, and we'll all be in the soup! No, let me handle it, I've got an idea. The squire's daughter wants a big sum of money all at once; she'll get it. Perhaps not as much as she thinks, because I haven't started bargaining yet, and she'll have to come down a bit! But once I've bought it, don't worry, I won't keep it all. I'm interested in the château, the pine wood and the grazing; I'll hand over the rest to whoever wants it. I've already got a hundred and twenty acres of my own or rented dotted about the place, I don't need any more land that I can't use.'

'Are you sure?' insisted Pierre-Edouard.

'I give you my word,' said Léon. 'You know my word's my bond. Our friends'll do well out of the sale of the château. But just for now, let me handle it, and don't tell anyone. Once, about forty years ago, I talked too much in your father's hearing, about the meadow by the mill, and he stitched me up. That was a lesson well learned.'

Mathilde had suffered too much from sharing her living space to be one of those mothers-in-law who believe they should transform a couple into a trio. She had therefore no wish to interfere in the young couple's household affairs. She forced herself to welcome her daughter-in-law as best she could, but she had to work to suppress the bad impression the hastily arranged marriage had made on her.

Despite the quietness of the ceremony, the lack of ostentation and limited number of guests, Mathilde had barely been able to swallow her daughter-in-law's audacity – marrying in white, and in her own parish!

'We'd never have dared do that in our day!' she confided in Pierre-Edouard.

'That's right, and not so long ago they'd have had to go to Rocamadour to marry, with just two witnesses. That's the way it

624

goes, we have to accept it's all changed; well, we'll have to make the best of it and take life as it comes.'

All went well for the first few months, but probably only because the purchase of the château land and Jacques' restored energy masked the petty differences, the divergent views and idiosyncrasies of all parties.

Michèle was gentle, kind, polite to her parents-in-law, but she had a will of her own, knew what she wanted, and gradually got into the habit of running the house her own way. She kept a different timetable for her work from Mathilde, happily left the evening's dishes to be done the next day, postponing the time for tending the animals and thus the midday meal as well.

These were trifles, so Pierre-Edouard and Mathilde tried to adapt. Most of all they did not want to disturb the obvious happiness radiating from the young couple.

Stimulated by his wife, who, despite her pregnancy was still as affectionate as a lamb, Jacques was in seventh heaven. Now that he was master of his own land and free to work it according to his own theories, he was bursting with confidence and new projects.

However, despite the pride Pierre-Edouard and Mathilde felt in their son's capabilities, and their good intentions, they never felt on the same wave-length as the young people. And what had at first been insignificant details grew into a wall of misunderstandings.

Seldom did Mathilde and her daughter-in-law hold the same opinion on any subject. Concerning religion, for example, Michèle made a point of avoiding it for, she stated quite candidly, 'Only bigots bother with Father Delclos!' It was partly true; he was growing old, crotchety, embittered, and his sectarianism alienated all the young people. However, Mathilde, although she could hardly bear him, felt it her duty to attend the services. Then to hear her daughter-in-law talk about bigots!

The two women also crossed swords on the question of money, for, even though they did not operate a joint budget, Jacques and Michèle's happy-go-lucky attitude was worrying. Pierre-Edouard and Mathilde had never borrowed without first calculating the rates of interest and the consequences. Jacques relied completely on the support of the Crédit Agricole, and already planned to borrow to the limit to purchase equipment. In this matter he clashed with his mother, and also with his father, who recommended caution and reminded him that with land, sowing and working it are one thing, and harvesting quite another.

'All right,' Pierre-Edouard said to him one evening, when he had talked of buying a second-hand van, 'your wheat is magnificent. I'd heard talk that this Vilmorin was good, and you've proved it to me. But it isn't threshed yet, nor sold, so don't count your chickens before they're hatched. Especially to buy a car, which will be nothing but an expense!'

'With your system, nobody would ever get anywhere!'

'Maybe, but it's thanks to that system that five generations of Vialhes have got you where you are! Anyway, you do as you want, it's your problem.'

Then came the absolute parting of the ways that Mathilde had seen coming for months. She was so looking forward to welcoming her grandson or granddaughter into the world that she was terribly disappointed when Jacques announced that Michèle was going to give birth in Brive.

'But why?' asked Mathilde, 'why not here? I'll be there! I'll help her!'

'I prefer Brive, it's safer!'

'Bloody hell!' shouted Pierre-Edouard, who also felt thwarted. 'Safer than what? Your mother was alone at Coste-Roche when you came into the world; she didn't die of it and you didn't either!'

'Michèle would prefer to go to Brive, she doesn't like Doctor Delpy very much.'

'And why's that?' Mathilde wanted to know.

'He's too old,' said Michèle at this point.

'Now that, dammit,' cried Pierre-Edouard, 'is the stupidest thing I've heard for a long time! Too old? He's only sixty-nine!'

'And you think that's young, do you?' mocked Jacques.

'You little squirt!' His father was beside himself. 'At least it proves that he's got experience!'

'Granted.' Jacques avoided the issue. 'In any case, she's going to Brive, it's decided.'

'Right,' sighed Mathilde. 'Well, I shall have to apologise to Dr Delpy, I wouldn't like him to think that we'd fallen out with him.'

And that evening, despite the door which separated the old building from the new, Pierre-Edouard and Mathilde understood that there was one person too many in the Vialhe household.

Dominique Vialhe, Pierre-Edouard and Mathilde's first grandson, saw the light of day in Brive, and not in the village of Saint-Libéral like all his father's forebears.

A beautiful baby weighing almost six pounds, he came into the world without complications, and justified Mathilde's conviction that her daughter-in-law had made a lot of fuss about a completely natural occurrence.

In spite of everything, and because she was deliriously happy, she thought this baby would restore serenity to the house, and couldn't wait for her daughter-in-law and grandson to return. But it was fated that the two women should never understand one another, for Mathilde lost her temper when she saw that Michèle, despite her generously rounded breasts, was not feeding her son herself.

'Why aren't you giving him your milk, isn't it any good?'

'Yes, but the doctor said that it was better on the bottle,' explaining the young woman.

'Your doctor is an imbecile, and you're a goose to have believed him! A baby should drink its mother's milk, and not any nasty old powder!'

Pierre-Edouard echoed her; Jacques joined in, and finished by saying coldly that he would not tolerate his parents' interference in things which were none of their business.

Pierre-Edouard gazed at him for some time, then looked over to his grandson and daughter-in-law.

'All right,' he sighed at last, 'we won't say any more. Come on,' he said to Mathilde.

'But where are you going?' she asked him, when she saw he was leading her out of the house.

'Come on,' he repeated, 'we need to take a walk and discuss this . . . That's it, we have to make another decision,' he said, when they had reached the track which climbed to the peaks.

She nodded her head, smiled a little sadly.

'Yes.'

'You've seen them; they're good children, they love each other, there shouldn't be quarrels because of us.'

'You're right.'

'Jacques is a fine, sensible chap, little Michèle is sweet, the baby is superb. They don't need us to be happy.'

He fell silent, broke off an elder twig and flicked it against his legs.

'And then?' pressed Mathilde.

'Well, you were right when you got me to repair Coste-Roche. When we did it, we thought it would be used by one of the children, but perhaps it's us who'll use it.'

'You want us to move up there?'

'Why not? I spent almost thirty years of my life fighting with my father, I don't want Jacques to be doing the same.'

'And wouldn't you mind leaving the house and village again?'

'Yes, I would,' he admitted, 'but if we stay together it won't work out. You know very well that you and young Michèle, I can feel it, you'll soon be fighting in earnest. So it's better to make peace before war is declared.'

'But what about the farm and the animals, all that? Coste-Roche is a long way!'

'We'll organise all that,' he assured her. 'You'll see, it'll be better for everyone.'

'All the same, the whole village will think we've fallen out.'

'People'll soon see we haven't. So we'll do it like that?'

'If you think it's for the best . . .'

'Then that's agreed. We'll tell them tonight after supper.'

'No!' said Jacques firmly, when his father had finished explaining his plan.

'Listen,' Mathilde said to him, 'it's for the best. We'll each be in our own home, we won't get on each other's nerves.'

'No,' now Michèle intervened, 'it's not you who should leave, it's us. And that's what we're going to do.'

'Exactly,' said Jacques. '*We*'ll move to Coste-Roche. It's what we should have done in any case when we got married, I should have listened to my godfather.'

Pierre-Edouard raised his eyebrows.

'What's the new squire of Saint-Libèral got to do with this business? That comes well from him, sticking his nose into other people's houses, now he's living in a château!'

'Jacques smiled.

'He said to me: "In a herd, if you put the young animals with the very old, it works, they tolerate each other. But if you mix the first-time calvers with cows who are still strong, they fight. It's normal, they all want to graze the same patch of grass!"'

It was Pierre-Edouard's turn to smile.

'That's a stock-dealer talking . . .' Then he grew serious again. 'Are you sure, wouldn't it be better for us to leave?'

'No,' repeated Jacques, 'we'll move up there. There's not much needs doing to make that house comfortable; with a motor-pump we could even have running water.'

'You're forgetting that there's no electricity,' his mother reminded him. 'You know, that wouldn't worry your father and me, but you . . .'

'That's a mere detail,' interrupted Jacques, 'there'll be electricity by the time we move in. I'll put in the request tomorrow and my godfather will push it through. Yes,' he expanded, 'we'll go up there, but not straight away, because of the work to be done there and the baby too. We'll be able to spend the summer here, together and without fighting, won't we?'

'Of course,' said Mathilde, 'but if it comes to alterations, why not change things here? We'll build a kitchen on our side, lock the door and each have a home.'

'No,' decided Jacques, 'Michèle and you'll be meeting in the yard all the time . . .'

'He's right,' said Pierre-Edouard, 'when you're apart you always want to see each other, but seeing too much of each other makes you want to get away.'

Later on, when Pierre-Edouard was undressing to join Mathilde, who was already in bed, she raised the matter again.

'You knew, didn't you?' she asked.

'What?' he asked, feigning astonishment.

'That Jacques wouldn't let us go.'

'I was hoping,' he admitted.

'No,' she insisted, 'you were sure of it!'

'Do you blame me for playing a little game? Well, you played it with me, because you were hoping Jacques would react like that too!'

'Of course,' she agreed. 'Well, I'm very pleased that Michèle said what she did, even before Jacques; did you hear her?'

'Yes,' he said, getting into bed, 'she's a fine daughter-in-law.'

She moved over and snuggled up to him.

'It's still a pity that it had to come to this,' she sighed. 'and I am a bit cross with you, you know; for a moment I believed you were giving up, and wanted to go to Coste-Roche for good. Now I know you were only pretending, and I'm annoyed about that too.'

'You're wrong,' he said, passing an arm round her waist, 'I very nearly did give up, really. I wasn't pretending. Believe me, I didn't know what to do. Still, we had to find a solution that wouldn't hurt anyone – well, not too much. So if I'd said to Jacques: "Go and move to Coste-Roche!" he'd have thought we were kicking him out. I said to him: "We're going," and it's he who doesn't want to drive us out. It's good of him, and I'm sure he's feeling quite pleased with himself this evening! It's what I was hoping for, but you know, you can make wishes but they don't always come true!'

He leant on one elbow, looked down at her, smiled and slid his forefinger over the little brown mark decorating her breast.

'It's still a teaser!' he joked, stroking her warm satin skin.

'Oh yes . . .'

'It's incredible, I've enjoyed it for almost thirty years and I'm not getting tired of it! And you, you're not bored, sleeping with a grandfather?'

'No, and I'll prove it,' she smiled, pulling him to her.

# PART SEVEN

## *The New Wine*

# 24

JACQUES and Michèle's decision to go and live at Coste-Roche had the immediate effect of defusing all the sources of conflict between themselves and their parents. Since they had only three months to live under the same roof, mother- and daughter-in-law made an effort to avoid any grounds for dispute. As for Pierre-Edouard and Jacques, they worked together all summer, and even Nicolas became talkative again.

He had been present without speaking at all the family fracas, and was very happy to see them come to an end. He even initiated Jacques into the secrets of bee-keeping, and helped him to set up five hives on the border of the little oak wood which lay behind Coste-Roche.

When September came and the young Vialhe family moved, nobody in Saint-Libéral was shocked by the separation. Many even thought that Jacques was sensible to settle closer to his land. Anyway, in the village it was no time for gossip. Added to a very unhealthy general situation – strikes were starting up again, as before the war, and governments followed one another in quick succession; there was spiralling inflation and the latest stupidity of the politicians, who could think of no better way to revive private wealth than to cancel all 5,000 franc notes – the very life of the village was threatened.

In August 1947, the month of his seventieth birthday, Dr Delpy had announced his retirement. He felt tired, he admitted, and they believed him; for several months everyone had noticed his pallid complexion, bent back and lack of interest in conversation. Therefore, so as not to succumb to the temptation of continuing his work, which he was convinced would be the case if he stayed in Saint-Libéral, he chose to leave, and move into his wife's family home, not far from Saint-Yrieix.

The news of his departure, set for 15 October, saddened the whole community, for the doctor was loved by everyone. But beneath the sorrow lay a worry: from now on Saint-Libéral would have no doctor. Who would be crazy enough to come and set up in a village in decline, which the young left for lack of work, where the population dwindled year by year: 1,092 inhabitants in 1900, 979 in 1914, 701 in 1920, 594 in 1930 and now 452, many of them over fifty.

'At this rate,' said Léon from time to time, 'in twenty years there'll ony be two hundred of us. I'm glad I won't be here to see it!'

Since nothing seemed to halt these death throes – already the markets were no more than a memory, Suzanne was talking of closing the inn, everyone knew that the ageing grocer would not be replaced – what did it matter that the Vialhe boy was migrating to Coste-Roche? At least he wasn't leaving the community, that was a bonus!

For the first time since their marriage, Pierre-Edouard and Mathilde found themselves alone. They were not accustomed to it, and had to make an effort to escape the incipient boredom. In unspoken agreement they threw themselves into their work and Mathilde, liberated from the burden of cooking and housework, returned to the fields full time.

She often needed to work herself to a standstill to deaden her anxiety for, whatever Paul might say in his letters, the news from Indo-China was not good. Nor was Mauricette's more encouraging. She was five months pregnant and had been forced to give up work, for she was supposed to stay lying down almost all the time. If no accident intervened she would give birth at Christmas, and Mathilde was gladly determined to be at her side.

Léon worried her a little too. While helping to load a cow into a lorry, her brother had been kicked full in the chest; he had remained unconscious for almost ten minutes and, although there were no physical repercussions, his spirits were affected.

'If you can't bloody well get out of the way of a kick from an old bit of gristle, either you need to learn your job, or it's high time you got out of it!' he said bitterly.

To help him think more optimistically, Pierre-Edouard and Mathilde often visited the château. At the beginning they had felt almost intimidated as they entered the portals of the grand building and walked on the walnut parquet of the huge rooms. Léon too seemed a little lost in this environment, as if he were not quite at home. Then they gradually got used to the size of the reception rooms, the mirrored walls, the sparkling chandeliers on the main staircase.

Since the château was much too large for two people, Léon and Yvette only used four rooms, five when Louis was on holiday: the kitchen, where they took their meals, a bedroom, an office and the billiard-room, where Pierre-Edouard and Léon enjoyed meeting around the green baize. The other rooms, unoccupied, empty of furniture, with closed shutters, gathered dust.

'If I'd known it was so big . . .' murmured Léon occasionally. 'Well, the boy will enjoy it one day!' That was about the only satisfaction his purchase gave him.

However, he did use the salons of the château to organise, on 14 October, a convivial farewell party for Dr Delpy and his wife. There was a crowd of friends and all the town councillors.

But it was a sad occasion; nobody had the heart to tell jokes. With the doctor going, the last personality in the village was disappearing – apart from the priest, who was a pathetic sight, and, poor man, had little charisma. Now, however, he would be the only one fulfilling a public role and an office worthy of some respect.

Formerly the teacher had shared that privilege, but no longer. He was still morally a little superior to the villagers, but his situation had lost its aura of brilliance; many of the young people who had left the village were earning a better living than he, and knew as much, if not more.

Jacques and Michèle were happy at Coste-Roche from the start. There at least they could live and act as they pleased, without having to worry about possible criticism or comments from Pierre-Edouard and Mathilde.

With hindsight his parents' opinions now seemed quite unobjectionable, possibly because they were no longer affected by them, and Jacques was sometimes surprised that they had succeeded in poisoning the atmosphere. But he was not sorry to be out of the village. Down there, although his father had always left him completely free to manage his land as he thought fit, his position was awkward, for even without intending to, Pierre-Edouard dominated him with his strong character, professional ability and reputation. Jacques had once thought that his father had been overtaken by events, was out of touch with modern techniques and set in his ways, but honesty obliged him to admit that he had been wrong.

Far from being ossified, or behind the times, Pierre-Edouard was proving once more that his courage and enterprise were still sound. But his age, caution and experience had at first been mistaken by Jacques for opposition to change. He understood now that it was simply the reflection of good sense, steadiness and knowledge, the fruits of so many years spent watching over the land, listening to it, and shaping it too; not with the rough and ready energy of a beginner, but with the patient, attentive love of a man whom life had taught the language of the seasons and the value of time.

So, now that he had achieved his own independence, Jacques

realised that he still had a great deal to learn. And it was no shame to admit this, for he had the feeling that he could also communicate to his father this new-found enthusiasm which was begging for an outlet. And because he felt a growing need for action on all fronts, he agreed to stand with Léon, his father and their friends in the municipal elections on 20 October 1947.

He was elected with a good majority, and unhesitatingly accepted the position of second deputy Léon offered him.

Pierre-Edouard laid down on the table the pages he had just been reading; it was a detailed plan of Jacques' proposed production.

'Well?' asked Jacques.

'Here,' said Pierre-Edouard, pushing them over to Mathilde, 'you read it too, you know as much about it as I do. Yes, it looks sensible,' he admitted.

'You see,' persisted Jacques, 'here, mixed farming is finished – that is, the old sort. With my ten little hectares, if I go on like that, I'll soon have to shove the key under the door and walk away, and you know very well it's not for lack of effort!'

'I know.'

In the three years that Jacques and Michèle had been living at Coste-Roche, Pierre-Edouard had never found fault with his son. He had truly done all he could, thoroughly applied the techniques learned in his captivity, tried different sorts of crops and worn himself out at the job. Michèle too: the burden of heavy work had resulted in miscarriage in September 1949. But despite all their labours, their income constantly diminished. Jacques was right, now the problem had to be resolved.

'Yes,' said Pierre-Edouard, 'your ideas look fine, but you should beware of taking specialisation too far; it's sensible to have several irons in the fire. Having said that, I'm sure you're right not to want to grow wheat any more. I'm going to stop it too, it really doesn't pay, and whichever way we do it, our output is too small. You're wise to give up the spring vegetables as well, they take up too much time and manpower. That leaves tobacco, and there you're wrong to want to abandon it. Tobacco's good insurance against a rainy day.'

'Maybe, but I'd never be able to do all the work!'

'We'll help you,' promised Pierre-Edouard. 'Nicolas and I still have some strength left in us. Believe me, you should keep the tobacco.'

'And what about the other projects?'

'Well there, you'd better not make a mess of it . . .' said Pierre-

Edouard, nodding his head. 'In his time your grandfather made a lot of money out of pigs, and he was thinking on a smaller scale than you! You're wanting to start off with at least forty sows – that's a lot you know, and they're greedy!'

'I know, but if I only plant crops for them I'll keep down the feed purchases.'

'On paper, yes . . . And then you'll have a big outlay on buildings!'

'I believe it could work,' said Mathilde, who had finished reading the plan, 'on condition that you keep the tobacco, of course, and that your second string is carefully organised.'

'You're thinking of the geese?' asked Michèle.

'Yes. You'll be looking after them, won't you? Well, you'll see, if you have the knack, they may bring in more than the piglets.'

'Good,' said Jacques, after lighting a cigarette. 'Now there's another problem, the biggest one, and it's not mentioned in my outline.'

'Oh,' Pierre-Edouard frowned, 'and what's that?'

'The time and the labour. Yes, I thought you'd overlook that. All the years you've worked, you've never counted your time or your trouble. The job was there and you did it, even if it meant a fifteen-hour day, including Sundays. We two have done exactly the same, up to now, but that's over; I don't want that kind of life any more, and neither does Michèle. It's nice to earn a bit of money, you need it to live – but that's just it, you need to live a little as well.'

'You'll have to explain more clearly,' said Pierre-Edouard.

'Our forty sows, our geese, various crops, our tobacco, since you insist on it – we couldn't manage all that except by working like beasts! And it's just not worth it.'

'And do you know any other way than by working?' asked Pierre-Edouard sarcastically.

'No, work is always work, but it depends what you mean by work, and above all, what you do it with! If we want to succeed, the way we mean it, we'll have to change, and for that I need your help. We need to buy a tractor and attachments.'

'Bloody hell!' exclaimed Pierre-Edouard, 'you think you're on a farm up in the north? A tractor? But that costs an arm and a leg, and it surely can't pay on our small acreage!'

'It'll pay its way,' Jacques argued, 'because it'll save us time, and you too. Yes, if you agree, you pay half of it; that way you could use it whenever you like. And instead of taking four or five days to plough one of your fields you'd finish it in less than a day, with much less effort.'

'I don't even know how to drive a car, let alone a tractor!'

'You'll soon learn, and you'll be so pleased with it, you won't be able to do without it. And your ploughing will improve as well!'

'How's that?'

'It'll be deeper.'

Pierre-Edouard smiled; he had given the same reason to his father when he bought his first pair of oxen.

'All the same,' he said, 'it's beyond our means.'

'Everything's expensive now, but money's not worth much!'

Pierre-Edouard meditated at length. His son's pronouncement was true, for even Mathilde, who always took care of the finances, and had known the inflation of the '20s and '30s, had difficulty in keeping pace with the astronomic scale of the figures. To the 1,100 francs Pierre-Edouard had paid Nicolas five years ago, he had been forced, as the years passed, to add more 1,000-franc notes: now, in April 1950, Nicolas was earning 10,000 francs! And a cow, previously a fair price at 3,000 francs, now cost twelve times as much! Léon had not been mistaken when he had urged them to buy land. As he had predicted, it didn't cost 30,000 francs a hectare any more, far from it! Their neighbour Maurice had just agreed on 120,000 francs for a patch of barely a hectare! Seen in that perspective, Jacques was right.

'Yes,' said Pierre-Edouard at last, 'I know money's lost its value, but I'm not like those good-for-nothings in the government, I haven't got a licence to print notes! And you know what your brother's going to cost us next year!'

If Guy passed his second baccalauréat, and all the signs were that he would not fail, he wanted to register at the School of Law in Paris in October. His parents had chosen Paris rather than Poitiers because Berthe had kindly offered to put up her nephew during his studies. With the price of a tiny room being what it was, that was an offer not to be refused: 'And I'll introduce him to people in Paris,' Berthe had said, 'that'll stand him in good stead.'

'Yes,' said Jacques rather bitterly, 'I hadn't forgotten that studying in expensive . . .'

'And this tractor, how much does it cost?' asked Pierre-Edouard.

'We need a twenty-five horsepower. With the equipment, it'll come to about nine hundred thousand francs, but I'll pay half!'

'And where do you think I'll raise the other four hundred and fifty thousand?'

'We'll find it,' said Mathilde quietly. 'Yes, think: if you buy a tractor, you won't need your oxen any more, so if you get them in good condition you might get a hundred and eighty thousand from the butcher. I'll find the other two hundred and seventy thousand . . .'

'If you go on dipping into your cauldron,' he commented sceptically, 'you'll end up scraping the bottom!'

'Yes, it won't be long . . .' she agreed. 'But just consider, in place of the oxen, you could feed four extra cows. Let's say it's only three, that still gives you three calves a year at forty thousand each; in a little over two years you'll have covered your investment.'

'Ever since I've known you, you've been counting your chickens before they're hatched!' he murmured.

'And with some success!'

'Yes, until the day you make a mistake . . . Now this tractor of yours,' he said to Jacques, 'I don't know much about it, but according to what I've read here and there, it eats too! And at almost fifty francs a litre for petrol!'

'Of course, but it's that or give up the struggle. Without this tractor I won't have the time to see to the sows and the geese, and Michèle won't be helping me. Yes, we wanted to wait a bit to tell you, but just so you understand: Michèle's expecting a baby at the beginning of November, and if we don't want the same to happen at last time . . .'

'That's lovely,' said Mathilde with a smile, 'really lovely; you were right to tell us, and we're very pleased. You'll be catching up with your sister – well, almost,' she joked. Mauricette already had two girls and was expecting a third child in July.

'Right,' said Pierre-Edouard, 'that alters the whole situation. You mustn't take any chances, and if you think this tractor will help you work better, with less trouble and higher returns, we'd better get it, even if it's expensive.'

'Yes, it'll make a world of difference to us,' said Jacques. He hesitated a moment, then smiled to soften his plain speaking: 'And it'll change everything for you as well, you . . . well, you're getting to the age when you shouldn't be crippling yourself with work, the way you've been doing.'

'Go on, say straight out I'm an old wreck!' protested Pierre-Edouard.

'No, no,' Mathilde calmed him with her quiet tone, 'but whether you like it or not, you're sixty-one and Nicolas is not far behind; it's beginning to get a lot for the two of you to manage! Jacques is right, this tractor will be useful.'

'Agreed,' he said. He sighed in amusement. 'After all, I moved on from the scythe to the reaper, from the sickle to the harvester, from the swing plough to the reversible brabant, from cows to oxen; I can change from oxen to a tractor. And I forget another thing: from paraffin to electricity! So it's just one more change in a long line!'

Jacques ordered a petrol driven Massey-Harris, fitted with a small detachable plough fixed by ten screws, and a cutting bar, also detachable. But he had to control his impatience and wait for delivery until the beginning of September.

That year, the severe frost which ravaged the surrounding area luckily spared Saint-Libéral, and Pierre-Edouard picked nine tons of plums which he succeeded in selling at twelve francs a kilo.

In July, Mauricette gave birth to a third girl, which inspired Pierre-Edouard to say, in his delight at being a grandfather again, that Mathilde's and Mauricette's features were like couch-grass, ineradicable – for the child, like her two elder sisters, was the image of her mother and grandmother. 'But,' he added, 'that's a weed I could wish on any man!'

Added to this good news came Paul's long-awaited leave; he had not returned since his posting to Indo-China. His arrival in Saint-Libéral did not pass unnoticed. Firstly because he turned up at the wheel of a splendid Ford Vedette, an indisputable sign of wealth; secondly because everybody very soon knew that he had just been promoted to captain.

Even Pierre-Edouard and Mathilde were impressed. Paul, matured and hardened by the preceding war, was now spare and chiselled, gaunt and nervous as a wild cat, always ready to spring, behind every glance the worrying little spark which shines in the eyes of those who have made war their first love. To him it was his *raison d'être*, his life and career, and his father – who himself had also fought ferociously – noticed with a certain alarm what differentiated men who were forced to defend themselves, not doing it of their own choice, from those, like his son, who married their warlike vocation body and soul.

Paul no longer strove to re-establish peace, but sought the thrill of battle. And Pierre-Edouard understood that he would search ever onwards for new conflicts: they were like a drug to him.

'But haven't you had enough of all this killing?' he asked one evening, when Paul had accompanied him to the Caput Peak to load a cart with heather for bedding down the animals.

'No,' said Paul, leaning on his fork. And because they were alone, man to man, he explained enthusiastically: 'This killing, as you call it, it's like love. There's all the build-up beforehand, that's very exciting in itself, and then the climax, when everything's let loose. With a woman you have the feeling you're dicing with a minor sort of death; in battle you're sure of it! Believe me, it's fantastic to know that you're flirting with death, and that she's always on the look-out for a moment's carelessness or a mistake which will win her the game! What I like about a battle is that you're not allowed the slightest weakness, you always have to do better than the time before, always prove that you're stronger! It's good, good like love!'

Pierre-Edouard shrugged.

'It's incredible, what rubbish you talk!' he said, 'and if it were only talk! Look, hearing you say you make love like you make war, I feel sorry for you, because love is more like peace. Yes, you'd have difficulty in extricating yourself from that hornet's nest, but then you don't want to, you like it. Basically it's what you were looking for fifteen years ago, when you wanted to leave for Paris: adventure, simply adventure.'

'Yes,' admitted Paul with a smile, 'it may be so, I've always had an insatiable curiosity.'

'I know, but what are you trying to prove?'

'Nothing. I live as I mean to live, that's all.'

'Oh, right, every man to his own taste. If that's how you see life, go on beating yourself unconscious, because one day you may wake up and realise that you've been fighting your own shadow, and you'll understand that no one has ever won that game!'

'Enough of this moralising,' said Paul with a laugh, 'you know I won't live long enough to wake up! So for the time being I enjoy my dreams – and believe me, they're superb, better than I'd ever hoped!'

Paul stayed three weeks in Saint-Libéral, helping his father in the fields and also with the large pig-unit which Jacques was constructing at Coste-Roche.

He even accompanied Léon to Brive market, for the pleasure of plunging into the atmosphere of his youth again, to hear the horse-dealers battling it out and to go and sit with them, towards ten o'clock in the morning, for a snack in one of those bistros on the Thiers Square which smelt deliciously of vermicelli soup, grilled meat, cheese and wine, and where the orders were given in dialect.

'I don't understand why you're going back there,' said Mathilde the day before he left. 'You've done your time, you could ask to stay in France!'

'In France? And do what? Work in an office? Teach kids how to dismantle a machine-gune and play at war with blanks and dummy grenades! No, thank you! You see, Maman, after the war, when I asked to be transferred to the Colonial Army, it wasn't so as to fall asleep in some town garrison.'

'But your confounded war in Indo-China will stop one day anyway!'

'Maybe, but the world is a huge place and the Colonial Army is all over it!'

And as he was about to continue, Pierre-Edouard placed a hand on her arm.

'Leave it,' he said, 'he needs his dreams.'

The arrival of the tractor at the Vialhes' attracted almost as many people as had gathered for the first demonstration of the mechanical reaper, bought by Jean-Edouard in May 1905.

Then a significant proportion of the elderly had at first regarded the machine with mocking scepticism, but nobody in September 1950 doubted for a moment that the tractor would prove extremely useful. Many even secretly envied the Vialhes, who had the courage and the means to acquire such a marvel.

It was magnificent, this Massey-Harris, with an impressive beauty and strength which made you want to touch the red bonnet, to stroke the swelling curves sculpted in the tyres, to climb on to the seat and gently handle the wheel.

As for its throbbing, both the soft, silky murmur of the pistons when disengaged, and the fierce growl of the cylinders exploding with energy, inspired respect, announced a power which had no equal amongst the best pairs of oxen in the community.

To test it, and also to prove that he was capable of steering and mastering it, Jacques decided to try opening a few furrows in the field called the Meeting. He had not driven a tractor since his captivity, and immediately appreciated the difference between the modern, manageable machine he had just acquired and old Karl's heavy, noisy Lanz.

Nevertheless, since he was being watched by all the neighbours, it was with some apprehension that he manoeuvred it to cut his first furrow.

'Will it work?' his father asked as he walked beside him.

'Yes, I think so. Well, we'd better see if the shares are properly adjusted.'

'Oh, don't ask me about that,' warned Pierre-Edouard, gazing at all the gadgets, 'I don't know a thing about it!'

Jacques lowered the right plough share, noted with a glance the proper opening angle, checked the distance between the coulter and the share and the correct slope of the mould-board.

'Fine,' he said, 'I'm starting.'

'That's right,' Pierre-Edouard encouraged him, 'let them see what you can do, and don't forget that some of them will have a good laugh if you bungle it!'

Jacques engaged first gear, pushed the accelerator and slowly let out the clutch. He noted the sound of the blades engaging, set his eye on a gate-post at the other end of the field which would give him the line, and powered the engine.

One glance over his shoulder was enough to tell him that the furrow was opening cleanly, the sods well turned, the depth even. Behind his back, hurrying their steps to keep up with him, all the neighbours were already crowding round with knowing and admiring looks. This ploughing elicited nothing but praise; it was a masterpiece of craft and speed that left them flabbergasted.

'Christ Almighty!' said Maurice. 'If he goes on like that all afternoon he'll have finished the field this evening! And he's a master at steering!'

'Yes,' said Pierre-Edouard with justifiable pride, 'he drives like a champion!'

Having reached the end of the field, Jacques lifted the plough, performed a fine loop on the headland, positioned the left front wheel of the tractor in the trench he had just made, lowered the plough and carved open his second furrow.

He experienced such satisfaction, such joy, that he cut four more before stopping. Then he jumped to the ground, admired his work and turned to his father.

'Come on,' he said, 'now show us what you can do.'

'You're crazy,' protested Pierre-Edouard, 'I've never driven in my life!'

'Of course not, but you're dying to!'

'Go on, Pierre-Edouard,' cried the neighbours, 'it's your turn! Climb up, and don't forget your goad, for when the tractor pulls to one side!'

'No, no,' he said quietly, torn between his desire to try out the machine and his fear of making a fool of himself.

'Yes, yes,' insisted Jacques, pushing him gently towards the tractor. 'Climb up; I'll stay beside you, on the mud-guard.'

'Don't upset your father, now!' interjected a rather worried Mathilde.

'Look, you see,' said Pierre-Edouard, delighted at the intervention, 'it'd frighten your mother. No, no, I'm not getting up on that!'

'Yes you are, they're all hoping you'll chicken out,' Jacques whispered to him, without believing a word of what he was saying.

'You think so?' asked Pierre-Edouard, happy to be able to use this completely imaginary excuse. 'Well, if that's the case, let's go!'

He climbed into the seat, pushed his beret onto the back of his head, and had it all explained to him. He very quickly understood the purpose of the two right-hand pedals, the brakes (which could be operated independently and each restrain one wheel at a time), and the left-hand pedal, the clutch. The gear-lever was soon mastered, and the throttle responded to his touch.

Then he started off and, happy as a child on Christmas morning, treated himself to a little test-drive around the field, to get used to the response of the steering-wheel and the play in the pedals. Then he turned slowly round and it was his turn to enter the trench.

'That's it,' said Jacques, who had just lowered the plough to make things easier for him.

'That's it? Are you sure? My God, it's fantastic,' he said, laughing with pleasure, 'fantastic!' He looked behind him. 'Bloody hell, what a piece of work! Have you seen what I've been doing! Look at that: it's at least twenty centimetres deep! My word, if I met the fellow who invented this machine I'd give him a pat on the back!'

He reached the end of the furrow, turned, resumed ploughing, came back, set off again, with growing enthusiasm and confidence in himself. Only after the eighth row did he finally stop.

'It's incredible,' he said, climbing down.

He admired the shining brown surface that he and his son had just created, walked on to the soft earth, gathered a fistful and kneaded it in his hand.

'I've never seen ploughing like that,' he said, 'never! And if you'd told me you could do it as fine and regular as that, I wouldn't have believed it. I'm happy to admit it, we were stupid to wait so long before buying this machine! With this, things'll really take off now!'

# 25

ONE more time, because the toddler had the knack of getting her to do what he wanted, Mathilde began to sing again, at the same time miming with her hands the words she was chanting, and once again the child burst into laughter when she got to: 'Your mill is turning too fast,' and speeded up her whirling arms. She smiled at Dominique, then rose from her cane chair.

'Right,' she excused herself, 'now I must see to your little sister.'

'She's always eating!' lisped the boy with a shrug.

'Well yes, that's because she's so little,' she explained, putting a pan of milk on the gas stove.

This was their latest purchase, and she was delighted with it. Thanks to this, it was no longer necessary to light the fire or the wood-stove every day, the sides of the pots were clean at last, and the cooking done more quickly.

In her moses basket, little François reluctantly released the toes of her right foot, which she had been sucking voluptuously for several minutes, and began to protest unrestrainedly about the slow progress of the bottle her grandmother was preparing. She would soon be eight months old, and was as chubby and dimpled as a brioche and louder than half a dozen magpies chasing an owl. The whole Vialhe family was crazy about her, and Mathilde was delighted whenever she was entrusted with her while her daughter-in-law went into town to do the shopping.

It was a wonderful afternoon in June, just right for haymaking; not too hot, for the north wind lent it freshness. Once again Mathilde savoured the ability to stay at home without a guilty conscience, to look after her grandchildren. Thanks to the tractor and the hayrake, she no longer needed to gather up the cut grass with long exhausting sweeps of the wooden rake. Now two men accomplished the task: Pierre-Edouard on the tractor, Nicolas on the tedder, and the work was done in a trice.

Then she thought of the coming holidays and felt happy, for Mauricette, Jean-Pierre and their three girls would be spending the summer in Saint-Libéral, in the enlarged house – it did serve a purpose, after all. Guy would also be returning from Paris, probably with Gérard and Berthe who, according to the latest news, had decided to spend at least two weeks in the village. In August Louise had promised to come too, with Pierre and maybe even Félix. And Mathilde was content, for she knew that Pierre-Edouard loved to see his family again.

She tested the temperature of the bottle by pouring a few drops of milk on to her forearm, bent over Françoise, who was now red with anger and running with perspiration, and took her in her arms. The child calmed down immediately with a great sigh of contentment.

'Crosspatch!' she called her, shaking the bottle to speed up the dissolving of the sugar, 'big bad-tempered Vialhe, I feel sorry for you, yes I do! Anyone would think you hadn't eaten for a week! Come on, my greedy love, feed yourself!' she said, stuffing the teat between the vainly sucking lips.

Holding the baby firmly in the crook of her left arm, she walked to the door to make sure that Dominique was being good and smiled to see him playing with the dog. The old mongrel displayed a touching patience with children. At the moment Dominique had passed a cord between his jaws, hung a rusty bucket round his neck and was sitting on his back. The dog cast Mathilde an imploring look, wagged his tail, then with a heavy sigh turned his head and licked the child's knee.

'Don't hurt him,' counselled Mathilde.

'We're having fun!' said Dominique. 'Look, there's Uncle Léon!' he called out suddenly, for he could see down the line of the main street from where he was.

'Léon?' she said as she emerged. 'What brings you at this hour of day?'

'Where's Pierre-Edouard?' asked her brother after kissing her.

'Making hay, on the plateau, why?'

'Ah!' he said in annoyance, 'I must warn him . . .'

'What about?'

'I'm just back from Corrèze market; it's full of foot-and-mouth disease up there, and it seems it's spreading all over the place!'

'My God,' she murmured, 'and you think we're in danger here?'

'Here like everywhere else! Which field is he in?'

'The lucerne.'

'I'll go up there.'

'Talk about a catastrophe if it spreads to this area!' commented Pierre-Edouard, as soon as Léon had relayed the news to him.

'You can say that again. Foot-and-mouth, that's fatal, you have to slaughter!'

'And what can we do?'

'I know what *I'*ll do,' said Léon with a meaningful look, 'but you – first you must sprinkle disinfectant in front of the cowshed, then you mustn't set foot near the markets. Believe me, that's where they catch it, that filth. And if your cows go to the bull, don't use Larenaudie, and I'll be saying that to everyone in the village.'

'But,' protested Pierre-Edouard, 'how shall I get my animals served?'

Since Léon had hastily disposed of his last bull two years earlier – the beast had almost disembowelled one of his workers – only Larenaudie, who lived in the locality of Fonts-Marcel, owned a breeding bull; an enormous Limousin with an evil eye and knotted shoulder-muscles, which, in return for the 350 francs pocketed by his owner, willingly and valiantly agreed to do the honours with all the cows in the area.

'You only have to apply to the artificial insemination service.'

'You think I should?' said Pierre-Edouard. 'That's what Jacques had been advising for a while now, but I don't like the idea. It seems a funny sort of thing to me, that insemination! And Larenaudie'll be cross if he loses all his customers!'

'I don't give a damn! I'm telling you what needs to be done to limit the damage, but if you really want your animals to catch that plague . . .'

'No, no, I'll do as you say. But what are you going to do?'

'Oh, me,' said Léon warily, 'I'm going to stop, that's all.'

'You mean to say you're going to leave off the markets and all that?'

'Yes, I've had a basinful . . .' Léon sighed, spat through his teeth. 'A basinful, do you understand? I'll be sixty-five soon, and I've had enough of running round the markets. This business of foot-and-mouth disease, it's basically a good thing for me. That decided it for me in the end, you know.'

'Bloody hell,' said Pierre-Edouard, 'you're not going to give everything up, just like that?'

'Yes, I am. I'm tired, I'm telling you.'

'But you'll die of boredom!'

'Oh no. I'll potter about a bit on my own land to keep busy, but not the rest, I'm giving up the lease. As for shifting animals, that's finished. Look,' he said lifting his trouser cuff, 'I got another nasty kick the other day; in the last six months I've collected more than my share! I'm telling you, I'm too old to find it funny.'

Pierre-Edouard examined the purplish bruise mottling the white skin of his calf.

'No, that's not very pretty,' he agreed. 'But you've got workers; they can take charge of the animals, you don't need to bother with them!'

'I know, but I enjoy touching the animals, that's what I like, you see. But if I get a thwack every time I feel one over, no thank you. And then, I've got animals all over the place, what if they catch the infection? No, no, I'm going to sell the lot, and have done with it!'

'It's your business,' said Pierre-Edouard. 'If you think it's best . . .'

He was distressed to see his brother-in-law sinking into depression, sliding into old age. For a long time he had felt this change coming; certainly it was partly due to age and fatigue, but there was more to it. In fact, Léon was disappointed in his son. Louis had passed his baccalauréat creditably, but had no desire to pursue any of the avenues favoured by his father. He was not interested in continuing his studies so, instead of taking advantage of a deferment, he had left to do his military service.

On his return he intended to set up as an estate agent in Brive, Tulle or Limoges. It was a profession which Léon considered too close to his own. Buying, selling, making money on the transaction; he had done nothing but that since he was fourteen years old and, although he liked his job, he did not consider it particularly honourable. To see his son embark in business was no comfort to him.

As he had just admitted, the foot-and-mouth was just an excuse. He had more money than he could spend, no longer had to pay for his son's education – if he was a worthy progeny he'd soon be earning more than his father! So what was the point of labouring on, and above all, who was he doing it for?

Anxiety plagued the village throughout the summer of 1951, for all the farmers felt the threat of the disease hanging over their herds.

Fortunately they received Léon's advice positively; sprinkled their cowsheds and dung-heaps with lysol, refrained from touring the market-places, and stopped taking their animals to Larenaudie's bull.

As Pierre-Edouard had expected, the stud's owner was appalled at being put in quarantine and deprived of a substantial income. Furious, he declared categorically that Léon was talking rubbish and that anyway, the precautions were pointless, as almost all the animals drank from the same communal trough. It was the plain truth, except for the Vialhes, who were fortunate enough to have their own pond in the farmyard.

This harsh reality had the effect of making everyone wary and men who had got on perfectly well until then caught each other casting suspicious glances at their neighbour's stock. The few hustlers who continued to frequent the market-places on principle were severely judged. They were roundly informed that if by ill-luck the infection should reach the village, the culprits would be quickly found and suitably dealt with.

Finally, with the first October frosts, the danger diminished. But they had all been so frightened and so vigilant that it took several months for people to stop wondering whether their next-door neighbour, their friend, would be the one to bring in the contamination.

True to his decision not to interfere in his son's affairs, Pierre-Edouard hesitated a while before deciding to act. He was compelled to in January 1952 when Michèle admitted, after a concerned Mathilde had pressed her with questions, that their money worries were reaching critical point.

Despite the workload they accomplished, they were not succeeding in reaching a threshold which would allow them to survive and repay their loans – and also, more importantly, to save.

Due to lack of capital, Jacques had not been able to purchase a sufficient number of breeding sows. He should have had forty and he was rearing fifteen! As for the geese, they had not fulfilled their potential and their livers, sold at the Kings' Market at Brive, had not realised half the expected sum.

'They overstretched themselves and went too fast,' said Pierre-Edouard, when Mathilde had told him that her fears were confirmed.

'No,' she maintained, 'they don't have enough land, it doesn't produce enough.'

'Not enough! Ten hectares? My God, my father brought us three up on that area, myself and two sisters! With our grandparents, there were seven of us! Yes,' he accepted with a shrug, 'it's stupid, what am I saying, that was fifty years ago!'

'Exactly. At that time the money coming in wasn't paid out, or very little of it. Whereas now, there's more going out than coming in . . . and it's not their fault, you know that. We don't live like we did years ago, nobody does, and then all these loans!'

'You could see it coming, eh?'

'Of course,' she said, 'but after all, you can't reproach them for fixing up Coste-Roche, nor buying a van, a few bits of furniture, and a wireless, nor the tractor and implements!'

'No, no, I don't reproach anyone for anything, except those

puppets up there in Paris, who don't care if everything goes up, except the prices we get!'

'What can we do for them?' she asked.

'Hard to know! Give them some money? We don't have the funds any more, and anyway, that's not the solution.'

'Perhaps if . . .' she murmured. 'I thought . . . We'll always have enough to live on, because as soon as Guy has finished studying, we won't be spending . . .'

'Yes, I see what you mean. We'll do that, that's the best idea.'

And, like two conspirators who have no need of words to understand each other, they smiled.

Pierre-Edouard climbed up to Coste-Roche the following day, and was welcomed by his grandchildren with cries of joy. Since the cold was penetrating, he gladly accepted the cup of coffee his daughter-in-law offered him, and enjoyed it by the fireside.

'Would you like a drop of something in your coffee?' suggested Michèle, bringing out a bottle of plum brandy. He hesitated.

'No – or rather yes, but first call your husband; perhaps he'll take a drop with me, and it's him I've come to see.'

'He's busy with the sows, but Dominique will go and fetch him,' she said, knotting a thick woollen scarf round the child's neck. And as the boy ran to the piggery she slipped on her coat. 'I'll take over from Jacques,' she said, 'then you can talk things over quietly.'

'No, you stay, it concerns you too. Come on, take off your coat and sit down.'

'Bloody hell, it's cold enough to bring the wolves out,' said Jacques, coming in a moment later. He stamped his feet and shook himself, poured a big bowl of coffee and made himself comfortable on the settle, opposite his father. The fire flickered at their feet. 'What brings you here?' he asked.

'You two; no, you four,' said Pierre-Edouard, pointing to the children.

'Ah,' said Jacques rather bitterly, 'I bet Mother's managed to get Michèle to talk!'

'Don't blame your wife for a little thing like that. Mothers are born to listen.'

'Well then?'

Pierre-Edouard had not come earlier because he suspected his son would refuse financial support; his pride would forbid it. At the outset he had allowed his father to settle some of the instalments on the loans because he was still feeling his way into the management of his land, starting out in the profession, and had not found it humiliating to be helped to get off the ground. Now that time had passed, he made it a point of honour to feed his wife and children without having to ask for handouts from anyone.

Pierre-Edouard took out his pipe and filled it slowly and carefully, as he did whenever he had a difficult problem to resolve. He drew a brand from the edge of the fire, and lit it.

'Well, it's true; your wife has been talking to your mother, and she was right. This business, it can't go on. And don't tell me that you're going to take another loan!' he said, raising a hand. 'Quiet now, let me talk. Yes, yes, that's what you wanted to do, run to the Crédit Agricole and say to them: "Let me put off this year's repayment until next year, I'll pay you just the interest and that way I'll have a few months' breathing-space." That's a bloody stupid way of doing things!'

'Maybe,' said Jacques calmly, 'but this year I'll have eight more sows, and I reckon that . . .'

'Not a hope! All that to sell the offspring for barely four and a half thousand francs a time; you'll go a long way like that! Let's stop pretending, my boy. This is what we're going to do, your mother's agreed. From now on, you are going to take over the Vialhe land, what came to me from my father, the old farm, you know. I'll have to keep the Long Piece and the Big Field and also your mother's land and what we bought together, but that still leaves you fourteen hectares, and they're top class! We, that is your mother and I, will be happy with what's left, it'll give us nine hectares counting Louise's Combes-Nègres. For you it's not enough; for us, at our age, it's quite sufficient. You need to progress, whereas we can tread water now. I'll go to the solicitor in Ayen tomorrow to get it sorted out.'

'But that's impossible!' protested Jacques. 'I'll never be able to make it up to the others! Where do you think I'm going to find the money?'

'Your brothers and sisters will wait; besides, they're not short of a few pennies! And what I'm handing over is only part of it – there's the rest of the land, the house, the farm-buildings. Come on, don't worry about that, take what I'm offering and make it pay. You'll see, it's good land, the Vialhe land – you know that, anyway! Only, just for this year, you let me have half the value of the crops on it; I need that to pay for your brother's education.'

'Oh no!' said Jacques, 'not half, two thirds. What's left will be enough to make ends meet. And, well . . . All the same, I'm . . . I suppose I want to say thank you, that'll save us.'

'But won't it be hard for you to do?' asked Michèle.

'You mean to let go of my land? No, it's not going out of the family, and that's the main thing. Besides, I had such a dreadful time waiting for a settlement which my father had no intention of making! And your husband won't kick me out if I go on working the land with him, will he?'

'No,' Jacques reassured him, 'just the opposite.' He thought for a moment, and smiled: 'You'll see, we'll make it more beautiful than ever!'

'I'm counting on it. Oh, by the way, as to the stock; I'll keep six cows, the four calves which are ready for sale, and the ewes. The rest are yours now.'

'That's much too much,' said Michèle. 'We can't accept all that!'

'Yes you can,' joked Pierre-Edouard, 'better that than a kick in the teeth, eh? And now, you know, I haven't enough acreage to keep all my stock! Oh, one other thing,' he said, looking at Jacques, 'your mother and I thought that if you wanted to come back down, we could arrange things so that we're not in each others' hair . . .'

'No,' said Jacques and Michèle in chorus. 'You see,' explained Jacques, 'we're fine here, nice and quiet, so we'd rather stay put.'

'I understand,' murmured Pierre-Edouard, with a look of nostalgia in his eye, 'and if your mother were here, she'd understand too. It was here, at Coste-Roche, that we were happiest. So since there's no reason for leaving, stay and make the most of it.'

Without the revenue provided by his new lands and, most of all, by the ten cows which his father had given him, Jacques would not have been able to keep his head above water in 1952. It was a catastrophic year, for drought set in during April and continued all summer, not ending until mid-September. But by then it was too late, the damage had been done.

The hay-crop was thin, the maize wretched; the beets dried in the ground and even the tobacco wilted. As for the barley, it yielded less than twelve quintals a hectare, next to nothing. Only the plums helped the Vialhes to weather the blow, and saved Jacques in particular from sliding into complete bankruptcy.

For in July, at the height of the heatwave, a bout of pneumo-gastritis developed in the pig-unit and, despite the speed with which he treated it, caried off twenty-three piglets of 15 to 40 kilos each. Added to that (for troubles never come singly, as his father resignedly reminded him), three of his sows in the space of a month, perhaps upset by the insupportable heat – or out of pure evil – devoured their young at birth. The first gobbled up eleven, the second swallowed nine; as for the last one, as she lay down she crushed the only survivor from a litter of twelve.

'That's done me out of almost a quarter of a million francs!' said Jacques to his father. 'Good God, I can see the day coming when I'll get rid of all these filthy sows! It's true: they're noisy, they're greedy, they stink and they die!'

He was more angry than depressed, for the setback made him want to fight, to cheat fate.

'Remember what I told you,' his father reminded him. 'On the land, you can't make plans. The only money you can count on is what you've got in your pocket. The rest, what you're expecting or hoping for, can't be relied on, it's like a drop of water on oilcloth; sometimes you catch it, often it runs off! But don't give up the pigs because of a thing like that. Who knows, maybe it'll get better next year . . .'

'It was only talk. I'm not looking to give them up, nor the rest of it!'

'The rest of it' was all the land which he was busy making productive by applying modern agricultural methods. Through the farming journals, he kept himself up to date with everything and already his voice had been heard at the meetings of the Departmental Union of Farmers' Cooperatives.

In the village itself, some were naturally jealous of him – he had the finest fields in the community, considerable livestock, a tractor, two beautiful children and a lovely wife – but others saw in him a worthy successor to his uncle and godfather, a leader in the mairie. For Léon, who now lived on his private income, made it plain that he would refuse the sash of office.

However, since he had stopped all his professional activities, he was bored. So to fill his time, he treated himself and his wife to trips to Paris, Nice and most often Mont-Dore, where Yvette took the waters. During his absences Jacques took care of matters at the mairie, for although his father was the first deputy mayor, he was quite happy to leave him to deal with ongoing business.

Jacques liked this work, did it conscientiously and with enjoyment, and he was preparing to take the mayor's seat when it fell vacant. If he succeeded in this, his dream was to revive the lost dynamism of the village. But he did not have too many illusions, and had already abandoned the idea of creating a study centre for farming methods in Saint-Libéral, through which he could have apprised all the members of the latest agricultural techniques.

But it was impossible, too revolutionary; that sort of thing upset

653

too many traditions, infringing on each person's privacy and individual ideas. Few and far between were the young people still working family land. Apart from Jean, Maurice's son, Louis Delpy, Delpeyroux's son-in-law; and himself, the youngest farmer in the village was Roger Vergne, and he was forty-six. All the others were in their fifties or older.

It was not possible to get through to them. Not that they were opposed to all things modern, but they were held in the straitjacket of their own routines and opinions. They were glad to try something new, but you had to let them take their time about it; and when, after careful observation, they finally decided to do something it was always so late that the advantage was lost.

Only Pierre-Edouard, Léon and possibly Maurice were enlightened enough to be aware that Jacques was right and to encourage him. But they were no longer involved; they were over sixty and looking forward to retirement rather than new ventures.

Some time in March 1953 Father Delclos, now aged seventy-four, developed severe pulmonary congestion whilst digging the earth for his onion-bed.

In the evening the old lady who did his housekeeping found him all shivery with a temperature, crouched by the fireside. His skin was flushed with the fever, and his eyes were already glazed. As soon as he was told about it, the doctor from Perpezac-le-Blanc put him in his car and drove him to Brive, where he had him admitted to hospital.

Contrary to all the villagers' predictions, the priest did not die and recovered quite rapidly; but he remained weak, frail, depressed. As a precaution, the diocesan authorities sent him to a retirement home and informed the parishioners that Saint-Libéral would no longer have a pastor; only a peripatetic clergyman would conduct the services.

The announcement that the parish would no longer have an appointed priest shocked everyone. God knows, Father Delclos, with his changing convictions, his inappropriate attitudes and opinions, had succeeded in emptying his church; for several years the gathering of the faithful had constantly dwindled, and even the children in the catechism class managed to cut their lessons quite frequently.

Nevertheless, everyone was aware of the gap left by the departure of the priest, for, quite apart from the man himself, the office which he represented proved to all that they were not forsaken and that, in spite of the exodus, the ageing population and the paralysis which was gradually numbing the village, nothing was really lost as long as the structures and framework which had for centuries governed the community of Saint-Libéral remained.

Deprived of solicitor, doctor and priest, the village felt forgotten, rejected. Maybe they were subconsciously inspired by an almost suicidal instinct, an introspection and nostalgia for times past, but at the council elections in spring 1953, instead of voting in a mayor who could halt the death-throes, the electors turned to an older man. And because Pierre-Edouard had retired from the contest, between Jacques who represented the future and Maurice who embodied the past, they chose the greybeard. He was honest and certainly competent, and they felt that his sixty-four years were a measure of wisdom, good sense and experience.

Jacques felt hurt, and almost resigned from his seat as councillor, which the electors had awarded him in spite of everything. Convinced that nothing could now save Saint-Libéral, he withdrew to Coste-Roche and, to get over his disappointment, devoted himself more than ever to his work on the land.

That year – when the world was relieved to see peace return to Korea; when in France the feeble-minded politicians elevated in-competence to an established art-form and ministerial crisis to a method of government, whilst demanding peace in Indo-China, calm in Morocco, a stabilised franc, regulation of the vintners' problems and the organisation of a European Defence Community; when they required thirteen ballots to elect René Coty as President of the Republic – Saint-Libéral, silently and without protest, sank into a coma.

Within twelve months eight young people between sixteen and twenty left the area, tempted by the jobs and wages offered in the towns.

That year again, for the third time running, the number of deaths in the parish exceeded the births.

Guy Vialhe had deferred his conscription, but the young pupil barrister at the Paris Bar was called up in July 1954. He was not keen to leave work which he enjoyed and a way fo life he appreciated in all its pleasures. Aunt Berthe, despite her age – she would be sixty-one in August – still managed the fortunes of her Paris couture house with a sure touch, now aided by Gérard. Thanks to her, Guy had discovered all the charms of Parisian life.

To him, Saint-Libéral and the Vialhe house were now no more than distant, tender memories and his parents charming, emotive representatives of the past. As for his brother Jacques, he remained an enigma. He never understood how someone of his intellectual weight could prefer the land, with its responsibilities and even trials, to any job in town.

However, Guy did like to visit his village, his parents. He felt a deep and sincere gratitude towards them, which amply repaid all their sacrifices. But his need to return to his roots did not stretch further than two weeks a year. After that he was overcome with boredom, and with it the desire to resume his work and a more exciting, eventful life, filled with friends and relationships.

He joined his garrison in Stuttgart two weeks before Paul, on sick leave – he was riddled with amoebic dysentery and recovering from two successive attacks of jaundice – finally quit Indo-China, which, since 20 July and the Geneva Conference, was no longer French.

Exhausted, looking older and a little bitter too, but still full of spirit, Paul arrived in Saint-Libéral at the end of August. He really rested up for two weeks, savouring with delight all the attention his mother lavished on him, the succulent little dishes she cooked with loving care, the infusions of herbs sweetened with honey.

Then one morning, because he was a man of the Vialhe stamp and idleness hung heavy, he followed his father and Nicolas and went to spread muck with them on the field called Léon's Letters. And in the evening, after having drunk the lime tea his mother handed to him, he went to his mess-chest in search of a bottle of cognac, poured some for his father, tipped a generous measure into his still-warm bowl, and talked.

He had not yet mentioned his long spell in Indo-China since his return. He evoked it now with an affectionate nostalgia which amazed his father, and opened his eyes to an unknown world, unimagined landscapes and incomparable smells. And Pierre-Edouard, who retained horrifying visions of butchery from the war of 1914, noticed with astonishment that his son preserved fond, almost loving memories. And this despite the ambushes, the slaughter, swamps, mosquitoes, leeches, the climate and all the lost comrades. To listen to Paul, however horrible it might have been, this war featured as one of the most gripping periods of his life, the richest and most exhilarating.

Thus words which up till then had been if not foreign, at least meaningless to Pierre-Edouard, Mathilde and Nicolas, were brought to life by Paul. With him they discovered the grinning coolies, the compliant women, smelt the fragrance of Chinese cooking, heard the bustle of Catinat Street in Saigon, stepped into the bars of Cholon and Hanoi, experienced the death-throes of Lang Son and all the battles.

Above all, they understood what Paul had left there: a part of himself, for ever. Whatever he did, for him Indo-China would now be a sort of paradise lost, and also probably an ever-open wound.

# 26

As soon as her grandson Pierre left for boarding-school, in October 1954, Louise felt overwhelmed by loneliness, idleness, and her age too.

Until then she had filled her time by trying to replace in some way the mother whom her grandson had never known. With Pierre gone she knew that Félix did not need her there; that she was possibly even in his way and preventing him from enjoying to the full that solitude he so loved, which he craved and lived for.

Through the years spent in the deepest forests, thickets and plantations, Félix had acquired complete peace of mind; this allowed him to live alone and not seek for company except amongst the oaks, beeches or hornbeams. To have as his only companions all the birds he so loved, which he observed and protected, and all those animals, both high and low, which filled the forest. He set off in the early hours and quite often did not return until evening, preferring to eat a snack at midday seated at the foot of a tree or the edge of a pool.

At first Louise was worried to see him withdraw from the world in this way, and had tried to jog him out of what she took for a state of depression. Then she had understood that, far from sinking into morbid melancholy, Félix sought and discovered in solitude the strength to live and be happy, showing his son the face of a man at peace with himself.

'Well now,' she said one evening in October, when the forest all around echoed with bending boughs as the east wind made it sing like an organ, 'now the boy has gone, I feel there's nothing left for me to do here.'

He pushed away the notebook in which he had been entering the results of his daily observations, looked at her and smiled.

'That's not a very kind thing to say. What about me then?'

'Oh! You! You haven't needed me for the last twenty-five years or more!'

'You want to go back to Saint-Libéral, don't you?'

She agreed with a smile, and he noticed that the mere mention of her birthplace rejuvenated her.

'You've always pined for your home,' he continued 'although

you've been living here for more than forty years, you should have got used to it by now!

'It's true, but this is not my land,' she said. 'Here it's too flat, you can't see far enough.'

'I know,' he joked. 'You Vialhes, I finally understood you while talking to my godfather down there, at your place, on the White Peak. You're not happy unless your eyes are level with the sky! You know, they say that in the past some knights had the right to enter churches without dismounting from their horses; you Vialhes don't like to have to raise your eyes to talk to God. I'm convinced you discuss things with him by getting up to his level!'

'Maybe,' she admitted, 'but that's not all I miss.'

'Your brother?'

'Him and the others. Everyone in the village. And the smells of home too; heather and bracken, the chestnut trees in flower and the black mushrooms you find beneath the oak trees. And the sun, the air, the wind – from the Auvergne with its taste of mountains, from the south with the feeling of heat, from the west with its odour of water and from the north bringing us the scent of fine weather. Here your wind smells of nothing, except mud!'

'To me it smells good, it tells me just as much as yours down there tells you. To understand it, you need to love it, but you never wanted to love it.'

'That's possible. I was just passing through here by accident.'

'Passing through for forty years, that's a long time!'

'Oh, yes! But now I want to return home; I'm old, tired. If I stay here, in this country full of forest and water, I'll soon lose the will to live. But down there, on our land, you'll see how we grow old gracefully! I'm going to write to Pierre-Edouard; I know he's expecting me and I think he may even say that I've left it too long.'

'Of course,' said Félix. 'But aren't you worried you may put them in an awkward position?'

'No,' she reassured him with a smile, 'I know there'll always be room for me in the Vialhe house as long as Pierre-Edouard is there, and even afterwards.' She nodded, and continued quietly: 'At the Vialhes' we only kick out the young ones, and only for a while. But the old ones always have the right to a home; none of us die except under our own roof.'


Despite the disappointment he had felt when the electors rejected him as mayor, Jacques did not feel himself beaten for ever. If for a while he devoted himself solely to his farm, the urge to operate on a wider scale, beyond the borders of his fields, did not desert him.

Intellectually, he had the need to grapple with other problems than those of his land and animals. So he attended the co-operative meetings more frequently than before, became known and respected within the Chamber of Agriculture, the Crédit Agricole and the Insurance Association.

But he was conscious that his age – he was only thirty-four – was a handicap to effective action at the heart of this rustic world, now controlled by a majority of men over fifty, who had no desire to relinquish to him positions or responsibilities which they wished to hold for themselves.

His first reaction was outrage at a state of affairs which ran directly counter to the revolution convulsing the countryside. Everything was on the verge of collapse. Already, here and there, mechanisation was arriving in force on the farms, speeding up methods of working in the first instance and even giving the illusion of prosperity. Then in the second phase it often accelerated the downfall of those who thought it was enough to acquire a tractor in order to increase their yields, and who realised, too late, that the expenses incurred would never be covered by the modest profits from their tiny farms.

When he understood that it would take him years before his point of view prevailed, Jacques changed his tactics and decided to go at it in a roundabout way, aiming for a role which would eventually allow him to expound his opinions. They were clear, and based on an analysis of the current situation.

He predicted, for everything pointed to it, that a certain way of farming had finally been superseded, and it was therefore necessary to work towards the development of competitive, modern agricultural system, regrouping with fewer men, and still producing more. But he wanted, at the same time, to control the cruel pace of the rural exodus. Without that, he felt, given the example of Saint-Libéral, entire regions would fall into decline, for lack of people.

It was to try to promote his theories in a practical way that he took the decision, at the beginning of October, to stand in the regional elections on 17 and 24 April 1955.

'You'll be beaten hollow,' forecast Pierre-Edouard as soon as Jacques informed him of his plans, 'and what an idea, to want to get mixed up with all those scoundrels!'

The older he grew, the less time Pierre-Edouard had for those who went in for politics. And he did not hesitate to say that every other one of them should be hanged, to make the rest put their hearts and souls into their work!

'Let your son alone, he's right!' said Léon, who had come to spend that evening at the Vialhes'.

'And after all,' added Jacques, 'the regional council, it's not real politics!'

'Much you know!' scoffed Pierre-Edouard. 'There are just as many toads in there as anywhere else! Well, if it amuses you!'

'Don't listen to your father, he's an anarchist!' said Léon.

Pierre-Edouard shrugged, and turned towards Mathilde to seek her support. But she was chatting with Yvette and Michèle by the fireside, and had not even heard the beginning of the conversation.

'Fine,' said Pierre-Edouard, suddenly serious. 'After all, why not, you're a cut above plenty of others I could name! But it's a far cry from that to getting elected!'

'I'm going to help him,' decided Léon, delighted at the thought of all the days he could fill supporting his godson. 'Yes,' he said, 'if you want to have a chance of succeeding, you'll have to get yourself known, everywhere. I know everyone, I'll introduce you. We'll go round all the farms, the markets too, and you mustn't be afraid to drink a glass or two, to talk and shake hands.'

'That's right,' mocked Pierre-Edouard, 'dance around, like that bear a gypsy promenaded through the village before the war – the 1914 war, I mean!'

'Don't listen to your father,' continued Léon. 'You'll see, as soon as you're elected, he'll be the first to say it was thanks to him!'

'Possibly,' admitted Pierre-Edouard, 'but in the meantime, who's going to look after the animals while he's running round the countryside?'

'Yourself and Nicolas of course,' decided Léon. 'You can do that, can't you?'

'Oh, I get it,' Pierre-Edouard smiled, 'while you two are stirring up a lot of hot air, Nicolas and I will be stirring manure and buckets of pig-swill! Well, I prefer my place to yours! At least my work serves some purpose!'

'What are you talking about?' asked Mathilde, who had only just started listening to them.

'Your son wants to stand as a regional councillor, and thinks he's already there.'

'He's right,' she said, 'and he should be elected, that would teach the people in the village who didn't want him as mayor! Yes, that would teach them!'

'Now look at that!' cried Pierre-Edouard. 'First Léon, now your mother! Well, my boy, I'll end up believing you could be elected, because with two Dupeuchs to support you, you'll see, everyone will vote for you, just to get rid of your uncle and your mother!'

'Don't pay any attention to your father,' said Mathilde, 'he doesn't believe a word he's saying! Right,' she pressed on in a serious tone, looking at her brother, 'you know the mayors of all the towns involved?'

'The mayors and everyone else.'

'Good. So before announcing Jacques as a candidate, you'd better find out the way they're thinking; what they want, what they're expecting, all that sort of thing!'

'*Miladiou!*' said Léon with a smile to Pierre-Edouard, 'there's my sister trying to teach me my job! What are you thinking of,' he said to Mathilde, 'getting your son elected, it's like selling a cow! You show all his good points and none of his faults! With him, I'm in luck; I don't even need to tell any lies – well, not too many, just a few for the fun of it, eh!'

Louise came back to Saint-Libéral for good on 29 October. She was greeted by mangificent weather which warmed her heart and threw her, overflowing with emotion, into her brother's embrace.

As she had said to her son, Pierre-Edouard and Mathilde had not hesitated for a minute to reply that she would be welcome; that her bedroom stood ready, and they would both be delighted to see her return at last.

That same evening, because she wanted everything to be above board, she suggested to her brother that she give him part of her pension to pay for her food. He rejected it outright.

'Keep your cash, you won't see the day when I allow my sisters to pay me for a room in the house where they were born!'

'Yes, yes,' she insisted, 'because if you won't take anything, I'll soon be embarrassed to be eating your soup!'

'Rubbish,' he interrupted, 'save your money. You'll need it if you're going go get that house built on Combes-Nègres one day.'

'Yes, but meanwhile I don't want my being here to cost you anything. And if you won't accept any money, I'd rather go and move into Suzanne's!'

'You'd have a job,' he said laughing, 'she hasn't kept any rooms for three years! Now she only runs the bistro.'

'Well,' decided Louise, 'I'll work with Mathilde on the farm, in the cowsheds, the garden, all over!'

'That I agree to; I can't argue with that.'

'And I'll go and mind the cows on Combes-Nègres, as I did in the past,' she added with a touch of nostalgia.

'You can mind them if you like,' he said, 'but it won't do much good; we closed off all our meadows a long time ago with barbed wire or Jacques' electric fence.'

'That's a pity,' she murmured in disappointment.

'Maybe, but it's more practical. Besides, who minds cows these days? You know, my dear, cowherds don't exist any more.'

Three days later, on 1 November, the news on the radio told of the tragic events which had plunged Algeria into mourning on All Saints Day. But in Saint-Libéral, as elsewhere, nobody paid much attention to these massacres. Algeria was far away, like Morocco or Tunisia, and there was always trouble with the Arabs, conflicts without apparent reasons.

And because the political situation was no worse than usual since Paul had been posted to Djibouti, and Guy was still in Germany, neither Pierre-Edouard nor Mathilde thought for a minute that a fresh war had just broken out.

Rejuvenated by the goal which he had set himself of getting his godson elected, Léon spent part of the winter running round the hamlets and villages. After considering the problem he had calculated, in agreement with Jacques, that it was unwise for a candidate to reveal his intentions and plans too soon, and thereby to present his competitors with the time and the wherewithal to attack him.

His judgement was correct, and he was jubilant when he realised that the majority of electors, as a result of seeing him beating about the countryside, firmly believed that he was preparing for his own candidature. Secretly delighted, he let them talk, amused to see his godson's future adversaries exhaust themselves by directing their blows at himself.

Then, when he had studied and researched the canton and learned everyone's needs – this village had no running water, that isolated farm was waiting for an electricity supply, others demanded surfaced roads – he faded into the background and pushed Jacques into the ring.

Even the people of Saint-Libéral were surprised at this dramatic turn of events. As for the other candidates, they were forced to change their target hastily, and look for arguments designed to denigrate young Vialhe. But just as it was easy to invent a hundred accusations against Léon – his former profession and his inordinate riches were a gift to his detractors – it was extremely difficult to attack Jacques. On his side he had the honesty and good reputation of the Vialhes; he was a serious professional, a pillar of one section of the farming world and of the young people in the Young Christian Farmers.

With all these advantages came an ease of expression and best of all, thanks to the information supplied by Léon, an excellent knowledge of particular situations.

Despite that, when all seemed set for him to gain a commanding lead at the end of the first ballot, he only came second, far behind an old war-horse who, as Pierre-Edouard said, had been lining his own nest for more than thirty years.

Sad and embittered, Jacques was within a fraction of abandoning the struggle.

'Out of the question!' said Pierre-Edouard, irritated by his son's partial failure, 'you have a week to climb back up the slope!'

'A slope of almost three hundred votes!' sighed Jacques, 'and I haven't even any money to pay for posters and leaflets!'

'Don't worry about money, that's my business,' cut in Léon. 'Starting tomorrow we'll go round all the farms again, and at the double! You'll see, the other old Arab is so sure of winning now that he'll sit back. We're going to get moving, and too bad if you're drunk every evening from buying rounds for everyone, I'll bring you home!'

'That's right,' Pierre-Edouard encouraged him. 'Look, we'll study the results, village by village; we'll have to give the ones who voted the wrong way a good working-over.'

'And then you must make a fuss of the women,' Mathilde reminded him. 'Well, what I mean is,' she said, smiling at her daughter-in-law, 'get them to vote, you know! They've had the right for ten years; tell them that now's the moment to exercise it!'

Jacques started his electoral campaign again on the Monday morning. He conducted it briskly, undertaking visits to the most remote farms and hamlets, never hesitating to walk into the fields to have a discussion with some elector busy sowing his beets or planting his potatoes.

On Wednesday, the day of Ayen market, he spent the morning in the market-place; strolled among the calves, gave his opinion on the heifers on sale and his views on the latest tractor models, agreed with everyone in deploring the lack of control over prices and the spiralling rise in the cost of commodities.

But to be forced to try to outbid his rival in this way depressed his spirits, and strengthened his impression that the battle was lost before it had begun.

'That's all very fine, but I really feel I'm prostituting my soul, and I don't like it one little bit,' he confided to Léon, when they went to recharge their strength, towards ten o'clock, by taking a bowl of soup with a little something in it at the nearest bistro.

Léon shrugged.

'Yes,' he admitted as he poured a generous measure of wine into the bottom of his soup-bowl, 'but your rival's doing the same, and not as well as you! So you may be in with a chance; when it's between two whores, it's seldom the poxy one that's chosen! Now, back to work. And don't be scared of making them promises!'

'Even if I were elected, I could never keep half the ones I've already made!' protested Jacques.

'Never mind,' Léon assured him, 'they know that perfectly well, but it's part of the game! Come on, my boy, let's go and get you the missing votes.'

It was on their way back to Saint-Libéral on Thursday evening that Léon was taken ill; a mixture of weakness numbing his left arm and a heavy-headed fuzziness in the back of his skull. Luckily he felt himself losing consciousness, and had time to stop the car before collapsing over the steering-wheel.

'My God!' What's the matter?' cried a worried Jacques as he supported him.

'Tired,' whispered Léon, 'take me home, quickly . . .'

'It'd be better to go to Ayen and see the doctor!'

'Home,' repeated Léon, 'you can call him from there. Drive on, my boy,' he muttered, sliding into Jacques' seat, 'drive on, it's getting better already.'

But the interior light revealed a pallor and an expression which contradicted his words.

'Go home,' he insisted.

'All right,' said Jacques, feeling more anxious than ever, 'but at the next village I'm going to call the doc.' And the Citroën roared off towards Saint-Libéral.

'A classic start to a stroke,' diagnosed the doctor, 'it doesn't surprise me, with that sort of blood-pressure! How old is he?'

'Sixty-eight,' groaned Léon.

He opened one eye, and looked at Yvette, Jacques, Pierre-Edouard and Mathilde who stood at his bedside. Then he noticed the young doctor.

'Who's this then?' he asked in a weak voice.

'The locum from Perpezac, the other one's on holiday,' explained Yvette.

'Right,' said the doctor, closing his bag, 'I've done what's needed for the moment, but he must be admitted as soon as possible. Do you have a telephone?'

'I'm staying here!' said Leon, trying to sit up. He realised that his left arm felt like cottonwool, and raised himself on his right elbow.

'Out of the question!' cut in the doctor.

Léon closed his eyes; he seemed to be gathering the remains of his strength.

'I'm staying here!' he insisted.

'Come, come, don't be so childish. No arguing! We'll take you down to Brive, you'll be very comfortable there. They'll nurse you and get you back on your feet in no time,' declared the doctor in the jocular, slightly patronising tone he reserved for his patients.

'Pierre-Edouard,' called Léon without opening his eyes, 'chuck him out, the young fool! Out!' he repeated in a remarkably firm voice, 'in memory of Drs Fraysse and Delpy . . .'

'Forgive him,' stammered Yvette.

'It doesn't matter,' the doctor assured her, although he was turning red, 'I'm used to sick people's peculiarities. Get your husband's things ready while I telephone.'

Pierre-Edouard looked at Léon, then at Yvette, and finally at the doctor. Suddenly he understood the strength and reputation of the old country doctors. They strove to treat the sick without removing them from their familiar surroundings, their homes and families, except in cases requiring surgical operations. Without depriving them of that reassuring, soothing environment, punctuated by the noises and incidents which chronicle the life of a farm or village; the whistle of the wind in the slates and the branches of the lime tree, the lowing of the animals in the barn, the children's shouts at playtime, the neighbours chatting beneath the window. And at night, punctuated by the solemn chime of the church clock, the dogs barking to each other, the plaintive whoop of the tawny owl, the screech of the little owl, and in the loft, the quick patter of mice suddenly halted by the cat springing from its ambush behind the grain sacks.

This was the life to which the sick clung, and even if the treatment given by the doctor was sometimes lacking, at least it was accepted with complete confidence and total faith in the man who hurried to their aid at any hour of the day or night. His presence alone was a relief, an immense comfort.

But all that was gone for ever. Saint-Libéral had no doctor now, and the stranger – possibly capable, possibly incompetent – who stood at Léon's bedside was dealing with a routine matter. To simplify things, and to off-load the responsibiity, he preferred to send this unknown patient to some equally anonymous treatment centre. Léon's wishes cut little ice with him; he was only one case among many, an old man whose name and appearance he would soon forget.

'Pierre-Edouard,' began Léon weakly, 'remember Dr Fraysse and Dr Delpy, they would have left me here; don't let them take me away . . . They'll kill me over there.'

He tried to sit up once again.

'I'm going to give him a light sedative,' said the doctor, opening his case, 'it'll calm him for the journey to Brive.'

'Leave him,' said Pierre-Edouard suddenly, 'and go. I've seen enough of you, too!'

'But . . .' protested Yvette.

'He's right, let him say it!' whispered Léon.

'Are you related?' asked the doctor coldly, delicately severing the neck of an ampoule.

'Yes,' said Pierre-Edouard.

He was conscious of the enormous responsibility he was taking. If Léon stayed in Saint-Libéral and died in the night, everyone would say it was for lack of positive treatment which, according to the doctor, he could only receive in hospital. But if he died over there, Pierre-Edouard would never forgive himself for having let him die alone and far from home.

Léon wished to stay under his own roof; he had a right to do so, his last right maybe. They should not betray him by disregarding it; it was unthinkable.

'Yes,' repeated Pierre-Edouard, 'since my brother-in-law doesn't want to go to hospital, no one can force him. He'll stay here.'

'I've never heard of such a thing!' protested the doctor. He observed Léon and pulled a long face. 'This man needs hospital treatment; he's already partially paralysed, any professional practitioner would tell you the same thing!'

'We don't give a damn about professional practitioners, we're not asking them!' said Pierre-Edouard. 'All we want is an ordinary doctor, a real one, who knows how to look after people without sending them off the devil knows where!'

'And what is Madame's opinion?' queried the doctor, turning to Yvette.

She looked at Léon, saw his imploring eyes and forced herself to give him a faint but reassuring smile.

'He'll be staying, I'll take the responsibility. I'll find a colleague of yours who'll agree to treat him here, and if need be, I'll get a home nurse in.'

'If you enjoy complicating things and taking risks!' said the doctor, throwing his syringe into his case and closing it briskly. 'I've done what I had to do; now, don't come complaining if the paralysis spreads to the whole left arm.'

'Bah!' spat Léon, placing his right hand on his stump, 'it's been half cocked-up for the last forty years, so . . .'

Watched over in turn by Yvette, Mathilde and Pierre-Edouard – Jacques had returned to Coste-Roche lest Michèle became anxious at his prolonged absence – Léon passed a peaceful night. He woke in the early hours, when the truck from the milk co-operative passed through Saint-Libéral with its churns clanging, saw Pierre-Edouard seated at his bedside and smiled.

'I was far gone, wasn't I?' he asked him.

'Maybe . . . How are you now?'

'Okay, but I think that little squirt was right, my arm feels like lead!'

'It'll get better but who's going to treat you now?'

'The doctor who looked after my father-in-law. He didn't stop the poor old fellow from popping off, but at least he died at home, in peace! Look, I'm hungry . . .'

'You're hungry?' explained Pierre-Edouard, delighted at this indisputable sign of recovery.

'Dammit, with this going on, I didn't eat a thing last night! Go down to the kitchen and fetch me a hunk of bread and a big bulb of garlic, I hear that's good for high blood pressure. I'd ask you to give the crust a good coating of lard and bring me a half bottle of white wine, but I don't think you'd do that!'

'No, I would not!'

'Well, go and get the slice of bread and garlic, we've got a battle to fight!'

'Yes,' Pierre-Edouard smiled, 'and we'll have the best of it, like in 1914!'

'Well?' demanded Léon anxiously, when Mathilde came to inform him of the election results.

'It's still neck and neck . . .' she said, holding out a sheet on which Pierre-Edouard, standing guard by the telephone at the mairie, had written the figures for the last known count.

Léon scanned the page, made a face and put down the paper on the bedside table, amongst the medicine bottles. He had accepted without protest the draconian course of treatment prescribed by the family doctor. He knew that he was ill and must take things carefully. That was logical. So, on condition that he was left in peace at home, he was quite disposed to follow the doctor's orders, which included, among other things, staying in bed.

God knows how much he had wanted to get up to go and vote, but Yvette was firmly opposed to it and even Pierre-Edouard had sharply reminded him of the threat hanging over him: at the next sign of trouble, it was into hospital with him!

'I'd rather die!' Léon had grumbled.

'You're not that bad yet,' Pierre-Edouard had reassured him. 'As for the election, one vote won't decide it.'

'Good God, no! But what if everyone did the same as me?'

'Stay in bed and be patient. Would you like something to read? I've got some magazines at home.'

'Go to the devil, you and your reading! You'd do better to go and watch the polling-station!'

'It's not open yet!'

Léon had been a bag of nerves all day, and now the results were arriving his fears were not abating. He picked up the figures again and studied them.

'Those bastards,' he said, 'they prefer a city type to a local lad!'

'That's to be expected,' said Mathilde resignedly. 'The countryside is growing emptier, people are forgetting about us. Right, I'm going back down to the mairie, maybe there's something new.'

'Wait, call Jacques on the telephone; maybe he knows more about it in Tulle.'

'No,' she said, smiling sadly. 'Leave him be, he wanted to be over there, at the préfecture, because he'd be calmer than here; we're not going to disturb him. And then, you know, if it's to tell him that even in this village he didn't do all he should have done . . .'

'You're right,' he agreed, 'go to the mairie, but come back as soon as you have any news!'

When she arrived in the council chamber, Mathilde felt that something had changed. There was not the same hubbub, and the looks she was getting were different. She saw that some were triumphant, others disappointed, and understood that one of the candidates was beginning to forge ahead.

'He's gaining!' Pierre-Edouard called as soon as he saw her.

Then she sighed with relief, rushed towards him and examined the figures.

'He's a hundred and twenty-eight votes ahead,' Maurice explained to her, 'it's fantastic! The other one can't make that up now; there are only two villages left and they're right behind Jacques!'

She looked at him and could not resist the impulse to tease their old friend, the good man whom the people of Saint-Libéral had chosen as mayor rather than her son.

'Well, well,' she said to him, 'I think, Mayor, you'll be seeing a regional councillor on your town council . . .'

'Yes,' he said, placing a hand on Pierre-Edouard's shoulder, 'and I'm proud of it. Not as much as you two, but almost. And Léon'll be proud too, and so will the whole town. You'll see; everyone'll be there to set up a maypole in front of the Vialhe house!'

'I'd better go and tell Léon,' she said.

But she stopped because the telephone was ringing. Pierre-Edouard lifted it, nodded his head.

'You can go now,' he said, putting it down again, 'that was the préfecture. Your son is elected with a majority of a hundred and eighty-seven votes!'

'Jacques has been elected!' shouted Maurice, and everyone there cheered with delight.

But Mathilde, beside herself with pride and happiness, was already scurrying through the darkness towards the château.

'He's won! He's won!' she called as she stepped into the hall.

She reached her brother's bedroom and stopped in amazement. Seated in his bed, well propped up against a pile of pillows, a beaming Léon was drinking a glass of champagne.

'What about your diet?' she stammered.

'Jacques telephoned us,' Yvette explained to her, 'so Léon absolutely inisted on toasting the good news, and since he was threatening to get up if I didn't bring the champagne . . . I thought it would be better if I served it up . . .'

'Come and drink to him!' he said, 'and give me a kiss, we can be proud, we have the right. Half an hour ago, the grandson of Jean-Edouard Vialhe and Emile Dupeuch became a regional councillor for the Corrèze!'

'Wait,' said Mathilde. 'I'll drink to it when Pierre's here, because without him there wouldn't have *been* a Vialhe-Dupeuch grandson.'

## 27

JACQUES and Germaine Sourzac, teachers in the village since 1932, finally left Saint-Libéral in July 1955. Since they had never mixed very much in the life of the village, except during election times, and had no close, long-standing friendships, the villagers saw them depart without any great regret. All the more so because it had been known for two months who their replacements were to be, and everybody was delighted to see them arrive.

When it was announced that Jean-Pierre Fleyssac, Pierre-Edouard's son-in-law, was to be the next schoolmaster, many people thought that Jacques had cleverly used his mandate as regional councillor to promote members of his family. He was at pains to deny it and confirm that his brother-in-law had applied for the post two years earlier, but the majority remained convinced that it was thanks to his intervention that Mauricette, her husband and three girls were able to move into the school in Saint-Libéral. In the end Jacques let them talk, for he quickly realized that far from reproaching him, they saw it as a sign of his power and effectiveness, and his electors respected him all the more. They could not, of course, know that Jean-Pierre had only been appointed to what was to be a single teacher school from now on – there were only twenty-one pupils – because Mauricette had given up teaching.

If the departure of the Sourzacs raised little interest, the same could not be said of the butcher; everyone understood that his dwindling clientele did not provide him with a livelihood, but people still lamented his disappearance. It was worrying, for if a man like him was forced to go and earn his living elsewhere – he was taken on as an employee by a meat-curer in Allassac – it stood to reason that the other shopkeepers would shortly be following his example. What was to become of Saint-Libéral then?

Already robbed of their priest, doctor and solicitor, more and more isolated, forgotten, the villagers foresaw the time when they would have to trek all the way to Perpezac, or still further, to buy the merest loaf of bread, litre of oil or three pounds of stewing-beef.

That summer of 1955 two other farmers in the commune acquired a tractor each; the era of working with cows or oxen was past. But during the same season five young people who had been helping on their fathers' farms left the village. Two set off for Paris, pleased to have been taken on as unskilled operatives by Renault; one enlisted in the army, and the last two went to work at the hinge-maker's in La Rivière-de-Mansac: they, at least, returned each evening to Saint-Libéral to sleep.

For Pierre-Edouard and Mathilde, Mauricette's return was a real joy. This happiness somewhat relieved their worries over Paul, who had been in Algeria since August, and over Jacques – despite all his effort and labour, the revenue from his land was not increasing as he had hoped.

The price of pigs was subject to incomprehensible and violent fluctuations; calves were hard to sell; cereals, given their yield, were no longer viable. As for fruit and vegetables, they did not stand up to competition from the citrus fruits and early produce from North Africa and the Midi.

Jacques still gathered in enough to support his family, but the accounts kept by Michèle were there to prove they were simply marking time; it was impossible to expand without taking out further loans.

'It's up there it's happening, in Paris,' said Jacques from time to time, 'they don't want to know about us, we're too small. I think they're hoping we'll disappear; some people don't balk at saying as much, too . . .'

And even Pierre-Edouard, who had long believed that the Vialhe land formed a great and untouchable holding, ended up assessing just how small, modest and vulnerable it was. Occasionally he was haunted by the idea that the time would come when maybe, despite the presence of his son to care for it, this property, fruit of the labour of five generations, would founder – just as in the past all those little small-holdings had gone under, the ones which his fathers and grandfathers, confident in their ten hectares, had considered wretched and without a future.

'It's not possible,' he told himself, 'for if we were to disappear, we who have the finest lands in the commune, who could then survive?'

Mauricette's return was therefore a great joy to him. It cheered him up, made him laugh at his granddaughters' pranks; he bounced them on his knees and in the evening wove baskets of willow or chestnut for them. Trifles for which they thanked him with cries of pleasure and kisses warm and wet as ash leaves after a June shower.

*

The winter of 1955–6 was treacherous and cruel, like an asp which pretends to sleep beneath the heather and coils with a hiss at the approach of a silhouette; you think it torpid and replete, but it reveals itself keen and ready to attack.

Thus January 1956 was mild, rainy, occasionally almost warm, even with the scent of spring some afternoons which deceived everyone. Even the bees were fooled when, on the 20th, a pale but pleasantly warm sun encouraged a few workers to leave the shelter of the hives and buzz about the shelf at the entrance.

'I don't like this weather,' said Pierre-Edouard to Nicolas one day as they were making up bundles of firewood. 'Look at that,' he said, pointing to the swollen buds of the sloe bushes, 'they're ready to burst, the fools; I don't mind if *they* get frosted, but I bet you the plum trees are doing the same . . . I'm telling you, the weather's going mad!'

'It's the atom bomb that's upsetting it!' joked Nicolas.

'It may be that,' said Pierre-Edouard, smiling. 'The trouble is, I remember winters just as crazy before the bomb! At that time, before 1914, people blamed it on the aeroplanes!'

The end of the month was wet and mild. On the evening of 31 January everyone fell asleep to the patter of rain-drops falling on the flagstones, but on the morning of 1 February the silence was astounding. A frozen, glacial silence. In the night, without warning, winter had fallen like an axe; the thermometer registered minus 12° at eight in the morning, and minus 14° by eleven o'clock.

Paralysed by the cold and amazed at the suddenness of the attack, the people of Saint-Libéral closed their shutters, stopped up the doors to cellars and cowsheds with great heaps of straw bales, and huddled in their chimney-corners around blazing fires.

The cold set in and, encouraged by a wind that cut like glass, tightened its grip. Even the snow, which fell in abundance from 10 February onwards, did not succeed in raising the temperature, which remained stationary at about minus 15°. On the 11th, the River Vezère froze over. But they had to wait until the 18th, Ash Wednesday, to experience a cold snap such as very few in the village had ever known. Even Pierre-Edouard admitted that the winters of 1899, 1917 and 1939 had not recorded such temperatures. Only a few former prisoners, like Jacques, and also Nicolas, maintained that they had seen worse; on the thermometer at the mairie the mercury fell to minus 24°. And the wind went on blowing.

It was because of this that Nicolas decided to go out in the middle of the afternoon. He was worried about his bees, for he feared that the wind surging from the east would tear off the thick wrapping of rye straw and jute sacks which protected the hives.

'Are you going out?' Pierre-Edouard was astonished to see him pulling on his fur-lined jacket. 'It's not time to see to the cows yet!'

'I know, but I'll be back soon,' Nicolas assured him, as he slipped on the thick woollen mittens which Mathilde had knitted for him the winter before. 'I'm going to the hives,' he explained. 'I'm afraid this infernal wind will rip away the straw,'

'Wrap up well,' advised Mathilde, 'it seems to me it's even worse now than this morning!'

He went out; the door was only open an instant, yet an icy blast swept through the room. Pierre-Edouard shivered and stoked the fire.

'By God,' he murmured, 'he's brave going over there in this weather!' Then he returned to reading his newspaper.

Nicolas was soon reassured. Even before reaching the apiary he noted from a distance that the straw was holding well; it was covered with frozen snow and was not moving under the buffeting wind. Nevertheless he climbed up to them, for the pleasure of contemplating the fine line of hives.

He was bending towards the first one when an agonising stab seared through his chest. Lashed by the pain he straightened up sharply, wavered for an instant, and collapsed like a tall poplar fells by the wind. And his hair, although so white, made a little patch of grey on the snow.

When Pierre-Edouard found him half an hour later, he could not even fold the arms across the body – they were already stiffened by the frost.

In the village they very quickly learned that death had struck at the Vialhes. And because everyone knew that Nicolas was almost part of the family, many came towards evening, despite the intense cold, to pay a last visit to the strange man who had landed up in Saint-Libéral a quarter of a century earlier and had made it his home, and the Vialhes his only family.

Even Jacques, informed by a boy, walked down from Coste-Roche, for the frozen snow rendered the track impassable by car. He came and was not surprised, any more than the neighbours were, to find his father dejected and his mother in tears. Their sorrow was heartfelt – and so was their gesture. For Nicolas, who in his lifetime had never wanted to leave his cubby-hole in the cowshed, now lay in one of the bedrooms of the Vialhe house.

For the two nights preceding the burial Jacques, Pierre-Edouard, Mathilde and Louise, but also neighbours and friends, took it in turns to watch over the mortal remains. Only Léon could not come; for him too the cold might prove fatal.

The weather broke on the day of the funeral and heavy rain accompanied the cortège, making the snow slippery and dirty and the red soil in the graveyard as sticky as grease. Despite that, the neighbours came in great numbers for, having been twenty-five years in the parish, Nicolas had eventually made them forget that he was a foreigner. Many were quite astonished to discover his name on the plaque which Pierre-Edouard had ordered to be engraved:

Nicholas Krajhalovic
30 juin 1893. 17 février 1956

For them all, he was simply Nicolas at the Vialhes'.

Nobody needed to wait for the complete thaw to discover the extent of the catastrophe. Besides a number of water-ducts burst by the frost – pipes can after all be replaced or repaired – not a single cereal field in the commune escaped destruction. But this loss, however burdensome, was not as devastating or far-reaching as what had happened to the walnut trees.

On every side were split trunks, gaping scars, through which their life would flow away as soon as the sap began to rise. And the damaged trees which might perhaps have survived would have their wounds open to every parasite, infection and fungus; attacks which would undermine the trees until they withered away in years to come.

With a heavy heart, when he foresaw the extent of the damage, Pierre-Edouard counted the victims. The frost of 1939 had cost him four trees; that of 1956 carried off another thirteen. Of the thirty-one walnut trees which he had planted long ago with his father, there remained only eleven. Eleven magnificent trees, in their prime, their beauty and value accentuated by the loss caused by the frost. Besides the harvest of nuts which the victims would have provided, their wood itself was spoiled. That wonderful wood for carving which, to the owner of a walnut plantation, is like a living investment, to be drawn on in dire need.

'How many?' asked Mathilde, when he came back down from the plateau. She had no doubt that the losses would be significant, but she wanted to know the extent.

'Thirteen,' he sighed.

She saw him unhappy, distressed by this fresh blow; Nicolas's death had affected him deeply, and the lost trees increased his sorrow.

'We'll have to replant,' she decided, 'this year. Promise me you'll plant some more!'

'Of course,' he said. 'What did you think, that I'm too old now to fight on?'

She smiled, held out her hand to him, and her small, delicate fingers were lost in his hard, calloused fist.

'No,' she reproached him, 'I didn't say that, but . . . in the long run, aren't you tired of always having to start again?'

'Yes, a bit,' he admitted, 'it's natural, I'm not twenty any more. But that won't stop me replanting our walnuts!' He turned to Louise, who was knitting by the fireside: 'Do you remember when we planted them, thirty-one of them, up there?'

'Of course! It was on St Catherine's Day, in 1901!'

'How old was Grandfather?'

'Oh, he was ancient, and his rheumatism was giving him a terrible time!'

'Yes,' she said, looking at Mathilde, 'he was seventy-one then. He still wanted to come up to the plateau on the last day of the planting. Well, I'm sixty-seven next month, so you mustn't think I'm going to sit about doing nothing! And I haven't got rheumatism – well, not much . . .'

The call-up for the class of 1952 in May '56, and the departure for Algeria of Guy, now a sub-lieutenant in the reserves, surprised and shook the Vialhes like a thunderbolt from the blue.

They suddenly understood, as did all the parents in the village with sons of an age for military service, that the so-called peace-keeping operations – as the politicians hypocritically named them – were a war; a new sort maybe, but a real war.

Until now, the people of Saint-Libéral had not taken much interest in the events in Algeria. They found them disturbing because they complicated and aggravated the political situation and the general malaise, and they could do without that, but they did not feel directly affected. Until spring 1956 it had never occurred to Pierre-Edouard, although he knew what was going on from Paul's letters, that his youngest son would one day have to face war.

Admittedly Paul wrote rarely, and his information was vague; but he had never given them to believe that it would ever be necessary to call up conscripts to subdue a rebellion amongst a few goatherds!

So the shock was severe for Pierre-Edouard, and above all for Mathilde; cruel and lonely because, beyond the first moment of amazement, those villagers who were not directly concerned – and they were the majority – continued their lives as if nothing had happened. But for the Vialhes and several others, the wait for letters began; the worry after reading a newspaper article reporting actions; the careful listening to the bulletins and, between the mothers, the exchange of news.

Mathilde, who had finally got used to the life chosen by Paul – he was a professional soldier, therefore, she thought, more capable of defending himself – suddenly felt very worried about Guy. He himself, stationed in Biskra, might sometimes forget to strike off the days which separated him from his discharge, but his mother certainly kept count of them. She calculated that her son had spent almost two years in Germany; the length of service was thirty months, and he would therefore be home to celebrate Christmas with them.

In September, Paul spent the last week of his leave in Saint-Libéral. Although Mathilde was secretly hurt when she learned that he had already taken three weeks' holiday in Paris without even telling them, she did not reproach him with it.

'You must understand that we don't mean much to him now,' Pierre-Edouard explained to console her. 'Here there's nothing to distract him; no friends, no cinemas, no bistros, no women,' he murmured almost to himself, 'and we're old . . .'

'There's still his brother!'

'Jacques? Yes, but you know they've nothing in common, you must realise that! Look how Paul lives, and what he earns! Poor old Jacques, in comparison . . . And then to Paul, Jacques' whole life is routine, peace and quiet, the family – everything he was trying to escape!'

For the first few days Paul talked very little about his life in Algeria. He made an effort to reassure his parents as to the risks Guy might run, but Pierre-Edouard was convinced that he was not saying what he was really thinking; that he was ill at ease when anyone urged him to talk about the war. So one evening, when Mathilde and Louise had gone to bed, he tried to find out.

'Now that the women can't hear us, tell me what's really happening over there?' he asked, as he watched his son pour himself another measure of plum brandy.

Paul inhaled the bouquet, swallowed a mouthful.

'Over there?' he said with a bitter grimace. 'It's foul, completely rotten. We comb through the Jebel Mountains, we trudge about, we lock people up. All that to pick up a few lousy vermin, and we don't know whether they're partisans by choice, or force! But we put a bullet in anyway, to clean up the countryside . . .'

He emptied his glass in one draft and refilled it.

'You're drinking too much,' commented Pierre-Edouard.

'Yes, I know; over there, we drink too much, what else do you want us to do? It's such a bloody mess, and we're doing such disgusting work! It's not a straightforward war, you see,' he continued fiercely. 'How can I explain it to you! The Viets were vicious, deceitful, but at least they were soldiers and in the field; when you could pin them down, there were real battles! Besides, over there, I knew who I was fighting against; against the Marxists, that was plain. But with the fellaheen, it's a complete shambles. You don't know who they are nor where they are, everywhere or nowhere, like shadows, you know! Bloody ghosts ambushing us and then disappearing. Or they're chucking bombs or grenades into the bistros and cinemas, poxy things, I'm telling you! Then we have to search through the hamlets, check the papers, drag about everywhere, interrogating questioning. It's a copper's job, that, and I'm no copper, but I'm doing their work!'

'You chose it,' his father reminded him.

'Yes, to make war, not be a policeman! And to add to it, now they've stuck these boys in amongst us, kids like Guy! It's not their job either to track down wogs! Those kids, all they want is their demob. You can't blame them; they don't give a damn about Algeria! That's natural, in France you don't care either, I soon saw that in Paris during my leave!'

'I care about it!'

'Of course, you've got two sons over there! But suppose neither Guy nor I were there. Come on, be honest, you'd do the same as everyone else, you'd wait for it to blow over!'

'Maybe,' admitted Pierre-Edouard. He relit his dead pipe, and sighed: 'And do you think it'll last much longer, this war?'

'How should I know . . . If they fought like the Viets, we'd soon have them on their knees! But the way they do things, it's not so simple.' Paul thought for a moment; contemplated his empty glass. 'Anyway,' he continued, 'we'll fight to the finish on the ground; over there we won't get screwed up in another battle like Diên Biên Phu, and they haven't got a leader like Giap either! Yes, we'll wring their necks, but I'm not sure there's any point in it!' he smiled rather sadly, and added: 'You see, I'm in a position to know that you can never hold on to those who really want to leave. You left the house a long time ago, and Aunt Louise and Aunt Berthe and I went away as well! And no person or reason could stop us. The Arabs will do the same — in fifteen or twenty years may be, but they'll be off. That's to say they'll kick us out, it amounts to the same thing! So we're already in a bloody mess, and the longer we wait the sillier we look!'

'So you think it would be better if we saved ourselves the trouble and stopped straight away?' asked Pierre-Edouard, surprised by his pessimism.

'Oh no!' said Paul pouring himself another half glass of alcohol, 'we've got this far, we might as well try to salvage something out of it; anyway that's what they're paying me for!'

'I thought you didn't want to do a . . . a policeman's job!'

'I know, but after the two bouts of jaundice in Indo-China and the amoebic dysentery, I shouldn't drink alcohol either, and still . . .'

Following Nicolas' death, Jacques lost several hours each day coming down to the village to help his parents look after the cows.

So in the spring, he reckoned that the most sensible and cost-effective course would be to take his own animals to Coste-Roche. And he would doubtless have moved them up there without more ado if the little byre attached to the house could have accommodated his fifteen Limousin cows, but it was only intended for three. He was therefore forced to consider the construction of a cowshed.

He talked to his father about it, and was surprised at his reaction. Without trying to dissuade him outright, Pierre-Edouard presented all the arguments which tended to demonstrate that this solution was neither the simplest nor the best. He spoke of the expenses of the building; assured him that Louise, Mathilde and he were still quite capable of seeing to the cows, and that he did not need to come twice a day if it took up too much of his time.

'And anyway,' he said, 'you're driving the children down to school and picking them up in the evening!'

'Of course, but as soon as they're big enough, they'll walk or bike it. No, really, it wastes so much of my time. And·it's not practical, nor good for the animals. Our land is up there, the cows tire themselves out climbing up to graze and again coming back down here; it's not viable. Besides, soon it'll be too small here; I've got to get to the stage where I keep more than twenty cows, and I'll get there.'

'If you move your cows to Coste-Roche, that means you'll never come back here,' said Pierre-Edouard finally.

And Jacques understood that this was the real reason for his reservations.

'Here or there, it's still a home!'

'Yes, but this is the real Vialhe house. Coste-Roche is different, and it's too small anyway!'

'That's no problem; as soon as I can convert the loft, I'll make three bedrooms there.'

'And who'll look after your mother when I'm gone?'

'You've got Mauricette, and after all, good God, we've still got time to think about that!'

'You never know . . . Well, if you prefer to stay up there for good, you'd better do it,' conceded Pierre-Edouard. He sucked his pipe, which had gone out, then smiled mischievously: 'Oh yes,' he said, 'I know what you like up there; that's where you were conceived and born. At heart you feel it's the new Vialhe home, for the young people. Here, with your mother, aunt and me, it's almost like an old people's home, just like the rest of the village!'

Pierre-Edouard let his son draw up the plans for his future cowshed, calculate the cost of the project and discuss it with the Crédit Agricole. But he would not compromise when, at the beginning of November, the moment came to plant the walnut trees, and Jacques proposed the establishment of a modern orchard, for quick returns and ease of working, planted with half-standard, fast growing trees.

'No, no,' insisted Pierre-Edouard, 'I saw you coming, I know what you want me to do, I've read about it somewhere, but I won't have it here! Do that on your land, if you like, I'm sure you're right, but leave me the satisfaction of planting real trees, the sort that take fifty years to reach their prime; at least they'll remind my grandchildren that I planted them for them! You're half-standards, with trunks like cabbage stalks – I don't want any of them, don't think I'm going to put them on my land!'

'But they're the most cost-effective,' attempted Jacques. 'You'll have nuts in less than ten years, whereas with the others you'll need to wait twenty-five! If they haven't been destroyed by the frost before then . . .'

'I know. If I were your age, I'd probably think the same way as you. You young people, you must work for yourselves, grow whatever gives quick returns and lots of it. And your sons'll have to follow the same system because you won't be leaving them much that's lasting; no big beautiful trees, no fine stone and slate buildings, nothing solid, you know, like so much wind . . . Whereas I'd like to leave behind some real nut trees, just for the sake of it. I'll never pick their walnuts but I don't care, because when I go, the trees you're going to help me plant will still be young. And if all goes well, in eighty years' time they'll be a memorial for me, and for you too.'

Since he was much younger than his brother, and in no way prepared for the hate, racism and violence, Guy was profoundly affected by the months he spent in Algeria. And he, whose vocation and profession was to defend the guilty – or the presumed so – discovered wit horror the law of retaliation, an eye for an eye, applied indiscriminately and immoderately. A corrupt law which escalated, quickly attaining a bloody and irreversible momentum of its own.

He saw its ravages in bodies torn by a grenade thrown at aperitif time between the legs of the drinkers peacefully sipping anisette. He measured its vileness as he watched the ragged fellaheen – maybe innocent, maybe real cut-throats – disappearing towards a mountain pass with doomed expressions and dragging step: they set off, well guarded by several squaddies in a deceptively peaceful way, on a supposed wood-gathering party, which would be suddenly interrupted by the long furious volleys of submachine-guns.

Immediately disheartened, he attempted at first to understand, to analyse, to plead for both sides equally, without differentiating between clans and races. He refused to choose between the young shepherd boy who, from sheer panic, fled at the sight of troops rather than coming towards them and was cut in two by a burst of machine-gunfire, and Private First Class Durand from La Ferte-Saint-Aubin or Calais, riddled with bullets twenty days before the discharge which he had looked forward to for twenty-nine months.

However, he very quickly understood that it was impossible to sustain the position of passive witness. It could only be maintained by those who were not at the heart of the tragedy, who did not experience it every day; those who far away, in France for example, had the opportunity to fulminate and argue – but at peace, without risk and among friends – and even to pronounce definitively on the facts of a situation of which they only saw one side, one tiny part.

Guy's arguments and ideas of one day were destroyed by the events of the next, for the clandestine execution of a suspect followed the mutilation or massacre of a comrade surprised in an ambush.

Because he was an unwilling participant in this terrible guerilla war, but did not want to succumb in his turn to the blind hatred, not to say sadism, of the torturers on both sides, he developed a melancholy cynicism. He compelled himself not to feel anything and, like many of his companions, tried to view the events and the corpses with the indifference of men who know that they are merely counters in a game which they have neither willed nor chosen; who submit to its demands and even inconsistencies, required only to obey, to act, and to remain silent.

Nevertheless, despite his wish to be only an unthinking tool – a position which prevented him from seeing war with the eyes of a real fighter, that's to say, to love it and live by it – he was aware of the conflicts within himself which he was forced to endure from the moment he noticed that, as a civilian disguised as a soldier, he was thinking and reacting like the lawyer he was to become, whilst behaving as the sub-lieutenant he now was.

Constant struggle between the man who rebels against a senseless war, and the Jebel scout who feels the heady exhilaration of the hunter, the instinct to fight. He was never one of those who rejoiced at the sight of enemies finally stretched out on stony ground – from that moment the game became a nightmare – but he did have to admit that he experienced a sort of barbaric satisfaction, participating in this horrifying game of hide-and-seek, where everyone knew the rules, and the stakes.

It made it impossible for him to speak of the war on his return to Saint-Libéral at Christmas, as his mother had expected. From now on it was a secret, an episode of his life, a memory to be shared only with those who, like him, had discovered all its facets, its occasional delights, frequent horrors, constant paradoxes. Civilians could understand nothing of all that, for on this matter they saw things with different eyes from those who returned from Algeria; they did not speak the same language.

Between them lay the chasm which isolates actors from audience; an unbridgeable orchestra-pit, crowded, for Guy and many others, with colonists who were not all exploitative, Arabs who were not all killers, beautiful *Pied-noir* women, tantalising but forbidden, the smiles and the glib chatter of the little shoe-shine boys, the smell of anisette, mint tea, burning spices, roast sheep and couscous. And behind it, on the stage – rendered all the more poignant by the incomparable brilliance of the sun – tragedy, in all its violence, horror and complexity.

The people of Saint-Libéral could not perceive any of that. They wanted everything to be black or white, good or bad; that someone should analyse logically for them a situation born of confusion and incomprehension and poisoned by a thousand nuances.

So they would have grasped nothing if Guy had told them that, despite the revulsion he still suffered at the memory of certain days, already a sort of nostalgia hovered within him, for a land which he had detested for its murderous fury, and loved so much for its gentleness, beauty and charm.

He only stayed a week in Saint-Libéral; was taciturn with his parents and grumpy with the neighbours, who all wanted to understand the inexplicable. They took him for a veteran, proud of his deeds and actions and happy to talk of them; he was no more than a man lost amongst them, almost a stranger.

Pierre-Edouard was worried about him, but remained silent. In former times he too, during a war, had measured the breadth of the wall which forever divides those who watch and comment from those who act and say nothing.

'But what's he been doing over there to have got like that?' Mathilde asked him, saddened to see Guy so distant and cold.

'Nothing,' said Pierre-Edouard; 'well, yes, he's aged, and that's a lot.'

# PART EIGHT

*The Gold Ring*

# 28

JACQUES installed his animals in the new stable at Coste- Roche in August 1957. All of a sudden the old Vialhe farm seemed really empty, almost dead. It was with nostalgic disappointment that Pierre-Edouard now tended the three cows which Mathilde and he had kept. Thanks to them, to the two sows, ten ewes, the hives and farmyard fowl, some fruit and vegetables, and also Pierre-Edouard's modest pension, they could survive without calling on either Jacques or Louise. Because they did not spend more than the absolute minimum, were almost completely self-sufficient and had finally paid off their debts, they even managed to put by some savings. The work provided by the animals, the cultivation of the last few hectares they had kept for themselves, and the help they gave Jacques, prevented the boredom which lies in wait for the idle.

Besides, Pierre-Edouard did not feel old, and although he no longer had the strength and dynamism of former times, at least he retained a clear, open mind, with a remarkable ability to adapt. So he understood and even approved, after a pause to consider and observe, the sometimes perplexing way in which Jacques managed his farm.

He therefore quickly realised that moving the animals to Coste-Roche was the best possible solution, and he appreciated all the benefits of it. With its short, easily cleaned stalls, metal tether rails, feeding passage, automatic drinking troughs, gulley for dung and urine, and accessible feed-store close by, the cowshed was beautiful, and the line of eighteen animals impressive.

During the two years that Jacques had concentrated on breeding, Pierre-Edouard had found the time to assimilate and appreciate the techniques which he cleverly applied. Even the tonnage of fertiliser which he spread each year no longer surprised him, and he ended up recognising that the results were spectacular.

Jacques now grew grass with the same care that his ancestors had formerly taken over wheat. Pierre-Edouard had been rather downcast to see his cornfields transformed into artificial prairie, but had quickly admitted, faced with the stretches of rye grass, cocksfoot and lucerne, that is son was heading in the right direction.

Only one shadow disturbed his complete peace of mind; he knew the total of his son's debts and was appalled by it, for he was also aware that his annual revenue was not increasing. The demonstrations, sometimes violent, which were currently shaking the countryside did nothing to reassure him.

They proved to him that Jacques, like hundreds of thousands of other farmers, was reduced to fighting a sort of rearguard action, an almost hopeless struggle.

Since he was bored, no longer had a taste for travel – on the rare occasions when he set out with Yvette, it was now she who drove – and was reluctant to hunt alone, Léon bought himself a television set in September 1957. It was the first receiver in the village.

For Léon and his wife, but also for Pierre-Edouard, Mathilde and Louise, who did not need to be asked to go and spend several evenings a week in the château, this acquisition was truly revolutionary.

Accustomed until then to learning the news only by reading the paper and listening to the radio; to considering the cinema, theatre and circus as luxuries reserved for townsfolk, they leapt straight into the world opened up by the screen, and were fascinated.

They, who had all known the era of the paraffin lamp – not to mention the cruse of oil with a wick poking out of it, for Léon and Mathilde – had experienced the arrival of the first cars and the clumsy flight of aeroplanes built of wood and canvas, marvelled at this prodigious wonder which allowed them, by simply pressing a button, to witness the life of the universe.

The television changed their entire existence. It offered them amusement every evening and, especially for Pierre-Edouard, Mathilde and Louise, who had never gone out as such, the unexpected chance to visit the cinema, theatre, circus, even the parliamentary chamber, without so much as leaving Saint-Libéral.

For several months they were regular, model viewers, to such an extent that the women hardly dared knit during the transmissions. Then, gradually, their interest in the pictures waned; Pierre-Edouard and Léon began to comment loudly on the news, to choose between programmes and even to criticise them.

Then, one evening, as *La Piste aux Etoiles* was beginning and the delighted women were comfortably settled in their armchairs, Léon tapped his brother-in-law's shoulder, tilted his chin towards the set and winked.

'What a drag, this carry-on! It's always the same!' he said

peremptorily.

'Ssh!' replied Yvette, Mathilde and Louise.

'Léon's right,' said Pierre-Edouard, getting up, 'it's fine for children, but we've got better things to do!'

And they went off to the billiard room where they had not set foot for six months.

'Television, it's like women,' declared Léon, 'shouldn't overdo it, it'll end up driving you off your rocker! Which reminds me, what would you say to a drop of plum brandy?

'Well, since you're not allowed it, I think. . .' said Pierre-Edouard, taking out his pipe.

'True: failing a cure, the quacks forbid things, that's all those charlatans can think of doing,' said Léon, grasping a bottle and two glasses, 'but a little brandy once in a while . . . it's like tobacco, eh? Come on, roll me a cigarette, Yvette's hidden my Gauloises again.'

'I'll get told off by your wife, and by Mathilde too!' said Pierre-Edouard, taking out his packet of Old Job cigarette papers.

'The women? You must be joking! They're much too busy watching that carry-on, reckon they won't be moving!' He inhaled the bouquet of the brandy and smiled: 'Say what you like, basically television's a bloody fine invention!'

Since he disliked both pandemonium and politicians, and was incensed by the government crises and incompetence of the fly-by-night personalities who succeeded each other in the political arena, Pierre-Edouard was amongst those who rejoiced at the return of General de Gaulle, following the events of May 1958. But his happiness was somewhat disturbed by the reserve with which his son greeted the arrival of the general.

Wisely, Jacques mistrusted the military; from 1939 he retained a much too sinister memory of them. In addition, he had not lived through the period of the resistance, was close to thinking that the general had the makings and ambition of a dictator, and had not hesitated, with the support of his wretched United People's party, to make a virtual alliance with the Communists. Consequently, unlike his father, Léon and so many others, he was not charmed or reassured by de Gaulle's character.

'But who put those ideas into your head?' grumbled Pierre-Edouard, when Jacques had communicated his scepticism with regard to the new President of the Council of Ministers.

'I don't need anyone to give me ideas! Your general, I don't trust him, that's all!'

687

'But, good God, you couldn't want it to go on like it was! You said yourself something had to give! Haven't you had enough of all those halfwits who've been ruining us since the end of the war?'

'Maybe there was a way of saving the situation without taking over by force!'

'What takeover? For goodness' sake, Coty sent for him, yes or no? And all those stuffed-shirt deputies agreed, yes or no?'

'Not all, not all. Well, time will tell, we'll talk about him some other day, your de Gaulle!'

'But dammit! Who the devil are you going to put in his place, eh? Can't you see we're in the soup? And with this war in Algeria to add to it! Here, you go and ask your Aunt Louise what she thinks of it! You'll see what she's expecting; that de Gaulle will stop his business, and Pierre and all the boys of his age will come home at last!'

'I know, but I'm not sure that he'll sort it all out the way you're hoping. Your de Gaulle's not God, you know!'

'That's for sure,' said Pierre-Edouard, 'but joking apart, who d'you want to put in his place? Find me just one decent person among all the dregs we've seen marching by for the last twelve years. Come on, I'm listening!'

Jacques shrugged his shoulders.

'They're not all dregs. It seems to me that someone like Mendès France, for example, or Gaillard or even Bidault . . .'

'Look, they've tried, haven't they? What have they achieved? Nothing, except regulating private distilleries and distributing milk in schools! And not forgetting the kicks up the backside we collected in Suez and Indo-China! Come now, trust me; with de Gaulle it'll change, and high time!'

But Jacques was not convinced, and for several months his father and he avoided talking politics.

Guy's marriage hurt Pierre-Edouard and Mathilde deeply, for although they accepted that their son had every right and was of an age to marry without their consent or presence, they viewed his attitude as a denial and rejection of his own origins.

'He's ashamed of us,' said Mathilde sadly when Jacques, in great embarrassment, told them that he had just seen the request for registration of the banns at the mairie.

'Bah,' scoffed Pierre-Edouard, to mask his disappointment, 'we wouldn't have been there anyway. But damnation, the little devil could have told us some other way!'

'Yes,' repeated Mathilde, 'he's ashamed of us, that's what it is.'

'I'd like to know what's going through his head! It may well be that he hasn't even old Berthe – although she wouldn't put him to shame, she knows how people live up there! And anyway, who's this girl? This Colette, where's she from?'

They had to wait three weeks for the arrival of Berthe to spend a few days' holiday in Saint-Libéral before hearing the details of the story.

'Well, I told him to write to you,' said Berthe with a shrug.

'Oh, we understood!' cried Pierre-Edouard, 'he was ashamed of us, that's all! He'd better not forget where he's from and who paid for his education!'

'That's not how it was at all!' she protested. 'Do you think I would have let him do it if that were the case? It's much simpler than that! Colette's parents didn't want anything to do with this wedding, so Guy and she married with two witnesses, that's all; I couldn't even attend, I was in Rome.'

'By God! You could have told us!' Pierre-Edouard was cross. 'We would have gone up ourselves for the ceremony! And why were her parents against it? Because Guy wasn't good enough for them? Because he's the son of peasants? Is that it?'

'Yes,' admitted Berthe with a smile, 'but it's not worth getting annoyed about it, those fools don't warrant it!'

'It doesn't matter,' said Mathilde sadly, 'he was ashamed of us too; the proof is, he didn't invite us.'

'But that's not how it is,' continued Berthe, laughing. 'Oh, you know, you two are amazing! Right, listen, let's be frank. We're in August 1958, not 1920; Guy and Colette have been living together for more than a year, that's all. So, as the girl's parents were opposed to it, they didn't consider it necessary to bother with a ceremony. You're not going to make a fuss about it, are you? It happens every day, marriages like that!'

'Ah!' gasped Mathilde, biting her lips. 'So she's expecting a baby, is that right?'

'Absolutely not! What are you thinking of! They wanted to regularise their situation, you're not going to complain about that!'

'No,' sighed Pierre-Edouard, placing his hand over Mathilde's, 'when you come down to it, he was right not to tell us, he knows us well; he must have thought we wouldn't put ourselves out. A wedding, that's a celebration; well, for us, it should be a great celebration. Regularising a situation, as you put it, is just a formality; they don't need us for that.'

'Now calm down and be happy,' said Berthe, to try to lessen their disappointment. 'You'll see, Colette's a fine girl, really nice, healthy and everything, and very pretty, too. You're bound to like her. And now she's a Vialhe, she's one of the family.'

'Of course,' Mathilde smiled sadly, 'she's one of the family, especially if hers has rejected her. But apart from Guy, will she want anything to do with the Vialhe family? At the moment, seeing the way she's come into it, you'd think she was trying to avoid it.'

Champing at the bit in an out-of-the-way post more than a hundred kilometres east of Beni-Ounif, Paul sought every chance to escape from the B2 Namous camp. One of those isolated stations, forgotten in the middle of the stony desert, established at the far edge of the *mesa* of El Medjbed, on the rutted track which led towards Benoud, Al Abiod and Brezina.

Pounded by the sun, which at the end of August maintained a temperature of 45° in the shade even at five o'clock in the afternoon, it was often scoured by fearsome, burning sandstorms, which blasted from the south with extraordinary strength and violence.

Paul was bored, and almost longed for his previous posting. In Kabylia, where he had spent more than a year, at least there was something happening; there was unrest, shooting, and the campaigns, even if they were dangerous and testing, made things lively and broke the monotony of the days. But here, nothing. Emptiness, absolute silence. Desert as far as the eye could see.

A natural hell into which even the fellaheen were not crazy enough to stray, especially in mid-summer. Despite that, it was still necessary to guard the sector; on principle, as a discipline, and in case, which was unlikely, the rebels from the mountains of Grouz and Antar, having broken through the frontier towards Benz Zireg – instead of crossing towards Figuig – tried to reach the mountains of Bou Amoud, Bou Lerhfad and the peaks of Ksour by the eastern route.

So, because it was in their orders, but mostly to keep the men busy, for they were ravaged by the heat and undermined by idleness, Paul organised raids; theoretically to detect possible rebels who might venture into this forbidden zone, but in fact to hunt gazelle, whose succulent flesh wonderfully improved their dreadful everyday diet. Besides these sorties he had to send three trucks, including a tanker, to Beni Ounif every ten to twelve days; they returned in the evening laden with stores, cases of beer and water.

On Monday 25 August, to amuse himself, escape the humdrum daily round and give the impression of doing something rather more useful than playing poker or dice, Paul decided to accompany the convoy.

He entrusted responsibility for the camp to Lieutenant Verriet, promised to bring back a good supply of cognac, anisette and cigars, and climbed into the cabin of the leading truck.

'Come on, roll it,' he said to the driver, 'let the lads behind us taste a bit of dust! And if you want me to buy you a beer when we get there, try not to shake up my guts too much.'

Pierre-Edouard put down the sledgehammer, stepped back to admire his work, and smiled at Mathilde and Louise.

'Not bad,' he said, 'not very big, but not bad, and with a fine view!'

To please his sister, who three months ago had made up her mind to have the house of her dreams built in the pasture of Combes-Nègres, and since the plans had arrived that morning, he had just marked out with four poles and a ball of string the ground where the building would stand.

'Yes,' said Mathilde, 'it'll be very good, due east.'

'It seems rather small,' noted Louise, as she stepped over the string into what was to be the kitchen.

'Don't go by that,' said Pierre-Edouard, 'like this it looks small, but wait until the walls go up and you'll see!'

'Anyway, just for me . . .' she murmured.

Pierre-Edouard shrugged, sighed, but kept his counsel. When the sister had talked to him of her project, he had tried to show her that it was quite unnecessary; from the moment Jacques had decided to move to Coste-Roche, Louise could stay in the old Vialhe house for the rest of her life. She was certainly not in anyone's way, but was good company. Besides, building a house, even if you owned the plot, was expensive, very expensive.

It was a waste of time; Louise had not wavered. She herself had contacted a small building contractor in Perpezac and taken all the necessary steps. She wanted her house, she could now afford to get it built, and nobody was going to rob her of the satisfaction. Faced with this stubbornness and determination, Pierre-Edouard had eventually understood and done nothing further to dissuade her.

It was not for herself that Louise desired this house; maybe she would never even inhabit it, preferring to continue to live under the roof where she was born rather than alone here, almost a kilometre from the village. But this house, she wanted it for Félix and Pierre, to leave them one day tangible, solid and lasting proof of all the affection she felt for them.

She had already devoted the greater part of her life to them, and wished now to present them with something which, after she had gone, would perpetuate her memory and her love. And to that Pierre-Edouard had no reply; had he himself not planted walnut trees for his great-grandchildren?

After two hours on the potholed track, which was choked with sand but passable, the little convoy of three vehicles reached the pass of Tamednaïa. Here the stony desert, stretching flat as a table as far as the encampment and even beyond, was broken by a huge, deep fault which overhung the valley where the dry Zousfana wadi sprawled like a fat grey snake.

The track tumbled down towards it in a multitude of breathtaking bends, of lethal sheer drops. It crept through the black scree, clung, twisted, coiled against the rock face, to emerge eventually thirteen kilometres lower down on the pebble plain which bordered the wadi.

Paul jumped to the ground. He had not needed to tell the driver to stop; Private Lavaud knew the road well. Here there was a compulsory halt. First to have a breather and a drink, but above all to work out the descent carefully.

It was crazy, so terrifying that even in the evening, on their return, after a climb of thirteen kilometres the convoy would stop at the same place and the men walked to the precipice to observe with relief what they had just survived.

Not only was the defile as dangerous as a mountain path; it was also well suited to all sort of ambushes, traps. There, fifty rebels could conceal themselves in a thousand different places and fire on the lorries as at a target. There one single fellah, just for the pleasure of christening his brand new weapon – made in Czechoslovakia – could dispatch the three trucks into the ravine; three drivers, three cartridges and goodbye, or rather *msa el khir*!

Since it was impossible to clear this pass as it deserved – that's to say with four platoons of well-trained men who would have taken hours to search through the smallest crannies – the convoy leaders threw themselves into it, foot on the gas, hoping, if it came to the worst, that the vehicles, launched like rockets, might perhaps have a chance of escaping; unless the driver miscalculated a bend.

'It really is a bloody filthy hole,' said Paul, lighting a cigarette.

'Would you like a drink, captain?' suggested the driver, offering a cool damp *guerba*.

'What a joke!' said Paul, grasping the goatskin. He drank deeply, then observed the trail. 'You see,' he said pointing to a bend, 'if I were the Viets – or rather, the fellaheen – that's where I'd hide, but they won't be there, too stupid! Ready, my boy? Right, off we go, and don't chuck us over the side!'

The three trucks rattled off and charged towards the incline.

The unexploded 105 shell, recovered four kilometres from the Duveyrier encampment, primed and buried in one of the turns of the track, detonated under the right wheel and pulverised the entire cabin of the heavy duty transporter.

It was only by the three stripes still clinging to the bloody, lacerated fatigues, that the horrified men in the following trucks could identify the body of Captain Paul Vialhe. He was thirty-six.


As soon as he saw them, all awkward and self-conscious, climbing slowly, as if reluctant, from their blue car, Pierre-Edouard understood. Before they had even spoken, he knew. And when the military police sergeant and his colleague, a corporal, still without having spoken a word, clumsily took off their kepis, he almost told them not to say anything.

He guessed what they were going to announce for, although he denied it time and time again, did everything possible to banish the insidious premonition which lurked within him, he had been expecting their visit for years. He dreaded it, but foresaw that it was inevitable.

His instinct had not deceived him: the two gendarmes who twisted their kepis between their fingers, looking at him with sad, guilty eyes, proved that the hour had come to hear the terrible news. He was so resigned, so shattered, that the policemen, although still silent and trying vainly to show their compassion, understood that they were the incarnation of death, and that this old man knew it.

'Good day, Monsieur Vialhe,' began the sergeant humbly, 'we are here to . . .'

'I know,' said Pierre-Edouard, 'but speak more quietly; Mathilde might hear us, and it's not for you to tell her about it.'

'Of course,' murmured the sergeant, shuffling from one foot to the other. 'I . . . Well, you may have some idea, possibly . . .'

'No, I know. When? How?'

'Yesterday morning,' stammered the gendarme. 'A mine, he didn't suffer at all, that was it.' He sighed. 'It'll take a week to bring back the body . . .'

'Yes,' whispered Pierre-Edouard, 'go away now, I've things to do. I must tell Mathilde, my dearest Mathilde, you understand?'

He turned on his heel and walked slowly towards the house. When he pushed open the door a flood of sun and light filled the room, but he knew that he was entering into darkness.

# 29

ONE supporting the other, responding to every sigh, look or burst of sorrow, with a determination full of consideration and a wealth of affection, Pierre-Edouard and Mathilde helped each other to emerge from the abyss. And since he believed himself stronger and better equipped to react than Mathilde, who thought herself the more robust, each persisted in wanting to carry the burden alone.

Pierre-Edouard compelled himself to suppress self-pity, to silence the mournful anger which thundered against this intolerable injustice: that he, an old man whose life was already so full and future so restricted, should survive his son. It was illogical, against nature, repellent. But he said nothing, for the sake of Mathilde.

And she, whose loins and flesh still held the memory of this son, she whose memory rang daily with his baby cries and childish laughter, she who had been so concerned yet so proud to see him become a man – she also remained silent, stifled her moans and hid her tears, for the sake of Pierre-Edouard.

So, in order not to increase their shared agony, each conquered their distress, attempted to stifle it, with the sole aim of shouldering their partner's pain.

Then gradually, because they had constrained themselves to conquer their sadness, they emerged together from the tunnel and the darkness lifted for them.

During this long period punctuated with pitfalls, setbacks, words and sighs which needed to be silenced – with worry too, at the thought of seeing the other stumble or fall – they were supported, watched over, surrounded. Besides, the help of Jacques, Mauricette and Louise, and even Léon, who himself was a sorry sight, they received comfort from Berthe.

She arrived in Saint-Libéral the day after the gendarmes' visit and with her, embarrassed at introducing themselves under such circumstances, but conscious of being in the right place, came Guy and his young wife Colette, to whom Mathilde opened her arms, quite naturally and without restraint.

Félix also appeared two days later and, as the women were comforting Mathilde, and Jacques and Guy did not know what to do for their father, he dogged his footsteps, hardly left him. He listened to the old man when he needed to talk, and knew to keep quiet when he sought silence.

Neither he, nor Guy and Colette, could stay long after Paul's interment. In contrast, Berthe, already semi-retired, moved permanently to Saint-Libéral. It was she who made sure that the Vialhe house was now always enlivened by the presence of Pierre-Edouard and Mathilde's grandchildren; she who encouraged her brother not to neglect his jobs, his hives, his garden, his vines. It was she, again, who placed a fat ball of wool and knitting needles in Mathilde's hands to begin the layette which Colette, one month pregnant, would need for her baby. Berthe again who, for Christmas, arranged for a television to be installed in the Vialhe house, since Pierre-Edouard and Mathilde, on account of being in mourning, did not wish to go and spend the evenings at Léon's – the neighbours would not have understood such behaviour.

She, finally, who, after Colette's confinement, succeeded in persuading her brother and sister-in-law to accompany her to Paris – where she had retained her apartment – to meet their grandson Jean and thereby prove to Guy and his wife that their offhand behaviour the previous year was forgiven. Pierre-Edouard and Mathilde had to be begged; they put forward the argument of their work, the care of the animals and the hives, and ended up accepting.

So it was that in May 1959 Pierre-Edouard, who had not set foot in Paris since 1918, helped Mathilde discover the capital which she had never seen. Mathilde, at fifty-nine, had never yet left the Limousin.

Elected mayor of Saint-Libéral in the polls of March 1959, Jacques had donned the sash of office with pride and satisfaction, but with no illusions as to his chances of reviving the community.

Everything indicated that it was without a future, without inner resources, in its death throes; deadened by its ageing population, deprived of strength by the haemorrhage of young people who, after their school certificate, fled to the towns to learn a trade, and it was never farming.

Saint-Libéral vegetated like very old chestnut trees which still grow a little greenery each spring, but the number of dead branches increases from year to year and the arteries of the whole framework harden. In Saint-Libéral now, the total number of full-time farmers did not exceed fifteen. As for the other local people, half-peasants, they cultivated their plots on Saturdays and Sundays, or in the evening, on returning from the work in town which was their only means of survival.

However, in the '60s Jacques regained hope, for, one after another as if Louise had taught them how, several houses were constructed on the edges of Saint-Libéral, on land sold by Louis, Léon's son, estate agent in Brive.

For a while Jaques believe in the resurrection – or rebirth –of the village, but he was quickly disillusioned. The new inhabitants, retired people on small pensions, or commuters, did not live within the community of Saint-Libéral, nor join in the life of the village. The former were there to sink into peaceful retirement, the latter came to sleep, or perhaps at the weekends to tend their gardens jealously. Some of them proved to be pleasant neighbours, but their mode of existence, their rhythm of life, created between themselves and the natives of the village a wall of incomprehension which was difficult to surmount.

As the years passed, Saint-Libéral changed in appearance and in character. Whereas not long ago everyone knew everyone else and greeted them daily (apart from quarrelling neighbours), now many villagers got to the stage of no longer bidding good day to individuals who, out of diffidence or pride, did not even respond to their greeting.

At the same time the spirit of mutual co-operation disappeared, which had been the strength and foundation of the whole community. Busy with their dual activities, the worker-farmers had neither the time nor the energy to help out their neighbours. As for the last farmers, they were forced to compensate for the vanished farm-labourers with the maximum number of implements, placing themselves further in debt without increasing their turnover to an equal extent.

Re-elected as a regional councillor in 1961, but disappointed to be unable to pull the village out if its slump, and worried also over the future of his farm, it was with a sceptical eye that Jacques watched the birth of the agricultural directives of 1960 and 1962. Certain aspects of these laws reconciled him somewhat to the existing government, but others reinforced his certainty that he was one of the rearguard of a fast-disappearing agricultural system, condemned because it was not sufficiently productive.

Nobody was interested in it any more, for it was practised by simple farmers who, whatever was talked of or decided, were incapable of transforming themselves into those business managers

697

who, it was claimed, represented the future on the land. Even Jacques, despite his abilities, knew that his modest enterprise, lost among a collection of tiny farms, many of them already in their death throes, was also on the slippery slope to economic stagnation, and therefore extinction.

Since he had a wife and two children to feed, was of the type which deplores passivity and surrender, and held fast to the idea that maybe the one who lasted out the longest would be the winner, he clung on to his land, cared for it, devoted all his energy to it. Thanks to his work, in the face of all logic, the Vialhe farm remained the finest in the commune.

He neither wished nor was able to retrench, he felt forced to rush forward, and therefore never hesitated when, in April 1964, the axle and gearbox of his first tractor gave up the ghost: he acquired a new machine, this time a 35 CV. He paid 25,000 new francs for it and, for good measure, since he was going to get into debt, he also bought a bailing machine for 9,500 francs. It had become as indispensable as the tractor and its accessories, for he and Michèle were now bringing in the hay alone. His father might well be strong still, but he was seventy-five; his help was not sufficient.

It was Léon who got wind of the business. He hardly went out these days – dabbled a bit in his garden, but mostly watched out impatiently for Pierre-Edouard, who walked up to the château every afternoon just after siesta time.

It had become a ritual. In former times they would probably have gone to the inn to talk, but it had been closed for four years, and the bistro previously run by Noémie Lamothe – the only one in the village, now, managed by her daughter Nicole – still had as bad a reputation as at the beginning of the century, at the time of Ma Eugènie.

Pierre-Edouard therefore climbed up to the château, kissed his sister-in-law, then joined Léon in the billiard room. The two men still played the occasional game, but more often they preferred to settle into the huge armchairs. There, with a conspiratorial air, although they had known for a long time that Yvette was not fooled, Pierre-Edouard rolled a cigarette for his brother-in-law – only one, but as thick as a finger! – whilst Léon poured a thimbleful of plum brandy into glasses. They then resumed their conversation of the previous day; commented on the local and world news, dissected the newspaper, discussed politics, evoked their memories and vanished comrades. They were well informed and interested in everything.

On that day 17 October 1965, despite his haste to tell Pierre-Edouard what he had just learned, Léon bowed to their customary ritual; only after he had lit his cigarette and placed the little glass of brandy in front of his brother-in-law did he announce:

'Louis came by this morning . . .'

'I know, he dropped in on us.'

'That's good,' commented Léon, happy to discover that his son was not neglecting his aunts and uncles. 'And he didn't say anything to you?'

'No.'

'That's good,' repeated Léon. 'I understand why he's successful in business, the devil: he knows how to keep quiet . . . And you know why he came?'

'Oh, that, yes! To check on the staking out of the three plots he's sold on the edge of the track up to the plateau!' grumbled Pierre-Edouard.

He did not like all these settlements of houses in the middle of the country. Up until the last few years, the plateau and the peaks had remained as he had known them in his childhood: wild, isolated, quiet, reserved for crops, herds, chestnut trees, collecting butterhead and chanterelle mushrooms, for hunting.

Then the road leading up there had been surfaced – likewise the one climbing up to Coste-Roche. And then the houses had appeared, incongruous eyesores ruining the countryside with the prominence of their tiled roofs and white roughcast walls; they frightened off the game, disturbed the silence, and gave the villagers the feeling of no longer being quite at home when they went out into their fields.

'I know,' said Léon, 'you don't like those shacks, nor do I, but you have only your son to blame; he's the mayor!'

'He believes it'll revive the village; well, he used to believe . . .'

'Never mind, I've something else to tell you,' interrupted Léon, anxious not to continue on this subject, for he viewed with a fairly jaundiced eye the way his own son was using the good ground which he had handed down to him.

'And what's that? Your son's going to do the same as Jacques and not vote for de Gaulle? I know that, he told me so this morning, the idiot!' said Pierre-Edouard sarcastically. His mood had clouded over at the thought of the new houses which would spoil his view.

'It's nothing like that! Let the young people vote as their fancy takes them, that won't stop the Big Fellow from giving the other rogues a good hiding! No, what he told me is much more serious: the Bouyssoux boy's selling his farm.'

699

'André Bouyssoux? From the Heath?'

'Yes, Léonard's son, that fool your father wanted as a husband for Louise!'

'Oh, bloody hell! And why's he selling?
'What else can he do? While Léonard was there, it worked; with him dead it's a right mess of a farm.'

'And his mother?'

'She's in hospital – and for a fair old time, if she ever gets out at all. Put yourself in André's place, all alone over there! Anyway, he's incompetent and bone idle, so the land . . .'

'That's a damn fine farm, at least fifteen hectares and almost all lying together!'

'Fourteen hectares, fifty-five acres,' said Léon. 'He wants nine hundred . . . no eighty, well, nine million in old francs! Now it's up to you.'

'You're crazy.'

'I wanted to tell Jacques.'

'I see,' murmured Pierre-Edouard thoughtfully. 'Heath Farm, yes; that would suit him down to the ground. But it's a lot of money, and a long way off!'

'Three kilometres from here, four from Coste-Roche. Going over the plateau with a tractor and these good surfaced roads, that's nothing!'

'It was Louis who tipped you off?'

'Yes, André went to see him at his office in Brive. So Louis thought that might interest Jacques. He hasn't said anything to anyone else yet.'

'We'd better tell Jacques, straight away,' decided Pierre-Edouard getting up.

'Yes,' smiled Léon, 'we'll go there; Yvette'll drive us. But first, let me finish my cigarette.'


'And where am I supposed to find nine million – ten even, with the fees! If I told you what I'm already repaying on loans each year, at your age, it could kill you!' commented Jacques ironically.

He felt bitter, for as soon as he heard, he realised that these fifteen hectares could save him, that they represented the chance, perhaps his only one, which he must seize no matter what it cost. But his enthusiasm quickly waned at the thought of the sum required to purchase it.

'You'll have to sort something out,' said Léon. 'First you can bargain on the price; in my opinion he needs to come down to seven million. That would be about half a million a hectare, which is fair. If you like I'll go and bargain with him myself, and I'll eat my hat if . . .'

'Dammit! Sort something out! You must be joking! I've no ready money!' cried Jacques, tapping his thumbnail against his teeth. 'And I'm fed up with always grubbing around for cash! The devil take your Heath Farm!'

'Calm down,' said Pierre-Edouard. 'This land, you absolutely must have it. First for you and later for Dominique, if he wants to come back one day.'

'Huh, he'd better not! Why do you think we've paid for all his education, and he's still costing us an arm and a leg? For him to come back and do what I do, work himself to death for damn all? Oh, no!'

'Be quiet,' said Pierre-Edouard brusquely. 'You don't know yet what he'll decide to do.'

This was a contentious subject between himself and his son, which they usually avoided mentioning. Dominique had followed in his father's footsteps, had passed two baccalauréats and was at present pursuing his studies at the college in Grignon, hoping to become an agricultural engineer.

Originally Pierre-Edouard had been very proud of his grandson, and had presented to him, on the day of his first bac, that twenty-franc napoléon which his own grandfather had given him for his school certificate on 11 July 1902.

Subsequently, Jacques' remarks and his grandson's choice of career had slowly undermined his contentment. He had realised that an agricultural engineer is not likely to return to clean out the pigsty, look after the cows, cart the dung. Although he was very happy about Dominique's achievements, the thought that one day there might be no one to succeed to the Vialhe land filled him with sadness. To overcome this he clung to the idea that, against all logic, despite his diplomas, his lily-white hands and head full of books, his grandson would – in his own time, but one day – return to the land.

'That's it exactly,' he repeated. 'You don't know what he'll decide to do later.'

Jacques shrugged. 'It'll never be to come and bury himself here! Not unless he goes mad first!' he grumbled.

'This business is getting boring,' cut in Léon. 'That's not the problem; it's this land at Heath Farm which we mustn't miss out on!'

701

'That's true,' said Pierre-Edouard. 'I hope time will take care of the rest. For the moment, you've absolutely got to buy,' he insisted in milder tone.

'I'd like nothing better, but I've no money, so don't let's talk about it any more!'

'We'll try to help you,' pleaded Pierre-Edouard, 'we could lend you some, er, not much, but a million perhaps . . . I'll need to speak to your mother, you know me and money . . . You must have this land. You've always said that you needed at least forty hectares; with Heath Farm you'd have them. Go for it, my boy, go for it! You should never let land go, never!'

'But you must understand that I don't want to spend my life paying for it! It's no way to live, in the end! All that to live poor and die rich!'

'Don't talk stupid,' Léon interrupted him. 'Your father's right: land, that's the only thing you can rely on. So, your problem, we're going to solve it. I say the older ones who can should help the young ones, that's about the only useful thing old beasts put out to grass like your father and me are fit for! So look: your parents can lend you a million, I'll add five to that myself. You give it back when you can, to me or to Louis, later, right . . . We'll put it on paper, that there's no hurry; because money, at my age . . . And believe me, if I could have, I'd have done more, but Louis cost me a pretty penny with his new agency he's just set up in Limoges! So, five million, will that do?'

'You'd do that? Really?' asked Jacques.

'I give you my word; right away, if you like!'

'Oh well, that changes things,' said Jacques. 'There's less than half left for me to find!'

'Yes, but where?' speculated Pierre-Edouard. 'From the Crédit Agricole?'

'Oh yes. It should work. Next year I'll have finished paying off my first loan, for the château land, so I'll reschedule it for the Heath. You see how it is,' he joked, 'when I said I'd spend all my life paying for my land! But that's less of a worry; four million's not a fortune!'

'Maybe,' said Pierre-Edouard, 'but if I were you, before going to see those gentlemen at the Crédit, I'd talk to Berthe; she gives sound advice, and maybe she'll lend you a few sous too.'

Once informed, Berthe never hesitated for a second, but took out her cheque book and smiled at her nephew.

'At least you make less of a fuss than your parents,' she said. 'Since I came back to live here, they haven't taken a sou from me. I even have to fight to go and do the shopping. Ah, that Vialhe pride! How much do you need?'

'Do you mean . . . ?' stammered Jacques in surprise.

'Here,' she said, and held out a cheque to him. 'You just told me that you were four million short; there it is, and don't mention it again.'

'The thing is, if . . .' he said, 'for the repayment, if you could wait a bit . . .'

'Yes of course,' she laughed, 'I'm seventy-two; if you can give it back in about thirty years, I think that will suit me fine!'

'But I'm not joking!' protested Jacques. 'Either I pay you back, or you keep your money!'

'Don't be silly, dear boy, you remind me of your grandfather Vialhe! Oh, I can see you've still got a lot to learn, and I hope you live long enough to understand that the value of money is only what it's worth to you. For me, it's a pleasure to write you this cheque, it's a little treat to myself, and it's not excessive, whatever you may think! For you, it sorts things out, so don't bore me with the rest. In my life I've earned lots of money, but I've never liked talking about finance. So don't make a fuss. Take this, but if it really bothers you, I'll tell you that when Guy and Colette got married, I helped them too. And then as now, it was a pleasure to be able to!'

Jacques became the owner of Heath Farm a month later. Since he was the only local buyer SAFER, the land development agency, did not intervene. It was therefore Léon who, by choice, bargained over it with the seller.

After a month of holding out valiantly, the vanquished André Bouyssoux laid down his arms, losing two and a half million old francs in the battle, but still certain that he had been the craftier; Léon had convinced him that the next presidential elections would bring a Marxist to power and that all fallow land – which his was – would be nationalised!

Thus, in return for six and a half million old francs, the Heath farmland, on which Jean-Edouard Vialhe had wished to establish his daughter about the year 1910, came into the Vialhe family in November 1965.

# 30

PIERRE-EDOUARD and Mathilde judged the events of May 1968 harshly, despite the explanations and justifications offered by Mauricette and Jean-Pierre, and Jacques' arguments – for without approving the form adopted by the movement he was with them at heart.

They disliked waste, civil disorder and strikes, and did not understand how people who enjoyed a comfortable existence, in comparison to what they had lived through, could have the impertinence to complain. They, who had spent their whole lives working, who in nearly fifty years of marriage had only ever taken ten days' holiday, listened in amazement to the demands streaming out from all sides.

It was not the demonstrations by working classes which shocked Pierre-Edouard the most. Since 1936 he had rather mistrusted them, knew they were quick to flare up and rarely satisfied, and, as he expected no good of the unions, he was not surprised to see them take industrial action. In contrast he was scandalised to his soul by the attitude of the teachers who sided with the protesting students.

He, who all his life had respected those who possessed knowledge, who had done so much and worked so hard to give his own children the opportunity to pursue their studies as far as possible, was outraged to learn that affluent and privileged children – they were students, after all! – not only had the audacity to spit in the soup, but also to create havoc in the streets, and that with the blessing of their professors.

'And is that what you find so good?' he challenged his daughter one evening, after watching the demonstrations shown on television.

Mauricette and Jean-Pierre had come to dine with their parents, as they did once a week, but, knowing their father's point of view on the current events, they carefully avoided broaching this controversial subject.

'You have to understand them,' attempted Mauricette, 'if you think their life's easy –!'

'Christ Almighty! You dare say that to me! Life has never been as easy as it is now! When I was the same age as those young good-for-nothings, I was working twelve hours a day, summer and winter, and my father didn't even pay me! Why are you laughing, eh? What's so funny about that?' he asked Berthe.

'Nothing,' she said, slipping a Gauloise into her cigarette-holder. 'But it's all very well you saying that: when you were their age, you wanted to break the system too! And that's what you did by leaving here, and me too, and Louise the same! When you think about it, we Vialhes were great anti-establishment types; that's what's making me laugh.'

'That has nothing to do with it!' he protested. 'Besides, we never preached revolution!'

'That's true, but we made it happen, in our own way.'

'That was quite different,' he insisted. 'In the first place we worked; they do damn all and demand the earth. Good God, what they deserve is a kick up the backside! And when I think that the teachers have sided with the little whingers!'

'It's not always easy to be a teacher!' pleaded Jean-Pierre.

'What's that? You're complaining too, are you?' mocked Pierre-Edouard. 'With your four months' holiday, your salary, your housing, your guaranteed pension, and all for looking after fifteen kids! You've got a nerve, my fine fellow!'

'I'm not speaking for myself – although I'm entitled to complain, having only fifteen kids to teach, in a village that's being left to die, abandoned by the state! Leaving that aside, I assure you that a number of my colleagues have good reason to demand changes!'

'Not at all!' contradicted Pierre-Edouard. 'A student who refuses to work is a scrounger, and a teacher who goes on strike is a jackass! You won't change my opinion about that!'

'Now, now,' Mathilde quietly intervened, 'we're not in the Latin Quarter now, or at the Sorbonne! I find it quite upsetting enough to see all those people fighting over silly things; so don't you do the same!'

'You're right,' said Pierre-Edouard.

But since he felt himself boiling with anger, and the May evening was still light and clear, he rose and marched to the door.

'I'm going to see my bees,' he called as he went out; 'at least they don't bloody strike, and they don't muck anyone around!'

Although from then on he avoided talking about the demonstrations when Jacques, Mauricette or her husband were present, Pierre-Edouard made up for it each afternoon with Léon. Together they followed the unfolding situation, and were appalled at the way it escalated as the days passed.

Léon remained enraged – even going so far as to advocate a good clean-up with heavy machine-guns and flame-throwers to get all the protesters off the streets – but Pierre-Edouard began to see things differently. After his first fury came mixed feelings, of sorrow, doubt and an inability to comprehend what motives inspired the young people, of an age to be his grandchildren, to act as they were doing.

'I don't understand any more,' he said one day to Léon. 'Either I've really turned into an old fool, or these youths are crazy. Did you see the TV last night?'

'Yes, they should all be shot!'

'But why did they do that? Why?'

'To make barricades, of course!'

'Maybe,' murmured Pierre-Edouard thoughtfully, 'but maybe to destroy everything that existed before them, too . . .'

Until that day, however scandalous he had considered the thoughtless vandalism which set fire to cars, broke windows and ripped up cobble-stones, however grotesque he had found the posturing of the politicians, at least he had seen nothing sacrilegious in all the madness.

He had even felt a tremor of fear when a few hotheads – there were some in the village – had declared that the real proletarian revolution and the time for settling accounts was fast approaching, but the attitude of those who hankered after purges had not surprised him. He knew these old enemies well. They were the sort who had failed to seize power in 1944 and aimed to make up for lost time in 1968. Although their threats called for a few elementary precautions – for a week he slept with the hunting rifle within arm's reach – at least they were logical, understandable, not to say obvious.

But since yesterday, what was to him an irreparable act had been committed; even Jacques, who was in the house, had muttered angrily when, on the television screen, they saw and heard the plane trees topple in the Boulevard Saint-Germain, briskly felled by the demonstrators.

That was the straw that broke the camel's back, the point of no return, the unpardonable crime; and for Pierre-Edouard, who had spent his life planting trees for the sake of his grandchildren, it was the parting of the ways with a generation crazy enough to destroy trees in their prime for pleasure and no other reason.

So, despite the relief he experienced when the crisis was resolved, after the elections on 30 May and in June, he remained hurt by this episode. It had compelled him to take real heed of a fact he had known for years without wanting to consider it particularly significant; that he was a man of the nineteenth century, and a chasm separated him from these youths who were preparing to confront the twenty-first.

It was not years which lay between them, but the sad image of the plane trees needlessly sacrificed on the Boulevard Saint-Germain.

In order not to wake Mathilde, Pierre-Edouard rose as quietly as possible, opened the big wardrobe by lifting the door slightly so that the hinges did not squeak, took his Sunday suit, a white shirt and a black tie, and shut himself in the bathroom.

There, having shaved and washed, he dressed with care, combed his white hair, moistened his temples with a few drops of lavender water, then crossed the bedrom, the living room, and finally emerged into the yard.

The night was just fading in the east and despite the time of year it was mild, with no wind. He examined the sky, and was happy to see stars, without the shadow of a cloud; the day would be fine.

Today, this Saturday, 21 December 1968, Mathilde and Pierre-Edouard were celebrating their golden wedding, and he was as excited as a young bridegroom.

Despite his shoes, which pinched a little, and to pass the time while waiting for Mathilde to wake – she would sleep another hour – he walked along the road, then turned off up the track which climbed to the plateau; the grit in the tar crunched under his leather soles. He strode along for five minutes, then stopped and turned round.

At his feet Saint-Libéral was barely awake, only the houses of those who were about to leave for work in Objat, Ayen, Terrasson, La Rivière-de-Mansac or Brive lighting up one by one. He noticed also that lights were on in the cowsheds of Maurice, Delpeyroux and Duverger; reckoned that it would not be long before Brousse's shone out too, and sighed to think that no other would ever light up again. In the village there were now only four herds, and in the whole parish just eleven farms still active.

'This area is like me,' he thought, 'it's old, worn out, tired, it's standing upright out of habit . . .'

He tried to banish these bitter thoughts, but did not succeed. The previous day Jacques had confided in him that he would only be registering three births in the year 1968, a miserable number. As for deaths, the least said the better; they were too numerous and too frequent.

So today Saint-Libéral, which seventy years earlier had contained almost 1,100 inhabitants, held no more than 322. Already, in spite of the protests and the intervention of Jacques – still a regional councillor – the administration had warned that the post office would be closed down from January 1969.

The rumour was also running round that the school would be closed, too, if the number of pupils remained so low. At the beginning of the school year in October Jean-Pierre had only welcomed eleven kids; if he nevertheless retained hopes of keeping his job, it was only thanks to the arrival of four Portuguese families – they had a swarm of young children whom Jean-Pierre counted on enrolling when they reached school age. And maybe, with a bit of luck, other strangers would move into the village.

There was no lack of empty houses, nor gardens in need of clearing.

Mathilde awoke as he entered the bedroom, frowned at first to see him so smartly dressed, then remembered and smiled at him.

'Happy anniversary, dear wife,' he said, bending over her.

'Happy anniversary,' she mumbled, offering a cheek still warm from the heat of the pillow.

He kissed her on the edge of her mouth and sat down beside her. And with his large hand, all calloused and knobbly, he gently stroked her face.

'Let me see your hand,' he said, 'the left one.'

She held it out, and he was moved to see the little wedding band of nickel silver which he had slipped on to her third finger fifty years before. The ring was quite worn away, as fine as wire.

Then, almost as awkwardly as fifty years earlier, he pulled a box from his pocket, opened it, took out a gold ring – a solid, broad, heavy one – and placed it on his wife's finger.

'I've been wanting to give you a gold ring for fifty years,' he explained; 'there it is, it was now or never.'

'You're crazy,' she murmured in delight, looking at the wide band with the little nickel silver ring almost invisible beside it.

'Yes, maybe,' he said, pulling her against him and stroking her hair, 'but it's lasted fifty years and I've got used to it now, and I like it very much.'

Her cheeks all pink from the champagne and her eyes sparkling with happiness, Mathilde leaned toward Pierre-Edouard.

'I'd really like us to go for a walk, in a few minutes, when the meal's finished,' she whispered in his ear.

'Like lovers, eh?'

'Of course, just us two.'

He smiled at her. 'Are you happy?'

'Oh, yes!'

'Well, so am I.'

Everything had been wonderfully organised by Jacques. Thanks to him, Pierre-Edouard and Mathilde had experienced one surprise after another, joy after joy.

First of all, as ten o'clock struck, Pierre-Edouard and Mathilde – who, for the first time in ten years, laid aside her mourning and wore a gorgeous cream ensemble presented by Berthe – had been summoned outside by a chorus of hooting. Then, because it was very fine, they had moved out into the sun and the steps and had seen at one glance that all the children were there, laden with flowers and presents.

Behind them stood Louise, Félix, as well as Pierre, his wife and their baby, and Gérard, too, with Berthe on his arm; finally, at the back of the group, Léon, Yvette and Louis. And one by one, in order of age, the families had approached the old couple, who awaited them arm in arm at the top of the three steps, their smiles trembling with emotion.

Firstly Jacques and Michèle, with Dominique and Françoise between them – real Vialhes; then Mauricette and Jean-Pierre and their three girls, Marie, Chantal, Josyane; and finally Guy and Colette and their four children, Jean, Marc, Evelyne and little Renaud, barely a year old; they were Vialhes, too.

And it was a noisy, happy procession which set off together for the church, where the vicar of Ayen, who generally only came to celebrate Mass every fortnight, had gladly agreed to officiate in honour of this venerable couple who, fifty years earlier in this same church on a cold snowy day, had sworn each other love, fidelity and support.

After the Mass, whilst the bells pealed out, Pierre-Edouard and Mathilde, like newly-weds, had shaken the hands of old friends and neighbours, and even posed for the two reporters whom Jacques had advised of the occasion.

Subsequently the whole family had assembled in silent meditation around the war memorial where, amidst so many other names, was engraved that of Paul Vialhe. Forcing a smile, for the day was not made for tears, Mathilde had placed a huge bouquet of roses at the foot of the stone cockerel which was crushing a pointed helmet, both flecked with lichen over the years.

Then they had all regrouped to the cemetery, where again

Mathilde laid flowers on the Vialhe tombs, that whole line of Edouards who had forged the family. Finally, before leaving, she had not forgotten to go and put a few white carnations on Nicolas' grave.

Under cover of the noise which reverbated around the village hall where the long table had been set up, Pierre-Edouard and Mathilde stepped discreetly towards the exit.

'Going to pick wild strawberries? At your age? Aren't you ashamed of yourselves?' Léon whispered to them with a wink.

'Jealous!' replied Pierre-Edouard passing his arm around Mathilde's waist. 'If you hadn't picked so many in your youth, you could still be gathering them!'

'Boasting again!'

'What are you saying?' asked Mathilde.

'Oh nothing,' Pierre-Edouard assured her, 'it's only that old man, your brother complaining about his age again!'

Outside peace and quiet welcomed them; even the church square was deserted, and they met only a dog as they walked up the main street. Shut up in their homes, the inhabitants of Saint-Libéral were watching television.

Still with their arms around each other they passed in front of the old Vialhe house, then quite naturally turned along the track which rose towards the peaks. They had no need to talk to know where their steps would take them.

Pierre-Edouard turned his head away as they passed the new houses which stood beside the track. There were now six of them; they ate into the edge of the plateau, and their positioning hinted that other buildings would shortly encroach upon the countryside.

They emerged eventually on the plateau. It was still magnificent, for the Vialhe land was spread out there luxuriant, rich, full of life. All the more beautiful now that it was gradually being encircled by fallow land, heath and even brushwood, which, since men had fled the land in disgust, was establishing itself firmly, and yet waging a losing battle against the inexorable march of the houses; much of this ground belonged to Louis, who some day or other would divide it up into plots.

'Come,' said Pierre-Edouard, pulling Mathilde along.

They walked on to their land, crossed the Long Field with its walnut trees, the very old and the very young, all beautiful, then the Malides – fine, fertile lucerne – Léon's Letters and At Mathilde's – thickly planted with rye grass, sheep's fescue and cocksfoot – and finally the Meeting Field, covered in a rye and vetch mixture, which petered out at the foot of the White Peak.

This had not changed, and the junipers, box, gorse and rush-leaved broom still covered its flanks, as on that day in September 1917 when Pierre-Edouard, on leave from the army, had met little Mathilde, all beautiful, impulsive and pure in her seventeenth year.

'Shall we climb up?' he suggested.

'Of course.'

Slowly, because his legs were no longer those of a young man, they scaled the peak.

'Look,' he said, stopping on mid-slope to catch his breath, 'it was just here that I came with your brother and Louise to empty the thrush snares. It was so cold! It was the twenty-fourth of December 1899, you weren't even born!'

'I know,' she smiled, 'you've told me a thousand times! And it was as you set off again that you heard the wolves and threw away your thrushes!'

'You're right, I'm rambling,' he said, sitting on a large flat stone.

'Don't catch cold on me now!' she worried, leaning towards him to tighten the knot of his scarf.

'No, no, it's fine. Sit down, there.'

She settled down beside him and they nestled against each other.

'Do you remember?' she asked indicating a clump of broom with her chin. 'That's where you stopped my cows. It's a long time ago, all that . . .'

'Oh yes,' he sighed, 'a very long time. And yet it's as if it were yesterday.'

'Don't be sad,' she said, for she knew how to interpret his every look and tone of voice.

'I'm not sad.'

She saw that he was gazing at the Vialhe lands; knew what he was thinking.

'Don't worry,' she insisted. 'Now, thanks to Heath Farm, Jacques is saved. They'll remain the Vialhe fields.'

He gently shrugged his shoulders.

'Yes they will!' she continued. 'Jacques is still young, he can hold them for twenty-five years.'

'And after that?'

'Dominique will be forty-six,' she calculated, 'maybe he'll be glad to have them.'

'Maybe . . . But you know, an agronomist, they don't like bending down.'

'*He* does!' she decided. 'And if not him, there are other young

711

Vialhes – Guy's children, Jean, Marc, Renaud, or perhaps even a son of Dominique's!'

'Perhaps,' he repeated. But he sighed once more: 'There'll be no more fields in ten years,' he murmured. 'They'll all be gobbled up by the houses!'

'Not ours, Jacques will keep them!'

'That may no longer be possible. He may well stop working for almost nothing on ground which is worth a fortune as building plots. Look,' he said, pointing his hand, 'from here you can already see the roofs sticking up. The wood pigeons never make a mistake; since the houses have come closer, the doves have moved further away, it's a sign. One day they won't fly over any more; then it'll all be finished, I mean the Vialhe land. Luckily I won't be here any more to see that . . .'

'Don't say that?' she protested, putting her arms around his neck. 'Don't say that! You must trust all our children; they'll guard it, just as we did. They've already taken over!'

He looked at her and was cross with himself on account of the tears which he glimpsed brimming in her eyes; it was he who had provoked them with a few bitter words.

'I'm nothing but an old ass,' he said. 'It's you who's right, as always. The children are there, they'll watch out, and others'll come along – I'm hoping to see you a great-grandmother. Forgive me for being so stupid on such a beautiful day. I have no right to complain. It's true, life is wonderful and basically we've had lots of luck, we two, and lots of love. Sorrow and hardship too, but who hasn't? Now smile for me. That's it,' he encouraged her, 'like that, yes. You're very beautiful.'

'No, old and covered in wrinkles.'

'Young to me, and beautiful,' he insisted, placing his large hands around her face.

He gazed at her, then, with his forefinger, traced the network of lines.

'You are beautiful, I love your wrinkles and I know them all, they're your very own medals. This one,' he said stroking a little furrow at the corner of her mouth, 'that's the first, it dates from 1917, when I returned to the front line, and my wound in 1918 etched it in. Those ones, those are from the children, their births and the worry they caused you. There,' he murmured, putting his finger in the middle of her forehead, 'that's Paul's, our dear Paul, the deepest one . . . And all the others – that's life; me, us.'

'Exactly what I was saying; it makes a lot of lines altogether!'

'What does it matter! Saint-Germain apples are covered in wrinkles too, when they've lain on the straw all winter. And you know very well that they're the best, the most wholesome and tasty, the ones I prefer above all.'

'You're saying that to please me. Anyone would think you wanted to seduce me, or eat me up!'

'Of course I'd like to! And that's nothing new, you know very well!'

She leaned towards him and kissed him.

'We're a bit ridiculous, aren't we?' she said. 'What if people saw us!'

'They'd say we loved each other, and at our age it's a good sign.'

'Come on,' she said, getting up, 'you'll end up catching cold. And down there, the children are going to worry if they can't find us. They don't even know where we are, perhaps they're looking for us already . . .'

'You said they'd taken over. Well, if they're worried, it's their turn now. I think we've done all we had to do, and we didn't do it too badly. So we've every right to rest a while or go for a stroll. Come on, let's climb to the top of the peak; from up there you see better, and further.'

Hand in hand, like two lovers who have an eternity before them and are careless of time, years or the weather, they ascended the heights of the White Peak.

Marcillac, avril 1979
– mars 1980

# Scent of Herbs

*For my grandchildren*

The Earth cannot end if one single man is still living. Have pity on the exhausted Earth, without love it would no longer have reason to exist . . .

*Jules Michelet (1798–1874)*

# PART ONE

*The Sleeping Village*

# 1

Saint—Libéral was sparkling, all the windows open in the September sun. With the new moon had come at last the stormy showers so longed for throughout two dry months. Too light and fleeting to soak the coarse red soil of the village thoroughly, they had nevertheless revived the green of the meadows and lucerne fields. In the woods the drab summer dust was at last washed off, and they resumed the dark, lustrous green of their summer foliage. However, here and there in the thickets of chestnuts and poplars, a few russet patches already presaged autumn.

In places, still scattered but all the more treasured and sought-after, the boletus mushrooms pushed up their brown or black domes beneath the bracken and heather.

Preceded by a dog still young and foolish enough to gallop and bound after butterflies and grasshoppers, Pierre-Edouard emerged from the chestnut grove which encircled the plateau. After two hours of painstaking search in familiar corners – the same ones over more than eighty years – he had found at least three pounds of beautiful cep mushrooms, healthy, young ones, and several dozen chanterelles. He made for the broad oak stump where he paused on each of his walks, and sat down with a sigh.

He was delighted with his collection, but weariness now dragged at his legs and the small of his back; a cruel ache gnawed at his shoulders too, where rheumatism had set in long ago. As for his heart, it was beating a little too fast, much too fast even . . . He had perspired so much that his shirt was wringing wet. He thought how Mathilde would, once again, scold him for his rashness. She might even force him to change his shirt and flannel binder, and make him promise not to venture out on such long walks any more.

I bet I'll have earned the right to a tirade about my irresponsibility, as she calls it! he thought, smiling to himself. Irresponsible, me? Yes, maybe, but if you can't be at my age! It's the same with the tobacco – he took his pipe and packet of shag from his pocket – not supposed to touch it! And other things as well . . . A pipe, and a little plum brandy, from time to time is very pleasant!

He shrugged at the memory of the recommendations made by the doctor whom Mathilde had called during his last attack of bronchitis, just before the summer. It was a young stranger who was acting as locum at Ayen, a pompous lad whom he had instantly disliked.

'This time, Grandad, you'll have to leave off the tobacco!' he had summarily announced. 'I've seen your file at Doctor Martel's. Firstly you have severe bronchitis, and on top of that a very much weakened heart. So from today, no more tobacco! I forbid it! I hope Grandma will watch out for that! And of course, no alcohol either, just half a glass of wine with meals!'

'What a little squirt!' grumbled Pierre-Edouard to himself, filling his pipe. 'Ten years ago I'd have kicked him up the backside and out through the window! Oh yes – but then ten years ago I had a strong heart . . .' he murmured, flicking his lighter.

He sucked at the stem with little puffs; pressed the tobacco into the bowl with his thumb.

'Never mind,' he told the dog, who had come to lie down in front of him, 'that's no reason for that pimply young incompetent to come reading me sermons! I know very well that I have a weak heart! And so, what's that to him, the little worm? It's my heart, isn't it?' He bent towards the dog, stroked it absentmindedly between the ears. 'You don't care; you're right. And after all, to finish like that, it's still better than poor Léon . . .'

Pierre-Edouard had taken the death of his brother-in-law two and a half years earlier in February 1972, very badly. And although he had so often seen death at close quarters – the carnage of the Great War was ever-present in his memory – he had been deeply affected by the loss of his old friend. A slow and painful parting, interrupted by that useless operation which Yvette, his sister-in-law, had not wanted to refuse, such was Léon's suffering from the stomach cancer which had finally carried him off. But after four extra months of hell!

'Bloody awful thing,' he murmured, shaking his head as if to banish those uncomfortable memories.

It was shortly after the funeral of his brother-in-law that he had experienced his first warning of heart trouble. Oh, nothing too bad! First this unaccustomed weakness and these twinges high up in the side of his chest. Sufficient symptoms for Mathilde to call Doctor Martel, their family physician, immediately: a real doctor, him, a good one, not some locum!

At least he didn't forbid me to smoke, he thought, sucking on his pipe. He knows that I've run most of my race already, and whatever I do, I'm in my eighty-sixth year! Since Léon's no longer here, I'm the patriarch of Saint-Libéral, a nice step up! Well, everyone makes a fuss of me, that's not unpleasant!

Not unpleasant, but occasionally annoying. He had quickly realised that Doctor Martel had recommended to all his household that he should be protected from strong emotions, and especially anything which caused anger. Since then it was a competition to see who would tell him the most lies, conceal the truth best, suppress everything which might shock him. Despite that, he knew everything, everything! He had an accomplice in the place.

Definitely not Mathilde! She depended on him too much, and did not want to risk causing a heart attack by revealing some bad news. Not Louise either; she also believed it was essential to cushion him from all surprises, and therefore to draw a veil over, among other things, the rash behaviour of certain members of his family. And God knows, some of them knew how to get into impossible situations!

However, despite these two mutes, there was nothing he did not know; every detail of all the matters concerning the family. He laughed about it to himself.

Yes, thankfully Berthe was there to keep him informed; to tell him day in, day out, everything which logically speaking he should know; was he not the eldest?

Since Berthe's return to Saint-Libéral some fifteen years earlier, a real bond had grown up between the two of them. This alliance could not have developed earlier, for Berthe had spent part of her life far from the village. She had led a life which had nothing at all in common with Pierre-Edouard's; a life which he had criticised severely for a considerable time. It seemed to him to have little to recommend it and to be unworthy of a Vialhe daughter.

But the war had intervened, then her incarceration, and Berthe had amazed them all. Full first of admiration for his sister, he now felt great affection for her, and in particular was grateful that she did not treat him like an old man. It was she who occasionally slipped a packet of tobacco into his pocket, warning him not to overdo it. Advice which astounded him, for his sister smoked like a chimney. Above all it was she who, each day during their shared walk up the track to the peaks or their chats by the fireside, kept him in touch with family life, the neighbours, the village. Thanks to her he knew it all. And if some of the news had caused him much sorrow, not to mention anxiety, none of it struck the mortal blow Mathilde and Doctor Martel feared. With age he had acquired great detachment. Only death touched his heart, especially that of someone near and dear to him, especially Léon's.

But as for the rest! Bah, that was life! You had to go along with it and keep telling yourself that nothing was the same as before, that you were only an observer, one of the last representatives of a vanished time, a defunct era. Everything became outdated, and most of the values which he had defended were no longer current. If you accepted that, it was all normal, logical, and Berthe was right not to hide anything from him.

What good would it do to conceal from him, for example, that his granddaughter Marie, Mauricette and Jean-Pierre's eldest, a maths teacher in Lyon, was filing for divorce after five years of marriage? Fortunately she had no children; but still, what a mess!

And her twenty-five-year-old sister Chantal, she was a one too! She had been favoured by Berthe, who had introduced her into the fashion house revived and managed by Gérard, her adopted son. Chantal, it seemed, was a resounding success as representative of the Claire Diamond label, but was also a hit with all the men who pleased her. And according to Berthe, who laughed about it, there were plenty of them . . .

As for Josyane, the third and youngest, she had suddenly thrown up her law studies one day and left to go round the world arm in arm with a little fool who purported to be a photographer. It was scarcely credible, such an I-don't-give-a-damn attitude! But according to Berthe, there was nothing extraordinary in all this.

Of course that was not the opinion of their parents, unhappy Mauricette and poor Jean-Pierre, who already had enough to worry about as it was. Jean-Pierre was still teaching in Saint-Libéral but was forced to fight each year against the threatened closure of his school. Thanks to some Portuguese he still had twelve pupils, but did not foresee the intake rising in years to come. On the other hand he was not of an age to retire and could not imagine, at forty-nine, leaving for a school in Brive, or still further away. Really, the poor fellow did not need his daughters to add to the complications of his life!

Pierre-Edouard was not supposed to be au fait with all that, so he never talked about it, except to Berthe . . .

Similarly he was not supposed to know that during his last visit to Saint-Libéral, two years earlier, his grandson Dominique had exchanged harsh words with his father. The culmination was that he had the audacity to reproach him for working himself to death for nothing on the Vialhe land! And he continued to say it in his letters. Dammit, who the devil had paid for the wretched boy's education? And who was still paying for his sister Françoise? Jacques, every time! And he would not see the end of back-breaking work on his fifty hectares until the girl had her veterinary certificate! But the younger generation were ruthless. Not content with finding a job with Arabs – as if there were not better things to do in France – that scamp Dominique had considered his father to be working too hard and inefficiently, his mother wearing herself out to earn a few sous, and that everything could be easier with good advice, better management and a well-organised development plan.

What a nerve, the rascal, thought Pierre-Edouard with a smile. He had a real soft spot for his eldest grandson, a true Vialhe.

Yes, cheeky as a Vialhe, that boy, but lost to the Vialhe land. An agricultural engineer and well on the way to success, if he decided to leave Algeria and return to his job in the company whose name Pierre-Edouard had forgotten. But Jacques assured him that it was a good firm and Dominique would have a very creditable situation in it.

Then he could help out his parents, which would be only fair. He felt slightly depressed at the thought. He knew that Jacques had recurring health problems. From working too long on his old tractor, a machine now ten years old, his back was ruined, his spine crumbling. Doctor Martel even said they might have to operate one day if he continued at that rate. But what else could he do? He was alone with Michèle to manage the farm, take care of thirty-five Limousin cows, ten sows and their litters for fattening. Added to that were the usual crops, especially grass and maize for forage. Also half a hectare of tobacco and double that of beets. So how could he stop when faced with such a burden of work! Not forgetting, besides, the time he devoted to his role as mayor. Saint-Libéral might well be in decline, but there were still three hundred and four inhabitants with expectations, and always plenty of forms to fill in.

Basically, Jacques had been right not to stand in the last regional elections. Firstly because he would have been beaten for certain. People don't want to be represented by someone from the land any more. They want town-dwellers who don't have calloused hands – doctors, lawyers, industrialists, but not farmers. Jacques had realised this. Better to go before you're kicked out, less upsetting. And then if by chance he had been returned, he wouldn't have been able to keep the farm going, and that . . .

To Pierre-Edouard, that was the essential point. Jacques was the last of a very long line of Vialhes. Of all those Edouard-Mathieus, Edouard-Benjamins or previous Jean-Edouards who had toiled over the Vialhe fields for more than two centuries. Like them all he was the eldest, the heir. But unlike them, his son was not preparing to relieve him. And that – yes, that gave Pierre-Edouard heartache.

The sunset was magnificent. Leaning on the rough trunk of an old tamarisk tree, Dominique Vialhe awaited the most beautiful, supreme moment. That dazzling flash of the last ray thrown out by the sun before being sucked below the deep purple horizon of the stony desert. Afterwards darkness would fall very quickly; magnificent, luminous, blue-tinged night, alive with all its fiery stars.

But for the moment, gold and crimson suffused everything. They shimmered on the black stones of the rocky plateau which opened to the north, and on the huge dunes of the great western desert which curled away to the east, soft and voluptuous as the pale thighs of a sleeping woman. They sparkled in the occasional, stagnant pools of water scattered in the pebbly bed of the river Guir. And the sight was so dazzling that Dominique felt he was experiencing one of the most beautiful sunsets in the world. One of the most perfect, the most delightful; and that despite the suffocating heat, the myriad fierce, pursuing insects and that sand dust which irritates the eyes and throat. A close of day such as he had never seen elsewhere. Not even when two years earlier, having fulfilled his national service as a voluntary overseas worker, he had treated himself to a three-month tour of the world before settling down in a job. A sunset which eclipsed those of Greece, Egypt, Indonesia or Australia; outshone those of Peru, Mexico, California or Quebec. Such an awe-inspiring sunset that it would even make you forget those of the Corrèze and Saint-Libéral! And God knows, those were magical indeed! Regal even, but not to this degree. Not to the extent that they filled you with such serenity, such happiness. Not to the point of inspiring tears on your eyelashes which were maybe not entirely caused by the dazzling light.

'We'll definitely have a sandstorm tomorrow,' predicted Dominique's companion as he turned over the spicy sausages sizzling on a bed of embers. And since his friend was still absorbed and did not reply, he continued: 'How much do you bet? At least three days' sandstorm. Bet on it, okay?'

Dominique watched the last rays, a little disappointed not to see that turquoise flash which occasionally, very rarely, flares up for a fraction of a second, and turned round. Now darkness would come very quickly.

'I don't bet anything at all,' he said, moving closer to the fire.

'What a try-on! I'd like to remind you that it's almost four years I've been living in your damned country, two years I've been ruining my health in all four corners of your Sahara Desert! Have to be an idiot not to see that damn sandstorm coming to destroy all our work! As if your buddies and the goats weren't enough! As if there weren't enough locusts! I tell you, I've had a basinful of it, your rotten dump!'

'You're just a dirty immigrant worker who does nothing but eat poor people's couscous and merguez!' retorted the young Berber with a laugh. 'Oh yes, a dirty immigrant, an evil, reactionary capitalist and colonialist!' he affirmed with a broad smile. He sprinkled the merguez sausages with a cloud of grey pepper, stirred the embers and continued: 'You haven't the slightest respect for the country and people who feed you with such generosity, we ought to deport you, pronto!'

'Funny guy!' said Dominique, sitting down beside the fire. 'Well, is it cooked? I'm hungry!'

When he had got to know Ali four years earlier, he had immediately appreciated his professional abilities. The young Berber, also an agricultural engineer, had a mission to benefit his people through his knowledge and to assist in the improvement of his country. After several months of contact with an administration which appeared to enjoy juggling with plans, alternative ideas, projects and other abortive attempts at action, he had retreated behind an impudent sense of humour which he shamelessly exploited.

'Joking apart,' he said, tasting a sausage, 'what have you decided? I really need to know whether I'm going to have to ask for another team-worker. Watch out, they're burning hot!' he said with a grimace.

'What I'm going to do? I've no idea. First take my holiday; there'll be plenty of time to see after that.'

That was untrue, and really a way of postponing the decision. An excuse not to choose between the profession he had pursued for four years in Algeria, and that tempting position offered by the huge and all-powerful multinational Mondiagri. On the one hand a life of liberty and the unexpected in a country he loved; on the other the rigours of research. On one side, real work as an agronomist, a livestock specialist, spending his time on down-to-earth experiments; on the other, a much better paid job which would probably take him to the four corners of the world, but also oblige him to spend more time in front of a typewriter or calculator than in the middle of a flock or a field of lucerne.

At present he needed the open air, space, the smell of grass and livestock – all that he had found here in Algeria, where his overseas work had brought him four years earlier. As a young agricultural engineer, he had found himself appointed technical assistant in the Algerian agricultural service where Ali was already working.

For two years they had laboured together in the fertile areas around Oran and Algiers, trying to establish both some flocks worthy of the name, and high-yield forage crops.

When his overseas service was finished, and after several months spent on holiday in Saint-Libéral and especially in travelling, he had accepted the Algerian government's offer and resumed his work with Ali for a further two years.

But they had both had to bid farewell to the rich soil of the north, and devote themselves solely to the agricultural development of the oases and semi-desert zones in the south. Unrewarding and frequently demoralising toil, consisting of attempts at irrigation and cultivation and the establishment of herds. Exhausting work as well, for it was carried out under a terrible, scorching heat, beneath a deadly sun, with devastating sandstorms and occasionally clouds of locusts which ravaged all the crops within a few hours. Difficult work, ultimately, for it was effected with the help of a workforce more inclined to take a siesta than to set to hoeing.

Despite that, Dominique was neither disheartened nor discouraged, and it was with continuing interest that he moved from one oasis to the next, from an experimental farm to a trial dam in the hills.

Stationed in Bouhamama for a week, he still had before him several days of lab and desk work – soil and milk analyses, crop evaluation, animal weighing, insemination and treatment plans to establish. He would then fill his last month with a brief final tour of inspection. First to the palm groves of Beni-Abbès and Tarhit, then the few small trial fields in Abadla where the production cost of a quintal of wheat was among the highest in the world. On to Béchar, just to dip back into the atmosphere of town life. Then by aeroplane sorties to the test areas around El Goléa, Ghardaîa, Touggourt, Laghouat, all those isolated patches which needed to be protected and saved despite the wind, sand, sun and at times even the incompetence, negligence or stupidity of men. Finally to Algiers, the transfer of authority and instructions to his successor, and then France. And above all the decision to be reached on which his whole future depended, Mondiagri, with his sights set on the salary and promotion they offered, or a further tour, without much future but still very attractive, of the Saharan oases.

'Shall I tell you something, you shouldn't talk so much while you're eating, it's bad for the digestion!' teased Ali, intrigued by his companion's silence.

'He who speaks sows, he who listens gathers the harvest; it was you who taught me that proverb!'

'And is the harvest good?'

'No, not particularly. But I have to say you're talking nothing but rubbish this evening!' laughed Dominique. 'Come on, don't get angry, I'm only joking,' he added, nibbling a merguez. 'I understand, you'd like to know who you're going to be working with!'

'Just a little, I wouldn't mind! We've put in some hard graft together, produced some good results, and we get on. But what if they send me a pen-pusher to follow you, a good-for-nothing? That'll be hard. So I'd really like to know what you're reckoning on doing, to be prepared.'

'I told you, first my holiday, then we'll see . . . Well, I hope I'll know how to assess things and choose . . .'

Ali shook his head, stoked the fire with charcoal, and set to cooking a few more merguez.

'What's your problem?' he asked eventually.

'You know very well! We've talked about it a hundred times! I'm twenty-seven: it's now or never. If I sign on again here, God knows how many years it'll be for! I love it dearly, your country, I really do. But I've no illusions, it's like a goat! It finishes by devouring people who stay too long. Look, I can't see myself suggesting to a woman that she wait for me in Oran or Algiers while I tour the oases. To tell the truth, I can't even see myself suggesting she move to Algeria for several years. Not unless she's pretty well used to Africa.'

'Filthy racist!' joked Ali.

'Okay, but you know I'm right.'

'Yes.'

'And besides, you have to admit that the professional future here is rather restricted, at least for a Frenchman. It's true. You know fine that your government is not rolling in money, and salaries . . .'

'I know. And yet you've been four years here, you've enjoyed it. You still enjoy it!'

'Sure. But I'm twenty-seven,' repeated Dominique, 'time's passing; if I wait too long, I'll have nothing left in France. And if I let Mondiagri's offer go . . .'

'So basically, it's a pointless discussion,' said Ali. 'You've already chosen. It'll be Mondiagri. And frankly, even if I'm sorry to see you go, I can't say you're wrong.'

# 2

JACQUES turned round to examine the rotavator's work and his face contorted. Although he had pulled tight the broad belt which supported the small of his back, the pain was still there, low down in the region of his kidneys, fierce and throbbing, radiating through his buttocks and into his legs. But if all went well it would gradually fade as the muscles and nerves were warmed by the vibrations of the tractor. And especially when the liniment had penetrated the painful area.

The trouble with this green-coloured, stinging counter-irritant supplied by a veterinary friend, was that it stank horribly and was so caustic that it transformed a scratch into a crater. However, lightly spread on unbroken skin it had unparalleled efficacity. As proof, it cured cows of injury-induced arthritis! It was therefore quite logical that it should bring relief to a human de-sensitised to the normal creams suggested by Doctor Martel.

For several years now Jacques had had little faith in the virtues of medicine. He had seen so many specialists – physiotheraphists, chiropractors, acupuncturists, not to mention the healers, manipulators, hypnotists and other charlatans – that he no longer had confidence in any of them. So when the pain came he treated it in his own way. But he knew very well that a day would come when he would find it impossible to get up. Meanwhile, he worked.

Thanks to some recent stormy showers the soil on the plateau had become pliable, less resistant to the prongs attacking it. Providing he did not attempt to set it too deep, the rotavator did an excellent job on this old, artificially sown pasture which he had decided to turn over. In its place, after a good winter, he was going to set spring barley, which should be a success. In this soil, rich in humus and nitrogen, which had not been exposed to the sun for six years, it would be surprising if barley did not do remarkably well.

'And make sure you don't overdo the fertiliser, watch out how you tip it on!' his father had said to him the previous evening. Attracted by the rumble of the tractor the old man had come to cast an eye over his son's work, the condition of the Vialhe land, and especially over the plot called the Long Piece. It had quite a history, quite a past.

Fertile and deep, it was this field that had, in 1901, received the thirty-one walnut trees which Pierre-Edouard was proud to have planted with his father. There remained only eight of these veterans; luxuriant trees with magnificent trunks which produced exceptionally fine wood for carving. Eight trees out of thirty-one, it wasn't a lot: the penalty of time, frost, storms and disease. Amongst them now grew eighteen of the twenty specimens Pierre-Edouard had replanted after the great frosts of 1956. But these eighteen were nowhere near equalling the old stock, their yield was still minimal; promising, certainly, but in ten or fifteen years. To tell the truth, if it had been up to him Jacques would never have chosen specimens with tall trunks which required twenty years to become profitable. He would have put in low, fast-growing ones, and already be harvesting a fine crop today. But his father had prevailed; he wanted to leave some real trees for his grandchildren.

Oh yes! They don't give a damn about trees, the grandchildren! thought Jacques. If I listened to Dominique and his agronomist ideas, I'd have to cut down every single thing which pokes its head up on the plateau, plum trees, apples, walnuts, the lot! and then – intensive farming! It suits him fine to talk about farming, the lout, the advisers aren't the ones who pay for it! As for his sister, the only thing she's interested in is technical research in zoology; apart from that, nothing!

He reached the end of the field, lifted the rotavator, turned on the headland, and set off again across the pasture on the old Massey-Ferguson. He noticed that the small of his back was less painful, less sensitive to the jolting, and increased the acceleration.

He had been distressed to witness the paths chosen by his three nieces. Distressed for them, because he loved them dearly and was afraid of seeing them unhappy; distressed for Mauricette. Neither his sister nor Jean-Pierre deserved that. They had done their best to bring up their children, to instil what they thought best, to prepare them for the future, to give them good jobs. And then, hey presto, the young people chuck it all away, morals and all. Goodbye parents and their outmoded ideas! The world is our oyster!

Now us, we've been lucky, we can't complain. Dominique is pig-headed and impudent but he's good at heart and a worker. As for Françoise, she's almost too serious, especially if you compare her with her cousins . . . But I prefer her like that!

He thought his brother Guy and sister-in-law Colette had also been lucky with their children. Jean, the eldest, was only fifteen, Marc thirteen, Evelyne eight and little Renaud a year younger. They were polite and never caused trouble when they came in the summer with their parents. Not for long, just a few days before heading for the beaches with their mother, whilst Guy went back up to Paris and his work as a lawyer.

He'd steered his boat cleverly, that one! You had only to look at his cars, always Mercedes, and his apartment too, nine rooms in the Avenue Bosquet, on the top floor, with a terrace and a pretence at a little garden! That was not the home of a poor man!

But what was so pleasant about him was that he was not ashamed to admit that he made a very good living, had an exciting job and was happy in Paris, surrounded by a wife who adored him and delightful children. Added to that he was generous, and made sure that his parents lacked for nothing. Jacques knew that he sent a cheque to his mother every month, and was grateful for it. He would have liked to do the same, but it was impossible, fate had decreed otherwise.

Occasionally he started to speculate bitterly what his life could have been like if the war had not intervened and messed everything up, spoilt everything. That was what had prevented him from becoming a veterinarian, as he had dreamed. It had virtually forced him to take over the Vialhe land. He did not regret it, not too much . . . And besides, today he was almost avenged, with his son an agronomist and his daughter soon to be a veterinarian; he had the right to be proud.

Mathilde could have managed without running down to the church square when the travelling grocer stopped his van on Wednesday afternoon beside the disused wash-house.

For the last three years Saint-Libéral had had no grocer; no baker any more, either. As for the butcher, he had closed his shop nearly twenty years ago.

So on Tuesday mornings Mathilde accompanied her daughter-in-law on her drive to the shops in Objat or Brive; Louise and Berthe frequently made the journey too. So nothing was forcing her to patronise a trader who, however pleasant he was, nonetheless marked up all his products by a fairly hefty sum; it was needed to pay for the petrol, the depreciation of the vehicle and for the service! Mathilde felt that she owed him this premium. To her, who had known the era when Saint-Libéral provided a livelihood for a baker, two grocers and a butcher, and even accommodated a market and livestock sales, this decent fellow represented the last meeting point. It was around him that almost all the women of the village gathered once a week. Because one might as well face facts: there was nothing else in the village to produce the slightest sign of life. It was a fair old time since the forge had rung out, since the wheelwright had died. As for the masons, carpenters and roofers, it was decades since they had disappeared.

Even the priest was seldom seen. He had an incredible number of parishes to serve, and could only come to say Mass once a fortnight. And more often on Saturday evening than on Sunday, which to Mathilde was not real Mass at all.

So where could they now meet their neighbours, get everyone's news, find out a bit about what was going on in the community, if it wasn't around the grocer's van? In addition, thanks to him, one heard the gossip from Perpezac-le-Blanc, Yssandon, Ayen or Saint-Robert. And as he visited the most isolated farms you could discover how your distant cousins and acquaintances were getting on in Laval, Louignac or Berquedioude.

Mathilde would therefore have felt guilty if she had missed the grocer. For two packets of biscuits, half a pound of coffee and a litre of oil she could, if she wished, have an hour's conversation with her old friends in the village. In addition, her attendance was a sort of thank-offering to a shopkeeper who had the consideration to come at sensible times, which allowed for a chat, especially in fine weather. Unlike the butcher, who arrived in Saint-Libéral at the end of his round, that's to say, late in the evening. What's more, his meat was not top quality. And he was rather surly and talked little.

As on every Wednesday afternoon, Mathilde laid down her work when the van's hooter sounded in the church square.

'The grocer's there, do you need anything?' she asked quite loudly, for Louise was getting a little deaf. As for Berthe, she was so absorbed in her sketches that she did not seem to have heard.

Her eighty-one years and her retirement did not prevent her from having just as many ideas as ever about fashions. She therefore drafted sketches of blouses, skirts and gowns which she sent to Gérard. Her taste was still reliable, and a number of lines at Maison Claire Diamond had first seen the light of day on the corner of the Vialhe family's table. She treated herself to a stay in Paris during the shows, and thereby kept in touch with everything.

'No, I don't need anything,' she said closing her sketch-book, 'but I'll come with you anyway, it's nice out. Look at poor Louise, she's getting more and more hard of hearing!'

In truth, busy with her knitting, the old lady appeared to have heard nothing. After living for several years in the house which she had had built on Combes-Nègres, Louise had returned to her childhood home six years ago. For however comfortable, pleasant and well-situated the new house was, she felt lonely there, too isolated. And on some winter evenings, when darkness fell so quickly and so early, she was afraid.

But she was glad, all the same, to have had it built when summer came. For, then her grandson Pierre and his wife Jeannette came to spend their holidays and with them – oh joy! – her two great-grandchildren: Luc, six years old, and Hélène, three.

And to see the children running and playing around the old chestnut tree which rose imposingly thirty paces from the house, filled her with a strange happiness. A joy suffused with nostalgia which had become very sweet over the years; poignant memories indeed, but mostly fond and tender ones. For it was there, under the chestnut which wore its three or four centuries well, its dense crown so luxuriant, so reassuring, its enormous trunk all bulging with callouses and burrs, streaked with folds and fissures, seemingly indestructible, that she and Octave had outlined their plans for the future some sixty-five years ago. A future which then seemed to belong to them, which appeared so beautiful and secure . . . It had not fulfilled its promise. Nevertheless, despite everything and against all odds, Octave Flaviens' great-grandchildren danced around it every summer; laughed and sang in the same spot where their forebear used to sit to watch the path along which Louise would appear.

The holidays over, quite rejuvenated by several weeks of children's laughter, Louise would close up her house again, already counting the months which separated her from next summer. For she no longer even opened it for her son. When Félix came, on average for about twelve days every three months – he had now retired, and could please himself – he also preferred to stay at the Vialhes. He knew that Pierre-Edouard greatly appreciated his company, his conversation, the walks they took together. The old man grew rather bored surrounded by three women, especially since the demise of Léon, with whom he had got on so well. He no longer had a friend, an ally, to comment on the news, criticise politicians and their politics, answer back to the TV journalists or simply evoke memories and count absent friends . . .

'The grocer's there, do you need anything?' asked Mathilde again, leaning down to her sister-in-law.

Louise stopped knitting, thought about it, shook her head but still got up.

734

'I'll come with you, I'll find some little thing to buy. And it'll give me some fresh air,' she said as an excuse.

Soon afterwards, taking short steps, the three old ladies set off in the direction of the church square where the housewives of Saint-Libéral were already assembling.

Berthe and Mathilde took Louise's arms and made sure that she avoided the cracked paving-stones; she was older than them. They walked without urgency, certain that the grocer would wait for them. He was accustomed to it, they always arrived last. Then there would be many more people, and a little more time to chat while waiting to be served.

'Instead of howling like a jackal, why not tell me about your *douar*!' insisted Ali as, with customary ceremony, he decanted the mint tea he was in the process of preparing, flavouring it with a sprig of mugwort.

As predicted, the sandstorm had been blowing for two days. Such a fierce wind that it rendered impossible Dominique and Ali's work: namely, to harvest in the normal way and then to weigh a crop of sorghum of which Dominique had had great hopes. Hopes which were evaporating hour by hour. For despite the protection of the oleander, prickly pear and palm hedges, and even wattle fences, he very much feared that the crop would already be burned by the sandstorm, lost.

Unable to fulfil their planned programme, Dominique and Ali had taken advantage of an apparent lull, that morning, to extract about fifteen soil samples, with a view to analysis. Subsequently the storm had resumed with greater violence.

Its fury was such that a suffocating reddish dusting of sand penetrated even inside the room where the two men were sheltering. For try as they might to plug the chinks in the doors and windows, the sand still got in. It drifted everywhere, insinuated itself, clung around their eyes in a stinging crust, crunched between their teeth, parched their throats. As for the noise, it was simply a long, deafening whistle which frayed the nerves like a stonemason's saw.

Although accustomed to phenomena of this sort, Dominique had difficulty in remaining good tempered and calm after several hours of wind. And here it had lasted two days. Ali, who knew his companion well, foresaw the moment when he would react in his own way.

Illogically, instead of trying to forget the storm by retreating into a soothing siesta, he would wind his turban cloth around his nose and mouth, tighten his sandgoggles to the maximum, strip to his underparts, and go out to face the elements. He would take a turn around the building for less than five minutes, but that was quite enough! He would walk until he could no longer feel his body, such was the force and sting of the millions of grains of sand launched at over a hundred miles an hour in a dry but suffocating shower. Afterwards, red as a pimento pepper, his skin almost raw, he would come back in, throw a bucket of water over his head and, his calm restored, would suggest that his friend try the experience. But Ali was in no way partial to that type of adventure. The wind hardly disturbed him. All you had to do was tell yourself that it would stop one day, and wait. Without getting irritated.

He poured himself a little tea, tasted it, and filled the glasses. 'Come on, tell me about your *douar*!' he repeated.

'Go and get stuffed!' muttered Dominique. 'My *douar*, I assure you has better weather than here! Over there you're not bored to death by sandstorms! Dead right! Oh dammit! I'll have to go out!' he shouted, getting up.

'Well go, then! I'll keep the tea warm for you! But take care,' warned Ali earnestly. 'Don't let the hut out of your sight: you can't see further than ten metres. If you get lost, you'll be cured for good! And covered in sand, too, for sure!'

'You must visit my village some day or other,' said Dominique later. His skin was on fire, but he had recovered his peace of mind.

However, not only had the wind not diminished; it had strengthened as darkness fell. By now, it was certain, apart from the root vegetables, tubers and melons, there would be nothing left in the experimental plots.

'Yes, you should come. Anyway, I've already told you that.'

'I know. I'll try to. One day, maybe.'

Ali did not know France except by reputation, and that was a mixed one. He retained detailed memories of his childhood close to Tizi-Ouzou. At that time France, and especially her army, was everywhere. It was often necessary for his parents – market gardeners and tree growers – to show their papers when they went to town to sell their produce, or to see friends.

And then, one summer's day, the three colours which waved above all the official buildings had been replaced by the Algerian flag – the real one, his father had told him.

Subsequently, according to those who spoke of her, France was completely evil, colonialist, murderous. Others, the more discerning, assured him that she was not so bad, rather fine even. No one remained indifferent to her. In any case, everybody agreed in saying that France was a rich country, very rich, and they lived well there.

As he grew older, Ali realised that it was all much less simple. By associating with Dominique and several volunteers, he had gained an insight into what the French might be like. But there again, he mistrusted generalisations, and vowed to go there one day to form his own opinion about the place. Meanwhile he stored away what Dominique told him about his country. And to listen to him, you were forced to believe that it really was a beautiful land.

'You'll see, I'll take you to the prettiest parts of the Limousin and the Corrèze,' insisted Dominique.

Saint-Libéral, for example?' joked Ali, who felt he knew each walk, each house, such was the stream of words flowing from his companion on the subject of his birthplace.

When he was in a bad mood, it was enough for Ali to touch upon his *douar*, as he called it, for him to launch immediately into a poetic description. What Ali found hard to understand, on the other hand, was that his companion could remain so long far from a land which he talked of with such fervour.

His attitude became even more blatantly contradictory since he envisaged, without any apparent problem, going away again when working for Mondiagri. And it was rather the same when it came to his relatives. If you were to believe him, he got on with them extremely well; spoke of his grandfather with great feeling and of his grandmother with touching affection. Ali was equally certain that he had a great deal of respect and regard for his father, but he did become less voluble when the conversation turned to him.

At the end of that afternoon it was perhaps out of devilment, or because he felt Dominique had relaxed after his sand shower, that Ali dared to go further.

'You're trying to tell me your village is the most beautiful, your family the best, and it's two years since you've been there. It doesn't seem to worry you very much!'

'There's a grain of truth in that,' admitted Dominique, after considering it for a few moments. 'I've taken a while to learn it, but I know now that there's no point in wanting to change a situation if you haven't the means to do so.'

'You've lost me.'

'Well it's simple. I'm in a rage every time I go there. I even manage to lose my temper in my letters. My father is killing himself, wearing himself out for nothing. The poor old thing really hasn't had any luck in his life. He found himself managing the farm by accident, and for thirty years it's sapped his spirit and health. First of all it was to enlarge the holding, then to pay for our education, my sister and myself, and to repay the loans too. And now he's struggling to reach retirement in ten years' time. But you may ask what state he'll be in when he gets there. And what annoys me is that I can't do a thing about it.'

'You mean to say that your father doesn't earn a good living? I thought you had a fine farm!'

'You know all these things are relative. Anyway, what's the use of a fine farm if it's badly managed? And it is. Well, my father looks after it as best he can, as well as he knows how, but his thought processes are twenty-five years out of date. That's the whole problem. And you see, when I go there, I notice how everything's deteriorating, that the equipment's worn out, that production's stagnant. And I don't need to be told that the income is diminishing, it's obvious. Like it's obvious straight away that my father's exhausting himself. And that makes me furious.'

'Why don't you tell him?'

'But I *have* told him! And do you know what he answered? "You've only to take my place, it's open, we'll see if you do better"!'

'I see, and that's not your idea at all?'

'You must be joking! I've got better things to do elsewhere! And look here, be serious, I'm not a farmer. No, what it needs is for my father to change tack altogether, to look for something different. But it's not very likely; at fifty-five you don't change your habits . . . Well, I understand him and it drives me wild. Do you get it now, why I don't often go to Saint-Libéral? It's so that I don't have a shouting match with my father. I know my mother can't bear our arguments, so it's damage limitation, okay? And if you add to that my grandfather sticking his oar in . . .'

'I thought you worshipped him! You always told me he was fantastic.'

'So he is! Only he thinks nothing of my degree in agronomy, nothing! The only thing he's worried about is finding someone to follow my father in looking after the Vialhe land. And he knows it won't be me! Oh, not that he reproaches me about it, no, but still . . . Look, even if I were appointed Minister of Agriculture, I bet the first thing he'd ask me would be: "When are you going to resign from that useless job and work on something serious, on the Vialhe land?" He's like that, Grandpa, a great character. What's so funny?'

'Nothing, nothing! When you talk about your land, I don't know whether it'll stay in the family; on the other hand, when it comes to character, in your case the succession seems to me to be assured!'

# 3

DESPITE the admiration and affection Jean Vialhe felt for his father, his relationship with him had changed in the last few months. It quickly became strained when the conversation turned to a subject on which neither wished to give ground. For, however much they agreed with each other on questions of sport, cars, films, books, or even politics, the dialogue became bitter-sweet when it touched on the future.

Almost a year ago, Jean had baldly announced to his father that he did not want to be a lawyer or a civil servant and that all the other supposedly 'good jobs' were a load of rubbish. He was going to be a stock-breeder, there was no other route possible for him!

He had understood that it came as a terrible shock to his father. All the more so because Guy had every reason to hope that his eldest son would follow him, if not in his footsteps at the bar, then at least by achieving a position in society as comfortable as his own.

For Jean was one of those pupils who, from kindergarten to graduation, seem to absorb knowledge like delicious sweets, greedily and with enjoyment. Always at the top of the class, he was about to enter his second to last year at school at the age of fifteen, and could thereafter quite reasonably aim for the highest qualifications.

At first Guy had thought he was playing the rebel, it was his age. After all, he had always been inclined to kick over the traces. Less than Marc, however, his junior by two years who proclaimed the need to reorganise the world from A to Z, gun in hand if it came to it. And without letting feeling get in the way! But given his age he could be forgiven for sticking up a photo of Che Guevara in his bedroom. Guy remembered it well, knew that everything changed at a great rate and you had to allow for what was in fashion. Since 1968, it had been protests.

So in the first instance he had not taken his eldest son's pronouncements very seriously. But he had begun to worry when he had discovered, six months earlier during Agriculture Week, that Jean was using every spare moment to go and admire the animals on the showground at Porte de Versailles. Annoyed, for he felt at a loss, he had talked to Berthe about it during one of her trips to Paris. The old lady had laughed until she cried.

'The genes, my dear Guy, the genes! There they are and in some strength too! Think of your parents! A Vialhe plus a Dupeuch, that's not going to give you a mandarin in the civil service. All the better!'

'And why not? None of us were born peasants! It was an accident that Jacques stayed on the farm. When he worked with Léon, Paul champed at the bit behind those cows. Mauricette wouldn't rest until she became a teacher. As for me, I left Saint-Libéral as soon as I could, you know that, you gave me a home in Paris!'

'Well, it's skipped a generation, that's all! Oh, if your father hears this, he'll be over the moon!'

'I forbid you to tell him, he'll do everything to encourage the boy in this mad idea! Stock-breeder, I ask you! When he has everything he needs to make a success of himself! Come on, joking apart, tell me what I could do to get this nonsense out of his head?'

'He hasn't talked about leaving school? So what's the problem? Don't spoil his dream, let it run its course.'

He was not convinced by this advice and felt it useful to relaunch the debate with his son:

'If I understand you properly, all you want to do is to copy those young fools who set off to live up-country in Larzac with three goats and two sheep, and would starve to death without daddy's cheques?'

'No way! I told you, I'm going to be a stock-breeder! The sort you're talking about are just mucking around. In the first place they don't know a thing about it. If they really wanted to raise livestock they wouldn't go there, where nothing grows except stones! I know, I've been finding out. It's one of the regions hardest hit by the rural exodus. Think about it, if the land were that good, the farmers would stay there! No, that's not where you need to go.'

His son's seriousness had rather shaken him. And he, who knew how to be so composed and calm when defending clients in court, had raised his voice:

'Oh, I see your drift! You'll be setting up in Saint-Libéral maybe?'

'If I could, yes, but there's not enough space free, I mean enough ground. But if one day Louis were to sell Uncle Léon's land, and not for building on, well yes, then it would be worth it.'

The wretched boy thinks of everything! thought Guy, gritting his teeth.

'Right, enough dreaming,' he cut in. I don't know who put these notions in your head, but we'll discuss it again later. At the moment I don't want to hear any more of the sort of rubbish you might expect from romantics like Giono or Lanza del Vasto! All those utopian ideas have already caused enough damage as it is! If at least you wanted to copy your cousin Dominique!'

'But I *am* reckoning on on doing the same as him! Only I want to set up on my own account, to rear stock.'

'Well that . . .' Guy had sighed, realising that the discussion was turning against him.

Instead of unsettling his son, as he had hoped, it had allowed him to formulate out loud what had perhaps until then been only a rather vague plan, poorly researched, barely thought out. Thanks to the soapbox inadvertently provided by his father, Jean had been able to explain his ideas, clearly and seriously, and had thus taken an important step forward in his commitment. Since then, Guy had avoided reopening a debate which he was no longer certain of controlling.

When informed of it, Colette, his wife, had supported him. She, too, hoped that time would cure everything, that their son would one day realise for himself just how impractical his idea was. She herself had suffered too much when her own parents had ostracised her on learning that Guy was the son of small-time farmers in the Corrèze. The breach had lasted until the birth of Jean. And now this brilliant child, pupil at one of the best schools in Paris, who could honestly call himself a Parisian, son of a lawyer and grandson of an antique dealer – there was no need to remember the other grandparents – was taking pride in referring to his country origins and wanting to go back to his roots? It was grotesque!

When Guy had sought to rent a shoot with a few friends three years earlier, he had considered that his cousin Félix would be well placed to advise him. He still lived a few kilometres from Mézières-en-Brenne in the forestry cottage, long ago bought for a token sum, where he had spent the greater part of his life. He therefore knew the area like the back of his hand, and had no difficulty in pointing Guy towards a very fine piece of land.

It had originally been part of the twelve hundred hectares belonging to the Château of Cannepetière, where Louise had worked for so long. The shoot now comprised six hundred hectares of woods, heath and thickets, all dotted with pools and marshes. A paradise for game, a delight for hunters who could shoot according to their tastes at roe deer, wild boar, pheasant, hare or partridge. But also, and most importantly, a selection of mallard, teal, shoveller and tufted duck; not forgetting the rail, woodcock and snipe.

During the hunting season, Guy went down once a fortnight for the weekend. He never omitted to go and say hello to his cousin – admittedly the shoot lay less than a kilometre from his house. Occasionally he even accepted the bed offered by Félix. Exhausted by a day's shooting in the fresh air, he slept soundly there, lulled by the song of the wind in the huge oak trees.

For the last two years Jean had nearly always accompanied him. Not to hunt – he was not old enough yet, and was not attracted by the sport – but to fish with Félix and especially to accompany him on long ornithological expeditions.

Félix had always felt a great affinity for birds; since his retirement they had become his obsession. He amazed Jean with his knowledge and the speed of his observation, which allowed him to differentiate in an instant a sedge warbler from a grasshopper warbler. So, whilst the shots and barking echoed in the distance, Félix and Jean, binoculars around their necks, practised a more peaceful form of hunting. During the last six months Jean had taken up photography and discovered how much patience, calmness and determination were needed to capture a simple coot with the lens.

What also interested Jean a great deal, and astonished him, was when Félix talked to him of the Vialhe family. He knew a lot about them and willingly related it. He seemed to know everything about the family circumstances, the important events, the character of each person, the tragedies, quarrels and reconciliations.

And when one day Jean had wanted to know how he had learned all that, he explained:

'It's true, the first time I set foot in the village I was already twenty-six! But thanks to your great-aunt – yes, your Aunt Louise – I was almost as familiar with it as I am with every little footpath in the woods around us. Your aunt told me all about the family, and the neighbours, the fields and meadows, the woods, the countryside of Saint-Libéral too. She was so unhappy here, poor woman. She told me, she pined for her village for forty years! So she used to re-read the letters which came from there. First the ones from your grandfather – she had a whole packet of them, which she knew off by heart. Then, after the war – the Great War I mean – it was your grandmother who wrote. And that went on until your aunt returned to live in Saint-Libéral in 1956, no, '55, October '55. Since then it's she who writes to me and tells me everything. That's how I know the history of the Vialhe family and the village, I should perhaps say the sagas . . .'

'So you know all about my cousin?'

'Which one?'

'Come on, you know very well: I mean Jo! Papa won't have her name mentioned at home!'

'Then I shan't talk about her either.'

'Is it true that she's gone off around the world with a boyfriend? Go on, you can say it, can't you? You can see I know!'

'Well you know as much as I do, don't expect any more. And the main thing is she'll be back one day. That's how the Vialhes do it. When they've a mind to it, they give up everything and go away for years to the devil knows where! And then one day they reappear in Saint-Libéral. It's hereditary. Your grandfather and your two aunts did it. And if your Uncle Paul didn't have time to do the same, it was because the heavens decreed otherwise.'

'You're sure it'll be like that with Jo? I hope so. She's nice, Jo. She lived with us before she took off . . . I remember, she wasn't stuck-up, *sympa*, you know! It was she who looked after us when our parents went out in the evening. Do you think we'll see her again?'

'Of course. Look, you remember those nightjars we saw last summer? They're migratory, they leave at the end of the summer, but they always return the following spring. The urge is overwhelming, they always return to where they were born, like the Vialhes. And they're similar in other ways too!'

'Oh, right?'

'Yes, they're very imposing. As a result they're often mistaken for small falcons or sparrowhawks; they pretend to be raptors, really! But they're showing off, you know, they only eat insects. And they have big mouths too! Can't stop puffing, churring, getting worked up, right! Don't you remember?'

'Of course I do!'

Jean recalled the whole scene. It was at the end of July. His father had come to shoot duck, and he had stayed with Félix, as usual.

At dusk, when thousands of starlings were whirling in search of a roost above the pools and reedbeds in unpredictably twisting, noisy clouds, Félix and he had set off walking across the heath. They were hoping to catch a glimpse of one of the two short-eared owls which were nesting there. Everywhere in the pools and ditches, in the slightest speck of water, toads were croaking. And now timidly, almost self-consciously, for the season for love was over, a few warblers were trilling from their perches in the bulrushes.

It was then that the shadow of a bird, seeming to shoot out of the ground in front of them, spun skyward, twisted round and immediately disappeared in a flurry of wings.

743

'Did you see that? Like a cuckoo or a kestrel, but smaller,' Jean had murmured as he stopped.

'Not quite, wait for it. The family lives there. Here, listen! Listen to the nightjars calling to each other.'

And suddenly, emerging from the night and diving straight back in to it, three other birds had circled round the observers for a few seconds. Then, following the repeated chucking call from one of the parents, they had all disappeared, swallowed up by the darkness.

'What are they looking for?' Jean had whispered, still surprised.

'The grasshoppers and moths we've put up by walking in the long grass. Usually they follow the animals, they disturb the insects too. See, that gives them their old name of "goat-sucker". Not so long ago I used to know some quite sensible people who firmly believed that nightjars came to suck their goats in the dark! Yes, they did! You'll be telling me they're the same ones who were convinced that adders and grass-snakes suckle as well!'

'But where do they come from?'

'From Africa, they spend all the cold months there. They arrive here at the end of April when they can find something to feed on. They nest and leave again. Those ones, well that family, I've known them since I was old enough to watch birds, that takes us back to the twenties! They lay in that heath-land every year, over there to the right, beside that aspen grove. You know, since I've been observing them that makes several generations of nightjars! One year, more than fifteen years ago, I ringed the two young; yes, they only have two per nest. They were magnificent. I don't know whether it annoyed them to know they were discovered, but it was three years before they returned! I saw some in other places, but not here. And then one evening at the beginning of May, they shot up like just now, they were back. Since then they've been there every year.'

'And you say the Vialhe family is the same?' Jean was amused.

'Yes, a bit, on account of their weird characters! But you don't need to go and tell you father and grandfather in Saint-Libéral that I'm calling them birds! You keep it to yourself, okay?'

Settling down at the far end of the Long Piece, Pierre-Edouard expertly evaluated the work accomplished by Jacques a few days earlier. His rotavator had worked miracles. Apart from a few green tongues which licked round the feet of the walnut trees, there was no sign of the old meadow. Cleanly scalped and turned under, it had given way to long smooth beds of rich, red earth. The clods were still too dry and brittle for ploughing, but a short day's rain would make it superb, ready to be opened by the share. And seeing it already so beautiful, Pierre-Edouard knew that the furrows would be smooth, regular. He was constantly amazed by the work modern machines were capable of producing.

In his time he would never have been able to obtain such results, make the soil so clean, so yielding. For even if his oxen had been equal to pulling the Canadian cultivator with its 'goose-foot' tines, the machine's prongs would have been broken by jamming between the interstices of the lucerne roots, which were broader than a man's thumb. Besides, in earlier times, even on pliable, damp ground, nothing would have pulverised the earth so well, mixed so thoroughly the humus, turf and that generous layer of limestone clay which made the Long Piece so productive.

And yet, despite this fantastic progress and all the care and manure lavished on it, the earth could give no more. What had nourished generations of Vialhes and, before them, over the centuries, other unknown generations, was year by year becoming less able to feed those who were maintaining it to an ever higher standard. From one harvest to the next, it grew weary of being forced to produce more each time, always give something extra. And what had been the yield of the century ten years earlier – and would have been inconceivable fifty years ago – now counted as a mediocre result, hardly sufficient to cover the costs of production. It was crazy, stupid. This was the outcome of the senseless dash forwards in which Jacques was involved in order to survive.

Over the years, like hundreds of thousands of his colleagues, he had been obliged to bend to the demands of the time. Producing more, always more, to try to compensate by increasing the volume for the losses caused by totally stagnant, or even falling prices. But how could he reach a target which was rapidly disappearing into the distance without running out of breath or courage!

Even during the worst periods of crisis, before the war, Pierre-Edouard had never seen such a mess, such a gloomy future for those who were clinging to their land. They clung on, for it was their only means of survival, their final struggle. They knew of no other way than to turn to it with loving care. But it was no surprise that as a result Saint-Libéral, which had counted 1,100 inhabitants at the beginning of the century, now harboured only 304, whose average age was over fifty! The dozens of little farms which formed its wealth, gave it standards and pride, were reduced to just eleven concerns.

They were of course much larger, more productive, more modern.

But what use was that since they seemed, despite this, less and less able to meet the needs of their owners? Moreover, the majority had no one to carry on the work. And everything seemed to indicate that they would not even attract purchasers when the last smallholder gave up. How would they find someone crazy enough to invest in such a marginal way of life?

And yet, *miladiou*, that's a bloody fine, rich earth we've got there, fulminated Pierre-Edouard, sweeping his eyes over all the Vialhe lands on the plateau.

He bent down with some difficulty, collected a fistful of earth, crumbled it, kneaded it. Then with a broad movement he cast in front of him, as sowers do.

Poor old Jacques, what with this and the fifteen hectares at the Heath, it gives him a fair old lot of work. And he's killing himself with it. Good God! he needs some help, a fellow like poor Nicolas . . . Or if that's hoping for too much, someone like that idiot my father employed in the years . . .? Huh! I've forgotten . . . And what was his name, that old cackler? Doesn't matter, I'll ask Mathilde, she has a good memory . . .

He reflected for a few moments, searched his memory to try to remember the christian name of the man whose inane and toothless smile he could still picture clearly, but whose name had faded away with time.

The devil with that ass! Never mind, even he would be of use to Jacques! But that's over! It's a long time since we've seen tramps passing with their bundles over their shoulders! Nobody wants to get their hands dirty any more. Besides, even if by some miracle Jacques discovered a rare pearl, he wouldn't have the means to pay him! Well, that's how it is, seems that's par for the course . . .

He pulled on his unlit pipe for a long time, knocked it against his palm, and continued his solitary walk. Above the Long Piece, not far away, a lone kestrel on the look-out for fieldmice hovered like the Holy Ghost.

Pierre-Edouard was at the edge of the plateau, at the foot of the White Peak, when he heard the Saint-Libéral bell strike eleven o'clock. He quickened his pace a little, for he knew Mathilde would worry if he were not home by a quarter to twelve. They had come to an understanding. Mathilde had long ago abandoned the idea of keeping him around the house, of confining him to the garden, main street or even church square, where everyone could have seen him and above all come to help him in case of need.

He had waved away the arguments she put forward to persuade him. Just as he had openly laughed when she had proposed, seeing he was bored at home, that he spend a little more time at the bistro – the last and only business in Saint-Libéral – still kept by Nicole, daughter of Noémie and granddaughter of Ma Eugènie, whose reputation as an incorrigible hussy was well-established. Naturally, she had suggested, it wouldn't be to drink there, but to talk things over with the last of his old friends, Edmond Duverger and Louis Brousse, who liked to meet there to share a hand of rummy.

'So now you want to send me to Nicole's? Well what d'you know, how times change! Only fifteen years ago you'd have scratched out my eyes if I'd stepped into her place! I was barely allowed to buy my tobacco there! And still you almost resented that!'

'No I didn't! You always exaggerate! I've never stopped you enjoying a game of cards if you felt like it! So now that you should be taking things easy . . .'

'That's it! Go on, say it, I'm allowed to see Nicole now that she's fifteen years older! Now she's as ugly as anything and I'm past it! But I don't want to call trumps. I don't particularly want to hang around with poor old Brousse, who's getting more and more doddery. Nor Edmond, who cries like a child over the slightest thing. I don't want to be with those dotards who are younger than me. I like them all fine, well, almost all, but they irritate me.'

What he craved was to walk in the woods and the fields, whatever the weather; to tend the last five hives he had kept; to take out his gun occasionally and try, without a great deal of conviction, to track and shoot a woodcock. What he loved was to see the Vialhe lands over the seasons, to admire Jacques' herd of Limousin cows and his enormous sows. What he wanted was to be free to climb as far as the White Peak one day, to the Caput Peak the next and another time up to Coste-Roche, to greet his daughter-in-law there and be given a cup of real coffee; Mathilde had a tendency to make it weaker and weaker.

But as he hated to see the ugly lines which worry etched on his wife's forehead, as he knew the extent of her fear for him, how she watched for the slightest sign of tiredness and stood ready to call the doctor, he had established a sort of system, a tacit agreement. Before leaving, he always revealed his itinerary and the aim of his walk. As for his timetable, it was fixed. Thanks to this, neither of them needed to express their thoughts. They both knew that this information would direct the search if one day he were to be a little late . . .

All the same he had smiled on discovering at the bottom of a pocket of his hunting jacket, the one he slipped on for his walks, a big whistle, which Mathilde had put in without saying a word, knowing that he would understand. He had refrained from telling her that he would have little chance of whistling into that tiny spout if his heart was causing him trouble. He knew just how short your breath was when that happened . . .

Thus for two years he had regulated his outings. And such was his understanding of her after fifty-seven years, he was persuaded that Mathilde knew where he was to be found at such and such a time. It was reassuring, for him as well . . .

On this day he checked with his watch that the church clock was right – since the electric chimes were installed, for lack of a sacristan, it had a tendency to wander – and stepped down the path which plunged towards the village. He took it carefully, for the slope was steep. He had known the track for over eighty years, was familiar with each turn, each hump, each big rock. Now, instead of running down it thoughtlessly and happily in ten short minutes, it would take him almost three-quarters of an hour. The key was to recognise and accept it, without resentment.

# 4

SINCE his first election as town councillor, Jacques had found no difficulty in getting re-elected at each ballot; he always won by a large margin in the first round. But that did not make his work as mayor any easier.

Firstly, Saint-Libéral was ageing at a catastrophic rate, the whole community was in a state of collapse and therefore lacked financial resources. Secondly, the representation within the council had changed since the last election, in March 1971.

It was not even politics which had set them at loggerheads. The relationship between the left and the right remained roughly the same, and as Jacques kept himself strictly aloof from all that, it was not the various opinions and their differences which gave him trouble.

Besides, it was a far cry from the battles of yesteryear. And it was really very amusing to see, seated side by side and promoting the same values, Jean Delpeyroux, Henri Brousse or Jacques Duverger. Thirty years earlier, the father of the first-named swore by Marshall Pétain alone, the father of the second took only Stalin as his model, while the latter's father never hid his sympathy for Léon Blum and his friends.

Today the sons were upset – and they were not the only ones – that they could not vote for Chirac, his constituency being too far from Saint-Libéral! So even if Peyrafaure or Delmas were susceptible to the smooth approach of a Communist like Duclos, political sparring did not present any problems for Jacques. On the other hand, a certain lack of understanding had crept into the council since the new arrivals in the village had been elected. It was not that they were unpleasant, far from it, but they were totally ignorant of the life of a rural community and its organisation.

Living for some years on the edge of the village, on the plots sold by Louis, Léon's son, they worked outside the village. Two of them were employees at the hinge-factory in La Rivière-de-Mansac, Claude Delmas and Alain Martin; another, Michel Lacombe, kept a small shop in Terrasson; the fourth, Mathieu Castellac, was with the electricity company EDF in Brive, and the last, Roger Peyrafaure, lived on his pension from the SNCF railway company.

Certainly their numbers did not give them the majority on the council, but the ideas they expounded, and which sometimes found a favourable echo with other councillors, frequently left Jacques speechless, they were so unrealistic. In fact, although living in a rural parish, the five newcomers expected to have the benefit of the services they had enjoyed in town. And they were not the only ones making such demands. So Jacques had to fight every inch of the way not to waste his already slender budget on trifles.

For to him, everything which was not absolutely essential was unnecessary. Unnecessary, and how costly, this construction of pavements at the beginning of the track up to Coste-Roche. Of course there were four recently built houses there, but their owners should consider themselves lucky to have the use of a surfaced and maintained roadway. So why the devil were they asking for pavements? To make out they were posher, and to be the envy of those in the village who had none?

Jacques knew full well that if he gave in on this point the fashion for pavements would gain ground in Saint-Libéral: everyone would want one, would demand it even! so, no! since the beginning of the century only the main street had had a pavement, and that was quite sufficient. There was therefore no question of embarking on new works.

Equally pointless, and even grotesque, the extension of street lighting along the track which led up to the plateau, where several new houses had been built.

'But, good God!' swore Jacques, 'they knew there were no lamp posts when they bought! And no main's drainage either! That's why they didn't have to pay too much for their land! Street lights in the middle of the country! I ask you! And what for, eh? For their dogs to pee up against, maybe? There are still plenty of trees hereabouts!'

It was also unnecessary, and unaffordable, to renovate and refit the inside of the youth club. It would have to do, old as it was. But what was the good of investing in a building shunned by the few young people in Saint-Libéral?

And yet, if there were one parish property which Jacques would have liked to see revived, that was the one. It embodied his entire adolescence. It was enough to think of it to hear once more the laughter of Paul, all his friends, of Father Verlhac; to remind himself of the vibrant, happy village it had been. A community where there were so many young people they had once needed a games room and a library of their own.

Today, the remaining kids were so few and far between that they could not even make up a football team!

After considering ongoing business, the discussion on the subject of youth did, however, resume in the council meeting that evening in October.

Jacques, already worn-out by a day's ploughing, realised that it would be a long time before he got to bed when Roger Peyrafaure began to speak. Not only was he as long-winded as a lawyer, but he loved the sound of his own voice. He knew too that his position as a civil service pensioner gave him a certain authority in the eyes of some, and he never denied himself the pleasure of holding forth.

'Messieurs,' he commenced, 'I regret to say that we are behaving extremely badly with regard to our young people. Extremely badly, and I choose my words carefully . . .'

He's got a nerve, the old crab, thought Jacques, massaging the small of his back. Our young people, he says! He never wanted any, if I'm to believe what his wife told Michèle!

'Yes,' continued the orator, 'one day they will judge us severely, will call us to account. And they will be right! For I pose the question, messieurs, what are we doing to prevent them jumping on their motorbikes every Saturday evening, and sometimes even during the week, to go all the way to Ayen, or still further, to hang about the cafés playing at some pinball machine or table football? I ask you . . .'

'Well, and so what?' interrupted Delpeyroux suddenly. 'What d'you want us to bloody well do about it? You can't tie them down, can you?'

He was the first deputy, and a friend of Jacques. Like him, he was one of the last farmers in the village, had spent all day picking walnuts, and was also in a hurry to get to sleep.

'But how can you say that, Monsieur Delpeyroux!' broke in Peyrafaure. 'Precisely! We have to bloody well do something, as you put it! Yes, monsieur!'

This too was a departure. Previously – friends or enemies, political adversaries or not – all the men of Saint-Libéral had called each other by their Christian name, or their surname, and used the familiar 'tu'. Only the very old had a right to the formal 'vous' and to be addressed respectfully, as père such-and-such. Nowadays, with the new-comers, you were almost always required to stick on a 'monsieur' as long as your arm and to juggle with 'vous'. But as Delmond had one day said with regret:

'Say what you like, it was much easier when you could say: "My dear old Jacques, you're really bloody stupid!" Nothing was inferred, you knew there was no harm meant! But today, if I say that to one of these fellows, using the formal "vous", he might take it amiss! And I'd be lucky if he didn't complain to the gendarmes!'

Jacques smiled, thinking of the anecdote, and decided to take a turn at moving the discussion along.

'Right,' he interrupted, 'I think we've all understood that there's practically nothing for the young people. But I believe I have explained my views. We cannot invest crazy amounts solely to keep a few adolescents amused. It's a pity maybe, but that's how it is. We are not rich, you know, so what would you suggest, Monsieur Peyrafaure?'

'Oh! It's very simple,' said the latter, drawing a Gauloise from his cigarette-case. He lit it slowly, to create the maximum effect, took a long drag and leant back in his chair: 'It's quite simple,' he repeated. 'I suggest we build them a tennis court . . .'

'A what?' breathed Brousse in alarm.

'A tennis court,' said Jacques, who had understood very well.

'That's not so stupid, that would allow some grown-ups to keep fit too,' approved Martin, with the manifest encouragement and support of Castellac, Delmas and Lacombe.

Jacques looked at his old friends, those born and bred in the village, and pictured them, racquet in hand, galloping after a ball.

'Listen,' he said eventually, 'I've nothing against tennis, it's an extremely healthy sport – well, I presume it is – but do you really think that we can afford this . . . this luxury? Yes, it is a luxury!'

'It's not a luxury! Other villages have built them, and everyone's very pleased,' Martin assured him.

'Well, those villages are richer than ours!' cut in Jacques, with a flash of temper. 'Those are villages where there are children! Where the average age is not over fifty, like here! Those are not retirement colonies!'

'There's nothing wrong with being retired!' cried Peyrafaure angrily, for he felt under personal attack.

'I wasn't thinking of you,' Jacques reassured him. 'But bloody hell!' he exploded, 'do I need to spell out just how meagre our budget is? We should be redoing the roof of the mairie and of the church; there's not enough money, even with grants! To buy a big mower, a proper one, to clear the verges, not enough money! Repair a section of the water piping, no money! No money, my God! And you come rabbiting on about a tennis court? Why not a golf course and a swimming pool while you're at it? Or a racecourse? Eh?'

'When it comes to money, all you have to do is ask your friend Chirac, it seems he's handing it out to all his buddies!' growled Peyrafaure, getting more and more annoyed.

Jacques shrugged. He knew that Peyrafaure was not of his persuasion. So sometimes, when the discussion grew lively, a few barbed remarks were thrown around. It wasn't serious. But he promised himself the satisfaction of returning a ball to hit Peyrafaure in the face one of these days, like at tennis, right?

'No, let's be serious, messieurs. I'm not denying that we need to consider the young people, and the not-so-young. But have a heart, don't talk about a tennis court any more, it's beyond our means! That's the situation and that's all there is to it,' he said, rising and so indicating that the meeting was closed.

'All the same, we'll have to find some idea to pull this village out of the doldrums!' cried Martin.

'Right, there I'm in complete agreement with you,' Jacques assured him. 'And believe me, that idea, I've been looking for it ever since I came to the council as second deputy. I remember it well, it was twenty-seven years ago this month! You were only just born, Monsieur Martin, for if I'm not mistaken, you're hardly older than my eldest son! Yes, I've been looking for it since the year he was born. And I'll have you know, the electors are aware of that and trust me. Because it's twenty-seven years they've been voting for me!'

Even as he told himself repeatedly that he had made the right choice, that it wasn't sensible to base his whole future in Algeria, Dominique felt rather like a deserter. He didn't enjoy that. So now that everything was decided he was in a hurry to finish, to climb into the aeroplane and draw a line under it. But, as ill-luck would have it, his Super Caravelle had already been delayed for two hours, and no one in the airport had been able to tell him what time they could hope for take-off. No one even seemed to know why the aeroplane was not there.

Good thing nobody's waiting for me at the other end, he thought as he watched the indicator board on which flight 108, his, had still not been announced.

'Say what you like, things still aren't up to scratch here!' he called to Ali.

The Berber smiled and shrugged resignedly.

'So it took you four years to find that out!'

He had absolutely insisted on accompanying Dominique and watching with him for the promised Caravelle. But neither had anything further to say to each other; the wait was becoming uncomfortable.

'Honestly, you could go,' suggested Dominique once more. 'It might be a long wait yet.'

'I've got plenty of time. And it'll teach the new boy some patience!'

'He'll bloody well need it, dealing with you!' joked Dominique.

As soon as he met his successor, he understood that all would not be going smoothly between him and Ali. Young Sliman was still a little too full of his agronomy course and all the theory in his studies. Too sure of himself and tactless, he had cut short the explanations which Dominique was prepared to provide. To listen to him, he already knew everything about Saharan agriculture, and had no need of a Frenchman's experience. His attitude displeased Ali, who had vowed to lick him into shape without delay. Dominique had no doubt that the matter would be sorted out quickly. One or other of them would have to give in, and it would not be Ali. But knowing that this youth might perhaps try to ruin his work annoyed him. In the same way he was troubled by a sort of regret, almost a bad conscience, which had haunted him from the moment of decision was taken.

'Look, maybe it's good news this time!' he said suddenly, hearing the display board clicking over. He watched it and turned to Ali. 'The bloody plane's ready at last; I hope they've tightened all the nuts and bolts! Right, I'll be leaving you then, mate. But don't forget you promised to visit.'

'Don't worry, I'll keep it in mind. And you, if your Mondiagri sends you anywhere near . . . Well, I mean, perhaps to Morocco; they've got a subsidiary over there, so . . .'

'You bet, I'll pop over here. Go on then, look after yourself, and hey, man, you watch our experimental fields. Don't let that junior muck up our work. Because between us we've done a bloody good job! You know, what annoys me about going is that I may never find such an interesting and useful job again . . .'

They shook hands, then Dominique turned on his heel and marched along the corridor to board.

Dominique adjusted his seat, stretched himself out more comfortably and glanced discreetly in the direction of his neighbour. He noticed immediately that she was young and good-looking, then that she was wrestling with her safety belt, which was much too long and all twisted up.

'Would you like some help?' he suggested.

'I'll manage, thank you,' she assured him as she got up.

She unravelled the strap, shortened it, sat down and fastened the buckle. Already the aeroplane was taxiing towards the runway.

When his eyes came to rest on his neighbour's hands, Dominique noticed that she was trembling. She was shaking so much that despite gripping the armrests with her fingers, her whole forearm was twitching. He observed her more closely, saw her closed eyes, mouth clamped shut, chin quivering. And despite her very deep suntan, two nasty pale blotches marked her cheeks.

He guessed that she was younger than him, and ventured in a joking tone: 'Is it malaria, fear, or both?'

She shrugged; gripped even tighter at her chair. Already the Caravelle was entering the final turn which would bring it to the beginning of the runway.

'If you're scared. I've got a trick to deal with it,' he reassured her, 'and if it's malaria, I've got what you need for that too.'

'Yes, I'm scared!' she blurted out. 'Now leave me in peace! Well, what's your trick?' she asked, biting her lips.

'Very easy. Look, as soon as the plane has switched to full thrust and begins to gather speed you start counting slowly. Or better still, you look at the second hand of your watch.'

'And what then?' she asked, smelling a rat.

'Well if we haven't taken off within forty seconds, at least we'll only be five seconds from heaven!'

'Oh, you think you're so clever!' she retorted and closed her eyes.

He saw that she was really very frightened. Already the sound of the jet engines was becoming deafening. He leaned over to her and offered a suggestion:

'It's not a joke! It works because it keeps you busy. But if you want to, you can hold on to my arm and squeeze as hard as you like, it seems that helps.'

He was surprised by the strength of the fingers which grasped his forearm and locked on. Pinned against the backrest by the acceleration and the Caravelle's amazing angle of ascent, he did not move so long as he felt the fingers digging into his muscles. Then the machine gradually levelled off and the hand clutching him relaxed.

'Please excuse me,' said the young woman. 'It's better now.'

'My, that's a really strong grip you've got there!' he said, pushing up his sleeve to view the red marks left by her nails.

'I'm sorry,' she said again, with a smile. 'I've flown often enough, but I'm still just as frightened at take-off. Silly, isn't it?'

'No more than being frightened of other things; that's just the way it is. And does it affect you at landing?'

'No, no. You're safe, I won't scratch you any more.'

'Oh, it doesn't worry me. Although it's common knowledge

755

that landing's more risky than take-off,' he added wickedly.

'It's so kind of you to reassure me like that!' she replied, leaning towards him to look out of the porthole which he was partially blocking.

He noticed that she had very beautiful blue eyes, an exquisite, delicate profile, but her extremely short, dark brown hair showed evidence of a disastrously unprofessional cut.

She did that herself and made a complete mess of it! he thought. Or one of her friends, not a very talented one!

'Would you like my seat?' he suggested.

'No, no,' she said, curling up in her reclining chair, 'it's over, you can't see anything any more, there are too many clouds.'

'Yes, you can,' he said. 'Look back there, you can still pick out a bit of the coastline.'

She leaned over once more, saw it, smiled and resumed her place.

'Well, that's it, farewell Africa!' she said.

'At your age, it's a bit melodramatic to be saying goodbye! You've got all the time in the world to go back to Africa!'

'Yes, probably. It's just a figure of speech.'

'Are you a teacher?' he asked suddenly.

'No, why? Do I look like one?'

'Not particularly. No, I was asking because I've met several Frenchwomen like you during my years in Algeria. They were almost all lecturers in something or other. The last one was a shrink and spent her time trying to understand the behaviour of countries recently released from the colonial yoke, her very words! A vast programme, don't you think?'

'And you, are you a teacher?'

'No, why? Do I look like one?'

'Not look, but sound – talk, talk, talk!'

'If that's all, there's nothing wrong with that. But come on then, instead of chattering away I'll nail my flag to the mast: Dominique Vialhe, agronomist, two years in Algeria, two in the Sahara.'

'Béatrice Laurignac, paediatric nurse, three years in Upper Volta.'

'Married?'

'Single.'

'Congratulations.'

'Because I'm still single?'

'Not at all, that's easy enough! But because of Upper Volta; that must be a tough job, down there!'

'You have to like it . . .'

'Of course. But tell me, your name comes from round our way.'

'Where's round your way?'

'The Corrèze.'

'That's in the north!' she said with a shrug. 'No, I'm from Agen.'

'That's not too bad,' he granted her. 'But tell me, why didn't you take the direct flight from Ouagadougou to Paris? What have you been doing in this dump? I may as well tell you that you were quite right to be frightened. You saw it, more than two hours delay we had! Seems they lost an engine . . . And just look at this cabin, it's rotten all through! If it were to rain, we'd be soaked!'

'Thank you for informing me so tactfully. I know very well that there's a more direct flight, but I had friends to visit in Algeria. There you have it. Any more questions?'

'No, that'll do. But please don't switch off. If I'm a bit too chatty it's because it's so nice to talk about something besides my job, especially with a fellow countryman.'

He looked at her, saw that she had closed her eyes, thought that maybe she wanted to sleep, and kept quiet. It was she who restarted the conversation after a few moments of silence.

'Are you leaving Africa too? For me, it's finished. And what about you?'

'Me too. But you said "It's finished", why?'

'Perhaps for the same reasons as you!'

'I bet you're going to get married,' he said, without really knowing why. 'Is that it?'

'What an idea!' she said with a laugh. 'But is that why you're going back then?'

'No way!' he retorted.

'Well why, then?'

'Oh, it's a long story!'

'Well tell me anyway, we'll see whether we've had the same experiences.'

'No, no, after you, ladies first.'


Dominique and Béatrice had not travelled the same road. Whereas one had worked in his younger days to reach the goal he had set himself – and it wasn't easy for the son of small farmers – the other had flitted happily from one thing to the next.

Daughter of a chemist, Béatrice had jogged along with classical studies up to her baccalaureat. Then, under the false pretext that the Universities of Toulouse or Bordeaux were less highly rated than Paris, she had persuaded her parents that her sudden enthusiasm for history deserved the best professors. That was in October 1967, and the only history which really interested her was her own!

She was then nineteen, and desperate to escape the smell, the tubes, creams, lotions and other patent products of the family chemist's shop. Anyway her elder brother was already preparing to succeed his father in the business, and she had no wish to compete with him for it.

From an attic shared with a girlfriend in the Rue Saint-André-des-Arts, she had gaily discovered all the pleasures of independence. And since it seemed quite natural that her parents should regularly send her a monthly allowance, she had no money worries.

She toyed lightly with the lectures in her course and developed a parallel education in theatre and cinema studies. As there was often a little time between two performances, she undertook to explore some museums.

It was not therefore to fill her spare time that she fell in with the protesting students; it was pure curiosity. She did not regret the experience, at least not at first.

She had discovered, in all those debates, meetings, shouting matches, controversies and good-natured chaos, a pleasant way of asserting herself and finding her own voice. And as she loved to take the floor, she had realised with delight that she could defend, with just as much determination, ardour and conviction, exactly the opposite of what she had advocated that same morning in front of a different audience! It was all very exciting. Much better than stupidly going out in search of a beating or a painful lungful of tear-gas, just for the childish pleasure of poking out your tongue at the riot police or calling them the SS.

However, since some of the listeners lacked the most basic sense of humour and the sneaks had told them that the little brunette with blue eyes had, two hours earlier, been proclaiming the opposite of what they had just applauded, she had been forced to abandon her career as an orator. Trapped at the end of a grimy corridor, she had understood that imagination and humour were not to the taste of the unyielding disciples and guardians of the new revolution; they were expressly forbidden.

'Right, you little bitch, you're busy sabotaging the movement! Is it that bastard Fouchet who's paying you?'

As she did not know the name of the Minister of the Interior, she had thought it was a joke and shouted back:

'No, it's Talleyrand!'

The clout she got brought tears to her eyes. But she had stood up to them, wrestled with them, striped her attacker's face with three sharp nails, lashed out with the toe of her shoe at the shin of another, and escaped under a shower of insults and threats:

'Stupid cow! If you come back we'll smash you up with crowbars!'

Considering the matter carefully, and not completely convinced it was absolutely necessary to sweep away a whole society and way of life which suited her very well, she had refrained from setting foot in the meetings or any of the other interminable discussions which proliferated everywhere. Since it was necessary to approach all this with the solemnity of a pope, it was not much fun. Likewise she had shunned all the demonstrations and marches which had followed throughout the whole month of May.

'That was it, shortly after all that fuss I changed tack,' she concluded.

'Funny, we might have met each other before during that period,' he said.

'Why? You were in Paris too?' she asked, switching to the familiar student form of address and using 'tu' without noticing.

'No, at Grignon. But I came and had a look.'

'Did you follow the events? Did you join in?'

'In the disturbances? No, I didn't have the time. And what's more I couldn't afford such luxuries! But you, after that, why paediatric nursing? Why Africa?'

'Because I like it, a great deal! As for Africa . . .' She fell silent, and shrugged. 'Why not Africa?'

'Well if you look at it like that . . .' he said. He watched her, saw that she seemed to be lost in memory, and continued, just as a joke: 'Africa wasn't to mend a broken heart, I hope? In Algeria I saw girls in that sort of situation. They were cured!'

'A broken heart?' she was amused. 'No, no, not especially. It was simply the first job I could find when I wanted a change of scenery, to make a break with my parents; give myself a bit of space, you know! But what about you, how did you get there?'

He looked at his watch and smiled.

'It would take too long to tell, we'll be landing in ten minutes. We'll have to meet again if you're interested in finding out. Shall we see each other again?'

'Who knows? . . . I believe in fate.'

'Why not! But we could still try to increase the odds a bit, couldn't we? Shall we exchange addresses? No obligation.'

'Okay, if you put it like that, no obligation. I mean we don't have to respond to a letter or call, right?'

'Well I certainly agree that gives fate more of a chance!'

# 5

SINCE Saint-Libéral no longer had a priest or a sacristan, Mathilde and Louise had committed themselves to looking after the church. They undertook to open it each morning, to close it after the evening angelus bell, to sweep it and set it to rights again after the few rare services. They made sure that there was always a good supply of candles, and holy water in the stoup.

Thanks to this, any old ladies who slipped into the church during the day did not have the feeling of entering an abandoned shrine. It was quite upsetting enough not to see the red lamp glowing above the tabernacle, empty of the blessed sacrament since Father Soliers had found the wafers all blue with mould after he had been away a fortnight. So, not being able to meditate in front of that, the female parishioners would kneel beneath the statue of Saint Eutrope, patron saint of the parish; Mathilde lit a small flame in front of it each morning.

For a long time now, a deep understanding had existed between these two. It was always at his feet that Mathilde came to draw courage when she had need of it. That habit dated from October 1917, after she had accompanied Pierre-Edouard to the train taking him back to the front line, when she had needed to feel she was not alone in the struggle against her overwhelming despair.

And then, over the course of the years, other events had brought her there, trustingly, to face the brightly painted statue. It was a very fine piece; thirteenth century, the experts maintained. Still well preserved, it had developed a sheen over the centuries and offered the faithful the rather tight-lipped but gentle smile of a man with a comforting expression and a beard of delicate ringlets. The hand raised in blessing had long ago lost the middle finger down to the second joint; in the other he held at his heart a thick missal embossed with a gold cross. Mathilde carefully dusted the statue each week, and used the opportunity to clean the niche where the spiders enjoyed weaving delicate haloes around the saint.

On this last Wednesday in October, two days before All Saints', Mathilde and Louise were happily chatting as they turned their steps towards the church. It was fresh but dry, and the day had begun pleasantly enough. But best of all was the news which delighted the whole family: Dominique had announced he would be arriving the next day. He had telephoned from Paris where he had been spending a short week sorting out some business with his new employers. According to Jacques, who was very proud of it all, he had secured an extremely interesting and very well paid job.

Unfortunately he would not be working in France, at least not at present. His first assignment would be to Guyana, which was not exactly a suburb of Saint-Libéral!

'Well, well, so that's it!' Pierre-Edouard had murmured on learning the news. 'That's his reward for wanting so many diplomas! Now they've sent him to a penal colony! Really, if you'd told my poor father that a Vialhe would one day go to Cayenne!'

But he too was very proud to know that his grandson had an important job. Anyway, Guyana was still better than Algeria. To Pierre-Edouard, that was the God-forsaken land where his son had died. He did not like it, and did not want his grandson to live and work there.

Well, the main thing is that he'll be here tomorrow, thought Mathilde, climbing the steps of the church. And as she was in a very good mood she decided to thank Saint Eutrope with a fat candle; a beauty, bearing that clever transfer of Notre Dame de Lourdes.

The empty niche was horrible, like an eyeless socket, obscene. Mathilde stood speechless, dazed, petrified to discover the cavity where there was nothing but a little heap of rubble and the pale outline of the statue printed on the grey stone, marking its presence there over the centuries. She jumped when she heard behind her the cry Louise emitted as she reached one of the two side chapels. It was the one where the altar housed the tiny casket containing the relics of Saint Eutrope, a fragment of jawbone. The reliquary had disappeared.

Then, all of a tremble, each transfixed by the same thought, the two women scurried to the other side of the apse, to the chapel of the Virgin Mary. And the same gasp of horror shook them when they saw that the magnificent door of Limoges enamel enclosing the tabernacle had been torn off.

'They've stolen everything, everything! How dare they!' Mathilde was incoherent, bitting her lips so as not to cry at such patent sacrilege. Then she saw, behind the great altar, a huge hole in the stained glass at the back of the church, giving on to the garden of the Vergnes' house.

'They've taken everything, everything!' she repeated, wandering to and fro.

Here, two big chandeliers were missing. There, the beautiful lectern of solid walnut, the eagle with outstretched wings on which the missal was placed. And in the vestry, horror of horrors. Everything had been pulled out of the cupboard through its broken door. Tossed into the middle of the room, there lay the capes and stoles, the old chasubles, the surplices. All those holy vestments which testified to the time when Saint-Libéral had its own resident priest, when the church was full each Sunday and Holy Day, and High Mass resounded with great pomp when His Lordship the Bishop honoured the church with his annual visit.

'Look,' whispered Louise, 'they've stolen it all . . .'

Stolen, the beautiful chalice donated in 1910 by Madame Duroux, the squire's wife, in honour of her elder daughter's marriage. Gone, the ciborium and the paten for the consecrated bread, the graceful crystal cruets for the wine, the ones they never dared to use because they were too fragile, and the monstrance. And even the old censer, which had not seen the smoke of incense for years, was no longer hanging from its nail.

'They got out that way . . .' said Mathilde, pointing to a little door, which had been unused for the last twenty years and led into the Vergnes' garden.

'Yes. We must call the gendarmes,' decided Louise.

'Of course, but first let me warn Pierre-Edouard quietly. It'll give him a shock, you understand.'

Carried by the postman from Perpezac – there had been no post office in Saint-Libéral for five years – the news had circulated around the village before it struck noon. Everyone, whether practising Christians or not, felt this theft like a violation. For by breaking into a holy place, it was rather as if the robbers had penetrated into the sanctum of every home. And everyone felt defiled by this incomprehensible act.

The oldest were the most shocked and scandalised. For even if some of them, especially the men, had not entered the church in years, it was still no less theirs. Within its walls all those born in the village had been baptised, taken their first Communion. It was there that many had been married. There, most importantly, had rested, for the duration of a service, the coffins of their parents, their friends, their partners, sometimes their children. There finally, before long, they too would be welcomed to begin their last journey. And those who had known an era when the church could remain open day and night without it occurring to anyone to desecrate it, were barely able to conceive of a person sufficiently immoral to plan and then carry out such a vile deed.

There was therefore a group gathered in the church square, reverberating with outraged and vengeful remarks, when the police car eventually arrived.

'They took their time!'commented Jacques.

'Yes, it must be more than three hours since they were called,' agreed his brother-in-law Jean-Pierre.

As teacher he naturally filled the post of secretary at the mairie, and was able to make an inventory of all the works of art the church contained.

'Come a bit quicker when it's a matter of confiscating a few demijohns of moonshine brandy!' said Pierre-Edouard sarcastically.

He had been in a bad mood ever since Mathilde had told him, and was cursing an era capable of producing individuals so foul that they would dare to sully consecrated ground.

Preceded by Jacques and Jean-Pierre, the two gendarmes entered the church, where Mathilde and Louise were waiting for them. Pierre-Edouard fell into step behind them.

'They must have come in through there!' said one of the gendarmes, after having examined the broken window.

Huh! No need to wear a kepi to work that one out!' grumbled Pierre-Edouard. He was growing angrier and angrier as he saw just how upset Mathilde was.

'Yes, they came in that way, the slobs!' he continued. 'And I can even tell you how! By climbing on to the lean-to by the Vergne house and jumping into the garden. It would never have happened when the house was inhabited! But that dump, with it's For Sale board to alert every passer-by, and it's been up more than a year, is almost an invitation to help yourself! It's like the empty presbytery – a signal for looters that's all!'

'Undoubtedly,' agreed the gendarme, turning to Jacques. 'And what have they taken?'

'Everything they could, but my brother-in-law will give you the details of the important pieces.'

'Here it is,' said Jean-Pierre, holding out a type-written sheet.

The officer read it and nodded his head:

'Very accurate description, but how did you know all that?'

'I helped with the inventory which the people from the Ministry of Cultural Affairs made five years ago.'

'Very good, we'll be able to circulate that,' said the gendarme, filing the document. 'But what I'd like to know is how they could do it without anyone hearing anything. And above all, how they got away so quietly.'

'By the vestry door which opens on to the garden,' explained Jacques.

'Look here, if you were a bit better at your job, you'd know that already!' interrupted Pierre-Edouard. He was aware of the two gendarmes' offended expressions, but took no notice. 'Exactly! If you came more often you'd know what was going on round here! Oh, I tell you, in the old days your colleagues weren't any cleverer, but they didn't need to ask questions like that! they would have known straight away!'

'Listen,' Jacques intervened, 'let the gentlemen do their work! We've come on a bit since the mounted constabulary!'

'And more's the pity!' Pierre-Edouard was carried away. 'I'm going to tell you,' he shouted at the gendarmes who were more and more discomfited by the attack, 'instead of your pretty blue van driving through Saint-Libéral once a fortnight, only when the weather's good and without stopping of course, if you were to walk about a bit you'd know that the Vergnes' garden backs on to the lane which goes down to the Combettes. Yes, there's a lane, and that's where the robbers' car must have been waiting. They won't have needed to walk more than eighty metres, and cool as a cucumber! There's no one left around there, or only a few old people. And they're not of age to go out in the middle of the night when the dogs bark. The old people know it takes you three hours to arrive! So they're not in a hurry to get bashed up waiting for you outside! That's what you ought to know!'

'Listen, monsieur, we're not here to be lectured! We're here to investigate!' cried the officer.

'A lecture; I'll give you a lecture if I feel like it! That's just it: if you came more often we wouldn't be robbed by the first thieves who turn up!'

'Calm down,' Mathilde put in. 'These gentlemen are doing what they can.'

'All right! Can't do much, those old jackdaws! This proves it, can't even prevent a break-in in the middle of the village! I'll tell you something, you won't be seeing your Saint Eutrope in a hurry. He's a long way off by now, poor fellow! And nobody's after him! Right, I'm off out for some fresh air. I can see that I'm holding up the smooth running of the investigation!' he hurled, as he strode towards the far end of the church.

He went out, and the noise of the heavy door slamming behind him echoed all along the main street.

'Well I must say, Mayor, your father's still in good form!' said the officer as soon as Pierre-Edouard had left.

'Oh, you think so?' Jacques smiled. Then he saw his mother quite downcast and sad, and his black mood returned. 'Yes, that's as maybe, but he's right – I mean about the route taken by our visitors.'

'We'll go and have a look at that in a moment.'

'And apart from that, what will you actually do?'

'We'll take statements from the witnesses, I mean these two ladies. We'll try to find out what time the robbery happened, look for tracks behind the church . . . all that, the usual routine.'

'That means there's no chance of getting anything back?'

'Sadly, your father's right on that count too,' sighed the gendarme. 'The stolen objects are several hours away by now. They're probably already in Paris, Lyon or Bordeaux. Or somewhere else just as distant! Or even sold already . . .'

'But who would dare to buy such things?' Louise intervened.

'What's that?' The gendarme was amazed. 'Anybody, my dear lady! You know, maybe I shouldn't say it, but since some priests have taken to selling statues and pictures which they no longer wanted in their churches, everybody's got used to finding them in the dealers and antique shops. So . . .'

'But . . . even the chalice? Even the ciborium?' Mathilde asked indignantly.

'Of course, madame! There are people who even enjoy using one as an ordinary dish, or as a vase!'

'Mon Dieu . . .' she murmured.

She was from an era when the worshippers had no right to touch the sacred vessels without express permission; it would have been a grave sin. And she felt so sad she could have cried as she pictured the Saint-Libéral chalice in impious hands.

'Well yes, that's how it is,' said the gendarme. 'It's a funny old world we're living in.'

It was then, and only then, that Mathilde realised how much times had changed, the world had turned upside down, for ever probably. Further proof lay in the fact that no one had yet thought to inform the vicar who served the parish. It was staggering, for that demonstrated that nobody in Saint-Libéral recognised good Father Soliers as the village priest. He was not and would never be more than a caretaker. Not unknown, naturally, but still forever a stranger, the vicar of other parishes, the one who could only come once a fortnight and not even on Sundays.

'We should perhaps tell Father Soliers,' she said eventually.

'Oh yes, that's true,' said Louise, 'but where is he?'

'Um . . .' murmured Mathilde as she considered the matter.

'It's Wednesday morning? He must be taking Catechism in Yssandon or Perpezac, at least I think so . . .' reckoned Jacques. 'But you're right,' he said to his mother, 'I'll go and telephone right away.'

He came back a few moments later to announce that the priest was neither in Yssandon, nor in Perpezac; he was at a meeting in Tulle, at the bishop's palace.

'So did you leave a message?' asked Mathilde.

'No, I didn't dare,' he said thoughtfully. He shrugged his shoulders before replying: 'They explained to me that he and his colleagues were discussing Christian activities in the rural framework. I didn't think it would be in very good taste to tell them what's happening here in Saint-Libéral, in the way of activities . . .'

It was almost midday before the gendarmes left the village. Mathilde watched the police car disappear, and turned to Jacques.

'They won't find anything, will they?'

'I'm afraid not . . .'

'And you, what do you think?' she asked her son-in-law.

'The same, sadly!'

'So they were wasting our time with their stupid questions. Pierre was right,' she said.

'I wouldn't be surprised,' said Jacques.

'Great!' she sighed. 'Right, it's time I went back, your father will be waiting for his soup and he'll be getting impatient. Especially as he's already in a bad mood . . . By the way, as he's not here, have you any news of the girls?'

She had a longstanding agreement with her daughter and son-in-law that she would continue to hear news of her granddaughters, whatever their behaviour, or misbehaviour, might be. She considered she had the right to know. So she kept herself informed whenever she got the chance, which was to say when Pierre-Edouard was not around. For although Mauricette dropped in on her parents every day, that was of course when her father was at home; and as they were supposed to keep it all from him . . .

'Marie telephoned yesterday evening, she's okay,' Jean-Pierre assured her.

'She didn't say any more about the problem with . . . uh . . .'

The fact that one of her granddaughters was prepared to break her marriage vows was heartrending for her, so that she did not even wish to say the word divorce; she was shocked by it.

'Yes, of course, it seems it's all done already,' said Jean-Pierre resignedly.

'Aah . . .' she breathed out. 'I won't ask you for news of Chantal. Aunt Berthe speaks to her on the telephone every fourth morning. I know she's very well. That is, if you like that sort of thing . . .' she sighed.

There again, the life led by her granddaughter was far from pleasing to her. All the while she consoled herself by telling herself that Chantal at least, if she went on the way she was going, would never need to get a divorce . . .

'And the little one?' she continued.

She had always had a weakness for Josyane. Of Mauricette's three girls, it was she who most resembled Mathilde. Lively and graceful, as she had been in her youth. But stubborn too, and deceitful if need be. And with a will of iron when it came to completing a project she considered worthwhile. To that she added an independent streak which Mathilde had understood. At least until the day when Josyane had gone too far. To leave like that for the ends of the earth, on an impulse, that was really unforgiveable! Well, almost . . . She saw that her son-in-law was delaying his reply, and asked again:

'So what about Jo?'

'We received a postcard this morning,' he explained. He seemed so unhappy that she should not really have enquired further. But she needed to know.

'She's well at least?'

'Oh! That, yes, seems to be! Well, you know, she never complains and especially not when things are going badly . . .'

'And where did this card come from?'

By now she was used to it. On account of her granddaughter, she had been forced to get down one of those old atlases out of the loft. A book dating from her days as a pupil with the nuns at Allassac, before the 1914 war. A completely obsolete work which showed the colonies, French and others, but which still allowed her to follow her granddaughter's movements a little better, when Jo thought to write.

After spending almost a year in the United States, she had headed straight for Mexico. Subsequently a postcard arrived from Colombia; then another from Peru. Three months later Josyane was in Rio. So it was hard to guess where the next message would come from!

'Come on, say it! Where is she now?' she repeated the question.

'In Tahiti!'

She needed several seconds to realise fully that it was a long way off, a long, long way . . .

'But what's she doing over there?'

'Who knows!' said Jean-Pierre with a shrug. 'I've given up trying to understand!'

'But doesn't she explain anything?'

'No,' he sighed. 'At least since she left she never has explained anything, why should she start now?'

The robbery from the church earned Saint-Libéral the attention of the local press. The afternoon had hardly started when a journalist from the Brive office stopped his car in the church square. Preceded by a dachshund which was nearly eaten by the first dog it met – a brute almost as big as a calf, which was always ravenous and belonged to Delmond – the man walked without hesitation to the door of the bistro and pushed it open. Here was a very fine professional who knew his area and his trade like the back of his hand. He reckoned on garnering a mass of information at Nicole's, all the details of the general atmosphere, which he was very keen to capture.

His disappointment was great when he found only two old men sipping coffee. As Edmond Duverger was as deaf as a post and Louis Brousse wary and disinclined to speak, the conversation did not even get off the ground. That left Nicole. But she had seen nothing and if she was, like everyone, aware of the crime, her information was second-hand, vague.

'Do you know whether Monsieur Vialhe is about?' asked the journalist.

'Which one?'

'Well, I only know of one, the former regional councillor, the mayor, you know! He's still the mayor, isn't he?'

'Yes. Maybe he's at the mairie.'

'Right, I'll go there,' said the man, carefully sniffing the beverage called coffee which he now regretted having ordered. 'But tell me,' he continued, 'it's astonishingly quiet here, what's going on? There used to be a few more people, didn't there?'

'At one time, yes, there were more people. But not now. It must be a long time since you've been here, eh?'

'Yes, I suppose it is if I think about it,' he said, fiddling with his Rolleiflex. 'Four or five years maybe. I was doing a report on a plan for redistributing the land.'

'Oh yes, that rubbish! But luckily the redistribution was never done! Just as well, it was only good for stirring up quarrels between neighbours,' explained Nicole. 'Yes,' she continued, 'redistribution, that costs money, even when it doesn't produce any!'

She observed him closely, searched her memory and then exclaimed happily:

'Now I remember you! One day you were taking pictures at Delpy's and his whole herd chased after you! We had a good laugh then, I'll say!'

'Yes, yes,' he tried to dismiss the subject.

'But tell me, you didn't have a beard then? Ah, I thought so! That made you look younger, yes, really! Although the beard's not bad either. Yes, I quite like it, it's soft, like being stroked . . .'

'So you're saying the village is always as empty as this?' he continued, indicating the completely deserted square.

'Huh, a few people turn up on days when there's a funeral, but otherwise . . . oh yes, and a few come for the grocer, but you're too early . . .'

He gave a little smile, for he was absolutely convinced that she was making fun of him, and returned to the reason for his visit.

'So you don't know anything of the theft?'

'Well, no, not much. Except it seems it's worth hundreds and thousands, what they took! All the church plate, you know! But what were they thinking of leaving all that stuff where it's never used? I must say, as far as I'm concerned, the church . . . I've got nothing against it. But I don't have anything to do with it either. Except for funerals . . .'

She regarded him eagerly; nodded her head:

'All things considered, it suits you, that beard. Yes, it does, it looks very attractive! And then, the best part is it hides the wrinkles, eh?'

She's well tanked up! Incredible, she must run on neat Pernod! he thought, contemplating the blotchy, swollen face of his hostess. He drank a mouthful of coffee and put down the cup.

'Well, I'll go and find out what the mayor can tell me,' he said, striding to the door.

'Aren't you going to take photos?

'How do you mean, photos? Who of?'

'Well, of me! Usually in the paper there's a photo of the people who have been doing the talking, with their names too!'

'Of course, you're right,' he said with a smile.

And since he was a kind man who would have been sorry to

disappoint Nicole, he took two photos of her, posing jauntily behind her bar.

'I'll send them to you,' he promised as he went out.

Still pulled along by his dachshund, who yapped himself hoarse on the end of his lead each time he caught sight of a hen or duck, he headed for the mairie.

Luckily he found Jacques and Jean-Pierre there, who supplied all the information he wanted. He constructed from this a very fine and moving article, illustrated with a photo of the broken window and the empty niche, which appeared three days later. However, he had been so struck by the silence and emptiness of Saint-Libéral that he began his piece thus: *In a village which seems abandoned, so sleepy and deserted as it is, the criminals were able to empty a church of its exquisite treasures with complete impunity . . .*

'So, now I'm the mayor of an abandoned village . . .' muttered Jacques, putting down the daily paper. He was a little annoyed, and almost telephoned the reporter to communicate his resentment. But he refrained; the man was simply making an observation.

Whether you liked it or not, even if Saint-Libéral was not abandoned, it was well and truly deserted and silent, motionless as a village about to die . . .

# PART TWO

*The Migrants*

# 6

FROM the moment he was old enough to think, Dominique had always done his best to look on the bright side of life. That did not preclude periods when he felt bad-tempered or discouraged; but at least he did all he could not to give in to these feelings.

He therefore reproached himself, after a week at Coste-Roche, with not being as happy as he should have been. Happy to see his parents again after an absence of two years, to plunge back into the world and the scenery of his childhood. Happy as a man taking a well-earned holiday. However, despite his pleasure at being with his family again, in a place he loved, he was not completely content.

He had expected to find that his parents had aged, but the reality was worse than he had imagined. His father in particular was worn out. What was more, he had the appearance of a man haunted by fatigue, whose worries had become his constant companions. Dominique might well remind himself that the break-in at the church had affected him deeply, but that was not enough to explain it all. Not enough to warrant his limping and obviously painful gait, his bent back and the deep lines etched in his face. Not enough to excuse the state of his land either . . .

Not that it was bad, but Dominique was too observant not to notice immediately that many of the pastures showed signs of depletion, and the majority needed to be resown. He had also too professional an eye not to register that the Limousin herd was ageing; many of them should have been culled and replaced. And he was not too blind to see that the plum trees on the Perrier field were no longer well tended. To cap it all, just about everywhere ugly fringes of brambles and thistles were springing up, all those weeds which take advantage of the slightest relaxation in the maintenance of the land.

But since he had decided before coming to say nothing which might upset his father, he was forced to keep his opinions to himself. Likewise he could not in all fairness blame his mother for having let herself go in her old age, and done nothing to alleviate its effects. She was only forty-nine but sometimes seemed nearer sixty. Lastly, he was saddened by the state of Coste-Roche.

For the house had an aura, if not exactly of poverty, at least of want. Here the shutters needed repainting; there a window with a broken catch no longer opened; here again a cracked downpipe poured all its water over a corner of the yard at the slightest shower.

And everywhere inside, yellowing wallpaper, sagging furniture, a collection of crockery which grew less well-matched and more chipped. There as elsewhere, as with the land and farm buildings, the gradual wear and tear caused by lack of maintenance and limited means. The thought that he was at last going to be able to help his parents a little – it looked as if his salary would be three times what he had received in Algeria – was not enough to improve his temper. He was not convinced that lack of resources was the only thing depressing his father.

'You're on the right track, my dear; what's eating your father is more serious than all the financial difficulties he's experiencing. And God knows he's got enough of those!' Berthe assured him.

She was taking advantage of a trip Dominique was making to Brive in his Ami 6 to accompany him and do a bit of shopping.

'They're very comfortable, these little cars,' she admitted, spreading herself out on the bench seat. 'You know, if I were still driving, this is what I'd have.'

'You should have gone on,' he suggested. 'You've never had any problem!'

'Exactly! It was to avoid any that I gave it up. I had always decided to stop driving on the day of my seventy-fifth birthday. That's what I did, and I don't regret it. Is it second-hand, this one? It doesn't look like it,' she noted.

'Yes, a bargain; it's a 1970 model but it only had thirty-five thousand on the clock. I took it right away.'

'You were right. At your age you need to lead your own life and be independent.'

'But I've decided to give it to Papa when I leave,' he continued. 'That'll allow him to get rid of the old Aronde; it's in a dreadful state, possibly even dangerous. This one will last him for a bit.'

'That's kind of you,' she said, patting him gently on the shoulder. 'Yes, very kind. Does he know?'

'No, it's to be a surprise when I leave.'

'And then it'll be a comfort to him after seeing you go, is that right?'

'I suppose so.'

'That's kind,' she reiterated. 'Slow down a bit, there are always loonies shooting out at these crossroads!'

He smiled, for he loved the rather slangy vocabulary his great-aunt liked to use, and took his foot off the pedal.

'So what's eating Papa, do you think?' he asked, resuming the conversational thread.

'Lots of things.'

'What in particular?'

'First of all, whatever he may have said and even if I think he was right, he's missing not being regional councillor any more. You see, there at least he felt he was achieving something.'

'You're sure he would have been beaten?'

'Yes. You know, it's all connected. He'd have been beaten because people nowadays don't want a small farmer to defend them. So that's one thing, that affected him deeply. He felt rejected. But that's not all. I hope you've been keeping in touch with what's been happening in France while you've been away. Well, you have to see things as they really are: nobody's interested in agriculture any more?'

'Well you have to admit that what's going on at our place . . .'

'That's not the point, it's your father's profession. He's already poorly paid, then people tell him he's useless as well! No, just look at that idiot, the speed he's overtaking us! What a wally!'

'And then what else is wrong with him?'

'Right, I could say his health. It's staring you in the face, his back's killing him, but that's almost by the by. No, what's eating him is not being able to jog Saint-Libéral out of its coma, not finding anything to revive the village. It's not for lack of looking or trying, but you get tired of it all . . .'

'I'm sure. But it's true, the village has got pretty gloomy. It's terminal, and I don't see any solution.'

'There it is, you can see the whole picture. All that stops him feeling happy. He's always taken everything to heart, and now he's frightened he'll end up without making a success of anything. Anyway, luckily there's your sister and you. That makes a difference. But you don't need him any more, Françoise only a bit, and not for much longer. Yes, your father needs to feel useful and to be successful. There's only the mairie to put his heart into, but as he has less and less hope . . .'

'And what could I do to help him?' asked Dominique as he slowed down to enter the industrial area of Brive. 'Just look, what a lot of development here! Bloody hell, not so long ago this was the middle of the country!'

'Yes, you see! It's developing here and dying thirty kilometres away, at home . . . The town is gaining ground and we're mouldering away. And everyone seems to think that's quite all right. So to come back to what you can do for your father? I don't know. Simply tell him he's right to fight on, even if it's apparently for nothing.'

'Better to find him something which would be worth fighting for, eh?'

'Of course, but have you got any ideas?'

'No.'

'So, you see . . .'

Never would Josyane have imagined that she could experience such a sense of relief as she did on seeing the Boeing transporting Gilles disappear.

And yet God knew how precarious her present situation was! Alone, more than twenty hours by plane from the mainland of France, with hardly enough to live on for a month, on an island where everything was arranged to fleece the tourist: not a very comfortable position. However, despite all that, she was happy, free.

Contrary to what her companion had perhaps hoped, it was not to try to persuade him to stay that she had accompanied him to Faaa airport, but to make sure he was actually leaving! He had tried that trick so often, saying, 'You're really too stupid, I'm going back to France!' that she had ended up wondering whether he would ever actually do it, and fearing he would not.

She had been fed up for a long time with the childish outbursts with which, like a spoilt brat, he greeted the slightest opposition. She had quickly realised that the impulse which had seized her when he had suggested she accompany him round the world was a monumental error; an idiotic whim which she was still paying for and regretting.

For although Gilles knew how to be pleasant and witty, although he was well educated and interested in everything, he was also often disagreeable, boorish, bad-tempered and spiteful. And always dramatically infantile. In fact when he had one day asked her to go away with him, it was not so much because she was a pretty, funny, jolly girl: it was to have someone permanently around to lean on. She had realised that as soon as they arrived in the United States, when, far from his own kind and already feeling lost, he considered jumping into the first available aeroplane to return to the calm of Parisian life!

She had also discovered that he was not much more of a

photographer than she was, that his journalistic projects were pipedreams based on vague contacts with an equally nebulous agency. Although she had quickly appreciated that he was inspired and athletic when the time came for tenderness and more energetic activities, she had also immediately observed that he was very lazy when he needed to earn his living. Always ready to escape to pastures new, as well! For it was he who, after a few months or weeks of little bits of work picked up by chance during their journeys, made a reverse charge call to his father, to get something sent for air-tickets so that they could change countries!

He declared that his father could easily afford to indulge his whims. He was a Member of Parliament, of fluctuating persuasion, who had grown grey but never blushed under two Republics and several different portfolios, without actually renouncing his profits from industry. Swept out in 1968 by a young tiger who had had the wit to chant 'Vive de Gaulle!' a quarter of an hour earlier than him, he now slumbered in the Senate and was in clover.

'I promise you it won't worry him to send us a bit of cash, he's got enough! I'm not joking,' Gilles reassured her, when she reproached him with the dreadful way he called for help the moment he felt bored or a little at sea. She had never accepted that sort of hypocrisy which consisted of declaring yourself free and independent, all the while reaching shamelessly into the paternal pocket! She would not stoop to that. So to draw the line, she had always managed to provide her share of the budget through her own work. But their differences of opinion on this matter had soured their relationship very early on.

Despite this, and all his other shortcomings, Josyane had not immediately envisaged cutting the ties and leaving him to extricate himself alone from his fits of depression, bad temper and fury. Wisely, she did not yet feel sufficiently confident to venture alone on the exploration of all the countries she wanted to get to know. And as he for his part was incapable of making any progress without support and clung to her like a toddler to its mother, they had remained together for almost two years, somehow or other, a strange couple, rather ill-matched.

But she had very quickly realised that it would all fall apart one day, that he would end up hating her for being made of sterner stuff than him, and she herself would tire of his outbursts, his insults and his cocksure arrogance, thinking he was irresistible the moment he slid his hand into her blouse. She had no doubt that there existed at least one other man in the world capable of satisfying her just as well as him, without being quite so emotionally disturbed. She only had to find him, or to wait for him.

The rift between them had been accentuated during their first week in Tahiti. The idea of visiting Polynesia was his. He wanted to make a photo-reportage for which the agency with whom he very sporadically collaborated would, this time, pay him a fortune! That was what he had given her to believe . . . But he delivered the same speech at each new foray, and she knew that he would be doing well if he even managed to get paid for the films! She had no more illusions about his abilities to earn his living as a photographer!

She was nevertheless happy to follow him to Tahiti, for her job as nanny to a rich family in Rio was beginning to weigh heavy. The three children she had charge of were really too badly brought up and in need of a cuff or two. Exactly what she was not allowed to give them! And after all, Tahiti – that was the ultimate destination, paradise on earth! She had quickly understood that it might be true for those who arrived with solid financial backing; lacking that vital ingredient, it was close to purgatory.

For despite the sun, the scent of mallow, the warm blue water and thousands of brightly coloured fish slipping through your legs, life was not simple for those who needed to earn their daily bread. Especially if they arrived totally unprepared, without any contacts, nor knowing who to turn to.

But Gilles and she had something to survive on for a while without too much trouble, and had therefore begun to snap away at a great rate. For she too had taken to the business, and often achieved better results than him. She had a superior sense of composition, of perspective, an eye for a fleeting image to be captured, for the light.

Their first serious row had arisen four days after their arrival. With all the pessimism of which he was capable, Gilles had decided that Tahiti was a real trap for suckers; it was tiny, you could get round it in an afternoon; two rolls of thirty-six were enough to photograph everything, and it was therefore imperative to leave such a miserable spot.

'Don't you think you're exaggerating a bit? We've only just arrived, and we've seen nothing of the interior!' she had said.

'The interior? You didn't think I was going to wade through that bloody jungle! There's not even a road! No thank you, to slog up fifteen hundred or two thousand metres for the sake of coming down the other side, not likely! No there's really nothing in this dump! Ah, except the girls! Their mugs could frighten the life out of you, but some lovely bums! And their boobs! Have you seen?'

'To me, you know, girls . . .'

'Right, it's not the article, I'm not staying here!'

'Where do you want to go?'

'To Bora Bora, seems it's worth a detour. And I'd like to pop over to Raiatea.'

'But you're crazy! You know our budget won't allow for that!'

'Yours may not, but mine will. You don't think I came here to sit around doing nothing!'

She had seen that he had made up his mind and knew already that he would make no allowances for her reservations. And as she was fed up with always having to make him see reason, she had given up the struggle.

'Fine, do as you like, I'm staying here.'

'You want to leave me?'

'Don't twist things; it's you who's leaving, not me!'

'Okay. Right, you muddle along by yourself then, old girl. Cheerio!'

'And to emphasize his displeasure, he had picked up his bag and camera and left the modest hut they had rented on the outskirts of Papeete.

She had then spent her first night alone since she had known him. To her great satisfaction, not only was she not frightened, she had actually slept better! As he had not reappeared the following morning she had set out at once to look for work in Papeete. Enquiring at every business, shop or enterprise run by Europeans, she had offered her services to each one either as a saleslady, or as an interpreter – she now had a very good command of English, could get by respectably in Spanish and Portuguese – or again as a secretary. And, as a last resort, as a nanny.

Demoralised by a week of futile searching, she was on the point of giving up hope when the manager of a travel agency almost flung her arms around her neck and at once adopted the familiar 'tu' commonly used in Tahiti.

'You speak American? This is really true?'

'Yes.'

'Well, you've come at the right moment, my dear! Oh yes! Our guide has been blackmailing us for a rise and I refuse to give in! I must say that's really not on here, because once you start . . .! Yes, she's Chinese, a beautiful girl, the sneak! And she speaks four languages! But that's no excuse! Is it really true, you can speak American with that authentic nasal accent?'

'Yes.'

'Great! Where are you actually from? I'm from Avignon. Well, we arrived one day, my husband and I, and we stayed. I really love this country, on account of the sun. Where did you say you were from?'

'From the Corrèze, but it's years since I left there. I've worked in Paris and in the United States too, a bit in Mexico, in Colombia and in Peru, and several months in Brazil. So if you need an interpreter, because, as for being a guide, I . . .'

'Sure I need you! We're expecting twenty-three Texans the day after tomorrow! You know all the atolls round about, I presume? Yes that's obvious, you're so nice and brown! Perfect, I'll give you a try. Come tomorrow, I'll explain everything to you.'

She had rushed in bewilderment to the nearest library and got hold of several works on Polynesia. By the early hours she knew Bora, Raiatea, Huahine and Moorea inside out, and was even familiar with Rangiroa!

All smiles, she presented herself to her employers. Only fantastic self control prevented her from bursting into tears on learning that she would not be getting the job.

'Well yes, my dear,' the lady from Avignon had explained to her, 'the Chinese girl's won, she's come back . . .'

'But I thought . . .'

'Yes, I know. But as I told you yesterday, she's pretty, that kid; my husband gave in, so . . .'

'So there's no work for me?'

'Well no, not at the moment. But come back in a few days. I haven't finished with this yet. When it comes to the locals, it doesn't worry me too much if my husband runs after them a bit. It's to be expected, eh? They're always wiggling their hips and rubbing up against anything in trousers! Fine. But if he starts with Chinese girls, then I shall have to say something, especially that one, she's the sort to take over my business and give me the heave ho! So if you haven't found anything in a few days' time, come back and see me, I'll deal with the Chinese girl myself . . .'

And now, as the Boeing heading for San Francisco was nothing but a silent, shining point in the distance, she was wondering rather anxiously how she was going to survive. But she was still very relieved to be alone at last and finally free of Gilles.

He had reappeared one evening after a fortnight's absence. He was not alone. At his side, a fat hibiscus flower in her ear, a Tahitian girl swayed languidly, her pareo accentuating her curves. She was magnificent, but Josyane had not experienced the slightest jealousy. On the contrary, she felt liberated: this girl proved that the break was final, that there was no point in discussing anything. They only needed to say goodbye to each other, without shouts, arguments or tears. It was much better like that.

'I'm going back to France the day after tomorrow, do you want to come?' he had suggested.

'No. I'll come back one day, but not with you.'

'You'll regret it. I tell you, you should stick with me.'

Then she had understood that he was actually hoping to resume their life together. The very idea of it revolted her.

'I'm staying here. But what about her, are you taking her to Paris?'

'You must be joking! No seriously, come with me. Come on, let's forget all the cock-ups and get going.'

'No way, and don't keep on about it, it's getting absolutely ridiculous, especially in front of this young lady. Come on, we'll part friends if you like, but it's over. And don't ever try to come after me again, I'd take a very dim view of that!'

He seemed genuinely upset, but she had often seen him like that and had no time for it.

'Right, will you at least come to the airport with me?' he had sighed. 'I'll be alone. I mean without her. She lives on Moorea and is going back tomorrow.'

'Okay, I'll come.'

And she had kept her word. But they had nothing left to say to each other and the wait had seemed long before his flight was called.

'So you're sure you won't come with me? It's not too late. I asked, there are still seats. I've got enough to pay for it.'

'Don't be ridiculous.'

'Have you got some money left? Do you want any?'

'No, I'll manage.'

'Look,' he had suddenly said, taking off the bag which held his Leica and lenses, 'at least take this; you could always sell it if you're really broke. And after all I owe you that much. I'm fed up with photography anyway, I don't ever want to hear about it again!'

He had passed the pouch-strap over her head, kissed her on both cheeks, and made off towards the boarding gate.

As she passed the shop selling souvenirs and postcards, she chose a sunset over Moorea. And having written her parents' address, she jotted down the first words which came into her head: *Love and kisses from Tahiti. It's all wonderful. Everything is fine*!

It was almost true.

Despite the doctor's advice, Pierre-Edouard could not resign himself to doing nothing all day long; his walks were not enough. He needed to make himself useful, or at least to pretend so to himself. He was still sufficiently aware to know that the tiny bits of work which he attended to were not essential, except to him.

Thus, for example, when the kitchen garden no longer needed careful weeding – he had cleaned between the carrots plant by plant as meticulously as a watchmaker – he busied himself raking the courtyard, trimming the old box hedge with the secateurs or, in season, shucking a few corncobs for Mathilde's geese and ducks. Sometimes too, when the late autumn sun permitted, he would sit on the steps by the door to shell walnuts or peel chestnuts which Mathilde would later blanch.

But what he also very much enjoyed was to set himself down in the woodshed. There, resting on an old oak log which had served as a seat for three generations of Vialhes and whose clawlike roots were cut short to form firm legs, hatchet in hand, he split the kindling for the kitchen stove. Of course he cheated a little in his choice of billets, rejecting any that were not of chestnut, or were knotty or too thick; he knew he would not be able to split them. But the rest, what joy!

Firstly they smelt nicely of good dry wood, cut in the right season, after frost, then properly stacked and left for several hot summers. Wood which held no more sap and would burn without spitting, but whose heartwood emitted a tang of old wine cellars as it split open; slightly acrid and bitter but pleasant, still living.

Then they were good to touch, just rough enough to grip easily without slipping, but never becoming too harsh or prickly. And finally they split without difficulty, giving a cheerful crunch, in long, even sections falling one each side of the blade. Small logs which it was a pleasure to divide again, then split once more, before piling them up beside him.

That morning it was the dry crack of the axe landing in the middle of a log which attracted Dominique to the woodshed. He smiled to discover his grandfather there. The old man – muffled up to the ears, for the cold was biting – was so happy and absorbed in his work that he made a delightful picture, like a child enthralled by his favourite toy.

'You'll catch cold, Grandfather,' he scolded him nonetheless.

'Hey! It's you! No, no, quite the opposite, it's keeping me warm!'

'Would you like a hand?'

'Not on your life! You can see I'm enjoying myself!'

In that case . . .' said Dominique, sitting down on a wide log.

'So, just like that, you're going off to the devil knows where? There are no jobs in France?' asked Pierre-Edouard, turning over a log to find the direction of the grain and so discover which end he should deliver the blow.

'Yes, I'll be off again, but not for a fortnight.'

'I know. But it still seems a pity that you have to go so far away.'

'Oh, it's not so far, only a few hours by plane.'

'Of course, it's not as far as Tahiti . . .,' smiled Pierre-Edouard, lowering his voice as if Mathilde, whose silhouette could be seen occasionally through the kitchen window, thirty feet away, might hear. 'Hah! It surprises you to hear me tell you that,' he said, amused. 'I'm not supposed to know what's going on! I know they take me for a feeble old stick who shouldn't be told anything! Well you see, I find out anyway! But don't tell your grandmother whatever you do, she'd have a fit! Promise!'

'Okay,' said Dominique, laughing.

'What do you think she could be doing there, little Jo?'

'Impossible to tell . . . But you really shouldn't worry about her, she always gets by!'

'That's so! Eh, she's as stubborn as a mule; she's a real Vialhe too, isn't that right? Talking of Vialhes, did you hear about your cousin?'

'Which one?'

'Jean.'

'Is he ill?' asked Dominique. Then he looked at his grandfather and continued: 'What's so funny?'

'You lot! Since you suppress any bad news which might reach my ears, you don't know anything yourselves any more! And I'm well informed! But don't tell a soul, not even your mother!'

'Tell what?'

'That your cousin wants to do the same as you, and I'm very pleased!'

'The same as me? In what way?'

'The same college, the same profession, that's what! All right, it's not exactly farming, but it's better than ending up a pen-pusher, eh?'

'Absolutely. But he's still young, he's still got time to change his mind!'

'I'd be surprised, he's pigheaded as well. No, that's not why I'm mentioning it to you.'

'Oh? Why then?'

'The problem is that his father won't agree to it. You know your Uncle Guy: he must have got it into his head that his son should be an ambassador, or a minister, or some other useless rubbish like that! So you'll do me a favour, won't you?'

'If I can, I will.'

'You're passing through Paris before you leave? Right. The thing is to explain to your uncle that there's nothing to be ashamed of in liking farming and wanting to do something with the land, like you are. And then tell the boy from me that he's right, he must stick to it, we need people like him! Will you tell him?'

'Listen, it's not that easy! Especially when it comes to my uncle . . .'

'Bunkum! I'm not asking you to lecture him! Simply talk to him about your job, in a casual way, about everything you do, your future, your salary . . . You can do that, can't you?'

'Not so easy . . . You have to understand,' Dominique hummed and hawed.

'Do it for me. If I were twenty years younger I'd see to it myself,' Pierre-Edouard assured him with a smile, 'but now, I really can't do a thing. Besides, you know, I haven't even been told about it! So . . .'

# 7

PREOCCUPIED and irritated by the mongrel's boisterous search, for it was too young to control its speed and enthusiasm when it found a trail, Jacques did not notice the hare getting up. Actually, instead of staying in its form until the last moment, then springing out straight ahead, the leveret, terrified by the yapping and over-zealous zigzags of the dog, crept from the tuft of ling under which it had taken cover at first light and slipped away. It was therefore fifteen paces ahead of the dog and forty from Jacques. And when he did make out the tawny arrow heading straight for the White Peak, it was much too late to aim his twelve-bore between the fugitive's ears. Nevertheless he hoped that Dominique, who was positioned by the mine-cutting, would understand the signal and let off a couple of shots to trim the tops of a few brambles.

'This dog is really useless!' he grumbled, shouldering his gun again after having ejected the empty cartridges.

With a bit of luck, although this confounded mongrel did the exact opposite of what was required and was at present barking away three hundred metres in the opposite direction from the hare's trail, their quarry would cut across the slope of the White Peak, traverse the plateau, then run back down, straight towards the mine cutting, to plunge into the valley of the Diamond. Unless Dominique sent it head over heels on the way.

All the hares flushed at this end of the plateau had followed the same track since time immemorial. And Jacques knew from his father that in olden days even the wild boar and wolves took this path. It was immutable.

So logically speaking, if Dominique was in a good position he would be able to take aim at the hare in the pass and stop it there, in the tumbled mass of reddish, iron-bearing rocks of the mine workings.

A broad chestnut tree, crooked and worm-eaten but still solid, stood twenty-five metres from the cutting; settling down at its foot, Dominique knew that he was well placed.

Ever since reaching an age to accompany his father on hunting expeditions, he had been familiar with all the good spots for game in the area; all the routes and haunts of partridge, pheasant or woodcock, the oak groves for pigeons and the broom bushes on the Caput peak where the thrushes lingered. Unfortunately that was not much use any longer, for the game had become very scarce for lack of opportunity to browse.

In fact the decrease in cereals sown had gradually limited the numbers of partridges breeding without any parallel diminution in the number of hunters. And the plateau, which formerly provided cover for eight or ten coveys of red-legged partridge, now harboured only one or two, and that was in a good year! As for the migratory birds, their numbers shrank from one season to the next, frightened away by the advancing houses which were popping up here and there on the edge of the plateau.

Added to that, car drivers were not slow to crush the few pathetic young hares which the hunting clubs persisted in releasing against all better judgement. And as myxomatosis had decimated the rabbit population . . .

The amazing thing was that none of this prevented the foxes, wild cats, civets, martens and other predators from multiplying at a great rate, but it did explain why it was becoming normal to beat around the countryside all morning without flushing anything.

It therefore grew to be almost the exception to fire a gun, and it was really to please his father, who was convinced that a hare was lying low at the end of the plateau, that Dominique had agreed to accompany him. But he was sceptical as to the outcome of their hunting expedition. What was more, he had the honesty to admit that he had little interest in what he was doing. There only remained just under a week of leave for him, but since the previous day the time had lost some of its savour; a few words had changed everything.

After serious consideration, having weighed the pros and cons, finally telling himself that he was a fool to wait, that his silence might ruin everything, he had made a decision. So, on the back of an aerial view of Yssandon he had written: *Wasn't the journey from Algiers to Paris rather too short?* and had then posted it to the address which Béatrice had given him.

That was brief, frivolous and harmless enough to allow for no response if the answer proved to be negative. But it could also be construed as an appeal. Especially as an appeal which might be answered. And it had been, by return of post. The single sentence conveyed on an aerial view of Agen had filled him with happiness: *Of course! But I didn't dare try a hijacking!*

Now he was floating on air, filled with elation which he wanted to share with the world, to proclaim to anyone who would listen. But he had not yet said a word to a soul!

And what amazed him was the discovery that none of the women he had previously met, and liked more or less, had made such an impression on him. Above all, the parting from one of them had never seemed so unpleasant, so difficult to accept. For, since he was sure that the feeling was mutual, the separation from Béatrice was becoming unbearable. And just as he had seriously considered and reflected on the matter before deciding to write, he now allowed his ardour the same rein.

Only the fact that he could not exactly recall the young woman's face clouded his happiness a little. Certainly he remembered her lively blue eyes, the short, brown, badly-cut hair, the rounded, tanned cheeks, but that was all. And much as he felt capable of recognising her in a crowd of ten thousand, he could not picture her exactly in his memory. He could make out the silhouette he had seen at Orly, disappearing in the direction of the bus, but he was frustrated by the vagueness of the little face when he tried to recollect it precisely. The smallest picture of her would therefore have delighted him and calmed his nerves. For he had to wait a little longer, be patient for two more days before taking the road to Agen.

Having received the card, he had rushed to the telephone to inform Béatrice that he was coming immediately, or almost. An anonymous and rather cold voice had brought him down to earth by informing him that she was away, would not be back for three days, and had not left a telephone number where she could be reached. Vexed, he could only grin and bear it and count the hours . . .

Although lost in tender thoughts, he still heard the two shots echoing from the plateau. Immediately on the look-out, he fixed his gaze on the path where the hare would shortly arrive if his father had missed it. But, treacherously, when he should have devoted all his attention to that particular corner of the mine cutting, the image of Béatrice, still cloudy but so comforting, floated before his eyes.

He raised his rifle briskly nevertheless, and aimed at the leveret as soon as he saw it. The animal, a fine beast weighing more than seven pounds, was trotting along unhurriedly since the dog had lost its trail, and was an easy mark.

With thumping heart he pressed the first trigger, the one for the right barrel. Nothing happened. Already the hare, having spotted him, was bounding away with lightning acceleration. He squeezed the second trigger and then remembered that, his thoughts being everywhere but on the hunt, he had forgotten to load his gun.

'The biggest fool on earth, that's me, I can't believe it!' he muttered in frustration.

Then he imagined the ironic comments which his father would surely aim at him on learning of his stupidity.

'That's bound to go all round the village!'

So, to cut matters short, preferring to be considered clumsy rather than a bashful lover, he slipped two cartridges into the chamber and let off a magnificent double in the direction of a fat cumulo-nimbus cloud which seemed to be mocking him as it hung motionless above the White Peak.

'I thought you were more skilful! Or you really have got out of practice in Algeria; isn't there any game there?' asked Jacques, crouching down to try to relieve the pains shooting through his loins.

'That wretched hare was too far away . . .'

'Get away with you! I hope at least you didn't wound it?'

'Oh, no danger of that!' Dominique assured him, trying not to smile. 'But where's the dog?'

'That idiot? God knows! I expect he's waiting for me by his feeding bowl. That's about the only thing he can do! I don't think I'll ever make anything of him,' said Jacques with a wry smile.

'Are you in pain?'

'Bah, no more than usual, no less; have to get on with it.'

'You should get some treatment.'

'Don't talk about that,' said Jacques curtly. 'Get some treatment, that means have an operation! So are you going to look after the farm while I'm in hospital? Are you going to take care of the animals?'

'No, of course not.'

'Well then, don't mention it again,' said Jacques, rising painfully to his feet. 'You see, if I seize up one day, I don't know what we'll do. Your mother wouldn't be able to hold out by herself. Okay, the neighbours would rally round a bit, the Brousses, the Delpeyroux', the Valades, but they couldn't do it all! So what would happen? Your grandfather wouldn't be able to help me either!'

Dominique nodded, and very nearly revealed the ideas which had been going round in his head about the farm. As his Aunt Berthe had realised, his spell away from France had not prevented him from following the development of the political situation in agriculture, in Europe or elsewhere; quite the opposite. And everything which he had been able to discover by reading the reports, articles, plans, theses and other projections had been painfully recalled since he had seen how his father was living and working. But his conclusions were so pessimistic that he now hesitated to relay them to him.

To tell him, for example, that he needed to look with fresh eyes at some modern ideas, to consider some projects which might perhaps seem crazy, but which were probably the only means of extricating the farm from this impasse.

To explain to him that everything was in a state of flux. That above all it was vital to understand that a farm like the Viahles', however good it might be, was viewed as a dead weight which the admirers of a certain sort of Europe, under American influence, had no wish to support. That those people were merely anxious to see the disappearance of all the rank and file in the farming world, whose work was of no interest to anyone. And those who said the opposite were liars and charlatans, for they were the same ones who defended and propounded the Malthusian economic theory current in Brussels! The same ones who, incapable of managing supplies, preferred to destroy them, when only three hours' plane-ride away children were dying of hunger!

And that a farm like the Viahles' was irrevocably condemned, from the moment the discussion included the malign schemes of individuals perverse enough to advocate the set-aside and the slaughter of milking herds! All these observations, painful as they were, only gave a brief glimpse of what awaited all the Viahle farms in France. Those hundreds of thousands of small units whose only mistake was to want to continue in a world which considered it much simpler and more economical to snuff them out, in the face of universal indifference.

If he, an agricultural engineer, had been so happy in Algeria and especially in the Sahara, it was because there at least he had the feeling of doing something useful; of putting his intelligence and skills at the service of an agricultural system which it was vital to develop. And he was pleased to be setting off again for distant parts for the same reasons. Reasons which he was not at all sure of finding in France . . .

But he remained silent, for he was afraid of further demoralising his father. Besides, for all he knew, Jacques had probably analysed the situation in the same way himself. Only he had maybe not the health or strength to draw the necessary conclusions. So what was the good of turning the knife in the wound?

'Incidentally, how do you think he's doing?' asked Jacques to break his son's silence.

'Who?'

'Your grandfather.'

'Rather well. I mean he's aged, naturally, but he's still just as scathing.'

'Ah that, yes! But he's got a weak heart, and in my opinion he doesn't look after himself properly!'

'You're a fine one to say so! I'm sure he feels the same about you!'

'Maybe,' admitted Jacques with a smile. 'Same family! Shall we go back? Hopeless to try to hunt any longer, there's nothing left. And without a dog . . .'

'But why the devil are you lumbered with a mongrel like that?'

'Bah, it was Delpeyroux who gave him to me. Well you need a hunting dog, and as old Frisette died . . . Anyway Delpeyroux assures me that the beast will improve with age; I rather doubt it myself . . .'

'Is Delpeyroux still a town councillor?'

'Yes. And a good thing he's there, with our friends, the ones born in the village. With them we're still just in the majority, but it may not last long! Have you heard the latest idea from the others? They want to build a tennis court! Can you credit it?'

'If it can be done at low cost, it may not be as stupid as all that . . .' considered Dominique.

He had got wind of this plan from Berthe, knew his father's opinion, and was aware just how carefully he had to tread so as not to clash with him.

'That's wonderful! You too? Have you all gone off your rockers or what?' cried Jacques.

He was surprised and a little disappointed by his son's reaction. In his eyes, that put him with the group living in cloud-cuckoo-land, the ignoramuses who would never understand the rural mentality, still less the financial difficulties of a small-town mayor. But as he did not wish to break off the conversation, he persisted:

'No, joking apart, can you imagine Delpeyroux and Brousse in shorts hitting balls to each other? There are others I could mention . . .'

'No,' Dominique admitted. 'To tell you the truth, apart from a few kids, I can't see many people in Saint-Libéral getting enthusiastic about it, although . . .'

'What? No, believe me, much as I need to find something to liven up the village, I must avoid making mistakes and spending money unnecessarily as well. So your tennis court – you jest! The people of Saint-Libéral aren't interested in that!'

They had reached the plateau, where the view reached in every direction, to each far horizon.

'I agree, that goes for the inhabitants of Saint-Libéral,' said Dominique, stopping to admire the countryside, 'but what about the rest? The ones who come for holidays over there, for instance!' He stretched his arm in the direction of a distant hill where lay the newly completed bungalows of a holiday village. 'Yes,' he insisted, 'think about the people who choose to come here in the summer! There's nothing in Saint-Libéral, so we must try to attract people who might come from elsewhere.'

'I've tried! Look at those new houses in the village. They're there because I did what was needed. Well, it wasn't a very good idea. I had people come who know nothing about our problems, our way of life as farmers. And yet there's a chance that they may take our places and decide how we should live! They're already asking for pavements, soon it'll be lamp-posts! Next thing they'll want a school bus! And if you listen to them, there's more than one who'd like to stop the cocks crowing because it wakes them up too early! Or who wants the church clock to break down, for the same reason! No, no, it was *not* a good idea!'

'I'm not talking about that sort of settlement,' said Dominique, walking on, 'and I grant you, it must be difficult to integrate them all! No, if I say a tennis court or something else of that sort isn't a bad idea, it's because that might encourage someone to spend an afternoon in Saint-Libéral without dying of boredom! Right now there's nothing! You can't even visit the church any more. Nothing left; no restaurant, no grocery store, not even a decent bistro!'

'And for a very good reason! Nothing begets nothing!'

'So we must think of something. And if you're allergic to tennis courts, imagine a pool, a ranch with horse-riding, a . . .'

'Stop!' Jacques interrupted. 'You'll end up suggesting a fair at harvest or threshing time, or some other pathetic tomfoolery, making us look like clowns! As long as I'm mayor I'll never ask one of my electors to make a spectacle of our work, and especially not the old ways of doing things! I'll never lower myself to pretend to feed sheaves into an old threshing machine when they've already come out of a combine-harvester! And all to amuse a few miserable idlers who are only too happy to look down on us! If you start that you'll end up like a theme park! Nothing doing! I don't want to see town children throwing me peanuts and chewing-gum one day!'

'I'm not talking about that sort of display,' said Dominique, 'and I'd be very disappointed too, if Saint-Libéral had to come to that!'

'Well you see the problem! Believe me, it's years now I've been thinking it over and I've found nothing acceptable, nothing!'

'That doesn't mean to say there isn't anything! If you don't want the village to wither away completely, there must at least be some people here in the summer.'

'That's easier said than done, without degenerating into quaint folklore! But believe me, I wasn't waiting for you to come along before I started considering all that!'

'I've no doubt. Well, all I can say is . . .'

'Yes, you come back every two years to give some advice!' Jacques laughed without the slightest bitterness, but not sorry to put things in their true perspective. 'By the way, I'm really surprised, this time you haven't made any comments about the farm!'

'What's the use!' said Dominique with a shrug, likewise keeping his remark casual. 'Anyway,' he added, 'I haven't said anything, but that doesn't mean I'm not thinking about it!'

'Right, then we're quits,' joked Jacques. 'By the way, are you really in such a hurry to go? Your mother told me you're leaving the day after tomorrow.'

'Yes, but I'll drop in again before I leave properly, at the end of the week probably.'

Dominique glanced at his father and was grateful to him for not persisting, for not trying to winkle out why he was going away or where he was going.

Then suddenly, without understanding quite why, he felt the urge to talk, to confide, to communicate all the happiness which filled his heart. And he was pleased that it was, rightly, his father who was at hand to be entrusted with his secrets.

'Must tell you, P'pa, I've found my wife!'

'What?' Jacques jumped. 'That's not what you're going away for, is it?'

Since his three nieces, who had been such good little girls, now rivalled each other in seeking independence and dissipation, he was ready to hear anything. And to tell the truth, he was sometimes amazed that he had so far escaped very lightly as far as his own offspring were concerned; but he knew that everything has to start somewhere!

'No joking,' he insisted, 'tell me that's not why you're leaving? You're not going to get married that quickly?'

'Get married? Of course not! I'm only going to ask Béatrice to go with me to Guyana.'

'Ah . . . Just like that, without any formalities! You don't bother about conventions, you young ones! Well, I must be getting too old to understand . . .'

He was disconcerted by his son's apparent irresponsibility in organising his emotional affairs. He felt like telling him that it was not very wise to plan your future in such a casual way, then thought better of it. Dominique was old enough to paddle his own canoe as he pleased, even if his technique seemed at first bizarre.

'You say she's called Béatrice?' he continued.

'Yes.'

'And you're absolutely sure in yourself? And of her?'

'Completely.'

'After all, it's your problem. Have you known her long?'

'It will be exactly a month the day after tomorrow. Yes, that'll be a month we've been apart, and it's damned long! You can't know how long!'

'Oh yes I can! I've got a good memory,' murmured Jacques. Twenty-eight years earlier, he too had realised that the young girl he had just got to know would be his wife. And from that moment the minutes separating him from her had seemed unbearable. Dominique was the proof . . .

'Your mother will be pleased,' he said at last. 'She's been dreaming of becoming a grandmother for ages!'

'Hold on! Not so fast! She'll have to wait a bit for that.'

True, what a stupid remark, and it really dates me! he thought. This generation can plan their children as they wish, without the slightest problem, and they don't hesitate to do so! Never mind, this great idiot wouldn't be here today telling me how happy he is if we'd behaved like that, his mother and I!

'Well, it's still a possibility in the future?' he continued. 'You won't be doing the same as your cousin Marie. Mind you, it's better that way if you're going to divorce after five years, like her!'

'Don't worry! You'll have your grandchild one day! What do you think, Béatrice is a paediatric nurse, so there!'

'Very good. Come on then, let's go straight to Coste-Roche and tell your mother. Afterwards we'll go down to the village to announce the good news to the senior Vialhes. Your grandparents will be over the moon! But go gently on them, don't tell them everything, there's no point, you understand? Introduce Béatrice as your fiancée, simply as your fiancée. Do you see what I'm trying to say? To them, that'll look better, more respectable . . .'

For the first two hours of their reunion, which had as its setting a restaurant not far from Agen, the two young people spent more time talking than eating. They had so much to say to each other! And so many lost hours to make up for!

'Are you serious, is it true? Did you tell everyone that we were engaged?' asked Béatrice, nibbling distractedly at a petit four.

'I actually boasted about it!' he assured her, lifting his forefinger to stroke one of the brown wisps which now framed the young woman's face.

In a month her hair had regrown nicely, and made her appear more graceful and feminine again. Dominique could not look at her enough, drinking in her image, engraving it on his memory. He had sought it for a month in vain and could not bear to risk forgetting it now. More, he was wondering what stupid reasons or arguments could have inspired him to wait three weeks before deciding to write to her. For his rational self obliged him to admit that she had made an impression on him from the first moment. And when he told himself, to explain his delay, that some more or less indifferent or unsuccessful experiences had no doubt counselled prudence, he was revolted by the idea of comparing Béatrice to the few silly girls he had previously known. They no longer existed, annihilated, obliterated by the young woman's blue gaze and the strength radiating from her.

'So as it stands, you've practically published the banns?' she joked.

'Almost!'

'You were so sure of yourself on the matter?'

'Yes. And of you too!'

'Why?'

'Because when you answered my card it wasn't just for the sake of starting an affair. Was I wrong to think that?'

'Of course not, stupid! Or rather, yes, you were wrong, to let me leave alone, that day at Orly!'

'Right on! I'm already cross with myself about that!'

'You know something? I really thought that you'd hardly seen me. Or rather, that you'd only seen my haircut!'

'Oh that, I must say it was rather a mistake. What on earth did you cut it with? A piece of broken glass?'

'Stop it! If you only knew! Three weeks before I came back, I woke up one morning with my head covered in lice! Ghastly! They were crawling all over the place! So, no quarter given! So, I was hideous, was I?'

'Yes, of course,' he teased her, 'and that's why I didn't say a word to you!'

She smiled at him, and crunched another petit four.

'Without getting all sentimental,' she said, 'seriously, it's great, what's happening to us, isn't it?'

'Yes,' he replied, placing his hand on hers.

'I think I should explain to you,' she said after a few moments' hesitation. 'I've had – how shall I put it, my fingers burnt. Yes, that's the right expression.'

'Me too. So we won't talk about it any more, okay? Unless you need to?'

'No.'

'So curtains, life begins from today. Does that suit you?'

'Very nicely.'

'We won't be parted again?'

'Why the question?' she said. 'Don't you dare say you were thinking of leaving without me!'

# 8

'YOU'RE not going out in this weather?' worried Pierre-Edouard when he saw that Mathilde, Louise and Berthe were preparing to venture out in response to the grocer's hooter.

'And why not? Didn't you go out yourself this morning?' cried Berthe, slipping on a heavy woollen coat.

'It's not the same for me!' he announced. 'I haven't got a cold like Mathilde! I don't complain constantly about my rheumatism like Louise, and I haven't got chronic bronchitis like you!' he added, totally insincerely.

'But of course, quite right,' cut in Louise, muffling herself in a huge cloak, 'you yourself are in strapping health, as everyone knows!'

'And that's why you took your normal walk this morning, despite the cold!' added Mathilde

'It's not the same for me!' he repeated. 'Besides, all I did was drink coffee at Nicole's!'

'Ah, right? Because mine wasn't hot enough, I suppose?' asked Mathilde.

'Now look at you!' he smiled. 'You tell me to go to the bistro and when I do you complain about it? Women!' he exclaimed, as he added a thick branch of hornbeam to the hearth.

Comfortably ensconced on the fireside settle, his feet warmed by the embers, he was arguing for the sheer pleasure of annoying the three women, for he knew that nothing would prevent them from going to make their purchases and, more importantly, have a little chat.

'Wrap up well then,' he advised Mathilde. She noticed the furtive movement he made to touch his waistcoat pocket, just to reassure himself that his tobacco pouch really was there, and called to him before going out.

'And don't you dare smoke like a fireman while I'm away!'

He shrugged, retreated into the seclusion of his corner by the fire and took out his pipe.

They can say what they like, it's no weather for going to chat in the church square! he thought, looking out of the window.

Driven by the wind which had just strengthened, the fine hail mixed with wet snow, which had been falling in showers since the morning, was beating on the windowpanes. The weather had taken a turn for the worse in the last two days, and whilst 1975 had begun gently in January and February, March was coming in with hoar frost, fog and half-melted snow.

Well, better now than in three weeks' time, he thought, drawing a brand from the fire. He lit his pipe, threw the spill into the flames. Yes, that'll curb the growth a bit and maybe prevent everything being frozen! But all the same, it's still awful weather! And since it's started like this it'll hold for the entire month, even if that doesn't suit the chatterboxes on the telly!

Although his son and son-in-law, and even his grandson, had explained to him that the weather forecasts were based on sound scientific data, he considered them extremely suspect, possibly misleading, ever since one of the lady announcers had laughed one evening when speaking about the moon. It had, according to that flibbertigibbet, no influence on the weather. To Pierre-Edouard, that was almost blasphemy! For if you not only violated it by walking on it, but also began to doubt its power, that boded no good! In a little while they would be saying that it did not affect the germination or growth of plants! Meanwhile, since the full moon, it had been cold enough to bring the wolves out!

'Aren't you all a bit mad to be out in this weather!' protested Yvette, as soon as she saw the three ladies from the Vialhe house struggling against the wind to reach the grocer's van. 'No, really! It's not very sensible of you!' she added. 'Especially you, with your cold!' she called to her sister-in-law.

'You're not going to take over from Pierre now?' said Mathilde. 'Good morning, I won't kiss you because of my cold.'

'Tell me what you three want, I'll get it for you. Go and shelter in the car,' suggested Yvette; 'the motor's running, it's warm.'

'Look at these young people!' joked Louise. 'Not even seventy years old and taking the car to go two hundred metres!'

'Exactly, and I'm not ashamed of it!' said Yvette. 'Go on, get in, all three of you, and we'll go and have coffee at the château afterwards.'

'In that case, we will!' said Berthe. 'I know your coffee is always good. Come on,' she said, pulling Louise and Mathilde along. 'The girl's right,' she added more quietly, 'it's not very warm, and besides, I'm sure a little company would do her good.'

Since she had been widowed, Yvette was living alone in the château. A Portuguese neighbour, who had moved into the village seven years ago, went up every morning to do a little cooking and housework in the three rooms still open. Louis came from time to time, but rarely, very busy, he assured her, with his work in Limoges. So Yvette was happy at each opportunity to break her loneliness.

She therefore hastened to make her purchases, joined the three women waiting in the car, and drove her DS up the track towards the château.

'As soon as we're up there, we'll give Pierre a call; it wouldn't do to worry him,' she said.

'Pierre, worry?' Mathilde was amused. 'I'm sure he'll have guessed where we're going already! Well, you're right, we'll still telephone, then he won't have to hurry so to finish his pipe!'

It was always with a slight twinge of sorrow that Mathilde returned to the château. To her it had previously represented the power, wealth and luxury in which the former lords of the manor lived. Those people inaccessible to her, whom she saw passing in the village when, as a child, she lived in a long-vanished hovel at the end of one of the seven lanes in Saint-Libéral.

Then everything had gradually deteriorated. After financial reverses had hit its owners, the château had responded with a rain of slates which slid the length of the roof before smashing to the ground; with pointing which crumbled, the ivy invading in its place; with shutters which rotted and leaking gutters which spilled their water over the walls. Then for a while, it had become really dilapidated. And finally, thanks to Léon – to the desire for revenge which had inspired him since his childhood, and above all, thanks to his fortune – the château, the park and the whole property had come to life again.

And Mathilde still remembered her feelings when she had first set foot within the walls which henceforth belonged to her brother. So now that he was gone, she always felt nostalgic when she returned. A little sad too, for Léon's laugh was no longer there to welcome her; because Pierre-Edouard had not set foot in the château since his brother-in-law's death; and because all those closed shutters on the rooms which now smelled of mildew and dust were enough to break your heart.

'Come into the kitchen, it's warmer there,' suggested Yvette, 'and sit by the fire. And you, Mathilde, phone Pierre.'

'It's lovely and warm here,' confirmed Berthe, taking off her heavy coat.

'Yes, it's all right. But it upsets me to heat everything when no one's living in it. But I don't want it to freeze, so I set the heating at the minimum, except in my bedroom and in here.'

'Yes, it's lovely,' repeated Berthe, sitting down in front of the hearth.

'And how's Louis?' asked Mathilde whilst dialling the number. She noticed her sister-in-law's worried look, was about to continue, and then heard Pierre-Edouard: 'It's me,' she said, 'yes, we're at Yvette's, she's making coffee for us. You expected as much? I know! See you soon. And stop smoking! What's that, I'm talking nonsense? I can smell it from here!'

She hung up with a laugh, and went to sit down by the fire.

'Now, what about Louis?' she insisted.

'I'm worried about him,' admitted Yvette.

'His problems aren't getting any better?' asked Berthe.

'No, just the opposite,' said Yvette, putting out the cups and a tin of biscuits.

She had no need to say more, for she knew that her guests had long been aware of the matter which was giving her so much anxiety at the moment.

'But really, what an idea to embark on something like that!' said Louise.

'He believed in it,' Yvette apologised for him. 'And then, it might have worked . . .'

But it hadn't worked and it wasn't going to! It was true that Louis had been dogged by ill luck. True, too, that his desire to distance himself a little from his father had driven him to take a route which he considered more honourable. For although he too was inspired by a desire to make money, he had always rather despised the trade which had allowed his father to amass so much of it. He had considered the label estate agent more respectable than that of livestock dealer. He had therefore not believed his father when he, whilst helping to set him up, had assured him that there were probably more rogues and swindlers in suits and ties than in market traders' overalls; and that the dung of the market places surely stank less than certain offices. He had quickly realised that his father was not wrong, but he liked the business and some smells did not worry him too much . . .

He had therefore made progress, attempted and succeeded in several good deals, and acquired a taste for large-scale operations. The first ones turned out to be as profitable as one could wish, the subsequent ones a little less so. As for the latest, begun more than two years ago, it was promising to be a catastrophe. For although he had been shrewd to bank on the expansion of a town like Limoges, and therefore to buy the maximum available land in the outer suburbs, he had been very unwise to mount such an operation with an associate not overburdened with scruples; a man who did not even know the word existed!

Then also unwise to invest deeply in preparing the plots, developing them, laying on services. For now that everything was poised to begin, not only were clients not rushing in, but it was raining bills thick and fast, sometimes overwhelmingly. As for the associate, he had departed without leaving an address, but not without money, the moment there was any question of sharing the costs of settling with the contractors, the surveyors, the architects, the suppliers . . .

And already, Louis knew, some kind souls were whispering here and there that he was running out of steam, that the bankers were jibbing at supporting him any further and his debts were approaching five hundred million . . . It was true, and even if it had only referred to centimes, Louis was aware he would be unable to raise them in a hurry.

In order to do that, he needed to be given time, and most of all for the rumours about his bankruptcy to cease, not to mention those about his imminent indictment for embezzlement and various frauds. Those were not true, but stories still circulated, and the creditors were growing more insistent.

He had been able to placate them so far by distributing the proceeds from the sale of some buildings he owned in Brive, and the money which his mother had given him as soon as she got wind of his difficulties. He had therefore tossed a few hundred thousand francs to right and left, a few morsels to quieten the loudest, the most dangerous.

But now he had nothing left. Nothing more which he could quickly convert into cash, for it was impossible to sell the forty-odd hectares of arable and pasture land scattered around Saint-Libéral and the plains of Varetz and Larche on favourable conditions. And if he had to sell them off cutprice, the exercise would serve no purpose. Besides, they were rented out, which lowered their value considerably. And then it was to be feared that the Land Development Agency would intervene and drag the business out.

As for the château, it was unthinkable to negotiate over it in a hurry. First of all because he could not come to terms with the idea of driving his mother out, and secondly because it represented too large a sum to find a cash client within a few weeks.

Since he had considered the problem from every angle, he now envisaged the moment when he would have to open his mind to certain propositions. They were abhorrent, but went beyond the stage of rumour, for one of the bankers had dropped a few words to him, just like that, without any apparent significance, to sound out the mood of the prey.

The solution was very simple, obvious even! As he could not settle with the businesses contracted to create the estate, others could do it in his place! On condition, naturally, that they took his place completely; that is to say, by becoming owners of the plots. Having agreed that and settled all his accounts, he would be left with nothing but a damp hanky and a ruined reputation, at least in this region.

In fact he could not see himself starting from scratch again: creating a new agency, restarting the discussions which would perhaps allow him to deal in seedy affairs for equally wretched clients. He was too accustomed to the comfort of plenty of money, to all it provided, to the happy trips to Paris accompanied by a one-night stand, or a one-month stand, those pretty girls always ready to help him empty a jar of caviare and a few bottles of Dom Perignon. Always ready to share a fortnight in Acapulco with him too, or more modestly in Monaco.

So to give up all that was unthinkable! Any more than it was possible to start driving a 2CV instead of a Porsche, to buy off the peg and not made to measure, to replace the Davidoffs with Gitane fags! And yet that was what was in store for him if he did not find a solution in the shortest possible time. He had not painted such a sombre picture to his mother during their last telephone conversation, but at least he had given her to understand that all was not going well.

'And yet it might have worked out,' repeated Yvette, as she served the coffee. She placed a plate of biscuits on the low table, passed round the sugar bowl, and sat down next to Berthe.

'So he has no financial reserves left at all?' asked the latter.

'You know, since he's been selling things all over the place . . . Léon was well off, and me too, but everything has its limit . . . You'll be telling me there's still a bit of land, the château . . .'

'You're not going to put that at risk?' protested Berthe. 'Look, you've still got plenty of years to live! You don't want to end up in a home, do you? You must be careful, my dear! I know how things go in business. When it gets difficult, it's often the fault of those who are in charge, and in that case, it's always too late to recover from the mistakes!'

'Listen, what if Louis needs me?' protested Yvette.

'I understand,' said Berthe, 'but do watch out, don't part with everything, or sign anything! Besides, believe me, the little you could do wouldn't be any use . . .'

'How do you know? Has Louis talked to you? Has he written?'

'Of course not!' said Berthe with a shrug. 'It's at least three months since I've seen your son! And he hasn't written to me either! It's my nose that tells me. But, trust me, before you do anything, promise you'll discuss it with me. And above all don't sign anything! Promise me?'

'No,' said Yvette, 'and I'm sure you're hiding something from me.'

'No, I'm not,' Berthe assured her. 'I assure you, it's my instinct guiding me. You know, my dear, if the house of Claire Diamond has branches all over Europe and the United States, that's down to me, because I knew at what point to do such and such a thing. Well, with what you've been telling us for some months about Louis' business, you don't have to be very talented to understand that he's not getting on well. That's all. So be careful.'

'I'll help Louis as much as I can!' insisted Yvette. 'Anyway, I don't need much to live on any more!'

'All right, you do as you wish, but at least you've been warned.'

'By the way, did you know that young Jo has sent some proper news?' Mathilde interrupted, for she now regretted having started a painful discussion which was embarrassing her sister-in-law.

'Little Jo?' continued Yvette.

'Yes, I saw Mauricette this morning. She had a letter in the post, a long one full of details. And what's more, she's given her address at last. That's good news, isn't it? But really, you could say she's given us a few grey hairs, that one!'

'Do you think it's going as badly as all that for Louis?' Mathilde asked Berthe that same evening.

She had waited until Pierre-Edouard had gone to bed, and was now in a hurry to hear why her sister-in-law had seen fit to be so frank with Yvette.

'Yes, I know it's going very badly. Louis is nearly finished, with a lot of debt. I was hoping he still had some substantial reserves, but since his mother assures us it isn't so . . .' explained Berthe, lighting a Gauloise. 'Do you remember, already last Wednesday Yvette was even more thoughtful than usual, so I made a few phone calls . . .'

'You did that?' Louise interrupted.

She was always surprised by her sister's way of managing problems. She faced up to them, threw herself into the thick of the fray; you had to admire her pugnacity.

'Yes, I did,' said Berthe, 'and I was right to. I'm very fond of Yvette, I'd hate to see her ruined by her son's mistakes.'

'Can you sort out Louis' affairs, do you have the means?' asked Mathilde, full of hope.

'You're joking? You know very well that I made over most of my business to Gérard, and he's in partnership himself now anyway! No, no, my income won't run to that sort of rescue plan, but that's no reason to leave poor Yvette in the lurch!'

'You said you made several phone calls. Who to?' asked Louise, who could not begin to understand how her sister could know so much about Louis without leaving Saint-Libéral.

'Oh, easy. I asked Gérard to pretend to be a prospective purchaser of some plots advertised by Louis. So his lawyer sought the information. Two or three calls to Louis' bankers were enough. The business is rotten, they're bound to foreclose before long. They didn't say as much, of course, but as I explained to Yvette, I've got an infallible nose for that sort of thing.'

'How can you be so sure?' insisted Mathilde. Ever optimistic, she was still thinking and hoping that her sister-in-law was painting a blacker picture than necessary.

'It's very simple. When someone who should be delighted to see the sale of a plot gives you to understand that it's vital to wait, that's because he's hoping to bring off a better deal later on . . . That, roughly speaking, was the bankers' response!'

'But what about Louis, then?' insisted Mathilde.

'It's sure to be bad. It must involve a very large sum. I didn't say all I knew to Yvette, I didn't want to put her in a panic, she's quite capable of doing something silly. You saw for yourself, she's ready to put the château up for sale! So we need to watch out that she doesn't find herself penniless without achieving anything. Because Léon would never forgive us for that!'

Since the evening which Dominique and Béatrice had spent with Guy just before leaving for Cayenne, Jean felt strengthened in his position and vocation.

First of all he was still under the spell cast by the young woman's eyes; he dreamed about her, and felt all weak at the knees when he thought of her. And it was not only her gaze which had affected him; he found Béatrice completely amazing! But apart from the satisfaction of having such a woman almost as his cousin, he had particularly noticed that Dominique's arguments had influenced his mother. Of course she still felt a certain reserve, not to say hostility, towards her son's plans, and had not despaired of seeing him change his mind. Despite that she had given in on several points, and it was now possible to discuss the matter without antagonising her.

Unfortunately the same could not be said for his father; with him it was like a brick wall. The more he was chatty and pleased when Jean told him of his marks and triumphs in class, the more he closed up like a clam as soon as his son talked of his future studies. At Grignon, the National Agricultural Institute, if all went well.

'We haven't got that far yet,' he grumbled; 'you're too young to know what you'll really be doing. For the moment keep working, and don't get carried away with crazy ideas, those are only dreams.'

'Dominique's not dreaming!'

'Don't worry about your cousin! Besides, I don't know whether his job is as good as he claims, or his salary as high!' threw in Guy, quite unfairly.

Doesn't matter, it's jolly interesting what he's doing in Guyana!'

'I don't think! All he'll bring back from his stay over there will be the runs and malaria! And all that for the pleasure of developing rice and sugar cane crops which cost the taxpayer an arm and a leg! Or trying to introduce some hare-brained cross between a humped Zebu bull and a Charolais whose offspring will die in the first epidemic that comes along, or be eaten by the alligators!'

'It's still interesting!' cried Jean. Then he changed the subject, for he did not yet feel strong enough to stand up to his father for any length of time. But he did not doubt that the day would come when he would have the intellectual ability and the courage to do so.

Jean did not like hunting much, especially not the sort practised by his father and his friends. However he was now of an age to take out a licence, and could have persuaded his parents to give him a gun. But he was much too independent and solitary to enjoy roving the countryside with the hunters who accompanied his father when he came to Brenne.

Jean despised those men. He found them inept, snobbish and, (an unforgivable fault in his eyes) worse than useless when they talked about birds, game or nature. They passed remarks which drove him mad, being the result of so much pretentious ignorance. And although Félix smiled, and sometimes even laughed out loud when he related some howler delivered by one of the party, he himself could not accept their conceit. He was not the right age to make allowances or be tolerant.

And when, to please his father and carry the game, he followed the valiant sportsmen for an afternoon, the account he gave of the expedition was never dull.

'You can't imagine it,' he said to Félix. 'Listen, the fat one, you know, the creep who's always sweating! The one with a Tyrolean hat and an over-and-under shotgun, you've seen him? The one who's always complaining that there aren't any women here! Well, at the Three Oaks crossroads we chanced on the track of a fallow deer. Magnificent, a beautiful hoofprint, sure to be a big second-year stag! You won't believe what he comes out with, the pretentious great wally, sounding like a professor of philosophy: "Look! It's a boar weighing at least eighty kilos!" With a bit of encouragement he would have told us its age. Well, even Monsieur Charles – yes, the banker, you know, the fool who nine times out of ten can't tell a hen pheasant from a cock! The one who fires at coots to keep his hand in – even he was embarrassed, listening to such stupidity! Rubbish, that's what they are! Rubbish! People as moronic as that ought to be barred from the countryside!'

'Let them talk. The main thing is that you know better,' Félix pacified him.

But at the age of just sixteen Jean was not inclined to be charitable. He therefore avoided going out with his father and his friends as much as possible.

On the other hand, through contact with Félix, besides an excellent understanding of nature, he had discovered and grown to like the art of fishing. And on this last Sunday in March, while Guy and his companions were hunting pigeons on the game reserve, Félix and he were fishing with live bait on the little pool at Souchet.

It was a lovely patch, three hectares of water and bulrushes, lying a few hundred metres from Félix's house. It was there, one terrible night in October thirty-eight years earlier, that Pierre-Edouard had joined Félix. But Jean knew almost nothing of that business, and it was better so.

'If you want my opinion, we won't get anything this morning,' said Félix after an unproductive half hour.

He had only come here to please his second cousin, for experience told him that the fishing would be poor, not to say hopeless. A light north wind had got up, which ruffled the water. The sun was not clear, but constantly played hide and seek behind the fat gloomy cumulo-nimbus clouds which were swelling for the next shower. The pool was as grey as a winter sky and even the water birds, the coots and grebes hiding in the rushes and sedge, seemed dull and somnolent, disinclined to be at all active.

'Nothing doing,' murmured Félix, nonetheless casting his lure towards an old willow stump rotting on the edge of the pool.

'I know what you're going to tell me,' let out Jean. '"North wind blows, sport all goes, fish will doze"! But that still has to be proved! And then why not wake them up? Look, that stupid thing's dead!' he observed, looking at the tiny carp which he had impaled on the end of his line. He reeled in again, removed the hook from the bait and threw it into the bulrushes.

'So shall we stop?' he asked.

'Come on, let's try one last cast,' Félix relented, holding out a fresh fish as bait. 'Take care!' he cautioned.

An unneccessary warning: Jean had known for a long time just how wicked the dorsal fin of a perch was. He neatly mounted the victim on the end of his casting-rod and resumed fishing.

'You know what I've decided?' he said after a few moment's silence.

'No.'

'I'm going to spend the whole of my summer holidays in Saint-Libéral, to help Uncle Jacques. It seems his back isn't getting any better.'

'Has your father agreed?'

'He doesn't know yet!'

'Oh, I see . . .' said Félix.

He was aware of Guy's attitude, and did not feel he had the right to stoke the flames of a dispute which he knew was about to flare up.

'What's that supposed to mean: "Oh I see"?' demanded Jean with a touch of belligerence.

'Nothing.'

'You don't think it's a good idea?'

'I didn't say anything of the kind!'

'But that doesn't stop you thinking it!'

'Don't get in such a state! I didn't say you were wrong! But is Jacques in fact aware of this?'

'No, not yet. But I don't see what the problem is,' pronounced Jean, casting his bait back out towards the middle of the pool. 'Anyway, Papa couldn't possibly say anything,' he decided confidently.

'Well now, and why not?'

'Because I'm going to finish up top of the class again, and that's an impregnable position as far as he's concerned! What do you expect him to say to me? You haven't worked hard enough, so you don't deserve a holiday? Impossible! So I'll go to Saint-Libéral. I've already worked it out, I'll arrive at the end of the haymaking, just before they tackle the harvest!'

'Still, it might be as well to mention it to the people concerned, don't you think?'

'Yes, I'll think about it! In any case, down there I've got one ally. You know what Dominique said to me when he came by our house?'

'Yes of course, you've already told me. He said your grandfather is on your side!'

'Exactly! And that's bloody important to me!' cried Jean slightly annoyed, for he felt he detected a tinge of sarcasm in his cousin's voice: 'Yes, it's important,' he insisted, 'however much you laugh – you are laughing, I can see it. But I don't care if you do laugh, that doesn't stop grandfather being somebody! He knows what he's talking about, he does!' he finished in a fury.

'In the first place I'm not laughing. Secondly, I agree absolutely when you say your grandfather is somebody! More than that, he's a great man. You'll find out more about that one day. But in the meantime, believe me, instead of driving your father into a corner, why not try to convince him that it's very healthy for a Parisian boy to spend his holidays working in the open air!'

'Yes, maybe. But to him, working on the land, it's degrading. You'd never believe he was born there!'

'Now don't go saying stupid things like that, damned pigheaded Vialhe! It's exactly because he was born there, lived and slaved away there, that he knows what he's talking about! Never forget that in his day, even if you were a good scholar – and he was – the holidays were spent in the fields. And if your grandparents weren't poor, they were still a long way from being rich, and they had to work hard! You have no idea how they worked! It's the memory of that which makes your father so difficult to persuade when you talk to him about agronomy. He managed to leave the land and create a very good position for himself, and it wasn't easy, believe me. For him, it's true, the land is a step backward. So it depresses him to see that one of his sons wants nothing more than to return to it!'

# 9

DOMINIQUE slid his hand under the mosquito net and caught hold of the bath towel hanging over the back of the chair. It was as wet as a dishcloth, but he still passed it over his chest to sponge off the sweat which was streaming down. He had been in bed for half an hour but already felt the need to get up again and take another shower to refresh himself a little and, above all, to rid himself of the sticky moisture which covered his body. He looked at Béatrice, lying beside him, and envied her ability to sleep so peacefully.

Naked, stretched out on her stomach, her arm curved above her head, she seemed impervious to the sweltering heat pervading the room. Nevertheless, perspiration stood in droplets all over her body, and he was almost tempted to wipe it. But he was afraid of waking her, and made do with using his fingertips to brush lightly the little dimples in the hollow of her back.

Never a day passed without him wondering how he could have survived at Bellevue without her – for after six months in Guyana, he sometimes caught himself counting the months to his return home. He who had almost felt annoyance at the contract sending him abroad for one year – he was ready to sign up for double that! – now rejoiced at his employers' caution.

It was not that his work was uninteresting, far from it. The responsibilities he took on delighted him, and there was no lack of variety. The several trial stations established by Mondiagri were scattered in different parts of the territory, the handful of coastal regions where it was possible to attempt to clear the ground without running into swamps or impenetrable jungle.

His main residence was on the experimental farm Bellevue Scree. Situated at the foot of Kaw mountain, some fifty kilometres south-east of Cayenne, it was aptly named, for the surrounding countryside was magnificent.

There, besides new varieties of sugar cane, of maize and pineapple, they measured the hardiness and productivity of a herd of cattle consisting partly of Zebu-Charolais crosses. As a loyal native of the Corrèze, Dominique was convinced that the Limousin breed could adapt very well to the land, and he was endeavouring to persuade his employers of this.

So it was not his occupation which weighed heavy. In contrast, he had a great deal of difficulty in adapting to the climate. For a start he did not appreciate the sense of humour of the geographer who had one day decided that there were two rainy seasons: the small rains from December to March and the great rains from April to July! To him, great or small, it was all water which poured down in torrents! And as he had not had time to experience what was supposedly the dry season, he was prepared to find it just as streaming wet as the previous ones!

After two years spent in the Sahara, where the smallest drop of water was of incalculable worth and was welcomed with joy and respect, the permanent hot, sticky humidity which he endured night and day tired him, wore him out.

Added to that were all the crawling, flying, stinging or poisonous creatures which swarmed on every side. The revolting babalous which proliferated in the marshes; the fat spiders, mosquitos and flies present everywhere; not forgetting the leeches, lizards, reptiles, amphibians and other creepy-crawlies which one always had to watch out for. So he did not conceal from his associates that he would not be spending one day extra in Guyana at the end of his contract. Fortunately he had Béatrice.

She bore the climate much better than he did, and was a marvel at making him forget the disadvantages of the country. It was difficult not to share her enthusiasm when she went into raptures at the beauty of a picturesque site, the luxuriance of the cattleyas or epidendrum (orchids), at a shimmering toucan or macaw. Despite the fact that he was called upon to travel during the week, she encouraged him to make weekend trips into the countryside, for the pleasure of it. As they had quickly found that, apart from the bizarre Palmists Square, Cayenne held no interest and oozed melancholy, and that the other conurbations were still worse, they plunged into the jungle, at least as far as the tracks and water courses allowed.

Since Béatrice contrived to make their bungalow as pleasant as possible, and knew how to change his mood when he was overwhelmed by bad temper – he had difficulty in coming to terms with the grinning nonchalance of the employees – in all fairness he was forced to recognise that he was the happiest of men; if it were not for this damned climate!

He sponged his chest once more and smiled as he looked at the young woman. She had just turned over and was in the process of snuggling up to him, without breaking her sleep.

Regretfully, he moved away. It really was too hot and humid to spend the night wrapped around each other.

If she could have been sure of finding another job, Josyane would have immediately abandoned the agency where she had been working now for six months. But she did not want to chase after shadows, and she still felt obliged to her employer. The woman had offered her work when she had exhausted all possibilities; she was grateful to her.

As she had predicted, the director of the travel agency had not given in to the Chinese girl who had turned her husband's head, and had dismissed her a few weeks after her attempted take-over. She had then kept her promise and engaged Josyane as guide and interpreter.

The first excursions filled her with enthusiasm. In fact she was not the sort of person to pretend to be blasé, and she still remained thunderstruck at the splendour of the countryside. Of all the atolls and islands the clients wanted to visit, it was difficult to say which was the most heavenly, the most beautiful! Difficult to choose between the vast beaches of white sand on Bora, the warm water and incomparable clarity of the lagoon on Rangiroa, or the breathtaking sites of the bays on Cook and of Opunohu on Moorea. Difficult to say where it was better to stay, for a few days. Only for a few days. For she now began to feel a weariness due to the enforced and repeated revisiting of places which ended up irritating by their perfection. Finally and above all, she became more and more allergic to the tourists in her charge.

The Americans most of all rubbed her up the wrong way, made her almost xenophobic! She had discovered most of them were a detestable variety of human. The sort who having paid, and extremely dearly, believed they had the right to demand everything, do everything, say anything, complain about anything, at opportune and inopportune moments.

Confident in the wads of dollars they had paid out, some were even sincerely convinced that she was part of the package, and it was therefore permissible to pat her bottom! As for the matrons who served as wives to these louts, she found them monstrous, fat as sows and much stupider. It was they who, in the middle of the night on Bora or Tetiaroa, began to bellow when they discovered an inoffensive grey lizard in their hut. They again who refused to touch the succulent grilled fish and coconut milk during some excursion into the enchanting motus, and loudly demanded hamburgers and Cola!

On top of all that, these people were blatantly mean. And since she had to serve as their interpreter when they wanted to buy a few souvenirs, she could not forgive them for the shame she felt when they asked her to haggle over a block of coral, a pareo or some shell knick-knacks.

Stingy to the very last day; they still had purses as fat as sea-urchins when the time came to say goodbye. But they accepted without apparent difficulty the Tahitian custom which maintains that all tipping is offensive, and pretended to believe that Josyane was a native.

But it is true to say that her satisfaction on seeing them depart was such that it compensated for the lack of gratuities and restored her good humour. Until the next batch saw her at the foot of the airline steps, with her little sign OROHENA TOUR AGENCY, around which her set of clients collected, while the airport rang with the welcoming songs of various swaying, beflowered Polynesians, paid for by the Tahitian Office of Tourism.

As a result, after six months she was dreaming of some less tedious work. But she did not want to take the risk of finding herself without a job again. Above all she was careful not to break into her savings, which would one day allow her to buy a one-way ticket to Paris. She was hoping now that it would be as early as possible.

As time passed, she became more aware of her isolation, and of the kind of prison Tahiti had become the moment she lacked the financial resources to escape it. A luxurious prison, certainly, full of flowers, birds and sun; without jailers, but nonetheless weighing on her because it was so deceptively soothing. A place of exile where it was tempting to let yourself slip into the prevailing mood of indifference. It was frightening, and she was as wary of it as of a drug.

So when the solitude and the distance weighed too heavily, she forced herself not to sink into that sort of somnolence in which the island dwellers took refuge when they were 'fed up'. She feared her senses would be dulled in that complacent and restful carelessness where any willpower, any desire to act was weakened, any impulse to escape even! She did wish to leave. That was her aim and she would have already quit the island long since if the possibility had existed.

But as she did not want to send out a cry for help to her parents – she would have felt ashamed of that – as she hesitated to sell the Leica donated by Gilles and her own Nikon, for she saw them as the ultimate insurance to be preserved come what may, she had no choice but to save month by month towards the price of her ticket home.

Thus, once she had decided to put an end to her peregrinations and return to the fold, her desire to see France again became ever stronger. And often, some evenings, she took to thinking with nostalgia and vague melancholy of Saint-Libéral. To remembering her childhood there, the adventures on the peaks with her sisters, the taste of the greengages in July, the chestnuts roasted in the open fire. To conjure up the picture of her parents, her grandmother Mathilde's welcoming lap, her grandfather's comfortable knees, and his rather rough cheeks which she liked to rasp under her fingers.

And, one evening, when the sun was dipping behind Moorea, forming a halo of fire around Mount Tohiea, whilst the group of Texans she was looking after were dutifully wallowing in rum and coke and trying to dance the tamouré, she had felt the need to write to her family; a proper letter, which begged for nothing but was nevertheless a cry for help. And it was without hesitation that she had given them her address. It was the first time since her departure. And as soon as the letter was posted, completely illogically, for she knew the time mail took, she began to expect the reply.

When Dominique had introduced Béatrice to them, to Michèle and himself, Jacques had hoped that the date of their wedding would at least be mentioned. There had been no sign of it. So he was a little embarrassed when his mother asked him for news of the couple. He knew that she was a stickler for morals and had a very low opinion of a situation which to her was not correct. It was not that she openly criticised Dominique's attitude, but he guessed she was distressed by it, as she was distressed by the behaviour of Mauricette's daughters.

He was also aware that his father did not think much of the eldest Viahle grandson living with his partner without marrying. That was not done, even on the other side of the ocean.

'I know very well that I'm out of date,' he had said to Jacques. 'You understand, I'm from the time when a girl who showed her calves was considered fast! Well, it's enough to see all those kids on the telly, or even here, showing their bottoms to everyone in their miniskirts, as you say, to know that I'm old-fashioned. That's obvious. So, all right, things change. But the boy shouldn't upset his grandmother. It grieves her, all that. So I don't like it!'

'I know. But what do you want me to do? Dominique's twenty-eight!'

'Well, yes. But you know, in my time, even at that age we

wouldn't have dared carry on openly like that. What I meant to say was, amongst people you knew, in the village, for instance! I'm not saying in the town . . .'

'Dominique is several thousand kilometres from here! Where he is, the people don't care! Anyway, I'm sure they don't know he's not married!'

'Your mother knows, that's enough for me!'

As for Michèle, Jacques knew that she felt in rather an awkward position with regard to her friends and neighbours in the village. For they had all had the opportunity to see Dominique and Béatrice strolling about, very much in love, during their visit to Saint-Libéral. And because Michèle had immediately announced that they were engaged, there were now certain good souls who expressed feigned amazement that the date for the wedding was not yet fixed!

Those gossips were often the ones whose daughters had begun to look at the wrong side of the sheets the year they got their school certificate, and sometimes even earlier with the more precocious ones . . . The same ones whose sons pawed the ground like billy goats when they spotted anything in a skirt! But it was still embarrassing to be within an ace of being lectured by them, embarrassing to be reduced to defending herself!

So Jacques was very happy to read the first lines of the letter Dominique sent. He had realised it was important even before he knew what it was, for Michèle had brought it to him whilst he was sowing maize for fodder in the Malides field.

First of all it announced that Dominique and Béatrice would be returning to France at the beginning of December, and that in itself was very good. Then, and this was even better, that they had chosen Saturday, 20 December as the date for their wedding.

'Wonderful!' he murmured. 'I know two people who'll be over the moon! Yes,' he added, seeing that Michèle did not quite understand, 'my parents were married on the twenty-first of December! That was in 1918! That will be fifty-seven years! What a celebration we'll have!'

'Probably less than you were hoping for, read what follows.'

'What do you mean?' he said, starting to read again. 'Oh damn!' he groaned at last. 'Just can't do anything like everyone else, those two!'

'I think myself that it's quite honest of the girl,' said Michèle.

'Yes, you're right. If she doesn't believe in God or the Devil, she's sticking to her principles. But I'm thinking of my parents. You know very well that for them there's no such thing as a civil wedding, it has no meaning.'

'They're not the only ones. Finish reading . . .'

'What else is there?' he worried. 'All right then! As I understand it, young Béatrice wants only a registry office marriage, because she doesn't believe in the church, and her mother, who is a religious bigot, refuses to hear of the registry office unless it's followed by a church ceremony! That should make for a cosy atmosphere!'

'You haven't finished reading. It won't make anything! They're going to get married in Paris, a quiet civil wedding.'

'I see,' he said, folding up the letter. 'But that doesn't matter, it's still a bit of good news! And I'm going to announce it at home. After all, if the young people do it in Paris, my parents definitely won't go up for it. So why tell them everything, eh? Come on, I'll pop down before lunch. It'll make them so pleased, I don't want to wait. In any case, *we'll* be there in Paris.'

Delighted and touched when Dominique had presented him with his Ami 6, Jacques had immediately traded in his old Aronde. Despite the pathetic state of the vehicle he had received an unexpectedly good price for it. But he had soon realised that his son's present was not without its drawbacks. However comfortable and convenient, the little car was totally unsuited to pull the big stock trailer, loaded with one or two calves or four pigs, which the wheezing old Simca used to drag, jogging along in a cloud of smoke, all the way to the market in Brive or Objat. So since then Jacques had been obliged to resort to Brousse and his trailer to go and sell his calves or pigs. It was embarrassing, for he did not like to abuse his neighbours' kindness.

That being so, apart from this inconvenience, he was absolutely delighted with his new car and took the wheel with real pleasure. And since Dominique's letter had put him in an excellent mood, he whistled as he covered the three kilometres which separated Coste-Roche from Saint-Libéral. He was still whistling when he drew up in front of the Vialhe house.

His cheerfulness waned as soon as he recognised the big muddy Peugeot belonging to Doctor Martel; when needs must, the doctor never hesitated to drive up the roughest country tracks to go and see some patient, and therefore considered it pointless to clean his car.

Worried, ready to hear the worst, for he could not forget that the youngest person living there was after all seventy-five, he pushed open the door and went in. On seeing his aunts Berthe and Louise in the hallway, he immediately thought his father was having problems with his heart. That surprised him a little, for he had seen him in top form, for him, the previous evening. But he was eighty-six and anything was possible . . .

'What's happening? Who's ill?' he asked.

'Your mother,' said Berthe in a low voice.

'What! Maman!' he protested. It seemed to him inconceivable, not to say outrageous, that his mother should be ill. She had never been ill in her life and was only seventy-five! 'What's the matter with her?'

'She felt faint a short while ago, she couldn't stand up at all. But don't worry, it's probably nothing,' said Berthe.

'Where's Papa?'

'With her, he doesn't want to leave her. Even the doctor didn't manage to stop him going in to the bedroom with him.'

'Well, this is a fine mess!' he said. 'But why didn't you phone right away?'

'We did, several times, but there was no answer,' said Berthe.

'Ah, that's right, Michèle had come up to see me on the Malides.' He almost said why, but decided that his parents should be the first to hear the news.

'Has the doctor been here long?' he continued.

'Getting on for half an hour,' said Berthe. 'We were lucky, he was near Perpezac. And as he has a telephone in his car . . . Whatever people may say about it, it's extremely practical!'

'Yes, yes,' he said distractedly.

'Don't you want to tell Michèle?' asked Berthe.

'I'd like to know a bit more first.' He heard the door of the bedroom squeak, turned, and saw his father. He felt sorry for him, he looked so worried, so lost: 'Well?' he asked.

'The doctor will explain it to you, it seems it's not serious. But those sort of people are nothing but liars!' said Pierre-Edouard, sitting down.

Jacques noticed that he was clumsily buttoning up his shirt.

'He listened to your chest too? Are you ill?'

'No, but it kept your mother happy, so . . .' Pierre-Edouard sighed as he tried to push the buttons through with a hand which trembled too much, far too much.

'Would you like me to help you?' suggested Louise, who was also worried about the old man's condition.

'I'll manage,' he assured her. 'And you, instead of fussing over me, go and see your mother, that'll please her,' he said to his son.

'Of course,' agreed Jacques, turning towards the bedroom. He moved aside to allow Doctor Martel to emerge, and greeted him.

'Don't leave without seeing me!' he requested, and went into the room.

It was a shock to see his mother in bed. He hoped his feelings did not show, that his face did not betray him at all, for he realised in a flash that the last time he had seen his mother in bed was at the birth of Guy, in 1932! He had been twelve years old then, and it had made a deep impression.

Since then he had never seen his mother other than upright, in sound health, for she had always considered that any attacks of flu or exhaustion she suffered were to be treated with contempt. What was more, in his memory there remained the picture of a woman still young, a little weary but blooming, happy, her breasts heavy with milk, smiling as she invited him, and Paul as well, to come and admire their little brother. Discovering that reddish doll, squealing and crumpled, lying at her side; whilst Mauricette, upset and feeling neglected, clung to her.

And now, forty-three years later, in place of the serene and beautiful young woman he remembered came the pitiful image of a little old lady; all thin, her body withered, her hands deformed, their skin transparent and speckled with brown marks, her face lined with wrinkles and fatigue. But still smiling.

'You're here already?' she murmured. 'It's good of you to come so quickly.'

'Are you feeling better?' he asked, kissing her.

'Yes, of course, it's nothing. My blood pressure is a little high, it's nothing to fuss about. I'll be up tomorrow.'

'Certainly not! You must rest!' he said.

'Don't worry about me, better to look after your father. You've seen him, he's feeling quite lost . . .'

'Okay, okay,' he said, 'don't get worked up. And right now, think about taking care of yourself. Would you like Michèle to come and look after you?'

'Of course not! Berthe and Louise can manage perfectly well, I don't want to cause any inconvenience to anyone. By the way, do you have any news of the children?'

'Yes. Françoise phoned last night, she's well. She'll be here in July. As for Dominique and Béatrice . . . Ah, I'd have liked Papa to be here! Anyway, I'll tell him in a minute, well . . .'

'They're going to get married?' she interrupted, full of hope.

'Yes,' he smiled. He noticed that his mother's gaze grew misty, but out of consideration and embarrassment he pretended to see nothing, and added: 'Yes, they're getting married, almost the same day as Papa and you, Saturday the twentieth of December.'

'Oh! That's good, that's very, very good,' she murmured, closing her eyes. 'They'll be having the ceremony at the girl's parents, of course,' she added. 'That's normal, eh? That's how it's done. Oh, we probably won't go ourselves. I mean your father and I. It's too far for him, it would be too tiring for him, I think . . . But it would please him so much, too . . . Well, we'll see. And then it doesn't really matter, the main thing is, it's great to hear. Go quickly and tell your father. Go on, I must rest anyway. Go and tell him the good news!'

'I'll come by again this evening,' he promised, kissing her. 'Look after yourself, and have a good rest.'

'So what exactly's wrong with her?' asked Jacques as he accompanied Doctor Martel to his car.

'I really can't say, exactly. Some tests will be to be done. At first sight it looks like no more than a bad attack of high blood pressure. Logically speaking, everything ought to return to normal quickly. But she must be made to rest.'

'Easier said than done!' replied Jacques, shrugging his shoulders. 'She insists on doing her vegetable garden, feeding her ducks and geese, looking after I don't know how many rabbits, hens and chicks, and even fattening two pigs! I ask you! Up there at Coste-Roche I raise more than eighty a year myself! But it seems they're worthless! Because of the meal I give them; nothing but chemicals, my mother says! And my father does nothing to convince her otherwise!'

'To be honest, he must be careful too, even more than her. I took advantage of my visit to listen to his heart . . .'

'I saw that, and so?'

'So it's absolutely essential that he sticks to his course of treatment! His heart is very weak, and it won't do just to muddle along! And besides, you saw what sort of a state he got into over the little fright your mother's just given us?'

'Yes.'

'Good. So for your father, it's the same old story. No excitement, no strain, and above all he must take his medicines. And as for your mother, I'll visit again tomorrow. But what about you for that matter, your back?'

'Don't talk about that,' Jacques cut him off. 'There's enough trouble as it is for today!'

'Please yourself,' smiled Doctor Martel, climbing into his car, 'but while I was here I could have done a third consultation! Go on then, till tomorrow. And watch your father, he's the one I'm most worried about.'

Pierre-Edouard came out on to the door step as soon as he heard the doctor's car drive off.

'Right, what did he say?' he asked Jacques, 'I don't believe a word of what he told me myself!'

'Well, for once you're wrong.'

'You're starting to lie to me like the others,' Pierre-Edouard reproached him as he filled his pipe. Jacques noticed that his hands were trembling less, and was happy about that.

'Don't go smoking right under Maman's nose, you know what she thinks of it,' he said.

'Mind your own business! It'd be better if you told me what that bloody quack said about your mother. I'm sure he's hiding something from me.'

'No, no, I give you my word. Maman has high blood pressure. Fine, that can be treated. They'll need to have some tests done to be quite sure, but it's nothing!'

'Tests?' Pierre-Edouard was worried.

'Well, yes, you know! Like you when you had your heart problem. It's nothing to make a fuss about, is it?'

'Oh, right,' said Pierre-Edouard. He lit his pipe, tamped down the tobacco with his thumb: 'Oh right, he's not going to put her into hospital then?'

'Of course not! Who put that idea into your head?'

'Good, that's very good,' said Pierre-Edouard. 'You know, they played that trick on poor Léon, and it did for him. And it didn't do me any good. So if your mother ever had to go, I'm sure I wouldn't hold out, this time . . .'

'Don't give it a moment's thought. Come and offer me a drink instead. I've some very good news for you, in spite of all this . . .'

'Really? News which will please your mother too?'

'She already knows it. I've just told her, and I'm convinced that hearing it almost put her on her feet again.'

'Ah! I bet I know what it is!' murmured Pierre-Edouard, sucking at his pipe. 'Let me tell you something,' he added with a smile. 'There are only two really important pieces of news she's expecting. First that young Jo has decided to come back from the ends of the earth, from her island over there! And then that your son stops this business of living together, it's uncivilised!'

'Don't get excited, it's not good for you!'

'I'm not getting excited! Your good news, I know what it is. I know from Berthe that young Jo's not on the way back yet. She's writing now, that's one good thing. So since it isn't to do with her, it must be my grandson who's finally decided to behave like a Vialhe. Come on, say it! The wedding, when's it to be?'

# 10

SEATED side by side in the shade of a plum tree laden with fruit which was filling the air with fragrance and driving the wasps crazy, Pierre-Edouard and Mathilde watched the huge blue combine-harvester rumbling and grumbling as it swallowed the barley on the Long Field.

As expected, the yield was superb, dense and tightly packed. The grain, nourished by the humus and nitrogen of the old lucerne, was heavy, rich. It flowed thick and fast into the trailer which followed the contractor's vehicle.

And Pierre-Edouard's happiness, already great on account of the fine harvest, redoubled when his eyes fell on the driver of the tractor. The young man who, concentrating as if handling a dangerous weapon, was steering the tractor exactly parallel to the combine.

For Jean Vialhe had been there a week. He did not begrudge his time or energy, proud to be of really practical use. Happy as well to prove to his Uncle Jacques, to his grandparents and all the people of Saint-Libéral, that he knew what to do and was capable of working like a proper man of the soil. Like someone whom neither city life nor education could divorce from his roots, who was instinctively rediscovering the behaviour and precise movements appropriate to each allotted task. For besides expertly driving the old Massey-Ferguson, you had only to see him grasp a pitchfork and handle the sheaves to understand the peasant stock working within him.

Pierre-Edouard smiled with happiness. And his joy was really complete. For just behind the combine harvester, there where the bales of straw fell out, more or less well tied by the small compresser, walked Françoise. In shorts, her loose blouse open over a nicely-filled, little blue bikini top, already bronzed like a peach, she looked magnificent. She was piling the bales into heaps of ten or twelve, and seemed to take a mischievous pleasure in moving faster than her mother and more especially her father, always hampered by his back.

'You know, they're simply fantastic, those kids,' said Pierre-Edouard. 'You see how beautiful the girl is? She looks like you, once upon a time . . .'

'Maybe, but I would never have dared walk about dressed like that!' Mathilde assured him.

'Not in the fields of course, but at home, you should have seen yourself . . .' he teased her.

She shrugged, but smiled conspiratorially and rested her head on his shoulder.

'Don't you want to go back?' she suggested, 'aren't you tired?'

'No, what about you?'

'I'm all right, quite all right now.'

It was true. After her lassitude had dragged on for several weeks, Mathilde had gradually got the better of it. Her blood pressure had returned to normal and her spirits revived, for all the tests were reassuring. But this was the first time, on this harvest day, that she had undertaken such a long walk.

'You're sure you're okay?' he insisted. 'If you like I'll tell Jacques to take you back; his car's down there.'

'No, no, we'll walk back quietly, we've plenty of time.'

He agreed absentmindedly, once more distracted by his grand-children, and repeated:

'Yes, they're simply fantastic, those kids. I'm so pleased about them. You know, I'm wondering whether their fathers, at that age . . .'

'But of course they did!' she protested forcefully. 'You're for-getting! Remember Jacques! The year he took his bac, in 1937, he helped us through the whole harvest! You remember that, surely!'

'You're right,' he murmured, after considering the matter for few moments. 'It was that year my father gave him a watch. Yes, we had a fine harvest and Jacques was there . . . And your brother paid for his trip to Paris . . . Dear Lord, Léon would be happy today too, if he could see this, poor old Léon . . .'

'Come on, don't think about it,' she said, sorry now that she had involuntarily reopened an old wound. She attempted to divert him from his sad thoughts and continued: 'And look! Think of Dominique! Whenever he could he came to help his father! And you said yourself he learned more in a month here than in a year at his college!'

He shook himself out of it and smiled. 'You're right. Anyway, if Léon were still here, he'd say the same as me!'

'What's that then?'

'That machine, that so-called combine may be very efficient, but it doesn't do such a good job as our old reaper!'

'Oh yes it does!' she teasingly contradicted him. 'I know your opinion! That machine makes a noise and lots of dust; it crushes the grain, it loses some, it doesn't cut off all the straw cleanly, and so on and so forth! If you go on like that you'll end up rambling on like your poor father! I can still hear him saying the scythe was better than the reaper! And it wouldn't have taken much to get him to declare that nothing was as fine as a good sickle!'

'Oh you! Give you half a chance and you're trying to settle old scores with my father!' he teased.

'That's not the point. Look, shall I tell you something? If there weren't all these machines, your grandchildren wouldn't be here either! I don't think they'd have left Paris and gone without holidays to break their backs and blister their fingers tying up sheaves by hand, like we used to. And be honest, you know very well that it wasn't all roses!'

Still quite deafened by the noise of the combine, grey with dust, weary to exhaustion, but happy with their day's work, Françoise and Jean set off towards Coste-Roche by a short cut.

Darkness had fallen, filled with the cries of insects and chirping of crickets, heavy with sweet fragrances, mingling the scent of greengages, flowering clover and still warm straw. A balmy night, illuminated by an almost full moon, glowing radiantly creamy-white. In the distance, moving along the track which cut across the plateau, bounced the yellow headlight beams of the tractor steered by Jacques.

'Go a bit further to the left, otherwise we'll run into Brousse's fencing,' warned Françoise.

'Towards the trees over there?' asked Jean. He was slightly lost, and would have had difficulty in reaching Coste-Roche by himself.

'Yes, those are the plum trees on the Perrier field, on our land, you know. After that we'll pass round the top of the mine cutting, going on into Delmond's meadow. Then we'll be on Mathilde's fields, and after that comes Coste-Roche. You'll see, we'll be there before Papa!'

'You're lucky,' he said. 'You know it all like the back of your hand!'

'That's nothing special. You know, we used to have some great games up on the plateau, with Dominique. Our cousins joined us and believe me, it was good fun! Watch out, you've got a ditch over there, along the side of Delpeyroux's land.'

'You know the owner of every plot and its boundaries too?'

'Just as well! Look, don't forget that my brother and I often had to drive the animals out to graze. It wouldn't have done to make a mistake!'

'Of course not,' he agreed.

He was full of admiration for his cousin. In the first place he found her breathtakingly beautiful. Disturbingly so; he hardly dared even look at her for fear of blushing when, to be more comfortable in her work and cool down, she unbuttoned her shirt and let it hang loose, thus revealing the charming spectacle of the little cups which barely covered her breasts. As for her cut-off denim shorts which clung to her bottom and set off her bronzed thighs, they were enough to drive you mad; especially when she bent down to pick up the sheaves – a stunning sight.

So to blot out and try to stifle the fantasies which threatened to overwhelm him, he kept telling himself that Françoise was his first cousin, almost his sister. Besides, she intimidated him. She was eight years older than him, with the maturity and confidence of a grown woman; he still wavered in adolescent confusion, full of doubts and uncertainties. To be sure he ran a razor over his cheeks at least once a week, but even his voice still betrayed him when it jumped suddenly into sharps more suited to a little boy; and that was always when he wanted it to be deep!

Finally, Françoise was confident in her Corrèze childhood which filled her memory. Confident in being at home there, on the land where she had taken her first steps and which was so familiar that she knew the ownership of each tree, each bush.

It was not that his own memories were unpleasant, far from it! They were different; he considered them less stimulating, more ordinary. For although it might have been very entertaining to crisscross the avenues of the Tuileries Gardens on roller-skates, or to sail your boat on the pool in the Jardin du Luxembourg, it was still less exciting than playing hide and seek in the caves of the mine cutting. Munching the neighbours' cherries, pears or strawberries for the sheer pleasure of scrumping, since there was no shortage of them on the farm! And then, despite it being forbidden, or maybe because it was, soaking your legs in the freezing water at the source of the Diamond.

Dominique, Françoise and his other cousins, Marie, Chantal, Josyane, had done all this. He had not. His visits to Saint-Libéral had always been too brief and the age difference too great, even with his closest cousins, Francoise and Josyane.

But now he was going to make up for that, properly explore Saint-Libéral, its fields, woods and views, create his own set of memories. And soon he would be confident, not only in the knowledge needed by young townies – especially those in the big cities – but would have in addition all that Jacques and the whole Vialhe family were eager to instil.

For his choice had been made. His holidays were going to be spent here, in the village and at Coste-Roche. And that was what he would tell his parents when they came, in a week's time. Inform them that he had better things to do than waste three weeks in Spain. Explain to them that the beach at Blanes held no attractions for him, neither did walks in the heart of Spain, nor the corrida, the flamenco or paella! Prove to them that his Uncle Jacques needed him on the farm, that his grandfather was counting on his help to bring in some wood and his grandmother was hoping he would pull up the two rows of Belles de Fontenay onions she had planted at the bottom of the garden. In short, that everyone was counting on him.

'To the right now: we'll cut across the land that's called At Mathilde's,' said Françoise. 'Just look, Papa has put in beets everywhere,' she remarked.

She had not been there since the beginning of her holidays, but recognized the broad leaves shining in the moonlight.

They were in the middle of the field when suddenly a bird flushed from a few steps in front of them, circled and then disappeared. Surprised, Françoise gave a little cry, then began to laugh.

'That stupid owl startled me!'

'That wasn't an owl,' he assured her, pleased by his expertise and also by this chance encounter, which he considered symbolic.

'Not an owl? Go on!'

'It was a nightjar! See, there it is again! Look! Look!' he whispered.

Dashing low over the ground, then swooping up vertically to swallow some noctuid moths, the bird skimmed past them, emitted a brief low churring, then disappeared.

'Super,' she said. 'So that's a nightjar? I've often seen them here, you know, especially when we bring in the cows in the evening, but I thought it was a sort of owl. Have to admit I'm not very up on birds. But you, how come you know them? Have you been observing them on the terrace at Les Invalides?'

'Yeah, sure! No, it was Félix who showed them to me. Hey, that'll be a year ago this month, we were at his place, in Brenne.'

'That's right, you often go there, don't you?'

'Yes. Félix is great!'

He was tempted to relate what his father's cousin had told him about nightjars, and the comparison he had made between them and

Vialhes. But he feared his cousin would misunderstand and laugh at him. He simply said:

'They're migratory birds, they travel a long way, as far as south-east Africa. But they always return to where they were born, like swallows. Great isn't it?'

On condition that his stay was brief, Guy always found great pleasure in returning to Saint-Libéral. First of all because he loved to see his parents and aunts again. Then because he enjoyed meeting his former neighbours, and even some of the men and women with whom he had learned to read on the benches of the same village school. The school now threatened with closure for lack of numbers, which had previously, in the 1940s, welcomed in fifty children each morning.

Finally he was happy to view his childhood haunts, even if they had changed. Even if, here and there, punctuating the countryside, new houses with unfamiliar tenants were appearing.

Despite all this, he never lingered long, especially in summer. He soon felt embarrassed at being there doing nothing, an idle stroller, whilst the last farmers of the village toiled from dawn to dusk. And as he was no longer fit nor keen enough to help his elder brother with the work in the fields, he always had the feeling of being an intruder there. Besides, the family home was too cramped to house him with Colette and the children; he was therefore obliged to move into Combes-Nègres, Louise's house. Now, although his aunt assured him that she was delighted to open her doors to him, he knew very well that she only maintained her home for Félix and for his son and family. He was therefore always worried lest his own offspring break a window, damage the furniture or trample the flower beds.

All these little considerations did not go so far as to spoil his pleasure. They simply encouraged him to take to the road after three or four days, before the social relationships, nature and way of life became too burdensome.

But during his visit, it was a real holiday – gargantuan feasts at his parents' and Mauricette's homes; evenings at Coste-Roche; excursions into the surrounding area, for the pleasure of introducing Colette and his children to all the rich diversity of his native land.

'And how do you find the parents?' Jacques asked him on the second evening of his vacation, when he and Colette had come up to dine at Coste-Roche.

The night was beautiful, warm, full of stars. So they had seated themselves outside, under the tunnel of vines, to round off the evening. Françoise had borrowed her father's car and gone to the cinema in Brive, with Jean, not a little proud to be accompanying such a beautiful girl! As for the children, Marc, Evelyne and Renaud, they were dozing in front of the television.

'Maman's aged a lot all of a sudden, hasn't she?' continued Jacques.

'Yes, but I was prepared for worse,' said Guy. 'She looks well and seems to be in good shape. Papa too, what's more.'

'If you think so,' said Jacques. 'I find he tires very quickly now . . .'

'It's his age, there's nothing to be done about it,' said Guy with a shrug.

He savoured the aroma from the little glass of plum brandy served by his brother, tasted it and nodded his head in approval.

'My hat off to you! Nothing in the best restaurants in Paris can compare with this!'

'Twenty-nine years old, that's what does it,' said Jacques. 'Do you remember? The still belonged to old Pa Gaillard. He set it up on the path to the Combes, just below the source of the Diamond. That's from the first barrel of plums I had distilled after returning from Germany. Do you recall it?' he asked Michèle.

'That was barely two months after we were married, we were still living down there with my parents.'

'Old Gaillard?' said Guy. 'Wasn't he the one who had a young fellow with a northern accent helping him? Papa always warned us to beware of him when we went to mind the cows on Combes-Nègres!'

'That's right!' agreed Jacques. 'He was a young fellow who'd had problems after the Liberation and who was under "resident supervision" in the Corrèze, as old Gaillard put it!'

He was about to continue with his reminiscences, then saw that his brother suddenly seemed rather preoccupied, rather worried, and feared that Jean was the reason for it. His nephew had announced the day before that he intended to spend his vacation working on the farm. Jacques surmised that his brother was not particularly pleased.

'You're looking worried, got problems?' he ventured to ask.

'Me? No. But you were talking about our parents' state of health; have you seen the way Aunt Yvette is?'

'Oh that! All the worry has aged her,' said Jacques. He sighed, shrugged his shoulders: 'Well as to that, you know what's going on with Louis!'

'Do I know what's going on?' replied Guy scornfully. 'Are you kidding or what? There's not a week passes but Louis spends an hour on the phone to me! And that's been going on for more than six months!'

'So you're dealing with his problems?'

'No way! I'm a lawyer, not a businessman. All I can tell him is that he's got himself into a dreadful mess!'

'I was well aware of that!'

'He is too, but he's pussyfooting around! He's just got to give up everything and start again from scratch. And not in the Limousin, he's blown it here, finished. If he wants to start another estate agency, I would advise him to go to the Dunkirk or Calais area! And yet, it may turn out that even up there they've heard of the crash . . .'

'Is it that bad?'

'Yes. He must settle all his debts and set up again elsewhere. If he doesn't, he'll really be needing a very good barrister to extricate him from all the lawsuits hanging over him!'

'He owes a lot?'

'You bet! What with the overdrafts, the unpaid interest mounting up, the bankers with their so-called "help", the loans to pay off other loans, he'll be owing not far off seven million!'

'What?' said Michèle, 'you mean to say seven hundred million old francs? Is that it?' she asked Jacques.

He nodded in agreement. He too was rather stunned at the vastness of the sum. Accustomed to managing a budget so small and fragile that it caused him many a worry, he had difficulty in grasping that an intelligent, capable man like his cousin could get himself into such a situation.

'Seven hundred million!' he repeated, 'But how the devil did he manage that?'

'Oh, it's easy! A slightly over-inflated idea of himself, lots of sharks around him, and then . . .' Guy stopped, made sure the children were still in front of the television: 'And then women, old chap,' he continued, 'he's been on a fantastic binge for years, you have no idea!'

'Is that really so?' said Jacques.

He could not come to terms with it. Certainly he had no doubt that his cousin rarely slept alone, but even so! There was a difference between chasing after a bit of skirt and living it up until you ruin yourself!

'Believe me,' Guy assured him. 'Look, ask Colette. To thank me for having won a case for them, some clients feel obliged to drag me around those stupid nightclubs where the more disgusting the champagne and whisky, the more they cost! So believe me, the girls you find there are exorbitantly priced too! Well, just think, we've often seen cousin Louis in that sort of bordello, as Papa would say. And Louis was never with one cutie, always with two or three! Isn't that right, Colette?'

'It's true,' she confirmed. 'It can't have helped his finances.'

'Ah well, now I understand better why poor Aunt Yvette looks so sad,' said Jacques pouring himself a nip of brandy.

'Don't tell me this is all news to you?'

'As far as the living it up goes, yes, but the rest, no, of course not. Aunt Berthe alerted me to it a long time ago, and Maman too. But I didn't think it was that bad! What can he do? Do you think he'll sell his land? Or the château?'

'You've got it in one! Just imagine, he offered it to me, to keep it in the family!'

'Seriously? The château and the land?'

'Yes.'

'What could I do with it? In the first place I don't want to get into debt buying property I have no use for. In any case, even supposing I were rich enough to pick up the tab, that wouldn't save him. He's really up to his neck in it. I told him as much on our way here.'

'You've seen him?'

'Yes, yesterday morning, on our way through Limoges.'

'And?'

'Well, he'll have to give up his whole business, that will pay it off. Christ, he won't have a single sou left afterwards, but that's better than landing up in the nick, isn't it? If he does that, I've promised to refer some prospective buyers for the château to him. I know a fair number of people who could come up with a million, no problem. The château's not worth more than that, you know. And even at that price, he'll be lucky to sell.'

'Well, well, I have to say it's a fine tale you're telling me,' murmured Jacques. 'And where does Aunt Yvette come in to all this?'

'Ah, there you have me! . . . She'll have to live somewhere. Or rather, he'll have to find her somewhere to live. You know he's already made her sell all the houses in Brive?'

'All of them? Are you sure?'

'All of them. There it is, now you know everything.'

'Yes,' said Jacques pensively, 'yes, but it's not going to help me sleep better tonight . . . First of all, as mayor I'm annoyed about the château, you never know who might appear. But that's not the worst part. No. For God's sake, Louis is our cousin, and for me he's the son of my godfather. Believe me, it really upsets me not to be able to help him! My God, you end up thinking poor Uncle Léon was lucky to be out of it and not see the carnage!'

'So it's true then, you're leaving the the boy with us for the whole of August?' Pierre-Edouard insisted on knowing as he stopped to catch his breath.

He had asked Guy to accompany him on his walk, and was glad to have done so. He felt rather weary, short of breath and with a weakness in his legs. But still he felt reassured, for he had a strong arm close at hand which he could hold on to if need be.

'You know,' he said, 'this path up to the plateau, it's not far off eighty-five years I've been using it, and believe me, I've a feeling it's getting steeper all the time!'

'We can go back down if you like,' suggested Guy.

'No, no, let's sit down a while instead. Look, over there,' suggested Pierre-Edouard, pointing to a large oak stump. Guy helped him to sit, noticing how stiff and unsure of himself he had grown, and remained standing.

'Sit down, you make me feel dizzy,' said Pierre-Edouard, taking out his pipe. He stuffed it with a few strands of coarse tobacco, lit it, and pensively contemplated the countryside spread out before them.

Nearest to them, at their feet, lay Saint-Libéral with its slate roofs shining in the morning sun. A peaceful village, silent, sleepy. A village slumbering in an apathetic coma which owed nothing to the early August heat.

And then, around it, the fields and meadows. Mostly meadows, for the arable land was gradually giving way to grass. The last farmers in the village no longer had the time to sink the plough into each plot. That was obvious, for even some of the plum orchards were half abandoned, not sprayed or pruned, with dead branches dangling and suckers feeding on their roots. Nor did the walnut plantations escape the men's loss of heart. Tortured by a torrent of hail on 3 August 1971, they were dying quietly, weeping a sticky sap which seeped from the stump of each branch broken by the wind. And on their calloused trunks parasites grew unchecked.

Fortunately, so long as the eye wandered and did not linger over details close at hand, the beauty of the countryside opened out before them, the sweetness of the fresh, green valleys, the harmonious curve of the hills worn down over thousands of years. And, yet further still, the uplifting immensity of the soft blue horizon stretching as far as the eye could see, climbing up towards the Auvergne and Cantal.

'You haven't given me an answer,' Pierre-Edouard reproached him.

'To what?'

'Young Jean, you're leaving him here . . . Is that right?'

'I said yes, that means yes!' Guy assured him, chewing a tender stalk of cocksfoot grass.

'It doesn't seem to give you much pleasure . . .'

'Of course it does! Well, his mother and brothers and sister would have preferred him to come on holiday with us . . . And me too! But okay, since he's chosen to work . . .'

'Why don't you admit you're not pleased that he loves the land?'

'Don't let's discuss that again, you know my opinion.'

'Yes, you're hoping he'll abandon the idea of copying Dominique.'

'We'll see . . .' said Guy, evasively.

He had no wish to quarrel with his father. No wish to tell him that he did not believe in the future of farming. No wish to explain to him that from all the evidence – and some studies proved it – it would have been much more economical for consumers to buy everything from the United States! That he was not the only person to work this out, far from it, and that one day, probably soon according to the specialists, only a few regions would remain predominantly agricultural; the Corrèze was not about to become one of them!

Nor did he wish to tell him that it was enough to see how hard Jacques worked and what he earned to be against his own son embarking on a similar treadmill!

'But *miladiou*!' cried out Pierre-Edouard, as if he had read his thought. 'You're exaggerating, farmers and agronomists will always be needed! Look in front of you, look all around, look at the fallow land gaining ground and the brambles spreading everywhere! That's because there's no one to control them! Do you think it should continue? If we go on fooling around like that, you'll see, one day our grand-children will be dying of hunger! Is that what you want, up there in Paris? Or on the other hand, you know, with a summer like we've had this year, it'll all be shrivelled up!'

'It hasn't come to that! Come on, don't get in a state about nothing!'

'It isn't nothing! It's because it grieves me to see land going to waste when it's begging to produce something!'

# 11

JEAN untied the calf. With one hand gripping the halter, the other its tail, he led it out of the van driven by Henri Brousse and waited.

All around them, locked in an indescribable jam, dozens of vehicles were unloading calves haphazardly on to the pavements and roadway.

Calmly, deaf to the gibes and insults flying around, a policeman was trying to convince the owner of a rusty 4L pick-up truck battered about by its cargo, that he could not possibly have any excuse for continuing to paralyse the entire road system. But it was obvious that he was not for one moment expecting to be heeded; the other man had better things to do!

Streaming with perspiration, brick red, close to apoplexy, his beret over his eyes, emitting long streams of Bloody-Hells and God's-Teeth and various allusions to some brothel with a divine manager, the man, kneeling in the back of the van, was trying to dislodge his calf, which was jammed across the box.

'Give it a push up the backside! Hey! You can see he's bracing himself against the door!' cried one spectator.

'Better to pull his head! That'll make him jump!' advised another.

'Shut yer mouths, dammit!' grumbled the owner, wiping his forehead with the back of his hand.

He did not seem prepared for conversation. His cord trousers were covered in urine and dung and his shirt was wringing wet.

'Right, now you must move on or I'll book you!' threatened the officer, waving his notebook.

The man shrugged, plunged back into the van, seized the calf's neck with both arms and twisted as it bellowed in terror. Free at last, the animal sprang on to the tarmac, charged towards the representative of the law, but swerved at the last moment, and stopped dead.

'Did you see that: animals don't harm their own kind!' called out a disappointed wag.

'Come on, move along now! Move, I said!' the policeman's tone was growing desperate.

A foolish hope: given the situation, it was obvious that no vehicle would shift a hand's breadth for at least half an hour if they were lucky!

'See you later at Pierrot's for a snack,' said Jacques to Brousse, who was still sitting at the wheel and philosophically reading his newspaper with the engine switched off. 'And you, don't let go of that calf!' he advised Jean.

Thiers Square was teeming with people and animals. And the din – a mixture of motor horns, rumbling engines, mooing, shouts, calls, swearing and laughter – was such that you needed to shout to make yourself heard. Already all the restaurants and bistros were full, their terraces black with famished customers; the air smelled of noodle soup, fortified bouillon, steak, camembert, wine and the cowshed. And on all sides the happy cries of neighbours or friends rang out, as they met and greeted each other with hearty backslapping.

'And make sure you hold on to that calf,' repeated Jacques. He was a little worried, for however strong his nephew might be, the calf was pushing a hundred and eighty kilos and had a tendency to pull on the tether. You needed a firm hand to control it, to lead it along the chains where several hundred animals were lined up, and to find it a space. But Jacques had been in such pain with his back for the last two days that he felt unable to hold the animal if it took it into its head to jump about.

It was a very fine Limousin bull calf of four months, top grade. Fed exclusively on its mother's milk since birth, kept in the quiet in the half-light of a box, it had knotted shoulders, a broad back and enlarged hind quarters. Moreover it would provide pale pink meat, as one could tell from the pallor of the mucous membranes in its mouth, the insides of its eyelids and its coat called 'leveret's fur', a pale covering speckled with greyish tufts.

'Shall we put it here?' suggested Jean, pointing to a place between two fine-looking animals.

'No, further down will be better,' decided Jacques, catching hold of the calf's halter.

Jean frowned but complied. He did not understand why his uncle was choosing a position in full sunshine, when the other spot had the benefit of the deep shade of one of the plane trees on the market place.

'We'll die of heat,' he said.

'Come on now!' Jacques smiled as he tied up the calf. 'Don't tell me you don't understand why I didn't want to stay where you were suggesting?'

'Well, no . . . we would've been in the shade at least, whereas here!'

'You've still got a few things to learn!' continued Jacques. 'I see you don't know the most important principle which your Uncle Léon never failed to apply: "Always present your produce as the finest at the market!" Do you get it?'

'Yes. Well no, not exactly . . .'

'Look where we are: there are nothing but "moles" all around us. Yes, Limousin-Friesian crosses. Not bad of their sort, but you know, next to ours they're real runts! Now, see how they sets ours off!'

'That's true,' admitted Jean.

'Up where you wanted to stop, we'd have been surrounded by animals just as good as him, so he'd look more ordinary.'

'I see . . . .' Jean agreed. He was discovering previously unknown side to his uncle, and it was very entertaining. 'And you try to do that every time?' he continued.

'Yes.'

'The same for the pigs?'

'Exactly. But you know, to be frank, it doesn't make much difference in the end; it's almost a game. The buyers aren't stupid, they know the system. And it's always the prices on the day which determine the outcome.'

'So we could've stayed in the shade!'

'Oh no! You must always work on the principle that you might chance on some young lad who doesn't know all the tricks . . . Hey! Cheers!' Jacques called to a man who was shouldering his way roughly through the throng of sellers.

'Cheers! Is this yours?' asked the man pointing to the calf, but not touching it. 'Ten-fifty when the bell goes' he said.

'You'd better be quiet!' replied Jacques. 'It's not open yet, so I haven't heard anything.'

'Ten-fifty on the bell!' repeated the fellow as he moved off.

'What was all that nonsense?' Jean was astonished.

'That was one of the scouts for old Jalinac, one of the biggest wholesalers in the area. As the market isn't open yet, he hasn't any right to buy. So he's making the rounds to pick out the best animals and prepare the ground. Your great uncle Léon began by doing that job. But he didn't stop at that.'

'Are you going to let it go at that price?'

'Of course not! And look here, if Jalinac is already deploying his troops, that means the Italians are here. Oh yes!' he explained, seeing his nephew's astonished expression, 'the Eyeties come as far up as here, or even further, into Haute-Vienne, to pick up anything they can. They fill their lorries up with calves; three or four hundred animals don't worry them. So you can imagine the dealers in this area are interested in keeping an eye on them. I myself don't trust them anyway, their cheques often bounce . . .'

'This is absolutely amazing,' said Jean. 'All they talk about is the common market, modern farming and economics and all that, and you're still selling like in the Middle Ages, it's crazy!'

'You're right, but I don't very well see how else it could be done. There is an agricultural intervention board in the département, but it doesn't operate at the top of the market, far from it! It works at the bottom end, picking up the unsold stuff and rejects! So here we are, myself and plenty of others, at the mercy of the wholesalers. You're dead right, the system's damnably out of date.'

'And what's more you're screwing up the whole town with this mess! All right, it's good fun, but for the tourist trying to get across Brive, it's bloody awful!'

'The mess will soon be sorted out at least. In six months' time the markets'll be held elsewhere, near the airfield, you know, on the road to Bordeaux. It'll be more efficient, but definitely not as pleasant . . .'

'Why not?'

'Because all the bistros you see around this square aren't going to be moving, are they? So I'm wondering where we'll be able to sit down with a glass of something, talk to our friends, mix some wine with our soup and have a bite to eat . . .'

Louis considered that he had payed dearly for the right to show off, to make those three louts who were ruining him believe he wasn't washed up yet. So it was with a firm hand that he initialled and signed each page of the deeds which discharged his debts, but which also divested him of his last centime, or almost. He even pretended not to notice the satisfied smiles of the new owners of his estate agency, and of the land in the process of being divided into plots where the construction work had forced him to capitulate – although, God knows, there was money to be made out of those lots!

The three crooks who had got the better of him, who had brought him to his knees, certainly knew that! They were going to triple their outlay in a few years and, whilst he was chewing over his humiliation and grovelling in poverty, those wretches would be making a packet at his expense! It was enough to drive you to murder!

Even the solicitor had an expression which incited homicide. He radiated contentment and seemed in such a hurry to see everything settled that his hand shook as he turned the pages of the dossier one by one.

Admittedly the operation was lucrative for him. And although he seemed as conceited and boastful as a turkey cock, it was obvious that he did not deal with matters of such importance every day. His expression betrayed him, showing just how much he was enjoying finishing a reputedly bleak month with such a lucrative session. It was well worth the trouble of working during August!

For that too was heart-breaking for Louis. The weather was wonderful, warm. A time for holidays, just right for lounging beside the water, a young thing with very little clothing or inhibitions in one hand and a scotch on the rocks in the other!

Instead of which he was shut up in this dark office which smelled of old dog, as cheerful as a dentist's waiting room, its walls covered in ugly grey paper in no way enlivened by the badly framed, incompetent scrawls of some depressed dauber. And worst of all, he was there to be legally stripped of everything. To sign his own extirpation and hand over what represented twenty-five years of his life, his business, to three sharks who were growing happier by the minute.

'Fine, right, that's it? Can we see the end of all this paperwork?' he said irritably. 'I have other things to do besides this, you know!'

'Nearly done. But you realise everything must be done according to the rules!' the lawyer assured him in a smooth tone. 'Here, initials there and there, and your signature to complete it,' he added with a smile. He had revolting, yellow, rat-like teeth and stank of tobacco. 'And there we are,' he said, carefully pressing a blotter over the signature, 'yes, the matter is settled.'

'Right, then we have nothing further to say to each other,' declared Louis, heading for the door.

'I hope you'll be our guest this evening, a nice little supper among friends,' suggested one of the buyers.

'Friends? What in hell's name do you think I'd be doing there! Keep your snacks, I can still afford to buy myself a proper meal!' cried Louis.

He ignored the outstretched hands, went out and slammed the door.

Louis spent the afternoon tidying his small flat in the Place Jourdan and piling his belongings into a corner of the corridor. He was no longer at home, for even these four rooms were included in the sale. Magnanimously, the purchasers had allowed him a month to sort himself out and move. But where to go, and more urgently what to do? He no longer owned anything or was anybody. And worst of all, he no longer had the will to fight on.

Fight for what, anyway? He had no child to feed, no woman worth making an effort for. His last mistress had dropped him at the beginning of July, when she had suddenly realised that he was virtually ruined. She had left for Saint-Tropez on the arm of a young man whose family were in kaolin and prided themselves on owning a twelve-metre yacht. Louis wished him a speedy shipwreck!

It was while emptying a drawer that he discovered an old photo of his father posing boastfully in front of the château of Saint-Libéral. He then realised to what extent he had failed, wasted it all, undervalued what had been entrusted to him. And he had been given a great deal, for fear that he should lack for anything!

His father had started with nothing, absolutely nothing, and had nevertheless succeeded in reversing his fortunes. At the age of twelve he had only disadvantages and not a sou to his name. But he had a compelling need to forget that body hanging in the barn, which he had bumped into one January evening in 1900, on 16 January . . .

Never had anyone in the family spoken of this episode to Louis. But he had learned by degrees, by putting two and two together. In Saint-Libéral, even after thirty-five years, the shared recollections were still alive. And the children in the village school were quite ready to make fun of the grandson of the man who hanged himself, to cut him down to size! A little matter of making him understand that his opulent leather satchel, his boots – an insult to all the clogs in the class – and his expensive clothes would never erase the memory of the contorted face and purple tongue of Emile hanging from the cross beam . . .

And even if a few sharp blows had silenced the slanderers, the gossips and the envious, he had forgotten nothing. Forgotten nothing particularly of the way his father had tried to eradicate that stain, that fault. He had fought, all the time, all his life. He had succeeded.

And me, I've really made a mess of it, from beginning to end, he thought with a shrug. I couldn't even be bothered to give Maman some grandchildren! That's all the poor woman was waiting for, she always believed that I'd do the same as Papa, that I'd marry late! Poor old thing, she hasn't even had the pleasure of cuddling a grandson! But it has to be said that of all the tarts I tumbled with, not one of them ever asked me to give her a child. They'd have preferred to get rid of it I bet! Well, to the devil with all that, he told himself, putting down the photo, you can't undo what's done, and at my age you can't wipe it all away and start again!

*

Louis dined alone in an establishment which he had frequented for a long time, where the cuisine was refined and the cellar respectable. The owner was almost a friend. Not quite, however; for some time Louis had felt him more reserved than previously, less ready to put on one side the bills which he settled at the end of the month. But this evening he was welcoming, there were very few customers.

'So, now you're going off on short holiday?' he asked as he offered Louis a vintage brandy on the house.

'Yes, I really need one.'

'You're going to the coast, I expect?'

'No, home, to the Corrèze, to Saint-Libéral.'

'Ah?' said the man, savouring the aroma from his balloon glass. 'By the way, how's business?' he asked carelessly.

'Very funny!' said Louis with a shrug. 'You know very well how I'm placed! Yes you do! Yes, you know, like everyone in this town with its stinking rumours! Never mind, I'll have the last word yet. That's what counts, isn't it?'

'Of course, anyway, I'm sure I . . .'

'Look here, give me my bill, yes, the month's total.'

'There's a little more than that . . .'

'Right, that's fine.'

'Um . . . I'd prefer cash if you have it,' said the owner, seeing Louis take out his cheque book. 'Because of the tax, you understand . . .' he said, lowering his voice.

'Of course, no problem,' Louis assured him, guessing that the tax was only an excuse: *That evil-minded squirt is just worried I might pass him a dud cheque! When I think of all the dough he's had off me over the years!*

He left the restaurant at half past twelve and took the road to Brive. It was at the top of the long slope leading down to Pierre-Buffière, which ends in the fearsome hairpin bend plunging down beyond the railway line where the crossing gates were always closed, that he made the decision. It all became so simple then, easy, no problems.

Suddenly relaxed, as he had not felt for months, perhaps even for years, he built up speed in his Porsche. Accelerator to the floor and engine running flat out, he hurtled down the hill at more than two hundred kilometres an hour, and launched himself against the broad metal posts which supported the level-crossing barrier on the Paris-Toulouse line. His neck broken clean through, Louis Dupeuch was already dead when the steering wheel crushed his thorax . . .

*

It was with a knot of fear in the pit of his stomach that Jacques lifted the receiver. It was barely three o'clock in the morning and that piercing ringing which frayed his nerves boded no good.

So, thinking that one of his aunts or his mother was ringing to tell him that his father had taken a turn for the worse, he raised the receiver to his ear.

'This is Sergeant Chastang, of the Ayen police. Is that Monsieur Viahle's house?'

'Yes.'

'Ah! Am I speaking to the mayor?'

'Of course, for God's sake! What's happened?' he asked, more and more worried and surprised.

'A problem, a big problem, sir ... We've been trying to call Monsieur Dupeuch's house, in Limoges, hoping that maybe someone ... but there's no reply, so ...'

'So what? Explain yourself, in God's name!'

'Well, we thought we'd better tell you first, you ... Our colleagues in Pierre-Buffière informed us as soon as they were able to read the documents ... So I thought that Madame Dupeuch being old, and that ... that ... There it is, it'll have to be broken gently to her ... She is your aunt, isn't she?'

My God, he thought, I bet Louis has done the same as Grandpa Dupeuch! That's all we need!

But still he asked: 'Break what to her?'

'An accident, a terrible accident ...'

'My cousin is dead, is that it?'

'Yes. He must have fallen asleep at the wheel, and as he hadn't done up his seat belt ... Oh anyway, the speed he was going ...'

'I see ...' murmured Jacques, thinking selfishly that it would be a little easier to announce to his aunt that Louis had had a car accident. He could not see himself telling her he had blown out his brains with a shotgun or hanged himself, like their maternal grandfather. Then he realised that the gendarme was still talking.

'Well, he's been taken to Limoges, but ...'

'Very good, you've done what's needed. Listen, if you would be so kind as to come to the mairie tomorrow, I'll be there at first light. We'll see about the details then, all right?'

'Very well, sir. But you will undertake to inform Madame Dupeuch, won't you?'

'Yes indeed. Until tomorrow.'

He replaced the receiver, turned round and saw Michèle standing in the bedroom doorway.

'Did you hear that?' he asked.

She shook her head and he realised she would be convinced that it was Dominique or Françoise who had had an accident. There had been no news from Dominique for almost a month, while Françoise had been back in Paris for a week.

'Is it serious?' she murmured.

'It's Louis . . .'

He noticed that she seemed relieved, but did not blame her at all. He too had felt less distressed on discovering that it was neither his son nor his daughter, but his cousin who had suffered an accident.

'Louis?' she prompted.

'Yes. A car accident. Killed outright . . .'

'Lord!' she whispered, closing her eyes. 'Poor Aunt Yvette . . . Does she know?'

'Not yet.'

'And it's you who's going . . .'

'Yes, someone has to do it.'

'And how are we to tell your father?'

'Oh that,' he sighed. 'It's not the sort of news that'll do him any good. Nor Maman either . . . Bloody hell, what a stupid mess! No, no, it's such a mess!'

He was simultaneously bitter and furious. Bitter because it was all too senseless. Because the death of a man in the prime of life was a shameful nonsense, gross stupidity! Furious because he could not forget that his own first reaction had been to believe that Louis had deliberately destroyed himself, and he still believed it. Furious, because he knew that he would never be rid of that idea, since it fitted in so well with his cousin's desperate situation.

For one thing was certain, if it was true that Louis loved to drive fast, and Jacques knew a bit about that as he had sometimes been to Brive with him, he was not the sort to leave his seat belt undone, and much less to fall asleep at the wheel. So . . .

My God! he suddenly thought, what's going to become of poor Aunt Yvette with all Louis' business to sort out? Well, it's a good thing Guy is back from his holiday; we'll certainly need his skills . . .

'With your father,' went on Michèle, 'it'll have to be Aunt Berthe who tells him, she'll find the words to say it, she knows . . .'

'You're right. But how can I get to her in the morning without bumping into my father?'

'I'll go, if you like. And you, while I do that, you go and see Aunt Yvette . . .'

'All right,' he sighed. He suddenly frowned and glanced towards

Jean's room. 'I think we've woken him. You'd better put something on,' he said.

She was barely covered by her thin short nightdress, for the night was humid, without a breath of air. She slipped quickly into the bathroom and came out pulling on a dressing gown, as Jean emerged from his room looking dazed.

'Hey, what's going on?' he asked uncomprehendingly.

'I'm afraid the last days of your holday are turning out badly. Your cousin Louis has just killed himself in his car . . .'

'Oh merde!' murmured Jean.

If he felt sad, it was more to do with the state Jacques and Michèle were in, and their distress, than any thought for Louis. He had met him no more than three or four times in his life, and he was rarely mentioned at home.

'Can you look after the animals for me tomorrow?' asked Jacques.

'Of course.'

'I'm going to have a rough day, and your aunt as well. So if you could possibly . . .'

'I'll manage, don't worry. But tell me, does Aunt Yvette know?' He was just appreciating how fond he was of the old lady. She was charming, always pleasant, gentle and concerned about everyone. He thought of the pain she was going to suffer and tears welled up in his eyes. 'And Grandfather? And Grandmother? Do they know?' he asked, forcing himself to control his voice.

'Nobody knows anything yet, except us three,' said Jacques, pretending not to notice his distress. He moved towards his nephew, grasped his shoulder and shook it:

'Don't worry, we'll tell them gently. Very carefully. One tragedy is enough.'

Contrary to what Jacques had feared, it was not his father who reacted most strongly, but his mother. To her, Louis was her only nephew bearing the Dupeuch name, her own name. With him gone, the Dupeuch branch of the family was extinguished for ever. Furthermore, Louis greatly resembled his father physically, and she saw in him a reflection of Léon whose disappearance had already deeply hurt her.

So this new trial affected her severely. And although she knew how to put on a brave face, she remained wounded, vulnerable. Less than her sister-in-law Yvette, of course, who seemed to age ten years in a few hours. And her bewildered, lost look worried Mathilde, Louise and Berthe so much that the three ladies decided to move her in to the

Vialhe house on their return from the cemetery. They made up a bed for her in Louise's room, and Yvette, distant, sealed in her sorrow, let it be done without saying a word. Without even crying, that was the worst. For everyone who saw her realised that the flood of tears which refused to flow was eating into her from within, like an acid, wearing her down, suffocating her.

'You know, you're going to have to find something to jog poor Yvette out of it. And to cheer up Mathilde too,' said Pierre-Edouard to Berthe a week after the funeral.

As every morning, he had asked his sister to accompany him on his daily walk, but it was the first time since Louis' death that he had broached this subject.

The announcement of his nephew's death had given him a shock, but much less than that of his brother-in-law three years earlier. In fact he had never been overly fond of Louis. He liked him well enough, but had little in common with him. Besides, Louis had built his life far away from Saint-Libéral, and his mode of existence and business had never drawn him closer to his uncle.

After all, Pierre-Edouard had reached an age where his memory was so full of the faces of those who had disappeared, and his heart so wrung by many a loss, that he came to the point where he no longer railed against death when it struck someone who, although not a stranger, was not very close to him either.

'Here, help me sit down,' he asked as they arrived at the old oak stump where he now rested during every walk. 'Yes,' he continued, taking out his pipe, 'you'll have to do something.'

'And what would you have me do?'

'How should I know! But you have to pull Yvette out of it, and Mathilde too,' he sighed. 'Poor old Léon,' he said after a few moments' silence, 'good thing he's not here any longer. What a mess! By the way, were you able to find out? Were Louis' affairs sorted out?'

'Yes, there's nothing outstanding. He'd signed everything the day before his death.'

'So why did he kill himself, the little fool!' He was suddenly angry. 'Because he did mean to kill himself, I know it! I'd swear to it! And that's what's eating at Mathilde, because she suspects as much!'

'Don't get worked up, you can't be sure of anything.'

'Sure I'm sure! He did the same as his grandfather Emile, that's what he did! And you know it's true too. Admit it!'

'What's the point?' she said with a shrug. 'Me, I believe what the gendarmes said . . .'

'All right,' he said calmly, 'all right, believe it if suits you. But in that case, try to persuade Mathilde! You see, she never knew her father, but she knows all about him . . . So she makes the connection with Louis.'

'There's no reason for it,' suggested Berthe. She herself was convinced of Louis' suicide, but did not consider it helpful or sensible to talk about it. Louis had chosen and that was his business, even if his decision was abominable.

'Right, fine, don't let's talk about it any more,' he said. He puffed slowly on his pipe, spat between his feet. 'You see,' he continued,' Grandfather was right . . .'

'Grandfather Edouard?'

'Yes. Do you remember what he always said to encourage us to be careful, so that we learned economical habits?'

'Yes, I've never forgotten that,' she smiled.

'"It only takes two generations to go from clogs to clogs"!' he recited. 'It's horribly true! Old father Dupeuch was the poorest man in the village, and it was touch and go whether he had enough to buy himself a pair of clogs. You hardly knew him, but I remember Emile well!'

'I do though. I was seven when . . . when he died.'

'Yes. Well there he was, so poor, but had a son who made his fortune! And then along comes Louis and devours the lot. Gobbles it all up. And it may turn out that he had barely enough to pay for a pair of clogs . . . And that's surely why . . .'

'Don't rehash all that, there's no point. Would you like to go back?' she asked.

'Not straight away, we'll walk a bit further. I want to hear you say that you'll look after Yvette. And Mathilde too. Because I don't know what to do any more, and it's tormenting me.'

# PART THREE

*In Memory of Léon*

# 12

Iᴛ was with a shrinking heart that Jean turned round and cast a last glance in the direction of Saint-Libéral. He fixed the image of the village in his mind as it lay bathed in sunshine, nestling up there on the side of the hill, then pretended to be interested in the road which curved away towards Brive.

He did not regret the last days of his holidays, although they had been disrupted by Louis' death. Firstly, because he had several times found himself alone at Coste-Roche, and so in charge of the farm, and he had managed that extremely well. Secondly, because his cousin's funeral had given him the opportunity to establish himself as a grandson worthy of the Vialhes.

Indeed, he had found himself the sole representative of all the Vialhe grandchildren, for Françoise had not been able to come down. As for the others . . . And he had also represented his parents, detained in Paris by pressing obligations. So he was proud to see that in the eyes of those who had come to the cemetery, he was recognised as a Vialhe, and that it was therefore right for him to be present beside his grandparents, uncles and aunts, to support the old lady with dry eyes standing rigidly by the open grave.

'Don't you worry,' said Jacques, seeing him look at his watch, 'you'll be there in plenty of time.'

'Oh, I'm not worried! Anyway, there are other trains!'

'Hey! No messing about! I told your parents you'd be arriving shortly after six o'clock, so . . . Considering you should have been in Paris at least three days ago! Seems you've done nothing to prepare for school and you haven't even anything to wear! Well, that's what your mother says.'

'Bah, I'll be ready the day after tomorrow, that's the main thing,' said Jean with a shrug.

He had not a single worry about the start of the academic year. He was not changing schools, would meet up with lots of teachers and mates he already knew, was not concerned about the course work to come and was even keen to tackle it. In fact, all would have been well if Saint-Libéral had not been five hundred kilometres from Paris! And if, instead of running senselessly round the cinder track in the stadium once a week to get some fresh air, he could have climbed each day amongst the stones of the White Peak, knocked down the walnuts on the Long Piece and led the animals out to graze!

Anyway, he thought to comfort himself, I'll go and see Félix as often as I can. And then who knows, maybe the parents would be happy to let me come down at Christmas . . .

He dreamed of seeing the village in winter, of exploring the bare landscape, walking on the ground hardened by frost, then plunging happily into the stable which had the chill taken off it by the animals, or warming himself up again beside the hearth, deep in the chimney corner.

But he made sure he did not speak about all that. He was aware that these wishes were the ones which strengthened his father's arguments. The ones which justified him in maintaining that it all arose from a rather affected sentimentalism, from a vision of the land as idealised as it was false. For daily life in the country, especially at minus ten or fifteen degrees or in persistent rain, was quite unlike a page from Giono, however sublime his romantic descriptions might be! And his father was speaking from experience.

Never mind, he thought, looking at his calloused palms these are also the beginning of experience! Because Papa may say what he likes, I worked till my hands bled in the first week at Coste-Roche, but it didn't put me off or make me give up!

'You've got real farmer's hands!' teased Jacques.

'Bah, they'll soon go.'

'There's nothing wrong with them!'

'That's not what I meant, just the opposite!' he said, reddening a little, for he was rather annoyed that his uncle had misunderstood his reaction. 'I'd prefer to keep them as they are; but you know, in Paris it's difficult to get hold of a pitchfork!'

'There's a time for everything. You'll see, in a little while you'll be glad not to be holding a fork to earn your living! Come on, young Vialhe, don't make such a face, and think about your bac! Any fool can have callouses on his hands, but not everyone has the luck to be born with academic abilities! Don't waste that! You see, you can even tell your father I gave you some good advice! Right?' joked Jacques.

'Yes, you're almost as smooth a talker as him! But it won't make any difference. First I'm going to do the same as Dominique, and then I'm going to be a stock-breeder! I don't know how or where, but I will be one day.'

*

846

Despite her age, Berthe refused to regard herself as an old lady, at least as far as mind and spirit were concerned. She was sufficiently intelligent and honest with herself to admit that her body, ravaged by the years and weakened by adversity, was that of an old person, which could betray her from one moment to the next. But she used all her willpower to think and act without allowing for the passage of time; as if no physical weakness should remind her that she was eighty-two.

So she quickly understood that Pierre-Edouard was right to be worried, and that it was vital to help Yvette regain her equilibrium. Without it Louis' mother, who was after all her junior by almost fifteen years, would sink into senility long before her!

It was as she made her way towards the grocer's van, as she did each Wednesday, accompanied by Louise and Mathilde, that she launched her campaign.

'Pierre-Edouard's right,' she said out of the blue, stopping in the middle of the pavement, and speaking quite loudly so as to be heard by Louise.

'What on earth's got into you?' replied a worried Louise.

'He's right!' she repeated. 'You're letting yourself go a bit,' she reproached Mathilde; 'and as for Yvette, she's on the way to turning into a real zombie. Yes, a sort of ghost of herself, if you like,' she explained, seeing that her sister-in-law had difficulty in understanding. 'We'll have to shake ourselves out of it, we'll have to give her a shake!'

'Easy to say, if you think it's amusing,' responded Mathilde.

'It's not a matter of amusing or sad! We must do something, that's all! And the first thing is to stop whining!'

'But we're not whining!' protested Louise.

'Yes you are! You're complaining! Secretly you're complaining! I know it!' Berthe was suddenly quite cross. 'With Yvette you spend your time shuffling through your worst memories, shaking the skeletons, like three little old ladies competing to see who's the unhappiest! Poor Louis is just an excuse to bring out all your old sorrows!'

'You have no right to speak like that!' protested Mathilde angrily. She had tears in her eyes, for the image of Paul was threatening to overwhelm her, the image of the vanished son whose presence had been felt more keenly since Louis' death. But to say that he was being used as a pretext! 'I forbid you to say such things!' she cried furiously. 'You have no right!'

'Let me finish!' said Berthe, her voice suddenly trembling. 'On that subject I have a right to speak as I think fit! I have the right because I should have been dead thirty years ago, I've had a suspended sentence for thirty years! Yes, I have the right! I have the right because I've seen more friends and colleagues die than you can ever imagine! All my sisters in the labour camps, all those who have gone before me, are telling me to say it! And I'm not going to betray them by not doing it!'

It was so unusual for her to evoke the months of hell spent in Ravensbrück that Mathilde and Louise were left speechless. Overcome by the incredible strength and determination radiating from this little old lady, so frail, so tiny, but whose voice was disturbing, appealing, and irrefutable. A voice full of life, spirit, hope.

'Yes,' she continued, 'all those I've seen go up in smoke – and there were some who were barely fifteen – give me the right to say that life is too short to be wasted on being unhappy! Too short to live with a cemetery in your head and a coffin on your back!'

She fell silent, shook herself and smiled:

'I'm sorry, it's stupid isn't it, to lose your temper. But it's true, you know! We must act! Even if it's not easy – especially when it's not easy! Are you cross with me?' she asked Mathilde.

'Of course not. Get away, I know you,' smiled Mathilde. 'You've always been the same.'

She could not forget that in earlier times, for months on end, her sister-in-law had helped her not to succumb, not to sink into a boundless sorrow; Berthe's strength had supported her then.

'And you, are you cross with me?' Berthe asked Louise.

'No. But you are hard on us, all the same . . .'

'Well I'm sorry. Forgive me, both of you,' she said, walking on. She smiled a greeting at one of their neighbours, Germaine Coste, who looked quite embarrassed to have witnessed the altercation.

'Don't worry,' she called to her, 'we were just exchanging a recipe! Well, are you coming? We'll miss the grocer!'

On the way back, after having devoted time to the traditional chat with friends, Berthe renewed her campaign.

'You're going to help me,' she decided. 'Yes, both of you, it'll buck you up, yes it will! And I'll ask Pierre-Edouard too, and Jacques and Michèle, to join in.'

'Help you with what?' asked Louise.

'We're going to take up Léonie Malpeyre's idea . . .'

'What?' Mathilde gasped. 'You want to launch a senior citizens' club in Saint-Libéral? You? But you always did your best to see it never happened! What a turn-up!'

'It's true,' added Louise, 'Léonie Malpeyre had organised every-thing with Julie and Fernande. It was all prepared. And you, you convinced us that it was ridiculous, silly, that it was something for doddery old people! It's true, even Pierre-Edouard joined in poking fun at the project! And now you want to . . . Well I never!'

'Exactly! I was right to oppose it. With Léonie, Julie and Fernande, it was a club for old women! And I don't want anything like that!'

'But she was younger than me by almost ten years!' Mathilde reminded her, amazed at her sister-in-law's nerve.

'With them, it would have been an old folks' club,' repeated Berthe. 'The proof is Julie and Fernande are dead and Léonie is senile!' she added completely unconvincingly. 'Fine, may their souls rest in peace. We'll revive the idea and arrange it so that Yvette is in the chair. That's the important thing! You see, that will force her to stir herself, to make plans, to organise excursions, visits to museums or châteaux, card sessions or knitting competitions, all those silly things, you know!'

'And what if she refuses?' ventured Louise.

'If we manage it properly she won't refuse,' Berthe was sure. 'First I'll begin by asking a favour of her, because that will drag her out of the dumps . . .'

'A favour?' persisted Mathilde.

'Yes. I don't have a car any more, and anyway I don't want to drive. On the other hand it's a bore and it tires me out taking the train when I go to Paris. Yvette has a car and she's a good driver, so . . .'

'And if she refuses?' reiterated Louise.

'Then we'll have to change our tactics until she agrees! But you're going to help me convince her that I must go to Paris at the end of the month, without fail!'

'Is it true? Do you really need to go there?' asked Mathilde, impressed by her sister-in-law's confidence.

'No, I have nothing to do there. And to be quite frank with you, the car tires me more than the train, but don't tell Yvette that!'

Yvette was not deceived for one moment. She understood immedi-ately that the entire Vialhe household had decided to support her at whatever cost.

Her first reaction was to protest, to tell them that she had the right to remain imprisoned by her grief. And if she wished to bear it alone, nobody should interfere. But the whole family's ploy was so heart-warming, so comforting, that she gave in, whilst pretending to see nothing so as not to embarrass anyone. She played the game and thus allowed her circle to share her burden, to help her carry it; she did not off-load it on to them, but it nevertheless seemed lighter, less painful to bear.

And little by little the game became a reality. Although she was secretly convinced that Berthe had no reason to go to Paris, she agreed to get her DS out of the garage and set off in the direction of Limoges. Attentive to every detail, Berthe made sure that they took Saint-Yrieix road and did not rejoin the RN 20 before Limoges. In this way they avoided passing the place where Louis had killed himself several weeks earlier.

It was on their return, after three days spent in Paris, where Berthe, helped by Colette and Chantal, walked her from restaurant to boutique and from department store to museum, that Yvette agreed to become the advocate, and most importantly, the organiser, of this senior citizens' club which it seemed was needed in Saint-Libéral.

'You understand, everyone feels the same, you can't refuse!' maintained Berthe. 'You can't refuse, in memory of Léon . . .'

'In memory of Léon?'

'Yes. He was a very good mayor for almost thirty years and in very difficult times. So now you must do your bit to carry on after him . . . Anyway, if he were here, that's what he'd be telling you to do!'

'Yes, maybe . . .'

'And if you want my opinion,' continued Berthe hypocritically, "senior citizens' club" isn't a very nice name, it smells of mothballs, it smacks of an old folks' home . . . If I were you, I'd call it something different. For instance . . . I don't know. The Léon Dupeuch Association . . . That has a fine ring to it, doesn't it? In any case it would be logical, because we'll really need a big room to meet in and it seems to me that the château has plenty of those . . .'

'You've worked it all out, haven't you?'

'No, not all of it. For example, I haven't prepared for the fact that you might refuse. If you'd said no, there wouldn't have been much else to be done for you . . .'

Yvette became chairwoman of the Léon Dupeuch Association two months later. Almost forty-five people from the village joined enthusiastically, happy to get together, looking forward to outings, excursions, meetings, games and meals.

If Jacques, as mayor, was pleased to see the village a little more animated, he did not cruelly draw attention to the fact that there were not enough young people in Saint-Libéral to form a football team, but the over-sixties could gather by the four dozen to fill their spare time . . . And even then they weren't all there, far from it!

Although she was beginning to get to know him, Béatrice was still amazed by some of Dominique's reactions. So she quickly noticed that he would not tolerate work being poorly executed by the agricultural staff. No deed was too small to escape his criticism if it concerned the land, the animals or the various experimental plantations for which he was responsible.

For example, one morning she had seen him vault over the bars of a pen, where two mulattos were unsuccessfully trying to control a three-hundred-kilo steer needing treatment against parasites.

Swearing like a trooper, he had sprung in front of the animal. Then, with his thumb and forefinger pinched in the bullock's nose, the other hand on its horn, he had subdued it and immobilised it in a corner, then had called to the two men:

'And now get a move on! Are you going to pull that head rope tight, or do damn all? I'm not going to hold on for ten years! That injection, is it coming? Have to do it all myself here!'

On another occasion, when visiting a cowshed with him, she had witnessed one of his more memorable tantrums. A cow was lying down, labouring to the limits of her strength, legs outstretched with the effort, in the process of calving. Or more accurately, in the process of trying, for her bulging, crazed eyes and her hoarse breathing showed how badly things were going.

Gripping a shiny, mucus-covered rope which disappeared beneath the animal's tail, two men were trying to extricate the calf. Surprised, for this was the first time she had witnessed such a scene, Béatrice had not at first understood what Dominique had shouted to her as he stripped to the waist.

'I bet you they haven't even checked!'

Then everything had happened very fast.

'Did you examine her internally before pulling like crazy?'

'Well, no, boss. Usually you pull and it comes of its own accord. The calf's big, that's the trouble!'

'For heaven's sake stop!' he had yelled.

On his knees in the soiled straw, he had plunged his arm into the animal, felt around, assessed the condition and position of the calf.

'Bloody imbeciles! You deserve to have *your* guts pulled out like that! And when I say your guts . . .'

'Why's that, boss?'

'Shut your face! The calf has its head folded back on itself, so you could pull forever!'

'Well, we saw the hoof sticking out a bit and as it didn't keep coming . . .'

'Idiots!'

His face contorted with effort, he had inserted his arm still further. And cursing them all the while, he had begun to push the calf back, to manipulate the neck into a normal position.

'And I'll knock the block off anyone who pulls before I tell him to!' he had threatened. 'My God, this is difficult . . . I can't manage it! Ah? Ah, yes I can! That's it! Pull, now. Not so hard, by God! They're cretins, these guys! There, gently. That's fine.'

And before Béatrice's fascinated eyes, more accustomed to childbirth than calving, the calf slid softly onto the bed of litter.

'And it isn't even big!' Dominique had ascertained as he cleaned his chest and arms with a handful of straw. 'Has nobody ever told you that you should never pull without knowing what's what?'

'Well, no, boss. We don't know much about it . . . That's what you're here for, after all!' one of the men had said with a good-natured laugh.

'These fellows drive me crazy!' he had shouted. But his temper had now cooled and he had politely asked for a bucket of water to wash himself.

After that performance Béatrice was no longer surprised when she saw him return to the bungalow covered in mud or dust. So that Friday afternoon, as Dominique and she sped down the track towards Route Nationale 2 which would lead them to Cayenne, Béatrice was not disconcerted when he suddenly stopped the Landrover on the edge of a field. Not far from them, rumbling smoothly, a huge John Deer pulling a three-share plough was opening furrows in the red soil.

'For God's sake tell me it's not true!' he muttered as he jumped from the vehicle. 'No, no, who's the bloody moron at the wheel?' He turned round, calling her to witness it: 'Do you see what I see?'

'Er . . . No,' she admitted. But she already suspected that her errands in Cayenne were in jeopardy, at least for the morning.

'But don't you notice anything?' he said as he took off his shoes. He dispatched his loafers to the back of the car, seized his boots and pulled them on. 'That fellow's ploughing without fixing the plough properly,' he explained as he stepped onto the turned strip and marched to the front of the tractor.

'Stop!' he yelled at the driver as soon as he drew level with him. 'Now come on, what sort of shambles do you think this is? Have you had a look at what you're doing, eh? What kind of work is this?'

'Well, it's ploughing, boss! It's going on fine!'

'Are you serious? So it doesn't worry you that you're ploughing three furrows thirty centimetres deep in one direction and fifteen deep in the other! And what's more the widths are all over the place! Now come on, it looks like a roller-coaster! You're not on a collective farm here, where anything goes! Come down from there!'

'Bah, it doesn't matter, boss!' said the driver, jumping onto the ploughed land. 'It's good soil, it'll grow fine crops! For sure, believe me!' he asserted with a broad smile.

'Matter! It matters to me! I don't like sloppy work, I'm paid to see it doesn't happen! Go on, get out your tool box . . . It won't take me long,' he reassured Béatrice who had just joined him, walking carefully across the stubble: she had no boots and did not want to spoil her town shoes. She smiled resignedly, for she already knew that he was going to get his hands covered in grease. Doubtless he would also dirty his trousers and shirt, and possibly even make a few serious tears in them!

'You've got some overalls in the car, do you want them?' she suggested.

He considered the work to be done, and shook his head.

'No it's not worth it, it'll only take five minutes,' he assured her. 'And you,' he said to the driver, 'hold that nut tight so that I can loosen the regulator. No, no! Not with that 22 spanner, it's at least 28! And you should be interested in learning how to adjust the hydraulic lifting system and how to use it! It's not just there for ornament, this lever! Nor to hang your lunch bag on!'

He busied himself with it for a few moments, judged it correctly adjusted, and climbed on to the tractor.

'Must test it . . .' he explained to Beatrice.

'Fine,' she agreed, 'I'll wait for you in the car.'

'No, stay there! You'll see the difference! Look what a properly balanced plough can produce!'

He engaged the gears, manipulated the hydraulic lifting system and started it rolling . . . He covered a dozen metres, made a face and stopped.

'It's not quite right,' he said, looking at his workmanship. 'Oh, it won't take much. The spanner!' he called to the driver, who was waiting patiently, sitting in the shade and smoking a small, bent-looking, foul-smelling, black cigar.

It was only after a further ten minutes that he considered himself satisfied. Then, for the sheer pleasure of ploughing, for the joy of leaving perfectly regular furrows in his wake in straight, shining, beautiful rows, he made three further trips up and down. He was almost sorry to return to Béatrice, who was reading in the car while she waited.

'It took a little time, but it was worth the trouble,' he assured her.

'A little time? That's your opinion!' she said, looking at her watch. 'It was only an hour and a half! Well, luckily I've got a good book!' she smiled, as she closed the latest historical novel by Troyat.

She saw that he was looking ashamed of himself, especially as he was so dirty that a return to the bungalow was imperative. 'It doesn't matter,' she comforted him, stroking his cheek with the back of her hand. 'You go and get changed. We'll go into town this afternoon. Or tomorrow . . .' she added.

Wisely, she realised that he could not help stopping the car if he chanced to notice some work which required him to intervene.

It was after returning from Cayenne, late in the evening, that Béatrice wanted to know. She wished to understand. Already bathed and refreshed, she had slipped under the mosquito net. She waited until he came out of the shower and called out:

'You'll really have to explain it to me, one day . . .'

'What's that?'

'Why you chose this profession?'

'You're joking?' he suggested, pouring himself a measure of rum punch which he diluted with sparkling water. 'Why I chose this profession? Because I like it! I even love certain aspects of it. But you're well aware of that! So you're teasing me?'

'Not at all. You know, I've been watching what you're doing, it'll be about ten months we've been here, that gives me time to notice things, doesn't it?'

'Of course. And so, did you come to the conclusion that I wasn't enjoying what I was doing?'

'No way! But I did notice that you're only really happy when you're hands on!'

'Explain.'

'It's obvious, isn't it? Well, tell me if I'm wrong: your job is to supervise the experiments, do the tests, analyses, reports, is that right?'

'Yes, what's the problem?'

'I haven't got one. It's you I'm talking about. I'll say it again, you're only really happy when you're on the land, like this morning on your machine. I saw you when you were ploughing; if I didn't know you well, it would almost have made me jealous!'

'But are you cray or what?' he said, lifting the mosquito net to see her better. He took the opportunity to stroke her breasts, and she gently slapped his fingers.

'Let down the net, I'll be eaten alive! That's exactly it, while you were ploughing, not only did you completely forget me, but it was almost as if you were involved with a woman!' she teased. 'To cut it short, I'm just trying to tell you that I'm worried,' she said, becoming serious again.

'But what's got into you?'

'We're going back to France in two months' time and you still don't know where your employers will be sending you. So, suppose they stick you in a purely administrative area, or even a laboratory, for example, what would you do?'

'I'd tell them to take two running jumps!'

'I expect you would. You need to be on the land, don't you?' she asked again.

'Yes.'

'So why aren't you working for yourslf on a farm? On your own farm, for instance?'

He was just taking a drink and she thought he would choke, he gave such a start. Then he let out a great laugh.

'On the farm? At Coste-Roche with Papa? That's the best thing I've heard this evening! No, that's impossible, my dear! For one thing the Vialhes have never succeeded in working together on the same farm! That's how we are, we each have our own ideas. I know it, Papa always said to me he couldn't have stayed long at Saint-Libéral with Grandfather. That's why he and Maman went and moved to Coste-Roche, for peace and quiet. And most of all so that they could be their own masters. And in my grandfather's time, I know that he didn't come back until my great-grandfather, Jean-Edouard, gave him a free hand. So you see why!'

'Possibly. But the main thing I see is that you might become impossible to live with if you happen to find yourself in an office one day!'

'Yes, maybe. But we haven't got to that yet! But tell me,' he asked suddenly, 'would you like to live on a farm?'

'You are fantastic, you know!' she said, smiling. 'What do you think we've been doing for the last ten months? And what's more, here it's not only full of creepy-crawlies and mosquitoes, but the farm and the land don't even belong to you!'

'All right,' he conceded after a few moments' thought. 'But you know, it's not really the same at all! Here, I have everything that's needed to conduct the experiments properly. I'm not saying that the purse is bottomless, but in the short term the profitability of the trials is not the chief problem. And what's more, here, even if it's often wayward, I have a considerable workforce at my disposal, and for free, at least to me!'

'That doesn't alter the fact that, in spite of your workforce, you're not happy unless you can get your hands dirty!'

'Agreed. And that's the best bit about the job! But it's not the most important part. Here, I'm on a salary and well paid. Thanks to which I can consider supporting a family. And I imagine it'll be the same as long as I'm with Mondiagri or any other company of the same sort.'

'You're trying to say that you'd die of hunger on a proper farm?'

'It would all depend on the farm. Anyway, I don't own one, and I haven't got the means to buy one either! And you know, even supposing – it's an incredible idea – that I set up with my father on the land in Saint-Libéral, it couldn't feed all of us! But I've already told you that.'

'Yes, but you still haven't told me what you'll do if one day you can't get your hands on a cow. Or, like this morning, jump on a tractor and enjoy some ploughing, even if it does mean forgetting me.'

'I haven't the faintest idea,' he spoke flippantly as he slipped under the mosquito net. 'Now while we're waiting for that unlikely day, I know what I'm going to do right away, so that you'll forgive me for forgetting you this morning.'

# 13

AFTER her painful experience with Gilles, Josyane vowed she would not let herself be fooled by smooth talkers again, especially if they suggested she go round the world with them!

Having burnt her fingers, she remained wisely on the defensive towards the males she steered from atoll to atoll. Although her steadily maintained reserve deterred the unwelcome, it brought her other surprises.

For instance, seeing her unresponsive towards men, a bisexual German woman with wandering hands invited her to share her hut. Another time, a Canadian woman shaped like a grizzly bear made her a direct offer, to 'set up home together' and come and move in with her at Fort Providence, on the shores of the Great Slave Lake! Josyane had not yet come to that.

Although she did not dislike her new way of life, she still found that on some days the loneliness was hard to bear. It was then that she caught herself re-reading all the letters which her parents were now sending regularly. Thanks to them she identified again with the life of the Viahle family in Saint-Libéral. And she realised just how important those ties of blood had become when, two months ago now, her heart sank as she read the first sentence of a letter from her mother:

> My dear Jo,
>     It is very sad news that I have for you today . . .

Mad with worry, she had immediately prepared herself to learn of the death of her grandfather or grandmother in Saint-Libéral. Her sorrow had almost prevented her from reading on, for she avowed a great love for the old couple who were so indestructible; to fear that this partnership might be broken was awful.

She had therefore felt somewhat ashamed at the relief she experienced shortly afterwards. For although the news was sad, Louis' death affected her less than the one she had dreaded. Not that she had ever disliked her cousin, but he was much older than her and did not live in Saint-Libéral. Besides, she had not seen him for years.

On the other hand, like Jean, she had been distressed to think of her Great-aunt Yvette, and was almost cross with herself for being so far away and unable to express all her affection. She had sent her a few lines, fearing they would have little effect on her sorrow.

But not all the letters were so tragic. Those from her Grandmother Mathilde for instance, were delightful, full of anecdotes, flavours of the Corrèze, titbits of news which it was nice to know. She spoke of the family, the neighbours, the fields and woods, the little crop of mushrooms brought on by the last rains, the walnuts which were beginning to drop. She also advised caution, rectitude, honesty. In short it was all evocative of times past, with an undercurrent of hope that she would soon be returning . . .

As for those from her Aunt Berthe, they were always full of spice, of advice which was never dogmatic, of humour and even slightly ironic asides on the advantages and disadvantages of celibacy! According to her, it was good to avoid shutting yourself away in solitude which might quickly become a burden. Equally good, after sowing your wild oats, going round the world, trying a little of everything, testing your character and trying your strength, not to forget that youth passes quickly and the time was coming when it would be important not to chop and change any more . . .

Josyane was increasingly convinced of this, and would have asked nothing better than to go and settle down at last in some corner of France. But her savings would not yet permit her to buy a ticket home.

She had been so pleased to find work in the Orohena Tour Agency that she had not even queried her salary, and besides, she had not been in a position to do so. It was low, for her employers reckoned that she was housed and fed by them during each trip. True enough, she had her bed and board on all the atolls the clients visited. By contrast she had to pay an exorbitant price to rent a hut, and also to feed herself, when she was staying in Papeete between two excursions; as a result there was not much left at the end of the month. She was therefore eyeing the two cameras more frequently, for selling them would probably allow her to fly off to France, so long as she did not let them go to the first Chinaman to come along!

On this particular day, resting between two waves of tourists, she was actually calculating the price she might get for them when someone knocked on the door. Thinking that her young Tahitian neighbour was making her customary visit – the teenager came for a chat as soon as she knew she was home – Josyane opened the door and almost bumped into a Bronica, the most beautiful camera in existence!

That gem is worth a fortune! she thought, before even looking at its owner. Then she realised there was a man, that he had a camera, and was immediately on her guard. The ghost of Gilles walked again!

'Are you Josyane Fleyssac?' asked the visitor.

She observed him without replying, found him very attractive, and decided to be still more cautious.

This fellow looks far too much like Paul Newman to be honest, she thought, without lowering her eyes. She was not going to let herself be influenced by this stranger's piercing blue gaze! She had seen others like it!

'Are you Jo?' he asked again.

'Josyane Fleyssac, yes,' she replied. 'Why?'

'I'm calling on behalf of your sister . . .'

This was increasingly incredible, and therefore dangerous.

'Which one?'

'Chantal, the one who works at Claire Diamond . . .'

'Chantal?' she murmured.

She suddenly felt very embarrassed, for there were tears in her eyes as she thought of her sister. She had not seen her for years and had not even written to her, except for two or three very bland postcards. Naturally she had news of her via Aunt Berthe, but it was overwhelming to discover that her sister was thinking of her to the extent of sending a messenger.

'A letter?' she stammered, forcing a smile to cover her disquiet.

'Yes,' he said, fumbling in his camera bag. She noticed an assortment of lenses, a Pentax, some boxes of film and the letter.

'I left Roissy airport last night,' he explained, holding out the envelope. 'With all the time changes, it's a dreadfully long journey!'

'Twenty-one hours, with a stopover in San Francisco,' she heard herself replying as she broke open the missive. 'Excuse me.'

'Of course.'

She sensed that he was watching her and was embarrassed yet again, for she had the feeling she was making a spectacle of herself.

'Sit down,' she suggested. 'And help yourself,' she said, giving him a glass and pointing out the bottle of fruit juice which was on the table. She needed him to stop watching her so that she could read in peace. She made sure he was no longer paying attention, and read:

My dear Jo,

According to Aunt Berthe, you're too hard up to return to the fold and too much a Vialhe to ask for help. Maybe Aunt Berthe is wrong, but I'd be surprised if she were, she has a nose for things, even at a distance. So, if you're fed up with playing the Tahitian maiden and dancing the tamouré, don't hesitate to cash the enclosed cheque. It will cover the journey. And don't be so stupid as to refuse. You can pay me back later. Try to be there for Dominique's wedding, we must make sure he celebrates it properly! See you soon.

Love and kisses,
Chantal.


P. S. Christian is an old friend, nothing more. I told him you could show him the good areas to get in the can. But don't bother if it's a nuisance, or if you really think he's an ugly pain in the neck.

Amazed, biting her lips so as not to cry for joy, she took the cheque out of the envelope. It was large enough to allow her to leave as soon as she chose. She noticed that her visitor was openly observing her, thought he looked mocking, and almost took a swipe at him.

But she was suddenly so relieved, so happy at the thought of her impending departure, that she crossed the three paces separating them and kissed him on both cheeks.

'To thank the postman! I'm so happy!' she gave as her excuse.

'So it would seem.'

'Do you know what was in the letter?'

'Some of it. From what your sister said, you must have been starting to find it a long haul. I have the impression that she's not far off the mark!'

'No, she's right.'

'At first sight it's hardly tough going here.' he said, indicating the garden full of flowers and birds.

'At first, no,' she admitted. 'And then . . . and then don't let's talk about it!' she decided. 'Are you a photographer?' she asked, suddenly remembering that she ought to be careful.

'Yes. That's why I'm here. I have an assignment to do on Mururoa. But beforehand I have time to cast an eye over Tahiti and a few of the atolls. They're worth seeing, aren't they? Your sister said you could maybe . . .'

'Of course. But it all depends what you want to see and what you can afford. Anyway, how do you know Chantal?'

'I take fashion photos too, I do everything!'

'Even porn I bet, you look the type!' she challenged him, remembering that Gilles had once told her it paid well. She had then advised him in no uncertain terms not to count on her as a model!

'No, not porn,' he said, amused. 'It's funny, your sister warned me, but you caught me out! Yes, she said: "Watch out; of the three of us,

Jo's the one who's quickest on the draw; like Butch Cassidy! You never know what she's going to come out with, or when!" '

'Do you know Gilles Martin?'

'No. Why, should I?'

'He's a photographer.'

'Which agency?'

'None, he works independently.'

'Gilles Martin?' he repeated. 'No, never heard of him. Although I've been almost fifteen years in the business, I don't think . . .'

'That doesn't surprise me, he's useless!'

'Well, if he's useless . . .'

'You just said that you've been a photographer for fifteen years?' she persisted.

She estimated that he must be older than he looked, and it was therefore important to be even more wary. For if, as well as looking like Paul Newman, he misled people about his age, he could be real trouble!

'Yes, I began in 1960, I was eighteen.'

'That's exactly what I was thinking . . .'

'Oh, right? I look that ancient, do I?'

'No, not at all! Well, yes! I mean . . . it doesn't matter. Eighteen, you say?'

'Yes, during the Algerian War. I enlisted. I was in the Army Film Unit. Photographer for the magazine *Le Bled*. I'm not making it up! Impressive, eh?' he joked.

'Well, in 1960 I was much younger.'

'I know. Your sister told me you're younger than her.'

'Oh, right. So Christian's your first name?'

'Yes, Christian Leyrac.'

'May I invite you to dinner? I owe you that much for the letter. We'll discuss what you want to see, okay?'

'Okay.'

'Which hotel are you at?'

'At the Taharaa.'

'Is that all? Every luxury!'

'What's the problem? My agency's paying!'

'So you must be a real photographer,' she decided. She examined him, nodded her head, realised that he wouldn't understand a thing she was about to say, but remarked all the same:

'Yes, a real photographer, that'll be a nice change!'

Jacques made sure that the ink had properly dried, closed the Civil

Register and shrugged resignedly. There were periods like this when everything conspired to undermine your morale.

For one thing his back was hurting, and even though that had become the norm it did not relieve the pain.

Then, yesterday evening, he had again clashed violently with Peyrafaure and those on the council who pretended not to understand that the village lacked money. He had nothing against them wanting to liven Saint-Libéral up a little, but he could not keep up with their schemes. For, following the tennis court, they were now proposing to compete with Ayen and create a holiday village on the plateau, no less.

In fact, Jacques knew for certain that Peyrafaure had his eye on his post as mayor. He was proposing an abundance of projects simply in order to be able to say, when the moment came: 'I myself suggested this and that which would have roused the community from its stupor, Vialhe rejected everything, he's incompetent!'

That loudmouth Peyrafaure is forgetting just one thing: the elections don't take place for another two years, and between now and then . . . And after all, the way things are going, there won't be many electors left! he thought, leafing through the Civil Register.

For it was not Peyrafaure and his babblings which worried him, nor his supporters; all of them would one day see that the Vialhes still had some backing and plenty of friends! No, the time had not come for Peyrafaure to don the sash of office. But what did it matter who was mayor if you were managing a cemetery!

That was the root of the problem. For the second time since the beginning of November, he had returned from escorting one of his electors to the grave. Two deaths in less than a fortnight, nine since the beginning of the year, without even counting poor Louis. It was getting frightening, worrying. And all the more so because there was not a single birth to inscribe in the register, and would not be in the whole of 1975. Given this situation, he looked a bit silly, Peyrafaure, with his tennis court and holiday village!

'He'd do better to start a funeral parlour, the fool!' he muttered as he rose.

He saw that his sister was regarding him with incomprehension.

'Don't worry, I'm rambling out loud!' he said.

Since her husband, who held the title of secretary, could not be there all the time on account of the twelve children attending the school, Mauricette acted as town clerk. She did not earn a sou for it, but found it more interesting to spend her time filling in a variety of administrative bumf or answering the telephone than to waste it by staying at home in front of the television. She dreaded inactivity and boredom in equal measures.

'What's the matter with you?' she asked. 'Is it your back?'

'Among other things. But if that were all! No, what gets me down is spending my life walking behind the hearse! I'm fed up with it, do you understand?'

'Of course, but maybe things will change!'

He nearly retorted roundly that she didn't know what she was talking about! That on the contrary, all the signs were that the situation would soon deteriorate, and if it continued in the same way, Saint-Libéral would be a ghost village in twenty years time! To tell her he was exasperated by the haughty indifference with which the public authorities left villages like Saint-Libéral to wither away, all over France! To share with her the bitterness which gripped him each time he had to write: *Deceased, on the* ... beside the name of a friend, a neighbour, an old acquaintance! To admit to her just how tired and demoralised he was, overseeing a community where the only really viable activity was the senior citizens' club! But he remained silent, for he did not want to spoil his sister's happiness.

During the last week, Mauricette had regained her *joie de vivre*, and so had Jean-Pierre. Their happiness since Josyane had announced her return was a delight to see. That was really good news for the whole family. It had elicited a gentle laugh from Berthe, lent Mathilde new energy, given Pierre-Edouard the excuse to pour himself a small glass of plum brandy, made Louise say that she knew young Jo would come back one day and roused Yvette to a real smile. A smile reaching her eyes which, for an instant, brought a little balm to the scar she bore on her heart.

'Yes, yes, maybe things will change,' he said, noticing once more just how much younger his sister looked.

'That reminds me,' she said, holding out a letter to him. 'You didn't tell me you'd been chasing up the Ayen police: it arrived this morning . . .'

'Ah? They replied?' he said, taking the document. He read it and shrugged: 'You can close the file, like the enquiry . . .'

'Surely that's not what they're saying!'

'No, but it comes to the same . . .'

'Did you write to them?'

'No, but I met the new inspector, the one responsible for the whole sector. He was at Objat the other day when Chastang received his Order of Merit for Agriculture. He was preening himself and boasting of all the cases he and his colleagues had chalked up for speeding or careless driving. You know, they had a special campaign on throughout the département. The great buffoon was really pleased to have trapped I don't know how many guys on the N89 road, and even on the 901!'

'I know,' she agreed. 'Marie-Louise Vergne got caught coming back from Terrasson: it made her really sick!'

'Exactly, he was irritating me, the fat sheep! So I told him that handing out fines was simpler and less tiring than finding church robbers!'

'You said it to him just like that?'

'Why shouldn't I! And can you imagine it, that nitwit wasn't even aware of what had happened! He listened to me, believe you me! The funny thing was, he didn't even know who I was. The sergeant from Ayen was killing himself laughing! He must have got a bawling-out later on. That'll be why he thought he'd better write. But you can close the file since it says *The enquiry is continuing* – It's hopeless, we'll never see poor old Saint Eutrope again!'

'Maman just can't accept that.'

'I know. But as we're talking of her, do you think she suspects anything?' he asked.

'About the wedding?'

'Yes. Do you think she's fooled?'

The closer it came to 20 December, the more afraid he was that his mother would discover there was to be no religious ceremony. He knew it was the sort of news which could ruin her happiness, and for a long time to come. And he had even written to Dominique conveying this. Not so that he would try to persuade Béatrice differently – he respected her opinion – but to warn him not to put his foot in it in front of his grandparents.

'Maman?' said Mauricette. 'Yes, I think she believes this story of a civil wedding in Paris on the nineteenth and the church one at Draguignan on the twentieth. But Papa, I wouldn't swear to it . . . I get the impression that he knows very well we're doing all we can to prevent either him or Maman being at the wedding!'

In truth, to avoid a fuss and having to explain to his parents why they could not possibly be at the wedding, since the journey was too long and tiring for his father, and therefore dangerous, Jacques had constructed one of those huge lies which would have left him blushing for the rest of his life, if he had not had the excuse of doing it all in a good cause. In collusion with Berthe, whom he really had to confide in as she had every intention of attending the wedding, he had explained that Béatrice had been born in the Midi, at her grandmother's, that the whole family were from there and it was therefore quite natural for her to marry there . . . As for the civil ceremony, since Béatrice was resident in Paris, it was logical to . . .

'Yes,' he said, 'I wouldn't bet my right hand that Papa is swallowing the story . . . I have the feeling that he knows much more about it than he's saying, and that goes for a lot of things!'

'But do you think he'd deny himself the pleasure of setting us straight?'

'No, of course not. But he keeps quiet for Maman's sake; well, that's what I believe.'

As soon as she had her ticket, and her seat booked on the flight on Thursday, 4 December, Josyane began to rediscover the bountiful charms of Tahiti. She no longer felt herself a prisoner, so life there became very pleasant again.

After informing her employers at the Orohena Tour Agency that she was leaving, she gave herself a few days' holiday. And, without dropping the guard she had sworn to maintain as far as Christian was concerned – this was not the moment to be ensnared by a photographer, even a real one – she agreed to show him the most beautiful parts of Tahiti.

It was on the evening of the second day, when he had invited her to dinner, that she agreed to accompany him to Moorea the next day. It was only ten minutes by plane or an hour by ferry.

'All right, that will let me make a last little pilgrimage, and of course it's so beautiful! But don't count on me after that. You're old enough to explore the other atolls on your own! Anyway, in three days' time it'll be adieu Polynesia for me!'

'I shall be bored!'

'I'd be very surprised! And I thought you were supposed to go to Mururoa.'

'Yes, that's the plan. But I'm waiting for my journalist friend. He's arriving at the end of the week, via Nouméa. So if you drop me tomorrow evening, I'll be at a loose end for three days, and that's the truth!'

'You're kidding! You don't look the sort who gets bored, wherever you might be!'

'I thought I was the sort who took pornographic photos!' he teased.

'Don't change the subject! Joking apart, if it's a girl you're after, you only have to say the word! That sort of person is quickly found in Papeete! And what's more, they love to be of service and give pleasure!'

'That's not what I meant,' he assured her.

'Yeah, that's what you say, but I don't believe a word of it!'

'Are you always as sharp as this?'

'Always!'

'Then I don't believe a word of it either! Anyway, that's your problem. Right, tomorrow we're going across to Moorea?'

'Yes, you'll see, it's worth the trip. Having said that it's like all the islands; you soon end up being bored by them.'

'Not as good as the Corrèze, eh?'

'No comparison,' she said with a shrug, 'and why do you say that, anyway?'

'Because of Chantal. She talks non-stop about that Godforsaken dump!'

'It's not a dump!' She cut in drily. She suddenly realised that he was teasing her, and smiled. 'It amuses you to make me lose my temper?'

'Aha! It's the same with Chantal; on that subject you can set her off in a trice, it's a real treat.'

'Do you know it?'

'What?'

'The Corrèze?'

'No. Well, yes, I've had to drive through, like everyone. But I must admit that I didn't notice anything special. Except perhaps that there are lots of bends!'

'You're a real berk, if that's all you're capable of remembering!' she shrugged dismissively.

'Don't get annoyed,' he said, placing his hand on hers, 'I was joking. I've promised myself I'll explore your region as soon as I can. Do you know why?'

'Because Chantal talked to you about it.'

'Yes, but not only that. Now I'm not joking when I tell you this next bit. My great-grandfather was born in the Brive area, but I don't know where.'

'Ah, that's where the name Leyrac comes from, then?'

'Probably. My mother told me that he was supposed to have owned a tiny farm south of Brive, not far from the River Lot. She didn't know anything else about it. She had that from my paternal grandfather.'

'And you've never tried to find out any more?'

'Well, no. I have to admit it's not that simple,' he said evasively.

She saw that he was hesitant about speaking, as if he feared to bore her with family stories.

'Come on then, tell me! That is, if you want to. After all, it's a free country! We can just as well talk about cooking or photography!'

'Oh, there's no secret,' he said. 'I don't know very much, because there's no one left to tell me about it, that's all.'

'Oh, I see . . .'

'Yes, my mother died five years ago, and she was the only one left who knew anything.'

'And your father?' she ventured to ask.

'He died in Dachau, in July '44.'

'Oh! I'm so sorry,' she murmured, placing her hand in turn on his. She drew it away as if she had burned herself: 'Excuse me,' she added.

'It's not your fault! I was just explaining. If he had lived, I'd have known where my ancestor came from. All my mother told me was that he went off to Chile, in the 1870s I believe. To seek his fortune! Can you imagine it? They had big ideas, those fellows then! But it worked! To prove it, it seems he ended up owning a hacienda of I don't know how many thousands of hectares! And he'd also earned a fair bit by going up to work on the Panama Canal! In short, that allowed him to pay for my grandfather's education. He was born out there. He came to France and left again as a qualified agricultural engineer, to take charge of the estate.'

'Oh, him as well!'

'Why him as well?'

'Because one of my cousins is an ag type, that's all. But why are you here, then? You should be Chilean!'

'Logically, yes. But would you believe it, my grandfather wanted to return to France to take part in the war in 1914! I'm telling you, they had grand ideas, those old people! He could have stayed out of trouble on his hacienda, but no: at the first shot from the guns, he reappeared! With my grandmother in tow. He set her up in Bordeaux and left to enlist, at the age of forty-two!'

'Maybe he knew my grandfather from Saint-Libéral,' she smiled. 'He served right through the war too. And then?'

'My father was born in 1915. My grandmother died of the Spanish 'flu, in 1918, in Bordeaux. As I understand it, my grandfather found a job as steward of some vineyard, one of the best vintages, I don't know where. That's it.'

'And he didn't leave anything behind, any documents?'

'No. I have to say he didn't like it much when my mother remarried in '48. He broke off all connection with her . . . Anyway, with my mother and her husband, we were living in Paris and he was in Bordeaux! He died in 1950, I was eight and I hardly remember it.

Pity, he could at least have told me which corner of the Corrèze the Leyracs came from! And my father, too, would have told me . . .'

'It's funny, all that,' she murmured. 'Oh, I beg you pardon!' she continued. 'That's not what I meant.'

'I know,' he reassured her.

'Yes, I meant to say: it's strange, families. We, on the Vialhe side, can trace our ancestors back through several centuries. We're all from the same area. On my father's side it's almost the same. When I'm over there, I'm really at home, on our land. What I'm saying is a bit pretentious, but it's true, whereas you . . .'

'Yes, but it's no big deal! I was born in Paris, like my mother, as for the rest . . . I certainly don't lose any sleep over it! But all the same, it's interesting that we're here in Papeete, in the French Antipodes, busy discussing the area the Leyracs come from, which I don't even know!'

Engrossed in her happiness at returning to France, Josyane decided that Christian's absence at Faaa airport was of no importance. Besides she really had done everything to prevent him feeling obliged to come and say goodbye before she left.

Obviously it was a little remiss on his part. He could at least have stirred himself to thank her once more for having introduced him to Tahiti and Moorea much better than he could have done it by himself. But his absence proved that he was just the creep she had thought, and that she had been right to mistrust him. Her instinct had not betrayed her; all was well.

Having checked in her baggage, she turned towards the boarding gate and was about to go through when she changed her mind. After all, maybe he hadn't been able to find a taxi?

But no, that was silly. He had hired a car. So he had no excuse. She looked at the huge clock in the hall, hesitated, then smiled suddenly as she spied him coming towards her with a fistful of shell necklaces.

'According to what I've been told, that's the custom here, when someone leaves!' he said, placing the garlands around her neck.

'Yes, that's the custom,' she murmured, blushing.

She was furious with herself. Furious for having waited for him and especially about the fuss he was making which, she felt, must be noticed by all the people there.

'It was high time,' she forced herself to say, 'I was just going to go through passport control.'

'I would have regretted it for the rest of my life!' he said, camping it up. 'No, but joking apart, I hate long goodbyes. So I always arrive at the last moment. Even if it means lying in wait in a corner and launching myself on my quarry at the last second!' he added, laughing.

'You're quite capable of doing a thing like that! But this really is the last minute! Listen: they're calling us for boarding.'

'Very good. But you'll still give me a kiss?' She did not have time to move and he placed a kiss on each cheek: 'And thank you again for the guided tour, it was perfect. Talking of which, if I come to the Corrèze and you happen to be there, will you act as my guide again? Yes?'

'In the Corrèze?' she murmured. 'If I'm there? Okay.' She fingered the necklaces adorning her: 'And thank you for these,' she said.

She gave a little wave of her hand, and walked away without looking back.

# 14

'DON'T you catch cold on me!' warned Pierre-Edouard, lifting his nose out of his newspaper. He made sure Mathilde was wrapping up warmly before going out to feed the ducks and geese, and called to Louise: 'And you too, wrap up well! My God! It's cold this morning, the pond is covered in ice. You're going to get frozen, both of you!'

'Don't worry so! We're not made of sugar!' Louise reassured him.

'Wrap up warm, I tell you!' he persisted. 'What an idea, to have such a flock to feed up!'

'Oh stop it! You don't say that when you take seconds of confit de canard or foie gras! Even though you're not allowed either because of your cholesterol!' said Mathilde, grasping the bucket of steeped maize which was warming not far from the hearth.

'The doctor's an ass!' he declared, immersing himself once more in his reading.

He waited until the two women had gone out, and glanced towards Berthe. Absorbed in doing her crossword puzzle, she did not seem to have heard him. That annoyed him and aggravated his ill humour. He had been very low for some time.

To begin with he had a cold, and Doctor Martel had forbidden him to go out, and also to smoke! He took no notice of that and, to get some peace and not hear the women's scolding, he went out in the courtyard whenever he felt the urge to smoke a pipe.

But the fact that he was unable to take his daily walk annoyed him a great deal. He missed his short hour of exercise, as well as the conversations with any neighbour he met and especially the confidences exchanged with Berthe. But she was complying with Doctor Martel's orders, and had refused to accompany him for three weeks now. It was infuriating, for he did indeed feel rather too weak to venture all alone up the steep path to the plateau.

'The doctor's an ass!' he repeated, impatiently folding his newspaper. He threw it on the table, immediately in front of his sister: 'Do you hear what I say? The doctor's an ass!'

'Yes, and so what? You say that twenty times a day. That won't start him braying, luckily!'

'And, what's more, all of you, you treat me like an ass too!' he shouted, getting up. He moved over to the window, checked that Mathilde and Louise were indeed in the barn, busy force-feeding the ducks: 'Like an ass! Absolutely! Are you listening to me, eh?'

For it was that in particular which was spoiling his temper; the near-certainty that something was being hidden from him, that someone was trying to deceive him.

It was Jacques and Mauricette especially who had started him thinking. Both of them were too eager to divert certain topics of conversation, to dodge his questions. At the same time they were also almost too cheery to be true. Certainly they had every reason to be happy. First little Jo was expected daily, and Dominique and his fiancée would be there in a week.

Despite that, Pierre-Edouard felt there was something mysterious going on, and he did not like it. Even Yvette seemed to have joined in hoodwinking him. She was feeling better, Yvette, that was very good: she had returned to the château, and spent a lot of time on the Léon Dupeuch Association. Yes, she was getting better. But that was no excuse for siding with those who wanted to take him for a ride. For he was almost certain that they were trying to fool him. And the worst of it was that even Berthe had gone over to the enemy, the guardians of the secret!

'I was speaking to you,' he said, seeing that she had returned to her crossword. 'Why do you take me for an ass?'

She sighed, smiled, and lit a cigarette.

'You know, you're a dreadful bore!' she said. 'Come on, make the most of my smoking to fill a little pipe, Mathilde won't be back for a while.'

'What a stupid idea, all those animals to force-feed! Now you answer me, right? I know you're hiding something from me. Is it so serious?' he asked as he lit his pipe. 'Is it so serious? Answer me, for God's sake!'

'No, no, it's not serious! That's exactly why I didn't tell you anything . . .'

'I really don't like that! Not at all! Who's got problems? Young Jo? She's not coming back? She's set off again for Patagonia or somewhere?'

'Not at all, she's landing tomorrow evening at Roissy.'

'So she's expecting a baby and the father has run off, is that it?'

'My poor Pierre,' she said, bursting into laughter, 'for donkey's years young people have only had the children they want! Even in my time all you needed was a bit of skill . . . So think of it now, them with their pill! No, she's not pregnant. Well, I don't think so. No, that's not it. All right then, it's not you they're trying to protect, it's Mathilde.'

'Mathilde? Come on then, it's that serious?'

'Mmm, it all depends how important you think these things are . . .'

'Right then, tell me straight out, that's enough beating about the bush!'

'It's to do with the young people's wedding. It's this – they're only getting married at the registry office, that's all.'

'Ah, I see,' he said, nodding his head. He meditated for a while, moved nearer to the fire to spit: 'That's why you don't want us to go to it, I understand! So okay, you're right. Mathilde mustn't know, it would depress her too much! And what about Louise?'

'The same, she doesn't know.'

'All right. Let's hope it lasts. But why are they doing that, the young people? Does it embarrass them to go into a church?'

'The girl doesn't believe in it, you can't force her!'

'Of course not,' he murmured. 'But Mathilde absolutely mustn't find out that they're marrying like heathens. It would spoil all her pleasure, you understand?'

'You're telling me, why do you think we're taking so much trouble to keep it from her!'

'True, true. But me, you could have told me!'

'Don't pretend it doesn't hurt you a bit!'

'Well yes,' he admitted, 'but all the same, I'd have preferred to know.'

It was true. Of course he was saddened to discover that his eldest grandson was not following in the Vialhe tradition. This held that men should go to church at least twice a year, celebrate their first Communion there, marry there, have their children baptised and be buried there. Everyone had abided by this until now, and with good grace. And here for the first time was a Vialhe breaking with custom; it was distressing. Despite that, he did feel in a better mood after his sister had told him. He considered he still had the right, and even the duty, to know everything concerning his family, even if it was not always very good for his heart . . . He drew a last puff, tapped his pipe on the top of the andiron, and subsided onto the settle.

'While you're at it, have you anything else to tell me?' he continued.

'No, isn't that enough for you?'

'Yes, it is.' He reflected, and then suddenly realised: 'But then, as I understand it, you're only going to Paris, not to the Midi?'

'Yes. Anyway, there's nothing happening in the Midi. When we talked of Draguignan, it was because that would be too long a journey for you. Paris is too near, you'd have wanted to go there, and as there'll only be a civil ceremony . . .'

'Well, well, you're a fine pack of liars! Oh, you villains! But who had the idea of this wedding miles away?'

'Jacques and Mauricette . . .'

'I see. Ye Gods! Such big liars, they get that from their mother! It's the Dupeuch side coming out! Yes it is! Léon was like that too. Ooh, the wretches! Right, not a word, Mathilde's coming,' he said, hearing the sound of feet on the steps outside.

'You were right, it's terribly cold,' she said as she came in. She shook herself, took off her coat and moved over to the fire to warm her hands. 'You, you've been smoking,' she said abruptly.

'Me? No, no! I give you my word! It was Berthe. Eh, it was you, wasn't it Berthe?'

'You know very well that Doctor Martel forbade it!'

'Martel is an ass,' he cut in.

He winked at Berthe and began to laugh quietly.

It was always with a certain regret, an underlying sadness, that Dominique left his work in progress. Already in the Sahara, fifteen months earlier, it was with a feeling of frustration that he had left to others the observation of his experiments and the trouble of continuing them properly. And yet over there he had had the time to watch the development of the crops and the growth of a flock, to test the validity of his plans, the accuracy of his predictions. He had been able to establish that his work was useful. But here, in Guyana, he had hardly had time to get used to the climate, the way of life, the mentality of the inhabitants. As for getting to know the land, its reactions and capabilities, it was impossible to discover its secrets in twelve months; he had barely even glimpsed them. It was annoying.

'You must understand, I do like to see the results of my work,' he explained to Béatrice whilst helping her pack. 'It's true, isn't it? What's the good of sowing if you can't reap it! And that's what's happening. What's more, my successor may chuck all my work away!'

'All the same, you need to sort out what you want,' she said. 'I don't think two days have passed without me hearing you moaning about this wretched country, the rain, the mud, the creepy-crawlies, just about everything!'

'Granted, I must say I've adjusted pretty badly to this dump,' he admitted. 'But you, I take my hat off to you! I've never heard you complain!'

'You know, after the bush clinic where I was working in Upper Volta, this is paradise!'

'So you've often told me. Well I hope there's a less humid paradise than this one waiting for us!'

'It'll soon be sorted out now.'

'Let's hope so!' he sighed.

That too did not improve his temper. He had a horror of uncertainty. For, despite his letters to Mondiagri's Paris office, it was still impossible to find out where he was to be sent. And as the firm had branches throughout the world, apart from the Eastern Bloc . . .

'They'll have to tell you something, won't they?' she said.

'Of course. But I've already explained to you, the annoying thing about these big companies is that they feel obliged to use a system which softens up the managers, by leaving them to stew without knowing where they're going! Okay, we're well paid, but that's not my style! And if they rub me up the wrong way any longer, they'll see what a Vialhe temper is like!'

'You know, I believe they couldn't care less! Come on, be a good boy, stop grumbling and help me close this trunk instead, I can't manage it.'

He came to her aid, pressed down their things and closed the lid.

'That's that job done!' he said, then walked out on to the terrace of the bungalow.

Night was about to fall, but he could still make out the huge man-made prairie in front of him, where a herd of cattle were grazing. And over to one side, the illuminated cowshed hummed with the motors of the milking-machines. Still further off the jungle pulsed, rustling with the animals and insects which wake at night. He sensed that Béatrice had joined him, and drew her close.

'You see,' he said, 'if it weren't for this damned climate, all this rain and those mosquitoes, it would be fine here. The soil is good and there's some good work to be done, isn't there? Look how beautiful that herd is!'

'Come on now! You're not going to regret leaving at this point?'

'No. What I regret is going away without having finished what I began . . .'

'If you stay with Mondiagri, that'll happen to you a few more times!'

'Bound to. But it's hard to come to terms with it, it's not in my nature.'

874

'Your peasant nature?' she joked. 'Yes, I've known you were really a peasant at heart for a long time now. Lots of qualifications, but still a peasant!'

'Probably. But I hope that won't stop you marrying me? Well, you can still reconsider!'

'Bah, look how I've compromised myself with you!' she teased, pressing against him. 'Besides, I want to. Yes, I'm really very pleased to be marrying someone whose expression and voice change when he talks of the land, it's reassuring.'

Josyane had felt cold for two days. Barely out of Roissy, in penetrating drizzle driven by a bitter wind, she had realised just how pleasant it was to wear light clothing and live in a climate which was always equable. The cold had taken hold of her and would not release its grip.

Even the comfortable two-room flat in the Rue de Berri where Chantal lived had seemed to her badly heated, which was far from being the case. Nevertheless, it had needed all her sister's warmth and welcome to bring her out of her shivering numbness, to revive her cheerful energy.

And yet their first contact had felt rather strange. Without immediately admitting it, they were neither of them as they remembered each other.

Josyane preserved the memory of Chantal as a tall dark girl with hardly any make-up, long hair, and sometimes a slightly timid appearance. She discovered a very beautiful woman, extremely soignée, with short blonde hair, impressively elegant, sure of herself. As for Josyane, Chantal had seen her leave almost four years earlier, still rather childlike and gauche. She returned radiating self-confidence, tanned, determined, very beautiful too, although dressed like nothing on earth.

'I don't know if I'd have recognised you in the street,' Chantal had eventually admitted.

'The same goes for me! You're blonde now, and what style!'

'And you, you used to be rather skinny and pale, you're so brown it shouldn't be allowed, especially in December. And just look at your figure!'

That evening, after telephoning their parents, the two sisters had chatted away until long past midnight. They had so much to tell each other, to hear about each other. Only tiredness due to the journey and the time change had overcome Josyane and stemmed the flow of her questions. On meeting her sister again she had discovered with emotion that her family ties were much stronger than before her departure. She had wanted to break them by going off on impulse one day, in order to liberate herself, to assert herself. She did not regret a moment of it, but realised now that some roots could not be torn up, and that was as it should be.

'Are you settling down or going off again?' her sister asked her the following evening.

Exhausted, Josyane had slept fifteen hours without a break and although she felt much better she was still permanently cold.

'No, I'm not going off again.'

'It was rather crazy, you know, to stay away so long, you gave our parents some grey hairs . . .'

'Sure . . . But you know, you need to be able to come back . . . You say they've aged a lot?'

'That's putting it mildly. But don't blame yourself, I played a part in it, and so did Marie . . .'

'That's true. I heard from Aunt Berthe. You know, I'd never have believed it, I'd have thought Patrick pleasant. But of course, I didn't know him very well.'

'Yes. And as Aunt Berthe says, it's not you who's involved with him! Poor Marie, she didn't deserve such a jerk! Dead boring, that guy!'

'I'd never have believed it . . .'

'But just imagine it! He spent the evenings counting up his retirement credits. "In thirty-two years I'll opt out!" he used to say. Stick-in-the-mud, that guy was, snoring away. And what's more, depressing, a real kill-joy! Well what can you say, an economics teacher!'

'You're exaggerating!'

'No I'm not! Heavens, I'm sure he thought of his retirement even when he was in bed. Marie had good reason to dump him! I wouldn't have put up with him for a weekend! But all the fuss didn't suit our parents. And as I contrived to upset them as well . . .'

'You? How?'

'Oh! Enough of that! I don't have to draw you a diagram, do I? To our parents I'm a loose woman, end of story. As Grandfather said to Aunt Berthe one day, it was she who reported it to me: "That Chantal, she needs a good hobble!"'

'Oh yes!' Josyane was amused. 'That enormous log that was hung from the cows' necks to prevent them jumping the fences!'

'That's it. Anyway, you've come back, that's the main thing.'

'Talking of which, I'm going to pay you back two-thirds of the fare right away, and if you can wait a bit for the rest . . .'

'I can wait for the lot. Pay me back when you have a job. But do you have any ideas about that?'

'Not a lot. Of course I could try to find a job in a travel agency, I've got to the stage where I know enough . . . After all, I could give the customers information about a fair number of countries . . .

'That's not very exciting!'

'Or I could launch into photography. I have some quite beautiful and original photos, I think. Well, I say that, but you have to find magazines or agencies who might be interested, and there . . .'

'Is it Christian who gave you that idea?'

'Not at all! I didn't wait for him to teach me how to hold a camera!'

'Don't be so touchy! Come on, admit at least that he's an attractive man.'

'Yes, rather too much so! And then he's old!'

'Old? Well . . . But he's nice, isn't he?'

'At first sight, yes. But I know him less well than you. I took him around a bit in Tahiti like you asked me to, that's all. Look, would you have a slightly warmer top, I'm freezing.'

And now that she was dozing on the train travelling towards Brive, Josyane wondered what had made her change the subject. At times she was almost annoyed with herself for having wasted a good opportunity to learn a little more about Christian. But on balance she was still quite proud of having kept to the code of conduct she had decided on – discretion.

When he had announced the date of his wedding and warned his parents that there would be only a civil ceremony, Dominique had also thought that it would be a small one. He was a little upset about it; if the decision had been his alone, he would have happily led Béatrice to the altar and invited the whole family to the celebration afterwards.

However, as he saw in his fiancée's decision proof of her honesty and her rejection of hypocrisy – she could have submitted to a religious ceremony and pretended to be as reverent as a child making her first Communion – he had not tried to talk her into it. Actually, he had been amazed to discover that she was more outspoken than him on many issues. In any case, it was not the concept of God she was rejecting, but the way men manipulated Him.

'When I was a girl,' she had told him, 'I already had great difficulty in accepting the moral precepts imposed on us. All right, I was already a troublemaker, but I always saw them as an expression of hypocrisy rather than faith. So I'm not about to support those sort of rituals now!'

She had understood that he was a little disappointed, and had continued: 'And now, be honest! You know very well we're living in fornicaton and sin in the eyes of those who've established the rules which I reject. And you're a damned liar if you dare say you regret it!'

'I don't regret anything. It's just that I think a religious ceremony which seals a promise is more serious than a boring administrative procedure, recorded by any old deputy mayor who doesn't give a damn about us, or we about him!'

'Possibly. But I prefer that to deceit; yes, deceit! If I believe my catechism, which is yours too, and if my memory serves me, to get married in church we'd need to attend confession. Well I've no desire to lie by going to tell some priest, preferably a deaf one, that I repent of cohabiting with you for a year, that I'm sorry I was in seventh heaven in your company without the approval of some father of the church! Count me out of that sort of masquerade!'

'Okay. All right, put like that, you're right.'

'So, what's the problem?'

'There's no problem. I'm thinking of my grandparents, that's all. They'll never understand your arguments. Well, my grandmother especially, and as I love her dearly . . .'

'Don't worry, they won't know anything about it ever.'

'And your parents?'

'My father doesn't care. As for my mother, she's considered me a tool of Satan since she discovered I was living in the sin of the flesh, that is, for ages now! But I don't bear a grudge against her. I'm sure that my position allows her to indulge her devotions even more and to pass for a saint, not to say a martyr, in the eyes of her friends! She's always enjoyed that sort of role, she adores spiritual improvement! So why deny her that pleasure!'

'Right, fine. But I hope you don't still want a wedding with all the trimmings?'

'No. As quiet as possible would be best. On condition, of course, that I don't deprive you of the pleasure of giving me a beautiful ring and a honeymoon worth the name!'

It was after this discussion that he had written to his parents and proposed that they alone should travel up to be present at the exchange of vows. So he was very surprised and moved when he discovered, on the morning of 20 December, that his Aunt Berthe, with the co-operation of Guy and Colette, had organised everything for a proper family celebration, fitting for the wedding of the eldest Vialhe grandson.

That added to his happiness and good humour. He had at last found out, two days earlier, that Mondiagri was sending him for three years to one of the experimental farms they owned in Tunisia. And that was a piece of good news.

Mathilde thought that the little saint looked rather ugly, and she turned him slightly to hide his injuries. He had a chipped nose, his right hand was cut off at the edge of the sleeve and his paint was flaking off. He was almost frightening, which was not his raison d'être!

With his arms raised to the sky showing amazement, and his angelic smile, he stood spellbound in ecstasy in front of the crib. In order to encourage all the faithful to imitate him. To invite them to worship the plump-cheeked doll which in four days' time would be lying on the straw, between the ox with only three legs left and the donkey minus an ear and a tail!

'Our crib is really like our parish: it's pathetic,' murmured Mathilde, arranging a few tufts of moss at the feet of the Virgin Mary.

Even she looked a little sad, for her colour had long vanished, allowing reddish patches of the terracotta she was made of to show through here and there. Only Saint Joseph, two shepherds and three sheep were presentable. On condition that they were never placed side by side. They were not to the same scale, and the good carpenter would be transformed into a dwarf and the lambs into fat curly calves as soon as they got near each other.

'And for goodness sake don't put down too much straw, you know what'll happen!' Louise reminded her.

'Don't talk of calamities!' interrupted Mathilde as she delicately dusted a shepherd's brown robe.

She had not forgotten. Twelve years earlier, the unfortunate fall of a candle had almost transformed the crèche into a blazing inferno. Luckily the fire had broken out during Midnight Mass and, as chance would have it, the large font was also full. The volunteer firemen had the blaze under control before it reached the big lumps of wrapping paper which were supposed to represent the rocks of Palestine.

However, the incident had completely disrupted the service and the children had taken the opportunity to run wild. As for old Julienne Lacroix, who had just entered her ninetieth year, she had been so frightened that she had to be put to bed immediately after the consecration of the host! Her robust constitution had quickly recovered from this, but she had nevertheless decided not to attend such a dangerous church any more. She had kept to her resolution until her burial four years later!

'Here, pass me the miller,' requested Louise.

'But my dear, you know that the kids in the catechism class broke him last year!' Mathilde reminded her, raising her voice, for her sister's deafness was not improving.

'Oh, that's right. The longer it goes on the smaller it gets. When I think of what it was like once upon a time . . .,' murmured Louise, contemplating the whole crèche with sadness.

For almost twenty years now she and Mathilde had taken responsibility for arranging the crib each year. They knew that the children would be impatiently waiting for it to appear, even if there were fewer and fewer of them grouped around it for the Christmas Mass.

And the last few parishioners also liked to meditate in front of the figures. For even if they were a little damaged, a little lame and always sparser on the ground, they were still the ones which they had marvelled at sixty or eighty years earlier, in the days when, in the crowded church, the Limousin Carol rang out at the end of the third Mass at midnight: *Awake you shepherds, leave your flocks to go to Bethlehem . . .*

Now only a few old ladies still remembered the words. But they did not dare even to hum them; they feared the priest would not understand.

And yet Father Soliers, who had served the parish for five years now, was a good man. To be sure, he celebrated Sunday Mass on a Saturday, began the midnight service at eight-thirty in the evening and completed it at nine-fifteen! He dispatched the burials and marriages at breathtaking speed. But at least he had never objected to the crib.

He was not like that clergyman who had turned up in the village in the mid 1960s. Certainly he had the excuse of being young, of having everything to learn about country ways and being responsible for six or seven other parishes. Very concerned to revitalise his flock and to announce to them that the moment for changes and reforms having come at last, he considered it necessary to sweep away a whole heap of antiquated customs . . .

But that was not sufficient reason to dress like a tramp and feel obliged to have two or three drinks at Nicole's, with the sole aim, he

880

assured them, of meeting the men in their normal suurroundings! No reason either to launch into long tirades of coarse language, and even some swearwords, when his little red motor-bike refused to start! No reason, in particular, to dare tell Mathilde and Louise one December day that he did not want a crib because it was a childish form of a faith forever gone, and smacked somewhat of fetishism, not to say superstition. True faith was expressed through involvement and action in the world, not through narrow-minded and repetitive devotions in front of plaster figurines, whose ugliness was rivalled only by their sickly sentimentality!

On that day Mathilde had seen red, as she had thirty years before, when Father Delclos had thought fit to meddle in matters which she considered private.

'I'm sixty-six years old! There has always been a crib in this church for me to see, here at the foot of our Lady of Lourdes. I've been arranging it for years! And neither you nor anyone else will prevent me from doing so! And if necessary, I shall call on all the men of the parish! They'll come and help me to install the crib, every single one of them!'

He had mumbled some vague comments about latent paganism still prevalent in the countryside, but he had not dared demolish the crèche when he had returned a week later. He had simply avenged himself meanly in his sermon by insinuating that Vatican II had come at the opportune moment, to sweep away all the retrograde and outdated practices which certain people confused with faith and felt obliged to perpetuate . . .

Luckily this reformer in grimy jeans and unbuttoned shirt had not lasted long in the area. He had disappeared one day, and nobody had been sorry.

Three years later Mathilde had happened to learn that he had married a girl of eighteen. She had been deeply distressed by this. God be praised, she had not had any further problems with his successors! Even if Father Soliers did not come often and kept strange hours, he had not objected to the crib any more than to the angelus bell or reciting the rosary; that at least was something!

Mathilde positioned a last tuft of moss and stood back to admire the crèche. All the little figures were in place, turned towards the empty, peaceful manager, which would soon be occupied by the Infant Jesus.

'Seen from a distance it's still beautiful,' she said.

'If you think so . . . But there aren't enough figures. Tell me, do you think we can use the sky again? It's all torn!' asked Louise, bringing out of the cupboard a large, dusty, dark-blue board sprinkled with stars.

'Of course! We'll clean it, and with a bit of sticky paper it will do!' Mathilde assured her optimistically.

Since the beginning of the month she had recovered her good humour and joie de vivre. It was enough for Jo to arrive one evening and come to kiss her, for happiness to reign once more in the household. For Jean-Pierre and Mauricette to shed their worried expressions, for Pierre to grumble a little less, and smiles to flourish again amongst all the Vialhes.

And the wonder was that it had all happened without any acrimony or bitterness, as if no one held it against Josyane for having stayed away so long. She was back, that was the main thing. The rest was no longer important, reproaches were no longer in order.

Admittedly she was so changed, so mature, that all the reprimands prepared and rehearsed over more than three years had become obsolete. The criticism which had built up was aimed at a girl who had left on the spur of the moment. It could no longer be applied to the returning adult. To want to do that would have been just as ridiculous and silly as scolding her for having pinched some jam fifteen years earlier!

Pierre-Edouard had immediately understood. And yet, if anyone was prepared to tell the prodigal that she had overstepped the mark, it was he. He had seen how her disappearance had affected Mathilde, and normally he could not bear her to be hurt. And he could not tolerate either that his daughter should have suffered such a long and demoralising wait.

Despite that, since he had guessed in an instant that his grand-daughter had already learned her lesson long ago, he had suppressed the choice sentences of biting irony which he had resolved to fire off as soon as he saw her. And it was without anger, but still with gravity, that he had welcomed her.

'So there you are, my girl? You certainly took your time on your little walk, didn't you?'

'Well yes, grand-père, it took me further than I thought . . .'

'But you didn't get lost because here you are. That's good. You know, there's nothing to stop you going a long way away, but the important thing is to find the road home again . . . And now come and kiss me. You've grown so beautiful and you look so much like your grandmother that I feel sixty years younger!'

Mathilde had been relieved that it all passed off in this way, and added to the happiness of having seen Josyane come back there was the delight in Dominique's return.

Naturally she would have been even happier if she could have attended his wedding. But that was really impossible, too far and too tiring. Besides, it did not matter whether she and Pierre-Edouard were at the celebration. What counted was that on that very day, 20 December 1975, fifty-seven years after his grandparents and twenty-nine years after his parents, Dominique Vialhe was finally marrying the companion he had chosen to accompany him on life's journey and perpetuate the Vialhe name. God willing!

# 15

WITH the arrival of spring, very early, Pierre-Edouard had recovered a dynamic energy which amazed him. Admittedly he had passed an excellent winter, without even a cold, and his spirits were in good shape. During the last fortnight, he had therefore resumed his daily walks all by himself. Wisely, he ventured much less far than previously, hardly strayed from the well-used paths, hesitated to step beyond the edge of the woods, and stopped frequently to catch his breath. But he then took the opportunity to revel in the scenery.

On this last Sunday in March the countryside was magnificent, ready to unfold, to embark on an orgy of greenery and flowers. Already the birds, deceived by the warmth of a balmy sun, were calling from bushes and groves, attempting trills and cantatas, showing off. Even the cuckoos and the hoopoes, which had arrived in the last two days, were competing with oft-repeated calls which echoed throughout the woods, spreading the news far and wide that spring was really here.

On all sides, in gentle touches which grew day by day, the tender green of the buds, sticky with sap, were prevailing over the pearl grey of the still leafless branches. And here and there, in the hollows of the little valleys, on the edge of the pools, or along the winding course of the Diamond, fat clumps of pale yellow willow shoots were bursting out, all bordered with catkins. Even the poplars were attempting some colour and holding up to the sun the slim and trembling fingers of their opalescent flowers.

Humming busily and as if confused by all the scents emanating from all sides, thousands of bees were launching an attack on the corollas, forcing them open sometimes, then slipping in to reach the stamens and feast on the constantly renewed supply of nectar.

'Tiens! Even they've arrived!' Pierre-Edouard smiled as his eyes followed the dizzy arabesques of a red-throated swallow. Then he watched a bee frantically trampling over a broad dandelion flower which had opened like the August sun. Already two fat balls of orange pollen sticking to its back legs were weighing it down, making its search rather clumsy.

He thought that he was going to have to ask Jacques for a hand to visit the hives, clean them out, mend some of the frames and maybe feed them a little if the brood cells were too numerous. With such an early, warm spring, there was the danger that the queens might have already started intensive egg-laying, so that if by ill-luck the cold should return . . .

'Because you can never be sure of anything until the Ice Saints' Days!' he always said.

So whilst happy to enjoy the mild temperatures and magnificent weather, he could not help fearing some damaging cold spells. The moon would be reappearing on the thirtieth, and if it took it into its head to play up, that would be a catastrophe.

Mustn't forget we're in a year with thirteen moons, and that's never great shakes! Still, when the cranes come over it's usually rather a good sign!

He had heard them passing over four nights earlier. A huge flight, without a doubt, which must have stretched over several hundred metres, for the harsh calls of the birds had echoed above the village for some minutes. He was not asleep, and could not help thinking of the old superstition formerly associated with the flocks of migrating birds which called them the *chasse volante* – the Wild Hunt. His grandmother and mother were terrified by them, attributed all sorts of evil charms to them, and brought out their rosaries at the slightest sign of one.

It's incredible what the old people could believe, and what nonsense they repeated! I hope I talk less of it than them . . . he thought as he resumed his walk.

He had decided to climb as far as the plateau, to rest there a while, then go back down without hurrying. By that time it would be half past eleven and Mathilde would not have time to get worried, that was the main thing.

Pierre-Edouard had barely covered fifty metres when he heard behind him, rising from the village, the deep tone of the church bell marking the hours. He counted out of habit, frowned at the twelfth stroke, and waited attentively for the second peal, meanwhile consulting his own watch. It indicated two minutes past eleven.

'Ten . . . eleven . . . twelve . . .,' he murmured. 'All right then! It's that stupid electric clock, gone and done it again! They work when they feel like it, these modern machines! And yet it cost hundreds and thousands! Old Fernand would never have got the hour wrong! Even drunk as a pig, he could still count!'

He sighed at the memory of the old sacristan, dead for many years, and continued his walk towards the plateau. It was then he suddenly remembered that Jacques had warned him the day before that the clocks were going to be changed. He had understood nothing of what his son had explained, but had declared that, in any case, the sun and he had no truck with anything decided by those morons in Paris!

'Change the clocks?' he had cried. 'And what next? They'll be asking the moon to rise in the west while they're at it, those asses! Don't expect me to accept such a stupid idea!'

'It's true, it's a load of rubbish!' he muttered, looking once more at his watch. Then he observed the sun again and was reassured. It was indeed five past eleven, no more.

And yet the church clock had struck twelve strokes . . .

'Ah, merde alors!' he exclaimed suddenly, understanding at last what Jacques had told him. 'Oh the buggers! They've foisted German time on us again! Why not say so straight off! But then, if it's midday, Mathilde must be getting worried! Oh, the buggers!'

Crossly, he turned on his heel and hurried as fast as he could towards the village.


'Couldn't you have said that it was today, the German time?' was his reproach the moment he entered the room where the three women were waiting for him.

'Where's your head, then? You only listen to what interests you! You were told yesterday, and this morning too!' Mathilde reminded him. 'Well, it doesn't matter, we guessed that you had forgotten.'

'I'll say I forgot!' he grumbled. 'I'm not going to clutter up my brain with all those nonsenses! No, it's true, it really is! You have to be crazy to dream up something like that!' he exclaimed, calling on his sisters to agree with him.

'Oh! They've already thought up plenty of others, worse ones! And I'm not even mentioning the stupidity of giving kids their majority when they're still sucklings!' cried Berthe angrily. 'No! But listen, remember the eighth of May last year!'

This she had never forgotten or forgiven. That they should dare to abolish the anniversary of a victory over absolute evil had disgusted her, wounded her. And she, the Resistance worker, the Gaullist, a former deportee, had insisted on going alone on the morning of 8 May to lay a huge bunch of wild flowers on the memorial to the dead of Saint-Libéral.

Nobody had mocked the frail silhouette, motionless in front of the stone pillar topped by a mossy old cock crushing a lichen-covered, spiked helmet. No one had laughed to see this old lady crying silently, who refused to forget and who, for the first time since the end of the war, had pinned her medals onto her white blouse.

It had taken this event for many people, even some of her own family, to discover that she was an officer of the Legion of Honour, decorated for her part in the Resistance; that she also had the cross for a volunteer in the Resistance and the medal for deportation and internment.

And nobody had seen her solitary demonstration as any condemnation of a people. The oldest inhabitants of Saint-Libéral knew that she had nothing against Germans, far from it! She had loved one and was preparing to marry him when the Nazis had assassinated him. And Gérard, her adopted son, had been born in Germany, to German parents. No, it was not a people nor a race that she had fought against in 1940. It was a system, a way of thinking, the Nazi order. And to learn that they were intending to court base popularity, out of stupidity therefore, to wipe away the date which commemorated the crushing of the swastika, had revolted her. Since then she regarded all those who had agreed to, not to mention applauded, this gesture, with extreme suspicion. As for the man who had instigated it, she despised him.

'Yes,' she reiterated to her brother, 'don't delude yourself, you can expect anything from that kind of people! And they'll do more!'

'I know. They don't know what else to dream up to annoy folks! But miladiou! I'd like to be told what the point is of changing the clocks?'

'It seems that it makes for savings . . .' suggested Mathilde.

'Savings? What sort of savings?' he shouted.

'You know very well, it's because of the oil, they say we won't have enough!'

'Well then, they only have to bring back ration tickets, same as during the war. And those who don't like it can walk, that'll stop them wrapping themselves round the plane trees!'

'Come on now, don't get in a state, it's not good for you,' ventured Mathilde.

'As for savings,' he continued, 'shall I tell you something? You could make some fine ones by hanging all bureaucrats in the ministries! All those officious little squirts! And while they're at it they could even hang a few ministers and deputies! Oh, by God, I wouldn't go into mourning!'

'Now, now, don't get worked up like that,' said Mathilde. 'And after all, you know, nobody's forcing us to change the clocks!'

'That's true,' he admitted. 'I don't want anything to do with German time, that's a collaborator's idea! Well, we'll stick to the old one. Besides, it seems it's past midday, but I'm not hungry! Right, that's decided, we won't bother with that Parisian notion.'

This decision calmed him. And it was in good spirits, laughing at the idea of underlining his independence, that he went to take a turn in the village during the afternoon, just to find out a little of what people thought of the new time. He returned to the house delighted, for all the people he had met were of his opinion and were preparing to take absolutely no notice of the official time, especially those who had animals to look after.

But he howled with rage and disappointment that same evening on realising that he had missed the television news and the beginning of a film he was looking forward to seeing. For if his watch and the light outside actually indicated eight o'clock, it was no less than nine o'clock official time. And that could not be helped.

'Well yes, my dear, whether you like it or not, if you want to watch the telly, you'll have to live on German time!' cried Berthe. 'I'm telling you, it's what you can expect from people like that! I think they're more stupid than wicked, but that's no excuse!'

Immersed in his accounts, which were far from pleasing, Jacques found the furious and incessant barking of the dogs increasingly irritating. The two mongrels were nice enough, but often barked merely for the pleasure of listening to themselves. Or again, when the wind carried the sound, they loved to answer their fellows giving voice three kilometres away in the alleys of Saint-Libéral, particularly as night fell.

'For pity's sake, shut up those yappers!' he begged Michèle. 'I'd like at least to finish my estimated balance in peace!'

The results were not inspiring. Since 1973, following an absurd decision by the public authorities, the prices for all cattle had fallen by twenty-five to thirty percent and were not about to rise again tomorrow! In fact France was importing beef from the Argentine and central Europe by the hundreds of thousands of tons. It was obvious that those responsible for such a ridiculous and pernicious commercial policy could not care less about the French breeders' situation. On the electoral level their influence was growing ever weaker, so there was no need to pander to them, let alone listen to them.

Jacques knew all that was normal. As normal as the collapse in the price of pigs. As normal as the huge question mark which rounded off his provisional accounts; everything was negative and forced them, Michèle and himself, to cut down on anything which was not absolutely essential. It was to be hoped things would go better soon, when Françoise had finally completed her studies . . .

'Good God! What's got into those mutts?' he asked.

'There's a car coming up,' warned Michèle after looking out of the window.

'At this time of night? You'll be telling me it's only seven o'clock by the sun, but with this dratted summer time!'

'It's Aunt Yvette,' announced Michèle, recognising the DS.

'Oh yes! She said to me this morning she'd be coming by! I'd completely forgotten,' he reproached himself as he closed his account book and filed away his bills. He rose and went to meet her.

'I hope I'm not disturbing you?' asked Yvette after greeting her niece.

'Not at all,' he assured her. Nevertheless he was a little curious, almost worried, for the ghost of Louis hovered not far off . . .

'Shall I make you a herb tea?' suggested Michèle.

'That would be nice,' said Yvette, sitting down. 'I wanted to come and see you here rather than at the Mairie, it's simpler and more discreet,' she explained.

'Is it the mayor or your nephew you want to see?' he asked. He was now really worried, for he did not understand his aunt's actions at all.

'The mayor and former regional councillor.'

'Would it perhaps be better if I left you two alone?' proposed Michèle.

'No, no! Don't be silly, go and make your tea and come back. Are the children all right, then?' inquired Yvette.

'Fine,' he said. 'Dominique and Béatrice seem to like it out there. Dominique has a job he's interested in and Béatrice has found something to keep her busy at a maternity hospital. As for Françoise, she's okay. She'll be here in two months, towards the middle of July. Right, you've got something to say to me? You know I always get straight to the point.'

'Yes, that's in the family! Right, this is it, I'm tired of being alone in the château, fed up . . . So I want to get rid of it . . .'

'Oh, I see . . .'

'I'd be very surprised if you did!'

'Have you found a buyer?' asked Michèle from the kitchen.

'No, I haven't looked for one yet. And it all depends on you,' she said to Jacques. 'Yes, on you, monsieur le maire!'

889

'I don't quite see how . . .'

'The château, you're going to take it over.'

'You're crazy! I wouldn't even have enough to pay for the upkeep!'

'I'm talking to the mayor,' she explained. 'This château, I don't need it. I'm bored to tears in it, I certainly don't have to sell it to live comfortably for the rest of my days. So I've decided to give it to the community, in memory of Léon. There, that's all.'

'Ah? That's all?' he stammered after a few seconds. He was flabbergasted. 'But where will you live?' he asked eventually.

'After Louis' death your mother told me there was a room free at their place. I get on so well with your parents and aunts. I'll be fine there. And then I'll look after them a bit, they're getting on, you know . . .'

'Yes, yes. But it can't be done just like that!' he continued. 'In the first place, even if it could be done, the village hasn't the means to take responsibility for a building like that. Then, more importantly, Léon has nephews . . . and don't misinterpret this: I'm not talking about Guy, Mauricette and myself, you know that! But what about the others? Look, I know of at least one. Yes, I've never told you this, but Paul and I made him drunk on your wedding day . . . Well, I'm sorry, but legally, he's Léon heir before you!'

'Go on with you!' she said, amused. 'You know, Léon taught me only to speak when I was sure of myself. The other nephews have no say in this matter. Besides, believe me, if they had hoped to pick up something, they would have come to his funeral. And to Louis' . . .'

'That's true, they didn't have the courtesy, but . . .'

'But nothing!' interrupted Yvette. 'The château is mine alone. Yes, when Léon bought it, in '46, it was as much with his money as mine. However, he absolutely insisted that it be in my name. In my name alone. And when we were married he wanted us to keep to the system of separate property . . .'

'Good heavens! I'd have happily bet the château was left to Louis!'

'You're right, it was really for him that we bought it, but he was too young at the time. And anyway, Léon didn't want it. He said to me: "If he believes he's lord of the manor at fifteen, it might go to his head, he'll think that money grows on trees . . ." Poor Léon, poor Louis . . .'

'Hey! Is that lime-tea coming?' called Jacques to Michèle, seeing that his aunt was about to succumb to tears. 'Right, fine, the château is yours, but you can't give it away like that!'

'Give it or sell it for a token franc, what's to stop me? Well, what does the mayor think of that?'

'We'll have to see ... I can't take the decision all alone, it's a weighty matter that you're putting to the community!'

'But you're interested?'

'Indeed! My goodness!' he exclaimed, 'I'll have to bring the chief executive of the council in on this, and we'll get together to look for some influential group to support the whole business. Just imagine, if we had the château, we could install, look, I don't know, ... a children's holiday home! Or something like that! Good God, that would liven up this dying community a bit. That would at least bring in some young people for three months of the year!'

'That's what I'm hoping,' smiled Yvette. 'You know, it's often depressing to be president of a senior citizens' club, even when it's called after Léon Dupeuch ... So I'd really love to see some children running about in the park ...'

'Fantastic,' he murmured, already lost in plans filled with children's songs, activities, life. 'Tomorrow I shall call a meeting of the council, and as soon as I have their agreement, we'll get going! But you've definitely decided? You're sure you won't regret it?'

'Certain. For several months I could have told you what I said tonight.'

'It'll be wonderful for the village if it works,' said Michèle, coming back with the lime-tea.

'Yes, but we'll need to pull all the stops out to do it,' he said. 'Just imagine! Now we'll really need a tennis court, and a swimming pool as well! And there, it will at least be used by someone! I can't wait for tomorrow evening, I'm dying to see the faces that moaner Peyrafaure and his mates are going to pull!'

After pondering far into the night the best method of realising their plan, Jacques awoke feeling a little less enthusiastic. He knew very well what difficulties he would have to surmount, what procedures to set in train, in order to transform the huge château into a building which could accommodate people.

First of all, there were administrative problems to resolve. Then, capital would have to be found to enable the château to be provided with all the infrastructure of a hotel. Finally, it was vital to interest a large firm in it by promoting the premises, activities, and a site which children would be happy to visit. None of that would be easy, and for the first time in many years he regretted that he was no longer a regional councillor. That would probably have enabled him to speed up the process. But he pushed aside the various pessimistic thoughts which assailed him when he considered all the work awaiting him, jumped in his car and set off to inform all the town councillors. He told them that the meeting would take place that very evening, that it was a matter of extreme importance and everyone should be present.

Then he went to visit his parents, but restrained himself from telling them of Yvette's visit. He had decided in conjunction with her to say nothing to anyone before the council meeting. Its members should be informed before anyone else, otherwise some of them might be annoyed and become fierce opponents, out of pure spite.

Right from the beginning of the meeting Jacques was glad that he had kept the secret, for it was obvious that some of them were in a black mood.

'I hope you haven't inconvenienced us for some trifle!' Peyrafaure went into the attack.

'Do I usually?'

'No, but there's a first time for everything! But maybe you're going to announce that you're resigning? That would be good news!' cried Castellac, in a tone which was intended to be pleasant and humorous but which still betrayed a latent animosity.

'Hey! Have you eaten something that's got stuck?' joked Jacques.

'You could look at it like that,' remarked Peyrafaure drily.

'Dammit! Speak your mind!' burst out Jacques.

'Don't get upset,' Coste explained to him with a laugh, 'with this meeting you're doing them out of a rugby match on the telly, and a great one too! So you can imagine how much they love you!'

'Oh, you should have said straight away! Well, I'm sorry gentlemen, but what I have to tell you seems to me more important than a match. I believe it is, anyway. It's this; my aunt, Madame Yvette Dupeuch, my aunt,' he repeated, 'has decided to part with her château . . .'

'It was only to be expected,' groaned Delmas, 'but we can't do anything about it, can we? Right, so what's the problem? If there is one, let's sort it out, and if we get on with it, we'll see the second half!'

'You're beginning to get on my wick with your game!' declared Jacques. 'There is no problem! My aunt has decided to give, I emphasise give, her château to the commune. I need your opinion before accepting.'

'Give? Well I'll be blowed!' whistled Martin. 'But why? She's losing by it!'

'That's right, on the face of it she's losing!' admitted Jacques.

'So what's the catch?' demanded Peyrafaure.

'There's no catch.'

'I don't believe it!' insisted Peyrafaure. 'You don't give away, just like that, a building worth perhaps . . . I don't know, at least . . .'

'More than that!' interrupted Jacques, who could feel his anger rising. 'I tell you there's no hidden snag, nothing! All we have to say is: yes, madame: thank you, madame! Dammit, it's clear enough! And it's free! Free!'

'Well, except for the taxes to be paid, and they won't be very small,' warned Peyrafaure.

'With a good lawyer that won't be a problem,' Jacques assured him.

'Granted,' said Martin, 'but what's the village going to do with that vast barrack of a place? Firstly it'll cost us a fortune to maintain and then, we've got nothing to put in it, so what's the point?'

'Firstly, I would reply to that you should never look a gift horse in the mouth,' said Jacques. 'Next, I shall make every effort to get the support of the sub-prefect to obtain favourable loans from the FAELG.'

'The Fa what?' rejoined Delmond.

'The fund to aid the equipment of local groups,' explained Jacques. 'And if that's not enough, we'll turn to the Crédit Agricole. In addition, I would expect to pick up a few grants here and there. Well yes, Monsieur Peyrafaure, it can be helpful to have friends in the right places . . .'

'If you don't mind going begging . . . And then, it's very fine, all that, but what purpose will your refurbished château serve?'

'Very simply, I hope to be able, not this summer but the next, to open it as a holiday home for children. And now, if you want to see the end of your match, we'll vote to accept my aunt's gift and you're released!'

'Why a holiday home?' persisted Castillac.

'Are you against it?'

'Bah . . . Not for it, particularly. Well yes, I am against it! It'll bring in a flock of kids! And kids make a noise and break everything!'

'Oh, right?' cried Jacques. 'You'd prefer a retirement home, maybe? An old people's home? They make less noise, old people! That's true! But don't you think we've got enough of those in Saint-Libéral? Eh? Our own aren't enough for you?'

'Castellac, my old friend, you're talking rubbish,' Peyrafaure intervened gravely. 'Monsieur le maire is right, for once. It's true, kids make a noise and break things, but at least they sing and shout and laugh, they're alive! I vote for the project!' he said, raising his hand.

He had scarcely completed the movement before every hand was raised, except Castellac's.

'Passed unanimously, minus one vote,' said Jacques. 'Gentlemen, I propose that tomorrow we immediately pay a visit to my aunt to thank her and to tell her that the château, whatever it's ultimate use, will be called The Léon Dupeuch Foundation. But of course, we will understand if the opposing party is absent . . .'

He looked at his watch, happy to ascertain that the meeting had not lasted long and that he had time to go and announce to his parents that Saint-Libéral would perhaps live again.

Dominique had felt at ease as soon as he arrived in Tunisia. Here, unlike in Guyana, there was no need for acclimatisation. It was more or less what he had known in the north of Algeria. And that also applied to some of the scenery, methods of cultivation and mentality of the local inhabitants.

The great difference was that he was working on much more fertile, productive land than that of the oases. He was not complaining about this. Established in the Mejerda valley, south of Beja and above the town of Bab el-Raba, he was, as in Guyana, in charge of an experimental unit. But the greatest change from his previous assignment was in the modest area of the operation. Here, it was obvious that Mondiagri had experienced difficulty in negotiating with the government to install an experimental farm.

In the 1960s, the management of the group had been out of step with theories applied by supporters of agricultural reform prevailing in the country. Although it was now obvious that this had ended in a resounding disaster which endangered the economy, certain of the work habits had persisted. For example, some people thought of the land, crops, flocks and the tools as collective property, and so did not bother to treat them well.

However, since the farm was small and the workers few in number, Dominique did not have too much difficulty in making them understand the importance of agricultural research and interesting them in it.

As he was not overburdened with work, and Beatrice's duties at the maternity hospital in Beja also left her with some free time, they filled this by setting off to explore the countryside. It had also been a great pleasure to meet with Ali again. He had turned up as soon as he had learned of his friend's arrival, and the two men had embraced each other, with a great deal of backslapping, before Béatrice's astonished eyes.

'Don't worry, it's our old bond as Saharan veterans,' Dominique had explained to her. 'We had such a rough time together on that bloody useless land in the oases! And you can't imagine what a merry dance he led me too, this rogue! A bigger coward than him doesn't exist! Didn't want to get his hands dirty, or to bend down, the lazy devil!'

'You bastard! Still just as colonialist and racist! Well, they were good times, after all . . .'

'Isn't it going well? Are you having problems?'

'Your successor is a little squirt and a boot-licker! He implements the plans and directives from our technical advisors down to the very last letter. Oh yes, we have that sort of scum amongst our lot too! So I'll leave it to you to imagine the results! With those types around you're heading straight for famine! Come on, let's talk about something different. So you finally got married!'

'Yes, a real gem!'

'And brave as well!'

'Wretch! Right, come and have some lunch. You're going to discover a cordon bleu cook who trained in the foie gras region!'

Since this reunion, Dominique was waiting for the opportunity to go and visit Ali. He was also looking forward to the idea of seeing once more the country in which he had spent four years of his life, and certainly not the worst ones.

Besides practising a profession which he enjoyed, accompanied by a very loving and attentive wife, he also greatly appreciated being close to France. Not that he was homesick, but he found it comforting to be only a few hours from Saint-Libéral, from his family. To be able to pop over to France if the fancy took them, for him and Béatrice to go and spend a weekend at Coste-Roche, or even in Paris.

He was delighted when a letter from his father informed him that the commune was now the owner of the château. That château encompassed his childhood and he was sentimentally attached to it, as were all the people of the village. And, like them, he caught himself saying 'our château'! It was there, solid, firmly planted above the village. And it belonged to everyone, like the wash-house, the church or the countryside. So to learn that from now on it really *was* theirs gave great satisfaction.

'And now, you'll see,' he said to Béatrice, 'it'll give my father a taste for the fight again. It's a good idea, a children's holiday home, isn't it?'

'Excellent. Your grandparents must be pleased as well!'

'You bet! And doubly so since Yvette has moved in with them. It's really funny, she must be in her seventies, but with her there's a bit of youth coming into the house!'

'I hardly know her, but she's obviously a very kind lady, so thoughtful.'

'That's true, but on that score she's nowhere near beating you,' he said, pulling her to him and holding her against his shoulder.

He knew that he would never forget the proof she had given him; he still felt quite moved by it. And proud too, to have a wife of such moral strength. Immediately after their marriage, on the afternoon of 20 December, he had not the faintest idea where she was dragging him off to when they had emerged from the town hall of the Sixth Arrondissement in Paris.

'A short visit to pay, and then we'll rejoin you at Guy's,' she had told her brother and sister-in-law (the only representatives of her family) and the much more numerous Vialhes. Then she had dragged him into a taxi.

'Stop in front of the Préfecture of Police,' she had requested. As he understood nothing, but particularly wanted to avoid giving the driver the chance to start a conversation, he had remained silent until they arrived there.

'Do you want to bring charges of assault and battery already?' he had joked. 'No, joking apart, what are you playing at?'

'Nothing. Come on, we're going to visit Notre-Dame, it will make me feel young again. I often used to come here to listen to organ recitals.'

'*You* are asking *me* to go into Notre-Dame?'

'Why not? It's one of the most beautiful cathedrals, isn't it? Listen, you know how I hate lying, I just can't help it. I'm aware of the act your parents have had to put on to conceal our decision from your grandparents.'

'And you disapprove?'

'Not at all. But if one day I have to answer a question from your grandparents about it, I want to be able to say to them "Yes, we went to the church." Maybe it's a play on words, but by doing that I'm lying much less than if I'd agreed to accept a religious ceremony. And then, apart from that, knowing you as I do, I'm sure you're very happy to make a short visit to this place, on this day, with me . . .'

Afterwards, he knew that he would always remember that visit to Notre-Dame.

# 16

JOSYANE went back up to Paris to look for work after spending a month in Saint-Libéral. She was aware that her parents would have preferred to see her settle locally. But although her urge to roam the world had now waned, the idea of accepting some modest job in the Corrèze was not immediately inspiring. She was twenty-five and already had a fair experience of life: she intended to make use of it.

'I could suggest that you work for the Maison de Couture,' Chantal said to her, 'Aunt Berthe and Gérard would be delighted, but frankly, I have the feeling that it's not quite your style . . . From what I know about you, you'll be snapping at the first old bore who appears, and as they form ninety-five per cent of our clientele, we'd get straight into a nasty incident, or bankruptcy!'

'Yes, I wonder how you can resist the temptation!'

'Very easily; I have no contact with them! My job is to organise and promote the Claire Diamond collections, in France and in Europe. But in that area, I really don't see what I can offer you either.'

'Don't struggle. Your rig-outs, even with the Claire Diamond label, are just not my kind of thing.'

'That's plain to see,' said Chantal sweetly: 'I'm coming to believe that your total wardrobe consists of one pair of jeans!'

'Almost! In any case, it's not work I'm asking you for, it's simply if I can sleep at your place, just until I find a room that's not too expensive. But if that'd put you out, say so. Well, I mean to say, perhaps you've got someone it might upset . . .'

'No problem,' Chantal said, amused, 'I never entertain men at my place. You see, if you do that, they soon start calling for their slippers the moment they arrive! So my flat is out of bounds, as a matter of principle. Out of bounds except to you, naturally.'

'Thanks, I hope I won't be in your way for too long.'

'Have you any ideas about work?'

'Yes, still the same thing. I'm going to begin by going round all the travel and press agencies. And if that doesn't produce anything, I'll look for something on the secretarial side; after all, I am trilingual, that may be some use!'

'Definitely. Look, as a matter of fact, someone's been asking after you . . .'

Josyane guessed that 'someone' had blue eyes and resembled Paul Newman, but she carefully avoided showing any reaction.

'Oh yes? Who?' she replied.

'Don't play hard to get with me, if you don't mind,' teased Chantal. 'You know very well who I'm talking about. I thought he was in a very strange state, poor old Christian, what did you do to him in Tahiti?'

'Absolutely nothing, I promise you!'

'Yes, that must be why he looked so ill. With your good little girl act combined with top-notch bodywork, you just turned him on and then slipped away!'

'I don't turn anyone on, that's not my style!'

'Thanks very much!' said Chantal with a laugh. 'All right, it doesn't matter. The fact remains it's Christian who asked me for news of you. That's nice, isn't it? Oh yes, and he also said that one of his projects was to explore the Corrèze. If I remember rightly, he once told me that his great-grandfather was from Brive, or nearby. You knew that, did you, did he mention it to you?'

'Vaguely,' Josyane replied evasively, 'but I didn't understand his story at all!'

It was a barefaced lie, but she expressed it with great élan.

'Oh, right. Well briefly, he's in Paris at the moment, if you feel like thanking him for playing postman . . .'

'No, that's already been done!'

'Golly, you do look fierce. Well, we won't talk about it any more if it annoys you. But if I were you, making the rounds of the press agencies I'd prefer to be recommended by someone from the profession, and someone well known! But you do as you think best . . .'

'Exactly! I shall manage by myself!' declared Josyane. She was suddenly in an extremely bad temper, for she knew this was not the best way of finding employment.

Exhausted by a testing and complex case, Guy decided to go and get some fresh air during the Whitsun weekend. Although he felt himself to be very Parisian and enjoyed living in the capital, he often needed to go and tread something other than asphalt. Needed to feel the earth beneath his feet, to breathe in the fragrance of the forests, to enjoy the greenery, and oxygen which did not stink of exhaust gases. Consequently, even when it was the close season for hunting, he did not think twice about going to spend twenty-four hours at Félix's. Down there he would forget his files, his clients and the smell of the courts.

In contrast to his eldest son, he was not very keen on fishing; got bored if the fish were slow to bite, often snagged his line in the branches of the willows and his hook in the roots of the water-lilies. But that did not prevent him from keeping Félix company when he decided to put buttered pike on the menu. For even if Guy often left empty-handed, the Souchet pool was so beautiful, so calm, that two hours spent on its banks was a real treat, a joy.

All the more so since Félix's conversation was never dull. He read a great deal, kept abreast of everything. Without feeling the need to give his opinion here there and everywhere, his judgement was sound when one requested it. What was more, as he was fascinating and inexhaustible when it came to questions about nature, it was a pleasure for Guy lead him onto that subject. It made a change from the futile and trivial conversations he was often forced to endure on his evenings in Paris.

However, this morning the two men turned their steps towards the Souchet pool in silence. Nature was so beautiful, so rich, and the chorus of birds so captivating, that it seemed sacrilege to interrupt it. It burst forth on all sides, amazing in its strength and variety. The raucous, repetitive call of pheasants was answered by thin piping from great tits, and the harsh drumming of greater spotted woodpeckers drilling into hollow trunks alternated with the singing exercises of lesser whitethroats and chiffchaffs.

The forest, still all damp with dew, was resplendent. The light was streaming in, and the oak groves, in the rich unfurling of their delicate, tender, spring greenery, drank in the sun in long draughts, gorged themselves on it.

'What a treat this morning,' whispered Guy as they arrived without a sound at the edge of the pool.

There, where a few wisps of creamy mist hovered over the grey-blue water, grebe and coot, moorhen, teal and mallard were preening and flapping, diving, calling, quacking. And amongst the rushes, cat's tails and reeds, enlivened by delicate touches of pale yellow flag, the sedge, reed and Cetti's warblers trilled with open throats.

Standing sentinel over them all, perched on a dead branch of an old, worm-eaten alder, a dignified purple heron kept an eye on the two men as they approached.

'We'll stay here, this is a good spot, and it would be a pity to disturb such a beautiful party,' said Félix, laying his equipment on the grass.

'Yes,' he continued shortly afterwards, 'you see, I know him, this heron, it's almost like a game between us. If we move forward another ten metres, he'll take off. Then it's goodbye to the ducks, moorhens and the rest. Everything will hide! Look, try this spinner, it's a new model, Pierre told me it was good.'

'He's well?'

'Very well. You should have arrived earlier yesterday, you'd have seen him. He was here with Jeanette and the children.'

Pierre Flaviens kept a small shop for fishing and hunting tackle in Buzançais. He often asked his father to test some new article.

'They're coming down to Saint-Libéral this summer?'

'Of course! If they missed it again this year my mother would be upset, poor woman! With the children's measles keeping them here last year, it was a tragedy for her! Well, almost.'

'And you, you'll be coming?'

'Probably; it will please your father, and my mother as well.'

'You can say that again! Oh blast!' Guy, suddenly irritated, passed his rod to his cousin. 'Fix this thing for me, I don't know how it's supposed to be attached!'

'Calmly,' joked Félix, as he deftly knotted the spinner on to the end of the line: 'There, and now no more playing around if you want to eat fish for lunch!'


It was Guy who made the first catch. After twenty minutes of struggling under Félix's direction, he succeeded in landing a pike of almost eight pounds on the bank, a magnificent, plump beast with the mouth of a killer.

'You can take that one away with you! He's much too big for us two,' said Félix. 'My goodness, a fine beast! But if you'd lost him, your son would have had a good go at you!'

'I wouldn't have told him!'

'But I would have,' teased Felix. 'Joking apart, he's well?'

'Yes, he's swotting for his bac.'

'But that's no problem?'

'No, not unless he breaks his legs the morning of the exam. Dammit, help me! I'll never manage to unhook this monster!'

'Yes, you're well on the way to losing your fingers!' advised Félix, deftly slipping his thumb and forefinger into the pike's gills. He retrieved the spinner and stunned the fish.

'And next year?' he asked, resuming his fishing.

'Oh ho! Don't you play games with me, if you don't mind! You know very well how the land lies!'

'Dammit! To listen to you, you'd think he wanted to become a guru in the foothills of Nepal or manager of a brothel! Seriously, there's nothing so dreadful about wanting to study agriculture!'

'He hasn't got that far yet! But the little wretch has already succeeded in extracting my permission to register for the preparatory course! And just imagine, he's turning his nose up at the holiday I was offering him too, for passing his bac. Yes sir! I suggested a trip to England, but oh no!'

'I know,' said Félix, 'he'd rather go and work with Jacques.'

'He told you so?'

'No, not this year, but I'm guessing. Okay, that's no big deal!'

'I didn't say it was! I'm simply saying that, gifted as he is, it's wasting his talent to want to launch into such a wretched profession!'

'Dominique's earning a crust or two!'

'Yes, I know. But Jean wants to be a stock-breeder, I ask you, a breeder! No less!'

'He has time to change his mind! Once he's an agricultural engineer, he could develop a career like his cousin.'

'He's so pigheaded, it would surprise me! Because you may know that monsieur has his own little plan for breeding. Indeed he does. And Dominique agrees with it, he may even be the inspiration! Oh yes! I was watching them at Dominique's wedding, they spent a whole evening chatting together!'

'That's rather a good sign, isn't it? That proves he's gathering information!'

'Oh Lord yes, the little devil! And monsieur isn't going for the economy model! Breeder yes, but in style!'

'How's that, in style?' asked Félix. He felt a bite, struck briskly. 'Look, there's our lunch,' he said as he reeled in. 'Shouldn't be too big, soon have it out . . . You say he's doing it in style?' he continued as he played with the reel-drag to tire his catch.

'Exactly! Monsieur wants to produce pedigree animals, registered Limousins, championship beasts. The finest of the fine, for export, right! And Dominique approves of it, or is advising him, hard to tell which! He says his father should have got into this a long time ago and he would have made a much better living from it!'

'That's not so stupid.'

'Get away! You're agreeing with Jean, as always!'

'No, no, quite the opposite! When he comes I spend my time

calming him down. Here, get the landing net ready, judging by the way he swallowed the hook, he won't slip off by himself. Are you ready?'

Félix pulled the pike dexterously to the edge of the bank, guided it into the net.

'That's good,' said Guy.

'It's a young one, no more than three pounds,' estimated Félix. 'So, you were saying he wanted to go in for top class breeding?'

'Yes.'

'That's not so stupid,' repeated Félix. 'No, it isn't: Oh, I know what you're thinking: if our economists and politicians go on the way they've started, they'll kill farming – well, our sort, the middling enterprises; the little ones are already dead! I see it clearly, the Brenne area isn't particularly rich anyway, but it's going from bad to worse. And it's the same in the Corrèze! That's our fault, we've left control to the eggheads who've never set foot out of the cities, except to go skiing or to the beach! So to them the country is just a bunch of yokels!'

'Well now, if after all that you have the cheek to tell me I'm wrong to worry about my son . . .!'

'Yes, you're wrong. I'd understand you turning grey if he wanted to work the way Jacques does at Coste-Roche. And yet he's a good fellow, is Jacques! But he was in the forefront thirty years ago . . .'

'There, that's exactly what I'm saying! Jean's going there this summer!'

'But not to do the same as him! Listen, the way things are going, you need to aim for the exceptional, the top of the range, as they say. There'll always be customers for the unusual. So for the dilettante, why not pedigree animals? After all, it was by developing into haute couture that Aunt Berthe raised her fashion house to where it is. It wasn't by selling aprons, blue overalls or tea towels that she created Claire Diamond.'

'Certainly. But right at the beginning I have to state that I have no land, not a square metre! You know that we came to an arrangement in the family and our parents left all the land to Jacques. That meant he had to take out a loan to compensate Mauricette. All right. I'll get the family home one day, but as for land, apart from the patch of garden . . . I've no complaints, it's fine like that. But really what I'm trying to say is, I've no desire to ruin myself now by buying a farm for my son. So, him and his cows, you get my drift!'

'If you look at it like that . . . But shall I tell you something? I'm not worried about Jean. After all, maybe his years in agriculture will teach him that there are other things besides stock-breeding.'

'Let's hope the gods hear you! You must admit the boy isn't choosing the easiest course!'

'Have you ever seen a Vialhe choose the easy way? I never have!' joked Félix. 'Come on, let's go back, we'll let this beast cook while we're taking an aperitif. What would you actually have liked him to be? A lawyer, like you?'

'Why not? It's not so bad. Or the ENA civil service college.'

'Why? Don't you think there are enough thick-heads coming out of there? I tell you, I'd prefer Jean to be interested in the land and stock-breeding. It's much less run of the mill, times being what they are. And what's more, less risky than having ambitions to govern the lives of the hoi-polloi like you and me, who don't want it anyway.'

'Maybe. But it has to be said, you're bloody subversive! I could be listening to my father!'

'Well yes, that's a Vialhe trait too, you have to live with it. Right, let's go, and don't forget your catch. For once you'll be able to impress your son!'

'Do you think so? Knowing him, he'll never believe I caught it all by myself!'

'I'll make you a certificate!' promised Félix, bursting into laughter.

Jacques had been worried for almost two months. He had felt that the month of April was abnormal – too beautiful, too sunny and in particular, too dry and hot. He had never forgotten the saying that his grandfather Jean-Edouard used to trot out whenever Paul and he had the audacity to complain about a wet April spoiling their Easter holidays:

'This month has only thirty days, but if it rained for thirty-one it wouldn't have rained enough!' the old man would declare.

Since then, Jacques had learned that he was right. April was when the last significant reserves of water filtered down into the subsoil before the hot summer days. When the plough-land, meadows and pastures drank it in, when the fodder crop was assured.

But the month had come to an end without heavy rainfall. And the new moon on the twenty-ninth had not brought any change. As for May, it was radiant: too much so, for the few stormy showers had hardly settled the dust.

Already the beets and maize had germinated poorly, and were wilting in patches. As for the man-made pasture, it was possible to discern, at the foot of the clovers and grasses, the granules of ammonium nitrate which had been spread at the beginning of the month and were still not dissolved.

By now, going on for mid-June, it was obvious that the fodder cut would be meagre, not to say non-existent on some plots. Even the cereals were suffering. They were already yellowing, and the ears of corn remained desperately empty, flat. Some of the fruit trees were also beginning to show distress, and to drop a few green, dry fruits which had shrivelled onto their kernels.

This morning of the 10 June, Pierre-Edouard felt he had the heart to walk up and cast an eye over the plateau. There, spotting Jacques reaping the lucerne crop on the Malides field, he pressed on, just to see what the cut was producing.

'If we have no thunderstorms in the next week, to unsettle the weather, you'll soon get the rest of your haymaking done!' he predicted. 'It's not up to much, is it?' he added, bending down to pick up a handful of fodder already wilted by the blazing sun.

'No, even the lucerne is sparse! As for the rest . . .'

'I've seen,' said Pierre-Edouard. 'It might be worth your while cutting it all straight away and, if it ever gets round to raining a little, you'd have a second cut.'

'I thought about it, but the density is still so poor! Mind you, we'll have to do something if this blasted weather stays stuck the way it is!'

'It reminds me of 1943,' said Pierre-Edouard. He reflected a moment, hesitated: 'Yes, it was '43. That was the year the reaper let us down. Yes, I took Guy to Brive to order another. What did I want to say now? Oh yes! We got the hay made quickly that year! You'll be telling me I had less stock to manage than you!'

'Well yes, I soon won't know where to graze them.'

'Have you got any hay left from last year?'

'Hardly any, maybe eight or ten tons, no more, that won't go far . . .'

'You're right,' sighed Pierre-Edouard. He suddenly felt very tired, and went to lean against the trunk of a plum tree.

'Are you not feeling well?' Jacques worried, and climbed down from the tractor. His back was hurting and he limped up to his father: 'Are you not well?' he asked again.

'Fine, I'm puffing a bit, that's all,' Pierre-Edouard assured him.

He observed his son who was pulling a face as he massaged his back, and laughed ironically:

'We're a fine pair, us two! You can hardly drag yourself along and I . . . Well I've got the excuse that I'm old, but we could do with someone to take over!'

'You shouldn't have come such a long way,' Jacques scolded, 'it's not sensible!'

'I know, but the devil with being sensible! I enjoyed seeing the plateau again.'

'I'm going to take you on the tractor as far as Coste-Roche. Then Michèle will drive you down in the car.'

'No, no, that'll be a waste of your time,' protested Pierre-Edouard without great conviction.

He was by now rather breathless and would gladly have sat down, for his legs felt heavy; but he hesitated to do so on the bare ground. It was so far down, and so difficult to crouch down without lying flat out. And then, afterwards, you needed to get up again . . .

'Come on, I'll help you climb onto the tractor. You can hold onto the mudguard, right? Can you get a grip?'

'Let me have a breather. I'll go back down by myself on foot, it's not far!' said Pierre-Edouard.

He felt unable to heave himself onto the tractor, and in particular to balance himself against the mudguard as far as Coste-Roche. But he would not admit it, not for anything in the world.

'Yes it is a long way! Too far for you!' insisted Jacques. 'Right,' he decided, 'don't move from there: I'll slip off to fetch the car and take you back down.'

'Well, all right, have it your way,' Pierre-Edouard gave in after a moment's hesitation. 'But promise me one thing; you'll drop me at the edge of the village. Promise, otherwise I'm going to walk.'

'But why?'

'Promise!' he said, making as if to set off.

'Right, okay.'

'It's for your mother's sake,' he explained, resuming his support against the gnarled trunk of the plum tree. 'Yes, if she sees me coming down in the car, she'll be worried. That'll make a whole lot of trouble, she'll want to get Martel, all that rigmarole, you know!'

'And she'll be right!'

'Get away with you!' said Pierre-Edouard irritably, before continuing: 'Whereas if I arrive on foot, thanks to you I'll be in plenty of time and she won't suspect anything. She's sensitive, you know, she doesn't show it but I know her. You have to be careful, worry isn't good for her. Go on then, go and fetch your car. You're right, I'm a bit tired now . . .'

Jacques kept his word and deposited his father on the edge of Saint-Libéral. But before returning to Coste-Roche, he wanted to be sure the old man was feeling better and decided to wait until he reached the main square.

Satisfied to see him walking away at a good pace, he nevertheless resolved to tell Aunt Berthe to keep an eye on his jaunts. For if, in addition to the weather conditions, his father joined in to complicate his life, things were going to get difficult!

He comforted himself by considering that Pierre-Edouard had some reason to be tired. After all, not content with climbing to the plateau – and the slope was steep! – he had pushed on as far as the Malides field, all under a lethal sun. That made more than three kilometres, a fine achievement for a man of eighty-seven with a weak heart.

And he was ready to return on foot, he thought admiringly. I wouldn't bet on doing as much at the same age, if I get there . . .

He waited until his father had disappeared at the end of the main street, and returned up the track to Coste-Roche. After all that, he had not finished cutting the lucerne. It was not critical, as, unfortunately, the weather was not threatening to break.

Some mornings, when she returned exhausted to her room in the attics of the Rue de l'Ouest, Josyane came close to thinking that independence was very dearly bought.

As she had forecast to Chantal, she had found a job. It was reasonably paid, and had therefore allowed her to reimburse her sister for the plane ticket and also to move into a little studio flat under the eaves. The only problem was that her duties corresponded very little with what she had expected. Certainly she was working in a travel agency. However, instead of welcoming clients and informing them about the charms of the Seychelles, the Carribean, Acapulco or any other supposedly enchanting spot, then organising their itinerary, she found herself forced to pilot groups of foreigners around the capital.

It was bearable when her stint was during the day, but very unpleasant when she had to guide some Japanese or Americans for an evening trip, from the Moulin-Rouge to the Lido, with a detour to the Eiffel Tower, Place de la Concorde and Notre-Dame for the illuminations, a 'typical' bistro and back to Pigalle! It was not only exhausting, but also devoid of any interest. What was more, as in Tahiti, she often needed to convince certain clients that she was not part of the 'Paris by night' package! Consequently she began to think Chantal had been right when she had tried to persuade her not to accept that sort of job.

Annoyed at first by her sister's remarks, she now considered them increasingly sensible, especially when tiredness forced her to collapse fully clothed on her bed at a time when normal people were beginning their day.

'I hope you're not crazy enough to accept that idiotic job!' Chantal had commented to her.

'It's the only one being offered to me at the moment! And, besides, there's no such thing as idiotic work! I have to earn my living, that's the bottom line!'

'But not like that! It's ridiculous. You deserve better! And why don't you want to ask Uncle Guy to help you? He suggested it. Good God, with the people he knows, I'm sure he'd find you a job in no time! And then, look, as soon as Gérard gets back from the United States, I'll mention it to him, if you like?'

'Certainly not! I won't ask anything of Uncle Guy, nor Gérard, nor anyone in the family!'

'But that's absurd! Then what's the point of having a family, in your opinion? We're there to hold together, to support each other, to help each other! Look, do you think Uncle Jacques hesitated before getting his brother in on the search for a firm which might be interested in the château? That's the way to do it, and no other way. Only fools don't grasp that!'

'That's your opinion. Listen to me: I set off one day for the ends of the earth to cut the cord, okay? So today I don't want to tie it up again, do I make myself clear? That's why I'm not asking anything of Uncle Guy, nor anyone else in the family!'

'Shall I tell you something? On the pretext of wanting to manage all by yourself and distinguish yourself from your family, you're behaving like a shopgirl! It's absurd! What are you playing at? A photo-romance in 'Nous Deux'? I was hoping your years of roving around would have knocked a bit of sense into your brain; I was wrong!'

'Don't you worry about my brain! Anyway, what's the problem? I've just found a job for now. That doesn't mean I'm going to devote my life to it!'

'Fine. Then let me at least ask Christian to put in a word for you with the press agencies, he's not part of the family, is he?'

'I forbid you to bring him into this, of all people! I made the rounds of all the agencies; none of them wanted anything to do with my photos! So there's no question of lowering myself now by getting your pal to intervene!'

'Well, my dear, I think you're going about things the wrong way!

You seem to be looking for a hard time. In fact you probably came back from Tahiti too soon!'

The two sisters parted very angrily, and Josyane waited more than two weeks before going back to see Chantal. Then, as always, they made it up.

And now, after three months of work, Josyane was beginning to think that her elder sister was right and the time had come to show some sense. Already she was contemplating swallowing her pride and going, as a first step, to ask her Uncle Guy's advice. But she still hesitated and deferred the decision. As she remained a little cool towards her sister as well, that did not improve her temper. For she was cross with Chantal, not for being sensible and realistic about her work, but for being incapable, until now, of bringing her together with Christian by one means or another.

And as there was no question of demeaning herself by requesting such a service, this fit of sulking with her sister was in danger of lasting, and even of getting worse if the situation did not resolve itself.

Josyane consulted her watch, calculated that she had four more hours of work before being able to sleep, and picked up the microphone again:

'. . . And on your right, you see the obelisk from Luxor. It was erected in 1836, in the reign of Louis-Philippe. At the same time the two fountains were built which . . .'

'And where are the Folies-Bergère?' interrupted a joker who was creating a rumpus at the back of the bus.

'. . . You can also see the eight statues which each represent a town in France: Lyon, Marseille, Bordeaux . . .' she attempted to continue.

Then she realised that no one was listening because, probably as a result of a dirty joke, the whole herd of Americans were guffawing and slapping their thighs.

'Give it a rest,' the driver advised her. 'They don't give a damn about your commentary. They're already as pissed as newts! If you want my opinion, we should drive them straight over to see the strippers: then they'll give us some peace for a while!'

She acquiesced. Exhausted by four sleepless nights – she had agreed to stand in for a sick colleague – she struggled manfully against encroaching slumber and forced herself to remain standing in order not to succumb. Despite that, she was not far from falling asleep, she was so tired, lulled by the gentle rocking of the coach, and she swayed as she gripped the support bar.

In good form after four brown ales, three cognacs, an armagnac and three glasses of champagne – a dreadful demi-sec which Josyane would not even have used to clean out her casseroles! – William B. Barlow, of Miles City, Montana, was fascinated by the rump undulating in front of him, within hand's reach. He found it so beautiful, exciting and graceful, squeezed as it was into the little blue skirt which accentuated its contours, that he could contain himself no longer. Alerting his neighbour with a knowing nudge of the elbow, he made the attempt. Not slyly or furtively, but openly, with cheerful vulgarity, burning to touch the soft warm skin he expected to find, between her thighs. He did not get far, barely above the hem.

'Filthy pig! Think you're on your ranch?' growled Josyane, turning round. And her hand shot out, like lightning; struck first one cheek then the other, before the culprit even had time to attempt a defensive movement.

'And you think that's funny, do you, you clot from Kansas?' she shouted at his neighbour, a gross, adipose redhead who was laughing fit to bust.

He too got the slap of a lifetime, but continued to choke with laughter just the same.

'Bunch of louts!' she exploded, going to sit on the little folding seat beside the driver.

'Now, now! If you start hitting the customers . . .' he murmured. He had heard it all and understood it all: 'Look, if they ever complain about you, you've had it!'

'Don't care, wish the buggers were dead! I'm getting out at the next red light!'

'Oh no! You can't leave the coach! Oh no! You're responsible for this horde of barbarians!'

'Don't give a damn! I resign, I have every justification! It's not stipulated anywhere that I have to let myself be pawed by drunkards!'

'Listen, let me at least drive them to the cabaret. After that you can do what you like. I'll take them back to the hotel all right by myself. Do that for me. Come on, be a good girl!'

'Okay, but as soon as they're off getting an eyeful, I'm leaving,' she vowed. And she took up the microphone again to announce: 'And here you see the Arc de Triomphe on the Place de l'Etoile. Begun in 1806, it was completed in 1836. Here lies the . . .'

'That's great, love, you'll see, you'll get used to it!' the driver encouraged her.

'Don't count on it!'

After sleeping like a log for half the day, she made for the house of Claire Diamond, located in the Faubourg-Saint-Honoré. She was anxious that Chantal should be the first to know of her decision to leave the agency.

# PART FOUR

*Held to ransom by the Fallow land*

# 17

IF it had not been for the drought, now catastrophic and tormenting, for there was no sign of an end to it, Jacques would have had every reason to be happy.

First of all, Françoise had been there for a week. She had succeeded brilliantly in her final year at veterinary college, and with her thesis. For a few weeks, before beginning work in the laboratories of the National Institute for Agricultural Research, she was free, and planning to spend part of her holidays at Coste-Roche.

Dominique and Béatrice were also keeping well. They wrote frequently, always sent good news, and even envisaged a trip to the Corrèze in September.

Another pleasant interlude: Félix had spent ten days in Saint-Libéral with his son, daughter-in-law and grandchildren. Thanks to all of them, there was no lack of entertainment within the family.

Added to that was the imminent arrival of Jean. As expected, he had passed his bac without any problem, and he was due at the end of July. He had eventually accepted his father's offer and set off to explore England. And there again, Jacques was pleased about this, for it was he who had, by telephone, begged him not to make an ass of himself and to take advantage of the offered visit.

'Besides, with the drought, there's nothing to do here! I promise you, it's true,' he assured him. 'So go and find out whether English food is as bad as people say. And don't think you have to bring back an English girl, your parents wouldn't appreciate that very much!'

Finally, another reason to be content: good, reliable tenants had at last been found for the château of Saint-Libéral, thanks to Guy. From July 1977, it would welcome children of the employees of the Franco-Belgian wireworking firm Lierson and Meulen. This was a large industrial group which produced thousands of kilometres of fencing wire in its factories, and was also involved in ironmongery. One of the directors was a friend of Guy's and went hunting with him at Brenne.

Lierson and Meulen's decision was excellent news, for with the children would come the support personnel; male and female group leaders, administrators. Jacques had undertaken to find a couple of caretakers who would live there permanently and maintain the château. It would therefore remain open and ready to receive guests. For the firm also planned to organise, in peace and quiet and during the off-season, some seminars for their representatives and salesmen. All this would give a great boost to Saint-Libéral. Already in the plans was the tennis court so eagerly demanded by Peyrafaure, and also a swimming-pool, without which the Lierson and Meulen group would have refused the lease.

Of course, all these developments brought enormous costs which the community was unable to meet alone. Jacques had had to knock on many doors to obtain subsidies, and in particular, long-term loans at very favourable rates. He knew that the management of the entire operation would not be easy, but never regretted for a moment that he had launched into this venture. For it was really cheering to see his friends, neighbours and fellow citizens preparing to join in the rebirth of Saint-Libéral.

Already, Brousse was planning to develop his market garden to supply everything the château kitchen was obviously going to require. As for Delpeyroux and Delmond, they were proposing to provide all the milk, cheese, eggs and poultry the residents might need. Even Coste was mulling over the idea of investing in the purchase of a few ponies and horses which the young people, and not just those in the holiday home, would be delighted to mount. He even saw himself opening a sort of ranch, with refreshments, various games, and pony trekking around the local lanes.

'All he needs is to hire a few Red Indians and arm himself with a Colt pistol and it'll be the Wild West!' commented Pierre-Edouard sarcastically on learning of the project. He did not regard the transformation of Coste into a sheriff very favourably, and dreaded seeing the track he followed for his daily walk invaded by hordes of riders, with or without bows!

'I shall bring out my twelve-bore again, the day that happens! And not just for the Redskins!' he had warned.

Despite reservations and comments of this kind, Jacques, as mayor, could only rejoice to see his community reviving.

Josyane almost did an about-turn when she saw, even before entering, that the Claire Diamond salon did not look as it normally did. She thought it was arranged for a fashion parade: nothing was in its customary place, and spotlights were standing ready to illuminate the grand staircase. Conscious that her threadbare jeans and rather faded T-shirt were likely to be out of place amongst the couture house's choice products, she was about to take to her heels when Chantal caught sight of her, and beckoned her in.

'Look, have you seen my outfit?' asked Josyane after kissing her.

'And? What's the problem? It's Monday, there are no customers!'

'Monday?' she calculated. As a result of going to bed in the early hours, she occasionally lost count of the days: 'Well what do you know, I hadn't realised yesterday was Sunday.'

'You don't look very well, you know?'

'That'll soon change, I'm stopping work with the agency.'

'Ah! That's good news!'

'Maybe, but I've no other work. Tell me, what's all this fuss going on here?' she said, with a nod in the direction of the spotlights.

'That? Just the photos for our winter collections. But guess who's upstairs? Yes! Our friend Christian! He must be busy flirting with Karine!'

'Idiot!' said Josyane, blushing a little, but also smiling, for she was suddenly very happy to have come. 'In the first place your Karine is called Josette! What's more she's as flat as a lemon sole, and I'd be very surprised if he were interested in a stick like that! And besides, she's sure to be a dyke!'

'Ah, right! You wouldn't happen to be a mite jealous?' Chantal was amused.

'And why would I be? And on what grounds? Your Christian, I haven't seen him since I was in Tahiti!' she said with a scowl.

'Well, go and say hello to him! He'll be delighted, he asked me again for news of you. You know the building, go up.'

'No. I'll wait here!'

She had decided once and for all that she would not take the first step, and intended to stick to the principle.

'As you like, nobody's forcing you!'

'Just as well! By the way, have you any news of the family?' she asked, simply to change the subject for she had received a letter from her mother three days earlier.

'Yes, last night on the phone. Everyone's fine. But it seems they're suffering terribly from the drought. Just imagine, the Diamond has stopped flowing and the spring has almost dried up. When I think that we're delighted with this super weather!'

'That's true, it's very pleasant,' said Josyane absent-mindedly as she glanced covertly towards the staircase.

'Are you sure you don't want to go up?' her sister teased.

She was highly amused, for, without her lifting a finger, everything was happening the way she would have organised it if she had wanted to intervene. She had known for months that Christian was not indifferent to her sister's indisputable charms and that he had not forgotten her. But she knew too that Josyane was still smarting from her previous experience. Consequently, so as not to spoil or rush things, she had decided to leave it to fate. And today, 26 July, fate seemed at last to be taking a hand.

'All right, then, come and have a drink in the office,' she suggested. 'In the meantime he'll probably come down . . .'

'Oh! Don't make so much of it, please!' smiled Josyane, who knew very well that her sister had guessed her secret long ago. 'And don't imagine I'm going to throw myself around his neck! What an idea!'

'I'm not imagining anything. So you've finally decided to stop your silly job?'

'Yes, it was really getting a bit much. And then, it was a killer!'

'And what will you do now?'

'Not the slightest idea,' said Josyane, placing herself in the doorway to watch the staircase. It was then that she saw him coming down, his Bronica in his hand.

He in turn noticed her, stopped, smiled. Then, as a professional reaction, because the young woman's outfit and her style were a magnificent challenge in this stuffy, affected, posh salon, he lined her up with his camera.

'Do you mind?' he said at the same time. And, without waiting for the answer, he photographed her three times.

'That's mean!' she said without moving. Then she waited for him to approach and exclaimed: 'You took your time coming back from Polynesia. Were you held up by one of the local girls?'

'One? You can't be serious! More like twelve! Anyway, don't tell me you've been waiting for me, I wouldn't believe it,' he joked. Then he noticed she was wearing one of the shell necklaces he had hung around her neck the morning of her departure from Tahiti. 'That's nice, you still have that trinket,' he said.

'Oh! It wasn't easy! I've already had to restring it twice, the shells cut through the thread,' she explained. Then she realised that she had just given the game away, and burst into laughter.

Motionless in the shade of the huge chestnut trees which encircled the pasture, where the reddish earth was cracking open day by day under the sun, the animals were waiting. Exhausted by the heat, debilitated by thirst and hunger, irritated by clouds of horseflies which attacked them incessantly, they were lowing pitifully whilst listening anxiously for the rumble of the tractor which would bring them water.

For more than a week now the spring which fed their pool had almost stopped flowing, although according to the old folk it was supposed to be inexhaustible. Now, on the bottom, baked by the heatwave, a blackish, stinking mud was thickening and hardening. Jacques was therefore forced to fill his tank every evening at Coste-Roche, where water was not yet scarce, and to cover the four kilometres which separated his farm from the fields and meadows of the Heath.

Despite all the time this wasted, he did not regret having taken his herd over there. For although the drought was just as dreadful as on the plateau at Saint-Libéral, there were woods and thickets here, where the cows could shelter from the sun. They succeeded in stilling their hunger a little by browsing on the lower leaves, the ling and a few dried grasses in the undergrowth, for there was nothing left on the pastures. Shorn and dusty, they no longer retained the slightest traces of greenery. As for the fields where tobacco, beet and maize should have grown, in the heatwave they revealed only the shrivelled skeletons of dead plants. It was a desolate spectacle.

And the worst of it was that there seemed to be no indication of rain. For the leaden blue sky was not relieved by the shadow of a cloud. And the sumptuously luminous sunsets were followed by sunrises all just as sparkling, harbingers of warmth and fine weather. The holiday-makers were delighted: the pools, lakes and river banks of the area were packed, thronged by the masses who had every reason to feel happy and lively.

But in Saint-Libéral and throughout the countryside there echoed the monotonous bellowing of thirsty cows. Everywhere too, from the break of day, taking up the response, the strident call of chainsaws and the heavy blows of axes sprang from echo to echo, as the oaks were pruned around which the cows and sheep crowded to snatch leaves and still tender twigs. Wisely, all the farmers were deferring the moment when they would have to broach their meagre stocks of hay. For if feeding had to start in August, what would be left in the lofts when February came? And yet it was essential that the animals were fed and watered!

Driven by thirst and hunger some of them, although quiet and peaceable until then, jumped the fences or crushed them. Then, mooing to their last gasp, cutting through by the shortest route, they bounded down to the bottom of the valleys where a semblance of greenery still clung to life. Or alternatively, and more seriously, they settled among the first vines they reached and nibbled them down to the stock. In the same way, attracted by the orchards, they pounced on and guzzled the leaves and fruit, at the risk of choking by swallowing big mouthfuls of green apples too quickly. Or again, guided by the smell of the little kitchen gardens which were watered somehow or other after a fashion, for they lay close to the houses, they gorged themselves on cabbages, carrots and beans. And even the strong, cloying smell of the tomato leaves did not deter them.

Fortunately Jacques' animals had not indulged in this sort of escapade. He really did not need that to take up his time. In fact, victims of the fierce heat prevailing in the piggery, three pigs weighing about a hundred kilos had succumbed, laid low by heat-stroke. Two sows, also within inches of apoplexy, had been saved in the nick of time by Françoise's initiative; she had performed a life-preserving bloodletting on each of them, then sprayed them thoroughly with cool water.

Since then, Jacques, Michèle, Françoise and Jean, who had arrived ten days earlier, took turns in the piggery, where the temperature was unbearable, to sprinkle all the occupants periodically. Jacques was very much afraid that water might now be cut off, rationed. Such an eventuality was quite probable and very worrying. For besides the pigs, he had to water his thirty-five cattle every day. With the heatwave, they each swallowed their fifty litres without difficulty. Now if, besides being underfed, they were to be short of water . . .

'You're right, those cows are hungry,' said Jacques to his nephew when he entered the enclosure that afternoon.

Busy with contractors' problems - the work on the château had begun a fortnight ago, but slowly because many of the workmen were on holiday – he had not had time to come the previous day and had left to Jean the task of driving the tank with its two thousand litres of water. He now had complete confidence in his nephew.

In one year Jean had changed a great deal; broadened out, grown seven or eight centimetres and acquired the build of a lumberjack. He had hands like carpet-beaters, shaved from necessity and not to be like the grown-ups, and had a fine voice, firmly fixed in the bass register. And above all he had become less impulsive, less dogmatic. He was prepared to accept arguments, no longer jibbed like a mule, and even went so far as to acknowledge that he could be mistaken.

Given that, he was still just as determined about his plans. With, however, one change which delighted his father. Although the idea of being a stock-breeder still gripped him, he admitted now that it would probably take several years before he could set up on his own account. And although he really hoped to achieve this one day, at least he declared himself prepared, for a while, to do the same as his cousin Dominique. On condition, of course, that it would be to manage a fine herd of pedigree animals. Jacques did not have the heart to tell him that such work was not so easy to find as he thought. He guessed his nephew would realise this for himself.

'You're right,' he repeated, climbing down painfully from the tractor, 'those beasts are hungry! Good God, look at that one there, how she's faded away! I know full well it's her calf killing her, but all the same!'

'We should at least bring them a few sacks of granules.'

'Hey, hang on! It's easy enough for you to say that! Do you know what they cost? And once you start . . . No, we're going to do the same as our neighbours; luckily there's no shortage of oaks here!'

'Where do we start?' asked Jean, catching hold of the axe which he had tucked in alongside the mudguard of the tractor.

'Remind me to bring the ladder tomorrow. But in the meantime let's tidy up this tree. You know how to climb, okay? Just leave the crown right at the top and prune as you come down. But mind you don't break your neck!'

'What an idea!' said Jean with a dismissive shrug. He slid the axe under his belt, sized up the tree, and climbed nimbly to the top.

The cows rushed over as soon as the first branch tumbled down. And it was such a pleasure to see them greedily swallowing the leaves and budding acorns that Jean stopped for a moment in order to watch them better.

'That looks great! They make me feel hungry!' he called to his uncle.

'Don't let me stop you! Look, tomorrow, remind me to bring them two or three blocks of salt as well. They've finished it all, natural in his heat.'

'Hey!' cried Jean, suddenly stretching out his arm. 'Have you seen over there? It's burning!'

'Where?' said Jacques looking in the direction he was pointing. 'Oh! Bloody Hell! My God, that's on the far side of the plateau, at the foot of the peaks, it's our place! Come on down, we'd better get over there, with this drought the whole plateau might go up, and the woods with it!' he said, quickly unhitching the tank. He waited while Jean climbed up beside him, and charged towards the black smoke which was already darkening a section of sky.

*

Starting from the edge of the track which wound towards the White Peak, the fire, driven by a hot east wind, leapt first on the bushes which covered the slope climbing up to the plateau. There you could make out the regular pattern of the little walls and boundary furrows which had formerly criss-crossed it, in the times when it was cultivated.

Well exposed to the spring sunshine, with an open aspect to the south, the plots which clung on there were rich with a soil suited to the spade; deep, easy to work, generous. Here, some sixty years earlier, succulent spring vegetables used to grow: the first extra fine peas, of an incomparable flavour, new potatoes with tender delicate flesh, juicy spring carrots, garlic and white onions, top quality green beans and even early season strawberries with a heady scent.

From there came the baskets and crates full of all that exceptional produce for which the wholesalers of Objat or Brive competed and paid the asking price, certain of making a great profit from the grand restaurateurs of Paris.

But for lack of manpower, and because the slope was much too steep to be cultivated mechanically, the gardens had been abandoned one after another. Then, very quickly covered by weeds, fleabane, broad-leaved dock and rye grass, they had subsequently provided a welcome for the first roots of bramble and dog rose. Encouraged by the richness of the soil, all the parasitic plants and shrubs had flourished, gaining on all sides, invading in giant strides with rhizomes, suckers and seeds, covering the land with an impenetrable barrier of thorns, spikes and creepers.

From a spark, the fire leapt to attack such a feast. Snapping up the blackthorn, brambles and bracken with crackling greed, it swelled up, spread out. And the red tongues, increasingly voracious, quick and long, swallowed in an instant the network of thorny brushwood, guelder rose, old man's beard and shrubs which emitted the sinister whine of boiling sap and splitting bark.

Its appetite whetted, strengthened by its first victims, it threw itself on the meadow spread out before it. This belonged to Yvette, but Jacques had rented it for years. Dry as gunpowder, it offered no resistance to the flames which darted now like grass snakes, jumped, flitted, busied themselves creeping in the layers of bent grass and the withered grey tufts of creeping soft grass.

Driven by the wind, fanned by its own force, the conflagration gained ground, spread across the plateau like a shifting blanket. And it was with the strength of a front which covered more than a hundred metres that the inferno, having crossed the Meeting field, attacked the White Peak. Eating into its flanks, with sudden high torches of flame it reduced to ashes the fragrant junipers, the twisted box trees, almost a hundred years old, and the great broom bushes which colonised the arid soil. The blaze then became terrifying. And its roar was so violent at the edges that it drowned the call of the bell in Saint-Libéral, at last tolling the alarm.

Monotonous, dismal, resounding from hill to hill, it appealed for help, begged all fit men to hurry along to try to control the wildfire up there, now encircling the White Peak with a moving crown, as stifling and evil as a stream of lava. And already, growing drunk on the stubble fields, feasting on the dead stalks of maize defeated by the drought, the fire grazed avidly on the plateau, homing in on the nut trees and plum orchards.

When Jacques and Jean finally arrived in the area of the blaze, a few villagers were already in position, trying to hold back the fire's progress on to the plateau fields. That was the only place where it could still be approached; for there, although the flames were lively and fast-moving, they were low. That was not the case with the ones devastating the peaks, which only tons of water might be able to control.

'Where are the others?' called Jacques.

'They're sure to come,' explained Delpeyroux. 'Us lot, and Valade, it happened while we were pruning the oaks on the slopes; so when we saw the smoke, you can imagine how we ran!'

'Bloody hell, we'll never stop it like this,' declared Jacques, observing how rapidly the fire was advancing, despite the furious, and exhausting, shovel blows which Valade, Delmond and Delpeyroux were dealing out to the flames devouring the stubble and dry grasses.

'And the fire brigade?' asked Jacques.

'Have been alerted!' said Bernical without stopping hitting. 'I did that myself, but by the time they get here from Ayen and especially from Objat! And then I gathered they had a job before this one behind Saint-Robert, towards Segonzac . . .'

He was already streaming with perspiration and tears, for the thick, acrid smoke was swirling all around, stinging the eyes, burning the mucous membranes.

'Right, can you manage to attach the rotavator?' decided Jacques, turning to his nephew. 'Then run and fetch it. Get Françoise to help you and come back as quickly as possible. Bring all the shovels you can find and remember, tell your cousin and aunt that women wouldn't be in the way, if we want to stop this inferno before it moves down to the village! Go on, hurry up! But mind you don't overturn the tractor!'

He did not wait for Jean to set off, but picked up one of the shovels brought by Bernical and rejoined his companions.

'Need to all get together,' he decided. 'And try to hold this corner, for the sake of the walnut trees. Because if it gets over there and takes a hold on the slope . . .'

The slope was the one descending towards Saint-Libéral. It was covered in wood, scrub, undergrowth. But above all, it was there that the roofs of houses showed above the treetops, the ones built in the mid-sixties, on the land which had then belonged to Léon and which Louis had sold as building plots.

'You're right,' admitted Valade, 'need to all get together in the same area.'

Elbow to elbow, trying to beat rhythmically to stifle the flames at the same moment, the men threw themselves head on at the blazing mass. Soon joined by ten, twenty, thirty volunteers, they had almost succeeded in controlling that small section of the fire when the wind veered, turned suddenly from east to north. It was only a brief change of direction, maybe a whirlwind created by the furnace roaring over the peaks. But however brief, the gust was so violent that it revived the blaze, renewed the flames' vigour and forced the men to retreat. Already, on their left a long flickering, red tongue was stretching towards Brousse's walnut plantation.

'My God! What are the fire brigade playing at? And where's Jean?' cried Jacques.

Like his companions, he was already crushed by exhaustion and on his face, now brick red under a mask of ashes, sweat and tears were tracing grey furrows.

'It's turning on us!' yelled Bernical suddenly. 'Over here, you lot! Over here! It's going into Duverger's tobacco! Dammit! We'll never hold it! Never.'

They rushed to the glowing front which was now attacking the tobacco, roaring like a wild beast. The plants, still green but withered by the drought, flared up, shrivelling and crackling. The smell of the smoke changed.

It was now half an hour since Jean had left for Coste-Roche to fetch the rotavator, and Jacques was worrying that he hadn't returned when he finally caught sight of him. He watched him and nodded his head in approval. Jean was doing the best possible thing.

Engine and clutch full out, he was moving parallel to the wall of flames, a few metres from them. And behind him, raising a cloud of red dust, the machine, its gearwheels humming as fast as they could go, was opening the ground, digging it up and, most importantly, scraping it thoroughly and burying the stubble. And the flames were suffocated and weakened on arriving at this band of almost bare earth; a few blows of the shovel finished them off.

'With him, we'll maybe hold it, at least on the plateau,' rasped Delmond in a hoarse voice. His mouth was so parched and coated that he could not even spit out the half-burnt cinders and dust which swirled around the men, choking them, burning their eyes, drying their throats and noses.

Almost a quarter of the tobacco was destroyed by the time Jean finally reached it. He stopped at the edge of the field, hesitated.

'Go on, boy, dig it up!' Duverger encouraged him. 'But my God, what a waste . . .!'

Leaning on the handle of his shovel, exhausted, he was disheartened, battered. This ruined, ravaged tobacco was a loss of thousands of francs. The drought had already greatly reduced the value of the expected harvest; the conflagration was wiping it out.

'Go on!' he repeated, 'dig, boy, don't think of the tobacco, dig! We've just got to stop this bloody fire!'

'Hey, listen!' said Jacques suddenly, 'here's the fire engine at last. I'd better go over there to find out how we should organise ourselves now. Make sure you tell Jean to go across a second time and watch the fire doesn't jump.' He delivered a last blow with his shovel to the sparks sputtering at his feet and moved off.

He could barely stand, his back was hurting him so much, and he was bent double as he walked towards the red truck which he could make out on the edge of the plateau, outlined against the high flames devastating the peaks. For the Caput Peak was also ablaze now, like an enormous pine torch . . .

'Right, if you don't drive me up there straight away I'm going on foot!' threatened Pierre-Edouard.

Standing in the doorway, his eyes fixed on the heavy, black layer boiling up wildly above the plateau, he was fidgeting impatiently. Furious at being there, stuck at home, powerless, he was commenting continuously on the advance of the fire. He knew the peaks and plateau so well that he could almost say, to within a metre or so, where the inferno was and on which bush or tree it was feeding.

He had wanted to dash up there the moment he had caught sight of the smoke, just after the first peals of the alarm bell. However, Yvette had unfortunately gone shopping in Objat, and as she owned the only car in the family . . .

He had then tried to get a place in Peyrafaure's old 403, as he was also going up to the fire. But his car was already filled with men still young and strong. Men who were needed up there, who were awaited.

So, because he knew perfectly well that he could do nothing, that he would be of no assistance in the battle, he had let Peyrafaure go without insisting. Conscious of his uselessness, he had not signalled any of the vehicles flying past towards the inferno. They too were full of men, women and even children who would be much more effective than him. And he had waited, seething with rage, his gaze fixed on the big cloud of smoke which was growing denser and larger by the minute.

At last, Yvette had arrived. But now Mathilde, Louise and even Berthe wanted to dissuade him from setting off.

'Be reasonable. You can't do anything, you're not going to go and get in the way of the ones who are working!' Mathilde had begged.

'I won't get in anyone's way! Bloody hell, those are our fields going up in flames! Our trees! Our hills! I have a right to be there. It's still my property, hell and damnation! And you, Yvette, if you don't take me up there straight away, I'm leaving on foot!'

And as she knew very well that he would do it, and that nothing could hold him any longer, Mathilde shrugged her shoulders:

'Fine, then, if it amuses you to make yourself ill!' she said. 'But don't come complaining afterwards!'

'Right, let's go, we've wasted enough time!' he said to Yvette as he marched towards the car. He was about to get in when he changed his mind: 'By God! I may not be able to take a shovel to bash the flames, but I've certainly still got the strength to carry a drink to those who are fighting! And you're going to help me, you women, because even at your age, you can still do that!'

'Why not,' agreed Louise.

'Yes indeed . . .' said Berthe, moving towards the sink.

'If you think . . .' said Yvette.

'You're right!' said Mathilde.

'Then fill the bottles, all the bottles, a quarter wine, the rest water. And the same in the jerrycan! Come on, get a move on! They're thirsty up there, I know it. They're waiting for us!'

# 18

ENCIRCLED on the plateau as night fell, the fire, having reduced everything to ashes on the White and Caput Peaks, launched itself into the woods and scrub leading down to Fonts Perdus. There stood three-hundred-year-old chestnuts, enormous, bulbous trees, often hollow but still living; they flared up like so much cotton waste. And the oaks, acacias, Scots pine and brushwood blazed in their turn in gigantic and billowing whorls of smoke, roaring like a stormy wind.

Broken with exhaustion, the men who had struggled to prevent the whole plateau being destroyed felt increasingly discouraged when they realised just how dangerous, not to say impossible, it would be to check the advance of the inferno. Settling like an enormous, red, fluid octopus into the woods which covered the dizzy slope plunging towards the valley, the blaze was unapproachable.

Even the firemen from Objat and Terrasson, finally arriving as reinforcements, did not really seem to know how to attack it. They feared, quite rightly, to venture into the gullies and amongst the fallen rocks, to be cut off there if the wind veered again. It had strengthened since sunset and remained changeable, unpredictable. It blew now from the east, now from the north, stirred the seat of the fire and, sometimes seizing in flight the highest flames, hurled them twenty or thirty metres further into the tops of the pines which then seemed to explode in enormous crackling firework displays. And the pine cones, shooting out like grenades, flew in all directions and lit new brushfires.

'Do you know which way we could get down there?' the leading fireman asked Jacques.

Dead on his feet, with his back aching all over, Jacques was seated on the mudguard of a Jeep and felt incapable of moving, barely able to speak. He looked at the firemen who were training their hoses at full force but without great result; at the volunteers, now almost powerless, for there was no question of extinguishing fifteen-metre flames with shovel blows, and shrugged his shoulders.

'I don't really know,' he murmured eventually.

'Yes, yes!' exclaimed Pierre-Edouard suddenly. 'You'll have to go and block it at Calvary Coombe, it's heading straight over there!'

'Ah! you're still here,' said Jacques.

He had not seen his father for more than an hour, and thought he had gone back down to the village. He had noticed him handing out drinks to everyone and even, for a few moments, taking a shovel from a boy's hands and attacking the flames; just to prove that he could still be of some use.

'Can you direct us there?' the leading firemen asked Jacques.

'Yes, if you help me to stand up and get into your Jeep,' said Jacques with a sad smile. 'But you,' he emphasised to his father, 'get someone to take you down to the house; it's irresponsible being here at this hour, Maman will be worried.'

'No, no,' said Pierre-Edouard, 'she's still over there, on the plateau, not far away with Yvette. You do as you think fit,' he told the fireman, 'but at Calvary Coombe you should cut down a swathe of trees and perhaps make a fire-break, or else don't stint with the water . . .'

'We'll see,' said the officer, stepping up briskly to support Jacques, who was staggering. 'Hey now, mayor, you're not in very good shape!'

'It'll pass,' Jacques assured him as he climbed in beside the driver. 'Come on, let's go. We'll cut through over there,' he decided, pointing to a grove of trees half way up the slope towards which the flames were extending. 'There's an old track which is just about passable,' he explained, seeing the driver hesitate a moment, 'the trucks will be able to get through there, but they mustn't hang about.'

'Don't be afraid to cut the trees, over there!' Pierre-Edouard shouted to them as they were already moving off. 'If you don't stop it there, it'll spread into Villac forest, and then . . . And mind you take care, there's enough damage done as it is . . .' he murmured, turning towards the plateau where the hissing skeletons of fruit trees were still glowing here and there.

If I'd been told I'd one day see that! he thought as he contemplated the extent of the damage. Despite the darkness, he could sense it all around him, for on all sides, on the peaks and the plateau, he could still make out a few men extinguishing the last small fires. He approached the group of women who were talking beside the cars, and noticed Mathilde and Yvette.

'You're still there,' he said.

'We were waiting for you,' said Mathilde. 'Do you think they'll stop it?'

'I hope so! They've gone off to wait for it at Calvary Coombe.

That's the only place they might be able to block it. Well, well, so you're here?' he called out as he recognised the pair of gendarmes from Ayen.

'Oh yes, Monsieur Vialhe, for the investigation,' explained one of the officers.

'Investigation? What do you hope to find? Everything's gone up in smoke!'

'One never knows,' the gendarme assured him. 'In this case, as the fire only originated in one place, I don't think it was due to criminal activity, more likely a walker's cigarette-end. It seems that some hikers did pass through the village this afternoon. They even visited the church before taking the path to the peaks, it seems . . .'

'They get the blame then, your hikers!' scoffed Pierre-Edouard. 'In my time, it needed more than a fag-end to light an inferno! Yes, in my time, there where it started there were nothing but gardens full of green vegetables! Nothing for the fire to devour, right! And the edges of the track were trimmed! You never saw a blackberry bush! You could sit down there without pricking your bum on the thorns! Yes sir! And there was no risk of fire catching hold!'

'Come along now, calm down,' said Mathilde, laying a hand on his arm.

But he was so miserable and angry that he could no longer remain silent, nor hide his pain.

'But now, with all these fields lying fallow, it's burning! And it'll burn again! And it's in the process of wiping out a chestnut plantation more than three hundred years old, and hundred-and-fifty-year-old oaks!' he said in a voice trembling with emotion. 'And do you want me to tell you why it's gone up in smoke? Because there's nobody left any more to stop the brambles taking over! No one to maintain the steepest hillsides any more! No one to prevent the brambles spreading and the undergrowth gobbling us up! But nobody gives a damn about that! And when you say someone should be looking after the land, you're treated like an old fool! Then the fire has all the cards stacked on its side! Oh Lord yes! Fine state it's in, our country. There they go, strutting about on the moon and leaving our countryside to go up in smoke! And this is only the start!'

'Come on, let's go,' insisted Mathilde, pulling him away. 'It's late, you know, we must go back down. You'll end up catching something on me!'

'The start!' he repeated. Then he shrugged his shoulders, climbed into the car and waited until nobody was watching him to wipe his eyes furtively . . .

As Pierre-Edouard had predicted, it was on the edges of Calvary Coombe that the men finally succeeded in mastering the fire. Drowned under torrents of water, encircled on either side and, above all, suddenly deprived of combustible material, it lost its arrogance, grew tame, then crept low and died with a prolonged damp hissing.

Stunned, dazed, hands and faces stinging, the men looked at each other at first without recognition, they were so dirty, covered in ash, stained with charcoal. In addition they had such dry mouths and throats, and lips so baked by the furnace heat, that each word was painful to articulate.

But unexpectedly, coming from one or other of the trucks, bottles of water made the rounds. Then, gradually, the men emerged from their stupor and became aware of the all-enveloping exhaustion which was almost paralysing them. Already, veiled by the layers of smoke, pale glimmers of the sunrise could be discerned in the east, beyond the black petrified trunks.

Starting out twelve hours earlier from the other side of the plateau, the fire had covered almost two kilometres in its longest thrust forward. Behind it, more than eighty hectares of ravaged woods, scrub, fields and meadows were still smoking . . .

Since she had found Christian again, Josyane was living in a state of bliss. She could not get over the fact that such happiness could exist, and was almost beginning to convince herself that her situation was unique, just as Christian was unique.

For even when she sought to reason with herself, to return to a semblance of objectivity, she was forced to admit that no other man she had ever known before would bear comparison with him. In the first place, she well realised, they were all kids. And the more they tried to play at being grown up, the more they made themselves look ridiculous.

In any case all of them, without exception, only thought of one thing, getting her into their beds as quickly as possible; the rest did not interest them. The worst had been poor Gilles, and she no longer understood now how she could have stayed such a long time with such a failure. She blushed at the memory! For she reckoned that Christian, next to all those pretentious little brats, was like an oak amongst saplings, a strength and certainty in the face of frailty, doubts and mediocrity.

'Right, go on, say straight away that he's the only man in the world, unique, the handsomest, tallest, cleverest, and let's not talk about it any more!' joked Chantal when her sister gave vent in front of her to impassioned hymns of praise.

'You don't understand!' she said dismissively.

But she was too intelligent not to recognise, in her heart of hearts, that her reply was stupid. When it came to men, Chantal had great experience, and she never hesitated to extend it! But that was no reason to underestimate Christian!

In the first place, he was reliable and always even-tempered, which was a great comfort, and very restful. What was more, even after searching thoroughly, she just could not find the slightest fault in him, which had the happy result of reducing her sister to tears of laughter.

'No faults, Christian? You're joking, surely? He's stuffed full of them – yes, and a good thing too! I know of nothing worse than men who try to be perfect! They're feeble, feeble in every respect!' Chantal assured her. She knew very well at the same time that Christian was someone on whom one could rely, hard-working, with not an ounce of boastfulness, honest, and also a very handsome man. But she so loved to hear her younger sister arguing that she took a mischievous pleasure in making her angry; with Christian as the target, it was really too easy!

'You can say what you like,' Josyane exclaimed in the end, 'Christian's not like the others . . .'

She would say no more about that, it was her secret. Nor about what made Christian so special, so different from the other more-or-less adult males with whom she had dallied, sometimes not without pleasure, but always without excitement. And she almost cried with happiness at the memory of the evening of their reunion during which, having invited her to an excellent restaurant, he had taken her for a stroll along the embankment, not far from the Ile de la Cité.

'There, now at last we can talk to each other a bit,' he had said as he leant his elbows on a parapet. 'There was too much of a crowd in the restaurant, and our neighbour was obviously ready to join in our conversation.'

'Yes, I saw that.'

'I wanted to ask: could we perhaps stop saying 'vous'? It seems a bit stiff, doesn't it?'

'Yes, rather, but it was you who began it!'

'Well, yes, I'm from another generation! But considering you nearly chucked me out of your hut the first time we met, what would you have done if I'd addressed you as 'tu'? Right, we'll say 'tu'?'

'Okay.'

'That's that. It's a bit crazy, what I want to say to you,' he had explained as he took her hand, 'but, if you want it as well, I'd like us to go a little way together. How do you feel about that?'

'I'm ready for that, but . . . How do you see it, this way?'

'As it should be. Just because I've waited till I'm almost thirty-five, it doesn't mean I don't believe in marriage.'

'Oh? Marriage? Straight off . . . well now . . .'

She had been taken completely by surprise. Firstly, because it was the first time in her life that such a proposal had been made to her. Secondly, because she had always thought whoever made it would use customary form and procedure. Yet Christian had neither wrapped up nor gradually introduced his remarks. His offer was clear, frank, straightforward; it was typical of him.

'Are you against marriage?' he had continued.

'No, but I didn't envisage things going in this direction so quickly.'

'There comes a time when decisions have to be made, a time to act. To prove to yourself, and prove to everybody, that you're changing course, changing your life even.'

'We hardly know each other . . .'

'And so, who's to stop us getting to know each other? I didn't say I wanted to marry you next week!'

'If you're so sure of yourself, to the point of announcing it to me this evening, when we've only just met up again, why did you wait so long before trying to see me? You could have got my address from Chantal!'

'I've had it since the day you moved! What are you thinking of, do you take me for a child?'

'And you did nothing? Why?'

'To be absolutely certain. Certain that I wanted to see you again, in a serious way, not for one of those easy affairs which everyone gets fed up with in the end.'

'And what's more, I might not have agreed to that sort of thing!'

'Exactly, I didn't want to spoil anything.'

'Oh, right . . . And what if we hadn't met again? And I'd thrown myself into the arms of someone else?'

'Rubbish! I knew very well you were waiting as well!'

'You knew it?'

'Of course, ever since I put that twopenny-halfpenny necklace round your neck. Ever since I saw you walking off towards the aeroplane, one morning, in Tahiti.'

'And you waited patiently for such a long time?'

'Is that a reproach?'

'No, but why so long?'

'Because Chantal told me that you needed to find your feet, on your own.'

'Oh? She's in on this, big sis?'

'No, no further than that. But she guessed it all, naturally. She's bright, your sister, you know!'

'And what if we hadn't met again at my aunt's just now?'

'I'd given myself until August the fifteenth before going to look for you! There it is, you know everything. So now it's up to you to decide.'

Her gaze fixed on the Notre-Dame illuminations, she had reflected for a long time before replying. It was not that she was hesitating, but she wanted to allow the seriousness of the situation to sink in. To grasp the idea that her life was about to change, in every way, irrevocably, and that she was mad with joy.

'Yes, I'd love us to make our way together, and for that way to be long – and very, very long!' she had said eventually.

'Then, our agreement should be sealed?'

'Of course.'

And she had thrown herself into his arms under the amused eyes of the walkers who were enjoying the sweetness of that summer evening, and its calm, for already Paris was on holiday.

Later on, when he had accompanied her back to the Rue de l'Ouest, she had once again got the measure of his real seriousness, his strength, his honesty too.

'Here you are, home. It is here, isn't it?' he had asked as he stopped his car below the block of flats.

'Yes; I see you really do know my address.'

'Did you doubt it?'

'Not for a second. Right, here we are . . . Do you want to come up?'

'No.'

'Why?'

'You know very well.'

Touched, she had smiled, then continued: 'Yes, I think I know, but I want to hear you say it. Go on, explain to me why you don't want to come up! I'm so ugly? I'm not your type? You think I'm frigid?'

'Oh yes, just like a furnace at white heat,' he had said, pulling her close to him. 'Ugly? Good Heavens no, you're almost as beautiful as my last conquest! Hey, don't pinch me so hard, you're making marks! No,' he had said, becoming serious, solemn, 'I won't come up this evening, nor tomorrow. After a while perhaps, yes, but not this evening. This evening must be marked out as different. It's not an affair we're starting. Or rather it is, but it begins with a capital letter. And if we don't want this one to be broken off, we'd better not manage it like others. So there it is, a nice kiss and we'll part until tomorrow, okay?'

He had placed a fleeting kiss on her lips, then leant over to open the door for her.

'Go on, go quickly, before I change my mind . . .'

She had got out of the car and almost run to the door of her flat, so as not to be tempted to make him go back on his decision.

It was all this that she could not explain to her sister; it was her secret, a huge part of her happiness. To know that Christian, in contrast to the posers she had met, was capable of waiting. Capable of patience, to prove to her that he considered her different from all the others, that she was to him unique.

After all the effort he had put into fighting the fire, Jacques could no longer climb onto his tractor, nor even take on very strenuous physical work; his back was torturing him. So, taking advantage of the presence of Françoise and Jean, he tried not to exacerbate the pains in the small of his back and only undertook the administrative chores at the mairie and those of the conversion work at the château. And there, it was not as easy as all that!

A dormitory, refectory and showers needed to be provided. Also bedrooms for the group leaders and a large kitchen: in short, the means to accommodate the sixty children whom the Lierson and Meulen company would be sending in two batches spread over July and August 1977.

But because the conglomerate had also announced that a week-long seminar would take place in April, it was essential to check that the various skilled workers were present each morning on the building site. That was not always the case, and as the project manager they had hired had other things besides the château to supervise, Jacques had then to fill in for him. A few telephone calls were sometimes enough to round up the absentees. But he was very often obliged to jump into his car to go in search of some craftsman or other, supposedly detained elsewhere by some urgent repair work.

Nevertheless, despite these additional tasks, he was happy to note how lively Saint-Libéral was in comparison to the preceding years. For not only did the workmen lend animation, but more, there were numerous inquisitive holiday-makers who came to take a look at this village which the whole region was talking about. And the fire had increased their number.

Now, the ravaged hills had become a place to take a walk. Jacques thought you really needed morbid taste to come and gaze on such desolation like that. For what with the drought which would not end, the plateau had turned into a lunar landscape. So appalling that even Pierre-Edouard did not wish to go up there any more.

'I'll go back there when it's rained,' he stated. 'Besides, I don't like all those walkers who come to gaze on our misfortune: I might say something rude to them . . .'

Jacques knew that the old man had, fortunately, other sources of satisfaction. Firstly, in July he had spent a good while with Félix. Now he was eagerly awaiting the arrival of Dominique and Béatrice. They had confirmed that they would be coming over in mid-September and everyone was happy about that. But at the moment, he was preparing in particular to welcome his granddaughter Josyane and her fiancé. For this was the great news in the family. Twelve days ago, that is on the day after the fire, Josyane had telephoned to announce her engagement to one Christian Leyrac. Mauricette and Jean-Pierre were deliriously happy. Truth to tell their youngest daughter had given them enough to worry about; now they had the right to relax a little. For according to Chantal, the suitor was really nice, serious, exactly what Jo needed. Only Mathilde was a little anxious. Jo was her favourite granddaughter and she had frowned on discovering that her fiancé was almost ten years older than her.

'Well, there, you've got a nerve!' Pierre-Edouard had exclaimed. 'And what about us then?'

'How do you mean, us?'

'So I'm not eleven years older than you, by any chance?'

'Yes. But in our time, it was quite different!' she had interrupted peremptorily. 'And you were only twenty-nine when you married me. And you would have done it earlier if it hadn't been for the war . . . This fellow, that'll make him almost thirty-six! If he's waited until now and he's not a widower, he must be a terrible fast-liver!'

'That's a fine thing to say about Léon!' Yvette had then joked. 'He was forty-three at our wedding!'

Disconcerted, Mathilde had blushed and then shrugged. She had no wish, especially in front of her sister-in-law, to support her arguments by citing her brother; until his marriage, Léon had never aspired to any award for virtue . . .

'All right, I haven't said a word,' she had concluded, 'but I'm dying to see this fellow. And if I believe he's not right for my little Jo, I shall let him know it; he'll be hearing from me!'

'You'll do nothing of the sort!' Pierre-Edouard had cut in. 'We know very well that Jo's your favourite, she's so like you! But that's no reason to interfere in her affairs! Anyway, don't forget she managed perfectly well all by herself for the three years she stayed away! So don't you go playing at mother-in-law, it'll be enough with your daughter in that role!'

'It's because I'd like so much for her to be happy . . .'

In fact, although she never mentioned it, Mathilde was still affected by Marie's divorce, and feared that Josyane might one day seek the same remedy if her choice turned out to be disastrous, like her sister's. She was therefore anticipating the visit of her grand-daughter and fiancé with some anxiety. They had said they would be arriving on 28 August. That was in another two days, and she found it still a very long time!

Too busy watching a sky that was still a delight to sun-worshippers, Jacques paid little attention to the change of government which marked the last week of August. For a long time, anyway, political jousting, from whichever side it came, had barely interested him. At the very most he merely smiled on realising that his father and Aunt Berthe were going to miss a chance to comment wickedly on the television news when they caught sight of the former Premier on it.

'When you've had the good fortune to make your début with the General you shouldn't team up with a Judas!' grumbled Pierre-Edouard, who could not forgive the head of state's treachery in April 1969.

'You can say that again,' added Berthe, who had not forgotten the suppression of the 8 May memorial service. 'I really don't under-stand how a man who appears to be intelligent could have associated with that other chap, the accordion player, Giscard d'Estaing. What's more, he plays like a pig!'

However if all this was mere trifling, the drought was no such thing. Now the damage had been done, the maize was lost, the tobacco dry before being ripe, the potatoes so ridiculously small and shrivelled as to be pitiful. In any case, the ground was so hard that it was impossible to lift them.

And the worst thing now was seeing the cows grow thinner day by day. Under-fed, thirsty, they had already acquired an ugly-looking, coarse, lifeless coat. As for their calves, even by buffeting fiercely with their heads, they barely succeeded in extracting from the udders, flabby as empty goatskins, a quarter of the milk they needed to put on weight. They looked like bean-poles, and there was absolutely no need to be interested in stock-breeding to understand that they would never regain those missing kilos. Like all animals for the butcher's trade, they were unsaleable anyway, for the market was now overloaded with stock which the breeders had got rid of in the hope that the sacrifice of one animal in three would enable them to maintain the rest. The calculation might have been valid if it had finally begun to rain.

But the sky was still superb, for holiday-makers and town-dwellers. Magnificent in its purity, it was full of promises of bathing in the coming days, of refreshing siestas, picnics at the water's edge, lovely, long, mild evenings in the garden, filled with the rustle of chirping crickets quite undisturbed by the chime of ice-cubes clinking in glasses misted with condensation.

But to those watching for clouds, to those awaiting the providential storm, the sky seemed so unmercifully set on drought day after day, that it became agonising, almost frightening, since there was no longer any hope of some development towards a change for the better.

So on this account as well, this desolation which afflicted the countryside and was so painful to contemplate, Jacques did not complain too much at being forced to take care of his back and not go out into the fields any more. But this was only temporary; Françoise and Jean would be leaving again before the week was out. At that point, fit or not, he would certainly have to look after his animals, go each day to lop oak trees for them and take them water. And whether he liked it or not, his back would have to hold out!

'And you say he was from the Brive area, in the south?' persisted Pierre-Edouard.

'Yes, that's what I've been told,' confirmed Christian, politely refusing another portion of *conflit d'oie* with mushrooms and sauté potatoes offered to him by Mathilde.

He could not eat another morsel! And he was amazed that they could dine on such luxurious produce without appearing to be aware how lucky they were to be able to take their fill like this of foie gras, cep mushrooms, *conflit d'oie*, omelettes with chanterelles, guinea-fowl and real farmyard chickens!

During the three days he had been in Saint-Libéral, he had swallowed more foie gras and other regional specialities than in the rest of his entire life! As a result he was beginning to wish for a plain

937

lettuce leaf as his whole dinner. But that was unthinkable. As Pierre-Edouard had said to him at the outset, handing him a plate of succulent, delicious-smelling smoked ham:

'You haven't come here to die of hunger! Tuck in! After that there's nothing much . . .'

Christian did not believe a word of it, but had felt obliged to serve himself a slice as thick as a hand. After that had come rillettes, then a joint of veal with green beans. And now he was absolutely unable to take more *conflit d'oie*; it was beyond his strength.

'No, really and truly. It's excellent, but . . . I'm not used to it, you see?' he said, passing the dish to Josyane.

She was seated beside him, and smiled at him. He guessed her thoughts and knew that she was happy to see him there, at her grandparents' table, with Mathilde on his left, Pierre-Edouard opposite him and the three aunts who were also observing him, weighing him up, watching his behaviour, reactions, remarks.

'If I understand things right, you're going to put me through one hell of an examination,' he had said to Josyane just before arriving in Saint-Libéral, three days earlier. She had painted a portrait of the whole family in detail, which did not make it sound at all reassuring, since it was obvious that nobody there lacked character and they would be checking that he had one as well . . .

'And then, you'll see, my grandmother Mathilde, I adore her. I'm supposed to look like her.'

'Then we'll get on very well, she and I.'

'But watch out. She's never at a loss for a quick retort either! And what's more she has sharp eyes, almost as bad as my grandfather!'

'They're not going to eat me alive, are they?'

'No, no, and besides you've got inner resources!'

Resources, without a doubt, but much less appetite than he should have had to do the meals the justice they deserved.

Apart from this drawback, obvious proof of lack of practice, everything had run very smoothly. First of all because he had immediately got on well with his future parents-in-law. Then because he had won over Mathilde from the first day. For it was indeed true that Josyane greatly resembled her; she had that same dark, piercing gaze, that same shape of face, with a small, slightly tilted nose and a very sweet smile.

So, without thinking, because he was moved to discover in that elderly, rather shy but smiling lady what Josyane would probably one day become, he had retained her hand in his and said exactly the right thing, just like that, in all sincerity:

'Jo said she looked a lot like you. It's true, I'd have recognised you anywhere!'

And the old lady's smile and eyes had told him that he was part of the family from now on, and very welcome.

'And you've never tried to find out more about him?' persisted Pierre-Edouard. He was extremely interested by what Christian had told them about his great-grandfather.

'No, it wasn't so easy.'

'I can imagine that,' said Pierre-Edouard, to whom Josyane had spoken of Christian's family, and especially about his father in the Resistance, who had died in the camp where Berthe's fiancé had disappeared, during the winter of 1939.

'I'll tell you a funny thing,' Louise intervened. 'On the railway workings here, in 1908, there was an old man who had worked in Panama too, on the canal. Yes, I remember it well,' she murmured, with signs of emotion. 'Octave often spoke to me about it . . . Don't you remember?' she asked her brother.

He reflected, then shrugged his shoulders with some irritation. He did not like to be made to lose the thread of his remarks.

'Not particularly, no. But it doesn't matter, it's interesting all the same that you have Corrézien blood in you. Usually it's not bad stuff. And you say your profession is taking photos? Just that?'

'Well, yes.'

'And that provides enough to feed a man?'

'That depends on the man!' affirmed Josyane, placing her hand on Christian's.

'For me, at present it does provide enough and I hope it'll continue to,' he said, cutting himself a minute slice of Cantal cheese, in order not to offend the lady of the house.

He noticed that Pierre-Edouard suddenly seemed absent-minded, distant, and almost jumped when he shouted at Louise:

'What was that you were saying, you, about Panama?'

She repeated the story to him, brought it all to mind again.

'Miladiou! Yes! Of course I remember that old man!' he said at last. 'He quite likely knew your forebear. There's a funny thing! Yes, I remember, he talked to us about the Americas, every evening at the Chanlats'. My father didn't really like me hanging around the inn, but when he'd gone to bed . . .'

He fell silent, became thoughtful again, lost in his memories.

'I see you don't like cheese, you haven't taken any!' he said suddenly to Christian, disconcerting him with his changes of subject. 'Now then, why don't you do the rounds of the solicitors? They'd be able to tell you!' he said, returning to his original idea. 'Why yes!' he continued, seeing that nobody understood. 'To find out where your ancestor lived! he's bound to have bought or sold something, that fellow, either him or his father! All that, it's written down somewhere! Or else in the christening registers . . .'

'I hadn't thought of that,' admitted Christian. 'Well, if I have the time, one day I'll try to find out which village Antoine Leyrac came from.'

'And you'll be right to do it,' said Pierre-Edouard. 'It's important to know where you come from, that gives you your roots. And say what you like, roots allow you to stand tall, and to withstand storms properly too! Ask young Jo: if she remembers what her grandmother taught her, she can tell you about the Vialhes as far back as my great-grandfather. That's not bad for a start, is it?'

# 19

WHEN Christian and Josyane embarked on the exploration of the Corrèze, it was for pleasure and not to discover possible traces of his ancestors. For despite the drought which disfigured it, lending its hills and slopes the russet tints of autumn's end, it remained beautiful in the valleys, harmonious. Bewitching, too, with its little blue-roofed villages nestling amongst the chestnut groves, its romanesque churches with their moss-covered stones, and remnants of castles, hidden by ivy, but still impressive, clinging fiercely to their crags.

Hand in hand, Christian and Josyane set out each morning and did not return till nightfall, exhausted but happy, their heads full of memories and country scenes.

But it was on visiting Saint-Libéral, lane by lane, that Christian had an idea he considered realistic enough to communicate to Jacques.

The evening before, Jacques and Michèle had come down to eat dinner with Josyane's parents. They were feeling rather low, for Françoise had gone away that same morning, while Jean had returned to Paris two days earlier. His absence was already being felt, for even though Jacques was improving slightly, his back was still making him wretched. Probably rather disheartened at finding himself alone again, he had fallen to doubting whether the château's new function would be sufficient to breathe fresh life into Saint-Libéral.

'You've got to understand: the kids will be great, but from the commercial point of view, I don't think they'll encourage shop-keepers to come and open up. What we need are adults. Even for three months, that would at least be something. Because we have to see things as they are; it's never going to be farmers who'll make the village live again, might as well look to holiday-makers right away. But how to attract them?'

'I thought you'd planned a swimming-pool and even a tennis court!' Josyane had said to him.

'Yes, but I doubt whether that'll be enough. And then, God willing, there'll be rainy summers too, so the pool and the tennis court . . .'

'Your uncle's right. Your village lacks excitement, life. Look at that boarded-up inn, it's so sad! And that lifeless grocery store! It's really off-putting to tourists!' said Christian as he dragged Josyane into the little road which led to the village hall.

'Look, they've refurbished it a bit,' confirmed Josyane after pushing open the door. 'Ah, I see . . .' she said, reading the plaques which adorned the walls.

In fact, for lack of young people to fill it, and since the château was no longer available, it was there that the Léon Dupeuch Association met, none of its members less than sixty-five years old . . .

'Not bad, this building,' said Christian, having made a tour of it. 'But, my goodness, it's gloomy! It already feels like an old people's home!'

'Yes, like the whole village. And when you see it in winter . . . It's frightful, I swear, dire.'

'I believe you. But there's sure to be something that can be done. Where the countryside is so beautiful, so welcoming, and where one eats so well, far too much but so well, you can't just stand by and wait for the village to die.'

'Easy to say! If you think that my uncle hasn't said all this to himself already, a long time before you!'

'Probably, but all the same I have a little idea. He can make of it what he will. We could go and give it to him straight away, if you like.'

'An idea? A sensible one?'

'I think so . . .'

'Come on, tell!'

'This!' he said, miming the movements of a photographer.

All the time he had been on holiday he had not touched his cameras, and she did not immediately understand.

'How, that?'

'Well now, here you have the premises, the countryside, as many subjects as you like! I think, if there were, in the summer, a permanent exhibition of the best photos by amateurs, that would bring in a few people. It should be aimed at holiday-makers. There are plenty round about; the problem is to entice them here. And as they all see themselves as first-rate photographers, they need to be flattered . . . All right, lots of them are actually rotten, but what of it, nothing venture nothing gain! Right then, with a bit of publicity, a few displays, a small lab, several joint first prizes, things like baskets full of local delicacies, that should attract the crowds. And, what's more, it would provide a good pastime for the kids in the holiday

942

home! Come on, let's go and see your uncle. Your dying village is getting me down!'

'It's not so stupid, your idea,' said Jacques, 'but the trouble is, I know nothing about photography myself, nothing at all!'

Christian and Josyane had found him at Coste-Roche, filling the water tank for the cows still confined in the woods at Heath Farm. As he continued to have great difficulty in driving his tractor, it was Michèle who was going to transport it.

However, whilst waiting for the tank to fill, Jacques, Christian and Josyane, seated in the shade of the porch, were refreshing themselves with a well-chilled beer, it was only four in the afternoon according to the sun, six by the clock, and the heat was suffocating.

'Yes,' repeated Jacques, 'I don't think I've taken twenty photos in my life!'

'It's not you who'll be taking them,' Josyane said, amused, 'so where's the problem?'

'The best ones will still need to be judged, the ones to be exhibited!'

'If that's all, we'll come and lend a hand,' promised Christian. 'All it takes, at the start, is to launch the idea. Afterwards it should run of its own accord. But to begin with, in my opinion, you need a specific subject which attracts people here, to the community. For example, the best photos of the village, the church or the old houses.'

'Not so stupid,' murmured Jacques. 'That would oblige the tourists to come. But they'd better not think they're in a zoo and take us for zebras. I have a few electors, among them my father, who would *not* appreciate that! And nor would I!'

'Easy', interrupted Christian. 'You stipulate in the rules that any photo including any person or group of people will be automatically eliminated, and there's an end of it; you have peace!'

'You know, young Jo,' smiled Jacques, 'I have the impression that you've found a resourceful fellow!'

'Yes, I feel it was worth the trouble of going to wait for him in Tahiti,' she joked.

'Enough flattery,' interrupted Christian. 'One essential is missing in this business.'

'Oh, what?' asked Jacques.

'Food!'

'How's that?'

'Yes, the people who come here must find something to eat. I'm amazed that nobody's thought to open a farm guest-house or something of that sort. They do it in other areas.'

943

'Easier said than done! You can't become a cook just like that!' retorted Jacques.

'Go on! We've been here eight days, and I've already put on at least four kilos! That's the sort of cooking to offer the summer visitors; real, solid stuff made with good local produce. You don't realise, but I know people who would make a detour of fifty kilometres to eat the way you eat at home at your sister's, or your grandparents, so there!'

'You don't imagine that I'm going to open a guest-house here?' Jacques smiled. 'As it is I never reach the end of all my work!'

'No, but there's an inn in the village and it's a real shame that it's closed. That's where something should be set up!'

'And why not . . .' murmured Jacques reflectively. 'After all, poor old Suzanne's daughter might be pleased to be able to rent out that barn of a place. It's been for sale since Suzanne closed down. That was in . . . I don't know any more, she died shortly afterwards, it must be more than ten years . . . Yes, for sale, but nobody's interested. Bloody hell, your ideas are worth looking into, and I'm annoyed with myself for not having thought of them before! I must be too old . . .'

'Not at all. You know, it's not always from close up that you take the best photos,' said Christian. 'You see too many of the irritating details and not enough of the subject as a whole. Personally, I like to step back a bit. As for your village, don't give me the credit, it's just that I see it from the outside, with all the necessary detachment.'

'Well then, I hope you'll come back often, to help me to stand back,' said Jacques. 'I'm bloody well in need of it. Or else, I'm too old.'


That morning, 4 September, Mathilde seized her chance while Christian was in conversation with Berthe – they were discussing the next catalogue for the House of Claire Diamond – to drag Josyane out to the kitchen garden. For a long time she had wanted to see her granddaughter alone, but had not yet found the opportunity.

'Look, isn't it miserable, all dried up, all dying,' she said, stepping into the little enclosure full of vegetables. 'What wrongs we must have done the good Lord, that he should send us weather like this!'

'It's more a question of an anticyclone,' smiled Josyane, 'but then, why not the good Lord as well!'

'I wanted to see you alone,' said Mathilde, instinctively lowering her voice. 'Here, help me pick the tomatoes, at least they benefit from the sun. Yes, I wanted to say to you first of all: I'm very, very pleased with your fiancé, I like him a lot.'

944

'Yes, I'm extremely lucky . . .'

'Definitely. Listen, I don't know how you . . . That is, how you two are living; that's not my problem. For a long time now I've understood that you, you young people, don't behave as we did in my time. We, you know, before we were married, well . . .'

'I know,' interrupted Josyane, a little confused and embarrassed to hear her grandmother tackling such a subject, 'but you mustn't worry!'

'I'm not worried! You know, Jo dear, I didn't wait for you, after all, to find out how good it is to be in the arms of the man you love! So I'm saying to you, you do as you like, as you see fit. I don't know whether it's better or worse than before, that's not my business. Anyway, it wasn't that I wanted to talk to you about. I simply want you to make me a promise, just one.'

'Right away, if I can!'

'Promise me you'll get married. I'm not even asking you to wear white, because . . . But promise me you'll get married!'

'Of course! Christian is set on it, and so am I!'

'No, you misunderstand me. Really marry,' said Mathilde, lowering her voice. 'Marry properly, not like Dominique and Béatrice . . .'

'But what are you talking about!' attempted Josyane, guessing that she was preparing to lie to no avail. 'Why do you say that?'

'Come on, don't take me for an idiot,' said Mathilde, with a trace of sadness in her voice. 'You know, you're the first and only person I've spoken to about this. And when you've promised me you won't do the same as your cousin, I'll never speak about it again, to anyone!'

'So you were in the know about Dominique?'

'No, I realised afterwards. But I didn't say anything, on account of your grandfather. If he knew, he'd be so unhappy, it would disappoint him so . . . Yes, it was afterwards I realised.'

'How?'

'Simple. When you marry in church, you always have the photos taken in front of it, in the doorway, with the whole family . . . I didn't see any photos in front of the church, none. There were only some photos taken at Guy's . . .'

'And that was enough for you to understand everything?' asked Josyane.

She was filled with admiration. And above all, overflowing with affection for her grandmother, now quite tiny, but still so strong, so clear-thinking. And above all so discreet, who suffered in silence because her grandson had not followed the normal course for a Vialhe. Who suffered but remained silent, so as not to distress her aged partner.

'It was enough for me to realise that Berthe was a bad liar ... So I want you to promise me that you'll get married in church, and I want to see the photos!'

'Listen, bonne-maman, listen carefully,' said Josyane, stepping nearer and placing her hands on her grandmother's shoulders. 'You won't need photos to be sure. We're going to get married here, in Saint-Libéral, and you'll be in the place of honour, with grandfather, both of you beside us. There, are you happy?'

'When?' murmured Mathilde, whose eyes had grown a little misty.

'Very soon,' promised Josyane. 'We haven't fixed the date yet, but very soon. Perhaps before the end of the year. Oh, you're not going to cry, are you?'

'It's nothing, it doesn't matter,' said Mathilde, turning away, 'I'll say I was peeling onions ... But why did Dominique do that?' she continued.

'Not say anything? That was on account of you two. Yes, grandfather and you, he didn't want to upset you. He knows you well, you see. And then, you can't make people believe! And Béatrice didn't want to play the hypocrite. The proof is, you must have seen it, she didn't have a white dress. There you are; personally I think that proves she's honest.'

'That's true,' admitted Mathilde. 'She wasn't in white, she's honest. And you say it was to avoid upsetting us that they said nothing?'

'Yes, the only reason.'

'Then they were right,' said Mathilde after a moment's reflection. 'Yes, it wouldn't have done for your grandfather to find out about that. You must have seen, he's growing old, poor thing, he's growing smaller, he complains. Sometimes he loses his memory a bit too. So, it's especially important not to upset him, he doesn't deserve it ... Right, now we won't speak of this matter again, of this ... this set-up, never again. And now, give me a kiss. I'm so pleased about what you've told me, so pleased! May I tell your grandfather?'

'Certainly, but it might be best if I tell Christian first!' said Josyane, placing two big kisses on her cheeks.

'He doesn't know?' Mathilde looked anxious.

'That he's going to marry me? Oh yes! It was he who brought it up first, he'd better not have changed his mind! But we hadn't decided yet to do it here. Now, it's definite, you can get the church ready!'

'Are you sure, really and truly?'

'Sure, Christian has no reason to deny me that. Come on, we'll go and ask him straight away.'

As they had both foreseen from the beginning, it was without forethought or calculation that Christian and Josyane put an end to the kind of test which they had voluntarily imposed on themselves on the evening of their reunion, almost two months earlier.

Since then they had never gone beyond the limits they had set themselves. Thanks to this, they had discovered the charms of tenderness and consideration, of suspense. And it was with amusement, on the evening of their arrival in Saint-Libéral, that Josyane had observed her mother's astonished expression when she had requested two rooms, without further explanation. Obviously her mother did not expect such prudishness on the part of a girl who had left on an impulse to travel the world on the arm of a boyfriend, not even her first! But she had asked no questions, and had taken two pairs of sheets out of the cupboard.

Since then, each evening, Christian and Josyane parted sweetly at their thresholds after several embraces which never went so far as to force an inevitable conclusion. Yet they were expecting it; it was just that each day they had made a sort of game of repeatedly putting it off.

It was two days before their return to Paris that everything moved on in a calm and logical progression. Before even admitting it to each other, they each deduced that the moment had come to begin a new stage, that the imposed period of waiting no longer served any purpose.

Less than an hour earlier, neither of them had planned that their walk should lead them to the other end of the plateau, away from the peaks, there where the fire had not penetrated. And neither of them had planned to go and sit in the shade of the pines bordering the field called Léon's Letters. Rather breathless from the hike, for the heat was oppressive, Josyane stretched herself out with a sigh at the foot of a pine, on a carpet of moss so dry that it rustled beneath her weight.

'What a heatwave! I'm sweating like a crock of water in the sun!' she said, peeling her soaked T-shirt away from her body.

He regarded her, smiling, and found her more beautiful than ever. He appreciated once again the firmness of the small round breasts, their swelling nipples pointed under the material, the flat stomach which ran down sweetly to the gentle mound of the pubis, shapely

947

under the skirt clinging with perspiration. A skirt rucked up far enough above the knees to reveal honey-coloured, lithe, exciting thighs.

She hummed as she stretched herself out, propping her head in her hands linked in a cradle behind her neck.

'It feels so good, here! You see,' she explained, 'here, we're at home! Well, at the Vialhes'. That's called Léon's Letters, I'll tell you why one day. When I was little, during the summer holidays, I used to come here with my sisters. We often met up with Dominique and Françoise, we used to make shelters. What fun we had! And in season, every now and then we went to scrump a bit from the neighbours' plum trees and even their apples! The apples were still sour; it sets my teeth on edge just to think of it!'

He sat down at her side and drew her to him.

'What I'd really like to do now is to eat you,' he said, placing a hand on her hip.

'Really eat me up?' she whispered.

He smiled, assented, and settled her head in the crook of his arm as she curled towards him.

'It's true, in the end it gets boring, this being sensible,' he murmured.

'Yes, very boring.'

'So shall we decide we've played long enough at the-first-to-give-in's-the-loser?' he continued.

'Yes. But there won't be any loser, quite the opposite,' she said. She briskly stripped off her T-shirt then unhooked her skirt fastenings:

'And now, don't waste any more time,' she breathed. 'And be very, very loving. This evening, now, I can tell you I've wanted you since the first day I saw you in Tahiti; that's ten months I've been waiting.'

'Me too, and it's been a very long time.'

The sun had just set when they came to their senses again, but the sky remained brilliantly radiant, still almost dazzling, so deep was the azure. Leaning over her, he saw that she was about to speak, and placed his forefinger on her lips.

'Ssh!' he smiled. 'You know what they say: the first one to talk after making love always says something foolish!'

'That's why you wanted to speak first?'

'Of course, to take responsibility for the folly.'

'That wasn't foolish,' she said, stroking his chest. 'And even if you've made me a beautiful baby, it wouldn't be! You know, I really hope you have created one! Yes, I do! I'd very much like to have your baby, straight away! Well, in nine months! After all, you did all that was needed, I think?'

'Well, I certainly didn't do anything to prevent . . . But you know, if it didn't work, don't get in a state, I'll be glad to try again whenever you like! Tell me, what's that?' he asked, placing his forefinger on a small brown mark which adorned her left breast. A little crescent-shaped mark which seemed to support the areola. 'What is it?' he insisted. 'A surprise present? It's absolutely delightful!'

'Oh, that?' she said, laughing. 'That's the family hallmark, seal of quality. It really is, it seems that my grandmother has one in exactly the same place! It was she who told me, when I was little. And it's because I take after her that I have a right to it. My sisters haven't got one. You have no idea how I used to infuriate them with it, when we were girls. I managed to make them believe it was they who had something wrong with them! Right, perhaps we should be thinking of going back?'

'Yes,' he said.

He gazed at her with tenderness, placed a kiss on the tip of each of her breasts, then helped her to slip on her T-shirt and remove a few scraps of moss from her skirt.

They walked down towards Saint-Libéral hand in hand. On their right, shining like a mirror, not yet full but already rounded, the moon was rising above the blue horizon.

Jacques turned the knob of the radio so forcefully that it almost came off in his fingers. For him, nothing was going as it should.

In the first place, the weather forecasts were all announcing the continuation of what the ignoramuses on the radio called the fine spell! He felt ready to put on a demonstration for them of this fine weather! Ready to invite them to come right here and see what things looked like – an orchard dying of drought, cows which could no longer bellow, they were so hungry and thirsty, and soil now grey, crazed, cracking open.

And, as if the weather forecasts were not enough to depress his spirits, the news had got in on the act. Now the commentators tried to outdo each other in finding fault with the farmers – those moaners who, not satisfied with evading taxes, were going to get money from the honest taxpayers, made to pay for the fine weather – perhaps it had lasted a little too long, but it was certainly less catastrophic than was being made out! And to support this type of clumsy lie, they had even produced some pedant who baldly stated on the airwaves that the peasants' tales of woe were without foundation! As proof, he maintained, France comprised one million three hundred thousand farmers who were the owners of one million three hundred thousand tractors! Well, if you knew the price of a tractor, did you not have the right to question the alleged poverty of the land-owning classes?

There again, Jacques was ready to issue an invitation to this loudmouth, just to let him see the reality of this luxury implied in his proof. In particular to let him know that many farms north of the Loire each owned half a dozen machines, or even more, which negated his theory.

Unfortunately, this fine orator was not the only one to spout. In fact it was open house to whoever could pour most scorn on those moaning farmers who were always complaining about everything and constantly demanding subsidies!

'Naturally, the moment there was the chance to muck things up, the morons governing us jumped in feet first! You couldn't find anything more pathetic than those technocrats!' he railed, each time that the television or radio news maliciously drew attention to the tax which some inordinately stupid, incurable halfwits had thought fit to impose; and christen the drought tax!

Like all his neighbours and friends, like all farmers, he felt it as a slap in the face each time a commentator mounted that hobby-horse again and attacked, repeating those two words: drought tax.

'For heaven's sake! The townies already turn up their noses at us, despise us because we're peasants; what'll happen now! But they're doing it deliberately, up in Paris, there's no other explanation! And for a start, they're perfectly able to help us without touching the taxpayers! Who does this bloody useless government think is going to believe they've got no more money? They know very well where to find it when it comes to bailing out the Renault Corporation!'

And as if all that were not enough to sap his morale, Dominique had informed them that he was deferring his arrival for at least a fortnight. Before coming it seemed he had to host several big noises from Mondiagri on a fact-finding tour. This change was obviously not a tragedy, but still, it was annoying. Just as it was extremely annoying that Michèle had to go out each afternoon to drive to Perpezac and take care of her mother.

The poor woman had slipped in one of the alleyways of the village and broken her hip. Without believing that she had deliberately stepped on a banana skin – it was difficult to imagine black ice! – Jacques could not prevent himself from grumbling whenever he thought of her. During the thirty years that he had known her, he could not remember a month having passed without her complaining of some bronchitis, flu, assorted aches, pains in the head, stomach, teeth, or ears, which obliged Michèle to step up her visits to Perpezac.

'You'll see,' he had often said to his wife, 'You'll see, just to muck us about, she'll break a leg one of these days!'

That was virtually what had happened! And, of course, Michèle was saddled with the work, as usual!

Since she no longer had the time to drive the tanker to Heath Farm, he had then been forced to mount the tractor again, despite the terrible pains that this induced. But as there was no question of constantly calling on his neighbours, and no question either of allowing the cows to die of thirst, he heaved himself onto his old Massey-Ferguson every evening and set off towards the woods at the Heath.

Very relieved to be rid of his visitors at last, Dominique did not even wait until their plane had taken off to climb into his car and take the road to Tunis.

If all went well, once he had got through the town, he would still have two full hours of driving before reaching Béja. Once there, he would collect Béatrice from the maternity hospital and return with her to their villa nestling amongst the date palms, tamarisks and oleanders of Bab el-Raba.

He felt much better since he had seen his visitors disappear into the embarkation hall. Not that the four men – a German, an American and two Frenchmen – were unpleasant, but they stank too much of greed, self-interest and ambition for him to wish to make friends of them. Very competent, no doubt – otherwise they would not have occupied the positions they held – they thought only of revenue, profitability, international markets, exchange rates.

When he had signed his employment contract with Mondiagri, Dominique certainly suspected that the word philanthropy was not part of the current vocabulary in the multinational company. The aim of the firm was not to teach the peons of Peru or Mexico better ways to cultivate their maize-plots. It was not to instruct the peasants of Black Africa how to avoid transforming their countries into deserts of beaten earth, nor the Egyptian fellaheen to irrigate better, or the unfortunates wading in the Indian rice-fields to protect their meagre harvests from rats.

Dominique knew all that. However, whilst he was in Guyana, that situation did not worry him because it it did not apply – or applied in a less obvious way – on French territory.

On the other hand, since he had been in Tunisia, his judgement had matured, and his critical abilities as well. He had therefore more and more difficulty in not bucking the system, such was his disapproval of the policies pursued by the brains of Mondiagri.

'It can only be one of two things,' Béatrice told him when he started talking to her about it, 'either you're incredibly naïve, or you were aware of it and didn't care when you signed the contract with them!'

'I didn't think it would reach such a level of hypocrisy. And then, admit it, in Guyana it wasn't so apparent!'

'No, of course not! But the fact is that you were working with equipment and techniques suited to all the Amazonian types of areas! By which I mean to say that everything you were developing on the technical side will be exported to northern Brazil, to Colombia – to Central America, and I don't know where else!'

'Stop! I'll begin to regret my job in Algeria. With Ali, at least we were genuinely working to help his mates feed themselves better, to make progress! But here!'

In fact, he knew very well now that the aim of the sharks managing Mondiagri was to increase their hold over the Third World. To set up research units almost everywhere, committed to creating or testing new varieties of seeds, animal hybrids, chemicals, to promote healthy plants and even equipment adapted to each soil, to each climate.

Next, and the faster the better, it was vital to persuade the governments to specialise in new forms of production and cultivation. As if by chance, Mondiagri would then suggest the selected seeds, the fertilisers, the animal feeds, the equipment and even the technicians to be responsible for setting everything up. Then, still paternally, the vultures of Mondiagri would also guarantee the purchase and export of the crops, at the lowest prices and after deducting various expenses, naturally!

Always ready to be of service, these same good Samaritans went so far as to sell back some of the provisions to those same countries, in order to allow them to feed themselves a little . . .

It was against all this that Dominique was rebelling. And yet he himself was only the advance guard, the reconnaissance scout, the pilot fish, the one testing the terrain. When his work was done the bulk of the troops would arrive, the lucrative government contracts, countless promises, bribes too. And always poverty. With as a bonus, for many peasant-farmers, the neglect or abandonment – if not the destruction – of their traditional agriculture which, however poor it was, still prevented them from dying of hunger one day out of two.

And the four mercenaries from Mondiagri whom he had just accompanied to the plane had come for just that. To make contacts, pave the way, to demonstrate, with the help of the experimental farm, that such and such a crop was exactly what the country needed. And to crown it all, they would no doubt be believed and even thanked, as saviours.

He avoided, at the last second, an absolutely decrepit Peugeot 203 taxi which had just shot out suddenly from the right. He hooted in rage, overtook the wreck and even cut him up. He was not in the mood to be intimidated by anyone. And especially not by a ruin of a taxi which smoked like a threshing machine and stank like an oil tanker.

'You look tired,' said Dominique, kissing his wife. He wrinkled his nostrils, for she smelled somewhat of ether and the delivery room: 'Have you been busy?'

'Yes, two births this morning and this afternoon a vaccination clinic. I won't describe the results, the mothers were wailing more than the kids! And how about you, is that it, have you sent off your VIPs?'

'Them, they can go to the devil! Anyway, they thank you for your hospitality, so welcoming, so French, in short, all that nonsense! But when I think that you served them foie gras from Coste-Roche! Those rogues didn't deserve that!' he said, turning on to the road which climbed towards Bab el-Raba.

'I was thinking of your promotion!' she joked.

'With foie gras like that, it's already settled! You'll be able to tell my mother, that'll make her happy.'

'Oh by the way, the post from France arrived this morning, just after you left.'

'And what's new?'

'I bet you'll never guess!'

He shrugged his shoulders, and changed down a gear because the slope was steep.

'So tell me?'

'Jo's going to get married, on the fourth of December, in Saint-Libéral . . .'

'What?' he exclaimed, laughing. 'Jo? Getting married? Is this a joke? Well, well, if anyone had tried to tell me! But who's the poor devil chancing his arm?'

'A photographer, a friend of Chantal's.'

'That's not very reassuring! Between Chantal and Jo, it would be difficult to say which has wreaked the most havoc! He's brave, that bloke! And what's more he'd better be in good health, because with Jo he'll need to deliver the goods . . .'

'Don't be unkind, Jo's very nice.'

'I'm not being unkind. I love her, you know that. But you're not kidding? She's getting married for real?'

'Yes.'

'Then that's absolutely the best news of the day! Well, we'll soon get some details.'

'Yes. You know, I'm thrilled we can leave at last. Even for a week, it'll cheer us up. And then maybe it'll put you in a better temper,' she added, seeing that he had resumed his sombre expression. 'Are you still thinking about your visitors?'

'No. Well, yes, I'm thinking particularly about the report they asked for; it seems it's urgent. And as we're leaving in three days . . .'

'They can wait! You're not going to take work home, are you? Your parents wouldn't like it! And nor would I, which is more important!'

'We'll see . . .' he replied vaguely as he drew up in front of their villa.

'If you play that trick on me, I can tell you it'll be bad news for you!' she warned, getting out of the car.

'Oh yes? You'll arrange separate rooms perhaps?'

'Right on!'

'Fine,' he said, moving aside to let her pass, 'so this evening, my only option is to get ahead beforehand. With my work, of course!' he said, patting her bottom.

Although engrossed in his work – the report which he had to prepare was long and detailed – Dominique lifted his nose from the page when Béatrice came out of the bathroom. He surveyed her from head to foot whistling softly, and nodded.

'Congratulations, lovely lady! You're magnificent! Yes, you are! And I know what I'm talking about . . .'

Still covered here and there with a few drops of water, with just a towel wrapped round her waist, which revealed one thigh to the hip, she was very attractive. He noticed once more that the semolina, frequently used in their diet, had a tendency to fatten her a little. But it was not yet a problem. Rather than thin, angular women he had always preferred the dimpled ones with rounded hips, soft to the touch.

'You're not going to work all night, I hope?' she asked, sitting down on the corner of the table.

'No; anyway, it's impossible under such dreadful conditions,' he admitted, placing one hand on her knee and lowering his eyes to the half-open towel.

'Well come on. That is if you want to get ahead in other ways than your work . . . But don't wait until I'm asleep!'

'I'm showering and coming,' he said, closing his file, 'and to hell with the report!'

He joined her shortly afterwards, and immediately forgot Mondiagri.

It was whilst he lay resting on her and they were still light-headed from their embrace that she whispered to him, her lips close to his:

'As your job seems to absorb you to the point of blindness, I'll have to point out to you that we've just been making love as a threesome . . .'

'What?' he jumped. He moved away sharply, observed her: 'Are you sure?'

'Yes. I'm way overdue now. And then, I am quite well placed to recognise the symptoms.'

'Wonderful!' he said, kissing her and hugging her once more, 'wonderful! But tell me, it must be only just? I may be absentminded and stupid, but all the same I'm not blind.'

'Yes, it's a little over a month, the baby'll be here at the beginning of May!'

'Well, what a thing . . .' he murmured, still in shock from the announcement.

Although, in the three months since Béatrice and he had decided to increase the Vialhe family, he had found time to prepare himself for the news she had just given him, he nevertheless felt strangely different from the person he had been half an hour earlier; he had altered. And his wife, suddenly also seemed changed; more solemn, more serious. Much more beautiful too, and strong.

'So that's what the semolina was . . .' he said.

'What are you burbling about?'

He stroked her hip and explained.

'Yes, I thought you'd put on a few kilos on account of the couscous,' he said, laughing and gently pinching her thigh. 'And these too, the same thing . . .' he said, passing a hand under her breasts. 'For a little while I've found them even more magnificent than usual, and that's saying something!'

'Ah? You noticed that. Naturally, whenever you can get an eyeful you do! But you didn't see that I was dead-tired every morning!'

'Er, no . . . But is that true? Are you feeling ill? Very ill?'

'No more than is normal,' she reassured him. 'And now I really must sleep, I'm tired. Are you going back to your work?'

'Oh no! Not now. This evening I'm staying with you. With both of you,' he continued, having placed a kiss on her stomach.

He turned out the light and snuggled up to her.

# 20

Jacques took his foot off the accelerator, left the tarred road, and turned up the steep lane which wound towards the woods of the Heath.

A thick cloud of very fine, red dust surrounded the tank and tractor as the tyre treads bit into the dirt of the track. This had become so dry, light and powdery that it covered and tinged with ochre all the withered grass and dry thorns which colonised the edges of the way; bitter and suffocating, it made the searing breath of the solar winds even more painful.

He slowed down again and prepared to change gear. He was nearing a hogsback which needed to be approached at full speed but in second gear, otherwise the hammer blow transmitted to the tank might throw it off balance. And it was unwise to forget the weight, and especially the force of inertia, in two thousand litres of water when shaken too violently.

When it eventually rains, and the soil is less hard, I'll have to level off this hump, he thought. But in fact, when it's rained I won't need to bring water to the cows!

He began to disengage the clutch and cried out, suddenly pierced by an uncontrollable pain which started in his left buttock, tore through his loins, and immobilised him.

Paralysed by a fiery stabbing which stopped his breath, it was so agonising, unable to move his legs and still less to press on the pedal, he saw the ridge approaching.

Too fast! I'll be thrown off! he realised in a flash.

Instinctively, he pulled on the lever which cut off the fuel. But the tractor had already bounced over the obstacle. Almost at the same time, Jacques heard at his back the terrific bang made by the water as it slapped around inside the tank. Then he felt the tractor tipping, dragged by the weight of the tanker which was sliding to the left, turning over as it twisted the coupling.

I've had it! he thought, seeing the right front wheel of the tractor already more than a metre off the ground.

Then, despite the hellish pain paralysing his legs, he clutched at the wheel guards, heaved himself from the seat with the strength of his arms alone, and threw himself to the right, praying that the wheel would not drag him under the machine. It struck him violently in the stomach and flung him to the left.

He just had time to tell himself that Dominique and Béatrice, arriving the next day, would be there for his funeral. Fireworks exploded in his brain. He lost consciousness.

Michèle was not worried by her husband's absence when she returned from Perpezac. Ever since she had been obliged to go and see her mother every afternoon, Jacques had fed the pigs alone, each evening. But as he also had to take water to the cows he had brought forward the feeding-time. Nevertheless, he did not leave until late in the afternoon, and only returned at dusk.

One thing was certain, he could not delay until it was completely dark; the tractor's lights had not worked for the last two months. And even for someone who knew practically every metre of the countryside, it was not wise to drive blind.

Convinced that Jacques would not be long, for the sun had just set, she was singing as she prepared the evening meal. The knowledge that Dominique would be there next day filled her with joy. He had not been back to France since his marriage and had most probably lots to tell, and Béatrice too.

Relations between Michèle and her daughter-in-law were good, but slightly ambivalent. Without admitting it, Michèle was almost intimidated by her. In the first place, Béatrice was from the town, which gave her an ease and confidence that was sometimes rather disconcerting. In addition, she took a lot of trouble over her dress and make-up. And there again, Michèle felt at a disadvantage when she compared her work-worn hands to those of her daughter-in-law, her face, coarse and reddened by the fresh air, to that of Béatrice, always smooth and delicately made up.

Also there was no doubt that Dominique adored her, doted on her. That was fine, but Michèle felt rather pushed aside not forgotten certainly, but a little less appreciated than before. She was intelligent enough to know that it was all quite natural, and the most important thing was for her son and daughter-in-law to be completely happy. However, even though she reasoned with herself, she still felt rather awkward in Béatrice's presence. The proof of it was that she could never manage to use the familiar 'tu' as Jacques had done from the start. That really simplified a relationship, made it less stilted.

I ought to try, from tomorrow, she promised herself, and I'll ask her to say tu to me as well; that is, if she doesn't mind . . .

She suddenly noticed that it was almost completely dark, and was surprised at her husband's lateness. Not yet very worried, but still, prompted by the need to reassure herself, she went to the doorway and listened out, hoping to hear the droning of the tractor. But only crickets were singing and bats squeaking as they chased mosquitoes.

'Now what's he up to?' she murmured to the dog stretched out in the courtyard dust. 'Hey, what are you doing here?' she asked in surprise.

Usually the animal was not tied up like its companion called 'the pointer', and enjoyed trotting along beside the tractor; it followed Jacques like a shadow. But the sun was still so hot when he left on the water run that you could understand the old mongrel's laziness.

If he leaves it any longer, he'll just have to walk back, she said to herself.

The moon was only in its first quarter: a tiny crescent quite useless for lighting the way. She took a few steps, went beyond the yard, listened again more carefully.

'No, nothing . . .' she remarked, biting her lips.

Now tormented by a little nagging fear, she tried once more to reassure herself. Then she suddenly made a decision, ran to the car and took the road to the Heath.


At first it was the smell which annoyed him. Still half-conscious, unable to understand why his bed was so hard, Jacques began to groan and wrinkled his nose. The stench of fuel and hot oil was unbearable and particularly out of place in his bedroom . . . or maybe it was the oil change he'd just done which had dirtied his hands . . .

No, no! It was more than two weeks since he'd completed that operation, he had even changed the diesel oil filter! Then why was it stinking so much, there, right under his nose, practically in his pillow which rustled as if it were stuffed with dry leaves?

He tried to turn over to resume his slumbers free from that nightmare stench, screamed in agony, and then regained consciousness completely. Gasping for breath because of the stabbing pains shooting through his back, he still took in his situation at a glance.

Above him, overturned on its side, the tractor was pouring out oil in every direction. It was flowing thick and warm from the engine and the axle, and forming a huge slimy pool which was now soaking into his shirt. And as the diesel oil had spurted out first and much more quickly, there was nothing surprising about the way he stank.

It must be at least ten minutes I've been lying here like an idiot! he reckoned, looking at the sun which was disappearing behind the trees. Then he suddenly realised how lucky he had been, felt himself pale, and thanked the Lord.

But for the big oak stump which was propping it up and had halted its spiral, the tractor would have turned over completely. As it was he lay almost underneath it, his chest against the big left wheel with part of the tread digging into his ribs.

'My goodness, I've had a close shave . . .' he murmured, gently feeling his head. He had a huge bruise above the nape of his neck, but it was not too painful. I knocked myself out as I fell, and if the tractor had continued its roll, it would have flattened me without my knowing! It could have gone up in flames, too, if I hadn't stopped the engine. Seems my time hasn't come . . . Right, I've got to get out of here.

It was then that he realised with anguish that he was incapable of getting up by himself. The moment he moved, the pain was such that he almost fainted away again. He could not even get his legs under him in order to lift himself up.

Good God, I must have bust something in my spine as I fell . . . Then he remembered that acute pain had paralysed him just before the accident: That's true, and that's why . . .

He forced himself to think it through, to reassure himself; carefully tried moving his toes, which obeyed, then his feet, which also deigned to respond.

Okay, it's probably something less serious than the spine . . . But as for getting myself upright all alone . . .

That was impossible, too agonising, beyond his strength. And yet I can't stay here with my nose in the oil! And then, good God, what if the batteries make contact, I'll be roasted like a pig!

He felt fear knotting his stomach at this thought and began to crawl, elbow over elbow, suffering the torments of the damned. It hurt so much that he was crying. Groaning and dragging his legs, he moved away from the tractor, crept through the dry leaves.

Exhausted, coiled like a foetus to try to assuage the searing waves eating into his back, he curled up at the foot of a chestnut tree. It was when he wanted to tighten his belt a notch to try to stop the ache at its source, there in his lumbar vertebrae, that he made one move too many. Overwhelmed by pain, he saw the sky revolving above him and the enormous branches of the chestnut toppling down. He thought they were going to crush him, and lost consciousness.

'Oh my God! No! No!' cried Michèle, as the headlights of the Ami 6 came to rest on the overturned tank and tractor. Her sudden braking raised a cloud of dust which whirled around in the lightbeams.

Her heart gripped in a terrible vice, she leapt from the car, rushed to the tractor and burst into sobs, convinced that Jacques could only be under the machine, since he was nowhere to be seen. And such was her relief, when she heard his voice emerging from the darkness, behind her, that her tears flowed twice as fast before ending in a nervous laugh when she understood that he was alive.

'You're there! You're there!' she said, kneeling beside him.

She touched him, stroked his face, kissed him, hugged him.

'Careful, careful,' he advised. 'I can't move at all, you'll have to go and get help!'

'But I can't leave you!'

'Go and fetch help! Phone Brousse, and Doctor Martel.' And as she seemed to hesitate, he continued: 'I tell you I can't move at all. You can't carry me even to the car, after all.'

'And if I support you?'

'No. I must have some bloody thing trapped in my vertebrae, it's hurting like mad! Go quickly and fetch help. Look, I've been here more than an hour, I can wait a bit longer . . .'

'I'm going to call the emergency services.'

'Not that! That would complicate everything! And then, by the time the ambulance arrives from Brive! No, no. Anyway, I don't want to go into hospital.'

'But what if something's broken?'

'Doctor Martel will tell me. Go on, get going. Oh yes, tell Valade too: he'll have to bring our animals something to drink, otherwise they'll break everything down, you can hear them bellowing from here already . . .'

'That's all we need, for them to escape!' she said.

'Yes, go quickly. You'll do the best you can, I know. But organise it so that my parents don't get in a panic.'

'Of course,' she said, leaning down to kiss him.

He sensed that she was crying, and held on to her.

'Just remember I was very lucky. Very,' he insisted. 'As my mother would say, the good Lord was with me. At this moment you might have been a widow! So unless you're crying because you're not one, stop it and go and get help.'

'You're right.'

She gave him a last kiss and ran to the car, where the motor was still running.

\*

Motionless in the darkness, concentrating on not moving so as not to exacerbate the gnawing pain paralysing him, Jacques stared at the few stars he could make out between the leaves. One of them, an enormous one, twinkled just above him.

That must be it, my lucky star, he thought bitterly.

He would have liked not to succumb to despondency, still less to despair. However, although he had escaped death almost by a miracle - he knew that tractor accidents were generally fatal - he did not manage to feel as pleased as he should have done at being unharmed.

And anyway, I'm not unharmed. Here I sit like a lemon, unable to move, confined to barracks. And how long for?

That was his main worry, his obsession. All would depend on the state of his back. Either it could be put right, and the accident would become just another unpleasant memory, or the damage was irreversible and would prevent any exertion. And then the farm would go to the dogs, for it was impossible for Michèle to manage it alone. And as for taking on a paid worker, you might as well hand in the keys right away. The herd, pigs and land did not bring in enough to afford such a luxury.

'It's been my fate to have really failed at everything,' he murmured, reproaching himself for voicing once more that dismal refrain.

It had lain on his mind for more than thirty years and he forced himself to banish it, to forget it, when he felt strong in health and spirits; he had a tendency to give in to it when fatigue and worries assailed him.

It's true! I wanted and was supposed to be a veterinary surgeon! That blasted war had to go and ruin everything! Six years lost, buggered up! And she makes the most of it by marrying the first little sod to come sniffing around . . .

There it was, one of his secret, painful thorns, stuck forever in a tiny corner of his memory, which sometimes sprang back to life . . .

She was called Marie-Louise, and had promised to wait for him, to marry him. And he had believed in it. No doubt she had too. But, there again, the war had come to destroy everything. Goodbye to Marie-Louise and his illusions! It was a real tear-jerker, like a magazine romance!

Bah, she was nothing compared to Michèle, he told himself, to banish the rather hazy but still touching image of a young girl before the war.

That was true. But even though Michèle had always been an excellent wife, a good mother and a dependable partner through life, she did not have the power to suppress for ever his lost dreams.

No more than Françoise's success could make him forget that he too, one day forty years earlier, had resolved to follow the same route. And, there again, goodbye to the fine plans for the future!

And now I'm going to end up the confirmed duffer. All because the ruddy war forced me to take over a farm which was already sinking into decline . . .

On this subject, too, he knew that he was not being objective, that he blackened the picture. In fact he had made the Vialhe farm extremely productive, and had been able to live off it and raise his family there. But what made him bitter was living always on the borderline of poverty, of collapse even. Fighting a losing battle, still having, at his age, frightening loan repayments. Having to row ceaselessly against the current, so as not to be swept away, swallowed up like so many others; it was wearing, exhausting.

And now that Michèle and I were finally going to breathe a bit easier, since the children don't need us any more, my body gives up on me! My God, I'm fed up with always having to fight on, fed up with struggling . . .

He wanted to turn over a little for numbness was creeping into his legs, but groaned with pain as soon as he tried to move.

Nothing doing, it's seized up . . . And what's more, now I'm dying for a pee! Still, not going to wet myself like a baby! I already stink of fuel and oil . . .

He managed to unbutton himself, turned a little on one side and relieved himself. But the proximity of the soiled leaves and moss annoyed him straight away. So once more, despite the pain and the weight of his legs dragging behind him, he crawled a little further off.

Well, what are they waiting for? What are they up to? He no longer knew how long he had lain there, his back against the warm earth.

He felt all his black thoughts returning, all those sombre reflections which he hated. Then, to chase them away, he tried to distract himself by contemplating the sky. He even ventured to count the stars which he glimpsed through the gaps in the foliage. He thought he had checked off sixty-three when he finally heard the noise of vehicles climbing the dirt track.

'Well, bugger me, you had a bloody lucky escape!' Delpeyroux whistled as he shone his torch on the tractor.

'Oh, is that you?' said Jacques. 'You're here? And you too!' he remarked, recognising Brousse, Coste and even Peyrafaure in the light of the car headlamps.

'Of course we're here, what d'you think? Wouldn't you have come if it had been one of us in your place?' said Brousse. 'It was the doc who told us to get together and come up, so as to move you more easily. We've even thought of a ladder, as a stretcher!'

'Where's the doctor?' asked Jacques.

'He won't be long,' Brousse assured him. 'By a stroke of luck, he was in the village!'

'Who with?' asked Jacques, immediately thinking of his father.

'At Antoinette's! Seems she got sunstroke coming back from the cemetery, that'll teach her! It's true, with this heat, that sort of thing could quickly land her next to that old fright she goes to visit there!'

Jacques managed a pale ghost of a smile. Old Antoinette was one of those rather bizarre but colourful characters who provided gentle amusement for the whole of Saint-Libéral. Widow for more than fifteen years of a lewd drunkard, who had been as bad-tempered as a sick pig and beat her black and blue almost every evening, she did not let a single day pass without going to pay her respects at her deceased husband's grave. There, after stirring the soil a little, pulling a few weeds and shifting the vase of artificial flowers, she murmured a few Ave Marias, then left again, at peace. At least that was what the charitable souls asserted . . .

Those less charitable, and they were more numerous, swore that the old woman's mutterings had nothing to do with the 'Hail Marys' or any other pious recitations. In fact, if old Antoinette made the effort to trot as far as the cemetry in all weathers, it was for the pleasure of being able to whisper over the grave: 'There you see, you old bastard, you're there, right underneath, and I'm still here, alive and kicking! And I'm trampling on you!'

'And Michèle, what's she doing?' asked Jacques suddenly.

'She's coming. She called on your sister and brother-in-law to tell them,' said Brousse. 'Now don't worry about your cows! Valade is just filling his tanker and he's taking them something to drink. Is that them I can hear bellowing like that?'

'Yes, they're waiting for the water,' said Jacques. 'Hope they don't break down the fence . . .'

'No, no, don't worry,' Delpeyroux reassured him, 'we'll take care of it all. And tomorrow, we'll come and fetch your tractor. My God, what a lucky escape you had!'

'Yes, you can say that again,' admitted Jacques. 'You know, you fellows, you're good mates, real mates.'

He was deeply moved to see his neighbours and friends around him. Touched to discover that even Peyrafaure had taken the trouble to come. And yet he had not always seen eye to eye with him.

'How did you know?' he asked him.

'Brousse told me as he went by my house,' explained Peyrafaure. 'But don't get in a state about that,' he added, anticipating Jacques' worry, 'we didn't raise a hue and cry. Your parents definitely don't know anything. There'll be plenty of time to tell them tomorrow, after you're sorted out!'

'That's it, tomorrow, and gently of course,' said Jacques.

Framed by his sister and brother-in-law, stretched completely flat on the bed, washed, clean, almost rid of the oily smell and best of all, relieved by Doctor Martel's injections, Jacques began to take a more serene view of life again. But that did not last long.

'Good, this time you can't get out of it,' the doctor told him, returning after discussing the matter with Michèle.

'Get out of what?' he asked rather curtly, for he had a premonition about the answer.

'It's the operation, or a wheelchair before very long. This time, you almost killed yourself. The next attack could come when you're in the car. And then too bad if there's a kid crossing the road when you can't brake any more . . .'

'Oh come on! You can stop that sort of argument, it's called blackmail! Look, I know my back is in shreds, but . . .'

'There's no but,' cut in Doctor Martel. 'You must be operated on as soon as possible. And as soon as possible doesn't mean in a fortnight's time! It means it's really urgent! Oh yes, just you wait till the effect of the injections wears off . . .'

'I know,' said Jacques wearily, 'I don't need you to tell me that it'll hurt! Right,' he sighed, managing a faint smile in Michèle's direction, 'how are we going to do it? I mean the farm, the cows, all that!'

'I'll cope,' she assured him.

'Come on, you know very well you won't manage all by yourself!'

'I'm telling you I'll cope with it! The neighbours have promised to come over. And Mauricette will help me, Jean-Pierre too.'

'Of course,' agreed Mauricette, 'we'll come.'

'You'll soon get tired of it! Anyway, Doctor, how long will it take after the operation?'

'Well . . . some time, yes . . . I'm not a surgeon, and . . .'

'You're a bloody hypocrite instead!' cried Jacques. 'Come on, give it to us straight, right! One month? Six months? How long?'

'It will certainly be necessary to avoid heavy work for several months, yes; but I do mean heavy work.'

'Like the tractor?'

'Oh, that! That's the worst thing for the vertebrae. So if you want a repeat of this evening . . .'

'Right,' sighed Jacques. He considered the matter, then decided. 'And where am I supposed to have the operation? If it has to be done, I'd prefer it to be by a good butcher, not one who does it with a knapped flint!'

'I know of one. Oh, I'm sorry!' the doctor corrected himself with a smile. 'Yes, I know a good specialist in Bordeaux. He's an old friend, a fellow student. If you like, I'll contact him this evening. Right away even, the choice is yours.'

'As if I had any choice!' grumbled Jacques. 'Go on, I'll give you a free hand. But from now on, the quicker the better! And don't feel you have to tell me it wouldn't have come to this if I'd agreed to have an operation earlier, I know that! So don't lay it on!'

'But I'm not saying anything, am I!' the doctor defended himself. 'Yes I am: where's your telephone?'

Although informed with great care by Mauricette, Pierre-Edouard still took the news of his son's accident very badly.

Actually until then he had been so pleased to be seeing Dominique again – Béatrice and he were due to arrive that same evening – that he was totally unprepared to hear bad news. It shocked him, left him speechless for several seconds.

'And is it serious?' he asked eventually.

'But I've told you, no! There's not even a scratch on him!' Mauricette assured him. 'However, he still has to be operated on.'

'And that's what you call nothing?'

'Now listen,' Mathilde intervened, 'you know very well he should have had it done a long time ago! So now he'll have to go in. But it'll be all right!'

She endeavoured to be reassuring, calm, but was concealing her anxiety poorly. She had never undergone a single operation, and regarded clinics and hospitals as totally unhealthy, treacherous places. You knew when you were going in and what for, but as for knowing when you were coming out again and in what state . . .

'And all his animals, eh, who's going to look after them?' he queried.

'The neighbours have promised to help us,' Mauricette assured

966

him. 'I'll go and give Michèle a hand as well. And Jean-Pierre'll come too, in the evening after school.'

'Your husband?' he said dismissively. 'He's never looked after an animal in his life. What are you rabbiting on about!'

'And so what? He can still help!' interrupted Berthe suddenly, who considered that the picture was being painted too blackly. 'It's not very difficult to feed pigs! Especially with modern equipment!'

'I'd like to see you do it!' he grumbled.

'Oh come on! Are you going crazy or what! I looked after them more often than you, our pigs!' she recalled. 'Yes sir! While you were chasing girls up near Paris, about 1910 on, I was carrying the pig-swill morning and evening! So if a teacher isn't capable of doing the same, what are we coming to!'

'Come, come,' Mathilde intervened, 'calm down, the pair of you; Mauricette's right, we'll manage.'

'You, I'm not letting you go up and work at Coste-Roche! You'd make yourself ill!' he cut in.

'Don't get so worked up! Maman won't be needed, don't worry!' said Mauricette. 'It'll all be fine. And then Dominique's arriving this evening. He's capable of helping, as well, isn't he?'

'No doubt,' he replied. 'But he's not staying very long. So afterwards, who's going to look after everything? And, what's more, in this drought, which means you have to take water to the animals! And then if Jacques has overturned, his tractor's had it! Oh my God, it all comes at once!'

He sighed and had to sit down, for he was suddenly very tired and very weary. And his heart was beating much too fiercely and too fast.

'You see, you shouldn't work yourself up into these states,' Mathilde scolded him. 'Look, don't you think we've got enough worries as it is?'

'You're right,' he admitted. 'When's Jacques leaving?'

'He's gone,' explained Mauricette, rather awkwardly. 'Yes, the ambulance was at Coste-Roche at seven o'clock this morning. Well, we thought it might frighten you to see it stop here . . . Jacques felt it was better to go without saying anything . . .'

'Of course, I understand,' he muttered. 'You wanted to hide everything from me, as usual, eh? But then who's at Coste-Roche with the animals?'

'Brousse and Valade,' confirmed Mauricette.

'Ah good, very good . . . So I can't help with anything?' he asked.

'You can help by not falling ill, that'll go a long way,' said Mathilde. 'Come on, don't worry any more, and best of all, think of this evening. Dominique and his wife should at least have the pleasure of finding you in good shape. Because if, besides their father being in the clinic, they see you with that dreadful expression, they'll be sorry they came.'

'And you say Félix has decided to come down? That's something!' said Jacques.

Operated on the previous day, and following a quite painful awakening, he was now recovering complete lucidity and even his strength. He felt in a particularly good mood, relieved. It was a relief to have it over with, and if, as the surgeon assured him, it had all gone extremely well, he would soon be back on his feet. Naturally he would have to be careful of his back for some time, but he didn't want to think about that yet. He preferred not to consider too deeply how he was going to organise things to accomplish all the work needed on the land . . .

For the time being, he wanted to be happy and show a suitably pleasant face to his son. For Dominique was there, strong and soothing, at his side. He had arrived an hour ago, and Jacques already felt quite cheered by his presence.

'Yes,' repeated Dominique, 'according to Grandma, Félix will be arriving tomorrow. But you know, I don't want to upset you, but I think he's really coming for Grandfather; this business has been a blow to him. I found him quite gloomy, worried. Félix'll cheer him up. And then together they can supervise what's going on at Coste-Roche.'

'But who told him?' asked Michèle.

She too was now relaxed, calm. She had been so frightened that she still had difficulty in believing it was all over, or almost.

'It seems it was Jean,' explained Dominique. 'According to his father, as soon as he heard about your accident he was ready to cut lessons to come and look after your animals. Luckily he's done no such thing! But it's a short step from that to suggesting Félix should pop down to Saint-Libéral . . .'

'Sure,' Jacques smiled. 'You know, he's great, that lad. He's got the bug, he believes in the land, we could do with lots like him. Which reminds me, are you staying for long?'

'Where? Here with you, or in France?'

'In France.'

'The whole week.'

'So I shan't see your wife,' said Jacques. 'I'm stuck here for longer than that . . .'

'Oh yes you will,' Dominique assured him. 'I thought it better to leave her in Saint-Libéral, she was rather tired from the plane – they gave us a fair old shaking, and she's just as frightened as ever!' he explained in a convincing tone. He did not want to announce the impending birth without Béatrice, and was anxious to find a good excuse for her absence.

'She'll be coming?'

'But of course! We'll come together next Wednesday, before catching the plane back.'

'Oh, good. That'll keep me happy.'

'I hope so!' smiled Dominique. 'Right, now you're going to explain to me what's to be done at Coste-Roche,' he asked his mother, 'I'll take charge of it, for these few days. With Brousse, there won't be any problem.'

'But I'm going there!' she protested vigorously. 'I am, right away, I'm coming back with you!'

'Out of the question!' he cut in. 'You're going to stay here with Papa. He needs you, and you'll have a chance to rest, that'll do you good, you look ghastly. Besides you can't leave; Françoise is supposed to be dropping by during the weekend, I had her on the telephone yesterday.'

'Oh, is that right?' said Michèle, delighted at the thought of seeing her daughter again. 'But as for Coste-Roche, you'll never be able to do everything!'

'That's it, say straight away that I'm incompetent, and then we don't need to talk about it any more. Fine, I'm listening, pass on the orders!'

# PART FIVE

*One Day in May*

# 21

SUPPORTED by Brousse on the first day, Dominique had no problem afterwards in caring for the animals. The work even made him feel several years younger, and reminded him of all the holidays in times past spent helping his father on the smallholding.

As a bonus, on account of the unusual events which left them the sole occupants of the house, Béatrice and he spent a wonderful week at Coste-Roche. Undisturbed, they enjoyed a sort of honeymoon which left them with only fond memories, and made them understand better why Pierre-Edouard and Mathilde always spoke of Coste-Roche with such feeling.

Truly the isolated house far from the village was a haven of peace, an island on which you could pretend you were at the end of the earth, far from constraints, free. In addition, as Dominique had remarked to his wife, who was quite ready to dream of just such an idyllic existence, the drought made any cultivation of the fields impossible and thus gave the impression of a very light workload.

In fact, with the slightest bit of know-how, the pigs were quickly taken care of. That done, there remained the lopping of the oaks for the cows. Dominique spent less than an hour on it each morning. He set off there in the cool of the morning, before sunrise, and returned to find his wife still in bed, all drowsy and languid, but already happy, thinking of the beautiful, sun-drenched day to come.

As for the water run, Félix took charge of that, pleased to be able to make himself useful in a small way. Jacques' tractor had only suffered minor damage. Once set upright, its tanks refilled and batteries recharged, it had started immediately. Carefully, and taking his time about it, Félix drove it at tortoise pace, which never failed to provoke jokes from Dominique.

'To see you, anyone would swear you were leading a pair of oxen!' he called out that evening, when he saw him returning from the Heath.

'Keep talking, my lad, I've got all the time in the world! Anyway, if your father still had oxen . . .'

'Hey, stop that engine and come and have a drink, it's time for a quick one!'

The sun was plunging into the red horizon and already foretelling that the following day would be just as beautiful and hot as all the previous ones, for the last four months . . .

'So, you're about to leave?' asked Félix, returning from the shed and seeing Béatrice packing her case.

'Well, yes,' she replied. 'A week passes quickly, especially under these circumstances.'

'That's right, funny sort of holiday! Your mother's coming back tomorrow?' he asked Dominique.

'Yes, and Papa the week after. I've asked Brousse and Valade if they could come and help maman with the animals.'

'I'll still be here myself,' said Félix, diluting the anisette Dominique had just given him.

'But you're not going to stay for ever, are you?'

'Certainly not! Well, we'll see . . .'

'What's up, then?'

'First there's your grandfather. He's not at all in good shape. I told you already, I thought he'd aged a lot. And then he's eating his heart out about here, the farm . . .'

'He has some reason to . . . It worries me too. I really don't see how Papa is going to manage. Or rather, yes I do know how he could, but to convince him . . . And what else is the matter, besides all that?'

'My mother. She's aged terribly as well! She's no longer interested in anything much, doesn't talk much any more, as if it tires her to join in the conversations. Admittedly she's getting increasingly deaf. Well, that's the impression she gives. But what can you do, she's almost eighty-seven and has been through so much in her unhappy life . . . So, as I know she's pleased to have me here, I'll maybe stay a bit longer than I intended. And then that'll give your father the time to recover a bit more.'

'That would be really nice if you did that, I'd go away feeling happier. In any case, we can never thank you enough for having come straight away!'

'Bah! You're making a big thing of it! But I'll never get here as fast as your grandfather came one day to help us, your aunt and myself, in October '37 . . .' murmured Félix, suddenly thoughtful. 'Right, and then I'm retired, aren't I?' he remarked, cheering up again. 'Have to say, too, that your cousin was so unhappy at not being able to come.'

'Jean?'

'Yes. He's a real dynamo, he'll go far!'

'I hope he does. But most of all, I hope Uncle Guy will finally accept the idea of having an agricultural engineer for a son!'

'Yes, it's coming already. I believe he's given up hope of seeing Jean follow him at the bar. But it hasn't all been easy going! And you, your work, it's okay?'

'My work on the land, yes, but the rest . . .' said Dominique, with a quick grimace which did not escape his cousin.

'Oh yes? You sound mad keen!'

'I'll explain it to you one day,' promised Dominique. 'In any case, for the time being I'm under contract to Mondiagri, so I've got to make the best of it. But that doesn't mean I'm married to them for life! That's the way it is. But mind you don't talk about all this to my parents, they're so pleased that I've got a good job! Here, are you ready?' he asked Béatrice. 'Yes,' he explained, 'we're eating at my grandparents' this evening.'

'I know, so am I, and believe me, knowing your grandmother's meals, I've been fasting since yesterday! Well, almost.'

The night was so beautiful, mild and bright that Dominique and Béatrice, leaning on the windowsill, could not make up their minds to go to bed.

It was so good to cool yourself in that gentle current of air from the north. So good, as well, to listen to the songs of the night, all humming with foliage rustling in the breeze, rodents pattering as they zigzagged through the dry grass, the calls of tawny and little owls, haunting as sobs; with sometimes, coming from an unseen and distant farm, the rather sad and poignant howls of dogs on leads, complaining of their chains to the moon.

'It's beautiful, admit it,' whispered Dominique. He spoke softly, so as not to break the spell and the peace of the night.

He sensed that Béatrice was agreeing, and pulled her against him.

'I think we did the right thing to speak out, it really made them happy,' he continued.

She nodded in affirmation, and he saw that she was smiling.

'You know,' she said at last, 'if you hadn't made me the baby already, it's here, in this house and this week, that I'd have liked to make it.'

'I've been aware of that,' he said. 'But it's true, it's been a really lovely week.'

He almost felt ashamed of it, for he could not forget that the peace, freedom and intimacy which he and Béatrice had enjoyed was due to his father's accident, his mother's absence.

'That proves that families should never live communally,' he said in reply to his thoughts.

'Shall we do it again?' she asked.

'What? Make a baby?'

'Sex maniac! Have a holiday like this, all alone here.'

'Yes, we could try to – send my parents on a trip, it'd be the first time they'd have taken one. But we won't be alone any longer, we two' he added, gently stroking her stomach.

'That's true,' she smiled.

'You know, I think we made them awfully happy!' he repeated.

'Definitely.'

They had not, however, consulted each other before the dinner at their grandparents. But they had suddenly realised the depth of Pierre-Edouard's melancholy and lethargy, and Mathilde's anxiety which one glance was sufficient to discern. Dominique had therefore announced:

'We wanted to tell our parents first, we'll do that tomorrow. But here goes – you're going to be great-grandparents. The next Vialhe is due in May!'

And those few words, which had suddenly softened all Mathilde's wrinkles, made Pierre-Edouard's lips tremble and blurred his gaze, had shown them that this announcement swept away everything else. It brushed aside Jacques' accident, all the worries and latent sorrow which Pierre-Edouard had been combatting less and less successfully.

'That, now, there's a piece of news, really good news,' he had eventually murmured, fingering his glass. 'You know,' he had said, smiling at Mathilde, 'that – yes, that makes me want to live a bit longer . . .'

He had got up, walked over to Béatrice, who was rather overwhelmed and did not know what to do, and had leant down to kiss her:

'And mind you don't get up, my girl,' he had said as he embraced her. 'Don't move, in your condition you've the right to stay seated in front of an old fossil like me!'

And, immediately, the lavish meal was enhanced by the smiles which sped from Pierre-Edouard to Mathilde, from Mathilde to Béatrice, already on intimate terms. By Berthe's jokes which declared that Taureans, like Gemini, were dreadful pests, of which Dominique was the proof, and that the next Vialhe born under one of those signs would surely break all records! By Félix's laugh, Louise's restored happiness, and the bottle of champagne which Yvette quietly went to fetch.

On coming to live at the Vialhes', apart from a few bits of furniture, she had brought the cellar patiently collected by Léon; Léon whose memory had unexpectedly hovered in the room.

'Maybe we should be thinking of going to bed,' suggested Béatrice, in the middle of a yawn.

'You're right. We've got to get up very early tomorrow and it'll be a long day, especially for you, 'he teased. 'Knowing how much you like aeroplanes! Well, it won't be easy for me either, I'm not sure my father will enjoy what I'm going to tell him! Let's hope the impending birth will calm him down . . .'


'That's it! You can look now, we're still alive! And don't feel you have to go on pulling off my arm!' joked Dominique, leaning towards Béatrice to kiss her.

She pinched him a bit harder, just to teach him not to make fun of her, then decided to open her eyes. The plane was already over a thousand metres and still climbing.

'Like a magazine?' he suggested to her.

'No, I think I'm going to sleep until we get to Tunis.'

'You're quite right. That way, if we explode in mid-air, you'll reach paradise without the slightest anxiety!'

'Just stop it!'

'Okay, sleep, have a rest,' he said, opening his newspaper. He skimmed through it distractedly, found it boring, closed it, and wondered yet again how his father was going to react now.

Béatrice and he had been agreeably surprised when they visited him. He looked marvellous, in very good spirits, was beginning to walk and starting to make plans again. Michèle had also seemed to them to be in much better shape, rested, relaxed. As expected, both of them had been extremely happy and proud to learn they were going to be grandparents. Already Michèle was talking of knitting the layette; as for Jacques, he pictured himself wheeling the baby right through the village, so that nobody should be unaware that the Vialhe's succession was assured.

It was a little later, when Michèle and Béatrice had left to buy a few bits and pieces which Jacques needed, that Dominique had initiated the conversation.

'I think, I'm sure even, you'll find the farm, pigs and cows in good condition. You can thank your neighbours for that, they're true friends. And Félix too. He won't be leaving before you return. But after that, how are you going to cope?'

'I don't know, have to manage . . .'

'Listen, Pa, you ought to use this accident as the opportunity to change tack completely. It's now or never to make the leap into the unknown.'

'Hah! I almost did that the other day! Once is enough, let me catch my breath, if you don't mind?'

'No. I'm not joking. I know fine that the drought makes all the fields, meadows and orchards look horrible, but still it's obvious that even then you couldn't do everything properly.'

'Oh . . . It's as obvious as that, is it?'

'Yes, it's obvious. Three-quarters of the sown pastures are too old, worn out, finished, need re-doing. Your plum trees are ruined. There are brambles on the edges of the land, and they're spreading. The walnut trees are full of dead wood, the . . .'

'Stop! I know, dammit! But I'd like to see you try and do it! Do you think it's fun for me? Well, try working with a wonky back! You've seen how that ends up, haven't you?'

'. . . And there are far too many cows which should be sent for slaughter in your herd,' Dominique had continued.

He knew very well that he was hurting his father, infuriating him even, but none of what he was saying was an exaggeration. He had not even said it all! The farm was going badly; a few more years and it would collapse, for lack of energy, initiative, strength, effective care. In fact, if it foundered, Jacques and Michèle would go down with it, becoming embittered, sinking into poverty filled with resentment, with hopes and dreams dashed forever.

Dominique refused to accept this conclusion, and so did Françoise. Brother and sister had organised it by telephone. Neither of them wanted to see their father an old man before his time and their mother wizened, faded, broken by work. Dominique had therefore decided to say all that had lain in his heart for years, which he had more or less suppressed until then so as not to fall out with his father.

But from now on, staying silent bordered on cowardice, amounted almost to failure to render assistance to an endangered person; at least that was what Françoise had said. Therefore, at the risk of unleashing paternal fury, he had decided to speak, to bring matters to a head.

'So you're still dying to lecture me?' Jacques had eventually retorted. 'It's your agronomist's diploma which makes you so impertinent, eh?'

'Oh come on! Stop that! I've no wish to lecture to you. I'm simply saying that if you go on the way you are, you won't even reach retirement, or you'll be in such a state! As for Maman, if you make her go on living this way, it'll be her you'll be sending to hospital! And that's not okay by me!'

'You think I enjoy seeing her killing herself by standing in for me?'

'Right, so consider something different, for her sake and yours. Listen; you keep yourself informed as much as I do, if not more, about what's going on in Europe! Good God! The minute you not only don't squash, but actually back, the creeps whose sole aim is to make two-thirds of agriculture disappear, the sort you practise is done for, finished! And I'll take all the bets you like: one of these days, those rogues or their successors will impose a freeze on farming, fallowing the land! They're already talking about it, they're preparing the ground! And already they're slaughtering dairy cows. So you're in a fine state with your little farm, your little crops. Already nobody wants any of it!'

'Here, I wasn't waiting for you to find all that out!'

'Sure. But you haven't drawn the conclusions from it! You know, when I arrived in France, I asked myself how our politicians could have been so stupid as to launch the idea of a drought tax. I thought it was one of those silly notions they're fond of, just one more! Well no way, I believe now that it was intentional, calculated.'

'Maybe not, but all the same . . .'

'Yes it was! They need to spoil the image of the all-providing, indispensable farmer. Make people forget that he's there to produce food. Get it into the consumers' heads that it would end up cheaper for them if all our grub was bought elsewhere, from the Americans for example.'

'Yes, that story's been going around for a while now!'

'That's just the start. But soon you, yes you, the small producer, you'll be called a pariah, they'll say you're subsidised to the hilt! They'll even blame you for the surpluses which our pathetic administrators can't be bothered to sell. Following that, they'll break you, in the name of the great European dream. Yes, a great dream which the incompetents are busy transforming into a nightmare, and mostly into an appalling mess! A Europe of bureaucrats, but most of all a Europe with a French desert, whole areas sacrificed, all the family farms killed off! And all that so that a few twisted brains can promote their evil idea of what agriculture should be in the year 2000! And that bearded fellow, the Minister of Agriculture, will be proved right; one day, in France, there'll be no more farming south of the Loire! So, Coste-Roche . . .'

'And after telling me all that, which doesn't teach me any thing new, you want me to change tack? You think I've the heart for it? Look, do you know how old I am?'

'Fifty-six! Grandfather was over sixty when you convinced him to buy a tractor and he changed practically everything on the farm . . .'

'All right. You win there; next?'

'Next? Given that all our useless experts and other myopic futurologists, not forgetting politicians of all colours, except may be the reds – that's the last straw – have decided to go for us, we've got to catch them on the wrong foot and refuse to play their game.'

'Easy to say! And what is their game, in your opinion?'

'That the smallest number should produce the maximum, as cheaply as possible! So we've got to do the opposite: stay in the last handful who produce less, as expensively as possible!'

'You say the first thing that comes into your head, don't you?'

'No. The aim is economic planning of production, which means second-rate from the taste point of view. Now, your milk-fed calves, which make so much work but are still the best, are in competition with the ones coming out of the factory farms. And as they're less expensive than yours and the customers have already lost their taste for fine produce, you're done for before you start if you don't switch to a higher gear. And it's the same for everything! Vegetables, chickens, eggs! And, believe me, the day will come when even the foie gras will be disgusting, like everything else. Disgusting to all those who still have any taste-buds. And those people will save you, because they'll be ready to pay very highly for quality.'

'Need to be a bit more logical, my lad! On the one hand you say it's done for, on the other, you assure me that it'll work!'

'You haven't quite got it. You need to eliminate ruthlessly all the produce which won't reach deluxe standard! Your pigs, for example, quite likely cost more than they bring in. That's to be expected, your little piggery is no match for the industrial concerns, but as you produce the same rubbish as them, you get paid what they're worth! So, you need to step outside the mainstream, aim for the top, specialise. At present you're doing too much of a mixture.'

'Yes, I know, and I'm doing it badly. That's it, isn't it? Go on, say it.'

'You're not going to get more annoyed? Right, we can't discuss it all day, I've a plane to catch. So this is what Françoise and I thought.'

'Oh, your sister's in on it as well, is she? That doesn't surprise me!'

'Will you let me speak, eh? Right: firstly, starting from now, Françoise and I will be sending you a cheque each month. Let me speak, I tell you! After all, we're only reimbursing you for our education. That money will allow you, Maman and you, to take a breather. And especially you, so that you don't climb back up on your tractor too soon. Secondly, I've asked Brousse and Valade, and they're ready to plough wherever you tell them to.'

'Look, don't you feel that's going a bit too far? I think we've taken advantage of the neighbours quite enough, haven't we?'

'That's for you to say; me, I'm telling you what I know. Thirdly, and don't go through the roof, you ought to give up the pigs, you're working for practically nothing, a waste of time. You'd do better to tell Maman to start feeding up geese again, like in the past, but no more than she can fatten alone and by hand, to produce a real deluxe goose liver; that'll always sell at a very high price, because it'll taste of foie gras and not of frozen fish! Wait, it's not over yet! Fourthly, whether you like it or not, your yields on cereals and maize are too low and cost you too much. Drop all that. And as for your livestock, start making silage. You ought to sell off half your cows and begin to go into it seriously, selective breeding, pedigrees, yes . . .'

'Oh right! You've taken over from your cousin, on my word! He's dreaming of one day producing show animals, for export he says!'

'He's right, it was me who gave him the idea! There, that's all. Don't answer now, but think about it at leisure. Look at it all with Maman. Oh! Another thing, I asked Aunt Yvette not to sell or re-let her land without talking to you . . .'

'You're crazy, aren't you? As it is I can't keep up with the work, and I haven't even finished paying for the Heath! I've got that for four more years!'

'Who said you should buy it? Don't I by any chance have the right to do that, myself? Or even your brother, yes, Guy, for Jean one day . . .'

'You're serious?' Jacques had murmured after a few seconds of silence. 'Guy, at a pinch, but you? Why? Don't tell me you want to take over Coste-Roche? That would be absolutely stupid, let me tell you!'

'In the next few years, it probably would. You know, I don't see myself working with you. But in fifteen or twenty years, who knows? Perhaps I'll want to invest in some land of my own and play the nightjar! Yes, you ask Jean for the explanation, he has quite an amusing theory about it! But, joking apart, it may be that one day I'll want to start stock-breeding, the sort I mentioned to you, of course! Then I wouldn't be sorry to have a starting-point at Saint-Libéral . . .'

'Well, if anyone else had told me that . . . But you mean it?'

'Yes. But don't forget: I said in fifteen or twenty years, perhaps more even. So you'd be well advised to take care of yourself if you want to hang on until then! That said, think about setting up a stock farm which is a bit out of the ordinary. One of those that's quoted as an example when breeders are talked of. That's the sort of standard you have to produce, and you can do it, because you've got the training, the technique. Because you know. There, mull over all that, calmly. And now I wish Béatrice would come back, or we'll end up missing our plane.'

'Look, one question: would you have told me all that without this dratted accident?'

'I don't know. But I've had it in my thoughts for a long time. In any case, it would have come out one day. It's done now. It's for you to judge. But remember I'd prefer to find a going concern rather than fallow land, if one day Béatrice and I move in up there.'

'That's practically blackmail! It's just to force me to change tack!'

'Call it what you like, but don't forget anything I've said to you. Dammit, I bet you our women are chattering away in some corner! And time's running out!'

'You're coming back for Jo's wedding?'

'No.'

'Pity, it's going to be a fine do. Why not come back? Just pop over, for the weekend?'

'Because I want to keep all our leave for May. Béatrice wants to have the baby in France, and I can understand that. So, since her mother doesn't seem to be in a hurry to see us or get to know me, we thought of coming to Coste-Roche at the end of April, if it's not too much trouble for you . . .'

'You devil,' Jacques had smiled, 'you little devil! You and your wife, you're really doing all you can to wrap us round your little finger! Ah, look! Here are our wives.'

'You know what?' cried Michèle as she entered. 'Well, Béatrice and I have decided to say 'tu' to each other, it's easier, isn't it? Well now, what's so funny about that?'

After clouding the sky for several days, hesitating and even attempting some minor sallies which were cut short, the rain finally made up its mind to return, to set in for good.

Driven by a west wind which seemed set to hold, it started to fall gently, fine, steady and mild. The whole countryside then began to smell different.

Casting aside first the dispiriting odours produced by four months' dust, it soon exhaled the slightly acid, bitter scent of humus gorged with water and the heavier, almost sensual one of the earth drinking, saturating itself, rediscovering its pliancy, its life.

From all the woods there soon rose the strong aroma of damp bark flexing, washing itself at last and emitting the perfumes of tannin, resin, sap and of foliage soaked through at last, restored to life and drawing breath. Very quickly, as if in a hurry to obliterate the huge, distressing grey and red blotches which spread their leprous scales everywhere, eating into the meadows and fields, infecting the woods, nature awoke in a sudden burst of verdure which transformed it within a few hours.

Born of each shower, a tender green, delicate as pastel strokes, crept from place to place, overflowed the valleys, flecked the pastures, dispelled the sad and earthy tints from the hills and far horizons. The first drops cleansed away the ash which enshrouded the plateau and peaks ravaged by the fire – they were the first to revive, to react by covering themselves with a carpet of minute grasses, soft as a downy quilt.

Comforting, steady, the rain fell for several days. Heavy but not violent, shower followed shower and autumn took on the colours of spring.

Overjoyed at the announcement of the imminent birth of a Vialhe boy or girl, reassured too by Jacques' homecoming to Coste-Roche and also by the weather returning to normal, Pierre-Edouard felt almost young and carefree again. Therefore, despite Mathilde's protests, he resumed his habit of going for a little walk each day.

He had not climbed back up to the plateau since the fire. The idea of seeing the ground scorched equally by flames and drought revolted him, put him in a bad mood. So he waited to take the track to the peaks until the countryside grew a little green again, became more welcoming, good to look at. And he would probably not have embarked on such a walk if Félix had not been able to accompany him. He felt safe with him; knew that his nephew, despite his sixty-six years, was still strong, sturdy, ready to help him to get up again if need be, and support him if the walk became too difficult.

That was no longer the case with Berthe for, although cheerful and lively, she no longer had the strength to steady him. She seemed to be shrinking ever smaller, like an apple which has faded and wrinkled after a winter on the straw. She was therefore unable to hold him if he faltered, or even to enable him to get up again if he felt the wish to sit down for a moment on one of the logs which punctuated his routes.

So with her he did not go beyond the last houses in the village or sometimes, when he really felt in good shape, the first two hundred metres of the track to the peaks. But with Félix, it was different. His presence was almost an invitation to adventure, to do something out of the ordinary.

'Well, you see, it's not my legs that are giving up on me, it's my breath,' he said to Félix that morning as they emerged onto the plateau.

They had, however, climbed quite slowly, without haste, stopping often to rest; and in particular for Pierre-Edouard's breathing to become less spasmodic, less wheezy.

'You're okay though?' Félix asked him. 'You know, you mustn't hesitate to say if you feel too tired. We'll wait here, quietly, and if we're not at the house by a quarter to twelve, Yvette will come up to meet us in the car, I asked her to.'

'You did that? You've got a nerve,' replied Pierre-Edouard. 'You all really think I'm on my last legs, don't you? Huh, basically you're not far wrong . . . Because frankly, it's true that it's beating a bit too hard down there,' he added patting the area of his heart with the palm of his hand. 'And don't annoy me by asking whether I'm taking my medicines, I'm taking them.'

'I didn't say a word,' Félix defended himself.

'Yeah . . . But don't think you need to repeat all this to your aunt, the poor little thing is already worried enough about me. Good heavens, what damage that fire did!' he exclaimed, surveying the countryside.

'Yes, we'll have to wait till spring for it to look better again.'

'Spring . . . That's it, spring . . .' murmured Pierre-Edouard. He slowly passed his hand across his face, then over his eyes which he massaged for a long time with his fingertips, as if to clear away some painful and irritating dust. 'Look, find me a stone to sit down on; I'm getting tired,' he said at last.

'Here,' said Félix, supporting him to a big rock.

He helped him to sit down, and noticed once more with sorrow his exhausted air, the dry and wrinkled face, and above all the stare which occasionally seemed to become vacant, to slip off into the distance, way, way beyond the horizon.

'I'm not sure it was a good idea to come up this far, it's too long a walk for you,' he said.

'No, no, don't worry! And if I don't make the most of you being here to help me! Poor Berthe can't . . . Tell me, don't you think she's getting awfully bent?'

'Berthe? Oh no, she seems to me in fine form.'

'It's true she's still young,' murmured Pierre-Edouard. 'She's only . . . wait . . . Seventy-three? No, eighty-three . . . Ah, still . . . So, you, you're off tomorrow?'

'Yes.'

'You could have stayed a few more days, your mother is going to miss you.'

'I'll come back for young Jo's wedding, and in the spring too,' promised Félix.

'That's good,' replied Pierre-Edouard, nodding his head, 'but the spring, that's a long way off . . . Well, for me . . . Listen, but don't repeat this to your aunt, sometimes I wonder whether I'll ever get to see Dominique's baby . . . It's so long till May, so long! You see, I'm frightened of the coming winter, yes I am . . .'

'Get along now! What're you thinking of! You'll see plenty more winters!'

'Not many . . . You know, at one time, I really loved the winters,' continued Pierre-Edouard. 'Mmm, especially when there was snow. Ah yes, just imagine, one year, we climbed up there onto the White Peak, me and Louise and poor old Léon, and . . .'

'I know,' cut in Félix, 'that was in '99, at Christmas! And on the way back you were frightened by the wolves which were ranging the area, you threw away your thrushes . . .'

'Oh? I've already told you that story? Oh right, I didn't realise . . . what was I talking about before that? I don't know any more . . . Oh yes, the month of May, that's it, it's a long time till May, a very long time . . .'

'Come on, don't talk rubbish, just because you've walked further than usual and you're tired, you don't have to ramble on! You're too old to talk nonsense!'

'It's not nonsense to say you won't last for ever . . .'

'All right, but would you mind talking about something else?'

'Huh, if you can't talk about yesterday at my age, nothing's sacred any more . . .' said Pierre-Edouard. He sighed, pressed his hand against his chest then rubbed his eyes once more, blinked his eyelids and stared hard at the eastern horizon.

'Miladiou! Look my boy, look!' he exclaimed in childish excitement, stretching his arm towards the hills. 'Look behind Yssandon! See how they're streaming towards Perpezac, see them! My God! What a mass! Can you see them? Oh, my goodness! It's years since I've seen such a big flight of pigeons! And look, look at the one coming behind! Can you see? And the other one after it, you see?'

'Of course,' murmured Félix after a few seconds of watching, 'they're beautiful, and so many . . . Well it's the season, it'll soon be Saint Luke's day! Yes, they're very beautiful,' he repeated, suddenly grasping why Pierre-Edouard was worried by the approach of winter and questioning whether he would ever see May again.

For in the grey sky, amongst the low, heavy clouds which foretold further showers, there was not the shadow of a pigeon, not even a tiny flock of starlings, nothing. And already, Pierre-Edouard's eyes seemed to have forgotten what he believed he had seen.

# 22

So as not to succumb to the temptation of climbing back on to his tractor too soon, Jacques chose to devote himself to his job as mayor. He knew that if he stayed at Coste-Roche the work which had accumulated due to the drought would push him to do something unwise, such as hitch up his Brabant and set off to plough.

Therefore, instead of biting his nails, he busied himself more than ever with village problems, and especially the refurbishment of the château. This had made good progress during his absence, and everything now pointed to the building being ready on the planned date. Besides the whole teams of artisans working on the inside, a contractor was already in the process of levelling the tennis court so dear to Peyrafaure's heart. When that was done he would tackle the excavation of the pool, then its construction.

However, the supervision of the various works and all the details to be sorted out here and there were not enough to blot out all the worries overwhelming Jacques. His father was not the least of these. Not that he was ill; he still kept on his feet and took his little walk each day with Berthe. But he had an increasing tendency to isolate himself in a deep and distant self-absorption which cut him off from the outside world. And although Jacques, unlike Félix, had not witnessed one of the delusive visions which sometimes afflicted him, that did not prevent him from dreading them. He was too accustomed to his father always being perfectly lucid not to be horrified at the thought of seeing him sink into a sort of permanent absence of mind or, worse, senility.

He still retained the memory of the last pitiful months passed by his grandfather Jean-Edouard, and constantly feared that his father might also come to such a lamentable end. And the rather unconcerned pronouncements of Doctor Martel, who attributed all that in broad terms to the medicaments, to some sudden but transient variations in his blood pressure or urea levels, to the weakness of an ageing heart and above all to the old man's approaching eighty-eight years, were no comfort to Jacques.

So, since his main occupation kept him in the village, he called every day — and twice more often than once — at the family home.

That was not very reassuring either, for unfortunately, when his father seemed to be on top form, it was his aunt Louise who gave the impression of losing ground! She was not actually ill, slept well and kept herself busy with knitting and sewing. But she was indifferent to everything, had no enthusiasm for anything. And, like her brother, she often gave the impression of being tired of finding herself faced each morning with a day which she had to endure without wishing to, like a burden, almost a duty.

Luckily, Yvette, Berthe and Mathilde were still there to help her to interact, and even to chivvy her. But Jacques preferred not to think too much about what might happen if his mother in her turn gave up the struggle, and if Berthe fell ill. Yvette could never cope with it all alone. She might well be in good health; she had still seen sixty-nine years go by.

And when you know that seven out of ten houses in the village are in roughly the same situation, it really makes you despair for the future of Saint-Libéral! he mused.

That was why he concentrated on the hope of a sort of community renaissance resulting from the conversion of the château. At the same time, he had not forgotten Christian's suggestions. Because of his spell in hospital he had not had the chance to discuss them in the town council, but he often thought of them.

After all, the people of Saint-Robert actually organise concerts, and that attracts people. So why not bring in some life with photos?

In the same way he was increasingly convinced that the opening of some sort of farm guest-house could be beneficial to the whole village. But there he ran into the problem of where it should be.

We'll need to discuss all that at the next meeting. After all, Coste's talking about starting a ranch, he could set his wife to cooking! I'll ask Michèle what she thinks. About that and all the rest, especially the rest . . .

'The rest' was what his son had said to him about the farm. He had still not mentioned a word of it to anyone. And yet not a day elapsed without him recalling Dominique's arguments. And each passing day confirmed the notion that his son saw things clearly, that he was right, and that the survival of Coste-Roche was going to depend on the decisions he would have to take. And take quickly.

Happy to continue the experiments which interested him, Dominique was glad to return to the trial farm at Bab el-Raba. Despite that, it took him very little time to realise that he would not be remaining in the employ of Mondiagri.

'You're going to think I don't really know what I want, that I'm vacillating and cultivate as many contradictions as varieties of hybrid maize, but I'm not going to make my career in the service of Mondiagri,' he said to Béatrice one evening.

She was already in bed, reading. She put down her book and smiled:

'You're forgetting you've already told me all that! The last time was two months ago, just after the visit from your supervisors,' she reminded him. 'But why are you talking about contradictions?'

'Because my work definitely interests me, because everything I do on the land gives me pleasure. It's afterwards that it comes unstuck! Look, if you like, it would all be fine if my work served some other purpose than to enrich the Mondiagri shareholders,' he said, coming to sit down on the edge of the bed.

'And to feed your wife and your future progeny!' she joked.

'I know,' he replied, stroking her face. 'No, seriously, I'd like you to understand.'

'Come on now, don't take me for an idiot! I can see, you know! Whether it's Guyana, here, or with even better reason in Coste-Roche, you're only really happy on the land. You need something concrete, some action. Anyway, I've already said that to you. So of course, when everything is reduced to simple experiments on little plots . . .'

'If not in tanks and test-tubes . . .'

'Exactly. Deep down, what you miss is a real farm, some land, some space, is that it?'

'Probably, but I'm not so naïve as to dream of the impossible, utopia was never in my line, so . . .'

'So?' she pressed him.

'So, since we're a long way from having the means to set ourselves up on a farm, but I don't want to grow bitter working twenty-five years for people whose outlook I don't like, I think I won't be renewing my contract with Mondiagri . . .'

'Which means to say you'll be finishing with them when we come to the end of your three years here? In two years' time, right?'

'Yes.'

'And after that?'

'I'd like to devote my time to a task which is really useful and in keeping with my training. Hey, for example, the sort of work I did in Algeria, with Ali. There at least we were teaching people to grow things better so they could feed themselves better! That was certainly more interesting than slogging away to fatten up Mondiagri. All right, it's less well paid and there's not much chance of making a career, but . . .'

'But it would be less distressing for you, wouldn't it?'

'Yes.'

'Well, for me too.'

'Is that true?'

'Yes, I don't like to see you constantly railing against your employers, it's unhealthy. So if it isn't working out with them, leave them and don't let's talk about it any more! But mind you don't set sail for some obscure country on the other side of the world! Remember there'll be three of us next year, or more if you've given me twins!'

'I promise. In fact, I haven't told you yet, but I really think that in twenty years' time I'll go back to try my luck in Saint-Libéral. Yes, at home, on our land at Coste-Roche. Would that suit you? You said you liked it a lot there.'

'It would suit me very well,' she smiled, 'and all the better if it's in twenty years' time, which leaves me a little while to choose the colour of the curtains, eh?'

'But I'm not joking!' he said, bending down to kiss her.

'Neither am I,' she assured him earnestly. 'And you know, quite frankly, I bet you don't wait twenty years . . .'

Whereas the idea of organising, in the following summer, a photo competition and exhibition was received with polite interest but not much eagerness by the assembled town councillors, that of trying to breathe new life into the auberge was by contrast welcomed enthusiastically.

'I'd go so far as to say we're fools not to have thought of it earlier! It's true, it was better when we could still go to Suzanne's!' sighed Delpeyroux nostalgically.

'You can say that again! Those were good times,' agreed Duverger, as he too began to dream of the fine pre-war period when, not content with serving drinks, the comely Suzanne allowed the young men of the village to ogle her generous cleavage. Sometimes even, when curaçao proved inadequate to relieve the bouts of depression provoked by the memory of her late and heroic husbands, she even allowed a lot more. And Duverger was now growing quite sentimental, thinking with what generosity, refinement and skill she then shared her sorrows . . .

'It's true, you lot wouldn't understand!' said Coste, with a tinge of pity, to the newcomers to the community, the Martins, Lacombes and Peyrafaures and others who had only ever seen the inn closed. 'Yes,' he continued, 'when Suzanne was here, the village looked different!'

He too had been a young man in Saint-Libéral and, if he added his testimony in praise of Suzanne, it was because he owed her a great deal. It was she who, one evening in August 1945, had tenderly helped him to grow up, to cross the threshold. She was then forty-nine years old, but immensely experienced and with boundless affection, and he, at eighteen, had a great deal of enthusiasm and imagination but no experience. He still felt a debt to her generosity of old.

'Have to say that Suzanne was . . .'

'Hey! Steady on, steady on,' interrupted Jacques, seeing that Delpeyroux was preparing to divulge his memories one by one. 'It's not a question of bringing Suzanne back to life or of replacing her, but of finding out whether it's possible to make use of the auberge, to set up a sort of guest-house there, that's all! Unless you know anyone who's willing to take over the whole thing, get it all going again, with a restaurant and rooms. Not forgetting that when Suzanne closed she'd had no customers for a long time, I mean to say customers for the inn . . .'

He had never himself helped Suzanne relieve her attacks of vague yearning, but knew that a number of men in the village, between seventeen and seventy, had considered it their duty not to leave her alone during her painful and grievous phases of melancholy. It was therefore to be expected that memories of her would still be so vivid, and that some would speak of her with a little tremor in the voice!

'Right then, explain!' said Coste.

'You're still wanting to invest in buying some ponies and horses?' Jacques asked him.

'Yes. That'll be a tidy sum to come up with, but it ought to bring in a bit all the same. Anyway, if it doesn't take off, they can always be sold again for slaughter, seems there's a shortage of that sort of meat in France. I don't like it myself, but if it sells . . .'

'Exactly. You've thought about feeding the people who'll be coming to play at cowboys?'

'Oh, that, no! I'm not a restauranteur!'

'All right, but your wife knows how to make an omelette? or warm up a jar of *confit d'oie*, eh? You ought to give that some thought!'

'No, definitely not!' Coste grouched. 'In the first place Paulette wouldn't like it. As it is she's not too keen on the horses . . . And then, if she cooks, I'm sure to lose all my customers! They won't come back a second time! Well that's how it is!' he protested, raising his voice to drown out his neighbours' laughter, 'grub's not her strong point! At home, it's mother-in-law who does the cooking and she complains, although there are only three of us! Think what a welcome I'd get if I told her she'd have to work for ten or fifteen! She's too lazy, the old girl! No, no, the ranch is okay, but snacks are out!'

'Well, don't let's talk about it anymore, 'said Jacques. 'I only mentioned it because it would liven up the village a bit, attract some visitors, that's all. Right, let's go on to other things, unless anyone has any ideas on this subject?'

'It might be possible. Well, have to see . . .' said Lacombe. He rarely intervened in the discussions, so everyone fell silent in anticipation of his comments.

'Have you a suggestion to make?' pressed Jacques.

'Maybe . . . But beforehand, we'd need to make sure it's possible to rent the auberge.'

'For that we only have to ask Suzanne's daughter. But why?' asked Jacques.

'Because my brother-in-law is retiring next year,' explained Lacombe. 'Yes,' he said, with an apologetic little smile, 'he'll have a warrant officer's stipend, that's not bad, you know. And then, he's not old yet. But you see with Indochina and Algeria, that makes some bloody fine increments and a good pension at the end of the month!'

'Okay, okay, but what's all that to us?' interrupted Peyrafaure rather curtly.

As a pensioner of the SNCF railways, he did not care much for the conversation turning towards the advantages enjoyed by former servants of the state. He had long known that his situation aroused some jealousy and had no wish to be used as scapegoat, should one of the council members start up the old refrain. The one saying that state employees, not content with doing damn all, were also scandalously overpaid. It wouldn't take much for a wicked old reactionary like Delpeyroux to say that civil servants shouldn't even have the right to vote, since no change of government ever challenged their position! What's more they were all irresponsible! Indeed, Peyrafaure was aware, from working in his kitchen garden, that it was even whispered behind his back that he had had to wait until his retirement to discover how exhausting work could be.

'Yes, what are you leading up to with your sarge?' insisted Martin. He was rather annoyed that Lacombe, whom he thought a good friend, had never spoken to him of this brother-in-law in the army.

'Oh, it's simple. My sister wants to come back to this part of the country,' explained Lacombe. 'Yes, like me she's a native of Terrasson. So she told me to look for something to rent in the area. And as I know my brother-in-law would like to supplement his pension a bit without overdoing it too much . . .'

'What a joke!' scoffed Martin. 'If he liked work he wouldn't be in the army!'

'You mean to say he'd be prepared to take over the inn?' Jacques intervened.

'No, not the whole thing! Certainly not the rooms, that is except for himself. But a bit of cooking in the high season. That yes, he knows how to do that, and do it well . . .'

'Hey! Is he a sarge by profession or a cook, your brother-in-law?' cried Martin.

'Both. Yes, for the last ten years he's been doing service in the officers' mess. Well, they need a manager in the kitchens!'

'Why didn't you say so!' put in Martin.

'And you think that might interest him?' continued Jacques.

'I believe so. That is if he can rent the inn. He could live there with his family and at the same time open a sort of table dot or something . . . Well, what you were saying just now.'

'Table d'hôte meals, that would be really great,' said Jacques. 'Wouldn't it?' he insisted, questioning his neighbours with a look.

They all agreed, especially those born and bred in Saint-Libéral, already happy at the idea of hearing again the bright tinkle which the little bell hanging above the door of the auberge used to make, in Suzanne's time.

'And that would give us a few people too . . .' added Lacombe.

'How's that?' asked Jacques, guessing that he had not told all.

'Well, yes, they have some little ones . . . That is, I mean their children! Six! That would be good for the school, wouldn't it?'

'What? Six kids?' gasped Castellac. He had raised one with great difficulty and was still suffering from it, so six!

'But how old are your nephews and nieces?' asked Jacques, also a little disconcerted.

'Hmm . . . They go from twelve, no eleven . . . I don't know, the last one's not walking yet, that must make him about seven or eight months.'

'Well, me old mate!' said Martin. 'Listen, it's not your brother-in-law who's in need of retirement, it's your sister! I understand, she wants to come back here for a rest cure! But with his pension, plus his family allowances, your brother-in-law has no need to burst a blood vessel to earn his crust! He's already done it by slipping off his pants, and jumping into bed!'

'No, seriously, do you really mean all that?' Jean-Pierre Fleyssac interrupted.

As secretary to the mairie and brother-in-law of the mayor, he had resolved as a matter of principle never to speak during council debates. His role was to take the minutes, no more. But this, six kids at one go, was a blessing for the school, postponing the closure which was discussed again each year. And for him, the teacher, a guaranteed future at Saint-Libéral until his retirement. He had to know about this!

'Yes, really, my sister has six kids,' said Lacombe. 'And she could still have more! After all, she's only thirty-four! And she likes it. Well, I mean, children . . .'

'Can't turn up her nose at making them either . . .' joked Martin.

'Six! Well I never,' Castellac started up again.

'But there may still be one little problem . . .' continued Lacombe in some slight embarrassment.

'Ah, that wouldn't surprise me, it was all too perfect!' griped Peyrafaure.

'And what's that, the problem?' insisted Jacques.

'Hum . . .' said Lacombe. He hesitated, then made up his mind: 'Have to say, I myself don't mind at all, but I know for some people . . . Well, it might be a surprise, especially here, eh? Have to admit it's not very Corrézien . . .'

'Come on, spit it out! We'll be here all night!' Martin urged him on.

'But make no mistake, through his father he's as French as you and me, right!' said Lacombe. 'Yes, he's French. But he's from Phnom Penh . . .' he blurted out at last, with a look to Jacques and Jean-Pierre pleading for help.

'What country's that, Africa, isn't it?' asked Duverger quietly of Delmond, who wisely limited himself to pursing his lips to avoid answering.

'You mean to say he's Cambodian, is that it? What's the problem?' said Jacques.

'Well, he's a mite yellow. And the children too . . . Less than him of course. But it's still obvious they're not from Terrasson, nor Brive!'

'Ah! That's why you never talked to me about him?' said Martin in annoyance.

'No, that wasn't why! It never came up, that's all! And now, if you don't like coloured people, say so!'

'I don't give a damn!' cried Martin, 'and after all, I'm not your sister!'

'Please, gentlemen!' interrupted Jacques. 'Right, in the event that this business goes ahead, which is my earnest wish, I hope that nobody will be so crass as to hold his origins against him, this Monsieur . . . Monsieur, what's his name, anyway?'

'Defort, Pierre,' said Lacombe.

'That's not a chink name, that!' said Peyrafaure, proudly displaying his knowledge.

'I told you his father was French!' shouted Lacombe, who had begun to lose patience.

'So then, he's only half yellow, your brother-in-law?' said Martin.

'Yes! Dammit!'

'No need to get in a state! It's not your fault! It doesn't run off – well I hope not, for your sister's sake!'

'Gentlemen, please,' repeated Jacques. 'Right, it goes without saying that we shall do our best to welcome Monsieur Defort, his wife and six children and . . .'

'Be seven or eight of them by next year . . .' whispered Martin.

'Quiet, please!' said Jacques in irritation. 'What we need now is to find out whether the auberge can be rented. You'll deal with that, Monsieur Peyrafaure? Yes, you'll know the best way to negotiate all that tactfully. We're relying on you. And if by any chance Suzanne's daughter doesn't want to let it, there are other empty houses in Saint-Libéral, and we'll find one! The meeting is closed. Good night, gentlemen!'

Michèle had not gone to bed when Jacques returned to Coste-Roche, but was knitting in front of the television. He smiled to see the little white vest which she often held out at arm's length in front of her, to appreciate its appearance and progress.

'You're not taking any risks, eh?' he teased. 'Neither blue nor pink!'

'Exactly,' she smiled, 'but white's really sweet, isn't it?'

'Very.'

'That's done? You talked to them about this photo competition and exhibition?'

'Yes, yes,' he said absentmindedly, taking the top off a bottle of beer.

'It wasn't to their liking?'

'Yes, I think it was; but to be honest, I feel it seems a bit rarefied to some of them. Well, the main thing is to get it up and running. But on the other hand, if you'd seen them when I talked about the inn!'

He filled his glass and described his evening while Michèle got ready for bed.

'And there you are,' he concluded. 'Eight years ago it was the Portuguese who brought some young blood into Saint-Libéral and prevented the school from closing. And again, you remember, fewer of them came than we were hoping for: four families and thirteen kids were expected, and only two with five kids came. I still remember poor Jean-Pierre's disappointment. If I hadn't still been a regional councillor, I'm sure they'd have closed the school. Anyway, if all goes well, next year we'll have seven Cambodians and a lady from Terrasson! And they'll save the school too; at least, I hope so. With a bit of luck, they'll revive the auberge as well and bring in a bit of life. But who knows what's coming next? Turks? Arabs? Blacks?'

'And that worries you?'

'No, it even seems to me logical, quite logical. Saint-Libéral is growing emptier, the old people are disappearing and there are no births to replace them. Then, like in fields which are left fallow, the wind carries in seeds from all parts, and here, some Cambodians have turned up. It's to be expected. You know very well nature can't abide a vacuum. So long live Monsieur Pierre Defort, his wife and six children . . . for the moment, as that clown Martin said!'

Josyane twirled gracefully in front of the mirror, assumed a few deliberately suggestive poses, then poked out her tongue at her reflection and shrugged her shoulders.

'Grotesque!' she said, unfastening the dress. 'With that on my back I look like a sack of potatoes! I wonder how you find sapheads who'll buy this sort of clobber off you! It's so corny!'

'What can I say,' sighed Chantal. 'Claire Diamond's customers don't have your tastes. And a good thing too! We'd have to shut up shop! Right, try that one; in any case, you're not leaving here without choosing your wedding dress! I don't want to fall out with my future brother-in-law!'

'I know,' Josyane was amused. 'He told me he didn't want me in jeans for our wedding. But as for insisting that I come and ruin myself in one of the poshest boutiques in Paris!'

'If Aunt Berthe could hear you!'

Wisely, knowing her sister well, Chantal had waited until all the vendeuses were gone and the doors locked to begin offering her model gowns. But the evening was turning out to be difficult, Josyane not wanting a classic wedding dress.

'If I dare carry even a white accessory, Grandma will have the sulks on me!'

And she was also refusing one of those excessively formal and dressy outfits for which the couture house was renowned.

'Look, just try that one,' suggested Chantal. 'By the way, did you manage to get in touch with Marie?'

'Yes, she hasn't made up her mind about coming,' said Josyane, regarding the dress with a critical eye.

'She's stupid!'

'That's just what I think. Right, okay, from what you told me she married a cretin, but hey, anyone can make a mistake! But I think she actually feels a bit embarrassed about coming back to Saint-Libéral without him.'

'That's true. She hasn't seen our parents or grandparents since her divorce . . .'

'Well that's just it! She ought to take the opportunity of our wedding to pop down there! That's what I told her. But you should phone her too, and insist on it, you know! I'm sure it'd be a treat for our parents.'

'You're right, I'll give her a call. Right, you're trying on this dress?'

'With that on I'll look like an old tart and Christian'll be furious!' decided Josyane.

'Try it all the same, he'll be really furious if I don't find you anything! No! Stop! The sleeve is here! Here! But be careful, don't pull like a lunatic! It does up down the back, there . . .

'Oh, you look wonderful!'

'Oh yeah!' said Josyane, looking at herself in the swing mirror. She turned round, took a few steps: 'Yes, all things considered, that one might do . . .,' she admitted after a few moments. 'Yes, it would maybe do,' she repeated, tracing out a dance step, 'but how much does a rag like this cost?'

'Never you mind! I'm under orders, it's on the house!'

'Whose orders?'

'Aunt Berthe's, of course.'

'That doesn't surprise me,' smiled Josyane. 'She's really something, Aunt Berthe.'

'You don't have to tell me! Right, hurry up and take that off. You did say that Christian was coming by to pick you up here? Well if he arrives now, it would be dreadful! Oh yes,' teased Chantal, 'you know very well that the fiancé shouldn't see his wife's outfit before the wedding day! But joking apart, you come back tomorrow for the alterations. Yes, that's not my job, I don't know anything about it.'

997

'You think it needs altering?'

'Yes, definitely, you're a bit better padded than our usual model girls. What's making you laugh?'

'Oh, nothing.' Josyane was enjoying herself. 'Well yes, I can tell you, the alterations don't have much chance of being useful for very long . . . A good thing we're getting married in a week's time!'

'Seriously?' said Chantal, who understood immediately. Then she burst into laughter. 'And when's this little Leyrac expected?'

'June.'

'You two didn't hang about!' replied Chantal after rapid calculations.

'Yes we did, longer than you think! Well that's it, all that to say this dress needs to be expandable if I want to have the use of it for a bit.'

'And naturally, our parents aren't in the know?'

'Oh no, not yet. And don't spill the beans, we'll announce it to them as a Christmas present. Yes, I know, at one time it would have created a scene: or rather, a premature baby of eight pounds! But as it is, I'm sure they're going to be over the moon. And tell you what, I even bet you Grandma will be quite pleased about it when she's told!' Josyane assured her. Then she thought for a moment, and smiled. 'But it's quite likely I won't have to tell her anything. She'll notice it as soon as she sees me next week!'

# 23

DROWNING in an icy fog which absorbed the slightest sound, veiling everything beyond ten metres, smothering the few rays of light filtering through the heart-shaped holes in the shutters, Saint-Libéral seemed as deserted as a ghost village, dead.

And the tiny black silhouette scurrying along the main street like a stray mouse was so frail, quiet and alone that she rendered still more poignant and melancholy the silence and emptiness crushing and paralysing the village.

Even the dogs held their peace. Curled deep in their kennels and barns, they had begun their slumber. For in defiance of the three strokes which were just sounding from the bell, darkness was approaching, already brought on by the fog which drowned everything in dirty cotton wool, gloomy as a dark colourwash.

And yet, despite the agonising loneliness which seeped from every corner, the deep silence and nightmarish façades of the houses distorted by the mist, Mathilde was happy. Happy because all the family would be here before the end of the evening; all except Dominique and Béatrice. Already, Josyane and her fiancé had been there since the previous day. And their shared happiness was such a pleasure to see that no one could resist the joy radiating from them.

Marie was there as well, a little embarrassed at first, for she was suddenly aware that Patrick's absence was still an oddity to her parents, her family. But Jo's liveliness was so infectious that everyone's awkwardness had quickly disappeared, melted away, engulfed in the enthusiasm of the reunion.

Besides, if black looks were due for those who had given their parents grey hairs, Chantal had also earned some sour expressions! She had not been back to Saint-Libéral for three years and had changed so much, looked so elegant and soignée, that Pierre-Edouard had not immediately recognised her; he had even felt a little shy when greeting her.

Finally, to the great pleasure of his mother and Pierre-Edouard, who seemed rejuvenated each time he saw him again, Félix was also there. As for the others, Françoise, Guy and Colette, Jean, Marc, Evelyne and Renaud, they were already in the train, the one arriving in Brive at six. Naturally, going to fetch them in this fog, Yvette and Jacques would do well to take care: the road to Brive was not going to be easy, especially on a dark night.

Oh, they'll drive slowly, that's all, thought Mathilde.

With a firm hand she pushed open the heavy door of the church. The creaking of the slightly rusty hinges echoed round the square like the wailing of a cat.

Mathilde shivered, surprised by the damp, cloying chill pervading the church. Despite the need to warm herself up as quickly as possible by sweeping up and putting the finishing touches to the arrangements before the next day's ceremony – she had come expressly for that – out of habit and courtesy she knelt down before the niche where, in former times, Saint Eutrope had smiled. A Saint Eutrope probably gone for ever, now sold to some unscrupulous heathens for whom hell would be too mild. In his place, for the empty niche was too sinister, distressing, Mathilde and Louise had installed a Saint Joseph previously relegated to a corner, on a wobbly stool next to a broom cupboard.

It is true that he was not exactly beautiful, poor man, and the years had not been kind to his plasterwork or colours, so bright and triumphant in the early 1900s, when he was young! Attacked by the damp, chipped here and there, he was a miserable specimen, for his nose, slightly broken in the middle, gave him the strange appearance of a bearded boxer.

But such as he was, Mathilde still loved him well. And since Saint Eutrope was no longer there to listen to her secrets, her wishes, Aves and also thanks, it was he who received them. And today, on Friday, 3 December, he needed to be specially thanked.

First of all, because the whole family, or almost all of them, were reunited, which was a great joy and a gift from heaven. Then, because for several weeks Pierre-Edouard had been well. To be sure, he was accepting without too much argument the new medicines prescribed by the doctor. Naturally his health was always fragile, subject to successive highs and lows which could no longer be evened out. Despite that he was in good humour, joining in the conversations in a lively and purposeful way. Moreover he was delighted to be seeing his granddaughter married the following day.

And it was important to give thanks for her, too. She had come back from so far away, little Jo! And she had been so lucky to find a man like hers, strong, able to help her, to support her when needed.

Of course, as she had chosen not to speak of it, one had to close one's eyes to her condition . . . Not to dwell on her hips, which had definitely spread since the previous summer, her much heavier breasts, already almost maternal, and her face, still smiling and youthful but now more solemn and serious. Yes, that was the way of it, she was expecting a baby before time . . .

And, all things considered, for that too thanks should be given. For according to the newspapers, radio and even the television – but should they be believed, when it was so astounding, incredible! – there was no need for Jo to keep it, this little creature! The law allowed her to cast it aside if she felt like it. And Mathilde shuddered at the thought that she might have been capable of parting with it, of killing it!

So, yes, give thanks! And too bad if a few neighbours took it into their heads to count the months . . . Besides, who paid any attention to that in the village now? Births were so rare, and were such an event, it never occurred to anyone to check on anything, not even if the father was the right one!

Her thanksgiving completed, she crossed herself and rose. She felt frozen stiff, and decided to have a good sweep to warm herself up again. Then she checked that everything was correctly in place, on the altar and in the nave, and especially that the big butane stove was working properly. To economise, it was never used except during services. But she resolved to send Félix, in the morning, to light it a good hour before the Mass, to warm the church a little and drive out that penetrating, icy damp.

And we'll put Pierre next to the stove, she planned, and Louise and Berthe as well; they mustn't catch anything on such an important day!

Pierre-Edouard tapped his empty pipe on his palm, smiled as he watched the dancing couples, and leaned towards Félix.

'Could you take me back to the house?' he asked him quietly.

'Yes, whenever you like. But is anything wrong?'

'No, no, it's just I'm getting a bit tired. And then all this wild music is too noisy, it's making me dizzy!'

He had had a hard day. It had begun at ten o'clock with the civil wedding, during which Jacques had made a very fine and moving speech. First of all reminding the young couple that if marriage – rather disparaged in recent years – had many attractions, charms and virtues, it also had duties and constraints. It was important to respect each other, if you wanted to have some chance of celebrating your Diamond Wedding one day, as the model couple here present were preparing to do, strong in their fifty-eight years of marriage. He had then described the fine qualities of Josyane's parents, and had stressed her father's enlistment in 1944 in the army of the Liberation.

After that, turning to Christian, he had also recalled his father's sacrifice of which he could be justly proud. For his battle, like that of the men and women who had chosen to fight and not accept, allowed them all to be there today, happy and free, in the Saint-Libéral mairie which had seen such a succession of Vialhes and, it was to be hoped, would see many more!

Then, in jest, he had warmly congratulated Josyane on having the wisdom, good sense, taste and intelligence to choose a man who, although a native of Paris, had his roots in the Corrèze, a guarantee of endurance, strength, courage and patience!

'And with Jo, my dear Christian, I'm telling you, you'll need plenty of all those! Take the word of her old uncle!' he had concluded amidst laughter.

Everyone had then set off for the church, where a beautiful and simple ceremony had been enacted. A little hurried, to be sure, for Father Soliers had a burial in Yssandon afterwards. And as they knew that he had another wedding in Perpezac that afternoon, it was understandable that his homily was kindly but brief, his blessing without embellishments and his Mass quickly dispatched. Pierre-Edouard had not complained about this for, despite the stove which blew its hot breath on his back, he was close to catching a dreadful chill on his chest; the church was as cold as the grave. Fortunately the village hall was very well heated, the meal and wines excellent, and the good humour universal.

But now, Pierre-Edouard felt weary. He had not touched the substantial cold buffet which the young people pounced on towards seven o'clock, nor the champagne. He wished for nothing more than to go and rest at home, in the peace of the chimney corner, his feet close to the warm cinders.

'I'm going to suggest to my mother that I should take her home too,' said Félix. 'Look at her, I have the impression she's in a hurry to get back as well.'

In truth, Louise, with Michèle and Mauricette on either side, seemed distant, far away, lost in some thought which made her nod her head occasionally, or smile, as if replying silently to an invisible questioner.

'Right, then we'll go,' said Pierre-Edouard. 'But the main thing is not to worry Mathilde, she must enjoy the celebration. Look how happy she is to be with her grandchildren! And did you see her dancing just now with Jacques and Christian? Like a young girl! So we won't spoil the evening for her. Just tell her that I'm going home because I feel like some soup with something in it! It's true, I miss my bouillon. And mind you say I don't need her and she shouldn't move from here. Otherwise I'll throw a fit!'

'Okay,' smiled Félix, getting up.

'Hey!' said Pierre-Edouard, holding him back by the arm. 'Tell little Jo and her husband to come and say goodbye to me as well. They're sure to be setting off on their honeymoon any moment now, so by the time I see the two of them again . . .'

A little out of breath from the last jive with his cousin Françoise – she danced like a dream! – Jean poured himself a glass of champagne and went to sit beside his uncle Jacques, who was in discussion with his father.

'Well talk of the devil . . .' said Guy.

'Oh yes?' said Jean warily.

His relationship with his father had much improved, but he wisely did nothing to provoke him. So, since his father now agreed to him following the same path as Dominique, it was really pointless to annoy him by mentioning the stock farm he hoped to own one day, later on, in several years' time; it would be soon enough to introduce that project when it needed to be financed . . .

'You were talking about me?' he asked.

'No, your father's joking, I was giving him the news of Saint-Libéral, and Coste-Roche too.'

'Oh yes, that's great! Christian told me you're going to launch a photo competition and exhibition! I'll join in, okay? Even do the presentation if need be!'

'Right, you never miss a chance to spend your summers here, do you?'

'Well, look! I love taking photos. I'll let you see the ones I took with Félix, at his place, super! And listen, I'll even bet you, if you organised photography courses, sort of improvement workshops, with processing facilities and everything, you'd get people. I have friends myself who'd like nothing better than to spend a week or two here! Especially with the swimming pool and tennis court . . . And if you found them a field to pitch their tents on as well . . .'

'So it's goodbye to helping your uncle!' joked Jacques. 'Well, too bad, I'll manage without you!'

'Oh yes,' agreed Guy joining in the game, 'goodbye to the cows, make way for the picture postcards!'

'Joking apart,' said Jacques, 'Dominique gave me some ideas concerning Coste-Roche, it happens they're the same as yours . . .'

'*What* a coincidence,' Guy said, amused. 'Yes, your uncle's going to cut the grass from under your feet, the last straw for a stock-breeder! He's thinking of going in for pedigree animals, but you know more about that than him, don't you?'

'Seriously?' said Jean, careful not to react to the final comment.

'Yes,' said Jacques. 'Well, I'm thinking of doing it gradually. Your aunt and I, it's high time we got ourselves better organised at Coste-Roche. And as I don't even know what sciatica feels like since my operation, we'd better make the most of it. Hey, go and fetch us something to drink, we're dying of thirst here!'

'No, but it's not a joke?' insisted Jean. 'It's true, Dominique managed to convince you? Bravo! When we last saw each other, just before his wedding, he told me your problem was not so much backache as stubbornness, worse than a dozen Arabian mules!'

'Ten out of ten for respect!' Jacques teased. 'Go on, you lout, go and fetch us a drink, we'll talk about it all again tomorrow, before you leave.'

'These young people have a nerve!' said Guy, watching his son move away.

'Bah! There was no shortage of that in our time either. Think, remember Paul . . .'

'That's true,' sighed Guy. 'When you recall he was hardly older than Jean when he slipped away to England!'

'Yes indeed! And if you think about it, Aunt Berthe had plenty of daring as well. And Aunt Louise, that wasn't bad either in its way. So they've got an act to follow, our kids!'

'That's for sure,' admitted Guy. 'So, you were saying we may be going to get some Cambodians?' he said, resuming the conversation interrupted by Jean.

'It's possible. Since Suzanne's daughter's not able to sell the auberge, she's quite happy to let it. So if our NCO is still agreeable, next year Jean-Pierre's school will have some young pupils with rather slanty eyes . . .'

'Incredible,' murmured Guy. 'But by the way, what does papa say about it?'

'You'll laugh, he thinks it's fantastic! "For myself," he said to me, "The Annamese" – yes he's still calling them that! – "the Annamese", I saw some of them during the war, the Great War. They weren't cowardly or evil. So I don't see why they should have changed!'

'Incredible,' repeated Guy. 'But he's in good shape, Papa, isn't he? Well, it seems so to me.'

'Yes, at the moment, it's all right. He accepts seeing the doc from time to time and he takes his medicines properly. And Maman's well too, so what more can you ask? You know, I calculated the average age in the family home, including Yvette and she brings it down, it was over eighty! So believe me, when I go down there each morning, I always wonder whether someone's going to be missing from the roll-call. Because I know very well everything's going to fall apart any day now, without warning. Like those old chestnut trees that have stood up to the worst storms, for two or three centuries, and fall over one day, toppled by a breeze . . .'

Despite the cold, fog and especially the darkness which made their escapade almost dangerous, Christian and Josyane sneaked quietly out of the village and wandered away up the road rising towards Coste-Roche.

They suddenly felt the need for peace, privacy. The need to be alone together for a few moments, just to exchange their impressions of the day, escape the rather too powerful sound system, get some fresh air before plunging back into the celebrations for a few hours longer.

Later, towards midnight, they would slip away and escape to the Black Truffle Hotel in Brive, where Christian had booked a room. Then, for twelve days they would conform to tradition with a honeymoon in Italy.

'Okay,' Christian had said at the time of booking the tickets, 'I admit that it's very petit-bourgeois and unimaginative, but that's too bad, it's worth the journey. Especially at this time of year, when there are fewer tourists.'

'You know, I don't mind tourists, now I'm not responsible for guiding them around! So long live the Bridge of Sighs and the gondolas!'

But meanwhile, they were there, walking slowly, clinging close to each other to withstand the damp chill engulfing the village. Christian stopped, pulled her to him and kissed her. She had deliciously cool lips.

'You see,' he murmured, 'if I believed in numbers and I was betting each way, there are two I'd tick, the four and the twelve . . .'

'Boring, a whole load of suckers play their wedding dates!'

'I know. But you've certainly got a short memory!' he said, stroking her cheeks with the backs of his fingers. They were all damp from the fog, downy as a peach on the vine pearly with dew. 'Yes, you have a short memory,' he repeated. 'It's a year today that I looped some shell necklaces round your neck and watched you go off towards the aeroplane. I was already missing you!'

'Are you sure? That was the fourth of December, like today?'

'Certain.'

'Well, you took your time about deciding to marry me!' she joked.

'There's one other thing I want you to know. And there's no need to tell me, in your usual way, that I'm lapsing into daft romanticism! Yes, you've already told me that! Right, so this is it: I do love your family, very much. Until now I've never really known what a family was. It's true, for an only son it's not easy to envisage. So there it is, I want you to know that I like yours a lot. And now, we ought to go back, otherwise they'll wolf-whistle when we go in!'

'That doesn't matter,' she decided. 'Let's walk on a little. It's good to be alone. But first, give me a big, big kiss, the way I'd have liked you to a year ago today! There, you see, this evening, I'm the romantic one.'

Softened by the increasingly impenetrable fog, the lively sounds escaping from the village hall echoed around Saint-Libéral. They reminded the very oldest inhabitants of the time when, almost every Saturday evening, waltz tunes used to resound in the alleys.

Occasionally, carried by the fitful breeze which sprang up in the church square and wafted down the main street, some muffled booming reached as far as the Vialhe house, right at the end of the village.

'There's nothing else I need; you can go back and join them again if you like,' Pierre-Edouard suggested to Félix.

Seated in his usual place, in the right-hand chimney corner, the old man, leaning towards the fire, gently stirred the embers with little puffs from the old bellows, its leather cracked and nozzle dented by the years.

'Don't you want to go back there? Now that your mother's in bed and I've had my soup, you can go!' he insisted, placing a few twigs on the still hesitant sparks.

'Later on, maybe,' said Félix. 'Berthe said she wouldn't be long coming back, so I'm going to wait for her.'

'I see, you're afraid to leave me alone with your mother? It's true she's not been doing so famously for some time, and I myself . . . Well, if you prefer keeping an old man company to running about with the young people . . .'

'You know, I'm like you, all that music tires me out in the end. I'm too old for all that noise.'

'Get away with you!' said Pierre-Edouard dismissively. He took his pipe from his pocket, tamped down a pinch of tobacco which he lit with a spill.

'And what do you think of the new fellow?' he asked suddenly.

'Which new fellow?'

'Young Jo's husband, I can never remember his name.'

'Christian.'

'No, I know that! His surname! It's from around here!'

'Leyrac.'

'That's it, it's a local name. What do you think of the young fellow?'

'I think he's really great, strong, just what the girl needs.'

'You saw how beautiful she is? You'd swear it was her grandmother when I married her!' smiled Pierre-Edouard. He was lost in memory for a few moments before exclaiming: 'But he'd be well advised not to torment her, like that other one with Marie . . . What, what did you think, that I wasn't in the know?' he continued.

'Well . . .' Félix said evasively.

He did not know exactly what the old man understood about his granddaughter's divorce, and above all did not want to have to explain anything.

'They wanted me to believe he had too much work to come to the wedding,' scoffed Pierre-Edouard. 'A teacher, too much work! Examinations, or something, they told me! Take me for an ass! Well, it's not so serious,' he sighed. 'But I pretend to swallow their stories, because I'm not sure whether Mathilde knows all about it, so I say nothing . . . You must understand, I won't be the one to tell her, poor thing, that would depress her so much!'

'You're right,' Félix approved.

He had always thought that wanting to hide anything from Pierre-Edouard or from Mathilde was a monumental error, a trap, even, for those who had chosen, out of consideration and care, to suppress certain things. This had created a delicate situation which was not easily resolved. Especially with Pierre-Edouard, who obviously took malicious pleasure in seeing his family circle tied up in knots.

'And Jacques, what do you think of him?' asked Pierre-Edouard suddenly.

'He seems to be in fine fettle. I'm pleased, his operation really was a great success.'

'Yes, maybe . . .' murmured Pierre-Edouard, suddenly pensive. He smoked in silence, and spat into the embers, which sputtered. 'Did he speak to you about his plans?'

'Yes.'

'Which ones? For Coste-Roche or for the village?'

'Both.'

'And? Do you believe they'll work, all these changes he wants to make?'

'Yes, why not?'

'Huh . . . I have my doubts,' grumbled Pierre-Edouard. 'Doesn't want to keep pigs any more, seems it no longer pays! Nor cereals, too much work for very little. Wants to pull up the plum and apple trees, there again, seems they're not worth anything any more! But then, what is worthwhile? Seems he wants to sell half his animals to replace them with better ones, talk about a mistake! And he needs to change his tractor too, you'll be telling me, with the other one doing a pirouette . . . And after all it's more than twelve years that he's been using the Massey! Even so, that's all money going out with no return!'

'He's bound to have considered everything before making the decision,' said Félix.

'And it seems it's Dominique who put all this in his head,' continued Pierre-Edouard without listening to Félix. 'I'm very fond of the boy, but I tell you: too much studying and these children end up talking nonsense! It's all very fine, education, I'm for it, we paid for Jacques and if Paul had wanted to . . . And then, look at Guy, and even Mauricette, we don't regret it. Education is good, but you have to know when to stop before you go barmy! Dominique must have gone on too long!'

'No, no, I'm sure he's right!' protested Félix.

'Bunkum! It's too many changes in one go, all that! And then Dominique, it's not him who'll be out of pocket!'

'Now you're not being fair! You know very well he sends his parents a cheque every month!'

'Possibly. But he's a long way from the land. He just talks, and his father breaks his back! And then all these projects, they're very fine, but you've seen how one lousy drought messes up your beautiful plans, haven't you?'

'Listen, you mustn't make yourself ill over this!' cut in Félix. 'Tell me, don't you think Jacques is old enough to know what he should be doing? You're forgetting he's about to be a grandfather!'

'I know fine! But all the same, all these changes worry me. Because, you see, I realise that sometimes I'm a bit soft in the head – yes, yes! Don't contradict me, I know it! But all the same, when I'm all right, when my memory's there, I think it all over. So I'm telling you, ever since Jacques has been on the farm, I've watched him chasing after something or other! He'll have spent his whole life haring about, poor fellow . . . Well, if *you* tell me there's no need to worry . . .'

'Yes I do. I tell you, everything'll be fine.'

Pierre-Edouard sucked on his pipe and became absorbed in contemplation of the fire in front of him, now hissing as it attacked a big oak stump.

'And what about the village?' he asked suddenly.

'Now what's the problem?'

'Do you think it's good, what he wants to set up? The château, the swimming pool, the Annamese in Suzanne's place, and I don't know what else? Oh yes, there's that one who wants to make a sort of ranch! Do you think that's a good idea?'

'Oh, that, yes! I'm sure of it, that'll make the village come to life!'

'Mmm . . . yes . . .,' said Pierre-Edouard sceptically. 'Come to life, you say! I've been told that before . . . Yes, when poor Louis began to sell plots of land for building. Yes, on the track leading up to the plateau. Well, at the time, Jacques said to me: "That'll give Saint-Libéral a new lease of life!" Oh yes! Now today, there are people here we don't even know! And who don't want to be known. Look at how some of them don't even say good morning! Well, if that's what a new lease of life is!'

'You mustn't let that worry you either! Look, I bet Jacques will still get through in the first round with seventy-five per cent of the votes!'

'Why are you talking about that now?'

'Hey, the vote's in three months!'

'For the municipal elections?' said Pierre-Edouard in surprise.

'Yes, of course! You know that!'

'Already the elections? Oh, miladiou! Why didn't anyone tell me? Nobody ever tells me anything round here!'

'There's been very little said about it as yet, that's why,' lied Félix, realising he had annoyed the old man by exposing his failing memory and alertness. 'But I'm telling you,' he stressed, 'Jacques'll get through in the first round, as usual, right!'

'Oh good, that's because the people really like him, because he's a good mayor,' said Pierre-Edouard rather abstractedly.

He suddenly felt tired, distant, and Félix understood that the time for rational, not to say heated, discussion was past.

'Wouldn't you like to go to bed?' he suggested to him.

'No, I would not! I'm not sleepy. And besides, if I go to bed at this hour, I won't sleep at all from three o'clock on, thank you very much. Anyway, I want to wait for Mathilde. But turn on the TV for me. It's not that I watch it, but it keeps me company. And then it's not tiring!'

After the three days of liveliness and jollity in Saint-Libéral, thanks to the wedding, the village sank back into its habitual torpor, apathy, silence.

The fog was followed by drizzle almost like fine hail, slippery, disagreeable, inducing people to shut themselves away at home, to huddle by the fireside. And when the grocer's van arrived on Wednesday, few clients were brave enough to emerge into the cold and face the easterly blast, cutting as a razor.

Therefore, as was his habit, Pierre-Edouard protested when he saw Mathilde slipping on her coat. He knew very well that she would do as she pleased whatever he said, but he would feel to blame if he did not warn her.

'You're not going out in this weather? It'll just make you ill!' he called out.

'No it won't! Anyway, I've already been out this morning to see to the animals. It's not as cold as it looks. And the forecast is for milder weather.'

'Pooh! The forecast! With them you're really well informed! Those chatterboxes must never put their noses out of doors!' he grumbled.

'Right, does anyone need anything?' she asked.

'No, no,' replied Louise and Yvette, without lifting their eyes from their knitting.

'Nor for me,' said Berthe, 'but I'd love to know what you're going to get, apart from a severe chill! Yvette did all our shopping the day before yesterday in Objat! We've got enough to keep us for a fortnight!'

'I know,' admitted Mathilde, knotting her thick woollen scarf.

'Right, so admit you're going out for your own amusement!' said Pierre-Edouard, seizing his chance.

He was in a grumpy mood, for he had been bored since Félix had gone home. So without going so far as to pick a quarrel with his wife, he still felt like crossing swords, just for something to do!

'Hey! Stop that, you two!' cried Mathilde. 'I'm going to the grocer's and that's that! Because if no one goes down when it's a bit cold, he'll end up not wanting to come, and he'll be justified!'

'That would be a great loss,' pronounced Pierre-Edouard with damning insincerity. 'He sells at ten times the price of other places!'

'All right,' she cut him off, 'but you don't say that when he fixes you up with tobacco! In any case, I really do need to go there. I haven't any spices left, and we forgot to buy any the day before yesterday. So, if you want the black pudding and grilled meat to be edible, don't waste more of my time! And you,' she threw at Pierre-Edouard, 'unless it's too tiring for you, or you don't know how to do it any more, instead of muttering, you'd do better to sharpen the knives! You should be thinking about that now, not tomorrow, when we'll be needing them!'

She impudently pulled a face at him and went out, not unhappy to have scored the last point.

# 24

DESPITE the pleas of her nearest and dearest, who constantly reminded her that her health could always play tricks on her again, Mathilde had not given up fattening two pigs. She also continued to feed up fifteen to twenty ducks and geese, raise half a dozen rabbits, and care for more than thirty hens and chickens.

And if Jacques happened to scold her for creating lots of work for herself, when he was very well able to supply her with eggs, chickens, ducks and pigs, she invariably retorted:

'All your animals raised on mixtures made of God knows what, they're worthless! They're only good for townies who don't know any better! Your father is much too fussy to eat just anything! And so am I! And even your aunts. Just go and ask Berthe what she thinks of your meal-fed produce! So you leave me to do as I think fit!'

And indeed, her way of fattening the two pigs destined for family consumption – and they were all beneficiaries, even those living in Paris – bore only a distant relation to the methods in use at Coste-Roche. For economic and therefore compelling reasons, Jacques was forced to aim for rapid growth. The granules, meal products, vitamins and different antibiotics which he dished out to his charges had the sole objective of making them reach optimum weight in minimum time. And the insipidity of the meat thus obtained hardly mattered. For a long time now, consumers had been accustomed to eating any old thing! They gulped down without a qualm chicken which resembled veal, veal you could take for pork, pork often mistaken for roast turkey. Not forgetting colourless eggs and fruit and vegetables without smell or taste.

Mathilde had an easy time ridiculing that sort of food. What she produced was on a different plane. So even if it did give her lots of work, she continued her varied stock-rearing.

'In any case, it keeps me busy!' she maintained.

Patiently fattened – in twice the time it took Jacques to get his battery pigs to the same weight – the piglets she cared for had the privilege of a first-class diet. A judicious mixture of steamed potatoes, barley meal and sunflower-oil cakes, with just a dash of maize flour. Not forgetting, of course, the refreshing cabbages and turnips spiced with artichoke peel. Finally, when the season came round, the happy guzzlers, already nice and plump, were entitled to succulent desserts of chestnuts, apples, beets and store carrots.

On a regime of this quality twice a day, with long and beneficial siestas and peaceful nights in the thick, soft litter of barley straw, the temporary quests developed, week by week, a succulent meat. Flesh which, when the time came, would be delicious-smelling, firm without being tough, without excess fat, just sufficiently marbled. Meat which would be fragrant in the cooking, refined, full of aroma; a treat, a delicacy.

And the hams, fillets, chops, shoulders and roasting joints, not forgetting the black puddings (made with chestnuts, apples or just plain), sausages, faggots, potted and grilled meats, the brawn, salt pork and trotters would be of such quality, and the pleasure of those who tasted them so great, that Mathilde would forget all her hours of work. And since the same went for everything she produced, since she was happy and proud to offer her family food of this value, she was not about to stop, despite the arguments and advice of her immediate circle.

What's more,' she would cry laughingly to conclude the discussions, 'if I were to take you at your word, you'd be the first to suffer! Deep down, you don't want me to stop at all!'

For a long time now Pierre-Edouard had been unable to help kill the pig. The effort required to hold the animal, which always seemed to sense the events to come, was too taxing. It needed too much strength and stamina. So he preferred to keep his distance from the sacrificial victim. He was not the only one.

To prove it, this year even Jacques refused to risk grasping one of the animal's hooves and clinging on. Even with the help of three other strong fellows, Delmond, Coste and Brousse, he no longer felt up to tossing the screaming beast on to the ladder resting on breeze-blocks, and holding it there until Delpeyroux plunged his knife into the neck and severed the carotid artery.

And that was not the end of it; for despite the torrent of blood spurting into the bowl, which Mathilde would stir after salting it, to prevent it coagulating, the beast would still have awful convulsions, spasms, snap furiously with its clashing jaws, ready to snatch at a hand and crush it.

It was only gradually that the death rattles and kicking diminished, grew more feeble, more sporadic. Then, whilst the muscles quivered with final tremors and the air bubbles, red and frothy, swelled and burst on the edge of the wound, the last rumblings sounded. Now the men could relax their efforts, wipe their hands and foreheads, then roll a cigarette.

From that moment on, Pierre-Edouard knew how to make himself useful. There was no need for great strength to run the lighted brand over the beast stretched on a temporary, crackling bonfire of straw, in order to burn off the coarsest bristles, those on the back, trotters and ears. Afterwards, when the pink skin was mottled here and there with sooty patches and the fire had become more harmful than useful, Pierre-Edouard could still scratch the hide with his knife, as the water poured by Yvette trickled over it.

'Bloody fine animal, must be about a hundred and thirty kilos!' commented Delpeyroux, passing his whetstone over his sticking knife.

Even though he did it well, always with perfect precision, he did not like this job of slaughterer very much. But the tradition was there, which had one day virtually forced him to take over from his father, who had grown too old, too debilitated to have a sure hand. As he had assisted him for years, and mastered the technique, he had agreed to replace him, to provide the service. And since then, come winter, when the bitter cold helped make the meat easy to handle, when the moon was old, and therefore favourable for preserving, he killed the pigs, without pleasure, but quickly and well.

'You say a hundred and thirty? A bit more, I think,' reckoned Pierre-Edouard. 'Must be over a hundred and thirty-five. He's heavier than his companion. But the other one's beautiful too, longer, maybe more meat on him.'

That one was destined for Mauricette and Jean-Pierre, but their daughters would have a share. And Guy and Colette as well, only too happy to enjoy a superlative ham.

'Talking of which, shall I do him straight away or begin the cutting up?'

'Straight away,' Jacques intervened. 'You know if you wait he'll get worked up, go crazy, get over-excited; it's not good for the meat.'

'Bet he's already worried,' agreed Pierre-Edouard. 'He's heard the bawling, and then the smell of the blood . . . You lot fetch him, I'll go on scraping this one; don't fuss, it's not difficult.'

He saw Mathilde coming back with the bowl, empty but still red-stained.

'They're going to do him now, I hope?' she asked.

'Of course.'

'Poor thing . . .' she murmured, for already the men were emerging once more from the shed, dragging and controlling the victim as best they could.

Wisely, Delpeyroux had muzzled the mouth with a halter. Yet the animal squealed, struggled, tried to bite, fought for its life.

'Poor thing,' she repeated.

'Hey! Come on, now,' said Pierre-Edouard, 'you don't want to keep him till he dies of old age!'

He was joking, but understood his wife's feelings very well. She had looked after and fed this pig for months, made a fuss of it every day, talked to it. So it was quite natural that she should feel a bit sorry for it. One could love black pudding without much enjoying the essential and only method of making it . . .

In front of them, the cries intensified as the men laid the beast on the ladder. Delpeyroux stepped nearer, Mathilde too. The blood spurted out.

Despite a still robust appetite, it was not the food which Pierre-Edouard appreciated most at the meal following the sacrifice of the pigs, but the reunion with neighbours. With those who had come to help and were invited to dine as a thank-you. And he was delighted to have around him Delmond, Coste, Brousse and Delpeyroux – whose fathers and grandfathers he had known – because it reminded him of the period when mutual help was so frequent, so normal, that not a month passed, or even a week, depending on the season, without friends meeting this way, at long and cheerful tables after work.

At that time it would never have occurred to a neighbour to refuse a favour – expecting it to be returned, naturally. That was the time when they would make up a 'troupeau' as it was called; six or eight strong, willing men who would undertake the heavy work together. Thanks to them, and at minimal cost, it was possible to tackle the deep ploughing of a fallow field, or break the subsoil of a future vineyard, the excavations and foundations for a house or barn, or set up their wooden framework; and, on the slopes inaccessible to machines, to harvest with scythes, or even sickles. And always, above all, marking out the seasons, the threshing machine, the grape-picking and the pig-killing.

But those days of work and interdependence which maintained friendly ties and united neighbours had long gone, disappeared, been forgotten even, except by the old.

Certainly, and Jacques' accident had proved it, neighbours still knew how to lend a hand to someone in need. But those were individual cases which required almost exceptional circumstances to inspire them.

In fact, because tractors had brought the possibility of decreasing the amount of work done by hand, the idea of helping each other had been eroded from lack of practice. Now only the day of the pig-killing could still unite four or five men and their wives around the same table.

On this day the house came alive again as in former times. It echoed happily with the chatter of the women as they prepared the potted meat and pâté, cooked the black pudding, cut up the hams and shoulders or watched that the heavy pots full of fat placed on the stove did not catch fire.

The house laughed too with the men, who, towards midday, came into the main room, bringing with them on their cords the smell of burnt straw and lightly-grilled crackling, absorbed around the fire. And at the tables where everyone sat together, laughter and jokes soon rang out, old stories were retold, heard a hundred times before but no less valued for that, and the past was brought to life. There, too, all the village news was commented on, ideas were exchanged, impressions of such and such an event. All that was over now, except for once a year.

So today, Pierre-Edouard was keen to play his part at the table as head of the family and he was enjoying it very much. Happy to see his neighbours, whom he met almost every day, but too fleetingly, during his walk in the village. For although he had nothing to do, that was not the case for those he greeted; it was therefore impossible to start a proper and satisfying discussion with them. It all went too fast.

'Bonjour, Père Vialhe. Lovely weather, that won't last! Right, it's not that I'm tired of your company but there's work waiting for me. Salut, Père Vialhe. And mind you look after yourself!'

Here at table it was different, one could forget the time. One could even allow oneself the luxury of some gentle teasing, and that Pierre-Edouard really loved.

After pouring a good measure of wine into a bouillon as meaty as one could wish for, and thickened with vermicelli, he turned light-heartedly to Pierre Coste, sitting next to him.

'So according to what Jacques tells me,' he said to him, 'you're planning to start up a ranch, just like that?'

'Oh, a ranch! Don't exaggerate, we're not the national stud at Pompadour, you know! What I want is just to keep some ponies for the kids coming to the château. And some horses too, for the bigger ones.'

'I see . . .' replied Pierre-Edouard. 'Here, help yourself,' he said, passing the dish of pot-au-feu. 'Some ponies and horses,' he continued. 'But do you know about these animals?'

'No, not too much,' admitted Coste. 'With me it's been mostly cows, as you know, so . . .'

'I see,' repeated Pierre-Edouard, serving himself in his turn. 'But you do know they give terrible kicks, those animals?' he said, thoughtfully contemplating a gherkin speared on the end of his fork. 'Kicks which kill you outright!' he insisted.

'My father's is always exaggerating,' interrupted Jacques with a laugh.

'What me, exaggerate? Tell me straight out I don't know a thing about horses!'

'Oh no! Nobody would dare say that, Père Vialhe,' Delpeyroux assured him. 'It's well known that you were an expert!'

He was old enough to remember the time when Pierre-Edouard had his horse and cart. He also knew just how much the old man liked to joke, and here his tone and expression were signalling a hoax.

'But Jacques says I don't know a thing about it!' said Pierre-Edouard. 'And yet, my lad, I had up to sixty horses to take care of morning and evening – yes, when I did my military service, I certainly did! Not to mention the percherons I had when I was working in the Brie area! Because I ploughed with horses, I did! To say nothing, either, about the ones which pulled our 75-millimetre cannon during the war! So, to hear that I don't know anything about it, and from my own son too!'

'The family always lets you down,' said Jacques. He knew his father well, and without guessing all the ins and outs, he saw the joke being constructed.

'Well, if I tell you that a kick from a horse can cut you in two, it's true,' said Pierre-Edouard, 'and the same with their teeth! They bite, those animals, you've no idea, worse than dogs! That's the only reason you put a bit in their mouths – and while they're chewing on it, they don't think of snapping up your arm!'

'Get away, they're not as vicious as all that!' replied Coste with a shrug. But he was nevertheless rather shaken.

'All right, but you just mind out. And if you pass behind them, allow at least . . . oh, three good metres! They can lash out as far as that,' Pierre-Edouard assured him.

'Oh no! There I don't believe you, that's a joke!' said Coste, laughing. He was relieved to have detected the trick in time.

'Okay,' admitted Pierre-Edouard, 'I'm exaggerating a bit, but it's just to make you careful.' He drank a few mouthfuls of wine, wiped his mouth before continuing: 'In any case, you'll do as you like, but on the treks, don't take the animals in the direction of Delpy's place, you know, into the valley.'

'But I'll have to go down there; the public road passes that way and it makes a very nice ride, you know that perfectly well!' said Coste. 'And anyway, why shouldn't I go there?'

'Have you thought about the pond?'

'The one Delpy had dug three years ago? Yes, and so what?'

'Any one can see you really don't know a thing about horses,' Pierre-Edouard reproached him. 'If you don't learn a bit more, you'll soon have lost half of them . . .'

'What?'

'Yes indeed! Has no one ever told you that they love to swim, those animals?

'Oh, no! But after all, even if . . . I don't see why . . .'

'And you've never been told, either, that mares shouldn't swim? Well it'll be all right if you only have geldings, but if you have mares . . .'

'Oh dear! That's right, that would be unforgivable!' commented Delpeyroux. 'It's common knowledge,' he insisted, 'a mare should never swim, never!'

'Well, how the hell can it harm them?' demanded Coste, more and more disconcerted.

'It's because they take in water, young man! Everybody knows that. All mares take in water!' said Pierre-Edouard in a tone which brooked no reply.

'And it doesn't do any good even if you hold their heads out of the water,' Delpeyroux went one better, 'because that's not the way they fill themselves up . . .'

'Huh! Now you're making fun of me, aren't you?' said Coste. But he was not really sure of anything and thought it wise to continue: 'So where does the water go in, then?'

'Tut, tut . . .' Pierre-Edouard sighed, glancing in the direction of the women at the other table, to make sure they were not listening. 'Think about it a bit, young man,' he explained, lowering his voice. 'Delpeyroux told you the water doesn't enter by the mouth, or the ears, okay? So . . .'

'Damnation . . .' murmured Coste, after a moment's consideration and an effort of imagination, 'damnation, I'd never have believed it! It's good thing you warned me! Well, well, I'd never have believed it!' he repeated.

'And yet, you need to know it,' said Pierre-Edouard, seeing that Jacques, Delpeyroux, and Delmond were about to explode with laughter. 'Yes, yes, young fellow, and I'll tell you something else — *I*'d never have believed that joke could still work!'

He had to raise his voice to make himself heard over Delmond who, his eyes filled with tears, was roaring with laughter as he delivered mighty slaps to his thighs.

'Do you know what?' continued Pierre-Edouard. 'That joke, we used it on the rookies coming from the towns, when I was only a second gunner and crew marksman in the Fifth Artillery Regiment in Besançon in 1909!'

'Good old Coste! "I'd never have believed it!" he said! The fool! The fool!' hiccuped Delpeyroux in a strangled voice. And his guffaws were so infectious, so heart-warming, that the whole table joined in.

As a result, nobody noticed that it was not laughter, but the memories of himself at twenty which now brought a few tears to Pierre-Edouard's eyes.

According to a tradition going back close on thirty years, Mathilde and Pierre-Edouard invited their children to share their midday meal on Christmas Day. And although it was exceptional for the Paris members, Guy and Colette, to be there, Jacques and Michèle, Mauricette and Jean-Pierre always kept the appointment.

Certainly the absence of young children made the celebration less boisterous, less noisy and cheerful, but everyone was still eager to forget for one day their worries, their little physical aliments, their work.

And in December 1976, nobody had need of forced jollity to bring some happiness to the Vialhe household. Mauricette made sure, during the aperitif, of cheering them with the hot news just telephoned through by Josyane and Christian: a baby was on the way for them, expected in June . . . So there it was . . .

'I knew it,' said Mathilde. 'Yes, I did, she'd changed too much all of a sudden, little Jo! Well, so it's June? All right . . . That's how it is . . .'

'Well, well!' smiled Pierre-Edouard, holding out his glass to Jacques for another drop of Banyuls wine. And, mischievously, he could not stop himself announcing: 'In our time, we weren't as smart as young people nowadays. If I remember rightly, you needed to allow at least nine months after the wedding to make a proper baby . . . But, there's progress for you, everything happens so quickly nowadays . . .'

'Stop it, will you?' Mathilde said to him; despite her pleasure, she was a little embarrassed that everything was not quite as it should be. And in particular, she was not forgetting that Jacques and Michèle had already, in their time . . .

'Oh, go on!' insisted Pierre-Edouard. 'Why shouldn't I say they've had Easter before Palm Sunday? That's how it is, we're not going to pretend to believe otherwise! In any case it's very good news: babies, you can never have enough of them!'

'Very good news,' agreed Jean-Pierre, who was bursting with pride at the idea of being a grandfather soon. 'Pity the baby's not being born here, with Dominique's; that would have made two more births in the village!'

'Yes, a hundred per cent better than this year . . . A fine feat!' said Jacques

'We'll talk about all that at table,' suggested Mathilde, 'because if you wait, the turkey will be too dry.'

It was while they were tackling the hors-d'oeuvre – a succulent home-made foie gras – with good humour and a little more good wine than usual bringing a sparkle to their eyes, that Mauricette launched the second piece of news:

'All right, Jo and Christian won't be having their baby here, but they will be having a house in the village!'

'A house? How's that? They want to have one built?' asked Jacques.

'They're not going to come and live here, are they?' said Mathilde.

'No, no,' cut in Berthe, who thought she understood, 'they only want a holiday home is that it?'

'Yes,' confirmed Jean-Pierre. 'They asked us just now to look for one for them; it seems that Christian feels more Corrézien than ever!'

'Do they want one in the village itself or in the parish?' asked Jacques, delighted at the idea of seeing some young people return to Saint-Libéral, if only for a few weeks a year.

'It doesn't matter to them. But Jo would like it to be on the plateau side, so not too far from the village,' said Mauricette.

'Are you going to tell me or not? I don't understand a thing!' Pierre-Edouard suddenly lost patience, and spoke with a brusqueness which surprised everyone.

He was vaguely aware of not having paid any attention to the beginning of the conversation, and was rather cross with himself. But on the other hand, it was sometimes so tiring, so exhausting just to keep track of everything being said! Especially when there was such a crowd and everyone was talking at the same time! That almost made you feel like doing the same as Louise, who no longer made the effort to listen to what was being related around her. It's true that it was often of such little interest . . .

On the other hand, not to know what people were talking about, that was annoying. Especially when you had the feeling that they were doing nothing to help you follow their discussion! That really was something to get cross about!

But there again, it was quite tiring, you always came away with the nasty impression of having fallen out over very little. For, actually, what they told you in the end, to calm you down, was of absolutely no importance, no interest at all!

But that was still no reason to leave you deliberately in ignorance of what they were saying. Because of course everyone deliberately spoke quietly, whispered, so that he heard nothing!

'It's true, by God! I never get told anything round here!' he cried in a voice filled with anger.

'Yes, yes, you do,' replied Berthe gently, placing her hand on his arm to calm the trembling. 'Right, what would you like to know?'

'Berthe's right, we'll explain everything,' said Mathilde, in a tone which barely concealed her sudden concern for Pierre-Edouard.

He seemed both exasperated and distant at the same time; the weariness which had swept over him in just a few seconds lined his features, distorted them. And at the end of his knotted fingers, all speckled with brown patches, the nails were turning purple.

'Now listen!' said Berthe. 'Jo and Christian want to buy a house in the village, to come and spend their holidays here. There, that's simple, isn't it?'

'Who wants to spend the holidays?' he asked.

'Young Jo and her husband,' explained Mathilde.

'Ah? Well, you could have said all that straight away, couldn't you? And so what's the problem?' he said, beginning to eat again.

'There's no problem,' said Jacques, noting with relief that his father seemed to be on an even keel again. 'And you know very well there's no lack of houses for sale in the area, sadly!'

'Ah yes . . .' replied Pierre-Edouard.

'And then, we'll need to know what sort of price before looking seriously,' continued Jacques.

'Not too expensive, I think,' said Mauricette.

'So that means they'll be coming here more often?' Pierre-Edouard intervened once more.

'Of course,' said Mathilde. 'It's good news, don't you think?'

'Yes, yes,' he said absentmindedly, as if all that was of no further interest. 'Yes, yes,' he repeated. And he sank into contemplation of his empty plate.

'Would you like to go and rest a while, take a little siesta?' suggested Mathilde, to try to break the awkward atmosphere which had fallen over the table.

'A siesta?' He reflected for a moment, passed his hand across his face, then frowned. 'A siesta? No, it's not time! And I want some turkey!' he said, his voice suddenly normal and firm again. He smiled at Mathilde, and continued: 'Say, if young Jo comes back more often, you'll be happy, won't you?'

'Of course,' she agreed, forcing herself to return his smile. But worry was etched on her face.

'No, I assure you, he's not in bad shape. Well, I mean to say, no worse than usual,' said Doctor Martel to Jacques after his visit the following day.

At the request of Mathilde, and although it was Sunday, Jacques had telephoned the doctor. But beforehand he had warned his mother that he ran the risk of finding a locum; a man whom Pierre-Edouard would not know and with whom he would have words. For he was very lucid again and less inclined to make allowances, especially for a stranger.

Luckily, Doctor Martel was on duty and had come as quickly as possible. And although Pierre-Edouard had not failed to complain that it was all being done just to annoy him, that he only wanted one thing, to be left in peace, he had let him sound his chest.

'Right, so, if we agree that he's no worse, what do we do when he seems . . . how shall I put it? . . . Yes, when he switches off?' asked Jacques.

'Oh, that! Only a genius could give you the answer! It's his age, and . . . But I think his heart misses a bit from time to time, so the brain is poorly supplied; that could explain his periods of absent-mindedness. Having said that, as you asked, I took the opportunity of my visit to examine your aunt, and there . . .'

'Let's have it! I've heard worse things!' insisted Jacques.

'She's declining fast, almost quicker than your father. And, as well as her mind not being very strong, she might be hatching a nasty surprise for us in the stomach area . . . You'll be telling me, at her age, it could take a long time . . . Then I must remind you to watch that your mother doesn't do more than she should; she seems well, but . . .'

'I know,' sighed Jacques, 'but what can I do? And you don't have to tell me that my sister and I may find ourselves with four old people on our hands! Because Aunt Berthe could come a cropper all of a sudden! And even Aunt Yvette isn't immune from the hard knocks of life!'

'And neither are you,' Doctor Martel reminded him.

'I won't forget. But all right, that's how it is. Our relatives are the way they are, we'll manage. It'll take as long as it takes. And then, as my father's said to me a thousand times, we must let things take their course, time will tell, it always does.'

# 25

WITH results which were nothing to be ashamed of, and what was more, with important projects about to be realised, Jacques could have saved himself the expense of an electoral campaign. His sash of office was not in danger. Despite that, he played the game.

First of all out of courtesy towards his fellow citizens – friends or enemies – and also to cock a bit of a snook at Peyrafaure; not too much, just enough to satisfy everyone. For even whilst certain of his victory, the electors would not have understood him leaving a free hand and a clear field to a rival as forceful as Peyrafaure.

The latter conducted his campaign in a frenzy of activity, multiplying meetings, interviews, interminable discussions and other consultations. He lacked neither courage nor audacity, nor that shameless dishonesty not displeasing to certain electors, who regard it as the height of political skill. Peyrafaure did not disappoint them.

Witness the fact that, having announced various sporting developments for the young people, amongst them a tennis court, he now declared that it was all going to cost a fortune, that Jacques had delusions of grandeur, that the community, already crippled with debts, would be ruined for fifty years to come and the taxes would be unimaginably high! Figures in hand, he forecast an intolerable tax increase, as never before seen!

Jacques did not take the trouble to refute this, for his visits to all the homes, even the most far-flung, gave him strength, proved that he had been right to convert the château and that the majority of the electors were delighted at the idea of soon seeing a flock of children on holiday there. Likewise, and he was pleased and surprised by this, people were gratified to know that the village was going to open itself to the outside world, to welcome visitors, to bring in new life thanks to the photo exhibition. Finally, everyone was now anxious to see the auberge opened again.

That was decided; Lacombe's brother-in-law, his wife and six children – four of them were already enrolled at the school – would be moving to the village before the summer. Lacombe also reported, and this was great news, that not only was his brother-in-law all set to open a fixed menu restaurant, but his sister, after studying the market, was contemplating keeping a small grocery store, with bread counter!

But there again, Peyrafaure found an excuse for spiteful gossip, when Lacombe was not there. Without daring to specify the colour of the impending arrivals, he insinuated that one did not know too much about the people one was going to be dealing with . . . Because, basically, who could stand guarantee for an individual who had spent part of his army career in the colonial wars and now trebled his monthly pension thanks to child benefit payments?

Peyrafaure would never have made such a suggestion three months earlier, when Lacombe was part of his team within the council. With Martin, Castellac, Delmas and himself, they formed the opposition. But, probably because that turncoat Lacombe wanted his sister and brother-in-law to start on a sound basis with the mayor, he had changed his tune and joined the camp of Jacques, Delpeyroux, Delmond, Coste, Duverger and Brousse; that is, of the majority!

And a majority which was going to be re-elected at the first ballot! An honour which Peyrafaure had no certainty of securing. He was therefore aggressive and vindictive, but not at all dangerous to Jacques and his team.

In any case, Jacques did not particularly resent his excesses. He did not forget that Peyrafaure was among those who had come running when he lay paralysed beside his tractor. That gesture really required him to turn a bit of a deaf ear at the time of an electoral campaign.

Besides, he knew that everything would subside again like a soufflé the day after the second ballot. As soon as the celebration wine toasting the elected members was swallowed, the council would return to its old ways, its monotony, with occasional rows and always Peyrafaure's grand perorations. It was fine like that.

Louise's condition deteriorated drastically two days before the first round of the elections. Although, like Pierre-Edouard, she had got through the winter without any great problem. True, the weather had been mild, the temperature kind. To such an extent that Pierre-Edouard had been able to go out almost every day with Berthe for his little walk in the village; not far, down to the church square; and sometimes even, when he was very bold, as far as Mauricette's, beside the school.

By contrast, Louise no longer went out, no longer moved. Rising early, which is to say soon after Mathilde, who was eager to be the first up to rekindle the fire, she drank the bowl of milk which now represented her main meal of the day. That done, she installed herself in the settle, and the few words she exchanged with Mathilde or Pierre-Edouard, he too an early-riser, grew less frequent, quickly becoming rather disjointed, joining in the conversation after too long a gap.

Thus, without appearing to suffer, she sank into an increasingly impenetrable silence and estrangement, although full of smiles, almost seraphic. She seemed to surface when Berthe sat down at her side to pass the afternoon. She then took some pleasure in her sister's prattling, as she commented on the newspaper, the television programme, the village gossip, and gave news of the family. And it was Berthe too who made sure that she fed herself a little; for she no longer even came to sit at table, but contented herself with nibbling a few morsels of biscuit which she dipped into half a glass of milk sweetened with a spoonful of honey.

When darkness fell, she left her corner by the fire without a sound, informing those around her quietly: 'It's late, I'm going to bed', and disappeared into her room until the following morning.

So on Friday, 11 March, Mathilde was worried not to see her up at her usual time. Apprehensively she entered the bedroom, turned on the light and understood.

Rigid in her bed, half her face deformed by a terrible grimace, Louise appeared dead. But Mathilde, upset as she was, prevented herself from uttering the slightest exclamation, to avoid any sudden shock to Pierre-Edouard. It was in leaning over her sister-in-law that she discovered she was still alive. Stricken by hemiplegia, the whole of her right side was frozen, inert. But her expression was alive, understanding everything, appealing for help.

Without hesitation, Mathilde continued into the next bedroom, that of Berthe. She always rose much later, having preserved her Parisian habits which often kept her up until midnight. Despite that, she woke as soon as Mathilde pushed open the door. Immediately lucid, understanding that a serious occurrence had caused her sister-in-law to burst in, she called:

'Is it Pierre-Edouard?'

'No, Louise.'

'Is she . . .?'

'No, paralysed.'

'That's all we needed,' said Berthe, rising and slipping on her dressing-gown. 'Have you called Martel?'

'Not yet.'

'Do it right away, tell him it's urgent! Does Pierre-Edouard know?'

'No.'

'I'll take care of that. We don't want anything to happen to him as well.'

Thanks to one of those letters, rather infrequent but very detailed, sent to him by his mother, Dominique learned of his aunt's health trouble and his grandfather's renewed cardiac alert at the same time.

His aunt, fortunately treated in time, seemed stable for the moment. But her paralysis, despite encouraging improvements, made a great deal of work for the household. To such an extent that Félix had come down to Saint-Libéral to give his aunts support for a while.

As for Pierre-Edouard, although exhausted and in defiance of doctor's orders, he demanded to be helped to rise every morning, to dress himself, to shave. Afterwards he installed himself on the settle, swallowed his bowl of milky chicory coffee, and waited until someone came to read the newspaper to him. That took him until the mealtime. He ate it at the fireside, then returned to his bedroom and had a nap.

Afterwards, weather permitting, he asked Félix to accompany him to take some air. Not far, a few steps outside the door, in exceptional circumstances into the garden. Then he came back in, had the television or radio turned on, and waited patiently in this way until it was time for supper. Only after that would he agree to return to his bed.

*But all that is very tedious for everyone* . . . explained the letter.

The same letter also announced that his father had been overwhelmingly re-elected as the head of the mairie. That the château had been opened with great pomp by all the invited dignitaries; and that, during the coming Easter holidays, the people from the Lierson and Meulen firm were going to meet there for a seminar.

Finally, to conclude, the information that his father was rearing his last batch of pigs. That he had at last found, for 25,000 francs, a very good second-hand tractor, a 55cv which only had 3,500 hours on the clock and could therefore do twice as many again without any problem. With the help of this machine, he was going to resow all his pastures, grub out the old plum and apple trees, set to work again on all sides. After that, cautiously, he would probably begin to turn towards the production of pedigree cattle.

'At last! Some good news!' sighed Dominique, folding up the letter again.

What she had told him at the beginning saddened him greatly.

Certainly he had known for a long time that his aunt was failing, but to picture her paralysed touched his heart. And he was also very distressed for his grandfather. And worried to such an extent that he could not help thinking that, perhaps, the latter would not await their return before joining Léon . . .

Actually, his mother's letter had arrived at an awkward moment, and he reacted badly. Already very annoyed about a series of failed experiments – it was not his fault, but that did not improve his temper! – he was also concerned about Béatrice. He found her tired, and would have liked her to rest much more than she did. Instead of which, she had not even stopped work at the maternity hospital. She considered she was better placed than him to know what she ought to do. All he could do was nurse his anger and count the days until their return to France.

'You can see the poor girl hasn't time to look after the garden any more,' remarked Pierre-Edouard, observing the beds where peas, carrots, white onions and garlic were growing.

Everything was flourishing, and well-advanced, but to those who knew about gardening, it was obvious that the crops were in need of attention. Lacking sticks, the peas were beginning to collapse, and weeds were invading the carrots. In addition, the ground prepared to receive the new potatoes was still empty.

'Poor little thing,' sighed Pierre-Edouard, 'we give her too much work. You should look after this garden a bit, just to help Mathilde. I'm sure it must depress her to see it like this.'

'Promise, I'll set to,' agreed Félix, who considered it useless to point out that he had already taken the trouble to hoe between the rows of onions and garlic.

'Ought to put in some chavignounes, they're a good sort of potato.'

'All right. And tomorrow, if it's fine, I'll stake the peas and you'll help me!'

'Oh, help you! Wish I still could! But I'll keep you company,' promised Pierre-Edouard.

'That's really what I meant. Do you want to go back in now?' suggested Félix. 'I wouldn't like you to catch cold.'

He had taken advantage of a ray of sunshine between two showers to accompany Pierre-Edouard, who was keen to see the kitchen garden. Actually they had not been able to go out for several days because Easter week, although not cold, had nevertheless been changeable and damp.

'Cold?' said Pierre-Edouard. 'No, it's fine. Listen to the cuckoos, how they're enjoying themselves, that's a sign of fine weather. Come on, help me get out of here, we're going to walk a bit in the main street.'

'You're not too tired, now?'

'No, no! And then all those nonsensical medicines and injections Martel gives me ought to be some use. Well, I can't complain, when I see your mother . . .'

On discovering, a month earlier, the state his sister had sunk into, Pierre-Edouard had felt his heart could not cope with this new emotion, this too-severe shock. And he suddenly felt as weak as a newborn babe, with somewhere in the top part of his chest a heaviness, a pain which constricted his breathing. Luckily, Doctor Martel was there looking after Louise . . .

'So you're sure, you want to take a turn in the main street? You feel fit for it?' Félix checked.

He considered it pointless and absurd to pretend to the old man that he was allowed to do anything and had never been in such good health. For although it was true his new treatment had alleviated the moments of absentmindedness or apparent delirium which were so disturbing, it did not permit him to remain standing for long, or to walk more than fifty metres without having to stop to gather his strength.

Besides, Pierre-Edouard was completely lucid and aware of his condition; he had no illusions about the little time he had left to live. With him, lies were useless. He had already seen so many, many people die, that he in particular could not be deceived in any way on that matter. Now, all he was hoping for was to see his grandson again. Jacques, knowing how much it would please him, had made him party to Dominique's plans: one day – maybe in twenty years' time, maybe more, but one day – his grandson wanted to come and live at Coste Roche, to work there.

And Pierre-Edouard wanted to hear that for himself, spoken by his grandson, to be certain. And then, God willing, but that was perhaps asking too much of him, and he hardly dared think about it, it seemed so far off, he would have loved to know that his first great-grandson – or daughter – had been born.

After that he would be able to rest at last and wait until his time came. It would come very soon. And nobody could do anything about it. And even the distress and love he read in Mathilde's eyes, when a bout of weakness forced him to swallow several life-preserving pills, would be unable to change anything at all. Even her prayers would be in vain.

But whilst waiting, and as he still had a remnant of strength, he wanted to take advantage of the burgeoning spring and this April afternoon full of such fine lilac blossom.

'Come on, help me,' he repeated, 'we'll walk a bit in the street. Ought to let everyone know that Père Vialhe is still upright!'

They were emerging from the garden when an old Citröen 2CV, its bodywork pitted by rust, braked behind them and then stopped on a level with them.

'Ah! It's you?' said Pierre-Edouard, recognising Father Soliers.

A month earlier, although very busy with all his parishes, Father Soliers had insisted on making a visit to the Vialhes as soon as he had been informed of Louise and Pierre-Edouard's condition.

His arrival had been a great comfort to Mathilde and Yvette; much less so to Berthe, who considered it premature and in very poor taste. It is true that her contact with consecrated places was barely more regular than Pierre-Edouard's. True as well that she was rather too independent a character to conform blindly to rituals which she considered were often questionable, not to say ridiculous. It was therefore rare for her to go to church more than three or four times a year.

Despite that, because she was well-mannered she did not remark to the priest that his visit was open to misinterpretation. Malicious minds might actually see in it, not a simple and friendly polite convention, but the opportunistic action of one who dispensed extreme unction and was suffering from a shortage of the dying.

However, since the only provisions Father Soliers had brought were a bar of milk chocolate and a packet of sponge fingers, and she had clearly seen a contented beam in her sister-in-law's expression, she had kept quiet. And now she behaved very nicely at each fresh visit by the priest.

He made the effort to come almost every week, and Louise always seemed happy to see him again. Always in a hurry, he only stayed a few minutes, time enough to note the progress made by the invalid and congratulate her on it. Then he assured everyone of his prayers, climbed back into his wreck of a 2CV and jolted along to the next invalid, often bedridden in the depths of some other distant parish.

'Well, well, Monsieur Vialhe, you seem to be in fine form!' he said, getting out of his car.

'Fine form? Don't exaggerate, but after all, I'll hang on a bit longer . . .'

'You're right! That's it, try to stay determined like that. Fine, I must go and pay my respects to your sister, I've still lots to do before dark.'

'He does what he can, the poor fellow,' said Pierre-Edouard as soon as the priest had entered the house.

'Yes, and it's good, what he's doing there,' agreed Félix.

'But all the same, it was a different matter in the time of Father Feix or Father Verlhac,' said Pierre-Edouard, advancing with short steps into the main street. 'Yes, when they went to see a sick person it was no trouble to them to spend an hour or two there.'

'They had the time . . .'

'Well, yes. That poor fellow, with all the parishes they've loaded on him, he can't keep up! But all the same, our old ministers were better. They didn't look at their watches. They were almost part of the family; he's just a visitor. That doesn't mean we don't like him, but he's just a visitor . . .'

Although so brief, Christian and Josyane's visit gave a great deal of pleasure to the whole Vialhe family. First, because the couple had come down from Paris to sign the contract for their future holiday home; there was therefore the assurance that they would be coming often. Then, because it was very comforting to hear Josyane's laugh as she responded to her grandmother's worries about her.

As a matter of fact, Mathilde considered that her granddaughter was behaving during her pregnancy with a detachment and casualness which bordered on rashness. So she never stopped warning her and commending the benefits of rest.

'You really should take care, my dear, an accident can happen in a trice! And you, Christian, you're not being sensible! That's a fair old step you're intending to cover, and it's uphill!' she considered it her duty to tell them, when she learned the couple were setting out to walk around the plateau. Truly this late April afternoon, filled with sunshine and perfume, was magnificent, but all the same!

'Now, now, bonne-maman, how dare you say that to me?' teased Josyane. 'To listen to you, anyone would swear you never worked in the fields or stables when you were expecting Maman and my uncles! So our walk, in comparison!'

'It wasn't the same for me! And then . . . It wasn't the same, that's all!' repeated Mathilde.

'That's right, tell me straight out I'm a weakling!'

'No, but I don't think you take enough care of yourself!'

'I love you, bonne-maman! Come on, don't worry, everything's fine, the baby's well settled in, everything's normal. And besides it's not an illness! That's what my gyno is always telling me!'

'You're talking about your doctor, are you? Those people, they trot out nothing but rubbish!'

'That's the first sensible thing you've said for five minutes!' Pierre-Edouard intervened.

He had insisted on sitting on the threshold. Propped up in a cane armchair, his head in the shade thanks to the porch, but his legs in the sun, he was feeling fine.

'Ahah! You see,' teased Josyane, 'even Grandfather thinks I'm right!'

'Naturally, the moment he gets a chance to contradict me!' replied Mathilde with a shrug.

'Don't listen to your grandmother, dear,' said Pierre-Edouard. 'When she gave birth to your mother, it was touch and go whether I could get her out of the cowshed a quarter of an hour beforehand! And if I'd let her, she would have been back there again that same evening!' he finished with a chuckle.

He coughed a bit and caught his breath, for even laughing was an effort to him now.

'You mustn't believe a word he says,' Mathilde assured her, bending over him to pull up the cover which had slipped from his shoulders.

'Do you hear her?' Pierre-Edouard called on Josyane and Christian as witnesses. 'Do you hear her?' He clung on to Mathilde's hand, held it between his own. 'You know,' he added, 'she always told me I was so full of mischief and tall stories, I'd end up in hell! Like poor old Léon did!'

'Stop it,' she smiled, 'you're still telling them!'

'And I always replied . . .' He coughed once more, squeezed Mathilde's hand and whispered with a little laugh: 'I replied: There's no chance of that, there's no one in hell. That's why the devil is bored and comes to torment us on earth!'

'And what's more you talk like a heathen!' she cried, without believing a word she said.

He smiled at her, let go of her hand and signalled to Josyane and Christian to come closer.

'And your little one, when's it due?' he asked.

'In June, six or seven weeks.'

'That's still a long time off, a long time . . .' he murmured.

'No it isn't,' Josyane assured him. 'We'll come and show it to you this summer. That way, with Béatrice's, you'll have one for each knee. And Christian will take loads of lovely photos!'

'That's still a long time off, all that,' he repeated. He coughed a little, cleared his throat: 'And what will it be called?'

'David or Marianne,' said Josyane, who had the tact not to remind him that she had given the same answer the previous evening.

'David? David? he murmured. He reflected, his brow furrowed: 'We hid a child during the war, yes, he was called David, him too. And his brother? His brother . . .?'

'Benjamin,' whispered Mathilde.

'That's it. They were nice kids, both of them . . . God knows what became of them . . . Well, that's the way it is . . .'

He shook his head, as if to banish some unpleasant memories, then asked:

'So, it's really true, you've bought Meyjonade's place, at Fonts Perdus?'

'Not Meyjonade's,' Mathilde intervened, 'I've already told you, his daughter married a Mouly. Anyway, you know full well it's Meyjonade's grandson who sold it!'

'It's the same thing,' he said irritably,'to me it's still Meyjonade's.' He fell silent, meditated: 'Before the war, that was a fine farm. The Meyjonades kept six or seven cows, yes, a fine farm . . . And then it's a beautiful spot, Fonts Perdus. Once upon a time, you always flushed at least two covies of red-legs there. And there were hares too. So, now it's yours?'

'Yes,' confirmed Josyane. 'It'll be lovely there. You must come and see us as soon as we've organised it a bit. Since it hasn't been inhabited for a while, there's some work to do . . .'

'And the fields?' he continued.

'You know very well that Valade and Duverger bought them a long time ago!' Mathilde reminded him.

'Ah, that's right,' he murmured, after thinking about it. 'That's true, it was good land . . .'

He pulled the rug around his shoulders, coughed a little and gestured to Mathilde:

'Help me get up, it's too cold now to stay outside.'

'Would you like Christian to help you?' suggested Josyane to her grandmother.

'No, Félix will come, he's in the vegetable garden. You go and take your walk,' she said, and she added quietly: 'It's beautiful and warm, make the most of it.'

If Dominique still had any illusions about his employers at Mondiagri, they were destroyed when he perused the letter he received a week before setting out for France. At first he did not believe what he was reading, then he checked the date and swore volubly:

'Jesus Christ Almighty! They're doing it on purpose! I swear they're doing it on purpose, the bastards!' he called to Béatrice.

She had at last stopped work at the maternity hospital, and was making the most of her free time by resting.

'What's up?' she asked, without moving from the chaise longue.

'That pack of exploiters at Mondiagri are bugging me, that's what's up! Talk about dickheads! They know fine in Paris that I'm taking my leave next week! I told them more than six months ago, the morons!' he shouted, brandishing the letter and pounding out each word heavily with his fist on the table.

'What's up?' she asked again patiently.

'I'm stuck here! That's what's up! And all because those buggers in Paris – because they're real buggers, those people! – are sending me two more idiots! Two hypocrites with the task of arranging a visit to the centre by the Tunisians responsible for food and agriculture! And all just to screw them as fast as possible! Because that's all they're coming for, those vultures!'

'If you'd kept calm, you'd have given me the dates of their visit by now.'

'The fourth and fifth of May! And our leave begins on the twenty-eighth of April! Oh, marvellous! I tell you, they do it on purpose! It's the second time they've played that trick on me! But this time they can go and get stuffed! I'm resigning!'

'There's no question of that,' she said without raising her voice.

'You don't think I'm going to let you leave and have the baby alone, while I'm here trying to convince the poor suckers that there's no salvation for their God-forsaken country besides Mondiagri! Are you out of your mind?'

'Not for one minute. To resign, you have to have the means! You have absolutely no safe place to go to in the immediate future. And just because Ali assures you they'll take you back whenever you like in Algeria, don't think it would be so easy. So no dreaming, if you don't mind? I'll leave on the planned date, and I'll wait for you before going into labour, promise!' she joked.

'No, no, no! That won't do! I'm not letting you leave alone!'

'Bah, there's two of me!' she said, patting her stomach. 'Come on,' she smiled, 'fetch a beer, that'll calm you down. I don't like it when you get worked up like that! And nor does the baby, it responds by pummelling me with its feet! And look, if it's any comfort to you, I'll go earlier and wait for you at Coste-Roche. Over there I'll rest even better than here. But I mean it, seriously!'

'I'm not going to leave you to have the baby alone.'

'Stop going on about it! You know what my gyno said, and I trust her, she's very competent: the baby will be there at the right time, no more and no less! So if you arrive on the sixth, that'll be fine.'

'Hey! Stop it with your infallible dates! That only works in books! Don't forget, as far as this is concerned, you're on the same system as cows. And that I do know about! Just because a cow is pregnant for two hundred and seventy-five days, it doesn't mean the calf arrives at that exact moment! So, stop talking nonsense, if you don't mind!'

'Thanks for the comparison,' she teased. 'Well, I escaped being like a goat, that's something I suppose!'

'One hundred and fifty-five days for a goat! Three months, three weeks and three days for a sow! A hundred and fifty-five days for a ewe! Do you want some more?' He saw that she was laughing and shrugged his shoulders. 'Fine,' he said, suddenly calmed down, 'after all, perhaps you're right. But you must admit these Mondiagri people are real bastards!'

'Why shouldn't they be? It works! The proof is you can't do anything but follow their directives, at least for the moment . . .'

'You did well to add "for the moment"! The time's not far off when they'll realise that Vialhes aren't sheep.'

Although everyone had been told to conceal from Pierre-Edouard that Domique would be at least a week late, he guessed the truth. Probably Yvette, Berthe, Mathilde or Jacques had said one word too many; perhaps someone had gone so far as to mention Béatrice, who was already at Coste-Roche and was staying put there.

As a matter of fact the whole family had been in agreement in telling her that it was pointless to go and visit the old man. One had to face facts, and recognise that it was not her he was waiting for. She had quite understood and was in no way upset.

But this delay played a great deal on the old man's spirits. He went into a rapid and devastating decline. This was all the more poignant since he remained clear-headed. It was just that, instead of calling early to be helped out of bed, he took to dozing there until the end of the morning. At that point, it was obvious he was calling on his reserves to drag himself from his torpor and this paralysing weariness which was crushing him. Then he would call to Félix or Mathilde:

'Have to get me out of here, it's high time,' he would say.

And then he would try to get down from the big wooden bed by himself. Afterwards, when Félix had shaved him, and he felt clean, he had himself brought to the corner by the hearth or, if there was sunshine, to a cane armchair placed in front of the window.

Once there, he waited until evening, punctuating the afternoon with long periods of drowsiness. He asked to be taken to bed as soon as darkness fell, but demanded each evening before lying down:

'Dominique's arriving when?'

'Very soon,' Mathilde would say, not wishing to venture a precise date.

However, on the evening of 6 May, as she leaned over to kiss him on the forehead, she could anticipate his question and announce:

He'll be there tomorrow, definitely. Do you hear? Tomorrow!'

He sighed, nodded his head and patted her on the arm:

'The devil, he's kept us waiting!' he said at last. But he felt immediately less anxious. And the night was peaceful.

Although shocked to discover Pierre-Edouard's condition, Dominique and Béatrice knew how to put up a good show when they came to visit him on the Saturday evening.

But there were too many people for Pierre-Edouard to feel like talking or even hearing what his grandson had to say to him. So, despite the evident contentment in his beaming expression, he did not say very much. He simply whispered to Dominique, just before going to bed:

'Come tomorrow morning, we must talk.'

'Promise. Well, unless Béatrice decides to go into labour in the meantime!'

'That would be good,' smiled the old man.

He squeezed Dominique's arm and went off towards his bedroom, supported by Félix and Mathilde.

'And now, don't think you have to lie to me!' she said to Dominique and Béatrice, when she returned after putting him to bed. 'I know very well that he's . . .'

'Come on, you can't possibly know,' attempted Dominique.

'Yes, I can,' she sighed as she lowered herself into the settle. She pushed several twigs into the flames, looked at Béatrice: 'So when's it to be?'

'Any day now.'

'The same as for him, then,' she murmured, 'the same as for him . . .'

'How is Aunt Louise?' asked Dominique, to change the subject a little.

Béatrice and he, arriving late, had not wanted to go and disturb her in her bedroom when she was probably already asleep.

'Better day by day,' said Félix.

'She's regained movement in her arm and leg,' clarified Berthe, 'and she's even beginning to try to speak. Oh, not much, but still. In any case, she was never very talkative!'

'But what about you, have you moved down here for good?' Dominique asked Félix.

'No. But I wasn't going to leave your aunt dependent on everyone else and sit around doing nothing. But I'll go back when she's improving.'

Later on, as Dominique and Béatrice were climbing back up to Coste-Roche, Béatrice wanted to know.

'Tell me, don't take it amiss, but just one question: it's the custom with you not to send the sick to hospital?'

'The sick, yes, when there's really nothing else to be done. Old people, no, never. And I think it's very good that way.'

'I didn't say it was wrong. I'm finding out, that's all. With you Vialhes, you learn something new every day!'


'So it's really true what your father told me, you'll be coming back to look after the land? That's definite?' insisted Pierre-Edouard.

'Yes. But I can't say when,' explained Dominique.

'That doesn't matter, the main thing is that you come back! And then you'll see, it passes so quickly, time, so quickly . . . So you'll be coming back one day? That's good,' smiled the old man, pulling his rug around him.

Despite uncertain weather, he had still demanded to go and take some air on the threshold. Not for very long, just a few minutes, to be alone with his grandson and hear what he wanted to know. And now he was calm, at peace.

'Tell me, I hope you've still got it?' he asked suddenly.

'What?'

'The napoléon I gave you I don't know how long ago . . .'

'Ah! The twenty-franc coin you gave me for my bac? Of course I've got it! Not on me, but I've got it!'

'Very good. So one day, you must give it to your grandson,' said Pierre-Edouard.

He was seized by a bad fit of coughing which exhausted him. And between gasps continued:

'You tell him you had it from your grandfather, who got it from his . . . For my school certificate . . . You tell him, eh? And then, talk to him a bit about me . . . And about your grandmother . . . Don't forget anything! It's important, to pass on memories, important . . . And now, help me back in. I'm cold. And afterwards, tell your father to come and see me.'

Jacques came down that same evening. As it was still quite light, he hoped to find his father up. But Mathilde informed him that he had already returned to his bed more than an hour earlier.

'Is he asleep?' asked Jacques.

'No, he's asking for you.'

'I couldn't come earlier, what with the animals . . .'

'I know,' she said, 'that's what I told him, he understood. But go and see him now.'

Jacques entered the room and approached the double bed.

'Ah, you're there,' said Pierre-Edouard, opening his eyes. 'Come closer.' He waited until his son was next to him and whispered: 'Go and send for the priest. Yes, I insist on it! That surprises you,' he said, with a ghost of a smile. 'Yes, you're surprised, I can see! But it's not for me . . .'

'I don't understand.'

'Yes, you do!' said Pierre-Edouard with an irritated gesture. 'I've nothing to say to him myself, the poor curé! We've never exchanged more than ten sentences since we've known each other! Not going to start today! But all the same, he must come and see me. You understand, it'll make your mother so happy . . . Call him, straight away.'

'All right, I'll see to it.'

'And mind you tell your mother that it's me who's asking for him, all my own idea. She'll be pleased that I thought of it. Go on . . . Ah, yes, perhaps you ought also tell Guy that . . . Well . . .'

'Don't worry, he phones every evening.'

'Oh, good . . . So he'll know all right to come when it's necessary . . . Now call the priest, it'll make your mother so happy.'

During the following three days, Pierre-Edouard remained in a stable condition. Obstinate to the end, he demanded that they continue to help him get up every morning. Then, slowly, step by step, he moved towards the cane chair which awaited him in front of the fire, where he spent the whole day dozing peacefully. He already seemed detached from the world.

But it was still he who reacted first when the telephone rang in the early hours of 12 May. Day was barely dawning. It looked fine, clear.

'That's it, that's Dominique's baby,' he murmured. He felt about quietly beside him, placed his hand on Mathilde's shoulder as she still slept, exhausted.

'That's Dominique's baby,' he repeated, gently stroking her cheek.

But Félix had already answered it. Awake at last, Mathilde rose, simultaneously worried and happy, and went out of the room to seek news. She returned at once, radiant, almost rejuvenated:

'It really is Béatrice. They took her to Brive in the night. She's just gone into the delivery room. That was Mauricette calling just now, she thought we'd already be up.'

'Help me to get up,' he said.

'Already?'

'Yes.'

She slipped him into his dressing-gown, pulled back the curtains, and supported him so that he could sit up.

'Call Félix,' he said, 'I want to go and take some air . . .'

'You're not to think of it!' she protested.

'Yes I am! It's beautiful, I want to see the sun.'

It took more than five minutes for Félix to help him walk as far as the door. The first rays of the rising sun welcomed them as they finally appeared on the doorstep.

'It's a really fine day,' sighed Pierre-Edouard. 'It'd be so lovely to climb on the peaks, things must be growing again up there . . .'

He screwed up his eyes a little, then leaned heavily on Félix again:

'My armchair,' he said.

He settled into it breathing heavily, pushed away the bowl of milk Mathilde offered, and began to wait, dozing.

He jumped when the telephone rang again towards ten o'clock. Rather confusedly, he made out the smiling, happy faces of Mathilde, Berthe, Yvette and Félix. And through a distant, woolly fog he heard Mathilde.

'He's arrived! He weighs 3.25 kilos! Béatrice is very well!'

Then he woke up properly, even tried to get up.

'Don't move,' said Mathilde, coming to hug him, 'you have a great-grandson. And he's called Pierre! Like you!'

'Pierre?' he murmured as he embraced her. 'Pierre, is that true?'

'Yes!' She said, leaning over him once more to kiss him again.

'Dominique just told me so. He said to tell you that his son is called Pierre, Jacques, Edouard Vialhe!'

'Oh, that's good, that's very good!' the old man smiled as he squeezed her hand.

Two days later, in the morning, when the sun was streaming in through the open window and a pair of cuckoos were calling to each other in the pinewood by the château, Pierre-Edouard announced to Mathilde that he would not be getting up.

*Marcillac, 6 mai 1990*